For more than a hundred centuries the Emperor has sat immobile on the Golden Throne of Earth. He is the Master of Mankind. By the might of his inexhaustible armies a million worlds stand against the dark.

Yet, he is a rotting carcass, the Carrion Lord of the Imperium held in life by marvels from the Dark Age of Technology and the thousand souls sacrificed each day so his may continue to burn.

To be a man in such times is to be one amongst untold billions. It is to live in the cruelest and most bloody regime imaginable. It is to suffer an eternity of carnage and slaughter. It is to have cries of anguish and sorrow drowned by the thirsting laughter of dark gods.

This is a dark and terrible era where you will find little comfort or hope. Forget the power of technology and science. Forget the promise of progress and advancement. Forget any notion of common humanity or compassion.

There is no peace amongst the stars, for in the grim darkness of the far future, there is only war.

LEGENDS
OF THE
WOLF
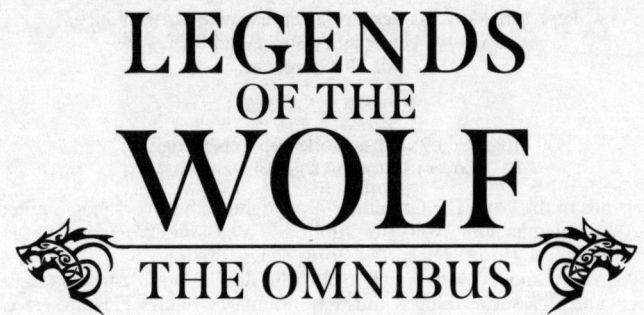
THE OMNIBUS

CHRIS WRAIGHT

BLACK LIBRARY

A BLACK LIBRARY PUBLICATION

'Kraken' first published digitally in 2012.
Blood of Asaheim first published in 2013.
Stormcaller first published in 2014.
The Helwinter Gate first published in 2020.
This edition published in Great Britain in 2025 by
Black Library, Games Workshop Ltd., Willow Road,
Nottingham, NG7 2WS, UK.

Represented by: Games Workshop Limited – Irish branch,
Unit 3, Lower Liffey Street, Dublin 1,
D01 K199, Ireland.

10 9 8 7 6 5 4 3 2 1

Produced by Games Workshop in Nottingham.
Cover illustration by Paul Dainton.

A CIP record for this book is available from the British Library.

ISBN 13: 978-1-80407-728-3

See Black Library on the internet at

blacklibrary.com

Find out more about Games Workshop
and the worlds of Warhammer at

warhammer.com

Printed and bound in the UK.

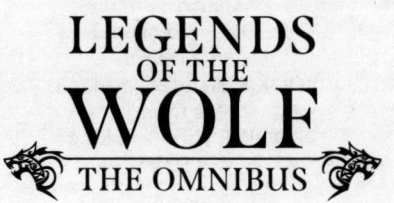

LEGENDS
OF THE
WOLF
THE OMNIBUS

More Warhammer 40,000 from Black Library

• DAWN OF FIRE •
BOOK 1: Avenging Son
Guy Haley
BOOK 2: The Gate of Bones
Andy Clark
BOOK 3: The Wolftime
Gav Thorpe
BOOK 4: Throne of Light
Guy Haley
BOOK 5: The Iron Kingdom
Nick Kyme
BOOK 6: The Martyr's Tomb
Marc Collins
BOOK 7: Sea of Souls
Chris Wraight
BOOK 8: Hand of Abaddon
Nick Kyme
BOOK 9: The Silent King
Guy Haley

LEVIATHAN
Darius Hinks

INDOMITUS
Gav Thorpe

• DARK IMPERIUM •
Guy Haley

BOOK 1: Dark Imperium
BOOK 2: Plague War
BOOK 3: Godblight

• WATCHERS OF THE THRONE •
Chris Wraight

BOOK 1: The Emperor's Legion
BOOK 2: The Regent's Shadow

• VAULTS OF TERRA •
Chris Wraight

BOOK 1: The Carrion Throne
BOOK 2: The Hollow Mountain
BOOK 3: The Dark City

CONTENTS

BLOOD OF
ASAHEIM

'You will be faster than they are, stronger, quicker to sense corruption and with full sanction to destroy it. You will be girded in the armour of gods and carry the blades of ruin. You will never age, never wither, never weary. And yet, in all of this, what remains your greatest gift?

'Only this: while you are a brotherhood, you are unbreakable. While you form the shieldwall, guarding your pack-mates as if they were your own kin-blood, you cannot be resisted. Solely by treachery can this power be undone, as we have learned. We emerge from the lesson stronger, tempered by the knowledge of how low our species can sink. We now know what waits for us should we fail, and that is well, for it is better to know your enemy's face than for it to remain hidden by shadow.

'Never forget this. When night comes again, as it surely will, only your brotherhood will protect you. Preserve it, and you will endure. Let it fracture, let it fail, and I tell you truly: our time, humanity's time, will be over.'

– The primarch Leman Russ
Words recorded on Ialis III, c.170.M31
Incorporated into *Liber Malan*; source-data lost

'The Wolves of Fenris? They will tire at the end. We will all tire at the end. What else is there, once war is eternal, but fatigue?'

– Attributed to the primarch Mortarion
Quoted in *Liber Infestus*
Date and source unknown

PROLOGUE

Blood rose in his gorge, foaming and flecked with bone, spilling from split lips and over cracked fangs. He stumbled down the walkway, feeling metal struts flex and snap under his limping tread. Gunfire, tinny and echoing, rang down from the airways above him. The noise was an irrelevance by then – a cluttered fury that signified nothing but the slow death of the drifting Arjute-class heavy troop conveyer. The Imperium would not miss it; it could spare a million of them and never notice.

He coughed up more blood, feeling the flesh of his throat constrict. He tried to smile, and the corner of his mouth ripped where the burns latticed against softer flesh.

It would miss him. The Imperium would miss Hjortur Ageir Hvat Blood-fang, Wolf Guard of Fenris, *vaerangi* of Berek Thunderfist: blood-shedder, beast-slayer, tale-teller. Sagas would mark his passing, declaimed in the icy vaults of home by skjalds who had feared and loved him, just as all in the Rout had feared and loved him.

He started to chuckle as he limped, and blood bubbled down his chin and into his clumped and matted beard.

He'd caused hell. He'd done some damage. He'd do some more before they brought him down, too. Blood of Russ, he'd make them all bleed a little more.

He stumbled, falling to his knees and feeling the mesh of the metal floor grate against his fractured poleyn-guard. He heard his breathing scrape and wheeze within the flickering mess of his helm's interior.

Above him the roof was a jumbled mass of burned-out pipelines, hanging like vines from the darkness. Somewhere up ahead a red light rotated in rhythm with a superfluous warning klaxon. He heard crashes from further back, further down: the resounding clang of iron-edged boots against metal, the hard clunk of magazines being loaded.

Hjortur pushed himself back to his feet. The enclosed corridor ran away from him, plunging down steeply, winding into the bowels of the conveyer's enginarium. The metal around him was hot. He staggered along it, reeling from the walls, breaking off shards of steel as his armour snagged against them. He felt enclosed, hemmed in, cornered.

He sensed a movement – twenty metres behind, stealthy like the others had been.

13

Not stealthy enough.

Hjortur twisted at the waist and squeezed a round away, watching the projectile streak off into the dark through blood-screened eyes. He couldn't make out his victim but heard the sounds of his death: the crack of breaking armour, the wet *schlick* of flesh parting, the stifled boom of detonation.

No screams. The hunters that closed on him didn't scream. He didn't know what they were. Human, perhaps. If so, they were heavily augmented and stuffed with bionics, for they moved liked he did and hit almost as hard. That was worrying. It shouldn't have been possible.

He started to limp off again, and the bestial phlegm-growl of his broken breathing hummed in his ears. His retinal display screamed at him, detailing pedantically just how badly he'd been torn up: two lungs gone, chest cavity flooded, seventy minor fractures and six big ones. His skin was a mess of partly-clotted plasma and slowly knitting tissue, all seething with a contradictory mix of stimms and pain suppressors.

Pretty bad. He was breaking up, just like the ship around him.

He heard more footsteps clattering down the corridor, then silence as the hunters crouched down into firing positions. He broke into a sprint, wincing as lances of white-hot pain shot up his shattered shins.

A second later and the corridor filled with solid rounds, crashing and cracking from the walls and filling the narrow space with spinning clouds of metal. He felt the heavy bang of projectiles thudding into his back, tearing fresh gouges in the weakened ceramite and burrowing down towards the flesh beneath.

He reached a T-junction and threw himself around the corner into cover, clanking against the floor and panting, waiting for the hail of fire to break off.

The junction was dark. The air tasted of engine oil and ship-bilge. He could hardly see five paces into the murk. When he blinked, blood cascaded down his cheeks.

The gunfire ceased. He waited two more seconds, enough for the first of them to get up and run down the corridor after him. He could smell them coming, sense their unfamiliar odour even over the stinking melange of the lower decks.

What are you? What kind of creatures are you?

As the first one approached he burst back to his feet, powering his huge, ravaged body into motion, swinging round into the corridor he'd just run down and flexing his claw-hand to gouge.

His pursuer skidded to a halt, suddenly confronted by a vast armoured behemoth rearing up out of the oily shadows. The hunter tried to scramble backwards, but his momentum carried him into lethal range.

Hjortur lashed out with his claws. Their disruptor field had long since burned out, but the dented blades still punched through the hunter's armour, skewering him. Hjortur lashed out, churning up the hunter's ribcage and flinging him hard against the nearside wall. The hunter's torso broke open into a flailing ball of skin-scraps and sinew.

Another one was too close. The hunter scrambled back out of claw-range, his black limbs skittering on the metal like an insect's.

Hjortur pounced, slicing his claw down and dragging the hunter back. The impaled warrior tried to turn, tried to get a weapon hand into position, but it was all far too slow.

Hjortur crashed his other fist down, mashing the hunter's helm, visor and skull into a glass-flecked soup of pulp. Blood splashed up along Hjortur's forearms, adding to the riot of streaks and stains already there.

He felt solid rounds crack against his armour again – one, two, three direct hits, rocking him backwards. A shot slammed between the gaping cracks in his breastplate, punching through flesh, grinding into the bone beneath.

Hjortur growled as he swung round, searching for a target in the dark, blinking to clear his vision of blood.

The first he knew of the frag grenade was a gentle *tink-tink-tink* as it bounced down the corridor.

If his senses hadn't been crushed, he'd have spotted it sooner. If his muscles hadn't been ripped apart, he'd have been able to leap clear in time. If his armour hadn't been carved open, he'd have withstood the blast.

It exploded. The blast-wave hurled him backwards, throwing him onto his back and sending him skidding into the far wall of the junction.

Hjortur's head bounced back savagely, prompting fresh spikes of pain from his twisted neck. He felt more sharp pops from within, the hot flush of fluids sluicing across his organs. A wave of sickly dizziness swept over him, and his hands went cold. He felt his bolter drop from numb fingers.

Blinded, reeling, he tried to push himself up. He dimly made out the silhouettes of more figures standing above him. He swung his fist clumsily at the nearest. A blade shot out from over to his left, severing his arm at the wrist. Hjortur felt the metal slide under his splintered forearm-guard, slicing agonisingly through what remained of his claw-hand.

More blades flashed in the gloom, plunging into his body, pinioning him to the metal deck. His back arched as they stabbed him, and a ragged, throaty gurgle of pain escaped his mouth.

The hunters kept up the assault. They worked as a team, moving sword-edges quickly, as if panicked by the thought that he might – *still* – get up. They locked his ankles down. They ran gouges along his torso, exposing glistening viscera. They threw chains across his legs and throat, yanking his head back against the floor.

By the time they had finished, Hjortur Ageir Hvat Bloodfang, Wolf Guard of Fenris, *vaerangi* of Berek Thunderfist, lay impaled on the lower decks of the Arjute-class heavy troop conveyer like an insect pinned to a collector's card. Twelve short swords held him in place, six adamantium-link chain lengths held him down, seven barbed gouges were lodged in his chest, each one standing at the head of a gushing fountain of thick, semi-clotted blood.

That was what it took to subdue him. Hjortur coughed up a wet, grim snort of satisfaction. He'd extracted his tally of pain.

How many hunters had he killed? Maybe a hundred. This had been a serious operation. They had come prepared.

The blurred black-clad figures withdrew. Hjortur tried to raise his head, but the chains pulled tight. His breath came in tight, short gasps. He could feel his armour systems gutter and fizz out. He could feel his body getting colder, shutting down, giving up the ghost.

Giving up the ghost. Hjortur felt delirious. *Giving up the ghost.*

A single hunter remained, hanging over his face like a vision in smoke. He could make out the fuzzy outline of a closed-face helm. He saw a cherubic device printed on the forehead – golden, spike-crowned against a sable ground. He saw plates of armour glinting, matt-black and rimmed with silver. He smelled the sooty aroma of a cooling weapon muzzle, and heard the faint whine of a power-pack winding down.

The world around him began to melt away. He concentrated, determined to look at his killer, right up to the end.

Fenrys.

The thought swam into his mind unbidden. He saw an image of the peaks of Asaheim, vast and snow-streaked, picked out in hard lines of frosty clarity. He knew then that he would never go back to them, never feel their knife-sharp air sting on his tongue. That knowledge pained him more than his hundred wounds.

The blurred figure swung closer, kneeling beside Hjortur and peering down at him. Hjortur saw his own face reflected darkly in a glassy visor, and barely recognised himself.

They will replace me, he thought. *The pack needs a leader.*

The hunter withdrew a tapered gun. It was a strange-looking thing – curved and sweeping and sculptural. Hjortur struggled to maintain focus.

I should have appointed a successor. Gyrfalkon? Gunnlaugur?

The hunter placed the muzzle's tip at Hjortur's fractured temple and pressed it through the flesh. Amid his cacophony of serried pain, Hjortur barely winced.

'Do you know who we are?'

The voice was heavily altered, filtered through a crackling vox-distorter. It might have been human; it might not.

Hjortur tried to answer, but the blood in his throat and mouth made him gag. He shook his head fractionally, making the needle in his temple tear at the flesh.

The hunter reached up with his free hand and depressed a switch at the side of his helm. His visor snapped up, revealing a gaunt face within, lit up by angry red internal illumination. Hjortur's killer leaned closer.

'Do you know who sent us?'

I could never choose between them. I should have chosen. What will Berek rule?

Hjortur tried to focus. It was difficult. The world had narrowed down to a gauze of pale mist, like ghost-frost spreading over glass.

The hunter opened his left palm. A little golden cherub's head nestled against the black synleather, surrounded by a spiked halo.

'Do you know who sent us?'

I should have chosen.

One more surge of effort, one final attempt to drag his faltering vision back into some form of clarity.

Then realisation dawned, as cold and sick as breaking fever.

'Yes,' said Hjortur, choking as he spoke.

The killer above him smiled – a thin movement of thin lips, perfunctory, frigid with wintry satisfaction.

'Good. It is good that you know.'

The hunter pressed the trigger, and the bolt slipped into Hjortur's brain. It was a theatrical gesture, an unnecessary accelerant to the death that was already overtaking him. The mercy stroke, it might have been called in another age; the assassin's courtesy.

Hjortur hung on for a few seconds more, trying to speak, his residual features rigid with shock.

Then, his body racked with starbursts of pain, his lone working heart swollen and weeping, his broken jaw lined with blood-thick drool, he died.

I
JÁRNHAMAR

CHAPTER ONE

After leaving U-6743 he took the Inquisitorial line cruiser *Obsession for Integrity* through the warp from Orelia – a long jump and a wearying journey. His dreams were bad, just as they always were when traversing the open hells of the void. He remained in his cell during that time, alone, refusing company and taking little food. The iron walls shuddered during the enforced diurnal cycle, over and over.

The cruiser dropped into real space at Nishagar, where he made his last and least formal rite of decommissioning to Inquisitor Halliafiore's transmission agent. Most of what he had still retained was surrendered then: everything, save for the onyx skull-pendant and his stalker bolter, a weapon he had come to prefer to the Godwyn-mark issue he'd carried previously. Losing the rest of it all – the devices, the kill-tallies, the armour decoration – made little difference to him, no more than waking from a long sleep with half-remembered dreams still clinging to the edges of memory.

After that it was a mid-range stint in an Imperial Navy frigate whose name he never learned. He scared the hell out of the regular troops with his brooding and grey-eyed stare. He didn't mean to do that. The fact that they couldn't master their awe depressed him slightly.

Only at Kattyak was he able to switch to passage on a Fenrisian vessel – *Yvekk*, a clunky system-runner with a full kaerl crew and a leaking enginarium containment shell. At least the attendants were able to speak to him in Juvykka. For a while even that made him feel awkward, having been confined to Gothic for so long. The kaerls weren't in awe of him, which helped, but they knew the proper forms of address and deference for a Sky Warrior, which also helped.

Only at the end, once they broke through the veil on the fringes of the Fenris system, did he take a little pleasure from the sounds of murmured Juvykka on the decks, the same sounds that he had heard as a child beside glowing fires, that he had shouted out on the ice when hunting, that he had listened to from the mouths of Priests after ascension. Not all pleasures of life were relinquished by service; those were the things that took him back, right at the end of the long transfer: the sounds, the smells, the textures of age-dried fur, of rune-etched steel, cured hide, lacquered hair in armour-compressed plaits.

During the final approach he came up to the bridge, standing on the observer platform while mortals and servitors scurried around him and prepared for orbital clearance.

The grey-white curve of the planet slowly filled the forward viewers. He saw snarls of dirty cloud drifting across the northern hemisphere, twisted into immense storm-curls. He knew what was under the shadow of those clouds. He imagined hammering columns of angled rain beating the sea down into a leaden mass, drenching the decks of the struggling *drekkar* until they listed nearly to the foam-line.

Seeing the violence of the planet from afar, having lived with it up close for so long – that was a strange and uncomfortable sensation. He had missed it, and that was a strange thing too.

The runner's captain, Rurik, a slab-faced man in snow-grey fatigues, shuffled up to him as he stood. Rurik had been trying to find an excuse to speak ever since the last tatters of the warp had slipped away behind them. It wasn't obsequiousness, exactly; just an understandable desire to make contact, to exchange words with one of the lords. Sky Warriors did not often travel on support craft like *Yvekk*; his own presence was an unfortunate consequence of him having dropped out of command structures for too long.

'Good to be back, lord?' Rurik asked, daring a smile.

Ingvar Orm Eversson, the one who had once been called Gyrfalkon, did not know the answer to that question. As he watched the planet growing in the viewer and saw the orbital defence stations swim up out of the dark, a whole host of emotions ran through him, none of which he was able to classify or analyse.

It was the same, and not the same; you never trod in the same river twice. Callimachus had told him that, passing on a saying older than the Imperium itself, a fragment of commonplace wisdom that predated it all.

Ingvar narrowed his eyes, as if he could peer through the scars of cloud and into the storm below. Somewhere down there was the ice, the place he had come from, the savage home that had forged him.

Good to be back?

'Land the ship,' he said softly, his grey eyes never leaving the viewer.

Once down, back with the granite of the mountain under his feet again, he noticed how different it smelled. Or maybe it smelt the same and he was different. Fifty-seven years was a long time, even for him.

Ingvar let the mix of aromas filter into him. His old human range of sensation had long been superseded by a richer, deeper, wider spectrum of awareness, and he picked up traces that even his old battle-brothers might have missed. All warriors of the Adeptus Astartes had their senses refined by the process of ascension; the *Vlka Fenryka* liked to believe that the process went further with them than any others.

Ingvar had learned to doubt such boasts. The Wolves of Fenris were a boastful breed, and his time away from the halls of the Aett had exposed their foundations.

Or perhaps not. He thought back to Onyx and its multiplicity of Chapters. Ingvar had always been sharper than Callimachus, picking up the scent of prey a fraction earlier than him. He'd been far quicker than Jocelyn too, though never really tested against Leonides. They had all laughed about it; the others had found his distended physiognomy both grotesque and impressive.

'If you can smell so much,' the Blood Angel Leonides had once asked, 'how come you wash so little?'

Ingvar remembered the laughter. He remembered joining in, playing along with his disjointed new pack of mismatched brothers, doing what every newly assigned Blood Claw had done since the days of the Crusade: finding his station, assessing hierarchy, doing what needed to be done to fit in.

If he'd been tempted to reply seriously, he might have pointed out that olfaction was an easily underestimated capability. It gave early warning of danger. It allowed a trail to be followed. It exposed corruption.

Would they have been impressed? It was difficult to impress an Ultramarine with anything: Blood Angels were nearly as bad.

Ingvar let his nostrils flare, and took a deep breath.

Old rock, damp with trace humidity. Mortal sweat, twenty metres down. Filter-engine lubricant, past replacement age. Cured leather. Embers, from a long way away. Bronze, etched in acid. Alien matter, recently introduced.

Ingvar smiled at himself.

That is me. I am an alien here, treading spores into stone from halfway across the galaxy. The Aett knows that I no longer belong.

He looked up. The doorway before him was barred by two bronze panels, each etched in a riot of knotwork dragons, krakens and seawyrms. Framing the doors was bare rock, as blunt and jagged as the half-worked walls of the tunnel he'd just walked down.

Typical Fenrisian juxtaposition: artistry the equal of any in the Imperium placed next to rude hackwork.

'Open,' he said, noticing the way his trial-hardened voice echoed dully from the stone around him.

The bronze doors slid smoothly apart. On the far side was a half-lit chamber, pungent with smoking brazier pans.

A figure waited for him in the darkness.

'Welcome home, Gyrfalkon,' said Ragnar Blackmane.

'So it's true?' asked Váltyr.

Gunnlaugur grunted. 'It is.'

Váltyr shook his head. 'When did they tell you?' he asked.

'Six hours ago.'

'*Skítja*,' Váltyr swore.

'He came in on a runner. They didn't send a warship. If they had, I'd have known sooner.'

Váltyr placed his slender hands together.

'Will he return, then?'

Gunnlaugur smiled wryly, a look that said, *Why would they tell me?*

The two were alone, hunched over a firepit and surrounded by lambent shadows. Gunnlaugur's chamber was high up on the eastern flanks of the Fang, close to the edge where the biting winds of Asaheim came over the Hunter's Gap. Ironhelmsshrine was within reach; on rare clear days, it could be seen from the narrow realview portal mounted on the external wall.

Out of battle armour, there were only marginal physical differences between the two warriors. Gunnlaugur, the one they called Skullhewer, was a fraction heavier-set, a finger's width shorter. His shaven head still had residual traces of flame-red hair in the stubble, though his beard was slush-grey and stiff with age. His features were the same tight, brutal ones that had propelled him to clan chief of the Gaellings when he had been mortal, only now filled out and made heavier by aggressive muscular augmentation.

He sat on a stone slab in front of the fire, massive and stooped, his shoulders draped in furs. He ran a dagger through his hands, playing with the killing edge, flicking it between thick, dextrous fingers.

'We are wounded, brother,' Gunnlaugur said. 'Tally it up. We lost Ulf on Lossanal, Svafnir on Cthar, Tínd to the greenskins.'

As he spoke, his dark eyes reflected the warm light of the coals.

'We're under strength,' he said. 'He'll have to come back, just to make us viable. And where else can he go? Who else will take him?'

Váltyr listened intently. His narrow face was hot, and the glow exposed the many scars latticed across his cheeks.

His hands were still. Váltyr never played with blades. His longsword, *holdbítr*, was strapped across his back just as it ever was. The weapon was only drawn to be used in combat, or for veneration, or for ritual maintenance, and even then he never left its side, watching the Iron Priests intently as they invoked the sleeping spectres of murder that dwelt within.

Blademasters – *sverdhjera* – were a strange breed, guarding their weapons as if they were children.

'He chose to leave,' said Váltyr. 'He could have stayed, and we would have welcomed him then. He could have contested for the–'

'You'd have made the same choice he did,' said Gunnlaugur. 'I'd have done it too, if they'd asked.'

He hacked up a gobbet of phlegm and spat it into the fire. Trace particles of acid made it fizz angrily against the coals.

'I could protest,' Gunnlaugur said. 'Blackmane has a Blood Claw waiting in the wings as well, one he's eager to give us to knock into shape. That would make us six – enough to hunt again.'

Váltyr snorted. 'That's what we're reduced to now?'

Gunnlaugur nodded.

'Plenty of packs are running with losses,' he said. 'Every Great Year more come back diminished. Remember when Hjortur died? Remember how shocked we were? Tell me truly, would you be shocked now to hear of a *vaerangi* dying on the hunt?'

Váltyr grinned.

'If it was you, yes.'

Gunnlaugur didn't return the smile. He stared into the fire, and the blade spun and flashed absently in his fingers.

'I'll take the Blood Claw,' he said. 'We need new blood, and he'll learn quickly from Olgeir. But as for him...'

Váltyr looked steadily into Gunnlaugur's eyes.

'Blackmane will choose,' he said.

Gunnlaugur nodded slowly. 'That he will.'

He stilled the movement of the dagger.

'Our Young King,' he said, rolling his eyes. 'Barely fanged. What in Hel are we coming to, brother?'

For a moment it looked as though Váltyr had an answer. Then the blade-master shook his sleek head.

'I really am the wrong person to ask,' he said.

Ingvar stood before Blackmane. Out of habit, his eyes ran over the Jarl's armour, scanning for weaknesses, assessing strength, gauging the likely route of attack. The process was automatic with him, as unconscious an act as breathing.

The experience was sobering. When Ingvar had last served as a member of the Rout on Fenris, he had barely known the name Ragnar Blackmane – a Blood Claw in Berek's Great Company, already tipped for an illustrious future, but no more so than many of the headstrong berserks they pulled off the ice.

Now, six decades later, the whelp had grown. Ragnar's face still had the supple bloom of youth but his armour was scarred as badly as any other Jarl's, draped with age-bleached trophies of a hundred kills and carrying the clenched-fist sigils of Berek's old company amid the howling wolfs-head device of his own. The blackmane pelt was slung over rune-graven shoulder guards, tight with weathering. A huge chainsword hung idle at his side, chipped and scratched from use.

Ragnar smiled, exposing short, sharp fangs. Glossy sideburns ran down each jaw, each as black as the long top knot that mingled fluidly with the pelt on his shoulders.

'I never knew you,' Blackmane said. 'I heard much, though.'

Ingvar bowed. He could feel every hair on his forearms standing up.

Why am I threatened by him?

'How does it feel to be back?' asked Ragnar, gesturing towards one of two stone benches. 'Strange?'

Ingvar sat on the nearest bench, feeling exposed without his armour. Even with *dausvjer* sheathed at his side, his grey shift and fur-lined cloak felt like flimsy protection against the Fang's permanent chill.

'Somewhat,' he replied.

Ragnar sat opposite. His movements were easy and unencumbered. The machine-grind of his suit's systems was barely audible. Something about him radiated confidence, ebullience, vigour. The Young King had none of the grizzled majesty of Grimnar, nor the raw elemental potency of Storm-caller, but now that Ingvar had witnessed him in the flesh he finally began to understand why he had been elevated so far and so quickly.

'I am curious,' Ragnar said. 'I served away from Fenris myself. What can you tell me?'

Ingvar didn't meet the Jarl's gaze.

'Little, I am afraid,' he said. 'Forgive me, lord, but...'

'...the Inquisition would have your lungs on a salver,' said Ragnar. 'And then mine. Very well, then – keep your secrets. But be aware: others will press you harder.'

'They are welcome to try,' said Ingvar. 'There's little to tell. The hunting was good. I learned the ways of others, they learned ours. After a while we worked well together. That surprised me.'

'But you were the strongest.'

Ingvar shrugged. 'I expected to be,' he said. 'Sometimes I was.'

Ragnar looked at him carefully.

'Service in the Deathwatch is considered an honour by many Chapters,' he said. 'Here it carries less weight. You broke your pack up when you accepted the summons to join them. I will be honest with you, Ingvar: if I had been Jarl when they came for you, I am not sure I would have given leave for you to go.'

Ingvar said nothing.

'Berek was indulgent,' said Ragnar. 'He had favourites, and he didn't care about appearances. Believe me, no one loved him more than I did, but we have to recognise fault when it appears. He saw something in you, Gyrfalkon, that much is certain, but you know what was on his mind at the time: Hjortur was dead, and Berek had no way of knowing what was intended for the pack.'

Ingvar listened silently, reluctant to hear old history recited again but unwilling to interrupt.

'Did it never occur to you that it looked like you were running away?' Ragnar went on. 'Gunnlaugur became Wolf Guard by default, without trial, without ever being pitted against you. You denied him that.'

Ingvar shook his head wearily. He had not expected an interrogation, and they were old allegations.

'I denied him nothing,' he said. 'The summons came and I accepted it. I would do it again. I am proud of what we did. I am proud of what my brothers did.'

'Which brothers?'

Ingvar realised that his fists had clenched tight, and relaxed them.

'All of them,' he said. 'All those who fought beside me.'

Ragnar nodded. 'Very good,' he said.

He cupped his hands. Ceramite clinked as he linked his fingers.

'Perhaps you think I'm being hard,' he said. 'I merely express sentiments that others will keep to themselves.'

'I can handle the others.'

Ragnar raised a ragged eyebrow over red-rimmed eyes. For the first time, Ingvar noticed that he looked tired.

'We have not escaped envy, up here in the realm of the gods,' Ragnar said. 'You think I am deaf to the whispers that run through this place? They say that I'm too young, that I should never have become Wolf Lord, that Berek was a fool to promote me.'

He smiled dryly.

'Berek had his weaknesses, but I do not doubt he was right. I have never doubted it. I have never listened to the whispers, but I know they are there. That was why I needed to speak to you. I needed to know that you were sure.'

'I don't understand,' said Ingvar.

'I feel certain that you do. But just in case, let me tell you what has taken place since you left us. Gunnlaugur has led Járnhamar pack with distinction. He has combined lethally well with Váltyr, but the whole group is strong. It has recovered from Hjortur's death and compensated for your absence. So now I have this dilemma: do I send you back to them? They could use another blade, but I fear for you there now. You were once a rival with Gunnlaugur for command – can you serve him?'

Ingvar looked up, directly into the tired eyes of the Jarl, meeting the gold-centred gaze.

'You shame me by asking that,' he said.

'I am not asking you anything. I am making up my mind.'

Ingvar felt his pride stir within him. It was hard to remember that Black-mane was elevated far above him in the arcane hierarchy of Fenris, that the Jarl's word was law, that if he ordered Ingvar into the maws of Hel then he was honour-bound to obey without question.

So young.

'Send me back, lord,' Ingvar said. The tone of his voice was less of a request and more of an insistence. 'Gunnlaugur was always ahead of me: he would have been *vaerangi* even if I had not left, and I would have followed him then. Nothing has changed. I belong with my pack.'

Ragnar's expression remained impassive.

'I did not know you then,' he said, 'so I cannot tell if the Deathwatch has changed you. They will know, though. If the Inquisition has turned your head then they will turn on you. Never forget what blood runs in our veins – we are wolves in temper as well as name.'

That was too much. Ingvar leapt to his feet, drawing his sword from its scabbard in a sweeping movement. He held it out, aiming the tip at Ragnar's throat.

'Do you know what this is?' he asked, his voice hard.

Ragnar regarded it coolly.

'It's a sword, Ingvar,' he said. 'I've seen plenty.'

He made no move to defend himself. Both of them knew how things stood: if Ingvar had truly been a threat to him, Ragnar would have killed him before the blade had left its sheath.

'It is *ancient*,' said Ingvar. He could feel his blood pumping in his temples. 'As old as this place. As old as the Annulus.'

Ragnar held Ingvar's gaze. 'This place is full of relics. What of it?'

'I was given this by Berek.' As Ingvar spoke, he remembered the events of decades ago with complete clarity. 'It belonged to him. Before him, it belonged to many others. It has passed through a hundred hands, each one leaving its imprint on the hilt. It has never been broken. The blood it has drunk would drown worlds. He honoured me with it, and I never used another, not even when they ordered me to take up xenos glaives that could carve Terminator plate like parchment. I carried it across the void with me, listening to its dry whispers of home, cleaving to what it reminded me of.'

The sword glinted in the semi-dark, its power field inoperative, the outlines of runes evident in thread-thin lines of silver.

'It has borne many names,' said Ingvar. 'Berek called it *fjorsváfi*. Others call it *helsverd*, and *blodstefna*, and *doomhringir*. Long ago it was *dausvjer*, carried by Ogrim Raegr Vrafsson in the age of legend. It is part of our life-blood. None but the elect will ever wield it.'

Ragnar's golden eyes flickered down to the point of the blade, and lingered there.

'Berek thought me worthy of it,' said Ingvar. 'The same who judged you worthy of elevation before your time. You trusted his judgement then.'

Ingvar held the sword level. The metal didn't move.

'I am a Son of Russ,' he said. 'I have nothing to prove.'

Ragnar's gaze snapped back up. For a moment, the two of them stared at one another. Blackmane's amber eyes scrutinised Ingvar's grey ones, narrowing fractionally, as if he somehow could penetrate into the soul beyond.

Ingvar felt the heavy pressure of Blackmane's countenance. Ragnar's stare was almost unbearable; it possessed an absolute conviction, a pure strain of certainty. No one, not Berek, not even Hjortur, had been able to project himself with such innate command.

The Young King.

Still the metal stayed level. Eventually, Ragnar shook his head wearily.

'Enough,' he said, gesturing for Ingvar to sheathe the sword again. 'This won't be decided by theatrics. Sit down.'

Ingvar did as he was bid. As he slid *dausvjer* into its scabbard, he suddenly realised how hard his primary heart was beating. He rested his empty hands on the cool stone of the bench.

'I like you, Gyrfalkon,' said Ragnar. 'I like your spirit.'

'Then send me back,' said Ingvar.

Ragnar smiled, but there was no warmth in it, just a wry grimace.

'Maybe,' he said. 'I'll reflect. You should do so too.'

Ingvar watched the Jarl carefully. Ragnar was a curious mix: insane levels of self-confidence coupled with a definite aura of fatigue. Perhaps command had proved harder than he'd anticipated.

'The galaxy is changing,' Blackmane said. 'Old Jarls lose their wisdom, young ones forget their strength. Stormcaller has dreams nightly that make him haggard, and he does not trouble easily. Even Grimnar laughs less than he did.'

The Wolf Lord placed his hands together again. Those deadly gauntlets, ones that had ended the lives of a thousand souls, formed a bulky pyramid.

'I would like to let Járnhamar remain here a while,' he said. 'They need to recover their strength. I would like to linger over this decision.'

Ingvar said nothing.

'But I cannot,' said Ragnar. 'We no longer have that luxury. We must keep fighting, all of us, without pause, and in such times wisdom is the first thing to fall away. I will make my decision quickly. You will know it soon.'

Ingvar bowed. 'And until then, lord? What I am to do with myself?'

'You still have your sword,' Ragnar said. 'Reacquaint yourself with the rites of your home world. Keep the edge sharp.'

Ragnar shot Ingvar a grim look. His youthful golden eyes reflected the light of fires wetly.

Confidence. Fatigue.

'Wherever I send you,' he said, 'you will have need of it.'

CHAPTER TWO

Hafloí ran.

He churned through the snow, throwing up sprays of crystal-white behind him. His hot breath condensed in the freezing air in plumes. His hearts hammered, his lungs burned. He felt the motive systems in his armour hum and boost, operating in perfect sync with his blood-flooded muscles.

The arc of the sky swung high above him, clear and vivid. Ahead of him lay a long sweep of fresh snow running down to the black line of the river. Tight clumps of *ekka* pines clustered over to his left, getting thicker towards the steep edges of cliffs beyond. This was hard country, traversed by gorges and broken rockfields, all hidden under glistening swathes of bridge-ice and powder snow. It was treacherous, frigid, lethal, exposed to flesh-scouring winds that screamed across the plains and scythed through shivering chasms.

Hafloí grinned savagely. All of Asaheim was hard country. That was the point of it. That was why he loved it.

He pushed himself harder, sprinting down the long incline towards the hard blue shadow-edge under the encircling peaks. His armour made minute adjustments as his boots crashed against the scree, compensating for ankle-turning crevasses, absorbing the shock of the uneven terrain beneath the pristine blanket of snow.

He ran like a hunted *skriekre*, pushing his enhanced body to the limit. He leapt clean over obstacles, crashed through waist-high drifts. His limbs pumped, his arms swung, his shoulders rolled.

For a few seconds more he was alone in the valley, charging down towards the rushing water, a lone speck of movement amid the glacial indifference of Asaheim.

Then the gunship crested the sawtooth ridge behind him, growling up into the air on a column of oily smoke. It lurched up, around, swinging over the lip of the rise and out over the valley floor.

Set against the majesty of the high plateau, the gunship was an aberration. It was heavy, blunt, crude, expending staggering amounts of energy just to stay aloft. Its engines roared with a thrashing, hungry growl, and it stank of burning promethium. Its wedged nose hung low as it surged forwards on a dirty bloom of heat-haze.

Hafloí heard it coming and kept grinning. He never slowed, just carried on racing. Already going at full tilt, he swerved and veered closer towards the riverbed, zigzagging wildly along the tumbling slope.

The gunship came after him, dipping its cockpit and plunging low across the snowfield. As it roared closer its heavy bolters keyed up, clanking as gigantic magazines were shunted into cavernous chambers. A second later and the linked barrels slammed into life, hurling twin lines of shells at the fleeing figure below.

The rolling barrage crashed into the ground in hissing furrows of exploding rock and vaporising snow. Hafloí bucked and darted left, dancing clear of danger, jerking round suddenly and haring off towards the rapidly approaching tree line. Splatters of blackened slush streaked down his armour as he rode out the onslaught before breaking free.

The gunship roared past him. It climbed quickly, banked hard and came around for another pass, trailing its filthy curtain of smog behind it.

Too slow, thought Hafloí with satisfaction, vaulting over a cracked ledge before powering down a slope of jagged rocks and ice towards the first of the pines.

He covered the ground quickly, hearing the grind of the gunship's engines grow louder with every stride he took. Just as he sensed the bolters click into firing positions he crashed into cover, shouldering through the dense, dark foliage as if plunging into water.

The trunks of the pines soared away above him like the pillars of some immense, shadowy cathedral. For the first time, Hafloí had cover. He ducked down low and slowed his pace, weaving through the snowy drifts piled high at the roots. The branches above him swayed in the wind, twisting back and forth and hissing at him.

Hafloí halted briefly, catching his breath, looking up into the branches. He could still hear the thudding whine of the gunship close by, but couldn't see it through the thick cover. He concentrated, filtering out extraneous factors, letting his superlative senses do their work.

'Oh, *Hel...*' he spat, suddenly realising where it was.

The trees around him blasted apart in a hurricane of splinters. Hafloí ducked and leapt, exploding back into action as the forest destroyed itself. He heard a crack, and another, as the massive trunks were brought down. One swayed towards him, toppling directly into his path as its base was blasted away by a flurry of bolter rounds.

He pounced out of its path, hearing the heavy whoosh of the trunk collapsing to earth behind him. More came down in a rain of severed branches and whirling needles. Gaps opened up in the canopy above, exposing the shadow of the hovering gunship and its juddering weapons.

Hafloí picked up full pace again, careering through the disintegrating forest. He vaulted over shattering stumps and ducked under collapsing beams. The air was choked with flying snow, rock shards and pulverised wood. He saw bolts impact on the earth around him and leapt out of their path.

He couldn't outrun the gunship, and with every passing second his residual shelter was being blasted away. As he ran, he swung his head frantically from right to left, searching for an alternative strategy.

'That'll do,' he muttered, spotting what he was after.

He skidded to a halt, throwing up a wave of scree and slush, then darted off to his right. The gunship adjusted course instantly, sending clattering bolt-rounds biting at his heels. Hafloí squeezed a few extra grammes of effort from his tortured limbs, sprinting hard down a steep bank as the remainder of his tree cover was ripped apart.

Then the land ended.

A dizzying precipice shot straight down, sheer and bald. Hafloí catapulted over the edge and out into the open. For a moment he was suspended in mid-air over a wide ravine, his legs and arms still pumping, wet debris showering over him from the exploding forest above.

He plummeted fast, dragged down by his heavy plate. Twenty metres below was a tangle of boulders, ice-plates and scrub. They all swept up to meet him with pitiless speed.

The gunship followed him over the edge, picking up altitude to break clear of the remaining pines before lowering its head again and resuming fire. Projectiles whistled past Hafloí's tumbling body, missing him by a hand's width.

Then he was down, crunching between two huge rocks the size of Rhino transporters. The impact was sharp, sending painful shudders up through his battered body.

He staggered, righting himself, and scrambled onwards, skidding and stumbling down narrow icy paths between the boulders, ducking into their cover as the fire from above fizzed and cracked around him.

The further he went the larger the rocks became. He'd entered a maze of overlapping stone slabs, the remnants of some massive earthquake or landslip. The boulders loomed up above him, capped with messy crowns of snow. The fissures between them were treacherous, clogged with glassy patches of ice.

Hafloí barged his way further down, scraping his shoulder guards against the walls of rock that surrounded him. He was soon enclosed on either side by bulwarks of stone. The sky above him shrank to a narrow strip of white.

The gunship thundered overhead, and the fire from its gun guttered out.

Hafloí allowed himself a smile. This was better cover – the granite boulders would take some shattering. He pressed on, going as quickly as he could in the labyrinth between the rocks.

The noise of the gunship faded into the distance, then grew in volume again as it came back around. Hafloí paused, listening carefully. He heard the telltale whine of a hatch door lowering while in mid-air, and the dull crunch of ceramite against stone as one of its occupants leapt to earth.

Hafloí drew his bolt pistol from its holster and kept moving. The icy corridors between the rocks ran like cracks across an ice-sheet – joining up, splitting apart, opening into open clearings or drying up altogether. He exchanged speed for stealth. He could hear dull footfalls running across the ravine floor: ceramite boots, crunching against gravel and frost, coming closer.

Too noisy, Hunter.

Ahead of him, Hafloí saw a narrow crevasse running in from the left and joining up with the one he currently occupied. Where the two fissures met was a small opening, no more than five metres across and overlooked by towering crags on all sides. The sounds of footfalls came down the left fork, getting louder.

Hafloí pressed himself into the shadow of the nearside boulder and aimed the pistol. A second later a huge grey-armoured warrior burst into view. He went helmless, exposing a shaven pate and black-streaked beard. He seemed to sense Hafloí's presence and turned to face him, lowering a boltgun.

Too late.

Hafloí fired, and watched the mass-reactive round spiral towards its target. The bolt hit the warrior square in the breastplate, sending him crashing into the far boulder.

'*Hjá!*' Hafloí crowed, drawing the sword at his belt and preparing to leap after him.

'Careful, now,' came a low voice at his ear.

Hafloí froze.

Gingerly, he looked down. A naked blade rested against his throat, barely touching the skin. If he'd have pounced, he'd have cut his throat open.

'And that makes you dead, whelp.'

His hearts still beating hard, he slowly let his hands fall to his sides. The blade was withdrawn.

The warrior he'd downed pushed himself away from the stone, moving stiffly. His big, ugly, snub-nosed faced was creased with laughter.

The second warrior stepped away from Hafloí, coming round from where he'd crept up behind him. The three of them – two Grey Hunters, one Blood Claw – faced one another. From some distance, the growl of the gunship could still be heard. The lower pitch of its engines indicated that it was coming down to land.

'*Skítja.*'

Hafloí spat on the ground. He slammed his pistol back into its holster.

Olgeir, the big one he'd managed to hit with his neutered bolt-round, the one they called Heavy-hand, came over to punch him on the shoulder. The gesture was possibly intended to be affectionate; it felt like a slug from a lascannon.

'Careless, lad,' said Olgeir.

Olgeir's gnarled face was encrusted in an impossibly dense mix of scar tissue, tattoos, ironwork piercings and curls of dark, stray hair. His streaked beard was full and unruly, cascading in snarls and braided twists over his full breastplate. For the exercise he'd reluctantly left his heavy bolter, the beloved *sigrún*, behind, and he looked strangely massive without it.

Olgeir's companion shot Hafloí a dry smile.

'You did well to outrun Jorundur,' he said, stowing his blade. 'He won't be happy about that.'

Baldr Fjolnir was easier to look at than his larger battle-brother. His beard was less ragged, his skin less tortured by burns and scores. He was lean, compact, with a mouth that tended to smiles and clear amber eyes. He wore his hair long, and it still bore traces of the sandy blondness it had had when he'd been in the Claws himself.

'You were waiting down here?' asked Hafloí, rubbing his neck ruefully. 'I only heard one of you land.'

Olgeir laughed again. His ugly face seemed made for it – a low, rumbling, throaty sound that rolled up from the curved barrel of his chest.

'Not too bright,' he observed.

Baldr was still smiling. There was no malice in the expression. The fair-haired warrior hardly looked capable of the extreme violence that his profession demanded, though Hafloí wasn't stupid enough to doubt that he was perfectly capable of it.

'We jumped together,' Baldr said. 'Make a note: that's something an enemy might try. They're unfair like that.'

Hafloí wasn't in the mood to be baited. As his body recovered, his pride slumped further into a low, surly frustration.

'*Morkai,*' he swore, letting his head fall back and rolling it around. As the adrenaline stopped pumping, he could feel a whole cluster of aches and pains gathering to assail him. He'd pushed himself hard that time – harder than ever. 'This is a joke. *A joke.* It's not possible.'

Olgeir raised an eyebrow. 'You think?' he said. 'So little faith – I think you'll do it.'

Hafloí rounded on him then. He was exhausted, driven to the edge by the endless drills, the ceaseless challenges, the days he'd already spent being tested by members of a pack he'd never even wanted to join. He hadn't done any proper fighting for weeks. He hadn't fired a proper gun, or run at a real enemy with a real blade.

'Fight me here, then,' he snapped. 'One on one – I'll break your fat neck.'

Olgeir chuckled approvingly. Baldr shook his head.

'No, you won't,' he said calmly. In the distance, Hafloí heard a muffled crunch as the Thunderhawk landed. 'You'll come with us, and I'll show you what you did wrong.'

The Grey Hunter looked at Hafloí, and his expression was serious. As he returned the gaze, Hafloí realised, as he had done a dozen times already, that he had no choice.

'Then we'll do this again,' said Baldr. 'And again. Right until you find a way to kill us, just like we asked you to.'

The air was hot, sweltering in a haze of seamy darkness. Clangs boomed through it, rhythmic beats like the drums on an ancient slave galley. Sparks showered, bounced and died on the stone floor, hurled from the glowing, gaping jaws of a thousand foundries.

Gunnlaugur looked up, away from the magma-light of the forge floor and up towards the distant roof. He couldn't see it. Thick columns of smoke swam up into the heights, pooling and drifting before being filtered up through hidden vents. The cacophony of the forging went with them – a discordant, overlapping strain of heat-softened metal being beaten into shape by ranks of vast, tilting hammers.

Molten steel ran down gullies like river water, spitting and frothing as it slopped over the sides. Bloated calderas tipped up, sending fresh gushes into waiting moulds. Conveyor belts of segmented adamantium rolled endlessly, shunting metal from bulbous cooling vats, to anvils, back to the furnace, on and on in a round of hammering, shaping, folding, tapering and tempering until the proto-weapons emerged, carried off reverently by dull-eyed servitors for the benediction and finishing of tech-priests and Iron Priests.

Above it all hung the silent images of the ancient forge gods, picked out in beaten bronze and mounted on pillars of stone. As the army of semi-human artificers laboured, those bronze images flickered and glowed in the sullen light of eternal fires, staring calmly and inscrutably across the shifting gloom of the Hammerhold.

Gunnlaugur looked away from them and strode past the ranks of machines. He had not been down into the depths for a very long time, but it looked much the same as it had on every previous occasion. The smell of it was oppressive – a sharp, acrid cocktail of smog, steam and sweat that lodged in his nostrils and wouldn't budge. There was barely room to swing an axe; none to run. It was claustrophobic, a vision of the underworld dragged up into the realm of the living.

Few Sky Warriors came to the Hammerhold without good reason. Gunnlaugur was no exception. It took him over an hour to find the one he was looking for, and it led him far away from the clamour of the main halls. Eventually retracing the routes he had taken last time, he slipped into side vaults and down cargo ramps, dodging the heavy crawlers that ground their way up from the deep-bore ore silos.

The booming clangs receded into a low murmur. A more modest vault awaited him – less than twenty metres in height, less than thirty wide. No icons of gods hung from the blackened ceiling, just bare stone worked into gothic arches. A single anvil rested in the centre of the chamber, black and heavy-set, shiny in the darkness. A furnace the height of two mortal men stood beside it, lit with shimmering coals that made the narrow opening shake with heat. A few other items stood beside the furnace – a rack hung with dozens of metalworking tools, a cauldron of water, iron caskets full of ingots – but otherwise the space was almost bare.

No servitors droned around that place; no conveyor belts brought raw materials to the hammer's bite. Less than one weapon a year left that anvil, and many more were destroyed by their maker before they reached the Iron Priest for blessing.

Few ironworkers would have had their painstaking energies so indulged by the Jarls. Arjac, though, the one they called Rockfist, was a special case.

The man-mountain stood over the anvil like a frost giant bearing down on a prone victim. His thick armour-plate shone blood-red in the light of the furnace, picking out the battered runes that ran down the length of his arms. His bald head hung low over his work, streaked with dirty sweat.

A blade lay on the anvil-top, shining with ruddy heat. Arjac worked it skilfully, using a light hammer to hone the edge down to a bite point. The image was incongruous – Arjac's immense body, bulked out further by thick sweeps of ceramite armour, tapping delicately at the sliver of metal before him.

Gunnlaugur said nothing. He remained in the shadows, watching respectfully. Arjac never looked up. The hammer rose and fell, glistening from the firelight, chipping out sparks as the impurities in the metal were beaten out.

Eventually Arjac snatched the blade away and plunged it into the cauldron. A swollen bloom of steam hissed up around it. He withdrew it and brought it into the light of the furnace. He turned it over and over, scrutinising what he had done.

The blade was the length of his forearm, ideal for a duelling gladius. Gunnlaugur looked at it appreciatively. His was no trained eye, but he knew how to use a sword, and it looked like he could use that one.

'Fancy it, stripling?' asked Arjac, never lifting his head.

Gunnlaugur smiled. 'For me?' he said.

Arjac let the metal fall back on the anvil.

'For no one,' he sighed. 'It'll be melted down, just like the others.'

'Seems a waste.'

'A waste? Of what – metal? There's more down here than we could use in a thousand years.'

Arjac straightened out of his stoop. Fully extended, his bulk was even more intimidating. Gunnlaugur, whose own physical presence was immense, seemed almost slight in comparison.

'A waste is sending a warrior out with a defective blade,' Arjac growled, rolling his great shoulders in slow circles. 'In any case, only an idiot goes into battle with a sword.'

Arjac's huge thunder hammer, *fomadurhamar,* hung from an immense iron frame at the rear of the chamber. Even powered down, it exuded a quiet air of implacable solidity – much like its master.

'Agreed.'

Gunnlaugur's preferred weapon was also a thunder hammer, one that shared his moniker – *skulbrotsjór* – safely stowed over the war-altar in his personal Jarlheim chamber. The two warriors shared a similar view of much in life, including which was the proper tool to break heads with.

Arjac came around from the far side of the anvil and approached Gunnlaugur. The furnace-light exposed a brawler's face, broad from tight bands of muscle, lodged deep amid stocky neck-sinew and his armour's fibre-bundles.

For a moment, Arjac looked straight at Gunnlaugur, appraising him as he would a newly-worked slab of metal. Gunnlaugur wouldn't have let many look at him like that – since being elevated to Wolf Guard, only Jarl Blackmane, the Priests and Grimnar himself had the authority to subject him to any kind of scrutiny.

Arjac, however, was different. Arjac was exceptional in every respect. His blood was that of an Iron Priest's, as was his temperament. Only his peerless skill at close range combat had kept him away from the lava forges where he longed to be. Gunnlaugur knew, just as everyone else knew, how much Arjac yearned to settle back among the true weaponsmiths, crafting artificer axe-heads and lightning claws among the silent, brooding anvil-masters.

But Arjac never complained. That generated a respect in the halls of the Fang. It had made him the first mentor Gunnlaugur had ever sought during his centuries of service in the Rout. To his surprise, Arjac had been receptive. Perhaps the Anvil of Fenris had seen something of himself in the raw Gunnlaugur. Perhaps, since he was rarely approached for serious counsel, he welcomed the chance to pass on some of his accumulated battle-lore.

Whatever the reason, the two of them always met on the rare occasions when both were present on the home world at the same time. Gunnlaugur had benefitted much from the exchanges. He hoped, perhaps optimistically, that Arjac had as well.

'You look bad,' said Arjac.

'As would you, if you'd been where we've been.'

'No doubt. How runs the pack?'

'Blooded,' Gunnlaugur said, truthfully enough. 'We're down to five. Losing Tínd caused us problems, but we did what we were sent to do, and most of us got back home.'

Arjac grunted. The big warrior seldom spoke much, and when he did he was curt.

'Glad you did,' he said. 'Now, why are you here?'

Gunnlaugur took a deep breath. His eyes flickered over to the anvil again, over to where the discarded blade lay cooling.

'We'll leave again soon,' he said. 'Blackmane wants us to take on a Blood Claw. He may want us to take Ingvar Eversson back too.'

Arjac raised a charred, stubbly eyebrow.

'The Gyrfalkon? He'll come back,' he said. 'Why pretend otherwise?'

Gunnlaugur shrugged. 'Because I do not know how to handle him,' he said. Anything less than full honesty was a waste with Arjac. 'Not any more.'

Arjac looked at Gunnlaugur steadily. His golden eyes were unwavering, the same eyes that could detect minute flaws in steel while it lay under the hammer.

'You really want my counsel?' asked Arjac. 'I'm not a Jarl, nor a Priest. You could speak to Blackmane yourself.'

'I could.'

'But you won't.'

Gunnlaugur shook his head. 'I don't think so.'

'You're a fool. One day you'll see why Grimnar thinks so highly of him.'

Gunnlaugur felt his heart sink. He didn't know what he wanted from Arjac. He didn't even know why the issue with Ingvar was exercising him so much. In the fifty-seven years since Hjortur had died he had never felt the burden of command weigh heavily at all; now, suddenly, it seemed like one of Arjac's anvils, shackled to his ankles and dragging him down into the abyss.

'I've built the pack around me,' he said, speaking half to Arjac, half to himself. 'Váltyr's my sword arm – I've learned to use him, and time has only made him deadlier. Baldr and Olgeir are as dependable as Freki. Jorundur is a sour old hound, but he's got his uses and flies a gunship like it's an ice-skiff. I'm proud of all this. I would not see it broken.'

Gunnlaugur shook his head.

'There's no room for him,' he said. 'Not now. He made his choice.'

Arjac's expression remained static – not judging, not scornful, not sympathetic. Like the rock that gave him his moniker, he was unmoveable.

'Then you must defy Ragnar,' Arjac said. 'But tell me truly, stripling: is that really what disturbs you?'

Gunnlaugur looked up. 'What do you mean?'

'You are Járnhamar's *vaerangi*. If your pack is your concern, then stand up to the Jarl over it – he may not bend, but he will respect you. But if *you* are the problem, if your weakness is the issue, then he will laugh in your face and cast you from his presence like a churl. I have heard the Young King likes to laugh – he will not need a good excuse for you.'

Gunnlaugur felt a flash of anger, a stab of the pride that always lurked just beneath the surface with him. Instinctively his right hand curled into a fist.

Arjac was quicker. The huge warrior shoved Gunnlaugur away from the anvil, pushing him hard in the chest. His expression flickered into something harder: contempt, spiced with the first spikes of combat-fury.

Off balance, Gunnlaugur stumbled backwards. He hit something as he staggered – a weapons rack – and metal blades and hilt-pieces clattered to the stone around him.

'What is it, Wolf Guard?' mocked Arjac, striding after him, his enormous fists poised to strike. '*Afraid* of the Gyrfalkon? Has your blood run cold since you last sparred with him as an equal?'

Gunnlaugur kicked back, thrusting himself at Arjac. The two of them crashed together, grappling like two old bears in a cave.

'I fear *nothing*!' Gunnlaugur roared. His arms clasped around Arjac's torso, and he pushed back violently. 'You *know* this!'

Arjac took the strain, and a strange sound burst from his mouth. Half blinded by rage, Gunnlaugur nearly missed it, already pulling his fist back ready for the punch.

Then he recognised the grating chortle, the closest Arjac's forge-dried throat ever got to genuine laughter.

Gunnlaugur halted, the momentum suddenly gone from his furious assault. He broke clear of Arjac, his cheeks flushed crimson, and spun away from the embrace.

Arjac regarded him tolerantly, smiling all the while.

'Good,' he said. '*Good*. For a moment I thought you'd lost it.'

Gunnlaugur caught his breath, his anger replaced, just as quickly as it had arrived, by shame.

Why am I so quick to wrath? he thought. *Why am I so easily goaded?*

Arjac returned to the anvil, still chuckling.

'You're letting this get to you, stripling,' he said, picking up the blade and looking at it again. 'Hjortur would have named you pack-leader if he'd lived long enough to choose. Blood of Russ, *I* would have done – you can hit hard enough when you want to.'

Gunnlaugur let his arms fall to his sides. He felt strung-out. One mission after the other, year after year; it would take its toll eventually.

'So what would you do?' he asked.

'With Eversson? I'd welcome him as a brother. I'd want a blade of his pedigree in the pack. If he challenged me, I'd beat him down. If he challenged the others, I'd foster it.'

Arjac ran his gauntlet along the edge of the anvil.

'A pack is a sacred thing,' he said. 'It has a life of its own, greater than ours. You cannot control that life, you can only guide it a little. If fate brings you and Ingvar back together, the pack will shape itself around both of you, one way or another.'

Gunnlaugur listened.

'Pride makes you strong, stripling,' said Arjac. 'Let it make you stronger – you deserve to be where you are – but do not let it blind you. None of us is greater than the pack. In the final reckoning, the pack is what must survive.'

Arjac's eyes lost their focus. It was as if he were addressing himself as much as Gunnlaugur.

'Remember this,' he said. 'You, me, Ingvar, the Old Wolf himself, we are nothing in isolation. We only live for the pack: that is what makes us deadly, what makes us eternal. Nothing else matters.'

Gunnlaugur bowed. He had his answer. He had what he had come for.

'I understand,' he said.

Arjac nodded.

'Good. Then you can leave me to work.'

'I can. My thanks, lord.'

Arjac scowled. 'Do not call me that. We are the same rank.'

Gunnlaugur smiled to himself. For a moment, he had genuinely forgotten.

'Of course,' he said.

Wolf Guard. Vaerangi.

Arjac took up a hammer again. That was the cue to leave, and Gunnlaugur turned back towards the distant roar of the Hammerhold. He walked slowly, turning Arjac's words over in his mind.

We only live for the pack.

They were familiar words, but it felt strange to be reminded of them.

That is what makes us deadly, what makes us eternal.

With every step he took, he felt a little stronger.

Nothing else matters.

CHAPTER THREE

The Thunderhawk *Vuokho* stood on the apron. Steam drifted up its ugly, chipped grey surface as the ice it had picked up on the way in evaporated in the heat of the hangar. Beyond it, further along the cavernous interior towards the entrance ramps, servitors and kaerl ground crew clattered and banged their way through a thousand menial tasks. The gunship hangars of the upper Valgard were never still; always the constant growl and whine of engines cycling up, or the tinny clunk of weapons being loaded, or the rumble of refuelling tankers crawling across the rockcrete floor.

Jorundur Erak Kaerlborn, the one they called Old Dog, looked over his pride and joy with a watchful, cynical eye. He knew every centimetre of its surface, and each fresh scratch or dent annoyed him a little more. He didn't care about the way the thing looked – given his own dark-eyed, sunken-cheeked visage, that would hardly have been reasonable – but he cared deeply about how it flew. *Vuokho* was as much a member of the pack as he was, a part of the whole, a component in the system. If it were ever lost then they would grieve for it as much as they had done for Tínd; perhaps more, for Tínd had been a difficult one, given to rages and with a fair slice of Gunnlaugur's fierce pride boiling away within him.

Jorundur didn't like taking *Vuokho* out on training missions. The machine-spirit hated the charade of it – it had been bred to hunt, just as they had been. If he had had his way he would have been left on his own with it more often, taking it out and up into the high atmosphere where the sky fell into nightshade-blue and the stars dotted the arch of the void. That was where its engines operated at the perfect pitch of efficiency, where the true power of its thrusters could be unleashed in bursts of furious velocity.

In space, a Thunderhawk was a clumsy, compromised thing, hampered by atmospheric drives it couldn't use; on land it was a bulky monstrosity, squatting against the earth like a deformed mockery of a prey-bird. Only in the inbetween spaces, the thin airs where void and matter met, only there was it unsurpassed.

'Brought it back safely, then,' came a voice at Jorundur's shoulder.

He didn't need to turn to see who was speaking. He carried on staring at the gently cooling chassis, moving his glistening, scrutinising eyes slowly over its outline.

'This time,' he replied as Váltyr drew alongside him.

Jorundur was not sociable. He had none of Baldr's easy manner nor Olgeir's generous humour. Of all of Járnhamar, Jorundur found Váltyr the easiest to rub along with; the two of them shared an appreciation of the colder side of killing.

'What did you make of him?' asked Váltyr.

'The whelp? He can run. I've seen him fight. He'll be all right.'

Váltyr nodded. 'We need new blood,' he said. 'Things have felt... tired.'

Jorundur gave a dry snort.

'That's because they are.' He drew closer to Váltyr, and lowered his voice. As he did so, lank grey-black hair fell around his face. 'Everyone is tired, blademaster. If they keep sending us out, year after year, with no chance to breathe or retrain or remember what we're doing, we will be more than tired – we'll be dead.'

Váltyr didn't pull away.

'Times are hard,' he replied evenly. 'What do you want? A soft bed and a weekly steam-bath?'

'I wouldn't turn it down.'

'No, perhaps you wouldn't.'

Jorundur was older than the next most experienced member of Járnhamar by a good hundred years. In the normal run of things he'd have shifted sideways into a heavy weapons squad a long time ago, taking his place amid the hoary old veterans with their gnarled gun-hands and *konungur*-tough hides. No one knew why he'd resisted it, staying in the ranks of the Hunters even as the chance for promotion to the Guard had passed him by. Some said it was because he lived for flying and would have missed the chance to pilot a gunship, others that he found the company of Long Fangs even more objectionable than that of anybody else.

Jorundur was happy with the speculation; he liked to keep people guessing and never explained himself. In any case he knew well enough that Gunnlaugur needed to keep him in the pack. Things had long been too straitened to countenance the departure of a seasoned pair of weapon-arms, no matter how pinched-faced and snipe-tongued their owner was. As things had turned out for him, that was good enough.

'So is this thing combat-ready?' asked Váltyr, moving away from Jorundur to inspect the flanks of the Thunderhawk.

Jorundur followed him.

'What do you mean?' he asked, feeling suddenly uneasy. 'We're going back out? Already?'

Váltyr nodded, reaching the first set of wings and running his finger along the thick leading edge.

'Like you said, they will keep sending us on these missions.'

Jorundur spat on the ground, shaking his shaggy head in disgust.

'*Morkai's teeth*,' he swore. 'We're not ready. Olgeir could spend three weeks with that whelp and we still wouldn't be ready. Who'll take Tínd's place? Arse of the Allfather, this is pathetic.'

Váltyr smiled. 'I knew you'd be pleased,' he said. 'They've given us two days, and this thing needs to be fully operational. They're loading up a frigate right now. I've seen it. It's a shit-bucket, but it looks fast.'

Jorundur spat again. He could do that all day.

'Where, then?'

'Ras Shakeh.'

'Never heard of it.'

'Two months away, on the fringes of protected space. Grimnar thinks we need to be pushing out a bit, extending our reach as others withdraw theirs.'

Váltyr reached up towards a cracked picter-lens embedded halfway up *Vuokho*'s cockpit armour, but Jorundur slapped his hand away.

'*Lunacy*,' hissed Jorundur, rounding on Váltyr and prodding him in the chest, pushing him away from the sacred adamantium. 'We need to retrench, not expand. Will someone ever tell the Old Wolf that we're all taking losses? Does he think that we can pick up the slack of every half-manned Chapter in the segmentum?'

'Actually, I think he does think that.'

'Then he's as stupid as he is stubborn.'

Váltyr sighed. 'Tell him that, then,' he said. 'Gunnlaugur will brief the pack when things are settled. I came up here because I thought you'd be pleased to see some real action.'

Jorundur paused. That was a reasonable point.

He looked up at the gunship's still-hot engines, mentally running down the list of repairs he'd intended to hand to the Iron Priest. Some of them might be possible in two days, and a few more could be carried out on board the frigate, but most would have to wait.

It was the incompleteness that irritated him, the constant harrying from one job to the next, never leaving enough time to work on something properly, always patching up, shifting out and making do.

Perhaps that was his age talking. Maybe that had always been the way, and he'd just tolerated it back then. Or maybe things really were getting worse.

'I'll get it fixed up,' he said, grudgingly. 'But tell Skullhewer it won't be in ideal shape. One big hit, and–'

'I'll tell him,' said Váltyr, already walking away. 'Just do what you can – I've a feeling Gunnlaugur has more pressing concerns right now.'

'Like what?' asked Jorundur.

'You'll find out,' said Váltyr, his voice as dry as ever.

Ingvar spun tightly on the ball of his right foot, thrusting out with *dausvjer*, sending the blade low and hard. Then he pulled it back, withdrawing, curling his whole body up tight, generating momentum, feeling his muscles respond.

He repeated the movement, then again, each time adjusting the pace a little, angling the point a fraction more, testing his stance. The repetitions went on. Firelight danced around him, making his sweat-covered skin shine. He heard the crackle and snap of fuel in the braziers, tasted the charcoal in the air, smelled his own hot, ripe scent as his body worked.

The physical exertion helped his mind relax. It purged the residual sickness of the long void-journey, purifying him, restoring his animal vitality.

He would have preferred to have sparred with a drone, something that would have fought back, something he could have smashed apart and left in a pile of sparking debris across the floor of the training chamber.

But the Wolves didn't use training drones, so he was alone, going through the motions on his own, rehearsing sword-thrusts with imaginary opponents in the dark.

'Why don't you use them?' Callimachus had asked him.

Ingvar remembered the Ultramarine's studiously polite expression. Callimachus had been trying hard to be diplomatic, but it had been clear enough what he had thought.

'A drone doesn't attack you like a minded creature,' Ingvar had said. Back then he had been fresh out of Hjortur's old pack, contemptuous of the skills of those he'd been thrown together with. 'It has no soul, and a warrior needs a soul. We fight each other. We fight the enemy. That's the way to learn.'

The rest of the squad had remained quiet. Back then, Ingvar had assumed they were cowed by his confidence, his ebullient manner, the proud heritage of Russ that he wore nakedly over his dull black battleplate. Now he couldn't be quite so sure.

Callimachus had shaken his head.

'Forgive me, but it makes no sense,' he'd said. 'Why not send your neophytes into war with the skills they need?'

'They learn the skills in real combat, or they die.'

'Indeed. Which is a tragic waste.'

'Conflict tests the warrior.'

'Quite so – but the drone-drills prepare him. They are more flexible, perhaps, than you realise.'

Ingvar hadn't believed him. He hadn't believed him even after two more weeks at Halliafiore's training facility on Djeherrod when the punishing regime had driven him into a level of exhaustion he had never known before, not even on the Long Hunt back to the Aett. He hadn't believed him during the sparring sessions with the other members of Onyx Squad, when he'd been taken to the limit by all of them.

He'd only believed it truly when he'd finally come up against a Deathwatch-conditioned drone – a titanium-clad monster of spikes and flamers and needle guns that had swooped around the cage like a trapped wasp, anticipating every move he made, reacting with astonishing speed, nearly taking his arm off and breaking several fused-ribs before he'd finally managed to put it out of action.

After that he'd been a bit more circumspect. Callimachus, true to form, had been painfully generous about it.

'I entirely respect your way of war, Eversson,' the Ultramarine had said afterwards, picking his words carefully. 'Truly, I respect it. But is it possible that there might be some virtue in learning from precedent?'

'You mean the Codex,' Ingvar had said, back then barely knowing of what he spoke.

'It does have some uses.'

Ingvar pulled out of the manoeuvre, letting *dausvjer* drop. He had been practising for several hours; even his body had its limits.

The exertion had done him some good. The burn in his biceps and quadriceps had a welcome familiarity about it. It felt good to be back on the home world, surrounded by the totems and sigils of the past, steeped in the harsh grandeur of the Halls of Asaheim. He was adjusting. He was remembering.

He would have preferred to have sparred with a drone.

'My lord.'

The kaerl's voice came from outside the locked and barred door to the training room. Ingvar pushed his shoulders back, letting his muscles unwind, before giving the order to unlock.

'My apologies for disturbing you,' said the man, bowing deeply as the door slid back.

'What is it?' asked Ingvar, reaching for a cloth and wiping the sweat from his face and neck.

'Jarl Blackmane wishes to inform you that he has reached a decision. He thought you should know as soon as possible, since time is always short.'

Ingvar felt a sudden pang in his stomach, an unwelcome reminder of how tenuous his fate had been since returning to the Fang.

'Fine,' he said, barely looking at the man before him. 'I'll report to the Jarl.'

The man stared at the floor, as if embarrassed.

'That will not be necessary, lord,' he said.

Ingvar looked at him sharply. 'What do you mean?'

The kaerl hesitated, aware of the awkwardness of the tidings he'd been asked to convey.

'I am commanded to inform you that you are to report to *vaerangi* Gunnlaugur. He will brief you prior to deployment to the Ras Shakeh system. Questions, supplementary orders and equipment requisitions are to go through him. The Priesthood has been informed and records amended. All has been done that was required to be done.'

The kaerl swallowed.

'Congratulations, lord,' he said. 'You are once again a member of Járnhamar.'

CHAPTER FOUR

When the pack convened it was in their old staging chamber, the one they always used before leaving Fenris. The place was in the Jarlheim, tucked away behind a shaft that ran clear down into the Hould, linked to the rest of the Aett only by a single-span bridge of cold stone.

Gunnlaugur had found it, years ago. No one knew who had carved it out, nor what uses it had been put to over the thousands of years since the fortress had been delved. That wasn't unusual. Millennia of constant war meant that the Fang was usually under-populated, and whole sections of it had collapsed, or were flooded, or simply unexplored. Every so often, squads of kaerls would undertake expeditions into far-flung sections, hoping to open them up to habitation. Sometimes they would succeed and new chambers would be cleaned out and put to use. Sometimes they would return bearing artefacts from the forgotten past that none but the Wolf Priests knew what to make of. Sometimes they never came back. That too was not unusual; the Fang was not, and never had been, a safe place.

Gunnlaugur had never disclosed how he'd found the chamber. It was a long way from where he had his lodgings, and a long way from where the majority of Blackmane's Great Company made their base. The room was old, that was clear. Stone carvings on the walls had been worn smooth by the whining wind and cracked by frost. Runes of a strange design were still visible near the arched ceiling, hacked into the granite by long-dead hands. More than fifty warriors could have been housed there comfortably, though why such a hall had been delved so far from the major transit shafts of the Jarlheim was a mystery.

A carcass lay along one wall, the skeletal remains of a sea-going *drekkar*. The longship's planks had ossified generations ago, leaving a crusted, stony shell behind like the ribcage of a slain seawyrm. The metal *drakk*'s-head prow had survived somehow. It reared up into the roof of the chamber atop a sweep of smooth hull planks, gazing with empty eyes into the gloom.

It must have been a daunting task to have carried such a ship so high, right up into the heart of the old mountain, bracing it against the frost-sear wind and powdery dunes of snow. Perhaps the *drekkar* had been dismantled at sea level and reassembled inside the chamber, though Gunnlaugur preferred to believe that it hadn't. He liked to imagine a torchlit procession of Sky Warriors hauling the ship up from the turbulent, iron-grey seas, dragging it into the high places and towing it on rollers into the heart of the Fang. There were tunnels big enough to accommodate it and hands strong enough to lift it.

That still left the question of why they had done it, and for that he had no answer. Perhaps it had been the whim of a timeworn Jarl, sentimental for his old life out on the open sea. Perhaps it had been brought there by the Priests as part of some obscure rite to placate the soul of the mountain. Perhaps it had lain there, slowly crumbling, since Russ had walked among them.

Whatever the truth of its origins, the *drekkar* and its strange tomb had fallen out of memory in the centuries since its entombment. Like so much else on Fenris, the place had become a relic, a half-lost fragment of a rapidly disappearing past. The Allfather alone knew how long it had been there, slowly mouldering and freezing and wasting away.

Now the ship's tomb was Járnhamar's place, the chamber they came to before embarking out into the sea of stars. It had come to seem appropriate, to make their final vows to one another under the shadow of the *drakk*'s head.

Hjortur had always enjoyed the conceit. He'd liked to leap up onto the fragile decking, crushing it beneath his boots, roaring out old sea-commands in a tribal dialect none of the others could understand. They'd laughed at that, watching him flail around amid snapping spars and planks and roaring impenetrable orders.

Gunnlaugur smiled at the memory. Hjortur had been good for a laugh. He'd led the pack with blood on his claws and a grin on his scarred face. He'd been a proper Son of Russ, that one, a bloody-minded hound, a reckless, startling monster of unrestraint.

'Come on, then,' said Váltyr, impatiently. 'Let's hear it.'

Gunnlaugur didn't reply at once. He took a moment to study the pack before him, the remnants of one that had once been larger, the broken heart of what had fallen to his command.

He saw Váltyr looking back at him, with his pale, querulous face and penetrating gaze. He saw the pent-up energy in the blademaster's limbs, the locked-in power that could explode without warning into a nerve-blinding whirl of steel. He saw the calculation, the coolly competent analytical mind, the strategeo's sharpness. He saw the edge of insecurity, too, and saw the neediness.

His eyes moved to Olgeir. The big warrior stood at ease, his unruly beard spilling over his armour, his scarred cheeks creased in readiness for a toothy smile or saliva-flecked bellow. Gunnlaugur saw the wholeheartedness in that one, the generosity, the commitment. Olgeir was the rock, the foundation; he could never lead, but he could guide, and he could encourage. The Heavy-hand wanted for nothing more than he had. That was a weakness, a lack of ambition, but it made him invaluable.

Next was Jorundur, the Old Dog. He was sidelong, sideways, twisted and warped by age. Gunnlaugur saw the marrow-deep weariness in him, the pride, the cynic's lip-curl. But he could fly. By Russ, he could fly. And for all his sourness, the Old Dog had seen plenty and done plenty. He knew where many bodies were buried, and what paths had been trodden to take them there, and where the shovels had been hidden and in what forges they had been made. When Morkai came for him at last, a thousand secrets would sink into the soil forever.

In Jorundur's shadow was Baldr. That one was an enigma. So pleasant, so easy, so amenable. His voice was soft when he read the sagas, recounting old songs with perfect, plangent clarity. No one hated Baldr Fjolnir. He went through life like a sleek fish gliding through reeds, effortlessly, slipping into the path of least resistance. And yet, when he killed, there was something else there, something guarded, something clenched, something buried. Yes, Baldr was an enigma.

And then there was the new blood, the whelp, the stripling: Hafloí, standing apart, still strung between nervy bravado and sullen withdrawal. His red hair caught the firelight, stained vivid. He looked painfully young, as raw as a gash, lodged awkwardly out of his element. Gunnlaugur liked what he saw. Hafloí would learn. His fangs would grow, his pelt would grey, his spikiness would soften. Until then he would be good for them all. They would remember what it had been like when they had been the same way, stuffed smart with puerile bellicosity, vigour, petulance, enchantment – and with the galaxy laid supine before them, begging for glorious conquest.

'So?' pressed Váltyr.

Gunnlaugur looked back at the blademaster.

'Not yet, *sverdhjera*,' he said. 'We are not all here.'

'What?' blurted Hafloí, speaking out of turn, not yet knowing his place in the order. 'There's more of you?'

Gunnlaugur looked up, over the heads of the assembled pack, back towards the low, arched entrance to the chamber. As his eyes fell on the armoured figure standing beneath it a brief tremor ran through him.

Fifty-seven years. Still, I would recognise that outline anywhere.

'Just one more,' Gunnlaugur said, his voice soft.

Baldr was the next to sense it. He whirled round, his eyes alive with joy.

'Gyrfalkon!' he cried, rushing over to greet the man under the arch.

Olgeir was next, shoving Baldr aside to envelop Ingvar in a crushing, armour-denting hug, dragging him into the chamber like a hunter hauling his prize.

Ingvar staggered out of Olgeir's rib-cracking embrace, laughing, emerging into the firelight only for the crowd of bodies to obscure him again. Váltyr approached and gave him an awkward handclasp. Baldr clapped him on the back. Hafloí hung back.

Amid all of that Gunnlaugur caught a clear glimpse of Ingvar's eye, just for an instant. It looked a little harder, a little greyer. Otherwise it was the same, the face he had spent mortal lifetimes in the company of.

'Enough,' he said eventually, stilling the noise and movement. Despite himself, a broad smile creased across his face.

Now that I see you, despite everything, it feels good to have you back.

Gunnlaugur walked up to Ingvar. For a moment, the two of them stared at one another, caught in the awkwardness of the moment. Gunnlaugur was the bigger, the broader, his armour more decorated with hunt-trophies and his pelts richer and more numerous. For all that, there was little to choose between them. There never had been.

'Brother,' said Gunnlaugur.

Ingvar inclined his head cautiously. '*Vaerangi*,' he replied.

No one else spoke. Baldr stopped smiling and looked warily between the two of them. Váltyr watched carefully. The air in the chamber seemed to thicken, like the humid precursor to a fire-summer storm.

Then Gunnlaugur moved. He flung his arms wide, grabbing Ingvar and pulling him into a rough embrace.

'We have not been whole without you,' he said, low enough so that only Ingvar heard him.

Ingvar returned the embrace, and the ceramite of his armour grated against that of Gunnlaugur. His gesture spoke of relief, of appreciation.

'That is good, brother,' he said. 'I yearned to hear it.'

Then he freed himself, stood back and regarded the pack before him. The hard lines of his face softened a little.

'But who is this?' he asked, smiling. 'We take on children now?'

Gunnlaugur gestured for Hafloí to approach.

'Careful,' he warned. 'The whelp has claws. Hafloí, this is the Gyrfalkon. He once served with us. Now he's back.'

Hafloí bowed stiffly. 'I know the name,' he said. 'You bear *dausvjer*.'

Ingvar inclined his head. 'So I do.'

'There is a wyrd on that blade.'

'That's what they say.'

'Then it should not have left the Aett.'

Olgeir took a step forwards, ready to cuff Hafloí. Jorundur chuckled darkly as Ingvar raised his hand, halting Olgeir.

'Perhaps,' Ingvar said, fixing Hafloí with dead eyes. 'But the sword goes where I go. If you have an issue with that, you may take it up with us both.'

Gunnlaugur rolled his eyes. 'Blood of Russ,' he said. 'Just introduced and already spoiling for a fight.' He shoved Hafloí away from Ingvar, sending the Blood Claw staggering. 'You'll fit in fine.'

Then he turned to the rest of the pack. Seven-strong, back to something like combat strength. They looked to him expectantly.

'We are complete,' said Gunnlaugur. 'Just as we should be. Now listen: here's what we're going to do.'

Ingvar tried to concentrate on what Gunnlaugur was saying. He felt his palms grow slick under the lining of his gauntlets. Hearing the old voices again, the old smells, it had hit him harder than he'd expected.

They hadn't judged him. None of them had the reproach in their eyes that he'd feared. Well, Váltyr perhaps, but he had always been a cold one.

It was hard not to watch them sidelong, to observe the way they related to one another, to examine them like he'd seen biologis adepts examine xenos corpses on dissection tables. They were relaxed in one another's presence, just as he had been once. Onyx Squad, for all its combined killing power, had always felt like an artificial creation. Járnhamar had once been home; for those who had remained, it still was.

Ingvar's wandering gaze flickered up to the head of the *drekkar*. That eyeless stare was as familiar to him as everything else. He remembered it watching over them before each mission, gazing coldly into empty space as objectives were outlined and timescales plotted. The *drakk*'s face had never been anything other than impassive to him then. Now, on his return, it seemed almost benevolent.

In the past it had been Hjortur's voice that had rung around the chamber. Hearing Gunnlaugur's growly tones in its place was odd. For a while, it felt like a violation. Only later, as Ingvar watched the others take it in their stride, did it come to seem natural.

Gunnlaugur spoke with a coarse, blunt authority. He had always been confident, but now it was different. A warrior spoke one way when his own life was at stake; when he had the whole pack to think about, his tone changed.

It suits you, brother, thought Ingvar. *You have grown.*

'Ras Shakeh,' said Gunnlaugur, flicking the switch on a palm-held device and sending a flame-red hololith spinning up into the air before him. 'Shrineworld of the Ras subsector. It is under the Ecclesiarchy with distant support from the Adulators Chapter, though our brothers have declared themselves no longer able to contribute to its defence. They are stretched, I am told, to breaking point.'

Jorundur snorted, shook his head, but said nothing.

'Before the Ras worlds were taken under the control of the Imperial Cult,' continued Gunnlaugur, 'it is said that an arrangement once existed between them and Fenris.'

'By who?' asked Váltyr.

'By Blackmane,' replied Gunnlaugur, tersely. 'And by Ulrik, and by Grimnar, and whoever else remembers what in Hel we were doing five thousand years ago.'

Gunnlaugur's tone gave away what he thought of what he was being asked to convey. Ingvar felt his spirits sag. After the euphoria of his return, it looked like the task ahead of them would not be glory-filled. It sounded perilously close to routine garrison work.

'This is not garrison work,' said Gunnlaugur. 'It is the beginning of an offensive, a multi-front assault into abandoned space covering three subsectors. We are to be part of it.'

Olgeir nodded in approval. 'Good,' he grunted.

Baldr looked thoughtful. 'Under whose command?' he asked.

'A warmaster will be appointed,' said Gunnlaugur. 'Don't get carried away. This will be years in the making. We are the advance wave, sent to secure worlds prior to major troop movements. For a while it'll be just us.'

Jorundur chuckled. 'That's not garrison work?'

'We won't be sitting on our arses,' Gunnlaugur insisted. 'There's enemy activity on the fringes, more coordinated than normal, more frequent. We'll have hunting to do.'

Baldr's expression hadn't changed. He looked pensive.

Ingvar could sense the wariness in the room from the others. They weren't stupid. They could tell when they were being shunted off to a nothing-mission.

'Who governs this world?' asked Baldr.

'The Adepta Sororitas,' said Gunnlaugur. 'The Order of the Wounded Heart.'

The silence of the chamber was broken by a collection of low growls, noisy expectorations and bitter-edged laughs.

'Enough,' snapped Gunnlaugur. 'They're servants of the Allfather.'

'They're servants of the Inquisition,' said Jorundur.

'They're crazy,' grumbled Olgeir. 'With no love for us.'

Baldr smiled softly.

'When did you last care about being loved, great one?'

Olgeir grinned, and patted the battered casing of *sigrún*.

'When I was given this,' he said. 'Not since.'

'The Sisters,' said Váltyr, acidly. 'They know it's us that's coming? They asked for us?'

Gunnlaugur sighed. 'They'd take anyone. They're hard-pressed, just like everyone else. But, yes, they know it's us. Grimnar's sent word to the canoness. Get used to it, brothers. This is who we'll be fighting with.'

Jorundur shook his shaggy head. 'I can cope with Sisters,' he said. 'I can't cope with garrison work.'

'Hel's *teeth*,' hissed Gunnlaugur. 'How many times? This is a combat mission.'

'Against what?'

'As yet unidentified. Possible cult incursions. We're waiting for more detail.'

Jorundur spat on the ground.

'Sounds terrifying,' he said.

Gunnlaugur looked distastefully down at the pool of spittle on the stone.

'We leave in less than thirty-six hours,' he said. 'Use the time well. Ensure your armour has been sanctified by the Priests and look to your weapons. Take the transit-time to reach combat fitness. That is all.'

An awkward silence followed. Ingvar remembered how it had been in the past, when Hjortur's exhortations would have filled the chamber with echoing roars, and they would have raised their weapons as one, slavering for the coming blood-terror.

It was muted this time. Olgeir did his best, with a low, rattling snarl, but no one else took it up.

Gunnlaugur didn't try to summon up more enthusiasm. His customary belligerence had a darker edge to it, something that Ingvar didn't remember seeing in him before. As he turned to leave the chamber, his eye caught Ingvar's.

'Not what you're used to,' he said. 'Work like this.'

It wasn't.

I have seen hive-fleets block out the light of nebulae. I have seen the spawning

fields where orks are born. I have seen metal legions rise silently from millen-
nial tombs. I have seen living starships orbit the hearts of forgotten empires.

Ingvar shrugged.

'There'll be hunting,' he said. 'I'm used to that.'

Before leaving, each one of the pack came up to Ingvar. They were curious, asking about what he'd done while on duty with *the others* – they never called the Deathwatch by its name – how many kills he'd made, what sagas he'd recorded for inclusion in the annals of the mountain. Váltyr asked him little, Olgeir a lot.

Jorundur enquired about the onyx skull pendant he wore around his neck.

'A record of service,' said Ingvar, clasping it self-consciously. 'That and the bolter – it's all I kept.'

They seemed to understand that he couldn't say much. They seemed pleased that he was back. As they spoke to him, probing for information, laughing at his stilted responses, some of the awkwardness between them faded.

'You'll have picked up bad habits,' said Olgeir, his eyes sparkling. 'We'll have to beat them out of you.'

'Try it,' Ingvar replied.

Gunnlaugur left the chamber first, accompanied by Váltyr. Before he left, he clasped Ingvar firmly by the arm.

'We'll speak properly, brother,' he said. 'When time is less pressing, we'll talk.'

Ingvar nodded. 'We should,' he said.

Jorundur was next, curtailing his questions to go and work on *Vuokho*, muttering as he left about the stupidity of taking it out so soon. He didn't smile exactly, but his bitter face lifted and the bruise-coloured lines under his deep eyes smoothed out just a little.

'He's not looked this happy in a while,' observed Olgeir.

'It's all relative,' said Ingvar.

'He'll never admit it, but he missed you. Hel, *I* missed you.'

'It's good to see you too, great one.'

Then Olgeir departed as well, taking the Blood Claw with him for yet more intensive training. Hafloí didn't say a word to Ingvar, but shot him a sullen look of challenge from over his shoulder.

That left Ingvar alone with Baldr. The heavy footfalls of the others faded into the darkness, and the chamber fell quiet.

Baldr smiled. It was a plain, easy smile.

'You've made an enemy there,' he said.

Ingvar spread his hands in a gesture of resignation.

'A fearsome one,' he agreed.

'So, then. Tell me what you see.'

Ingvar hesitated. 'What do you mean?'

'Járnhamar,' said Baldr. 'Tell me how we've changed.'

'Tínd is gone. Ulf and Svafnir are gone. I'll be honest, I never liked Tínd, but I'm sorry for the others.'

Baldr raised a sceptical eyebrow. 'Is that all?'

Ingvar sighed. 'Fjolnir, do not do this. Not now.'

Baldr smiled. 'Forgive me,' he said. 'You are newly returned. There will be time for questions later. But you do not deceive me: you see what I see.'

'And what is that?'

Baldr looked serious again.

'You see Váltyr hanging in Gunnlaugur's shadow, unwilling to stay in it and unable to leave it. You see Jorundur turning in on himself, bitter at missed chances for glory. You see Heavy-hand's laughter becoming thinner since he no longer has Ulf to spar with.'

Ingvar sighed. He had no appetite for hearing how the pack had been ravaged in his absence.

'And what of you, Baldr?' he asked. 'I suppose nothing troubles you.'

For a moment, something flickered across Baldr's face – a faint play of unease, whispering around his golden eyes.

'There's trouble for all of us,' he said. Then he smiled again. 'I knew you were coming back. Something told me you were. Why is that? It's been decades, and I knew you were coming back.'

'Lucky guess.'

'There's no luck. There's fate, and there's will. If the will is mightier, then you carve out a life for yourself. If fate is mightier, then you're carried along, twisting like a spar on the flood.'

Baldr stopped talking, suddenly tense, as if he'd said more than he'd planned to.

'I knew you were coming back,' he said again. 'Why is that?'

Ingvar tried to shrug off the question, though Baldr's manner unnerved him. There was an intensity to him that he didn't recognise.

'You sound like a Priest,' he said. 'Stop it.'

Baldr reached for a pendant hanging around his belt then. He held it up: a bleached avian skull suspended on links of metal. Iron bearings had been hammered into the eye sockets, and a rough rune – *sforja* – scratched on the bone.

'Do you remember this?' Baldr asked, letting the hanging pendant turn slowly.

As Ingvar's eyes rested on it, he felt a sudden pang of memory. He reached out for it, letting the fragile skull clink against the palm of his gauntlet.

'I had forgotten,' he said softly. 'By Russ, I am sorry, brother. I had forgotten.'

Baldr lowered the pendant into Ingvar's hand, letting the iron links coil around one another.

'Don't be sorry. Take it back. You were right – it has a wyrd on it. It has protected me, and a part of me lives in it. For all that, it knows you are the owner.'

Ingvar took it and held it up against the red light of the braziers. He remembered giving it to Baldr as a token of their friendship on the night he'd left Fenris. Back then he'd had no expectation of seeing it again. It had been a piece of his life in the Rout that he'd left behind, a splinter of his being that wouldn't follow him into his new life.

A *sálskjoldur*; a soul-ward, a fragment, a remnant, something to cling on to against the coming of Morkai.

'I had not felt myself,' Ingvar said, gazing at the bone as it spun before him. 'Not until now. This is the final piece of me, the presence that I left.' He looked back at Baldr. 'It was given freely. I have no right to take it back.'

Baldr nodded. 'I know,' he said. 'But what are rights between brothers? It has been calling to you. It is yours.'

Ingvar regarded Baldr carefully.

'You asked me what has changed,' he said. 'You have. You are more solemn, more serious.'

He collected the coiled pendant in his fist and placed it around his neck. It hung down across his breastplate, nestling next to the onyx skull amid the crevasses of his embossed armour.

The two symbols occupied the same space uneasily: one a totem of Fenris's strange and ancient magic, the other a symbol of clandestine Inquisitorial power.

'But I thank you for this,' Ingvar said, taking Baldr's hand and clasping it firmly. 'We have always been shield-brothers, you and I. We shall be again. Of all of them, I suffered your absence the most.'

Baldr returned the grip firmly, almost hungrily.

'We have suffered without you, Gyrfalkon,' he said. 'We need you back. You will make us whole again.'

Ingvar released his grip. Talk like that made him uneasy; Gunnlaugur had used the same words.

'We shall see,' was all he said.

CHAPTER FIVE

The storm howled up from the Hunter's Pass, bringing snow-swollen clouds boiling over the sheer passes. The mountain's shoulders were lost in a haze of churning ice-white, piling up drifts against the old causeways and choking the ravines below.

Only at the summit of the Fang, high above the surrounding peaks of the Asaheim range, was the air clear. Thunderheads circled below the Valgard landing stages, angry and majestic, buffeting and snagging against the granite cliffs like breaking black-foamed waves.

Gunnlaugur studied the maelstrom remotely from the shelter of *Vuokho*'s cockpit, still waiting on the hangar apron.

'A big one,' he observed, watching the sweeps of brume and blizzard rotate on the auspex.

Jorundur, strapped in beside him, flicked the final launch controls on the console.

'Fenris always gives a send-off,' he said, frowning as he concentrated on the pre-launch sequence. 'She never likes to see her children leave.'

Gunnlaugur grunted, and sat back in his seat. Valgard hangar 34-7 stretched away from them, perched right at the pinnacle of the mountain and open to the elements at the eastern end. A maze of red lights blinked on and off, half hidden behind the veils of gusting sleet that spilled in from the entrance. He could hear the grind of refuelling tankers running clear, and the shouts of kaerls as blast-hatches were slammed and locked.

'Try not to kill us on exit, eh?' came Olgeir's cheerful voice over the comm. 'Nice and smooth now, Old Dog, nice and smooth.'

The rest of the pack were in the aft crew hold, below the cockpit. Gunnlaugur could hear coarse laughter in the background. That improved his mood. For all their complaints about the mission, the pack were glad to be under way and doing something, and that was reassuring.

'You want to fly, *hálfvit*?' replied Jorundur, his voice sour. He activated the main drive system, and a throaty, sclerotic roar broke out from below.

Olgeir's bellow of laughter made the comm-link crackle with feedback.

'Any signal from the frigate?' asked Gunnlaugur, shutting off the feed and watching the last of the ground crew scuttle out of view. The whole structure of the gunship shuddered as the engines gunned into their hammering rhythm. A messy tide of oil-speckled, fire-dotted smoke poured across the apron from the exhausts.

'Not a thing,' said Jorundur, easing power to the atmospheric retros. With a jerk, *Vuokho* lurched up from the rockcrete floor, buoyed by a raging cushion of flame and smog. 'But it'll be there. Believe me, no one else will have taken it.'

The lumen-bank mounted over the hangar entrance clicked off, and a whole series of indicators on the gunship's control console went green. The cockpit's head-up display flickered into life, overlaying a jumble of runes and vectors across the grimy viewers. The whine from the main drives intensified, ready for the explosion of energy that would hurl them clear of the mountain.

'It's a decent ship,' said Gunnlaugur, bracing for detonation. 'Blackwing-class.'

'That what they told you?' Jorundur laughed. 'I've seen it. It's a heap of shit.'

Before Gunnlaugur could reply, Jorundur switched power to the main thrusters. *Vuokho* pounced forwards, blazing down the short hangar length before thundering clear of the mountainside. They cleared the cliff face in a bloom of evaporating snow and engine backwash. Jorundur took the gunship out wide before banking hard, bringing the prow up and feeding more power to the main thrusters.

Gunnlaugur glanced down out of the port viewer. Below, already receding fast, was the pinnacle of the mountain, crusted with a dirty layer of sensoria towers, pockmarked hangar gates and defence batteries. The summit speared up through the moving layers of bruise-dark cloud, a lone bastion of rock and ice amid a continent's-worth of seething squalls.

It looked besieged. It looked as if the rage of the planet had closed in on it, throttling it, sweeping up to grab it by the neck and snuff the life from it.

Gunnlaugur knew the history of the mountain, at least as it was related by the overlapping and semi-legendary saga-tellings of the fire halls. He knew that the Fang had been besieged more than once: by the forces of the great enemy, by armadas sent by the Ecclesiarchy in the civil wars of the past, by the Inquisition itself.

Sky Warriors still boasted of those battles, chanting them in ritual war-rites or hearing them declaimed by the hot light of burning torches. Gunnlaugur loved them. He'd learned the Bjornssaga from the skjalds, word by word. He knew other legends by heart, other songs, some of them older than the Fang itself, their origins lost in the violent years of humanity's first stumbling amongst the stars.

He smiled as he remembered the stanzas. Even as the landscape dropped far below him, dwindling into a white haze, his mouth moved silently, speaking the eternal words soundlessly.

The sun turns black, earth sinks in the sea,
The hot stars down from heaven are whirled;
Fierce grows the steam and the life-feeding flame,
Till fire leaps high about heaven itself.

Seeing the proud spike of the mountain below made his hearts swell. That place was eternal, founded by gods and guarded by savage angels, an inviolable citadel amid a darkening galaxy. It had stood for millennia before his birth and would do for millennia after. Other worlds might fall into corruption or ruin, but the Fang would remain unsullied forever.

That was what he had always believed. That was what he still believed.

So it ever has been, he breathed, watching the sweep of the planet's atmosphere drop into a glistening curve. *So it ever shall be.*

Gunnlaugur knew that he could never have done what Ingvar had done. He was body and soul of the *Fenryka*: the most deadly, the most faithful, the most potent of the Allfather's many servants. No others compared with the Wolves of Fenris. No life compared to that of the Sky Warriors, lived without compromise or quarter, thrust into the white-hot core of combat, gifted the mightiest weapons of humanity, charged with its ultimate defence where all others faltered.

Gunnlaugur respected his brothers in other Chapters. He had fought alongside many of them, and recognised their skill and devotion. He had fought with mortal men too, many of whom had fallen with honour.

But they were not *Fenryka*. They were not Russ's sons.

Much do I know, and more can see.
The fetters will burst, and the wolf run free.

Gunnlaugur smiled. War was coming again. He was leaving the Fang, taking murder out across the sea of stars. Whatever else had transpired, that was good. It was the proper state of things.

'Clearing the grid, *vaerangi*,' said Jorundur, his voice barely audible over the roar of the engines. 'We'll get visual in a moment.'

Gunnlaugur looked out ahead. The milky grey of the sky had faded to black as the atmosphere thinned to nothing. Familiar constellations emerged into pure clarity, obstructed only by dozens of gunmetal-grey defence platforms in orbit above the planet. The closest of them was less than a kilometre away and hung massively in the void, the marker lights on its gun turrets blinking in the dark.

'I don't see the ship,' said Gunnlaugur, scrutinising the view forwards as the platform slipped by beneath them.

'I've got a fix,' said Jorundur. 'We're not at full tilt yet. You know this thing shouldn't even be flying?'

Gunnlaugur ignored the snipe. For as long as he'd known Jorundur he'd been complaining about the readiness of the ships he flew. He'd have found something to complain about if Russ himself had given him *Hrafnkel* to pilot.

'There it is,' announced Jorundur, gesturing to a glowing rune on the viewer display. 'Take a look at the realview. How sharp are your eyes?'

Gunnlaugur narrowed them, scanning the velvet darkness. For a long time, he saw nothing. Hundreds of vessels, from tiny system runners to gigantic capital ships, occupied the Fenris system at any one time, but few lingered for long in the planet's shadow.

Then he saw something glinting in the empty gloom like a sliver of alabaster. As Jorundur steered the Thunderhawk closer, details emerged.

It was small for a frigate, of an old design. The engine-level on it looked big; its weapons array looked small. Its shell was black, with old Rout images painted on the flanks in chipped yellow and grey. Its bridge was set lower than usual, surrounded by charred bulkheads. Faint plumes of gas vented from something jagged and reflective under its hull.

A single word, *Undrider*, had been etched along its side.

Gunnlaugur pursed his lips. 'That's the one?'

Jorundur nodded, bringing *Vuokho* to approach speed. As he did so, hangar doors on the receiving ship slid slowly open, spilling warm yellow light into the void.

'I'm told it's fast,' Jorundur said.

Gunnlaugur felt deflated. 'Right,' he said.

Jorundur smiled in vindication.

Heap of shit.

'Welcome aboard, lord,' said the *Undrider*'s master.

Gunnlaugur grunted acknowledgement, barely looking at him.

The master, an experienced kaerl rivenmaster named Torek Bjargborn, used to the perfunctory ways of Sky Warriors, didn't miss a beat.

'We're ready to go, on your order.'

Gunnlaugur's eyes roved around the command chamber. The pack stood alongside him. None of them looked impressed.

It was a small, cramped place by the standards of interstellar craft. The captain's throne was surrounded by concentric banks of cogitator stations. A dais had been raised behind it on which the pack had congregated. The floor was polished black marble. Cracks in it had been repaired with a dull grey aggregate.

Beyond and above the throne was a dome of bronze-lined crystal viewers, thick with tarnishing. As on all such ships, a low murmur of machine-clicks and human muttering provided a constant accompaniment to the grind of the sub-warp engines. An aroma of sacred oils rose from the deck, spiced with an undertone of human sweat and engine lubricant. Servitors, many hard-wired into consoles, clattered away at menial functions. There were more of them than usual, and fewer human crew.

'What's your complement status, master?' asked Jorundur.

Bjargborn didn't hesitate.

'Twelve per cent down, lord. But we do have extra servitor provision. Demands on the fleet are heavy, I'm told.'

The look on Jorundur's face said all that needed to be said.

Gunnlaugur turned to Váltyr. He gave a half-shrug.

'It only has to get us there,' he said.

'Can it even do that?' replied Váltyr.

Bjargborn had the stomach to look affronted.

'It will, lords,' he said. 'And back again. It may not look much, but it's voidworthy, and it's fast.'

'Yes, I'd heard that,' said Gunnlaugur. 'Very well, master, you have the order. Take us out to the jump-point. We'll cross the veil as soon as we can.'

Bjargborn thumped his chest, bowed, and resumed his seat in the throne. Around him the machine chatter picked up in volume.

Jorundur's nostrils flared. 'This ship stinks.'

'All ships stink,' said Baldr.

'Not like this one.'

'I've known worse.'

Gunnlaugur ignored the conversation. He walked slowly away from the throne, under the observation dome, looking out and up at the stars. The constellation of the Hewer was visible, framed by bronze.

In a few hours that view would be gone, replaced by heavy lead shutters to blank out the madness of the empyrean. On arrival at Ras Shakeh it would be replaced by an alien set of constellations, each with its own name in another language.

The underpowered ship irritated him. It pricked at his pride, wearing at it like acid on metal.

We cannot be that short-handed. It is an insult.

He flexed his fingers, trying to let his annoyance flow out of him. It would be some time before he could exorcise the emotion through combat.

Hjortur would have railed against this. He would have howled the Fang down until he got what he wanted.

He closed his fists, squeezing hard against the inner membrane of his gauntlets.

He could be a poor judge. There will be a time to howl; this is not it.

Gunnlaugur felt the floor beneath him vibrate as the frigate began to power up. That did something to ease his mood, and he felt his clenched hands relax a little.

At last.

For what it was worth, for what little it meant to him, the mission was underway.

Ingvar didn't sleep.

Warp travel always had the same effect. He felt nauseous, unquiet, unable to meditate, unable to think, unable to do much beyond prowl back and forth in his cell, his fangs bared.

A long time ago, back when he'd been a Blood Claw, he'd asked Hrald, the Wolf Priest, why passage through the empyrean affected him so badly, whether it spoke of some taint or flaw within him. The old hook-nosed warrior had looked deep into his eyes for some time before clapping him roughly on the shoulder.

'Who knows?' he'd said. 'The warp – it's Hel. You should hate it. Only worry if you come to like it.'

Ever since then he'd suffered in isolation, keeping himself locked away, breaking off contact with his brothers until the cramps and the dizziness faded.

Jocelyn had been scornful of that. The Dark Angel had been the one he'd had most trouble with in Onyx. The others had all rubbed along together well enough, but the pale-skinned son of Caliban had been difficult: proud, high-strung, close.

'Why does it make you sick, Space Wolf?' Jocelyn had asked him during a jump, his deep eyes suggestive of mockery as much as curiosity.

Distracted by his sickness, Ingvar had growled at him involuntarily. That alone had been a minor humiliation. His squad-brothers needed no extra inclination to think of him as bestial.

'Why does it *not* make you sick, Dark Angel?' he'd replied. 'Unless your kin feel at home here. I've heard that said.'

Jocelyn had laughed that off, not deigning to show anger. Later, Ingvar regretted the exchange. Matters never came to a head between them after that; equally, they never succeeded in breaking down that fog of early suspicion.

They became stereotypes of their Chapters with one another: the snarling Wolf, the haughty Angel. They should have done better, perhaps. It would have been nice to transcend expectations.

Ingvar reflected on that, alone in the practice cages of the *Undrider*, blade in hand, his stomach churning. He moved the sword back and forth, turning it under the harsh light of the lumens, finding some solace in the familiar rituals.

He wondered where Jocelyn was now. Perhaps he still served with the Deathwatch. Perhaps he was back on the Rock, rediscovering the ways of his old Chapter, just as he had done. Perhaps he was dead.

Ingvar would never know. He had no special access to information, no back-channel route to the Inquisition. They had severed things completely, rendering him as ignorant of future operations as he had been before they'd first come to Fenris to take him.

For all that, Ingvar found it hard to conceive of the universe without Jocelyn's sardonic presence in it. The Angel would be fighting somewhere, just like the others. All of Onyx Squad would be, scattered to the six corners of the galaxy, alone again, trying to relearn old lives, trying to forget what they'd seen together.

'Still don't like it?'

Ingvar didn't turn around. He'd not heard Váltyr enter the cage-room. That had been sloppy.

He completed the manoeuvre. His blade flickered in the semi-dark.

'Nothing changes,' he said, watching sidelong as Váltyr moved into his field of vision.

The blademaster wore his armour but went helmless, just as Ingvar did. *Holdbítr* was sheathed at his side.

'I couldn't sleep either,' said Váltyr. 'This ship creaks and moans like a skiff in a gale.'

Ingvar said nothing. He moved into another manoeuvre, one taught him by Leonides. It was a complicated, difficult switch, something that would seldom be used in real combat, mainly a means of training the mind to work with the blade. The Blood Angels had an interesting philosophy on close combat. As in all things, they valued the aesthetics of a gesture as much as its effect.

Váltyr watched him as he worked, peering through the wire of the training cage.

'You've learned new tricks,' he said. 'That was not taught on Fenris.'

Ingvar let *dausvjer* fall away.

'Too artful for the likes of us.'

Váltyr smiled. 'Don't let Gunnlaugur hear you say that,' he said, reaching for the door to the cage. 'May I?'

Ingvar nodded, though he had no appetite for it.

Why are you here? To prove you can still best me? Or worried I've moved beyond you?

Váltyr closed the metal door behind him and drew *holdbítr*. The blade was longer than Ingvar's – straight, double-edged, rune-etched, spell-wound and with its edge honed down to a vanishing point that would hew a Rhino's hide.

It was a fine weapon. It wasn't *dausvjer*.

'I was bored, in your absence,' said Váltyr, swinging the blade around him lazily and taking up position. 'Baldr can handle himself, but it's all hammers and bolters with the others. I missed our sparring.'

Ingvar pulled his sword into guard. He hadn't missed their sparring. He'd always been able to appreciate the skill of the blademaster, but had never loved going up against him. Váltyr's fetish for the weapon was something that disturbed him. A blade was for use, not for worship.

'Nothing too strenuous,' Ingvar said, watching the tip of *holdbítr* warily. 'Just loosening the arms.'

Váltyr nodded, and started to circle him. His lean face caught the shadows, and the pinned black in his golden eyes seemed to shrink into nothing.

'Your stance has changed,' he said.

'Has it?'

When Váltyr moved, it was characteristically quick. He seemed to have the facility to leap from total immobility into action with nothing in between. It was a fearsome talent, made all the more lethal by his habitual coolness. Ingvar had seen Váltyr eviscerate opponents before they'd even known he was planning to move.

Holdbítr swooped, and *dausvjer* flickered up to meet it. The two lengths of metal clashed, sparking from one another.

Váltyr didn't press the attack. He pulled away instantly, dancing back, resuming guard.

'Who fought best?' he asked. 'Can you tell me names? Chapters?'

Ingvar kept his eyes fixed on Váltyr's hands. Watching the blade was an error; the hands were where the attacks came from.

'I learned that such things are meaningless,' he said, shadowing carefully. 'We all had our gifts.'

Váltyr looked disappointed. 'Diplomatic,' he said, before bursting into a flurry of attacks.

Ingvar met them all, and the swords spun around one another.

There was a kind of raw perfection there. They were alone. No one witnessed their skill, their neatly matched violence. In the past, Ingvar would have found that a waste; boastful Fenrisian souls liked the open display of prowess. After long years fighting in the shadows, locked in a quiet world of enforced secrecy, that urge had abated.

He wondered if Váltyr felt the same way. The blademaster had always celebrated purity. That might have been the key to him. Or perhaps it was something more. Perhaps Váltyr needed the reassurance of it all, the gentle, repeated reminders of his uniqueness.

Holdbítr jabbed down, held double-handed. Ingvar darted away from it, letting the accumulated power in the strike dissipate. Then he pressed in close, swinging *dausvjer* hard.

It didn't trouble Váltyr. Nothing seemed to.

'I don't think you're any faster,' Váltyr observed, his voice as calm as ever as he worked.

'Speed is not the only thing,' said Ingvar.

Those words were Callimachus's.

'But it *is*, Gyrfalkon. Move fast enough, and the gods themselves will bleed.'

Váltyr demonstrated the point. He came back at Ingvar in a spinning, dazzling series of rotations and cuts.

For the first time, Ingvar struggled. He let the blows jar against his parries, attempting nothing more than defence, retreating back across the cage step by step, riding out the storm.

'Blood of Russ,' hissed Ingvar. 'Does this have to–'

Váltyr silenced him with a vicious left-right swipe that nearly hurled *dausvjer* from Ingvar's grasp. Then he piled in again, mixing up standard thrusts with the chaotic, freeform bladework he loved.

'Just keep up,' he said. 'If you can.'

Ingvar crashed against the wall of the cage, scraping along it as he fended off the incoming storm.

So that's what this is, he thought. *You are here to remind me of the order of the pack.*

Ingvar shoved clear of the cage edge and moved back towards the centre. Keeping *holdbítr* at bay took up every last dram of his physical skill. Facing Váltyr's expertise again was a chilling experience.

'Show me something new, then,' said Váltyr. '*Unnerve* me.'

That was when it happened. The moment was over in less than a heart-beat, less than a thought, but the clarity of it was breathtaking.

Ingvar saw the gap, opened by Váltyr's enthusiasm. Leonides would have called it a half-breach or *sotano*, the sudden thrust upwards at a three-quarter angle, jutting past the guard and beneath the breastplate.

The twist to get there was excruciating, too narrow and confined for all but the sharpest hands. But he knew, in that instant, that he could do it. He knew he could stab the blade through, blooding him, throwing him off, ending the fight.

Ingvar had never beaten Váltyr before, not truly, not when he was concentrating.

So when he pulled back, the fact that he hadn't made the move was a choice, not an omission. It was not a mistake. He had not erred. Another decision had been made.

Váltyr hammered away at him, his sword-edge smearing into a silver gauze of movement. Two, three more strikes, and Ingvar was rammed against the cage-edge again, his room for movement closed down.

Ingvar looked down. *Holdbítr* was pressed against his throat, lodged up to the skin.

Váltyr smiled. 'Close, this time,' he said. 'You still know how to move.'

He let his blade fall away, leaving a thin line of blood against Ingvar's flesh. Ingvar reached up to feel it, wincing.

Váltyr strolled away from him, swishing his sword idly through the air. Ingvar watched him go.

'You missed something, Eversson,' said Váltyr. 'I made a mistake, right there at the end.'

Ingvar sheathed *dausvjer*.

'Didn't catch it,' he said. 'You were too fast. Again.'

Váltyr laughed. 'We should do this more often. Perhaps you could teach me some of those Blood Angels tricks.'

Ingvar nodded. 'Surely. When this is healed.'

Váltyr bowed, with a victor's gratitude. 'Perhaps I'll sleep now,' he said, opening the door to the cage and stepping through it. 'You should do likewise.'

'I'll try.'

Ingvar watched Váltyr go. There was a slight spring in the *sverdhjera*'s step – barely perceptible, but definitely there.

Alone again, Ingvar drew his blade and looked at it for a moment. Then he stepped into guard and executed the *sotano*. Perfectly.

I could have done it. I could have halted him.

Callimachus came to mind again, soft-spoken, courteous, reserved.

'Why didn't you strike him?' Ingvar had demanded, back when Jocelyn had initiated yet another challenge to the squad leader's authority.

Callimachus had looked at him with a tolerant, cautious eye, as if weighing up whether a Wolf of Fenris could really be expected to understand such things.

'I was taught this,' he'd said. 'Do not win every battle that you can, only those that you must. I did not wish to shame him.'

'He'll think you're weak.'

'What does that matter? I am not.'

Ingvar looked up, out towards the door that Váltyr had taken.

The decision had been the right one. Váltyr did not need another reason to resent his return; the inevitable tension between them would be eased by his victory.

For all that, frustration burned away within him. He was too much of a Fenrisian not to chafe against defeat, real or imagined. Before Onyx, he would never have willingly lost a fight.

Before Onyx, he would not have had the skill to avoid it.

These contradictions will grow, he thought. *I will become a contradiction.*

He knew he wouldn't sleep. The hours would pass in wakefulness, made sharper by the knowledge of his concession to another's pride.

He started to move again, forcing his aching muscles back into practice strikes, making them move faster than before, more savagely.

I could have done it.

The sword danced in the dark, tracing tighter arcs than ever, propelled by his sullen anger.

He imagined Váltyr's face before him, not bright with triumph, but open-eyed with surprise.

I could have done it.

Baldr woke suddenly. His eyes snapped open, staring into perfect dark.

He lay on his back, breathing heavily. He could feel the layers of sweat on his skin, chilling rapidly. Both his hearts were working hard, beating out a tremulous pattern that he could hear as well as feel.

'Lumen,' he whispered.

A single globe flickered into life, casting a bleached glow over the narrow cell. It showed up pressed metal walls pocked with bands of rivets, a mesh floor, a low ceiling and a single bunk, worked out of a solid slab of stone.

Baldr didn't move. He watched, he breathed, waiting for his body to recover.

He could still hear the echoes. The voices were very faint, hovering just on the edge of hearing, but they were still there. He hadn't been able to understand them even in his dreams. Now they ran through his waking mind, cycling in an incessant babble of half-sensical syllables and phonemes.

He reached up for the warding pendant at his chest, only then remembering that he'd given it to Ingvar. His fingers closed over emptiness.

That may have been rash.

The grind of the engines hammered away far below, thrumming up the walls of the cell and making them shiver. The hum of it was maddening after a while unless you could tune it out, which he couldn't.

That is surely the problem. I cannot tune them out. I must learn to ignore them.

Baldr knew he should have sought out Stormcaller while on Fenris. The problem had become too intrusive, too frequent, and he'd long since passed the point where guidance had become necessary.

He wasn't even sure why he'd resisted it. Not fear, not of a straightforward kind. Perhaps caution, or maybe an unwillingness to trouble the great ones on account of half-remembered nightmares and unidentifiable inklings.

It was worse when in the warp. Many minds had strange dreams while in the warp. Baldr knew that Ingvar suffered, and he had considered confiding in him. Years ago he would have done so without hesitation, but now, after so much time and space had come between them, things were not so easy.

He opened his mouth, taking a slow draught of cold air. His second heart stopped beating. His first returned to its normal rate.

He could hear the activity of the ship on the decks around, above and below him. Kaerls trudged down corridors, filtration units wheezed as they pushed recycled air around, slaved stabiliser systems ticked over gently, emitting occasional chittering bursts as the *Undrider*'s machine core instructed them to adjust some parameter or other.

It felt like being in the belly of a single giant organism.

He pulled himself up onto his elbows. No more sleep would come to him that night. His clammy hair fell in lank strands around his face. He lifted a hand up to his eyes, and saw sweat glistening on the flesh. He watched a line of moisture run down the curved surface of his palm, leaving a thin trail like rain on glass.

Things would be easier once out of the empyrean. Perhaps a stint of garrison work, leavened with manageable combat missions, would be beneficial. Dull, perhaps, but restorative.

Baldr let his hand fall back to the bunk. The sweat on his skin evaporated fast, chilling him. He didn't reach for a cloth to wipe it clear – his body was more than capable of adjusting. In any case, the cold would do him good. It would introduce some clarity.

He lowered himself back down, resting his head again. His open eyes stared, defocused, up at the ceiling.

Dull, but restorative.

I should not hope for such things.

It would be easier once out of the empyrean.

CHAPTER SIX

'We are coming through now, lord.'

Bjargborn's voice betrayed some measure of relief. Gunnlaugur guessed it hadn't been easy for him sharing a cramped, poorly equipped frigate with a pack of prowling, unsatisfied Sky Warriors. He'd done well, all things considered.

'Very good, master,' said Gunnlaugur, slicking his beard down with lacquer ready to receive his helm. 'Bring us in close.'

Gunnlaugur liked mortals. He liked their simplicity and prized their bravery. Kaerls were a tough breed even without genetic manipulation – they stood their ground, they followed orders, they knew how to hold an axe when the situation demanded it. Bjargborn was a good example of the type.

The master swung round in the throne to direct the break back into real space. Ahead of him the lead panels on the observation dome creaked and snapped, ready to withdraw when the bolts were pulled.

The seven members of Járnhamar stood on the dais behind the throne, just as they had done at the start of the warp transit. All of them wore their armour. Gunnlaugur could sense their eagerness to have earth under their feet again. It was most palpable in Baldr, for some reason. He'd lost his habitual air of unconcern, and looked drained by the warp passage.

'The veil is breaking,' reported Bjargborn. 'Navigator reports that your desire to come in close will be satisfied.'

The *Undrider*'s hull creaked, as if braced against crosswinds. The low grumble of the warp engines cycled down, ready to be replaced by the imminent roar of real space drives.

'Let's get a look at this place, then,' breathed Gunnlaugur, his eyes fixed on the observation dome, ready for the withdrawal of the shields.

A crack echoed up from the frigate's bowels, and the deck trembled. A sound like an elongated scream shuddered across the command chamber, followed by a rushing hiss.

The void drives thundered into life. The ether-screens slammed back into place. For a second, the viewer panes were smeary with snags of false colour. Then they clarified into the deep velvet of the void, punctuated by a pinprick-sharp starfield. In the centre of the display, dead ahead, was a rust-red world scarred by iron-black birthmarks.

The cogitators around the throne burst into life as screeds of data suddenly flooded into the sensoria. Servitors started up their swollen-tongued chattering, and banks of bronze-ringed lights flickered. The *Undrider* was once again in the world of physics and matter.

'Bring her up to approach speed,' ordered Gunnlaugur calmly, walking forwards to Bjargborn's side to get a better look at the view ahead. 'Anything on the auspexes?'

Bjargborn worked smoothly, his fingers running over levers and dials set into the arms of his throne.

'Nothing yet, lord. Translation has been affected with ninety-two per– Ah. We're getting something. Are we getting something? Yes, I've got ship signatures.'

Gunnlaugur felt the hairs on his neck stiffen.

'Show me,' he said.

Behind him, he heard Olgeir's low growl. The sweet tang of kill-urge suddenly pricked in his glands.

'Unencrypted traffic picked up,' reported Bjargborn, flicking a switch to send the feed to bridge-wide audio. 'No location yet.'

Speakers set on either side of the command throne crackled into a fizz of white noise.

Ingvar drew up alongside Gunnlaugur. His grey eyes fixed steadily on the blood-red orb suspended in front of them. His expression was taut.

'Do not broadcast that signal,' he said.

Bjargborn's hands moved to comply, but it was too late. For a few seconds, the fizz dissolved into recognisable word shapes, thick with phlegmy distortion.

'–sccrxxscrt... sfccgh... skeerrs... talemon mon mon morrdar ek'skadderjjul... nergal alech frarrjar... ach h'jar nergal–'

The feed broke off.

'How many ships?' Gunnlaugur demanded.

'One, lord,' said Bjargborn. His face was white. He didn't understand the words, but he knew what kind of mouth uttered them. 'I think.'

Gunnlaugur turned round to face the pack. He felt his blood already beginning to pump.

'Ensure full power to the weapons.' He seized his helm from his belt and lowered it over his head. 'Maintain full speed.'

Járnhamar were moving too. Jorundur took position by the throne, his eyes sparkling with sudden excitement. The others donned helms, twisting them into place with a series of tight hisses.

Gunnlaugur glanced up at the observation dome, scouring the starfield. His animal spirits were active already, priming his muscles, making him alert, speeding his thoughts.

'Find it,' he snarled. 'Then kill it.'

Void battles were strange and varied things. Most were settled over unimaginably vast distances and conducted via the statistical feeds of locator machines, neither captain ever setting eyes on his opponent. Some lasted for months, with ships dropping in and out of the warp in a drawn-out attempt to gain positional advantage. Some were brutally simple – a rammed hull cracking apart in a destructive orgy of engine detonation, an overloaded shield generator causing a cascade of ruinous chain reactions. The variables to consider were immense, the variety inexhaustible.

Which was why Jorundur enjoyed it. No motive cogitator had the imagination, the *flair*, to take on void war. It was left to flesh-and-blood captains, men and women who knew the tolerances of their ships like they knew the limits of their own bodies, souls who could eke out the last gramme of power and aggression while the universe exploded in fire and blood around them.

This situation, of course, was different. Jorundur had no more understanding of the *Undrider*'s finer-edged capabilities than a newly inducted ensign. It would have been prudent to leave matters in Bjargborn's hands, trusting in the mortal's experience of his vessel's powers.

But that would have been no fun. And, despite what many believed about Jorundur, his capacity to find enjoyment in his work had not been entirely lost over the centuries.

'There it is,' he said, pointing at a fast-moving blob on the forward auspex picter. 'Give me hololithic local space. What are the shields doing? Speed to maximum – we need to close it down.'

Bjargborn complied without hesitation. A three-dimensional matrix flickered into life above them, glowing in lines of red and gold, dominated by the globe of Ras Shakeh. It showed the position of the *Undrider* closing fast on the planet. Another signal emerged from the far side of the world, moving directly towards them to intercept.

Jorundur had no idea what the ship was doing there. He could hear Gunnlaugur trying to establish comms with the world below and failing. All he knew was that it was there, that it was commanded by something unholy, and that it needed to die. The circumstances of its presence could wait until its carcass was burning up on re-entry.

'What are we facing?' he demanded, watching the signal race into range. 'Give me something to work with.'

'On screen,' said Bjargborn, switching long-range scanner readings onto a picter mounted next to the command throne. A three-dimensional schematic sheered into life on the hololith, spinning around its axis.

'Archenemy,' said Gunnlaugur immediately.

'A destroyer,' confirmed Bjargborn, watching fresh columns of data running down the hololith boundaries. 'Its weapons are powering up.'

Jorundur scrutinised the flickering image rotating before him. The bridge around him ran with shouts and orders as weapon systems were brought online and the void shields raised. The lumens overhead dimmed, replaced by the dull red glow of combat lighting.

'Can we kill it?' demanded Gunnlaugur. 'Decide now.'

Jorundur growled. He needed more time. The outline of the destroyer was... odd. Its guns looked misshapen. It might have been Idolater-class, but if so then something bizarre had happened to its hull. The *Undrider* was probably faster, but his hunch was that it was weaker and packed less of a punch.

'Ashamed you even asked,' he growled, fixing his eyes on the hololith and gauging distances. 'Maintain speed and course. Prepare for drop to nadir on my mark, ten thousand kilometres.'

Bjargborn scurried to comply. Warning lights strobed across the picter array, warning of energy spikes out in the void.

'Lance strike!' shouted a kaerl from the sensoria station.

'Too far away,' breathed Jorundur. 'They're too–'

Space ahead of them exploded into a blaze of harsh, caustic light. The *Undrider* slammed to port-zenith, sending unsecured crew members tumbling across the marble floor. Klaxons blared out, and the combat lumens flickered twice before resuming.

'Evasive action!' ordered Bjargborn.

'Do not *dare*,' threatened Jorundur. 'In closer.'

Gunnlaugur, still on his feet, looked at him sharply. 'Closer?'

'We can't hit it back at this range,' snapped Jorundur. 'All we've got is speed.'

'Hits to forward voids,' reported a servitor. The voice was dry and empty of concern. 'Damage on dorsal plates. Repair crews dispatched.'

Ingvar approached the throne and stared hard at the hololith image of the enemy ship. Jorundur ignored him.

'Down now, *hard*,' he ordered. 'Scrape the planet's edge, find us some more speed.'

The *Undrider* plunged towards the world below, and the huge orb began to fill the real space viewers. As it did so another energy beam scythed past, missing the crenelated spine of the frigate by less than a kilometre. The growl of the engines swelled to a howling whine and the deck trembled beneath their feet.

'This is hurting,' warned Bjargborn, as more warning lights blinked on across a dozen consoles.

The structure of the bridge started to rattle. The sound of something shattering echoed up from a lower deck, followed by a diminishing run of sharp cracks.

Jorundur ignored all of it. Proximity indicators rattled down in front of him, tracking the shrinking gap between the two ships. They were still too far out, and the enemy had the range on them.

'Open fire, master,' he ordered.

'We don't have–'

'Open fire or lose your teeth.'

The *Undrider*'s forward lance sent a shard of sun-white light arcing into the void. Banks of lascannons opened up all along the prow, briefly flaring up against the dark before disappearing in a hail of scattered beams.

The barrage caused no damage, but the enemy adjusted trajectory, just by a fraction, enough to postpone the next volley. By then the *Undrider*'s course across the fringes of Ras Shakeh's atmosphere was hurling it onwards even faster. Continents blurred by underneath them in smudges of red and black.

A few seconds more...

The enemy barrage hammered in again. The destroyer opened up with ship-to-ship las-fire and the *Undrider* took hits all along its exposed starboard flanks, making the shielding buck, flex and crackle.

'Losing voids!' shouted a kaerl from the cogitator banks, seconds before a hard bang made the chamber shake. The *Undrider* swung keenly down and to port, lurching off course just as a baroque cluster of cabling exploded overhead, showering the floor in bouncing, tumbling sparks.

'And that's enough running,' said Jorundur, standing defiant and unconcerned against the ship's yawing tilt. 'Now we return the favour.'

He caught sight of the enemy in the realview portals then – a bruise-black, bulbous destroyer, swinging in closer for another pass. Its forward lance was already blazing white, ready for the next spike. The telltale glitter of void shields shimmered across its outline, still intact.

A fresh salvo scythed out from the *Undrider*'s cannons. The crews had a good aim – as the glare faded Jorundur saw a swathe of hits across the enemy underside. Something blew up under the dagger-sharp prow, knocking the lance up out of position and sending a splash-pattern of static across the ship's shields.

'Closer now,' hissed Jorundur, his fists clenching. '*Rake* them.'

The *Undrider* shot upwards, sheering a little and trailing debris, still fast enough to evade most of the hail of las-fire aimed at it. The engines laboured, sending stuttering impacts vibrating through the bulkheads and gantries. Biting detonations along the hull tipped it over several degrees but didn't slow it.

For less than a second it passed right beside the enemy, close enough to see its glistening, tumorous hide through the crystal of the realviewers. Banks of lascannons snapped out in unison, hurling a thicket of deadly neon-bright spears across the gap. The return barrage was just as vicious – two walls of heat and light slamming through and past one another, cracking into the swimming energy of the void shields, bursting through and boring down to the metal below.

Explosions crashed out all along the length of the *Undrider*, punctuated by the scream and snap of expiring void generators. The whole ship reeled as las-beams carved into overheated conduits and burned through metre-thick plate. The engines coughed and flared, beating erratically as if having a sudden coronary.

'Away now, evasive manoeuvre *jorva*,' ordered Jorundur calmly, all the while watching the hololith whirl and flicker.

The structure of the ship shivered as the *Undrider* launched into a steep, cork-screwing climb. More explosions thundered out, bombarding the bridge crew with debris. Cracks cobwebbed across viewports, quickly shuttered. Kaerls staggered to and fro across the chamber, labouring to reach nascent fires and douse them.

'Status, master,' Jorundur asked, all the while monitoring spatial positions.

Bjargborn, who'd nearly been knocked out of his throne by the repeated impacts, scrambled for data.

'Starboard weapons gone,' he reported. 'Lance gone. Six, no seven, hull breaches. We're leaking atmosphere.'

'What's this thing made of?' muttered Jorundur. 'Paper?'

Gunnlaugur braced himself against the steepling deck, compensating for malfunctioning grav-generators.

'And the enemy?' he demanded.

The destroyer had shot wide, battered by the brutal broadside exchange. It was coming round for another pass, but more clumsily than before. A long trail of gases plumed from its underside.

'Its voids are down,' said Bjargborn, scanning the auspex data. 'Still got weapons. Still got engines.'

'It can kill us,' said Ingvar quietly. 'We can't kill it.'

Jorundur whirled around.

'I'm just getting started,' he glowered.

Ingvar turned to Gunnlaugur.

'We have to withdraw, *vaerangi*,' he said. 'We can't fight this.'

Gunnlaugur looked back at Ingvar.

'Withdraw?' he asked. His voice betrayed astonishment. For a moment, it looked like he had no idea how to react.

More explosions hammered out from the lower decks. A whole row of cogitators exploded, their screens flinging shattered crystals across the decking. A choir of warning klaxons broke out, overlapping one another in a discordant hymn of despair.

'There's no shame in this,' Ingvar said. 'We might still outrun it, but we can't kill it. We have no weapons left.'

At that, Gunnlaugur gave a grim laugh.

'You've been away too long,' he said. 'We have plenty.'

He glanced briefly at the hololith, calculating, before turning to Jorundur.

'Take us in again, close as you can, fast as you can. Then burn like Hel away from it. Don't care where, just don't die on the way in.'

Jorundur grinned knowingly. 'That is understood.'

Gunnlaugur turned to face the rest of the pack. They looked back at him expectantly, sealed in their suits of armour, draped in pelts, daubed with ritual bloodstains, etched with runes, hung with wolf's-teeth, wyrd-totems and fate-forged blades.

'Come, brothers,' he said, his thick voice snagging with anticipation. 'I wish to show you something.'

Gunnlaugur jogged down the corridors leading to the frigate's hangars. The lumens failed before he got halfway; his helm compensated instantly. The broken thuds of his pack's massed bootfalls resounded down the narrow space after him. He filtered out the incessant klaxons and warning beacons, only hearing the clinks of weapons against armour, the ragged, expectant breathing, the tinny grind of power armour servos.

The *Undrider* was, in all but one respect, a substandard vessel, something that he should have been ashamed to go to war in. It had one thing, though – one thing that made it more than useful.

'So what is this?' came Váltyr's voice over the pack-wide comm. 'What are we doing?'

He sounded uneasy, like he should have been informed. Váltyr was always on the look out for slights.

'We're here for this,' said Gunnlaugur, reaching a pair of thick security doors. He punched a switch, and they eased open with a scrape of pistons.

On the far side of the doorway was a yawning chamber the size of the Thunderhawk hangar. The metal of the walls was blackened, as if lined with carbon. Huge lifting claws hung from the roof, shaking slightly as the *Undrider* took more hits.

In the centre of the chamber was a slingshot launch mechanism – two hundred metres of track-lined tunnel heading straight out into the void, softly illuminated by a heart-red glow.

At the far end of the track stood two closed sets of armour-plate doors. At the near end, sunk into floor level and squatting amid scorched rockcrete buffers like a lumpen, ugly twin-hulled avatar of the Imperial brutalist aesthetic, was the reason they'd come.

'Blood of Russ,' breathed Baldr.

'A Caestus,' said Olgeir, sounding impressed. 'Glorious.'

Gunnlaugur laughed as he strode over to the control console and activated the remote launch authorisation.

'Strap in quick,' he said. 'Jorundur's sending us out, and he won't like waiting.'

A Caestus Assault Ram was a common sight on Adeptus Astartes capital ships, rarer on escort-class vessels like the *Undrider*. Unlike the versatile Thunderhawk gunships, which were almost three times as large, a Caestus was built around a single operational principle. Its twin hulls were heavily armoured and reinforced with plates of ceramite, ridged and braced to absorb enormous impacts. Its chunky thrusters had afterburners designed to hurl it into blistering straight-line speeds. Its weapon complement – twin-linked heavy bolters, wing-mounted missile launchers, magna-melta heat cannon – all faced ahead, concentrating their destructive power into a single point.

A Caestus, launched into the void and carrying its full complement of ten Space Marines, could survive a direct hit at full speed with the unshielded hull of any battle cruiser in the Imperium. That was fortunate, as it could do very little else. It was less a vehicle, more a projectile.

The two embarkation ramps clanged open. Ingvar and Baldr clambered into one; Váltyr, Olgeir and Hafloí the other. Gunnlaugur took his seat in the tiny cockpit, set back at the rear of the ungainly craft. It was an awkward, cramped fit, doubly so once the metal ribs of the impact cage descended across his chest.

The hull booms closed with the hiss and snap of locking bolts. Gunnlaugur primed the engines, feeling the whole vessel shudder as the thrusters broke into life.

The launch chamber rocked again, buffeted by more incoming fire from the void-battle outside. One of the lifting claws separated from its supports and came crashing down beside them, crunching into a tangle of metal fingers and cracking the rockcrete floor.

Gunnlaugur glanced down the long launch tunnel, watching as the external blast doors opened, one after the other, exposing star-flecked blackness beyond.

'Brace for launch,' he ordered, seizing the rudimentary flight controls and tensing for the explosive launch. Piloting a Caestus in such conditions was like riding a whirlwind – he'd be able to nudge its trajectory a little before impact, but not much more than that. 'The Hand of Russ be with–'

The ram exploded into movement, leaping forwards as if kicked. Its engines swelled into a crescendo of flaming, roaring thunder, deafening even over his helm's aural dampeners.

Gunnlaugur slammed back in his seat. The launch tunnel screamed by in a rush of motion-blur and the Caestus shot clear of the *Undrider*'s hull. Stars wheeled before them briefly, marred by trailing fronds of smoke and fire.

Then the destroyer's bloated hull swept up to meet them, racing into range at frightening speed. Jorundur had timed the burst well – they were heading straight amidships, angling under the jumbled forest of armour plating and into the engine levels. A storm of las-fire cracked around them, some of it impacting on the Caestus's hull, rocking it even as it careered towards its target.

Gunnlaugur prodded the vessel's course down by a fraction, aiming for an already damaged section of hull-plate. He let loose with the missile launcher, then the heavy bolters, blazing away at the projected impact site.

The sun-hot magna-melta was the last weapon to fire, just as the destroyer's bulk overshadowed them, racing up out of the void like a cliff-face of adamantium. For all his conditioning, Gunnlaugur couldn't resist gritting his teeth together, clenching his jaws tight as the hull hurtled in close.

The smash was colossal. The Caestus blazed into a raging core of melting, boiling metal. For a microsecond it plunged straight through the magma, barging aside disintegrating columns and armour plate. Then it rammed square against a solid bracing rib and reared upwards. Momentum dragged it onwards, scraping and tearing through chunks of steel and adamantium, boring away into the reeling heart of the destroyer's wounded flank.

Gunnlaugur was hurled forwards in his seat, barely held in place by the thick metal bars across his chest. Massive, fleeting explosions flared up around the assault ram, turning the forward viewer into an orange soup of flame.

The bracing rib bent, twisted, then broke, bringing a fresh mass of crumbling superstructure raining down on the still-moving assault craft. Its engines cut out suddenly, and their roar was replaced by the shriek of tortured metal and the whistling rush of escaping air.

Slowly, grindingly, the Caestus slid to a halt, wedged deep within the bowels of the enemy ship like a bullet lodged in the muscle of its prey.

Gunnlaugur released the cage and blew the door-locks. More incendiaries went off, clustered around the hull booms to clear a space for the descending crew ramps. His cockpit hatch flew open and he clambered out, reaching for his thunder hammer as he scrambled free of the Caestus's upended chassis.

Around him lay a collapsing, howling, blazing maze of destruction. The Caestus had blown a huge hole in the side of the destroyer, carving away whole chunks of hull structure and exposing the ragged ends of broken decking. A gale of oxygen rushed over him, extinguishing the myriad fires that laced the collision site. Shattered lumens flickered and swung from severed brackets, throwing grotesque and leaping shadows over the ruins.

Behind them, back at the end of a cone-shaped tunnel of molten iron-work, was the void. In front of them was the ship they had come to murder.

Gunnlaugur activated *skulbrotsjór*, and blue lightning arced across its adamantium head.

'Time to go,' he growled, hoisting clear of the Caestus and grabbing hold of a section of broken decking to brace himself.

The rest of the pack emerged from the hull booms. They hauled themselves away from the upended Caestus, seizing what spars and braces remained intact around them and climbing upwards through the devastation. The air had gone but the ship's artificial gravity remained, allowing them to orientate themselves and pull free of the tangled wreckage.

They formed up again on the next deck, the first place that retained some semblance of a floor, walls and ceiling.

'That was... invigorating,' said Olgeir, shaking a crust of debris free of his shoulders. *Sigrún* sat comfortably in his two hands, sweeping the area in front of them casually. The rest of the pack fanned out, their helm lenses glowing red in the unsteady gloom.

A large open space stretched away from them, echoing and empty. What parts of it remained intact had the look of a cargo hold – the floor was rock-crete and the walls were iron. Dark, fluted columns studded the expanse, each one terminating in pointed arches against a ridged ceiling. The vacuum made it silent and as cold as Morkai's breath. Nothing lived, nothing stirred. The faint vibration from the engines against their boots was the only indication that this wasn't a dead ship already.

On the far side of the chamber, thirty metres away, were six huge cargo shafts, each one barred by reinforced shutters.

Baldr knelt down, peering at the floor. He scraped a patch of still-glowing dust clear.

'Tank tracks,' he said, looking up at Gunnlaugur. 'A vehicle depot.'

Gunnlaugur nodded, swinging *skulbrotsjór* back and forth and rocking his head from side to side. The cramped passage in the assault ram had compressed his spine – he needed to flex his limbs.

'To the bridge, then,' he said.

As he finished speaking, one of the shutters began to rise. A sickly green light, lurid like marsh-gas, tumbled out from under it, dissipating quickly in the darkness. Black shapes, blurry through the fog, moved back and forth on the far side.

'Not just yet,' said Váltyr with relish, spinning *holdbítr* in one hand before bringing it up into guard. 'Here come the crew.'

CHAPTER SEVEN

Jorundur staggered, keeping his feet with difficulty. The mortals around him did less well. Those strapped into their chairs were flung viciously against their bonds. Those who were unsecured were hurled from one wall to the other, landing with the crack and snap of broken bones.

A sheet of flame rippled across the observation dome, overloading half the hull-mounted sensoria and masking for a moment the horrendous punishment the *Undrider* had just taken on the close pass. A gallery on the far side of the chamber twisted and sagged as its supports cracked. Shouts, some of pain, some of urgent command, blended into the background noise of explosions and disintegrations.

'Assessment,' Jorundur commanded, gripping the back of the command throne as the *Undrider* tilted precipitously.

Bjargborn struggled to speak. Something, shrapnel perhaps, had hit him in the face and his cheeks streamed with blood.

'Uh,' he mumbled, his speech slurring. 'M-multiple impacts. Hull breached on four, no five, levels. We're depressurising. No, we're not. Not everywhere.'

Jorundur glanced at one of the few functional pict screens, taking in its data quickly.

'Did we hurt it?' he asked, more interested in the damage he'd done than that which he'd sustained.

Bjargborn called up the sensoria reports. His hands trembled, but he was working hard to hold it together.

'We did,' he reported. Even in his battered state, he sounded proud of that. 'Pretty bad. See for yourself.'

Bjargborn switched the rear-view feed to the throne-mounted screens.

Jorundur saw the destroyer falling away from them, its nearside flank bursting with quickly-extinguishing spot fires. Whole sections of hull-plate had been driven in. A swarm of sparking fragments tumbled around it in the void. It looked like it was having trouble coming around, and rolled awkwardly in space like a beached *hvaluri*.

'And the assault ram?'

'They're in, lord,' said Bjargborn. 'Out of locator range, but they're in.'

As the master spoke, Jorundur caught sight of the ingress wound made by the Caestus – a jagged hole in the destroyer's side, laced with glowing shards of molten metal.

He felt a small surge of satisfaction. He'd aligned the ram well. Gunnlaugur had better remember that when it came to the mission assessment.

'We've done what we had to,' he said. 'Now get us away from that thing.'

Around him the command chamber slowly returned to something like a functioning space. Men still lay prone on the floor, streaked with blood, but the servitors just kept on working. Kaerls, many of them limping or cradling broken arms, moved to douse the fires and shore up the worst of the damage.

For all that, Jorundur knew the situation was still balanced. The *Undrider* had gone into the broadside in worse shape than the enemy and had come out of it badly mauled. The damage it had sustained already might well prove fatal, even without the continued attentions of a pursuing ship.

He felt the broken judder of the engines kick in again, thrusting the *Undrider* away from the combat zone. The movement felt sluggish, as if only half the usual levels of power were online.

Bjargborn read his mind.

'They've holed the enginarium,' he said. He'd managed to find a rag to wipe his face with, and blood smeared across his chin. 'We won't outrun them for long.'

Jorundur nodded and glanced at the hololith tactical display. The enemy was recovering too. The destroyer began to turn, angling back to match course with them. Its speed had been dented too, but not by as much.

'Give me what you can, master. Stay within range of the planet. Any weapons still functioning?'

Bjargborn gave a hollow laugh.

'A few,' he said. 'Enough to chip their war-paint.'

Jorundur didn't find that amusing.

'We'll trust to speed, then. Find it from somewhere.'

Bjargborn turned back to his pict screens, a furrowed look on his bloody face. He knew their only chance of picking up speed lay with the hundreds of enginarium workers down in the forge-hot belly of the vessel, striving against hope and reason to restore the titanic drive mechanisms to health. For all he knew they were already dead, their bloated corpses tumbling through space in their wake.

Jorundur kept watching the ship-signal on the hololith as it completed its turn and came after them.

'Out of interest,' he asked, feeling like he already knew the answer, 'can we still make warp?'

Bjargborn smiled sadly. 'Without a Geller field?'

'Just asking.'

It had been a hypothetical question; while the pack was on board the enemy ship there was no question of leaving them. Jorundur liked to know all the options, though, just for the sake of completeness.

Whatever you're doing in there, he thought, watching the destroyer's shadow loom larger on the hololith, *do it quick*.

They had once been human. They weren't any more.

They still had the carcasses of human flesh, and still wore the robes and uniforms of human soldiers, but they had passed beyond their old state and into something new, something abhorrent, something debased.

For Ingvar, the most striking aspect was the smell. The fighting soon took them beyond the ruined vehicle depot and into pressurised areas of the ship, and after that the stink of it pressed in on him. A thousand aromas jostled against one another like swine in a herd – decaying offal, mould, pestilence, the rich tang of recent death, the metallic stench of old blood. He could pick out every strand. He could taste it like sour milk at the back of his throat.

Over the past decades he had become used to xenos fighting. The smell of an alien was always so utterly bizarre that disgust barely registered; engagement with it was a rational matter, something to be processed and filed away for reference.

And so he had forgotten the uniquely sickly fug of fallen humanity, the cocktail of scents that hovered on the edge of familiarity before plunging into chasms of filth, all of it too close to home to be indifferent to.

A human wore his scents like an autobiography, describing his journey through the labours of sanctioned life and into damnation. It picked out traces of old ways – the fabric of uniforms, the sweat of mortal glands, the rotten breath swirling out of mouths black with caries. There were smells of the descent – the flush of fear, the frothy residue of mad euphoria, the dull ache of coming malady. Then, finally, the stink that came with the falling itself: pox, bloat, sore, tumour, pus-streak, glisten-tight sac, ulcerous gobbet of slime, residue of bile, liver-green effluent of gristly, metastasising organ. It all piled up on top of itself, multiplying like a nest of blowflies on a corpse, intensifying in the dark and the wet, redounding to the glory of the false god that revelled and rolled in such muck.

The ship was pregnant with bodily horror. In every chamber, down every corridor, behind every bulkhead and compartment more of it lurked, ground hard into the spongy mass of the floors and dripping like afterbirth from the sagging ceilings. The creatures that had once been human waded through it all to meet them, dragging scrofulous limbs through slurries of liquidised flesh and breaking the scum-crusts that floated atop standing pools of fermenting saliva.

They had lost much, those once-humans. Their eyes were milky orbs, shuttered with cataracts or clawed into blindness by frenzied fingernails. Their exposed skin was grey and vomit-yellow and clustered with berry-red sores that wept trails like bloody tears. Their distended stomachs swung low and heavy, wobbling free of chafed leather belts and spilling over knock-knees and bowed legs. Their jaws lay slack on blubbered necks, laced with sulphurous, trembling strands of viscous spittle. Clouds of biting flies swarmed over them, clogged in the fatty clefts of their quivering hides, tumbling out of sleeve-ends to buzz and plop into the liquid below.

But they had gained much, too. Their rotten muscles were strong. Their addled flesh sliced without bleeding, closing up on wounds instantly. They gurgled and murmured as they came, immune to fear, immune to pain, lost in a universe of syrupy infection. They had forgotten what it was like to yearn for health and cleanliness, for all that remained was the sticky embrace of plague. They cavorted in it, sweeping up the filth and waft and musk in both hands until nothing but a blurred miasma of cankerous foulness remained, swirling around them in billows of seamy vapour.

They had forgotten their names, their ages, their purposes.

They were the lost. They were the damned.

Ingvar raced through the twisting corridors alongside his brothers, charging into the oncoming horde with clean, fast strokes. Grey hands reached out to him and he cut them clear at the wrists. Fingers tugged at his armour, grabbing the pelts that flew around him, scrabbling to get at the joints of his helm and gorget.

He kept moving, kept working. His sword dripped with a thick layer of mucus that clung to the metal, weighing it down. Plasma and creamy dollops of fat splattered across his armour, slowly dribbling down the overlapping curves of ceramite.

The others laboured just as hard. He could see Gunnlaugur ploughing on ahead, hurling the head of his thunder hammer around, crashing it through semi-living flesh, annihilating it in bloody bursts and plastering the walls with scraps and flecks. Váltyr fought more clinically, aiming *holdbítr* for the neck, the eyes, the skull. The corpses that tumbled away from him did so cleanly, their released heads splashing into the knee-deep slime, their outstretched hands scrabbling at nothing.

Over on the flanks, Olgeir reaped whole swathes of corpses, firing in disciplined bursts from his heavy bolter. Diseased flesh exploded into spinning fragments, laced with clots and cysts like biological frag grenades. Baldr and Hafloí used their bolters, backing up Olgeir's volleys with pinpoint strikes that burst skulls, punched chests, spilled mottled guts.

Progress was slow. The once-humans could be cut down, only to drag themselves back up. They clogged the claustrophobic corridors and access routes, shambling into battle in close-packed crowds. Some hefted blunt hand weapons – mauls, warhammers, spiked clubs – and others carried guns. They were outlandish things, those guns: rusting, oil barrel-shaped blasters with glowing cabling and feeder vials of toxins. Others hurled gas grenades, each stuffed with nerve-agents and flesh-eaters. The poisons they used were potent, strong enough to melt the walls around them in hissing pools of steam, but still they marched through it all, wheezing and streaming but staying on their feet.

Ingvar hauled his blade around, swinging it two-handed, barely registering as it ended the tortured existence of another glass-eyed mutant. More came to replace it.

'This is taking too long!' he warned Gunnlaugur.

The Wolf Guard didn't seem to hear him. Gunnlaugur fought on, scything his hammer upwards and hurling broken bodies into the ceiling. They fell back to the floor in a slapping rain of body parts. Further back, the echoing roar of *sigrún*'s discharge picked up frequency. Olgeir was having to expend more bolter rounds than he wanted.

Váltyr swivelled on one foot, kicking a stumbling mutant in the face. His boot wrenched the creature's spine clear of its shoulders in a shower of fractured bone and fluid. Then he switched back to the blade, gutting two more before taking a single stride forwards.

'How many of these things,' he asked, his breath getting short, 'does it take to run a ship?'

Ingvar nodded grimly.

Thousands. Tens of thousands.

They would be crawling down from every deck, leaving their stations and slithering into creaking transit shafts. They would be shuffling up from the bilges, thick with oily slime on their fingers. They would be emerging from demented apothecarions, their organs hanging out and their faces bandaged with dirty swaddling. They would just keep on coming, unable on their own to seriously threaten the armoured giants that walked among them, but capable of slowing them, holding them up, throttling their progress.

'Too many,' Ingvar said. 'We need to speed this up.'

He reached for a frag grenade at his belt, cleared space around him with a vicious blade-sweep, then hurled it down the corridor. It sailed over the heads of the oncoming horde, bouncing from the slime-slick walls before falling among them.

The explosion rocked the confined space, crashing out and hurling severed bodies in all directions. The blast wave swept along the corridor, slamming dismembered corpses headfirst into the foaming effluent. A wave of whirling gore flew back at them, dropping around them in messy, liquid slaps.

That broke the horde's momentum. The front ranks staggered, dragged down into the slime by the weight of those falling behind them.

Olgeir stepped up to take advantage.

'Watch your backs, brothers,' he warned, then opened fire.

Sigrún thundered out, vomiting a thick hail of mass-reactive rounds. The bolts punched deep into the reeling mass of pustulent flesh before detonating in a ragged line of destruction, ripping diseased meat apart in bleeding slabs.

As the echoes died away, Gunnlaugur surged back to the front, ploughing into the shaken heart of the enemy, immense and battle-roused, his hammer whistling around his shoulders in incisive arcs. Váltyr and Baldr were close behind, crashing through what remained of the mutant horde with growing space and freedom.

Of all of them, though, it was Haflói who went in hardest. He sprinted right into the press of once-humans, screaming battle-cries through his helm-vox. His bolt pistol bucked in his right hand; the left clutched a double-bladed axe. He leapt straight past Gunnlaugur, slamming bodily into the morass of corruption beyond, lashing out like a berserk of the Old Ice.

Olgeir struggled to keep up with him.

'Whelp!' he roared furiously, trying to summon him back.

It did no good. Even Gunnlaugur laughed to see it – the Blood Claw, limbs flailing, giving into his bloody rush of primordial kill-urge.

'*Fenrys!*' Haflói cried, pounding and slaying with artless abandon.

The mutants broke then, assailed on all sides and faced with the twin storms of Gunnlaugur's massive presence and Haflói's crazed one. Those that had survived the initial assault began to limp away, shrinking back into the stinking shadows or sinking into the murk at their feet.

'*Hjolda!*' roared Gunnlaugur, wading after the fleeing horrors.

The pack hunted the remnants down the corridor, following its organic twists and turns as it snaked into the heart of the corrupted ship. The retreat became a rout, a killing ground, an exercise in raw butchery.

They fought on until reaching an intersection with a vertical transit shaft, running up from the lower levels and soaring away into the heights. The iron doors that had once guarded it from the corridor were shattered.

'They've destroyed the lifters,' observed Baldr calmly, wrenching the head of a milk-skinned mutant from its rash-red body.

'So they have,' replied Gunnlaugur, shaking his hammerhead free of a ropey necklace of entrails. 'Then we climb.'

'Hel,' swore Olgeir, preparing to hoist *sigrún* across his back. 'How far up?'

Váltyr kicked out with his boot again, driving in the eggshell-thin skull of a blinded, crawling mutant.

'Not far,' he said coolly, walking up to the shaft. 'But rein in your protégé. He's getting carried away.'

Hafloí had ignored the transit shaft and had surged ahead down the corridor, lashing out to either side of him with bolt pistol and axe, shrieking and cursing.

Ingvar was closest, and went after him, grabbing him by the shoulder and dragging him back. Hafloí whirled on him, for a moment looking like he'd take on anything.

'*Easy*, hot-blood,' warned Ingvar, keeping *dausvjer* en garde. 'Don't make me use it.'

Hafloí stared at the sword for a moment, bristling with aggression, before finally lowering the axe.

By then Gunnlaugur had moved into the shaft, swinging clear of the broken gates and into the red-tinged darkness beyond. The others followed him, leaping like grey ghosts into the abyss.

The shaft was immense. It dropped away below them into an angry crimson swirl of choking fumes. The deep boom of the destroyer's engines drummed up from its base, echoing eerily from the many-columned walls. Iron gargoyles stared out across the void, their leering, daemonic faces warped into grotesque, bloated expressions of loathing.

Pipework, rusting electronics, mouldering mounts and braces all crisscrossed the metal-plate surface, affording plenty of handholds. Everything was draped in a slick, sticky layer of slime, making the surface treacherous. For all that, the pack surged up the shaft like rats running up a hawser, going quickly even as the fragile ironwork cracked and crumbled under their armour's weight.

'*How* far up?' repeated Olgeir, falling behind as his heavy bolter slowed him down.

Gunnlaugur gave him no quarter. The pack clambered up the levels. Eerie noises pursued them: moans, creaks of tortured metal, whispered voices just under the edge of hearing. The filth in the air got thicker, making their helm filters strain. A pale green mist tumbled down to meet them, emerging from beast-mouthed outlets protruding from the shaft walls.

Gunnlaugur reached the summit first. Massive, twisted iron cables hung from the roof of the shaft, swinging and clanking in the rising stink. They would once have hauled elevator cages up from the depths; now they dangled free, like nooses.

Near the top a narrow ledge jutted out into the abyss, above which were a pair of heavy doors surrounded by two swollen pillars of warped and cracked stone. Gunnlaugur grabbed hold of the ledge and dragged himself up on top of it. He seized his thunder hammer, pulled it back and hurled it two-handed at the join.

The doors crashed inwards in an explosion of blue-white lightning. Gunnlaugur charged through the gap, closely followed by the others as they reached the ledge and hauled themselves over the top.

On the other side of the doors was a huge chamber. Its roof was curved like a ribcage of burnished bronze and glazed with translucent crystal. Beyond that was the void, half visible through smeary panes. Pillars of veined marble jutted up from a floor swimming in greasy, bubbling matter. Gantries ringed the central command throne, all dripping long lines of clear fluid from rust-edged walkways. It was stiflingly hot, and the air hummed with the drone of corpse-flies.

On an Imperial frigate, a bridge that size could have accommodated over two hundred crew members. On that ship, only one remained at its station. No room was left for anyone, or anything, else.

Perhaps once the creature had sat on a command throne like a normal human, legs planted on the floor and hands resting against the arms. Maybe the mutations had burst out quickly after that, blooming like overripe fruit and tumbling forth across the available space. Or maybe it had been sitting there for centuries, slowly bulking out, slowly consuming everything around it, squeezing all other life from the chamber until it alone squatted there, wobbling with sores and lesions, hemmed in on all sides by the creaking walls of its starship cage.

Whatever the process, it had become colossal. Its lower limbs had long since been swallowed up by its expanding girth, the bulk of which rippled like gelatine across the floor. Webs of ink-dark veins pulsed under the trembling surface of its skin, pumping sluggish blood around its gigantic structure. Waves of blubber folded up against grimy cogitator banks, surrounding them, enveloping them, sinking down over them. Strands of sinew stretched directly from its obese flanks and locked into signal connector nodes. The frail network of tendrils shivered as the thing drew shuddering breaths.

It no longer occupied the bridge. It *was* the bridge.

And it stank. It stank of suppurating fat, of boiled fish, of rotten fruit, of confined and intensified putrescence. When it moved, waves of foul odour wafted across its vast body. Fluids glistened in the crevices between fatty tissue. Mucus spilled across slick patches of taut skin and bubbled over scabby patches where abscesses had ruptured.

A tiny head still surmounted the mountain of blubber, a vestigial remnant of a human skull and face. It was eyeless and hairless, with flared nostrils and a long whiplash tongue. It screamed at them, and flecks of yellow spittle splattered down a cascade of trembling chins. Tiny arms, wasted and scrawny, thrashed against its sides.

Baldr gazed up at it.

'That is impressively foul,' he murmured.

Ingvar stood at his shoulder. *Dausvjer*'s energy field spat and shimmered, throwing electric light across the face of his armour.

'Then we end it, brother,' he said, bringing the blade to bear in unison with his pack-brothers, 'and send one more lost soul back to Hel.'

'Energy spike, lord!'

The kaerl's report rang out across the command chamber. On the realview feed, Jorundur watched the destroyer's forward lance power up, sparkling like ball-lightning in the darkness of space.

The *Undrider* was racing as fast as its savaged engines would carry it, but the enemy had clawed back much of the space between them. Las-fire flickered from its forward array, too inaccurate to cause much more damage, but with increasing intensity.

It would soon find its range. After that, the brief game would be over.

'Any signal from the pack?' he asked.

'Nothing,' said Bjargborn.

The man's voice was tense. The pressure of the chase was telling.

'Then we are out of time,' said Jorundur. 'Give the order.'

Jorundur had only partial faith in the plan they'd concocted. Enginseers working down in the weapons levels had somehow managed to dredge up a semblance of a working weapons grid. He had no idea how. He'd heard Bjargborn over the comm talking about re-routing the output from the lance mechanism to burned-out lascannon coils under the warp core, which had meant precisely nothing to him. Whatever they'd done, it had been difficult and dangerous. He'd heard the screams of the tech-priest himself as one attempt had failed, incinerating an entire generator module and blowing lumens on every deck in the ship.

Now, though, they had it working. A single volley, that was all – a lone burst of shots sent spiralling away aft, hoping against hope to score a decisive hit on the destroyer's forward lance housing. If they managed to disable that, then they had a chance to live a little longer. A small one, but a chance.

Jorundur had waited until the last moment before authorising the strike. The odds of even hitting the destroyer's lance were low, but if they somehow managed it, an infinitesimal risk existed that they would do more than just knock out the weapon itself. A starship lance was a huge repository of volatile energies – a direct hit might cause an overload, sending mutually reinforcing explosions rushing back up into the vessel's innards and destroying the whole thing.

That would save the *Undrider*, but wipe out six-sevenths of Járnhamar. The decisions were fine ones, each soaked in danger.

'Order all non-weapons crews to prepare for saviour pod evacuation,' said Jorundur, his eyes fixed on the glowing hololith before him. 'If this fails, tell them to move quickly.'

'By your will, lord,' said Bjargborn, his fingers dancing over the throne's controls as he distributed the instructions down the chain of command.

One of the few surviving servitors, plugged into a terminal close by, turned its pallid, slack face towards them.

'Weapon primed, lord,' it intoned dryly.

Jorundur's eyes never left the hololith.

'Fire,' he commanded.

A crackling boom rang out from the lower decks, echoing up from the depths as if something huge had collided with the frigate and was now ploughing up through the ship, deck by deck. The command chamber shook, dislodging a stone image of Russ from the ceiling. It shattered on the floor in a cloud of shards, nearly killing the kaerls working nearby. Red lights flickered across the consoles, reciting a baleful litany of overloaded relays and burned-out translocators.

That was the price of a final, defiant volley. Jorundur watched as the makeshift array opened up, stabbing a tight cluster of las-fire aft towards the closing destroyer. For an instant the barrage blazed brilliantly, a nano-second's worth of hard, clear energy, then it was gone.

The *Undrider* shuddered. The arrhythmic growl from the engines cut out entirely, then shakily resumed. Cracks ran up the walls around them, and more loosened debris scattered across the marble.

'Did we hit it?' demanded Jorundur, peering intently at the viewers.

The destroyer hadn't lost speed.

'We did, lord,' reported Bjargborn. He sounded like he barely believed what his auspexes were telling him. 'Direct hit, forward lance.'

A second later, and the damage became obvious through the realviewers. The destroyer's prow was burning, masked by an inferno that raged in defiance of the vacuum around it.

'Blessed Allfather,' breathed Jorundur, gazing at the destruction. He turned sharply to Bjargborn. 'I want detailed readings on that ship. Power build-ups, secondary damage. You get *anything*, you tell me.'

He was already planning what he'd do if a chain reaction took hold. He might be able to get the *Undrider* in close again, but only if the enemy had lost control of its remaining weapon batteries. They couldn't survive another broadside. He started to calculate the distances, the relative speeds, what remained of his hull armour.

'Energy spike, lord!'

The report came from the same kaerl as before, in exactly the same tone.

'That's imposs-' started Bjargborn.

Jorundur's head snapped back up. He looked out at the realview feed.

'They can still fire,' said Jorundur grimly.

The gap between the ships had closed further. Jorundur saw the energies snap and fizz across the lance's muzzle, only temporarily disrupted by the volley they had sent into it.

Bjargborn's face was locked into horrified unbelief. Part of him was still searching for something – some mistake, some reading that had eluded him. Anything but the truth that now confronted them.

The chase was over. The *Undrider* was seconds from destruction.

'We can source more power,' Bjargborn said, his fingers and eyes moving quickly. 'We can–'

Jorundur laid his gauntlet heavily on the mortal's shoulder, silencing his desperate attempts to find a last-gasp solution.

'They're firing,' he said. 'Get to the pods. Now.'

Bjargborn looked up at him for a moment longer, his unwillingness to leave evident.

Then his shoulders slumped.

'This is the master,' he announced over the ship-wide comm. 'Leave your posts. Leave your posts now. Take the saviour pods. Go swiftly, and the hand of Russ be with you.'

Jorundur released him.

'Well said. Now *run*.'

The chamber was already emptying. Kaerls unstrapped themselves from their stations and sprinted across the deck, streaming towards the lifters that would carry them to the banks of saviour pods.

Bjargborn made to do the same. The chamber shuddered as the first stabs of las-fire cracked into the *Undrider*'s structure.

'And what of you, lord?' he asked, still deferent even as the ship began to come apart around them.

Jorundur smiled, already moving.

'Look to your own, master,' he said. 'I can handle myself.'

Then the lance fired – a brief, silent stab of immense energy out in the void – and everything turned to fire.

CHAPTER EIGHT

Gunnlaugur *roared*.

The bellow of raw aggression made his lungs burn and the bridge around him tremble. He whirled his hammer around his head, picking up tremendous amounts of momentum before loosing his fury at the horror before him.

Around him, his pack did the same. He saw Hafloí launch himself into action with typical reckless abandon. He saw Ingvar and Váltyr work off one another, the two of them forming a seamless wall of swordplay. A rain of bolts punched into the creature's bloated withers, puncturing the translucent skin and exploding in wet, muffled slaps.

Fighting it was like fighting a sea of living fat. Sword edges snagged on it, gripped by the cloying matter. Hafloí's pistol-rounds seemed to do no more than pockmark it. Only Olgeir's heavy ammunition made much headway – his relentless barrage had carved a vast, weeping gash in the mutant's putrescent hide.

Gunnlaugur's thunder hammer was the next most effective weapon. Its charged head could shear swathes of juddering flesh away, ripping it up and throwing chunks clear. He felt like a reaper of old, striding into the mouldering heart of the beast and carving his way towards its heart.

The sensation did him good. He could lose himself in his battle-anger. The doubts and trials of the past few weeks meant nothing in the heat of combat; all that existed for him then was his fury, unleashed on the flood.

Hjortur had been the same. The old Wolf Guard had been an immense presence to fight alongside. He'd howled to the sky while charging in close, his axe whirling. It had looked messy, but that was all artifice. No Sky Warrior fought inexpertly, not once they'd emerged from the testing ground of the Blood Claws. The battle-cries, the posturing, the bravado, the howls and growls, that was all to chill the blood of the enemy, to stir the ancient spirits of murder, to loosen the amber-eyed wolf within.

To kill, kill and kill again. That was what he had been bred to do. That, in the end, was what they had all been created to accomplish. A Space Wolf was an axe-blade, a sword edge, a hammer's head. Life offered nothing finer for those who understood that; only misery awaited the Son of Russ who queried that purity of purpose.

His gripped the handle of *skulbrotsjór*, relishing the familiar weight and heft of it in his armoured hands.

'*Deyja, hrogn af Helvíti!*' he thundered in battle-cant, hacking and sweeping, feeling the muscles of his mighty arms sing.

The creature responded. It did so blindly, erratically, all the while screaming from its grotesquely tiny head. New growths burst out from its innards, glossy and shining like embryos. Polyps emerged from pores, bursting in clouds of foul-smelling gas. Ragged jaws opened up all across its body, splitting the skin and exposing concentric rows of black teeth.

One bursting polyp caught Haflói full in the face. He staggered back, clutching at his facemask, hacking uncontrollably. Baldr got himself entangled between two snapping pairs of flesh-jaws, and a mountain of blubber rose up over him, quivering with the anticipation of drowning him in a tide of corpulence.

Ingvar broke free immediately and waded towards Baldr, slicing through sweeps of jellied meat with his lightning-arced blade. That blunted the effectiveness of Váltyr's attack, and the blademaster was forced backwards before a snaking forest of barbed, poisonous feelers.

Gunnlaugur snarled. The pack's momentum was faltering.

The head. Always strike corruption at the head.

He glanced up, spying the raging, wailing skull of the creature as it flailed around in a spittle-laced fit. Three metres away, and nothing but jaws and adipose horror in between.

'Russ guide me,' he whispered, crouching down and tensing. The pistons in his power armour geared up, responding to his physical and mental cues. He gripped his thunder hammer two-handed, feeling the shaft vibrate as the lightning-crowned head whined up to full power.

He launched himself into the air, propelled by his enormous strength and boosted by his armour. As he swept towards the creature's shrunken head, he raised *skulbrotsjór* high.

At the last moment the creature sensed the danger. Its blind head snapped towards him, screaming hatred.

Then Gunnlaugur landed. The thunder hammer plunged downwards, cleaving straight through the monster's skull and boring through what remained of its upper body. Gunnlaugur heard bones snap and organs splatter. The screaming broke off abruptly, replaced by the sick splat of watery flesh-sacs bursting and the stench of disruptor-scorched skin.

Gunnlaugur's weight carried him down. He plummeted into the heart of the beast, cutting through with the still-burning *skulbrotsjór*. Waves of blotchy, greasy fluid crashed over him, dragging him under, enveloping him in a clutching swamp of sucking, ruined tissue.

He kept fighting, feeling the pressure of the beast's headless carcass press against him. Curtains of visceral slime washed down his armour, smearing his helm lenses. It felt like being thrown into an ocean of slops and foetid offal.

The pressure built up. Gunnlaugur felt his grip on his hammer slip and struggled to hold on. The tide of blubber rose over his head, burying him in cloying, suffocating bulk. Moving his limbs became difficult, like swimming against a riptide. He raged on, hearing his thunderous battle-cries become muffled as slick nodules of flesh pressed against his helm.

Then, just as it was getting tricky, the pressure released. The walls of fat and stink abruptly shivered, quaked, and began to fall apart. Gunnlaugur heard the snarls and howls of his pack coming for him. His hammer whipped around in front of him, cutting cleanly through the rapidly diminishing press of bloody brawn and sinew.

His head burst free, dripping with gore-flecked sludge. He saw Olgeir wading towards him, the great one using his bulk and strength to rip the creature apart.

He was using his *hands*. That made Gunnlaugur laugh – a brutal laugh of joy in battle.

'*Hjá*, Heavy-hand!' he roared, greeting the arrival of the heavy weapons specialist with a slopping salute of his gristle-dripping hammer.

Then he saw the others, all cutting and slicing their way towards his position. In the face of that combined assault, what remained of the vast creature melted and shuddered away, sliding into a foaming, bursting morass of shapeless tallow.

Olgeir extended his gauntlet to Gunnlaugur, seizing him and dragging him clear.

'That was a mighty leap, *vaerangi*,' he said.

Gunnlaugur broke clear of the last of it, his armour caked in gobbets of slime. Now that the thing was dead, the euphoria of the kill was waning fast, giving way immediately to a fresh sensation of danger. The floor under his feet was trembling.

'What of the ship?' he asked.

'This *is* the ship,' said Baldr grimly, standing knee-deep in a bubbling pool of blubber. 'We need to leave.'

Even as he spoke, that truth became obvious. The horror's residual flesh was blackening fast, hardening and stiffening as if scorched by fire. The tendrils it had used to link to the ship's corrupted spirit snapped, severing the arteries of control.

Marsh-gas lumens above them flickered and died, plunging them into darkness. From far below, the destroyer's engine-growl halted, restarted, then halted again, as if the entire vessel were having a massive coronary. Corroded pipes running up the glistening walls of the bridge burst open, showering the space in oily spurts of coolant.

Gunnlaugur shook off the last stringy lengths of sinew and started to move.

'The whelp?' he asked.

'He'll live,' said Ingvar, supporting Hafloí as the pack began to withdraw. The Blood Claw's helm was cracked half open, exposing a raw mass of bloody flesh beneath. He was breathing, though, and the wound was already clotting.

'Can we make the Caestus?' asked Baldr, bringing up the rear as the pack hastened out of the bridge and into the gloomy corridors beyond.

'We'll see,' said Gunnlaugur, picking up the pace as the bridge around them began to convulse. 'But if we can't, pray that Old Dog's still flying the *Undrider*.'

* * *

The *Undrider* was broken, impaled by a scything column of energy. Whole sections of hull peeled free, shearing clear of the stricken core and rolling slowly planetwards. A fuel tank breached, causing a fireball to roar through the containment cages and sweep through the lower decks, raging thirstily as it destroyed ammo dumps and power storage cells.

Some of the crew had made it into saviour pods, jettisoning free of the dying ship even as the lance-strike burned through it. The cloud of tiny vessels – little more than teardrop-shaped caskets of adamantium – burned their way into Ras Shakeh's atmosphere, lighting up like torches as they spiralled down to the surface.

Jorundur saw none of that. His last clear view of anything had been Bjargborn's head being blasted apart by a leaping crackle of electric discharge. Then the command chamber had collapsed around him, bursting into a sun-hot cloud of flying crystal shards and powdered marble.

His armour absorbed much of the impact, but he didn't go unscathed. The servos in his right leg-plate buckled, and he crushed his left wrist against something heavy as he landed, twenty metres away from where he had been standing. The impact was bone-jarringly hard, sending radial judders down his spine and causing him to black out momentarily.

He moved like an automaton after that. His survival instincts propelled him even as his mind remained blurred and sluggish. He clawed his way free of the wreckage, somehow finding the half-destroyed doors at the rear of the command chamber and dragging himself through them.

The escaping atmosphere howled around him into the burning void, dragging detritus with it. Jorundur crawled onwards, his senses gradually returning to clarity. He could feel pain burning all over his body. His retinal display listed all the ways his battleplate had been battered and dented. The only important factor was its airtight seal, which appeared to be intact. Jorundur's breath echoed raggedly in his helm, and he could already taste the staleness of the oxygen recycled through his suit's filters.

More crashes rang out, roaring up from the flame-ridden bowels of the frigate. Everything around him seemed to be in motion – the walls of the corridor shook, rolled and buckled. Wall sections further down broke open, revealing the glow of swelling fires beyond.

Jorundur clambered to his feet and started to run. Keeping his feet on the rolling deck was difficult, even with his preternatural balance. He slammed into the nearside wall, staggering away from it. Then the floor began to give way.

He leapt ahead, landing heavily on a firmer patch as the metal walkway tumbled into ruin. Gouts of fire-flecked smoke poured up from where the floor plates had been, filling the narrow space with choking waves of smog.

'Hel,' he spat, feeling his body protest as he pulled himself back into motion. 'This is *absurd*.'

He limped, crawled and lurched onwards, buffeted by the raging destruction around him. The corridor gave way to an intersection, then to an access tunnel, then an open hallway with a crumbling roof and jagged crevasses snaking across its floor. Explosions shook the walls, multiplying into an overlapping orgy of demolition. Bodies were everywhere, hurled on top of one another, stuffed into blocked service hatches, hanging from stairwells, all beginning to burn as the growing flames lapped at them.

When Jorundur finally reached his destination he barely recognised it. Sheets of blue-tinged fire coursed down the melting entrance passage. A whole segment of outer hull had peeled away over to his right, exposing dizzying patches of emptiness. He had a brief glimpse of stars striated with flying lines of wreckage. There was no sign of the enemy destroyer, and he briefly wondered why it hadn't closed in for the kill yet. The ground beneath him rippled like water, snapping pressed-steel panels as if they were made of glass.

He broke into a limping run, racing over the disintegrating floor and skirting past igniting piles of fuel tanks. The ship was coming apart around him. He felt his footfalls growing lighter as the grav-generators gave out.

'*Skítja*,' he swore as he tumbled forwards, careering into a pile of ammo cases and sending them flying. Unable to arrest his forward momentum, he blundered on, slewing through the half-open shutters of the entrance passage and into the huge space beyond.

Once through, he skidded along a wide, open patch of buckling rock-crete. He had the vague impression of an enormous vaulted roof above him, zigzagged with growing cracks. The lack of air made everything strangely balletic – a choreographed dissolution in total silence.

Ahead of him was the gulf into the void. He saw the starfield beckoning, broken only by lines of spinning debris. He'd made it to the outer skin of the *Undrider*, beyond which there was nothing but empty space.

For a moment he thought he'd be carried straight out, shooting clear of the collapsing structure and somersaulting into vacuum.

He avoided that by a hand's breadth. He shot his intact left hand out to catch the trailing edge of the landing gear as he sailed past it, grunting from the effort. His gauntlet closed over the metal strut, arresting his out-ward trajectory with a jerk. Once secured, he began to haul himself back up, struggling against the hurricane of flying wreckage.

He looked up, seeing a familiar grey cockpit looming over him. For all its bulk, it was already beginning to slide towards the void as the docking clamps holding it in place twisted and snapped.

Jorundur grimaced, and started to pull himself towards the entrance hatch.

'No you don't, you ugly bastard,' he said through gritted teeth. 'Not... *yet...*'

The plague-ship was dead and drifting, locked into a steadily accelerating tilt towards the planet below. The animating presence lurking at its heart was gone, and like a vast body suddenly bereft of its brainstem the whole vessel began to go haywire.

Ingvar ran hard, keeping Haflói on his feet and trying not to lose ground with the rest of the pack. Together they tore through the warped labyrinth of the ship's gruesome interior, going as swiftly as the cramped space and treacherous footing would allow. The route they'd taken to reach the bridge was closed to them – blocked by a furious, acidic inferno belching out of the ship's tortured innards – and so they'd been forced to make their way down through the narrow capillaries of the destroyer's crew decks.

It was hard to believe that the ship had once been designed by the hand of man. Once, many thousands of years ago, it would have been a creation of iron and adamantium, proudly bearing the insignias of the Imperial Navy on its golden prow and commanded by mortal officers bearing the sacred aquila on their breasts.

After millennia of corruption, little remained of that. Every surface had been warped and twisted, curled away from its original purpose and compelled into new, troublingly carnal forms. The narrow airways were thick with spores, and the spongy floors were clogged with filth. Every metal strut and beam was thick with oxidisation. The machinery, all of it ancient and arcane in its own right, had morphed into bizarre techno-biological hybrids, quivering with organesque appendages and glossy with cascades of dribbling fluid.

When it started to break open, it did so like a body. Blood coursed down from the sagging ceilings; pus pooled in the torn gaps between wall sections, oozing like infection across a scabrous hide.

'No signal from the *Undrider*,' reported Baldr, leaping over a dissolving patch of hissing floorspace. 'Nothing at all.'

The plague-ship suddenly lurched hard, throwing them against the pulpy walls. The narrow tunnel started to shiver more violently.

'Out of interest,' asked Váltyr, struggling to keep his feet, 'how close are we to re-entry?'

'You had to ask,' grunted Olgeir.

The pack pressed on, going as fast as the treacherous conditions permitted. With every step, the stench and filth intensified around them.

Eventually they burst out of the tunnels and into a larger domed chamber. It had been set into the side of the ship, and its exterior wall was entirely taken up by a multi-faceted window in the shape of a giant eye. The place might once have been a viewing gallery, built in an age when starships carried more than purely military crew.

Now it was a charnel house, a rotting canker of accumulated foulness. Death-bloated corpses hung from the roof on rusting hooks. Maggots carpeted the floor, wriggling across a sickening floorspace of mouldering cadavers. Bleached skulls protruded from the festering mass, barely visible under the clouds of flies that droned around them.

As they entered, the heaps of putrescence stirred. Bodies, clad in robes of mildewed sackcloth, twisted to meet the intruders. Their cowled faces were masked by obscenely long rebreathers, and their round eye-lenses glowed lime-green in the dark. Like the mutants they'd seen earlier they carried toxin weapons in their bony hands. Oblivious to the slow doom encompassing their ship, they limped towards the pack, chattering to one another in half-breathed, sibilant voices.

'Slay them!' thundered Gunnlaugur, kicking aside the heaps of decaying body-parts to get at them. 'Slay them all!'

Olgeir's bolter opened up again, sending severed limbs spinning and bouncing across the chamber.

Ingvar didn't follow the order. Dozens of the creatures had already risen; many more were stirring. There would be hundreds before long, drawn from every stinking hole and pit in the ship by the sounds of battle.

They were running out of time. Soon the ship would begin to roll into the planet's atmosphere and the whole structure would burn. Gunnlaugur would never admit it, but they'd left it too late to reach the Caestus. They'd still be fighting their way towards it when the first flames began to lick along the destroyer's hull.

Hafloí struggled to free himself from Ingvar's grip. Though still spore-blind and bleeding, he wanted to fight. Ingvar didn't let him go.

'Bastard,' Hafloí slurred groggily.

Ingvar ran another sweep via his helm-mounted sensors, searching for some sign that the *Undrider* had survived.

He got nothing: the frigate was gone. Ingvar felt his heart sink. Gunnlaugur's gambit had been too risky; they should have withdrawn when they'd had the chance.

He was about to give up, to return to the fight, when something suddenly registered. He picked up a signal in the void, moving fast, closing on their position.

The way it flew was familiar. Ingvar smiled.

'Brothers!' he roared, dragging Hafloí over to the huge window. 'We have to leave! We have to leave *now!*'

They didn't listen. They couldn't listen. They were already hard-pressed by hordes of grave-mutants. The whole chamber crawled with them – snaking down from the meathooks, burrowing up from the butcher's piles, shuffling into the chamber from corridor orifices.

Ingvar turned to Hafloí, and activated *dausvjer*'s disruptor.

'Hold your breath, whelp,' he said. 'This is going to hurt.'

He lashed out with the blade, shattering the window. The sword's energy field exploded and the iron frame cracked outwards. Foul air exploded through the breach, wrenching the rest of the window free and blowing the contents of the charnel chamber out into the void.

Ingvar was ripped out first, shooting clear of the destroyer's hull in a tumbling rain of crystal and iron. He kept a tight grip on Hafloí's cracked helm, squeezing it tight in his gauntlet and trying to stem air-loss.

A messy spume of spinning bones and cadaverous flesh shot out after them. Among the spreading fog of decay tumbled the grave-mutants, clutching wildly at nothing and gasping for air through their useless masks. The armour-sealed Space Marines came along with them, protected from the shock of exit and oxygen loss though powerless to halt their ejection.

'What in *Hel*?' demanded Gunnlaugur over the comm, sounding choked with rage as he rolled clumsily through space. 'What are you *doing*?'

'Look up,' replied Ingvar calmly.

Vuokho swooped in close, manoeuvring expertly on its retros as beams of las-fire flickered around it. It hovered over the expanding cloud of falling bodies, swivelling on its axis and opening the frontal crew-bay doors.

'Six of you,' came Jorundur's sour voice on the pack-wide comm, dripping with irritation. 'This could take a while. For Russ's sake, try not to thrash about.'

The two vessel-corpses carved their way into Ras Shakeh's upper atmosphere, lighting up in vivid trails of flame.

One was the *Undrider*, barely more than a semi-coherent collection of melting metal plates.

The other was the plague-ship. Its core integrity remained intact until the full force of re-entry hit. Its swollen underside began to glow rust-red, then orange, then eye-watering white. It exploded shortly after that, spreading a network of burning debris across the skies of the planet below.

Gunnlaugur watched both ships burn from the sanctuary of *Vuokho*'s cockpit. Since being recovered, his mood had blackened. He'd always found it difficult to come down from the fearsome endorphin-high of combat. This time, though, it was doubly hard. Jorundur had sensed it, and for once attempted no acerbic comment. They sat together in silence, watching the wreckage below them twist and blaze.

All across the control console, *Vuokho*'s machine-spirit sent them angry warnings of imminent systems failure. The gunship had taken a lot of damage from the enemy's close gunners. Just making planetfall would be an achievement.

The whole pack was subdued. Hafloí had nearly died. Váltyr shared Gunnlaugur's anger with Ingvar, convinced that they could have fought their way to the Caestus before it was too late to launch. Baldr and Olgeir had said nothing about it, though even Heavy-hand had found little to smile about after his recovery.

It had been victory, of a sort. They were alive, the enemy was dead. Somehow, given the carnage, given how close it had been, it was hard to see things that way.

He overruled me.

Gunnlaugur suppressed the thought, knowing where it would lead. Dealing with Ingvar would have to wait

He turned to Jorundur. The two of them were alone, sitting side by side; the others had remained in the crew compartment below.

'So,' he said. 'Tell me. What was that?'

'Only guesses, *vaerangi*,' said Jorundur.

'Any signal from the planet?'

'Still silent.'

Gunnlaugur looked down at the Thunderhawk's scrolling auspex readings. He saw patterns of conurbations down on the surface – sprawls of industrial cities, web-like traceries of roads, the puckered mass of mountain ranges. Some of it was burning; trails of black smoke stained the atmosphere across a whole band of urbanised terrain.

'No orbital defences,' he said. 'One ship couldn't have taken them down. There must have been others.'

Jorundur looked sceptical. 'Then why aren't they still here?'

'They did what they came for – landed forces, then moved on. We saw empty depots on the destroyer. It stayed behind. A sentry, perhaps, over-looking the planetary assault.'

Jorundur nodded slowly. 'Perhaps.'

Gunnlaugur scrutinised the auspex feeds. Their resolution wasn't enough to make out much detail, but the damage on the surface was hard to miss.

'There's fighting down there,' he said. 'Movement. I can see it. If we're getting no readings, then they're being jammed.'

'We have to land,' said Jorundur. 'We're losing power. Soon we'll lose our hull. Here are the drop coordinates we were given.'

Gunnlaugur watched as the picters scanned across to them. He saw a blurry urban splash of pale grey against red earth. He saw two concentric walls, and what looked like massive defensive installations arranged in ter-raced rows. There was no burning around those walls; the nearest sign of destruction was hundreds of kilometres to the south-west.

'Looks undamaged,' he said. 'Take us down. Broadcast encrypted landing clearance on the secure comm. I'll get Olgeir up here to man the guns – we might need him.'

Jorundur started to move the heavy control columns, and the gunship's battered muzzle dipped towards the world's curve.

'What are you expecting?' he asked, trying to lighten the oppressive atmosphere.

'I don't know,' said Gunnlaugur, sinking back into his seat and falling silent. 'I really don't know.'

II
THE WOUNDED HEART

CHAPTER NINE

Sister Uwe Bajola rose before sunrise, as she always did, and went to the west-facing wall of her cell, as she always did.

In the hour of deep-red shadows, before the full day's heat properly arrived, her mind was clear and her body was calm. Routine calmed it further. She had always appreciated the familiar rhythms, the mechanical purity of repetition. In times of trial they had a particular value.

She opened the gahlwood door and padded out onto the balcony. She took a deep breath. The air was already warming. It tasted of sand.

Bajola leaned on the balcony and felt the last of the night's breeze press against the cotton of her shift. That was pleasant, for the short while it lasted. Though raised on a world of unrelenting sun, her melanin-rich skin as black as her battle-armour, she had never quite come to terms with Ras Shakeh's climate. Something about the sunlight was wrong. It burned, but did not warm; it dazzled, but did not illuminate.

She bowed her head, running a hand absently over her cropped hair. Such thoughts, such ingratitude, were unworthy.

Cleanse my soul, she mouthed, reciting the words in her head, remembering how they'd looked on the parchment when she'd first learned them.

> *Cleanse my soul;*
> *Clear my mind;*
> *Enable my body.*
> *Grant that my station may serve;*
> *Grant that my strength may suffice;*
> *Grant that my life may give honour;*
> *Grant that my death may earn it.*

They were beautiful words. They comforted her; they always had. She closed her eyes for a moment, enjoying the quiet of the pre-dawn. In the distance she heard the *erh-erh* of klohawks. The scents of the city rose to meet her: gently warming rockcrete, dried spices, burning oil, gahl trees turning their speared leaves to face the rising sun.

Only in the hour before dawn was the city of Hjec Aleja restful. As the flaming orange sunrise tipped over the western horizon, the manufactories would start up again, the dust-crawlers would begin to move, the garrisons would empty and refill as the watches were cycled.

Until then, she could watch the place sleeping, cooled by the long night, the toils and strains and nightmares subdued for a while, if not forgotten.

Her balcony was high up, near the summit of the Third Spire of the Cathedral of Blessed Alexia, so she could see a long way. Her deep brown eyes ran over the cityscape as it unfolded below her.

She saw tight-packed streets with tiled roofs, arranged in a haphazard maze of overhanging eaves. No thoroughfare in Hjec Aleja ever ran straight. When she'd first arrived she'd assumed that was an accident. Only later had she discovered the myriad superstitions of the planet. A straight road let in mirage-spirits, she had been told. Keep the way crooked, and they can't find the thresholds.

Stupid beliefs they were, probably heretical, but tolerated for so long that opposing them had long ago been abandoned. Bajola knew that de Chatelaine would have loved nothing more than to purge the world of its theological untidiness – it was a shrineworld, after all – but even she had to bend when faced with something ground so deep, so, impervious, like the endless red dust that you could never scrub from your fingernails or keep from caking on your lips.

Besides, the people of Ras Shakeh worshipped the Emperor fervently enough. They could be forgiven their eccentricities, which even the canoness allowed were harmless.

In any case, now that the horror had arrived, such things had ceased to be important. Bajola screwed her eyes up, gazing into the rusty haze of the horizon, wondering when that empty land would first fill with the cloud-blight of marching soldiers.

Soon. All the strategeos told them that, shaking their heads as they looked into their tactical projections. Progress had been astonishing since the landings: unreasonably fast, unreasonably brutal.

When she had been younger, newly inducted into the Orders Famulous and sent out into the void on her first diplomatic missions, Bajola had been troubled by what she saw of the Archenemy's work. Why, she had wondered, did the Emperor, the omnipotent Master of Mankind, permit such terror to exist in the universe? He must have been capable of destroying it, just as he had once destroyed the heresy of his greatest son.

The error of that thinking had led to castigation fairly swiftly. Canoness Reich, her first superior in the Order, had been unequivocal.

'What do you want, child?' she had demanded, fixing her with those biting, ice-blue eyes. 'A life of comfort? What d'you think would become of us then?'

She'd leaned over to Bajola, jabbing her in the chest with her bronze augmetic finger.

'We'd become fat. We'd become corrupt. Conflict keeps us lean, fit, pure, the way we were meant to be.'

Bajola had been more easily cowed then. Reich had been a formidable woman.

'He orders the universe as it should be. Welcome the test, child. Welcome the knowledge that the void harbours terror. Without terror, there are no heroes.'

It had been easy to say, and easy to believe. Now, watching the sun rise over a doomed world, waiting for the ranks of terror to close on the last city, the aphorism felt hollow.

Bajola was not so easily cowed now. She was capable of making her own mind up.

Grant that my life may give honour;
Grant that my death may earn it.

A first sliver of gold broke over the distant ridge of the Djarl peaks. Almost immediately the air began to feel hotter.

She could have stayed there for a long time, gathering her thoughts before the day's labours began. When her comm-bead disturbed her, buzzing into life as she watched the first amber rays of sunlight angle through the mountains, it was an irritation.

Early, for a summons.

'Bajola,' she acknowledged, moving away from the balcony and slapping the railing's dust from her hands.

'Sister Palatine,' came the response. It was Callia, one of de Chatelaine's aides. 'The canoness demands your presence. Hall of the Halicon, twenty minutes.'

Bajola smiled. Typically terse.

'On my way,' she said. 'Did the canoness say what it was about?'

The link cut dead. Either Callia was being rude, or she was ferociously busy. The latter was more likely.

Bajola walked back into her cell. Not much to look at – a narrow bed with no covers, a devotional pict of Saint Alexia, a metal-bound chest containing her robes, a bolter hung on the wall from iron brackets and draped in embroidered benedictions.

Her eyes lighted on the weapon. It had an ugly, blunt aspect. Even though she'd long since left the Order Famulous behind and embraced the way of the Wounded Heart, she'd never learned to love the core tool of her adopted trade.

Get over it, she thought to herself, pulling the shift over her head and starting to dress. *You'll be using it again soon.*

When she arrived at the Hall of the Halicon, the place was in a frenzy of preparation. That was unusual. Ever since fighting had broken out, the grand ceremonial space had been virtually unused, its marble surfaces surrendered to the drifting, gritty air.

Now hundreds of labourers were at work, polishing statuary, rolling out long crimson carpets, hanging banners with the bloody symbols of the Wounded Heart sewn in crimson and gold thread.

As soon as she saw that work, Bajola's spirits rose a little. She knew who had been summoned. So perhaps they had made it. Perhaps it would be a whole battle company of them. That would be something worth seeing; it might even turn the tide.

She couldn't see the canoness. She walked up the wide stairway, feeling the first pricks of sweat at her neck, trying to catch a glimpse of de Chatelaine in the milling crowds.

The Hall was an obscene place, a vulgar display of power and indulgence that sat uneasily with Ras Shakeh's windswept emptiness. Bajola hated it, the canoness hated it, everyone who worked in it hated it. Unlike the white-walled structures in the rest of the city, the Hall had been constructed from a dark-veined stone that sucked in the sunlight during the day and made the interior shimmer with close, sweaty heat.

Its bulk was out of all proportion to the older buildings around it. Rings of corded pillars supported an ornate panelled ceiling of stuccoed cherubs and milk-faced saints. Incense burners swung from the vaults above, staining the patterned floors with saccharine aromas. Golden statues of heroes stood in ranks down the echoing aisles, their melancholy, smug faces turned to the starry heavens for inspiration.

The Order had not been responsible for the Hall's construction. Cardinal Tomojo-Kech had built it seven hundred years ago, demolishing a more suitably austere priory that had stood on the site since the Order had first come to Ras Shakeh in the 37th millennium. No one knew how much it had cost to ship such huge quantities of precious commodities to such an isolated place. Perhaps the extravagance had been what had cost Tomojo-Kech his head during the Jericar Purges; perhaps not. It was always hard to know.

His legacy had lasted, though. The Halicon citadel, of which the Hall was the major part, dominated the mountain city of Hjec Aleja, squatting atop the rocky outcrop at its heart and gazing out across the plains with overblown grandeur. All roads in the city led there, sooner or later, snaking up the narrow causeways and switchbacks until they emerged at the Plaza of Triumph, two hundred metres above the ochre plains and baking under the sun.

Bajola preferred the cathedral, her own demesne, set outside the inner walls of the city and placed within the teeming outer hab-districts. It was where it ought to be, close to those who needed it, allowing the priests to minister to the faithful rather than sweat away in Tomojo-Kech's folly up on the mountain.

Bajola pushed her way through the crowds, smelling their odour of sweat and incense, before catching sight of the canoness at last.

Alexis de Chatelaine saw her coming and nodded sharply in what passed for acknowledgement with her.

'You're late,' she said.

'Forgive me,' said Bajola, bowing. 'The streets were clogged.'

De Chatelaine pursed her lips. 'Word has got out already. I don't know how. The masses will always find a way. If we could tap that, turn their ferreting curiosity into something useful, I would not fear losing this war.'

The canoness was a clipped, severe figure. Her silver hair, cut into a sheer razor-bob, framed a hard-edged face made old by a lifetime of devotion. Her lips were thin and her flesh was roughened from both the sun and age. De Chatelaine scorned cosmetic treatment and so looked every year of her one hundred and forty-two winters. For all that, her movements gave away her essential vigour. She could still fight, and Bajola knew her will was as starkly unbending as ever. She dominated the space around her, tall and spear-lean in night-black armour plate, trimmed with pale ermine and decorated by the crimson cracked heart device in pearl and ruby.

'They heard more than I did,' admitted Bajola.

'Then I shall enlighten you, child,' said de Chatelaine. 'Emperor be praised, our summons have been answered. I could almost have given up, but that would have been a failure of faith, would it not? The Wolves of Fenris have sent their forces, just as their Great Wolf promised. The timing is propitious. They have already given battle to the enemy and have emerged victorious. Now we are tracking them. They will be here within hours.'

Bajola placed her hands together and bowed her head. A mix of emotions surged through her – she had begun to insulate herself against the possibility that they might not come.

'How many?' she asked.

'I do not know. I fear not many. But recall this – a single warrior of the Adeptus Astartes is worth a hundred Guardsmen. In the cause of morale, his value is even higher. They will kill at a rate that even our Celestians cannot match.'

'So I have heard. Let us hope the stories are true.'

'Of course they're true,' she snapped. 'I've fought with them before. Watch your thoughts, Palatine.'

Bajola bowed in apology. It was something she'd become used to, when speaking to the canoness.

'I mean no disrespect,' she said. 'But our service has been with the Adulators, who are steeped in our ways and are on close terms with the holy orders of the Ecclesiarchy. These are the Wolves. I have heard... things.'

De Chatelaine's expression softened a little.

'So have I,' she said. 'Who has not? But these are the instruments the Emperor chooses to make available to us, and so, by necessity, they are the right ones.'

Bajola sometimes found de Chatelaine's ramrod faith touching, almost juvenile. To admit that, though, even to herself, was dangerous.

'That is so,' she said. 'I look forward to meeting them.'

'You will do more than that. I wish you to work with them. You will be our conduit. I trust that meets with your approval.'

Bajola felt a brief twinge of surprise. 'Of course,' she said. 'But, I–'

'You were of the Famulous before you joined us,' said de Chatelaine. 'The diplomats. I take it you have retained some of those skills. We will need them.'

The canoness lowered her voice, moving her head closer to Bajola's.

'Matters have not always gone well between the Church and the Wolves,' she said. 'You know this, and they will not have forgotten it. I am not a fool, Palatine: I am aware of the potential for strife, and I wish to limit it. We will have to find some way of working together if we are not to end our days on this dust-blown rock.'

She placed her gauntlet over Bajola's hand. It was a strangely protective gesture from a battle-hardened woman.

'Do not let me down, Uwe,' she said. 'You will be the voice of calm that smooths the way between us.'

Bajola swallowed her discomfort. Working with the Wolves directly had not been something she'd considered. Unlike the canoness, she had long since got used to the idea that they weren't coming. It was a complication, though maybe one she should have foreseen.

She bowed. 'By His will,' she said.

When she raised her head again, de Chatelaine was no longer looking at her. The commotion in the hall was growing. From the Plaza outside came the noise of Shakeh Guardsmen shouting something in Haljeha, something about an incoming ship on the horizon.

'Earlier than I expected,' said de Chatelaine, fixing her green eyes on the ornate entrance gates as if she could peer through them. 'Perhaps I should not be surprised.'

She took a deep breath, and released Bajola's hand.

'Prepare yourself, Palatine,' she said. 'The Wolves approach.'

They were, and they weren't, what she'd imagined.

Seven of them strode through the Hall gates, shaking the dust from their armour as they came. De Chatelaine had used what little time remained to her well, and the audience chamber was as clean and well ordered as could have been hoped for. Lines of Guardsmen stood to attention along either aisle, their uniforms scrubbed clear of the worst of the grit and bloodstains.

Squads of Battle Sisters stood beside them, far more imposing in their pristine black power armour. Bajola felt a swell of pride just looking at them. Some of her Sisters had returned from the front mere days ago, carrying stories of horror with them. They stood to attention in neat ranks, eyes gazing straight ahead, betraying nothing but rigid, silent resolve.

De Chatelaine waited for the Wolves at the far end of the chamber. A marble dais of wide steps led up to a blood-red leather-upholstered throne surmounted by a gaudy tableau of angels and writhing serpents. The canoness had chosen not to make use of that, but stood at the base of the stairs, clad in her regulation battleplate. A small coterie of aides, including Callia and Bajola, clustered around her.

Bajola watched the Wolves approach. She surprised herself by feeling a faint tremor of unease. Not fear, exactly; more like tension, as if an attack were imminent. The warriors in grey exuded a palpable atmosphere of intimidation. It rose from them as they moved, flowing from their limbs like musk, hanging in the air behind them.

She studied them as they neared, moving her eyes from each one to the next, soaking in as much information as she could and storing it away, just as she had been trained to.

Observe. Retain. Scan for weakness; watch for strength.

Their leader was obvious. He walked with a fighter's rolling gait. He wore his full armour minus the helm, and it made him massive. His head was bald and marked with tribal tattoos. A matted grey beard tumbled across his breastplate. The hair looked filthy, as if it had been dipped in a bucket of boiling lard and the slops had been left to dry.

They were all dirty. They stank of rotten meat. Their chipped battleplate was smeared with blood and grease and grime. They were hirsute and grim-faced, save for one: a younger-looking warrior with flame-red hair and a raw weal running crossways the length of his face. That one could almost have passed for human.

She had expected them to look savage. She had expected the grinding whine of power armour, the clanking bone-totems, the back-slung weapons with runes carved finely on the blades.

She hadn't expected the stench. She hadn't expected the sheer aura of belligerence, the thick expressions of surly violence in their amber eyes.

They were beasts. They were beasts clad in the rags of humanity, given a veneer of civilisation to mask the deep animal within.

As she was wont to, as she always did, she found herself wondering why the blessed Emperor would have created and given sanction to such things.

The answer came to mind almost immediately.

Because they are needed.

Bajola noticed that one of them carried himself differently to the others. His eyes were grey, not golden. His exposed face was equally marked by scarification and tribe-marks, but he walked taller, with less swagger. He was contained, wrapped up in himself. The others let their souls spill out in front of them, betraying their essential core of menace, glorying in the dominance they so casually projected.

The grey-eyed one did not.

Once, a very long time ago while serving with her old Order, Bajola had witnessed a squad of Ultramarines accompanying an Inquisitorial retinue. She'd been awe-struck by them – their discipline, their confidence, their reserve. The grey-eyed warrior carried himself a little like they had done. That was strange. She wondered whether anyone else had noticed. She even wondered whether the rest of his pack had noticed – such subtle signals were hard to read and easy to miss.

The leader drew up before de Chatelaine. At close quarters he was immense, a mountain of brutal energy encased in dirty ceramite.

'I am called Wolf Guard Gunnlaugur,' he announced. 'Of the Great Company of Ragnar Blackmane, of the Rout of Fenris.'

His voice was harsh, a grating thrum of pit-deep hazard.

'You are welcome, Son of Fenris,' replied de Chatelaine. Her voice was dry and clear. If the canoness felt any uneasiness in his presence, she didn't show it. 'We are grateful to the Great Wolf for sending you. We are grateful to you for coming.'

Gunnlaugur grunted. 'Glad you're pleased to see us. That ship up there wasn't.'

'You destroyed it,' said de Chatelaine. 'That was your first great service to us. We shall not forget it – it was a mighty deed.'

'Mighty? I lost my own. That is a great shame to have hanging on my shoulders. We were not expecting to have to fight our way down.'

The canoness gave him an apologetic look.

'Yes, I am aware of that,' she said. 'If there had been any way of warning you–'

'There wasn't?'

'If we had been able to reach you, to help you, do you not think we would have done it?'

Bajola appreciated de Chatelaine's skill. The canoness spoke evenly, matching the Wolf's blunt challenges with calmness. It was not easy to quarrel with one who would not rise to it.

Gunnlaugur fixed her with his black-pinned gaze for a long time, assessing, appraising. Bajola half expected him to start sniffing.

'Tell me what has happened here,' he said at last.

'I fear you will not like it,' said de Chatelaine. 'You have landed in the middle of a war, Wolf Guard. Until you had arrived, I would have said it was one we could not win. Even now, I am not sure how long we have left.'

Gunnlaugur didn't look troubled by that. If anything, Bajola thought she caught the gleam of something like excitement in his eyes.

'We are here now,' he said. 'Anything is possible.'

After that, the conversation moved to the canoness's private chambers. The troops in the Hall dispersed, sent back to their barracks and bunkers where they could exchange wild theories about what they had just seen. Only de Chatelaine and her entourage – a dozen officers and officials – and the seven members of Gunnlaugur's pack took their places in the heavily shielded room behind the dais.

The ornamentation was less elaborate there, though the chairs had gilded backs and the polished table was formed of a priceless darkwood that didn't grow natively on Ras Shakeh. The walls were scrubbed plain and the floor was bare stone. Sunlight angled in from rows of half-blinded windows. Even with screens in place, the glare added to an already uncomfortably hot space.

The two parties took up places on either side of the table. The chamber had been fitted out with the largest, most sturdy set of furniture they had been able to find, but still the Wolves looked almost comically ill at ease when seated. Bajola guessed that they would have preferred to stand, but they didn't insist.

In their own way, they were making an effort. That was encouraging.

'So, the situation,' said de Chatelaine, pressing her hands together on the tabletop. 'The Adulators withdrew their defensive presence from here six months ago. By that time the cover they offered us was little more than token. We frequently went for months with no significant strike force within range. I was unhappy with the situation, as was the Chapter Master, but it became apparent that no easy resolution existed. The Ras subsector contains over thirty-nine inhabited worlds and has a population in excess of ninety billion souls, so merits more than cursory attention. But the Adulators have many concerns, and I believe that garrison work does not greatly appeal to them. Perhaps that is true of other Chapters too.'

Gunnlaugur listened intently. Bajola watched him drink the information in. She'd heard that Space Marines possessed eidetic recall. Then again, she'd heard many things about them, not all of which could possibly be true.

'You will be aware of plans to use this subsector as a staging post for a new crusade into lost space,' she went on. 'When I first learned of the proposals, I knew the process of organising such an undertaking would last decades. Nonetheless, the idea put us on the stellar cartograph, so to speak, and gave me leverage in my quest for more permanent defensive arrangements. Ancient pacts between the Ras subsector and the Fenrisian zone of protection were uncovered. I was informed by my scholiasts that the treaties had no current validity. I responded that anything was worth a try.'

Despite himself, Gunnlaugur smiled. It was a curious gesture. The Wolf Guard had an elongated jawline, crammed with overdeveloped dentition, especially the canines. His smile was more like a dog's growl, with the lips pulling back and the fangs jutting forwards.

Even their expressions of amusement, it seemed, served as a challenge.

'My motives were sound,' said de Chatelaine. 'We are not immune to the blights of heresy and sedition here. The problem has been growing, and my Sisters have been fully occupied over the past few years. We destroy one nest, another emerges. These heretics worship sickness. I have witnessed men expose themselves to crippling disease, revelling in their decay. The appeal of that eludes me, but then we do live, do we not, in a fallen galaxy?'

At the mention of plague-cults, a low murmur of recognition passed among the Wolves.

'The heretics,' Gunnlaugur said. 'They brought the war.'

'No, not them. They kept us occupied, but we never let them flourish for long. Do not think that my Sisters are afraid to use their flamers, Wolf Guard, for they are not.'

Gunnlaugur smiled again. Against all expectation, he and the canoness seemed to be finding each other's company agreeable.

'The enemy came from outside the subsector,' said de Chatelaine. 'The cults here did nothing more than prepare the ground for them. The ships must have arrived in-system before we sent our request for aid to you, but back then we had no inkling of their presence. It was a large fleet, and our defences were so paltry and undermanned that we stood no chance. We quickly lost what orbital grids we possessed. We prepared our cities for bombardment, assuming that destruction was what they wished for. It was not so. They landed forces – we do not know how many – and the majority of the fleet moved on. The ship you encountered was the only one they left behind. As we speak, dozens more are no doubt ravaging the rest of the subsector.'

Bajola watched de Chatelaine's expression grow tighter, more self-conscious. The canoness had taken the blame for the war on her own shoulders, and the ruin of her world pressed heavily on her. The fact that she had acted with the utmost propriety at every stage made no difference. De Chatelaine had exacting standards, and did not exempt herself from them.

'It happened so quickly,' she said, almost to herself. 'Too quickly. They have already overrun our industrial heartland. We have lost our population centres, our manufactories. A few hold-outs remain, but we receive word of capitulations every day. This planet is going dark. Two weeks ago I ordered the withdrawal of all remaining forces to this zone. We have succeeded in holding the city since then, but we know they are coming for us. Everyone here knows it.'

She smiled dryly.

'This is the planet you have landed on. I had hoped to show you an exemplary shrineworld, one from which the legions of the Emperor would march out to fresh conquest. Believe me, I am sorry that I cannot do that.'

Gunnlaugur leaned back in his seat, and the wooden chair creaked alarmingly under him. He hacked up a gobbet of phlegm, leaned over and spat on the floor.

'War has a way of following us,' he said. 'Truth be told, we like it that way. We get bored without it.'

De Chatelaine's advisers looked disapproving. Bajola could understand why – they had all suffered enormously; the savage in front of them was making light of it.

She stole a glance at the grey-eyed figure sitting at the far end of the pack. As her eyes lighted on him she caught him looking directly at her. She averted her gaze quickly, half embarrassed, half irritated.

He is studying me, just as I am studying him. Do I seem as outlandish to him as he does to me?

'If war is what you wish for, you will have no shortage of it on Ras Shakeh,' said de Chatelaine. Her expression had become severe again. The canoness disliked flippancy in most things; in the face of the horror that had come to her world, it bordered on obscenity. 'Though perhaps I have not adequately conveyed the scale of what faces us.'

She turned to Callia.

'Replay the footage from Jedaj,' she said. 'That may prove instructive.'

Callia nodded, rose from her chair and moved over to a wall-mounted projector. She adjusted the controls and the blinds slid down the windows. At the far end of the chamber, against a bare whitewashed wall, a picter image flickered into life.

'We retrieved this material six weeks ago,' explained de Chatelaine. 'It was taken by a defender of the ore-processing plant at Jedaj, five hundred kilometres south of here. I am not sure why he took it, nor why it survived. Perhaps he wanted a record of what had happened, or perhaps the enemy wished us to see what they are capable of. My first inclination was to destroy it, but I decided against it. It is not easy viewing, but then I am sure you are used to such things.'

As she finished speaking, the footage crackled into life. It was shaky and motion-blurred, as if the images had been shot from a helmet-mounted picter. The first pictures were dark and grainy, indicating night-vision enhancement.

Bajola hadn't seen the footage before. She'd been offered the chance when it had first come in, and had declined, guessing what was on it. She shifted in her seat, watching the images with a heavy heart. She had no great wish to keep watching.

A few seconds afterwards, an audio track kicked in: a man's breathing, heavy and panicked. The picter-view leapt around wildly as he moved his head. It showed an industrial complex at night – tangled pipes, rows of generator-coils, huge cooling towers. The dark sky beyond was mottled with smoke, the kind of dense, greasy pall that comes from burning promethium.

The man with the helmet-picter was running, making the picture shake and jerk. Others ran with him, all in Shakeh Guard uniforms, all carrying lasguns two-handed.

'Holy Emperor,' the man mumbled, snatching the litany between his ragged breaths. 'Holy Emperor. Holy Emperor.'

It wasn't clear where the men were running. Explosions sounded in the background, muffled and tinny on the recording; no doubt deafening to them.

Other shouts intruded – men's voices, curdled with fear and disbelief.

'Holy Emperor. Holy Emperor.'

The Guardsmen opened up with their weapons. Bright lines of las-fire scored the night, overloading the pict-stream and blanking the feed. When the images resumed the men were running again, faster this time.

Something flitted across the picter's lurching visual field, just glimpsed for a second: a bloated face amid the far darkness, pale as corpse-light, grinning, stalking towards them.

'Holy Emperor. Holy Emperor.'

The man's panting got more urgent, more uncontrolled. More las-beams flashed off.

The view swept round suddenly. A semi-ruined wall emerged from the smog, gaping with black holes where munitions had exploded. Unidentifiable shapes were moving in the shadows beyond, twitching and rocking and jabbering.

'Grenade!' screamed one of the Guardsmen, out of view.

The picter lurched to the floor. A riot of static hissing broke out as explosions maxed-out the audio filters.

Then the man started moving again. Audio resumed. He was whimpering from fear.

'*Holy... Emperor... Holy... Emperor...*'

Someone screamed from behind him, a garish sound of animal horror, high-pitched and keening. The Guardsmen all started sprinting, their formation gone, firing off random rounds into the dark, leaping and stumbling over blast craters underfoot. One of them was hit by something. The view jerked over to him for an instant – his face white with terror.

'Don't leave me!' he squealed. Something with spidery limbs was crawling up his leg.

'*H-holy... Emp... eror!*'

The men kept running. They stumbled through what looked like a bombed-out manufactorium. Huge machines were still running inside it, clanking and spinning and roiling in the darkness. Screaming started up again, a whole chorus of it. It seemed to come from all directions, from the mouths of all of them, echoing from the jagged wall-remains.

Objects hung from the roof, twisting in the grainy gloom. The view briefly slewed upwards, exposing a shaky snapshot of man-shaped bundles suspended on corroding meathooks, some shuddering like marionettes, some glistening wetly.

'H-h-ho... Hol...'

Bloated, grinning horrors crept up out of the shadows. Las-fire downed some of them, knocking them back to the ground with gurgling pops. Others kept on coming. They had swollen faces in the flickering light, the skin stretched tight and held in place by iron pins. They laughed as they scampered, a low, throaty *hurr hurr hurr.*

The picter was shaking badly now, shuddering so hard it was hard to make out what was going on. The horrors must have got in amongst them. Everything dissolved into a jumbled succession of sickening images – flesh being cut, eyes being pulled, stomachs bursting.

In a brief flash of clarity, a devilish face reared up dead centre, laughing so hard its lips split open. Its eyes stared wildly, cat-yellow and weeping with pus. It reached out with needle-tipped fingers. The whine of a circular saw started up somewhere close by.

'Ho-! Hol-! Empe-! Ach! Nnngh!'

The Guardsman's frenzied litany collapsed into a jerking, frothing shriek. Blood splashed across the picter's lens, coating the image with a splash of red. It shook violently, rocked back and forth by its bearer's spasms.

Then it went dead, replaced by a fizzing wall of white noise.

A few seconds later it resumed.

The image was swinging back and forth like a lazy pendulum. The sound had gone. Blood on the lens made everything smeary and indistinct. The viewpoint was higher up, as if the picter were suspended a long way above the floor.

It showed a manufactorium crawling with movement. Hundreds of enemy troops scuttled between machines like swarms of roaches, clambering over one another, chittering and cavorting. Huge, distorted creatures stalked among them, stomachs ballooning and flesh glimmering with corpse-light.

Something else approached the lens. A single, glowing eye peered up, lodged in the centre of a rusting, tusk-jowled helm. Massive pauldrons rose up out of the murk, each one studded with gleaming entrail-loops. The edges of twin cleavers could be made out, glistening, steadily dripping.

For a moment the armour-clad titan just stared at the picter. Then it reached up. The last image was of a gore-splattered gauntlet closing over the lens.

After that, static.

Callia cut off the feed. The window-blinds slid up, letting sunlight flood back into the chamber.

Bajola looked down at her hands. They were damp with sweat.

'That is what our troops have been fighting, Wolf Guard,' said de Chatelaine. 'They were heroes just to stand their ground, do you not think?'

Gunnlaugur gazed back at her steadily. He didn't look entirely unmoved by what he had seen. That was to his credit, Bajola thought.

'They were,' he said.

The atmosphere in the chamber was subdued. One of de Chatelaine's counsellors, a scholarly man named Arvian Nomu, looked faint, and gripped the edge of the table tightly.

'That thing at the end,' Gunnlaugur said. 'You know what it was?'

'I do,' said the canoness.

'How many of them have landed?'

'That is our only confirmed sighting.'

Gunnlaugur snorted, his nostrils flaring. He looked pensive. 'Your troops can't kill it,' he said.

De Chatelaine nodded. 'I know. I hope yours can.'

Gunnlaugur didn't smile that time, which surprised Bajola. Until then, his casual confidence had seemed inexhaustible.

'We can kill anything,' he said. 'That's what we do.'

He turned towards one of his warriors, a lean-faced killer with a long-sword strapped to his back. They exchanged a brief, significant glance.

'Just depends how many there are,' he said bleakly.

CHAPTER TEN

Three hours later, with the sun burning high in the sky, Váltyr walked up a tight spiral stairway, his shoulder guards grinding against the stone walls. He emerged onto a small square platform at the summit of one of the Halicon's many towers. The city and its surroundings flowed away from him in every direction, falling down the long, broken mountain ridges before giving way to kilometres of featureless ochre plains. The distant horizon was hazy, masked by a pale screen of dusty grey.

The arch of Ras Shakeh's sky was a deep, royal blue. Its earth was dull orange, like rusting iron. Everything shimmered under a beating, constant wall of heat. No breeze stirred the air. No animals called and no birds sang.

He paced over to the battlements running around the edge of the platform. Olgeir was already there, peering over the edge, his huge gauntlets gripping the sides.

'Planned it out, great one?' asked Váltyr, coming to join him.

Olgeir didn't reply immediately. His amber eyes ran across the warrens of streets below. His cracked, pierced lips moved soundlessly, as if he were calculating angles, strengths, numbers.

The Halicon squatted at the summit of the mountain city. Beyond its walls lay the upper city, an orderly collection of red-tiled chapels, memorials, habs and admin blocks. Groves of spear-leaved trees grew in shaded courtyards and the sound of running water could be heard from under their eaves. The sigil of the Wounded Heart was prominent on the larger edifices, hanging limp on unmoving banners. A few landing stages were dotted amid the tight-packed buildings, ringed by defence lasers and servitor bays. *Vuokho* sat on one of them, still leaking smoke, still looking barely functional.

The upper city was protected at its perimeter by a winding circuit of high, thick walls. Defence towers studded the battlements at fifty metre intervals, each one bristling with lascannon turrets and swivelling missile launchers. Only one gateway broke the enclosure of those walls – the Ighala Gate, a blunt bastion of adamantium and granite that hunkered darkly to the west of the Halicon's bulk. The Gate was a mini-citadel all on its own: dank, angular and forbidding. Just like the towers on either side of it, weapons clustered all over it. Some of the bigger guns looked like recent additions, cannibalised from overrun installations and bolted into place for the attack they all knew was coming.

Beyond the Ighala Gate was a narrow bridge that stretched out across a plunging, debris-choked gully. The ravine was a natural cleft in the mountain that ran around the upper city, dividing the two halves of the settlement and adding to the effective height of the inner wall. The cleft was too deep for infantry to negotiate unaided and lay tightly under the shadow of the tower guns. Váltyr grunted with approval when he saw that. It was a killing ground, a formidable barrier for any army to cross.

On the far side of the ravine was the lower city, a much larger straggle of far shabbier buildings. That was where the bulk of Hjec Aleja's population lived their lives, clogged up against one another in close-packed hab-towers. The urban landscape ran down through a series of terraces, each one teeming with jostling, multi-storied estates. Váltyr could see very few major transit arteries; the streets were narrow, winding and overlooked.

Few structures of note existed in the tangled morass of stone beyond the inner walls. Only one caught his eye – the Cathedral of St Alexia, a gothic basilica with three gargoyle-encrusted spires. Its trio of spikes rose up into the clear air, casting long shadows over the houses below.

Much further out, tiny with distance, was the outer perimeter wall. Like the inner barrier it was buttressed with defence towers and studded with fire-points. A second armoured gatehouse stood on the outer rim, as lumpen and gun-covered as the Ighala Gate.

After that, nothing – just desiccated scrubland, dissolving slowly into rust-coloured desert. A lone road wound steadily westwards, its broken rockcrete surface marred by blown dust.

Váltyr looked at it all carefully, taking his time.

'This is no fortress,' said Olgeir eventually.

'No,' said Váltyr. 'It isn't.'

'You know how many troops they have here?'

'Tell me.'

'Thirty thousand regular Guardsmen. A few thousand armed militia. Less than a hundred Battle Sisters. A few dozen tanks and walkers. One crippled Thunderhawk. And us.'

Váltyr nodded, chewing over the figures. All that was left of a planet's defences after just a few months of war. Not much to boast about.

'Arm the civilians?' he suggested.

'They have been armed,' said Olgeir, in a voice that gave away how useful he thought that would be. He leaned over the parapet, hawked and spat. The spittle flew a long way down before hitting anything. 'I've seen better defended asteroids,' he concluded.

'We should strike out,' said Váltyr, running his eyes along the horizon. 'Blood them before they get here.'

Olgeir grunted in agreement.

'Gunnlaugur's already planning it. The canoness is unhappy. She wants everyone behind the walls, waiting for them to get there.'

Váltyr looked down at the inner ring of defences.

'We could hold this upper level, perhaps,' he said thoughtfully. 'The bridge is a choke point, and those walls look solid. But the outer rim... I don't know.'

Olgeir nodded. 'There's no way we can hold the perimeter. Too long, too low. But she wants to, all the same. They won't let the cathedral fall without a fight.'

Váltyr couldn't blame them for that. It was their cathedral.

'We're going to need to clear some space, then,' he said. 'We can't move anything through those streets.'

'Aye,' said Olgeir. 'I've been planning it. They've got earthmovers and plenty of manpower. We need trenches, ones we can get burning. The one thing they'll do is keep on coming. We could soak up thousands if we organise it right.'

Váltyr didn't say what he thought.

It won't be enough.

'Do they have flyers?' he asked.

'Apparently not.'

'That's something.'

The two of them fell into silence again. Váltyr felt himself sweating under the relentless glare of the sun. He could have put his helm on and let it regulate his temperature, but that felt like an acknowledgement of weakness. De Chatelaine had said that most of the fighting on Ras Shakeh had taken place at night, and he could see why. Even the damned would struggle to march under that unbroken heat.

'I tell you, Heavy-hand,' he said at last. 'I already hate this place.'

Olgeir chuckled. 'That bad?'

Váltyr thought for a moment.

'Actually, it is,' he said, letting his irritation get the better of him. 'I mean, what in Hel is this? This is a backwater, a rock. If we're going to die here, I want to know why. We won't get a saga for this. Not a decent one. Why would *anyone* fight for this?'

Olgeir shrugged. 'Can't answer that, brother,' he said. 'But you can see it as well as I can. This isn't just a raid – they're here to take this world. Others, too. This is organised. There's method in it.'

'What can be here that they would possibly want?'

'Something worth sending a fleet for. Seems to me this is about occupation.'

Váltyr shook his head. Olgeir's judgement was normally good, but that felt wrong.

'The Sisters,' he said, changing the subject. 'They sent distress calls?'

'For weeks, they say,' said Olgeir. 'They don't know if any got through. We're months away from anywhere with an army.' He chuckled darkly. 'Face it, we're on our own.'

Váltyr pushed back from the railing and stretched his arms out, feeling the muscles flex.

'Then I need to get out of here and find something to kill. I'd just started to find my rhythm.'

Olgeir nodded appreciatively. 'You and me both,' he said.

Váltyr looked into the distance, and the empty land gazed back at him. To the west, the horizon's haze had taken on a faint greenish tinge, like mould spreading across water.

'That's where they'll come from,' he said.

Olgeir nodded. 'I can smell them already.'

Váltyr felt an itch run across the palm of his sword-hand then. It missed the weight of *holdbítr*.

'Soon, then,' he said softly, clenching his fist tight and gazing intently at the pall of sickness on the world's edge. 'Very soon.'

Gunnlaugur sat alone. The chamber he'd been given by the canoness was the finest in the citadel: the walls had been hung with silks and the floor had been covered in a series of finely woven deep-pile rugs. He'd had them strip all that away, exposing the stone and plaster. Only two chairs remained; the rest had gone.

He struggled to shake his black, surly mood. He'd arrived at Ras Shakeh expecting no greater enemy than tedium. Though he would only have grudgingly admitted it, even to himself, a little tedium would have been welcome. It would have given time for the pack to bed in, for Ingvar and Hafloí to find their places, for everything to settle into the old rhythm.

Instead they had been plunged into a world on the edge of ruin. The *Undrider*, with its thousands of loyal souls on board, had been lost. Those that had made it to the saviour pods had crashed down onto a planet enveloped in a nightmare. None of them had made contact since *Vuokho* had landed at Hjec Aleja. That disaster alone wore away at his conscience. In the scant moments he'd had to himself since making planetfall, he had run the events of the brief orbital battle over and over in his mind. Perhaps he could have handled it better. Perhaps his desire to get into combat may have overruled tactical sense.

Or perhaps not. The choices, and the time to make them, had been limited. It was always easy to second-guess decisions made in the heat of battle.

So why am I so troubled by this one?

He knew the answer.

A soft chime sounded at the door.

'Come,' he growled.

Ingvar entered. The warrior's expression was hard to read. Not contrite, exactly; not spoiling for a fight. He must have known what was coming, but he made no concessions to it.

He came to stand before Gunnlaugur. His face was a mask of calmness. That alone pricked at Gunnlaugur's pride.

You are a Son of Russ! Show some mettle!

'So why did you do it?' Gunnlaugur asked, looking up at Ingvar from under heavy lids.

'I tried to warn you,' said Ingvar. 'It was the right thing to–'

'It was not your call.' Gunnlaugur's voice remained low, animated by a low, snarling threat-note.

Ingvar took a breath. 'I saw Jorundur approaching,' he said. 'It was the right thing to–'

'Blood of Russ, don't treat me like a fool!' Gunnlaugur swept up out of the chair. They stood facing one another, barely a hand's width apart. Gunnlaugur's face was hot with anger; Ingvar's remained still.

'What has *changed* in you, brother?' Gunnlaugur growled. 'You spoke against me on the bridge. You didn't want to attack that ship.' As he spoke, as he remembered it, the whole thing became harder to understand. 'We had a chance – one chance – for the kill. Why would you not take it? Why would you *ever* not take it?'

Ingvar's grey eyes didn't flinch.

'I didn't speak against you,' he said. 'We had to consider alternatives. The tactical options had not closed down.'

That was not language Gunnlaugur had heard from Ingvar before. It was not language he had heard from any Sky Warrior.

'Speak plainly,' he muttered.

'We could have withdrawn. We were faster. They had seen us before we saw them, and so had the advantage. Given space, we could have used our speed to more effect. An alternative to boarding might have presented itself.'

'You're saying I was wrong.'

Ingvar shook his head. 'No. You are *vaerangi*. But it was my duty to point out alternatives.'

Gunnlaugur looked at him with furrowed brows. The language Ingvar was using, the tone of it, it was all unsettling.

He wouldn't raise his voice. He wouldn't fight him.

'You've changed,' he said again.

'You say it like it's something to be feared.'

Gunnlaugur looked away, spat on the floor, then rubbed his hands through his matted mane. Something like sickness churned within him.

'I fear nothing.' He flexed his fingers, as if to clutch at his weapon. Fighting was easy, straightforward. That was what he knew how to do. 'Do you remember Boreal V? Do you remember how we ravaged that world, you and I? That was fighting. That was how I remembered you, when you were gone.'

As he spoke, Gunnlaugur let the memories revive within him. He saw Ingvar and he alone amid a sea of howling, tearing blood-cultists. His hammer had whirled with abandon that night, hewing at the damned in droves. Ingvar's sword had never moved faster, never slain with more deadly accuracy. They had stood back to back, isolated in a sea of death-lust as the sky burned above them, fighting in the purest way possible – two battle-brothers, their lives in each other's hands.

Gunnlaugur had expected to die then. He had not been sad about it: a death on Boreal would have been a fitting end. Sagas would have been sung of two Sky Warriors, elbow-deep in the blood of the fallen, their sacred duty discharged and their honour unstained.

When Hjortur had eventually fought his way to their side, raging and flailing with the others in tow, it had almost been a disappointment.

'I remember all our fights, brother,' said Ingvar. For the first time, his voice had something like emotion in it.

'Then *act* like it,' said Gunnlaugur, whirling back to glare at him. 'Act like you're back amongst your own kind, like you belong here.'

Ingvar's grey eyes were unmoving. 'I would die for Járnhamar,' he said, his voice intense. 'I always would have. You know this.' He took a step towards Gunnlaugur, his own fists twitching as if he wanted to clench them.

Your anger is stirring. Good.

'But I learned *so much*,' Ingvar said. His eyes flickered strangely, as if his attention were elsewhere. 'I thought that I would learn nothing, but I was wrong. We think of ourselves as the bravest, the fastest, the strongest. We laugh at the others. We're wrong. We blunt our own weapons. There are other ways. Some are better.'

Gunnlaugur listened with disbelief. 'Better? That it? Better than the savages from the ice-world who bred you?'

'You're not listening,' Ingvar snarled. Another spark of anger flickered across his face. 'Your mind is closed. It has always been closed.'

Gunnlaugur swept in close, fangs bared, his whole body bristling.

'Do not *dare* to lecture me,' he warned darkly, his hot breath on Ingvar's face. 'We are not equals, Gyrfalkon, ready to brawl in the straw to settle this. This is my pack. You will accept that, or by the blood of the ancients I will *break* you.'

They stood, face to face, both of them tensed for the first move. Gunnlaugur felt his blood pumping around his system, ready to flood into primed muscles. He could see the fury in Ingvar's expression, the desire to lash out, the pungent spike of kill-urge.

Heartbeats passed, thudding heavily in rib-fused chests.

Then, slowly, Ingvar backed down. His eyes lowered. His gauntlets uncurled.

'You are right,' he said quietly. 'You are right. I recognise my failing. I will be sure to correct it.'

Gunnlaugur watched him pull back from the confrontation. For a moment, he couldn't believe it. He had been ready to fight, poised for the explosion of movement. It was a struggle to come down from that. His blood still thundered in his arteries, thick and vital.

I was ready to humiliate him. I was ready to prove myself.

With effort, he forced himself to relax.

Would I have won?

It was hard to find the right words. For a moment longer, they faced one another in silence.

'Listen, brother,' said Gunnlaugur at last, making his voice ebb, pushing it to lose its edge of violence. 'We can fight together like we used to. I want this. But it cannot be the same. I need to know that you will follow an order. I need to know that you will follow me.'

Ingvar nodded. He looked suddenly withdrawn, unsure of himself, as if he'd got close to blurting something out and had only hauled it back at the last minute.

'You are *vaerangi*,' he said again. 'I never challenged you for that.'

Gunnlaugur suddenly felt like he'd missed something, like he'd mistaken Ingvar's meaning somehow.

But it was too late to argue back. He'd stamped his authority, just as Hjortur would have done. That was the important thing.

'Then we are clear,' he said. 'We understand one another.'

'We do.'

Gunnlaugur took a deep breath. In another age he might have reached out then, clapping Ingvar on the shoulder with his gauntlet, behaving like the battle-brother he'd once been. Now, though, the gesture felt strangely inappropriate. He kept his distance.

The air hung heavily between them, tense and febrile. It pressed against his temples. Nothing would clear it; not anger, not remorse.

'We need to work with the Sisters,' Gunnlaugur said, moving awkwardly on to strategic matters, hoping that would salve the nagging unease in his mind. 'They've been working hard on the defences here, but there are too few of them. They don't understand what's coming here.'

Ingvar listened carefully, saying nothing more. He looked chastened, but with an edge of defiance still in his bearing.

'There are things we can do, ways we can strike back,' Gunnlaugur went on. 'But the canoness has her own priorities. The cathedral is one. It's madness to try to hold it, but they won't pull back. I want you to go there, see how defensible it is, assess how viable a stand would be.'

Ingvar nodded. 'By your will,' he said. 'But that isn't all, is it?'

'The Sister Palatine. That's her domain. You saw her observing us at the council, thinking we didn't notice. She's the liaison the canoness has chosen. If they want to observe us, then we can do the same.'

Gunnlaugur looked at Ingvar seriously.

'It won't be easy, working with them,' he said. 'We both have a hundred reasons to distrust one another. So get close to the Palatine, learn how they operate. By the time the enemy get here I want us to be working like hand and gauntlet. You understand?'

Ingvar bowed. 'It will be done,' he said.

Gunnlaugur nodded. 'Good. And after that we'll fight together, you and I. That will cleanse all this bad blood. It will be like Boreal V again – pure, uncomplicated, as it ought to be.'

He could hear himself sounding forced, trying to erase the memory of his anger. It didn't convince him; he doubted it would convince Ingvar.

To his surprise, though, the Gyrfalkon looked at him almost gratefully, as if he'd been handed a way back. That was something to seize on.

'I would like that, *vaerangi*,' he said. 'Like Boreal again, you and I.'

Vuokho stood on the landing platform, its shell blackened from re-entry. The length of its blocky hull was scored with damage taken on the approach to the plague-infested destroyer. Even while their warship had been dying around them, the enemy gunners had maintained a thick defensive barrage, one that had sorely tested Jorundur's skills in evasion.

He cast an expert eye over the damage, and his face wrinkled in disgust.

'How do they *do* it?' he asked, talking to himself. 'They can hardly see, hardly breathe, their hands are tentacles. How can they pull a trigger, let alone hit things?'

After the void-battle, the descent into Ras Shakeh's atmosphere had been difficult. One system had blown after another, gradually knocking out all of the gunship's flight aids and turning it into little more than a wedge of gliding wreckage. By the time he'd finally got it down, *Vuokho* was more dead than alive.

'So will it fly?'

Jorundur turned to see Haflói walking towards him. The Blood Claw's face was a mass of scabs and inflamed flesh. Even his enhanced body had struggled to cope with the poisonous wound he'd taken, and his short trip into the vacuum hadn't helped.

But he was healing well. Gunnlaugur had been right – the whelp was tough.

'No, it will not,' said Jorundur, turning back to the pitiful heap of wreckage before him. 'I've seen the tech-servitors here and what they can do. We may as well start building a new gunship from scratch.'

Haflói joined him and gazed along the Thunderhawk's long flanks.

'Doesn't look too bad,' he said.

Jorundur laughed in his dark, throttled way. 'Fine,' he said. 'You try to fly it.'

Haflói bristled. 'I might,' he said, his scabby chin jutting.

Jorundur snorted, a grim sound that cut out abruptly.

'Listen to me,' he said, jabbing his fist at Haflói's chest. 'You do not *touch* it. You do not go *near* it. You do not even think about going near it. Gunnlaugur himself wouldn't take it without checking with me.'

Haflói looked shocked for a moment, then laughed in turn.

'You're serious?' he asked. 'You think I want to fight you for this heap of junk?'

Jorundur scowled. 'It's not at its best,' he said. 'It was never ready.'

Haflói turned back to face it. 'We could still use it,' he said, musingly. 'Get this in the air, and we'd murder them. You know the enemy doesn't have flyers?'

Jorundur rolled his eyes. 'I see. Perhaps, then, you'll tell me where we can locate a replacement drive chain, and thruster housings, and retros?'

Haflói didn't rise to the bait.

'I've seen these things fixed on a battlefield. This city has workshops.'

'Crewed by morons.'

'How do you know? You just got here.'

Jorundur shook his head. Haflói's persistence annoyed him. The whelp was young, full of the confidence and optimism that youth brought. He hadn't been part of the pack five minutes and already he was offering his counsel.

Had he been like that himself, once? It was centuries ago. Hard to recall.

'Why are you so interested, anyway?' Jorundur asked irritably, walking up to the frontal wings and running his hand along the chipped metal. 'You'll be on the front line with the others, shrieking and hollering like you did on that destroyer.'

Haflói grinned. 'Maybe,' he said, following Jorundur. 'Or maybe I'll be right here with you, in the cockpit, running the battle cannon.'

Jorundur snorted. 'You could handle that?'

'I've been trained.'

Jorundur looked at him scornfully.

'Training's one thing. If you can keep your aim while the gunship's being shot to shards and the air's burning and your dying crew's screaming in your ear and you've got blood running down your chest and arms, then I'll be impressed.'

He patted *Vuokho*'s chassis.

'This thing has taken down Titans,' he said proudly. '*Titans*. Don't tell me how to look after it. I'll work on it, even if I have to rewire those servitors myself.'

Hafloí nodded. 'Then I'll fly it,' he said.

Despite himself, despite trying hard not to, Jorundur laughed out loud.

'*Skítja*, lad, no you won't.'

He looked up at the cockpit. The metal around the armourglass panes was cracked. He knew that most of the instruments inside were burned out and that the machine-spirit had been reduced to a barely perceptible flicker haunting the automatic motive system.

'It'll be a miracle if we get it ready in time,' he said. 'A miracle. And, believe me, despite all the saints and angels haunting this place, I'm far too old to believe in miracles.'

Hafloí smiled.

'You might be,' he said, his voice full of arrogance and confidence and challenge, just as it should be. 'I'm not.'

CHAPTER ELEVEN

Baldr didn't know where he was. *Away* was the best approximation, and that was good enough for him. The pain in his temples, hammering away since the engagement on the plague-ship, had become a problem.

Lack of sleep had exacerbated it. A Space Marine could go for days without sleep, using his catalepsean node to prolong that even further. That didn't mean that it was comfortable. Given enough time the symptoms of sleep deprivation kicked in just as they did with mortals. Fuzziness, heaviness in the limbs, slower reaction times, poor judgement.

He needed to rest. Escape from the warp hadn't helped as he'd hoped it would. It might do, in time, but Ras Shakeh's hot, dry air didn't make it easy. The sunlight was harsh, reflecting painfully from the deep-coloured landscape and flashing from glass and metal.

So he'd gone down, right into the bowels of the Halicon. Below the ostentatious entrance halls, the citadel's chambers became cooler and darker. The lumens were set low and many had been turned off, pooling shadows in the corners of the corridors. To begin with there had been plenty of people around – robed officials, Battle Sisters hurrying from one duty to another, Guardsmen. Now, deep in the basement, the numbers had thinned out.

He was alone again. It felt good.

That fact surprised him. For as long as he could remember, Baldr had revelled in the close fraternity of Járnhamar. They had welcomed him when he'd joined, Ingvar in particular. He'd slotted in well. He couldn't match Váltyr for swordplay or Gunnlaugur for brute force, but his aim with a bolter was the best of them. There had been times on the battlefield when it had felt like he'd known where each enemy would be before they did. On his day, Baldr's shells found their marks with uncanny, unerring precision. It was all so easy, all so effortless.

So his torpor, his lack of self-command, that concerned him. For a brief time, during the fighting on the plague-ship, he'd been able to forget the pain throbbing behind his eyes. Only on the descent to the city, with the Thunderhawk shaking and rattling around him, had the pain returned.

Contemplating such weakness angered him. He would have to learn to master it. He was a Son of Russ; pain should be easily overcome.

He kept on walking, descending dusty stone stairs, striding down long, bare corridors, passing by empty doorways leading into empty rooms.

Motion helped. Coolness helped. Being alone helped.

He heard the whimpering late. If he'd been in his right mind, he would have detected it far earlier. As it was, his senses blunted by the angry throb in his skull, he nearly missed it entirely.

He stopped, listening carefully. It came from further down. At the end of the corridor a tight spiral staircase descended through a circular well-shaft of stone. The tiles on the walls around it had come loose; several had shattered across the floor. Dust lay heavily on the remains, a thick, undisturbed layer. No one had walked that way for some time.

He heard it again. A faint, breathy exhalation, ripe with pain.

He tensed. Something about the noise made the hairs on his body stand up. He drew his bolter silently and moved towards the stairs. Getting down them silently was impossible – the metal railing snagged against his armour. Before he'd reached the bottom, he heard something scuttling away from him.

The dark closed in. His eyes compensated immediately. He moved away from the stairs and walked further into the shadows.

He was in some kind of basement vault. The arched roof was low, barely high enough for him to walk without stooping. The floor was bare earth, old and loamy. He guessed he'd reached the foundations of the citadel. A familiar stench – sweet, cloying – hung in the dusty air.

He moved his head carefully, sweeping the space ahead of him. The earth was disturbed, as if an animal had suddenly stirred and raced off into the dark. The nearside wall was clear, but the opposite end of the basement was piled with old metal crates, most of them broken and gaping.

Baldr paused, listening, sniffing.

It was behind the crates. It didn't make much noise, but it had to breathe. He heard its lungs straining, pulling hard on dank air.

He guided his bolter muzzle over to where the sound came from, and fired.

The explosion of the shell's release broke the silence. At the same time, the crates burst apart, hurled away from the walls as something broke from cover. Baldr's round detonated harmlessly into the wall, blowing a crater in the stone.

He had a brief glimpse of something running at him, scampering across the floor like a giant, bloated insect. It moved incredibly fast.

Baldr fired again, hitting it this time. It flew back away from him, its limbs splaying, a thin shriek echoing around the vaults.

He went after it, stowing his bolter as he moved. It twisted around and leapt back up at him. He saw a grey, gaunt face leer up out of the dark, snapping at his own with black jaws.

His fist shot out, seizing it by a scrawny, stringy neck and pinning it to the floor. He felt sinews break and bones snap under his grip.

It still lived. Its hands clawed at him, scraping his armour in a frenzy of useless scratching. It spat at him, sending a stream of thick, lumpy spittle into his face. It thrashed, screamed and writhed under the pressure of his gauntlet.

Baldr looked at it in disgust. Its flesh hung in flaps from its bony frame, withered and wasting. Sores clustered thickly around its lips, tight and pus-filled. It was almost naked, its exposed skin covered in lesions and tumours. Its eyes were sunk deep into an emaciated skeletal face, both dull with cataracts. Its tongue was long gone, chewed away in the wretch's madness, and its screams were formless and choking.

For all that, it had once been human. Baldr recognised the remnants of a scholiast's robes hanging around its loins.

He squeezed his fingers together. For a moment longer the thing hung on, its blind eyes popping, its hands clawing.

Then it went limp. Baldr withdrew, wiping the smear of stinking spittle from his face. He could almost taste the corruption in it, like long-rotten fruit.

He drew himself up, gazing down on the crumpled corpse of the scholiast. Its mouth hung slack, exposing inflamed gums and the blackened stump where its tongue had been.

It reeked.

He activated the comm-stud in his armour collar. The link, which he'd severed earlier, sparked back into life.

'Fjolnir,' came Gunnlaugur's voice. He sounded preoccupied and irascible. 'Where have you been?'

'Clearing my head,' said Baldr. 'Where are you now?'

'With the canoness. My chambers.'

'I'll see you there,' said Baldr, stooping to scoop up the remains of the diseased cadaver. He turned back to the staircase, his tread heavy. 'She'll want to see this too. Warn her that we have a new problem.'

He cut the link. As he climbed, tucking the limp bundle of limbs under one arm, he could already feel his headache getting worse.

Ingvar walked down the narrow streets from the Halicon citadel to the cathedral. To do so he had to pass through the Ighala Gate, jostling with the crowds that milled under its narrow portals.

The experience was uncomfortable. Mortals disliked being in such close proximity to him – they pulled away when they saw him coming, staring with open mouths as he passed – but under the shadow of the enormous arches there was too little space for them to escape.

He ignored their stares, partly for his own comfort. Decades of operating on secret missions with Onyx had desensitised him to unaltered human presence. He had become more comfortable with the select few who, like him, had been elevated into positions of prominence: Inquisitors, Imperial agents, senior Adeptus Mechanicus priests, his fellow warriors of the Adeptus Astartes.

Mortals were different. Whenever he caught their expressions they showed the same thing: fear. They were terrified of him. Children ran away, screaming. Adults worked harder, but he could see the anxiety clearly enough in their staring eyes, their trembling fingers, their sudden, pungent aroma of fight-or-flight.

Ingvar knew Gunnlaugur wouldn't have worried about that. Perhaps he was right not to. In any case, it was just one more difference that had grown up between them.

He strode down from the gate, over the bridge and into the lower city. The streets there were hotter and closer than those above the Ighala bastion. The buildings were shabbier, though more brightly decorated. Pennants displaying the Hjec Aleja coat of arms hung limply from doorways, their colours fading as the sun beat down on them. The smell of spices – cloves, cumin – rose from the baked earth, as if generations of use had stained it forever. Voices rose and fell from hab-units around him. The conversations sounded brief and subdued. Very little laughter rang out from the narrow windows. An atmosphere of tension, of low-level fear, of weariness, had sunk into the entire place.

People went about their business as they must have done before war had come, but their tight, febrile movements betrayed their anxiety. Ingvar had seen such things often on other worlds and in other battlegrounds. Humans would maintain a familiar rhythm for as long as they possibly could, pottering around, concerning themselves with trivialities while the forces of Hel crouched just over the horizon. The pretence could only ever be half successful – they all knew their world was about to change – but then what else were they supposed to do? Food still needed to be prepared, water needed to be fetched, clothes needed to be laundered.

Eventually the press of crooked streets opened up into a wide square. On the far side of it rose the sheer walls of the cathedral, sweeping up into the sky in a series of ever-narrowing layers of stony gothic ornamentation. Its three spires jutted dramatically, soaring far above the roofline of the houses around, thrust up from the overlapping tumble of slate and stone like an immense iron-tipped trident.

The courtyard at its base was shaded and thronged with people, all of whom were waiting patiently in long, huddled queues. At the head of those queues stood priests of the Ecclesiarchy in earth-brown robes. One by one the people received a blessing from them and were sent away. Ingvar watched them bow before the clerics, their heads bobbing low over the ground. They had the sign of the aquila waved over them and a few words of High Gothic muttered. Then they went away, a look of quiet satisfaction on their otherwise haunted faces. They slipped back into the shadows of the narrow streets, quickly disappearing.

Ingvar watched the process repeat itself. The mortals paid him little attention here. Their attention was fixed on what they were doing; if they caught sight of him watching them, they didn't show it.

'Do not despise them,' came a woman's voice.

Palatine Bajola drew alongside him. She wore her ceremonial robes – ivory cotton, trimmed with red and gold. Her ebony skin stood in stark contrast.

'Why do you think I would?' he replied.

'You are superhuman,' she said. 'They are human. They suffer fear. I am told you do not.'

Ingvar watched the queues shuffle. Just as at the gate, he could smell the undercurrent of uneasiness.

'How often does this happen?' he asked.

'Priests are here every day between dawn and dusk. They are kept busy the whole time.'

'And it does some good?'

Bajola paused before replying.

'If you mean that those people sleep a little at night and are able to go about their business without falling prey to waking nightmares, then yes, it does. If you mean that the Emperor will spare them from the coming horror and allow them to live their lives in peace, then no, it does not.'

Ingvar turned to face her. 'Do you receive the blessing?' he asked.

Bajola smiled. 'They wouldn't dare. They assume I have all the faith I need.' She gestured towards the cathedral. 'You are here to see me, I take it. We should go inside.'

'And do you?' asked Ingvar, staying where he was.

'Do I?'

'Have all the faith you need?'

Bajola hesitated.

'We will find out, I guess,' she said.

The interior of the cathedral was cool even while the streets outside sweltered. Its vast nave ran north-south, lined with dark rows of basalt columns. Sunlight angled in through narrow stained-glass panes depicting stylised images of saints and warriors, throwing intense coloured swatches on the chequerboard marble floor. The high altar was simple – an obsidian block of stone over which hung war-banners of the Wounded Heart and the Shakeh Guard regiments. An imposing cast-iron representation of the Emperor Manifest on Earth smiting the Great Serpent Horus had been mounted above that, glinting wetly in the gloom.

Few people moved around in the dusty shadows: scholiasts, a priest, an old penitent crawling towards the altar on his knees. The faint sounds they made were amplified amid the soaring spaces. Aromas of incense and human sweat rose from the stone.

Ingvar took it all in. He could appreciate Bajola's pride in the place. It was a serious building, a place of devotion, unlike the grotesque pile of the Halicon that the canoness occupied.

She led him through a side door and up into her private chambers. The room they ended up in was high on the south-facing front, lined with crystal-paned windows that gazed out over the city below. Several chairs stood waiting, all of which she ignored. That was considerate; Ingvar guessed his armour-clad weight would have cracked most of them.

'They call you the Gyrfalkon,' she said, leaning against the far wall and smiling at him. 'What is that? No one has been able to tell me.'

'You cannot guess?'

'A bird, I would have said.'

'You would have said right. One of the few that can dwell on Fenris. It has grey plumage, thick against the cold. They are good hunters. Then again, everything on Fenris is a good hunter. If it is not, then it dies.'

Bajola looked amused. 'So why you?' she asked. 'Because you are a good hunter? Or is it some dark secret of your Chapter?'

Ingvar shrugged. 'My brothers are not overly imaginative,' he said. 'My eyes are grey. I had a reputation for speed with the blade, once. They liked the sound of it. I don't know.'

Bajola nodded, as if he had confirmed some suspicion she had of him.

'You are not quite like your brothers, I think,' she said.

'They might agree with you,' he said. 'Why do you say so?'

Bajola evaded the question.

'Tell me about yourself, Gyrfalkon,' she said.

'What purpose would that serve?'

'The canoness asked me to get to know you,' she said. 'You have been asked to get to know me. If you like, we could dance around one another for days, trying to gather information by stealth. Or we could put aside those games and talk. Enough, at least, to keep our superiors happy.'

Bajola had a polished, worldly air that Ingvar had not seen from the other Battle Sisters. She and de Chatelaine, it was obvious, were cut from very different cloth.

'You are not quite like your Sisters, I think,' he said.

Bajola laughed. It was deep, spontaneous laugh, almost like a man's.

'That much is true,' she said. 'But tell me of the Wolves. If we are to die here together, I'd like to know who I'm dying with.'

Ingvar looked away from her, past her shoulder, out through one of the windows. Ras Shakeh's deep blue sky shone with heat and light. A world more removed from Fenris would have been hard to find.

'We are Járnhamar,' he said slowly, as if to help himself remember. 'That is the pack-name. A pack may last for many generations, and we have fought together for a long time. Gunnlaugur, Olgeir, Váltyr, Jorundur and myself are the surviving founders. Baldr came later. Hafloí, the pup, barely yesterday. That forges a bond. It is not easily broken, though it can be strained.'

'I noticed,' said Bajola. 'You and your leader, you see things differently.'

Ingvar shook his head.

'Not really,' he said. 'Not about the essentials.'

He snapped his head towards her suddenly, baring his fangs, snarling. He was pleased to see that, for all her poise, she started.

'We are both of the blood of Asaheim, Sister,' he said, smiling at her hungrily. 'Neither of us is tame.'

'I never thought you were,' said Bajola, recovering herself and looking irritated.

'Gunnlaugur has led the pack for fifty-seven years,' Ingvar went on. 'Longer than the lives of most of your Guard captains. He knows what he's doing. I would trust my life to him. I have done, many times.'

'Still. You see things differently.'

Ingvar's eyes narrowed. Bajola was bold. He couldn't decide whether to be impressed by that.

'He's proud,' he said. 'He's got much to be proud about. But time changes things. It changes perspectives.'

'What changed yours?'

'I have been away from the home world. Our old Wolf Guard died while on campaign. I left Fenris before Gunnlaugur took over from him. It was a long time before I came back.'

'How long?'

Ingvar smiled wryly, calculating. 'Nine weeks ago.'

Bajola let out a long breath. 'Holy Ophelia.'

'We're adjusting.'

'I don't doubt it,' she said. 'What happened to your old Wolf Guard?'

'Greenskins,' Ingvar said, simply.

She didn't need to know the details – the long assault on the chain-fortresses of Urrghaz, the void-pursuit, the final confrontation with the orks above the gas giant Teliox Epis. She didn't need to know that Hjortur's body had never been found – an insult unworthy of the old warrior and a sad loss of gene-seed. At the time, that detail had seemed strange; now it was just a piece of history, embedded in the archives of the Valgard and mourned in the sagas.

'I'm sorry,' she said.

Ingvar shrugged. 'Don't be. It was his time. He lived a good life, a warrior's life.'

Bajola looked thoughtful. 'You are a fatalistic people,' she said. 'I have heard this before, from others who have had dealings with you. Now that I meet you, I believe it.'

'We live amongst death on Fenris. From birth we are surrounded by it. It comes suddenly, the crack of an ice-sheet, the gush of flame. You cannot defend against such things. You learn to accept it: the way of things, fate. The wyrd.'

'I could not live like that,' said Bajola. 'I have a... problem with fate.'

Ingvar didn't reply immediately. Bajola watched him all the while, holding his gaze with her brown eyes.

'I've been doing all the talking,' Ingvar said. 'This has been an uneven bargain.'

Bajola smiled, and lowered her eyes. 'Fair enough,' she said. 'What do you want to know?'

'I could ask you the same things you asked me,' he said. 'You sit ill with your comrades. I have never heard one of your kind talk like you do. I wonder what forces created you. I wonder what forces brought you here. You are as unlikely a presence on this world as we are.'

Bajola gave a slight nod of acknowledgement, as if to say *Well read*.

'I was trained by the Ordo Famulous,' she said. 'I accompanied Hereticus Inquisitors on high-level missions and arbitrated in the disputes of planetary governors. If you're interested, I speak twenty-nine dialects natively, six hundred more via lex-implants. I learned to read the state of a man's soul through a single gesture. Once you read a man's soul, you control him. At least, that was what the Inquisition taught me.'

She sounded almost wistful as she reeled off her accomplishments.

'I assume, though,' she said, 'that you think little of the Inquisition.'

'It is always dangerous to assume,' said Ingvar. 'Your story is half-told. The Order of the Wounded Heart is militant, not ceremonial.'

Bajola looked weary. 'Ah, yes. The Wounded Heart prides itself on its burn-tally.' She looked down at her hands, pressing her fingers together in a loose cage. 'Why did I join them? It was not enough, in the end, to spend my days talking. I felt that I was wasting myself. I saw the effects of wars but never participated in them. I was a mouthpiece for others, never speaking for myself.'

She looked back up at him. An edge of defiance danced around the edge of her expression.

'I was advised against the transfer,' she said. 'They told me I wasn't right for the Militant Orders. But there are ways of getting what you want if you try hard enough, even in the Adepta Sororitas.'

'So I see,' said Ingvar. 'And you never regretted it?'

The defiance in Bajola's face faded, replaced by a more familiar resignation.

'I regret plenty,' she said. 'I regret that this world is so damn hot, so damn arid. I regret that it will soon be put to the sword, and that so many will die. If I had stayed in the Ordo Famulous my life would have been easier, and probably longer.'

Then she flashed a smile at him again – a knowing smile, one that spoke of a capacity for mirth that had not yet been extinguished.

'But do I regret standing on my own two feet and learning to fire a bolter?' she asked. 'No, not at all. Turns out I'm good at it.'

In that instant, in those few words, Ingvar felt he knew all he needed to know about Uwe Bajola. It was hard not to be impressed, given the circumstances.

'That makes two of us, then,' he said.

'Where did you find this?'

Gunnlaugur could hear the low fear in the canoness's voice. The corpse lay twisted on the pristine floor of her chamber, stinking of rotting fish. Its unseeing eyes glared up at the ceiling, already beginning to decay from the inside. Its neck was swollen, bruised and oozing.

'In the foundations,' said Baldr. 'Right under your feet.'

To Gunnlaugur's eye, Baldr didn't look too good either. He seemed tired, distracted. His hair hung lankly around his forehead, which was strange. Of all of them, Baldr was normally the one who looked least like a savage.

First Ingvar, now him, thought Gunnlaugur. *What is wrong with them all?*

The canoness turned her face away from the corpse, her nose wrinkling.

'It is – it *was* – Scholiast Geriod Nerhm,' she said, drumming her fingers together. 'He's been missing for several days. I had assumed... Emperor forgive me. I had assumed that he'd deserted. Some have tried that, knowing the heat will kill them quicker.'

Gunnlaugur studied the heap of suppurating flesh at his feet. The signs of virulence were familiar enough; the scholiast's body could have been lifted straight from the corrupted heart of that plague-ship.

'Had Nerhm been exposed to the enemy?' he asked.

De Chatelaine shook her head. 'He was an official,' she said. 'He never left the citadel.'

'What of the rest of your troops?' asked Baldr, running a tired-looking hand across his forehead. 'The ones you pulled back?'

The canoness looked lost for a moment.

'I– I suppose so,' she said. 'We have regiments extracted from the warzone, brought here to resupply. What was I supposed to do – leave them to be annihilated?'

Gunnlaugur pursed his lips. 'Have you seen any cases like this?'

De Chatelaine shook her head. Her expression was distraught.

'None,' she said, weakly. 'We didn't think to–'

'No, you didn't,' said Baldr, his voice accusatory. 'You've been fighting these things for weeks. There should have been quarantine for anyone coming from the front. Do you see what you've done?'

'Enough,' snapped Gunnlaugur. He had no idea why Baldr was behaving so harshly. Blame was pointless; given the speed and severity of the outbreak of war, it would have been impossible to screen everyone.

De Chatelaine's face, though, had gone pale.

'No, he is correct,' she said, looking haunted. 'We thought it was the right thing, to pull them back. We thought we were saving them. Oh, Holy Emperor...'

Gunnlaugur shot a furious glance at Baldr.

'It matters not now,' he said. 'We still have time. What medicae complement do you have?'

The canoness struggled to focus.

'Sisters Hospitaller, a few squads,' she said. 'The Sisters have training. We can run checks, set up quarantine for those in the garrisons.'

'Good,' said Gunnlaugur. 'Do those things. Are the gates sealed?'

'Not yet. We had hoped for reinforcements. The Twelfth Guard battlegroup, heading north from the ruins of Bagahz. From reports, they're two days out.'

Baldr rolled his eyes. 'Do you not understand?' he said wearily. 'They *allow* them to survive. Carriers walk among them. You cannot let them in.'

'They cannot be abandoned.'

Baldr shot her a dark look. 'There are millions of people in this city, canoness,' he said. His voice was low but insistent. 'Some of them will already be infected. If we act now, we might keep it down, but if you let more in, this thing will spread. You will have dozens, *hundreds* of living corpses within the walls. Is that what you want?'

De Chatelaine looked down at the corpse, her drawn face riven with indecision.

'Seal the gates,' insisted Baldr, looking briefly to Gunnlaugur for support. 'Allow none to pass in or out. Then start the purges. You'll need flamer teams – everything contaminated must be destroyed.'

Still de Chatelaine hesitated. For the first time, Gunnlaugur noticed the deep lines of fatigue around her eyes. She'd been fighting without pause for too long.

'He's right,' said Gunnlaugur quietly.

Slowly, very slowly, de Chatelaine's chin lowered.

'It will be done,' she said. 'Leave it to me. We have allowed this into the city, we will purge it.' She sighed deeply. 'So they have got what they wanted. We will be cooped up here, unable to strike out, waiting for them like rats in a trap.'

'No, we will not,' said Gunnlaugur fiercely. 'We – the pack – we can still fight. We'll hit them on the plains, blood them, show them what manner of warrior defends the city. It'll give you some time.'

De Chatelaine looked unconvinced. 'I had hoped you would help us here,' she said.

'Right now they fear nothing on this world. When we have done with them they will fear plenty.' He grinned coldly, baring his long hooked fangs. 'It's what we're bred for.'

On another day, perhaps she might have resisted longer. The toll of her workload, though, combined with guilt, seemed to dilute her will.

'You will do what you judge best,' she said, her eyes flickering to the corpse lying on the floor before her. 'But if you go, just make sure you hurt them. Hurt them badly. For the first time since this thing began, I find myself wanting to see them truly suffer.'

She stared at the scholiast's body stonily. Then she recovered herself, and looked back up to the Wolf Guard.

'I have much to do,' she said. Her voice had recovered some of its steel. 'Purge-teams will be dispatched. We will root this out.' She shot him a wintry smile. 'If there's one thing we know how to do, it's burn.'

Gunnlaugur nodded. 'You will not be alone,' he said. 'While the sun shines, we fight here. After that, the pack hunts.'

De Chatelaine bowed. 'So be it,' she said. 'While the sun shines.'

Then she turned, pivoting sharply on her heel, and strode out of the chamber. Her boots clinked against the marble, echoing from her heavy tread.

After she'd gone, Baldr made to do the same. Gunnlaugur prevented him, raising a hand before his chest.

'Brother,' he said. The tone he used was firm. 'Speak to me.'

Baldr looked back at him. His complexion was pale, his eyes dull. He did not look sick, exactly. Drained, perhaps.

'About what?'

'You are not yourself.'

Baldr's eyelids twitched. 'I'm fine,' he said. 'The warp passage was... difficult. I will recover.'

Gunnlaugur didn't release him.

'Ingvar suffers like that,' he said. 'I have to worry about you both now?'

Baldr smiled. It was a distracted, snatched gesture. 'Don't worry about either of us,' he said. 'We're not children.'

Gunnlaugur's gaze didn't waver. 'I don't like to see you like this,' he said. 'It's enough that Jorundur is forever in foul temper. You were always the one I could rely on to keep your head. If something is amiss, tell me.'

Baldr hesitated. For a moment, he looked unsure of himself. His dull eyes flickered up to meet Gunnlaugur's, then away again.

'Seriously,' he said. 'Just warp-sickness. It will pass.' He took a deep breath, and rolled his shoulders. 'I need to hunt. To hunt properly. Void-war is one thing. It doesn't match the chase. You feel it too.'

Gunnlaugur nodded. He let his hand fall away. 'When night falls, brother,' he said.

'Good.' Baldr's eyes alighted on the corpse. 'For now, though, work to do.'

Gunnlaugur grunted distastefully. 'Aye,' he growled, looking at the pile of pustulent matter at his feet. It would be the first to enter the furnace. Many more would follow. 'Summon the rest of them. Time we got started.'

CHAPTER TWELVE

Ahlja Yemue woke up. Her eyes opened lazily, bleary with mucus. It was hard to open her eyes. She would have preferred to sleep. Sleep was all she had wanted to do for a while. The pain was less when she slept, even though the dreams were bad.

But she couldn't sleep. Not now. The itching compelled her. It made her limbs restive and her mind fractious. She needed to move. She had something to do.

Ahlja pushed her coverlet down. It smelled bad and was heavy with sweat. The mattress under her was damp and hot. The room around her was thick with flies.

That wasn't good. She didn't like flies. Why were they there? She should have cleaned up. She was a good cleaner, the most fastidious in her hab.

At some point the flies had got in and they hadn't left. She didn't remember when. Remembering anything was hard. Why was remembering anything hard?

She swung her feet over the edge of the bunk and tottered upright. She was thirsty. Her throat felt furry and baked. Swallowing was painful.

Ahlja looked at the window and winced. Strong sunlight burned away at the edges of the blinds. It looked like late afternoon outside. She shouldn't have been sleeping in the day. There was work to be done. It was lazy.

Work to be done. Work to be done.

Her mind seemed to run in circles. Whenever she tried to think of something new, the same old thoughts would cycle around and around.

Get up. Get up. Get up. Work to be done.

Ahlja shambled into the washroom. Her feet ached. They looked swollen. She wouldn't be able to squeeze them into her shoes. She'd have to go outside barefoot. That would be embarrassing. Helod would see her like that. She'd gossip about it. Hateful Helod. Why were her feet so swollen? Some misfortune must have occurred.

She reached the basin and stared into the cracked mirror above it. She didn't remember it breaking. It looked as if someone had thrown something at the glass, trying to shatter it.

Ahlja looked at herself.

Holy Throne. I look...

Get up. Get up. Work to be done.

She looked away. It wasn't nice, seeing all those things on her face. She rubbed her hands across her belly, feeling the flesh sway and bulge.

She was running to fat. Really, badly, running to fat.

She felt sick. She need to drink something. She needed to eat something.

She stumbled into the next room. No food there. Just her living area, tatty and smelly and buzzing with flies. The floor was covered in stains. One corner had a pile of drying, caking vomit in it. Other parts were worse.

I should clean this up. Very soon. Just need to find the time.

She kept walking, swaying heftily under her nightshirt, wincing as the material scraped across her lesions. Her feet trod through puddles of sticky liquid.

No time now. No time now. No time now.

She ran her hands over her hips. She felt the swollen curves there, pressing up against her nightshirt. So bloated, so uncomfortable, like something was trying to push its way out. How long had it been like that? She couldn't remember.

She did remember the man, though, the one who'd been helping her. He'd been nice. What was his name?

It doesn't matter. Work to be done.

She'd appreciated his kindness. He'd been very good to her, offering the balm that soothed the worst of the rashes and making the spiced tea that had cleared her head a little and patiently winding the bandages around the sores on her calves and arms and neck. He'd been there for her ever since she'd first got sick. He'd never left her. So attentive. So kind, even if he'd always smelled strange.

Perhaps that tea had made her stomach swell.

Ahlja pushed open the door and limped down the stairs. The air was cleaner outside her hab-unit. The communal corridor was free of all the muck on her floor. That was shameful. The others had got ahead of her. Helod would be gossiping already, holding her nose and pointing at her doorway with spiteful eyes.

It doesn't matter. Work to be done. Work to be done.

She reached the outside door and pushed against it. Sunlight flooded over her, blinding her, making her head throb. She felt dizzy and leaned against the frame. She could hear people talking and jostling around her.

They were in the street, those people. She'd gone out into the street wearing her nightdress. Why was she doing that? It was indecent.

It doesn't matter. It doesn't matter.

She kept walking. The sunlight hurt her eyes so she kept one hand over them. It was hard to walk. The stones in the street cut her skin. She felt the sores on her soles burst, popping open and spilling their fluids. She felt her belly sway. Throne, she really had got fat. It was embarrassing.

She heard people gagging around her. She opened her fingers a little, just a crack, to see what was going on. They were running away from her, or pointing at her with disgust on their faces, or laughing.

That almost made her stop. Why were they laughing? Why were they disgusted? Should she go back, clean herself up? Why was she even in the street in her nightshirt?

It doesn't matter. You have work to do. You have important work to do. They do not matter. They do not matter.

She kept going. She didn't like it when her mind cycled. If she just kept going, her mind cycled less.

Then she heard shouting. She heard a woman screaming, and she heard men crying something over and over again. She didn't like that. It upset her. She broke into a run, which was difficult on her cut feet and with her sagging belly.

Do it now. Do it now. Do it now.

Do what? Why was her mind cycling again?

She picked up speed, bumping and jostling against the walls around her. She stumbled over a drain-cover, nearly pitching headfirst into the dust of the road. The sunlight made it so hard to see. She didn't know where she was. Near the cathedral? She hoped so – she liked the cathedral. The priests had blessed her there, three times, maybe more. So hard to remember.

'Stay where you are!'

The voice was like a woman's, though horrifying; monstrously loud. Ahlja spun round, opening her fingers.

She saw a monster coming at her, running after her: a huge, tall monster, clad in black armour and wreathed in fire. She saw the monster carrying an enormous metal weapon that smoked and spat from its muzzle. She saw the people scattering away from the monster, breaking away from her, sprinting up the street, screaming and falling.

Do it now. Do it now.

Do *what?* She got very scared. The monster was almost on her. She dropped her hands from her face, squinting around her, trying to work out where she was.

She saw a holy brass aquila, hung up over the lintel of a doorway. She heard the hum of machinery behind rockcrete walls. She saw narrow, barred windows.

Then she knew where she was. She was outside the power plant, the sub-station that fed the district, no more than a hundred paces from her own little hab.

Do it now. Do it now.

The monster skidded to a halt in front of her. It was less than five metres away. Ahlja saw the horrific mask over its face, the swirling cloak, the cracked heart on its breast. It lowered its gun at her.

Suddenly, Ahlja knew what was going to happen. After so long being sick and bleary and muffled, she knew exactly what came next. She tried to swallow it down, but it was too late.

Well done.

Sister Honorata was thrown back as the subject exploded. The fat woman's foul body, riddled with its diseases and unnatural tumours, blasted apart with horrifying speed and force. Bile-laced flames cascaded up and over the walls around her, shattering brickwork, cracking metal, hurling masonry in all directions. The streetscape briefly became a blizzard of debris and fractured rockcrete.

It took a few moments for the carnage to clear. Smoke billowed up from the blast-centre, fed by smouldering piles of rubble. Puddles of blood boiled and bubbled amid the destruction. The power plant wall remained intact, though only barely. A gouge ran across its length, exposing metal shielding within.

Honorata picked herself up from the floor, tasting blood in her mouth. Her vision cleared. She hefted her flamer in bruised hands and advanced carefully towards the charred crater-edge.

'Notify,' she voxed into the comm, sweeping the muzzle of her flamer across the blast site. At either end of the street, terrified civilians were already emerging from behind whatever cover they'd been able to find. 'Another bomb-drone. Rejez district power plant, intersection of Yemn main-route and south-west cathedral approach.'

'Understood,' came the reply from the Halicon. The comm-operator's voice was clipped. She sounded stressed. 'Damage report? Did you get it?'

'Negative.' Honorata stepped through the wreckage, listening and watching carefully. The equipment within the plant seemed to be working. The whine of the generators might have been a bit more strained than usual, but she was no expert. 'Target managed to detonate. Minimal damage, but get a tech-team down here. If this thing blows, we do have a problem.'

'Acknowledged. Support on its way. Remain in position, Sister.'

A fresh commotion broke out at the far end of the street. Honorata looked up. Some of the civilians had started moving again. Fresh shouting broke out.

Her eyes narrowed. She blink-activated her helm's zoom-lens. A crowd was forming, spilling into the street from the mouth of a big hab-unit further down. One of the civilians was moving strangely, reeling unsteadily on bowed legs. His grey tongue lolled from an open mouth.

'Negative,' she snapped, thumbing the flamer back into life. 'I've got another one. Just get that team down here.'

Then she broke into a run, screaming at the crowd to get out of her way, aiming the flamer carefully and judging when to fire.

She'd erred back then. She'd cared too much about collateral damage to open fire when she should have done. The time had passed for such sensitivity – things were getting out of hand. Plague-carriers were emerging from everywhere, bursting out of their stinking dens as if summoned by silent, coordinated commands.

So Sister Honorata ran harder this time, feeling the flamer weigh heavily in her gauntlets. Her jaw clenched, her finger rested easily over the trigger.

This time would be different. This one wouldn't live long enough to swallow.

Ingvar heard the distant explosions go off before Bajola did. He stiffened immediately, gauging direction. As he did so, another one detonated, closer to the cathedral, near enough for her to pick up.

'What is–' she started, but Ingvar was already moving.

'It's started,' he said grimly, striding over to the doorway.

Bajola came after him. She was out of her armour and carried no weapon.

'Already?' she asked. Her unguarded voice betrayed a note of unease. 'Last report said they were days away.'

Ingvar paused before the lintel and shot her a dry smile.

'Fought the plague-damned before, Sister?' he asked.

Bajola shook her head.

'They carry weapons other than cleavers,' Ingvar said. 'The contagion spreads. They'll plant seeds of sickness here, hoping they'll take root. They'll pump toxins into the air and poison your water. They'll recruit the slack-minded with whispered promises in the dark. They'll reduce this place to infighting and disease before they come in sight of your walls.' He reached for his helm. 'I've seen it before. This is where the battle starts.'

He lifted his helm into place and secured the seals. He saw proximity markers scroll down his retinal display overlaid with moving pack runes. His brothers were already on the prowl.

Strange. Gunnlaugur hadn't summoned him.

'Then I'll need my armour,' said Bajola, her expression hardening. The uncertainty in her gestures faded quickly, replaced by a tight, disciplined resolve.

'You will,' said Ingvar, turning away from her and striding out of the chamber. The stairs wound down in their well, twisting into darkness. 'You should seal the cathedral. You should clear those crowds too.'

Bajola followed him down.

'If you wait, we could fight together,' she said.

Ingvar halted. He turned to face her. Bajola looked suddenly self-conscious.

'I mean, we...' She trailed off. 'My armour takes time to fit.'

Ingvar gazed down at her. In his battleplate he towered over her. She was a slight, slim woman. In her robes she looked impossibly frail.

He felt a strange impulse then, the first stirrings of something like... protectiveness. He felt that if she should come to harm he would regret it.

Unusual, to think that. Possibly unworthy.

'The fight has started,' he said, turning back. 'I cannot wait. If given leave, I will come back.'

Noises of running, of consternation and alarm, were already filtering up from the cathedral's nave.

Bajola hurried after him.

'We could use you here, Space Wolf.'

Ingvar winced. He was *Fenryka*, a Sky Warrior, a Son of Russ. *Space Wolf* was what off-worlders called them, transfixed by their totems and fang-tight jawlines and black-pinned eyes.

'If Hjortur were alive to hear you say that,' he said, 'he'd knock you cold, mortal or no.'

'Who?'

Of course. He'd not mentioned the name.

'Hjortur Bloodfang. The one who used to lead us. The one I was telling you about.'

Bajola stopped walking. Ingvar glanced over his shoulder and caught the look of surprise frozen across her features. For a moment, her ebony face looked almost grey.

'Mean something to you?' he asked.

Bajola shook her head. As she did so, another explosion rang out. It felt like it came from just the other side of the cathedral walls. The stone around them shivered, and lines of dust trickled down from the ceiling.

'You're right,' she said, pushing past him and hastening down the stairwell towards the doors at its base. 'This thing has started. We've talked for long enough.'

Ingvar followed her. He wasn't a fool. That had been recognition on her face. Such a thing was not quite impossible – Járnhamar had fought across hundreds of worlds and with dozens of allies – but it was almost vanishingly unlikely.

Bajola reached the doors and shoved them open. Just as she was about to go through, out into the body of the cathedral, she swivelled to face Ingvar.

'You got here just in time,' she said. Her voice had a strange, sardonic edge to it. 'Just before the fighting started. Strange, eh?'

Ingvar drew *dausvjer*. He could hear growing commotion from beyond the cathedral confines.

'It was my wyrd to be here,' he said. 'Just as it was yours.'

Bajola smiled dryly. 'Maybe you're right.' She looked squarely up at him. Her expression was an odd mix of defiance and amusement. 'I do need more faith.'

The smell of burning rose up into Ingvar's nostrils then, barely filtered by his helm's intake grille. Screaming broke through the bustling tumult of the crowds outside. He felt his heart rate begin to pick up, already preparing for the exertions to come.

Her manner had become strange. There was no time now, but he would need to speak to Bajola again.

'When I am gone, seal everything,' he said. 'Begin your siege preparations. Kill any among you who show signs of plague. And clear those damn crowds.'

He pushed past her, out of the doors and into the nave beyond. Already his helm-display was giving him targets.

'And you'll come back?' Bajola called out after him.

'Count on it,' he growled, kicking *dausvjer*'s disruptor into life and breaking into a run.

Váltyr paused for a moment, driving the tip of *holdbítr* into the soft earth and leaning on it. The sun began to dip over the roofs of Hjec Aleja, presaging the end of the long, hot afternoon.

For all the sweat and grime that caked his exposed skin, he wasn't tired. He wasn't close to being tired. With the steady lessening of the heat the streets had become good hunting grounds. The contagion was in its first stages – still sporadic, still isolated – and its victims hadn't succeeded in grouping together in any numbers.

Still, the process had only just started. Parts of the lower city were already burning, sending dirty columns of smoke into the clear sky. Plenty of plague-nests still existed, fomenting filth and pestilence in forgotten corners. Váltyr knew, just as they all knew, that they were ready to burst, scattering their foul incubated contents into the seamy air.

Ahead of him stretched a series of tumbledown, metal-framed warehouses, all in various states of disrepair, all huge and blunt against the deepening sky. The streets between them were sunk in shadows and thick with brown dust. Their walls were caked with a scouring patina of drifting sand that lodged in the detail of the metalwork. Váltyr had already uncovered one cluster of plague-carriers nestled within the district; he was sure there were more. In such semi-derelict, barely patrolled parts of the lower city the conditions were ideal for the incubation of proto-mutancy.

He inclined his head a little, stilling his breathing, letting his armour-hum die down with inactivity, listening.

He didn't pick it up immediately. The noise was just on the edge of detection, buried deep, muffled by walls and hanging dust and distance.

But his ears, like those of all his brothers, were sharp. He smiled, bringing *holdbítr* back into guard, watching the metal glint as the blade whirled into position. Then he started, silently, to move.

He slipped along the narrow alleyway between two warehouses, and the shadows slid over him like liquid. Twenty paces ahead to his left a wall section was broken. He saw a corrugated metal panel peeled away from its housings, hanging like a flap of skin from a wound and shivering in the cooling air. The noise became clearer as he neared the source – rattling breath, irregular and rheumy, the soft brush of clammy skin against cloth. More than one pair of lungs was working. Bodies were huddled together, clustered tightly on the far side of the damaged wall.

Váltyr paused and sniffed, flaring his nostrils. The note of honeyed decay was unmistakable. Mortal sickness did not have that stench, not even when gangrene had set in or the flesh had turned rotten. The sufferers of such unnatural illness learned to love the sweetness. They no longer wanted to be cured. They would caress their own lesions and pustules, squeezing them gently and watching the bile ooze thickly between their fingers. Once that stage was reached, all they really feared was death. Death brought the end of the blissful pain, the suffering they'd come to love. Even in the misery of plague-raddled weakness they would fight to stay alive, just to stretch the odorous agony a little longer, just to revel in it for a moment more.

Váltyr crouched beside the breach in the wall, moving carefully, estimating numbers. A dozen, maybe, all close at hand, all unaware of his presence.

Easy prey.

With a sudden jolt from his armour, he pounced, bursting through the ragged gap and plunging into the cavernous interior. The clang of falling metal echoed as pieces bounced around him. He whirled around, catching sight of a cluster of plague-thick bodies huddled against the near wall, wrapped in filthy bandages and nuzzling against one another like a brood of rats. As soon as they saw him they broke, scampering and scuttling away on all-fours.

He was far, far quicker. The first one to die never made a sound – *holdbítr* cleaved her from head to waist in a single flashing stroke, carving through her ribcage and scattering it in a clatter of bones.

Another one darted across the floor at his feet, panting like a dog, frantic with fear. Váltyr twisted back to jab, and the mutant's swollen head rolled into the dust, neatly cut from his bloated body.

He never stopped moving, switching from one stroke to the next in the space of a thought, lashing out smoothly as more of the plague-bearers scurried for cover. Every strike was perfectly aimed and weighted: cleaving necks, cutting muscle, going for the efficient kill, the swordsman's deadly figures. The only sounds were his victims' strangled cries, ringing out into the darkness in an overlapping mess of surprise and terror.

'Nineteen,' he breathed, adding to the tally of the day. 'Twenty. Blood of Russ, more than I thought.'

The floor became sticky with blood. He slaughtered with ruthless speed, felling most before they'd got more than a few paces away from him. Only a few managed to break clear of the initial assault, racing off into the dark, squealing like startled swine.

He went after them, loping across the cracked rockcrete floor, holding his blade low. There was nowhere for them to go. Their shuffling, stuttering footfalls echoed into the open spaces, giving their location away. Váltyr swooped on the first runner, a man with weeping white eyes and a glowing rash around his obese neck. *Holdbítr* flickered and he collapsed to the ground, his sore-tight stomach carved open in a single gaping slash.

Váltyr swept across the warehouse interior like a vengeful spectre. He knew he was almost invisible to them in the dark, picked out only by his helm lenses, which hovered in the shadows, and the shimmer of his blade as it whirled.

He liked that. He liked to think of his enemies convulsing with terror even before he came into cutting range.

Three more were struck down in the next few seconds, their cries ended in sudden, gurgling coughs of blood-choked surprise. After that only one set of running feet still rang out across the floor towards the far walls. Váltyr sprinted after it, fixing his eyes on a lone, shambling mutant ahead.

He came within blade-range, hearing the plague-damned man wheeze with fear even as he drew his sword round for the killing blow. He could smell the man's corruption, his fear, his desperation to escape.

He brought *holdbítr* down savagely, fast as ever, watching the mono-molecular edge whistle towards its prey's spine...

...and miss.

Unbelievably, the plague-ravaged man leapt clear at the last moment, scrambling away from the blade. The killing-edge snicked his robes, slicing free a scrap of dirty fabric, but didn't cut into flesh.

Váltyr almost lost his footing. It was inexcusable. *Embarrassing.*

'I would have killed you *quickly*, little man!' he roared, thundering after his prey's scuttling outline. 'Now you *suffer!*'

The man moved incredibly quickly. His flesh looked wasted, all skin and bone under flapping robes. He reached the far wall of the warehouse and frantically scrabbled for a way out. He found one – a corroded metal door hanging by its hinges. He slammed into it and the lock broke open; then he tore through the gap and out into the alley beyond.

Váltyr spat a curse and followed him through. Once outside he swung around, expecting to see the man scampering down the narrow streets ahead of him. Instead the plague-bearer's body lay at his feet, twisted in the dust, his robes dark with blood and filth. Standing over the corpse, towering into the darkening air, was a warrior in pearl-grey armour carrying a mighty warhammer one-handed.

'Careless, brother,' admonished Gunnlaugur, shaking the blood from the hammer's head.

Váltyr bristled, his blood still pumping. 'He was lucky.'

Gunnlaugur gestured towards the warehouse. 'All cleansed in there?'

Váltyr nodded.

'Good,' said Gunnlaugur, sounding satisfied. 'I'll summon a burn-team.'

He pressed his boot to the man's sore-mottled skull, and pressed down. The bone caved in with a limp crack, splattering white-flecked gore across the dust.

'Walk with me, *sverdhjera,*' he said, moving off down the alleyway.

Váltyr followed him. The two of them strode back through the warren of dusty streets around the warehouses. Ahead of them, golden in the failing light, reared the outcrop of the mountainous upper city.

'Outbreaks everywhere,' said Gunnlaugur grimly. His armour bore the evidence of fighting – streaks of wind-dried pus and slime across his gauntlets and breastplate. 'It'll get worse once night falls.'

'The Sisters can cope,' said Váltyr.

'I'm sure they can.'

Gunnlaugur stopped walking and lowered his head.

'Have you spoken to the Gyrfalkon since we made planetfall?' he asked.

Váltyr shrugged. 'Not much.'

'What do you make of him?'

Váltyr hesitated before replying. Since the practice-duel on the *Undrider* he'd not given much thought to Ingvar.

'He fights like he used to,' he said.

'You think so?' asked Gunnlaugur. 'That's not what I saw.'

Váltyr sighed. 'What do you want me to say? If he's changed, we all have.'

Gunnlaugur remained motionless. It was impossible to read the expression behind his bloody helm-mask.

'I wouldn't have blamed you if you'd spoken against him. Yours was the only rune-sword in Járnhamar. Now there are two. You need to know this, though: you are my blademaster, my right arm of vengeance. That has not changed.'

Váltyr didn't know what to make of that. He hadn't asked for reassurance. The fact that it was being offered at all gave him pause.

'Glad to hear it,' he said.

Gunnlaugur started walking again.

'We've got to get out of this city,' he muttered. 'Hunting this scum is weary work.'

'Just say the word, *vaerangi*,' said Váltyr, following him. 'We'll all follow you out.'

'No.' The finality in Gunnlaugur's voice was sudden. 'Not all of you. I don't want Ingvar with us. I don't want him questioning orders. I don't want him slowing us down. *Skítja*, I don't want him there at all.'

Váltyr didn't like hearing that. It was not the way of the pack. Ingvar had behaved strangely since his return, sure, but he had been back only a few short weeks. There was time for that to change, for his old self to re-emerge.

'Are you sure?' he asked. Gunnlaugur answered him with a snarl.

'It is my judgement,' he said. 'You, me, Olgeir, Baldr and the whelp – we'll conduct this raid. Ingvar can stay here with Jorundur and stiffen the resolve of the Sisters. Russ knows there's plenty to keep them busy.'

Váltyr shook his head. 'He won't like it,' he said.

'He doesn't have to.' Gunnlaugur swung his hammer menacingly as he walked. The head of it rolled like a pendulum in the gloom. 'But I need you to support me. I have your word?'

Váltyr didn't like that either. In fifty-seven years Gunnlaugur had never asked him to support anything. He'd just gone ahead and acted – that was the way of things. Now, without warning, that seemed to have changed. It was as if all Gunnlaugur's certainty, his famed pride and justified battle-arrogance, was eroding before his eyes.

For a moment, Váltyr felt like protesting, arguing Ingvar's case, standing up for the unity of a broken brotherhood.

But he didn't. He looked across at Gunnlaugur, noticing the pent-up frustration in the warrior's shoulder-roll, the over-tight grip on the warhammer, the almost imperceptible stiffness in his long stride, and thought better of it.

Perhaps it was for the best. A hunt – a clean hunt with no dissension – would clear the air.

'You always have my support,' said Váltyr, haltingly, trying to inject more certainty into his voice than he felt.

'Good,' said Gunnlaugur bluntly, sounding like he'd been given what he needed. 'Then let's get it over with. We meet at the Ighala Gate.'

'And then?' asked Váltyr.

Gunnlaugur let slip a low, snagging growl.

'Then we break out of this shithole,' he said, 'and bring Hel to the enemy.'

CHAPTER THIRTEEN

The great sun sank towards the western horizon like a smouldering ingot of gold, turning the sky bronze and setting the world's edge alive with fire. Shadows streaked across the rust-red of the plains, rippling over runnels of sand and merging in their broken lees. The air lost its heaviness; it remained hot, but the searing, beating oppressiveness of it lightened just a little.

In happier times, dusk was magical on Ras Shakeh, a time to light candles under the lintels of the doorways and file towards one of the city's one hundred and twenty-nine chapels to perform rites of devotion. Scents of cinnamon and gahl-oil would rise from braziers and thuribles, intermingling with the murmur and hum of voices lost in prayer and wonder.

Now, though, the coming of night was far from magical. Hjec Aleja burned with unholy fires now, punctured across its expanse by the immolation of plague-addled saboteurs. Pyres constructed before the chapel doors now smoked from the charred bodies of the damned. The roast-pork stench of smouldering human flesh hung like a cloud over the narrow roofs and winding streets.

Burning the infected was the only way to limit the damage. Keeping the flesh intact created foul cradles for the blowflies and maggots that spread the sickness. The Sisters worked methodically through the city's many districts, dragging those with signs of infection from their habs and administering the Emperor's Mercy. Civilians looked on sullenly, only partially aware of the dangers posed by the plague-carriers in their midst, resentful of the savage measures taken to keep the healthy intact. Rumours filtered up to the Halicon of riots in the poorer quarters, of families sheltering mutants in cellars and under floors, and fighting to keep them hidden from the burn-teams.

They were only rumours, but this was just the beginning. All knew it would get worse.

Olgeir stood on the ramparts of the Ighala Gate, just under the shadow of one of its many defence towers, and gazed out over the cityscape below. Unlike his brothers he had taken no part in the hunt. His energies had been devoted to the city's defensive preparations: shoring up wall sections, excavating fire trenches, demolishing paths through the tangle of buildings to allow the passage of arms. He'd worked tirelessly throughout the day, hauling and lifting alongside the mechanised transports, roaring at the mortal labourers and exhorting them to greater feats of sacrifice. Many of the men were already exhausted, thrown into construction work straight from active tours on the battlefronts to the south and west.

Olgeir felt pity for them. He recognised their sacrifice, he could see the pain in their faces, he knew what some of them had already faced.

He gave them no quarter. Time was short, and the storm front was closing. With the Sisters preoccupied with containing the infection, much of the task of improving the defences had fallen to him. He'd embraced it, throwing himself into the heavy, draining labour as if he alone could somehow refashion the entire city in the few days that remained. He'd trudged up and down the lines of sweating labourers between the inner walls and the outer gate, marshalling them, bellowing for more supplies, physically clearing blockages and barriers when mortal endurance failed.

But even his strength was not infinite. As the last of the sun's rays sank below the horizon, he leaned on the stone walls of the soaring inner wall and felt the sweat rising from his body like steam from a horse's flanks. Every muscle in his huge body throbbed painfully, chafing at the input nodes where his power armour interfaced.

He let his shaggy head fall back and pulled in a long, long draught of night-warm air, feeling the smoky taste of it against the back of his throat. Above him, the stars gazed down, points of brilliant silver in a field of darkening nightshade.

'*Hjá*, great one,' came a familiar voice from further down the parapet, towards the Ighala gatehouse where more lascannons were being slowly winched into place.

Olgeir smiled as he turned to face Baldr. 'Good hunting?' he asked.

Baldr grinned. His face was speckled with gore and his long hair hung unplaited around his neck. His helm had been locked to his belt and his blade was sheathed.

'They're everywhere,' he said, drawing alongside Olgeir and looking out over the city below. 'Kill one, another runs from cover. It's thirsty work.'

Olgeir looked at Baldr carefully. He looked better than he had done when they'd made planetfall. His eyes had their old intensity back, like soft orbs of gold. Perhaps his cheeks looked a little more sunken than they should have, but his voice had recovered its calm, easy assurance.

'It suits you, brother,' he said. 'I'd begun to worry.'

Baldr leaned heavily against the stone railing.

'No need,' he said. 'But nice to know I have a nursemaid.'

Olgeir let a rumble of laughter escape his chapped lips. It felt good to let his lungs expand after so much heavy lifting. He stretched his arms out, feeling the muscles pull, loosening the stiff layers of hard flesh.

'Don't relax too much,' he warned. 'We'll be heading out again soon.'

Baldr nodded, looking eager enough. 'Aye,' he said, softly. 'Can't wait.'

He meant it. His face had a hungry look to it, one that hung around his grey features like a scent. He stared out across the twinkling cityscape as the dusk-lights were lit, beyond the outer walls and across the wine-dark plains beyond.

'You've been working hard,' Baldr said, scanning the earthworks that scarred the route down the outer gate.

Olgeir snorted. 'We could have weeks and it wouldn't be enough.'

'Still. You've done plenty.'

Olgeir shrugged. 'The main gates are rigged with incendiaries,' he said. 'Once they break in, we'll burn their entire vanguard. After that they've got three layers of trenches to get across. We'll pump promethium into them once this thing starts – it'll take them a while to wade through all that. And this place has twice the armaments on it now. I diverted a whole stash they'd been planning to mount on the Halicon walls. No point keeping them there. If they get that far we'll all be dead and rotting.'

Baldr nodded thoughtfully.

'Good,' he said. 'Good. Much more to do?'

'Depends how long we've got,' said Olgeir. 'When the Sisters aren't burning plague-carriers they're training the civilians to shoot straight, which is worth doing, but they won't do much more than slow the advance.'

'I don't know. I've seen mortals learn to fight. These ones are scared enough. They know there's nowhere else to go.'

'True enough,' said Olgeir grimly.

Baldr's fingers drummed against the parapet railing. He pushed himself away from them, grasped the hilt of his sword, then released it again. His movements looked nervy, impatient.

'Where are the others?' he muttered, almost to himself. 'We should be going.'

Olgeir watched him warily. Perhaps his earlier assessment had been too optimistic. It was strange to see Baldr so transformed, so removed from his usual self.

'They'll be here soon,' he said cautiously. 'Brother, I mean no disrespect, but are you sure you're feeling...'

He didn't finish the sentence. He'd got so used to Baldr's calmness, his lack of fuss or drama, that finding the words to express concern was difficult.

Baldr looked back at him for a moment. It looked like he was going to say something, to unload some long-clutched anxiety.

'Heavy-hand!'

Ingvar's clear voice rang out across the parapet. Baldr spun round, the moment gone, his expression clearing.

'Gyrfalkon,' he said, clasping Ingvar's hand as he came to join them.

Olgeir greeted him in turn. Ingvar looked pleased to see both of them.

'Others not here yet?' he asked. Like Baldr, his face and armour were speckled with dried gore. He hadn't wiped it off his matted hair or skin; the Wolves wore the blood of their enemies as marks of pride.

'You were always faster,' said Baldr. 'Many kills?'

Ingvar nodded. 'Crawling all over the cathedral district.' He patted *dausvjer*'s scabbard. 'Not any more.'

Olgeir shook his head with disgust.

'That blade shouldn't sully itself with filth,' he said. 'The Sisters should have nailed this down themselves – they've had weeks.'

'They've done plenty,' said Ingvar. 'This is a shrineworld, the garrison here is tiny. Don't judge them too harshly.'

Olgeir chuckled. 'So she's got to you,' he said. 'You've gone native.'

Ingvar smiled. 'Not yet,' he said. 'But they can fight. You'll see.'

'We'll all see,' said Baldr.

The noise of more boots crunched along the parapet. Three more warriors emerged from the shadows of the Ighala Gate tower. Gunnlaugur and Váltyr marched together; Hafloí trailed behind. The Blood Claw bore almost no trace of the wound he'd taken on the plague-ship. Váltyr's expression was hard to read. He seemed tense, as if already preparing for the combat to come. Gunnlaugur's burly face was expectant and heavy with kill-urge. He looked ready to burst out of the walls, ready to plunge into the oncoming horde and smash it apart single-handed.

'Now listen,' he said, looking across the assembled pack. 'Here's what we're going to do.'

Vuokho's innards spilled across the blast plate, patchily lit by scaffold-mounted flood-lumens arranged around the perimeter. Whole engine sections lay on the rockcrete, stripped down and exposed to the night air. Oils and lubricants stained the ground in splatters. The landing stage hummed with the low buzz of machine tools, the whine of drills, the thud of rivet guns. Welders threw dazzling arcs of blue fire across the scene. Between it all, dull-eyed labourers shuffled into place to lift, clamp, cut and fit.

They were all servitors, and they crawled over the gunship's carcass like scavengers picking at the bones of a fallen giant. Some looked almost species-normal, with only puckered grey skin and augmetic limb-units giving them away; others were more machine than human, with mere fragments of muscle and sinew stretched between jointed tracks and thickets of cabling. They slaved silently, ignoring the sparks from the welders as they burned against unprotected skin, never slowing, never hurrying.

Jorundur clambered out of an inspection pit under the gunship's huge underbelly and wiped his forehead. His skin was covered in streaks of inky engine oil, his beard singed from the hot metal of the thruster housings. He'd removed his armour and wore a filthy brown tunic that exposed the burnished sweat of his arms.

He seized a rag from one of the more human-looking servitors and ran it over his neck. His hair and beard hung lank about his gaunt face.

'Progress?' he asked.

The servitor looked back at him vacantly.

'Task at phase alpha, lord. Estimated completion: five local days. Parts missing. List follows: two fuel-line regulator valves, three boost-plug sleeves, one–'

'Spare me,' sighed Jorundur, throwing the rag back at the demi-human workman. It slapped the creature full in the face and slid down to the floor. The servitor didn't flinch.

'Blood of Russ,' swore Jorundur, limping around the apron to get a better look at *Vuokho*'s flanks. He felt stiff and awkward, a result of hours spent hunched over piles of crackling component-bundles. 'Hopeless.'

He stomped around to the cockpit. Its angular nose hung above him, still covered in re-entry burn and cracked from projectile impacts. One of the panes of armourglass was a shattered mess. That had been fun when it had happened, still barely into Ras Shakeh's troposphere and with the gunship falling fast.

He stood back, hands on hips. *Vuokho* was far from flight-ready. It was even further from combat-ready. Deep in his heart, he knew it would play no role in the battle to come. Even if he could somehow restore limited drive-function, the weapons would overload the second they were fired.

His time would have been better spent with the pack, hunting the plague-damned before their foulness spread further.

For all that, though, he couldn't let it go. It was all he had, his peerless mastery of airborne combat. Take that away, and it was hard to mask the truth: he was old. He'd missed his chance for the Wolf Guard, he'd missed his chance for the Long Fangs. All that remained for him was death in Járnhamar, no longer fast enough to evade it, no longer strong enough to see it off.

He could feel Morkai panting down his neck. At night, in the scant moments of sleep he allowed himself, Jorundur could feel the dark wolf's foul breath running down his spine. Only when he was in the air, wheeling and banking through the hammering fire-lanes and letting rip with the battle cannon, did the sensation leave him.

He hawked up a bitter gobbet of oil-tainted phlegm and spat messily.

'You and me,' he snarled, looking up at his beloved *Vuokho*. 'Ice and iron, I'll get you in the air again.'

He heard a faint cough, and whirled round.

A Battle Sister stood before him. She was dressed in full ebony armour, though her head was bare. Like all her Sisters she wore her hair clipped short. Hers was silver-blonde, shorn close to pale skin. Frost-blue eyes looked at him uncertainly.

'What do you want?' Jorundur growled, irritated at the interruption. Being surrounded by mind-dead servitors was one thing; having living mortals sniffing around was another.

The Sister bowed.

'Callia, at your service, lord,' she said. She proffered a regulation food-tin, vacuum-packed with protein extracts. 'The canoness sent me. She thought you might have need of sustenance.'

Jorundur looked at the tin doubtfully. He could smell its bland contents through the metal. He briefly remembered the supplies that had been destroyed with the *Undrider* – raw meats of Fenris, blood-heavy and slick with fat; whole vats of *mjod*, frothing in the cold and as thick as bile.

He started to salivate, and swallowed it down.

'My thanks,' he muttered, snatching the tin from her. It looked meagre in his oversized hand, barely enough to sate a moment's hunger.

But she was right, and it had been good of her to come. He'd lost track of time and had little idea how long he'd been working.

Sister Callia looked up at the half-dismantled Thunderhawk. Her cool eyes soaked up the damage.

'It's not as bad as it looks,' said Jorundur, a little quickly, unable to stomach criticism of it even when it was half ruined and broken open.

'A mighty machine,' murmured Callia. Her quiet voice held no trace of sarcasm. 'Even before the war destroyed our few flyers, we had nothing so grand.'

She started to walk around it, heading under the cockpit's overhang.

Jorundur put the tin down and followed her. He couldn't decide whether to be annoyed or flattered by her interest.

'Four centuries,' he said, staying close. 'That's how long it's been in service.'

Callia turned to face him. 'And will it last a little longer?' she asked. Her face held a certain sadness, as if she'd long resigned herself to the destruction of all she cared about and now only concerned herself with making a decent fist of the last stand.

Jorundur rubbed his chin. 'Perhaps,' he grunted. 'Get me some better servitors, I might get it flying again.'

Callia gave a rueful smile. 'You have our best already. But I'll talk to the canoness.'

'Do that.'

Jorundur turned away from the gunship and looked at Callia. Her armour, though beautifully cared for and polished, bore the marks of recent use. Her greaves and cuirass were chipped down to bare metal. Like her Sisters, she had been in action for a long time.

Callia noticed his gaze and seemed to guess what he was thinking. 'Burn-team duty,' she said bluntly. 'Next rotation in two hours.'

Jorundur nodded. He'd smelt the pyres.

'Did you get many of them?'

She nodded sadly.

'Too many.' She pursed her lips. 'Your brothers kill faster than we do. I saw them in action. They laughed when they returned, covered in blood they didn't bother to wipe from their armour.'

She looked down.

'I cannot laugh. These are my people. A month ago we were ministering to them. We told them a new dawn was coming, the start of a crusade. Even when the plague takes them I mourn that so many must die. I wonder at the way you Wolves delight in slaughter.'

Jorundur shrugged. 'Don't expect us to be like you,' he said. 'We were made this way. That's why you wanted us here, was it not?'

Callia looked back up at him, unabashed. 'The canoness wanted you here. Others of us – I will not mention names – were opposed. You have a reputation.'

Jorundur chuckled. 'A cultivated one,' he replied. 'You speak plainly, Sister. I like that. I'll return the compliment. Until I got here I thought you were all stuck-up bitches, wearing a pale mockery of our sacred armour and pretending to fight like we do. I thought you were pious and arrogant.'

Callia suppressed a smile. 'Stuck-up bitches,' she said, amused. 'That's... candid.'

Jorundur shrugged. 'I try to be. And don't be surprised – our memories are long. Fenris has been attacked by your kind more than once.'

'Not in living memory.'

Jorundur snorted. 'In *our* living memory. You may have forgotten, but we have not. We tell sagas of it. We sing of how we sent your priests home, their robes stripped from their backs and their warships breaking open around them.'

Callia sighed. 'I'm sure you do,' she said. 'But then you are a warlike people. Fenris has been attacked by the Inquisition too. You make enemies easily, it seems.'

'We make no enemies but traitors and xenos. If others choose to get in our way, that's their business.'

Callia nodded, as if confirming something to herself. 'Perhaps that is what I meant.'

Jorundur paused then, suddenly concerned he'd caused too much offence. He wouldn't normally have been worried, but Gunnlaugur had given them all strict orders to keep the peace.

'But I speak loosely,' he said, smiling awkwardly and exposing his curved yellow fangs. 'You understand that? Forgive me. We are just savages – savages from an ice-world that breeds us cold and rude.'

Callia looked amused again.

'I'm not some prim schola maid,' she said. 'But thank you. I had not expected such concern for my sensibilities. Especially as we are all such – what were the words you used? – *stuck-up bitches.*'

Jorundur laughed out loud, hacking up phlegm from his dry throat and coughing on it. He clapped Callia hard on the shoulder, and the slap of unguarded flesh against power armour made his palm sting.

'I like you!' he exclaimed. 'Blood of Russ, has the galaxy no end of wonder?'

Callia looked less sure.

'Maybe not,' she said, moving away from him smoothly. 'But I do have duties waiting. I'll talk to the canoness about the servitors.'

Jorundur bowed, still smiling. 'It can wait,' he said. 'My work is drawing to a close for today.'

Callia raised an eyebrow.

'You need rest?'

'No, no. My brothers have had the hunting in this city all to themselves. They will be heading out into the dark soon, and it is time I took up the burden on their behalf.'

Callia looked at him distastefully.

'You will relish killing our people as much as they.'

Jorundur gave her a crooked, semi-ashamed grin.

'Maybe more so,' he confessed.

Ingvar watched Gunnlaugur intently. The Wolf Guard spoke to them all but wouldn't meet his gaze. He'd looked at all the others, but not him.

He's putting something off. Something he doesn't want to tell me.

Ingvar felt his hearts sink. He'd hoped the exchange in the Halicon, as difficult as it had been, had cleared the air between them. A state of continued tension suited nobody.

But then Gunnlaugur had always been proud. He was a born warrior, only happy with bolter in hand and prey in sight, never knowing how to handle anything but combat. It wasn't so much that the Wolf Guard didn't tolerate differing points of view, more that he didn't understand how they could exist. The way of Russ, the brutal life of the hard ice, the exalted state of the Sky Warrior, that was all there was for him. Just as the Sisters fervently believed in the perfect godhood of the Emperor, so Gunnlaugur believed in the perfect heritage of the primarch, frozen into the annals of Fenris and sanctified by millennia of war.

Ingvar couldn't blame him for that. He'd thought the same once. It had taken a lot to shake that faith.

Tyranid-breed xenos, millions upon millions, turning the void into a living hell, burning with hive-malice, dousing the light of Terra. The ships! They are like worlds, vast and swollen, disgorging living contents in columns of twisting, slavering frenzy.

We cannot fight them. They will come at us, again and again. There is no end to it. Callimachus, there is no end to it!

Ingvar forced himself not to remember. He forced himself not to see the Ultramarine's face turning towards him, stoic to the last, ready to enact the order he'd been given by Halliafiore. He forced himself not to see the agony in that face, hidden by Callimachus's peerless conditioning, his reserve, his unimpeachable honour.

The things they made us do.

He curled his fingers together, concentrating on the present.

'The canoness has restored partial mid-range auspex scans,' Gunnlaugur was saying. 'We have readings coming at us from all directions. The city is at the centre of a closing circle. Numbers are hard to estimate.'

'Take a guess?' said Olgeir.

'Thousands,' said Gunnlaugur sourly. 'Many, many thousands. The plague has spread. De Chatelaine thinks most of their troops are defenders who've succumbed and then mutated. That's why this thing's happened so fast. Every city they've taken has swollen their ranks. They conquer, they get stronger.'

'She was right: they do not wish to destroy this world,' said Baldr. 'They wish to possess it. For what?'

Gunnlaugur looked at him irritably.

'We don't need to know.' Still he avoided Ingvar's eye. 'Survival is the first task, vengeance the next. The armies have fractured as they near the city. Discipline is weak on the fringes, and one armoured column has come too far up the defiles to the south. That's the one we'll take.'

Olgeir grunted. 'What are we talking about? Mortals? Plague-bearers?'

'Both. Perhaps more.' A glint of anticipation lit up Gunnlaugur's features, sparking in his amber eyes. 'De Chatelaine picked up strange readings, ones they couldn't decipher. Something... interesting travels in that column.'

Ingvar felt mounting unease. A raid was one thing – taking out enemy troops before they could take up position made sense. Going after unverified targets was another.

He said nothing. It would only antagonise Gunnlaugur. The Wolf Guard had taken a blow to his prestige by losing the *Undrider*; a feat of arms against a worthy foe would redress the balance.

'How far?' asked Hafloí, flexing his fingers absently. His voice gave away his eagerness – he was chafing at the leash already.

Gunnlaugur gave him an approving look.

'If we leave now and move fast, we can engage before dawn.'

'No speeders?' asked Olgeir.

'Nothing that could carry us. We'll run.' Gunnlaugur grinned. 'Think of it, brother: close pursuit, under the stars, nothing but the scent of fear between you and the enemy.'

Olgeir nodded slowly, a smile creeping across his scarred, ugly face.

'Pure,' he murmured.

'We kill them all,' said Gunnlaugur. 'Destroy everything. Hit hard, then withdraw. Allfather willing, that'll give the bastards pause. They already know something destroyed their ship – we can work on that doubt. It might even slow them, give us more time to cleanse the city.'

'They won't slow,' said Ingvar. The words came out of his mouth unbidden; he hadn't meant to speak. Immediately his eyes flickered up towards Gunnlaugur, but the Wolf Guard still avoided contact. Váltyr, standing to Gunnlaugur's right, looked uncomfortable.

'It'll hurt them,' said Gunnlaugur. 'And what's the alternative? Hole up here until they're clawing at the walls? Not the way of the *Fenryka*.'

Olgeir and Hafloí both growled in agreement. Ingvar could almost smell their hunt-readiness.

Gunnlaugur pulled himself to his full height. The runes on his armour flickered in the soft lights of the city, playing over the ceramite like tongues of flame. Despite the blood and slime that still caked his battleplate, he looked savagely magnificent, the very embodiment of a *vaerangi*.

'We were brought here for a reason, brothers,' he said. 'Time to show them what it was.'

'And Jorundur?' asked Ingvar.

Only then did Gunnlaugur look directly at him.

'He's staying here,' he said. 'As are you, Gyrfalkon.'

For a moment, Ingvar didn't believe it. He felt sure he'd misheard.

'You mean–' he started.

'I mean you're staying here.'

Gunnlaugur's voice was cold. His amber eyes didn't waver.

Ingvar felt sweat break out across his palms. For the space of a heartbeat he couldn't say anything, sure that if he tried he'd unleash something he'd regret.

'Why?' he asked thickly, keeping himself under control with difficulty.

'The plague worsens. The Sisters need help.'

That was ridiculous. The Sisters had been trained for such work; they were very, very good at it.

Ingvar looked over at Váltyr. The blademaster averted his eyes.

'Is this your doing?' he spat. The anger in his voice rose to the surface.

Váltyr stirred then, looking like he wanted to rise to the challenge. He was cut off by Gunnlaugur.

'Enough,' he said, letting threat-notes bleed into his speech. 'The city is burning. I will not abandon it.'

Ingvar crushed his fists into tight balls.

It was a humiliation. Punishment for what happened on the plague-ship. *I need to know that you will follow an order.*

Or a test.

Ingvar stared directly at Gunnlaugur. For a moment their eyes met, one pair golden, the other as grey as winter sleet. When he spoke next, his voice was sharp with bitterness.

'You want me to waste my blade here on filth that can barely stand? So be it.' Ingvar raised his chin, looking proudly back at the Wolf Guard. Jocelyn himself could not have expressed such disdain. 'I will scour the citadel. When you return, expect to find it cleansed and ready for your arrival.'

He swept his gaze across the rest of the pack. Olgeir was dumb with surprise; Baldr almost distraught. Hafloí returned his gaze coolly. Váltyr looked torn between shame and defiance.

Then he turned, not waiting for Gunnlaugur to dismiss him, and strode away from the pack, back towards the defence tower. He could feel his cheeks burning from the fury that coursed through him, bubbling under the surface like magma under a thin crust of rock.

After he'd ducked under the doorway and started to descend the stairway down to the next level he heard footsteps clattering on the stone behind him. For a moment he thought, or hoped, they were Gunnlaugur's. When Baldr grabbed him by the shoulder it was a disappointment.

'You have been wronged,' said Baldr.

Ingvar twisted round to look at him. Baldr's face was white with shame. His eyes looked sunk deep into his flesh and an unhealthy pallor hung in their shadow.

Ingvar wondered how he'd not noticed that earlier.

'It is nothing,' he said.

'Olgeir is arguing with him. Come back. Fight with us.'

Ingvar smiled, despite himself. He could hear Heavy-hand's booming voice from the parapet above, remonstrating futilely.

'You are my true brother,' he said. The worst of his anger subsided, giving way to a low, sullen feeling of misuse. 'But do not do this. He is *vaerangi*. It is his judgement, and his anger is with me, not with you.'

Baldr looked pained. 'It is unjust.'

'It is not.' Once the first flush of humiliation had passed, Ingvar began to see what Gunnlaugur was doing. It was not the way that Callimachus would have run his squad, but it had a certain, brutal logic. 'Follow Gunnlaugur, just as you have done. You do not help me by defying him.'

Baldr hesitated. He looked lost.

'I do not understand,' he said. 'You were like blood-kin.'

'We were. We may yet be again.' Ingvar reached down to the soul-ward at his breast, the *sálskjoldur*, and lifted it up. 'But *this* is the mark of brother-hood. I cherish it. Do not fear for me.'

Baldr's eyes followed the pendant as it twisted in Ingvar's grasp. He looked suddenly wistful, as if part of him regretted losing it.

'This is one raid,' he said. 'One raid. After that the true battle begins, and we will come together then: you, me, Gunnlaugur, like it used to be.'

Ingvar nodded. 'I yearn for it,' he said, with feeling. 'For now, though, let him have his way. Blood the enemy, just as he wishes. He needs a victory, one that will banish the shades of the *Undrider*. Deliver that for him and he will forget his pride.'

Baldr reached up for the soul-ward and pressed it back against Ingvar's breastplate. His grimace was wry. When he looked at Ingvar, the meaning in his expression was plain.

It should have been you.

'As you command, though it pains me,' he said. 'Hunt well, Gyrfalkon.'

Ingvar bowed. 'Hunt well, Fjolnir. I will look for you with the dawn.'

Then Ingvar turned, hastening down the stairs and away from the pack. As he did so, despite his words to Baldr, a part of him hardened, tightening with a resentment that he knew would not easily unravel.

CHAPTER FOURTEEN

The pack left the outer gate as the first moon rose. It cast a fragile silver sheen over the still-warm landscape. They broke into a run as the massive doors clanged closed, loping easily in loose formation. The city quickly fell away behind them, retreating into the north as they sped. The five warriors dropped into a steady rhythm, their limbs working in unison, each casting a deep-black shadow on the dust beneath them.

Gunnlaugur set the pace. He'd strapped *skulbrotsjór* to his back, lacquered down his straggling hair and beard and donned his helm. Like the others, his battleplate was still layered with the patina of combat. The rune of destruction, *turza*, was still visible on his helm's forehead, cut deep by the Iron Priests and inlaid with iron. In the moonlight it glowed dully, making his snarl-masked visage seem marked with the sign of ancient magick.

He drove the others hard. The physical exertion helped to clarify his mind. He felt his hearts beating in slow unison, fuelling the huge furnace of his body. He drew air into his barrel-chest in long draughts, feeling the gritty dryness of it drag deep into cavernous lungs.

The pack went silently. Olgeir was brooding, still angry at Ingvar's exclusion. Váltyr was similarly unquiet, though he'd voiced no objection. Hafloí was the only one in high spirits. He'd let out a whoop of battle-joy on leaving the city, but hadn't repeated it after no one else had joined in.

'What's the matter with you all?' he'd grumbled once they were under way. 'Lost your voices when your hair went grey?'

That had made Baldr laugh, but it had been a stifled sound. After that they had run without speaking. They might have been predators indeed, grey-clad and draped in strange hides and bones, striding out across the wide emptiness in search of victims.

Gunnlaugur didn't blame Hafloí for his irritation. Back when he'd been a Blood Claw himself he'd raced into battle with death-oaths thundering from his hoarse throat. He'd laughed as readily as he'd cursed, exuberant at the raw power unleashed within him by the Helix. Hjortur had been the same, and under his leadership Járnhamar had been a raucous, brutish juggernaut of noise and hot blood.

Gunnlaugur didn't remember when that exuberance had begun to fade. Perhaps it was fatigue – the pack had been on engagement after engagement for nearly a century with only snatched periods away from the front. Even the furious energy of a Sky Warrior had its limits.

Gunnlaugur found himself growling as he ran, his hot breath snagging throatily. It was an animal sound, a primeval note of slow-burning frustration. He had found it hard to endure words of reproach from Olgeir, who was the most generous of them, the one most ready to laugh off tension and still dissent with a cuff or a laugh. It had been hard to endure Baldr's weary looks and Váltyr's doubts.

For all that, he couldn't regret his decision. Ingvar had to learn his place in the hierarchy. It was a matter of precedence, of power. From Járnhamar, to Blackmane's Great Company, to the Rout, to the Imperium itself, everything depended on hierarchy, on the establishment of command. Without the iron gauntlet of discipline everything fell apart, leaving the defences open to the predations of the enemy.

In time, things would be more like they had been, but only once order had been re-established. Matters had been left to drift. He was *vaerangi*, the inheritor of an ancient and noble battle-role. Even if he wanted to loosen things a little, to cut the others some slack, he couldn't.

It wasn't personal. It wasn't about self-doubt, jealousy, or the spectres of the past. It was about duty, about leadership.

Above all, it wasn't about Ingvar. He was certain of that. It wasn't about Ingvar.

I'd want a blade of his pedigree in the pack. If he challenged me, I'd beat him down.

Arjac's words came into his mind unbidden, like a waking dream. He remembered the way the Rockfist had spoken to him: like a father to a son. The memory affected him strangely. He couldn't remember his birth-father at all. It was all so long ago.

If fate brings you and Ingvar back together, the pack will shape itself around both of you, one way or another.

Ah, but there was the rub. Gunnlaugur had to control the pack. He had always needed to control, to fashion, to mould, just as Rockfist moulded soft metal into his killing blades.

Pride makes you strong, stripling.

Yes, that was so. It had always been so. It had been the cause of his rise from the mass of other warriors, the thing that had first caught Hjortur's eye. His pride did more than make him strong. It made him unbreakable.

We only live for the pack. That is what makes us deadly, what makes us eternal. Nothing else matters.

And that was also true. Gunnlaugur had always known it. He had always lived it. What had Ingvar done for Járnhamar, compared to him? It was Gunnlaugur who had held the pack together after Hjortur's death, making it stronger, tempering it and keeping a grip on the raging spirits within. Could Ingvar have stood up to Tínd when the black temper came on him? Would Ingvar have kept Jorundur's bitterness in check, or managed Váltyr's need for validation at every turn?

But this wasn't about Ingvar.

Ahead of him, the plains stretched away into darkness. Gunnlaugur checked the locator readings on his lens-display, blink-clicking to cross-reference with the coordinates de Chatelaine had given him. On the southern horizon the land began to pucker up like scar tissue, breaking into a mass of higher ground riven by snaking gorges. The wind from that place had a taint of foulness.

Gunnlaugur checked proximity readings. Just on the edge of sensor-range, he saw the cluster of runes he'd been hoping for. They glowed red against the filtered darkness of the desert around him.

He adjusted course and picked up speed. The pack swung automatically along with him. He could hear their low breathing, the dull thud of their boots against hard-packed dust.

'That one,' he said, pointing over to the mouth of a wide defile that opened out onto the flat land. It was thick with shadow, unlit by the low moon.

They would come through there. They would come incautiously, believing the land cleared of defenders. They would stride proudly out, waddling from plague-distended torsos, wheezing from corruption, living only to spread the infection that fizzed and coursed through their swollen veins. They would bring their engines of war with them, each one laden with long-forbidden biological weaponry and marked with the ruinous symbols of dark gods.

Gunnlaugur kept running. His breathing picked up, not from fatigue but from expectation.

Skulbrotsjór felt light across his back; it would feel lighter in his hands.

Ingvar walked through the empty streets, his mood as black as the sky above him. The boom and clang of construction still echoed into the night as more guns were hoisted into position and more streets were cleared of clutter for supply-lines. Few mortals left their hab-units after dark; those that did so wore the tabards of the Shakeh Guard or the battleplate of the Wounded Heart.

Ingvar ignored them. He went quickly, descending from the Ighala Gate and down into the lower city. The stars were vivid, masked only by drifting smoke from the pyres. He could still hear noises of combat from all over the city, distant and unremitting. The Guards' las-weapons were silent, but the sporadic reports of the bolters and flamers used by the Sisters broke the tense blanket of fear like hammer-blows.

Hjec Aleja was gripped by foreboding. The smell of death was every-where. Civilians, Guardsmen and Ecclesiarchy officials all suspected one another, hurrying to report every observed flesh-sore, overheard cough or suspected rash. It made for a wild, drum-tight air of interlocking suspicion.

Ingvar cared for none of that. The canoness could worry about the city; he had other concerns.

The cathedral reared above him into the night. The lights around it had been doused, making it ghoulishly forbidding. The courtyard where pilgrims had queued for blessing was empty, the stone flags carved up by the tracks of crawlers. Heavy bolters had been mounted up on the spires, jutting out from the stonework like huge snout-nosed gargoyles. Sandbag walls had been heaped around the doorways, all of which were braced with bands of steel and ringed with hastily thrown-up defensive barricades. Shakeh Guardsmen manned all those entrances, huddling around tripod-mounted lascannons and squat-throated mortars.

They shrank back as Ingvar approached the main gates, not daring to challenge him. They could see the grim look in his eyes as he emerged from the cloying darkness.

He pushed the doors open and walked into the echoing nave. It was deserted. His footfalls echoed down the long space. He could smell mouldering incense, left unburned in caskets or strewn across the stone. Ahead of him, hung in darkness, was the statue of the Emperor.

Ingvar's eyes lighted on it for a second. The representation was highly stylised. The Allfather's face was hidden behind a golden mask carved in the likeness of a young man. It was handsome, almost cherubic. That might have been Imperial orthodoxy – the Emperor in the prime of vigorous youth striking down the upstart Warmaster – but Ingvar doubted it had any basis in fact.

Then again, who alive could know what had taken place in those days of fire and loss? Who was to say the Emperor had not worn a mask of gold as he prepared to face Horus the Betrayer for the first and last time?

History had faded into myth, just like the sagas of Fenris told over and over in the firelit halls of the Aett. No one outside the inviolate sanctums of Holy Terra had set eyes on the Emperor for nearly ten thousand years. Perhaps even the fabled Custodians did not see him as he truly was. Perhaps they only saw a shell of what he had been, or a screen of illusion projected by his indomitable will, or rushing visions of glory and redemption streaming from his immortal throne.

In the Cathedral of St Alexia on the shrineworld of Ras Shakeh, though, he would always be just as he was in a million other gloomy temples of the Ecclesiarchy: young, vital, indestructible.

Human.

Ingvar looked away and headed to the stairway leading up to Bajola's chambers. He could already smell her presence; she had been on the stairs recently. As he neared her rooms, he heard the clamp and drill of armour being put in place.

He pushed the door open and swept inside. Bajola whirled round to face him, shock written across her face. Her attendants, three young women of the Sisterhood in black robes, reached for their weapons.

'Leave us,' growled Ingvar, staring at Bajola.

He hadn't drawn his blade. His hands were empty. Bajola's attendants trained laspistols at him; one of them aimed at his head, the other two at his hearts.

Surprise ebbed quickly from Bajola's face. She clipped the last buckle of a replacement cuirass into place, then placed a calming hand on the nearest of her attendants.

'You may go,' she said. Slowly, they lowered their weapons.

Ingvar waited for them to leave. His eyes never left Bajola as they filed past him and into the stairwell beyond.

'If you wished to resume our conversation, you could have picked a better time,' said Bajola, reaching for her helm and checking the connector bolts.

'What do you know of Hjortur Bloodfang?' asked Ingvar.

This time there was no recognition in Bajola's features, no brief flicker of guilt. Instead, she shot him a weary look.

'Not now, Ingvar,' she said.

'You recognised the name. It meant something to you. Why was that?'

Bajola shook her head irritably. She reached up and fixed the helm over her head, twisting it in place with a hiss of seals.

'Not now.'

In her armour, she cut a very different profile to the last time he'd seen her. The battleplate bulked her out, making her both taller and broader. The plates of ebony ceramite were lined with silver and picked out with blood-red detailing. The power generator at her back let out a grinding hum of electronics, just as his did. She carried a boltgun, just as he did.

Ingvar blocked her passage.

'Did you serve with him?'

Bajola exhaled in exasperation. 'I need to leave,' she hissed. 'Get out of the way.'

'You were shocked. I saw fear in your eyes. You're not the only one trained to recognise deception.'

Bajola blurted out a cynical laugh. 'Oh really? Who taught you? Some ranting shaman?'

Ingvar didn't move an inch.

'The same people who taught you. Don't test my patience, Sister. It has been a trying night.'

Bajola's finger strayed to her bolter's trigger. Ingvar found himself wondering just how fast she was.

'You are–' she started, but never finished.

The floor rocked suddenly, and cracks sped across the stonework. A muffled boom broke out from far below, followed by another.

'Throne, Space Wolf, get out of the way!' she shouted, looking ready to open fire on him where he stood.

He hesitated for a second longer, but then more explosions went off, all from far below, shivering the walls.

'We'll take this up later,' he said, finally standing aside.

'Fine,' she said, pushing past him and heading into the stairwell. 'For now, make yourself useful.'

Ingvar followed her.

'What's going on?' he asked, breaking into a jog to keep up with her as she raced down the spiral of stone.

She didn't turn, just kept her eyes fixed ahead. When she replied, her voice was cold.

'I don't know yet,' she said. 'But whatever it is, it's in the crypt, and it's started.'

Baldr crouched down low amid the rocks, his head hammering, his palms sweaty, his breath shallow.

The short-lived respite had ended and the pain had returned. Sealed in his armour, he was able to conceal it from his brothers, but the sensations were getting worse; it felt like something was stretching his muscles and pulling them from the bones. At times he had to bite down not to cry out.

He clutched his bolter two-handed, willing something – *anything* – to happen. He needed to move, to burst into action again, to force his aching limbs to stretch. Bodily exertion helped. Combat was even better. It allowed him to direct the pain away from him, to focus it onto the enemy and turn it into something useful.

He didn't know why the pain ebbed and flowed, but he could guess, and those guesses made him uneasy. In the warp he had been close to the raw stuff of the ether. In the city it had been strongest while in the presence of the ether-blighted; only when their unholy contagion had been staunched did the agony abate a little.

Now, as the enemy crawled towards them once more, searing needles of fire in his temples were blazing again. The touch of the ether would be heavy on them too. Baldr remembered what Gunnlaugur had said.

Something interesting travels in that column.

Not for the first time he thought of the soul-ward he had given to Ingvar. He'd been fighting with it for so long that he'd still not got used to its absence. The pain had got worse since he'd given it up.

He didn't regret handing it over; it had been the right thing to do.

Still, the pain *had* got worse.

He clutched his bolter more tightly, pressing the outline of his gauntlets into his weapon's grip. He could feel his flesh push up against the inside of the ceramite. His armour's inner membranes felt hot, even in the coolness of the desert night. His tongue was swollen in his mouth, and his throat was raw.

'Here they come,' warned Hafloí over the comm.

Baldr stiffened, peering into the darkness. His hearts were already drumming from the pain. Their rate picked up further, fuelled by hyperadrenaline seeping into his system.

His body knew combat was close; as ever, it worked to make him ready.

Like the others, Baldr was perched up one side of the ravine wall, half covered with rock and rubble. Gunnlaugur and Váltyr were on the far slope, lodged amid piles of chest-sized boulders about ten metres up from the gorge floor. Olgeir was crouched on the same side as Baldr, further back and higher up, the better to get an angle for *sigrún*'s deadly delivery. Hafloí was at the forefront, his young eyes employed to get advance warning of the approaching column.

All of them were virtually invisible. They had dug in deep, and their matt armour blended with the stone of the ravine sides. Even though Baldr knew where his brothers had concealed themselves he could barely make out their outlines against the stone. Only his helm-display showed their location: glimmering red runes overlaid on the fractured, tumbling terrain.

'Hold position,' growled Gunnlaugur. His comm-filtered voice was thick with anticipation. He wanted to move. When he did so, it would be like a dam bursting.

Baldr gritted his teeth. Sweat ran down his cheeks.

Then they came into view.

A few hundred metres to the south of the pack's position the ravine took a sharp turn to the west. They emerged from around that corner, creeping across the level valley floor like a slowly encroaching swarm of bilge-vermin.

Baldr narrowed his eyes, letting his helm's lenses zoom in and pick out the detail.

The troops in the front ranks were lightly armed. They were mortal, with poorly-fitted carapace armour pieces bolted over civilian uniforms. Some went helmless, exposing bald, grey-skinned scalps to the atmosphere. Others wore heavy iron gas masks. Pale green illuminations swam behind their visors, glowing in the dark like bobbing corpse-lights. They came in loose bands, walking unguardedly and swinging their weapons. The squads were small – twenty, thirty troops.

More detachments followed. Soon hundreds of them had entered the ravine, some limping, some misshapen, all of them carrying hulking carbines or strange canister-fed gas-guns. They filled the valley floor from side to side, kicking up clouds of dust as they tramped onwards.

Baldr winced as the stench of them assailed his nostrils. His eyes watered, and he felt his gorge rise uncomfortably.

Let me slay them. By Russ, let me slay them all.

More troops followed the vanguard. Some of those were clad in heavier armour. Banners swung above the host, rocking to the rhythm of the march, each one clanking with necklaces of skulls. Fell symbols had been bleached into the tattered fabric. Baldr made out three leering, bloated death's heads nailed to an iron frame; three circles, riddled with worms and shedding maggots; the eight-pointed star drawn in dark brown blood.

Those symbols made his head worse, and he looked away.

'Hold position,' repeated Gunnlaugur.

The first of the gas mask-wearing troops began to draw level with Hafloí's position. They marched onwards without pause, not one of them looking up. Baldr started to make out the *hurr hurr* of their massed phlegmy breathing. Those whose faces were exposed displayed nothing but a blank, semi-blinded torpor. It looked like they were sleepwalking into battle. Insects buzzed around their shoulders. The stink of old vomit rolled around them in a cloud of drifting spores.

Then, back at the turn in the ravine, the first of the chem-tankers crawled into view. Another emerged, following in convoy, then another. Their huge tracked chassis were lit up by marker lights that slowly blinked in the darkness. They churned along at walking pace, their enormous engines throwing up clouds of red-tinged soot from rusting smokestacks. The cylindrical tanks they carried were crusted with corrosion and streaky with leaking lubricant.

Slowly, grindingly slowly, the tankers crawled onwards. More followed, each as bulky and cumbersome as the first. They were vast, towering over the hordes of infantry around them and swaying laboriously atop immense tracks. Steam gushed from bronze valves jutting along their flanks. Tangled masses of piping ran all over every rusting surface, twisting and clogging like a jumble of varicose veins splayed across muscle. They belched fumes and retched smoke, wallowing and grinding as they hauled themselves towards the front line. Their spines were serrated with the bronze-spiked maws of cannons and flail-launchers.

As they drew closer, the earth began to tremble underfoot. Six tankers in total ground their way down the ravine, each one surrounded by hundreds of mutant troops. Baldr saw hideous growths on some of the marching guards – obscene flopping bellies bursting open with disease, lashing tentacles spilling out of the cracks between armour plates, hooked hands dripping with trembling lines of fluid.

Baldr heard Gunnlaugur's heavy breathing over the comm.

'When the lead tanker draws level, we break,' he ordered. 'Váltyr and I'll take the first, Haflói and Baldr the second. Olgeir in support. Then we work down the line, one by one. Understood?'

The confirmations came in order. Baldr barely whispered his response, fearful his tight-clenched jaw would give him away. It felt like his blood was boiling in his arteries.

The first chem-tanker inched its way towards the invisible line Gunnlaugur had drawn across the gorge. Baldr watched it come, willing it to move faster, feeling his innards churn and his temples throb while his body remained static. The glowing lights of its drive-unit swam closer, surging up through the clouds of smoke and spoor, juddering and leaking, trailing acrid tangs of chemical poison. Every riveted panel of it, every piece of armour plate or looped tubing was raddled with decay and degradation. It was a wonder the thing moved at all. Lurid flickers strobed along its straining bulk, exposing stringy lattices of mucus hanging from each joint and piston-housing.

Finally the leader passed Haflói's vantage. Baldr's breathing got faster. He heard the faint clunk of Olgeir bringing his beloved *sigrún* into position. He detected movements on the far side of the ravine as both Váltyr and Gunnlaugur adjusted stance, ready for the pounce.

He felt sick. In the final few seconds that remained, he scanned the host marching in the valley below, scouring it for the source of his sickness.

Something interesting travels in that column.

He saw nothing but rank after rank of shuffling plague-bearers, their sore-puckered mouths hanging open, their feet dragging in the dust, their empty eyes fixed ahead. Some of them wore the remnants of Shakeh Guard uniforms.

Then Baldr heard the comm-link crackle open. When he heard the order, the relief was overwhelming.

'The Hand of Russ be with you, brothers,' said Gunnlaugur, his savage voice alive again. 'Slay freely.'

Ingvar and Bajola descended quickly, bypassing the cathedral's nave and heading deep into the underground levels below. Bajola led, travelling swiftly and surely through the switchbacks and twists. Her lighter armour was an advantage in the cramped tunnels of stone, and more than once she nearly left Ingvar behind.

The chambers and passageways under the marble floor formed a labyrinth of dank, claustrophobic spaces, thick with old dust and mouldering with the stale air of centuries. Ingvar caught fleeting glimpses of age-withered statues set in arched recesses. He saw leathery purity banners hanging over granite altars, barely moving even as he brushed past them.

'How in Hel did they get down here?' he asked, working hard to keep up.

A fresh storm of bolter-fire snapped out ahead of them, fractured and overlapped by the echoing chambers. They were close.

'Throne only knows,' said Bajola, her voice tight.

She swerved around a many-columned pillar crumbling from age. A dull red glare of firelight swept over her, turning her black armour the colour of old blood.

Ingvar rounded the pillar after her, drawing *dausvjer*.

Ahead of them lay carnage. An arched chamber stretched away from where they stood, its vaulted roof lost under a pall of smoke and under-pinned by lined ranks of granite pillars. Flames roared furiously from its far end, licking up along blackened walls and rippling across the floor like spilled liquid. Huge, squat objects stood between the pillars, as square and solid as devotional altars. They were all on fire, sparking and raging like igniting melta bombs. Portions of the roof had fallen in further back, and metal struts dangled precariously amid the roaring blaze. Gouts of thick smog curled up against the arches, raining flakes of soot.

Two Battle Sisters had arrived before them. They were retreating in the face of the inferno.

'Where are they?' roared Bajola, grabbing one of them by the shoulder and hauling her round to face her. Her voice was furious.

The Sister nodded towards the fires.

'Dead already, Palatine,' she reported grimly, nodding to a scattering of blackened bodies lying on the stone near the edge of the fire.

Bajola edged over to one of the corpses, keeping her bolter raised, raising one hand against the heat. She kicked it over with her boot. A flabby, slack-skinned mutant rolled onto its back, its sightless eyes staring up at the ceiling. One whole side of its body was burned into scarring from the flames. Its eyes were gone, leaving empty orbits. Even in death, its blub-bery face retained a brutish expression of fervour.

Ingvar drew alongside Bajola.

'How did they get in?' he asked again. He could feel the tremendous press of the flames even inside his armour.

Bajola shook her head. 'Did you not hear me the first time?' she said. She squatted down beside the plague-bearer's corpse and looked more closely into its face. 'I have no idea.'

More Battle Sisters arrived. Orders for dousing agents were shouted back up the line. The stone roof above them began to crack and blister.

'We cannot remain here,' said Ingvar, watching the growing wall of flame lick up across the vaulting.

'Too late,' breathed Bajola, no longer listening. Her voice was distant, broken. 'All destroyed.'

Ingvar stared into the heart of the inferno, letting his helm-lenses adjust to the light and heat. More bodies lay amid the flames, crackling and bursting. Some were little more than slivers of flesh, blown apart by the bombs they'd been carrying. Others, more intact, lay amid the altars like slaughtered cattle. Sparks flew from the boxes as they burned, interspersed with flickering arcs of electrical lightning. The iron sheaths that had encased them were melting, buckling and distorting.

'What is this place?' Ingvar asked.

Bajola clambered to her feet, shrugging off his outstretched hand irritably. Her helm-masked face turned to his. Even though her expression was shielded by the black ceramite, he could sense her frustration.

'If you had not delayed me...' she started, then trailed off.

More explosions sounded at the far end of the chamber, fuelling the firestorm. Fragments of granite fell from the ceiling nearby, shattering as they slammed into the ground.

Bajola gazed one more time into the inferno.

'Too late,' she said, sounding defeated. 'Damn you, Space Wolf.'

'What is this place?' Ingvar pressed.

'What does it matter now?' she said, her voice a hoarse whisper.

She turned away from him and started to walk.

'All destroyed,' she said. Ingvar watched her go. 'All destroyed.'

CHAPTER FIFTEEN

Gunnlaugur broke, flinging himself from the fragile skin of debris that had sheltered him. His hammer lashed round, leaping into his grasp as if alive, and the disruptor field snarled into life.

Váltyr broke from cover beside him and burst down the slope. He went silently, swiftly, uttering no battle-cry.

Gunnlaugur's momentum carried him down. He leapt and skidded down the long scree incline, swinging the hammer in arcs to build momentum. He felt his blood pump in his temples, swelling the veins with heat and fervour. The need for secrecy had passed; he could unleash his true self.

'*Fenrys!*' he bellowed, and the sacred, battle-sanctified words echoed from the ravine walls and called back to him in a dozen new, overlapping voices. '*Fenrys hjolda!* Cower and scream, slaves of darkness, for the blades of the Wolves are upon you!'

He heard Olgeir answer him with a slamming volley of heavy bolter rounds. The explosive shells lanced into the front ranks of Guardsmen, immediately causing havoc around the lead tanker. Dozens of troops went down, clutching at their exploding bodies futilely and tumbling into the dust. Some of them tried to respond, scrabbling for their weapons and looking for something to fire back at.

By then it was too late. By then the pack was among them.

Gunnlaugur crashed into a knot of milling troops, hurling half a dozen of them into the air with a single blistering sweep of *skulbrotsjór*. Their broken bodies thudded back to earth before they'd even had time to cry out.

'The Blood of Russ!' he roared, scything the hammerhead back and throwing more corpses into the night. He swung *skulbrotsjór* two-handed, leaning into the devastating strokes, whirling on his axis like a typhoon of destruction, carving his way deep into the mass of marching bodies.

The still of the night exploded into a rage of flashing las-light and clattering bolter-fire. Gunnlaugur saw Váltyr turning and leaping, veering past incoming lines of fire effortlessly as he sliced through the meagre defences. He left piles of twitching corpses in his wake, each of them mortally cleaved by a single stroke.

Gunnlaugur grinned. That was astonishing skill. It was arrogant. It was *beautiful*.

By then the rest of the pack had joined in the carnage. He could hear

Hafloí's echoing cries of rage and frenzy. He could see the Blood Claw's favoured axe glittering in the moonlight, already flinging blood around it in long splatters. He saw Baldr break from cover and charge, his bolter thundering, screaming ancient death-curses from the Old Ice as he rampaged. His voice was the most terrible of all. It sounded almost demented.

The defenders loosed off rounds into the dark – panicky shots, poorly aimed and badly timed. Some were already scrabbling up the ravine edges, desperate to escape the sudden, horrific attack of the grey terrors that had exploded into them.

Gunnlaugur turned on his heel, slamming *skulbrotsjór* hard into the midriff of a wide-eyed plague-carrier. The force of the blow ripped through the mutant, sending remnants of its bisected body tumbling backwards in a cloud of blood and spores. Gunnlaugur switched back savagely, taking the head off another one. They couldn't get away fast enough – there was no room. The thunder hammer became heavy with strips of gore, the flesh cooking into frazzled slivers on its sparking disruptor. Gunnlaugur waded through them like a reaper of old, slaying in crushing strokes, spinning and crushing and cracking. He towered above them, his heavy power armour making him twice the bulk and heft of even the largest of them. His hammer flew freely, travelling in unstoppable arcs, moving around him in a halo of annihilation like those of the mythic Iron Gods.

Váltyr was the first to gain a foothold on a chem-tanker. He sprang up from the clutching hands of the mutants, kicking out as he rose and breaking the jaw of a reeling cleaver-carrier. He seized on a railing that ran along the swollen flanks of the toxin tank and clutched it fast, his boots searching for purchase.

By then the enemy had begun to respond. They surged towards the invaders, swarming around the beleaguered chem-tankers. Their aim got better, and Gunnlaugur felt the hard jab of las-beams glancing from his breastplate.

He roared with laughter, shrugging them off like rain.

'That's better!' he thundered, crashing through the press of bodies around him, flattening any who came within the ambit of the thunder hammer. Another half a dozen hapless mutants were crushed, smashed or ripped apart, their bloated entrails sent spinning into the night. 'Try harder! Come on, try *harder*!'

They did. They screamed at him, hurled their corroded blades at his face, clutched at his ankles as he trod them into the blood-clotted dust, grabbed at his arms as the hammer-blows blurred past, loosed thick barrages of las-fire to try to bring him down.

The task was hopeless. Olgeir's withering torrent of heavy ordnance blew apart any nascent defensive positions. Hafloí's assault cut deep into their reeling ranks, preventing any rally further back. Váltyr's terrifying efficiency was just unanswerable.

But the one that really scared them was Baldr. Gunnlaugur, busy with his own slaughter, only caught snatches of what was going on, but it sounded like Baldr had gone completely berserk. He heard him shrieking like a banshee of legend, and the sound of it chilled his blood. He wondered what it was doing to the enemy.

'What in Hel's wrong with Fjolnir?' voxed Váltyr breathlessly, working his way along the tanker's toxin-cylinder, swatting down the defenders that crawled all over it and beginning to climb higher.

'He's certainly having fun,' replied Gunnlaugur, kicking through the stomach of an obese waddler and vaulting over the corpse. The chem-tanker's tractor unit loomed through the dust-flurried murk, its cab-lights glowing like a cluster of insectoid eyes. 'Concentrate: let's bring this down.'

He lashed out with the hammer, clearing a two-metre circle around him. Three mutants were sent spinning under the tracks of the tanker. They had plenty of time to scream as the treads slowly ground them to a pulp.

Gunnlaugur leaped, pulling clear of the crowds and landed on a coolant duct on the tanker's muzzle. It was riddled with oxidisation, and whole chunks of it came free in his grip as he climbed up to the cab. Gunnlaugur whipped his hammer round and mag-locked it to his back, hauling himself up the front of the titanic vehicle.

Some of the enemy tried to follow him up, but most were picked off by Olgeir's ever-present curtain of supporting fire.

'My thanks, Heavy-hand,' voxed Gunnlaugur as he reached the cloudy armourglass of the cab windows. He was enjoying himself.

'Bring them pain,' replied the great one cheerfully.

Gunnlaugur reached up with his fist and smashed the closest pane. A bloom of thick, green smoke tumbled out, streaming down the front of the tractor unit like spilled sick.

He grabbed the frame and hauled himself up. Inside, the chem-tanker's crew were hard-wired into fleshy command thrones. Eight of them sat in a cramped space stuffed with throbbing, pulsing mountains of semi-tissue and pseudo-machinery. Tentacles ran from rheumy glands, interfacing with thickets of dirty metal cables. Fluids gurgled in translucent sacs, filtered through pinned-open bodies and sent churning down long tubes into the innards of the vast machine.

The crew turned to face him as he clawed his way inside, letting fly with screaming wails of impotent hatred.

'Right, then,' he snarled as he pushed himself through the shattered windscreen and thudded to the cab's floor. He drew the thunder hammer. 'Who's first?'

They screamed at him in unison. With a shrug he started to swing, crushing what remained of their mortal skulls and punching through their etiolated innards. They shrieked as they died, locked into position, forced to watch as Gunnlaugur worked his way down the line. As each one died the whole chem-tanker shuddered. The growl of its engines became a stuttering whine, and the clouds of smoke billowed ever higher. As he neared the end of the line Gunnlaugur felt the chem-tanker change direction, reeling on its axis and starting to crush its way aimlessly across the ravine floor.

'Time to leave, *vaerangi*,' came Váltyr's voice over the comm.

'Already?' asked Gunnlaugur, breaking the neck of the last shrieking crew member and pushing his way to the far side of the cab. 'Hel, you work fast.'

He glanced back at the carnage left in his wake. Fluids, pink with blood and blotched with inky lubricants, swilled across the metal-mesh floor. Eight raw carcasses slumped amid a tangled mess of fizzing cabling and shattered ironwork. The last of the pale marsh-gas drifted loosely away, no longer fed by its belching feeder valves.

Gunnlaugur grunted with satisfaction, then smashed through the far end of the cab wall, pummelling a huge, ragged hole in the armour plates. He thrust himself through the gap, hanging clear of the cab-edge. The huge machine was still ploughing onwards, though its progress was now directionless. Dozens of milling defenders were dragged under the tracks as they tried to get out of the way. He could still hear Baldr's frenzied screams and Hafloí's battle-cries. The two of them had already destroyed their chem-tanker, which blazed in a mass of lurid chemical flames against the far wall of the ravine.

Gunnlaugur saw Váltyr leap from the tanker's lurching spine, hurling himself a long way clear and landing expertly amid a swarm of glow-eyed mutants. Gunnlaugur tensed, ready to do the same.

Then the krak grenades went off.

Váltyr had clamped them all along the toxin-tank, just as Gunnlaugur had ordered him. They exploded in sequence, rippling along the bulbous sides of containers, spraying the noxious contents in all directions.

The chem-tanker bucked, shuddered and ignited, hurling Gunnlaugur clear of the cab. He crunched heavily to the ground several metres away, his shoulder guard driving deep into solid rock, his helm cracking against blood-wet rubble.

He picked himself up in time to be doused in a spray of flesh-eating acid from the broken chem-tanks. It cascaded down his armour, instantly dissolving the blood and slime from the surface and eating through the pelts that hung from his shoulders.

The mortal troops around him were not so well protected. They screamed in chorus as their flesh was scoured from the bone, a riot of shrieking, gargling sobs that only ended when the acid ate down to the vocal cords.

When the torrent finally died out the scene around the smoking tanker was horrific – bodies in all directions, skinless, eyeless, with exposed bone and shrivelled flesh. A thick soup of dissolved organic matter, tinged grey with foamy scum, lapped over the rocks of the valley floor, bubbling and babbling as it drained deep into the dry earth.

The chem-tanker itself, driverless and burning, swayed on, finally crashing into the far side of the ravine and bursting into toxin-edged flames, just like its companion further down the gorge.

Gunnlaugur shook the last of the acid from his burly frame before striding out to find Váltyr. As he walked, his boots crunched sickeningly through half-eaten bone. The silence from Olgeir's heavy bolter told him that Heavyhand was climbing down to join in the close combat. Four tankers remained before their night's work was done.

Gunnlaugur was glad of that. He was enjoying himself.

'Ahead of schedule, bla–' he started, just as something huge went off over by Baldr's position. It was an explosion of sorts, but it lit up the ravine edges with corpse-glimmer and sounded like a strangled scream. He tensed immediately, the hairs on his arms rising.

Then Hafloí's voice came over the comm. It didn't sound like it normally did – it was urgent, tight, serious.

'Support,' Hafloí gasped, his words clipped with pain. 'Blood of Russ, support *now*.'

Gunnlaugur took up *skulbrotsjór* again, his mood switching instantly. Even before Hafloí had finished he was already running.

Ingvar and Bajola stood facing one another in her chambers, just as they had done on their first meeting. The night was old by then, heavy with smoke and the fatigue of a city under siege. Lights could be seen from the vantage of Bajola's spire-windows, bleeding across the whole expanse of the lower city. They were not wholesome lights – they were pyre-glows, or searchlight beams, or the sudden flashes of las-volleys in the dark. Those lights were accompanied by similarly unwholesome sounds: crackling flesh, the thudding of running feet, screaming in the dark.

Unlike at their first meeting, Bajola did not remain standing for long. She slid into a hard wooden chair, scratching it with her armour as she slouched wearily. She let her unfixed helm fall from her hands, and it rolled across the stone floor.

'When did you last sleep?' asked Ingvar.

'I don't remember. You?'

'Four days ago.'

Bajola snorted. 'Explains your mood.'

Ingvar walked across to the far side of the room, near one of the narrow windows.

'This place was meant to be a respite.' He smiled to himself. 'Garrison work.'

'You want to sit?' she asked.

'I'm fine.'

Bajola gave him a sardonic look.

'Always on duty, never at rest,' she said. 'You *never* get tired? You never just want to stand back, for a minute, to look away from it all and forget that you're the Emperor's finest and that you're needed all the time and every-where because, well, we're all so much weaker than you?'

Ingvar leaned against the stone wall behind him. In truth, he wasn't immune to fatigue. If things had been less straitened he would have welcomed the chance to recover himself, to reflect on how to handle Gunnlaugur when he returned, to prepare for the trials ahead. But those things were luxuries.

'What was that place?' he asked for a third time.

Bajola's face fell. 'The archive room. Not something you'd think much of – just a bunch of datacores and repository banks, sealed and categorised.' Her brown eyes went hollow. 'The history of an obscure shrineworld, its succession documents and transaction records.'

She looked up at him.

'It was our story here,' she said. 'One of the things I was charged with defending. Now all gone, and before the enemy has even arrived at the gates.'

'Could it not have been moved to the Halicon?'

'It would have taken a whole convoy of heavy transports, and they had all been assigned other tasks.' She shook her head resignedly. 'I made my decision. De Chatelaine will ask the same questions when she hears of it. It will be one more failure in her eyes. She was never convinced of the wisdom of taking me on, this will reinforce that view.'

Ingvar found himself surprised by Bajola's deflation. When they had first met she had seemed so lively, so defiant. It was strange. In her fragile robes she had been strong; encased in power armour, she was diminished. Perhaps she might have been better off staying in the non-military cadres.

'They're only records,' he said. 'None of your troops were hurt.'

Bajola let slip an empty laugh.

'Only records,' she said. 'I don't suppose you keep any, on Fenris.'

'We do.' He tapped the side of his helm. 'The skjalds recite the sagas. We commit them to memory. We pass them on. Every one of us knows the myths of the past.'

'Myths.' Bajola's tone was scornful.

'All of us use myths, Sister. Some are stored on data-slates, some come from the mouths of skjalds. Your way has its strengths. Its weaknesses are obvious.'

Bajola smiled wryly. 'Nice.'

Ingvar clasped his hands before him. The blood on them had blackened from the heat of the archive chamber.

'You know why I came,' he said.

Bajola nodded. 'You think I'm keeping something from you.'

'You recognised his name.'

Bajola reached up and rubbed her scalp with her gauntlet. Her short, wiry hair was flecked with ash.

'I did.' Some of her old defiance glistened in her eyes.

'How?'

Bajola laughed.

'You think he kept it secret?' She shot him a sidelong glance; it was almost flirtatious. 'You are a boastful people, Space Wolf. You brag about your conquests from one end of the Imperium to the other. Do not be surprised if others hear you.'

'It had significance,' said Ingvar. 'You had heard it before.'

For a second longer, Bajola held his gaze. Her dark skin, the same ebony as her armour and sweaty from exertion, glistened in the low light of the chamber.

Then she lowered her eyes.

'I have seen many secret things,' she said softly. 'Never intended for my eyes, but one does not spend so much time with the powerful and not catch glimpses of their affairs.'

Ingvar listened intently.

'It is said that Fenris makes enemies easily,' said Bajola. 'You do not know the tenth of it. There are inquisitors who would gladly see your world virus-bombed into poisonous slush if they could only find a way to do it. Other Chapter Masters, too. And, yes, the Ecclesiarchy harbours some with no love for your brethren. That is no secret. Our forces have clashed before, they may do so again.'

Bajola's voice was low but firm. She spoke like an agent delivering a report to her superiors, much like she must have done many times while in the Orders Famulous. Ingvar remembered how he'd been required to speak when in Halliafiore's presence, and how long it had taken for him to knock the rough cadence of Juvykka from his speech. The results had been much the same.

'There was a document,' Bajola went on. 'I only saw it once, but I was in the business of memorizing things then. It had names on it, most of which are irrelevant. Hjortur Bloodfang was among them. I remember thinking the name was absurd, but that was before I had had dealings with others of your kind.'

'What was it for?'

'A briefing note, prepared for the senior cardinal of my jurisdiction, one of dozens that would pass his desk every night. Such things had many purposes. It might have been in relation to diplomatic embassies – unlikely, in this case – or problems with military liaison, or some clandestine matter that I would not have been aware of.'

Her voice was steady, calm, assured.

'That's all?' Bajola nodded.

'My guess is that it related to communication between Fenris and the Ecclesiarchy that was kept quiet. Such things exist, you know. Perhaps Hjortur was the conduit.'

Ingvar remembered how Hjortur had been – his frothing bravado, his thundering anger – and almost laughed out loud. Subtlety had not been his strong suit.

'I find that unlikely.'

Bajola looked equivocal. 'Well, you knew him,' she said. 'But at some point his name came to the attention of a cardinal of the Ecclesiarchy, one who wielded considerable power. I have seen stranger things in the galaxy, but not many. If you do not know why that is, then I cannot help you.'

Ingvar drew in a long breath, tasting the last of the soot that still clung to his vox-grille. He turned Bajola's words over in his mind. Silence fell across the chamber, broken only by the sporadic noises of trouble still rumbling across the city outside.

'There is no lie in your voice,' he said eventually. 'But you are not telling me all you know.'

Bajola half smiled – a strange, almost melancholy gesture – and leaned back in her chair.

'You're wrong,' she said. 'But even if you weren't, I won't take lectures from you about that.'

Ingvar raised an eyebrow under his helm. 'Which means?'

'You understand me,' said Bajola. 'The Imperium we both serve and love is built on secrets. We use them to clothe ourselves, to wall ourselves in, and I swore vows never to disclose the secrets I was given to guard. I swore never to reveal the identity of those who conferred such privilege on me, nor those whom I was charged with protecting. Those vows were not lightly made. The secrecy that binds me is as sacred to me as your sword is to you.'

She looked at him, and her eyes sparkled knowingly.

'You are no stranger to secrets, Ingvar,' she said. 'You did not tell me what took you from Fenris for so many years, though I can guess, and if I am right you could not tell me even if you wished to. No force on this planet could compel you to speak, no matter how much I might desire to share the terrible sights you keep locked in your never-forgetting mind.'

She leaned forwards in her chair. Her face lost its spectre of dry amusement and became earnest again.

'For all that, I do not doubt that you are a servant of the Emperor and a loyal ally. You could extend the same courtesy to me.'

Ingvar didn't respond immediately. He watched the way her body moved – the confidence of it, the heaviness of her limbs, the comfort of knowing she was in her own demesne and surrounded by her own kind.

Her chin jutted proudly. She held his gaze, looking up into his death-snarl mask fearlessly.

A rune-signal flickered into life on his retinal display. Jorundur wanted to see him about something. Ingvar dismissed it. The Old Dog would have to hunt alone for a little longer.

He reached up, released the air-seals and twisted his helm free. He mag-locked it to his belt and ran his fingers through sweat-stiff hair. The long tresses flopped over his armour's gorget.

He pushed himself away from the wall and advanced on Bajola. The disparity in their sizes was almost comical: his bulk, augmented by thicker plate and heavy pelts, dwarfed her slender frame.

He stood over her and lowered his head towards hers.

'I have no doubt of your loyalty,' he said. His voice was a low murmur, one that resonated in his chest and echoed from the stone around him. 'If I had, you would be dead where you sit.'

His eyes bored into hers. For the first time, he saw a flicker of fear in her sleek features.

'I will fight alongside you, Sister,' he said. 'I will serve the cause of this world as if it were the cause of my own, and before the end of this thing you will learn truly why I bear the name I do and what it means.'

His grey eyes went flat.

'But know this – my brothers are more than blood-kin to me. If I discover your silence has led to harm befalling them, I will come after you. Wherever you are, I will hunt you, and what the *Fenryka* hunt they find.'

He grimaced, his leathery flesh creasing away from his fangs.

'You would not like me as much then.'

To her credit, Bajola retained eye contact. She blinked once, then again, but never looked away. When she replied, her voice wavered but did not fail.

'Then I thank the Throne I have nothing to hide,' she said.

CHAPTER SIXTEEN

Hafloí fought with two weapons, just as he did whenever he could, his axe in his right hand and his bolt pistol in his left. Older warriors, those who had honed their craft over centuries, would eventually settle on a preference for blade or ranged work, but he intended never to specialise. He enjoyed the interplay between axe-strike and pistol-kick, doling out death in equal quantities as he rampaged through the enemy. He relished the thick cut-and-drag of the metal on diseased flesh; he took delight in the action of the bolt pistol as it tore up body armour and ripped through vehicle plate.

He'd opened his throat since Gunnlaugur's order, giving in to the urge that he had always had to shout and holler and whoop with the raw joy of killing. That had been how it was in his old pack, all of them flame-haired neophytes led by the brutal *vaerangi* Oje Redclaw. They'd taken joy in their work, laughing like savage children in the heart of battle, pushing every limit that was set for them, racing out to be the fastest, the most deadly, the strongest, the best.

Járnhamar was different. He'd known it would be, but still the shock of it had been hard to get used to. From the long, hard training sessions back on Asaheim he'd learned just what it took to be a Grey Hunter. Olgeir was as strong as a mountain, Váltyr as quick as a snake, Jorundur as wily as an ice-drake. One on one they were all more than a match for him. Their sinews had hardened, their muscles had tempered, their combat skills had been honed and honed again.

And yet, for all that, they were missing something. Their joy had gone. They had all been fighting too long; the Long War had made their spirits shrivel even as it had toughened their bodies.

Hafloí kicked out, plunging his boot into the reeling forehead of another plague-bearer. He loosed a single shot to halt the charge of another, jerked his axe-blade round harshly to decapitate a third. Flecks of blood circled him like debris swirling around a star, thrown up by the vicious hack, thrust and fire of his relentless movement.

One chem-tanker already smouldered, its fuel tanks ruptured and its toxin-cylinder leaking. He could hear that the other one – the one taken on by Gunnlaugur and Váltyr – was reeling. The hordes of plague-raddled mortals had shaken off their shock and now lumbered into combat, but they had little with which to combat the unleashed wrath of the Wolves.

'*Hjá*, brother!' Hafloí roared to Baldr, leaping clear of a las-volley before blasting the firer's head open with a return shot. 'The next one waits!'

Baldr was worrying him. On Fenris, Baldr had always been serenely, irritatingly in control. Olgeir had called him the quiet one, the calm presence at the centre of the pack.

Now Baldr was shrieking, ripping into the enemy with a stark energy that surpassed even his own. Hafloí had never seen another *Fenryka* fight like it. Baldr's movements were fast, too fast, careless and slapdash. If the enemy had been more competent he might have been in trouble; as it was, his sheer brutality was enough to daunt the trapped and panicked host of misshapen and plague-twisted. They were terrified of him, falling over themselves to flee his haphazard sword-strokes.

'Forget this filth!' Hafloí called out again. 'The tanker!'

No answer came over the comm. Baldr's breathing was thick and wet, more like the wheezing of a dog than a man.

Hafloí spun round, swinging his axe to clear space amid the milling host of mutants, looking up briefly to gauge the shape of the battle.

Further down the ravine the remaining four tankers had slowed, grinding to a near halt as the gorge-slopes descended into chaos around them. Their towering drive-units reared up above the swirling melee, underlit by eerie green glows, their engines churning as they struggled to change course.

Hafloí glanced over at Baldr one last time. He remained busy slaughtering those around him, lost in a mist of blood and fury.

'*Skítja.*'

Giving up on him, Hafloí kicked into movement, sprinting after the next chem-tanker, firing at any plague-bearers who barred the way ahead and cutting down any who got too close. He wasn't sure what he'd do when he arrived. He might vault up into the cab and take the tractor-section down, or maybe go for the engines with kraks. In any event it would be a worthy kill to add to his name, something that might gain him a little more respect from the warriors around him.

He'd like that. For all their lack of mirth and vigour, for all their dreary fatalism, he'd still like their respect.

He was barely ten metres away from the chem-tanker when he saw the Traitor stride out from the shadows. If he'd been more experienced he might have sensed him earlier, though the fug of human filth clogging the ravine floor made it hard to pick out individual aromas. He might, though, have noticed the ever-heightening terror in the mortals he cut down so easily and seen that they weren't just scared of him. As it was, consumed by the combat around him and fixed on the target ahead, he only saw the Traitor once he had lumbered into range.

Once, he must have been like Hafloí, a loyal Space Marine of the Imperium decked in blessed power armour. Now he had been altered, had grown, bloating and twisting as the slow arts of the warp had worked their baleful influence. His ceramite plate was thick with poxy encrustation, like polyps of dirty coral layered over rotting stonework. He trod ponderously on huge, cloven hooves, and necrotic flesh burst through wound-like gouges in his breastplate and cuirass. A sweaty stink of fear hung over him, and hosts of flies followed his every movement, billowing around him like a shroud.

Inexperienced as he was, Haflói knew well enough what he faced.

Plague Marine.

His helm had once been an old Mark I issue but it had been ravaged almost beyond recognition. A dull green light spilled from hollow lenses, leaking across the decaying snarl of the vox-grille. A fused mass of tortured ironwork rose up over his shoulders, studded with loosely nailed skulls and pulsing with the ghost-flicker of unnatural energies. He carried a heavy glaive two-handed, and phosphor-dim witchlight glimmered over the pocked blade.

As soon as he saw the Traitor, Haflói felt his battle-joy transmute to blind rage. Deluded mortals were one thing; fallen brothers were another.

'Allfather!' he roared, charging towards the Traitor, loosing a hammering barrage of bolts from his pistol and twisting the axe-head to swing.

The Plague Marine did not move fast. He could not match Haflói's pace and energy, and his reactions were sluggish.

But he did not need to move fast. As the Blood Claw closed in on him, cracking a dozen rounds against its fist-thick battleplate, the Traitor raised his glaive and levelled the point at him.

'*Maleficaris nergal,*' he whispered in a glottal, sibilant wheeze.

Haflói never saw the bolt hit him. He had the briefest impression of savage fire bursting across him, tinged with lime-green flickers and stinking of ethanol. The next thing he knew he was on his back, hurled five metres away, his armour half embedded into the earth below. His bolt pistol had been knocked clear and he only barely clasped on to his axe.

He tried to rise and instantly felt agony flood through his limbs. Witchlight rippled across his armour, playing across it like mercury sliding on steel. He felt his flesh tighten, his energy draining away. He tried to cry out, but his mouth had dried to a husk. Through a filmy haze of pain and disorientation he saw the Plague Marine loom over him, pointing the tip of the glaive at his neck. A hot-metal stink of fell magicks competed with the rank odours of decay.

The Plague Marine gazed down at him. His gestures were laborious, made as if wading through tar, but the power he exerted was crushing. Haflói weakened further, his lungs burning as he tried to breathe. He felt his axe fall loosely from his grasp.

'Just a child,' whispered the Traitor, musingly.

His voice was extraordinary – gurgling thickly through bubbling layers of saliva and mucus, broken into overlapping tones and breathy echoes as if a thousand other voices jostled for prominence within his blank helm. No particular malice permeated it, just a kind of long, tired sadness. The air itself seemed to sag in his presence.

Haflói couldn't move. He stared up at the Plague Marine, watching the glaive hover above his neck. He could feel his skin creasing under his armour, crinkling with unnatural weariness. He fought against it, tasting sorcery at the back of his throat like a bitter gall, swallowing it down and coughing, but the vice did not loosen.

Hafloí knew then the measure of his foe: a witch, steeped in the twisting, changing ways of the warp's touch, a warrior as far beyond him as he was to the milling crowds of diseased cattle that marched alongside the chem-tankers.

'Just a *child*,' repeated the sorcerer, shaking his head sadly before pulling the glaive back to swing.

The rain of bolter shells came from hard over to the right, peppering the witch's armour plate and rocking him back on cloven heels. He staggered, lost in a bursting torrent of splintering ceramite. The glaive was knocked out of position.

'*Fenrys!*' came a bellowing, half-demented voice.

With the sorcerer's hold broken, Hafloí managed to lift his head a little.

Baldr was charging across the ravine floor, his sword drawn, his bolter blazing. Tattered scraps of pelt flew around him as his limbs pumped.

The sorcerer responded, moving as slowly as before. His rotten armour seemed to absorb the power of the bolts, rippling like sludge as the shells detonated. The impacts clearly hurt him, but still he was able to lumber around to face Baldr's attack.

Hafloí could barely move. He felt as if centuries of ageing had taken place in seconds, making his limbs frail and his bones weak. He tried to retrieve his axe, and the effort made him gasp.

Baldr closed in on the witch, and the two of them fell into combat. The Plague Marine's movements were still slow, but somehow he managed to parry Baldr's flurry of expert strokes. It was as if time itself sloughed to a halt around him, dragging everything down into a pit of torpor.

'You are no child,' observed the sorcerer softly, gurgling away as Baldr's sword clanged against the rusty glaive.

Baldr ignored him, cracking him back several paces. His strikes were wild and florid. He'd discarded his bolter and now threw his sword around two-handed.

The sorcerer levelled the glaive and the Hunter smashed it clear in an explosion of sparks. Baldr's movements were still erratic, but some dark, urgent fury seemed to animate him.

'You should not be here,' said the sorcerer, pushed back again and parrying sluggishly. 'Why are you here, Son of Russ?'

Baldr pressed home the attack, cutting and lashing. Hafloí could hear his grunts of effort, the heavy breathing. He was fighting furiously just to stay alive.

Hafloí reached again for his axe, dragging himself across the rocky ground towards it. As he crawled nearer, he saw the first pair of glowing eyes emerge from the gloom. A plague-mutant stood before him wearing a heavy gas mask over its sore-thick face and holding a spiked morning star on a looped chain. More of them shuffled into view, edging forwards nervously, clutching flails, cleavers and meathooks in liver-spotted claws.

Hafloí managed to snarl, to clench his fists and clamber to his knees. That forced them back, squealing with fright, but they didn't break. Hafloí knew that if they rushed him now he'd be in trouble. He tried to snarl again, but the noise died in his throat as his energy drained away.

Then, from behind him, the ravine suddenly exploded into light, a riot of lightning-white illumination that raced up the rock face on either side and threw everything into eye-watering definition. Hafloí was briefly dazzled by it before his helm-lenses darkened; the mutants fell back, clawing at their faces and shrieking madly.

Hafloí twisted round to see the sorcerer bathed in a sick corona of vivid energy, cracking and curling around him like a billowing cloak. Baldr was suspended in mid-air above him, wreathed in the same whipping coils of power, his whole body clenched in spasms of pain. His head had jerked back, locked in a silent scream, and his arms were thrown wide. The sorcerer held his glaive up, using it to feed more power into the ether-summoned aegis.

'Do they even know what you are?' asked the witch, sounding genuinely curious. 'Why have you never told them?'

Hafloí watched as Baldr writhed in pain. He tried to rise, to run again, to do *something* to break the deadening fatigue clamped on his limbs.

He failed, his strength giving out, and fell back to his knees.

'Support,' he gasped into the vox, forcing the words through clenched teeth. It was all he could do to spit them out, let alone rise again. 'Blood of Russ, support *now.*'

Gunnlaugur sped past the broken shell of the tanker, his boots churning the earth as he sprinted. He needed no locator mark to spy Baldr's position – he could see the witch-lightning crackling around a silhouetted core of brilliance. The stink of sorcery hummed in the air, rank and putrid.

'*Hjolda!*' he thundered, charging directly towards the source.

Váltyr and Olgeir tore along beside him, their blades flashing brightly in the unnatural light.

The sorcerer saw them coming. Gunnlaugur thought he heard him speaking – a whispered voice saying something to Baldr – but then the corroded helm swivelled to stare directly at him. The swathe of ether-energy surrounding Baldr gave out and the Hunter crashed to the ground, his head lolling like a corpse's.

The sorcerer angled the glaive at Gunnlaugur, and the Wolf Guard felt the sudden build-up of dark power.

It was too late. Gunnlaugur pounced, his hammer held high and spitting with raw plasma. His enormous body, still streaming flecks of burning acid from the tanker's immolation, coursed through the air, massively, unstoppably.

Gunnlaugur slammed *skulbrotsjór* down. The warhammer connected with the sorcerer's helm, shattering the diseased ceramite and driving on in.

The witch reeled, bludgeoned to the ground. He tried to swing his glaive up but Váltyr darted in close, lashing *holdbítr* around and severing the sorcerer's arm at the elbow.

Olgeir piled in next, throwing wild, heavy blows with both gauntlets, pummelling in a blind rage. He was screaming death-curses; in such a fury he was all but unstoppable.

Gunnlaugur swung again, hurling *skulbrotsjór* across hard, working it like a pile-driver, pistoning the energy-wreathed hammerhead into the Traitor's throat and sending him sprawling on his back.

The Plague Marine was incredibly tough. Even in the face of that onslaught he somehow hung on. He reached for his glaive with his remaining hand, scrabbling after it as the blows came in.

Váltyr worked as smoothly as ever, switching hands and dancing in close. He chopped down on the sorcerer's free arm, cutting the sinews cleanly and ending his desperate reaching for the glaive. Olgeir seized the witch's broken legs and hauled him across the ground towards Gunnlaugur, pinning him face-up.

That left Gunnlaugur to land the killing blow. The Wolf Guard swept the hammer up a final time, gazing with disgust into the bloody mass of what had been the Plague Marine's head. He could see a puckering mass of warty flesh looking back up at him, as pale as milk and rimmed with red. He saw one filmy eye blinking and the remnants of a crushed jawline hanging loose. Blood bubbled up from under torn flaps of crusty skin, dribbling down into a shattered gorget.

The Traitor tried to speak.

'You don't know–'

Gunnlaugur brought the hammer down, and *skulbrotsjór* cleaved the sorcerer's skull with a thunderous clap of discharged energy. A sheet of pale flame shot up, raging across all three warriors before gusting out with a boom and rush like storm-wind.

The sorcerer's body shuddered, spasmed and slumped into stillness. The three Wolves broke away from it, panting hard, weapons raised, watching for any deception.

None came. The Traitor's body lay broken, its eerie light gone, its throaty breathing stilled.

Gunnlaugur turned away, moving quickly to where Baldr lay. He stooped down, cradling the Hunter's head in his hands.

'Brother,' he whispered. 'Fjolnir. Speak to me.'

Váltyr crouched down beside them. He withdrew a handheld auspex from his belt and ran it over Baldr's limp form.

'Alive,' he said. 'But unconscious. The Red Dream has him.'

Olgeir limped to join them. He was still breathing heavily and one gauntlet was cracked and sparking.

'What's that on his armour?' he asked.

Baldr's breastplate and helm were coated in a film of luminous slime. It glowed in the night, an after-echo of the storm unleashed by the sorcerer. Olgeir leaned down to wipe it clear.

'No,' said Gunnlaugur, grasping Olgeir's wrist. He could hear Baldr's shallow heartbeat, just on the margins of detection. Morkai circled closely. 'Not yet.'

He looked up, searching for the whelp, and saw Hafloí crawling towards them. The Blood Claw's plate was scorched white, his pelts and totems ripped away.

Váltyr went over to him, hooking a hand under his armpit and dragging him to his feet.

'What happened here?' he asked.

Hafloí tried to answer but the words were just a mess of croaking. His head lolled loosely on his shoulders, his boots scraped for purchase in the dust.

Olgeir started to move, fingers flexing, bristling for more violence.

'Four left,' he muttered darkly, watching the remaining tankers slowly reversing down the length of the ravine, putting as much distance as they could between them and the Wolves. Their mutant entourage retreated with them, going warily with their weapons raised, staring nervously at the carnage they'd stumbled into. 'Give me leave, *vaerangi*. Give me leave to take them.'

Gunnlaugur followed his gaze. His first instincts were the same. A cold anger seized him, spurring him to take up the hammer again. They had killed the sorcerer. All that remained were the witch's vermin, ripe for slaughter.

He glanced at Váltyr. The blademaster slowly shook his head.

Gunnlaugur drew in a deep, reluctant breath. Váltyr was right. Baldr was teetering on the edge of death; the whelp was out of action. The hunt was over.

'No, Heavy-hand,' he said, his voice catching with frustration. 'No, not now.'

He laid Baldr's head on the ground and got to his feet.

Around them, the valley floor was a scene of pure devastation. Scores of bodies lay draped over the rocks, broken and bleeding by the Wolves' assault. Two toxin-carriers had been destroyed. What remained of the enemy detachments were hurrying back the way they came.

Gunnlaugur's gaze settled on the Plague Marine's corpse. The body smelt even fouler in death than it had in life. Maggots dropped, still wriggling, from the gaping chasm of a shattered chest. The witchlight had died, sinking into nothing with the death of its master.

'We'll burn the gene-seed,' said Gunnlaugur bleakly, reaching for his thunder hammer. 'Then we return. Olgeir – you and I will bear Baldr. Váltyr will take the whelp.'

Olgeir started to protest. Gunnlaugur ignored him. He withdrew a long dagger from a sheath at his thigh and stalked over to the sorcerer's corpse. As he walked, he heard the crackle of flames and smelled the chemical tang of boiling toxins.

It was destruction, but not what he'd hoped for. The pack's resources were limited; he had damaged them further.

Pride. All for pride. The Gyrfalkon should have been with them.

Hafloí staggered up to him. The Blood Claw could barely stand, let alone walk.

'My thanks, *vaerangi*,' he rasped, blurting the words out from behind a heat-whitened vox-grille.

Gunnlaugur nodded curtly. He should have said something in reply, but the shame, the sick guilt of it, prevented him.

They would have to leave soon. They would have to trawl back across the desert, going as fast as they could, fleeing before the wrath of the pursuing host. That wasn't victory; that was disgrace.

All for pride.

He bent over the sorcerer's stinking cadaver, gripped the knife in his fist, and started to cut.

The night's hunt had come to a close and the dawn was close. Ingvar walked up onto the walkway atop the city's inner wall and leaned against the rock-crete parapet. He looked west, out across the encircling plains. The night sky was dark still, a cool, near-black purple studded with stars. Behind him the upper city rose up in tiers of glimmering light, pockmarked by smoke from the pyres. At the summit, proud and ugly, hunched the Halicon fortress, floodlit gaudily as the siege labourers crawled over it.

His body ached. Soon he would be entering his fifth day without sleep. He'd noticed his reactions slowing, just a little, probably imperceptibly to mortal senses but clear enough to him.

That wasn't good enough. He'd have to work harder.

He rested his weight against the rough-cut stone and smelled the cool air. The scent of the city surrounded him – dust, sweat, spices, embers. He smelled the leaves of the trees as they swayed in their courtyards, and the oily burn of crawlers hauling material down to the bulwarks, and, faintest of all, the slowly growing tang of corruption, wafting across the plains and over the walls.

They were closing in, coming at the city from all directions, their ranks swollen with the newly-dead and plague-infested. By the time they arrived the air would be thick with their filth, buzzing with clouds of blowflies and making the citizens cough and retch.

He sniffed again, trying to guess distances.

Close, now. This would be the last night that the air was clear.

A locator rune blinked softly on the edge of his retinal feed indicating the presence of Jorundur climbing up to meet him. Ingvar smiled to himself. The Old Dog had been busy during the night, stalking through the shadows after the infected with a brutal zeal. Some life in him yet, it seemed.

Ingvar strolled along the parapet towards the nearest defence tower, wondering whose tally was the higher. He guessed his was, though you could never tell with Jorundur, who had a habit of surprising.

Jorundur emerged from the tower's doorway and sloped onto the walkway. He went helmless, just as Ingvar did, and his lean face carried a rare grin of enjoyment.

'Thirteen,' he announced.

Ingvar bowed his head. 'Eleven,' he replied.

Jorundur laughed. 'Had trouble finding them?' he asked.

'The Sisters have been busy,' admitted Ingvar. 'I think this thing has finally been contained.'

Jorundur grunted dismissively. 'Until the rest of them get here,' he said, leaning heavily on the parapet edge, just as Ingvar had done. He stared out at the pre-dawn dark, wrinkling his hooked nose and frowning. 'Any signal from the pack?'

Ingvar shook his head, resting his elbows beside Jorundur's. Being reminded of the rest of Járnhamar out hunting, pursuing the genuine threat rather than mopping up the last dregs of sabotage, was still an irritant. He hid it poorly.

'Still sore, then,' noticed Jorundur. 'Ice and iron, I don't envy Skullhewer.' He laughed again, his more usual cynical snort. 'All your egos, jostling together like pups in a litter. Who'd try to command you? Not me, even if they begged.'

Ingvar smiled. 'I think your time may have passed,' he said.

'I think you might be right,' said Jorundur. 'Allfather be praised.'

He spat on to the parapet and sniffed noisily.

'So how's your friend?' he asked. 'I made a friend of my own this night, you know. I reckon I could learn to stop despising the Sisters, given a little more time.'

'Palatine Bajola is fine,' said Ingvar. 'The cathedral was hit. She took it personally. Her troops burned a lot of things to make up for it.'

'Careless,' said Jorundur. 'Is she sloppy? Will she be a liability?'

Ingvar pursed his lips. 'I don't know,' he said. 'The Battle Sisters are tough. They'll fight like wildcats to keep the enemy away from the Halicon. But her? I'd like to think so.' He paused, thinking back to their exchanges. 'I don't know, though. She's a strange one.'

Jorundur snorted, as if to say *you can talk*.

'How bad was it hit?' he asked.

'They got into the crypt. Took out the archives, wiped everything out. That was it.'

Jorundur gave him a sidelong look. 'The archives?' he asked.

'Yes. What of it?'

Jorundur thought for a moment, his hollow cheeks bulging as he ground his fangs together. 'Nothing.'

Ingvar turned to face him. 'Speak to me.'

Jorundur shrugged. 'Perhaps they just got lost.' His old, shrewd, yellow eyes glittered in the dark. 'But you never asked yourself why, given the choice, they went for a bunch of scrolls in a basement?'

As Jorundur spoke, Ingvar felt a sudden pang of unease. He didn't reply.

'I mean, that place is covered in guns,' Jorundur went on. 'Really big guns, ones we'll need. The bomb-drones, they've all been directed towards the sites that would hurt us – ammo dumps, power plants, comms towers. Think about it. You get a gang of them inside that cathedral, what are you going to tell them to do? Head up to the batteries and bring them down, or torch the archives?'

He shook his shaggy head.

'Maybe that's what they wanted,' he said. 'I just find it surprising.'

Ingvar felt a sick sensation in the pit of his stomach. He gripped the edge of the parapet, and the fingers of his gauntlet sent hairline cracks running across its surface.

'They were trapped,' he said. 'It was their only target.'

Jorundur looked unconvinced. 'If you say so.'

Ingvar pushed back, away from the edge.

'I should go back,' he said.

I swore vows never to disclose the secrets I was given to guard.

Jorundur reached out, grabbing him by the wrist and holding him back. 'And do what, Gyrfalkon?' he asked.

Ingvar whirled to face him, but couldn't find the words to reply. He had nothing concrete, no suspicions, no theories, just the renewed sense of missing something important.

It was my wyrd to be here. Just as it was yours.

'I don't know. Yet.'

He started to push clear of Jorundur's grasp when his comm-feed crackled into life. De Chatelaine's voice emerged over the non-secure channel.

'Warriors of Járnhamar,' she said, sounding both concerned and angry. 'Your presence is requested at the Halicon. Urgency, please, would be appreciated.'

Ingvar paused. 'What is it?' he asked.

'Communication from Gunnlaugur. He's coming in now, carrying casualties. The apothecarion is prepared. We will do what we can.'

Ingvar shook his head furiously. '*Skítja*,' he swore.

Jorundur was already moving, his cynical face hardening as he made his way to the tower portal. Ingvar hesitated for a moment, torn between conflicting priorities.

Gunnlaugur, you fool.

'Can you give me more information?' he asked, lingering on the parapet. 'What has happened?'

He heard de Chatelaine exhale impatiently.

'Forgive me, but your brothers can inform you better than I,' she said, her voice sounding almost peevish. 'I have many things to detain me. You are on the walls? Look up, Space Wolf, and I'm sure you will understand.'

The link cut out abruptly. Startled by her tone, Ingvar turned and peered out across the night-shrouded plains. Jorundur, halting before the portal, did the same.

Right on the edge of vision, across to the far horizon where the wide, flat landscape broke into ravine country, the perfect dark had been broken. A long, thin line of green polluted it, glowing softly in the night. It hadn't been there a moment ago. Even as Ingvar watched, it grew in intensity, as if hundreds of tiny candles had been lit in the shadows.

It was still far off, but clearly visible. The faint strand seemed to stretch from north to south without a break.

'So many,' breathed Ingvar, everything else forgotten for the moment.

Jorundur drew alongside him.

'Aye,' said the Old Dog, his expression grim. 'So they're here at last. Now it gets interesting.'

III
THE BLIGHTED

CHAPTER SEVENTEEN

Gunnlaugur lowered Baldr's torso onto the metal-slab operating table. Olgeir swung the Hunter's legs over the far end, arranging them on the stainless steel surface with painstaking care.

A man in a white tabard hurried up to the table, his hands stuffed with a thick bundle of cutting equipment.

'Leave him!' snarled Gunnlaugur, twisting round and shoving the man away. The mortal fell heavily, upending a metal container full of empty syringe cases. 'This does not concern you, human.'

His mood was black still, fuelled by shame. The long trek across the plains had been hellish – a limping, straggling race in the dark, every jarring step risking more damage to Baldr's battered body. As the night had waned the lights had started to follow them: a few at first, then hundreds more, always a long way behind, but growing like a canker across the horizon.

He'd longed to turn then, to bare his fangs and charge straight back into the pursuing horde, losing himself in the pure exertion that would help him forget.

Instead he'd set his jaw and staggered onwards, his arms hooked under Baldr's shoulders, the dead weight of his battle-brother dragging him down.

None of them had spoken during the journey back. Olgeir's harsh breathing had become more and more strained as he'd struggled to haul Baldr's bulk on top of *sigrún*'s. Váltyr had had his own hands full keeping Hafloí on his feet. Between them they had cut a sorry sight, limping back to the safety of the city with the pursuing stench of the enemy curling at their heels.

Now, back in the Halicon, they were surrounded by fussing, useless mortals, stumbling over one another to offer their fussing, useless assistance.

The apothecarion was cramped and cluttered with equipment. It had six operating bays, each one designed for human dimensions, all reinforced for power armoured occupants thanks to the Sisters' presence. Baldr lay on one, Hafloí on another. Pristine white tiles reflected the glare of overhead lumen-bars, pitilessly picking out the damage on their battleplate. Hafloí's armour was the colour of bleached bone. Baldr's was mottled and streaked with dark green growths, as if lichen had sprouted from the joints.

'Get out,' ordered Olgeir, gesturing to the remaining mortal staff. All four of them, including the functionary Gunnlaugur had knocked to the floor, scurried to comply. The apothecarion was then occupied solely by Wolves – Gunnlaugur, Váltyr, Olgeir and the two invalids.

Váltyr twisted his helm off, hurried over to Baldr and began to work. He was no Wolf Priest, but of all of them he had the deftest hands and greatest knowledge of the Apothecary's art.

'He lives still,' he said, gently prizing the vacuum seals from Baldr's helm and unlocking the catches. 'I can feel his primary heart beating.'

Gunnlaugur started to prowl back and forth, unable to stay still. He felt like a caged bear, bursting with energy but unable to do anything. He removed his helm and shut off the comm-line to de Chatelaine. He yearned for answers, but knew asking for them would be futile. Váltyr needed to work at his own pace, undisturbed and unhindered.

Olgeir remained unmoving, his huge arms crossed, brooding. For once he had no words of encouragement to offer.

Hafloí, left alone on the next slab along, pushed himself up onto his elbows and peered over at Váltyr's work. The whelp was still weak but had already regained some measure of control. He could speak again, and his strength was gradually returning.

Gunnlaugur no longer worried for him; Baldr was the concern.

'This... *stuff* is resistant,' said Váltyr, grimacing as he tried to clear the residue of slime from Baldr's facemask. 'It has some life of its own. It's got under the seals somehow, I think he's absorbed a lot of it.'

He withdrew a steel cylinder from his armour, unclasped it and took out a long scalpel. Working quickly, he cleared the algae-like filth from the gorget-join of Baldr's armour, where the torso met the helm. The lumpy substance clung to the armour, stringing out viscously against the blade edge.

'He was not himself,' croaked Hafloí, still sounding disorientated. 'He was screaming, Gunnlaugur. Did you not hear it?'

Gunnlaugur said nothing. He remembered how Baldr had been during their last conversation. He remembered how he had been on the warp transit.

Should I have probed more, asked more questions?

If so, it was too late now. The knot of guilt in his stomach tightened.

So many errors, one after the other.

'I'm removing the helm now,' said Váltyr. 'We can't leave it on him, the airways are all but clogged fast.'

Gunnlaugur stopped pacing. He came over to the slab and rested his knuckles on the metal. Olgeir stayed where he was, silent, watching intently.

Váltyr pulled gently, releasing the helm's locking mechanism. It came free with a dry hiss of escaping air.

Gunnlaugur felt his hearts sink. Baldr's face was the colour of his armour – pearl-grey, sinking to black under his open eyes. His mouth was open, revealing a dark tongue lolling loosely amid gaping fangs. His breath was sulphurous, making Váltyr gag as he withdrew the diseased helm. Sores had broken out around Baldr's white lips, tight with pus and ringed with angry red inflammation. His cheeks had sunken, and his clammy skin had a greenish tinge to it.

'That is not the Red Dream,' said Olgeir slowly.

Váltyr said nothing. He looked even paler than usual.

Gunnlaugur sniffed, flaring his nostrils and drawing in the noxious stench. Corruption was generally easy to detect – it was over-sweet, layered with the subtle flavour of the warp.

He couldn't be sure. Baldr looked much like any of the plague-bearers he'd killed in the city. That thought alone made his stomach tighten.

'Speak to me, Váltyr,' he said.

The blademaster ran his hands through his hair, smoothing down the sweat-matted mass of grey. His movements were stiff; like all of them, he was tired.

'I don't know,' he said eventually. He looked up at Gunnlaugur. 'If he were mortal, then... But he's one of us. I don't know.'

Olgeir growled in frustration and uncrossed his arms, balling his great fists impotently.

'*Skítja*,' he snarled. 'I've seen filth like that on men I've killed, and–'

Haflói tried to get to his feet, and failed.

'He was *screaming*, Gunnlaugur. Something was wrong. He was–'

'You don't know–' started Olgeir.

'Enough.'

Gunnlaugur's stare swept around the apothecarion, cutting them short. Silence fell, broken only by the soft workings of the chamber's equipment.

Gunnlaugur's chin fell to his chest. It was hard to clear his head, to think what to do – emotions boiled away within him, still too raw to dismiss.

'No one enters this room but us,' he said at last, his voice deliberate. 'One of us remains here at all times, watching over him. We say nothing of this to the canoness. As far as she is concerned, we are tending to a fallen brother's wounds.'

He looked up, fixing each of them in the eye.

'For now, we do nothing. We watch, we wait, we hope. But if he is taken by plague, if his spirit turns...'

He hesitated, then drew in a deep breath.

'If he turns, I will do it. I began this, I will end it. That is my judgement.'

He continued to stare at the others, as if daring them to disagree. Haflói was too weak to object; he seemed to go limp again, resting his head on the slab. Váltyr looked gaunt, but nodded.

Olgeir held out the longest. His scarred, ugly face remained twisted by unhappiness. He looked down at Baldr's diseased features, then up at Gunnlaugur, then back to Baldr again.

Then even his mighty shoulders sagged. He nodded resignedly.

Then the door to the chamber slammed open. They snapped round as one. Váltyr drew *holdbítr*; Gunnlaugur seized the hilt of his hammer.

Ingvar halted where he was, framed in the doorway, shocked by the reaction.

'What's this?' he asked.

'Close the door,' hissed Gunnlaugur. Váltyr sheathed his blade. Olgeir pushed past Ingvar and Jorundur, shutting them in. Only then did Ingvar catch sight of Baldr's body on the slab.

'Allfather,' he swore, rushing over to the table.

'Don't touch him!' warned Váltyr.

Gunnlaugur interposed himself between Ingvar and Baldr's body, grasping the Gyrfalkon's forearm.

'He is in the Red Dream, brother. Be careful.'

Ingvar's eyes went wide as he saw Baldr's face.

'That is no Red Dream,' he said. 'What happened?'

Gunnlaugur maintained his grip.

'They had a sorcerer,' he said. 'Baldr bore the brunt. He may yet recover.'

Ingvar angrily shook off Gunnlaugur's grasp and shoved his way to the slab-edge.

'Recover? Blood of Russ, he's infected!'

'We don't know that,' said Váltyr.

Ingvar rounded on him.

'What more evidence do you need, blademaster?' he asked, his voice wild. 'Look at him!'

'We will wait,' said Gunnlaugur, watching Ingvar carefully. 'He may yet–'

'What did you *do*?' demanded Ingvar. 'Why was he taking on a witch unaided?'

Gunnlaugur suppressed a flare of anger. Ingvar's face was lurid with accusation; it provoked him, but he knew the cause of that.

'Watch yourself,' he warned, pinning the words on a low, growling note. 'You weren't there.'

Ingvar laughed out loud, though the sound was bitter.

'No, I was not! You saw to that. Why was that, *vaerangi*? What did you fear from my being there? That I'd show you up again?'

The room burst into movement. Olgeir came over, hands spread, trying to calm the others. Váltyr muttered something inaudible, glaring darkly at Ingvar. Hafloí tried to speak, but his dry throat betrayed him.

Gunnlaugur rounded on Ingvar, keeping his temper in check by a hair's breadth. He could feel his heart-rate picking up, his blood pumping angrily.

'Say no more, Gyrfalkon,' he ordered, glowering menacingly. 'If you value your hide, say no more.'

'Not this time!' cried Ingvar, eyes staring. 'I held my peace before, I walked away twice – not again.'

He shrugged off Olgeir's restraining hands and squared up to Gunnlaugur.

'You *knew* there was something hidden in that column,' he said, his eyes blazing. 'You knew it! But still you went after it, hungry for the glory you needed.'

Gunnlaugur felt his restraint slipping. Ingvar's mood was febrile and his words pricked at him like dagger-tips.

'Damn you to *Hel*, Skullhewer,' Ingvar raged. 'You *killed* him. Are you proud now? Has that sated your need for bloodshed?'

Ingvar swung in close, so close that the spittle from his invective flew into Gunnlaugur's eyes.

'You killed him, you *fool*.'

The dam broke.

Gunnlaugur launched himself at Ingvar, barely even feeling Váltyr's futile attempt to rein him in, throwing himself forwards and butting him viciously on the forehead.

'You *want* this?' Gunnlaugur roared, throwing a punch with his left fist. It connected brutally, hurling Ingvar back and sending him reeling. 'You *want* me to destroy you?'

Ingvar crashed into a trolley full of medical instruments. They spun and clattered to the floor as he careered on backwards. Gunnlaugur went after him, fists swinging, aiming for the head.

Ingvar pushed back, shoulders down and arms wide, crunching into Gunnlaugur's waist. Ingvar wrapped his arms around him and heaved, arresting the Wolf Guard's momentum and nearly upending him.

They rocked back, locked together, smashing machines and sending them skidding into the walls. Gunnlaugur twisted out of Ingvar's embrace and hurled him aside. Ingvar slammed heavily into the apothecarion's far wall, cracking the stone and spitting blood onto the floor.

Before Gunnlaugur could close, Ingvar came back at him, fists whirling. The two of them traded a flurry of bludgeoning punches, each one landing with the force of jackhammers. Ingvar was quicker, cracking two ferocious blows against Gunnlaugur's right side, but Gunnlaugur fought as if possessed, his eyes blazing with a dark, enraged energy.

He crunched a deadening strike into Ingvar's face, hurling him back against the wall. Then he piled in, lunging madly, roaring curses as his arms flailed.

By the time Olgeir and Váltyr finally dragged them apart both of them were panting hard and covered in blood. Gunnlaugur's forehead carried a long gash and streaks of deep red coursed freely over his beard. Ingvar's face was swollen and purple, his lips split and one eye half closed.

For a moment they both stared at one another, breathing heavily. Gunnlaugur felt his whole system blazing with energy, urging him back into the fight. The veins at his throat throbbed. His fists were still tight-clenched, aching to fly again.

Haflói's jaw hung open, as if he couldn't quite believe what he'd seen. Váltyr looked weary of it all; Olgeir concerned.

Only Jorundur was unmoved. His sour laughter broke the heavy silence.

'It happens at last,' he said dryly. 'Better now than when the walls are on fire. So is that it? Can we move on now?'

No one had any appetite to answer. Gunnlaugur remained poised, his fists raised and blood pumping. The discharge of fury had felt good while it had lasted. It had been building up for days, poisoning him, polluting everything he did.

Ingvar glared back at him. He'd taken a battering; brawling had never been his strong point. He was still angry, but something else lurked behind those stony features.

Shame, perhaps. Or maybe sorrow.

He glanced momentarily towards Baldr's unmoving body, and something seemed to snap within him.

His shoulders slumped.

'Brother, I–' he started.

'Say nothing,' ordered Gunnlaugur, still primed, still snarling. He pulled himself to his full height, ignoring the slowing trickle of blood that ran down his cheek. 'Say *nothing.*'

He turned his gaze to Hafloí, who still wore an expression of shock. No doubt he was used to Blood Claws settling things in such a way, but Hunters were another matter.

'Can you walk yet, whelp?' demanded Gunnlaugur.

Hafloí seemed briefly uncertain, but nodded.

'Good,' said Gunnlaugur. His senses were returning. He felt clarified. 'The canoness will be wondering where we are. We need to go.' He shot a savage look at Ingvar. 'We'll settle this later. For now, survival.'

The pack looked back at him. They listened. In a strange, primitive kind of way he'd established his authority again.

Is that the best we can do? he thought to himself, not knowing how he would answer that, if pushed. *Is that really – still – how these things are done?*

'Stay with Fjolnir,' Gunnlaugur ordered Ingvar. 'Let your blood cool while you're in here. He needs guarding, and I'll not have the Sisters discovering this.'

Ingvar nodded curtly, his expression torn between residual belligerence and the sullen acceptance of defeat.

Then Gunnlaugur swung round to the rest of the pack. The flow of blood raging around his system banished the weariness of the night's work. There would be time to reflect on his choices later; for now, battle called again.

'The rest of you, with me,' he said, reaching for his helm. 'We have a war to fight.'

With the departure of the pack, the apothecarion fell into near silence. Baldr remained prone on the slab, his face grey and pallid. Unseeing eyes stared up at the ceiling, their pupils shrunk into mere specks of black. Even the golden irises, normally so vivid and reflective, looked washed out.

After a while Ingvar came over to stand beside him. His own face, a criss-crossed mass of bruises and lacerations, scarcely looked healthier than Baldr's. He stooped, resting his hands on the edge of the table and bringing his head down closer to his brother's.

Grief marked his severe features. He felt suddenly older, as if the cares of centuries had only then chosen to etch themselves on his genhanced flesh.

'Brother,' he whispered, as if speaking to him could bring Baldr out of the grip of his deep coma.

If he died there, it would be a terrible death, one every Son of Russ would shudder to hear of. No glorious last charge, no defiant stand, just slow capitulation to corrupting poisons within the walls of a mortal fortress.

Ingvar's body ached. He could feel the blood on his skin thickening into scabs. Already the brawl seemed like a trivial, stupid thing; something born out of grief and guilt, something to be put aside and forgotten.

Some things, though, were more important.

'Brother,' said Ingvar again. He reached for the soul-ward at his breast. Despite Gunnlaugur's furious assault it remained intact, as did the onyx skull beside it. 'You should not have given me this. It was yours, and I should not have taken it back.' His eyes lowered. 'But it was freely given. Is that not the way of our kind? To seal blood-debts with trinkets? I thought it was a way back for me. That was why I took it.'

Ingvar's eyes flickered out of focus, their gaze uncertain.

'I believed I could come back. I truly believed it. I wear them both now – my two lives, intertwined, interdependent. I thought I could keep them in balance.'

He looked around him then, as if suddenly nervous others might be listening. The apothecarion gazed back at him, deserted, echoing with antiseptic emptiness. Baldr's blank expression registered no change.

Ingvar lowered his head further, keeping his voice to little more than a hiss.

'I have to tell someone,' he said. 'If we are both to die here, far from the ice and unmourned, I have to tell someone. You will not remember. No vow is broken.'

Baldr's face was unmoved, locked in the rigid grip of paralysis. His sickly features seemed carved from granite.

Ingvar paused, poised over what felt like a precipice. Heartbeats passed; his own strongly, Baldr's almost undetectably.

'I no longer believe, brother.'

Ingvar's voice almost broke as he spoke those words. His hands gripped the side of the table. Horror filled his heart, horror that he had spoken such a thing out loud. Until then he had never done so, not even in the privacy of his cell's solitude. The psycho-conditioning of the Adeptus Astartes was so ferociously strong.

But not unbreakable.

'I no longer believe,' he said again, more firmly.

It was less terrible the second time. Like unlocking a door into a hidden chamber of forbidden secrets, more thoughts spilled out, tumbling after the first one. He had broken the taboo; the totem had been cracked. After that, anything was possible.

'We were seven,' he said, no longer staring at Baldr's static features but seeing things far away. 'Just like Járnhamar, we were seven. Callimachus of the Ultramarines, Leonides of the Blood Angels, Jocelyn of the Dark Angels, Prion of the Angels Puissant, Xatasch of the Iron Shades, Vhorr of the Executioners, Ingvar of the Space Wolves. We were Onyx Squad.'

Ingvar smiled softly.

'We did not call ourselves that. Halliafiore gave us the name. He gave us our missions. He gave us plenty.'

As he spoke he heard the faint noises of the apothecarion machinery working around them – the hum of rebreathers, the drip of saline valves, the slow click of medicae-cogitators. The chamber itself seemed to be listening to him.

'For a while I held on to the past. I kept to the old ways, I walked the path of the ice. I learned to doubt slowly. Callimachus was patient. I think he liked me, for all the pain I gave him. He believed I would see the virtue of the *Codex* if I could be shown how it worked. He was right about that, at least at first. It was painful to see myths unravelled. Do you remember when we used to laugh at other Chapters? Of course, *we* were different. Nothing so hard, so cold, as the soul forged on Fenris.'

Ingvar bowed his head lower. He stared at his own clenched fists.

'To do what we do, we have to believe. We have to believe there is no alternative, that our destiny is sacred, set apart from the start. That is what we are told in every saga and forced to learn by every Priest.'

Ingvar reached up for the soul-ward again, clutching it tight and straining the chain around his neck.

'But what if the myths are broken?'

He remembered Bajola's contempt.

Myths.

'I have seen things, brother. I have seen star systems burning. I have heard the screaming of a billion souls. All of them, screaming. We couldn't shut it out. I still hear them.'

Ingvar's right hand started to shake. He let go of the soul-ward and clamped his gauntlet firmly against the steel.

'There are weapons, Fjolnir, things you would not believe. There are devices so powerful that even to speak of them outside the Deathwatch is to earn execution. Only Callimachus could have been trusted to give the order to use them. He would have done his duty even if it meant tearing out the heart of his own primarch. Could I have done it? I do not know. But he did. He gave the order, and we used those things on our own kind, burning them into atoms so that the Great Devourer would not be able to feed on their corpses.'

The cogitators ticked gently. Baldr's chest rose and fell. The rebreathers hummed.

'Then we had to watch it come. The Shadow, so vast it might have been another star system in motion. We had to watch it move over us, blind to our presence, day after day, huddled away from its wrath, watching its living ships ply across the void, watching them crawl into the warm heart at the centre of the galaxy.'

Ingvar shuddered at the memory.

'Endless,' he whispered in horror. '*Endless.*'

Baldr's ashen face showed no tremor of recognition. He lay limply, locked in a sealed world of pain.

'After that, after seeing that, I no longer believe,' Ingvar said again. The third time, it was almost easy.

He straightened slowly, pushing himself away from the slab.

'If there is to be victory, brother, I cannot see it. I cannot remember how it feels to keep my blade in hand, glorying in my service to the Allfather. All I see is the living ships. All I see is what they made us do.'

His voice cracked again.

'I thought I could come back. I thought I would remember again once I was among you. I do not blame Gunnlaugur for pushing back, he is as lost as the rest of us. I blame myself for hoping.'

He smiled again, a pinched, wistful narrowing of the lips.

'And I blame you, Baldr. You fed my hope. As long as you remained as you were in my mind's eye – so calm, clear, so noble – coming back did not seem impossible. But it is. I understand that now.'

He wiped a thickening trail of blood from his upper lip. He could feel his broken skin beginning to swell.

'You must fight this. You still have a place here. If I fight for anything now, it is for that. I would see you restored before the end.'

Ingvar leaned down again for a final time, bringing his lips close to Baldr's ear, ignoring the stink of putrescence.

'Remember how you were. Remember the way you smoothed the way between quarrelling brothers. You always commanded your animal spirits so much better than we did. Remember that strength. Do not die here, brother. Remember yourself.'

Baldr made no response. His open eyes stared sightlessly at the ceiling, their lustre gone.

'Remember yourself,' he said again, his voice a quiet urging. 'I no longer believe, but you must. For the sake of what is left of this pack, you must believe.'

As Ingvar spoke, he felt the first spike of tears at the corner of his eyes.

It might have been fatigue. It might have been shame, or frustration. It was weak, out of character; but then so much of what he had done had been out of character, and for as long as he could remember.

Ingvar bowed his head.

'For the sake of us all,' he said, his voice soft and pressing. 'Come back.'

CHAPTER EIGHTEEN

They came with the sun. As the sky turned rust-red, then flesh-grey, then a clear, deep, cloudless blue, the plains began to fill with the armies of ruin. Slowly at first, as the advance units crawled across the dust, then with growing frequency as the main detachments caught up and the day waxed towards noon. They went warily, watchfully, before finally digging in several kilometres clear of the walls.

Canoness de Chatelaine watched them from atop the fortifications of the Ighala Gate. As the hours passed, she watched the air turn brown from the clouds of dust they threw up, and smelled the hot, putrid stench of their bodily corruption. The sun beat down, making her sweat even within her armour.

Callia stood beside her, as well as six of her Celestians in their dark battle-plate. All along the walls, running away from the gate-bastion in either direction, Guardsmen and Battle Sisters had taken up positions behind the battlements. The Guardsmen wore full-face gas masks and sealed carapace armour. Few of them spoke. Few of them moved. They stood quietly, expectantly, nervously, watching.

'Word from the Wolves?' asked de Chatelaine, her eyes fixed on the gathering army out on the plain.

'On their way, canoness,' said Callia. Her voice was more nervy than usual.

'Their wounded?'

'One warrior. He remains in the citadel. The others will fight.'

De Chatelaine nodded. 'Good. For what it is worth, good.'

She couldn't summon up much more than a token enthusiasm. This day had been coming for months. It had filled her dreams every night since the plague-ships had first appeared above her world. In her heart she had never believed victory to be possible. Now, seeing what the enemy had created and was capable of deploying, that belief became a certainty.

Privately she had always doubted that Gunnlaugur and his savages really understood just what volume of horror had been unleashed on Ras Shakeh. Perhaps their raw confidence was just an act, a show of defiance in the face of inevitable defeat. Perhaps they truly believed they could turn the horde back. In either case, their arrogance had only a superficial charm.

'Nothing remains to be done,' she said coldly.

It was true. The outer walls were fully manned and the defence towers stocked with huge quantities of ammunition. The engineering works in the lower city had been completed. Fire lanes had been gouged through the interlocking network of shadowy streets; pits had been dug in concentric lines ready for the promethium that would be pumped into them at a moment's notice. Explosive lines snaked their way through the hab-units and gun-clusters, ready to be ignited as the enemy reached them.

De Chatelaine felt a soft swell of pride as she cast her eyes over what had been achieved. Her Sisters had laboured well, keeping the spread of contagion down and mobilising the workforce. The Wolves, particularly the big one with the scars, had accelerated the work enormously, but the bulk of the lifting had still been done by mortal soldiers under her command. Given the time they had had to work in, and the conditions, it was an achievement worth taking pride in.

She ran the numbers through her mind one last time. Twenty thousand Guardsmen were on the outer perimeter, almost all stationed along the walls or in the defence towers. Sixty Battle Sisters stood with them in ten-strong squads to stiffen their resistance. A reserve line of ten thousand Guard and militia, plus the few mechanised units they possessed, were posted within the terraces of the lower city in staggered detachments. Six Sisters were billeted in the cathedral with Palatine Bajola, with the remainder of the Sororitas contingent up in the Halicon, together with the final five thousand Guard troops, ready to oversee the withdrawal to the citadel should they be forced into a last stand at the summit.

De Chatelaine lifted her helm and looked out again at what faced them. The enemy had dug in several kilometres out, far beyond the range of the guns on the perimeter wall. Her helm-lenses zoomed in as she squinted into the hot light.

Their formations were huge. Battalions of infantry, each one many hundreds strong, marched up out of the dust. They arranged themselves in ragged squares, each one headed by contagion-mutated command squads bearing rough-hewn standards and skeletal trophies. The air around them was thick with a screen of dust and spore-clouds. The troops wore a motley collection of armour – rusting iron plates, looted Guard uniforms, strangely warped and merged creations of bolted metal and stretched sinew.

De Chatelaine couldn't zoom in close enough to see their faces, though she knew well enough what they would be like: listless, bloated with tumours, the flesh pressing out from the stitched joints in their leather hoods and gas mask helms, stained green from the clouds of filmy murk that swam behind their eyepieces. Some of those troops would have been landed from the plague-ships; others were new recruits, infected and enslaved during earlier fighting. They were all equally lost now; only death, in some cases for the second time, would release them.

Already the host of plague-bearers comfortably outnumbered the defenders on the walls and more regiments were arriving all the time. She saw huge, slab-sided troop carriers smoking and rolling into position, vomiting more diseased soldiers from their flanks before shuddering back away from the front line to ferry more in. Plumes of noxious smog rolled and boiled amid the drifting dust, staining the clear blue of the sky with a wash of swimming filth.

De Chatelaine swept her gaze back and forth, scouring the front line for signs of more formidable fighters. She knew they would be there, somewhere, stalking amid the endless ranks of mortal fodder. She'd seen footage of great striding horrors, each three times the height of a man and almost impervious to pain or damage. She'd heard stories of hovering drones that buzzed across the battlefield spreading gouts of flesh-melting blooms, and swarms of fist-sized insects that latched on to faces and bit through flak jackets.

She saw none of those things. They were being held back at the rear of the gathering host, ready to be unleashed when the defences were reeling under the weight of attacking numbers.

De Chatelaine smiled thinly. It was what she would have done, given the luxury of such overwhelming force.

And of course there was the matter of the Plague Marines. She knew that one had been destroyed by the Wolves; she doubted it was the only one. Perhaps only a handful had been landed, or perhaps dozens had.

No way of knowing until the fighting started.

'We've been waiting too long,' said Callia grimly. 'I find myself wishing for it to begin.'

De Chatelaine nodded. 'Which is why they will linger.'

'Maybe this time will be different.'

'No. They wish for our fear to grow.'

Even as she spoke, a strange, half-audible noise drifted across the plains towards them. At first it sounded like the eddying drift of the desert wind. Then it clarified – a whispering chant, hissed through broken lips and filtered by spore-thick rebreathers. Thousands of voices were murmuring in unison, mournfully repeating the same words over and over again.

Terminus Est. Terminus Est. Terminus Est.

'The end,' said Callia. 'They are telling us that this is the end.'

De Chatelaine listened. 'Maybe,' she said. 'Or perhaps it has some other meaning. Who knows?'

She spoke deliberately lightly, as if it mattered not what jabbering nonsense those pustulent mouths spat out. For all that, the mournful repetition quickly became grating. It preyed on the nerves, irritating like the sting of a gadfly. The army kept up the chant, whispering and chattering like ghouls.

She straightened, pushing her shoulders back and keeping her spine straight. That was how she intended to stay until the fighting began – standing tall, looking the enemy in the eye.

'Ensure the mask drills are broadcast,' she ordered. 'Check the secure comm-lines to Bajola and the perimeter. And unfurl the standards – it is time we matched their faithlessness with the symbols of devotion.'

Callia bowed, and hastened to obey.

De Chatelaine let her go. She would have to think of more things to give her to do. She would have to think of more orders to issue to all of them, keeping the entire city busy lest it lapsed into a fearful paralysis. In truth, though, there was nothing left to do. Everything that could have been done had been done; all that remained was to wait.

Terminus Est. Terminus Est.

De Chatelaine edged forwards, making sure she was visible on the parapet to the troops lining the terraces below her. It would be important to stay visible, to give them a signal that she was with them.

The air around her felt muggy and oppressive, even more than usual, as if thickened and curdled by the poisons leaking from the enemy.

Terminus Est.

The words were strangely familiar, though she couldn't quite think why. She turned her mind from them, trying not to listen. It would be important not to listen.

Terminus Est. Terminus Est.

She gritted her teeth, forcing herself to think of other things.

All that remained was to wait.

Váltyr hurried down through the streets, heading for the outer walls. Olgeir went with him, striding in his purposive, unhurried, rolling gait.

The pack had split. Gunnlaugur had gone to the Ighala Gate to consult with the canoness. Hafloí and Jorundur were heading to the northern edge of the perimeter zone to stiffen the defences there. Váltyr and Olgeir had been assigned to the southern half. With the city surrounded on multiple fronts, the defenders were stretched thin.

Váltyr briefly wondered if it had been the same in every city that had been destroyed. Perhaps each of them had put in place hasty defences, working until their fingers bled to erect barricades and fire-trenches, hoping against hope that it would be enough.

As the two of them moved towards their positions, loudspeakers blared out repetitive messages to the populace.

Keep your gas mask on at all times. Ensure your armour is sealed. Check your fall-back routes and muster points. Do not leave your post unless ordered to do so. The Emperor protects the faithful. Remain strong, and the righteous will prevail. Keep your gas mask on at all times. Ensure your armour...

Olgeir had spent the time since leaving the apothecarion cleaning and oiling his heavy bolter. Huge loops of ammunition hung from his burly frame, interspersed with graven rune-totems promising destruction for the faithless. His battleplate still bore the acid-burns from the ravine but he'd stripped the tattered remnants of his pelts from his back.

'You are quiet, great one,' said Váltyr as they walked.

Olgeir sniffed. 'Not much to say.'

His rolling voice was subdued.

'Perhaps not,' said Váltyr.

Neither of them wished to speak of recent events, though in truth there was little else on their minds.

They passed quickly from the shadow of the Ighala Gate and down through the cathedral zone. Mortal soldiers scurried around them the whole time, hauling ammo gurneys or hefting lasguns. They had stopped staring at the Wolves a long time ago. Their faces were hidden behind masks, but their movements were hurried and anxious.

'How long do you think this perimeter will hold?' asked Váltyr as they approached the lowest terraces. He tried to keep his tone light, but it sounded forced. 'You helped build it.'

Olgeir snorted. 'If we'd had more time, maybe a day or two,' he said. 'As it is? A few hours.'

Váltyr looked around him.

'Aye,' he said ruefully. 'Looks about right.'

They strode across what had once been a narrow, tree-lined courtyard. The hab-units around its edges had been demolished to clear space for a lascannon emplacement on the northern edge. Old tiles and cobbles had been dumped in a rough embankment around the lascannons. Shakeh Guardsmen crouched on the far side of it, surrounded by stacks of lasguns and spare power-packs. Some were methodically going through their last weapon rites in order to placate machine-spirits. Others were praying. Others just squatted in the heat, their limbs listless, waiting for their world to come crashing in on top of them.

'It will be hard on them,' said Olgeir, halting for a moment.

Váltyr nodded. 'It will.'

Olgeir gazed around him. The surviving walls of hab-units and personnel bunkers seemed to shake in the heat.

'I worked with them,' Olgeir said. 'They are good people. I think they will fight well enough.'

Váltyr listened warily, wondering where he was going with this.

Then Olgeir shook his head dismissively. 'It is a shame they will die,' he said. 'I could have done things here. With more time, we could have made them as tough as kaerls.'

As he finished speaking, a low, brushing noise broke out across the city. From every tower balcony and gate lintel around them, banners suddenly unfurled, sliding down the stone and hanging limply in the unmoving air. Váltyr looked over his shoulder, back up at the imposing bulk of the Ighala Gate, just in time to see two immense standards unroll on either side of the yawning entrance arch. Each one was black, lined with pearl-white and gold. One displayed the emblem of the Wounded Heart in deep crimson; the other had the Imperial aquila emblazoned in gold.

Similar devices unfurled across the entire city. Hjec Aleja was a cere-monial site, full of processional hangings, regimental standards and ritual tapestries; when they were unravelled all at once the effect was startling: blank stone and rockcrete were replaced by a rippling sea of ebony, white, gold and crimson. The immortal images of the Imperium and the Ecclesi-archy came into being, picked out starkly by the unforgiving sun, staring out defiantly at the sea of blasphemy beyond the walls.

For a moment, faced with that spectacle, Váltyr forgot the reality of the tactical situation. He saw the dazzling array of icons, all of them created by a world whose only purpose was to venerate the Imperial order. He saw the pride that had gone into their making. Ras Shakeh was not a rich planet, it was not a beautiful one, but it had always been pious.

Olgeir grunted with approval.

'Good people,' he said again, as if that had proved his point.

The two of them started moving again, Olgeir striding out, Váltyr following on, his hand on the hilt of his blade. He felt a mix of emotions, including ones he rarely indulged. For once, the forthcoming combat was not something he looked forward to as an abstract exercise. With Baldr's fall, it had gone beyond that, becoming something more personal.

Most strangely, and against all the odds, he found himself sharing some of Olgeir's sentiments. As things had transpired, he regretted the ruin that would come to Ras Shakeh. They had already fought hard for it; they would fight harder for it before the end came.

The people had earned that. With their dogged resistance, their artistry, their loyalty, they had earned the right to one last battle.

He remembered hating the planet, and found he could no longer do so. *It is a shame they will die.*

Haflói limped along behind Jorundur. They were near the outer walls, surrounded by the bunkers and resupply depots of the perimeter defence forces. His limbs still felt like they were atrophied inside his armour. Váltyr had told him it would pass. Haflói wondered how he could be so certain.

'You could slow down,' he complained.

'And you could keep up,' Jorundur retorted, not changing his pace. 'I thought you were capable of fighting?'

'I am,' said Haflói sullenly. 'This is walking.'

Jorundur stopped and turned to face him.

'They're linked,' he said acidly. 'Tell me truly, whelp. If you can't swing an axe up there, you're no good to me.'

Haflói scowled under his helm. 'I can swing an axe fine,' he said. His voice held a growling edge to it, just as Gunnlaugur's so often did. 'Just get me into position and let them come to me.'

Jorundur looked at him for a long time, as if judging whether that was wise.

'Your armour's burned white,' he observed. 'That's not going to change. Perhaps we should give you a name to remember it by. Witch-marked? White-pelt?' He shook his head. 'Never been gifted at such things. Baldr would have known what to suggest.'

Haflói felt a twinge of pain. 'Deed names are for heroes,' he said. 'I won't take one.'

The memory of what had happened in the ravine was still raw. He'd fought a thousand times against the scions of the Dark Gods and had never been so easily swatted aside. If he'd just been a little quicker, a little wilier or a little more experienced, Baldr might not be lying on a slab in the heart of the Halicon.

He expected Jorundur to respond with sarcasm. To his surprise, the old warrior reached out to him, resting his gauntlet on his warp-whitened armour.

'You're young, whelp,' he said. His dry voice was as warm as it ever got. 'You fight well. Váltyr told me he'd have struggled against that witch if he'd been up against him. It took three of them to take him down. *Three.* And one of them was Gunnlaugur, who can kill anything that lives. So you have nothing to be ashamed of.'

The kindness was so unexpected, so unusual, Haflói didn't know how to respond. For a moment he thought Jorundur might still be mocking him somehow, masking a jest with honeyed reassurances.

'Doubt is the killer, Haflói,' Jorundur went on. 'Let it under your guard, and it will murder you. I've seen you use your axe, and you've got a mighty future ahead of you.' The Old Dog's voice drifted a little, as if he were remembering something else. 'Don't doubt. I'd hate to see you not fulfil your potential.'

It was then that Haflói knew he wasn't mocking him. He watched Jorundur standing before him, somehow hunched and crabby even in his ancient battleplate. Those last words had been heartfelt.

Then Jorundur withdrew his gauntlet and started walking again.

Haflói hurried to keep up with him, feeling the muscles in his calves throb. He struggled to think of something to say.

'So what of *Vuokho*?' he asked, suddenly remembering the Thunderhawk sitting up in the citadel.

Jorundur laughed. 'Still hoping, eh?' he said. 'Forget it. It's back in one piece, but we ran out of time. It wouldn't get off the landing pad. And if it did, it would crash soon after.' He chortled darkly to himself. 'A shame. I'd have enjoyed opening up with the cannon.'

Haflói sighed. 'Aye,' he said. 'And I'd have enjoyed flying it.'

That made Jorundur laugh again.

'Where is this nonsense coming from?' he asked. 'You're a fine warrior, but you're no pilot. Trust me, I've trained plenty. You've got muscle where your brain should be. You'd burn a Thunderhawk into the ground as soon as look at it.'

Haflói began to feel reassured. That was more like it – the old sarcasm was back.

'So you think,' he said, wincing as his damaged muscles protested against the work he put them to. 'I'd have enjoyed proving you wrong.'

As he spoke, they reached the broad expanse of cleared earth on the inside curve of the walls. Dozens of Shakeh-liveried troops milled around at the base of the fortifications, hauling materiel or barking orders to one another. Ladders ran up from the ground level towards the summit, more than twenty metres up. Haflói could see figures moving between the various gantry levels on the walls' inside faces. Long chains ran down from the parapets above, ready to lift the heavy ammo crates chewed through by the fixed bolter turrets on the battlements. Everything was in motion, a bustling energy that spoke of nerves and resolve. Haflói could smell the sweat of the workers even through their sealed armour and rebreathers. They would be sweltering in their chem-resistant outfits.

Jorundur moved to one of the many ladders leading to the parapet, then paused as he gripped the metal.

'Last time I'm asking,' he said. 'Are you fit for this?'

Hafloí briefly saw Baldr's grey face, laid out on the slab, eyes open but unseeing. *They* had done that to him. He hadn't been strong enough to prevent that then, but there was always vengeance.

He flexed his arms. Still painful, but some of their old suppleness was returning.

'Think I'd tell you if I wasn't?' he said. 'But worry not, old one.'

He drew his weapon and hefted it loosely.

'I can swing an axe fine.'

De Chatelaine smelled the Wolf Guard's approach before she saw him. His aroma hadn't improved with the passing of time. The musk that always hung around him had been added to by the remnants of those he'd killed. She could detect the dry tang of crusted blood, the slowly decaying residue of slaughtered flesh, the musty stench of residual acid-eroded furs, so incongruously worn in the full heat of the sun.

She waited for him on the platform above the Ighala Gate, standing where she had done since the first enemy troops had crawled onto the plains before her. She heard his heavy tread coming up the stone steps behind her. She knew that Space Marines could move stealthily when they chose to, but for the most part their movements seemed to her heavy, almost clumsy.

They were such crushing, blunt instruments. Each individual among them was capable of slaying hundreds of lesser troops. They had passed so far beyond the capabilities of mortality that they were more like living tanks than lone soldiers.

And of all the Chapters that might have answered her summons, the Wolves were the most incongruous of all; a weird mix of mutation, superstition and backwardness that would have long since been purged from the Imperium if it hadn't been for their other qualities: unshakeable loyalty, terrifying combat prowess, sheer bloody-mindedness.

De Chatelaine smiled silently to herself. Despite everything, despite all she'd expected, she couldn't help but appreciate their uniqueness. Dealing with the Adulators had been easier. They had been courteous, predictable and efficient. But – Throne forgive her – they had also been mordantly dull.

'Canoness,' came Gunnlaugur's greeting.

De Chatelaine turned away from the vista before her and inclined her head gracefully.

'Wolf Guard,' she answered. 'How fares your wounded warrior?'

Gunnlaugur drew alongside her. The two of them stood together at the Ighala's summit. Below them spread the tumbling face of the lower city. Beyond that sprawled the enemy army, now bloated into a foetid sea of bodies that lapped in all directions, staining the earth into blackness. Their numbers had long since become uncountable.

'He lives,' said Gunnlaugur. His expression was masked by his helm. 'One of my pack tends him.'

De Chatelaine placed her hands together before her.

'Good,' she said. 'Then your raid was a success.'

Gunnlaugur didn't reply immediately.

'They had a witch with them,' he said. 'A sorcerer. We killed it.'

'So I heard,' she said. 'The first such abomination to die on this world. Let us hope it will not be the last.'

Gunnlaugur growled his assent. 'Trust in that.'

Out on the plains, the low whispering had never stopped. It still rolled across the thickening air, repeated in overlapping, husky, phlegm-thick voices. The sound was impossible to get used to; de Chatelaine couldn't block it out or forget it was there. That was, presumably, the point. She forced her mind not to fixate.

'*Terminus Est*,' she said. 'Does it mean something to you?'

Gunnlaugur nodded slowly. 'It does,' he said. 'It is the name of a ship.'

As soon as he said it, de Chatelaine knew he was right. She dimly recalled stories, old stories, legends of drifting hulks in the deep void crewed by nightmares.

'So why do they say its name?' she asked.

'I do not know.'

De Chatelaine looked at him shrewdly. 'You do not know, or you will not tell me?'

Gunnlaugur seemed to consider that for a while. Eventually, he spoke again.

'The mutants that pollute your planet are scions of Mortarion,' he said. 'The Traitor Marines that walk among them are of his Legion, the Death Guard. Their captain has many names and many faces. Some are legendary, some remembered only by the souls of those he has slain.'

Gunnlaugur's voice dropped low, audible only to her and the Celestians in attendance.

'In the annals of our order he was once Calas Typhon of the Dusk Raiders. Now he is called Typhus.' The contempt in Gunnlaugur's voice was almost physically tangible. 'The *Terminus Est* is his flagship.'

'Why do they call out its name?' asked de Chatelaine. 'Is he here? Is that it?'

Gunnlaugur made a strange, twisted noise. For a moment de Chatelaine thought he was choking on something. Then she realised he was laughing.

'If he were here, Sister, this world would already be smouldering ash,' he said, before turning his dust-lined lenses to her. 'They say I am proud, but I am not stupid. Some foes are beyond all but the mightiest of us.'

He looked back out over the plains.

'No,' he said. 'His brothers lead this attack, but he is not with them.'

The canoness couldn't draw much comfort from that. The forces against them were so immense that the presence or otherwise of one warlord, no matter how dreadful, seemed to make little difference.

'Then I do not understand why they chant,' she said.

'Neither do I,' said Gunnlaugur. 'But if his name is invoked here, then this battle is a part of something larger. The *Terminus Est* has been hunted for millennia. Whenever it draws clear of the warp it is the harbinger of some great terror.'

His tone was sombre. The ebullience that had coloured his words on arrival seemed to have faded.

'I have the sense of something unfolding,' he said. 'I have the sense that long-prepared plans have been mobilised. This world – your world – had the misfortune to be in the way of them.'

'Misfortune?'

'Fate, then.'

De Chatelaine unclasped her hands. Absently, her right strayed to the grip of her holstered bolt pistol.

'Nothing you say makes me optimistic, Space Wolf,' she said. 'For a long time, even after they began to march on us here in Hjec Aleja, I was optimistic. I prayed that some outside force would come to deliver us. When you arrived, I thought it might be you.'

Gunnlaugur snorted in amusement. 'We haven't started on them yet.'

'But you yourself do not believe it.'

'Oh, I do,' said Gunnlaugur, at last injecting some resolve into his deep voice. 'We all believe. That is what makes us who we are.'

He held up his gauntlet and turned it in the sunlight. The grey ceramite was criss-crossed with scratches, scorches, gouges, chips and bloodstains.

'These are just tools,' he said. Then he tapped his finger against his chest, just over the angular markings on his breastplate. '*This* is what makes us *Fenryka*. We believe. If any one of my pack wavered in that, even the closest of my battle-brothers, I would disown him. When the urge comes on us, when we enter the fight, none of us doubts. Not for a second. That is Russ's legacy.'

He clenched his fist before lowering it.

'Some things are eternal,' he said. 'When this thing starts, I will enter battle in the full certainty that I will crush them utterly.'

De Chatelaine laughed. She wasn't sure whether that was because his words inspired her or because they were ludicrous. In any case, it felt good to release some small portion of the tension she had carried with her for so long.

'And you would say the same even if this Typhus were here?' she asked.

Gunnlaugur nodded. 'I would. And you would see then what contradictory creatures we are.'

De Chatelaine inclined her head amusedly. 'I already see that,' she said.

They stood together after that, watching the clouds of dust drift across the plains. The sun was at its apex, hammering down over defender and besieger alike. Smoke wafted lazily up from the enemy lines. It was hard to make out what they were doing. In the far distance, the hazy outlines of huge vehicles could just be made out. Some looked like bloated artillery pieces, others like massive fuel tankers.

'So Typhus is not among them,' said de Chatelaine, musingly. 'But they are led by one from his Legion. Who, I wonder?'

'Do not worry on that score,' said Gunnlaugur, his voice bleak. 'We will know soon enough.'

CHAPTER NINETEEN

The first sign of change came with the sounding of klaxons out on the plain. A few blared out, braying tinnily, then others joined them. The banners hanging over the legions of diseased troops twitched, then started to sway as their bearers broke into the march. Great booming gongs rang out from beaten hammers of brass. The cloud of drifting soot split and severed, fractured by the sudden movement of thousands of troops.

All along the battlements, Guardsmen immediately tensed, hoisting their lasguns onto the parapet edge and staring through the sights. The twin barrels of the bolter turrets swung into position, angling at the terrain before the walls. Warning chimes sounded throughout the city, echoing along what remained of the narrow spaces and courtyards below.

Váltyr watched it unfold with a calm, expert eye.

'The first wave,' he murmured, watching the front ranks of mutants start to creep across the dust-pan towards the outer gates.

More dust kicked up as the legions picked up momentum. The entire expanse of desert seemed to be shifting. Regiment after regiment began to move, lumbering heavily into motion, still whispering the same words, maddeningly repeated far beyond the tolerances of mortal sanity.

Terminus Est. Terminus Est.

Shielded behind the front ranks of infantry came the crawling siege engines. They hauled their way through the muck and murk, belching smoke and venting gas. Some carried rusty toxin vats on their backs, just like the ones destroyed in the ravine; others dragged along multi-barrelled artillery pieces, their snouts corroded and dry with ancient rot and metal cancer; others were tottering creations of iron scaffolding and ramshackle ladders, topped with grapple-claws and chain launchers. Dozens of them emerged out of the preternatural fog, then dozens more.

Stand firm, defenders of Hjec Aleja!

The recorded voice blasting from the vox-casters along the wall was more hectoring than reassuring.

The Immortal Emperor protects! Aim true, hold fast, and no creature of darkness shall pass these walls! Preserve your power-pack! Fire only on command!

Olgeir grunted. 'If they don't kill that man, I will.'

Váltyr didn't smile. 'They're coming within range of the wall guns,' he said. 'So slow. This'll be a slaughter.'

'Aye. But it'll soak up bullets.'

The enemy host picked up some speed, stumbling from a limping stagger into a half-paced jog. They never launched into battle-cries, just kept up the eerie, incessant chanting. As the heavy sun slammed down on them, feeding the sweaty, stale fug of their sickness, they hissed and wheezed in unison, their dull eyes gazing stupidly.

All along the parapet, lascannon feeder units whined up to full pitch. Their long barrels swivelled into position alongside the squat heavy bolters.

Váltyr glanced over his shoulder, up to the Ighala Gate fortifications in the distance. He could see the canoness standing at the summit of the gatehouse. Gunnlaugur had left her side, no doubt heading down to the perimeter before the storm broke against it. De Chatelaine looked isolated up there, her cloak hanging heavily in the airless heat and the metal lining of her battleplate glinting. She raised her arm, and a thousand pairs of eyes all across the city waited for the signal.

For a moment her fist hovered motionless, raised above her like a salute. Then it fell.

The wall batteries opened up. The stone beneath Váltyr's feet trembled as serried lascannons, heavy bolters, sabre platforms and mortar launchers unleashed their contents. Blinding spears of energy lanced out from the city's edge, shooting clear of the smoke-choked discharge of missile launchers and heavy ordnance.

The front rows of enemy infantry disappeared behind a rippling wave of exploding earth. The cracks and booms of secondary detonations rang out, drowning out their whispering and replacing it with a hammering chorus of mechanical devastation.

More volleys followed, loosed in a steady rain of destruction, tearing through the oncoming horde and miring its advance into a bloody, dust-swirled morass.

Hundreds died in those opening seconds. They just kept marching through it, swinging their scrawny arms even as they staggered into the heart of the maelstrom. Not one of them turned back, not one of them hesitated.

Váltyr felt disgust rise in his gorge. He had seen men used callously on battlefields by the Imperium in the past, but the rank slaughter in front of him went far beyond that. There was malice in it, a casual destruction ordained by powers that loathed humanity and delighted in its degradation. Somewhere, in some forsaken vault of eternity, ruinous intelligences laughed to see such wanton suffering inflicted on their own servants.

For all that, the tactic was not mindless. The lascannons had to pause between barrages to allow the power units to be recycled. Bolter turrets needed reloading, mortar arrays took time to replenish. The crews worked quickly, getting their weapons firing again as soon as they could, but the tiny gaps created opportunities. Enemy infantry, their masks glowing with a dull-edged resolve, clambered across smouldering blast craters and trod down the sagging bodies of the slain. They kept on coming, inching closer with every pause in the firing. Eventually the gun crews were forced to angle their barrels down, ratchet-notch by ratchet-notch. The filthy tide of broken bodies and tangled metalwork edged closer, metre by clogged metre, their progress bought dearly amid the hammering rain of las-beams and bloody bolt-shells.

Through breaks in the growing screens of dirty smoke, war engines could be made out, grinding towards the walls in the wake of the sacrificial infantry. Their heavy treads rolled over the corpses, crushing the stacked cadavers into a slurry of brown-frothed slime. Every so often a lascannon would get a clear shot and one of them would burst into green-edged flame, collapsing into ruin as other weapons zeroed in. But for every one that was downed many more crept nearer, slowly crunching and snapping their way through the pools of twitching, necrotic flesh.

Váltyr drew *holdbítr*. Olgeir hoisted *sigrún*. The two of them stood on the wall's edge, watching the first of the big machines draw into range. Alongside them on the parapet's length, mortal troops held their lasguns tightly, blinked into their sights and tried not to seize up too much. The few Battle Sisters among them stood silently, patiently, like ebony statues of lost saints.

'The Hand of Russ be with you, Heavy-hand,' said Váltyr.

Olgeir nodded. 'And with you, blademaster. Reap a swathe.'

Váltyr flourished his blade. Even in the dull, smog-thick air the metal flashed brilliantly, polished to a glass-clear sheen.

'I intend to,' he said.

The dusk was hours away but the sky darkened swiftly. A dilated pall the colour of sour plums soared up from the horizon, blotting out the light of the sun. Rearing towers of airborne ash snaked out, bleeding up from the skirts of the boiling hordes as they advanced. Lightning, picked out in lurid green, flickered under the ragged hems of the racing clouds, closely followed by the dull roll of unnatural thunder.

The air, already hot, became stiflingly humid. Insects swarmed up from the plains and began to plague the battlement level of the walls. They clustered around the air intakes of the Guards' chem-suits, buzzing furiously as their swollen abdomens jammed in the mechanisms. Gun crews began to leave their stations, choking, slapping and clawing at their gas masks. The intensity of the defensive barrage fell away.

'Stay where you are!' roared Gunnlaugur, striding up to the edge of the broad gun platform that perched over the outer wall gatehouse. He was surrounded by hundreds of Guardsmen, all manning one of the dozens of bolter-mounts that lined the ornate bulwark. Despite the droning mass of biting insects they laboured on as best they could, dragging fresh crates to the gaping gun-breeches and spinning elevating wheels two-handed.

By then the enemy had almost reached the walls. Their losses were still incredible, but with every passing minute the gap closed by a few paces more. Some of the mutants even managed to loose grappling hooks or hurl spiked incendiary bombs up at the defenders. Such futile attempts did little more than scrape the foundations of the city's perimeter, but the fact they'd got so close, and so fast, was sobering.

Gunnlaugur grasped the lip of the platform's railing and leaned out over the raging tumult below, craning for a better view. The siege engines were getting closer, wrapped in thick coats of oily smoke. The first flickers of enemy las-fire started to spike upwards from ground level. As bigger guns were dragged into range, that trickle slowly grew more disruptive.

Hjec Aleja was completely surrounded. The plague-host stretched away in all directions, devouring the open land and turning it black. The pale stone of the city turned scab-brown under the gathering smog and the golden lining of the banners lost its lustre. Lumen banks began to flicker into life across the walls and defence towers, but their light was quickly muffled in the dense murk.

Gunnlaugur stood defiantly above it all, poised atop the beleaguered gates like some ancient sea captain at the prow of his wave-cutter.

Ahead of him, vast and wreathed in underlit gouts of steam, a tottering mobile tower rig emerged from the gloom. It reached up to the level of the battlements, dwarfing the ranks of marching mortals before its huge segmented tracks. Its flanks were formed of an intricate skein of interlocking iron webs. Banners of crudely stitched human hide fluttered in its wake, still bloody and unscraped, bolted to the scaffold with metal pins. As Gunnlaugur watched, a row of bronze-throated cannons rolled out along the tower's top tier, each one already smoking from its baleful contents.

'Bring it down!' he thundered at the crews around him.

They tried to. Two lascannon stations found their target, sending beams tearing through the superstructure and nearly sending it crashing back to earth. Somehow, the siege tower kept on coming, teetering and rocking.

Then, with a glottal roar, the tower's cannons returned fire. Shells screamed across the exposed gun platform, whistling across the space at head height. Gunnlaugur, ducking under the barrage, saw Guardsmen hit full on, hurled into shreds of flesh as the barbed missiles exploded. Metal shards flew out from the shells in bursting clouds of spinning debris, scything through body armour and cutting into stone. Trails of vomit-yellow mucus flew out from the exploding ordnance, clinging to whatever it splattered across and eating at it like acid.

In that single volley half the gun stations had been taken out. The rest of them had mauled crews and only slowly scrambled to respond.

Gunnlaugur kicked back to his feet. He raced over to the nearest heavy bolter turret – an open platform with a single twin-linked gun mounted on a swivel-plate. He grabbed the two-handed grip, spun the barrels round and opened fire. Twin columns of mass-reactive shells blazed straight back at the tower's approaching summit.

The line of cannons blew up one after the other as the stream of bolts flew into their gaping maws. Skeletal figures clinging to the tower's structure fired back at Gunnlaugur, concentrating las-beams at his position. Those shots that hit him glanced from his armour, scoring it but not penetrating. Gunnlaugur weathered the storm, firing all the time, holding firm as the long chain of shells spun through the bolter's feeder mechanism.

By the time the heavy bolter clicked empty the other gun crews were recovering. Stark white las-beams and solid projectiles hammered into the reeling siege tower. With a sighing crack, the spine of it broke, sending the top level crashing down to the smoke-filled plains below. Ammo dumps stored inside ignited with a whooshing bang, and a thick bloom of orange flame raced up the tower's cracked sides. It reeled on its tracks, hanging precariously for a moment, then toppled, breaking up into burning shards as it disintegrated over the jostling throngs below.

Gunnlaugur looked around him. Three more war engines were approaching, each as large as the first one, crushing and tearing their way through the legions that pressed around them. At ground level, heavily armoured plague-bearers in dull black armour were hauling what looked like huge bomb carcasses towards the barred gate entrance. The volume of fire aimed up at the battlements was growing all the time.

He drew his bolter grimly, trying to gauge just how long the defences on the perimeter could hold before retreat became inevitable. The task was already nearly hopeless, like trying to hold back a storm-tide of the Helwinter.

'Hold fast!' he roared defiantly, picking his next target out and opening fire again. The familiar hammering clatter of his bolter rang out across the growing cacophony of the battlefield, adding to the steady crescendo of rage and fury. 'In the name of the Allfather, hold fast!'

Ingvar heard the blasts from far off. In the sanctuary of the Halicon's apothecarion they were little more than dull rumbles. Some of the larger impacts made the walls vibrate, sending hairline cracks along the cement between the tiles.

He started to pace around Baldr's table, his fingers twitching. The mood of despair that had fallen over him following the brawl with Gunnlaugur had faded, replaced by a burning impatience.

He should be out there, standing with his brothers. Watching over Baldr in the Halicon was a waste.

He paced some more, resisting the urge to draw his blade. The sterile air of the apothecarion tasted stale as he breathed it.

I should be out there.

He blink-clicked a comm-link to Olgeir.

'How goes the fight, brother?' he asked.

The feed was crackly and static-filled. He heard the thin background buzz of what must have been explosions, the low roar of bolter shells loosing.

'Ingvar?' Olgeir's voice was strained. 'What do you want? We're a little busy here.'

'Where are you? I should be with you. I'll come to your position.'

The feed broke off briefly, overloaded with white noise, before re-establishing.

'...ere you are. Blood of Russ, Gyrfalkon, do not leave him. You saw what he looked like.'

Ingvar clenched his fists in frustration, glancing over to where Baldr lay, as immobile as ever, his flesh as torpid as rotting meat. There had been no change. If anything, he looked worse.

'This is madness,' hissed Ingvar, starting to walk again. 'Send the whelp back. You need my blade there, brother.'

Olgeir didn't reply. The link boomed briefly with more explosions, followed by a series of drawn-out screams. Ingvar heard a mortal voice shouting something in the background.

They're coming through! Throne, they're coming through!

When Olgeir finally spoke again, his thick voice was punctuated by panting, as if he'd broken into a jogging run.

'Do *not* leave him,' he said, breaking off to fire another hammering volley before starting to move again. 'You hear me? At this rate we'll be back with you within the hour anyway – they're all over the walls. Stay at the Hali–'

The link snapped out.

Ingvar cursed, his fists still balled. He drew in a deep breath, trying to stay calm. It was hard to resist the urge to move, to prowl across the confines of his prison like a caged beast, to do *something*.

He glared at the door. The lock mechanism could be crushed from the outside, sealing Baldr in. He hesitated, torn between duty and desire.

He looked back at Baldr. The fallen warrior's cheeks still bore a greenish hue. It seemed to be intensifying, as if whatever filth had been shoved into his system was breeding away within him.

That was an uncomfortable thought.

Ingvar went back over to the slab, studying Baldr's pale face. Flecks of foam had collected at the corners of his mouth, speckled with blood. They shivered as his shallow breaths came and went.

Ingvar sniffed. Just as before, the tang of the warp was clearly detectable. That, though, could have been down to the residue of the sorcerer's art, clinging to the armour like bloodstains on a corpse. In itself, it was no proof.

If Baldr had been mortal, Ingvar would have killed him without another thought.

But he wasn't mortal. He was one of them.

As Ingvar stood there, his mind racing, more muffled booms rang out from far away, making the floor shudder. They seemed closer than the last ones.

'Forgive me, brother,' said Ingvar, straightening. 'But could you stay here, knowing the battle had come at last? I will return for you.'

He started to move away, then hesitated, looking over his shoulder. For a moment, just as he'd turned his head, he thought he'd seen a flicker of movement in Baldr's eyes – a momentary tremor of peeled-back lids.

He stared for a little while longer, scrutinising Baldr's prone outline.

Nothing. Baldr lay as still as a graven image in the halls of the Jarlheim. The algal tinge around his cheeks and jawline remained as unsettlingly deep as before.

Then Ingvar grasped his helm from his belt.

'Forgive me,' he said again, backing towards the exit as he donned the red-lensed, snarling facemask. 'If Gunnlaugur wanted one of us to sit this out, he should have chosen the whelp.'

I need to know that you will follow an order.

He paused at the doorway, his fingers resting on the stone frame.

'I *will* return,' he said.

Then he pushed the door open, and headed out into the dark.

The volume of incoming fire steadily cranked up. It became intermittently dangerous, then solid, then devastating. As fast as the enemy artillery was knocked out by the defenders, more guns were hauled into place. Brass cannon-pieces, their barrels carved into snarling devil maws, bludgeoned the walls remorselessly, hammering away with incendiary bombs, shrapnel-bursts and tumbling vials of toxic sludge. The last were the worst – when they exploded amid the defenders their contents ate through armour with terrifying ease, melting flesh and popping eyes.

The parapets were aflame, burning in all quarters where the torrid mix of accelerants and chemicals ignited. The air shimmered with heat and noise and fear. Gouges had been blown out of the upper levels by the artillery barrages, cracking open the reinforced rockcrete and sending blocks of it crashing into the city beyond. Teams of enemy sappers, covered by ferocious quantities of las-fire and spore-grenades, had already gained the base of the walls and were pitilessly hacking away at the foundations. Several siege towers had reached their targets, cranking open drawbridges and spilling hordes of masked horrors onto the battlements. Each sally so far had been repelled, but more towers kept on coming, emerging out of the poisonous smog with remorseless frequency.

Jorundur stood on the battlements, firing his bolter two-handed. He worked stoically, almost in silence, fully absorbed in what he was doing. The mortals working alongside him continued to fight even as the defences crumbled around them. They all knew the cost of surrendering the walls and clung on to them tenaciously, firing in disciplined barrages while their comrades were cut down by the rain of chem-bombs and shrapnel bursts.

Hafloí was different. He marched up and down the parapet, firing his bolt pistol with abandon and brandishing his axe flamboyantly.

'That all you've got?' he roared, spreading his arms and taunting the enemy. '*Skítja*, you *disgust* me! Come up here and test your arms on *me!*'

Jorundur had seen the mortals break into laughter as Hafloí had strutted past them, despite the unfolding horrors around them. His relentless rain of insults, challenges and expletives was having an effect on them. They saw his brazen lack of fear, and some of it rubbed off on them.

Jorundur smiled wryly. That was good. He swept his bolter muzzle around, looking for targets in the murk. Down on ground level he saw a huge, slack-bellied monster lurching towards the walls, its yellow skin hanging in bags from an obscenely stretched skeleton and what looked like a massive limpet mine cradled in its arms. Claw-fisted infantry shambled along in its wake.

He took aim carefully, adjusting the bolter a fraction as the walls shook beneath him, and fired. The creature's head exploded in a burst of bone and jellied matter. The mine crashed to the floor at its feet and went off, sending a shuddering boom radiating out through the troops around it.

Even as that assault crumbled into disarray Jorundur searched for the next one. His concentration was distracted, however, by a horribly familiar surge and crackle from behind him. He immediately pushed back, leaving the battlements and moving to the inner edge of the walkway. The stink of discharged ether filtered up from the city below, mingling with the myriad other stinks polluting the smoggy air.

Hafloí had heard it too and broke away from his posturing. He seemed to be moving freely again.

'You sense that?' he asked, his voice tightening. 'I thou–'

'Hush,' snapped Jorundur, listening carefully.

He didn't have to wait long. From below, down at street level in the lower city, a chorus of screaming started up, punctuated by the wet rattle of bolter-fire.

'They've teleported behind us,' said Jorundur grimly, slamming a fresh magazine into his bolter and preparing to jump. 'Stay here and hold the walls.'

But Hafloí had already leapt, throwing himself clear of the parapet and plummeting down to the ground below.

'Damn him,' muttered Jorundur, following him down. He hit the earth hard and staggered from the impact. His armour servos whined as they compensated, pushing him back upright.

The scene on the ground was fluid. Ahead of him, twenty metres away, rose the nearest buildings. In between them and the walls was the wide area cleared by the engineers, clogged with barricades, ammo crates, spare weaponry and reserve defence squads. Men were running back from the line of buildings, turning to fire sporadically. Something was in the maze of alleys beyond – Jorundur could hear the noise of walls collapsing, mortals crying out in terror, gunfire rattling.

Hafloí sprinted towards the source of the noises, his axe already whirling. Jorundur struggled to keep pace with him.

'Wait!' he roared, knowing it would be pointless but fearing what the Blood Claw would do. Hafloí was hungry to make up for his failure, and his blood was up. That was a dangerous combination.

Hafloí disappeared into the shadows of the streets. Jorundur raced after him. By the time he caught up, Hafloí was already in combat.

Jorundur burst into a steep-sided courtyard overlooked by burning habs. The floor of it was a cracked mess of rubble and bodies, strewn with torn limbs and crushed weapon barrels. In the midst of it stood a lone Plague Marine, his armour still swimming with shimmering ether-residue, his power claws nearly black with boiling viscera. Two pale green lenses glowed in the murk as he swung round to face the raging Blood Claw.

Jorundur aimed his bolter but Hafloí blundered into the way. Jorundur circled round to the left, closing in to try to get a clear shot.

He never had the chance to fire. As he watched, stunned into inaction by what he was seeing, Hafloí took the Plague Marine apart.

Hafloí's speed, his fury, his power – it was phenomenal. He fired with the pistol at close range, chipping and cracking the monster's crusted power armour, all the while hacking with the twin blades of his hand-axe. The Traitor was strong, just as all his kind were, but he had no answer to the sheer pace of the attack. Haflói's movements became a blur of velocity, a whirlwind of hammer-blows and axe-bites.

The Plague Marine tried to respond, hauling his bloody claws in broad sweeps, but Haflói never gave him a chance to bring his greater strength to bear. He ducked under the lunging claws, thrusting up and twisting his axe round in a tight arc. Then his body spun around, propelling the blade across in a glittering line. It severed the Plague Marine's neck just above the gorget. The strike was perfect – angled between the hard armour plates and dragged through the flesh beneath with staggering power.

The Traitor crashed to the earth, his lopped neck oozing a thick mixture of pus and heartsblood. Haflói stood in triumph over it, his boot crunched onto the enemy's swollen breastplate, his axe raised high.

'*Fenrys hjolda!*' he roared, throwing his head back and howling to the fiery heavens.

Jorundur found himself momentarily lost for words.

'Blood of Russ,' he breathed, stalking over to Haflói and gazing at the damage he'd done. 'A mighty kill. Where did you learn to do that?'

'From watching you,' replied Haflói, his voice savagely cheerful. 'You're a miserable pack, truth be told, but I've learned a few tricks.'

Jorundur was about to reply when fresh screaming echoed out into the false night. He looked up, over the roofs of the buildings to where the walls loomed.

Plague-bearers had got onto the parapet at last. He could see them swarming along the battlements and grappling with the Guardsmen, overwhelming them through sheer force of numbers. Further along the walls, gouges had been opened up in the stonework as the big artillery found its range. Flames coursed up the flanks of the beleaguered defence towers, snapping and writhing like nests of serpents. The stink of warp energy remained strong, indicating that other Plague Marines had been dropped behind the defensive lines. Above it all boiled the clouds of flies and chem-spores, whipped up into a thick airborne pall of madness and disease.

The line was breaking. Once that truth became evident the vox-casters blazed out again, matched by the shouted commands of the surviving unit sergeants.

Fall back! Back to the inner walls! Fall back! Back to the inner walls!

As soon as they heard the order men began to pull away from their posts, trying not to break into a headlong run, firing steadily in retreat at the hordes of bloated, twisted mutants that swarmed through every gap and breach in the burning defences.

Jorundur stowed his bolter and drew his power axe. He thumbed the disruptor field on and its blue-edged crackle snarled into life.

'Time for blades, I think,' he said, striding back towards the approaching enemy. 'Your axe and mine, White-pelt.'

Haflói laughed harshly, falling in behind.

'Fine,' he said. 'But you *have* to think of a better name.'

CHAPTER TWENTY

Gunnlaugur did not leave the gatehouse until it was falling apart around him. The walls on either side were breached and broken, and the ground beneath the arches was teeming with a crush of enemy troops, all hacking at the heavy metal doors and stacking piles of explosives against them. Las-blasts lanced up at the parapets, undeterred by any return fire now that the last of the bolter turrets had been taken out. Grappling hooks were flung up; siege towers clunked heavily against abandoned wall sections and disgorged their contents onto the walkways.

Still Gunnlaugur stayed where he was, his feet planted firmly on the keystone of the gate's central arch, his hammer swinging around him in bloody curves. He was alone; the mortals who had stood with him had either fled or had died. Mutants, plague-bearers and blight-skinned cultists all rushed at him, lashing with flails, morning stars and meathooks. He cut them down in broken droves, hurling spine-snapped bodies from the battlements and sending them crashing back down into the sea of straining flesh below.

'For the honour of Russ!' he roared, crying out each time *skulbrotsjór* connected. '*Heidur Rus!* The hammer of the *Fenryka* is among you!'

They were not daunted. Oblivious to the carnage being reaped among them, they kept on coming, crawling on all fours just to get their blades into striking distance. Clouds of pestilence buzzed and droned about their heads, the insects feeding on the gaseous flesh of the dead as eagerly as they sucked on the blood of the living.

Only when the gates were finally broken did Gunnlaugur fall back at last, sweeping the parapets clear with a final, mighty strike of his crackling thunder hammer. He felt the basalt columns beneath him shudder as the gate's adamantium doors were driven in, and heard the thick crack of stone coming apart amid the rush of explosions.

In a final act of defiance, he stood atop the crumbling archway and brandished *skulbrotsjór* to the lowering heavens. The sky was as dark as night, broken by green lightning dancing along the underbelly of unnatural thunderheads. The stench of fear hummed in the burning air, but Gunnlaugur Skullhewer stood tall, silhouetted against the raging flames that now whipped along what remained of the walls.

'I *defy* you!' he thundered, swinging *skulbrotsjór* in ritual sweeps of denunciation. 'Only death awaits you! I, Gunnlaugur of the Rout of Fenris, will bring it down upon you! For the Allfather! For Fenris!'

Then the gatehouse started to collapse, reeling on its supports even as a straining tide of plague-bearers began to surge through the cracked doors.

Gunnlaugur backed away, retreating to the inner edge of the ruined archway as it yawed and buckled beneath his feet. He flung himself clear, falling hard and crashing into the throngs of mutants that had already broken through, crushing several under his heavy armour and scattering many more.

Then he started to run, slamming aside any laggards who got in his way. Behind him, the archway slowly collapsed in a sighing, slipping landslide of stone and metal, sending up thick plumes of dust and glowing from within as the fires took hold.

A low roar of triumph rose up from the host still on the far side of the walls. They swarmed over the broken and burning masonry, trampling their own just to be in the forefront of those breaking in.

Gunnlaugur never looked back. He had held the line for as long as possible, giving time for the mortals to fall back to the next circle of defence. That was how it had been planned – staged withdrawals, each one extracting as much pain from the attackers as possible.

He ran along the wide thoroughfare that Olgeir had helped excavate, hearing the broken patter of thousands of calloused feet as the horde swept after him. Ahead of him lay the first of the trenches. He could see defenders on the far side of it manning the spewing promethium ducts. They were waiting for him to cross before igniting the blaze.

'Do it now!' Gunnlaugur roared, picking up his pace and sprinting towards the defensive cordon. 'Light it now!'

They complied immediately. Flamers angled down into the trenches and opened up. Jets of fire kindled in a clap of acrid ignition. A swaying wall of flame shot down the length of the trench, swiftly rearing up into a surging barrier. The valves stayed open, pumping promethium into the inferno and feeding the conflagration.

Gunnlaugur felt the enormous heat pressing against him as he neared the trench. He put on a final burst of speed, building up momentum, before leaping through the glowing furnace and bursting clear onto the far side. The few remains of flammable material still draped across his armour exploded into flame.

He ripped them free, letting the final sparks die on the ceramite. He could hear screams of frustration coming from the far side of the barrier as the pursuing horde skidded to a halt, suddenly cut off.

Gunnlaugur turned to the lines of Guardsmen waiting in ordered ranks behind the veil of fire, their weapons poised and ready.

'Do it,' he snarled.

The front line released their volley in perfect unison, sending a wall of las-beams lancing through the sheets of flame. The screams of the damned rose in intensity as shots found their targets. Even when firing blind through the inferno, the press of bodies in the street beyond made it impossible not to hit something.

With the barrier secure for the moment, Gunnlaugur walked away from the lines of Guardsmen, letting them rotate ranks to keep up the pressure. As he moved clear of them he saw Váltyr waiting for him. The blademaster's armour was blackened from fire.

'Dramatic,' Váltyr said.

Gunnlaugur grimaced. It was as close as he was likely to get to a smile. 'Speak to me,' he said.

'Plague Marines are inside the walls. Olgeir sighted one and went after it. The whelp killed another.'

Gunnlaugur started. 'Hafloí?'

'He's bragging about it already.'

Gunnlaugur shook his head wearily. He let his hammerhead lower, barely noticing the disruptor-cooked flesh-slops sliding off it.

'These won't hold them long,' he said, looking over his shoulder at the burning trenches. 'Are all fronts falling back?'

Váltyr nodded. 'We need more time. We killed obscene amounts on the walls, but they just keep coming.'

'Then I'll stay down here with Olgeir and the Old Dog. We'll make them pay for the passage of the lower city. Go to the Ighala Gate and put it in readiness. Call Hafloí back too and get him to replace Ingvar on the watch – the Gyrfalkon's stewed in there enough and we'll need his sword.'

Gunnlaugur glanced up at the distant Ighala Gate, towering precipitously above the burning city.

'That's the key. If we can hold the bridge a while this is not yet over.'

Váltyr gestured towards the cathedral, looming into the smog over to the left of their position. Its triple spires still spat with mounted gunfire. Once the last of the defenders pulled back to the inner walls it would be a lone island in a sea of ruin.

'What do we do about that?'

Gunnlaugur shrugged. 'That's up to the Sisters. If they've got any sense they'll pull out while they still can, and I'd welcome having their flamers with us on the inner walls.'

'And if they try to hold it?'

Gunnlaugur hefted *skulbrotsjór* once more, swinging it loosely around him. The noise of battle was already growing again.

'Not my concern,' he said, striding back towards the raging front line. 'I have Traitors to hunt.'

Bajola crouched down beside the altar, her bolter ready. The six surviving Sisters of her detachment did similarly, cradling flamers. The roof shuddered as incoming fire speared into the cathedral defences. What remained of the Guard units assigned to the place had withdrawn inside the doors, taking up positions within the aisles and nave.

Bajola said nothing. She had given all but one of the orders she would give. Her troops had fought with commendable resolve, slaying far more of the enemy than she would have predicted possible, holding them back from the precincts even as the surrounding barricades had been destroyed or were abandoned. Her Sisters had been in the forefront of every bloody melee and firefight, remaining in position until the last of the regular troops around them had been slain and the enemy was swarming through the breaches.

Sister Jerila had been the first to die, surrounded by clouds of exploding toxin-grenades and assailed by arm-length blood leeches that cracked her armour open and slithered underneath. Sister Honorata had been next, charging headlong into a whispering knot of grotesque plague-bearers, giving time for the Guard units with her to retreat into the cathedral's nave. Sisters Alicia and Violetta had both fallen during the final assault on the great gates, cut off at the last and swarmed over by hundreds of grasping, tearing claws.

Bajola had never truly been proud of being a member of the Wounded Heart. Her feelings about the militant order had always been complex, defined by the compromises she had made to leave her old life behind.

No longer. As she waited for the final assault every fibre of her body was proud. She saw the faces of the slain in her mind's eye, their fierce beauty and their unbending will, and felt like one of them at last. At last she had no doubts, no regrets.

Well, one regret perhaps: that she had not broken her vows and told Ingvar the truth. The Space Wolf deserved to know, even if the knowledge would only pain him and could not possibly do any good now. But that moment had passed; Ingvar was gone, no doubt fighting along with the rest of his malodorous brothers somewhere in the burning ruins of the lower city. She had made her choices, and had learned a long time ago not to give in to the corrosion of remorse.

In any case it was too late for remorse. The end was coming.

Grant that my station may serve.

Her lips moved slowly as she silently ran through the motions of the litany. At the end of the long nave, fifty metres away in the dark, she could see the gates still standing closed. The noise of the battering rams crashing against the barred metal tore at her heart. Every strike was like a body-blow, knocking the life out of the place she had never truly loved before that day.

It was ironic. Only on the verge of its destruction had she fully appreciated the austere majesty of the structure she had been charged with defending. There was a lesson in that, somewhere. Something for one of de Chatelaine's homilies; a pity, then, that there would be no more of them.

Grant that my strength may suffice.

The doors shuddered again, cracking along their full height. Another strike hammered home, cobwebbing the struts and beams with spreading fractures.

Bajola crouched lower, shifting her gun's muzzle a little, gauging where the first break would come. She could feel the sick tension in those clustered around her. They all knew this was the last line of defence; no further fallback positions existed. Above them, hanging high in the shadows, the golden mask of the Emperor gazed serenely down on them, untroubled by the carnage unfolding under His spreading arms.

Grant that my life may give honour.

Another strike landed and the right-hand door was driven in, shattering and swinging back against the pillars. The jabber and hiss of mutant troops burst into the cold serenity of the interior. She heard the roar and crackle of flames, smelled the foetid reek of plague-riddled flesh under decaying armour plate.

Grant that my death may earn it.

As the horde spilled through the broken doorway at last, tumbling into the sanctified space of St Alexia's holy precincts with the sick light of debauchery in their weeping eyes, Bajola spoke at last. She gave the final order, the one she had been saving for the final extremity, the one she had been preparing in her mind over the last hour of desperate fighting.

'The altar will not be surrendered,' she said calmly, fixing her aim on the first of the horrors to break the holiness of her domain. 'Die well, Sisters. Our bodies may be broken, but our souls are secure.'

Scholiast-Majoris Iaen Rahmna hurried along the corridor between the Halicon's prayer-scroll librarium and the incense stores. The canoness's private chapel was running low on supplies, and with nine scheduled services on the slate there was a faint chance future ceremonies would have to be truncated.

For some people such an apparently trifling matter would not have seemed important, especially given what was happening in the city at large. Some people, not blessed with Iaen Rahmna's meticulous attention to detail, would have long since ceased to care about the niceties of ritual. They might have seen the armies of darkness eating their way slowly through the lower urban zones and despaired of ceremonial propriety. They might even, in their weakness, have taken up a weapon and turned it on themselves, knowing that their life's work was now useless and decades' worth of careful prayers to the immortal Emperor of Mankind had been in vain.

Thankfully, no such people were in charge of the canoness's ecclesiastical affairs. Under Rahmna's management the thirteen chapels and sanctuaries dotted all across the citadel still worked faultlessly. The world might be ending around them, the Sisters might all have been called away to the battles outside, but the rituals would carry on. If the cardinal himself were to walk through Rahmna's gilded doorways and into one of his thirteen chapels and sanctuaries, he would witness a perfectly orchestrated suite of devotional chambers, all perfectly stocked, all ready for the priests to undertake their solemn ministry.

And of course the familiarity of the routines was a distraction. It helped Rahmna to function. It helped to keep him from giving in to the fear that threatened to suffocate him every time he heard the echoing boom of the explosions getting nearer. It prevented him from remembering that he hadn't slept properly for two weeks, or that three of his staff had succumbed to the plague and had been executed by Sisters Felicia and Calliope before his very eyes.

Keeping busy was important. It staved off the worst of the nightmares. It kept his hands occupied and gave him no time to think about retrieving the laspistol he'd stowed under his bunk for emergencies.

That was the coward's way out. And for all that Iaen Rahmna was officious, prim and completely in thrall to routine, he was no coward.

The corridor was empty. His robes rustled softly as he walked. Aside from the diffuse hum of noise coming from outside the citadel, no other sounds disturbed his mechanical thought processes.

The only departure from orthodoxy was the route: he'd had to take a detour, heading deep into the lower levels to avoid Sergeant Ehre's squads milling about in the assembly rooms. The Guardsmen were making a fearful mess there, overturning priceless cabinets and dragging their heavy equipment across polished marble towards the doorways. Rahmna didn't really understand why they were bothering. If the enemy got as far as the Halicon citadel then surely it was all over. Better instead to remain faithful, to attend to the services, to pray.

He went as swiftly as he could. The lower levels smelled bad and the lumens flickered every time a big explosion went off. Rahmna wasn't even sure what the chambers down here were used for. Food storage, perhaps. Or maybe medical facilities for the Halicon staff. Yes, that was it – the chambers on his left were part of the medicae's domain.

Ahead of him he saw a door hanging loosely on its hinges. He slowed down, unsure what to make of it. He could hear the dim humming of medicae cogitators from the other side of the wall.

He stopped walking. Something about the open doorway unnerved him. The metal panels bore long, raking marks, as if huge claws had been dragged along them.

He looked over his shoulder, his heart beating. Then he looked back. He wondered what to do. It would take him a long time to find another route.

He pressed on. His imagination had always been vivid; his superiors had castigated him for it many times in the past and he had laboured hard to curb the excesses of his mind's eye.

He went as quickly as before, padding softly in sewn leather shoes. The open doorway approached, framed by the angled outline of the broken door.

He passed by hastily, not daring to look inside. He could smell a thick aroma of something like human sweat, though it was rancid and laced with other more musky elements.

Rahmna almost reached the far side before his eyes flickered involuntarily to the left. It was just the merest glance, a fleeting vision of what lay within.

He didn't scream. The shock was too great for that. A knot of panic twisted in his stomach and burst up his throat, choking off the cry of surprise that he wanted to make.

'L-lord,' he managed to blurt, wondering, despite it all, if the etiquette was to bow. 'I did not–'

They were the last words Iaen Rahmna ever spoke. A flailing storm of green-tinged lightning forked out at him, catching him in the face and bursting his skull apart. His headless body slammed into the far wall of the corridor. For a moment the corpse hung there, impaled on sparking fronds of ether-energy, twitching and kicking, before the lines of force finally snapped out. Rahmna's corpse slid to the floor, crumpling into a heap of smoking robes.

A little later, Baldr emerged through the doorway, breathing heavily. His eyes were glassy, his skin pallid and greasy. Thin lines of drool ran down from the corners of his mouth, viscous with clotted mucus. His gauntlets glowed with a pale witchlight, dancing across the armour plate like a will-o'-the-wisp. His battleplate had darkened, crusting with scab-like patches that throbbed and pulsed. His head drooped low, his jaw hung loosely, his arms were limp.

His feet dragged along the ground as he moved; his breath vaporised in foul trails of mist as he breathed. He seemed unaware of where he was or what he was doing. He looked up and down the corridor, halting before moving off again.

Only when he limped back in the direction Rahmna had come from, stepping carelessly on the dead man's legs and crushing the bones, did his sallow-eyed stare pick up something a little like resolve. A lime-green lustre kindled under his heavy lids. Strands of phlegmy saliva trembled on his lips.

'*Terminus*,' he breathed, his voice as dry and whisper-quiet as corpse candles gusting out. '*Terminus Est.*'

When Váltyr reached the Ighala Gate it was lit red by fire. The bulwarks and gothic fortifications danced with the flickering light of flames, turning the stone into a seething patchwork of shadow and reflection. The twin banners on either side of the main archway leading into the upper city were torn and punched with holes from long-range ordnance. Guns arranged along the embattled parapets drummed a heavy return rhythm of fire, throwing round after round back into the contested suburbs below.

Váltyr paused at the head of the bridge, watching the last of the retreating columns of soldiers hurry across the span and into the shadow of the gates. They looked exhausted, their feet dragging and their shoulders hunched. Five hours had passed since the outbreak of hostilities and there had been no let-up since, just a grinding, hammering, relentless assault that had kept on coming no matter what resistance had been put in its way.

He turned away from the bridge and looked back the way he'd come. The land immediately in front of him had been cleared to give targets for the wall gunners. It ran gently downhill without obstruction, a bleak, open plain of rubble, dust and blast craters.

Half a kilometre further down, the surviving buildings of the lower city started to cluster tightly together. They fell away from Váltyr's vantage in ranks of terraces that ran over the uneven slopes of the mountain. Olgeir's concentric rings of trenches were all lit far below, throwing their fuel-laced blaze into the mix of raging fires from incendiaries and las-blasts. The lower circles had already been breached, in some places by plague-bearers throwing themselves into the fire in such numbers as to create bridges from their smouldering carcasses. Those barriers that remained would not buy the defenders much more time; the enemy was advancing on every front, creeping up through the ruins like a cancer penetrating a body. Only in a few isolated places, where squads of Battle Sisters or individual Wolves had taken them on in counter-attacks, did the advance halt for more than a few moments.

As Váltyr watched the encroaching devastation, Hafloí strode up out of the flame-licked darkness, limping across the broken landscape. He looked weary, and his bleached armour bore signs of recent damage.

'*Hjá*, whelp,' said Váltyr. 'You gained a skull for your weapon belt.'

Hafloí snorted disgustedly. 'Wouldn't touch it,' he said. 'Smelled worse than the Old Dog's breath.'

Hafloí drew alongside Váltyr, turned and looked out over the same vista. His breathing was heavy, his movements stiff. For all the Blood Claw would never admit it, he was at the limit of his strength and still affected by the wounds he had taken in the ravine.

'You know what the *vaerangi* wants of you now?' asked Váltyr.

Hafloí nodded. 'For me to take my turn by Baldr's side. To free up another rune-sword for the final fight and sit the rest of this out.' He shook his head. 'Don't worry, blademaster. I know it must be done.'

Váltyr looked at him quizzically. 'You're not going to fight it?'

'Would it do any good?'

'No.'

'There you are, then.'

Váltyr laughed. 'You're growing fast, whelp,' he said. 'You surprise me. Soon your hair will be as grey as ours.'

'When Hel melts,' muttered Hafloí, turning away and stomping up the slope towards the bridge.

He was one of the last to cross it, still limping slightly but with his shoulders back and his spine erect. He was even learning to walk like a Grey Hunter.

Váltyr smiled to himself. The new blood was welcome. Of all of them, only Hafloí still had the unconscious, arrogant assurance that a Sky Warrior ought to have. Olgeir retained much of his old bravado, and Gunnlaugur in the right mood was still an unstoppable kill-engine, but even they had learned to temper their fury as the centuries had played out. Baldr had never lost his aura of self-command, not until this mission, but that was moot now.

Váltyr himself had never possessed that innate confidence. Despite all the psycho-conditioning, all the training, all the long decades of success, he had never quite been able to convince himself that he deserved his place among the honoured of the Rout. His matchless prowess with the blade didn't mask that. He knew he pushed his reputation too far, testing it too often, forcing others to take him on. He was aware that they resented it, thinking that he delighted in humiliating them and proving his superiority.

They were wrong about that. The duels, the tests – they were a compulsion rather than a desire. He had even begun to wonder whether he wanted to be beaten, just once, just so he could look himself in the eye in the mirror and know truly that his limits had been reached.

That was the strange thing about success. It was useless in disproving the nagging, whispering notion he'd been unable to shake ever since ascending into the Blood Claws: that he was a fraud, that he wasn't quite as good as his results indicated, and that one day he'd be found out; that one day, when it really mattered, he'd let the pack down.

Váltyr, like all his brothers, was immune from fear in battle, but he'd never been immune from that anxiety. No matter how hard he trained, no matter how deadly he became in the practice cages, the quiet voice in his mind would never quite go away.

It is good that we are always forced to fight, he thought grimly to himself, watching the city burn below him. *It prevents us spending any time with ourselves.*

The last of the mortal troops, some dragging their wounded behind them, crossed the bridge. The enormous doors under the central arch slowly ground together, leaving only a narrow gap for the Wolves to slip through. After that, when they were all in, the breach would be sealed.

Váltyr walked down the shallow slope, away from where the bridge met the cleared land. Ahead of him, still a long way off and half shrouded by smoke and night shadow, lay the jagged, toothless line of buildings. Many were little more than skeletal ruins, bombed empty and glowing like angry coals. The rest were deserted, dark and hollowed out, their old inhabitants slain or cowering behind the inner walls. From beyond their see-saw profile came the dull roar of battle, a distant sighing like the surge of the ocean.

He sniffed. Something unusual laced the air, mingled amid the melange of foul smells rising from the lower city as if purposively concealed there. The hairs on his forearms rose.

He walked further down, his boots crunching through the rubble, drawing steadily closer to the line of ruins. Visibility was poor, even with his superb eyesight; the air had been turned into a miasma of spores and smoke.

'Whelp?' he voxed into the comm, wondering how far Hafloí had moved away.

No answer came. The Blood Claw's channel was unobtainable. That was strange; perhaps interference from the electrostatic in the air.

Váltyr drew to a halt, sword in hand, peering into the gloom. For a few moments more he saw nothing beyond the penumbral silhouettes of the ruins backlit by a lurid red-green sky.

'Will you stand against me, I wonder?' came a voice from the darkness.

Váltyr tensed. The voice was astonishing – a thick, wet purr of indolent malice that seemed to rise from the ground around him. It was like Gunnlaugur's, only deeper and more throatily resonant. After-echoes of the words hung amid the spores, whispering on in a faint chorus of weary mockery.

'Show yourself,' snarled Váltyr, keeping his blade raised.

'And it is a question to be asked,' slurred the voice, 'what valour still resides with the Emperor's lapdogs?'

The curtains of darkness seemed to sigh aside. A brume of ash and filth shuddered away, exposing a lone warrior standing beneath the shadow of the ruins.

As soon as Váltyr laid eyes on him his hearts started thumping. Kill-urge surged through his bloodstream, spiking his muscles. His pupils dilated under his helm and his lips pulled back in a fang-thick sneer.

'Contact,' he voxed over the pack-wide channel. 'Ighala Gate. One got past you, Skullhewer.'

He had no time for any more.

The Plague Marine lumbered closer, emerging from the darkness like a sepulchral leviathan hauling clear of the deeps.

The Traitor was huge, far taller and broader even than Olgeir. His armour might once have been Terminator plate, though the centuries had ravaged, swelled and altered it. The plates had fused together and thickened, merging into a leathery hide of scaly, semi-jointed segments. Raw flesh pushed and burst through the remaining gaps, bleached and glistening like fat. A long cavity ran across the monster's torso exposing glossy loops of entrails within. Every surface was crusted with a bizarre mix of rust patches and angry lesions, as if the substances had fused halfway between organic and inorganic matter and become prone to the infections of both.

The creature strode through the rubble on two massive cloven hooves, and each cumbersome tread sank deep into the earth below. Two immense fists carried thick-bladed cleavers. One blade ran with a constant drip-feed of blood; the other slopped viscous trails of pus. Cloaks of black-bellied insects swirled around the blades like shrouds. Two long tusks curved out from the creature's distended jawline, each one wet with thin layers of saliva. A single eye sat amid a domed helm, glowing green through a jagged frame of broken ceramite.

Váltyr recognised the profile. This was the monster that had been in de Chatelaine's vid-footage.

'We had not expected Wolves here,' the Traitor said. Just as the witch in the ravine had done, he sounded only marginally interested. 'Your presence, though, makes this turgid exercise just a little more consequential.'

Váltyr held his ground. He wondered how long it would be before Gunnlaugur could respond to the summons. He guessed that the Death Guard champion far outmatched him. He might outmatch all of them.

'We were fated to be here,' said Váltyr calmly. He let his muscles fall into their habitual loose state of readiness. He would need to be as fast as he had ever been. *Holdbítr* trembled momentarily in his grip, like a stallion eager for the hunt. 'We were fated to halt this.'

'Perhaps,' said the creature, coming to a halt a few metres before Váltyr. He loomed above him, bloated and immense. 'You were always fatalistic souls.'

Váltyr studied his enemy closely, trying to spy weaknesses in its twisted armour.

'Know this,' he said proudly, seeing none. 'I am called *sverdhjera* of Járnhamar. A thousand souls have been extinguished by my blade. When you greet your gods in the cold tombs of Hel, tell them Váltyr of Fenris was the one that ended you.'

The monster bowed.

'An honour, Váltyr of Fenris,' he said, with no obvious irony. 'To return the courtesy, I am named Thorslax the Blighted, exalted of the plague-host of the Traveller. I have walked both mortal and immortal planes since the days when your ruddy-cheeked primarch drank oaths to the Throne of Terra and pretended to be more savage than he was. I too have killed more men than I could ever count.' The creature chuckled mordantly. 'It grows tedious, after a time. Everything grows tedious. That is the curse of this war. I long for it to be over.'

He raised his twin cleavers and they shed their gruesome coating like runnels in a storm.

'And it *will* be over, Space Wolf,' he said. 'Do you not guess what is happening here? This is the beginning, the first stirrings of the plague that will consume the galaxy. You cannot stop it now. It starts here, and on a hundred other worlds, but it will all end in Cadia. All that remains for you is the slow death that follows the sickness. You have all been sick for too long. Let us end the agony.'

Váltyr allowed the abomination to speak. He had heard such screeds before and paid the detail little heed.

'Finished?' he asked, assuming the stance, bringing *holdbítr* into guard. 'Then make the first move.' He smiled coldly, feeling the first pulses of joy in his lethal craft. 'I always allow my prey the first move.'

CHAPTER TWENTY-ONE

Ingvar tore through the night, veering between the ruins at full tilt. Since passing under the Ighala Gate and breaking into the lower city he'd only had one destination in mind. It reared above the houses as it always had done, vast and forbidding, striking up into the roiling clouds like a three-pronged claw.

The streets belonged to the enemy now. The serried tides of the damned crawled up through the burning remnants of what had once been Hjec Aleja's main urban zone. The main body of the enemy host marched relentlessly towards the Ighala Gate, driving in huge columns through the devastation. Fringe detachments peeled off from the main assault, loping through the wavering firelight and looking for defenders still breathing under the rubble.

Ingvar skirted around all of that, hugging the shadows and keeping to the lesser paths, breaking into combat only when he had to. When it came, his fights were quick and brutal – a dozen precision strikes from the spitting edge of *dausvjer* leaving the burst corpses of the damned lying face-up in the gutter.

Only as he neared the cathedral did the volume of enemy troops increase again. They had swarmed across the supplicants' courtyards and broken through the main doorway. Most of them were glass-eyed, shabby plague-bearers, still clad in the rags of their old Shakeh uniforms, but some, the ones who had landed from the plague-ships, were more heavily mutated, their outlines now only faintly human.

They didn't see him coming, occupied as they were with trying to push inside the cathedral to join the slaughter.

Given space in which to work, Ingvar picked up speed, leaping over the smoking remains of a gun emplacement and burning through into the courtyard beyond.

'*Fenrys!*' he roared, and his hoarse voice rang out into the night.

Taken by surprise, the enemy troops scattered before him. Only the most corrupted, those whose minds had been turned into slurry by the long, numbing years under the sway of dark gods, had the will to turn and fight.

It did them no good. Ingvar ripped through them, unleashing the full flood of his fury for the first time since boarding the plague-ship. He whirled around, punching a broad furrow into the midst of the crowds, breaking ribcages, cutting through paunches and snapping scrawny necks. *Dausvjer's* energy field blazed, throwing electric-blue sparks dancing across the morass of slack-skinned, pox-gnawed bodies.

He hewed a bloody path towards the gates, his progress barely slowed by the knots of fighters around him. More of them ran, scampering back into the shadows to huddle out of sight of his wrath; those that remained died quickly. As he passed under the shadow of the cathedral's ornate frontage, Ingvar kicked the last of them aside and crashed headlong through what remained of the doors.

The scene inside the nave was one of rampant desecration. Sacred icons had been ripped down and trampled over. Graven images of primarchs and cardinals had been cast to the floor, shattering against the marble. Smears of vomit and excreta were strewn over the walls, belched up by obscene, obese mutants with tiny piggish eyes and orbicular bellies. Shakeh's regimental standards had all been shredded and fires had been started all along the aisles, kindled on the flesh and fabric of the slain and catching on the timber of candle-racks and portrait frames.

Mutants ran amok, careening over upturned fonts and altars, shrieking, spitting and laughing in high, gurgling voices. Insects swarmed noisily over the growing pits of filth, scuttling freely across the stone, spilling from the eye-sockets of corpses and bursting from their stomachs.

Only at the high altar was there still a flicker of resistance. The banner of the Wounded Heart had been nailed to the pillar behind the dais, just under the baroque sculpture of the Emperor defeating Horus. It was riddled with bullet-holes and charred around the edges, but the black and red sigil could still be made out. Heaps of bodies, the majority of them mutated or swollen with disease, piled up high on every side, a testament to the tenacity of the defenders' last stand.

'For the Allfather!' Ingvar bellowed. His voice surged up into the vaults, echoing in the dark spaces and resounding down the long aisles.

The mutants turned from their slaughter. When they saw him coming – crackling with the tight burn of his energy weapon, his lenses blazing red like fresh-cut heartsblood, his massive armour plates smeared with the liquid remains of their fallen comrades – they broke into a feral mass of shrieking. They surged towards him in a tumbling, crashing wave, ignited into sudden terror, hatred and bloodlust.

Ingvar thundered into them, his blade whipping around him in wide sweeps. His body arched and swayed as he moved, thrown into a whirl of power and poise. *Dausvjer* ceased to be a weapon and became a part of him, an extension of the killing potential he'd unleashed. It rose and fell, danced and flickered, tearing up rotten flesh and carving through atrophied bones. He crunched, stabbed, crushed and shattered, throwing the tattered remains of the slain away before piling into the wavering throngs that remained.

The gangs of mutants and cultists held firm while their numbers remained, but as he sliced through their ranks their green eyes began to waver. Fear shuddered through them like a wave, and the weakest began to peel away and slink back down the long nave.

'Flee while you can!' cried Ingvar, cutting more down with every two-handed swipe of his rune-sword. '*Death* has come among you!'

The rump of the horde broke then, finally giving up on the prize of the altar and scampering away from the unleashed kill-machine in their midst. Ingvar pursued the greatest of them, a needle-toothed monster with oyster-grey skin and flapping, barbed hands, plunging *dausvjer* into its neck and ripping it out in a grisly flourish. He spun round, primed for more slaying, only to see the rest racing away from him.

He switched weapons, pulling his bolter from its holster and firing one-handed. Shells sprayed across the nave, exploding and splintering against pillars and thudding wetly into the backs of the retreating horrors. Dozens fell under that ear-splitting barrage, adding to the heaps of mouldering bodies already staining the floor.

The barrage only stopped when the last of them had fallen. Ingvar released the trigger and the cathedral slowly fell silent. The results of his epic butchery stretched away from him – rank upon rank of twitching limbs, carpeting the marble in a melange of sagging, clotting meat.

By then he was close to the altar. He strode slowly towards it, scanning the corpses at his feet for any yet living. He saw the bloodied uniforms of Shakeh Guardsmen mingled among the sore-raddled limbs of the damned, locked together in death as they had been in combat. It looked like they had held their positions until their ammunition had run out, resorting at the last to their knives, their lasgun-butts, their fists.

The bodies of five Battle Sisters were slumped amongst the slain, each one lying a little further up the steps of the dais. They had fallen back as far as they could, their empty flamers and bolters discarded on the way. Each of them was surrounded by a knot of corpses. They had killed dozens upon dozens; an honourable tally, one that reflected credit to their order.

Ingvar waded grimly onwards, seeking the one he knew would be there, whose fate it had been to defend her domain to the last. When he saw her at last, half buried under the grey hands of a fly-masked mutant, he thought she was dead. Her helm was gone and her dark skin was a mess of lacerations.

Ingvar crouched down, lifting the weight of her dead assailant from her and pushing it away. It was then that she drew in a faint breath. Her eyes flickered open, bleary at first but then clarifying.

Bajola looked up at him. She smiled.

'Your fate,' she croaked. 'To be here.'

Ingvar nodded, clearing more space around them, assessing the damage. Her breastplate had been punctured in three places. A jagged shard of iron protruded from a gash under her ribcage. Blood still oozed from the wound, pooling on the stone in thick dark slops. She didn't have long.

'As it was yours,' he replied, but his voice was bleak.

Hafloí descended into the bowels of the Halicon, his limbs throbbing. The pain still radiating across his body was an embarrassment, a constant reminder of the dark power that had shut him down so contemptuously.

Even after his return to combat he knew he was not yet himself again. The weight of the witch's magick still plagued him, needling away at him like the memory of failure.

As he passed through the long trains of tunnels and twisting corridors, the ceiling-mounted lumens flickering as the big wall guns boomed, he was struck by the almost complete emptiness inside the citadel. The few remaining civilians too old or young to fight huddled inside bunkers dotted around the upper city. Everyone else manned the inner walls or the snaking battlements of the citadel. He'd walked past teenagers tottering under the weight of bolt-round cases, old women working in gangs to carry the bodies of the wounded to the field hospitals set up in chapels.

Once Hafloí might have felt contempt for that effort, but no longer. The mortals were making as much of a fight of it as they could. He'd seen the respect that Olgeir had for them and that had rubbed off on him a little. Perhaps he was growing up at last.

He kept moving, removing his helm as he went. Only then did he notice the damage done to his comms array. It looked burned out, eaten away by some stray gobbet of acid.

Hafloí smiled. Having some time to himself would be no hardship. Given what he intended to do, he might have been tempted to shut down the incoming feed in any case.

He looked down the long passage leading towards the apothecarion where he knew Baldr and Ingvár waited for him. The lumens along there were very dim, as if some localised power drain had taken the area grid down. He listened carefully.

No sounds at all; just the dim, ever-present roar of the battle taking place outside the walls.

He hesitated for a moment, doubting himself right at the last.

It would be easier to do what he'd been ordered to do. He certainly owed it to Baldr, not least for saving his life in the ravines, and Gunnlaugur's orders had been clear enough. The Gyrfalkon's blade was second only to Váltyr's in deadliness – it was needed on the walls.

So he almost did it. Hafloí nearly went on down to the medicae bays to take up his place watching over the stricken Fjolnir. Only at the last moment did he exhale his defiance, shake his head and ruffle his slicked-down hair, restoring its rust-orange spikiness.

He had never been good at following orders. The day would come when that rebelliousness was curbed, but it had not arrived yet. Battle called, and he intended to be a part of it.

Working hard to suppress a mischievous smirk, Hafloí turned on his heel and strode off in the opposite direction.

'So close,' he muttered to himself, disbelieving, now looking forward to more of the action that made his blood burn and his hearts pump. 'Really. I nearly did what they told me to. Blood of Russ, what am I turning *into*?'

Váltyr moved with all the perfection of his long training. His body flowed like water, propelled further by his armour, darting and wheeling with a velocity that belied his ceramite-heavy bulk. *Holdbítr* snaked around him, flashing in the firelight, the blade blurring with speed.

His opponent was not fast. Thorslax moved like his arms were weighed down by lead chains. His body swung around cumbersomely, sloughed in the bloody mud that sucked at his hooves. His twin cleavers were hurled about, seemingly at random, with careless, ill-aimed strokes. The stinking cloud of spores and insects spiralled around him, drifting in the wake of the blades.

For all that, Váltyr's rune-wound blade made little impact on the monster's hide. Thorslax barely tried to evade the strokes. He angled his huge body into the path of them, gurgling with delight whenever Váltyr managed to slant a cut in.

'Well *done*,' he would chortle. 'Very quick. Very nice.'

Váltyr kept his head. He worked methodically, avoiding the trajectories of the cleavers, staying close to his enemy and seeking the vulnerable spot. Despite unbroken hours of combat he felt alert and poised.

His foe's almost cheerful boredom was something he had encountered before. The Death Guard had learned to revel in their degradation. If some small part of them retained a sense of horror at what physical depths their primarch's treachery had forced on them, then it was deeply buried under layers of superficial contentment. They had ceased to suffer under the onslaught of the diseases that ravaged and wasted their sinews; they had *become* those diseases.

That no longer appalled him. It didn't enrage him. Váltyr was not a hot-blood like his brothers; he sought a way to use it, to lever the knowledge against the creature he faced. There would be a weakness; there was always a weakness.

Thorslax took a heavy stride forwards, his whole body shuddering as the hoof landed. His swollen arms flailed as he hurled the bloody cleaver in at Váltyr's shoulder. Váltyr ducked away, leaning out of danger before plunging in again, aiming his blade at Thorslax's gut-spilling stomach. The point punched deep, sliding between nests of polyps, doing no damage that he could see.

Váltyr wrenched it clear just as the pus-dripping cleaver hammered down. He spun out of the encounter, feeling the metal's edge hiss past his shoulder guards. Then he was back in tight, dancing through more heavy blows, probing for some way to do damage.

'So can you hold me here until your brothers arrive?' mused Thorslax, his voice a moist drawl. His single eye glanced up at the distant bridge, then back down. 'And even then, would it help you?'

Váltyr redoubled the flurry of strikes. As fast as he worked, Thorslax's defence responded. Though his individual movements were slow, the Blighted seemed able to anticipate what he was going to do, as if part of his soul somehow existed fractionally ahead of time.

Despite that he almost connected with a blistering sideways swipe, a blow that would have surely sliced Thorslax's chest-cabling away, but the bloody cleaver jammed down, clashing with *holdbítr* in a shower of sparks.

'Fast,' Thorslax observed appreciatively. 'You're really very good. Were I younger I would toy with you for longer.'

Váltyr charged back in, hauling his blade around two-handed, hacking at the creature's implacable defence. His blade bounced from Thorslax's hide, barely scratching the corrupted flesh-plates. The impact rocked him, though; it pushed the creature back down the slope, forcing him to use his weapons in defence.

'But I am not younger,' Thorslax remarked. 'I am *so* old. And you have become boring.'

Suddenly, his movements changed. His fists flew out, far faster than before. Váltyr saw the change and adjusted, bringing his blade into guard. The metal connected with a radial shudder, sending Váltyr rocking backwards. The green light bleeding from Thorslax's eye-socket flared. He seemed to grow even larger, swelling and bursting with grotesque, bulging growths. The swarm of flies reared up over him like a wind-whipped cloak.

Váltyr didn't flinch. He corrected his stance and brought his blade round for the parry, twisting the metal before him in a tight, glittering curve. Thorslax bore down, loosing a torrent of cleaver-strikes in quick succession. Váltyr parried the first few but the rain continued, flying in with deadening force. The impact was incredible – jarring, dense blows that cracked the ground beneath them and sent the rubble skittering.

Thorslax grunted. He sounded surprised.

'Very good,' he murmured, pressing the attack. 'Really very good.'

But then one got through – a cleaver thunked into Váltyr's breastplate, biting through the armour plate and deep into the flesh beneath. Váltyr twisted away, ignoring the pain and keeping *holdbítr* moving.

The wound unbalanced him, though. His left shoulder fell, opening up a gap. Thorslax pounced, hurling the pus-drenched blade in hard. It connected with Váltyr's neck, cutting deep and severing the shielding under his helm.

Váltyr's vision went black. He pressed forwards, feeling his hands go numb but still seeking the elusive way through. Blood ran down his breastplate, cascading across the runes graven across his chest and sinking into the channels.

Thorslax had stopped talking by then. He was fighting hard, wheezing through his rusty vox-grille, concentrating furiously. His cleavers, now both dripping with Váltyr's own blood, flew up and down, hacking and chopping. Both fighters landed blows, and for the first time Váltyr's strokes seemed to hurt. Each of them piled on the pain, locked together in a brutal close-range dance of hew and counter-hew.

'Enough!' Thorslax cried, raising both fists up and slamming them down on Váltyr's reeling defence.

Váltyr got his sword up just in time, bracing the blade against the impact, but his strength was gone. *Holdbítr* broke asunder with a hard clap like thunder, its rune-strength broken. Thorslax's cleavers plunged down, burying themselves deep into Váltyr's chest and puncturing both hearts. The monster then ripped them out, dragging trails of blood and flesh with them.

Váltyr stayed on his feet for a few moments more, his chest torn open, his arms limp. His vision was gone. The pain had left him, replaced by a cold nimbus that raced up his limbs towards his brain.

Thorslax withdrew without saying another word, already turning to face new enemies. Dimly, as if from a long way off, Váltyr could hear the battle-cries of Gunnlaugur closing in, as familiar to him as his own voice. He'd heard that cry across the war-torn continents of a hundred worlds. He could hear Olgeir's cries as well, and Jorundur's. The pack had arrived.

He collapsed to his knees, watching his lifeblood drain from him. His shattered sword, the weapon he had carried for over a century and whose soul he had come to know better than any living man's, lay before him in the gravel.

None shall wield it but me, he thought with a final, grim satisfaction, seeing how irreparably the sword had been destroyed.

They had died together. That, at least, was fitting.

Then, his consciousness draining away into darkness, Váltyr toppled forwards, crashing atop the shards of his beloved *holdbítr*, and moved no more.

Ingvar held Bajola's broken body carefully. She felt impossibly fragile. He could feel her heart beating, shallow and fluttering like that of a trapped bird.

Her skin was grey. The ebony richness of it had faded and it looked matt and grainy in the gloom.

'They will come back soon,' she warned.

'When they do, I will kill them.'

Bajola nodded wearily. 'That is what you excel at.'

'Of course. Someone has to.'

Bajola's eyes momentarily lost focus and her head lolled. She recovered, but the spirit was draining out of her quickly.

'You said you'd tell me what your name meant,' she said.

'Now?'

Bajola nodded.

'Gunnlaugur gave it to me,' Ingvar said, speaking softly, feeling like he was wasting precious time. 'He called me that on the eve of my departure from the home world. He decreed it would be my pack name, since I had no other.'

Ingvar remembered the way Gunnlaugur had been then: wounded by his decision to leave even though he'd striven to hide it. A strange look had lit up Gunnlaugur's eyes in those last days. Unhappiness, certainly, but something else. Envy, perhaps.

'And by that he wished to bind you to him,' said Bajola.

Ingvar paused, surprised that she knew so much of their ways.

'The gyrfalcon always comes back,' he said. 'It ranges far but always returns. That was what he was telling me, that I had to return.'

Bajola looked at him with an indulgent smile on her dying face.

'Oh, Ingvar,' she said. 'You did return, and it has not given you what you hoped for.' She swallowed painfully. 'But at least you killed with honour here. That is why you were bred. Or do you choose?'

'Choose?'

She swallowed again. Blood collected on her lips.

'To be what you are, or to be mortal.'

It was so long ago. He had been selected when near death, pulled from the ice by the Priest with the wolf-mask. After that, all he remembered was pain, instruction, and fear.

'I do not think so,' he said.

Bajola's lids looked heavy.

'I chose,' she said. 'I could have been anything. A scholar. A diplomat. I excelled at it all. But I chose the Sisterhood. Why was that? At times I think I wasted myself. Or maybe I didn't choose at all. Maybe it was my... What do you call it? Wyrd.'

Ingvar felt her heartbeat grow weaker as he held her. Time was running out.

'Why did you destroy the archives?' he asked.

By then Bajola was too weak to bother hiding the truth.

'Secrets,' she said.

'Of your Order?'

'No, not this one.' She tried to lift her head. Ingvar lowered his. He could smell the copper of blood on her neck and face. 'Pointless, no? We were always destined to die here. But old habits. They made us thorough. Completeness.'

Her voice got fainter with every breath. Ingvar had to crane his neck to hear the words over the distant crackle of flames.

'Hjortur's name was stored in there. On a list. A kill-list. A list of those to be killed.'

She was beginning to ramble.

'Hjortur was killed by greenskins,' said Ingvar gently.

'No,' said Bajola, smiling again. 'No, he wasn't. He was killed by the Fulcrum.'

'The what?'

Bajola's face creased into a mask of concentration. She was slipping away. Every breath she took added to the trickle of blood that ran down her chin.

'Look up,' she rasped.

Ingvar did so. The golden mask of the Emperor stared back down at him. Its face was cherubic, surrounded by a spiked halo. The expression on the mask was oddly mournful.

'Their mark has been here all along,' said Bajola. Wincing from the pain, she reached down to her weapon belt and withdrew a small golden bauble. She pressed it into Ingvar's hand. When he looked down at it, he saw a miniature facsimile of the golden mask – a thumb-sized cherub-face ringed with spikes.

'Do you really want to know this truth, *Fenryka*?' she asked, teasingly using Juvykka as if born to it. 'You will be honour-sworn to avenge him, will you not?'

Ingvar said nothing. The golden-faced cherub smiled stupidly at him, its metallic surface glinting in the firelight.

'You think you know so much,' she said, as mockingly as her frailty would allow. 'You are the thinker among them, the one who has learned to doubt. You, out of all your brutal brothers, might understand that some wars never show themselves.'

Ingvar felt frustration rise within him. He needed her to speak plainly, but in her delirium she was drifting into incoherence.

'I didn't want you here,' she mumbled. 'I argued against it. The Adulators posed no problem; they were dutiful and unimaginative. But Wolves? On Ras Shakeh?'

Bajola let slip a bitter laugh, and more blood bubbled up between her lips.

'Once that argument failed, I should have destroyed the archive. I don't know why I didn't.'

Ingvar caught the first faint sounds of enemy troops creeping back towards them. It would not be long before they forgot their fear and re-entered the nave.

'I cannot save you, Sister,' he said softly. 'But you can make our meeting on this world worth something. Tell me what you know.'

Bajola looked up at him. Her deep brown eyes moistened. Some resolve returned.

'More of you will die,' she said. 'They are coming for you now, and they will never stop. They will never tire, never forget. You will not even know you are being hunted. Killed by greenskins, lost in the warp, turned to darkness – those are the stories that will find their way back to Fenris. You make too many enemies, Space Wolf.'

An explosion went off within a few hundred metres of their position. The pillars around them shuddered. The dull thud of mutant feet falling echoed out across the nave, still distant but circling closer.

'Tell me,' growled Ingvar, feeling her go limp in his hands, growing impatient with the evasion.

Bajola smiled at him, her eyes losing their focus and growing dim.

'I did tell you,' she croaked loosely. 'The *Fulcrum*, Gyrfalkon. Take the name, take the golden face. Use them.'

She tried to lift her hand and failed. Her breathing slowed to nothing.

'Against my judgement, I liked you,' she said, her voice little more than an expiring sigh. 'I hope you survive.'

Then her body stiffened, going taut. Her spine arched, holding in place for a heartbeat.

She went slack, her mouth falling open.

Ingvar held her for a while longer, staring at her. The rest of the battle became an irrelevance. He felt as if he'd been on the cusp of something, prevented at the last by Bajola's intransigence, or perhaps just frustrated by time slipping away.

He opened the palm of his gauntlet and looked at the tiny golden face resting there. It gazed back at him, smiling benignly. It looked like any pilgrim's trinket: nothing special, nothing rare or valuable.

The Fulcrum.

It meant nothing.

Ingvar heard her last words echoing in his mind.

They are coming for you now, and they will never stop.

Who? Why?

You make too many enemies, Space Wolf.

The noise of boots rang down the nave. They had got close by then, edging forwards, hugging the walls.

Ingvar rose, lowering Bajola's head carefully to the stone. He placed the cherub's head safely in a clasped capsule at his belt. Only then did he turn, thumbing *dausvjer*'s energy field into luminosity. Ahead of him, perhaps twenty metres away, a crowd of cowled faces jostled against one another, their pale eyes shining in the dark. For once they looked scared, torn between a desire to kill and the knowledge of what they faced.

Ingvar started to walk towards them, swinging his blade lazily to free up his arm. His mind was still racing, trying to digest what Bajola had told him. The presence of plague-bearers in the cathedral was an irritation he could have done without.

'A bad time to take me on, filth,' he snarled, lowering his gaze and picking the first one to die. 'A *very* bad time.'

CHAPTER TWENTY-TWO

The lower city was gone, lost to the enemy, now little more than a haunt of unrestrained slaughter and madness. The last of the trenches had been breached and the hordes of mutants, cultists and pestilence-ridden foot soldiers tramped up from the depths, their cold eyes fixed on the summit. The Halicon citadel reared up above all of them, still inviolate despite the bruise-purple pall that swirled above it, its flanks lit a dull crimson by the wavering light of a thousand fires. Down from the citadel's extravagant battlements stood the precarious ring of the inner walls, still held by the city's defenders. The battered Ighala Gate endured at the centre of that defensive line, bursting with anti-infantry weaponry that flashed and burned into the spore-heavy night.

If the advance had been quicker the gate might already have fallen. As it was the hosts of plague-damned still moved slowly, trudging up through smouldering ruins with their stumbling, ill-directed gaits. Hundreds of them had drifted into the shadows, distracted by isolated pockets of survivors and the prospect of feasting on fresh flesh. Others had succumbed to the virulent contagion that coursed through their veins, collapsing to the ground as their stomachs burst asunder or their hearts gave out. The gifts of the Plaguefather were capricious things, as likely to curse as they were to bless.

So it was that in answering Váltyr's call, Gunnlaugur was able to outpace the closing circle of invaders and sprint clear of the advancing battlefront. Olgeir, fresh from a hard-fought victory over the third Plague Marine down by the outer perimeter, joined him in the chase. His armour had taken heavy damage during the encounter and he'd discarded his heavy bolter.

'Tough kill?' asked Gunnlaugur, running heavily.

'They always are,' spat Olgeir, working hard to keep up. 'Pox-ridden bastards.'

Jorundur joined up with them as they neared the cleared wasteland before the Ighala crossing.

'So what is this?' the Old Dog demanded, his strained voice betraying a rare tightness. 'Did he say?'

Gunnlaugur said nothing but ran hard, his hearts thumping viciously.

One got past you, Skullhewer.

Váltyr's voice had been almost resigned over the comm; whatever it was that had broken ranks and pushed ahead to the bridge had knocked the kill-relish out of him. That was almost certainly bad.

'I see it!' roared Olgeir, his voice suddenly thick with kill-urge.

The landscape of ruins gave way before them, opening out into the charred and desolate wasteland just within sight of the bridge. Directly ahead of them, out on the trawled mounds of debris, was the object of Váltyr's summons – a vast and engorged champion in a distended mockery of Terminator plate. He must have teleported ahead of the rest of his sluggish minions, aiming to break the defence at the gates before the defenders had time to rally behind them.

An arrogant decision, one that spoke of misplaced confidence.

'*Fenrys Hjolda!*' thundered Gunnlaugur, swinging *skulbrotsjór* wildly around him as he tore up the slope.

Olgeir and Jorundur joined in the chorus, hurling battle-challenges out like berserks of the Old Ice. They could all see Váltyr being hammered backwards, his armour taking heavy damage from repeated cleaver impacts.

For all their speed, for all their blistering rage, they arrived too late. As Gunnlaugur sped into contact, he could only watch as Váltyr's blade was broken and the *sverdhjera*'s chest was ripped open.

An explosion of grief surged up from his breast. Black fury blazed out of him, kindled in the furnace of his pumping hearts and emerging as a strangled roar of revulsion. Gunnlaugur charged towards the monster like a Rhino careering along at full tilt, lost in a maelstrom of horror and loosed ferocity.

Thorslax turned slowly to face him, his body moving with ponderous clumsiness. His single glowing eye stared down at them, spearing through the murk of the seamy night.

'*More* of you,' he murmured.

The three Wolves hit him almost in unison, crashing into combat with the force of a hurricane, limbs tearing, blades flashing. All four warriors clashed under the lightning-laced storm clouds: one enormous and reeking with millennial corruption, three as vital and vivid as sun-dazzled snow. They ripped into a spinning, crashing cacophony of fearsome blows, each strike landing with the power to crush bone, to dent armour, to pulverise flesh.

Gunnlaugur was ahead of the others by a hair's breadth, his hammer scything imperiously. Olgeir was next, his short blade spiralling, clasped tight in both burly hands. Jorundur brought up the rear, adding his axe-head to the driving wall of steel.

Thorslax was hurled backwards in the face of that coordinated mass. His arms pumped like the pistons of a great war engine, parrying the furious rate of incoming strikes and hitting back with punching cleaver-blows of his own.

Though outnumbered and off guard, his huge bulk gave him a telling advantage. His strength, like all of his kind, was virtually infinite. He absorbed a whole barrage of blows, any one of which would have ended a lesser warrior. *Skulbrotsjór* crashed into his leathery armour plates, driving in the warped ceramite but not breaking it. The Wolves' blades bit deep but did not draw blood. Thorslax was pummelled, battered, beaten back – but not wounded.

As the shock of the first assault was absorbed, Thorslax began to reassert himself. His cleavers cycled with greater intent – not just in defence, but into the attack. He towered above his assailants, and began to use his greater heft and reach. Jorundur was the first to be thrown out of the attack, his right shoulder guard gouged open.

'*Fara tíl Hel, svikari!*' bellowed Gunnlaugur, rolling onwards, hauling *skulbrotsjór* in monstrous arcs. The air seemed to ignite in the wake of the blazing hammerhead. His massive body was a blur of wanton movement. He swung heavily before piling in deep, every gesture loaded with lethal intent. He and Olgeir pressed on, each working seamlessly around the other.

Thorslax uttered no words. He laboured hard at the heart of the breaking storm, striving not to be overcome by it. Gunnlaugur landed a searing crack on his turning spine, causing him to roar out loud. Olgeir leapt into a rare gap in his defence, chopping down deep into his thigh, finally producing a jet of oil-black blood from the wound. Jorundur regained his feet and staggered back into range, his axe held ready.

For all their skill, though, for all their strength, Váltyr's judgement had been right. Thorslax was a foe beyond them. His body had been ruined and changed by the slow arts of the Eye, fused with his living armour and shot through with the undiluted virulence of the Plaguefather. His hearts beat with the slow, grinding rhythm of millennia and his blood coursed with the slurry of infinite mutation. No mortal weapon, no matter how skilfully wielded, could break through the aegis of foulness that swept around him, knitting together his rotten thews and animating his disease-riddled organs.

He was an avatar of the plague, suffused with all its poisons and its delights, as indomitable as mortality, as invincible as the dragging entropy that wearied all living things.

He was despair. He was fatigue. He was the essence of mortality in all its putrid, failing imperfection.

Thorslax punched out, throwing Olgeir clear, sending the huge warrior grinding into the rubble on his back. Then the cleavers whirled, beating Jorundur a second time. The Old Dog fell to his knees, clutching at his mangled shoulder.

For a little while longer Gunnlaugur and Thorslax fought on alone, hammer and cleaver battering away at one another, splintering armour and denting metal. The Wolf Guard fought with all the bull-hearted resolve of his conditioning, giving no quarter, powering on after his prey with both speed and power. When *skulbrotsjór* made contact, the sharp crack of the energy field discharging was like the snap of lightning forking down from the heavens; when Thorslax's cleavers connected, the dull boom was like Arjac's hammerhead striking the iron anvil. The two of them like gods duelling at the fire-wreathed end of the universe, outstripping all other powers in their extravagant, unrestrained wrath.

As they hacked and hewed at one another, unnoticed by any of them, the city's ruins behind them slowly filled with green points of light. Mutants limped out of the gloom, their gas masks bulging and deflating as they drew in the airborne miasma. They hung back amid the cover of the shattered rockcrete, unwilling to break cover entirely. With every passing second, though, more of them gathered in the shadows. The vanguard of the enemy host had caught up with its standard bearer.

Olgeir scrambled to his knees, cursing. Jorundur rose more slowly, his armour covered in blood. They started to limp back into range, both moving stiffly.

Neither of them was unable to prevent the strike that floored Gunnlaugur. Thorslax lashed round with uncharacteristic speed, catching the Wolf Guard in the throat with the blunt edge of his blood-cleaver. Gunnlaugur, off balance and moving too late, was hurled clear of the bulbous mutant and sent sailing through the air in a bloody swathe, his limbs splayed. Thorslax lumbered after him, striding across the scorched earth like a vengeful Titan.

'And so it ends,' he slurred.

The pack had thrown everything it had at him, and had still come up short. Thorslax was barely wounded; all three Wolves were prone, exhausted and bleeding. The champion of Mortarion stalked across to Gunnlaugur for the kill, his throaty voice wheezing from exertion.

He raised his cleavers, holding them both high, but then the guttural noises died in his calloused throat. Ahead of them all, dim at first under the walls of the besieged upper city, something had broken across the tortured landscape, lighting up the earth beneath it with a sick smear of witchlight. A new fire burned brightly in the night, though its flames were lurid rather than vivid.

As Thorslax watched, his interest suddenly piqued, a lone figure swept down from the bridge towards them, his limbs dark against the raging backdrop of illumination.

Thorslax looked dumbstruck. Then, as the strange warrior drew closer, he relaxed, and a moisture-damp laugh finally broke from his cracked lips. The fire-cloaked newcomer slowed down, striding awkwardly across the craters and ruins, swathed in a dirty corona of whipping green flame.

'Welcome, brother,' said Thorslax bowing in greeting. 'I see that our ranks are set to swell again.'

Gunnlaugur twisted round blearily, still reeling from the blow that had felled him. Olgeir and Jorundur did likewise.

Baldr stood before them, panting slurrily. Trails of saliva hung below his sore-mottled chin, trembling as his loose-jawed face stared out sightlessly into the night. Snaking lines of ether-force scurried across his marsh-grey armour. His eyes were pupil-less and blazed with a pale silver light. Swirling skeins of energy obscured his features, though the lesions clustering around his lips and eyes could still be made out. Silver flame spilled from the corners of his mouth, as if he were filled to overspilling with the blinding power of the warp. His clenched fists crackled and twisted with a growling aegis of witchlight.

'Brother!' cried Olgeir, his voice thick with surprise and horror. He staggered towards the flaming outline.

Baldr didn't turn to face him. He extended a fist in Olgeir's direction and a fork of diseased lightning, black-edged like tarnished steel, cracked into the big warrior's chest, throwing him back to the ground again. Olgeir landed awkwardly, his back arched in pain, flickers of lightning blistering and dancing across his battleplate.

Thorslax chuckled. 'A corrupted Son of Russ,' he murmured. 'Quite an achievement.'

He walked towards Baldr, stretching out his massive hand.

'My bro–' he began.

He never finished the sentence.

Baldr exploded. His fists swung around and thrust out before him. Blazing arcs of black-edged lightning leapt out, latching on to Thorslax's neck and twisting into it like an electric current. The Traitor froze, locked in place by columns of witchlight. His limbs went stiff; his cleavers dropped to the earth.

Baldr never said a word. The boiling clouds above him broke open and spears of the world's lightning, as green-tinged as the clouds of warp essence around his eyes, licked and flickered against his slime-crusted armour.

Thorslax tried to retreat, to pull away from the shimmering spikes that impaled him, but Baldr hauled him back, sending shards lancing into his enormous body. Dagger-edged flickers snaked under the Traitor's battle-plate, ripping it up and exposing blubber-pale flesh beneath. Thorslax's limbs jerked, pierced by glimmering lines of plague-green and warp-silver, locked down amid a nimbus of blazing energies, just as Baldr had been in the ravines.

The Traitor champion tried to fight it. As flakes fell from his armour, crisping and burning amid the veil of lightning, he tried to break free. He managed a single step, crying out from the effort as his huge, swollen leg swung through the fizzing electrical storm.

Baldr hardly seemed aware of what he was doing. His blazing, mono-chrome silver eyes glared wildly. His fists stayed extended, feeding on the lashing columns of tainted warp energy.

Thorslax held on for a moment longer, outstretched fingers trembling. Then, with a sick crack, his helm fell open, briefly exposing a twisted and blood-blotched face locked in a scream of unbearable agony. Pus-filled lesions burst apart, spewing their yellow contents across his blistering armour plates. His skin stripped away, melting and crisping as it was devoured. Cracks shot up his battleplate, latticing like atrophied bone. Fragments of it burst clear, shattered into dust by the raw ether-matter that coursed across and through it.

The silver fire consumed what was left, burning through raddled skin and metastasised tissue. Organs popped open, shedding greasy gouts of bile and plasma. Thorslax's screams died away into chokes as his throat was eaten away. His chest caved in, his limbs twisted and snapped, his eyeballs liquidised.

When the storm finally died out, all that remained at its centre were a few thick chunks of burned ceramite. Baldr finally let his hands drop, and the last pieces of Thorslax's war-plate toppled over, half buried in a heap of smoking, rotten meat-chunks.

For a few moments, no one moved. Baldr rocked back on his heels, his arms hanging limp, his unseeing eyes staring emptily. Olgeir remained on the ground, still transfixed with pain. The crowds of plague-mutants congregating in the shadows held their positions, seemingly uncertain whether to fall at Baldr's feet or flee from him.

Jorundur moved first, gingerly inching towards Baldr.

'No,' hissed Gunnlaugur, ignoring the blaze of pain under his shattered gorget as he moved. 'Do not approach him.'

Baldr seemed not to see either of them. His breathing was heavy and snagging.

Gunnlaugur kept his distance, taking up his thunder hammer carefully, watching Baldr the whole time. Conflicting intuitions ran through him. Part of him, driven by his warrior instincts, urged him to take on the abomination, to end it before it consumed them all. He knew he should have done it when he'd had the chance.

But it was futile. If Baldr – or whatever had taken over Baldr – was capable of ripping through the Traitor champion with such ease then the idea of *him* taking him down was ludicrous. The raw power coursing through Baldr's diseased limbs was a force beyond anything he'd seen before, save perhaps in a master of the elements like Njal Stormcaller.

So Gunnlaugur stayed where he was, his weapon held tightly, breathing hard, waiting to see what Baldr would do next.

He did not have to wait long. As the last remains of Thorslax smouldered down into embers, Baldr suddenly looked up. His silver-flamed eyes stared out, past Gunnlaugur, past Olgeir and Jorundur, out into the burning mass of ruins beyond.

Baldr threw his head back. He cried out once – a horrifying, shrieking skirl of inhuman pain – and kicked off again into a limping run. He swooped down the slope, arms hanging loose, reeling madly. Flickers of unholy fire streamed behind him. He looked like a deranged spectre of ice-myths, a fragment of old nightmares conjured up into the world of the living.

The mutants scattered before him, letting him plunge unmolested back into the depths of the lower city. Powerless to prevent him, Gunnlaugur watched him go. A few last scraps of silver witchlight glimmered for a while in the dark, before they too faded into nothing.

With Baldr's departure, the scene around them returned to one of empty desolation. Olgeir managed to drag himself back to his feet, though his every movement looked shot through with pain. Jorundur had been mauled.

'What in Hel was that?' grunted Olgeir, his clipped voice giving away his torment.

Gunnlaugur gazed in the direction Baldr had fled. Only then did he feel how hard his hearts were beating.

'I do not know,' he said. 'And answers will have to wait.'

With the departure of Baldr the enemy had started moving again. They crept out from under the eaves of empty hab-shells and up from the shadows of blast craters, edging into the open along a long, ragged line that stretched across the entire battlefront. First dozens, then hundreds, then thousands became visible, all trudging up the slope towards the Ighala Gate with the same mute determination they'd shown since the opening hours of the siege.

In the face of such numbers the Wolves fell back, crossing the strip of cleared wasteland and backing up towards the bridge. For the first time since the battle had started, Gunnlaugur felt weariness lying heavily on his limbs. Olgeir could barely walk and Jorundur was in poor shape too. They had fought for three days with almost no respite and the battle against the Traitor champion had nearly finished them all. Though Gunnlaugur still hefted his hammer, it now felt cripplingly heavy in his hands.

'A last stand on the bridge?' suggested Jorundur dryly. 'Worth a saga, perhaps.'

'We can hold them there,' growled Olgeir, optimistic as ever though his heavy breathing gave away his pain. 'I just need... a few moments.'

Gunnlaugur kept moving, watching the enemy spill out of the ruins and trudge up after them. A broad vanguard of mutants coalesced before him, driving out from the lower city and homing in on the walls. They never hurried, never speeded up, just murmured softly as they came, repeating the same inane whispering mantra they had always done. Gunnlaugur forced himself not to listen to it.

It was only then that he realised something about the situation was wrong. As he came under the shadow of the inner walls, falling back towards the bridge itself, he realised what it was – he shouldn't have been able to hear them at all.

'Why are the wall guns silent?' he asked, looking over his shoulder to the towering bastions of the Ighala gatehouse.

As soon as he looked up, the huge doors on the far side of the bridge began to open to the full, grinding heavily along on metal tracks. Out of the gap, marching in close-packed ranks, issued de Chatelaine's army.

They were the surviving regiments the canoness had held back for the final siege. Ranks of Guardsmen strode confidently out across the single span, all of them heavily swathed in chem-suits and hefting lasrifles. Among them marched a whole phalanx of Battle Sisters – heavily armoured Celestians with black cloaks and flamers, followed by the remaining Sororitas garrison. More Guardsmen followed in their wake, emerging in ordered ranks from the heart of the upper city.

Thousands had come – de Chatelaine was emptying the bastion. Battle standards swung up into place above them, displaying the Wounded Heart symbol proudly.

'Blood of Russ,' murmured Olgeir, watching the mortals draw up in assault formation on the near bank. 'They're breaking out.'

Jorundur started to laugh darkly.

'Excellent,' he said, buckling his axe to his belt and drawing his bolter. 'We'll all die together.'

At the sight of the sortie, Gunnlaugur felt his fatigue suddenly ebb. He strode closer to the bridge, seeking out the canoness.

De Chatelaine, her face masked behind her ebony helm and surrounded by her bodyguard, saw him first.

'Enough cowering!' she shouted, marching alongside her Sisters. Her voice was tight with determination. 'Now we end this, one way or another.'

Gunnlaugur raised his hammer in salute.

'So be it,' he called. 'Our blades together.'

He turned back, looking across the wastes to where the enemy was advancing. They far outnumbered the defenders but their progress now looked strangely directionless. They were moving across the wasteland by instinct, driven onwards by their urge to attack the living, but no longer held together by a single intelligence.

With the champion gone, their will looked to be fragile. For all that, their sheer volume remained intact. De Chatelaine's gamble was a perilous one.

Gunnlaugur gathered himself to his full height, reactivating *skulbrotsjór*'s disruptor in a sharp fizz of energy.

'Come, brothers!' he snarled, feeling the kill-urge kindle in him again. 'One last push.'

Jorundur fell in alongside.

'We'll need to hit them hard,' he said doubtfully.

'Aye,' said Olgeir, brandishing his blade and glowering down the slope. He looked like he was missing *sigrún*. 'We could really use some firepower now.'

As the words left his mouth, a thunderous, grinding roar suddenly broke out from behind them, briefly drowning the rush and crackle of the fires. The earth shook, rocked by the ignition of something massive far above them. Thousands of faces, defender and Traitor, turned in shock, gazing up to see what dreadful new engine of war had been unleashed on the city. Only the Wolves, as familiar with the sound of a Thunderhawk's engines as they were with their own voices, knew what had happened.

The gunship swooped down from the Halicon landing stages and flew low over the upper city, held precariously aloft on a dirty smudge of trailing smoke, its engines coughing sclerotically and its fuselage tilted heavily to one side. It lurched over the dividing gorge, barely clearing the inner walls and shedding huge gouts of flame from its labouring thrusters.

'The little *shit!*' breathed Jorundur, his voice heavy with outrage. 'He's taken *Vuokho!*'

Hafloí's voice crackled over the pack-wide comm.

'*Hjá*, flat-feet!' he crowed, laughing in triumph. 'Follow me down!'

Then *Vuokho*'s spine-mounted battle cannon boomed out, hurling a withering barrage of shells deep into the heart of the enemy ranks. As they exploded in a rolling pall of conflagration the gunship's bolters opened up, bursting earth and splintering flesh. The barrage only lasted seconds, but a Thunderhawk could unleash a frightening amount of ordnance in that time. The entire vanguard of the enemy disappeared under a rolling cloudbank of shattering armour and flying shrapnel.

Then something broke open on *Vuokho*'s battered undercarriage. The gunship slewed violently to the left, dropping like a stone.

'He's killing it!' shouted Jorundur, furious now. 'Gods of ice and iron, I'll *murder* him!'

Vuokho dived steeply, its guns still hammering, until it crashed right into the heart of the horde, crushing hundreds of fleeing figures beneath its bulk as it ploughed deep into the earth and skidded messily down the slope. Its engines raged away for a few seconds longer, hurling streamers of blue flame into what remained of the plague-bearer vanguard. Even after being grounded its wing-mounted bolters continued to judder away, cutting bloody swathes through the shell-shocked troops reeling away from it.

Gunnlaugur laughed ferociously, lofting his hammer high and roaring his humour to the heavens. It felt like a long time since his lungs had opened up in mirth.

'The whelp shows the way!' he thundered. 'Now *charge*, faithful of Ras Shakeh! *Break* them, and do not relent until you consign the last one of them to Hel!'

With a massed cheer the defenders surged down the slope towards the downed Thunderhawk. The mingled army of Guardsmen, Battle Sisters and Wolves swept across the ruinous landscape, on the front foot at last and with the light of vengeance in their eyes. Gunnlaugur and Olgeir burned along at the forefront, their wounds forgotten, their weapons swinging into position again.

For once, though, they were not the fastest. At the head of the army, moving faster than he had done in more than a hundred years of warfare, came Jorundur Kaerlborn, his limbs flailing and his battle-axe whirling around his head.

'He *killed* it!' he roared, his voice as baying and strident as all the unshackled hounds of Morkai. 'Blood of Russ, I'll *flay* him!'

CHAPTER TWENTY-THREE

Ingvar sped between burning buildings, pausing only to slay those unwary enough to stray into his path. The air around him was thick, a soup of toxins that lowered visibility to a few metres. Shells of hab-units loomed up out of the murk, their empty innards glowing.

None of the filth that tarried in the remains of the lower city was much of a threat to him – the biggest and most organised contingents of infantry had pushed ahead up the slopes, their eyes fixed on the summit. The scattered warbands that remained behind were sufficient to slow him down, though; they kept his blade busy in a series of bloody encounters. Ingvar had been fighting ever since leaving Bajola in the cathedral – fighting to get out of the despoiled nave, fighting to clear the courtyards, fighting to force a passage through the broken streets and rejoin the pack.

Only now was he making good progress. Something seemed to have rattled the enemy troops – they were scrambling up towards the citadel faster than ever, heedless of anything but the need to get out of the burning terraces of the lower city.

Ingvar ran along in their wake, loping purposively, keeping clear of the bigger detachments. He'd heard Váltyr's summons but after that the comm had died. A series of dull booms from beyond the Ighala Gate lit up the cloud-heavy sky, indicating something big had gone off, but otherwise he had little idea how matters stood at the inner wall.

He cleared the cathedral district and started powering up the main route to Ighala when he heard the first scream break out. The noise was a grotesque amalgam of human and unhuman, as if mortal throat-cords had been wound around a core of daemonic madness; more than one voice raised in terror – the plague-damned were shrieking in panic along with... something else.

Ingvar hesitated, listening carefully. He recognised some of the strains within them, and that familiarity chilled him.

Ahead of him ran the thoroughfare that led, after many twists and switchbacks, to the upper city. On either side of him sprawled the maze of alleyways that tangled out across the burning urban zone, all of them sunk into shadow even as the flames licked through the shattered rockcrete around them. The screams came from inside that labyrinth of derelict masonry, fractured and echoing like dancing tomb spectres.

After a moment of indecision, he veered off into the darkness. It didn't take him long to discover the origin of the terror. A narrow passageway zigzagged into a warren of smaller paths, all of them narrow and tightly overlooked. Those led in turn to an octagonal courtyard surrounded by many-storeyed hab-blocks.

In the centre of the courtyard rose a slender tower of dark stone, ringed with skull-pattern friezes and ribbed with iron bands. The pillared icon of the Adeptus Ministorum adorned the lintel of the main gate, surrounded by tattered scraps of old battle standards. Twin doors hung from their hinges, shattered and gaping. A glimmer of ghoulish green light spilled out from within. Corpses, all of them tortured by plague, littered the courtyard. Their exposed skin was scorched black.

Ingvar kicked his way through the bodies and plunged inside. He was immediately struck by the foul stench – a noisome cocktail of decay, excreta and stale sweat. More bodies lay across the stone floor, each one stinking of charred flesh.

The tower interior was gloomy, unlit except for slit windows that ran around the circular walls. An old altar lay in the centre covered with broken candle-stands, vestment caskets and censers. A spiral stairway hugged the stone wall, snaking up to the floor above. The glimmer came from up there.

Ingvar vaulted up the stairs, keeping *dausvjer* unsheathed and activated. Its electric-blue light burned brightly in the dark.

Four levels up, past a series of rooms streaked with bloodstains and thick with corpses, a final chamber opened up in front of him. It had once been the private sanctum of the Ministorum adepts and was strewn with their paraphernalia: robes, scrolls, thuribles, ceremonial staves, polished skull-pendants.

Ingvar barely noticed any of that. His eyes were drawn to the stricken figure cowering against the far wall, hunched over as if dry-retching. Flickers of corpse-gas rippled across dull grey armour plates, flickering eerily in the obscurity.

He froze. For a moment, his mind would not let him believe what he was seeing. Only slowly did he reconcile the data given him by his senses with what must have been the case.

It was Baldr. Or rather, it was the thing that had once been Baldr.

His armour had darkened, as if a shadow had been draped across it and had somehow fixed to the ceramite. Glints of pale light, insubstantial and wavering, leaked out of every joint and opening. Liquid dribbles of it ran across the curved plate like globules of mercury, slowly fading to black and withering away. The illumination was piercing but somehow unhealthy, as poisonous as gall.

Ingvar stayed still. He kept his blade in position; its dull hum was the only sound aside from Baldr's desperate gasping.

Baldr never looked up. His flaming eyes remained fixed on the floor in front of him. His sore-edged mouth looked twisted in pain.

When Ingvar finally spoke, as softly as he could, it felt like he was breaking some kind of sanctity.

'Brother,' he said, taking a single step towards him. 'Fjolnir.'

Baldr's head snapped up. His empty eyes stared directly at Ingvar. For a split second his face betrayed a childlike confusion, the innocent agony of a soul adrift and in pain.

Then it twisted into fury. Baldr's fists clenched and silver-black lightning kindled quickly on the gauntlets.

Ingvar interposed his blade, backing away.

'Do not do this, brother,' he warned. 'You are not yourself.'

Then Baldr *screamed*. At close range, the sound was even more horrifying than it had been before – a keening, pining, unearthly screech of fused souls grappling within a single body.

Baldr raised his fist and clenched it tight. Forks of vivid lightning shot out, slamming into *dausvjer* with the force of a stormfront hitting and sending stark white streaks of light wheeling across the walls.

Ingvar skidded backwards, expending all his strength just to keep his blade in the way. The rune-sword absorbed the inflow of ether-twisted matter, but keeping it in place was crushingly hard. Ingvar felt sweat burst out across his body, his legs bracing, his arms burning.

'Baldr!' he cried, sliding back against the far wall. 'Do you not know me?'

Baldr uncurled himself and straightened up, all the while pouring more fell energy into his lances of dark-edged lightning. The chamber filled with the stench of ozone and the hot crackle of warp discharge.

Ingvar felt his arms buckle. He set his jaw and pushed back, watching the blade before him shiver under the stress. He was forced down to his knees, his arms locked rigid, his whole body trembling with effort.

Baldr took a shaky step towards him, then another. His eyes spilled silver fire, and the residue ran down his blotchy cheeks like tears. He stared out crazily, drooling from an open mouth.

Ingvar felt his strength begin to fail. His hands struggled for grip on *dausvjer*'s hilt. Baldr staggered up to him, standing barely two metres away, his gauntlets still blazing. Lines of virulent force snapped and licked across the entire chamber, fizzing against the stone and leaving snaking weals.

Ingvar sank down further, his backpack pressed against stone. He could feel *dausvjer*'s grip worming free of his fingers, pushed towards him by the deadening force of the incoming barrage.

'*Brother*,' he hissed again, his teeth clenched. Baldr's face showed no recognition. It was unrecognisable from the cool, amiable face that he'd been so pleased to see again when he'd returned to Fenris.

We have always been shield-brothers, you and I. We shall be again.

Ingvar suddenly saw the exchange in the *drekkar* chamber, flashing across his mind's eye like a vid-pict.

It has a wyrd on it. It has protected me, and a part of me lives in it.

He took one hand from the sword hilt and grabbed at the soul-ward. Just as he lost control of the blade, he wrenched the totem out in front of him, thrusting the crow's skull in front of Baldr's tortured face.

The effect was immediate. The stream of warp lightning suddenly snuffed out, plunging the room back into darkness. The stink of ozone subsided.

Ingvar's blade fell from his hand, clattering emptily against the stone, blackened and burned out.

Ingvar held the *sálskjoldur* aloft, dangling it before Baldr's eyes. Baldr watched it spin, his face locked in something like recognition.

'This, at least, you know,' said Ingvar, breathing heavily.

A soul-ward, a fragment, a remnant, something to cling on to against the coming of Morkai.

'It *was* a part of you,' he said. 'It protected you, warding you against *maleficarum*. Your soul cleaves to it.'

The rune *sforja*, cut deep into the bone totem, flickered in the dim light. Its empty eye sockets rotated, catching the dull red glow of the fires raging outside the tower.

Baldr watched, transfixed. His arms slumped to his sides. His head hung lower. The silver flames on his body died out, guttering and flickering across his pockmarked skin.

What remained was grotesque. His skin, once tight and glare-tanned, had sagged. Deep bags hung under his red-rimmed eyes. Clusters of lesions and open boils nestled in every fold of flesh. His breath, which came in shallow gusts, was foul.

He tried to say something. His rheumy eyes flickered up to meet Ingvar's, then back down to the soul-ward. The blind fury was replaced by something else: confusion, recollection, pain.

'Bad... dreams,' he rasped, his voice dry.

Then he teetered, losing balance, toppling to his knees. Ingvar caught him and held him up.

Baldr looked up at him, his expression pathetically grateful. His face, criss-crossed with lines of blood, pus and drool, bore little resemblance to the clean visage of the past. It was still his, but only just.

'I had terrible dreams,' he slurred again.

Then his eyes fluttered closed and his body went limp. Ingvar, supporting his weight, lowered him onto his back, watching him carefully all the while. Then he pulled clear and retrieved his sword. *Dausvjer*'s blade was coated in a layer of sooty carbon, obscuring the protective runes engraved along the flat.

He sagged back against the wall, utterly drained. As he looked down on his brother's ravaged face he felt sick. He lifted his sword again, holding it in position. A quick down-stroke would do it – between chin and gorget, cutting the jugular and biting down into the spinal column beneath.

He held it there for a long time, his mind working hard. He was exhausted, weary of the slaughter, weary of not knowing what to do.

Eventually he put the blade down again. Baldr lay unconscious before him, his sallow cheeks hanging loose as he breathed.

'Not dreams, brother,' he breathed, taking the soul-ward and fixing it around Baldr's neck. As the crow's head clinked against Baldr's armour, a faint smile flickered across his diseased face. 'I wish they had been.'

Ingvar stood up again. He felt nauseous, and went over to one of the narrow windows. The glass in it had long since been shattered. He leaned against the frame, letting his head rest against the stone.

He could see across a broad sweep of the lower city. Fires still burned in all directions, but the sounds of battle sounded closer than they had been. As he watched, he saw plague-bearers and mutants running down the streets below him. They were no longer advancing; they were fleeing.

He narrowed his eyes, peering up towards the Ighala Gate. Even his senses failed to make much headway through the rolling clouds of muck.

He could hear enough, though. He could hear the roar of flamers and the battle-cries of the Celestians. He could hear the shouts of Guardsmen trying to keep their spirits in the face of the horrors around them. Loudest of all, cutting through the shifting walls of sound, he could hear the curses of his brothers. He heard Olgeir's deep-chested bellows, Haflói's whooping, Jorundur's strident fury, Gunnlaugur's ferocious war-cries. Only Váltyr's voice was absent, but then he was always quiet in combat.

Hearing the sounds of the pack back on the hunt triggered mixed emotions in him. On the one hand, it meant that the enemy was falling back – a fine achievement for Gunnlaugur's command. On the other, he had played little part in that victory, forced into the margins by his *vaerangi* and distracted by hunts of a different kind.

Worst of all, the reckoning for Baldr would come quickly now. His condition could no longer remain hidden. Death surely awaited him; perhaps worse.

Ingvar glanced over at his motionless body. Baldr's breathing was regular again, deeper than it had been before. The green tinge around his eyes and mouth had lessened. Whatever force had possessed him had been banished, at least for the present.

'I should never have left you,' said Ingvar, speaking softly, just as he had done in the apothecarion. 'I achieved nothing and learned little.'

The noises of fighting grew louder and closer. He felt the familiar nagging urge to participate, to race down the winding stairs and throw himself into the heart of it.

He resisted. If he had remained with Baldr in the Halicon as ordered, perhaps the madness would never have reached such terrifying depths.

Ingvar moved away from the window and crouched down beside his battle-brother. Baldr was locked in the Red Dream. The coma seemed somehow healthier than it had done before: deeper, and with none of the stench of corruption about it. His skin looked to be healing even as Ingvar watched, its genhanced mechanisms slowly combating the toxins lodged beneath.

Or perhaps that was wish-fulfilment. Some corruptions were impossible to expunge.

'I will remain,' he said. 'I owe you that much.'

As he watched and waited, though, his thoughts turned to Gunnlaugur.

And what will Skullhewer do when he hears of this? he thought. *What will he decide?*

There was no rout, no disorderly scramble, no massacre. The enemy, bereft of its champions and having taken heavy losses at the Ighala Gate, pulled back steadily, retaining its cohesion. De Chatelaine's spearhead pursued them down from the inner walls and back into the smouldering morass of the lower city.

The fighting remained furious and bloody. Clouds of toxins still hung low over the rooftops, blotting the sky like water-spiralled ink. The bands of mutants still retained their powers of fear and infection, and many units of Guardsmen were lost in sudden counter-attacks or ambushes. After the first push down from the gates the advance soon clogged into resistance again.

For all that, the upper city had been secured. The attacking army had lost its momentum and many of its most dangerous troops. For the time being, the Halicon's survival had been won.

After hewing a bloody passage down towards the warehouse zone, Gunnlaugur caught sight of the canoness and her command squad moving up to join him. He pulled back and waited for them. They met up on a spear of bare rock that jutted out above the lowest terraces of the city. Far below them the outer walls lay in ruins, surrounded by dug-in units of plague-bearers. Straggling formations marred the desert beyond, studded with isolated siege engines and the smoking carcasses of vehicles.

'This is as far as we go,' said de Chatelaine grimly, standing alongside him and looking out across the desolate vista.

Gunnlaugur hoisted his thunder hammer over his shoulder. His arms were weary from swinging it. He knew she was right, but found it hard to admit. In the heat of battle, charging with his brothers amid the rush of flame and blood, he had briefly entertained visions of driving the enemy back out into the dust, of chasing them into the burning sands to shrivel and wither.

Too many still lived for that. They were in disarray but were already recovering. Like the poisonous cells of a recurrent cancer, they were grouping, coalescing, clustering together in the shadows, preparing to hold the ground they had won.

He nodded grudgingly. 'So now what?' he asked.

De Chatelaine holstered her bolt pistol and put her hands on her hips. Her bearing was still regal, despite her exhaustion.

'We have wounded them,' she said, her voice giving away a fierce pride. 'They will not breach the inner defences now, not without reinforcements. We should consolidate while we can.'

She gazed out to her left, over to where the dark profile of the cathedral still burned. Its triple spires sent twisting cords of inky smoke up into the foul sky.

'Perhaps we should have done so earlier.'

Gunnlaugur grunted. That had always been his counsel.

'What's done is done,' he said. 'Every street was fought for. That satisfies honour.' He looked over his shoulder, up the steep ranks of terraces leading to the upper city. 'But you are right. They will not break the citadel now, not as they are. Give the order to your troops. My brothers and I will guard the retreat.'

De Chatelaine bowed. 'This is your victory, Space Wolf,' she said. 'I should have trusted the hand of providence. You *were* our deliverance.'

Gunnlaugur shook his head. 'You commanded this.' He smiled under his belligerent helm. 'You may yet get the crusade you dreamed of.'

De Chatelaine stood on the outcrop for a little longer, her cloak hanging limply in the thick, unmoving air.

'They will come at us again,' she said. 'This is only one army. We know they have others. Plague Marines may yet live. What have we bought here? A few days?'

'A few days are worth having,' said Gunnlaugur. 'The Imperium will answer your calls in time, and our task is to remain alive until then. We have made a start.'

De Chatelaine inclined her head in apology. 'Forgive me,' she said. 'I learned to suppress my optimism. Perhaps I shall have to unlearn that again.' She laughed. The sound was weary but clear. 'Learning from a savage. That such things are possible.'

Then, ahead of them, out to the south over the wide dust-flats, the low covering of clouds broke open. The rift was fleeting, just a tattered break in the plague-pall that soon covered over again. But for a moment, sunlight shafted down on the battlefield, thick and golden, sweeping across the rusting, burning debris lining the road to Hjec Aleja.

Both Gunnlaugur and de Chatelaine watched it. Even after it had passed and the scene had resumed its preternatural gloom they said nothing.

It would not be the last such break, though. The clouds were thinning.

'I had not realised dawn had come,' de Chatelaine said.

'Nor I,' said Gunnlaugur. 'But it has, and we are alive to see it.'

He looked across the devastation, thinking of Váltyr and Baldr, reflecting on what had been sacrificed.

'Give the order to fall back,' he said gruffly, avoiding such thoughts. Much work remained. 'Let's finish this.'

As Ras Shakeh's natural daylight began to wane, the last of the toxin clouds thinned and drifted clear of the Halicon. In the deepening twilight, underlit by residual fires still growling away amid the wreckage of the lower city, the battlefield could at last be seen to its full extent. The outer walls had been half demolished, their smooth curve cracked open. The buildings closest to the perimeter had been hit hardest – huge areas had been reduced to black swathes of ash, gently smoking as the flesh, metal and stone all cooled.

The enemy withdrew beyond the walls, drawing up in sombre ranks out on the dust. Their numbers had been depleted by the assault but still remained formidable. The whispering stopped. They moved slowly, sullenly, like a vast beast withdrawing to lick its wounds. Their stench remained thick on the air, fuelled by the sweet tang of decaying offal left behind inside the walls.

The defenders pulled back to the inner walls, drawing closed the Ighala Gate doors and repopulating the long ramparts. The wall-gun magazines were reloaded, and materiel salvaged from the ruins of the perimeter defences was stowed, ready for use when needed. During the final withdrawal heavy lifting equipment was hauled down from the upper city to drag the wreckage of *Vuokho* back inside the walls. Hafloí's haphazard flight had destroyed all of Jorundur's repair work and caused fresh damage to the fragile hull, but what remained was judged worth retrieving by de Chatelaine's surviving tech-adepts.

The Wounded Heart standards still hung on either side of the Ighala Gate. Many other battle-flags remained in place, albeit with rents and burns marring the holy icons. The Halicon had escaped largely undamaged, and still reared its baroque profile up against the far horizon. Though marked by missile-fire and stained from airborne filth, much of the upper city was intact, a final island of defiance amid a world of ruins.

Between the defenders' redoubt and the enemy encampment on the plains stretched a wide swathe of no-man's-land – a waste-zone of contagion studded with the remains of empty hab-shells and hazy with smoke. That was the buffer between the two forces over which artillery pieces gazed and troopers watched. Like a huge circular scar, it ran down from the gorge and out to the shattered perimeter wall, slowly greying and festering, devoid of all sounds but the hissing breeze.

Gunnlaugur and Olgeir stood on the Ighala ramparts watching over those wastes, their helms removed and their weapons sheathed.

Olgeir's mood had improved after he'd managed to recover *sigrún* from a retreating warband of mutants. As they'd died under his fists he'd broken into laughing and hadn't stopped until he'd withdrawn back to the bridge. Even now his ugly face was twisted by a half-smile.

Gunnlaugur, on the other hand, had fallen into brooding. The withdrawal from combat always turned his mood dark.

'Any news from Old Dog?' he asked, his eyes fixed on the ruins below.

Olgeir snorted. 'Not since he dragged the whelp back to the hangars to put right what he did. For a while I thought he'd kill him.'

Gunnlaugur smiled. 'Haflói can look after himself.'

'He can.' Olgeir looked satisfied. 'He's a good fighter. You know who he reminds me of?'

'I was never so foolish.'

Olgeir chuckled. 'You were. And as arrogant. When his hair starts to grey he'll be a formidable Hunter.'

'If he lives long enough.'

Olgeir's smile faded. He looked down at his burly hands where they grasped the parapet edge.

'And Ingvar?'

Gunnlaugur's chin slumped against his gorget.

'He lives,' he said quietly. 'He says he's found Baldr's body, and will return it.'

Olgeir looked up at Gunnlaugur. His face betrayed his disquiet. 'Fjolnir was destroyed?'

'I do not know. Ingvar would not tell me. He told me he'd explain when he was back.'

'So you two are speaking again.'

'We *will* speak,' said Gunnlaugur, his voice heavy with weariness. 'I cannot feel anger with him, not now.'

'He disobeyed you.'

'He did. But was the order just?' Gunnlaugur turned to Olgeir. 'Have I persecuted him, Heavy-hand?'

Olgeir shrugged. 'I'm no *vaerangi*. But the bad blood between you cannot continue.'

Gunnlaugur nodded, then lowered his head again.

'I hoped he would be how he used to be, but I see the change in his eyes. I see that damned onyx skull around his neck and I know he carries his past with him like a ghost at his back. At times I wonder if something's possessed him.'

Olgeir made the ritual gesture against *maleficarum*.

'Do not jest.'

'Even so.'

Silence fell between them. The first stars appeared above, pricking silver into the veil of dark blue. The smells of cooking fires wafted up from the buildings behind them, the first wholesome aromas that had been detectable since the enemy had arrived. Although battered and surrounded, Hjec Aleja still clung to life.

'Baldr cannot be suffered to endure,' said Olgeir at last, his deep voice sombre. 'You saw what he'd become. He is as much a brother to me as he is to you, but we should have ended him when we had the chance. You know this.'

Gunnlaugur didn't look at him.

'If we had done so, then we would all be dead and the Halicon would now be the throne room for that monster,' he said. 'Perhaps it was his wyrd to be there. Perhaps he can still be saved.'

As he spoke, a figure emerged from the ruins below and moved across the wasteland. It went haltingly, dragging something along. Only slowly could its shape be made out – a warrior in pearl-grey armour hauling another behind it. The two of them stumbled up out of the desolation and towards the bridge.

Gunnlaugur watched their progress bleakly.

'You will let him pass?' asked Olgeir.

Gunnlaugur remained still for a long time. All along the parapets, defence towers locked on to the moving figures, primed to fire on his order.

He remembered Baldr's own words to the canoness, back when the first of the infected had been discovered.

Do you not understand? They allow them to survive. There are carriers among them. You cannot let them in.

His amber eyes held steady in the failing light as he watched Ingvar struggle under the dead weight of his unconscious brother.

Allow none to pass in or out. Everything contaminated must be destroyed.

'He is one of us,' Gunnlaugur murmured. His voice betrayed his doubt, but it brooked no argument. 'The Gyrfalkon would not have brought him back if he thought Baldr had gone beyond redemption.'

Gunnlaugur took in a deep breath. The air was still foul in his nostrils.

'I must learn,' he said. 'I must change. I must find him a place, now that Váltyr is gone.'

He leaned forwards on the parapet, his brows furrowed.

'I must learn to trust his judgement, Heavy-hand,' he said. 'Open the gates.'

CHAPTER TWENTY-FOUR

Canoness de Chatelaine knelt before the altar and watched the memorial fires burn in their brazier pans. Dozens had been lit, each one marking the soul of a fallen Sister. The smoke, pungent with incense, twisted up into the chapel's vaults.

As the thin columns rose the choir sang a low, cadenced dirge. The music was a blend of traditional Shakeh death-chants and sanctioned Ministorum melodies. The words had been written by Sister Renata of her Celestian bodyguard. Like so many others, Renata was dead now, her body lying somewhere unmarked in the smouldering ruins of the lower city.

De Chatelaine bowed her head. The rites of remembrance gave her a little comfort. So many of those she had lived with for years were gone, their lives ended in cruel and ignominious ways, but as long as the rites endured some measure of dignity could be restored to their legacies.

As each brazier was lit, a chime sounded and a priest declaimed the name of the fallen. As the list neared its end, ordered by rank in the Imperial way, only a single brass pan remained empty.

An iron-masked acolyte walked up to the remaining station with a flame cradled in his metal-gloved hands. As he reached up to the pan and the coals kindled, the chime sounded a final time.

'Sister Palatine Uwe Bajola, of the world Memnon Primus, of the Orders Famulous, afterwards of the Order of the Wounded Heart. Confirmed slain in the conduct of righteous duty. Gathered into the bosom of the Emperor of Mankind. Blessed are the martyrs. Their souls remain inviolate.'

The canoness listened sadly. Bajola had always been a mystery to her. De Chatelaine had never understood why someone with the Palatine's gifts had wanted to take up a station in such a remote world. The pleasures and rewards of ministering to a devoted populace were not something Bajola had ever seemed to feel deeply. De Chatelaine had always felt that her rest-less spirit would have been better employed elsewhere; perhaps in one of the bigger Orders, or perhaps in the Famulous chambers where she had come from, with all the glamorous system-spanning work that entailed.

She remembered how Bajola had been on the day she'd arrived on Ras Shakeh. De Chatelaine had admired the younger woman's poise, her calm manner, her quiet application. Only later had she been troubled by the amount of time Bajola had spent in the bowels of the cathedral, how disconnected she had been with the work of the other Sisters. When Bajola had so vociferously opposed the decision to seek protection from the Wolves of Fenris, for reasons de Chatelaine had never fully understood, a rift had threatened to open between them.

That had never happened. Now, after so much bloodshed, it seemed pointless to even think of such things. She was gone, and any secrets she had were gone too.

It would have been good to talk before the end. If the Palatine had not been so obsessed with that damn cathedral, perhaps they would have done. But that was in the past now. Perhaps one day it would be rebuilt and a shrine dedicated to her heroic defence of it. It was always comforting to think of the future.

With the last of the pans lit, de Chatelaine got to her feet, bowed a final time towards the altar, and turned back down the chapel's central aisle. As she walked towards the doorway she heard the scurrying footsteps of aides. They kept to the shadows of the aisles, cloaked and hooded. Some were flesh and blood like her; others were at least part mechanical.

As she pushed the heavy gahlwood doors open and stepped into the cool of the night, one of them came up to her, bowing and genuflecting.

When he raised his bald head, displaying an age-lined face and blank white eyes, de Chatelaine recognised her Master of Astropaths, Ermili Repoda.

'Could it not wait, master?' she asked.

Repoda bowed again in apology. 'You commanded me to inform you if the Choir received anything.'

Despite herself, de Chatelaine felt a twinge in the pit of her stomach. It was dangerous to hope.

'And?'

Repoda swallowed drily.

'I do not wish to give you grounds for false optimism,' he said. 'But since that... thing was killed, we have been getting intermittent scraps. Nothing as solid as I would like, and mostly from the acolytes who are not yet trained to interpret soundly.'

De Chatelaine drew in an impatient breath.

'I think we were heard,' he said, his face oscillating between doubt and expectation. 'I do not have a reliable name, nor a time, but someone has been trying to reach us.'

'No more detail?'

Repoda looked uncertain. 'Perhaps. A title, maybe. The Wolves may be able to tell you more. My people interpreted it differently: one of them came up with gibberish, another the title *Stormcaller*. I do not know what to make of it.'

De Chatelaine pursed her lips thoughtfully.

'*Stormcaller*,' she said slowly. 'I will speak to Gunnlaugur of this. It sounds like something he would recognise.'

Repoda bowed again. His hands twitched nervously. He looked on edge. Everyone around her was on edge, driven into a state of fragility by what they had seen and lived through.

De Chatelaine gave him a kind look, not that he would have seen it.

'Do not despair, master,' she said. 'I had almost given up, and then our prayers were answered. The Wolves will not leave their own kind. More will come, and when they do our survival here will count for something. They will find this city still defended, ready to receive their warriors for the crusade we hoped for.'

Repoda tried to smile, but his old face produced little more than a grimace. 'I hope you are right, canoness,' he said.

De Chatelaine drew in a deep breath. The airs around the Halicon were purer than they had been.

'If I had learned to doubt, master,' she said, 'then I have unlearned it again. The Master of Mankind does not desert souls who remain true to Him. That is what we need to remember, is it not? To *believe*.'

She smiled at him again, more for her own benefit than for his.

'After what we have seen,' she said, 'surely even the most lost of us has remembered that.'

In a forgotten corner of the upper city, cloistered away from the overcrowded chapels, converted hab-units and medicae stations, shaded by spear-leaved trees and open to the deep night air, a fire burned.

It was larger than most, a heaped pile of wooden slats stuffed with torn fabric and doused in oils. Váltyr's body lay amid the roaring flames, lying on his back with his open eyes gazing up into the sea of stars. About the pyre were set his warrior's artefacts: his armour pieces, what remained of his pelts and trophies. Set at his feet, hanging from an iron frame and sheathed, was *holdbítr*. The blade looked mournful. It would no longer draw; the pieces had been retrieved but only a smith with the skill of Arjac would be able to reforge the blade.

Gunnlaugur watched the flames consume the corpse of his battle-brother and friend. He knew what Váltyr would have wanted: the sword to be destroyed with him, to perish completely so that none but he would ever wield it.

That would happen in time, but the pyre would not be sufficient to harm it. A greater furnace would be needed to melt the imperishable metal and break the wards of the runes along the blade.

His eyes moved away from the flames and scanned across the pyre's watchers. Four others had gathered before it, each standing silently, each lost in their own thoughts.

Olgeir was closest. He stood proudly, his huge shoulders pushed back, his snub nose and gnarled beard silhouetted against the pyre's glow. His deep-set eyes stared into the heart of the fire. He had not been close to Váltyr, but Gunnlaugur knew they had respected one another. Baldr's affliction had hit him harder. Though Olgeir had argued for giving Fjolnir the Emperor's Mercy, he had done so with pain in his eyes. Since Baldr's entry into the pack they had fought together like kin-brothers, their bolters ringing in unison. If Baldr died, Olgeir would mourn long. If he lived but did not recover, he would mourn longer.

Beside him stood Jorundur. The Old Dog, if anything, looked slightly less hunched than he had done on past campaigns. His fury towards Haofloí had abated; even he could see how *Vuokho*'s last flight had turned the shape of the battle. Gunnlaugur suspected his wrath had never been full-hearted in any case. An odd relationship had developed between those two, as if Jorundur saw something in Haofloí worth protecting or encouraging. If that were so, then it gladdened his heart. Jorundur, for all his bitterness, was a priceless asset to the pack, a repository of knowledge and experience that outstripped even his. It would be good to see him fighting again with his old assurance.

Next was the whelp. Haofloí watched the dancing flames with only perfunctory interest. Death to him was like life: ephemeral, fleeting, of little importance when set beside the raw pleasures of the hunt and the kill. He had not had time to develop a deep connection to either Váltyr or Baldr and did not pretend to mourn more than he ought. His ruddy face was thrust out belligerently, as if chafing at the necessity to mark the passing. Gunnlaugur smiled with bleak foreknowledge. Haofloí would learn to mourn, should he live long enough. He would learn what it was to lose a soul-brother, one whose life had been shared amid blood and fire. For now, though, he was just as he should be: fearless, alive with boundless energy, uncaring of anything but the feat of arms.

Finally, set apart from his brothers, stood Ingvar. The shadows hung heavily on him, part-masking his stone-grey features. His expression was hard to read. Gunnlaugur knew that Váltyr and he had always chafed at one another, vying for the mantle of the pack's deadliest blade. If Váltyr had become the more lethal swordsman, Ingvar, to his mind, had become the more complete warrior. Now, though, such contests were irrelevant, and Ingvar's face betrayed nothing but grief. If he had stayed in the Halicon as ordered, he might have arrived in time to save him. Or perhaps he too would have died. Gunnlaugur could see the doubts preying on him even as the lambent red light played across his battered armour. Those doubts would not leave him quickly, adding more layers to his already conflicted soul.

Gunnlaugur's eyes turned back to the pyre. Váltyr's body was almost gone, slowly being reduced to whitening ashes. The wounds he had taken had been burned away. Gunnlaugur hoped that, at the last, the blademaster had found some measure of peace in what had been a restless, doubting life. He would have deserved that.

Moving slowly, he raised the heavy shaft of *skulbrotsjór*, lifting the weapon in salute against the glow of the dying pyre.

As silently as he, the others did the same – Olgeir raising his sword, Jorundur and Haofloí their axes, Ingvar his rune-blade.

No words were spoken. The four of them held vigil as the last of Váltyr's mortal remains were consumed. Only when the flames had died and the embers were cooling did they lower their weapons again.

'The thread is cut,' said Gunnlaugur softly.

Olgeir was the first to leave, nodding to Gunnlaugur as he stalked off, his face tight with emotion. Jorundur and Haofloí were next, both heading back to the hangars to work on *Vuokho*. Haofloí looked eager to be away; Jorundur pensive.

That left Ingvar and Gunnlaugur alone again, separated only by the smoking ashes. Ingvar made no move. For a while nothing passed between them but the low crackle and spit of oil-soaked wood.

'How is Fjolnir?' asked Gunnlaugur eventually. He tried to keep judgement out of his voice.

Ingvar stepped into the circle of fading light. Gunnlaugur noticed that the soul-ward pendant he'd worn since leaving Fenris no longer hung around his neck, though the onyx skull still did.

'The Red Dream has him,' Ingvar replied. His voice was wary. 'I believe him to be recovering.'

Gunnlaugur nodded. Baldr had been restrained, clapped in adamantium shackles and buried deep within the Halicon's dungeons. Doors a metre thick locked him in. Even if he woke to madness again, there would be no escape from the citadel.

'I hope you're right,' said Gunnlaugur. 'I took a risk, accepting you both back. The gates had been sealed.'

Ingvar bowed. 'I know,' he said. He needed to say nothing more; the gratitude was evident.

Gunnlaugur hoisted his thunder hammer, locking it across his back.

'I still don't know if I was right,' he said. 'Even if he recovers he will be tainted. You saw what he did.'

Ingvar sheathed his blade.

'I share your doubts. I nearly killed him myself.'

'What stopped you?'

Ingvar hesitated. 'Callimachus would have killed him without a thought. Jocelyn would have done it, as would the others. But we have never been a Chapter for rules, have we? We have always acted as our souls warned us.'

Gunnlaugur didn't recognise those names, but he could guess well enough what Ingvar meant.

Ingvar looked directly at him. Weariness scarred his grey visage.

'For better or worse, I am *Fenryka*. I doubted it for a time, but a wolf does not shed its pelt. I would give him a chance.' He lowered his eyes. 'If you permitted it.'

Gunnlaugur considered the words. As ever, something about Ingvar's tone unsettled him. Perhaps he would just have to get used to that.

'Váltyr never argued for your exclusion,' he said. 'You should know that. It was me. And you were right. That was for pride. I am shamed by it.'

Ingvar looked surprised. For a moment, he didn't reply.

'Thank you,' he said, his eyes flickering briefly towards the pyre. 'I had assumed–'

'Váltyr was not jealous. He warred with himself. It was never about you.'

Ingvar nodded slowly, taking that in. At length his grey eyes rose again.

'So what now, *vaerangi*?' he asked. 'We have survived. We have been blooded. What comes next?'

Gunnlaugur rolled his shoulders, feeling the deep-set fatigue in the muscles.

'The canoness received word of reinforcements,' he said. 'If she's right, then Njal is on his way.'

'Stormcaller?' Ingvar looked impressed. 'Our hides are worth that much?'

'Not ours,' he said. 'But this is more than one lost world. Hundreds are ablaze. This is a new war, one that has only just begun.'

'At least not garrison work,' Ingvar said wryly, working to raise a smile. The effort was weak, but Gunnlaugur did his best.

'No, at least not that.'

Ingvar looked thoughtful then.

'I have much to tell you,' he said. 'I learned things from the Palatine before she died. It may have been for those alone that fate brought us here. There are things about Hjortur we were never told.'

'We shall speak of them,' said Gunnlaugur. 'Truly, we shall. But not now, not while the ashes of our brother are still cooling.'

He looked down at his hands.

'I was wrong, brother,' he said. 'Your presence wore at my pride, and I let it govern me. Now Váltyr is gone I have need of counsel like never before.' He looked back up. 'Can the river flow cleanly between us again?'

Ingvar came towards him, grasping him by the arm.

'We were both at fault,' he said fervently. 'I forgot myself. Never again, brother. I swear it.'

His eyes held steady – two orbs of flecked grey, like the plumage of the raptor that had given him his name.

'I told the Palatine we were both of the blood of Asaheim,' he said. 'I am not sure I meant it then. Now I do.'

Gunnlaugur took Ingvar's hand and gripped it in his own gauntlet. The two of them stood before the glimmering light of the pyre, alone at the summit of Hjec Aleja.

'I am glad,' he said.

For the first time in a long while he looked at Ingvar's face and saw no challenge there, real or imagined. A future presented itself: their twin animal spirits, as lethal as any in the galaxy, working in tandem, no bitterness dividing them.

'For Fenris, brother,' he said proudly. 'Our blades together.'

Ingvar closed his eyes then, as if some terrible, crushing weight had been lifted from his shoulders. For a moment, he made no reply. When he spoke again, his voice was thick with emotion.

'For Fenris,' he said quietly, his head bowed.

EPILOGUE

The chamber was carved from a dark, glossy stone that reflected the light strangely. It wasn't even clear where the light came from; it seemed to spin out of the air between ebony pillars, each one rough-cut and many-faceted, just like the walls and floor. The place looked like it had been carved from the heart of an asteroid.

Which it had. The room was a single node within Clandestine Station U-6743, operating under the auspices of the sub-adjutant proximal command group Theta-Lode-Frier, one of several thousand outposts placed at the disposal of Deathwatch kill-teams and scattered throughout the galaxy.

Seven Space Marines stood in the centre of that eerie, echoing space. Callimachus of the Ultramarines, Leonides of the Blood Angels, Jocelyn of the Dark Angels, Prion of the Angels Puissant, Xatasch of the Iron Shades and Vhorr of the Executioners had already received their skull pendant, the mark of their service during the incident in the Dalakkar Belt in which forty-six billion souls had died. They remained silent, their unmoving armour-shells as black as the stone that enclosed them. The atmosphere was one of resigned stoicism. None of them had enjoyed seeing the results of their last mission, not even Xatasch, whose humours were dark.

Only Ingvar remained. He stood among his brothers, his left shoulder guard as grey as dirty snow and bearing the insignia of Berek Thunderfist's Great Company.

Callimachus, helmless like the rest of them, approached him. The Ultramarine tried to smile reassuringly. It was hard for any of them to smile after Dalakkar, but he did so for the sake of form. His Chapter placed much store by the manners of occasion.

'Last of all, the Son of Russ,' said Callimachus, holding the pendant before Ingvar.

When he had joined Onyx, a mortal lifetime ago, Ingvar would have resisted bowing his head to anyone, let alone a Space Marine of another Chapter. Now such inhibitions had melted away. The long years, each one filled with strange horror-breeds and murderous missions in the dark, had changed him. He had studied the Codex with Callimachus. He had learned the beauty of sword-craft from Leonides. He had learned advanced void-war tactics from Jocelyn, the use of battle-shield variants from Prion, ancient methods of infiltration from Xatasch and closerange bolter techniques from Vhorr.

Like all of them he had become an amalgam, a lethal mix of different martial orders. At times that made him feel stronger than he had ever felt; at times it felt like he had lost his soul.

So he bowed before the Ultramarine, ready to receive the mark of his duty and, as he saw it in his darkest moments, his shame.

Callimachus placed the pendant around his neck.

'You have had the longest journey,' he said.

Ingvar felt the iron chain settle on his flesh. Once he had been used to bearing all manner of totems and charms on his battleplate, such as the soul-ward he had given to Baldr as a token of their unbreakable friendship. Now, like so much else, adorning his sable armour seemed strange, like rehearsing the moves of a half-forgotten dream.

'We have all travelled,' he replied. Little difference existed between his voice and that of Callimachus; even their spoken Gothic, once thickly differentiated by accent and idiom, had merged into similarity.

'And now we must travel again, but apart,' said Callimachus. 'I grieve to lose your friendship. When we first met I thought you nothing better than a barbarian. Now I know you have a warrior's heart and a scholar's mind. I learned a lesson from you, Ingvar, one I will take back to Macragge.'

Ingvar bowed. 'Our paths may cross again.'

Callimachus smiled. 'If they did, we would be honour-bound to say nothing. I would look on you with haughty eyes, and you would snarl at me with contempt, and our brothers would approve.'

'Because they are ignorant.'

'Because they are pure.'

Callimachus looked solemn and regretful. He always looked solemn and regretful, like a statue carved from pure-grain nobility.

'We have become mongrels, forever destined to bestride two worlds. It will be hard to return. It will be hard to become what we once were.'

'But we will.'

Callimachus gave him a hard look. 'Will you, Ingvar? Will you forget what you have learned when you tread once more on the cold plains of Fenris?'

Ingvar held his gaze. 'I intend to forget nothing.'

'Do not expect to find your home world as you left it. Do not expect your battle-brothers to be the same as they were. You may never tread in the same river twice.'

'So you said to me before,' Ingvar said. 'But you forget, brother, I am still a Son of Russ. We are the arrogant ones, the boastful scions of a boastful primarch, and we do not respond well to being told what we may or may not do.'

Ingvar smiled then too. It was a warped smile, one that reflected the infinite horrors he had witnessed, one that still betrayed a certain guilty pride.

The onyx skull hung against his breastplate, dark against the sable ceramite. Already it felt like a repository of secrets.

'With us,' he said, 'anything is possible.'

STORMCALLER

PROLOGUE

Always cold.

Cold at the moment of dawn when the red sun slid above the fields of ice like a clot of blood. Cold at the heart of the day when the ice cracked under grey, feathered skies. Cold in the long nights – bone-aching cold, cold that sunk under the skin and lodged fast.

Men could go mad from it, weeping as their fingers blackened and softened. When the pain grew too much, they would scream their hopelessness at the stars, and that brought beasts to the flickering circles of the fires. Screams always brought beasts, as lean and hungry as those who huddled at the flame-pits. Once you let the cold make you scream, that was the end. Fenris ended the weak quickly.

It was near the end of the long winter-spell when he was born, bloody and motley, wailing before being silenced by rags as the wind made the tent walls drum. The highlands were cracking by then, opening up like parted flesh. Faer told them change would come before the fire-summer, so they had to move, packing hide tents onto sleds and skiffs and wrapping them hard with leather twine.

Ana, his mother, was fifteen seasons as the Terrans reckoned it and as tough as knucklebones. When the dawn came she was ready, wrapped in furs, her face swathed from the blast-wind, her pale hands clutching the cords of her back-strapped cradleboard.

They walked in teams, dragging goods on long sleds, heading south towards the long, grey firth where the *hvalari* snorted and dived. The skies were low and stone-grey, blurred by fine rain that felt like ice when it hit. Mountains rose up in the north, bleak and dagger-sided, kindling thunder. Those mountains had no name, for they had stood less than a child's lifetime. Only one range on Fenris had a name. Only one range endured more than a mortal span, and the Ascurii knew of that range only through the sagas of Faer.

They went three days before the land ahead of them changed. Ice cracked underfoot, spreading like uncurling dark fingers as their leather-wound feet kicked through the slush. Ana gritted her teeth, bending against the weight of the bundle on her back. She suckled the infant on the move, pulling him round, trudging, staying silent.

He never cried. No infants on Fenris cried once the immense cold first washed over them – they kept their mouths clamped shut, their fists balled, their black eyes staring. He stayed swaddled tight on the cradleboard, limbs pressed to his body to retain heat, covered in a thick layer of deer pelt and grass, only his eyes and nose exposed.

Faer halted on the morning of the fourth day. Totems rattled under his arms, swinging from lengths of twine. The Ascurii stood in straggling groups around him, huddling under the shade of bony *furu* pines. They numbered no more than sixty by then, worn down and harrowed by the Long Winter. The men's skin was drawn tight over bone and wrinkled dry like cured fish. The women's faces were chapped from the wind, blotched red and white, their eyes narrowed. Their breath steamed in the morning mist, catching on furs and cloaks and drifting into the white sky.

Faer looked out over the firth as it stretched away towards a lowering horizon – lead-matt, crested with the froth of choppy water, studded with drifting ice. In the far west rose the sky-blue wall of a glacier, and beyond that the piled-high landmass of the Greater Island.

That land might survive for a dozen seasons, or one, or none. It looked sturdy enough, but no one could tell. The world was in constant change from one Great Year to the next, and that was the way of it. None complained, for none knew any different – you might as well complain about the bloodpox, or the golden-eyed wolves that roamed the islands like ravenous shadows, or the ravens that squatted over cooling corpses after the gore had sunk among the stones.

Faer's eyes narrowed. It wasn't far. They could rebuild and refit the boats within the week, and be over to the other side in less than a day. If the storms held, it would be no more perilous than when they'd last crossed the deep.

Jorund clumped over to stand by him. The big headman pulled his cloak tight around his burly shoulders, sending a shiver of snow rattling down his back.

'We go?' he grunted, watching what Faer was watching.

The shaman nodded, and his straggling beard pressed up against the folds of coarse fabric at his neck.

'Others will be there, too,' said Jorund, doubtfully.

Faer nodded again. 'Ice and iron,' he mumbled.

'We are weak.'

'We cannot stay here,' said Faer, turning his milky eye towards the headman. 'You want to stay? The land is fire-cursed. It will crack soon.'

Jorund's grey eyes scanned the firth. A month ago it had been solid with ice, thick enough for a heavy skiff. Making the boats ready would be backbreaking.

He looked up at the glacier. The land beyond was dark with trees, needling up against the horizon in tight rows.

It was a big island, a solid island, with deep roots. Many would contest the land – it would have prey under the branches, and predators watching the prey.

As Jorund thought and watched, the ice around him sighed and creaked. He looked down to see a fissure opening between his feet, just a finger's-breadth wide. The gap filled with water.

'We go, then,' he growled, stepping away. He turned to the others. They stared back at him, expectant. 'We go,' he told them, clapping his frozen hands together to get the blood flowing.

Ana looked up at him. Her round face was shiny with fatigue. Her trothed man, Aesgir, stood at her side, supporting her with one hand, dragging his sled with the other.

They knew the danger. The child might not survive the crossing. Ana was weak still; she might not, either.

'Have you named him?' Jorund asked Ana.

Ana shook her head.

'Name him,' he said. 'The gods must know him.'

Ana nodded, understanding.

Then she turned and began to unload tools from the sled. No one said anything more. One by one, the Ascurii got to work.

Only two boats foundered on the way over, tipped up by the crash of surf against floes; the rest scraped home against the icy gravel of the shoreline. The survivors clambered up a long incline towards higher ground. Once the boats were hauled high onto the glass-ice and stone, the men took up flat-bladed spears and throwing axes. They crept up into the rocky uplands, hanging together, their bodies crouched.

Jorund was wrong – there were no others there before them. They climbed up above the shoulder of the glacier, crouching against knife-hard winds from the open ocean. Immense forests stretched away from them, pine-dark, close like fur. The ground was the colour and density of steel.

Faer went quickly, confidently, guided by his visions. The tattoos on his withered skin looked bright blue in the hard light, like veins. He pulled on his old staff, and the bones and vision-trinkets jangled.

At the summit of the massif above the glacier's southerly flank, he paused. He lifted his wiry arms into the air, and his filthy rags fell from them, exposing skin to the ice-bite.

'New land!' he shouted. His voice echoed flatly. A broody forest line glared back at him, and the wind scoured across empty stone and milk-white ice and the obsidian shade of the deep wood.

Ana clutched her child close to her, listening for the rattle-growl of beasts. She had the keenest hearing of the Ascurii.

Nothing yet, but they would come. They would already be uncurling in the dark, sniffing, salivating, stretching.

Aesgir came to her side. 'Anything?'

Ana shook her head, but said, 'Baldr,' quietly, lest Faer hear.

'For the boy?'

Ana nodded, and Aesgir smiled, exposing the half-toothed jaw he'd carried ever since the fighting against the Gyeths.

'Yes. Baldr. He is awake?'

Ana wrenched the cradleboard around from her shoulder, exposing the infant swaddled within. Two dark eyes peered from the straw and leather, steady, unmoving, solemn.

Aesgir grinned again and ran his fingers over the boy's face. 'Always awake. Never sleeps.'

Ana pulled him away, hoisting him back onto her shoulder. 'What is there to sleep for?'

Aesgir looked at her, irritated that she'd pulled him away. He was about to speak when Jorund strode past, axe drawn.

'Further up,' he grunted, beckoning the others on. He glared at Ana for a moment. 'Night will come.'

Then they were moving again, dragging the boats with them, the sleds, the leather sacking and the spear-bundles, clattering it across scree and moss, searching.

Above them, the white sky stretched, remorseless, empty, like a void.

They did not name the place they built, for it would be gone soon enough, just like everywhere else, so it was just the settlement, the hearth, the fire, the *aett*. Jorund drove them hard. They raised a stockade, first using the wood of the boats they had brought, then trunks felled from the forest. They hammered the beams in, digging out the frost-rimed earth with picks. The women worked with the men, hauling, tying, hacking. By the time the sun set, all of them were shining with sweat.

The fire was lit on the first night. It roared with a blaze the height of a skiff-sail, throwing bloody shadows across the snow and turning it to grey puddles. The warriors stood guard, all of them, none sleeping, fingering axes watchfully.

Jorund was the tallest, his heavy grey cloak hanging stiffly, his frost-crusted beard jutting from under a low hood. Ana watched him from the fireside, where she was nursing Baldr. She couldn't see Aesgir – he must have been on the far side. Faer mumbled somewhere in the shadows, squatting and rocking in his visions.

As the sun went down, shadows crept out from the eaves of the forest. The air chilled fast, searing against sweat-cooled skin. Stars pricked into the sky, vivid like the jewel-belt of the gods.

Ana heard them first, as always – low, gurgling growls. They were a long way off, drumming along the earth from far away, deep away. The sounds echoed in the gathering dusk, making the hairs on the back of her arms rise.

Baldr stirred in her arms. He broke from her. His dark eyes glistened in the fire-glow, wide and unafraid. He listened.

Ana smiled at him. 'The wolves, Baldr,' she breathed, wiping a droplet of milk from his sombre mouth.

By then, the others had heard. The men tensed as they stood around the fire, their bodies black against the half-built stockade. Long spears swayed as their bearers peered into the night. Blades were drawn from leather-bound scabbards, each inscribed with scratch-runes by Faer.

Ana rocked the child, though he needed no comfort. 'The *wolves*,' she whispered again.

He was not looking at her. He twisted his head, trying to see where the noise was coming from.

'More fire,' ordered Jorund, his voice tight. Logs were thrown on, spitting and cracking, sending sparks spiralling into the frigid night.

Baldr didn't like the light; he screwed his eyes against it, smearing balled fists over his ruddy face. But the sound – the purring, damp, hot catch of clustered lupine throats – *that* made him listen.

Ana watched it, and her heart warmed.

It was a good sign. A sign of the god-marked, of the iron-hearted.

'Listen to them,' she told him. 'Listen. They will kill you, if they find you. They will tear you apart if they catch you before you are made strong. They will hunt you, run you down.'

She grabbed his head and turned it to her.

'But if you live, Baldr Ascurii, if you *live*...' She gazed at him with a hungry, desperate love. 'You will hunt *them*.'

It was a hard first year. Johana died when with child, and Beorth was gored when he got separated from Jorund's hunt-party. After, the Summer of Fire came, burning across the boiling seas like a fever, and pox ravaged the Greater Island, sending ten to the neverworld, their faces stark and staring with fear. They would not have been afraid to die with axe in hand, but a sickbed promised no glory.

Baldr lived. He thrived as the months passed, growing strong on milk and hunt-meat. Aesgir fed him blood from the meat of slain *konungur*, and he lapped it greedily, licking stringy matter from the sinew.

Ana watched him shoot upwards, tottering on his bent legs as the Summer faded, learning to hold a hilt as the Long Winter gripped the land again. She watched as he spoke the first word – *axe* – and the second – *father*. She watched him as Jorund showed him how to fish, to stalk, to handle a blade, and she watched him as Faer initiated him into the mysteries. Baldr's expression never changed: his dark eyes followed his teachers, drinking in their knowledge. His sombre face remained still. When the others ran the hunt, roaring their fear out and their fury, he stayed silent, like a shadow in daylight, grey and ephemeral.

He listened to Faer most closely. He would crouch at the man's feet, silent as the tales of old wyrds and deeds were mumbled into the flickering flames. He would watch the bones spiral on their cords, and reach out for them, as if he could pull them all to him.

'Is he marked?' Ana asked Faer once, after seeing Baldr scratch the outlines of runes in the dirt, intent and obsessive.

Faer's mouth creased equivocally, making the rings in his nose jangle. 'He is a hunter. A strong one.'

That satisfied her. She wrapped her cloak about her and felt the cold stir in the air again as the winter came in.

It was no life, to be among the runes and the knucklebones. Better to have spear in hand and run with the packs, to eat meat and drink blood and become a warrior of the *vlka*.

Baldr was quiet. He was placid. He would have to learn to be angry soon, for Fenris did not shelter calm souls.

So she watched him, and waited for the fire to come. She knew it would do, that it must do, but did not know when.

Four more Great Years passed. More were born, more died. The wolves took Aesgir one night, as they often did when hunters became too bold or were too unlucky, and so Ana kept hearth alone. The *aett* did not flourish. Wind blew hard across the highlands, scraping at the wood and making the hide tents shiver. Faer's vision had saved them from the cracking earth, but it had not led them to plenty. They hacked a living from the iron-tough earth, hunting the skirts of the forest, cheating what prey they could from the dripping maws of greater predators.

Baldr took his father's place in the hunting pack, adopting the axe. Faer gave him the hunt-mark on his shoulder. Baldr made no sound as the ink-needle went in, piercing flesh and giving him the icon of the *fjolnir* – the nightjar.

He went with them after that – thirty men of the Ascurii, clad in furs, each bearing spears or axes. His was the only beardless face, as smooth as a nut-shell; he was brown-haired, clean-featured.

They walked in file, heading up the path of a half-frozen river into the jagged country west of the great glacier. Water had run clear for the long summer but was now steadily choking as the ice stretched down from the peaks. Baldr's fingers were stiff with cold as he clutched his axe, his breath steaming.

The air thinned as they climbed, taking them up winding paths and into the heights. The trees were old by the standards of the ever-changing world – a dozen Great Years, perhaps – and their bark was oil-dark and gnarled like rope.

Jorund paused, crouching low, sniffing, and the party waited silently. The headman's flinty beard brushed against the ground as he stooped. Eventually he got back to his feet. He was moving stiffly. Baldr watched him move, and wondered how long it would be before a challenger tested Jorund's mettle.

'Higher up,' Jorund grunted, and they set off again.

The trees rose up on either side, vast as pillars, covering the land in dark-ness. Snow piled high against the trunks, glowing a soft blue in the darkness, and the paths silted up with it. Baldr strode with the others, axe clutched tight.

Hours passed, marked only by the trudging steps, the brush of snow against leather, the drip and crack of the deep forest.

Then Jorund got wind of something, and beckoned the others to halt. He sniffed, holding his grizzly head high into the oncoming wind. He stayed motionless for a long time.

Baldr sniffed too, taking care to draw the air in silently.

Musk, he thought. *Tilbrád. Far off. Meagre.*

He'd got better at it, honing his senses, learning from the others.

Jorund tensed. He said nothing, but his hands began to move. The hunt-signals came fast – flickering fingers, gestures. On his final signal, the hunt-pack burst into movement.

They ran as one, softly, loping through the snow with high, silent strides. None of them spoke. Baldr kept pace easily, and the pack spread out, sweeping under the pine eaves. Soon each hunter was only visible to his counterpart on either side, and the net spread wide. The prey – tilbrád – were wary and agile, and far faster than a man if given a start.

Baldr stumbled as he ran. Swallowing a curse, he picked up his pace, veering past a giant trunk and ploughing through a deep drift that lapped up to his knees.

He was falling behind. The others were older, stronger, more used to the chase. Baldr pushed hard, hearing his breath echo inside his close-tied hood. He stumbled again, tripping on something beneath the snow, losing his footing and staggering against the curled root of another tree.

He couldn't match the speed of the pack, no matter how much he pushed himself. Flushing from shame, panting like a dog, he kept going, reeling and tripping as the hunters pulled away from him.

Baldr didn't know how long he'd been running before he heard the growl.

He froze – his head whipped round, his heart thumping. Tree trunks marched off in all directions, black like obsidian against the gloom. The terrain rose and fell in snow-covered clumps, broken by the jagged teeth of moss-clad rocks.

For a few terrible moments, he saw nothing. The echo of the growl resonated through the forest, low and quiet, like the soft crack of earth breaking. Baldr stared back and forth, peering into the dark, his axe-blade poised.

Then, slowly, as if resolving from the smoke of a fire-pit, he saw twin orbs of amber in the night. They were a long way away – thirty metres, across a tangled mass of snow-laden briars. They did not blink. They shone dully – black pupils, golden irises, fixed, steady, unmoving.

Baldr felt as if his limbs had been run through with lead. He heard the purring growl again, running along the ground, making the hair on his neck rise. He smelt it for the first time – musty, wet, dog-thick. The beast had come from upwind, just as they were doing to their prey.

Baldr squeezed his fingers on the axe-heft, terrified, his blood raging in his temples.

Why doesn't it move?

His eyes adjusted further. He saw the huge, ridgebacked spine curving over the briars' edge. He saw grey fur, claws sinking into the snow, ludicrously muscled shoulders bunching and flexing.

It was twice his height, a dozen times heavier, draped in a thick, dark mane. Long jaws pulled back into a snarl, sending beads of saliva glistening down to the snow.

It seemed to be regarding him as closely as he regarded it. Its huge nostrils flared. Its massive paws raked the ground before it. The beast was fighting against something – some pull, some drag.

Then it *roared* – a massive, throaty, throttled bellow that shook snow from the branches above it. With a twist and a thrust, it pounced, shouldering clear of the briars and bounding towards him.

Baldr held his ground, almost paralysed with fear, his axe-head clasped stiff. The beast ate up the ground between them, gaping its obscenely long jaws to reveal rows of yellowing, blood-mottled teeth.

The first spear came in from Baldr's right, hurled hard so the shaft trembled as it hit. Another whistled in from the left, *thunking* into the creature's withers.

The beast yowled and skidded to a halt, throwing up slush. More spears hurtled from the trees. They all hit – the hunters of Fenris who lived to adulthood had superlative aim.

The beast thrashed back and forth, caught in a crossfire of hurled barbs. Baldr suddenly felt the vice of fear lift, and hefted his axe.

The beast stared at him, golden eyes wide with pain and fury. Baldr threw, sending the axe head-over-heel, watching as it cracked into the creature's shoulder, biting deep, sending a fountain of wine-dark blood jetting.

Then he was running, scampering into cover again, weaponless in the face of the creature's wrath. He heard great echoing roars as the hunters loosed more spears. He heard the scrabble of claw on stone, and the crack of branches as the beast charged at its tormentors.

He kept running. His lungs burned, his muscles protested, but the thrill of danger, the stink of fear and exhilaration, kept him moving.

He slid to a halt under the lee of a felled trunk, twisting round to see if he was being pursued.

He saw men running between the trunks, some to throw spears, some to withdraw. He didn't see the beast. He heard its yowls and its barks, muffled in the snow and the trees. The noises grew fainter as the pack drove it off. They couldn't kill it – even Baldr knew that – but they could give it enough pain to lope away, slinking back to lick its sores and gashes in the hollowness of some meat-rotten den somewhere.

Baldr fell to his haunches, still breathless, feeling the burn of the cold air as he forced it into shocked lungs.

Jorund found him later. The headman laughed gruffly, grabbed him by his furs and hauled him to his feet.

'Got a shock?' he asked, smacking the snow from Baldr's shoulders and making him stand upright. 'Stumbled on a real killer?'

Jorund grabbed his chin and forced his gaze up to meet him. Baldr stared ahead blearily.

'Throw your axe first,' Jorund said, not letting him go. 'Fear will kill you quicker than the cold.'

Baldr nodded, shamed. He could still feel the pull of terror around his heart, and knew that was weak.

'Why did it wait?' asked Jorund thoughtfully, studying him hard. 'Never seen that.'

Baldr didn't know what to say. Jorund was handling him roughly, like a piece of carcass to be dragged over the fire-pit.

'Maybe you're marked,' said Jorund, lightly, shaking Baldr and slapping him on the shoulder. 'Or maybe it had eaten already.'

Jorund dropped him, then tramped over to the others. The hunters were retrieving their spears. Once they had weapons in hand again they pulled together, respectful of the shadows.

Baldr had lost his axe. For all he knew it was buried in the wolf's flank, sticking from its hide like a trophy.

He looked back into the trees, back into the depths where it had retreated. His heart-rate had slowed to something like normal.

Why did it wait?

Jorund called the hunt together. They had lost the trail and scared any prey far out of reach. Another failed trek, another hungry night.

'Back to the *aett*,' Jorund ordered, not looking at Baldr, not waiting to witness the looks of disappointment from the rest of the pack.

Baldr fell in with the others, keeping to himself, ignoring the mutters and glares that came his way. Once they started marching again, in line just as before, weapons kept ready, the monotony of the walk took over.

They fell silent. He remained so. The snow kicked over his boots, the blood of the wolf froze and crystallised on the ground.

Why did it wait?

Winter came in, blasting from the north as the last vestiges of health bled from the land. Prey became harder to find, and the iron pots that hung over the fires contained little more than dried tubers and boiled grass. More of the Ascurii died, and Faer spent his days in visions, trying to plot a path through the maze of the future. He emptied the last of his rattle-bags, scraping the strands of fungi from the leather and burning them, inhaling the god-smoke to make his visions true.

The days shortened, down to a few hours of grey light around noon, bordered by the long, frigid nights that forever threatened to gust out the fires and plunge them all into oblivion. Jorund showed his age, Ana showed hers. Lives were short on the death world – short and vigorous, driven by the eternal cycle of ice and fire.

It was at the nadir of the Great Year that Faer foretold the coming of others. Jorund sent scouts up to the headlands every day, watching for sails. The seas were closing up with ice, so passage by boat would soon be impossible.

Weeks passed, and nothing came. Some began to mutter against Faer – that his visions had led them nowhere, that they would starve before the next summer, that they should have stayed in the old lands.

Baldr never joined in. He sat with his mother and sharpened his new axe. He hadn't missed out on another hunt, and his young limbs had grown supple and strong. He hadn't lost his nerve again, and his axe and spear had accounted for two kills – a good tally for one of his age and stature, and much needed.

Hrom was the one to see them first. He came running to the *aett*, out of breath and with his hair hanging wildly around his face.

'Sails!' he blurted, panting.

'How many?' asked Jorund, standing grimly before him.

'Four,' said Hrom. 'More, maybe. Fog's heavy.'

The hunters stirred themselves. Jorund sounded his bronze horn to summon the other scouts back, and the Ascurii girded themselves for fighting. The Greater Island wasn't much of a home, but neither was anywhere else during the Long Winter, and the newcomers would not be coming to barter.

The Ascurii could muster only thirty warriors by then, more than half of them longbeards with unyielding joints and wasted muscles. No one questioned Baldr's presence among them. Aegnor was even younger, barely able to lift the throwing spear he took to battle, and no one questioned that either.

The warband marched back up to the headland where they had first landed. By the time they reached the vantage, the boats were already fighting through the swell to reach the beach. Fog rolled in from the ocean, breaking across rocks like summer sea-foam. The invaders waited until the last moment before jumping clear and hauling on the ropes.

Baldr hung back. He had never seen men of other nations. They looked almost as fearsome as the beast had done – huge, pelt-clad, covered in unfamiliar totems and war-tattoos. One of them was a bear of a man with a thick black beard that spilled down a metal breastplate. He carried a double-bladed axe in two hands, and swaggered through the icy surf. Others came after him – thickset fighters with throwing axes and blunt hammers and iron rings piercing their faces.

Jorund watched them come, gauging numbers. 'As pinched as we,' he muttered, fingering his own axe impatiently. 'We can take them.' He turned to Bolg, his cupbearer since Aesgir had been taken. 'Now. Before they clear the beaches.'

Bolg nodded curtly, thumping his own warhammer into an empty palm. 'I count twenty.'

The Ascurii broke into a run, careering down the steep path towards the shoreline. As he ran, Jorund bellowed his defiance, soon joined by the others. Baldr raised his voice with them, running as hard as they did, whirling his axe around his head. The fear left him, replaced by a growing excitement – a yearning to get into the fight, to crack the iron into flesh and bone. Together, the Ascurii tore across the stone-land, their leather boots thudding on the ice and granite.

Jorund was first among them, hurtling down onto the beach and barrelling straight into the oncoming newcomers. Bolg was next, then the others, all sprinting, whooping as the blades came to bear.

Baldr darted among them, faster and shorter. A man with long red hair lunged at him with a spiked cudgel, trying to catch him on the nape before lumbering after more serious prey.

Baldr dodged the blow. He lashed his axe-head across, not aiming, just swiping. It connected with the man's trailing wrist, and the edge cut clean through, taking the hand off at the bone.

The man screamed and collapsed, clutching at his pumping wrist, trying to staunch the torrent that sprayed from the wound. Blood splashed against Baldr's chest and face, blinding him. He staggered back, wiping his eyes, only to see his enemy slump onto his back, writhing in agony.

A fierce pleasure blazed through him. He spun his axe about and buried it in the man's chest, ending his yelps. Then Baldr whirled around, ready for the next one.

By then the stony beach was riven by cries and screams, by the clang and thud of metal blades clashing and finding their targets. Blood dotted the air like kicked chaff. Men ran at one another, shaggy locks flailing, arms pumping. Jorund had beaten his man and was grappling with another. Bolg had had his legs chopped from under him and lay twitching in a slick of gore.

The tang of blood made Baldr heady. He flung himself at the nearest newcomer – a boy not much older than him, hefting a long maul. The boy squared up, long sandy hair flying across his face. He bared his teeth like an animal, and ran at Baldr.

Baldr waited for the maul to swing in, jerking out of the way at the last moment. He darted back with his axe, hoping to catch the boy's leg, but missed by a hand's width.

The boy was as quick as he was, slippery as a worm. They circled one another, lunging and feinting. Baldr rushed him, hammering the axe down, but the boy got his maul up to parry and the weapons banged together.

Baldr pressed the attack, working the axe around to thrust it up at the boy's chest. The sandy-haired fighter fell away, retreating, keeping his weapon raised.

'Had enough?' taunted Baldr. The boy didn't respond – only then did Baldr realise he didn't speak the same tongue.

They clashed again. The boy swung his maul at Baldr's head – a wild lunge, full of venom. Baldr nearly didn't dodge it, and felt the rush of air as it swished past his face. Before he'd had time to feel the shock of the near hit, he was twisting at the waist, backhanding the axe across at chest height.

The blade bit deep, cracking bone and carving the muscle open. Baldr's opponent screamed, dropping the maul as his limbs spasmed. Baldr hacked again, severing the boy's neck and dropping him.

Before the body had even hit the stones, Baldr was roaring in delight. He could feel the heat of the blood on him. All around him, men fought desperate battles – eyes were gouged, skin was ripped, throats were throttled.

He whirled, looking for fresh kills. As he did so, his eyes suddenly caught the top of the headland, a long way off now and part-masked by drifting fog. For a moment, just a heartbeat, he thought he saw a hunched outline on the summit. He thought he saw two golden eyes, ridged fur, a long maw.

He kept moving, but the sight distracted him, so he didn't see the man bearing down on him, fresh from beating an Ascurii hunter into the bloody surf. This man was bigger than the first one he'd killed, wearing snarled furs that made him look half animal. The man rushed Baldr, giving him no time to swing his axe.

Baldr ducked, aiming to pounce clear and get space, but something hit him on the back, followed by a hot, sick rush across his head and spine. He crashed to the ground, tasting salty grit in his mouth.

He tried to rise, to get to his feet, but something heavier cracked across his back, flooring him. His vision blurred, and the pain came on – astonishing pain, radiating out from hot wounds.

Somehow, he pushed himself onto his back, axe still in hand. He tried to rise, to find some way to fight back before the lather of blood in his mouth choked him.

The man didn't come after him – he was standing, mouth open, looking up at the sky. The clouds were churning, tearing like fabric. Baldr thought he saw the shadow of some enormous bird swooping out of the emptiness, but then his eyes failed him.

He arched his ravaged back, racked in agony, feeling his heart racing out of control. Still he clutched the axe in his hand. He heard a booming roar, like the sea coming in, and heard men's voices raised in alarm and terror.

Then he was out, lost in a crimson world of pain and madness.

He slept for a long time. At times he half roused, and realised that he was not dead. The world was filled with sounds and smells he didn't know. Everything was thundering, swaying, tilting.

It was hard to open his eyes. Something had been done to them – it felt like wires across the lids.

He managed it, during one of the rare times his awareness returned, just briefly, before the pain pulled him back under.

He was in some kind of chamber, square-sided, smooth like the face of an axe. Men towered over him, draped in matted furs. They looked like giants. They smelt like wolves. They didn't look at him.

He twisted his head. He was lying on the floor, and it felt as if the earth were shaking. Far off, he saw a door, open to the white sky. The clouds seemed to be racing past it impossibly fast.

He didn't know what he was seeing. He didn't know why the floor of the chamber was vibrating and juddering like a seer in a fit, nor why the air was so painfully thin, nor where the thunder-roar came from.

His head cracked back, he felt groggy again and knew he was going under. Just as he did, the clouds ripped apart, showing him the face of a mountain through the narrow door.

He was *above* it. He was *above the mountain*.

Baldr passed out then. The rush of oblivion embraced him, dragging him down, sucking the last warmth from his battered, bloody, hacked body.

He slept.

It would be a long time before he woke, or saw that mountain again, or saw or felt anything else. In his sleep, unbeknown to him, came healing, and change, and augmentation. Whispered voices came and went like dreams.

When he woke, much later, nothing was the same. It would never be again. Only the name remained, the one he had been given on the ice-crossing so the gods would know his soul.

Baldr. Fjolnir. God-marked.

I
THE CARDINAL

CHAPTER ONE

'He will wake,' said Ingvar.

Gunnlaugur looked sceptical. 'How long?'

'A few days.'

'You're sure?'

'Olgeir says the same. Fjolnir dreams again.'

Gunnlaugur looked down at his hands. A thick cloth hung between his fingers, black with cleansing oils. His massive thunder hammer, *skulbrotsjór*, leant against one knee, its ornate gilding half swabbed. The old detail was coming through again, obscured for too long by blood and filth. Cleaning it away was cathartic – a reminder of old rhythms.

The sun beat down into a narrow courtyard. Dawn had broken less than an hour ago and already the heat was oppressive.

'If he dreams, he will wake,' agreed Gunnlaugur, resuming the painstaking cleaning of his weapon.

Ingvar was clad in a grey tunic, and his lean, muscled body glistened in the amber light. Soon his blond-grey hair would be slicked down, ready to take his battle-helm again. His armour would be hoisted and drilled into position, cladding him in the cocoon of murder, and he would take up *dausvjer*, cleaned and given rites of restoration.

The respite had been hard won, but it had given them time to breathe.

'What news of Njal?' Ingvar asked, strolling across the enclosed space like a caged animal, flexing his arms absently.

Gunnlaugur spat on the stone. 'The star-speakers here are *skítja*. They scrape at their dreams.' He shook his close-shaven head. Flecks of red lingering in his dirt-grey hair caught the sunlight. 'They don't know.'

'She wants to wait for him?' asked Ingvar, leaning against a whitewashed wall.

'She wants to fight,' said Gunnlaugur, his voice growling with approval.

Ingvar shared the Wolf Guard's sentiments. The Battle Sisters who had survived the assault on Hjec Aleja deserved their survival. They had fought hard for the walls, for the Cathedral, for the approaches to the last bridge. Even when the tide of plague-damned had threatened to overwhelm the entire city, they had kept fighting. Their devotions were strange, their manner alien, but in combat they showed their worth.

'Then everything is ready,' Ingvar said.

'Pretty much.'

Gunnlaugur held his weapon up. The sunlight caught the edges of the disruptor, sparkling like gold nuggets on the iron-grey of the hammerhead. He narrowed his eyes, scrutinising for flaws.

'I wanted to seek your counsel,' said Ingvar. 'About Bajola.'

Gunnlaugur didn't look away from the hammer. 'It can wait.'

Ingvar made to speak again, but Gunnlaugur held up a warning finger. His amber eyes never left the runes on his weapon. 'A long time, since I had to restore this myself. Feels good, to push the dirt out with my own fingers.' He looked up at Ingvar. 'Stormcaller will be here soon. We'll break bones before then, you and I. That is all that matters.' His savage face cracked into what passed with him for a smile. 'I am not ignoring it. Just not now.'

'When it is over–'

'When it is over, we'll talk. How's your own blade?'

Ingvar smiled dryly. 'The rites have been sung. It'll bite.'

Gunnlaugur ground his cloth into the thunder hammer's recesses.

'It'll need to,' he said.

De Chatelaine leaned against the balcony, high up in the hall of the Halicon. Her armoured fingers pressed against the limestone surface. She'd felt tense for a long time, and every gesture she made seemed tighter, more cramped.

Hot morning air wafted against her face. Sweat had broken out on her forehead, tiny beads that would only grow.

Below her, the city sprawled away in its unregulated, tangled messiness. The streets had always been crooked. Now they were choked with barricades, locked in a semi-ruined network of tumbled stone and half-dug pits. Smoke hung over the outer walls, distant across the wasteland beyond. The old Cathedral, Bajola's place, rose up from the debris like a spike of rusted iron, still smouldering long after the fires had exhausted themselves.

Beyond that, beyond the warren of occupied districts, the endless plain burned under a clear sky. The enemy army milled around in the heat-haze, their standards swaying drunkenly, half hidden by the clouds of filmy dust they kicked up. Other clouds roiled lazily amid that natural grime – masking clouds, sensor-defying murks.

More fallen troops had joined them since their first attempt to storm the inner walls. Augur readings indicated thousands more tramping across the deserts to swell their numbers. The entire world was wallowing in corruption, and the enemy had whole cities of ruin to draw on. If any other bastions of purity had endured, they had long since stopped transmitting signals. The planet was infected now, and only Hjec Aleja remained, a lone outpost of Imperial rule surrounded by seething shores of disease.

The canoness preceptor lifted her severe chin, scanning the ruins below her vantage. The Ighala Gate stood, just as it had throughout the entire siege. She could see the cloaks of her Sisters as they strode across the parapet below her, tiny with distance. Alongside them were the hunchbacked outlines of the big lascannon emplacements and rotary guns, most still in operation despite repeated assaults from the enemy.

Her people remained crammed inside the defences like rats trapped against rising water, pressed together and jostling in the shadow of the citadel. Food was not yet a problem, but water would become one soon. The wells were running dry. One of them now foamed green, like bubbling bile. They had somehow got to it, injecting toxins from the tankers that prowled the wasteland edges. Those who'd drunk unwarily died in excruciation, their innards turned into a fizzing slurry before the end. She'd seen the bodies afterwards, locked in contortions, drenched from the bloody voiding of every orifice. The poisons had not been designed simply to kill, but to inspire terror.

She would have hated the enemy enough without that – they didn't need to give her fresh reasons.

De Chatelaine heard a faint noise behind her then – a shuffle of silk on stone. Ermili Repoda, her Master of Astropaths, was waiting. His glassy eyes gazed unerringly at her, as if they were as sighted as hers.

'What is it?' she asked.

Repoda came to stand beside her. 'He's close. The Stormcaller. *Njal.* That's his name – the aether's alive with it.'

'You do not know when, though.'

'The art does not work in that way, canoness.'

'Do they try to speak to us?'

'They do not know whom to speak to. Perhaps they think we're already dead.'

'How many come with him?'

'More than one squad,' said Repoda. 'Maybe more than two.'

'We are honoured.'

Repoda smiled thinly, and his lined, pale face looked desiccated in the sunlight. 'You seem relaxed about his coming.'

'Should I not?'

'This is an Ecclesiarchy world.' Repoda inclined his head a fraction, perhaps in equivocation, perhaps in apology. 'The people look to you. They fear the Wolves almost as much as–'

'Then they're fools,' said de Chatelaine. 'They know. They *know* what waits for them out there.' She turned on him. 'We've worked *so hard*, the Wolf Guard and I, to clamp down on these fears. I won't have them intruding, not now.'

Repoda bowed. 'I merely report.'

De Chatelaine breathed in deep, tasting the smoke that hung over the entire city. It felt as if the lower reaches had been turned into a sacrificial offering, as charred and useless as a carcass on pagan flames. The stench was an accusation: *This is your failure. This is your defeat.*

'When the Stormcaller gets here, I will bow the knee. You will bow, all my people will bow. We don't get to choose our deliverers.'

De Chatelaine brushed her hair back from her face. The enemy never left her thoughts, even when out of eyesight. Now, thronged on the far horizon, seamy and massive, it dominated all else.

'We hold out,' she said. 'That is our only task. When the Stormcaller comes, he will find at least this: we did not submit.'

* * *

The servitors were crawling all over it like lice on a corpse, their grey flesh pulling at its innards and hauling them out onto the ground.

Jorundur watched them, wincing with every tug and wrench. *Vuokho* stood on the landing pad, half gutted, its flanks as black as *Undrider*'s had been, covered in scorch-marks and las-trails. Its huge engines loomed up into the sky, burned out, their systems fused. The armourglass on the cockpit was cracked, the undercarriage bent and twisted. Now that the gunship was hoisted on giant service racks designed for big cargo lifters, the full extent of the damage was visible.

He was rapt, lost in the detail of the work, though, like all his warrior kin, never fully off-guard.

'I can smell you, Sister,' Jorundur said out loud, sensing Callia's presence before she became visible.

The Battle Sister, de Chatelaine's deputy, emerged from the shadows. Her armour was as battle-worn as ever, and her face carried fresh scars – long raking lines down a smooth left cheek.

'You've been busy, Space Wolf,' she said, looking up at the gutted internals.

Jorundur sniffed. 'It'll fly again. That bastard didn't destroy everything on it. Just nearly everything.'

Callia's gaze ran across the blunt angles of the gunship. It was a huge machine up close – big enough for the void, and carrying weaponry enough to gut a small army.

As it had done, of course.

'When can you get it airborne again?' Callia asked.

Jorundur snorted. 'Days. Many days. If I am called to murder, then longer.'

Callia looked disappointed. 'We could use it.'

'You said that to me before. We all could.'

Jorundur liked Callia. She'd been there since the start, marshalling the long retreat, keeping her flamers raised the whole time. He'd seen her in action right at the end, when the enemy finally stormed the gates. Jorundur had been first into the vanguard, but she hadn't been far behind.

'They tell me more of your kind are coming,' Callia said.

'Don't trust star-speakers. They pipe all kinds of *skítja.*'

'They tell me a whole fleet's inbound.'

'*Fekke.* You thought *Undrider* was a whole fleet.'

'It was enough,' said Callia.

Jorundur shook his head sourly. 'You trust too much,' he muttered. 'It sticks in the craw.'

'Ah, but you believe in something.'

'My blade. My brothers.'

'You just give it a different name.'

'You name a thing, you control a thing. The Priests taught me that, at least.'

'So many priests,' mused Callia, her eyes bright with jibing, 'and so little faith.'

'Ever met a Rune Priest?'

Callia shook her head.

'You will do,' Jorundur said.

'Stormcaller is a Rune Priest, then.'

'It is one of his names.'

Callia shot him a curious, half-guilty look. 'I've seen psykers at work. I could sense the divine will in them. I could *feel* it. It must be the same. The same source, even with your war-shamans.'

Jorundur croaked out a harsh laugh. 'The source? *Skítja*, I don't care.' He grinned at her – an ugly, hooked grin that made the metal studs in his face clink. 'I saw a Priest rip a gunship in two, just like this one, and burn everything inside it like paper. They've slaughtered armies, they've scraped worlds clean. *God-marked.*' He looked up at the Thunderhawk again, knowing he needed to get back to the work of restoration. His fingers moved, itching to get among the entrails of the machine. 'They're just like the rest of us – butchers. That's all you need to know.'

The smoke rolled ahead of them, drifting and breaking across derelict buildings. Ahead, the street twisted away, heavy with dust, streaked with long-dried stains on what had once been white walls.

Hafloí applied pressure with his fingers, gently, smoothly. The mortal neck enclosed within them flexed, then burst. Hafloí's other hand remained clamped over the mutant's face, stifling its screams. Its legs stopped kicking, its swollen hands stopped trying to clutch at his armour. For a moment longer its body twitched, locked in muscle-rigidity. Then it flopped into torpor, leaking a mix of blood and infected fluids over his gauntlets.

'Quiet,' observed Olgeir, crouching beside the two of them. 'Nicely quiet.'

Hafloí relaxed, letting the corpse slide to the ground. He shook his hands free. 'They shouldn't be this strong.'

'Plague. Gets into the muscle.'

The big Wolf's armour was covered in blood, some of it ritual markings, some of it evidence of recent kills. His beloved heavy bolter, *sigrún,* had been left up in the citadel – this work required silence – so he carried a long-handled, twin-bladed axe with knotwork wyrms' heads engraved on the metal faces.

Hafloí kicked the corpse away from him, and drew his short blade – a leaf-shaped dagger with the rune *hata* etched on the blade. Then he looked ahead, down the street, to where it ended in a high stone wall.

Olgeir's helm lenses whirred faintly as he ran a scan. 'Fifty metres. Stay close.'

He set off, keeping his body low. For such a giant, Olgeir could move both fast and quietly, barely stirring the grime beneath his boots. Power armour made its own distinctive grinding noise, but there were ways to dampen it.

Hafloí followed, keeping a careful watch. The lower city had been a haunt of horror ever since the first attacks. The main enemy army had withdrawn beyond the walls, but the old suburban zone was still occupied by mutants too addled or stubborn to leave. The residuals stumbled through the ruins, hunting for flesh that was now scarce, cradling bulbous stomachs and weeping scabrous tears.

Hafloí paused at an intersection, looking down a long alley running transverse before ghosting across it. The lower city was quiet, darkening slowly as the short dusk gathered pace. Brown-blue shadows crept across the dust, running up the sides of the tight-packed hab-shells.

It smelt foul. Corpses rotted in the heat, buzzing with flies. Icons had been daubed on the standing walls – three circles, picked out in dirty green. Some lettering lingered here and there: *Terminus Est*, scrawled across any heap of stones big enough to accommodate it.

The hunt had been meagre – stabs from the gloom, neck-twists, gut-kicks. Quiet killings, just enough to clear the path, to get them where they needed to be.

Olgeir reached his destination – a tower, half demolished, its metal skeleton visible where the render had come down. Hafloí caught up with him, slipping under the cover of the blown-open doorway.

'Really?' he voxed. 'Nothing better?'

'It will do,' replied Olgeir, pushing ahead.

They entered a narrow corridor built for mortals. The ceiling was low, barely above their helms. It sagged in places, stained brown, and watery gurgles came from above them. They reached a stairwell, running in zigzags up the floors. It was as dirty as everything else and strewn with the detritus of war – bloodmarks, bolt-shells in the rockcrete, scattered possessions dropped in the hurry to get out.

Hafloí sniffed for targets as he climbed. The proximity markers in his helm were of limited use – the walking dead would not show up on them until they were actually moving – so hunt-sense was superior.

They reached the top level, and the damaged floor creaked under them. Hafloí tensed as he left the stairwell, sensing something up ahead. Olgeir responded immediately, moving silently down the corridor towards a locked door at the end. Hafloí went with him, blade in hand. He reached the door first – a single push broke the lock, sending the metal panel swinging open.

Hafloí slipped inside, blade ready. The room beyond was unlit and clogged with rubbish. Fabric sacks piled high, bursting with rotting foodstuffs. Insects scuttled over every surface, bloated and glossy.

A single figure faced him, scrabbling back across the floor, eyes wide. He was emaciated and sore-ridden. It looked like he had been gnawing on something from one of the sacks, and dark fluid dribbled down his chicken-scrawn jowls.

Hafloí strode over to him, keeping his blade raised.

'Angels!' blurted the man, wedging himself up against the far wall and looking up at him, terrified. 'At *last*.'

Hafloí paused.

The man got to his knees, his face trembling with fear and emotion. 'Is it over?' he shuddered. 'Throne, say it's over. Get me out of here. Please, for the love of the Emperor, get me *out*.'

Hafloí glanced at the sacks. He kicked the nearest, and it spilt open. Joints of meat, crusted green with putrescence, tumbled out. He recognised a thigh, a calf, a hand – five-fingered and curled tight into a desperate claw.

The man panicked. 'I *had* to! You have no–'

Hafl07's blade punched through his neck, killing him instantly.

Olgeir walked past, heading for the doorway into a connecting chamber beyond. 'You hesitated,' he said. 'Don't hope. They're all long gone.'

Hafl07 gazed down at the man's body. Sores had clustered around his mouth. Some of them were moving, as if tiny creatures writhed under the tight-stretched skin.

'Long gone,' he muttered.

He followed Olgeir. The chamber beyond must have once been the man's dorm-unit. A single bunk stood against the far wall, its grey sheets soiled. The walls were smeared with what looked and smelled like excrement.

Olgeir moved to a floor-to-ceiling window on the west-facing wall. The glass was cracked and daubed with grease, but still intact. He pulled a catch, released the lock and hauled the window open on to a balcony outside.

The two of them took up position behind the outer railing. Ahead of them, less than a hundred metres distant and on a level with their position, stood the upper edge of the city's walls, semi-ruined and tumbled into piles of rubble.

Hafl07's helm lenses switched to magnocular vision, scrolling out over the rim of the walls and filtering the fading light beyond. Green wireframes flickered over the terrain, indicating troop formations, buildings, vehicles, all standing within a kilometre of the shattered perimeter.

He scanned from left to right, gradually extending the range out across the plain. Positioned high up on the very edge of the city, hard under the lip of the sensor-baffling clouds, the detail was better than it had been up in the citadel.

'Tell me what you're getting,' said Olgeir.

Hafl07 extended the reach again, letting his armour-mounted auspexes do the work.

'Infantry formations,' he said, passing over several big contingents. The soldiers were arranged in loose phalanxes, basking in the heat, mouths slack, ready for the long desert night. Fires had been started, massive ones, adding to the pall of smoke that hung over them. 'Six... seventeen chem-carriers. Big ones.'

The massive tanker-juggernauts stood in a makeshift compound behind the first of the infantry lines, towering into the murk and underlit by pale green marker lumens. Their engines were running, fuelling the chemical furnaces in the tanks behind.

'They've dug in,' added Olgeir, marking the trench patterns.

Hafl07 ran his augmented gaze along earthworks topped with coils of razor wire. Gun-towers had been built along the ridges, constructed from huge rockcrete blocks and carrying heavy, snub-barrelled cannons on rotating bases. Each tower was protected by dedicated units of gas mask-wearing troops in thick carapace armour. More lights blinked on and off in the gloom, tracing the outline of bigger edifices beyond.

'Prefabs,' said Olgeir, indicating points along the defence lines. 'They landed them, or looted them.'

Hafl07 remembered the empty depots they'd seen on the plague destroyer in orbit. He ratcheted up the scale again, and his helm zoomed in further. He swept over lines of infantry, some loosely formed up, some in deep-dug positions overlooked by more earthworks. A few rust-encrusted tanks rumbled between formations, belching smoke. Their hulls had been defaced and covered in corpse-racks, all of which buzzed with insect clouds.

'Until I saw this world,' murmured Hafloí, 'I would not have believed so many flies existed.'

Beyond the tank columns, the land rose. The magnocular range reached its limit, and the images became less defined.

'That's it,' said Hafloí.

More razor wire ran around the base of the incline, arranged in layers. Scaffolds were everywhere, all slung with swaying gibbets. Green marker lights peered fuzzily through the miasma, blinking on and off.

'Get a loc-reading on that,' said Olgeir.

Hafloí had already done it, storing the positions of kill-zones, ingress routes, choke-points. 'They've got something big in there.'

'Wall-breakers. Focus more – you can see them.'

'We can take it,' Hafloí said.

'Perhaps,' said Olgeir, his voice as deep and calm as ever. 'With Njal, certainly.'

Hafloí let his vision lapse back into short-range. 'You fought with him?'

'I saw him. From a distance.'

'And?'

'And what?'

'What's he like?'

Olgeir kept up the scan. Hafloí could hear the faint clicks as his helm-gear registered picts. Then, before he could reply, something broke out below them – a crash, a long way down, followed by a series of thumps. The walls of the building shook.

Olgeir clicked his lenses back into focus and took a deep breath. 'We've been detected.'

Hafloí smiled inside his helm. 'Good.'

Olgeir turned and walked back into the hab-chamber, hefting his wyrmblade axe loosely. 'Don't let your blood get hot. We clear them out, then back to the citadel.'

Hafloí followed Olgeir. He hoped there were lots of them – a whole herd, something worth drawing a blade for.

'Fine,' he replied, feeling the first spikes of kill-urge stir. 'Just leave a few for me.'

CHAPTER TWO

Baldr's nostrils drew in breath again. His eyes twitched as he dreamed. The ghostly pallor had left his skin, replaced by Fenrisian colouring – pale, like stone under winter sun.

Ingvar looked at him. Baldr lay on a metal slab under bright apothecarion lights, face up, limbs slack. Shackles grasped him at the wrists, ankles, neck and waist.

The door to the apothecarion was criss-crossed with sensors. A second blast-door had been rigged in the room beyond, primed to slam closed if anything disturbed the contents of the inner chamber. Pict-feed lenses dotted the ceiling, flickering intermittently as they shunted their feeds direct to Gunnlaugur's helm-display.

Olgeir had inscribed a rune of warding over the medicae-cot, scratching it crudely into the brushed metal of the lumen-housing. A Rune Priest would have done a better job, but it had been a long time since one had accompanied Járnhamar on the hunt. There were fewer of them now, they said. They were overstretched, burnt out, kept busy by Grimnar's remorseless war-calling.

Ingvar didn't know the truth of that. He'd seen the condition of other Chapters, though, and knew well enough the trials that faced them all. Every Chapter Master from Terra to the Halo Stars was feeling the strain – they couldn't train new aspirants quickly enough, the rate of attrition was growing and the weight of ten thousand years of ceaseless combat was catching up.

If there is to be victory, I cannot see it.

But he had vowed not to think such things again. He drew a vial of liquid into a long syringe, watching as the dark red matter foamed. He discarded the vial and flicked the air bubbles from the syringe.

Then he moved close to Baldr. Feeling for the vein, he inserted the needle. He had to push – mortal instruments had trouble penetrating the skin of a Sky Warrior. As he depressed the plunger, he watched the tincture enter Baldr's system. His eyes flickered a little and his mouth tightened a fraction, then he relaxed.

Ingvar withdrew the needle and discarded it. He was no Apothecary, far less a Wolf Priest. It was one thing to keep a brother warrior alive on the battlefield – every Hunter knew the basics of chirurgy – another to shepherd Baldr through whatever horror had overtaken him.

At least the visible taint of corruption had faded. For a long time Baldr's saliva had retained a green hue, like algal scum at the edge of summer-hot pools. Lifting his lids had exposed bloodshot eyes, unseeing, the irises shrunk.

The breathing was more regular now. The rancid stench had gone, replaced by the healthier smells of perspiration. The Red Dream still had him, but the other sickness had retreated. Whether it was truly gone or simply dormant he had no way of knowing.

'Gyrfalkon,' came Gunnlaugur's voice over the comm. 'Anything yet?'

'No change,' Ingvar replied.

'But he will wake soon?'

'I cannot say.'

Gunnlaugur grunted. 'Re-seal the chamber, then. The canoness has news.'

'By your will.'

Ingvar severed the comm-link. He reduced the lumens, keeping the observation lamps over Baldr's body on full. He ran a final check, activated the locks, then left the chamber. The door clanged closed behind him, followed by the hiss of bolts sliding home. The metal briefly glittered as the detector-field swept over it.

Baldr was sealed again, as secure as one of Ras Shakeh's ancient gods, locked in the cool under the desert floor and waiting to be stirred once more.

He lay on the slab, breathing shallow, eyelids flickering.

'This is the moment,' said de Chatelaine, allowing a little pride to sink into her voice. That felt good – it had been a long time since she had done so. 'This is the time we have been holding out for.'

She stood in one of the marble-and-gold antechambers running clear of the Halicon's main hall. The war had hardly intruded there: ivory and ebony statues of the primarchs still stood proudly on lozenges of veined stone. Thick drapes warded the force of the sun outside, though bars of light still angled in, twisting with dust.

Callia stood by her, as did others of her Sororitas command retinue. Five Wolves faced them, making everything else in the chamber look fragile.

Gunnlaugur had scoured the worst of the combat-grime from him, and de Chatelaine had been surprised to see the extent of the glorious fine work around the edges of his armour. He seemed animated by a fierce, almost febrile energy, even when standing. Perhaps he thought he hadn't performed well enough, hadn't slaughtered quite as many as he should have. De Chatelaine couldn't share that view, but then she only had the scantiest of insights into the battle-culture of Fenris, and what counted for satisfaction with a Wolf Guard.

The other one, Ingvar, remained at one side, though some of the separateness she had detected in him at the start had ebbed – he now stood amongst his brothers at greater ease. Olgeir and Haflói had come to the chamber fresh from their scout mission to the walls. Jorundur, the darkest, had remained alone with his gunship.

'You have new tidings?' asked Gunnlaugur, looking at her sceptically.

'A flotilla, on the cusp of the veil,' said de Chatelaine. 'Your brothers.'

'Fleet markers?'

'Repoda is in no doubt.'

Gunnlaugur shared a look with his brothers. 'If Njal's bringing a pack, a large one, then this battle's already over.'

'Then, after it, we take it to the sector,' said de Chatelaine, her eyes shining. 'The beginning. This is the crusade we sought.'

The canoness activated a large hololith column. A battle schematic hovered in glowing lines over the marble face, picking out the perimeter of the city, the terrain beyond, and what they had discovered of the enemy positions.

'When your forces detect our beacon signal,' said de Chatelaine, 'they can make planetfall on the open plain, surrounding the enemy. We will break out then, and they will be caught between the two fronts. Caught, and destroyed.'

Gunnlaugur scrutinised the schematic. He sniffed sceptically. 'They won't wait.'

Olgeir nodded. 'They've not moved for a while, but this looks complete now.' He pointed to a low hill, two kilometres to the south-west of Hjec Aleja's ruined outer gates. 'They've brought wall-breakers. We ran deep augur sweeps while down at the wall's edge.'

'And Plague Marines,' added Hafloí. 'The last ones left. We've been waiting for reinforcements, and so have they.'

'Then we need to hold out,' said de Chatelaine. 'Just a little longer.'

'They have had all the time they needed,' said Gunnlaugur, shaking his head. 'They have dragged those guns halfway across a continent, and now they are ready to use them.'

Olgeir leaned over the column and gestured to the landscape immediately behind the fortified incline. 'The wall-breakers are there. Couldn't get a good look, but if they fire, we'll know all about it.'

It was de Chatelaine's turn to study the schematic. As she did so, her brow furrowed in concern. 'We can't launch a sortie that far out.'

'*You* can't,' said Ingvar.

'And you can't wait for those guns to fire,' said Gunnlaugur. 'They're ready to go. We have to move first.'

De Chatelaine pursed her lips. The Wolves always relished the reckless attack, but that didn't automatically make it the right tactic. 'The mortal troops aren't like you – they won't last long in the open desert, not against those numbers.'

'They don't have to,' said Gunnlaugur. 'You just need to retake the outer walls. Get their attention. Seize the towers by the main gate and you'll give us all the cover we need.'

'And you'll take on what's left.'

Gunnlaugur bowed. 'For as long as needed.'

Callia shook her head in disbelief. 'Even for you, that's–'

'Possible,' said Ingvar. 'We don't have to hold them forever – just hit them before they move.'

'They won't stand still,' added Gunnlaugur. 'Wait longer, and the city will be in flames before Njal makes orbit.'

De Chatelaine hesitated. She scrutinised the hololith again. 'You go out there, in plain view, and they'll rip you apart.'

Gunnlaugur snorted. 'Do it in plain view, and we'd deserve to be.'

'What's the readiness of the city garrison?' de Chatelaine asked Callia.

'Full readiness,' Callia said.

No hesitation, no shade of doubt. That gave de Chatelaine some comfort. 'And this is your only counsel?' she asked Gunnlaugur.

The Wolf Guard shrugged, making bone totems clatter against his armour. 'We'll take the guns out anyway. Better to do it with cover, but it's your city.'

De Chatelaine smiled. 'So it is.' She turned from the hololith, giving the nod to Callia. 'We will need time to prepare. I shall notify you when all is ready.' Then she looked back at Gunnlaugur. 'And *I* will give the order, Wolf Guard. As you say, it is still my city.'

Gunnlaugur inclined his head. 'We will aim to keep it that way,' he said.

Five hours later, Callia stood under the arch of the Ighala Gate as the sun set, casting deep orange shafts across the darkening sky above. Towering toxin-clouds glowed in the dusk, vivid and spectacular. The heavy twin defence-doors loomed up ahead of her, bolted and barred as they had been since the final hours of the last assault.

Around her stood the remains of Ras Shakeh's Celestian contingent. The remaining Battle Sisters of the Wounded Heart lined up behind them, their ebony armour glinting with the last rays of the dying light. Beyond that stood attack squads of Ras Shakeh Guard, arrayed in the mixed uniforms of hastily combined regiments. Some of their gear was in good condition, some of it looked barely capable of resisting a determined bayonet strike.

She didn't like to think too closely about numbers. They had mustered a few thousand, all told, with a skeleton reserve to follow them down and an even thinner defence force to man the wall-guns. Still, it was good to be on the front foot again. Huddling behind the gates waiting for the inevitable assault was not what she had been trained for.

Her comm-bead crackled.

'You have clearance, Sister,' came de Chatelaine's voice. 'Go with hate, and the Emperor guide your aim.'

Callia smiled. 'And yours, canoness preceptor.'

The bolts on the gate began to grind open, sending sparks flying from the adamantium sheaths. On the walls above, lascannons swivelled on their mounts, holding fire for now but already picking targets. A hundred sharpshooters mounted on the parapets crouched down, resting long muzzles on the hot stone.

Callia tensed, clutching the grip on her bolter. She could feel her heart-rate pick up, slipping into the pre-combat state she cherished.

Cleanse my soul.

The words came to her unbidden. Callia couldn't remember who'd taught them to her. Bajola, perhaps.

Clear my mind.

The last of the bolts powered home, sliding into the wall-mounts on immense pistons. A thin line ran up the centre of the two doors, and dust showered down the joint.

Enable my body.

With a jolt, the gate-engines kicked in and the two doors parted, grating slowly apart and exposing the bridge beyond. Las-beams whickered out into the gathering gloom, angled down from the parapets to lay a covering wall of fire. A wide, empty expanse stretched off, cleared of buildings during the first siege and home to nothing more than broken earth.

Callia advanced, the Celestians on either side of her, until they were directly under the arch. The narrow span of the bridge ran ahead of them, empty, before terminating on the far side of a deep gorge. In the distance, hidden by both gathering darkness and smog, ran the jagged outlines of the lower city, its habs now bombed-out and derelict.

'With me,' voxed Callia to her retinue. She strode out into the foetid air beyond the gate. More las-beams scythed out above her, whining into the line of buildings in the distance. The volume picked up as the gunners found their targets, aiming to give the infantry a clear run for as long as possible.

Callia glanced upwards, looking back over her shoulder. The face of the gate bore the tattered remains of Wounded Heart banners and iconography. Though scorched and ripped, the symbols of the Imperium still endured.

'Forward,' she ordered.

The vanguard broke into a run, leaving the cover of the Gate and charging out across the bridge. For a few moments they were totally exposed, running across the open span with no cover of any sort. Then they reached the far side and split into four columns, fanning out across the wasteland. Battle Sister squads headed each unit, followed by the more numerous Guard detachments, all heading straight towards the forbidding line of silhouettes ahead.

For a while, there was no return fire. The lascannons on the high wall behind them kept firing, briefly lighting the scene before them in stark flash-frames. It was eerily silent, save for the echo of breathing in their helms and the crunch of boots on gravel.

Callia ran hard, her movements boosted by her power armour, her head low and her bolter trained on the lines of cover ahead. They rapidly closed the gap between the Gate and the first ranks of ruined hab-blocks. Her column took the central path, the one cleared by the Wolves to aid the passage of arms down to the outer wall. The other groups split off, one to the left and two to the right, moving swiftly to take up positions in cover before the fight down to the perimeter.

A las-beam from the Ighala formation hit the remnants of a big tower ahead of her, scything clean through the weakened masonry and sending bricks cascading to the ground. More hit, crowning the shattered ruins with blooms of incandescence.

The lead group reached the line of buildings and kept running. Callia leapt across a tangled line of razor wire and felt her boots thud onto rockcrete on the far side. The serrated outlines of the lower city rose up on either side of her, enclosing the night sky like two walls of a canyon. The street ahead was littered with wreckage – blast-rubble from the walls above, the carcass of a Rhino transport, the cracked edges of craters where ordnance had hammered down during the worst of the previous fighting.

Her Celestians ran alongside her, sweeping their weapons two-handed as they searched for targets. Callia could hear the clatter of boots as the Guard units worked to keep pace. They would already be looking for ways to bring heavy weapons teams down to tactical points to cover the onwards advance.

Still no return fire. The Celestians tore down the main thoroughfare, hugging the shadow of the buildings on either side, their armour dark against dark and their robes fluttering about them like death-shrouds.

'Where are they?' voxed Callia's subordinate Djinate, advancing hard on her right flank.

'Watch the habs,' replied Callia, running, angling her helm up to the broken rooftops. 'It's only a matter of–'

The first stabs of light lanced out of the dark before she'd finished speaking. Callia didn't break stride, weaving across a patch of shattered brickwork as the barrage of small-arms fire came in. Her Sisters did the same, scattering across the open ground, using what cover the battlefield gave them and losing no momentum.

Callia let the targeting lines on her helm intersect, pinpointing a location ten metres up in the empty heart of a multi-storey hab-tower.

She took aim, compensating for her own movement, and loosed two shots. Then she kept running, barely hearing the crack and subsequent blast of bolt-rounds obliterating the sniper-nest. By then, other Sisters had opened up on their own targets and the air filled with the resounding roar and crack of bolter discharge.

'The flanks,' warned Callia, spotting another sniper position and dispatching it with a single bolt-round. 'They'll be coming around.'

The thoroughfare they ran down was broken up with the intersecting streets of the lower city, all overshadowed by the close-packed hab-blocks. Even as Callia spoke, enemy units broke from cover some twenty metres back from her position, streaking out of the dark and engaging the Guard units following in her wake. The enemy troops were wearing gas masks, and their bulbous eyes glowed softly in the dark. Grenades started to fly, detonating with puffs of toxic smoke.

The Guard responded, and the staccato growl of a tripod-mounted autocannon opened up from back up the street. Whisper-snaps of las-fire followed, crackling into the bands of mutants emerging from the gloom.

Callia pressed on, confident in the main Guard contingents to hold their own. Speed was the main thing – to secure the outer gates before the enemy could muster a full defence and drag them into street-to-street combat. Locator runes cycling across her helm-lens showed the positions of the other Battle Sister units – they were closing on the lower city edge, pushing rapidly, giving the enemy no time to form up before they reached the target defence points.

Callia swung her bolter and squeezed off another round, watching as the shell shot into the maw of a shadowed intersection to her left. She heard the wet grunt of impact, followed by the rip of explosion, and a bloated mutant staggered out in front of her, stomach spilling, gas mask ripped from its neck.

Still running, she launched a kick at its reeling face, breaking its neck before she'd landed. More mutants emerged in its wake, some with close-combat weapons, a few with projectile cannons.

Callia charged into them, firing from the waist with one hand, lashing out with her blade with the other. She was far too fast for them – a few seconds of fury, and they lay at her feet, coughing up blood and phlegm.

These were the outriders. The real enemy lay beyond the outer perimeter, holed up in their vast complex of tunnels, trenches and gun-towers. She knew they would be stirring now, roused by the sudden break from the inner gates, preparing their terror weapons again and priming the launchers. If the vanguard couldn't make their objectives before the enemy responded, this sortie would be very short-lived.

'Maintain pace,' she ordered, kicking away the last choking mutant and breaking back into a sprint.

It was good, thought Callia, to recover land they had given up after such heavy bloodshed. Her helm-display showed each assault column driving towards their objective, supported by Guard units that made good ground and seized strategic intersections. Some of the devotional buildings around them were half intact, showing the old emblems of the Wounded Heart amid the filth and desecration. This push might be little more than temporary, but it felt like a reclamation of sorts.

Another autocannon opened up from behind them, sending a heavy rain of shells rattling into the night and cracking into the buildings ahead. The Guard were getting faster at bringing them into position, securing the path back up to Ighala and clearing the long transit routes of the enemy.

Callia's bolter clicked empty and she slammed a new magazine in, barely pausing. The air was now falling away to perfect dark, shrouded by the ever-roiling clouds of smoke piling up from enemy positions beyond the walls. The ground became slimy with old chem-weapon discharge, glistening with ophidian dullness under the muzzle-flares of the massed bolters and lasweapons.

They tried to make a stand up ahead of her. Callia saw them massing across the width of the street, trying to haul drum-barrelled guns onto heaps of refuse and get some kind of fire-line established.

The Celestians needed no orders – they assaulted it in unison, laying down a curtain of bolter-fire before picking up the pace and charging head-on. The surviving enemy troops managed to get a volley of return las-fire clear, but it barely slowed them. Callia charged up the earth slope of the bulwark, drew her blade, then leapt into the mass of bodies beyond. Her sword flashed out, jamming under the neck of a grasping mutant before slicking away and cutting deep into the outstretched arm of another.

Then her Sisters were with her, whirling, cutting, blasting, crushing. Sororitas power armour didn't quite have the juggernaut impact of full Adeptus Astartes plate, but it was still formidable, capable of seeing off all but the most determined impacts and hugely augmenting the physical movements of its wearer. The barricade was smashed apart, its defenders crushed and bludgeoned aside and trodden into the shattered earth beyond.

Then the outer walls loomed, battered by past bombardments but partially intact. Callia located the target tower on her forward view – a squat rock-crete structure built up against the wall itself, just over two hundred metres north of the ruined outer gates.

'Objective sighted,' she voxed, firing all the while. 'Follow me in.'

The Celestians streaked across the last of the open ground, trading shots with the scattered resistance holed up in the buildings around them. More heavy weapons fire broke out from behind them, testament to the growing security of the Guard positions.

Callia reached the tower entrance on ground level – a gaping hole where doors had once stood. Bodies, fresh with hot blood, slumped over the jagged edges of metal plates. Djinate slammed against the wall on the far side of the entrance hole, priming a frag grenade and hefting it one-handed.

Callia nodded, and Djinate hurled the grenade into the dark. A second later and the interior of the tower filled with a boom of heat, light and screaming. Callia ducked inside, her helm-lens compensating for the swirl of smoke burning across her visual field. Disorientated mutants stumbled into her path, clutching at shrapnel wounds or gasping from severed chem-tubes, and she dispatched them one by one.

'Get a Guard squad at the breach,' she voxed, racing for the spiral stairway with Djinate close behind. 'I want this one secured first.'

She took the stairs two at a time, racing up around a tight spiral. The enemy defenders seemed to have clustered, foolishly, at the base of the tower, and she encountered no more living until reaching the summit. Half a dozen mutants tried to rush her then, tearing across the open-roofed platform at her as she emerged.

Callia charged straight into them, blade in hand and already spiralling. She jabbed it up, impaling a porcine maul-carrier under the chin, then pulled it round, severing the neck of a three-eyed horror with flailing jowls. The edge flashed in the night, catching the now-vivid glow from the piled-high toxin-clouds, and the savage beauty of it made her laugh out loud.

By the time Djinate caught up, the tower summit was heaped with bodies and Callia stood alone at the epicentre, her breathing heavy, her blade slick with diseased gore.

'Objective achieved,' observed Djinate.

Callia strode over to the parapet facing towards the lower city. Lines of tracer-fire scythed out from the fixed gun positions, cracking against the bulwarks where enemy warbands still hunkered down. Guard units were dragging heavy weapons down the cleared thoroughfare, and a long las-cannon barrel was being hauled along on the back of a half-track, ready for lifting up to the tower top where it would be mounted.

They were moving efficiently, going fast, taking care to clear out the remaining pockets of resistance. Other towers and bulwarks along the city's perimeter were rocked with explosions prior to being seized, cleared and occupied.

Callia turned around and walked over to the parapet's outward-facing edge. The tower she'd taken ran up the inside curve of the outer wall, cresting the upper edge by a few metres and affording a clear view of the plains outside.

Just a few dozen metres out, and the madness began. Hordes of glow-eyed mutants were advancing out of the night, roused by the clamour of combat from within the city. The front ranks looked as ramshackle as those the Sisters had already swept away, but behind them came more organised units – plate-armoured and carrying more lethal weaponry. The throttled growl of vehicle engines keying up rumbled across the plain, out of sight behind the shifting curtains of smog but not far away.

Callia leaned against the parapet edge. More Sisters emerged from the stairwell and took up position on either side of her.

The enemy encampment was vast. It was like a miniature city in itself – a huge, rambling collection of trenches, infantry detachments, tank squadrons and luminous, belching chemical works. Toxin-clouds blossomed above it all, blotting out the stars in swirling columns of virulence.

It was like kicking an ant's nest. Now the enemy was stirring, sending out its gathered strength. The defenders of Hjec Aleja had provoked it, forcing the assault early in order to buy the Wolves some breathing room, but set against the advance of such a huge, brooding mass of slaved warriors, the gamble now felt perilously fine.

'So, we've done our part,' Callia breathed, leaning against a rockcrete battlement and angling her bolter. 'Now, Sons of Fenris, do yours.'

CHAPTER THREE

He no longer remembered his name.

For a while, after the sickness had first come, he'd remembered it. After that, when he'd torn his uniform to get at the sores and his skin had started to pucker, he'd still remembered it. During the long nights in Hjec Morva when everything seemed to be dissolving into a long, sweaty frenzy of contagion he'd repeated it to himself, over and over, together with his rank and his regiment, as if by mouthing the syllables he could stave off the horror that was already combining and multiplying within his body.

Now, much later, he remembered doing that, but he no longer remembered why. His name was long gone, as was his old military grade, as was caring about either.

He pushed at the pustules clustering across the back of his neck and smiled as they burst. Milky fluid leaked down his chest and gave off an interesting smell – like fungus, or rotten boot leather.

Orders came to him in different ways now. Sometimes the Masters sought him out in person, lumbering through the trenches in their gloriously distended battleplate, speaking to him in a language he knew wasn't Gothic but that somehow made sense. Other times his duties would just become clear to him, formulating in his mind as if crystallised from a dream.

This was one of those times. He pulled himself out of what had been a shallow, dream-filled sleep and hoisted his autogun into position. His uniform – what remained of it – was crusted with dusty mud from the trench floor. His weapon-casing was already beginning to rust. Once, that would have appalled him. Now he just didn't care and nor did it seem to have any effect on the operation of the gun.

He adjusted his helm, biting down against the rebreather that pressed against the inside of his mouth, then climbed up, grabbing hold of the wooden ladder that ran up the inside wall of the trench and out to the world of fire beyond.

Others came with him – his men, the ones who had followed him into damnation right from the start. Just like him, their movements were heavy, their reactions dulled by the mucus that seeped from their ears and nostrils. Some carried autoguns like him, others had resorted to meat-hooks and rusty spikes laced with the special nerve-toxins the Masters gave them.

In his more lucid moments, he wondered why the Plaguefather had afflicted them in so many different ways. He wondered why, if the gods of decay desired his service, they hadn't made him faster, more deadly, more skilful. To lace his body with such gurgling rottenness seemed like a strange choice. But then the Father's ways were hardly likely to be transparent to him. All things considered, it wasn't worth worrying about overmuch.

He reached the lip of the trench wall and heaved himself over the top, and the full vista of war stretched out and away, glimpsed through bleary gas mask-lenses. The whole camp was moving. The charred desert ahead of him, thrown into perpetual twilight by the churning smog, crawled with a steadily growing carpet of advancing men. It was a strangely awesome sight – like the planet itself stirring to excise the last remnant of those who opposed the Father. He dimly felt his small role in that, and a swell of something like satisfaction grew in his rheumy chest.

Far away, he saw the outer walls of the city. He saw bright flashes of weaponry igniting along the parapets, tiny and blurred in the distance. He saw the army of the Masters marching to respond. He saw thousands of warriors, all like him, picking themselves up, dragging themselves out of the earth, falling into loose assault formations. He saw the big tanks grind into motion, gouging up desiccated earth under their tracks. He saw artillery pieces crank into firing angles, and gun-crews working to deliver the payloads of chem-bombs and incendiary canisters.

Then he was marching himself, shambling like the others over the broken, dusty ground. His men fell in around him, dozens of them, faces hidden behind their black rebreathers. They did not follow the infantry heading for the city. They had their *own* duty, up on the earthworks guarding the Masters and their glorious Machines. They would not be hurled up against the inferno of the wall assault. They would stay amid the gun-towers and trenches, forming the final line of defence that would keep the Machines guarded.

They were needed, those Machines. They had been hauled across the pitiless sands by a hundred thousand blessed drone-slaves, their barrels anointed with pungent oils, their innards infected with the most virulent scrapcodes, their mechanisms augmented with the living sinews of sacrificial thralls, their kill-range extended through the occult rites of the Masters' red-robed, half-metal servants.

As he marched, dragging his newly bulging body up the incline towards the earthworks' summit, he envisioned the blessed slaughter to come. The barrels would be winched onto scaffolds and the breeches would be filled with flesh-burners and stone-breakers. Then, finally, when the blood of the sacrificed boiled on the iron shells and the hooded ones had doused the fire-pits with fresh spoors, the thunder would begin.

He reached his designated place in the defence lines, high on the earthworks, facing south, away from the desperate battles already breaking out across the city walls. The attention of the entire host was turned to the east, towards the fragile battlements, the slender lines of defence that dared to oppose the inevitable.

He reached his assigned trench and dropped down beyond the leading parapet, landing on the firing step and turning to take up his fire position. All along the defensive bulwark his fellow warriors did the same, dropping heavily into the protective earth-bank and slotting autoguns and lasguns into targeting grooves.

He looked out into the night, and wondered why he'd been stationed so far back from where the fighting would come. Defensive duties were surely no longer required.

The first clue came with a low growl, running along the earth like a tremor. He stiffened, looking back and forth, seeing nothing.

He pondered voxing a warning, but couldn't quite remember how to use the comm-bead. His mind was sluggish, as if in a fever.

Another growl, closer this time, emerging from the smog-filled night – everywhere, nowhere.

From further down the trench, he saw las-beams flicker out soundlessly, followed by the clatter of projectile fire. He heard short, strangled cries, like animals having their necks wrenched.

He stood back from his fire-point. To the north was the inner defence cordon guarding the blessed machines. The earthwork ran around it, manned by hundreds of gunners, each protected by hard-packed walls and backed up by gun-towers every hundred metres.

As he peered into the gloom, some vestige of fear stirred in his sluggish soul. Marker lights were going out along the length of the trench, one by one. He saw a gun-tower open fire just a hundred metres away, spraying a curtain of explosive shells into the dark, before a dull explosion took that out too.

He couldn't see what was doing it. He couldn't see where the noises were coming from.

More growls, closer now, snickering in the air, punctuated by savage-sounding cracks and crackles. The remaining hairs on his neck stood up stiffly, as if an old race-memory lurked at the base of his brain-stem, not quite driven into abeyance by the plague.

He stood down from the firing step and advanced slowly along the trench floor. Others came with him, sharing his caution. For a moment longer, he saw nothing solid – just toxic dust swirls spilling into the trench shaft, spiralling away in the night, lit red from chem-fires.

Then something burst along the trench towards them – a grey ghost, massive and blurred by speed. He only had time for the briefest of impressions – the dull boom of machine-armour moving, a blade snarling in the dark, two red eyes blazing like afterburners. It was *huge*, it was *fast*.

The ghost bounded across the packed space of the inner trench, slaying as it came. Its victims died so quickly they had no time to scream, no time to react, just time to be spliced open as an energy-spitting blade ripped them into meat-chunks.

He aimed his autogun. He even managed to get a shot away. He saw it splinter from the creature's shoulder – a burst of ice-white against the roiling dark.

Then it was on him – a hurricane of movement, a deafening snarl, a jackhammer impact. He didn't feel the bite of the blade, just a smash of a huge iron-bound fist, hurling him high into the air. His head cracked back, shattering his helm.

He landed with a snap of bone. Something burst, and hot liquid sprayed across his hands. He tried to get up, but his legs would no longer work. The air was filled with bestial noises – growls, tears, bellows of rage. He half saw more bodies flung across his field of vision, trailing gobbets of blood.

Then it was on him again. He stared up at something he vaguely recognised from old devotional vids – a warrior-god towering over him, a grey-clad titan, a force of winter elements hurled out of the night and made into hellish, feral reality.

Just then, in a blaze of clarity and terror, he knew what it was. He remembered his humanity. He remembered what had happened to him. He remembered his old name.

I was Jevold.

Then the sword plunged down, slicing clean at the neck, and the misery of existence was ended.

Ingvar leapt away from the headless corpse, swaying clear of a row of incoming las-impacts and tearing down the earthwork's boundary trench. *Dausvjer* whirled around him, lacerating flesh and ripping through armour plates. The trench defenders charged at him in clumps of bodies, moving slowly as if in some dreadful dream.

He tore through them. He kicked out, pulverising torsos and breaking limbs. He punched, smashing skulls and cracking atrophied ribs. He hacked with the blade, biting into tumours and organs and spilling their contents out across the earth. The hordes clustered around him, swarming him with weight of numbers, before being broken and hurled away, tumbling through the air in a ballet of spiralling limbs. The carnage was voluminous, remorseless, implacable.

Ingvar wanted to *roar* – to open his throat and declaim the name of the Allfather, of Russ, of Fenris. He wanted to bellow at them as he slaughtered, relishing every splash of blood against his armour.

For now, though, he was silent. The Sisters had done their work, drawing the attention of the enemy towards Hjec Aleja's walls, and the need for stealth was still acute.

The Wolves, all five of them capable of bearing an axe, had sprinted out of the city just as the assault on the outer walls began, breaking clear of the Ighala Gate and ghosting through the deserted suburbs, heading down and away from the growing fighting and finding passage through the dark. Once beyond the city's southern limits they'd pulled around, running fast through empty lands before angling back up towards the enemy encampment. The few scouts they'd come across had been murdered swiftly. Like a deadly riptide, the Wolves had swept up out of the gloom and into the maze of trenches, spreading out across a wide front and kindling blade-weapons as they came. By the time they hit the main defence-lines, their momentum was unstoppable.

Ingvar heard a muffled *crump* as one of the pack – Gunnlaugur, he guessed – took out another gun-tower. Ingvar kept moving, barrelling down the jagged line of the trench, cleansing it, harrowing it, purging it. A big mutant swayed into his path, its fists crowned with grafted spikes, its heavy helm bleeding marshlight from nine iron-ringed lenses. It lunged at him, gurgling through a clutch of breathing tubes and going for his throat.

Ingvar severed the tubes with a tight swipe of his blade, spinning out of range of the spike-thrust before backhanding the mutant with the heel of his sword, breaking the creature's neck and driving its jawbone up into its skull. As the creature toppled into the dust, Ingvar spun to face three more warriors. They lumbered towards him numbly, firing a mix of las-beams and bullets from corroded weaponry. Ingvar charged straight into them, arms wide as if in an embrace. He bore them down with him, crushing ribcages and smashing limbs. Then he was up again, grinding the remains into the bloody mire at his feet, sword crackling, helm scanning for more targets.

'Target located,' came Olgeir's heavy voice over the squad-comm.

Ingvar switched to Olgeir's loc-reading – forty metres to the north, up amid the big tank formations and heading into the heart of the encampment.

He smashed aside a grasping claw, ducked under a hastily aimed thicket of green-tainted las-beams, and started running again. He leapt up the far side of the trench wall, boosted by his armour, and sprinted across open ground.

Enemy troops swarmed at him from the poison-clouds, throwing themselves at his feet, hurling spiked grenades into his path, trying to land a shot, do some damage.

It barely troubled him. Ingvar raced through it all, speeding like a loosed cannon, veering and swerving out of danger and annihilating all that remained in his path. His armour ran with blood – it slopped away from him as he moved, thick and glistening. He went noiselessly, quietly ratcheting up the kill-tally as he burned towards the hunt's focus.

The ground rose up steeply towards a crater-edge summit, laced with lines of razor wire and broken by the shafts of more concentric trenches. Each defence-line was stuffed with mutant soldiers, all now aiming at him as he came.

If he'd moved like a mortal moved, they'd have hit him – even power armour could be cracked by sufficient concentrations of incoming fire – but Ingvar moved like no human mortal had ever moved. He accelerated far too fast, then displaced himself, then checked back and loped back to full charge. It was impossible to track, to latch on to, to cope with. By the time he reached the crater's lip he was attracting whole webs of incoming shots, criss-crossing over one another in a desperate attempt to bring him down.

'Whelp – faster,' Ingvar voxed to Hafloí, who wasn't closing in at the rate of the others. Hafloí was a natural slayer, but he was decades younger and still had things to learn.

Then Ingvar reached the summit and vaulted through the final defences before hurtling down the far side of the ridge, down to where the objects of the hunt had been dragged.

They rose up, ruinous and magnificent, each one the size of a Warhound

Titan and angled steeply into the toxin-boiling night. The four wall-breakers stood at the crater's wide, flat base, each surrounded by vast throngs of attendant slave-workers. Long telescopic barrels glinted in the light of explosions, stained dark green and bearing the ornate livery of blasphemy. Furnaces growled away at their bases. Tubes slung and bubbled, conveying skin-melting compounds to the delivery shells. Plague-burst corpses hung from the lips of the gun-muzzles, twisting in the hot smoke from exhaust vents.

The guns were nearly ready. Segmented belts churned towards snarl-mawed entry points, carrying payloads of ruination to the firing chambers. Gangs of shackled and blinded slaves hauled on chains, each link the size of a man's torso, cranking the firing angles a little higher.

Ingvar sped towards the nearest. The time for secrecy had passed – he heard Gunnlaugur's blood-chilling war-cry echoing out into the darkness. Frag explosions suddenly kicked out, and the night erupted into a ripple of pyrotechnics.

Ingvar grabbed his bolter from its mag-locked hold and opened fire. He heard Olgeir's heavy bolter breaking out on the far side of the compound. The pack was converging, bursting through the defences en masse, hitting them all at once and overwhelming them.

Ingvar cleared a whole swathe before him. It was all about speed now – sudden, overwhelming force applied to a single point. The whole enclosure held thousands of mutant warriors, and sooner or later those numbers would wear down even a Space Marine. Járnhamar had to achieve the immediate task quickly, then cut their way back to a more defensible position and hope Callia was still keeping the larger part of the huge army busy.

Ingvar neared the first of the artillery pieces, and its huge shadow fell across him. The breech section loomed out of the smoke, as tall as a Rhino, clad in thick blast-armour and vomiting palls of ink-black fumes.

He mag-locked his blade and pivoted on his heel, firing all the while to keep the enemy from him. His magazine clunked empty, and he leapt up, latching on to the jagged edge of the breech casing. He climbed fast, ignoring the rain of las-beams that pinged and snapped around him. Once he reached the top of the armour-casing, he flung himself onto an angled roof. The metal beneath him rocked and shook, boiling away like some infernal oven. Just ahead of him, the barrel-base itself soared up into the night, five metres in diameter and ringed with chains.

'They're good to fire,' voxed Gunnlaugur. 'Gut them. Now.'

Ingvar glanced up, seeing the Wolf Guard clambering across the breech-chamber on the wall-breaker across from him, less than twenty metres distant and barely ahead of a pursuing horde of screaming mutants.

Ingvar reached for melta charges and clamped them to the sides of the huge barrel, fixing six of them in quick succession, before hearing the first clang of mutants scrambling up after him onto the armour-casing.

He placed the last charge and whirled to face them, slamming a fresh magazine home just as the first of the enemy hauled itself up onto the roof of the breech section.

'*Fenrys!*' Ingvar thundered – the sacred word felt like catharsis as it flew from his fanged mouth. He let loose with his bolter, blasting the way clear of bodies, then raced along the spine of the breech-chamber housing. As he went, he mentally counted down the timer.

Ten seconds.

Just as he was about to leap clear, a horrific shape dragged itself clear of the metal grille in front of him. It seemed to emerge from the bowels of the machine itself, and its metal limbs pulled stickily out of a morass of boiling, glowing putrefaction. Six eyes flared at him, pulled back from a noseless, fang-lined face.

Ingvar kept firing, sending bolts thudding into the creature's emerging chest. The rounds went off, popping dully as if doused in magma. The creature dragged the last of its flame-licked body free of the machine, and flung itself at him.

The mech-mutant was as big as he was, multi-limbed, clad in oxidised armour plates and glistening with bio-augmetics. It carried twin power mauls, semi-enclosed in iron gauntlets. It charged him, skittering across the roof of the breech-chamber and screaming in overlapping vox-channels.

'Get *clear*,' warned Gunnlaugur over the vox.

Ingvar grabbed his sword, activated it and slung it wide – all in one movement – and the strike severed the thing's armour plates. Its momentum carried it forwards, though, and both mauls slammed down against Ingvar's shoulder-guards.

Five seconds.

The impact was heavy, forcing him back towards the steep-sloped chamber roof. The creature swung again wildly and pressed on towards him, but Ingvar punched his blade out point-first, snaking it between the two oncoming mauls and embedding it directly between the horror's snapping iron jaws.

Dausvjer's energy field exploded into life, lashing tendrils of disruptor-force against the mech-mutant's mottled skin. Ingvar grabbed the hilt two-handed and heaved the impaled creature over the edge. Then he whip-snapped the sword away, cleaving the creature's head in two and sending its body plummeting to the dust. Hearing the final *tick-tick* of the charges, he switched back to a sprint and tore back down the length of the breech-chamber roof. With a powerful lunge, he catapulted himself free of the armour-housing, only to hear the *whoomp* of the meltas going off behind him.

The blast was horrific – a maelstrom of heat and noise and kinetic force that snatched him up like a leaf in a storm and flung him hard through the air. Other charges on the other guns went off in tandem, cracking open all four artillery pieces in an orgy of rippling flame and spinning shrapnel.

Ingvar crashed to the ground some twenty metres from the gun-chassis he'd blown open. His head slammed forwards against the inner curve of his helm, and he felt the hot burst of blood spraying across his face.

Ignoring it, he pushed himself to his feet, and was hauling his armoured body up from the trench he'd carved in landing when an armoured fist grabbed him by his forearm and dragged him higher.

He tensed to strike, fingers tight on *dausvjer*'s hilt, before Gunnlaugur's familiar voice crackled over the comm.

'That was too close,' the Wolf Guard growled, yanking Ingvar upright before turning to face the mutants still on their feet and already coming at them.

Ingvar shook his head to clear it. 'Plenty of time.'

All four of the massive artillery pieces were cracked open and burning, riven asunder by the power of the massed meltas. Four vast columns of smoke churned up into the tortured sky, glowing angrily from within like nebulae. Sparks whirled and danced across the face of the inferno, thrown up from chain-exploding ammunition. The entire crater floor was in ruins, its defenders scattered, maimed or dazed, its war machines reduced to tilting shards of flaring metal.

Ingvar stood back to back with Gunnlaugur, his blade spitting defiant energy-stars. Those mutants not killed by the explosions began to gather again, dragging themselves up from the dust and searching for the source of their pain.

'What now?' asked Ingvar, watching them come.

Gunnlaugur nodded towards the crater's northern edge, where the concentration of enemy troops was thickest. 'They're not alone.'

The horde moving down the broken terrain towards them was not just composed of mortals. Ingvar saw flame-glints reflecting from the curved shoulder-guards of power armour. He saw single-horned helms, and pale green lenses, and reapers lifted high.

A cold rage burned instantly. 'Plague Marines.'

'I see six.'

Ingvar scanned across the compound, assessing distances, judging numbers. Olgeir, Jorundur and Hafloí were scattered across the crater floor among the corpses of the guns, out of position, isolated. More mutants were spilling into the crater from the north, adding to the horde already coming at them.

'We should pull back,' Ingvar said, pointing to a jagged outcrop of sandstone high up on the southern slopes, close to where he'd broken in. 'We could hold that.'

He fully expected to hear Gunnlaugur's growl of disdain then, followed by the command to charge into the heart of the horde, to cut a bloody swathe towards the Traitors before weight of numbers finally bogged them down.

'So be it,' said Gunnlaugur, defying expectation. 'We hold the ridge.'

Both of them started to move. A host of mutants was already racing towards their position, opening fire again in a ragged wave of las-beams. Ingvar lowered his boltgun, picking the first targets amid a sea of warped faces.

Before he could fire, though, a new roar kindled across the cloud-cover, louder than the residual furnaces of the ruined artillery or the yowls of mutant voices. It was thunderous, like main-drive starship engines gunning to full thrust. A crimson bruise spread out across the boiling brume of toxic smog, glowing angrily. Above it all came a familiar machine-howl – the whine of drop pod engines straining to break precipitous descent velocities.

Gunnlaugur laughed then, staring up at the heavens and lifting his arms wide.

'He's *here*,' he snarled, infusing the words with hunt-fervour. 'The sky cracks!'

All eyes looked up then, buffeted by the sudden storm of massed thruster down-force. The clouds split open, speared in a dozen places. Massive, fist-shaped transports lanced down from the skies, trailing smog and flame in their wake.

Ingvar watched the nearest pod make planetfall. The impact was horrendous – an earth-breaking smash that sent dust flying in a bow-wave. Cracks shot out from the epicentre, hitting the damaged foundations of the nearest wall-breaker and shivering what remained. Every mortal within fifty metres of that collision was ripped from their feet by the blast-radius and slammed hard against the churning earth.

Gunnlaugur kept laughing – the harsh laughter of impending slaughter. 'The wrath of Fenris!'

Ingvar kept watching. As the dust cleared, the shape of the pod became clearer. It was huge, far bigger than a typical Adeptus Astartes lander. Its flanks were not the slate-grey used by the Wolves, but arterial red and banded with black. Ornate gold and bronze chasing enclosed panels bearing baroque skull-icons.

'That's not Njal,' said Ingvar.

As the pall of fire and debris cleared around the drop pod, its door-bolts blew. Vivid red light bled out from the interior, wreathed in exhaust fumes, part masking a hulking shape within.

Only when it moved did the truth emerge. A towering walker stomped clear of the pod, limping out into the open on awkward, switch-backed, pistoned limbs. Heavy arms swung round, each capped with a flamer slung over a chainblade. It was more than three times the height of a man, a nightmare fusion of mortal flesh and machine artifice. Its engine shrieked like a caged ghost, its smokestacks vomited gouts of flaming gas-vapour, and its enormous segmented feet trod down the dust of Ras Shakeh, crushing the carpet of roasted limbs that surrounded the landing site.

By then more drop pods were coming down, dozens of them, slamming into the ground and opening up with halos of flamer-discharge. More bizarre war machines streamed out from them – quadrupedal walkers with underslung flame-cannons and swollen vox-emitters screaming war-curses; half-tracked cannons with gun-servitors lurching in escort; hovering gun-drones bristling with trailing hook-lines and segmented chain-flails. Crimson-armoured mortal troops marched in the war machines' wake, all bearing the same black skull devices on their closed-face helms.

Gunnlaugur looked on, his battle-joy quickly turning to shocked disgust. 'The Church,' he snarled. 'The *Church*.'

Ingvar scanned for the Plague Marines they'd sighted earlier. This changed everything – with allies crashing into the heart of the enemy army, the odds were evening up rapidly. 'I think they're on our side,' he said.

'*Who* is?' demanded Gunnlaugur, outraged. 'Who commands?'

Ingvar activated *dausvjer*'s energy field.

'Find out later, brother,' he said, starting to move again. 'For now, be glad they hunt with us.'

CHAPTER FOUR

De Chatelaine stood at the summit of the Ighala Gate, watching as the sea of flame lapped up against the walls of her city. The platform on which she stood was broad and open, containing only her and twenty ceremonial Guard soldiers, and it felt like being isolated on a pinnacle over a universe of blood and torment.

She'd watched her Battle Sisters spearheading the assault down to the perimeter, noting with pride how swiftly and how skilfully they had retaken lost ground. She'd watched as the big guns had been hoisted into position, remounted on the old defence towers and angled at the huge mobs outside the walls. She'd watched as the enemy had responded, stirring lazily at first, then hurling its vast resources at the fragile barrier, hammering at the gates, surging up against the defiant line of defenders.

It had been difficult to witness from a distance, condemned by her rank to remain an overseer of the carnage rather than a participant in it. One of the towers had been overwhelmed less than an hour after being retaken. Waves of mutants clambered up the walls, poured through the demolished sections and surrounded the pockets of reclaimed defiance. De Chatelaine had been tempted to order a fighting retreat back to the inner walls. She could see her meagre troops being surrounded, and it felt like throwing away everything they had worked so hard to win.

She held firm. Most of the bulwarks survived, reinforced by a constant stream of troops and materiel sent down from the upper city. They were besieged and isolated, but fought on defiantly. As time went on, the precarious salient drew yet more troops out from the sprawling enemy encampment, dragging them across the poisoned desert and into the meat grinder of combat.

When the four gigantic explosions rocked the foundations under her and sent intertwined columns of burning smoke rearing high over the entire battlefield, she knew the Wolves had done what they had promised – the enemy had been blooded, its fangs drawn.

'Come back now,' she breathed, leaning out into the night air. 'No pride, no glory – you've done what was needful and now we need you here.'

But then everything changed. The sky above her burned. The roar and clamour of the battle was replaced by the thunderous crescendo of landers coming into range.

She looked up, gazing at the film of lurid pollution that had overarched them since the first days of the siege, and saw it glowing from above, lit vividly by starbursts of crimson and silver. Then drop pods broke through, hurtling down into the wastes beyond the broken walls.

As she watched them fall, de Chatelaine's sudden joy gave way to unease – they were not Space Wolves drop pods. Though hard to make out in the particulate fog, the war machines looked blood-red, their death's-head insignias surmounted by baroque crests of gold.

'Canoness,' murmured one of her guards, hovering at her side. 'Please, now, you must withdraw.'

Her bodyguards had been trying to persuade her to retreat to somewhere more secure for over an hour, but now, for the first time since taking position on the Gate, she felt suddenly exposed.

'Captain, I do not–' she started, but her voice was immediately drowned out by a fresh clamour.

Six columns of actinic energy shot down around her, surrounding her and making the platform blaze wildly as if in full daylight. She reached for her sidearm, just as the eddying distortion guttered out and threw the platform back into fire-flecked gloom.

Standing before her, glistening from the residue of warp-translation, were six figures, each looking at her dryly as if they owned the planet and she were some kind of interloper.

'Put your weapon away please, canoness preceptor,' said one of them, a slender man wearing sable robes and holding a tall, aquila-tipped staff. His voice was soft, and his skin was as pale as milk. 'If we were here to harm you, by the Emperor's will you would already be dead.'

De Chatelaine stared back at him for a moment, her heart thumping. She kept her bolt pistol raised, holding it two-handed. 'This is my domain,' she said. 'I would know who treads here.'

Another of the newcomers shuffled forwards then, pulling at the robe of the speaker and gesturing for him to make way.

This one was different, his skin oil-slicked and golden. Voluminous robes swaddled a corpulent frame, picked out in brocade of gold and red and black. Armour glinted from under gaps in the robes, itself richly decorated and studded with rococo flourishes. He too carried a staff, but it was far grander, carved from gold and studded with garnets, emeralds and carnadines.

His eyes were dark, almost white-less, and had the dead-stare certainty of a man who routinely controlled the fate of worlds. When he smiled, his thick lips pursing fleshily, it was with the awareness of what honour the gesture bestowed on the beholder. There was no joy in that smile, just a smooth, practised command of indulgence. He lifted a limp hand, heavy with bands of gold, and glided towards her.

'Of course you would,' he said, extending the hand in her direction. 'But I trust you know me now?'

De Chatelaine dropped to one knee.

'Lord Cardinal,' she said, grasping his hand. She kissed the golden ring of his middle finger – a weighty band of gold surmounted by a ruby in the shape of a skull. 'Forgive me, I did not–' 'Rise, my daughter.' He gazed down at her tolerantly. 'This is war, and you were cautious. Now it is over, and the Church comes to reclaim its own.'

De Chatelaine did as she was bid, and holstered her pistol. Drop pods were falling from the skies, lancing down into the thick of the fighting beyond the walls. She could hear the crescendo of intensifying combat, pocked with the familiar rush of flame-weapons being deployed.

'We had no idea,' she said. Repoda had given her no warning, no *inkling*, that Ecclesiarchy forces had come into range of Ras Shakeh.

The Cardinal nodded. His every movement was feline.

'We can move carefully when we wish to,' he said. 'But you were clearly expecting help from somewhere. A rash assault to make, I think, if you were not.'

'The Wolves of Fenris,' said de Chatelaine. 'A pack of them fights with us, and more are due.'

At the mention of Space Wolves, the man in the sable robes stiffened. The Cardinal sniffed, as if a minor foul aroma had just wafted into his otherwise perfumed presence.

'They have an old claim on this place,' he said. 'Like half the worlds in this sector.'

As he spoke, a heavy troop lifter emerged from the clouds, far out over the plains. It was immediately strafed with flickering lines of las-fire, while labouring on a throbbing cushion of engine down-blast. The ship was huge, far larger than the drop pods, and must have carried hundreds of troops within its swollen crew bays.

'What strength do you bring?' asked de Chatelaine, observing the lifter fighting its way down.

'Enough.'

'My lord, they have Traitor Marines. The Wolves–'

'Space Marines are not the Emperor's only weapons.'

'No. No, they are not. Even so...' She trailed off.

The Cardinal gave de Chatelaine a disapproving look. 'This is *our* world. We can use the Wolves if we must, but when this filth is cleared away, they will stay or leave by our command.' He shot a glance at the sable-cloaked man, who nodded fervently in agreement. 'I may have been remiss in fortifying this sector, but there are so many for us to ward, all with mouths to feed and souls to shrive. You must forgive me, canoness, for leaving you to the mercy of savages.'

'They have died for us.'

'Which is the least of the many services a man may render. And, for them, who are not even men in the true sense, what else is there?' He reached into a deep pocket in his robes and withdrew a small ivory box. He flicked it open, retrieved a pinch of what looked like coal-dust, placed two dabs of it against his nostrils, inhaled, then replaced the box. 'There is a reckoning for all things. We are all held accountable for our service, one way or another.'

The Cardinal behaved as if the warfare thundering around them all were somehow a trifling affair, the business of others. By now, the lifter had made planetfall and was busily disgorging its contents onto the plains around it.

De Chatelaine saw battle engines striding amid the carnage. Most were Sentinel-class walkers, adorned with Ecclesiarchy colours and bearing flamers slung under their chassis, but there were other assault machines among them, some with a darker genesis.

It had been a long time since she'd witnessed a Penitent Engine at war. The memory of the first time was still raw in her mind.

'So this is deliverance,' she said quietly. 'I had assumed it would be them. Better that it be my own kind.'

'It matters not who wields the blade,' the Cardinal said, sniffing again, 'so long as it finds a neck to bite.' He looked around him, casting dead eyes across the carnage. 'Perhaps you will show me to the Halicon now. I wish to instruct you on what is to come.'

De Chatelaine hesitated. 'My forces are engaged.'

The Cardinal smiled coldly. 'Do not concern yourself with that. You have laboured for long enough, and your service will be recognised.' The fleshy lips twitched. 'We are here now. That is all that matters.'

Down on the battlefield, the volume of fire was incredible. Penitent Engines hurled out vicious streamers of flame, catching on the enemy and exploding in promethium-laced clouds. Phalanxes of closed-helm troopers in red segmented armour stalked through the carnage, laying waste to everything before them. Most destructive of all were the Battle Sisters, hurled into the thick of the fighting by precision drop-strikes. They, too, were clad in deep crimson battleplate and bore the sigil of a teardrop surmounted by flames. Like their counterparts of the Wounded Heart, they fought with brutal commitment, charging in close before unleashing a torrent of flamer weapons.

The entire battle-plain was now a furnace of brutality. The enemy remained as stubborn as ever, fighting with the sullen, semi-conscious violence they were known for. Tides of mutant soldiers charged into hurricanes of incoming fire, overwhelming oncoming troops with weight of numbers. Twisted horrors limped out of the depths of the army, swollen with stimm-enhanced grotesquery and laying waste with chem-weapons or poison-tipped flails.

Out of all of them, though, the most formidable were the Masters – the Plague Marines, centuries old and hardened into instruments of destruction. They strode through the clogged battlefield, reaping as they came and leaving ditches of severed limbs in their wake. Las-fire glanced harmlessly from their crusted armour, blades turned from their rust-pocked breastplates, and flames coursed over them, leaving nothing but surface charring. While they lived and fought, the battle remained in the balance.

'For the Allfather!' bellowed Gunnlaugur, charging to be the first into contact. Ingvar, Olgeir, Jorundur and Hafloí charged with him, howling and bellowing death-curses as they cut their way towards their fallen brothers.

The Plague Marines lumbered to meet them, striding across the flame-laced battlefield in grim silence. They carried thick-bladed power scythes, their twisted blades running with filth. Their immense armour power-packs had distended, fusing into the plague-pale flesh beneath and latching on to coils of bunched cabling.

When the two forces clashed, the impact cracked out across the battle-field. The pure fury of Fenris thundered into the pure corruption of Barbarus, shivering the earth and blasting away any combatants foolish enough to dare to intervene.

Every blow was perfectly aimed, lashed out with crushing weight and infinite hatred. Hammers and axes thudded into the curved blades of the scythes, exploding in showers of disruptor-sparks. Boltguns blazed, blasting shards from power armour.

The Wolves were faster. Up against real opposition for the first time, their speed became truly phenomenal – they hacked and shot, roaring and snarling, totems flying about them like satellites. *Skulbrotsjór* arced wildly, cracking into corroded armour with deadening force. *Dausvjer* thrust, catching the light of bloody flames on its rune-carved length.

The Plague Marines responded with equal fervour. Eerily silent, their movements were suffused with the wearing power of eternity, absorbing impacts and turning them back on the bearer. They thrust and parried with their scythes, meeting the hammer blows and blade strikes and hammering back. Green-edged energies rippled down their corrupted blades, flaring as they hit and sending webs of aetheric power dancing like ghosts.

One of them, a monster with one bulging eye-lens and a bursting abdo-minal armour plate, was smashed bodily to the ground by Gunnlaugur, his death mask driven in to reveal a bloody mass of flesh beneath. Jorundur was mauled by another, his axe slammed away by a power scythe before the hilt cracked into his gorget-plating. The Old Dog hit the earth, cursing even as Olgeir raced to support him. Hafloí became locked in a frenzied duel with a tusked adversary covered in clanking skulls. Ingvar took on two at once, working his sacred blade with preternatural speed and dexterity.

Each warrior, Traitor and Loyalist alike, remained so focused on the fight, so locked into the pure state of combat, that none noticed the wind pick-ing up around them. The blows continued to land, the boltguns continued to drum. They fought on as the earth at their feet shook and electric arcs crackled around them. They were fighting even as lances of power shot down from above, outshining the crackling roar of the flames and sending shadows leaping across the battlefield.

Only when the Plague Marines were encased in fields of writhing ball-lightning and lifted clear of the battlefield did the pack finally pull clear. Gunnlaugur checked a hammer swipe, seeing his opponent held rigid within a vice of rippling translucent force. The six Traitors were transfixed, locked in midair by snaking bolts of silver fire.

Gunnlaugur withdrew along with his brothers, hackles rising, primed for the next assault. As soon as he saw the origin of the battle-lightning, though, he let the head of *skulbrotsjór* fall. The rest of the pack, free from the grip of combat, fell back, their ragged pelts rippling in the howl of wind and dust.

More drop pods had come down, this time in grey livery with yellow-and-black chevrons. They studded the battlefield like granite monoliths, steam-ing from their atmospheric plummet. Two dozen Grey Hunters surrounded the pods, bolters lowered, their rune-daubed armour limned red by the fires. They remained motionless, every barrel of every gun aimed at the stricken Plague Marines.

The Hunters were not alone. Before them stood the living legend.

He towered over all else, clad in hulking Terminator plate that made him look like some storm-giant of Fenrisian myth. Runes glowed on its surface, throbbing like open wounds, and the air around him ran with static. A heavy red-mane wolf-pelt hung over the curve of his thick psychic hood, pulled by the unnatural wind that eddied around him. His staff, a thick stave of ebony, snarled and shimmered as if alive, crowned by a bleached skull whose eyes flared with pooled aetheric matter. His flame-red beard, unfaded to grey despite hundreds of years in service, spilled out across a huge barrel chest. Two frost-blue eyes stared out, perfect in their clarity, fearsome in their intensity.

He said nothing. Lines of force lashed and snaked from his staff, swept up by the circling winds and feeding the coronae that enclosed the locked Plague Marines. The very stuff of the elements seemed drawn to him, and the dust drummed and rippled around his boots.

He raised his left gauntlet, encrusted in ice-rimed ceramite, and a black shape flapped down out of the tortured air. A sleek raven, half the size of a mortal man, its night-black plumage laced with the cables and iron bands of the Iron Priest's trade, alighted on his wrist, folding semi-metal wings, cawing once, then glaring out at the battlefield.

Njal Stormcaller issued no war-cry. He lifted his immense staff, and lightning forked out, bounding across the earth before snapping into the Traitors suspended in their auras of psychic fire. Tempests howled around him, whipping up blood and smoke and grime, and hurling them into vortices of destruction. The *noise* of it was incredible, as if the planet's soul were being harrowed before their eyes and remade anew.

One by one, life was strangled out of the suspended Traitors. Their limbs twitched, then flailed, then spasmed, as if invisible hands had reached up to their throats to choke them. Their armour cracked, splitting with snaps of silver brilliance, revealing pox-thick flesh within, as pale as bone and puffed up with lesions. Layer by layer, their fallen magnificence was stripped away, scorched and consumed, withering in waves of coruscation. They screamed, but the sound was snatched away by the scream of the wind. When nothing was left of them but husks, as black and fragile as coiled paper, their carcasses thudded back to the ground. Remnants of their ceramite shells rolled away, held together by inky strands of tar-like residue.

All but one. The largest of the Plague Marines, the monster Gunnlaugur had felled, still hung intact, immobile, locked by the esoteric forces that played across his armour. He fought against the coils and spiked webs of aether-force, but the dazzling lattice clamped him tight, shrinking onto his tortured frame like throttle-wire.

Njal walked slowly up to his captive, his boots crunching across the bones of the battlefield. As he moved, the raven at his wrist issued a harsh vox-caw of denunciation. Crackles of lightning continued to dance and flicker around the Rune Priest's colossal frame, as if leaking out from the furnace of power contained within.

'You,' Njal rasped, gazing up at his prey. His voice was ice-sheer, as raw and jagged as the wyrd-storm that raged around him. 'You will live. For now.'

Gunnlaugur, until then held rapt by Njal's imperious presence, remembered himself and raised his thunder hammer in salute. The rest of the pack did likewise with their blades.

'*Hjá, gothi!*' they cried.

Njal turned to look at them, maintaining the force-aegis over the Traitor with ease. It was hard, even for Gunnlaugur, to meet the stare of those eyes, laced as they were with flickers of deep aether-fire. Something about the way they burned – the inflexibility, the *acuity* – was impossible to endure.

'Grimnar sent seven to this world,' said Njal.

'He did, *jarl*,' replied Gunnlaugur. 'Váltyr's thread was cut.'

'The sixth?'

'The Red Dream.'

Njal's gaze moved towards Ingvar, as if he knew, instinctively, who was responsible for Apothecary duties. 'He will recover?'

'He will,' said Ingvar.

Njal nodded curtly, then looked out beyond the protective circle of Grey Hunters. Ecclesiarchy battle engines were by then running rampant, driving out into the reeling heart of the enemy horde. More forces were being landed all the time, hammering down into the battlefield on roiling columns of thruster-burn. With every crash-landing came the slam and recoil of lander-ramps, followed by the charge of booted feet. The air was filled with the whine of mortars, the rush of flamers, the roar and crack of bolter weapons.

In the distance, the enemy was already falling back from the city's outer walls, and Battle Sisters clad in both black and red were leading the counter-offensive. Penitent Engines swayed and burned among them, many carrying the tattered banners of the Ministorum above the carapace-shells of their agonised occupants.

'No honour in allies like these,' Njal murmured, watching a squad of what looked like men with metal flails in place of arms and thick iron plates bolted over their faces.

His raven watched it all with dark, reflecting eyes. It cawed again – a harsh vox-scrape – then turned its long-beaked head away.

'Know this!' cried Njal then, whipping up more stormwind as his huge voice boomed out into the night. 'The Rout is among you now! *Fear* us! *Flee* from us! We come only to slay, and before the red dawn rises, our axes will be black with your blood!' His pelts flared out from his shoulders, buoyed by unnatural wind and crowned with the thorn-pattern of lightning shards. 'Run while you may! Plead to your gods! Nothing remains for you but *death!*'

Njal's raging aura exploded into a sunburst of raw light, streaming out into the gloom with eye-burning intensity. Given their cue, the Grey Hunters of his retinue broke out of the cordon and charged down the retreating mutant hordes. Járnhamar charged with them, spurred into fresh combat-fury by the arrival of their battle-brothers. With a massed howl that cut through all else on the battlefield, the Wolves of Fenris tore back into combat, driving the enemy back into the desert and breaking the grip they had exerted on the city for so long.

Birthed in fire and fury, the final deliverance of Hjec Aleja had begun.

CHAPTER FIVE

When dawn came, the sun rose over a bleak scene of devastation. The city remained enclosed in a pall of rising smoke, part chem-filth from the enemy's ample reservoirs, part smog from the broken tanks and fuel depots. A sprawl of tangled metal and armour ran out from the ravaged walls far into the desert, marred by deep gouges where the drop pods and bulk lifters had come down. Bulbous lander-craft squatted amid the ruins, some hollowed out by gunfire, some intact and operating. Reclamator machines crawled down the long embarkation ramps equipped with lifting gear and purge-flamers. Those who still walked amid the wreckage went warily, their faces covered and their environment suits tightly sealed.

The fighting had raged through the night, gradually moving away from the city's edge and further out into the wilds. The Traitor forces had been eviscerated by the initial assaults but had not yielded easily. There was no break, no panic, just a grim, futile resistance that had lasted for hours. Even as the sun climbed into the sky there were pockets of defiance – knots of mutants too steeped in mind-breaking corruption to recognise the impossibility of victory and who just kept on doing what their combat-implants told them to.

The Ecclesiarchy troops, once landed in sufficient numbers, had been horrifyingly efficient. They had swept across the battlefield in ordered zones, burning everything, responding to the terror-weapons of the Traitors with terror-weapons of their own. Fear meant little or nothing to them – it had been bled out by psycho-conditioning or neural extraction. They were reinforced by their arcane bestiary of biomechanical creations – every conceivable combination of human–weapon interface seemed to have found a home in the forces of the Cardinal.

None of them, though, had quite matched the bolstered forces of the Wolves, who had pushed deep into the heart of the enemy formations and ripped out the command centres. Caught between the fury of the Space Marines and the systematic advance of the Ecclesiarchy, the contest descended into industrial-scale slaughter. The dust of the desert thickened with blood, turning black-brown and curdling underfoot. Flames were poured across every conquered metre, sanctifying the corpses of the faithful fallen and atomising the bodies of the stricken traitors.

When the first rays of sunlight angled through the miasma, they revealed a vast circlet of ruins around a tiny epicentre of survival. Above it all, spear-leaved trees still grew in the sheltered courtyards, and the citizens still breathed untainted air behind the atmosphere-sealed chambers, but they were alone amid a swathe of destruction.

Ingvar stood in the ornate great hall of the Halicon. He remembered the first time he'd laid eyes on it, fresh from the destruction of *Undrider* and with the situation on the ground unknown. It looked little different – the real fighting hadn't reached this far up. Gaudy monuments to the Immortal Church stood in the alcoves, carved from alabaster and marble and bearing golden crowns above penitent faces. The heroes of the Adeptus Ministorum always seemed to be penitent. The edifice was *built* on penitence – an entire species held in thrall by it, locked into fear of error, transfixed by the guilt of crimes committed, planned or imagined.

Perhaps that was necessary. Halliafiore, the inquisitor who had commanded Onyx, would have agreed readily: mortal humans were wayward, prone to congenital weakness, and only their sanctioned guardians, those given the most rigorous psycho-conditioning ever devised, could hope to face up to the universe without stricture.

'My Lords of Fenris,' came the Cardinal's voice, ringing out from the throne he'd occupied. He was used to the grand occasion. 'Welcome, in the name of the Deified Master of Mankind, to the delivered shrine world of Ras Shakeh.'

The Cardinal had decreed that the deliverance of the city required imme-diate ceremony. His acolytes had laid on all the trappings of a celebratory service – a triumph, overseen by the servants of the Ministorum and accom-panied by all the gilt-edged finery he could muster. They had done well in a short time – the Halicon chamber had scarce looked, or smelt, more opulent.

Such ostentation could almost have been calculated to antagonise the Wolves, who wished for nothing more than to capitalise on the tactical advantage and drive the remains of the enemy further into the desert. Still, Njal had ordered them all to attend, even if only for a few moments while Delvaux said his piece. The two forces would have to work together to cleanse the world, and so would have to find ways to accommodate each other's idiosyncrasies.

Njal himself stood in the very centre of the capacious chamber, his Ter-minator armour flecked with the muck of the battlefield. He dominated the entire hall – a man-mountain of ceramite and animal-hides, crowned with graven imagery and draped with bone icons. In the blistering sun-light, refracted through the lenses of a dozen crystalflex chandeliers, the scarce-contained brutality of his heritage was even more evident than it had been during the night. His every gesture dripped with an almost uncon-scious menace, underpinned and reinforced by the constant hard hum of his armour's power units.

By comparison, to Ingvar's eyes, the Cardinal looked ludicrous. Delvaux had been smoothed and primped with aggressive rejuvenat, making his sleek jowls shine. His finery was extravagant beyond reason, a level of splendour that seemed calculated to amaze or offend, depending on the audience. He spoke casually of the Emperor's godhood despite knowing Njal would not share that belief. His voice was soft and smooth, though it carried well enough throughout the hall. A vox-distributor, perhaps, lodged somewhere in the man's throat.

When Njal spoke, the contrast was stark – his unfiltered voice was like the low crack of thunder, tempered by an extended lifetime of constant warfare. He had communed with Traitors, xenos, the vilest of the neverborn, and had lived to perform rites of destruction over their corpses. Alone among the occupants of that hall, Njal could most closely claim to have experienced the terrible scope of true divine power, and the knowledge of it lent his every gesture the grim weight of innate dignity.

When the Stormcaller spoke, all listened.

'This is just the start,' Njal rasped, looking with poorly disguised contempt at the Cardinal's sumptuous throne. 'We must take the war back to the enemy.'

The Wolves of both Járnhamar and Njal's retinue stood around the Rune Priest in a semicircular honour guard. De Chatelaine stood at the right hand of the Cardinal, decked in what ceremonial finery she could lay hands on. Sister Callia, the most senior of her command still alive, remained at her side, as did forty of the Sororitas of the Wounded Heart.

Ras Shakeh's Guard regiments took up most of the rest of the space. Many had come straight from the field and bore the grime of the fighting openly. For all their fatigue, they stood as firmly to attention as they could. They were devout men, and to witness the Cardinal in their midst was more than most would have hoped for in their brutally short lifetimes.

The rest of the assembled throng came from the Cardinal's forces: storm troopers and assault troops in crimson armour, flanked by Battle Sisters of the Order of the Fiery Tear. The Cardinal's command group was the most striking. Standing at the prelate's shoulder was a thin man in black robes. A couple of cherubs hovered around him, grinning inanely and belching incense. The man's eyes flickered back and forth, searching through the throngs before him. He looked nervous.

Beside him stood a menagerie of warped biomechanics. A Battle Sister lurked imposingly among them, her entire left arm refashioned into a bronze-clad flamer housing. Cables looped up and around it, hung with devotional icons. Her face was similarly augmetic, clustered with arcane sensor bundles that obscured her otherwise alabaster-pale features.

The Cardinal sniffed. He did that a lot, Ingvar noticed.

'Of course, you are correct,' Delvaux said. 'We must fight again soon. But for now, let us remember the source of our salvation.' He smiled thinly. His flesh looked unusually supple, flexing like fat slopped over gauze. 'We are all servants of the same power. It was by His will that we found ourselves brought here.'

Njal grunted noncommittally. Ingvar could sense the impatience coursing through every muscle of his lethal body.

'And you are to be thanked, my lord,' the Cardinal went on. 'Without the assistance of your fine warriors, this world would have been lost before we arrived, and we would have taken orbit over a dead city. So on behalf of the Diocese of Hvar Primus, please take my gratitude back to your Great Wolf. Their – and your – service shall not go unrecorded.'

The psyber-raven perched on Njal's shoulder extended its wings, as if itching to rake at the Cardinal's eyes. 'Record what you wish,' said Njal. 'I care not, and nor will Grimnar. We must speak of battle.'

'So we shall. I have already ordered the pursuit. There are other cities – dens of corruption, gripped by the dead hand of contagion. They can be recovered.'

'Recovered?'

'Purged. Cleansed. Whatever word does the labour justice.'

Njal's scarred lips tightened in irritation. 'This whole *sector* is at war. Pause now, even for an hour, and they will recover.'

The Cardinal bowed. 'Correct, and my strategos are already at work planning further deployments.'

'So you have more forces inbound.'

'We do,' confirmed Delvaux, 'though they will be in the aether for months. What of your brothers?'

'When they can be spared. For now, no.'

The Cardinal extended his arms wide then, exposing more fabulous detail on his brocade robes. 'Then let us – please – take this brief hiatus to rest in a little thankfulness. Let us dwell, for a *moment*, on the deliverance of this place. The Emperor does not abandon the faithful. He will *never* abandon the faithful.'

At that, members of his command group stepped forwards. Cherubs emerged from somewhere behind the throne, pumping incense into the Halicon's upper reaches. Clanging started up, a rhythm beaten out by hooded acolytes with sutured cymbals for hands. It was smoothly orchestrated, drawn straight from the Ministorum's millennia-old patterns of devotion.

The crowd responded instantly, almost involuntarily. Ingvar turned to see fighting men, their features drawn with fatigue, suddenly spark with a kind of desperate gratitude. The Sisters bowed their heads, their lips moving in prayer. The entire place began to sway with the dull rhythm of devotion. Soldiers who had endured terror for weeks suddenly began to break down, tears streaming down grimy faces.

Njal remained where he was for a moment, his frosty eyes locked with the Cardinal's. The prelate gazed back at him, a touch of defiance, laced with impudent trepidation, playing across his bland features.

'You may join us, if you wish,' Delvaux said. 'None are refused.'

Njal snorted a short, acerbic laugh. 'Not for us,' he said, and gestured towards the chamber doors. His Fenrisian honour guard immediately turned and headed for the grand doors. Before he joined the exodus, Ingvar caught a small look of amusement the Cardinal shared with his black-robed deputy.

'As you wish it,' called out Delvaux, as robed menials in gold masks shuffled up to attend him. They brought ewers full of boiling water, and braziers glowing with hot embers, and ritual scrolls filled with tight-curled sacred scripts. The clanging cymbals grew in volume, filling the chamber with a cacophonic dirge. 'Though we shall remember your souls.'

By then Njal was striding down the aisle towards the daylight beyond, bristling with irascibility, his staff striking the marble heavily. 'That's good to know,' he muttered.

Ingvar, Gunnlaugur and the others fell in behind the Rune Priest.

'This is going to be interesting,' remarked Ingvar, under his breath.

Gunnlaugur nodded sourly. 'Very.'

The Wolves convened as far away from the Halicon edifice as they could. The bulk of Njal's warriors were still engaged in the final stages of Hjec Aleja's cleansing, so only the pack leaders met with their master to plan the next stage of the hunt.

Njal had brought three packs of ten with him on his Gladius-class frigate, *Heimdall*, each one headed by a veteran Grey Hunter. The first was Steinn Fellblade, a sharp-faced, sleek-eyed killer with a jagged, wolf's-head-engraved broadsword strapped across his armour. The second was Hauki Long-axe, whose favoured twin-headed blade hung from his belt on iron-studded straps. The third was Kjarl Bloodhame, who bore a blackened flamer under the blood-red, age-hardened pelt that gave him his moniker.

Alongside them stood Álfar the Cold, Njal's Wolf Guard and shieldbearer. His armour was ancient and gunmetal-dark, marked with icons of Morkai. He carried a storm shield with a wolf's fanged skull set at the centre, as well as a massive chainsword marked with the ice-rune *hjarz*. He glared out at the world with heavy-lidded eyes under a frame of long, slush-grey hair. His tattooed face looked liable to crack if it smiled.

They had gathered away from the sun, deep in the shadowed chambers of the city where the air was cooler and the stone rough hewn. Only Gunnlaugur had been summoned from Járnhamar. He took his place alongside the others, his armour even more battle-ravaged than theirs, his features darkened by the pitiless Ras Shakeh sun, his restored thunder hammer freshly marked with evidence of kills.

Each one of those warriors was a truly deadly practitioner of Fenris's murderous arts of combat. Each one of them was capable of rendering whole regiments of mortals to waste, of tearing down cities and stripping starships clean of life. And each one of them, without hesitation or rancour, bowed his head in submission as Njal entered.

The Rune Priest came among them, ducking under the low stone archway. The runes on his heavy Terminator plate remained dark, but power hummed from them like heat-wash over an engine. His eyes glittered as if lit by an inner flame, blue as the seas in the Season of Fire. The psyber-raven, Nightwing, perched atop his left wrist. As the Rune Priest took his place, it hopped from his hand and into the shadow of a stone alcove, where it stared out, silent and watchful.

Njal didn't speak for some time. He rested his chin on his armour's gorget, and his flame-red beard fell across the ceramite in matted snarls.

'They know what they're doing,' he said at last, his deep voice echoing from the stone. 'They will build a new Cathedral on the ashes of the old. They will drag pilgrims to their shrine and fill them with new fears.'

Álfar nodded slowly in agreement, but said nothing. No others dared speak. Njal seemed lost in his own deliberations, and none were going to interrupt those.

Eventually, the Rune Priest lifted his head and bared long fangs in a cynical half-smile. 'Loathsome. But they are here, as are we.' He turned to Gunnlaugur. 'So, Wolf Guard. This is the time for tales. Tell me what happened here.'

Gunnlaugur did, leaving nothing out. He told of the landing, the destruction of *Undrider*, the arrival in Hjec Aleja and the defence of the citadel. He spoke quickly, covering the ground with no embellishment. Váltyr's death was reported just as it would be in the annals of the Fang. 'He died with blade in hand.'

Njal nodded in satisfaction. 'And the other one?'

'Baldr. He was...' Gunnlaugur hesitated. 'Changed. A madness took him. He slew the enemy champion, tore him apart, then we lost him. Ingvar brought him back, but the Dream has him now.'

Njal looked at him sceptically. 'Madness? The Wolf?'

'He used... the way of the storm.'

'And you didn't cut his thread.'

'No.' Gunnlaugur looked defiant. 'There is no taint now, not that we can sense.'

Nightwing turned its half-steel head to face Gunnlaugur and stared at him inquisitorially.

'That is not your judgement to make, Skullhewer,' said Njal.

'I judged when there were no others to do it.'

Njal considered that. 'And now I am here,' he said. 'Which may be a sign, or it may not. In either case, you will bring him to me for examination.'

Gunnlaugur bowed.

'And what of the canoness?' Njal asked.

'Brave. I trust her.'

'Good. We have to work with these people. Fenris will not be sending more strength here, not soon. Battle has come to a hundred systems at once and the Great Companies are all engaged. They are even pulling forces back from Armageddon. We are just the start, the arrowhead before the shaft.'

'To what end?'

'That is what we must discover.' Njal turned to his shieldbearer. 'Álfar, tell him what we know.'

'The Cardinal is named Giorgias Delvaux,' said Álfar, in a voice as cadaverous as his appearance. 'His power comes from the hive worlds of the Hvar Belt, bordering this subsector. He has issued edicts calling for a crusade and started drawing together what he needs. He commands a Grand Cruiser, the *Vindicatus*, in orbit above us.'

'Reputation?' asked Gunnlaugur.

'Brutal. Orthodox. Fiercely ambitious, and he has the ear of those at the top of the Church.'

'That's encouraging.'

Álfar's face didn't so much as twitch. 'They were unprepared for this. They don't know what brought plague here, and they can't fight it alone.'

Njal snorted derisively. 'That won't stop them wishing they were. They number thousands, we less than forty, so we must find a means to drive this our way.'

'What of the Plague Marine?' asked Gunnlaugur. 'The one you took from the battle?'

'He lives,' said Njal. 'Just. We have him on *Heimdall*, and secrets will be wrung from him. We need more, though. The Cardinal will purge this place before taking up arms again, and we need to be faster.'

'There were deep-void listening stations on the system edge,' said Álfar. 'Dead to augur-sweeps, but they might have picked something up before being overrun.'

Njal turned to Gunnlaugur. 'You still have your Thunderhawk?'

'Just about.'

'Use it,' said the Rune Priest. 'Anything we can find before they do will give us an edge.'

'It'll barely get off the ground,' said Gunnlaugur.

'We can fix that for you,' said Álfar.

'I'll speak to Jorundur,' said Gunnlaugur, looking like he didn't relish it.

'For now, though, we have prey to run down,' said Njal. 'The Cardinal has this right – this city will not be secure until we've purged every settlement, and we can do it as fast as they.' He reached out to Nightwing, smoothing its feathers absently. The psyber-familiar half closed its eyes and angled its head back. 'But I don't want to stay here longer than I have to – the sea of stars calls.'

He looked around him, at the hot, dusty stone, as far removed from the icy wastes of Fenris as it was possible to be.

'And I already dislike this place,' he said.

Ingvar picked up Gunnlaugur's summons soon after the war council had concluded, and headed in from the wasteland to the upper city, passing through streets where reconstruction was already under way. During the first phase of fighting, the Wolves' very presence had been enough to provoke terrified gapes from the populace, but after witnessing so many horrors in turn, the packs' power to shock had diminished. Citizens and soldiery bowed as Ingvar passed them, respectful but no longer overawed.

Ingvar preferred that. It was wearying to be treated like a god.

'Is he as you expected?' he asked Gunnlaugur once they'd met up at a heavily guarded and blast-shielded entrance to the lower Halicon levels.

Gunnlaugur passed inside, and Ingvar followed him into the long corridor that led to the apothecarion. 'He is a Priest. What should I expect?'

'I don't know. That's why I asked.'

They went down, heading deeper into an underworld of old, musty tunnels. Ceiling lumens were replaced by flickering torches, set deep into the bare stone walls.

'His anger already burns hot,' said Gunnlaugur. 'He does not like to be beaten by anyone, let alone a man like the Cardinal.'

Ingvar smiled dryly. 'De Chatelaine will flay her astropaths.'

They reached the apothecarion's outer doors. Gunnlaugur pressed the entry rune, and held his face up to the scanner. A red line ran down across his right eye, before clicking off.

Heavy bolts clunked free, then slid open with a hiss. Lumens flickered on in the chamber beyond, illuminating banks of medicae supplies. Most of the shelves were bare – testament to how low materials had run.

'What would Njal have done if Delvaux hadn't turned up?' asked Ingvar, as they entered.

Gunnlaugur made straight for the inner door, disabling the proximity alarms as he went. 'Killed them all himself.' He threw a hard glance in Ingvar's direction. 'Doubt he could?'

Gunnlaugur repeated the entry procedure on the inner doors, unlocking the medicae chamber beyond. Baldr lay where he had been left – on his back, bound tight to the metal bunk, his forehead clustered with wires and probes. His eyes were closed.

'I never like to see this,' said Ingvar.

They moved closer. Just as before, no taint remained on Baldr's face. He was breathing more deeply now. The cogitator systems, all of them designed for mortal physiology, beeped and clicked around him.

'What do you think?' asked Gunnlaugur.

'That we need a Wolf Priest.' Ingvar reached for a handheld bio-scanner. He ran a series of tests, checking the results off against what he'd expect to see. 'He's just cycling now, held under by sedatives.'

Gunnlaugur rested his knuckles on the bunk-edge. 'Any advantage to keeping him under?'

Ingvar shook his head. 'His body's recovered. He's as he was.' He stared at Baldr's face, intently this time, scouring for more than the faint flicker of eyelids. 'As far as I can see.'

'He should go to Njal awake,' said Gunnlaugur grimly. 'If he's going to be judged, he should face it standing.'

'And what if the judgement goes against him?'

Gunnlaugur drew in a long breath, then looked at Ingvar. There was rare uncertainty in his warrior's eyes. 'He's one of us,' he said eventually. 'He's Járnhamar.'

'That's what I meant.'

'Just do it.'

Ingvar reached for the vial of clear liquid hanging over Baldr's forearm. He cut off the flow, then pulled the tube from the flesh. It withdrew with a faint pop, followed by an upwelling of blood, quickly clotted.

Then he reached for one of the last of the syringes, drew a stimulant into it, and found a vein. He depressed the plunger, then discarded it.

Nothing happened. Baldr's breathing stayed the same, his eyes stayed shut.

'You think–' started Gunnlaugur.

'Wait,' said Ingvar, his eyes narrowing. 'He wakes.'

Baldr's finger twitched. Then his whole hand moved. His mouth opened a fraction, exposing his fangs. He breathed more deeply, making his chest rise.

Then his eyes snapped open – two orbs of amber, marked by the black pupil in the centre, as dilated as a Space Wolf's eye ever got.

Baldr stared up at the ceiling. Neither Ingvar nor Gunnlaugur said anything – it wasn't clear whether Baldr could even see them.

Suddenly his hands clenched, pulling at his bonds. His head snapped up, the blood vessels in his neck sticking out. The metal shackles flexed, but held. Baldr stared at them, his gaze wild.

Gunnlaugur took a step back, his hand straying to the grip of his bolter. Ingvar remained where he was.

'Do you know us, brother?' Ingvar asked.

Baldr gaped at him. A flash of panic ran across his face. He thrashed against his bonds again, making the bunk rattle in its brackets.

'Then know yourself,' said Ingvar, calmly but firmly. 'You are Baldr Fjolnir, of Járnhamar pack. Of Blackmane's Great Company. Of Fenris.'

Baldr stopped moving. He looked down at himself awkwardly, as if surprised to see he had a body at all. His head fell back against the metal. He licked dry lips, and swallowed painfully.

'Why am I shackled?' he croaked.

The voice was just as it had been, only roughened from lack of use.

'You don't remember?' asked Gunnlaugur, still ready to draw.

Baldr's forehead creased. He shifted his body in its bonds, and a bone pendant secured at his neck slipped across his chest.

'This is... Ras Shakeh,' he said, slowly.

Ingvar looked at Gunnlaugur. 'Anything else?'

Baldr looked groggy and exhausted. 'What happened?'

Gunnlaugur's hand left his weapon. 'You killed a lot of people.'

Baldr closed his eyes again. 'Better tell me everything.'

'You should try to remember,' said Gunnlaugur. 'There is someone you need to meet. He will have a lot of questions, too.'

CHAPTER SIX

This time, the repairs were made properly. *Vuokho* was covered in dozens of servitors and kaerls, most brought down from *Heimdall* following Njal's return there. The gunship was hoisted on massive cantilevered struts, exposing damage even Jorundur hadn't discovered. Pipework-encrusted hunks of the engine train were pulled clear, cleaned and restored, before being slotted back in by whole gangs of tech-crew.

'Pointless,' Jorundur muttered, watching the progress like a hawk. 'No need to replace half of this.'

Hafloí snorted, standing beside Olgeir and Jorundur and picking gobbets of blood-clumped dust from his armour. The respite from the work of clearing the wasteland beyond the city was brief, but in the punishing heat of Ras Shakeh's sun it was welcome enough, even for a Space Marine. 'You should be pleased they're doing it.'

'*Heimdall* has its own gunships,' said Jorundur. 'They could use one of those.'

'*Vuokho*'s fast,' said Olgeir in his even, low-rumbling voice.

'Do we have a location yet?'

'The system edge.'

Jorundur spat messily. 'It'll be dead, just like everything else out there. Waste of time.'

'It'll be hunting,' said Olgeir.

'So we're always promised,' said Jorundur.

'*Skítja,*' said Hafloí. 'Don't you ever stop?'

Jorundur ignored him and looked over towards the edge of the apron, to where the first buildings clustered. Troops were moving all around the perimeter, some in Guard uniform, most bearing the signs of the Cardinal's entourage.

'This won't end well,' he said in a low voice, watching them march to their stations. Repair work had already started in the inner walls, and dozens of purge-teams prowled the lower city, flushing out infected zones, reducing anything living to ashes before moving on.

'What won't?' asked Olgeir.

'The Sisters are one thing. These... people. They're another.'

Hafloí followed Jorundur's gaze. 'They can fight.'

'You know what those bastards would do if they had the stomach for it.'

Jorundur looked at the whelp darkly. 'We're *devils* to them. They'd haul Grimnar up before the Lords of Terra and mind-wipe every kaerl in the Fang.'

Hafloí looked derisive. '*If* they had the stomach.'

'They've tried.'

'And failed.'

Jorundur shook his head wearily. 'You look at that cardinal. What do you see?'

'Fat,' observed Olgeir.

'Weapons. A Grand Cruiser. They got here quickly. Very quickly.'

'When's that damned gunship going to be ready?' asked Hafloí, shaking himself down and preparing to leave. 'If I have to listen to any more of this–'

But Jorundur was no longer listening. He walked over to the Thunderhawk's carcass, his attention caught by some minor infraction committed by one of *Heimdall*'s service crew. 'No. *No.* Have you ever *seen* inside a power train?'

Hafloí watched him go. 'Is he getting worse?' he asked.

'Not that I've noticed,' said Olgeir.

Hafloí drew his axe and turned it in his hands. The blade shone in the heat, flashing as it rotated. 'He needs to fight again.'

'We all do.' Olgeir drew his own blade – a shortsword with a sickle-hilt. 'You won't have to wait long. *Vuokho* will be ready in a few hours. We should spend the time well – improving your aim.'

Hafloí bristled. 'There's nothing wrong with–'

Olgeir's blade moved like a scorpion strike, snapping out and latching under the hooked edge of Hafloí's axe. The axe ripped from his fingers and clattered on the stone two metres away.

'Always room for improvement,' said Olgeir, smiling. 'There are chambers in the citadel that would serve.'

Hafloí retrieved his axe. 'So be it,' he said, a dangerous look on his ruddy face. 'Let's work on my aim.'

The Plague Marine hung in a holding cell deep within *Heimdall*'s hull.

Stripped of his armour, he looked like a side of rotten meat. His stomach was grotesquely split, glistening with entrails under a glossy sac. The skin of his pinned limbs was saggy and wrinkled, as if age had sunk deep into the bone. His head lolled against its bonds, marked by a single weeping eye, and his broken jaw dangled loosely, exposing the sinews of his facial musculature.

Njal stood over him, towering in the dark. Álfar was to one side, reaching for another drill. The cell was pooled in darkness, lit only by red lumens set in a distant ceiling. The walls trembled with the close grind of engines.

'You are resilient,' said Njal, lifting the Plague Marine's bloodied chin with a single armoured finger. 'I could admire that, in a different cause.'

The Plague Marine gazed up at him groggily. His lone eye rotated in a chafed socket, and blood ran down from the torn edges of his mouth. 'Endurance,' he rasped.

'For what?' asked Njal.

'Not a means.' The Plague Marine attempted to smile, and more flesh cracked. 'An end.'

Njal took the drill from Álfar and looked at it bleakly. He depressed the trigger, watching the spiked bit whirr. 'So how long are we going to have to do this?' he asked, the weariness in his voice perfectly genuine. 'Hours? Days?'

The Plague Marine coughed up a glut of blood. 'It's just pain.'

Njal nodded. 'That it is.' He primed the drill to the slowest setting, and moved towards the Plague Marine's pinned fingers. 'We'll start with the name *Thorslax.*'

Despite himself, the captive tensed, his breath becoming rapid and shallow. Just as the blades were about to bite, a chime sounded. Njal held steady.

'What is it?' he voxed to Derroth, *Heimdall*'s mortal shipmaster.

'The Cardinal, lord,' came the reply. 'You wished to be notified as soon as he arrived.'

Njal shut the drill off. 'Send him down.'

'By your will.'

Álfar shot Njal a quizzical look. 'You permitted him to come here?'

Njal shrugged, putting the drill back amongst the other instruments. 'He's entitled. Hel, he's welcome to take over.' He reached for a cloth to wipe his gauntlets. 'I did not come here to butcher rotten meat.'

The Plague Marine didn't seem to hear. Exhausted, his body slumped against its bonds. A few moments later, and a second chime sounded, this time just outside the doors.

'Come,' said Njal.

The doors slid back, revealing Delvaux and his black-robed deputy. The Cardinal stepped carefully into the cell, pulling his robes above his ankles to stop the hem trailing through the muck running across the floor.

'My lord Rune Priest,' he said, bowing.

'Cardinal,' replied Njal, not bowing. 'I do not know your shadow.'

In the confines of the cell, the physical disparity between Njal and the Cardinal was even more pronounced than it had been before. Delvaux, next to three huge, grisly, blood-spattered, armoured figures, looked both diminutive and flabbily corpulent.

'This is my confessor,' Delvaux said. 'He is called Klaive. Bow to the Wolf, Klaive – this is his domain.'

The sable-robed man inclined his head gracefully. By contrast with his master, the cell seemed to suit him. His pale flesh and neat, precise movement made him the image of an excruciator, and he balked at neither the stench nor the sights.

'Have you learned much from the subject?' asked Delvaux, searching around gingerly for the least besmirched place to stand. Álfar watched him with a cool mix of interest and contempt.

'He calls himself Falvo,' said Njal. 'He is of the Death Guard. All of which we could have taken from the armour pieces before they went to the furnace. Aside from that, he doesn't even scream.'

Delvaux regarded the prisoner with eager appreciation. 'Then this will be a long and messy business. Klaive? What do you think?'

Klaive glided up to the Plague Marine, running violet eyes over the contours of his broken flesh. 'I think there are things we could do,' he said.

'What do you mean?' demanded Njal.

Klaive withdrew a long casket from his robes – a slender wooden case the length of his forearm, inlaid with silver. 'May I?' he asked.

Álfar looked at Njal, who nodded, and Klaive opened the box. Inside was a dagger with an iron hilt. A script ran down the blade, etched in miniscule and swaying across the metal like a serpent. Klaive discarded the box and held the blade up before the Plague Marine. It glinted dully in the red light.

'Cutting won't hasten this,' said Álfar. 'We tried it.'

'I do not intend to cut him,' said Klaive, running his finger along the edge of the blade. 'But he knows what this is – look at his eye.'

The Plague Marine stared at the blade as it neared him, going rigid in his bonds. Sweat broke out over his bone-pale hide. 'Where did you get that?' he slurred, bloody saliva foaming over his split lower lip.

Klaive drew closer, reaching up to hold the blade just over the Plague Marine's forehead. 'It is a rather fine story,' he whispered. 'I could tell it to you, if you wished, but I would rather hear yours.'

Then he pressed the flat of the blade against the Plague Marine's skin. Immediately the prisoner writhed in agony, shrieking with pain. The smell of burning filled the chamber, curling up from the crisping edges of skin. The Plague Marine spasmed against his bonds, jerking and kicking out, opening up fresh wounds where iron coils bit into his wrists and ankles.

Then Klaive withdrew the blade, letting the Plague Marine recover. The confessor had a strange, eager light in his violet eyes, and his breathing was a little faster than it had been.

'Tell us, Falvo, what was your task on Ras Shakeh?' Klaive asked.

The Plague Marine regained his breath, still sweating in rivers. He shot a look of pure hatred from his single eye, his nostrils flaring. Pus, mingled with blood, dribbled down from the open weal on his forehead.

When no words were forthcoming, Klaive smiled and took up the blade again.

'Very well, if you will not–'

'I was under the Mycelite,' blurted the Plague Marine, staring at the blade with undisguised anguish. He panted heavily. A thick look of self-loathing rippled across his ruined features.

Klaive gave the two Wolves an assured look of triumph. 'Well then. I think we may make progress now.'

Njal looked down at the dagger with distaste. Everything in the cell made him feel sullied, and that wasn't the worst of it. 'What is on that blade?'

Klaive held it up to the light, turning it slowly. 'Words,' he said. 'Ancient words. We have discovered, in our researches, that words may be used for all sorts of purposes.'

Silently, Álfar's hand had strayed to his weapon, something neither Klaive nor Delvaux had noticed.

Njal had. In an instant, sickened by what surrounded him, he was tempted to let the shieldbearer use the chainsword, and damn the consequences.

Then, wearily, he shook his shaggy head.

+Time is against us,+ he sent, implanting the words into Álfar's mind. +A warrior cannot always choose his weapons.+

As Álfar relaxed, Njal turned back to the Plague Marine, who now looked up at him with real terror. 'I do not wish to see that thing used again,' said the Rune Priest, his voice a low growl. 'Neither do you.'

Njal leaned forwards, until his beard was almost brushing against the captive's face.

'So we will start where you did,' he said. 'Who is the Mycelite?'

The lander from *Heimdall* came down on the plains south of the city, far from the main deployment zones for Delvaux's forces. Ingvar, Gunnlaugur and Baldr slipped out of the city to meet it, hardly noticed by the crowds of menials and reclamators still at work.

Baldr walked haltingly, as if remembering how to use his muscles from scratch. The bright sunlight made his eyes water, just as the ice-glare had once done before the Helix. He felt heat rising from the packed earth, making him sweat under his loose robes.

In time, such things would cease to register with him – his physiology would return to its chameleonic adaptability, his strength would return, his animal spirits would roar back into immediacy. For the time being, though, he felt as frail as a mortal.

You killed a lot of people.

He remembered so little of it. Every so often, flashes of memory would return – a leering, joyful face burning amid a corona of green fire, a bone pendant spinning in the dark. His hands were still sore from where his skin had burned. Scars puckered the flesh, marring the smoothness of his old skin.

Ingvar and Gunnlaugur said nothing. The antagonism that had needled away between them on the journey out to Ras Shakeh seemed to have abated, replaced by uncertainty over how to deal with this new problem.

I have become the poison at the heart of the pack. Baldr smiled to himself wryly. *They fear me now.*

In truth, he feared himself. Though he detected no trace of the madness, there could be no denying what had happened. On the balance of probabilities, death waited for him on *Heimdall*. Stormcaller was not a sentimental soul, and had cut the thread of more heretics and witches than most inquisitors.

So be it. Better to end now than face corruption.

The grey-sided lander waited for them on the desiccated earth, surrounded by drifting clouds of dust, its ramp down. Two dozen kaerls stood before it, all in blast armour and with their helms on. The squad leader slammed his fist against his chest in salute.

Baldr looked at them. 'Surprised he didn't send more,' he said.

He turned, looking over his shoulder. The desert wind skipped and eddied across the plains. The air was clearer than it had been. A charred smell of burning flesh lingered from the pyres, and there was an undertow of plague-sweetness that hadn't quite been eradicated. The spires of Hjec Aleja glinted in the sun, though the blackened shell of the old Cathedral spoke of the tremendous destruction that still had to be cleared away.

All in all, the place had a stark beauty to it now. He could understand why pilgrims had come here. The pious always sought deserts, the pagan the ice.

'Until we fight again, brother,' said Gunnlaugur.

Baldr nodded, at him and at Ingvar, then turned and walked up the ramp into the lander's crew bay. Once he'd taken his place, the kaerls piled in after him, averting their eyes as they filled the vacant spaces. The lifter engines started to whine, and the ramp lifted noisily.

It slammed closed, locking him within a shaking metal shell. For a moment, he remembered how it had been the first time, dragged from battle and spirited away to Asaheim. He remembered how he'd felt the steel panels tremble, and how he'd been unable to work out where he was or what had happened or whether he was even alive at all.

Then the main thrusters fired, and the lander swayed up into the air.

Ingvar watched it go. The craft's atmospheric drives angled round on thick ball-and-socket housings, and it gained loft quickly, propelled on a white-blue cushion of engine-wash. Once high above the city, the orbital thrusters kicked in, hurling it up into a fast-dwindling ascent. After only a few moments, it was lost amid the relentless blue of Ras Shakeh's open sky.

'So what do you think?' asked Ingvar.

'Didn't sense a thing,' said Gunnlaugur. He ran his hands over his bald pate, wiping sweat from the tattooed skin. 'You can *smell* it, normally.'

Ingvar knew what he meant. The plague-mutants all had it – that faint stench of rotting fruit, lodged deep in their being, hovering over the human stink of illness. You couldn't disguise it, couldn't scrub it clean.

'He is free of it,' Ingvar said.

'You trust him, then?'

'It is not up to me.'

They turned away from the landing site and started to walk back towards the city perimeter. Over to their left, a few kilometres distant in a haze of heat and kicked-up dust, an army of labourers was working to clear and secure the battlefield. The acrid smell of promethium laced the air, the after-effect of fuel-spills and burn-teams at work.

'We could not have kept it secret,' said Gunnlaugur, striding out with his swaying, belligerent gait.

'I know.'

'But you think we should have tried.'

Ingvar felt a spike of annoyance, and pushed it down. Gunnlaugur had done the right thing, *was* doing the right thing. 'I'll say it again – what if the judgement goes against him?' he asked.

'It won't. You said it yourself – he is restored.'

'Njal may think different.'

Gunnlaugur stopped walking. 'He's *gothi*, brother. He carries the Law engraved on his staff. If we tried to keep Baldr from him–'

'I know,' insisted Ingvar. 'Still, if he is to be damned...'

He stopped before saying the words. There was no point, not until they knew the outcome.

Gunnlaugur sighed, screwing his eyes up against the glare. By now the lander had passed out of view, leaving the sky empty and trackless.

'You wanted to speak to me,' he said. 'About Hjortur.'

'You need to know.'

Gunnlaugur nodded. 'I have kept you waiting long enough.' He started to walk again. 'But not here. Come with me to the city. When we are back under shadow, you can tell me everything.'

De Chatelaine had to admit that the reconstruction, its speed and its completeness, had been remarkable. The Cardinal's troops had swamped the ruins with earth-moving crawlers and atmospheric lifters. Walls had been shored up, hab-blocks purged and made fit for reoccupation, defence towers restored and crowned with fresh ranks of operational weaponry. Temples had been cleansed of filth, their icons scrubbed clean and their statues replaced. Fresh images of the Blessed Primarchs and the Saints of the Ministorum were carted in, drilled into place and unveiled before the populace.

The people flocked back to the altars, falling prostrate before them. The scars of the conflict were close, and they wept openly during the ceremonies giving thanks to the Emperor. Thousands had died, perhaps three out of every four citizens according to some estimates, and those who remained were still in a kind of mass shock, plucked from the brink of annihilation just as all hope had faded.

For the survivors, it was a simple fact – He had delivered them. The faith that had sustained them through the worst of the long night flourished like a plant bursting into flower after drought.

The Cardinal's agents were everywhere, scouring the ruins of the Cathedral, pulling material out of every last remaining chapel, working their way through the Halicon undercroft. Their attention to detail was phenomenal – they worked as if in perpetual fear of some flaw in their labours being discovered. If some agents took certain liberties, and extended their control into areas where they had no strict right to, then few of the survivors were going to make any kind of complaint. They were too busy praying, and working, and weeping.

De Chatelaine glanced at her chrono. She had lost track of time. The marble surface of her pedestal desk was piled high with papers and data-slates, all of it bearing the skull-invested 'I' of the Ministorum. Delvaux's servants were assiduous, recording everything they did with almost compulsive completeness.

She rose, adjusting her robes over her armour and reaching for her ceremonial sword.

'Sister Callia,' she voxed, setting off for the short walk that would take her to the audience chamber where Delvaux had set himself up since returning from *Heimdall*. 'It is time.'

Callia joined her just as she reached her destination.

'Canoness,' Callia said, bowing. 'If I may, what is this about?'

'The restoration of authority,' said de Chatelaine, smiling. 'The Cardinal wishes to update us on progress. We should consider ourselves fortunate. Have you ever seen the city in such blessed fervour?'

Callia looked at her uneasily. 'No. Never.'

De Chatelaine gestured to the guards standing on either side of the two gilt doors, then strode through as they opened.

Inside, incense billowed across the polished floor, carried by servo-skulls trailing lengths of clanking chains. The sun had been filtered out by heavy fabrics, making the hall within glow with a dull, suffused light. Crimson-armoured Battle Sisters stood motionless amid the twin ranks of pillars running down each aisle. The air felt humid, fuelled by glowing brazier-pans.

The Cardinal was seated at the far end of the hall atop a towering throne, crusted with gold-leaf and flanked by helical columns. Cherubim buzzed lazily over an elaborate dome, dusting it with more incense, squabbling and blundering into the stonework. A low dirge of devotional chanting came from vox-emitters set in the high roof.

The Cardinal waited for the two of them to approach. He looked somehow larger than he had on their first meeting. His heavy robes flowed in thick folds over a substantial belly. He slumped in the golden seat, his eyes heavy-lidded, his fleshy fingers drumming on lion's-head armrests.

'My lord Cardinal,' said de Chatelaine, bowing.

Delvaux gazed down at her disinterestedly. 'Canoness,' he replied, his voice flat.

'You have been busy, I see.'

'These things?' Delvaux said, looking around absently at the finery. 'Brought down from *Vindicatus*. You had nothing suitable here.'

As he spoke, de Chatelaine noticed a Battle Sister move to his elbow, leaning up from the throne's stepped edges to whisper something in his ear. With a twinge of distaste, de Chatelaine saw the extent of the Sister's augmetic alterations – the entire left-hand side of her body was encased in bronze plating. Her half-concealed arm was bulky and stiff, ending in a blunt metal clump under a fabric glove. It looked like a flamer.

'You do not approve of Sister Nuriyah, canoness?' Delvaux asked, as the Sister withdrew again.

'Not at all,' said de Chatelaine, wondering at the Cardinal's changed tone with her. 'I commend her diligence.'

'She is most diligent. She performs every task I set her, even to the gravest extremity. The galaxy is not a forgiving place. It asks sacrifices of us all.'

A servo-skull swooped in from the aisles then, bearing a gold platter. It hovered over the Cardinal's lap, and he took a piece of peeled fruit from the platter before it swayed away.

'My lord, did you–' started de Chatelaine.

'I return from interrogating the fallen,' Delvaux said, still studying the fruit. 'Judgement comes to all. Or did you not preach that doctrine on this world?'

'We preach the Imperial Truth,' de Chatelaine said, stiffly.

'But there is more to our task than the truth, is there not? There is guidance. There is discipline.'

De Chatelaine bristled. 'My lord, if there is anything you find remiss, then I trust you will speak of it.'

Delvaux took a bite of the fruit, and red-purple juice ran down his chins. He chewed, dabbing at the runnel with a silk napkin. 'You were in command throughout the invasion?'

'I was.'

'Then you bear responsibility for what happened here.'

'I do.'

Delvaux nodded, taking another bite. 'Investigations continue. My people have spoken to many of those who served. We hear things.'

De Chatelaine's impatience began to get the better of her. '*Things*,' she said, coldly. 'Perhaps you will elaborate?'

Delvaux lifted a finger. From the shadows of the aisles, masked by the rows of pillars, de Chatelaine heard a shuffle. A second later, two Battle Sisters of Nuriyah's contingent emerged, their faces hidden behind white masks. They dragged a bundle of rags between them. Only as they emerged into the pool of dusty light before the throne did de Chatelaine see that the bundle was a man, pulled by slack arms, his head hanging between his shoulders.

The Sisters threw him to the floor. He lay prostrate, as limp as sackcloth.

'Tell us your name,' said the Cardinal, chewing the last of his fruit.

At the sound of Delvaux's voice, the man's head snapped up. Two wide eyes glared in terror from sunken cheeks. De Chatelaine saw the unmistakable signs of agony in his bearing.

'Velash, lord,' he said, his voice panicky. 'Velash! You asked me this.'

De Chatelaine looked at Delvaux stonily. 'By what right was this man put to the trials?'

Delvaux ignored her. 'Tell us what you told Sister Nuriyah, Velash.'

The man stared around him, though it wasn't clear if he was able to focus any more. 'They let them in! They let them in. They came across the desert, and they let them in.'

Delvaux nodded sympathetically. 'That is what you told us, yes. Who gave the order?'

'The canoness.'

De Chatelaine felt a chill run through her heart. This was a distortion – a grave one. 'Some mistakes were made,' she said. 'We had regiments returning from the front. Quarantine was not perfect.'

'What happened next, Velash?' asked Delvaux.

The man grinned. It was a manic, deranged grin – the grin of a man whose mind has turned. 'They came for us. The plagued. The flesh-eaters.'

'This is in my report,' said de Chatelaine, feeling as if she were hardly there.

'How many died?' Delvaux asked Velash.

Velash smiled wider. 'Thousands,' he said, gleefully. '*Thousands*.'

'Thank you, that is–'

'They kept coming!' Velash shouted, dragging himself up to his knees. De Chatelaine saw the way his legs bent under the fabric, and winced. 'They could not be stopped! The dead! The dead were eating the living!'

Delvaux motioned to his Sisters again. One of them cuffed Velash across the forehead, silencing him, before they both dragged him away. A trail of something liquid remained on the marble where he'd been.

'You had no right,' said de Chatelaine, her voice tight with anger.

'Did he speak the truth?' asked Delvaux.

'He is a citizen under my protection. Under the protection of the Church.'

'Did he speak the truth?'

'How many others have been questioned?'

'Did he speak the truth?'

The Cardinal's face was a slack mask of superiority.

'You know he did,' said de Chatelaine, quietly.

Delvaux rubbed his stained fingers on his napkin. 'This planet was nigh consumed. The Wolves were needed to save it. The *Wolves*. I have just spent time with this Stormcaller, and I have seen the way he behaves. I have seen how his trained beasts fawn over him. They believe in nothing. Their souls are the souls of animals. You should have done better.'

De Chatelaine looked about her, finding it difficult to believe such things were being said in her citadel. The red-armoured Battle Sisters of Delvaux's entourage gazed back at her from the margins, their faces blank with steady hostility.

'We… *fought*,' said de Chatelaine, struggling to find the words. 'We fought. My Sisters died. My… people died.'

Delvaux considered her as if she were something he had found lurking in the salty dregs of a ritual goblet. 'You were appointed to make hard choices, canoness. The reward for success is a record of glory, the price of failure is penance. What would you say happened on this world? Did you succeed? Is that what you think happened?'

De Chatelaine could sense Callia on the cusp of intervening then, and spoke quickly to prevent that.

'My lord, you were not here,' she said, speaking as steadily as she was able. 'If you had been, you would know that we did everything in our mortal power.' She pushed her shoulders back, feeling her armour flex as she stood straight before the throne. 'None could have worked harder. We were alone. We resisted, right until the end. We would have done so for as long as our bodies drew breath. You may conduct whatever investigations you wish. My conscience is clear.'

The Cardinal regarded her for a while longer, masticating. A thin trail of juice lingered on the pulpy underhang of his lower chin.

Then he stirred himself, reaching for a casket secreted within his robes. Just as before, he withdrew a pinch of powder and dabbed it under his nostrils.

'So you say, canoness,' he said. 'And your word counts for much, even with me.' He sniffed heavily, causing his eyes to water. He replaced the casket, adjusting his position on the throne, and a deep flush came to his cheeks. 'Our investigations will continue. Those who remain faithful receive the benedictions of the Ecclesiarchy, those who fall short receive its castigation. You know to what I refer.'

De Chatelaine remained defiant. 'I do,' she said calmly.

'Then let us hope that the testimony we uncover reveals a favourable truth.'

'There can be no doubt.'

'That is all, then. We understand one another. You may go.'

De Chatelaine stayed where she was for a moment longer. Then she turned to Callia, whose face was a tight mask of fury. 'Come,' she said.

The two of them walked back down the long nave, observed in silence by Nuriyah's Sisters. The doors closed behind them with an echoing clang that took several seconds to die away.

'He *dares*–' Callia started, but de Chatelaine held up a warning finger.

'He is the Hand of the Emperor,' she cautioned. 'Say nothing that will damn you.' She looked up to the ceiling, her eyes roving for vox-detectors. Callia took the hint, and fell silent.

De Chatelaine sighed then, and smiled – a forced smile, but it was important to maintain appearances. 'Have faith, Sister,' she said. 'This will be resolved.'

Then they started walking again, back along the corridors to their own chambers. As they went, de Chatelaine's mind worked furiously, gauging how many of her troops would remain faithful, how many would speak against her, how many would be taken for the trials.

She remembered the last words she'd shared with Gunnlaugur.

It is still my city.

Back then, it had been.

CHAPTER SEVEN

The void was lit virulent green, like a spiralling glut of ink poured into the dark. The dust-cloud towered through the well of space, sending fronds arching in a slew of vivid translucency. Asteroids cycled past it in procession, ink-black against the swathe of colour, held in place by the distant pull of Ras Shakeh's young star.

Vuokho ghosted in close, engines working on low burn. Jorundur steered it deftly, angling under a mammoth ball of tumbling rock before applying a little more power, sending the gunship skimming towards the central mass of asteroids beyond.

'Getting anything?' asked Olgeir, voxing from the forward hold below the cockpit.

'Just as they said,' replied Jorundur, tilting the Thunderhawk to starboard to dip below the field-plane. 'Coordinates were perfect.'

Amid the stellar rubble, one asteroid loomed closer – a mid-sized rock, ten kilometres in diameter, as black and cratered as the others. Jorundur locked on to it, running a brief scan to confirm the target.

'How does it look?' asked Hafloí, also from the hold.

'Like the rest,' said Jorundur, noting the results of the auspex run and checking it against what he'd been told to expect. The asteroid showed no power readings and no more than a trace heat signature. If he had not been given the precise location by de Chatelaine's strategos then he would have skimmed right on past. It was perhaps too much to hope that the enemy had done likewise.

He nudged *Vuokho* nearer, drifting to fifty metres over the asteroid's pitted surface. Retro exhausts fired, and the gunship came to a semi-stop, pulled along for the final few metres by residual momentum.

'I've got some damage on the outside,' said Jorundur, peering down at the gently scrolling landscape. 'Blast marks? Probably. Faint power readings. You might have gravity, might not.'

'Understood,' voxed Olgeir. 'Just get us there.'

Jorundur angled the Thunderhawk to the left, dipping the nose. *Vuokho* skimmed a few metres above the ash-grey outer crust before coming to rest just above a jagged pit, five metres across and ringed with black. Metal glinted down in its maw, charred and broken.

'This is it,' voxed Jorundur. 'Opening doors.'

The forward hold ramp bolts clanged back and the heavy armoured bow of the gunship swung open. Jorundur held *Vuokho* steady, making use of the retro thrusters to hold it in position.

He switched to the external viewers and watched Olgeir push himself down the ramp, still shackled to the gunship's interior by a length of metal cabling. Hafloí edged down after him. It was impossible to look graceful in zero gravity, even with the reactions and poise of a Space Wolf, and they looked like lumbering giants.

Olgeir reached the lip of the ramp and ran a scan of the pit below. 'Blast damage,' he voxed. 'Melta charges. All armour doors blown. You're right – no power.' He chuckled dryly over the comm. 'Done much zero gravity work, whelp?'

Hafloí held the anchor cable loosely, balancing casually further up the gunship's lowered ramp. 'How hard can it be?'

Jorundur rolled his eyes. 'Move faster,' he voxed, watching the incoming patterns of space-rubble on the scanner. 'I need to pull up.'

Olgeir pushed himself out into the void, unlatching the cable as he drifted clear of the hold. Hafloí followed, going a fraction too fast and nearly hitting the edge of the ramp. Olgeir touched down ahead of him, just on the lip of the pit, bending his knees to absorb the impact and grabbing hold of a twisted-up sheet of adamantium to gain purchase.

Jorundur deftly pulled *Vuokho* higher, taking care not to blast the two Space Wolves with his thruster-fire. Then he powered further away from the rock, adopting a position away from the rolling clouds of debris. He ran a quick check on the gunship's bolters, just in case, for all the help they would be. As soon as Olgeir and Hafloí dipped below the surface, they would be on their own.

'Good hunting,' voxed Jorundur, watching on the real-viewer as Olgeir dragged himself down into the shadow of the pit, followed by the jerkier movements of Hafloí.

Then he pulled *Vuokho*'s prow around, hovering above the asteroid like a jealous raptor over its nest, and stood guard.

'Sister Bajola told me,' said Ingvar. 'She knew about Hjortur. His name was on a kill-list, and she claimed she'd seen it.'

Ingvar and Gunnlaugur were back in the apothecarion, one of the few rooms in the Halicon still off-limits to the Ecclesiarchy staff. The place looked oddly empty without Baldr lying on the slab.

'Hjortur was killed by greenskins,' said Gunnlaugur. 'We were *there*, brother.'

'None of us saw him die.'

'What did she say killed him?'

'She mentioned a group: the Fulcrum. Then she died.'

Gunnlaugur winced. 'De Chatelaine told me she was strange. She was mortal. Dying does strange things to mortal minds.'

'She said they were coming after the Chapter. She said there were others, powerful figures, targeting more of us.'

'Any names?'

'No, though she gave me this.' Ingvar produced the golden cherub-face Bajola had given him, still spotted with her blood. 'Some kind of icon.'

Gunnlaugur took the cherub from Ingvar and held it up to the light. He studied it for a while, then handed it back. 'I've seen this before.'

'Where?'

'On every Cathedral, every Navigator house, on every inquisitor, and everywhere I've ever been.'

Ingvar smiled wryly, and stowed it back away. 'I see.'

Gunnlaugur sighed. 'Are you taking this seriously, brother?' he asked.

'We have a blood-debt.'

'*If* she was speaking the truth.'

'She had no reason to lie.'

Gunnlaugur's expression became serious. 'Give me a *name*,' he said. 'Just one name, and I'll pursue it with you to the limits of the galaxy. Until then, we have war snapping on our heels.'

'There is more hidden here,' insisted Ingvar. 'On this world. Bajola knew it, and she destroyed the archives in the Cathedral to hide it. Did you not wonder why the Church was so quick to get here? We were told there were no other defenders in this sector, but the Cardinal got here soon enough.'

'So what are you going to do? Interrogate them?'

'They're lifting kill-teams out into the desert, moving ahead of Álfar's packs. They say they're taking back overrun outposts.'

'They are.'

'Yes, but what else? I could run with them. It would be good hunting.'

Gunnlaugur looked at him sceptically. 'We will be moving off-world as soon as we have a spoor. Njal is itching to leave.'

'Not until *Vuokho* returns. There is time.'

'What are you going to find, brother? It is a wasteland.'

'It can't all have been destroyed. In any case, it will keep my blade sharp.'

Gunnlaugur drew in a weary breath, exposing his long fangs. 'What if I said no?' he asked. 'What would you do then?'

Ingvar stiffened. The tension between them, almost dissipated since the last days of the siege, still lurked, ready to flare up again. 'You are *vaerangi*.'

Gunnlaugur snorted out a harsh laugh. 'True enough, but you'd defy me. I'd have to floor you myself to keep you leashed.' Then he looked at Ingvar levelly. 'Tell me you are certain. Tell me this is blood-debt.'

Ingvar returned the look, his face intent. 'Hjortur was killed, and not by greenskins. Someone here knows why.'

Gunnlaugur studied him for a long time, then nodded. 'So be it. Just find me a name.'

Ingvar looked fiercely grateful. 'I will do it. The Ecclesiarchy is a den of secrets, but they can't hide them all.'

'And go *quietly*,' urged Gunnlaugur. 'They disgust me as much as you, but we need them. Njal wants the peace kept – he'll need that Grand Cruiser, if nothing else. So we tell no one.'

'And you?'

'My duty is here. De Chatelaine and I need to speak again. Of all of them, I'd fight by her side again.'

Gunnlaugur was about to move away then, when Ingvar grabbed him by the arm. 'They have struck at the heart of us,' Ingvar said. 'Whatever happens, once we have a name, we move.'

His tone was fervent. There was a fire there, one that had been missing for too long.

'You have my word,' said Gunnlaugur.

'And Baldr?'

Gunnlaugur's expression darkened. Baldr's fate remained in the balance, and there were some paths even a Wolf Guard could not travel.

'We are all Járnhamar, brother,' Gunnlaugur said, shaking loose the hold. 'When the time comes, the decision will be mine.'

The chamber was metal-lined, hammered with runes and bitter with the stink of ash. Animal skins hung from hooks in the flickering dark, some from the Old Ice, some from worlds as far-flung as the curve of the galaxy. Tall, narrow windows let in only a little artificial light, angled through iron lattices onto a floor of rough stone.

Baldr breathed deeply as he entered, drawing in the familiar aromas, the familiar sights. After Ras Shakeh, *Heimdall*'s air felt almost frigid, and he liked that. His grey shift, cloak and bound leggings did little to keep out the chill, just as his meagre furs had once done on Fenris itself.

He walked into the centre of the chamber, pausing before the great fire-pit at its heart. Embers glowed like angry stars, heaped high and raked with iron tongs. Each of the lining stones had a rune picked out on it – *sfar, zhaz, rhozan*. All of them, he knew, were wards against *maleficarum*, powerful symbols that dampened and dispersed the corruption of the underverse. Everywhere he looked he could see more spiky, angular etchings, half glimpsed amid the heavy shadows.

It was like being back in the Fang. When the Space Wolves took to the sea of stars, they took their home world with them, carved out of the shell of their iron-boned ships and hammered into every surface.

Baldr rolled his shoulders, trying to relax. His muscles ached from the final stages of the Dream, as tight and wound hard as weather-stiffened leather. Spikes of pain still ran down his spine, his eyes still smarted and the flesh of his hands was raw and covered in scabs.

All things considered, though, he felt more *himself* now. Time would only heal further. He stood, alone, watching the coals crack and darken in the fire-pit. Old flames licked across them. The rest of the chamber, filled with instruments and items even his acute sight could not pick out, was shrouded in frigid darkness.

He considered his position.

Would I have permitted it, he wondered, *if it had been another one of us? Would I have let him in, or cut his thread? I do not know.*

The doors hissed open again, throwing a thin bar of yellow light across the stone. Baldr turned to face it, and for an instant saw the same pair of eyes staring at him as so long ago – twin globes of amber, crouching in the snow-thick briars, slavering but not moving. With a lurch, he was straight back there, alone and unarmed, facing the wolf in the darkness of the primeval woods, and his hearts picked up in an involuntary threat-response.

Then the doors slipped closed, and the illusion faded, though the eyes remained. They were not the amber of most *Fenryka*, but ice-blue, like mortal eyes.

Njal stepped into the glow of the fire-pit. Baldr's sense of raw intimidation didn't fade. He was a seasoned warrior, used to facing every horror on the battlefield, but facing the Stormcaller in his own lair was something else. Njal wasn't just *a* Rune Priest, he was *the* Rune Priest, custodian of the deepest lore of the Chapter and confidante of the Lords of Fenris. The air around him seemed to drop in temperature, as if ice were always on the cusp of forming across his thick runic armour. Every surface of his ancient battleplate was engraved in esoteric sigils, each one etched over decades by the finest loresmiths of the Hammerhold.

They said Njal was the greatest *gothi* of the *Fenryka* since Odain Sturmhjart. They said he had more sagas sung of him in the Aett than any but Grimnar himself, and that each told of the destruction of such maleficent foes that the skjalds struggled to find words to describe them. They said that he knew secrets dating back to the Age of Wonder, and that his own vaults in the Valgard contained artefacts carved in the childhood of the Imperium when the Allfather yet walked alongside Russ and the ways of the void were pure.

Looking up at him for the first time, Baldr could believe all those things. In the semi-dark, lit from below by the angry glow of brazier coals, Njal loomed like a shadow of a half-forgotten past, vast, mythic, and potent.

The Rune Priest took his place on the far side of the fire-pit. He stood there, studying Baldr silently. That scrutiny felt like knives pressed against flesh.

'So,' he said, finally. 'You are the one. Here to be judged.'

Baldr lifted his chin. 'I am, *jarl*,' he said.

'Then we begin,' said Njal.

Olgeir drew his bolter. *Sigrún* had been left behind for this mission, replaced by a more practical standard-sized Asaheim-pattern weapon. He activated his helm's night-vision, and it picked out a long circular shaft below him, a few metres in diameter, running straight down into the heart of the rock.

Olgeir felt the impact of Hafloí touching down behind him on the asteroid surface, scuffing a little as his boots scrabbled for purchase. Olgeir leaned down and grabbed a metal hoop embedded in the shaft's wall. He pulled himself down into the shadow of the pit, moving hand over hand. As he went, he scanned the surface around him.

'Las-fire damage,' he voxed to Hafloí. 'Lots of it. Approaching inner doors now.'

The inner doors had once been adamantium and half a metre thick. Now all that remained were bulbous metallic outcrops of melta damage. The interior curve of the shaft was dented back into the rock by the force of explosions.

Haflói followed Olgeir down more slowly. He collided with the wall, rebounding awkwardly before steadying his descent.

Olgeir smiled to himself, nudging himself further towards the base of the shaft. His helm-display showed no targets, no movements. The interior was utterly lightless, too cold even for infrared, so the way forward was picked out by his helm-lumens.

'I'm getting nothing,' voxed Haflói from above him.

Olgeir coasted down into what must once have been the main entry chamber – a spherical capsule about ten metres across, accessed by a hatch at the top and exited via a pair of standard blast-doors on his right-hand side. He arrested his fall and touched down lightly on the bottom of the chamber, sweeping his bolter-muzzle up at the empty open doorway in front of him.

'Nothing here either,' he replied.

There was evidence of fighting – las-marks on the metal interior walls, blown hatch controls, scratches on the bulkheads, but there were no bodies. Aside from the sound of his own breathing and the interior hum of his power armour, the capsule was vacuum-silent.

Haflói touched down beside him. 'How big is this place?'

Olgeir recalled the schematics taken from the archives in Hjec Aleja. 'Twenty crew. Twenty-nine rooms, augur-chamber, power plant, shield generator. This won't take long.'

He pushed off, gliding through the open doorway. He skimmed down a long circular connective tube beyond, filling it out and grazing the edges with his armour. The spaces narrowed down, small even by mortal standards, claustrophobic for Space Marine bulk. His lumen-gaze moved over everyday remnants of the station's working life – devotional imagery set into the walls, prayer-beads, duty rosters. The further in he went, the more signs of violence emerged. Long, dark trails ran across the concave floor. Olgeir sniffed by instinct, as if somehow the smell of corruption could penetrate sealed battleplate.

He passed an open hatchway to his left, blasted open like the outer doors had been, and ran a lens-scan. The chamber was big, more than ten metres cubic, dominated by a floating cluster of ruined machinery – brass spheres, metal coils, crystal transistors stamped with the icons of the Ecclesiarchy. Winged iron angels drifted amid the wreckage, gazing up at the roof with empty eyes.

'Comms array,' said Olgeir. 'Still no bodies.'

Haflói pushed past, taking point and tumbling further down the corridor. 'They've stripped it clean,' he muttered. 'There's nothing here.'

Olgeir followed him. The walls bore down on them, tight and clad in thick shadow. It felt like they were being dragged deep into the heart of the asteroid. More blood-smears appeared on the walls, thick and mottled with desperate handprints.

Suddenly, Olgeir felt the hairs on the back of his neck prick up, pressing against the inner seal of his gorget. 'Sense anything, whelp?' he voxed, watching Hafloí's boots disappear around the corner ahead.

'Another shaft,' Hafloí reported. 'No targets. I'm going further down.'

By the time Olgeir had followed him round, pushing against the corridor walls and roof to propel him along, Hafloí had gone ahead through another hatch opening, diving in headfirst. Olgeir did the same, squeezing his bulk carefully through the aperture. This shaft was smaller than the first, the space limited by a metal-ring ladder running down one side, and he grabbed the rungs to haul himself downwards. His breathing felt close and rapid inside his helm.

The chamber at the bottom was carved from bare rock, no more than five metres across. Smashed equipment rotated gently in the cramped space around them, rolling away when pushed.

Olgeir emerged through the ceiling and twisted awkwardly to right himself.

'Nothing,' Hafloí voxed, arresting his spin against the rough wall. 'Nothing at all.'

Olgeir let himself rotate, studying the chamber carefully. It looked like a storage area lodged down at the bottom of the station. The skull device of the Ecclesiarchy had been stamped over the entrance, though since gouged out with thick claw-marks.

He wished he could use his sense of smell.

'Might be right,' Olgeir voxed, scanning for heat-sources just to be sure. Nothing came back from the blank, crudely cut chamber edges.

'We should go,' said Hafloí, kicking back towards the shaft entrance.

Olgeir paused. He shoved himself over to the far wall of the chamber and pressed his gauntlet up against it. For a moment, there was nothing.

Then, fainter than breath against the wind, he felt it – vibration, brushing against the far side. His pupils immediately narrowed.

'This is sensor-shielded,' he said. 'Hold position.'

Hafloí halted at the base of the exit shaft, twisting around and training his bolt pistol.

Olgeir ran his hands along the rock. He found a small change in texture, almost undetectable – a strip of stone that felt marginally different from that around it. He called up the schematics given to them by the Ecclesiarchy. There were no rooms marked beyond their position.

'Secretive bastards,' he muttered. He pulled a krak charge from his belt, clicked the countdown and clamped it to the stone strip. Then he pushed himself away, drifting back to the far wall. Hafloí drifted over to join him.

'Ready yourself,' Olgeir said, bracing himself against the wall and training his bolter on the clicking krak charge. 'Fire through the detonation.'

Hafloí locked position, wedging himself into the corner of the chamber to secure a firebase. Then the charge exploded in a stark, silent bloom of light, driving in the wall and filling the chamber with a blaze of swiftly extinguished flame. The far wall dissolved into dust and rock fragments, raining against the two Wolves' armour.

They opened fire in unison, pumping bolt-shells into the breach. As the rounds went off, the loosened wall section crashed away, breaking free from the bolts holding it in place. A howl of escaping air rushed past them, making the debris in the grav-free chamber rock and slam into the walls.

'Now!' ordered Olgeir, thrusting powerfully against the stone behind him.

Haflói did the same, and they crashed through the disintegrating wall section, weapons firing. With the escaping atmosphere came the high-pitched scream of semi-human throats on the far side, suddenly roused in throttled fury.

They were no longer alone.

There were many wolves on Fenris, just as many as there were warriors in the Halls of the Fang. Most snarled and roared with feral abandon, given over to the frenzy of the hunt. They slavered with the scent of prey in flared nostrils, they crashed through the snow in pursuit of agile prey.

The Dark Wolf was different. It curled around the shadows, back arched, head low, hugging the frigid depths of the eternal pine-woods. It padded through the dream world of the underverse, following the spirits of the dead, escorting them deeper into the cold, cold tombs that waited prior to the battle at the end of the world. It never roared, and its soul was silent.

The Dark Wolf knew many secrets. It had seen the galaxy decay, turning from magnificence into atrophy. It had seen the fires go out, one by one, snuffed into oblivion by the crawling march of the Annihilator. The Dark Wolf had watched the compromises being made and had listened to the lies being told. It knew the sources of those lies, and where they sprang from, and upon what date the untruths would catch up with their utterers.

Njal had felt the Dark Wolf on his trail from the earliest of times. He remembered listening to its panting while still on the ice. Even in the Fang, the mightiest of fortresses, he had sensed it treading around the walls. In the utter night, when the vaults and tunnels of the Mountain were drenched in sleep, he had heard it snuffling in the outer twilight.

The Dark Wolf had always been his companion, and they both shared the secrets of aeons. One day, Njal knew, they would meet. He would look up, and see the eyes of his mirror-self staring back, and know that the hour had come.

There were times when he dreaded that meeting. There were times when he yearned for it. Neither dread nor yearning would hasten the day, though – it would come at the appointed moment, when his wyrd was accomplished and there were no more deeds ahead of him.

Grimnar was the joy of the hunt, the roar of triumph and the tang of blood in the air. Ulric was the fury of the kill, the shake and rip of flesh tearing. Njal was the echo of death, the aftermath of murder. That was his lot, and it was as sacred and unbreakable as the Annulus itself. Such was the way of the universe. There was no pity in it, just the tight grip of fate.

'I am the Law of Fenris,' said Njal, feeling the eyes of the Wolf resting on him, as always, when he spoke. 'You are bound by it, just as you were when you took the Helix.'

Standing before him, the Grey Hunter Baldr nodded in response. Given what he had endured, he looked ready enough to fight – his eyes were clear, his stance solid. If he had not been told of what had happened, Njal would not have guessed he'd been under the curve of Morkai's claws for so long.

'This is a test of corruption,' said Njal. 'You know what that means.'

'I do.'

'You are Baldr, called Fjolnir, of Blackmane's Great Company.'

'I am.'

'Fjolnir. The nightjar. What does that signify?'

'It is a hunt-mark, from the ice. The mark no longer exists, not since the Rite, but the name I kept.'

'Who gave it to you?'

'The *gothi* of my tribe.'

Baldr spoke clearly. As the words left his mouth, Njal listened for the faint stirrings of falsehood under them. A traitor had a thousand ways to give himself away, and the Rune Priest was a master of detecting them all. His psychic sense extended gently across the chamber, alert to the harmonics of *maleficarum*. The words spoken were a part of the examination, but there were other tests as well, hidden ones that only he would be aware of.

'Did this *gothi* have you marked out?' asked Njal. 'To follow him?'

'I do not know.'

'Did he ever speak to you of the way of the storm?'

'No.'

'What age were you taken by the Priests?'

'Five, of the home world.'

Nightwing, who had remained hidden up until then, stretched out its pinions. It was perched high up above the fire. Njal, if he chose, could use the creature's artificial eyes to see with, just as he did on the battlefield. The psyber-raven was a shrewd judge of souls, though, and seemed content enough. Had Baldr been obviously tainted, the raven would surely have gone for his eyes already.

'Do you remember what happened to you on this world?' Njal asked.

'No.'

'Nothing?'

'I remember sickness, during the crossing. It lingered after we landed. I put it out of my mind.'

'Describe the sickness.'

Baldr paused. 'Like a fever. I did not sleep. I had pain, often, here.' He pointed to his right temple. 'I performed battle-rites to remain of service. I thought it was warp-sickness.'

'You suffered before?'

'A few times. Never as bad.'

'You never raised this with a Priest?'

Baldr smiled faintly at that. Njal could understand why – he was a Sky Warrior, a member of the Rout of Fenris. What was he supposed to have complained of? Headaches?

'Tell me your last memory, before the sickness took you.'

'We were in a gorge, out from the city,' said Baldr. 'We attacked an enemy convoy. Hafloí, a battle-brother, was in combat with a Traitor. A witch. I charged it. After that, nothing.'

'Nothing.'

'My next memory was waking here.'

Njal nodded. The fire-pit spat as a coal rolled from the heap. He considered all the answers. He considered the way they had been given. He considered the psychic resonances within the chamber, the echoes of a deeper reality under the one his mortal senses picked out.

The Wolf made its presence felt again, like the aroma of bloody breath hanging over a kill.

'Listen to me, Baldr,' said Njal. 'When you arrived at the Fang, when you were five Great Years of age and your body was as fragile as a twig, you were tested. You were under the eyes of the Priests for a long time. We rebuilt your body, we peered deep into your mind. We took it apart. We stripped it down, scoured it clean. We were looking for a sign – any sign – of aptitude. None was found. I say this with certainty. If it had been, you would have been given instruction. You would be a Rune Priest under me, or you would be dead. There are no alternatives.'

Baldr listened carefully, taking it in.

'And yet, here we are,' Njal went on. 'If you were the only one, then I might leap to one conclusion. But you are not. Some secrets are not talked about openly, not outside the Annulus. Tell me this: do you know the word "awakening"?'

Baldr shook his head.

'For a long time,' said Njal, 'it meant nothing to me. I do not willingly keep the company of inquisitors, but on occasion I am forced to suffer their presence. When they talk, I listen, and so a thousand stories reach my ears. Some talk of awakening, some of veil-cleaving, some of soul-latching. They all mean the same thing.

'The galaxy grows old, Baldr Fjolnir. It withers, and it cools. Barriers that have existed for ten thousand years wear thin, like skin stretched too tight over bone. Things are leaking into the realm of the senses that never did before. I see it on every battlefield – men going mad, or bursting into flame, or rising into the air. Some hail these things as miracles. I do not share that kind of faith.'

Njal grimaced a little as he spoke that word. *Faith* had always been a painful concept for him, too redolent of the fanaticism of allies, and nothing like the warrior fatalism of the Fenrisian creed.

'There have been visions on Fenris,' Njal said. 'Ulric tells me the years are racing towards their conclusion. He thinks the End Times are here. We hear names whispered that have not been so much as thought of since the Fell-Handed fought alongside Russ. These are not idle fears, just as every mortal dreams of in the dark, but the visions of the Lords of Men.

'We have come to recognise that some things long accepted as true may no longer be. We have been forced to see that some old protections have lost their power. We have no new ones. All that remains is the strength of our blades, and even they grow blunt.'

For the first time, Baldr looked uneasy, as if those words hurt him. 'Then, lord, do you–'

'I said listen. These are possibilities, no more. You may be awakened. I do not know. From what you say, from what I see, from what I sense, I still do not know. There are ways of delving deeper. If we were in the Mountain, I would submit you to the trials, and Ulric and I would strip your soul bare before our eyes. That, at least, would bring certainty, if you survived it.'

Nightwing emitted a thin vox-caw then, as if the creature somehow objected to that.

'What I can do here is limited,' said Njal. 'It would be safer to end you now, just to be sure, but to throw away a warrior on the eve of battle... In these times, in this place, that is a hard choice to make.'

Baldr drew in a deep breath. 'Anything, lord,' he said firmly. 'I will submit to any test. If you find fault, I will do the deed myself – my blade is sharp enough.'

Njal maintained the gaze of scrutiny, his eyes boring out into the darkness. 'What do you *feel?*' he asked. 'What does your blood tell you?'

Baldr thought for a long time before answering.

'It tells me I am restored,' he said. 'I would say I am cured. I would fight again, with my pack, just as I did before. But if you discovered any taint – *any* taint – better to end it now, and not to linger with a curse hanging over me.'

Njal nodded. They were good words. He could understand why Gunnlaugur wanted Baldr back in his pack.

'Well said,' he responded.

He raised his staff then, kindling fresh fire from the skull-tip. The shadows of the chamber lifted, shrinking back from the fire-pit like oil sliding from steel. Shapes were revealed – metal framed cages, stone thrones, brass orbs hung from the chamber roof and wrapped in a filigree of needle-thin wires.

'There are tests we can perform here,' said Njal, walking over to the nearest of the devices and beckoning Baldr to join him. 'You recognise these things? They are like those used when we first brought you inside the Mountain. Sit.'

Baldr took up position on a long stone bench. Above him hovered a spidery collection of probes suspended from a looped coil of cabling. As he pulled himself onto the stone, the tips of the probes glowed into life, glistening like tiny jewels in the dark. A machine began to work close by, gurgling and thrumming.

Njal moved to the far side. Nightwing flapped awkwardly over to the other end of the chamber, taking position atop the heavy stone doorframe and observing intently. Baldr lay back.

'Prepare yourself,' said Njal, resting one hand on the housing of the machine, using the other to hold his staff.

A faint crackle ran down the ebony shaft, like static discharging. Soon the veil around them would thin, and matter would run perilously close to non-matter. The entire chamber would be dangerous.

Other visions would come, then. Other times, places. Two amber eyes would be trained on him, lost in an ancient world of dreams, stalking through the void for eternity.

'This will hurt,' he warned, then threw the first switch.

CHAPTER EIGHT

'*Hjolda!*' roared Olgeir, firing hard as his momentum propelled him into a disintegrating storm of rock and racing, churning oxygen.

The chamber's wall had cracked and broken into a cloud of debris, blasted outwards by the explosive force of the released atmosphere behind it. The station's unnatural silence rushed back into a whirl of howling sound, punctuated by the massed screams of mutant throats.

Olgeir was first through the breach, and slammed straight into a spinning crowd of them. They clawed at his armour, piling on top of one another, scrabbling at the battleplate to get their teeth at the flesh beneath. They were everywhere, like locusts, flailing and jostling in the pitch-black zero gravity. Despite the rapidly depressurising chamber, they kept up their shrieks of bloodlust, lost to anything but the sudden prospect of slaughter.

Hafloí piled through the gap next, careering into a knot of writhing bodies. He fired his bolt pistol as he came, punching into the solid glut ahead of him. Olgeir kept up his volleys but the detonations were muffled, clamped down by the pressure of skin and limbs around them. Blood speckled out from the impacts, spinning in glutinous droplets and spiralling in the whooshing air.

'Blades!' roared Olgeir over the vox, struggling to free himself from the dozens of claws scrabbling for his throat. The space was pitch black, confined and clogged with bodies, and gaining orientation while weightless was a nightmare – every push sent him spinning into fresh tangles of mutant legs and arms.

Hafloí somehow hauled his axe from his belt and lashed out wildly, rolling headfirst and clung to by scores of screaming mutants. Fresh blood-slicks rolled out, slapping incongruously into the bodies around them.

Olgeir resorted to his fists, punching blindly into the mass of the plague-damned. He cracked the first skull clean through, shattering the fragile bone amid a cloud of pulpy, red-blotched matter. He swung again, bursting the ribcage of another, then jabbed his elbow back, feeling the crack and snap of more bones.

More mutants came to replace those, hands swimming up out of the gloom like shoals of diseased fish, lashing out in a frenzy of claustrophobic hatred. The attacks came from every direction, all in a confused welter of jerky movements. Olgeir felt a blade scrape across the armour-joint at his knee, cutting into cabling, and kicked out against it.

Both Space Wolves were entirely smothered by then, covered in a ball of raging, calloused, desperate bodies. Olgeir felt himself driven back into the nearside wall. Able to brace against something at last, he lashed out harder with his punches, ripping a narrow space just ahead of him. The mutants' screams were the worst he had ever heard – amplified and fractured by the rushing howl of fast-escaping air.

Hafloí was dragged down, his axe pressed against him. Even as Olgeir kicked off from the wall to aid him, he was hauled back by a dozen hands. He twisted, using his bulk to crush a few more against the chamber's edge. He kicked again, feeling his boot drag through muscle. It was like fighting a single, amorphous mass of decaying meat, albeit one with a hundred biting maws and stabbing blades.

In the end, the vacuum tipped the balance. The last of the air ripped away, dissipating out into the breached station. The mutants began to gag, coughing on the thinning air as it whistled out of reach. Their eyeballs swelled, the cords of their necks strained.

'*Heidur Rus!*' roared Hafloí with real rage, sensing the change.

Then the sounds around them shredded away into the eerily silent dance of void-combat. Olgeir saw the jaws of the mutants screaming at him soundlessly. He smashed into them with greater freedom, using his gauntlets and bolter-grip. Gasping in oxygen-starved panic, their bodies were slammed away, cracking against the walls with back-breaking force.

'Further in,' growled Olgeir, angrily discarding the last of the clutching mutant hands around him and pushing on towards the chamber's far end.

Hafloí finished off the mutants around him, and followed, pushing aside the final choking, tumbling bodies. The chamber terminated in a circular hatch at the lower end, two metres in diameter, still sealed and powered. Faulty lights flickered around its edge. The metal rim was a mess of gouges, all full of blood, as if the mutants had mutilated themselves in their frenzy to get through the final barrier.

Olgeir scanned it. There was another air-pocket on the far side, and light, and some heat. 'This is where they ended up,' he said, looking for some kind of vox-unit to use.

Hafloí stared at the portal. 'Really think there's anything beyond that?'

'*They* did.' Olgeir pulled open a panel next to the hatch-rim, his armoured fingers clumsy in the zero gravity. He punched some buttons, and connected a vox-cable to his helm. 'Respond,' he said. 'Any survivors?'

A crackle came back over the comm, seething with static. Then it cleared. 'Thank the Throne,' came a trembling human voice.

The sun was high, a white hole in the sky, burning away with pitiless strength. The land extended in all directions under it, nearly flat, broken only by rust-coloured ridges of stone on the far northern horizon. There was no shade, nowhere to hide, just an endless expanse of shimmering, shaking heat.

Ingvar crouched down behind the low rise. Fifty storm troopers of Delvaux's command crouched with him. Their colonel, a man called Rigal, who wore the full crimson carapace armour of his order, lay on the earth next to him, magnoculars pressed to his visor.

Two hundred metres away rose the ruins of Hjec Falama, one of the satellite settlements that had once guarded the long road to the capital. The burned-out shells of troop transports littered the landscape around them, rising like carbonised skeletons from the topsoil. A few thin columns of smoke rose from the cover of the buildings, though with less intensity than other enemy positions they'd already purged. The defensive line started with a long, low earthwork, crowned by razor wire. Behind that rose the sawtooth lines of hollow, roofless buildings.

'Tell me what you see,' said Ingvar.

Rigal initially hadn't wanted the Space Wolf to join the kill-team, though Ingvar hadn't given him much choice. After the first few assaults, the colonel had changed his mind. Ingvar alone killed more than the rest of the team combined, and such strike-ratios went a long way towards changing attitudes. For his part, Ingvar studiously deferred to the colonel's authority during operations. He'd served with storm troopers before, and knew how their minds worked.

'They're dug in beyond that first line,' Rigal replied. 'A few hundred. Three artillery pieces, some heavy weapons. After that, the usual rabble. They know we're here.'

Ingvar knew all that, but it did no harm to let the colonel tell him. 'It's your command,' he said.

Rigal stowed the magnoculars. 'I'll take any guidance, lord.'

Ingvar studied the approach, using his helm-lenses to zoom in and pan across the hardscrabble vista ahead. Rigal might have been too conservative in his estimates – there were plenty of defenders in position. Behind them, though, there was movement. Fresh plumes of smoke were blooming from some way back into what remained of the settlement. He thought he caught the outlines of troops running across patches of open ground between the carcasses of shelled-out habs.

'Any other forces in this zone?' he asked Rigal.

'Just us.'

Ingvar nodded. 'I can break the line. Once they've started panicking, begin your advance.'

'With pleasure.'

'Begin your bombardment,' said Ingvar, unholstering his boltgun.

Rigal gave the signal and his two mortar-squads prepared to launch. Ingvar hoisted himself up onto his knees and crouched for the sprint.

'We'll be right on your heels,' said Rigal, shuffling further up the rise and resting his bolt pistol on the earth ridge.

Seconds later, mortar trails arced high into the air before thudding down behind the enemy positions. The crews had aimed them well, and explosions burst out all along the line. Reloading took place quickly, and more trails streaked out above the enemy.

Ingvar burst into motion, kicking out into the open and running hard.

He was a big, bulky target and his grey armour gave him no camouflage. Las-fire started to flicker in his direction immediately, skittering across the open desert like flashes of sunlight off glass.

He kept low, zigzagging across the open terrain, picking up speed and twisting unpredictably. A few sharpshooters had taken position up in the habs, though most were clustered at ground level, hunkered down behind the barricades. Rigal's troops opened up a covering barrage from the flanks, pinning some of the bolder defenders behind the earthwork.

Ingvar selected the point to strike. Las-beams pinged from his shoulder-guards and drilled into his breastplate, doing little damage. Solid rounds puffed up the dust at his feet, fruitlessly trying to catch him as he raced into contact.

He fired as he ran – a short brace of pinpoint shots, each aimed from instinct, each one finding its mark with a wet pop, followed by the messy slap of bodies being ripped apart. He seized a frag grenade from his waist and hurled it ahead of him. It bounced over the barricades and into the semi-walled space beyond, exploding in a messy, spiralling boom.

Then he was at the barricades and smashing through the razor wire. Those still on their feet raced away from him, firing steadily.

'*Fenrys!*' roared Ingvar, laughing with savage pleasure. He unsheathed *dausvjer* with his right hand, firing his bolter with his left, then charged them.

They kept their lasguns levelled and their mauls and flails in hand. Ingvar swept through them like a desert wind, ripping down the length of the barricade and bringing terror with him. Even the plague-damned fell back in the face of the furious assault, limping away from their posts and shambling back into the blasted townscape beyond.

That was the cue for Rigal to advance. His storm troopers moved from cover and charged across the open ground. The last of the mortars, angled for long range, whistled overhead and crashed into the ruins, blowing up amid cohorts of retreating enemy soldiers.

Ingvar went after them, saving bolts in favour of cutting their legs from under them. Rigal's forces were quick to catch up. They split into two squads, spreading out along either flank of the barricade and coming at the remaining defenders in a pincer movement. Their carapace armour – superior to the flak-plates worn by Ras Shakeh's Guard regiments – gave them good protection from return fire, and their hellguns sent better-aimed, more focused beams into their targets.

Caught between Ingvar's lone devastation and the disciplined push of Rigal's forces, the enemy line shattered entirely, breaking into bands of retreating warriors. Once they lost their shape, the storm troopers went after them remorselessly.

Ingvar pulled ahead. Like a grey ghost he flitted through the dust-kicked sunlight, pouncing on his prey before tearing it to pieces. Soon he had penetrated into the heart of the old settlement. A few big buildings still stood, blackened by fire and windowless, but with their walls largely intact. A wide courtyard ran away ahead of him, bordered on one side by a large municipal edifice with granite columns and a domed belltower. A huge Imperial aquila lay on the ground before it, broken in pieces.

Ingvar skidded into the open, catching a retreating mutant by the neck and lashing him against the stone. Dozens more fled ahead of him, stumbling over the shattered rockcrete.

His instinct was to race after them, taking down as many as he could reach before they dispersed into the ruins. Just as he was about to sprint after the nearest, though, he caught the snap and fizz of las-fire coming from the far side of the square. Some of it hit the fleeing mutants, causing them to crash to earth.

Ingvar's helm picked up multiple targets hidden in the buildings on the far side, some positioned higher up amid the hollowed windows. He raised his bolter, training it on the first such position. His finger slipped over the trigger, and he lined up the shot.

It never came. More las-fire scythed down from the cover of the buildings, cutting down more plague-mutants. The aim was good – professional, not wasteful.

As Ingvar hesitated, Rigal's troops caught up. The storm troopers pushed on, making cover and aiming their hellguns at the buildings beyond.

'No!' roared Ingvar, holding his blade up.

Rigal gave the order, and the entire square fell into echoing silence, the dust settling slowly over the corpses.

Ingvar strode ahead, looking up at the windows ahead of him. As he emerged into the open, a cry broke out from the far side. The language wasn't native to Ras Shakeh.

'*Fenrys Hjolda!*' came the cry, repeated over and over from hoarse throats.

Soldiers emerged from cover, encrusted with grime and bearing a motley assortment of lasguns and improvised weaponry. All of them wore grey uniforms, though covered in thick layers of caked dust and dried blood. Their hair was long and shaggy, many of them blond or red-headed. They laughed raucously as they advanced, saluting Ingvar with the fist-against-chest gesture.

Ingvar watched them come, dumbfounded for a moment. Only when their leader approached, pushing those around him to one side, did he realise the truth.

'Bjargborn,' Ingvar said. 'How, in the name of–'

Torek Bjargborn laughed. All of them laughed. The sound was one of relief, the release of long-coiled tension.

'We waited, lord,' said the old master of the *Undrider*, grinning. 'We held on.' He fell to one knee then, as did all those around him. There must have been more than eighty of them, all in grey Fenrisian garb.

Rigal joined Ingvar. He, like the other storm troopers, regarded the newcomers with suspicion, and kept his weapon levelled.

'Is all well, lord?' Rigal asked.

Ingvar reached down to Bjargborn and pulled him back to his feet. His fanged mouth broke into a smile.

'Better than well, colonel.' He looked up, gauging how much of the settlement remained infested, then turned back to Bjargborn. 'First, we fight,' he said. 'Then, when this place is clean again, you can tell me how in the name of Hel you're still alive.'

When Baldr came round, his vision remained blurred for a long time. For a few moments he had no idea where he was. Grey shadows loomed over him, shifting like candlelight. He heard a metallic cawing, and boots scuffing on stone.

Recollection came back slowly, along with the pain. It ran down his back like cold fire. He reached up to his forehead, feeling bloody scabs on his temples.

'Welcome back,' came a familiar deep voice from the shadows.

Baldr lifted his head, blinking thickly.

Njal was still there, towering over him. The smell of burning filled the chamber, as if he'd been cooking meat.

Baldr pushed himself up into a seated position. His head hammered as he moved. He was desperate to ask, but the words wouldn't come.

Njal prolonged the agony for a few more moments.

'Nothing,' he said at last, putting his instruments away and coming to stand by his side. 'Nothing at all.'

Baldr swallowed thickly, tasting his own blood in the bile. He wasn't sure whether he fully believed it. 'No corruption?'

'None.' Njal fixed him with his frost-clear gaze. 'I sense nothing, I see nothing. If I had, you would not have awoken.'

The Rune Priest reached for a ceramic cup and filled it with water from a ewer. He handed it to Baldr. 'When you return to the city, restart your training. Work hard. You have lost muscle mass, and I want you fighting again as soon as possible.'

Baldr nodded, draining the cup. His throat remained parched and sore.

'I have done nothing but interrogate since I got here,' said Njal irritably, turning back to his instruments. One by one, he cleaned them and put them away, treating the devices reverently, like an Iron Priest with his tools. 'First the Plague Marine, now you. This must be the end of it.'

At the mention of the Traitor, the pain burning at the base of Baldr's neck briefly flared, as if in sympathy with old memories. 'Did you discover anything from the Traitor?' he asked, before remembering it was not his place to ask.

To his surprise, Njal merely nodded, and carried on with his work. 'We have names now. The Mycelite. This one is new to me, but there is another which is not: *Festerax*.'

Baldr flexed his fingers gingerly, feeling the blood slowly flow back into the arteries. 'Another Traitor?'

'A ship. A hulk. It has been in the annals of the damned for millennia.' Njal smiled grimly. 'This is the enemy. Once this world is purged of the last dregs, we will hunt it down.'

'Where is it?'

'We do not know. Not yet.' Njal put the last of the devices away in leather-lined caskets, clicking the locks closed firmly and making the sign of warding across the lids. 'We'll know more if the deep-void stations can be trawled. If not, we're in the dark over their movements. I don't think our prisoner knew more than he told us. At least, while he still had a tongue.'

'Does he live?'

'I killed him.' Njal opened a heavy iron door in the chamber walls. 'The Cardinal seemed happy to keep going indefinitely. I was not.' He retrieved something from behind the door, and closed it again. 'Not good for the soul, that kind of work. Ulric has more stomach for it, but even he takes no pleasure. We were made for the clean kill.'

Njal returned, carrying what looked like a torc. It was white, carved from ivory or bone, and covered with lines of tiny runic script. Baldr found his eyes drawn towards it uncomfortably. As the torc emerged into the light, Nightwing became agitated, hopping from one foot to the other.

'To the fight in the open, blade to blade,' Njal said. 'That is what we aspire to, yes?'

Baldr nodded. 'Where possible.'

'Yes, where possible.' Njal turned the torc in his gauntlets, studying the script carefully. 'You still present me with a problem, Baldr Fjolnir. From the stories I've heard, a mortal would already have been burned for less. Do I risk you living? All for an extra claw in the pack? Gunnlaugur kept it secret, but will it stay that way?'

Baldr found it difficult to look away from the torc. The collar seemed to suck in the meagre light around it, making the runes blacker than night.

'If the Cardinal finds out, he'll come after you,' said Njal. 'Once this is over we can go back to loathing one another, but for the time being we need him.' He held the torc up, looking through its hollow interior at Baldr. 'So this is a precaution. It won't kill you. It won't dull your instincts. Physically, it won't affect you at all.'

Baldr felt an almost overwhelming urge to pull away from it, and resisted. 'What is it?'

'A dampener. A null-collar. If you have any aptitude at all, even something undetectable by my devices here, it will quash it.'

A sick feeling curdled at the back of Baldr's throat. He'd been surrounded by warding runes ever since entering the Mountain, but something about those on the collar appalled him.

'Is it permanent?' he asked.

'I can remove it. No others can – it is bound to my soul-pattern.'

'If they tried?'

'It would end you.'

The collar was slender – a few centimetres thick and perfectly smooth. It would slot between the armour plates of his gorget and helm, hidden away from view.

'I thought...' started Baldr, then trailed off.

'Say it.'

'I thought that the power came from Fenris,' he said. 'From the soul of the world.'

Njal raised an eyebrow. 'And?'

'I had always believed... If a warrior had it... I believed that nothing could interfere with it.'

'All strength is finite. Everything can be countered.'

'So, where does it come from?'

Njal looked at him. 'Runecraft? Where does it come from?' His icy irises glittered in the dark. 'You think you are ready for those secrets?' He let slip a grim laugh. 'You are inches from damnation, Grey Hunter. This is not the time to be asking.'

He held the null-collar up high, rotating it as if it were a crown of conquerors. Baldr tensed as it was lowered over his head. Njal rotated it so that the open section of the torc was at the front. Two dragon's mouths, intricately carved from what looked like iron, gaped at one another across the narrow gap.

'So you are bounded,' said Njal applying pressure to either side.

There was a faint sound of hissing, and the two dragon's mouths clamped together. A ripple of heat ran across his skin, quickly dissipating. Baldr felt his breathing speeding up, and quelled it. He remained unmoving, his mind working to detect any change.

'You will not feel anything,' said Njal. 'If your pack-mates ask, it is a rune-ward. For luck. I see you already carry one.' He reached for his staff again, taking it up. 'And that is the end of this. You may go. But you know, of course, that it is not the end. I'll be watching you. Your pack will be watching you.'

Baldr felt other eyes on him, and caught sight of Nightwing staring at him from a lone obsidian ocular implant. The raven's head was eerily still.

The Rune Priest raised his staff, and the wolf-skull shadow fell over Baldr.

'You will never be out of our gaze again, Fjolnir,' said Njal. 'Best you get used it.'

CHAPTER NINE

Hafloí watched Olgeir fumbling with the airlock release controls, but the danger had passed. Behind him, open-mouthed mutant corpses twisted in the zero gravity, bumping up against the chamber's sides.

That fight had been closer than he was ever likely to admit. In such a dark, confined space, with no room to bring his superior agility to bear, the odds had been too tight. For a long time after his solo kill in Hjec Aleja, he'd gloried in his unrestrained way of war, and looked with some scorn on the older warriors of the pack. Since then, things had become steadily harder. His pack-mates took it all in their stride, but it was becoming slowly clear to Hafloí that there was still much to learn. There were other ways of fighting, not all involving pure speed and strength. Already he found himself wishing to fight in the void again, knowing that his movements would be quicker and smoother the next time.

For now, he let his breathing recover and watched Olgeir try to gain entry.

'You have air in there?' Olgeir asked, using the vox-cable again.

More static from the other side. 'The what?'

Hafloí snorted his impatience. 'Just open it.'

Olgeir persevered. 'There is a vacuum on this side,' he explained to the occupant of the chamber beyond. 'You have breathing gear?'

'Breathing gear, yes,' came the response. 'I'm wearing it. Are you of the Church? What is your ident? What diocese?'

Olgeir pushed back and raised his bolter towards the door's locking mechanism. Hafloí, seeing what he intended, moved out of range.

'Get back,' said Olgeir. 'We're coming in.'

'Wait,' came the voice. 'What is your–'

Olgeir leaned back against the wall and fired, blowing up the lock-panel in a blaze of light. Crackles of electricity ran around the hatch rim, quickly snaking out.

Then he drifted in close again and seized the edge of the hatch door. Gripping with both hands, he pulled. For a moment, the door-bolts resisted.

'A bit harder?' said Hafloí, enjoying watching the big warrior struggle.

Olgeir heaved, his power armour servos geared up, and the bolts sheared. The hatch sprang open, blown out by air pressure on the other side. Olgeir shoved the hatch door aside and hauled himself through the gap, working against the rush of escaping oxygen. Hafloí followed him in.

The chamber was lit by a single lumen lodged in the ceiling. It was less than four metres square and lined with banks of flickering cogitator equipment. Three bodies hovered at the rear, two with their uniforms ripped and bloodstained. The other teetered on his feet, swaying uneasily in the zero gravity, wearing a sealed helm and a red voidsuit. He levelled a lasgun at them, backing away and rising as they came in. Olgeir scanned for the man's vox-caster, and locked on to it with his helm's counterpart.

'Come no further!' the man shrieked over the vox-link. 'I will fire!'

Hafloí ignored him and moved to study the cogitators, most of which looked operational. 'Might get something out of this after all,' he mused.

Olgeir floated over to the mortal, his hand held open, his boltgun lowered. 'Are you the only one?'

The man backed up against the rear wall, his weapon still raised. The bodies of his companions bumped away from him. 'Get out!' he screamed. The muzzle shook as he gripped it. 'Get *out!*'

'We're not your enemy,' said Olgeir, keeping his distance.

'These are augur records,' Hafloí murmured, running his finger down the tall, boxy cogitator units.

'Leave now,' the man blurted, 'or, or, by the Emperor's will, I *will* end you!' As he spoke, he switched the aim of his lasgun between the two of them.

'That is unlikely,' said Olgeir. 'Just tell me–'

The man opened fire. A tangle of poorly aimed las-beams hissed into Olgeir's breastplate, scoring the ceramite and making the chamber flash with freeze-frame light-bursts.

Olgeir shrugged off the impacts, pushed himself closer to the terrified man and grabbed his lasgun. With a twist of his armoured fingers he cracked the barrel and pushed it aside. The ruined weapon tumbled across the room, ricocheting from the walls before finally lodging up against the ceiling.

'Your mind has been damaged,' said Olgeir, speaking steadily. 'Hel, how could it not be? Remain calm. We need to know what happened.'

For a moment the man stared up at him, trembling, hovering halfway up the chamber wall with his boots twitching. Then he reached for the mouthpiece of his helm and wrenched it off. Olgeir lunged for it, but the survivor ripped it clear and threw it away.

His face went red, instantly bloodshot as the air in his lungs burst out. Olgeir tried to grab him but the man somehow scrambled away, gagging and retching, coughing up blood from a ruptured windpipe. By the time Olgeir had seized him there was no way back. The man looked up at the Space Wolf with anguished triumph in his staring eyes.

Then his body spasmed, and went limp. Disgusted, Olgeir let it float free, turning gently amid floating dots of blood.

Hafloí looked on, unimpressed. 'Strange decision,' he said.

'He must have been down here for days,' said Olgeir. 'Listening to them all outside, trying to get in.'

Hafloí sighed. Olgeir's perennial tolerance of mortal weakness could get wearing. 'At least the hunt wasn't wasted. We can withdraw these data-cores. If they picked up anything before the station was taken, we'll have it.'

Olgeir pushed over to the nearest cogitator unit. Faint lights still played across its complicated surface, lost amid a filigree of valves and coolant tubes. He felt the cases whirr and click through his gauntlets, a constant rhythm in the airless cold.

'Start clearing them out,' he said. 'I'll head back up and vox the Old Dog.'

'And once we're done?'

Olgeir looked back over his shoulder, out past the circular hatch where the bodies of the plague-damned drifted in a soup of blood-spores.

'Burn it,' he said, pushing off again.

Gunnlaugur strode through the halls of the Halicon. Menials, servitors and cherubim scurried to get out of his path. The Cardinal's troops were everywhere, refitting and restoring. Golden altars had been hammered down over the older stone ones the canoness had used. Devotional picts of the Wounded Heart had been removed and placed with icons of the Fiery Tear.

It was good to see the citadel being made strong again, but little else pleased Gunnlaugur. The gold, the incense, the chanting – all of it set his fangs on edge. He went as quickly as he could to the upper levels, shoving his way past any of the robed prelates too slow or clumsy to see him coming.

Njal remained on *Heimdall* with Baldr, and the rest of the Wolves had been assigned to kill-teams operating in the wastes. The entire planet had a breathless air of preparation. All knew they would be back in the void soon, though the destination remained obscure. Only one firm message had come in, typically curt from Jorundur – *Datacores retrieved. On our way.*

Gunnlaugur had tried to find the canoness to consult on strategy, but her aides seemed to have gone missing. Everywhere he went, the servants of the Cardinal seemed to have assumed the functions of governance, displacing men and women who had stood in position before the siege. It was getting hard to find anyone who knew anything about anything.

He reached de Chatelaine's private chambers in the Halicon's eastern wing. The doors were unguarded, which was strange – there should have been two Battle Sisters on duty at all times.

Inside, the chamber was empty. The canoness's desk was piled with papers. Two long glass doors stood open on the external wall, the drapes hanging limply in the afternoon heat. A half-empty goblet of water stood on the arm of a throne.

Gunnlaugur moved over to the desk and looked over the paperwork. All of it was stamped with the Ecclesiarchy icon, and looked like routine business – munitions movements, resupply plans. He wondered about leaving her a sign to contact him.

He was about to turn away, when the doors to the chamber swung open again, and Sister Callia came in. When she caught sight of him, she froze.

'My lord,' she said, recovering herself. 'I was looking for the canoness.'

'As was I,' said Gunnlaugur.

Callia's gaze darted around, as if de Chatelaine might somehow be hidden somewhere in the chamber. 'She is not answering requests for audience.'

'I noticed.'

Callia closed the doors quietly behind her. Gunnlaugur thought she looked hunted. 'They should be locked,' she said, and headed towards the nearest of the glass panels. The open panes led out to a balcony overlooking the upper city, and she slipped out onto it.

Gunnlaugur followed her. The space outside was narrow, barely wide enough to accommodate a single power armoured warrior. As he stood next to her, Callia closed the glass door behind them.

Hjec Aleja ran down away from them steeply. From that vantage, the scale of the reconstruction could clearly be seen. Ecclesiarchy-liveried landers were still coming and going in a steady stream. The streets milled with bodies, most clad in carapace armour or the crimson plate of the Fiery Tear. Out on the plains, Sentinels prowled. The noise of reconstruction hammered out from every corner.

'What is it?' Gunnlaugur asked.

'I have not heard from her in hours. She answers on no channels, not even those private to the Sisterhood.'

'Is she with the Cardinal?'

Callia's expression tightened. 'I have not asked him.'

'Perhaps you should.'

'Where is your Stormcaller?'

'On *Heimdall*.'

'He should come back.'

Gunnlaugur gave her a warning look. 'He doesn't answer to my summons.'

'Then this is...' said Callia, glancing up at him. 'I don't know.'

Gunnlaugur waited for her.

'His *severity*,' said Callia, eventually. 'His methods are not those we are used to. We were faithful, were we not?' Callia's expression was oddly trusting.

'You were,' said Gunnlaugur.

'He has been handing out penance,' said Callia. 'I have tried to see the justice in it. My instinct is to *believe*. It is a strong instinct, but... even so.'

Gunnlaugur sighed. 'This is your business, Sister.'

Callia looked at him intently for a moment, as if deciding whether to say more. 'Why did you wish to see her?'

'I've had word from *Vuokho*. We need to confer.'

Callia nodded. 'When I locate her, I will tell her you're looking for her. She will be pleased. It is what we have all been waiting for.'

'Just tell her where I am.'

Callia paused then. She suddenly reached up to her collar and withdrew a small comms-bead. She handed it to him. 'This is aligned to a secure channel, used by our Sisterhood,' she said. 'It might prove... useful.'

Gunnlaugur looked at it steadily. 'I can use the open vox-net.'

'Please, take it,' said Callia.

Close up, Gunnlaugur saw the hunted look in her eyes again. He took the comms-bead, stowing it securely. 'As you wish.'

'Like I said. It might prove useful.'

Then she pushed the glass door open, and walked back into the chamber. She gave Gunnlaugur a parting bow, and was gone.

Gunnlaugur watched her leave. As he was pondering what to do next, a comm-burst from *Heimdall* came in.

'Njal summons you, *jarl*,' said Derroth. 'Landers are dispatched.'

'By his will,' Gunnlaugur responded, absently, noting the loc-fix of the incoming shuttle. He took a last look around the empty chamber. De Chatelaine's absence was strange. It was out of character, and it would be good to have her back soon.

Then he left, heading down towards the city's landing stages.

It took many more hours before Hjec Falama was cleansed. Its defenders had nowhere else to go, and so they fought on, grimly clinging to what passed for life.

As the sun set, a boiling ember in the rapidly darkening sky, the deep dark crept across empty, dusty streets. Shadows swayed and flickered against the remains of old walls, made to dance by the bonfires on every corner. Though the heat of the day was fading, Hjec Falama would remain hot well into the night, warmed by the crackle and spit of crisping flesh.

Rigal secured the perimeter, sending his men out in teams to patrol. The storm troopers had evaded joining the Fenrisians in combat, keeping to their own disciplined patterns of attack. Bjargborn's troops had been typically reckless, and Ingvar had hunted with them. Ingvar kept his bolter stowed, using a blade just as the kaerls did. They all killed in the old way – face to face, watching the eyes of the enemy as he died.

After the killing, they fell back to the central courtyard and sat around fires, wholesome ones, and did what the Sons of Russ always did after battle – ate, drank, told stories.

Ingvar watched them, holding their battered ration packs over the flames before devouring the freeze-dried gloop and savouring it as if it were *konungur* flesh. A raw happiness played across their drawn faces. They had all lost body mass since their service on *Undrider*, but could still crack a grin.

'So,' Ingvar said, turning to Bjargborn, who sat beside him in the circle of ruddy light. 'Tell your story.'

Bjargborn chewed, nodding. 'Your battle-brother, Jorundur,' he said. 'He ordered us to the saviour pods. I ran down from the bridge as the destroyer hit us.' He shook his head ruefully. 'Everything was on fire. It nearly caught me. By the time I got there, most of the pods had gone. I jumped into the last, pulled the hatch, hit the controls. The explosions hit just before the docking-clamps blew, and I thought my thread was cut. Next thing I know, I'm out, and the planet's swinging round me like an ice-skiff.'

'How many got out with you?'

Bjargborn's expression darkened. 'Half the complement? A lot of us made it down. The pods scattered, half of them stuck out in the deep desert. I don't know if any of those made it. We had no comms, weapons, nothing. I remember kicking the hatch open and thinking the thrusters were still burning. Then I realised how hot it is here.'

Wide smiles around the fire. The kaerls listened, just as they might have listened to a skjald as the ice-wind howled.

'Some of us had come down close to cities,' Bjargborn said. 'At first, we thought we were the lucky ones. Then we found out what lived there. That was nearly the end of me, too.' He looked over at the flames. 'You don't see it coming, not at first. You catch their eyes too late, see that they're not really alive, and then they're all over you.'

'How many are left?'

'Ninety of us, here.' Bjargborn's expression held a flicker of pride, an old stubborn arrogance that didn't retreat easily. 'If they didn't catch you at the start, there were things you could do. They were careless. They could hardly see, and daylight made them slow. Once a few of us made contact, we could organise. At night we hunted for others like us, by day we hunted them. We got hold of guns, armour pieces. There was some food left – old ration packs, water. They didn't touch it.'

'Any other groups like yours?'

'There might be, down past the big manufactories.' He looked at the others, but they didn't meet his gaze. 'But I don't know. Probably not.'

Ingvar nodded. 'Then your wyrd was a lucky one. You evaded the Ecclesiarchy, too, and they've landed thousands.'

'We know. We saw them in action, before you got here.'

'Storm troopers?'

'Yes, and battle engines. They were heading west, going fast.'

'You met them?'

'No, not up close.' Bjargborn looked contemptuous. 'They weren't here to take anything back. They were looking for something. By the time we'd worked out what was going on, they were gone, leaving us with all the plague-damned they hadn't killed.'

'What were they doing?'

'No idea. They went through some of the old temples. They stripped one out – I saw them carting crates away. Not the big, grand ones. Just one or two, out on the edge of the desert. It was done quickly, then they were gone.'

Ingvar pressed his gauntlets together pensively. 'You didn't see any more than that?'

One of the other kaerls spoke up then. 'I saw them leave,' he said.

'He is Aerold,' said Bjargborn.

'They were led by a man in black robes,' said Aerold. 'A priest. He was overseeing them all, even the Battle Sisters. I couldn't get close, but I don't think he wore any armour. He walked around unshielded, like he feared nothing. Like it was all his.'

Ingvar stared into the fire and smiled wryly. 'Maybe it is,' he said.

The kaerls waited for him to say something more, looking expectant. Ingvar suddenly thought of the halls under the Mountain, the fire-pits in the vaults, the weapons hanging on chains, the bone-breaking cold. He remembered the skjalds and the Priests declaiming the old sagas. He remembered the smell of it – the charred meat, the oil-thick *mjod* swilling.

'You will come back with me,' he said, reaching for more food. 'All of you. The pack has no Aettguard – that needs changing.'

Bjargborn bowed proudly. 'We live to serve. We can still fight.'

'So I can see.'

'We remained *Fenryka*,' said Bjargborn. 'You can't get the ice out of your blood, not even here.'

Ingvar thought on that. He remembered how it had been just after rejoining the pack – a kind of madness. The desire had been there, to go back, to be again what he had been before, but the ability was not. His old self had become foreign to him, almost unintelligible.

We have become mongrels, Callimachus had told him, in what felt like another life. As always, the Ultramarine had been right.

Now, though, it felt different. The more time passed, the more Ingvar felt the half-buried savagery return. The fire-circle, the sharing of tales, the laughter in the shadows, it all slowly came back.

You can't get the ice out of your blood.

'Lord.'

Ingvar stirred to see Bjargborn looking up at him.

'They say the Stormcaller is here,' the kaerl said. 'Forgive me, if this is forbidden, but we wanted to ask. You fought with him?'

'Briefly.'

Bjargborn turned to his comrades, smiling in vindication. 'Then, if it is not too much... If it can be asked for...'

'You want the tale.'

They were hard-bitten soldiers of the Aett, survivors of the horrors of Ras Shakeh and veterans of a hundred battles, but they nodded.

Ingvar unlocked his gauntlets. It had been a long time since he had been called to be skjald, and then only to battle-brothers of the Great Company. Other Chapters would scorn such rituals. He would have done himself, fresh from Onyx with the sarcasm of Jocelyn in his mind.

But the wind had changed. It was fresher now, cleared of the filth that preyed on the soul and made it defensive.

'This is how it was,' he began.

The Chamber of the Annulus was buried in *Heimdall*'s dark heart. It was a mere echo of the original, but still it soared up into the vaults of the starship. Its curved walls were hewn from granite, held aloft by rough pillars crowned with the heads of beasts.

A single stone, six times the height of a man, stood at the heart of it, jutting up from the iron deck. The stone bore age-weathered runes on its rough surface. The hand that had carved those runes was long gone, for the stone had been old even before Russ first came to Fenris. It had been taken from Asaheim and lodged in the heart of a starship, surrounded by the creak and crack of metal rather than the eternal howl of the mountain gales.

Njal stood before the stone. He felt like one of the old *gothi* of memory, gathered under the lee of ancient rock circles. The quiescent runes in his armour glimmered with fire-reflections.

Others stood around him: Álfar of his retinue, Gunnlaugur of Járnhamar, Fellblade, Long-axe and Bloodhame with their packs. All wore their armour, fresh from the last of the hunts on Ras Shakeh, marked with new kill-tallies.

The dust had not yet been cleaned away, though the stink of the planet had been replaced by the harder aroma of hearth-coals and weapon-oil.

'Brothers, our fight on this world is over,' Njal said.

As he spoke, Nightwing preened itself absently. Every so often, the raven's head would lift to stare at one of the warriors, then it would return to its work.

'The Traitor spilled some truths before he died,' Njal went on. 'The Death Guard Legion is here. He mentioned the Traveller – his fell hand will be shown at some point. And he mentioned another: the Mycelite. I do not know this name. Perhaps some champion, perhaps one consumed by maleficarum. The name was repeated more than the rest, so he, if anyone, is master of these forces we have seen so far. And there is a ship: the *Festerax*.'

'Where?' asked Gunnlaugur.

'The datacores your warriors brought back have been studied. We compared void-markers with those in the annals of the damned. Some were unknown, others too small to pose a threat. Then we found a match. The *Festerax* is known to the Imperium, and appears on the augur-logs. It is a legend of darkness, sighted on a hundred worlds across nine thousand years. Now we know where it is headed.'

Njal raised his gauntlet, and a spinning star of energy formed in front of him. The nimbus resolved into a collection of star-system runes, glowing into a slowly rotating lattice. Carving its way through the heart of the network was a green slick – a jagged spear of lurid light-points. As it progressed, the slick split up, spreading out across the volume of the void and angling towards unconquered worlds ahead.

'They are moving faster now,' said Njal. 'They know we are here. Half the subsector veers on the edge of desolation – if enough worlds are infected, there will be nothing left to save.'

Njal gestured, and the schematic zoomed out. Neighbouring star-systems swept into view, each identified with floating rune-markings.

'That is their aim,' Njal said. 'To scour these worlds. This takes strength away from fortresses closer to the real target.'

The star-map kept zooming out. The fringes began to glow with curls of red matter, like licking flames at the edge of parchment.

'The Eye,' said Njal with grim finality. 'Below the Cadian Gate. If they succeed in driving ruin this far, it will be one more wound to absorb on the flanks of the Praeses.'

'They're clearing the tribute subsectors,' muttered Fellblade. 'The ones that supply the front line.'

Njal nodded. 'They are.'

Gunnlaugur studied the schematic. 'Are these positions accurate?'

'As much as anything is.'

'We can't run them all down,' Gunnlaugur said. 'We don't have the ships.'

'No. We have to make choices.'

The star-map zoomed in again, cycling through subsectors, narrowing down to a single vector of the enemy incursion. The rune-markers spread wider and slipped off the edge of the projection. Soon only one remained.

'Kefa Primaris,' said Njal. 'Hive world, significant forge capability, situated at the nexus of several warp-lanes. Take it, and the subsector is torn open. Hold it, and you have some chance of salvaging a remnant. They know this, and they know we're on their trail, so they've sent forces ahead. Once they break that world, it's over.'

Njal watched the slowly spinning system-figure float into focus – a lone planet orbiting a giant red star.

'Speed is not the issue,' said Njal. 'Only the *Festerax* itself is in range of Kefa Primaris, and both *Heimdall* and *Vindicatus* can overtake it. If this were a standard battleship, there might be little issue – Kefa is not undefended, and we have our own weapons – but the *Festerax* is not a standard battleship.'

The projection narrowed down to a single ship – a vast, hunched, bloated ball of amalgamated hulls and prows, jumbled together like a gobbet of molten slag.

'It is a hulk. A living hulk. Its origins are unknown, though they are ancient, maybe even pre-dating the Betrayal. It has been engaged by the Imperial Navy on seventeen occasions, each time destroying its attackers or evading capture. Its gunnery is meagre, but it can take immense amounts of damage. Seven hundred years ago, it was engaged by the *Bellicosa Extremis*, an Emperor-class battleship. The engagement lasted for seven days, during which *Bellicosa* hurled everything it had at it. By the end, its torpedo tubes were empty, its void shields burned away, and the *Festerax* had slipped into the aether.'

Njal closed his fist, and the projection rippled out. 'This is what heads for Kefa Primaris. This is what we must bring down.'

Gunnlaugur let slip a low whistle. 'A fine target.'

Bloodhame laughed. 'So it is. We are boarding, then?'

Njal nodded. 'If *Bellicosa* could not crack it, then nothing we have here will either. But we've seen monsters like this before, and we know how to slay them. Get into the heart of it, into the drive-halls, lock thermal charges. When enough of those go off, every methane chamber in the hulk will ignite.'

The Wolves around nodded appreciatively. A low, barely audible growl ran around the chamber – pack-wide kill-urge taking root. It was all they ever asked for. A target.

'We will need the Cardinal,' said Njal. 'The *Festerax* will have escorts, and his ships can take those on long enough to give us a way in. *Heimdall* will support. Apart from that, we will be on our own.'

Fellblade snorted. 'He's busy scourging the planet below.'

'He will see reason. But remember this: he loathes us. His creatures loathe us. They will provoke, they will protest. For now, it is up to us to keep the peace.' Njal swept his gaze across them all, as dark as the vaults over the stone. 'Do nothing to break faith with them. *Nothing*.'

One by one, the Wolves bowed in submission.

Nightwing cawed then, a thin sound like mocking laughter. Njal looked up, and extended his wrist. The psyber-raven flapped down from the chamber's heights, landing heavily, its metal-pinned wings extended.

'So we have our prey, brothers,' Njal said, fangs exposed as he bared them in the old threat-gesture. Every spirit in the chamber kindled, quickening like flame on oil. 'The wait is over. Now we take the fight to the enemy.'

CHAPTER TEN

Gunnlaugur left the Annulus Chamber as the others did. The atmosphere of *Heimdall* did him good. It smelt *right*, like a starship should, with its ritual skulls and rune-wards engraved on every panel. Still, he could feel himself on edge, unable to give in fully to the impending battle-joy.

There was much to prove. He had failed against Thorslax. He had managed Ingvar badly. The pack under his watch was not the fluent weapon it had been under Hjortur. He knew it, and his brothers did, too.

More than that, though, were the uncertainties. Was Ingvar's suspicion founded on truth? Where was de Chatelaine? And, most of all, what was the judgement on Baldr, the one he had chosen to preserve, knowing the risks?

'*Vaerangi*,' came Njal's voice from behind him.

Gunnlaugur felt a chill run through him. He turned and bowed. 'Something else, *jarl*?'

'Come with me,' said the Rune Priest, stalking off down the corridor.

The two of them set off, heading up towards the next level. Njal's boots clanged heavily as they hit the deck, weighed down by his thick Terminator plate.

'How runs your pack?' asked Njal gruffly, his staff-heel thudding as he walked.

'They're prepared,' said Gunnlaugur.

'But you had trouble.'

Gunnlaugur bristled. 'Nothing I couldn't master.'

Njal looked at him sidelong. 'There's no shame in it. You lead warriors. Some bad blood will flow.' His cracked lips twisted in a thin smile. 'On the ice, the warrior-kings were killed by their flag-bearers. That's the world we come from. Nothing changes,' he said, tapping his chest. 'Not under here.'

Gunnlaugur kept his mouth shut, wondering where this was going.

'I spoke to Baldr,' Njal said.

Again, the chill.

'I found nothing,' said Njal. 'He will return to you, but be watchful. The first sign of any change, tell me. We have all lived too long to be unwary.'

Gunnlaugur bowed his head, hoping the relief flooding over him wasn't obvious. 'I'm glad,' he said, gruffly. 'He was a good warrior.'

'He *is* a good warrior. He will need to be, as I want him on this hunt.'

'He's ready?'

'We will need every blade we have,' said Njal. 'More than that, I want him *close*. I want him back among us again.' He shot Gunnlaugur a cynical look. 'I want him away from this world, and I want him away from the Cardinal.'

Gunnlaugur nodded. 'By your will.'

'This is what he was bred for, Skullhewer. His speed will come back once he's got blade in hand.'

The two of them kept going, clanking up a shallow metal stairway. Kaerls saluted as they passed, averting their eyes and clenching their fists against their chests.

'So, can it be done?' asked Gunnlaugur as they reached the next deck up.

'The hulk?' Njal exhaled a bleak laugh. 'We'll see.'

'They killed my blademaster,' growled Gunnlaugur. 'I've not yet slain enough to avenge him.'

'You won't be short of skulls to crack. Not in there.'

They passed along a long, open gantry, flanked by crew-cells and refectory chambers. The life of the ship hummed around them, raucous and echoing.

'The Cardinal is the key,' said Njal. 'We cannot break into that hulk without him, and he knows this. He's powerful in his own kingdom, but powerful enough to refuse a request from a Lord of the Adeptus Astartes? In his theology, we are the Angels of the Emperor.' Njal shook his head, mystified. 'If he practises what he preaches, he will not refuse.'

They left the crew quarters behind and moved into a broad thoroughfare leading up to the flight decks. The smell of promethium and engine lubricants spiced the air.

Njal paused before a barred iron door at the end of the passageway, its lintel carved with an elaborate knotwork bestiary of winged sky-wyrms. 'I could choose to go to him in strength,' he said. 'But that would send the wrong message, so it will be just the two of us. You understand this?'

Gunnlaugur nodded. 'Perfectly.'

Njal raised a finger and the doors slid open. Beyond them stood the antechamber to *Heimdall*'s primary shuttle hangar. Servitors clattered to and fro across a rockcrete deck. Through armourglass viewports Gunnlaugur could see into the cavernous shuttle-bay beyond, where a fleet lifter in slate-grey stood on the apron, surrounded by refuelling cables, its thrusters venting.

'We don't have much time,' Njal said. 'Let us make this as quick as we can.'

Gunnlaugur followed him, reaching for his own helm as the blast-doors ahead started to grind open.

'No argument from me,' he said.

Vindicatus was an immense vessel, only surpassed in void-displacement by the line battleships of the Imperial Navy. Its hull was ancient, laid down as an Exorcist-pattern Grand Cruiser millennia ago. Perhaps it had originally been intended for use in Navy patrols, taking its place alongside the thousands of war-vessels in the standing Imperial fleet. At some point, though, it had shifted purpose and found its way into the service of the Ecclesiarchy, who had taken it and changed it.

Its exterior armour was covered in gold, from the jutting prow to the ranks of slab-sided weapon housings along the flanks. A mighty skull-device, a hundred metres across, had been carved into the hull, grinning out into the void and lit with a circlet of blood-red flood-lumens. The whole vessel hung in the well of space like a gaudy, opulent altarpiece, glinting from the light of Ras Shakeh's vigorous star.

Gunnlaugur peered out of the shuttle's viewports on the way over, watching the baroque flanks slide closer, wondering just how much blood and treasure had been squandered to give the cruiser its skin.

The interior of the cruiser was no less extravagant. The two Wolves were greeted by an honour guard of Battle Sisters, led tersely by the half-bionic Sister Nuriyah. They passed through halls of polished mirrors and crystalflex domes, all filled with devotional items encased in golden reliquaries and guarded by white-masked gun-drones. Heavy fabric drapes hung from ceilings fifty metres up, dusted by the meandering flights of incense-cherubim. The air was thick with cloying fragrance. Unlike on *Heimdall*, there were no mortal voices raised in laughter or cursing. The entire interior echoed to the low drone of endless chanting, piped through vox-emitters hung from gothic arches like battle-trophies.

Delvaux received them in his private audience chamber, which was large enough to house an entire Guard company. He wore thick crimson robes lined with ermine, and his pudgy fingers were studded with jewelled rings. A lone column of gold-tinged light shone down on him from a lumen-cluster directly above his throne; otherwise the room was heavy with darkness. On either side of the dais stood two huge Penitent Engines, their motors idling and their smokestacks fouling the drapes around them. Stranger creatures flitted around in the gloom – servo-skulls dragging litanies of duty with them, cowled priests muttering benedictions and supplications, penitents shuffling on bleeding knees amid the velvety splendour.

'My lord Rune Priest,' said the Cardinal, lounging casually.

'Lord Cardinal,' replied Njal.

'So there is a hulk. The *Festerax*. You think it possible to destroy it.'

'That is so.'

'You are mistaken.' Delvaux shifted slightly on his cushions, lifting a thick arm and hitching up the sleeve. 'We analysed the data you sent, and that hulk cannot be destroyed, not by the power we have here.'

'Not by our ships,' agreed Njal. 'But I command thirty-seven warriors. Get us close enough, and we can disable it from the inside. Its skin is thick, but its heart is rotten.'

'Very bold,' said Delvaux. 'But there is a thin line between boldness and delusion. There is a better way.'

Gunnlaugur studied the surroundings silently as the two conversed. The chamber was soaked in hostility, as if the sanctified stones themselves protested over the boots that trod on them.

'We know what they are doing,' Delvaux went on. 'They infect worlds with mass spore landings, causing waves of contagion that turn defenders into plague-bearers. On a hive world, that canker will spread even faster than it did here. If a hulk that size releases its spores, there will soon be nothing left to fight over. Better to starve the beast.' He placed his hands together on his lap, pressing the fingers together as if in contemplation. 'This vessel is equipped with nucleonic torpedoes. We can overtake the *Festerax* and wreath Kefa Primaris in holy fire. The sacrifice will buy us time, and deprive the damned of the prize they seek.'

Njal said nothing for a moment, taken aback. When he next spoke, it sounded as if he were struggling to process the suggestion. 'You're serious?'

'Very,' said Delvaux. 'They are here for recruits. Once the contagion latches onto Kefa Primaris, they will add billions to their army. We can prevent that.'

'The planet can be saved,' insisted Njal. 'We can destroy the hulk before it makes orbit.'

'And if you fail?'

'It will be done.'

'Well, yes. So you say. But you would, wouldn't you?'

In the face of such studious sarcasm, Njal remained implacable. 'What you propose is forbidden. Only the Inquisition may launch Exterminatus, and even they wouldn't try it with us around.'

Delvaux smiled tolerantly. 'Give it a different name, if that makes you feel better. *Quarantine*, perhaps.' His expression became serious. 'My lord, you have seen what is at stake here. Ras Shakeh is one thing – a world we cherish, but home to fewer than a million souls. A core planet is another. It must not be allowed to be claimed.'

'Billions will die,' said Njal, softly. 'All able to take up arms. All healthy.' His eyes held the Cardinal's. 'I will not allow it.'

The Cardinal's face did not flicker. 'This is not a question of *allow*. We are discussing options. Or did you come to my ship to give me orders?'

'All we need is the firepower to get us in,' said Njal. 'The hulk will be shielded. This ship, working with mine, can crack those shields, just for an instant. We can do the rest. That is all I ask.'

Delvaux smiled coldly. 'I never thought I would live to see it – the Wolves of Fenris asking for help. That is what you are doing, is it not? Tell me, just so I am sure.'

Gunnlaugur tensed, feeling Njal's frustration emanating like kill-pheromone from his armour. When the Rune Priest replied, his voice was like a rusty axe-edge being dragged across stone.

'I am asking for your help.'

Delvaux left the words hanging, enjoying them. 'Well, then,' he murmured. 'We must accommodate what we can. Here is my proposal. We will inter-cept the hulk together, just as you suggest. Our weapons will be used with yours to break the shields, and we will get you on board the vessel.' He spoke casually, as if setting out the orders of promotion in a Cathedral. 'But the price for my agreement is this. My ship will overtake the *Festerax* once Kefa Primaris comes into strike-range. If the hulk reaches orbit, even if on the edge of destruction, I shall launch my quarantine. I will give you all the time necessary, but no more. This is the condition of my assistance.'

Having said his piece, Delvaux placed his hands back on the armrests of his throne. His face took on a satisfied, almost beatific glow.

Njal waited a long time before replying. 'I have your word?' he asked eventually. 'No deployment of your payload before the hulk reaches orbit.'

'If it makes you feel better, yes, you have my word,' said Delvaux, amused. 'Saints, I am a cardinal of the Emperor's Holy Ministorum. I will swear on the relics of the saints in our keeping, if that will seal things for you.'

'Your word is enough,' said Njal, weighing the words deliberately. 'On Fenris, the oathbreaker is lower than a beast. He is hunted unto the ends of the world.'

'How charming.' Delvaux leaned back. 'Then we have an agreement. Time is pressing, if your augur-scans are to be trusted. My ships will be ready to break for warp within the hour. Yours?'

'*Heimdall* is prepared. My warriors on the surface are being recalled.'

'Good,' said Delvaux. 'I will leave a garrison from the Fiery Tear on Ras Shakeh. They can carry out the work of restoration in our absence.'

'What of the canoness?' asked Gunnlaugur.

Delvaux turned to him, surprised that he had spoken. 'The canoness comes under my jurisdiction, Wolf Guard. Her part in this does not concern you.'

'She fought with me,' said Gunnlaugur. 'She wished to form part of the crusade. I would welcome fighting alongside her again – she was a fine warrior.'

'You thought so?' Another wintry smile flickered across Delvaux's lips. 'But see, we have a rigid code in the Ecclesiarchy. De Chatelaine knew it, just as all the Sisters in my service know it. There are prices to be paid for failure, and her leadership was found wanting on Ras Shakeh. I have made arrangements. The Order of the Wounded Heart will be folded into the Order of the Fiery Tear. The rites can be completed once we are in the warp. A change of leadership will do this world good. A new governor will be found, one more amenable to taking the hard decisions necessary in a fallen galaxy.'

The hairs on the back of Gunnlaugur's neck rose. 'Then the canoness is on this ship?'

'She is.'

'I would speak with her,' he said. Then, from grudging lips, 'If you allowed it.'

Delvaux spread his hands magnanimously. 'Of course. You may speak to her whenever you like. Though whether she will able to reply to your satisfaction is another question.'

He clapped his hands together. One of the Penitent Engines behind the throne hissed, sending gouts of steam from its reverse-jointed legs, then lurched into the pool of light. Its massive feet clanged on the marble floor, and it towered over the two Wolves at the centre of the lumen-beam.

Gunnlaugur looked up to see a woman's body suspended amid the gears and electro-shackles. Her head was covered with a white cloth, obscuring her features. Two muscled arms had been clamped wide, locked into the mechanisms of the Engine's giant weapon-limbs. The rest of her body was half lost in a tangle of implants and cables, the tendrils swaddling more bloodstained robes. From under the cloth drape, the soundless howl of a permanent scream could be made out, imprinted on the fabric.

Gunnlaugur's hand swept to his hammer. He unlocked it in a single movement, activating the crackle of the energy field.

'You *dare...*' he began.

He didn't get anything else out. His limbs locked, his jaw froze. He stood, half poised to strike, raging against inertia.

Only then did he realise the situation. Njal had lifted his staff, pulling him back, enclosing him in a vice of power.

Delvaux looked on, unsettled and unamused. 'This is my place, Space Wolf. Raise a weapon in here again and I will end you.'

Gunnlaugur felt his muscles straining against Njal's bonds, and a ball of agonised frustration rose up in his gorge.

+Stand down,+ came the Rune Priest's voice in his mind. +Strike him, and I will slay you myself.+

The vice lifted. Gunnlaugur staggered, catching himself before falling. The Penitent Engine stood over him, its infernal machinery ticking over. He looked up at it, his thunder hammer growling. If de Chatelaine retained anything of her self, she was not capable of responding to him any longer.

Gunnlaugur swept a heavy-lidded gaze up towards Delvaux, keeping his hammer raised. He took no step towards him, made no threatening move, but the Cardinal still blenched.

'Deactivate your weapon,' Delvaux said, a little quickly, his voice rising.

Slowly, deliberately, Gunnlaugur clicked the energy field off. Then he withdrew, keeping his black-pinned eyes fixed on the Cardinal the whole time. Delvaux shifted agitatedly in his seat.

'Is this what we can expect from your warriors, my lord Rune Priest?' Delvaux asked, rearranging his robes in a pretence at nonchalance.

'It is,' said Njal, his voice stony. 'That is why I remain proud to be one.' The Rune Priest looked up at the Penitent Engine, sharing Gunnlaugur's disgust. 'We have said all we came to. I will send word when we are ready to make for the veil.'

'I shall wait with eagerness.'

Without saying more, Njal turned on his heel and stalked down the chamber's central aisle. Gunnlaugur relocked his thunder hammer, never releasing Delvaux from his stare as he did so, before doing likewise. The two Wolves strode down the length of the audience chamber, their footfalls echoing.

'He is mad,' voxed Gunnlaugur as they cleared the threshold.

'Not mad,' replied Njal, sweeping through the glistening finery.

'She did not deserve–'

Njal whirled on him, grabbing him by the throat. Even for one of the Rout, the movement was incredibly quick. '*Never* lose control like that again,' he hissed. 'Did *nothing* I said register in your mind?'

Gunnlaugur clenched his fists instinctively, shocked by the sudden move. 'I recognise my failing,' he said.

Njal released him, but remained furious. 'Let him run rampant,' he voxed, 'and he will do to whole sectors what he has done here. We must tie him to *our* will.'

Gunnlaugur nodded, humbled. 'I see it.'

'She did not deserve it,' Njal said, his voice quieter. 'None do, who end up in those things, but put your wrath aside. There will be targets for it soon enough.'

'But when this is over–' Gunnlaugur began.

'Hel, when this is *over*,' said Njal, starting to walk again, his staff-heel striking the floor harder than it had done, 'I will hand you the hammer myself. Until then, keep it locked.'

Gunnlaugur bowed. The stink of the incense felt even more repugnant in his nostrils, and the chanting even more offensive. As he walked, he couldn't get the image of de Chatelaine's agonised face out of his mind. His hearts felt sick.

She did not deserve it.

That she didn't. For the time being, though, Gunnlaugur swallowed his fury, kept his fists closed, and followed his master back to the shuttle-bays.

Once the order was given, things moved quickly. Those wolf-packs still on the surface were brought back to *Heimdall* by a succession of lifters and gunships. Ingvar had already made contact, passing on the news of the recovered units of kaerls, and a series of shuttles was sent down under Álfar's supervision. It took some persuasion before Bjargborn's troops were accepted – all were aware of the possibility of contagion, a lesson that had been learned the hard way at Hjec Aleja. In the end, quarantine chambers were isolated on *Heimdall* and medicae-sealed shuttles were allowed to head off-world with them. They were Sons of Fenris, and had fought for too long to be abandoned.

Ingvar came up with them. As the planet's rust-orange landscape fell away in a hail of dust, the sky intensified into a deep blue, and the desert dropped down into the haze of distance. As the shuttle rose higher and the colours bled away to darkness, the trails of other voidcraft scored the starfield. Most bore the red livery of the Ecclesiarchy, some with the Fiery Tear on their hulls, others with the skull device of Delvaux's diocesan command. Ingvar watched a cluster of vapour-lines arcing out from the deep wasteland, and remembered what the kaerls had told him of black-robed officials moving out from temple to temple.

Then the shuttle rolled over, angling for the docking run. The slate-dagger profile of *Heimdall* swooped closer. The Wolves' ship was far smaller than the majestic *Vindicatus*. Its towers were close-clustered, its lone forward lance nestled sharply amid jowls of ice-white armour plate. *Heimdall* was a strike cruiser, and had an old and proud pedigree. It was fast, and tough, and brutally aggressive, just as it should be for the transport of the Stormcaller.

Once docked, the kaerls were greeted by armed medicae teams in environment suits and led away to their observation cells. Ingvar headed down to his assigned quarters, pulling his helm off and freeing his ash-blond hair, rubbing the last of the oil from it as he went.

The whole ship was in the throes of pre-launch activity. Kaerls ran down the corridors, seemingly chasing the klaxons that burst into life at every intersection. Bulkheads were pulled closed, hatches hammered down. Void engines were keyed up, sending growls juddering from the lower levels. Battle-brothers of the Rout passed him on the way to their own musters and he saluted them, clasping his fist to his chest.

He reached his destination, and pulled open a heavy blast-door. The rest of them were waiting for him, standing in a loose circle in the chamber beyond. Jorundur somehow looked hunched even in his battleplate. His hollow eyes lifted as Ingvar entered. Hafloí acknowledged awkwardly; Olgeir was effusive.

'We send Gyrfalkon to the desert and he returns with kaerls,' the big warrior said, chuckling. 'Give him longer, and he'd find Russ.'

Ingvar smiled. 'Good void-hunting, Heavy-hand?'

Olgeir shrugged nonchalantly. 'It proved useful.'

Ingvar turned to Gunnlaugur and bowed in acknowledgement. 'Vaerangi,' he said.

'Gyrfalkon,' said the Wolf Guard, looking amused. 'Last back, as ever.'

'Wouldn't want to disappoint.'

It was then that Baldr moved into the light of the lumen. He looked drawn, his armour bulky around a thinned-out body. His eyes still had deep black rings under them, and his lips were grey. For all that, he moved much as he used to – compact, economical. His face had lost some of the tightness it had carried on the last warp jump. If anything, he looked... healthier.

Ingvar regarded him warmly. 'So you can hold an axe again, brother?'

'Pretty well,' said Baldr.

'And Njal pulled your mind apart?'

'Feels like it.'

Gunnlaugur looked at them all, one by one. 'Reunited.' He bared his fangs in a savage smile. 'As it should be.'

The smile was infectious. From that point the savagery would only grow, building up over the short warp-stage as they trained and sparred and drove themselves into the full pitch of combat readiness.

'Our course is set, our prey is marked,' Gunnlaugur went on, setting up for the briefing to come. 'Now. Here's what he wants us to do.'

Two hours after the pack's war-council, with *Heimdall* running deep in the warp, Ingvar and Gunnlaugur met on their own in a chamber down in the darkened lower decks. Gunnlaugur stalked over to the dormant fire-pit at the centre of the chamber and poked at the coals. Ingvar hauled the hatch closed behind them and sealed it.

'What did you find?' asked Gunnlaugur, getting a weak flame to shiver over the embers.

'They were active on the surface,' Ingvar said. 'At least three teams, all led by the Cardinal's man, Klaive.'

'Active. What does that mean?'

'They went ahead of the main purge-squads, striking into enemy territory before it was cleansed. They were hunting for something – targeting the temples, then moving on.'

Gunnlaugur grunted. 'And you think?'

'Datacores, just like the ones in the Cathedral.'

'You didn't find any?'

'They worked fast.'

Gunnlaugur kicked his boot through the coals again, raking up a gut-tering tremor of fire. 'I'd like to rip their *throats* out,' he snarled. 'I'd like to gut them all, one by one, and hang the corpses from their own spires. De Chatelaine's been put into an Engine. You know that? If he can do that, he can do anything, and he *wants* to burn that planet. I could see the look in his eyes. Give him a cause, and–' He took a deep breath. 'Njal isn't stupid. The Cardinal's word means nothing. He wants to send Olgeir ahead of the battle-group, to the planet, just in case. There's a system-runner docked in *Heimdall*'s berths. There's no time to evacuate the entire world, but the Guard regiments at least must be saved.'

Ingvar looked doubtful. 'I'd rather have *sigrún* with us on the hulk.'

'As would I, but the ruling's been made. I'll speak to Heavy-hand – he'll understand.'

Ingvar thought for a moment. 'We could use this,' he said. 'Klaive remains on the cruiser. He is the one we seek.'

'Brother, you told me I did not need to worry...'

'And you do not. We will follow our orders, but if the oath is broken...' Ingvar held Gunnlaugur's gaze steadily. 'Then we take Klaive.'

Gunnlaugur paced, prowling the narrow chamber like a caged animal. 'Njal already watches us. He watches Baldr. If we slip the leash, he'll have our eyes. We need good kills, brother. We should have done better at Hjec Aleja.'

'We did what we could.'

'It wasn't *enough*.' Gunnlaugur stared moodily at the embers, grinding his fangs as his mind worked. 'I'd have welcomed fighting with her again. *Skítja*, these allies are poorer.'

Ingvar couldn't disagree. 'We'll be rid of them soon enough. I feel the old rages – they're coming back. We have Njal with us now, a whole hunting-pack at our shoulder.' He grinned. 'What is better? What more is there?'

Gunnlaugur nodded. Ingvar's enthusiasm was infectious.

'Nothing, brother,' he said, thinking ahead to the slaughter and feeling acid saliva quicken in his mouth. 'There is *nothing* better.'

II
THE MYCELITE

CHAPTER ELEVEN

Four hours before *Heimdall* broke the veil, the Wolves gathered in the ship's main assembly hall. Ancient war-banners of the Chapter hung from the distant ceiling, each one charred at the edges. Columns of alabaster and granite soared up into the smoky heights, banded with iron and studded with red-tinged lumen-beads.

Njal stood on a stone platform at the far end, flanked by the two Wolf Guards Álfar and Gunnlaugur. A fire burned behind them, mounted on a granite altar and sending a column of thick soot twisting up at his back. The symbol of the Priesthood – a wolf-skull against an angular lightning bolt – had been graven into the far wall and lined with bronze.

The rest of the warriors, Járnhamar included, stood facing the platform. The fighting force was divided into four packs, all Grey Hunters. Only Járnhamar had the distinction of fighting with a Wolf Guard at the helm; the other three pack leaders – Fellblade, Long-axe and Bloodhame – carried the same silver-and-black pauldron devices of their brothers.

'So we come to it,' announced Njal, his harsh voice ringing through the hall. 'All of you know void-work. All of you know your craft.'

As he spoke, a glowing representation of the plague-hulk, drawn from the Chapter datacores, spun into existence in front of the watching warriors. The profile was ugly and bulbous. Long, jagged stalactites of fused metal hung underneath it, jutting beneath scarred carapace edges and tangling as they speared into the void. The semi-intact hulls of a hundred space-vessels protruded from its back, rusted and deformed as they were slowly interred within the heart of the corrupted giant.

'We know the spoor of this from the records of those who fought it before,' said Njal. 'Maleficarum has birthed taint in the hulk's innards. It will treat us like a wound treats infection. We will be its disease.'

The glittering hololith zoomed in.

'The skin of the hulk will endure our ships' weapons, and it has void shields. The best we can hope for is a narrow strike, taking out enough to send boarding torpedoes into the underbelly. From there our only path is to destroy the furnace at its centre. The hulk's atmosphere is methane rich, stinking like an auroch's gut-line. We will set off charges in the enginarium core and the blast will eviscerate the entire vessel. It will test us, but it can be done.'

The assembled warriors took in the schematics quickly, scanning the lithcast, orientating themselves and committing the profile to memory.

'Getting out will be fun,' grunted one of them – a scarred, bionic-eyed veteran from Bloodhame's pack called Aesgrek.

'We will have to kill fast,' agreed Njal. 'We won't have long.'

Some of the others snarled under their breath. The danger of it appealed – if any of them got out again, it would be worth a saga back at the Aett.

'Who is on the ship?' asked Fellblade. 'Do we know that?'

'We have names,' said Njal. 'There will be mutants in their thousands. Remember, though, it is not a battleship – it is a weapon, a vessel for the plague-spores in its belly. That is its only task – to disperse them into the atmosphere.'

'So it'll have fleet escorts,' said Hauki.

'It will. *Heimdall* and *Vindicatus* will keep them busy. We have three Thunderhawk gunships also, but we will need every ranged gun for the hull-breach.'

Gunnlaugur stole a glance at Jorundur, and caught the Old Dog's satisfied expression. He'd be in command of *Vuokho* again, out on his own, just how he liked it.

'We keep together when we are inside,' said Njal. 'We keep moving. This is about *speed* – if we get slowed down inside then we will never get out.' The Rune Priest stared at the hololith, his expression eager. 'This is the filth we were bred to cleanse. Sharpen your blades. Ready your claws. No greater prize for us exists in this war.'

He bared his fangs in a challenge-gesture, and glared at them all.

'But it is *ours* now. We have marked it. Its fate is fixed.'

Two hours before *Heimdall* broke the veil, the six members of Járnhamar assembled on the deck of one of the ship's five hangar bays. A sleek system-runner stood on the rockcrete. It was less than ninety metres long, with a crew complement of just a few dozen mortals. A hawk-sharp prow jutted towards the distant external doors, dwarfed by the collection of oversized drives clustering along its ventral hull-edges. Njal's device had been painted on its nearside flank, just under the icon of the Chapter. Steam vented from a dozen thruster-housings as the last checks were made on the void drives. A few loader-bay hatches were still open, swarming with masked menials and loader-gurneys.

'How is it named?' asked Gunnlaugur, looking at it doubtfully.

'*Hlaupnir*,' said Olgeir, casting his own expert eye along the ship's length. 'Njal says it's fast.'

'I can believe it,' said Jorundur, nodding in appreciation. 'They laid these down on Ryza. Not a touch of Mars on them. You don't see many.'

'You will miss the hunt,' said Ingvar to Olgeir.

Olgeir shrugged. 'Njal gives the orders.'

'You won't have long enough,' muttered Hafloí. 'What does he expect you to do?'

'What I can,' said Olgeir. As he spoke, the loaders began to trundle away from *Hlaupnir*'s undercarriage. 'I don't mind it. If this goes to *skítja*, I'd rather die among mortals than those fanatics.'

Jorundur grunted in agreement.

The last of the fuel-cables clunked empty and detached from the runner's hull, carried away reverently by tech-servitors. The kaerl crew members clambered up the open ramps and into their stations. Warning horns began to blare, and the hangar cleared of support staff.

'Go with Russ, brother,' said Baldr to Olgeir. His voice was stronger than it had been.

'And you,' said Olgeir, cautiously. 'You'll remember how it feels, once the axe whirls again.'

Then he saluted the rest of the pack, turned on his heels and strode towards the ship. As he neared the ramp he started to call out orders. Between now and the entry into the Kefa Primaris system there was still much to do to get it ready for its mission.

Gunnlaugur looked at the others. 'This is it, then,' he said.

They turned and marched away from the apron and towards the corridor that would take them down to *Heimdall*'s torpedo chambers. As they reached the blast-doors, Jorundur peeled off towards *Vuokho*'s berth.

'Keep the pack-vox open, brother,' called Gunnlaugur after him. 'Stay close to the hulk.'

Jorundur rolled his eyes. 'Where else am I going to be?'

'You have Callia's device? The one I gave you?'

'You need it, I'll find it.'

Then Jorundur was gone, stomping down the narrow corridors towards the Thunderhawk hangars. That left the four of them – Baldr, Ingvar, Hafloí and Gunnlaugur.

The lumens in the corridors switched to red combat lighting. The drum of running boots and slamming bulkheads swelled up through the ship's innards. Far above them, the cruiser's weaponry was being rolled out and powered up.

'I want us at the *forefront*,' insisted Gunnlaugur, his gait now rolling, assuming the belligerent swagger that the kill-urge kindled. 'I want the axes of Járnhamar at the edge. This is *our* war.'

The others matched his pace and mien. Each of them was primed now. Their bodies were restored, their minds refreshed, their spirits keen. Ingvar drew his blade, looking down the length of it and seeing how the red light caught the edge of the runes.

It thirsted again, just as he did.

With a burst of ionised energy, the veil broke. *Heimdall* was first through, tearing into real space through an expanding corona of torn aether-energies. Its void drives exploded into life a second later, ricocheting it into the icy vacuum as if hurled from a slingshot.

Vindicatus crashed through a second later. Its impact wave was far bigger – a violent splash-pattern of torn reality, resolving almost instantly into the fire-wreathed profile of a jagged Grand Cruiser of the Ecclesiarchy. Its real space drives thundered into life, throbbing crimson like burst veins. As it surged forwards, its turrets and spires left streamers of flickering luminescence behind them, guttering away as the wound in the universe snapped closed.

The inky starfield of the Kefa Primaris system sprawled away from them. The planet itself was still out of visual range, only barely detectable on the high-gain forward augurs.

Both ships had speared into reality with precision. Dead ahead, already visible through the armourglass real-view blisters, burned the *Festerax*.

Its bulk was staggering – a vast, fist-shaped tumour of dark metal, underpinned with knife-sharp stalactites and crowned with ridges of the ship-hulls that had been drawn into its necrotic embrace. Its bulk blotted out the stars beyond, casting a shroud of ruin across the void. It was surrounded by its own petty fleet of lesser craft – gunships and assault boats, shepherded by two Infidel-pattern raiders.

Both Imperial vessels powered up to intercept speed. *Heimdall* was faster, and pulled away from its counterpart in a blaze of neon-white thrusters. Before its void shields snapped fully into place, it disgorged four craft from its launch bays. The first, *Hlaupnir*, broke away immediately, spiralling down out of the battle-plane and igniting its engines to full burn. It was soon powering clear, locked on to the coordinates for the planet far ahead. A few of the enemy escorts started in pursuit, but as soon as it became clear it was heading away from the combat-sphere they pulled back.

That left the Thunderhawks – *Vuokho*, *Kjarlskar* and *Grimund*. They stayed in close formation with *Heimdall*, powering alongside it but not straying far from the cover of its mighty gun-ranks.

By then *Vindicatus* was catching up. It released its own squadrons of escorts – Fury-class interceptors in the blood-red livery of the Ecclesiarchy. They spun out of the launch bays and streaked towards the enemy escort-cordon, outpacing the Thunderhawks and pulling into the vanguard. Twenty-four of them dropped into formation, arranged in six squadrons of four.

The Infidel raiders were the biggest threat – savage assault vessels with serrated jawline prows, macrocannon batteries and prow-mounted torpedo launchers. Both took up position above the hulk and opened up with a flickering barrage of shells. The Furies evaded the worst of it, ducking under the fire-lanes and angling upwards at the more lumbering enemy assault craft. Tracer-lights sparked silently into the void, creating a sphere of crackling energy around the hulk's retreating profile.

The vast plague-ship itself did not pick up speed. It maintained course, barrelling through space with a fearsome, implacable momentum, unconcerned by the gnat-like movements of the lesser ships in its wake. Its array of engines glowed dully under the segmented layers of outer hull, flecked with angry snarls of plasma-discharge.

Still out of range of the hulk's massive broadsides, the Imperial flotilla closed in on the escort ships. Once within gun-range, *Vindicatus* stood off, rolling starboard to present its twin-ranked rows of broadside cannons. The

Fury squadrons, acting as part of the prearranged plan, pushed clear of the front wave of enemy assault craft and dropped low to the battle-sphere's nadir.

The Cruiser's guns opened up, and a blinding flash of light ripped across the void. Enemy escorts caught in the withering assault exploded in sequence, their shields overloaded and their engines detonated.

Even before the corpses of the destroyed had spiralled out of contact, *Heimdall* hove into view, sweeping down from its vantage above *Vindicatus*'s fire position. It loosed torpedoes, each one already primed for the enemy raider coordinates. They tore off towards the targets – six trails of flame, three for each target.

The enemy flotilla, still forming up, raced to fend off the barrage. One of the Raiders was caught amidships by *Heimdall*'s torpedoes and fell out of the defensive pattern, venting heavily. The other one was saved by a suicidal squadron of enemy craft, interposing themselves in a scatter of tight explosions. Three assault craft were destroyed outright, winnowing their numbers down further.

By then the Furies and Thunderhawks had re-engaged, swooping up through the broadside-cleared approaches and opening fire. The three Wolves gunships barrelled up the centre of the engagement, letting loose with battle-cannons and linked lascannons. The Furies angled and twisted in their wake, adding thickets of las-fire to the intense bursts spearing out from the gunships.

The combination was intensely destructive. An entire wing of enemy fighters was immolated, caught in a bow-wave of combined fire. A dozen survivors pulled clear of the engagement, heading for the doubtful cover of the lone Infidel.

By then, the engagement-zone had drifted into range of the hulk itself. As the distance narrowed, the true scale of the monster became apparent. It soared away into the endless void-night like a cliff-face, gouged, scarred and ancient. Its sheer flanks dwarfed even *Vindicatus*, casting a heavy shadow across the Grand Cruiser as it passed between it and Kefa Primaris's sun. The crushed outlines of impacted starships, each one a colossal voidgoer in its own right, twisted and jutted across a landscape of ruined immensity.

With a shudder, the plague-ship loosed a volley of ship-killing energies. The barrage was as misshapen as the vessel was – a combination of las-arcs, cannon-shells, torpedo trails and plasma bolts. Some gun-trails came from the dozens of wrecks accreted to the hull, others from deep within the corrupted structure itself, launched from forges and fire-halls lodged in the beast's unfathomably ancient core.

The impact was punishing. *Vindicatus* strayed too close, and took a scything run of lascannon beams along its golden flanks. Its void shields flexed and crackled, stressed to near-breaking by the collisions. Several Furies were caught up in a wave of solid-round fire and exploded into clouds of fast-moving shrapnel.

Emboldened by the carnage, the remaining Infidel escort spearheaded a counter-offensive, burning in hard at the exposed Imperial craft and sending a wave of fighters ahead of it.

By then, though, *Vindicatus* was able to launch its second broadside. Despite the damage sustained by the hulk's attack, the rejoinder was even more ferocious than the first. The battle-sphere blazed white again as every cannon on *Vindicatus*'s nearside flank opened up. A wave of solid, dense destruction flew out at the approaching assault craft. The Infidel was caught up in the radius – it held out for a few seconds, firing all the while, before its shields overloaded and it blew apart.

The Thunderhawks and remaining Furies closed in on what remained, taking out the ragged wings of enemy assault craft. The void clogged with glowing scraps of metal as the wreckage swirled out from the kill-zones, bouncing from speeding hulls amid the criss-cross of lascannon beams.

Amid all of it, *Heimdall* drew in closer to the *Festerax* itself, braving the ferocious torrent of incoming fire to position itself under the hull's shadow. The plague-hulk's trailing underside stalactites hung close, glinting in the flashes of las-fire, each one as immense and crustaceous as a hive spire.

Green-edged beams arced out at *Heimdall*, striking it across its snarl-prow and knocking it out of line. Torpedo trails curled out and sped towards it, but *Heimdall* remained in position, firing back from all points along its facing flank. Soon the reason for its positioning became clear – a dozen Caestus assault rams blazed out from the outward-facing hull-edge and swept round under *Heimdall*'s keel. The Wolves cruiser pulled away immediately, firing hard to cover the attack run of the boarding craft.

The assault rams' boosters ignited in unison, sending them hurtling, arrow-straight, towards the looming edge of the *Festerax*. One was taken out by a snarled lattice of incoming fire, another slammed off-course by a torpedo hit, but the remaining ten made it into range and loosed missiles against the hulk's tangle of outer plating.

At the same time, the retreating *Heimdall* and *Vindicatus* loosed a coordinated barrage from all available weaponry. The move had been pre-arranged – thick columns of coruscation lanced in at the same point, just under the curve of the *Festerax*'s hull where the underhanging spires jutted. Every cannon on the two ships, every remaining torpedo tube and plasma launcher, every las-barrage and missile station, was aimed at the same zone. The repeated volleys smashed against the hulk's void-coverage, cracking against it with a scream of nova-hot energies.

Just as the first of the assault rams neared the designated impact zone, *Heimdall* finally loosed its main bombardment cannon, and *Vindicatus* followed suit with its ventral lances. The Grand Cruiser's gunners found their range, and the combined maelstrom slammed in amid a hurricane of blazing, spitting energies.

Under such an immense hammerblow of mingled fire, the plague-hulk's void shields guttered out in a blaze of static, exposing a narrow section of mottled hull beneath. Just as the barrier ripped away, the assault rams scythed clear through the rent's flame-edged maw, plunging into the heart of the newly carved rent. It was a tiny gap in the void-umbrella, but just enough.

As they screamed towards the *Festerax*'s flanks, the assault rams loosed their fore-mounted melta weapons. Glittering wreaths of vivid orange fire shot out, slamming directly into the fast-closing hull. The impact was crushing, driving in thick layers of adamantium plating, burning through it and dissolving the struts beyond.

Then the assault rams hit, one after the other in a ragged line of head-on collisions. A rip, hundreds of metres wide, was cut into the flank of the *Festerax* as the reinforced prows of the rams plunged deep into its hide. Secondary explosions went off, rippling along the plating as the rams burrowed in further.

By then, though, the volume of return fire had become apocalyptic. The *Festerax* opened up with a vast array of arcane weaponry, vomiting lasspears, spiked incendiary shells and sensor-disrupting clouds of greenblooming gases. *Heimdall* took a series of heavy impacts as it tried to roll clear, tearing up its ventral plating and forcing it to disengage. *Vindicatus*, which had remained further out during the combined assault, endured a similar battering, and lost a whole ridge of gun-towers when the shielding above them overloaded.

The *Festerax* seemed to have an infinite number of guns, and unleashed them all. With its escorts burning or fleeing, it was free to open up with everything left in its offensive arsenal. The void around it shimmered with the rolling barrage, and both Imperial ships were bludgeoned further out of range. The remaining gunships and interceptors hared for cover, aiming to dock with the larger craft before being overcome by the tidal wave of destruction.

Heimdall and *Vindicatus* finally pulled clear, ravaged and broken. They gained position just beyond the edge of the hulk's main range, absorbing a reduced level of punishment just to remain in contact. *Heimdall*, having run closest, was in the worst shape, and it was all it could do to maintain position. *Vindicatus* was able to launch a few retaliatory strikes, but did little more than pepper the *Festerax*'s immense profile with glancing hits.

Contemptuous of such threats, the plague-hulk maintained trajectory towards Kefa Primaris, its escorts destroyed but its integrity almost perfectly intact. The contagion-spores still survived, locked in the launchers deep in its core. Its weaponry remained potent, and the only real damage done to it was restricted to a tiny pocket on the immense tracts of its lower hull, the product of all the Imperial forces' combined might in arms.

It was a minor wound, no more than an insect bite in the hide of a sauroid. Within that wound, though, bodies stirred, blades were drawn and oaths were sworn.

Deep in the darkness, the Wolves were already moving.

CHAPTER TWELVE

The impact of the assault ram hitting was all-consuming – a tearing, burning, juddering collision that threw its occupants hard in their pistoned restraint mechanisms. Ingvar's mind immediately shot back to the assault on the plague-destroyer over Ras Shakeh. The hit was greater this time, though – the hulk's outer hull-plate was far older, and far thicker.

The rams drove and ground their way far inside, crunching onwards through walls of solid metal as the melta-tipped prow burned. Ingvar gripped on just like the others, thrown around by the immense shocks striking the ram's exterior.

The speed, the roar of the engines, the tortured scream of shearing adamantium – it made him want to *roar*. Even as the thunder-rain of jolts juddered down the shock absorber columns, he found himself straining at his bonds, desperate for the crew bay doors to slam open.

Baldr was shackled ahead of him, swaying jerkily.

'Ready for this, brother?' Ingvar voxed over the crashing echoes.

Baldr laughed eagerly. '*Craving* it.'

Every time Baldr spoke, he was more like the old warrior he'd been. The dryness, the cracking, was going.

The assault ram's momentum finally slowed. The shrieks and cracks fell away, replaced by a howl of escaping air and a thunder of flame.

They had lodged deep, wedged at an acute angle. Bolts and brace-rods slid back from Ingvar's armour, freeing him up to move again. With a wrench of tortured ironwork, the doors at the front end of the assault ram crashed down. A caldera-hot wave rushed over them, flecked with spinning motes of ash and rust, followed immediately by the echoing roar of racing atmosphere.

Gunnlaugur was first out, shouldering through a tangle of twisted support struts. Baldr followed him, then the rest, spilling from the melta-hazed prow of the assault ram and levelling bolters.

A ruined chamber stretched away from them. A part was lit by flickering green lumens while the rest was ink-dark and stinking. The assault ram had demolished the inner wall it had come through and was now wedged amid a heap of smouldering wreckage. Fire still ran across its back, catching on the white-hot edges of seared metalwork.

Gunnlaugur took point, hefting *skulbrotsjór* and activating the hammer's energy field. Electric light spilled from it, picking out the gloomy surroundings.

Baldr and Hafloí took up bolters, Ingvar his power sword. Four other warriors burst from the ram's second crew-berth, all marked with the insignia of Bloodhame's pack.

Ingvar activated his helm's proximity sensor. It was dotted with rune-locators from other ingress points. Some were just a few dozen metres away – a deck up, or across. Others had come in far out of position. He saw Njal's signal several levels up and fixed on it.

Gunnlaugur moved out. The pack fanned across the chamber behind him, keeping close on his heels, scanning as they went. Eight pairs of glowing red helm-lenses pierced the shadows.

The chamber ran for ten metres before terminating in a heavy-set wall of iron. Every surface was thick with glistening slime, pooled over rusting pressed-metal panels. It could have been in the hold of any Imperial vessel in the fleet, only given over to the ravages of corrosion in a way that no ship of the line would ever be. Blooms of rust spread everywhere, gnarled and pocked and glinting in the faint light of the Wolves' power weapons. The glare from their blades illuminated pools of oily water on the decking, rippled from the howling wind and streaked like blood-splatters.

From far below them came the dull rumble of weapons-fire. The hulk's ordnance was still active, sending recoil judders through the entire structure.

Gunnlaugur reached the door and pressed himself against it, listening. Then he pulled the hammer round, smashed the bolt-lock, and pushed through the splintered gap.

The corridor beyond was narrow and clogged with filth. The Wolves jogged down it, heading for Njal's marker signal. As Ingvar moved, he caught glimpses of old Imperial iconography on the walls. They had broken into one of the old ships that made up the *Festerax*'s hull – it might have been a Navy frigate by the pattern of aquilae on the roof, though impossible to tell through all the grime and corrosion.

'Target,' reported one of Bloodhame's warriors.

Ingvar picked it up a fraction later – a cluster of runes on his helm-display, closing fast. He ran his tongue over his fangs.

'Here they come,' he breathed, almost to himself.

The eight of them broke into an iron-walled octagonal chamber lined with moisture-slick chains. Other corridors led off in the four cardinal directions, and a deep well-shaft ran down from the centre.

Gunnlaugur looked up. The chamber was roofless – the base of a larger shaft that seemed to run up for at least several decks. The chains swayed down from unseen heights, clanking together and dripping with liquid.

'We climb,' he said, seizing two chain-lengths and hauling upwards. The steel links took his weight, and he kicked off, climbing fast. Bracing against the walls, each warrior followed suit, grabbing a handful of chain-lengths and ascending quickly.

Just as they did so, a cluster of bodies broke into the chamber below – the first inhabitants of the hulk they'd seen. Ingvar was barely a few metres up when he saw them. They were full-helmed, mortal fighters, clad in rags and carrying drum-barrelled projectile weapons.

'Mine,' voxed Ingvar, letting go of the chains and plummeting back to the chamber floor.

He took two of them out as he landed, kicking out with his armoured boots and crushing them against the chamber wall. *Dausvjer* whipped around in a lashing arc, spraying blood across the grimy decking.

Something heavy crunched down next to him, and he whirled to face it.

It was Baldr. He opened fire, and a storm of bolt-rounds surged off into the darkness, punching into the press of bodies. Baldr then aimed up at the lintel and destroyed the metal housing, bringing the corridor ceiling down in a crash of heavy panels. There were a few high-pitched screams, then the debris settled, silencing the defenders and sealing the ingress point.

Ingvar grinned under his helm. Baldr fought just as he always had – calm, clean, effective. Ingvar leapt back up for the chains and started to climb, slamming his boots against the shaft's inner wall for purchase.

'So you *are* ready,' he voxed.

'Just the start, brother,' Baldr replied, following him up.

Jorundur brought *Vuokho* up and out of a potentially ruinous spiral, gunning the engines hard and boosting clear of danger. All around him, space was filled with the tumbling carcasses of destroyed assault craft, most of them bearing enemy insignia on their ripped-up hull plating. A few had survived the inferno and were harrying the bigger warships, so his hands remained full. Keeping alive during the initial assault had been the hardest task, but he wasn't out of the woods yet.

'Shut that down,' he snapped to his co-pilot, a female mortal from Njal's retinue named Morven. She was good – as good as any mortal – but it was irritating not to have fellow Sky Warriors handling the support functions of void-combat.

Morven nodded smartly, working to close the fuel-loop to the gunship's damaged spine section. They were still leaking promethium into the void – a perilous thing to be doing when half of the space around them seemed to consist of plasma explosions.

The two other crew, also mortals, worked furiously at their stations. Beor was a competent enough navigator and had kept them out of the most obviously suicidal points on the battle-sphere, and Terrag, the gunner, already had a brace of kills against his name.

'Incoming enemy, *fyf-un* vertical,' reported Beor.

Jorundur pushed the gunship harder into its climb, wondering how long it would be before *Heimdall*'s guns came back online. He caught sight of the incoming ships – two skinny-looking interceptors with missile-underslung wings, thrusting clear of the Fury squadrons and heading up after *Vuokho*.

'We can outrun them,' said Morven, still working hard to plug the leak.

'Of course we can,' snapped Jorundur, calculating angles. He punched a series of coordinates into the cogitator. 'Gunner, you can handle that?'

'Affirmative,' said Terrag, running his fingers over the firing mechanism.

The Thunderhawk abruptly lost momentum, falling back towards the approaching interceptors. Seeing that they were going to overshoot and stumble into *Vuokho*'s fire-angle, the interceptors spun away to starboard, using their agility to pull out of the attack.

As they did so, though, Jorundur kicked the drives back to full power and swung the gunship hard about, swinging neatly onto a parallel course and opening up a shot for the starboard heavy bolters.

Terrag performed ably, working both mounts at once and sending twin lines of armour-shredding shells lancing out into the void. One of the interceptors took heavy damage to the rear engine quarters. Its fuel tanks were punched open, after which the igniting bolts detonated the promethium stores and destroyed the ship in a cloud of spinning metal. The second took hits all along the facing flank, forcing it to climb rapidly in an attempt to break away.

Jorundur calmly hauled *Vuokho*'s prow after it, keying up the lascannons as he did so. 'There you go,' he voxed to Terrag. 'All lined up for you.'

Terrag punched the controls and the lascannons cut the interceptor cleanly in two.

Vuokho sailed through the wreckage, smashing the fragments apart and driving back up to full battle-speed.

Jorundur stole a glance out of the cockpit armourglass, looking up to where the curve of the plague-hulk's hull filled his visual field.

It was almost like atmospheric combat, fighting so close to such a massive object. The detail on its surface was clear enough – a forest of interlocked and embedded ship-corpses, tied together by strands of ossified matter. Tiny lights glowed like marsh-gas amid the arcane tangle of gothic buttresses and ancient hangar bays. Somewhere under all of that accumulated carnage was the original structure, the forgotten battleship that had started the whole millennial process, now buried under kilometres of detritus.

'Power spikes detected, all along underside batteries,' reported Beor.

Jorundur switched his attention back to the near-range augurs. 'They're gearing up to fire again,' he growled, judging distances and feeding more power to the main thrusters. 'Run for *Heimdall* – those lances will end us.'

The crew got to work – calmly, coolly, obeying his orders without a second thought. *Vuokho* swung around, pitching through a glowing debris-zone and boosting down away from the range of the hulk's fearsome guns.

Work quickly, brothers, Jorundur thought, already spying his next targets and working the controls hard. *This grows difficult.*

Gunnlaugur reached the lip of the shaft and hauled himself over the edge, emerging into a vast open chamber lined with iron pillars. The thick gloom was oppressive and dank – a near-perfect dark, broken only sporadically by flickering lamps or faulty strip-lumens. The environment was hot and close: a heavy cocktail of methane and carbon dioxide with an aftertaste of more exotic chems.

He loped across the chamber floor, his boot-falls echoing with dull clangs. Behind him came his brothers, spilling out of the shaft, their helm-lenses glowing. Njal's location-beacon glowed on all their helm-displays – still several levels up and already moving deeper into the heart of the hulk.

An archway towered up ahead, thirty metres high and ten across. The lintel was engraved with old Gothic, now worn away and unreadable in the murk. He picked up echoing booms, just on the edge of hearing, like distant detonations in the deeps. Either the hulk was still firing, or something was stirring in its labyrinthine innards.

Then he heard it for the first time.

Scuttling.

'Getting that?' voxed Ingvar, going swiftly, his head low as he ghosted through the archway.

'They are gathering,' growled Gunnlaugur, watching proximity points on his helm-scanner converge. 'Make your kills swift.'

As Gunnlaugur ran, he had to duck under a collapsed bulkhead before powering onwards, his shoulders hunched low, his hammer held two-handed. Blooms of gas hissed from shattered pipework, gusting across the tortured floor panels in luminous snarls. The spaces constricted into tight, claustrophobic capillary tunnels.

Then he caught sight of the first mutants, up ahead where the ways grew even more confined. Their eyes glowed in the dark – many eyes, like insects. They surged towards him, scrambling on four limbs over every surface, scampering along the walls, the decks, hanging from the sagging tunnel roof on hooked hands.

The tunnel filled with the whoosh of bolt-shells, followed an instant later by the dull crack of explosions. The mutants were blasted from their perches and sent spinning across the width of the passages.

Then Gunnlaugur was among them. He struck with his thunder hammer, crushing the head of one and sending it slamming into a knife-sharp wall section. He caught another, smashing it against the roof where its spine severed with a wet snap. He ploughed on, tearing through the horde of defenders, driving into them with brief, efficient strokes.

The rest kept pace. Ingvar remained at his shoulder, working his blade with ferocious speed. Bodily fluids slapped and sprayed across the narrow passageway, bringing with them the screams of the dying. The pack-members kept close together, forming a wave of grey-edged steel that tore down the twisting tunnels, never dropping speed, never pausing.

Eventually they burst out into the open again, and the tunnel walls gave way entirely to a new set of surroundings – bone-white matter. The new terrain curved away from them in sinuous arcs, glimmering softly in the deep night of the hulk's interior. A vast plain extended into the gloom, studded with sculptural undulations like some frozen sea.

Gunnlaugur nearly slipped as he ran. The mutants were everywhere, spilling out of crevices like blowflies clustered on rotten meat.

'This is... unusual,' he muttered, pivoting on one foot to send the head of *skulbrotsjór* into the midriff of a mutant. The screams echoed strangely, rebounding from the immense void above them. It felt like they'd stumbled into some bizarre hololith world.

A distant roof soared away from them, towering like the sheer flanks of the hive spire. More ivory matter curled and twisted in a mesh of buttresses. It all glittered softly, as if studded with tiny crystals.

'Xenos,' said Ingvar coldly.

As soon as Ingvar said it, Gunnlaugur saw the truth of it. He'd fought the eldar before and should have recognised their architectural excess. He'd never been inside one of their warships, though. The colossal chamber had the stench of ages on it, as if it had been incorporated into the hulk's warped menagerie an unimaginably long time ago.

He checked the tactical map – Njal was close now, and above them. More mutants emerged from the tangle of eldritch spires and walkways, defiling the ground over which they scurried like rats.

'I do not know what is worse,' snarled Gunnlaugur. 'This filth, or the ones that built this.'

'I do,' said Ingvar grimly, following him into battle again.

Hlaupnir was nearly as fast as Njal's boasts – a long, lean system-runner that wouldn't have looked out of place in a Naval formation. Olgeir liked it. It had a good smell, like charred stone, and its engines burned hard and clean.

He sat in the command throne. The hewn-stone chair was set at the rear of the bridge atop a low metal platform. Ahead of him, the main sensor station ran in semicircular ranks, interspersed with servitor pits and bulging logic engines. A large iron-framed portal, elliptical like a stained-glass eye, formed the main real-viewer, and took up nearly the entire forward wall of the bridge chamber. The crew worked at their positions, clad in Fenrisian grey, bent over pict screens or sensor tubes.

Olgeir checked the augurs, seeing how far the *Festerax* had already fallen behind. None of its escorts had come after them, which was something of a disappointment – it would have been good to exercise *Hlaupnir*'s guns a little before breaking for the planet.

'How long, Hanek?' Olgeir asked.

The sensorium officer – a burly kaerl with an unruly beard – pulled up the figures.

'Entering extreme augur-range now, lord,' he reported. 'I'm getting some ghosting on the fore array – either we're picking up some static from the battle, or they've seen us.'

'Broadcast our position marker. Sooner we make ourselves known, the better.'

Kefa Primaris was still some distance from visual range. Ahead of *Hlaupnir* ran an empty-looking starfield. Its lingering void-trail signatures were perfectly standard for the planet's grade – plenty of bulk carriers, a few light cargo freighters, the odd military patrol. All those ships had plied the incoming space-lanes to the planet recently, their spoor hanging in the vacuum like animal scent.

No doubt they were hanging in orbit over Kefa Primaris now, surrounded by clusters of unloading barges, refuelling and refitting after the warp-stage. Reaching those berths would seem like reaching sanctuary, with prayers of thanksgiving to be offered to the Emperor and the saints after the turmoil of the aether. They could have no idea what was heading their way.

'We need more speed,' Olgeir said.

Thraid, the navigation officer, looked up at him. 'We're already operating at far beyond–' He saw Olgeir's expression, and shook his head resignedly. 'I'll see what I can do.'

Olgeir grunted in satisfaction, resting his gauntlets on the armrests of the throne.

'You do that,' he said. 'Stormcaller wanted us on Kefa twelve hours ahead of the hulk.' He smiled broadly at Thraid, enjoying the challenge. 'Make it sixteen.'

Ingvar climbed fast, speeding up the smooth curves of the terrain around him. His boots crunched into a brittle surface, cracking it in tiny patterns. He grabbed at trailing lengths of it, hauling himself higher, immersing himself ever further in tangled trails of alien psycho-substance.

It was like being immersed in a vast, static cataract. All around him, dirty white matter stretched upwards in twisting trunks sweeping towards the cavern roof. The Wolves raced up it, grabbing on to outcrops for handholds and wedging their boots into intersecting forks and platforms.

Ingvar had encountered wraithbone first during Onyx's raid on Craftworld Nyo-Fae. Halliafiore had taken care to brief the squad on its properties.

'Harder than ceramite,' the inquisitor had told them, hefting a piece, 'yet lighter than honeycomb. And it's saturated with the warp. Break it open, if you can, and for an instant you're staring into raw aether.'

The wraithbone on the *Festerax* was different – it was dull, lifeless, riddled with cancerous pocks and patched with mould growths. On Nyo-Fae it had been magnificent, swirling into arches of such purity that it hurt the eye to look on them; here, it had no more lustre than the scattered bones of a decaying mortuary.

The eldar warship had paid a heavy price for being dragged into the heart of the hulk. Nothing could survive millennia inside such a ruin-ark and not succumb eventually, and he felt the fragility of it all around him, like desiccated flesh stretched too long under a beating sun.

The creatures that screamed at them were no eldar, though. They were the same plague-zombies as before – human in origin but now twisted and distorted into grey-fleshed monsters. Ingvar caught scant glimpses of their faces in the dark before he killed them – jaws pulled wide, eyes staring from bloodshot rims, cadaverous flesh glistening clammily. They burst out of the wraithbone like roaches and scuttled down the long fronds, throwing themselves at the climbing Wolves in a disparate tide.

They were not hard to kill, not for warriors of the Rout, but every wave of defenders slowed them down. Just like all his brothers', Ingvar's helm displayed a ticking chrono on his inner lens, incessantly reminding him of the shrinking window for completion.

'Faster!' roared Gunnlaugur from up ahead of him, smashing aside four shrieking mutants with one vicious hammer-blow, dislodging them from their precarious handholds and sending them sailing into the emptiness.

The pack fought its way high above the surface of the wraithbone plain, racing up dozens of undulating pillars and cross-spans. The threading walkways led ever upwards, rising towards a single oval orifice at the summit of the chamber. Gunnlaugur made the lip of the passageway, leaping from a wraithbone platform to land on its rim. Three ragged mutants sprang at him, and Gunnlaugur punched them aside, cracking their backs and sending them tumbling over the edge.

Then he was through, charging into the dark. Ingvar raced up after him, stamping aside the snagging fingers of a half-buried zombie before clearing the last of the wraithbone fronds. A thin frame of pale stone ran around the orifice, lined with flowing runes in the xenos tongue, much of it faded and mutilated.

Ingvar plunged through it, and into a second wraithbone chamber. The previous one had been big; this one was colossal. Vast wraithbone sculptures rose up into smog-streaked gloom, each one pitted and worn with age. Sweeping columns soared up towards an obscured and distant roof. The chamber's floor-level ran away from him, strewn with the broken eddies of some arcane, flowing design. Empty-eyed, lissom statues lined a series of avenues running into the darkness, blank-faced and passive.

The whole place already rang with the noise of battle – a jarring, percussive hammer of boltguns and projectile weapons, underpinned by the roar of hundreds of voices in overlapping, distorted waves.

A few hundred metres ahead of him, more than twenty Wolves had taken position. They crouched behind the cover of broken statuary, firing steadily out into the shadows. Beyond the defensive line, everything was shrouded in murk.

Ingvar spied Gunnlaugur's marker. He ran up the front line and skidded into cover, stowing *dausvjer* and pulling his bolt pistol from its holster. Next to him, the Wolf Guard was firing short, deliberate volleys into the smog.

'Why do we not run at them?' Ingvar hissed, taking aim himself.

'Njal is here,' Gunnlaugur voxed, firing steadily all the while. 'He has sensed something.'

Ingvar picked his targets, and opened fire. More Wolves emerged from adjoining chambers to join them, racing up to add their firepower to the fragile defensive perimeter. Ingvar spied Njal's own contingent fifty metres to the left, clustered around the base of one of the hall's gigantic supporting pillars. Further down the line, Bloodhame's squad were already creeping slowly up the left extremity, taking position for flanking fire.

Just then, Njal suddenly broke from cover himself, surrounded by warriors of Fellblade's pack. He lifted his rune staff high and cried out words of power. A clap like thunder boomed out, filling the entire hall, making the miasma shudder. Howling winds spiralled out of nothingness, shearing away the oppressive heat and pushing back the roiling banks of smog. Harsh light suddenly leapt up the faces of the pillars, illuminating for a moment the intricate carvings still visible on their surfaces.

That was not all it illuminated. Njal's lightburst flooded out across the emptiness, dazzling the hordes of approaching mutants. Beyond them, several hundred metres out, rose a further pair of columns, each one as wide as a Titan. Beyond those columns lay a chasm running transverse across the full width of the chamber. A single span crossed the divide, gently curved.

Something massive was crossing that bridge. Huge, cloven feet cracked against the dusty floor, crushing the lesser creatures beneath it. Gangling legs shot up, bulging in xenos-tainted curves. Long, grasping arms hung down from armoured shoulders, almost human in scale, but deformed by eldritch slenderness. A curved blade of dull, black metal swung rhythmically, balanced by a segmented fan-shaped shield on the opposite arm. A tapered, faceless head swept back and forth, lolling as if intoxicated.

It was fully fifteen metres tall – a giant of xenos tech-witchery, towering far above even Njal's Terminator bulk. Every heavy stride brought it several metres closer. The mutants around it yelled and goaded, lost in terror and awe, oblivious to those of their number it killed with every crunching footfall.

Ingvar narrowed his eyes. He had seen such sorcerous engines before. Imperial strategos had given them a name fitting their spectral appearance: wraithknight. Under normal circumstances the war machines were shimmering, elusive monsters of combat, sweeping across battlefields, glittering brightly from the energies coiled deep within their ghostly cores.

The thing before them was different. It strode clumsily, as if blind or maimed. Its curved shield was corroded and punched with black-edged holes where projectile fire had once stabbed through. Muddy-green fluid leaked from plated joints and cavities, dribbling across pitted wraithbone. The pregnant swell of its head-unit was fractured and smashed open, revealing intestinal growths spilling out of what had once been the pilot-chamber.

The wraithknight was true xenos no longer: just a shell over a deeper corruption. The black blood now boiling through its artificial veins had once hummed with esoteric harmonics. The Ruinous Powers had turned it into a tool of their own, slaved to the very powers it had been built to fight.

'Hel's teeth,' breathed Gunnlaugur.

By then, Njal was already moving. Heedless of the ravening hordes tearing across the emptiness, he strode out into the preternatural dark, his staff blazing with light and fire. Mutants raced towards the searing light, dying even as their addled eyes caught sight of it.

'To *me*, brothers!' Stormcaller cried, his old voice choked with kill-urge. 'In the name of Russ – *bring it down!*'

CHAPTER THIRTEEN

The crystalflex viewer still filled with intermittent light, dazzling from discharged lances, though the mortal danger had passed. *Vindicatus* had pulled back to agreed coordinates, holding position parallel to the plague-hulk and remaining just on the edge of its mainline gun-range. The cruiser's shields fizzed and guttered as the tech-adepts struggled to restore them, but otherwise damage had been containable – just a few hundred casualties along the macrocannon-ranks; nothing to lose sleep over.

The Cardinal's throne dominated the centre of the bridge. Its seat was high-backed, ridged with gold and lined with blood-red leather. A domed silk canopy hung over him, held up by the grunting efforts of twelve skull-faced cherubs. Incense filtered out through grilles in the throne's side-panels, dribbling across the marble dais in filmy swirls.

Hundreds of bodies moved in the spaces under the gaze of the throne. Most wore the crimson livery of the Grand Cruiser's bridge crew, their faces tattooed with the Cardinal's emblem and their tabards draped in devotional screeds. Others were tech-priests, spared the most egregious symbols of the Ministorum and given a wide berth by their superstitious counterparts. A few were of Sister Nuriyah's battalion, towering over the non-power armoured, their cloaks swishing softly as they strutted.

The crowds moved with a purpose, tracing pathways across the enormous bridge expanse. Data-slates were passed from hand to hand and orders were conveyed in soft whispers. *Vindicatus*'s command stations echoed with the hum of earnest tactical consultations. With its towering columns of bronze and its glassy seas of polished marble, the bridge looked a little like one of the great cathedral precincts of Holy Terra, and that was not entirely accidental.

Delvaux rested his elbows on his lap, and considered the situation. He hardly noticed any of the finery. He had hardly noticed it for many years – opulence was the water in which he swam, as transparent as the seas around a shark. His gaze fixed on the floor-to-roof observation panels at the far end of the bridge. Immense facets of armourglass, framed by curved metal fixings in the shape of angels' wings, gave a superlative view of the void outside. Ocular implants in his left eye superimposed fleet markers over the polished surface, delineating the patterns of combat still taking place in the vacuum.

He gloomily watched the surviving wings of his interceptors taking their chances against the last dregs of the plague-hulk's escort. He watched *Heimdall* stay riskily close to the enemy ship's lance range, continuing to loose its weapons with reckless defiance. He watched the three slate-grey gunships wheel and dive, shadowing the hulk like raptors harrying prey too big for them.

For a long time he did not stir, lost in his thoughts, knowing none of his servants would so much as dare to look up at him.

None but one.

'What do you make of it?' asked Klaive.

Delvaux twitched, and looked down. He hadn't heard the confessor approach. Klaive was out of armour, wearing his favoured black robes, velvet stole and soft slippers. The man's ivory skin shone under the bridge's intense light, and his wet gaze was unsettlingly unblinking, just as ever.

'Make of what?' Delvaux asked.

'The attempt,' said Klaive, coming to stand just below Delvaux's left armrest. 'Can you detect the Wolves?'

'Intermittently. The deeper they go, the harder it gets.'

Klaive nodded. 'Let us hope they are preserved. Such *fighters*.'

Delvaux shot him a scornful look. 'You admire them.'

'Of course.'

'I detest them.'

'For shame. They are the Emperor's instruments.'

'Preach at me here, confessor, and I'll stuff your tracts down your throat.' Delvaux felt the urge to reach for more snuff, and resisted. He was getting bad at resisting things. There had been a time, long ago, when he'd not needed stimulants to get through the diurnal cycle, when he'd fervently believed the things he was required to say. It was hard to remember that, now.

Klaive examined a broken nail. 'How long do they have?'

'Seventeen hours.'

'And you're going to give them that long?'

'That was the agreement.'

'Was it? You were generous.'

Delvaux turned to glare at Klaive. Something about the man had always made him angry. Perhaps it was the calm, otherworldliness of him, like the saints were always supposed to be. Klaive never got angry, never raised his voice. That was unnatural.

'Did you find what you were looking for on the surface?' Delvaux asked.

'Some of it. The rest will turn up.'

'Anything of interest?'

'Not really. Wasted effort, for the most part, I'm afraid to say.'

Delvaux studied his face carefully. 'Archives, you told me.'

'That is right.'

'A lot of trouble you went to. For archives.'

Klaive smiled thinly. 'Such things are important, lord. Records, transactions, documents of succession. When this war is over, they will be needed. Ras Shakeh was a small outpost of your diocese, but not an unimportant one.'

'It was a blasted rock,' Delvaux muttered. 'I still cannot quite believe you persuaded me to take it back in such force.'

'It was but a detour, lord. The real prize lies ahead.'

With that, at least, Delvaux could agree. Kefa Primaris was a colossal world, one harbouring billions of souls. To send it to the flames – that would be an act of supreme commitment. It would send a message, not just to the enemy, but to those who had begun to doubt his zeal.

The Ministorum had its own games of power, ones that cardinals were compelled to play just like everyone else.

'And what of you?' Delvaux asked. 'What odds would you give them?'

Klaive pondered the question. 'I am not sure that is the right question, lord,' he said. 'The true question is this: can we risk giving them time for the attempt?'

'I have made my judgement,' snapped Delvaux. 'Their Rune Priest knows my limits.'

'He is out of contact, at least for the moment. You are an honourable man, my lord, but do not lose sight of the danger.' Klaive's eyes flickered around the bridge. 'A whole world given over to ruin. Billions of new souls for the faithless. Once that is started–'

'Say no more. I know the consequences.'

But Klaive's speech nagged at him. He could already envisage the torpedoes being launched. It would not be hard to outpace the *Festerax*, to thunder into range ahead of it, gain optimal orbital position, deploy the life-eating virus-bombs. By the time the hulk made orbit, Kefa Primaris could be a scoured rock, as barren as the void itself.

No one would blame him. On the contrary, he would be commended. What were a few billion lives compared to the security of the entire sub-sector? These were the calculations a *statesman* made, one with the nerve to rise to the very top.

'I have made my judgement,' Delvaux repeated coldly. Beyond the armour-glass viewers, the void-battle raged on silently. 'Let that be an end to it.'

Klaive bowed, though his faint smile lingered a little longer, hanging on his face like the reflection of gold on glass.

'As you will it, lord,' he said.

The xenos engine soared up into the gloom, huge and corroded. Njal could sense the heart of corruption beating within it. Something, just a sliver, of the pilot remained buried inside, wretched and agonised, locked in millennial torment and bound to the machine it had once commanded.

The machine sensed him, too – whatever gestalt mind still functioned within its eldritch body could respond to the power of the runes. Its shattered head swung towards him and it took a heavy stride clear of the bridge. Its curved blade glowed with a dull green light, sick as poison gas, and it swung low across the horde at its feet like a reaper.

At that moment, Bloodhame's pack opened up with a barrage of long-range bolter-fire, scything in from the left flank. A rain of shells smashed across the wraithknight's body in a shower of explosions, rocking it and making it stumble. Tracer-lines speared out in the flickering dark, cutting through billowing smog. Raw flame-bursts spread across the xenos's torso, washing over the curving breastplate and shoulder-arches.

The xenos engine wasn't hard to hit – it moved slowly, its joints leaking gas and fluid with every staccato movement – but physical rounds wouldn't be enough.

Njal whipped his staff around, building up a whirl of speed. Rune-energy lashed around him, snaking up to his clenched fists and rippling along the length of his skull-staff. The bone-totems tied to his weapon-belt clanked and jolted as the storm ramped up. He extended his staff, aiming the skull-head directly at the xenos engine. Vast arcs of lightning crackled out, snapping against the pillars.

'*Heidur Rus!*' he roared, and the echo of the war-cry rang from the pillars around him.

The wind suddenly flared into a full-blown gale. The temperature in the hall plummeted, collapsing into extreme, bone-breaking cold. Ice-crystals surged up the edges of the columns, fracturing and freezing.

Njal's Wolves streaked out ahead of him, carving a bloody path through the half-blinded mobs of mutants standing between them and the bridge. Glowing blades hacked and danced in the shadows, all locked in a cacophony of snarling, roaring and tearing. Bloodhame's pack secured the left flank, piling on more long-range ordnance. Long-axe's warriors fought their way up to a shallow stairway on the right flank and held position there, lancing fire in hard at the wraithknight. Gunnlaugur and Fellblade drove up the centre, their packs gouging a path of ruin into the heart of the enemy.

Njal spoke again, and gusts of the searing wind surged across the battle-field. Mutants froze in agony, their skin instantly blackening in frostbite. Their weapons shattered, their muscles seized up. Knife-hard blasts ripped through them, throwing them from their feet and sending them spinning and slamming into ice-rimed columns.

The xenos engine limped towards Njal, its carapace already glittering with a thickening coating of hoarfrost. It *shrieked*, a sound like metal shearing from its fastenings. Its shoulder-mounted weaponry spun around and opened fire. The Wolves in its path leapt and pounced from danger, veering and darting around the impacts before charging back into the fray.

Njal laughed out loud, as wild and brutal as a *gothi* of the old ice. Tethered skulls cracked against his armour, snapping and writhing like serpents. The storm-gale intensified, ripping wraithbone from stone and sending it flying into a vortex of whirling debris. The aether-ice gripped fast, cracking every-thing it coated. The Wolves fought on, in their own savage element, while the hordes of the damned were driven into submission by the void-cold maelstrom.

Only the wraithknight weathered the storm, absorbing wave after wave of impacts. Its shoulder-weapons were blasted from its hide, its greaves driven in, and its faceplate cracked further, exposing a brain-like mass of glossy folds underneath. Throughout it all, it kept lumbering towards the Rune Priest, swinging its immense blade as it came. A single sword strike ripped through Fellblade's pack. Another swipe scattered Hauki's. None of the Wolves got close to the creature.

'Face *me*, then!' roared Njal, feeling his whole body blaze with elemental forces. A kind of ecstasy of power thundered out, making the runes on his armour burn with a furious, cold coruscation.

The ice-wind became ruinous. Massive chunks of the hall's wraithbone structure dislodged, crashing to the ground and sending up great clouds of dust. The wraithknight staggered, hammered by ball-lightning strikes and ravaged by the frigid gales. It stretched out a clawed hand, as black as coal amid the sheeting ice. Its tortured head emerged once more, surrounded by gouts of steam. It tried to take another stride towards the Rune Priest, to grasp at him.

'Your body is *broken!*' bellowed Njal. 'Your soul is *shriven!*'

Njal swung around, his staff whistling through the air as it churned up yet more power. The hurricane overflowed from him, bleeding from the joints in his ornate armour. The air roared, thundered and sped, chilling and cracking, as irresistible as glacier-grind. Nightwing, riding the squalls high in the vaults, shrieked defiance at the monster below.

'I name you *xenos!*' Njal boomed, grasping his staff two-handed, planting his feet, and jutting the skull-tip at the creature's head. The wraithknight towered over him, surrounded by the spinning cloud-patterns of the aether-whirlwind. 'By the will of the Allfather, you are *ended!*'

Storm-fury lashed out, crashing into the monster's midriff with an echoing explosion of multi-hued lightning and spinning ice-shards. Radial shockwaves shuddered outwards, ripping away in the deafening wail of the tempest. Every loose object in the chamber spiralled wildly around the icy vortex, dragged into the heart of the Stormcaller's summoned devastation.

The wraithknight, reeling in the eye of the gale, tried to get a sword strike away, and hauled its massive blade upwards. The dark metal surface, latticed with thick hoarfrost, glinted amid a blizzard of driving sleet, then swooped down. The wickedly curved edge tore towards Njal, swift as the raven's flight, perfectly aimed and weighted with massive kinetic force.

Njal swung his staff to meet it, bracing himself for the impact. The sword hit, and he was driven down into the cracking wraithbone underfoot. He felt his arms jar, his vision go black with stars. Around him, the blast-wave crashed out, flooring any mutants still standing.

Njal gritted his fangs, pushing back against the colossal pressure, feeling his staff flex as the strain took. Sweat burst out across his brow, veins throbbed in his bulging neck. The crushing power of xenos tech-sorcery came up against the bottomless well of Fenris's world-soul, and the epicentre raged like the heart of a star.

Amid all the ice and spiralling magicks, Njal looked up at the monster. It towered over him, vast and corrupted, bleeding raw pain and madness. Every surface was coated in a thick rime, as tight and frigid as the grasp of Helwinter. The diamond-bright carapace glowed with a harsh white light, and crackles of lightning flickered across the face of it.

The frost was lethal. It was spun from utter desolation, drawn from the airless chill of Fenris's utmost unforgiving heights, and no power, be it mortal or divine, could withstand its gnawing power forever.

At the end, it only took one word. As Njal uttered it, gasping through a clenched jawline, he even managed a grim smile.

'*Shatter.*'

The creature's sword burst apart, smashed into a thousand flying shards. The wraithknight stumbled, caught by the pull of gravity. The hoarfrost coating it contracted viciously, cracking wraithbone and driving deep. Wraithbone spars shattered, blown apart as cracks raced up the creature's armour plates.

The wraithknight screamed a final time, frozen in its death-lunge, bludgeoned by the ice-wind and racked by the clinging frost.

Then it exploded, flinging shards across the entire hall. The gales whipped up the debris and hurled it into the heights. A crack of released warp-essence rushed out, shaking the columns and making the floor tremble. The wraithknight's body disintegrated entirely, lost in a flailing tempest of crackling lightning and tearing ice-winds. Its meagre remains, harrowed by the ice into nothing more than withered scraps of flesh and metal, crashed to the ground in steaming chunks.

Njal pulled his head back, spread his arms, and howled. His warriors howled with him, charging with fresh savagery into the remaining hordes of mutant footsoldiers.

'*Gothi!*' they roared, en masse, and the sound of it made the chamber shake anew. '*Stormurstjórn! Hjá, gothi!*'

Buoyed by the surging hurricane, the Wolves cut through the cowering surviving mutants in a frenzy of unfettered bloodlust. Blades whirled in blurs of silver-edged speed, cutting deep into the reeling masses of the damned.

Njal's whole body still rang with storm-magic. Every muscle blazed with pain from where he'd met the creature's blade, but his blood still ran fast with hyperadrenaline. The last forks of lightning still sparked across his amour, vital and dagger-sharp.

He kicked free of the wraithknight's downed corpse and started to move again. The chasm's edge drew nigh. On the far side, Njal could see the wraithbone architecture give out, replaced by a vast wall of rusting iron. Grotesque gargoyles, huge and crusted with the patina of ruin, glared out over the chasm amid riveted panels the colour of dried blood. A high portal gaped open, its interior velvety dark. Across the gate's lintel were carved words of ruin in a language that no mortal had ever spoken.

As he gazed at the portal, Njal felt the aura of absolute decay wafting out through the gateway. It was like a portal into the maw of Hel.

'To the bridge!' he commanded, his voice raw, striding out into the sea of bodies.

The Wolves surged forwards alongside him, driving the mutants over the chasm's edge. Bloodhame's pack came in from the flanks, with Long-axe's not far behind. The squads went swiftly now, unhindered, killing freely.

'First test passed,' Njal gasped, under his breath, before joining them in the slaughter.

* * *

Kefa Primaris filled *Hlaupnir*'s forward scopes. The globe was dirty grey and striated with lines of earth-brown cloudbanks. Even from the extremes of the orbital approaches, the massive urban coverage was clearly visible – vast geometric patterns of transit clusters and ground-level shield patterns. On full magnification, augurs showed up the core spire zones, the tracts of power-gen stations, the furrowed wastelands seething with chem-effluent.

Lights glinted in the shadow of the solar terminator – trillions of them, sparkling in the void with a beauty of abundance.

Olgeir left his throne and walked up to the railing around the command platform, gazing intently at the armourglass portals. 'Signals, Hanek,' he said.

'Standard system traffic,' the sensorium officer replied, scouring his pict-feed assiduously. 'Several hundred carriers in high orbit. No military-grade warp-capable vessels. We're not... Oh, we are. We're being intercepted.'

As Hanek spoke, Olgeir saw it for himself – six fighters burning towards them in formation. They were smaller than Imperial Navy Furies, with what looked like lone prow-mounted lascannons and limited missile tubes. Each had navy-blue livery on angular wings marked with a white hawk's head.

'Calm them down,' said Olgeir.

Hanek broadcast the standard approach codes as Thraid pulled the *Hlaupnir* two points away from an intercept course and dipped the cockpit towards Kefa Primaris's orbital holding zones.

'Unauthorised vessel,' came a tinny order over the ship-vox. 'Stand down or be disabled.'

Olgeir glanced at Hanek, raising an eyebrow. 'Are they serious?'

'They're powering up, lord.'

Olgeir shook his head in irritation. 'Get me a visual link.'

Hanek's fingers ran across his console. 'Shunting to your throne now.'

Olgeir went back to his command throne and sat heavily in it, clicking a rune on the armrest panel. A thin translucent screen spun out from the holo-cast projector revealing a pict-feed of a helmeted pilot in a cramped cockpit.

'Can you see me?' Olgeir asked, addressing the image.

There was a brief delay, a visual freeze, and the transmission juddered into life again.

'I... Yes. Getting a signal.' The pilot rapped the side of his helmet, as if checking to make sure his view was genuine. 'Lord,' he added hastily.

'Good. Then you know what I am, you have our codes, and you know what I will do to you if you fail to power down and fall into escort formation.'

The pilot looked briefly uncertain. 'I have orders–'

'Here are your new orders. You will escort us to the zone above the capital spires. You will send ahead orders for a lander to bring me to the governor. You will make sure he is ready for me on arrival.'

'It will be done, lord. It is... I mean she is...'

Olgeir sighed. Mortals were no use when they let their awe get the better of them. 'Do it now.'

He cut the link. Out in the void, the fighters pulled out of their attack run and split into two groups. They turned expertly and took up flanking position around the *Hlaupnir*.

'We have our coordinates,' reported Hanek. 'They're guiding us in.'

Olgeir leaned back in the throne, watching the arc of the planet swell in the forward viewers. He already knew how it would be – hyper-urban, towering habs, thick layers of industrial smog, crammed with worker-souls like insects in their nests. They were the greater part of the Imperium's teeming quadrillions. They were the backbone, the template, the standard pattern of human existence in the galaxy.

It was a depressing thought.

'Take us in,' said Olgeir, grimly.

Baldr ran with the pack across the bridge, glancing up at the towering cliff-face ahead. Bolt-rounds still fizzed out from the chasm's edge, but fewer than before. All blades were bloody now, caked with the thick residue of mortal fodder. He was still exhilarated from witnessing Njal's true power. The spectacle had been magnificent, though all of them knew sterner tests would lie ahead. The most powerful denizens of the plague-hulk would be stirring now, uncurling from whatever dark pits they were spawned in, slowly reacting to the intruders within the vessel's vast body.

We will be its disease.

Njal's words still echoed in Baldr's mind. He hadn't liked hearing them the first time – too close for comfort. He could feel the collar chafing at his neck as he ran, jostled by the cables running up the inside of his gorget. At times, the circlet felt hot, at others, rough, like uncured hide. He could never quite forget that he wore it, no matter how close the fighting became.

The portal loomed above him. Already the vanguard had fought through it, hurling frag grenades into the dark before racing after them to clear out the corridors beyond. Baldr was part of the second wave across, close on Álfar's heels, just ahead of Ingvar and Gunnlaugur.

He could hear his breathing echoing harshly inside his helm. He was pushing himself hard, just as he had planned to do, all to show his brothers that he was back to full fight-potential. Only in combat could he truly shake off the sense of shame that marked him, just as the torc marked him. There could be no shame in the rush of the hunt, and so he hurled himself into it, caught up in the bloody-mawed embrace of his heritage.

Once through the portal, the air instantly changed. The musty atmosphere of the eldar warship gave way to a close, hot, humid bloom of gaseous vapours. The tunnel closed down around him quickly, collapsing in on itself until barely more than head height. The dark shadows of his battle-brothers charged up ahead, forging a path into the eternal gloom. Ahead, the iron-ribbed lengths of twisting tunnel walls grew ever tighter.

'More targets,' reported Álfar from up ahead.

A second later, Baldr received the same data. Runes blinked into life on his helm-display, homing in from all directions. It was near impossible to gauge distance and orientation – the paths twisted quickly into sweeping curves, before branching off into dozens of alternative routes. The metal outlines of the walls dissolved into what looked like pus-coloured layers of fleshy matter. Baldr saw bulbous polyps throbbing amid the slime, glowing softly, and his boots sunk deep into gurgling pools of liquid that splashed up against his greaves as he ran.

He risked a look over his shoulder. The bulky outline of Ingvar's power armour was visible a long way further back. Beyond that, nothing. Locator runes for the rest of the packs seemed caught in some kind of lag, and didn't report true.

The tunnel snaked around to the right, angling sharply. Long trails of saliva-like ooze ran from the low ceiling. False colour patterns imposed by his helm did nothing to disguise the essential darkness, the claustrophobia, the foulness.

Then he heard bolter-fire from up ahead, followed by Fenrisian curses coming over the pack-vox.

'Flamers!' came a furious order – Baldr couldn't tell from whom.

The tunnel around him shuddered, rocked as if by a quake. Baldr nearly plunged headlong into the filth at his feet, and skidded to a halt. He saw Álfar up ahead; he had stopped running.

'Something just… shifted,' the shieldbearer said.

A sucking sound ran along the tunnel walls, like skin being ripped from flesh.

'Keep moving,' Baldr voxed, breaking back into a run, scanning the tunnels around him as he went.

Álfar joined him, and the two of them raced through the narrow, switchback tubes. The second time the shuddering came, there could be no doubt – the flesh-like covering of the walls had come loose. About ten metres ahead, a tumbling mound of translucent skin detached, slipping down like an eyelid drooping.

Álfar fired instantly, punching two holes in the barrier, but the bolts popped harmlessly within the thick curtains of glutinous matter. With a rip and a splurt, the ceiling started to sag. Thick walls on either side of them sucked closed, sealing them off in both directions.

Baldr joined up with Álfar in what space remained. Both of them maglocked bolters and took up blades. Álfar punched his longsword into the quivering bulk ahead, drenching himself in watery pink fluids. Baldr joined him, hacking into the thick blubber and pulling the edges apart. The first cut revealed a brief glimpse of the tunnel beyond, but it was quickly obscured by more folds of glistening fat.

'Grenades,' voxed Baldr, reaching for a krak charge from his belt.

Before he'd had time to prime it, a shattering explosion burst out from behind him, filling the narrow bubble with flying, gore-splattered debris. Baldr was thrown hard to the tunnel's far side, impacting with a wet crack of ceramite against iron. Álfar was hurled further back, his armour charred from the blast.

Baldr struggled to his knees, reaching for his bolter again. One entire side of the tunnel wall had been driven in and stood in a tangled ruin of metal struts. As smoke boiled from the molten ruins, six power armoured figures emerged out of the smog, their eye-lenses glowing pale green.

Álfar was the quickest. With a growl of aggression, he leapt at the lead warrior. He got his longsword up into its face, hacking into the bulbous helm and biting deep. The two of them crunched together, trading hammer-blows that tore shards from their battleplate.

Baldr opened fire, striking one of the intruders and sending him staggering. Then the bolt-rounds came in. Álfar was smashed back against the tunnel walls again, his armour pitted and cracked. Baldr was hit before he could get another shot away. One bolt crunched into his shoulder, spinning him around, then another exploded into his side.

He scrambled away, firing back, keeping the shots low, aiming to topple one of the advancing Traitors. One of his shots must have connected, as he heard a throaty grunt of pain and the wet snap of corrupted ceramite breaking.

That was drowned by a strangled bellow of pain from Álfar – he'd felled his first adversary, but a second had closed him down. The Traitor plunged a power maul into Álfar's bolter-ravaged torso, driving through the armour with an explosive burst of disruptor energy. Álfar fought on, hacking out wildly, but the maul lashed round, striking him in the throat and nearly severing his head entirely.

Baldr charged at the closest enemy, his bolter kicking in his grip, his sword crackling with energy. He lashed out, driving his blade into a pockmarked chest and twisting it. The Traitor collapsed, and more of his shots drove home, fragmenting armour and sending another to his knees.

Then he took a direct hit, this time to the helm, blinding him. Another hit exploded against his breastplate, sending ceramite fragments spinning. He tried to rise, to get another shot away, but a power scythe hit him hard, whistling in at chest height and driving him down onto his back. He felt a heavy boot clamp on his neck, and the agony of a blade-edge pushing through his cracked breastplate. His wrist was stamped down, his sword ripped away from him.

For just an instant, he caught the smeared outline of a Plague Marine helm hovering above him, expressionless and splattered with blood. He saw a power fist clench up, crackling with worm-like energy, and could do nothing to evade it.

'The one,' he heard, filtered through a rust-laced vox-grille.

Then the fist beat down, smashing into his damaged helm, shattering the lenses and pushing the faceplate inwards, and he knew no more.

CHAPTER FOURTEEN

Heimdall's structure shook as the impacts ran along it. Deep inside, confined to the medicae observation cell, Bjargborn could do nothing but listen.

'We're not thralls,' said Aerold, bitterly.

'There's a reason for it,' said Bjargborn.

'We deserve more.'

Bjargborn turned on him. 'Deserve? What are you talking about?'

The rest of the retrieved kaerls sat or lay about them. All ninety-two had been crammed into the same cell, one that had been built to accommodate a little over half that number. There was food, water, medicae supplies, and not much else. Overhead lumens flickered every time the cruiser took a hit.

'We never stopped fighting,' muttered Aerold.

'We didn't.' Bjargborn ripped a piece of reconstituted meat-stick from its packing and chewed. 'Too stupid to do anything else.'

Aerold looked at him darkly. His beard was straggly, his flesh still unwashed since the lifter from Ras Shakeh. They all still bore the mark of the desert on them, and the stink was oppressive.

'Then why don't they let us?' Aerold asked.

'Because they know what happened down there,' said Bjargborn, working his jaw methodically. It felt good to eat proper rations again – the food, at least, had improved. 'So do you.'

Aerold pulled the sleeve of his tunic up to the elbow and brandished his arm. 'See any signs?' he asked. He pulled his collar down and bared his neck. 'Any sores?'

Bjargborn shrugged. 'You'd need a full scan. We were lucky they didn't leave us behind.'

'Lucky.'

'Yes, lucky.' He leaned closer to Aerold, lowering his voice. 'This is a lucky wyrd. Fate smiles on us.'

Aerold didn't look convinced. 'I wish to *fight*. They're short-handed.'

'*You* know you're healthy. I know you are. They don't. They can't. Rest up. When they come for us again, you'll remember this as a good dream.'

Other kaerls looked over at them. Some had the same belligerent expressions as Aerold. They'd taken it hard, being accused of carrying plague after fighting for as long as they had.

Bjargborn glared back at them all. 'You heard me! What are you going to do? Forget your vows?' He shook his head in disgust. 'Remember who you are.'

They turned away again. They were a long way from revolt – they were sons of Fenris, committed by blood and conditioning to fight for the Sky Warriors until death took them. About the only thing that would shake that faith was the idea, even the suggestion, that their loyalty had become somehow questionable.

Whatever he said to the troops to keep them in line, Bjargborn could understand their resentment. Despite himself, a fragment of it burned away inside him. When he'd seen the Grey Hunter emerge from the haze, he'd imagined battle would call again soon, this time alongside the masters.

Instead they had confinement, suspicion, followed no doubt by the gruelling examination of the apothecarion once the void-battle was over.

He ripped another slice of meat from the pack and rolled it up in his fist. The walls of the confinement chamber shuddered again, either from *Heimdall*'s macrocannon batteries firing or from taking another hit.

It would have been better to be out there, manning a gun-station or a tactical console.

That wasn't going to happen. The only choice now was to wait it out, to sit idly until the chance to prove themselves came again.

'A good dream,' he said to himself, and started to eat again.

Gunnlaugur raged at the bio-matter around him. The walls had come sucking in on him just as they had all across the capillary tunnels. His hammer ripped through the screens of flesh, driving them back against the rotten metal substructures that underpinned them. The decking underfoot pulled at his boots, the sluice of fluids ran down his helm. Everything dragged at him, weighing him down, tying up his arms, wrenching him deeper into the fleshy entrails.

'*Fenrys!*' he bellowed, lashing out double-handed. His hammerhead flew wildly, eventually breaking through a final tattered skirt of pulsating blood-vessels. Staggering from released momentum, he burst into the open again, dripping with bloody residue.

A gruesome chamber opened up ahead of him – a stomach-shaped bowl of bile-flecked effluent. The walls themselves were contorted into organic nodes and folds, each one popping with fluids. Further chambers could be glimpsed beyond, each one similarly draped in pulpy bio-residue. Flamers roared in the dark, illuminating the flesh-sheets with flares of crimson.

Others had broken through ahead of him – he saw Fellblade, and Hafloí and Hauki, all hacking at the retreating walls of blubber and torching what remained. More emerged at every moment, crashing through the retreating flesh-piles from a dozen different orifices. The sudden contraction of bio-matter had caught them off-guard, but the application of blade and flame was driving it back with ruthless efficiency.

Njal stalked through the chamber, his huge armour-shell coated in the burned remnants of tunnel-bile. He looked furious.

'Too *slow!*' he thundered at the warriors around him. 'We cut it out, then we *move!*'

Gunnlaugur came up to him. 'Losses?' he asked.

'Three to the xenos-construct, three in here,' Njal snarled, the numbers clearly angering him. 'Six is too many. They're wearing us down.'

Gunnlaugur looked up, to see Ingvar emerged from the next chamber along, his blade-edge still running with semi-cooked phlegm-gobbets. 'Eight, *jarl*,' he reported flatly. 'Baldr is gone, as is Álfar.'

The word *Baldr* hit Gunnlaugur like a blow. For a moment, the news seemed to rock even Njal. The Rune Priest stared back, and in that instant, for all his immense power and bulk, he looked wounded.

Then Njal lifted his head, and drew in a deep, rasping breath. 'Enough. We keep moving.'

Ingvar remained where he was. 'Was he ready, *jarl*?' he asked.

Gunnlaugur couldn't believe it. It seemed the Gyrfalkon had not changed as much as he'd hoped.

Njal turned his red-lensed gaze back to Ingvar slowly, astonished that his decision would be so much as commented on, let alone questioned. Ingvar glared back up at the huge Rune Priest, holding his ground.

'You play with danger, Grey Hunter,' Njal growled, his old, deep voice grating with an instinctual threat-note. 'You are here to fight. Now, *move on.*'

For a moment, Gunnlaugur feared Ingvar would not comply. He could feel the rage emanating from his pack-mate. He knew how hard Ingvar had worked to keep Baldr alive on Ras Shakeh, and how dark and strange his fervour could be.

Then, slowly, Ingvar backed down. 'I recognise my error,' he said, bowing stiffly.

Nightwing, mounted on Njal's shoulder, extended its pinions and screeched out denunciation. Njal turned away from him, shaking his head in disgust. 'There is ironwork ahead,' he said to Gunnlaugur. 'Multiple tunnels, all leading down.'

As he spoke, the rest of the Wolves fell into their pack formations again, clustering in the blood-streaked chamber.

'Then we are getting close,' Njal announced. 'I sense the core. We press deeper.'

Njal shot a brief glance at Ingvar before turning his deathmask helm back to the path ahead.

'And no more delays,' he snarled.

It had been hard for Callia to ensure she remained stationed on *Vindicatus*'s bridge. Since taking on duties as part of the Order of the Fiery Tear, she had been pressurised into assuming a more junior position elsewhere in the warship's lower reaches. Nuriyah didn't trust her, and nor did the other Sisters of the Cardinal's entourage.

Once battle broke out, though, there had been no time to let the issue come to a head, and even Nuriyah could not argue with her combat-rank and experience. In the end, Callia's presence was tolerated on the command level, perhaps out of a lingering sense of unease over what had happened to de Chatelaine, perhaps for more pragmatic reasons.

Once the void-strike had got under way, Callia had glanced up at the huge Penitent Engine as little as possible. The last time she'd walked under its shadow she'd risked a proper look, daring to hope that somewhere amid the gears and pain-nodes and cabling the canoness might still be able to respond to stimuli.

Yet Callia had seen nothing but that frozen scream, hidden under a sheet of pure white linen. De Chatelaine, for all her loyalty and valour, had ceased to exist. What remained was a mechanical thing, a bringer and an endurer of pain.

Delvaux kept the Penitent Engine close to him at all times, perhaps as some kind of trophy. Together with its counterpart, it stood guard behind his throne. Every so often, servitors would shuffle up to the two Engines and apply some sacred oil to their joints or whisper some prayer for the continued shriving of the souls at their hearts.

Callia maintained her distance after that, attending to the many small duties that her position gave her. The plague-hulk loomed on *Vindicatus*'s forward viewers, just as staggeringly vast as ever. The volume of exchanged fire had fallen away sharply since the Cardinal had given the withdrawal order. With the last of the escorts destroyed, *Heimdall* still risked attack runs, but the shared task now was a limited one – keep in watching range, ready for when the Wolves gave the signal to re-engage.

Callia wondered how likely it was that they'd ever receive that signal. She yearned to see it appear on the consoles, vindicating boldness over pragmatism, remembering Gunnlaugur's almost casual bravado towards the task at hand.

She looked over her shoulder, back up towards Delvaux's throne. As her eyes alighted on his corpulent robed form, an involuntary spike of hatred rippled through her, quickly pushed down again.

That is unworthy. He is still the Cardinal.

She walked over to a cluster of navigation stations just below the throne platform. As she did so, she heard Klaive enter the bridge. Huge slide-doors at the rear of the bridge chamber hissed closed, and the confessor padded up to the Cardinal's throne.

Callia lowered her head, making a show of studying the pict screen closest to her, listening carefully.

'Back again,' remarked Delvaux to Klaive, unenthusiastically.

From the corner of her eye, Callia watched Klaive make himself comfortable on the steps leading up to Delvaux's seat. The Engine that had once been de Chatelaine stood silently over him. She could have crushed him with a single stride, if any of her will remained.

'We have had communications,' said Klaive. 'From... Well, you know.'

Callia always found Klaive's tone with Delvaux surprising. It was overfamiliar, not tinged with the fawning attention to precedence that coloured all the others' dealings with the Cardinal. If there was a reason for that, she'd not discovered it yet.

'And?' asked Delvaux.

'They judge the Wolves' ambition overreaches itself. I told them of your proposal. They approved.'

Delvaux pursed his lips, causing his jowls to wobble. 'Did they, then?' He looked out through the forward viewportals. *Heimdall* was just visible, far out into the void, holding station as close to the hulk as it dared. 'But they are not here. I am.'

'Their views are hardly insignificant.'

'Of course not.'

'And there is the question of reputation.'

'So you have often reminded me.'

'Such things are important.'

Delvaux smiled at him coldly. 'Enough. You can save the arguments you came to make. The matter is already decided, so your presence here comes after the event.'

Callia tensed. Klaive raised an eyebrow. They both waited.

'Then you have–' Klaive started.

'What did you think, that I'd let them burrow away until the End Times? This is madness. I have changed my mind.'

Klaive bowed, unusually respectfully. 'You have come to the right decision, lord,' he said. 'Though the Stormcaller...'

'You think I *fear* him?' Delvaux's lips curled in outrage. 'You think I fear the bone-rattler and his entourage? He can howl as much as he likes – it will change nothing.' His cheeks reddened. 'I have given them long enough. The Throne knows I have. Let this be an end to the madness.'

Klaive folded his arms, satisfied. 'Then shall I pass on the order?'

'You do not give the orders. You never have. Just watch, and keep your counsel to yourself.'

Callia turned away, looking back at the pict-feed before her. Already coordinates were scrolling down the lens aperture, updating a matrix of movement vectors for the enginarium to act on.

As she saw them, her heart sank. He was really going to do it.

'Can we still outpace the plague-hulk?' she heard Klaive ask Delvaux.

'Of course. The margins have been calculated.' She heard Delvaux sniff. 'By the time the vessel reaches orbit, the last flames over Kefa Primaris will already have died down.'

'A noble sacrifice,' said Klaive, softly, as if awed by it.

'A necessary one,' said Delvaux.

Callia felt the bridge deck vibrate as the engines powered up. Lights flickered on all across the tactical stations, warning of imminent course change.

Somewhere down below, she knew, the life-eater canisters would be being shunted into torpedo casings. The priests would already be reading benedictions over their deadly cargo.

On another mission, she might have swallowed her unease at that. She had performed many difficult tasks during her service, not least the destruction of plague-bearers on Ras Shakeh, and it was part of her conditioning to obey.

But loyalty worked both ways. She glanced up at the Engines again, seeing de Chatelaine's frozen scream impacted on the linen.

She moved smoothly away from the navigation station, keeping her demeanour natural. Silently, she activated the comm-bead at her collar. Once out of earshot of the throne, she opened the secure channel she'd given Gunnlaugur access to.

'Space Wolf,' she voxed quietly, noting the successful connection. 'I think we need to talk.'

The primary urban cluster on Kefa Primaris was called Kallian Hellax. It contained two billion inhabitants divided between twenty major hive spires and a heavily built-up hinterland of sprawling hab-units and communal manufactory clusters. The city core had existed for seven thousand years, having been added to and augmented dramatically during nine separate expansionary phases.

As big as it was, Hellax was only the largest of many such hive complexes arranged across the planet's temperate zones. No one had ever been able to survey accurately just how many workers lived in the full tally of towers – even the logic engines of the Mechanicus had their limits. However, it could be ascertained with reasonable certainty that the figure ran into the trillions, a factor commensurate with the sizeable levy the planet contributed to the Imperium in both tithes and manpower.

All of these things Olgeir knew due to the databursts sent over by his escorts on their way down through the upper atmosphere. The statistics were impressive enough, but the actual sight of the hyper-cities emerging through the bands of cloud underwrote the cold facts.

Hellax was wreathed in night-shadow. Great spikes of adamantium and rockcrete thrust out from the planet's surface like blades, glittering with electric light and surrounded by a halo of moving aircraft. The entire pattern glowed with activity – furnaces, industrial venting, neon display-patterns on spire-summits, transit-spans carrying closely packed megatrains and bulk cargo streams.

Hlaupnir had been left behind, hanging far above them in a stationary orbit and still flanked by the same void-fighters that had ushered it in from the outer limits. Olgeir now piloted an atmospheric lander down to the landing stages. Thraid had come with him, leaving Hanek in command of the system-runner.

As they plummeted, military aircraft in royal blue livery soared up to meet them, dipping their wings in salute as they approached. The escort operation was slick and well organised, just as their orbital encounter had been once credentials had been established. Kefa Primaris, it seemed, was well governed enough.

'Lord, if it pleases you,' came a pilot's voice over the lander's comm, 'follow the course-markers being sent to your ship's cogitator. The governor has been informed of your arrival and awaits you in her chambers.'

The governor: Praesidia Magisterial Lujia Annarovea, two hundred Terran years old, the Imperial authority on Kefa Primaris for seventy-nine. Olgeir studied the data on his pict screen carefully. It was hard to gauge much from the brief bio-note attached to the planet's propaganda material, but he liked the way she looked in her image – stern, clear-eyed, standing tall in a military uniform of black trimmed with the same royal blue her fighters carried.

'Lead on,' he replied over the comm, easing the lander downwards and following the angled flight of the fighter wing.

The tips of immense spires loomed under him, their outlines luminescent with heavy shielding. Olgeir's lander glided towards a docking platform near the summit of the largest, situated on a narrow rockcrete apron just below a tall copper dome. An imposing Imperial aquila decorated the dome's facing surface, picked out in golden lumens. Rain bounced and whipped across the exposed apron, where an honour guard of sixty Guard troopers in leather greatcoats waited.

The lander touched down, hissing gently as shock absorbers contracted. Thraid activated the door-release mechanism.

'Remain here,' Olgeir told him, extracting himself from the pilot's seat. 'No one touches this vessel, no one moves it.'

Thraid bowed. 'By your will.'

Gull-wing cockpit doors cracked open, easing down on long pistons. Olgeir clanged down the ramp, mag-locking an axe to his armour as he emerged into the elements.

At the end of the twin rows of honour guards, a lone figure waited for him. She looked much as she had done in her pict – silver hair cropped severely short, a thin face, straight shoulders. She wasn't wearing the ceremonial uniform of her calling and carried no aquila devices on her jacket, but was dressed in some kind of long gown of shimmering pearl-silver.

Olgeir walked up to her. 'Governor,' he said.

Annarovea bowed in acknowledgement. 'Lord,' she said. A slight tightening of her jawline gave away her tension. 'This is an unexpected honour.' Olgeir glanced at her gown, and she caught the look. 'You'll forgive the dress. Ceremonial dinner for the One Hundred and Forty-Fifth Regiment Kafjian Lanciers.'

'Sorry to call you away.'

'It wasn't you,' said Annarovea. 'They pulled me out three hours ago to monitor long-range augur signals. Something's inbound. Something worrying. I can only assume your appearance is in connection with it.'

'We need to talk, somewhere secure.'

'I had a chamber prepared as soon as I received notice of your arrival. Please, come with me.'

Her voice was calm and business-like. Olgeir decided he liked this governor.

'That's good,' said Olgeir, walking with Annarovea out of the rain and under the cover of the dome. 'Though I warn you, you're not going to like what I have to say.'

Vuokho powered smoothly under the vast shadow of *Heimdall*'s starboard flank. Jorundur worked the controls, readying the gunship to dock. The two other Thunderhawks, *Grimund* and *Kjarlskar*, had already gone in, their work done and their damage taken.

Jorundur looked out at the cruiser's edge, noting the heavy damage sustained all along the facing hull-line. The flickering void shield coverage looked close to ripping away. Intermittent bursts of las-fire still belched out from the distant plague-hulk to test it, but *Heimdall* had finally pulled out to long range and was spared the full intensity of the vessel's firepower.

'We have clearance?' Jorundur asked, watching the marker lights blink on along *Heimdall*'s hangar edges.

'We do,' said Beor.

Jorundur grunted. He'd hung in the void for as long as possible, reluctant to give up the freedom of his own craft in exchange for the corridors and fire-pits of *Heimdall*. All there was to do on Njal's ship was wait for news or fresh orders, neither of which appealed.

'Then we–' he started, then broke off. The comm-bead Gunnlaugur had given him suddenly signalled an incoming feed.

'Lord, do you wish to make preparations?' asked Beor.

Jorundur waved the question away, feeding the bead's input to his helm system.

'Grey Hunter,' came a message, crackling with distance and interference. 'I think we need to talk.'

Jorundur sat back, surprised. 'Sister,' he replied. 'There are easier ways of getting in touch.'

'None so secure. You need to know this – the Cardinal is making his move.'

'He can't be. We are far from orbit.'

'Klaive convinced him. You need to warn your brothers.'

'*Skíthof.*'

'Be in no doubt, he will do it,' said Callia.

Jorundur quieted the comm and leaned towards Terrag's station. 'Run a scan on *Vindicatus*. Tell me if you detect course change.' Then he reactivated the link. 'Why are you telling me this, Sister?'

There was a static burst – perhaps the germ of a bitter laugh. 'My service is to the Imperium and the Order. One has gone mad. You are what is left of the other.' Her voice lowered. 'He is set on this. It must be stopped.'

Jorundur checked the augur readings on his console. The Cardinal's huge warship still occupied its allotted position, holding a parallel vector to the hulk at a similar distance to *Heimdall*.

'He wouldn't break an oath to the Stormcaller,' he muttered. 'He's not that stupid.'

'It's already happening,' said Callia. 'Once we're under full thrust and out of lance-range, you will not be able to overhaul us.'

Terrag looked up from his station. 'Detecting power build-up in *Vindicatus*'s void drives, lord. It'll be moving soon.'

Jorundur exhaled in disbelief. 'Can you do anything to hold this up?' he asked Callia.

'There's only a few of us left. Nuriyah controls the ship, so it won't be much. If you want to stop this thing, you'll–'

'Yes, yes.' Jorundur balled his gauntlets, assessing options. 'I'll do what I can. Sister, you have...' He swallowed. It was difficult, even then, to force the words out. 'My thanks.'

He cut the link and turned to Terrag again. 'Can you reach Njal?'

Terrag shook his head. 'Not at this range.'

Jorundur smiled thinly. 'Thought not.'

Beor turned to him. 'We're cleared to dock, lord.'

'We're not going in,' said Jorundur, running a careful eye over *Vuokho*'s vital signs. As ever, the gunship looked half ready to fall apart. Every time the thing was patched up, it was sent right back into the warzone.

Just like the rest of us.

'Signal *Heimdall*,' he said, preparing to plot in a new vector. 'Tell them to shadow *Vindicatus* and not let it out of range. Then run a course back for the hulk.'

Beor hesitated. 'The hulk?' he asked.

Jorundur nodded grimly. 'Aye,' he said. 'Njal needs to hear this, so we need to close in again.'

Morven cleared her throat. 'Lord, just so you know, I'm required to inform you that we're in no shape to go back out there.'

'And?'

'Just doing my duty.'

'So you should,' growled Jorundur, pulling the control column round and dipping *Vuokho*'s cockpit below *Heimdall*'s keel. 'Now get ready to do some flying.'

CHAPTER FIFTEEN

Ingvar could feel Gunnlaugur's gaze on him. He kept his head down and ran along the corridor with the rest of them, not wanting to have it out with him now.

Gunnlaugur had other ideas. He caught Ingvar's shoulder, just as they were about to break back into the next intersection.

'What was that?' he hissed.

Ingvar shook off Gunnlaugur's gauntlet. 'Baldr should have remained on the ship,' he said, using Járnhamar's closed channel. 'I know it, you know it.'

'He's gone, brother. We still have the hunt.'

Ingvar knew the truth of that, but it still burned at him. Whatever canker had overtaken Baldr's body and mind had been *beaten*: to see all that progress snuffed out, so soon, filled him with a fury born of both pain and frustration.

An octagonal hub intersection loomed, now populated by the jostling of warriors as they assembled before the push into the core.

'We are shield-brothers,' Ingvar said, angrily, just before crossing the threshold into the chamber.

'You *were*,' growled the Wolf Guard. 'All there is now is vengeance – fix on that.'

Then he pushed past, into the chamber beyond, and Ingvar followed. Njal already stood at the centre of it, his huge battleplate streaked with blood. The Rune Priest was barely lit by the clusters of red helm-lenses glowing around him.

'We are close,' Njal said, turning his head up to the low ceiling, as if sniffing out a scent. 'From now, keep locked on the main energy spike – that is the target. Gunnlaugur, Fellblade – your packs run with me. We will break through the centre. Bloodhame – stay back and hold the core gate. Long-axe – spread wide through the side-tunnels, sow fear in those that come at us.' His severe glare swept back to them. 'They know we are here. Now, more than ever, *keep moving.*'

There were low growls of assent from the assembled warriors. They shook the bile from their weapon-edges, keying themselves up for a plunge deeper into the dark. Just as Njal looked ready to lead them in, a crackle of static burst out across the pack-wide vox.

'Stormcaller,' came Jorundur's voice over the link, thick with white noise and barely audible. 'Do I reach you?'

Njal halted. 'Speak.'

'Signals from *Vindicatus*. The Cardinal has broken his oath. His ship is powering up. Ordering pursuit.'

Njal swore. 'He has moved yet?'

'Still in position. *Heimdall*'s preparing intercept.'

'What is *Heimdall*'s status?'

'Heavy damage. It can fight. Just.'

Njal's whole body bristled with anger. 'Bring him *down*,' he ordered. 'Full sanction.'

'Do you need extraction, lord?' Jorundur asked.

Njal looked torn for a second. If *Heimdall* was drawn too far away or was destroyed, their chances of getting off the hulk were zero. In any case, the Wolves frigate was a poor match for the massive *Vindicatus*, even without the extra damage it had taken.

'Negative,' he snarled. 'We are finishing this.'

'Understood,' came Jorundur's reply. 'The Hand of Russ be with you.' Then the feed crackled out.

'This thing is not over,' snarled Njal, turning back to the packs. His staff flickered with slithers of lightning, as if his own rage were spilling out of the dark shaft. 'We will *destroy* this place. We will tear it apart from the inside and cast the fragments to the void. *Then* we will destroy the oathbreaker. He cannot run forever.' He lowered his staff tip towards the archway, and the skull-head burst into flame. 'The hunt must be completed.'

With Njal at their head, the packs loped into the dark, pelts swirling, heads low.

Ingvar, though, held back.

'Brother,' warned Gunnlaugur wearily, seeing the hesitation. 'No more of this.'

'We can't let him go,' Ingvar said.

'What do you mean?'

'Klaive is on that ship. We lose him now, the scent dies.'

'*Now?*'

Ingvar backed away, inching towards the chamber exit. 'There is still time. Jorundur is in close. I can get to him.'

'They will tear you apart.'

The last of the hunting packs slipped into the tunnels, leaving Gunnlaugur and Ingvar alone.

'We have to do this,' said Ingvar. 'You know why.'

For a heartbeat, Ingvar thought the Wolf Guard would reach for his thunder hammer and drag him to heel. Gunnlaugur, though, did not move.

'Njal will not forgive,' the Wolf Guard said.

'You lead the pack, not him,' said Ingvar. 'You asked for a name. Klaive can give us one.'

Gunnlaugur remained poised to strike – poised to haul him away and shove him back into the fray. Then, slowly, he relaxed. The need for vengeance had never been questioned, only the means of obtaining it. 'You are actually serious,' he said.

'Njal will need you,' urged Ingvar. 'Hafloí, too. But let me go.'

The distant roar of battle echoed up from the tunnels ahead, growing in volume, capped by the stark bellow of Njal's kill-rage. Gunnlaugur's helm twisted away, angled towards the battlefront, over to where he belonged.

He glanced back at Ingvar. 'Go, then,' he said. 'Hunt him.'

Ingvar bowed. '*Vaerangi*, I will not forget.'

'*Succeed*. That is all.'

Gunnlaugur clamped his fist against his breastplate in salute, then followed the rest of the pack down into the darkness. As he ran down into the tunnel, he unlocked his hammer, its head kindling with energy as he disappeared into the endless shadow.

With Gunnlaugur's passing, Ingvar felt a final spasm of doubt – a flicker, as ephemeral as the curls of lightning running across the Stormcaller's staff. There would be no way back from this, nor forgiveness for it.

This will damn me.

He drew his sword. Its edge glowed keenly in the dark.

So be it.

He broke into a run of his own, heading the other way. Already he could hear fresh movement in the cloying dark – remnants of the hordes they'd battled through, coming together for the lone, mad soul they could sense heading back towards them.

'Old Dog,' Ingvar voxed. 'In range?'

Another hiss of static, then the link burst back into fractured life. 'Gyrfalkon?' came Jorundur's irritated voice. 'Not for long. We are being flayed out here.'

'Hold position,' said Ingvar, picking up his pace. 'Lock on to my signal – I am coming out.'

'*Skítja*. Coming *out*? You know what you're asking?'

Ingvar's helm-lenses were already giving him targets – runes in the dark, zeroing in on hunched shapes in the shadows. He didn't break stride.

'Surely, brother,' he said, picking up speed, angling *dausvjer* for the first strike. 'This is but the start.'

The Cardinal hunched in his throne. He had an almost unbearable urge to gnaw on his fingernails. The habit had been with him ever since infancy, and even after so long occupying the high offices of his order, it had never quite been banished.

There were many other things that ought to have been banished. He should have put aside his appetites for food and drink, for the pleasures of his sensor-shielded bedchambers, for the daily influx of narcotics that stimulated his nerves and dulled his mind. All these things should have been limited, freeing up the time for him to do what his followers expected of him – to be a *leader*. A prophet. A Prince of the Church.

The problem was, of course, that since rising to the highest offices of the Ministorum there had been no external pressures on his conduct. None of his retinue would dare to so much as query any foible, much less question an order. He could click his bejewelled fingers and Nuriyah would bring him a fresh platter of cortex-snuff, or a salver of hydroponic-grown grapes, or a handsome slave fresh off the tithe-shuttles. She would never say a word. Ever.

Who, save a saint, could have resisted that kind of indulgence for long? But that, of course, was the point. He was supposed to *be* a saint, or something like one. His billions of followers revered him as such, fed by a ceaseless propaganda missionaria and desperate for hope in a darkening galaxy.

He had told himself for so long now that the reform would come soon – that he would cast off the ephemeral trappings of luxury. He would undertake penance. The petty flashes of vindictiveness would cease, and he would lead a *real* crusade. In the higher echelons of the Ministorum there were, he knew, voices raised against him. Stories of excess had filtered their way back to Terra and Ophelia VII. He needed to prove himself. He needed a grand gesture, something to still those wagging tongues.

His mournful gaze flickered up to the great crystal viewscreen. The planet was out there somewhere ahead, unsuspecting, unprotected.

It was a high price to pay to restore his position, but there were other justifications, ones that the Wolves would never accept. Klaive had always been right – even the *risk* of letting the world fall to the Ruinous Powers was not worth entertaining.

So it was not all about him, not just about his faltering vocation. There were reasons. Good ones.

He sniffed. The temptation to chew on his nails became overwhelming. 'Lord Cardinal.'

Delvaux stirred out his reverie. Harryat, *Vindicatus*'s bridge-captain, stood at the base of the throne's dais, bowing. He was a broad-chested, square-jawed man in a trim crimson uniform – the best of the Ecclesiarchy's officer cadre.

'What is it, captain?' asked Delvaux, placing both hands in his lap and curling them into fists.

'Communication from *Heimdall*. They're asking for confirmation that we intend to hold position.'

Delvaux felt a twinge of panic. *So quick. How do they know?*

'How soon before we're ready to move off?' he asked.

'The engines took some damage,' said Harryat. 'We're working on restoring full power. It will not be long. An hour, no more.'

Delvaux drew in a frustrated breath. 'An hour is not good enough. I gave the order. I expect it to be complied with.'

Harryat didn't flinch. Unlike most of the others, he could look Delvaux in the eye while giving bad news. 'If we ignite the main drives now for a full burn, the damage will be permanent. The work can be done swiftly – I have three hundred crew working on it.'

'Thirty minutes,' said Delvaux. 'That is all I will give you.'

Harryat looked like he was going to protest, but then his gaze shifted up to the two Penitent Engines standing behind Delvaux's throne, and he changed his mind. 'We will do what we can,' he said.

'No, captain,' said Delvaux, fixing him with a heavy stare. 'You will do what I tell you. In thirty minutes this ship will be headed for Kefa Primaris, at full burn.'

'And the Wolves?'

'Tell them the agreement stands. Tell them they've detected rogue energy spikes while we repair the main power system.' Delvaux rolled his eyes. 'Love of the Throne, tell them whatever you want – just keep them quiet. They should be concentrating their efforts on the hulk.'

Harryat nodded brusquely, but for an instant his face gave away a flash of what he really thought.

He wishes to stay, to fight alongside them.

'And do not forget, captain,' said Delvaux, his voice darkening, 'where your loyalty lies. The beasts can howl at shadows all they wish, but our task is the safeguarding of souls from corruption. Better to die in the flames than succumb to damnation, is that not so?'

Harryat drew in a curt breath. 'It is just as you say, my lord.'

'Now go,' said Delvaux, dismissing him with a wave, 'and do not return until you have given me what I need to destroy that world.'

Baldr's eyes flickered open. He tensed immediately, going for his weapon, but his limbs did not obey him. He tried to move, to struggle against whatever force held him in place, but he remained stubbornly immobile.

His mind felt cloudy. Pain – hard, unyielding – throbbed all over him. Sluggishly, he realised that he was not wearing his helm. The rest of his armour was intact, but he was breathing the unfiltered air of the hulk's interior. It was foul, like ingesting faeces, and he felt the gag-reflex at the back of his throat kick in.

The space around him was jet-black and as hot as blood. Without the aid of his helm-lenses, it took a while for his eyes to adjust – even his occulobe-enhanced optics struggled without any kind of light source to latch on to.

He blinked heavily, staring out into the utter blackness. He made out the faintest hint of darker edges in the gloom. The sound of something gurgling thickly echoed close by. He tried to move again, pushing hard against his bonds, and failed.

Then, a long way ahead of him, a soft green light bled out of the darkness. It was the first chance Baldr had to orientate himself – he was upright, suspended less than a metre above the floor of some narrow, low-roofed chamber. His arms and legs appeared to have been absorbed into the walls around him – thick knots of organic material clamped him in place, twisting over his body like tree roots.

The light continued to grow. The floor was illuminated by its creeping progress, exposing fungoid nodules clustered tightly together. They thronged like a carpet of spores, thick and bulbous, glistening faintly as the crepuscular light-shafts slipped through the murk. Long, stringy tendrils hung in loops from vaults above, each one swollen with trembling pustules.

Baldr tensed his arms, pushing against the bonds that held him in place. Whatever the roots were made of, they were incredibly strong – he forced one of them to flex, just by a few millimetres, before having to relax his muscles again in exhaustion.

By then, the greenish tinge had sunk across the whole chamber. A shadowy figure clarified at its far end, slowly hobbling. Baldr heard wheezing breath. He smelt a fustiness, like long-mouldered bread. He saw cloven hooves treading down the fungus, sinking into the deep layer of milky softness underfoot.

Slowly, the outline of a Plague Marine appeared. Unlike any uncorrupted Adeptus Astartes, he hunched over almost double. His shoulders bulged with growths. His ancient armour, pitted with jagged holes, hung from a warped frame, and flesh as pale and grey as Baldr's own livery protruded from the gaps.

The Plague Marine carried a staff – a gnarled thing, knotted like a vine. The green light came from a hollowed-out human skull at its tip. The creature's own head was helmless and withered. Vaguely human features competed with knots of tumours. Two deep-set, heavy-lined eyes looked up rheumily at Baldr.

'Welcome, Son of the Wolf King,' said the creature.

The voice was quiet, and old. There was a kindness to it, as if the speaker knew what suffering had been caused to bring him there and regretted it. Nothing about that voice suggested the speaker had once been a Space Marine, and yet the armour was there to prove it – dull grey-green, still bearing the forbidden marks of Mortarion's old Legion under a thick layer of rust and dirt.

Baldr felt the ancient hatreds kindle quickly. It was automatic, primed by a lifetime of *gothi* warnings and augmented by decades of psycho-conditioning.

Traitor.

Baldr bared his fangs instinctively. The hunched Plague Marine moved close enough, so he spat, tasting acid on his curved teeth as he sent it into the grey-skinned face before him.

The spittle sprayed across the Plague Marine, fizzing as it impacted. The stooped figure wiped it away with a hooked, arthritic finger. He sucked on the fingertip, musingly.

'A long time,' he muttered. 'A long time since one of you got close enough to spit.'

Baldr raged again at his bonds, straining to get a weapon-hand free.

'Rest,' the Plague Marine urged. 'Please. You will only damage yourself. Do you think we would have placed you in bonds you could break?'

Baldr's amber eyes narrowed. 'Know this,' he snarled. 'I will die before I give you anything you value.'

'No doubt you would, if that were an option.' The creature smiled sadly. His voice remained soft, almost melodically so. Two moist eyes shone in the dark, peering out from a ruined, sepulchral face. 'But I do not wish to hurt you, Space Wolf. On the contrary.'

Baldr's eyes roved across his surroundings, looking for something – anything – that he might use to extricate himself. There were always features of an environment that could be used. The Archenemy were powerful, but also capricious, and their desire to prolong agony rather than go for the swift kill was a weakness he had used before.

'What are you?' Baldr asked.

The Plague Marine raised a scab-covered eyebrow. 'That is a question,' he wheezed. He limped over to a natural outgrowth in the chamber's walls – a rock shelf in a fungus-filled grotto – and painfully sat down. The experience of watching him move was unsettling, for he carried himself like a decrepit old man, his breath rattling, his hands shaking. After seating himself, he slumped, letting the curve of his spine drag his head down even further. He kept hold of the skull-staff, though.

'What answer would satisfy you?' he asked. 'You would not believe much that I tell you. It will all be the truth, of course. Those of my Legion rarely tell lies. An old habit. We left the lying to others.' He chuckled dryly. 'What use is a lie? It gains you a little advantage, but this is the Eternal War, and eternals have no use for little advantages.'

Without meaning to, Baldr found himself listening, and cursed himself inwardly. The Plague Marine's voice remained quiet, almost tremulous. There was no threat in it at all – no bombast, no defiance. It wasn't even resigned.

'My name was Jeshua Ben Gur. I was born ten thousand, two hundred and sixty-nine years ago, by the reckoning of Terra. I grew up in sight of the Imperial Palace. That is more than you can boast, scion of the ice. I do not remember much of it, though – they took me for the Legion when I was eight, even before the primarch had been found. Younger than you were when they came for you, I expect.' He drew in a tremulous breath. 'I recall golden spires. I never saw them again, not even when the Siege came and we ran at the Gates in a world of fire. Sometimes I dream of those spires, and those flames. I no longer know if my memory of them is even reliable. Who knows? They are long gone now, and there is no going back to check.'

He coughed, bringing up a lumpy gobbet of phlegm. He spat it out and it landed, bloodily, on the chamber floor.

'After that I was called many things. I have lived a long time. Not, of course, for ten thousand years – the Eye melds time in strange ways – but long enough. When Calas brought the change with him, I changed too. I learned new things and forgot old ones. I learned that every situation brings its opportunities. I became a *gardener*. Do you believe that? A cultivator of forgotten things. I discovered that some lives will flourish in the dark. Some harbour their own light, inside themselves, cradled in phosphor, needing no sun or starlight to warm them.'

Baldr couldn't stop listening. A warning voice in his head screamed at him to plug his ears, to recite some litany against corruption, but he was unable to comply. He felt his muscles relax in their bonds. Even his wounds, which had been angrily painful, felt numb.

'There are organisms that thrive on decay, Son of Russ. There are creatures that lap up the matter of the dying and transform it to sustain themselves. Do they have no place in the galaxy? Do they have no beauty of their own?'

He chuckled sadly. 'They need their champions, too. It cannot all be ice and iron, talon and tooth.'

The Traitor looked up directly at Baldr, and the light from the staff fell across his face. His skin was impossibly lined, like a reptile. Glossy sores bunched around dry lips, swollen with dark blood.

'The name I took in the Garden was the Mycelite. I lived for a long time there. I sat at the feet of the caged goddess and listened to her weeping. That taught me pity. I determined that striving against the inevitable was a peculiar kind of cruelty. It has to be ended. The War, everything, the whole meandering story – it has to be ended. And it will be, thankfully. It has started at last, and the whole carnival will finally pass into the long night again. Everything – all the striving, all the contests, they'll all slide away. It'll start at Cadia – you know that? The threads are pulling together there.'

The Mycelite's speech flitted from subject to subject, but as Baldr listened to the sibilant tones in the warm dark, he felt as if there were some truth there, ready to be grasped if only he could glimpse it. Nothing he heard made him angry any more – only curious.

'Is that why you are here?' Baldr asked, surprising himself as he heard the words leave his mouth.

The Mycelite shook his head. Every gesture he made had a kind of sorrowful benevolence to it, like a weary grandfather gently correcting the errors of a wayward protégé.

'Matters have gone awry,' he said. 'You responded swiftly, and your Rune Priest already burns his way towards the heart of my kingdom. Perhaps he will halt my spores landing, perhaps not. I have sent my servants to hinder him, but it no longer much matters to me, truth be told. The Traveller will be here soon, and then the tide will be rising faster than even your rune-witches can handle.'

He got to his feet once more, leaning heavily on the staff. Rasping from the effort, he limped up to Baldr again.

'But surprises can still be found – flowers amid the filth. That is another thing I learned.'

The Mycelite extended a withered hand and ran it down Baldr's cheek – gently, like a caress.

'*You* are here,' he breathed, as tenderly as a father. 'And, amid all the ruin, I could not have asked for more than that.'

For a long time, Hafloí had doubted the sagas recounted by the Grey Hunters around the fire-pits. He had fought well with his old pack of Blood Claws, charging recklessly into the oncoming storm alongside his battle-brothers, whooping and howling as his bolt pistol kicked and his axe whirled. He'd existed for nothing else. Combat had been a rush, thumping in his temples, fuelling the white-hot furnace at his warrior's core. His brothers had all been the same – flame-haired, hot-blooded, short-fanged and short-tempered.

They were called Blood Claws for a reason. At times, it seemed that his gauntlets were never free of it. He revelled in the killing, each time testing himself a little further, seeing just how far he could push the immense gifts he had been given. There was nothing finer, nothing purer – to be young, and vital, and given the power of a demigod to use in the cause of humanity.

The summons to leave that existence and join Járnhamar had been a shock, and an unwelcome one. Packs of young bloods were expected to fight together, to grow older and tougher together until their locks greyed and their fangs curved. After taking the Helix, that is what he'd been told would happen.

'You will be shield-brothers until death takes you,' the old Wolf Priest, Aesde, had told him, his ancient yellow eyes glowing in the firelight of the Aett. 'Mark the names. They shall stand with you at the End Times when fire consumes the galaxy and Russ comes again.'

It had been difficult to leave after that – to be joined to an older, colder band of brothers. Grey Hunters were tempered and harrowed by time. Each one of them had been beaten into something tougher and harder, and the flames within them had shrunk with it. From the beginning, they had looked down on him, and he had looked down on them. The two of them might as well have been different breeds.

If times had not been so straitened, if the entire Chapter were not stretched as thin as throttle-cord by the Long War, then it would never have happened. Ragnar had told him as much when he'd delivered the order. He'd done it in person, at least. That ought to have been a rare honour, but the tidings were too bad for him to see it.

'Everything is changing,' Ragnar had said, back on Fenris. 'The old order is eroding. You will have to learn faster than those you leave. Your new pack will test you, and you will rage against them.' Ragnar had gazed down at him impassively, giving nothing away. 'But you can learn from this. If you weather the storm, you will rise even faster than I did.' A wary smile. 'And I never fought as a Hunter. So we are both misfits.'

At the time, Hafloí had listened in silence, part awed by the Wolf Lord standing before him, part sullen from the news. Now he saw what Ragnar had been trying to tell him. If he had not been so thick-headed, so stuffed with rage and kill-urge, he might have appreciated it at the time.

Járnhamar fought so differently. Each one of them, taken individually, was far stronger than him – far wilier, far more experienced and far more adaptable. He'd seen it on Ras Shakeh, on the plague destroyer, and now within the hulk itself. For all he'd boasted of his Traitor kill on Hjec Aleja, he'd always known he needed to overachieve just to keep up with his taciturn, grim-faced brothers. He could boast, and they would indulge him, but every one of his new brothers had kill-tallies far in excess of his.

So it was that, as Hafloí sprinted through the arteries of horror in the depths of the plague-hulk, his breathing was ragged, his heart-rate was dangerously high, and his muscles were shrieking with pain. The packs had been fighting non-stop for hours, lost in the swirling hordes of mutated enemy soldiers. Since the passage of the bridge, they had been attacked constantly. The mutants never stopped coming. At times they burst from the walls like larvae from pupae, scattering into the open with embryonic fluids still trailing from their diseased flesh. There was never room to properly *fight*, only to hack and kick and claw them back into submission before treading their remains into the knee-thick filth.

Throughout, the Hunters around him fought on with undiminished fervour. Their endurance was phenomenal. Hafloí stayed close to Gunnlaugur for most of the descent, and for the first time he truly saw what it took to become *vaerangi*. The Wolf Guard hewed with undiminished heft and purpose, roaring out his defiance even as the air around him hummed with heat and hatred. The raw fires of the underworld could have rippled across him and he would have shouldered them aside. He was immense – unbowed, furious, unstoppable.

The rest of the pack-brothers were scarcely less formidable. They entered combat low and fast, swinging and pivoting to bring their blades to bear. They smashed heads, ripped open torsos, punched through spines. Even before their fists had stopped moving they were pouncing onto their next prey. Their armour ran with trails of gore, slapping around them like flails as they moved.

Hafloí laboured to keep up. He drove his axe with as much speed as his burning arms could muster. He fired his bolt pistol into the dark as accurately as his mind would allow. He leapt to the aid of his brothers on the rare occasions when their guard was broken, just as they kept watch over him when his judgement faltered.

Once, during the long, horrific fight down from the hub towards the hulk's core, he'd spotted the desperate lunge of an eyeless terror as it pounced towards one of Fellblade's pack. Hafloí got to it first, sending it tumbling with a pistol-shot before eviscerating it with two crosswise swipes of his axe.

The warrior he'd saved, a grizzled old fighter named Eir, nodded at him, once, before loping off after fresh prey.

By then Hafloí was sprinting again, never resting, always heading further down. The bodies of his battle-brothers loomed around him in the dark. He could smell their acrid hunt-scent – sweat, armour-coolant, the sharp tang of overloaded disruptor fields. The humidity was incredible, bearing down on him like a vice.

You will have to learn faster.

His breath became rapid. His vision clouded at the edges. His axe strikes became erratic from weariness, but still he kept his feet, maintained the pace, ran with his brothers in the very maws of Hel. All that was left was to *keep going*.

'Maintain speed,' came Njal's vox-command again from up ahead, somewhere in the clogged mass of twisting tunnels. 'The core approaches.'

Hafloí kept his head down and his legs pumping hard. A bloated mutant swung down at him from the sagging tunnel ceiling and he lashed out with his axe, severing it diagonally. Another loomed up out of the murk from the left, grasping at his waist with tentacled arms, and he sent a lone bolt-round into its scabrous torso.

Down they ran, further down, and the environment became even more febrile. Echoing screams ran up the tunnels, the sound of whole crowds of blood-maddened damned roaring up to meet them.

When the break came, when they burst through into the open once more, Hafloí barely noticed the change. The shrieks echoed differently, but for a few moments nothing else altered – it remained corpse-dark, fever-hot and stinking.

Then Njal's staff lit up. Hafloí saw that they had charged into a vast space again. Actinic light lashed up into the void, rebounding from soaring walls of iron. As the storm-lightning kindled, green-tinged flames thundered into life ahead of them, surging out from deep pits in the floor.

For a fraction of a second before his conditioning kicked in, Hafloí didn't exhale. The sheer scale of it was hard to get a grip on. Ranks of obsidian columns soared into the high roof. The pits between the walkways boiled and seethed with unholy fires, sending smoke roiling up in thick pillars. At the far end of the chamber, half lost in a miasma of drifting soot, was the target – the impossibly huge engines that powered the entire hulk. Each one was cast in bronze and iron, towering up in terraces of twisted pipework and organ-like heat exchangers. Dull red flames growled away behind thick metal grilles the size of Reaver-class Titans. Colossal, eyeless, multi-limbed statues stood sentry about the drive units, hewn from granite and depicting obese and foul deities of ruin.

Huge arcs of energy snapped and snaked across the surface of the enginarium chambers, briefly throwing flares of putrid green light across the fiery shafts. Enormous wheels turned slowly in the depths, driven by linked-iron chains and shackled to hab-sized gearing mechanisms of beaten adamantium.

Every surface glistened with corruption. Every metal component was thick with rust, and every exhaust vent belched toxic sludge. The whole edifice looked liable to collapse in on itself at any moment, driven apart by the incomprehensible levels of power thrumming through its cancerous structure.

In that split-second moment, just as he looked up at the full extent of the drive chamber, Hafloí realised for the first time just how potent its destruction would be. His armour-readings of the power contained in the coils and fusion chambers were off the scale – if its shell could be cracked, the blast would be world-endingly huge.

But the enemy knew it, too, and had pulled all of its strength back towards the ship's ancient heart. The space between the Wolves and the engine gates swarmed with legions of mutants. Among them strode greater horrors – figures twice the height of a mortal man with clawed fists and elongated, muscle-bunched arms. Demented vermin scuttled and shrieked across every surface, their eyes shining in the fire-flecked dark. Traitor tech-priests stalked among the hosts, their tattered robes exposing bizarre biomechanics of contaminated flesh and bolted augmetics.

But beyond them all, by far the most potent of all the terror troops assembled in that cathedral of ruin, were the Traitor Marines. Their armour swelled and cracked as they stood sentinel, massive and unmoving, under the engine gates themselves. They carried power scythes and snub-nosed boltguns. Some wore armour from forgotten ages, with angular vox-grilles and heavy ceramite plating. Others stood in Mark VI or VII variants plundered from more recent campaigns, slung with skulls and surmounted by blunt spikes. In every case, their helm-lenses glowed pale green, glimmering spectrally as the hordes of Chaos howled before them.

They would wait there. They would let the filth before them absorb the brunt of the attack before taking the field themselves. Only when the packs had waded through the deranged masses at their feet would the scythes be taken up. Then the real test would come – equally matched, equally potent, each driven by an equal hatred nurtured over ten thousand years of endless war.

Hafloí wasn't blind to the extent of the test. All things being equal, this chamber would see the death of all of them. Even the fury of the massed packs had little chance of penetrating such deep and eternal corruption.

But things were not equal. One factor tipped the balance.

Njal strode into the open, his outline already shimmering with storm-energies. His heavy Terminator tread cracked against the stone, his staff lifted high. Lightning spilled from the runes on his battleplate, fierce and eye-watering. A chill, steel-hard wave of intimidation radiated out from him, as pitiless as Helwinter. When facing the xenos-construct his rage had been wild and free, the exuberance of the hunter. Now, with the deaths of Álfar and Baldr, it had become a thing of pure, distilled hatred, and even Hafloí was taken aback by its intensity.

'*Heidur Rus!*' roared Njal Stormcaller, summoning the storm-wind once more. His cloak snapped and billowed, and silver forks of lightning blazed from his staff's tip. His runes flared, and he stood, inviolate and immense, a pure shard of defiance against the limitless nightmarish hordes.

'*Gothi!*' the Wolves roared in unison, thrusting their blades high into the flame-edged dark. '*Stormurstjórn!*'

Hafloí roared his soul out with them, forgetting fatigue, revelling in the raw potency of the battle-challenge. Flames flared up again, greater than before, rippling like walls of plasma. The mutated denizens of the engine core yelled and bawled their defiance, and surged across the cavern floor towards the thin line of steel-grey. The Wolves thundered out raw death-oaths, levelling their axes just as the tribes of the iron seas had done since the age of legend, choosing those whom they would slay in the name of the Stormcaller, the Allfather and the Wolf King.

Then they charged.

CHAPTER SIXTEEN

'We have ships. They are already prepared for launch. Let us fight it.'

Annarovea's tone was defiant. She sat in a high-backed chair at the head of a long table. The walls of the narrow room around her were black and glossy. The table was black. The floor was black. Every surface reflected dully from the few low-power sodium lamps set into the ceiling.

Olgeir faced her at the opposite end of the table. Annarovea's staff sat along both sides: General Galx Favel, the commander of the Joint Guard Regiments; Marshal Brejial Hagh, controller of the orbital defence forces; Lord Commissar Selucius Morfol; Hamoda al-Yeshiv, Mistress of Astropaths; Salvia Verdello, Senior Judge of the Adeptus Arbites.

They had all had their say, and had all voiced similar sentiments. Hagh estimated he could have twelve of the planet's void-fighter wings out of their orbital hangars within ten minutes. Eight more wings could be called from reserve within three hours. Favel judged he could mobilise six armoured divisions for the main spire zone, thirteen more for the rest of the planet's urban territories. They could, he claimed, hold out for weeks. Morfol agreed – Kefa Primaris was a well-defended world, a linchpin system: it had reserves, munitions, supplies. It had raised nine Guard regiments, six of which had garrisons in-system.

Olgeir admired the sentiments. As the mortals spoke, he tried not to show impatience, even though the chrono in his armour-collar kept ticking down steadily. If he had been in their position, he would have argued the same way. They were cogent, measured, defiant.

'You have heard all this, lord,' concluded Annarovea. 'Only hours remain. We must give the order now.'

Olgeir still liked her.

'No order will be given,' Olgeir said. 'You're getting off the planet. Guard only, no civilians. You can't defend against this. As many as you can, all into deep void.'

His words stunned the chamber into silence. Commissar Morfol, who had welcomed Olgeir effusively on arrival as a fellow zealot for combat, looked as if he'd been kicked in the stomach.

Annarovea's jawline dropped a little, only to be swiftly clamped shut again. 'Is this some jest, lord?' she asked.

Olgeir shook his head. 'I wouldn't insult you.' He leaned forwards, resting his arms heavily on the tabletop. 'You can't stop it. Line battle cruisers would not stop it now. It'll make orbit whether you launch your fighters or not. It's already mauled ships with more firepower than your entire defence grid. Once it comes into range, it'll launch contagion spores. Millions of them. You'll take a hundred out, but when the rest hit, they'll burn through your cities. A few of you will be able to take refuge, the rest will be infected. They'll begin to change. They'll look sick, but they'll be far stronger than your best warriors. They'll overrun every defence-line you have. They'll keep coming. You'll empty ammo-dumps at them, and they'll keep coming. Your own troops will begin to change. You won't be able to kill them fast enough.'

Olgeir looked at Favel. 'Hold out for weeks? Not against this. You'll have a few days. Once the spores are in the atmosphere, it's over. The infected don't die. They'll take any voidcraft you have and they'll launch for other worlds. More plague-ships will come here once your defences are down and they'll pick up more. The army will swell, getting bigger with every conquest. This place will be the source, then. It'll be the *incubator*.'

He returned his gaze to Annarovea.

'You wish to serve?' he asked. 'Get off-world. Every battalion you can pull out of the system is another battalion that will fight again. That's the truth, governor. There are no other choices now.'

For a moment, no one spoke. The lamps burned away in their brackets; the air-filters hummed behind mesh grilles. Olgeir remained where he was, letting the news sink in. It was a strange thing, being a diplomat rather than a killer. In other circumstances he might have enjoyed the challenge. As it was, the words he was forced to speak made him feel hollow.

Morfol was the first to respond. 'I had *dreamed* of meeting one of you,' the commissar said, holding his emotion in with difficulty. 'And now, you come here, and tell us...' His voice trembled with fervour. 'We have ships. Guns, fighters. What kind of... *cowardice* is it that–'

'Enough, Morfol.' Annarovea's voice – calm but steely – cut him dead. Her cool grey eyes remained fixed on Olgeir's, as if trying to work out whether he was some kind of horrific fraud. 'This cannot be right, my lord. We have the resources of an entire world ready to deploy. There must be something we can do.'

'Nothing you have would get close to it,' said Olgeir, flatly. As he spoke, he felt a dull ache run through his body. Morfol was right – it felt like betrayal. 'This thing is no ordinary ship. Such vessels leave the warp once in a thousand years, and even a full Navy battle-group would struggle to halt it. It is your misfortune that it came here, but something can yet be saved. There will be other battles, and your guns will be needed for those.'

Annarovea's eyes never left his. Her defiance slowly gave way to understanding. She took it in, absorbing the bitter truth.

'Is there nothing, then?' she asked.

'My brothers have already boarded it,' Olgeir said. 'They fight towards its heart. A Rune Priest is with them, as well as more than thirty warriors of my order. That is the last hope for this world. They will kill it or they will die in the attempt.'

Hagh perked up immediately – before that, he had been slumped in a kind of mute state of denial. 'Then it is not all lost,' he said.

Olgeir made no mention of Delvaux. There was no reason to – it would not help their resolve to know that if the Wolves failed to destroy the hulk then the Ecclesiarchy stood ready to immolate the planet instead.

'Not yet,' Olgeir said. 'But it will be soon.' He flexed his gauntlets, ruefully wishing they clutched at an axe-shaft rather than air. 'So, then. This is the situation. We need to stop talking, and you need to start moving. I have your word of command?'

The disillusionment in Annarovea's face was still heavy. A lesser soul might have been crushed by it. Slowly, though, the hardness of her features reasserted itself.

'If there is no other way,' she said slowly, sitting erect in her chair, her back straight in defeat, 'then there is no time to lose.'

She turned to her staff.

'Begin the evacuation.'

Jorundur had flown gunships for longer than most mortals had been alive. He felt their every tremor, their every yaw and shudder, and knew just what they meant. At times he could almost imagine the machine-spirits whispering in his ear, summoned up from the coils and logic-boards buried deep in the sacred heart of the vessels.

To fly a Thunderhawk was a privilege and a joy – the only true joy he felt any more. The heavy vibration of the engines thundering away at full blast, the immense power of the main cannon, the surprising manoeuvrability of such a huge and cumbersome object – they were the things that stirred his withered soul.

To take such a thing into the edge of annihilation, then, was a test of nerve. He held no fear for himself, nor for the mortals around him who struggled stoically to keep the machine in one piece. His fear was reserved for the thing of beauty that would depart the universe forever should the near-infinite gunnery of the plague-hulk catch up with it.

His rage at Hafloí for nearly destroying it on Ras Shakeh had not been feigned. To see it cut apart by the guns of some plague-addled star-behemoth would infuriate him far more than the likely prospect of his own demise.

'Are you getting him yet?' he snapped, pulling *Vuokho* out of a steep plummet, just in time to evade a ship-killing brace of las-beams.

The hulk's impossibly gigantic hull soared away from them, a cliff-edge in space, scarred and tangled with the patina of the warp. *Vuokho* danced and shot across the ruinous vista, darting among the lines of incoming fire. There was no point in firing back – nothing the gunship carried would so much as scratch the hulk's surface. All they had to keep them alive was speed and guile.

'Negative,' said Beor. The faintest note of accusation hung in his voice. The attempt was becoming more than suicidal, and even the loyalty of Fenrisian kaerls had its limits.

'Coming round again,' said Jorundur, working the controls as deftly as he'd ever done. Projectiles and energy-lines shot silently past the gunship as it corkscrewed and thrust. So far they'd only taken glancing hits. That couldn't last.

'If we maintain course–' began Terrag.

'We'll run into those macrocannons,' finished Jorundur, well aware of the make-up of the hulk's nearside weapon arrays. 'Keep monitoring for signals. We can give it one more pass.'

As he pushed the Thunderhawk's tortured frame harder and faster, he glanced at the close augur readings. *Heimdall* was already crawling towards *Vindicatus*, but slowly. The frigate looked badly mauled, and its engines were bleeding into the void. On its own it wouldn't last much longer against *Vindicatus* than *Vuokho* would against the *Festerax*. The Cardinal's flagship was still stationary, but its main drives were demonstrably keying up. Time was fast running out.

Jorundur coaxed an iota more power from *Vuokho*'s straining drive-train, sending the gunship skimming across the face of the plague-hulk. More fire scythed in at them, launched from the hundreds of emplacements embedded in the *Festerax*'s grotesque underbelly.

Jorundur checked back out of a dive, rolled hard, and pushed up towards the hulk's nearest stalactitic vane before shoving mercilessly down back into the void. The gunship's structure cracked and shrieked, causing red warning runes to flood across the cockpit consoles like bloodstreams.

We are the prey here. An unfamiliar sensation.

'Are you getting anything?' he demanded again, working the control columns hard.

'Nothing,' reported Beor flatly.

Jorundur cursed, and prepared for another hard dive.

Just as he did so, something hit *Vuokho*'s ventral plating. Hard.

The gunship slewed violently, tilting away and losing speed. A warning klaxon sounded, and tiny stress-fractures spidered out across the armour-glass viewscreens.

'Hull breach below,' reported Morven calmly. 'Losing pressurisation.'

'Clamp it down,' snapped Jorundur, fighting with the controls. *Vuokho* locked into a steep plummet, driven by blazing engines that no longer responded. The trajectory took them straight at the vast face of the nearest descender vane.

'Control system's gone,' growled Terrag, reaching up for a lever and yanking hard. 'Switching to backup.' As he pulled down, a hard clank rang out from the gunship's innards, followed by an explosion of sparks across the cockpit's right-hand side.

It did the trick, though – *Vuokho* immediately responded, pulling high and gaining power again. Projectile rounds followed them, peppering the dorsal armour and making the whole craft spin and buck.

'Leak plugged,' said Morven. 'For now.'

'Good,' snarled Jorundur, still wrestling to keep the racing gunship from tearing itself apart. 'Keep it that way.'

A shimmering criss-cross of las-fire streaked out into the void ahead of them. Jorundur hauled on the control columns, pushing *Vuokho*'s nose up and out of their path, but it wasn't quick enough. A brace of beams impacted, burning through the multi-layered hull-plates and spearing through the far side. *Vuokho* reeled again, its lower crew bay carved open and venting freely.

'We can't stay in this, lord,' said Beor, quietly.

Jorundur rounded on him, ready to tell him what to do with his advice, but the words died in his throat. More dire metrics ran across the consoles, heralding a fresh barrage from the hulk. The void was filled with energies, snarling and spearing across the dark in a dense web of destruction.

'You're right,' Jorundur snarled, checking *Heimdall*'s position and calculating whether they could race back to its shadow before destruction overcame them.

Beor twisted in his seat, as if wanting to be sure. 'Did you–'

'You heard me,' Jorundur said, pulling *Vuokho*'s trajectory away from the incoming storm and back out towards the deep void. 'We're getting out of this.' He glanced back at the retreating hulk-face, feeling the sting of failure.

'You left it too late, brother,' he breathed, watching the immense slab-side of twisted metal flash and swing in the light of macrocannon discharge. 'You're on your own now.'

'Tell me of your childhood.'

Baldr struggled not to respond. He willed his mouth not to move, to remain clenched shut in defiant silence, but, just as before, the muscles relaxed before he knew it.

The Mycelite's power was in his voice. It was soft, almost mournful. The ruined Traitor Marine looked as fragile as a hollowed-out tree-bole, but Baldr could feel his strength burning away, filling the air, heating it and making it thicken.

Njal could have resisted that voice. Gunnlaugur, too, perhaps. Any of his brothers with greater strength of will would have remembered their vows and stayed quiet.

Why could he not?

'What do you want to know?' Baldr replied.

'Your life on Fenris. I have heard many stories of your wild planet. Who in the galaxy has not? I am genuinely curious.'

The words spilled from Baldr's lips like blood from a wound. Once he started talking, it became harder and harder to stop.

'I was born on the ice,' he said. 'I only remember the later days, just before they took me.'

'They watch your combat, taking the valiant. Is that so? That is what I heard.'

'The Wolf Priests do. They draw the dead from the red ice. They re-knit their bodies and remake their flesh.'

'And you were among the dead.'

'A long time ago.'

'They take you into the Mountain,' said the Mycelite, his eyes rapt with fascination. As he sat, hunched like some vast toad in his squalor, dull rolls of noise rose up from the depths. Baldr knew those noises meant something, but it had become hard to even conceive of a world outside that dark chamber. 'They test you there, yes? They make you pure before they give you an axe.'

Baldr remembered what Njal had told him, back on *Heimdall.*

We were looking for a sign – any sign – of aptitude. None was found.

'What does "pure" even mean to you?' Baldr countered, dredging up some scorn from somewhere.

The Mycelite smiled wryly. 'Something different to your Priests, I admit.' He stirred himself, extending the staff and making its skull-tip loom closer. 'Let me tell you something. You won't believe me, but I will tell you anyway.'

He pushed his battered body from its seat and got to his feet. The effort made his breath scrape and whine.

'You are remarkable, you Sons of Russ,' he said. 'Every other Legion has faced the truth. One by one, they have all acknowledged the way of the universe. They have accepted that the warp runs through them, boiling in their blood, turning them into the thing that they hate. They can ring it with wards, they can bind it with rituals, but still it is *there*, the reminder of their failure. Every time a Librarian closes his eyes, it's grinning back at him.'

He lost his smile. 'The warp,' he croaked, as if the word pained him. 'We must perforce use the tools of our own damnation. The irony was not lost on your Imperium's architects. They tried to excise the whole charade, once, but by then greater forces were already in play, and Nikaea was always doomed.'

The Mycelite shook his head in wry wonder. 'After that, we all had to swallow the bitter taste of truth, sooner or later, but you – the attack dogs of Fenris – never did. You told yourself stories about your home world, and its storms, and the magick of the runes, and convinced yourself that you, and *only you* among the Eighteen, had no need to use witches on the battlefield.' He laughed hoarsely. 'Ha! Such story-weavers. The best in the galaxy, even if you told your tales only to yourselves.'

Baldr listened, unable not to. Some of what the creature said made no sense to him. The events he referred to were thousands of years ago and lost in the fog of legend. 'I have seen runecraft,' he said, maintaining at least the veneer of resistance. 'It draws from the world-soul. What you do is... different.'

The Mycelite nodded wearily. 'No doubt you truly believe that.' He shuffled closer to Baldr, and extended a withered hand. The gauntlet that had enclosed it had long gone, revealing atrophied flesh stretched over a network of bone. 'You see this? It was once as firm as your skin, and just as strong.' He turned his hand in the gloomy half-light, watching the lines and wrinkles move. 'You would hardly know we were forged from the same gene-coding, yet we have your Corpse-Emperor's trickery embedded within us both. That's the thing, Baldr Fjolnir: we *look* different, but that's all on the surface.'

He withdrew the hand, moving stiffly, as if, despite himself, some part of him was still capable of registering shame.

'Runecraft *looks* different. It *sounds* different. You can tell yourself as many stories as you like about how it *is* different. I admire you for doing so. But, deep down, even your Stormcaller knows it's all lies. He knows that he drags his power up from the same place we all do. He can call himself a Priest if he wants – I've heard worse titles for our kind.' He shuffled close again, lifting his reptilian face up to Baldr's. '*Our* kind. You, me, him. We are all locked in the same prison. Some of us are a little more honest about where the walls are.'

Baldr stared down at the creature before him. 'You have made this place a living Hel,' he said, quietly, fixing the Mycelite with a mask of contempt. 'We are nothing like each other. The *Fenryka* chose to keep our oaths.'

The Mycelite snorted. 'Chose? *Chose?* What did you *choose*, young hunter? You were not even allowed to *die* on your own.' He spat on the floor. 'This is the only time you have truly had a choice to make in your life, and I am the one to give it to you.'

Baldr watched him carefully. 'You can give me nothing.'

'So sure, for one so merely on the cusp of knowledge.' The Mycelite reached up with his staff, resting the tip of it on Baldr's breastplate. The skull clinked against the ceramite. 'I sense the collar you wear,' he said. 'Your mentor knows his art. To remove it would kill you. Possibly me, as well. While it remains in place, I can only show you a fraction of what I had hoped to.'

Baldr tensed, feeling heat building up before him.

'As I said, you cannot–'

'Hush,' whispered the Mycelite, closing his eyes. 'No more words.'

Baldr tried to speak again, to defy the order, but the two empty eye-sockets before him suddenly flared into green-edged life. He felt a huge pressure bearing down on him, as if he'd been plunged deep underwater, and the dim light around him snuffed out. For an instant, it was as if the entire universe had been erased, replaced by a black, muffled wall of infinite weight and density, but then the crushing mass ripped away.

He realised he had closed his own eyes, and carefully opened them.

'Where am I?' he asked, too lost in surprise to remember any defiance.

The Mycelite's voice still rang in his mind – just as soft, just as seductive.

'Everywhere,' said the creature, chuckling as he spoke. 'Do you see it? You are *everywhere*.'

Ingvar ran.

He strained with every sinew and burned every muscle, forcing his body into new extremities of raw speed. In the foetid plague-hulk, everything was tight, clogged and enclosed – rammed with screaming, jostling armies of the damned. They emerged in droves from crevices and cracks, shrieking and blind, thirsting only to lay scab-encrusted hands on him and bite into healthy flesh. The only response was to keep ahead of them, to keep his limbs driving and the sword-edge dancing. As the enemy came after him, time and again, the runes on *dausvjer*'s edge ran black with clots of blood and bile.

Ingvar sprinted back through the halls of the eldar starship, fighting his way across the bridge and past the stricken outline of the downed wraithknight.

He hewed his way across the wraithbone plains, and he fought his way, stride by bloody stride, back into the outer core where the impacted voidcraft lay thickly atop and within one another.

As he neared the surface levels, weariness began to slow him at last. His genhanced arms burned, his chest spiked with pain. Sweat ran down the inside of his armour, trickling down the back of his neck and pooling around the carapace nodes in his spine. They got closer with every attack, scrabbling at his armour with their talons before he could kick or swipe them away. They launched themselves from hidden roof-vaults, they burst up from compartments in the floor, they spilled out of void-dark culverts and air-cycling tubes. They were like locusts, covering every pressed-metal floor panel and grease-streaked wall section, scuttling and skittering and hissing in the penumbral gloom.

After a final, blood-drenched push, Ingvar broke out into a high-roofed hall, gothic-arched and encrusted with defiled Imperial iconography. At the far end rose a soaring gateway marked with old rune-identifiers for fighter hangars. It was as good a destination as any – one of the thousands of void-facing apertures that would give him a chance to make contact with Jorundur.

The mutants knew well enough what he was doing, and came after him with even greater frenzy. Hundreds surged into the hall behind him, all thirsting to pull him down and back within the hulk's dark embrace. Ingvar felt a clawed hand grab his arm, and wrenched its owner from its feet. Three more dropped down from the vaults above, wailing as they plummeted. Ingvar punched out as they fell, still running, breaking their bones as they thudded and bounced from his armour.

The impact made him stagger. If he lost his footing now, they would be on him, dozens of them, then more, piling on so fast he'd be buried alive. He forced his limbs to keep pumping, to keeping powering on through the fatigue.

The hangar entrances rose over him, vast enough to accommodate Valkyrie gunships being lifted on claw-rails. He gained the launch-zones beyond and raced across them, his boots finally striking rockcrete again. Ranked launch bays stretched off on either side, empty of the craft that had once lined them. Up ahead, two hundred metres off, void-entrance gates glittered from the exposed starfield beyond.

He was close, now – desperately close.

'Jorundur!' he voxed. 'Fix to my loc.'

No reply – the comm-link hissed with static. Ingvar tore onwards, sprinting towards the closest of the void-gates, and the mob followed him like a breaking wave. One clamped a fist around his trailing leg, another nearly speared his shoulder with a heavily thrown blade.

'Jorundur,' voxed Ingvar again, seeing nothing on his armour's scanners. 'Are you getting this?'

He neared the far edge of the launch bay. There was nowhere else to go.

With a cold lurch in the pit of his stomach, Ingvar contemplated, for the first time, the possibility that Jorundur had not been equal to the firepower of the hulk's outer guns. Perhaps even the Old Dog, the finest pilot Ingvar had ever fought alongside, had succumbed to the barrage.

As the lip of the hangar approached, Ingvar let out an echoing roar of rage, skidded around and faced his pursuers.

They careered into him, carried into contact by the huge momentum of the crowd. Ingvar ripped into them, hurling bodies clear in all directions. He hewed and blocked with ferocious, blinding speed, carpeting the apron in fresh gore. He lashed out in the baresark way, worked his blade two-handed, blurring the edge with velocity even as they pushed him back towards the edge of the void.

'For *Russ!*' he roared, time and again. 'For the honour of the Wolf King!'

Not since leaving Fenris for the Deathwatch had he fought like it. There were no Blood Angel strokes in his hammering display, no Dark Angel tricks or Ultramarine restraint. The mutants died in swathes, thrown against the glittering arcs of his vengeful blade and broken asunder by its wrath.

In the face of such limitless ferocity, even those hordes fell back. They scrambled and clawed to get away from the blue-edged sword.

The hangar fell silent. Ingvar stood on the very extremity, the open starfield at his back, panting heavily, his armour red from the gore that covered it, his head low.

There were still hundreds of them. More streamed into the halls with every passing second. Ingvar's blood still boiled with the war-fury, but it could not last forever. It was only a matter of time before they summoned the courage to rush him again, and this time there would be no victory.

Gunnlaugur had been right. It had been a foolish effort, one born of overweening pride. He would die on the hulk, alone, with Klaive's secrets still hidden in the depths of *Vindicatus*.

Ingvar smiled wryly under his battered helm. Callimachus would never have approved.

But I am a true Wolf again, he thought. *That, at least, has been proved.*

He angled his blade at the face of the nearest mutant, feeling the energy field spit with relish.

'Who will be first, then?' he cried, challenging them all. 'Who will have the honour of this scalp?'

At that, the spell broke, and the front rank of mutants rushed him again, stumbling in their haste and panic, driven by the swell of the hundreds pushing behind.

Ingvar bellowed a fresh war-cry, tensing for the almighty impact.

The row of mutants before him exploded in a sequential line of blasted flesh and armour-shards, blowing up as columns of bolt-rounds thudded into them. A thunder of thrusters filled the hangar space as something huge and furnace-hot broke the atmosphere seal over the hangar's exit.

Ingvar looked up to see *Vuokho* labouring hard to maintain loft. Its entire underside had been ripped to pieces, and it looked like the heavy bolters were about the only thing that still functioned on its entire chassis. It turned on a thick downdraught, laying into the hordes of plague-damned as it circled about.

'Gyrfalkon,' came Jorundur's furious voice over the pack-comm. 'You have two seconds.'

Ingvar grinned, and leapt up to grasp the mangled remains of the lower crew bay door.

'What kept you, brother?' he asked, hauling himself clear of the hangar floor.

'I changed my mind,' said Jorundur, sounding very angry about it.

Then Jorundur wheeled the Thunderhawk around and pointed its charred muzzle back towards the void outside. The engines fired, and both gunship and passenger tore free of the *Festerax*'s interior, back out into the las-beam-crossed storm beyond. Ingvar hung on, clambering up into the crew bay even as the Thunderhawk powered into the void.

Behind them, the screams of the damned lingered – furious, rabid, but impotent.

CHAPTER SEVENTEEN

Gunnlaugur felt the blood in his throat. Every time he roared out a fresh battle-cry, the pain flared up. He ignored it, and kept bellowing. His armour made his voice swell out across the entire space, filling the fire-hot hall with the sound of his wrath.

His brothers did the same, howling raw fury at the enemy. The combined effect was electrifying – it made his hearts surge and his mind sing. Even in the midst of almost infinite ruin, the cries of the Wolves were chilling. Deep in the depths of the plague-hulk, a fragment of immortal Fenris had lodged, and with every stride it worked its way further into the flesh of its prey, ice-cold, steel-hard.

Gunnlaugur and Haflói had spearheaded the charge on the right flank of Njal's advance. With Fellblade's surviving warriors, they carved a bloody trail out across the pit surface. Bloodhame held the left flank, while Njal pushed up the centre, bolstered by his own retinue and Hauki's fighters.

The warband cut a diminished aspect from the numbers that had broken into the hulk on the assault rams, and now fewer than thirty remained. Set beside the forces ranged against them, those numbers were pitiful. Laughable.

Yet no one laughed. The mutant tides yelled and bawled their defiance. Monsters in their midst lumbered into contact, their minds slushed by pain-amplifiers and thick layers of disease. At the rear of the horde, the bloated Plague Marines waited patiently, immobile and inscrutable.

'*Russvangam!*' thundered Gunnlaugur, decapitating the mutant closest to him with a broad sweep of his hammer. He lurched back into the counter-swing, punching the crackling weapon-head through the bodies of another two.

Ahead, half shrouded by drifting smoke-lines, loomed a greater test. It might have once been an ogryn, a grotesque abhuman many times the size and strength of an unaugmented mortal. Its swell-veined muscles bulged unnaturally, bursting out from under ramshackle plates of beaten iron. As it came on, it laid about itself with a crackling power maul. Its roars of challenge were nearly the equal of Gunnlaugur's own, though thickened by madness into a bestial, slurring mess.

Gunnlaugur barged his way through a squad of lesser fighters to get to it. The plague-ogryn saw him coming and ploughed its way straight at him.

As Gunnlaugur crashed and bludgeoned his way closer, he saw the metal tubes punched through the monster's corpse-white skin, each one gurgling with combat-stimms. Lodged among the overlapping armour plates were vials of sludgy bile, fizzing from some toxic combination of battle-poisons.

Then the two of them collided, and the impact was shuddering.

Skulbrotsjór scythed, smashing against the jangling gourds and sending them clattering. The ogryn slammed its power maul down, aiming to crack Gunnlaugur's trailing pauldron. Gunnlaugur evaded the blow, then launched another crushing hammer strike at the creature's midriff.

The smashes came in thick and fast after that – heavy, driving blows that dented ceramite and tore up iron plating. Gunnlaugur was faster, hauling his hammer around him in speed-blurred arcs, but the tainted ogryn was taller, bulkier and immeasurably strong. Both of them took bone-breaking impacts. Gunnlaugur's plastron was nearly sheared in two from a sharp maul swing, while the ogryn's right leg was virtually cloven open by a sharp switchback from the thunder hammer. Blood, both post-human and abhuman, spiralled out from the epicentre of the combat.

The plague-ogryn worked to shut the Space Wolf down, bearing over him and cracking the maul down two-handed. Gunnlaugur responded instantly, ducking low and thrusting up under the creature's guard. As he did so, he fed a sliver of extra power to *skulbrotsjór*'s energy field, making it roar like a voidship's thrusters.

The impact was explosive, lifting the colossal mutant from its feet and sending its power maul flying. The wounded ogryn tumbled away, disorientated and nearly disembowelled. Gunnlaugur pounced after it.

'For Russ!' he roared, leaping high, then smashing the hammerhead down on the ogryn's forehead.

The creature's skull blew apart, drenching both of them in cranial slime. The ogryn tottered, headless, for a few moments more, its fists still clenched and its legs braced, before crashing backwards.

Gunnlaugur thrust his thunder hammer high and howled his triumph out. '*Heidur Rus!*'

His every pore streamed with sweat, his muscles screamed from the effort of wielding his great weapon, both his hearts raced to keep his genhanced systems from overloading, but still his spirit raged and his eyes blazed.

This was what he had been desperate for. Around him, his battle-brothers raced forward, echoing his howl of triumph with savage whoops of their own. He was where he had always been destined to be – at the heart of the tempest, slaying freely for the Allfather and the primarch.

As the last echoes of his kill-cry rang across the chamber, Gunnlaugur burst into movement once more. Over to his left, Njal was striding out, wreathed in snapping wyrd-lightning. The warriors of the Rout tore into the hordes like the predators they were, leaping across the pits to get at the enemy, driving in low and forging gore-soaked paths through whole knots of mutated troops.

Step by step, blade-swipe by blade-swipe, they were cutting their way towards the objective. The colossal heat-exchanger towers loomed closer.

It was then that the Traitor Marines began to move, hefting their scythes and striding down from the portals. Gunnlaugur detected twelve of them.

Back on Ras Shakeh, right at the thickest of the fighting, the Plague Marine champion had bested him. Now he latched on to the greatest of those who marched under the fires of the enginarium, and bellowed out his challenge.

'You!' he thundered, and his hoarse voice cut through the mass of screams and roars to reach its target – a huge monster with a lone-eyed helm, bearing an armour-fixed scythe blade in each hand. 'I claim *you!*'

For a moment, Gunnlaugur could not be sure that the Plague Marine had heard him. Then the Traitor paused. His corroded helm swept the battlefield, and his gaze alighted on him. The two of them stared at one another – twin titans of slaughter, separated by a raging sea of lesser warriors.

Then the Traitor nodded, acknowledging the contest, and strode out to meet him.

Gunnlaugur grinned under his helm, licking hot blood from his fangs, and broke into the charge.

Challenge accepted.

Dawn broke over Kallian Hellax. The sunlight was weak, and struggled to push through thick banks of violet-tinged cloud. The vast sprawl of the spire complex rose up through layers of mist like islands in a milky sea, drear and immense.

On the far northern rim of the conurbation, landers came and went like clouds of metal insects. Requisition orders had streamed out of the command centre during the night, rousing divisional commanders and stirring them into action. Regimental barracks were given red-alert warnings, and whole battalions now marched into the waiting maws of orbital lifters. Huge troop-carrying craft squatted obesely on rockcrete aprons, their hulls open and glowing with red-tinged light.

It all looked orderly enough – long lines of marching men in uniform disgorging from ground transports and heading for the cavernous craft interiors. Every ten minutes, one of the big lifters would haul its doors closed, prime its engines and take off in a blaze of smoke and thruster-fire, swaying heavily up into the gathering dawn sky. Every time a space was cleared on the landing stages, another troop carrier would emerge from the clouds above and take its place on the grid, ready to absorb another detachment of living cargo.

'You have done well, governor,' said Olgeir, watching the progress from a balcony high on the southern edge of the compound. He'd taken a skimmer over to the complex with Annarovea an hour ago.

He hadn't slept. None of the planet's high command had done so. Organising a lift involving such vast numbers of soldiers was no easy task, even more so in the time they had been given. Some orders, inevitably, had been mangled. One regiment, stationed in the equatorial city of Bennafela, had somehow decided that the planet was in revolt and had taken over the local levels of control. Others had wasted precious time querying the orders and demanding to know under whose authorisation the evacuation was being enacted.

But they were the exceptions. The bulk of Kefa Primaris's many millions of registered Guardsmen were now being lined up for redeployment, drummed into shape by their commanders and commissars and prepped for orbital lift. Every voidcraft in the planet's orbital zone had been pressed into service, giving them a huge potential capacity.

Annarovea, standing beside Olgeir, smiled resignedly. 'I am glad you approve.'

'This is just the start, you realise. News will get out.'

'Verdello is very thorough.'

'Even so. Talk will have started. Your people are waking up.'

Annarovea ran a tired hand across her face, massaging the skin. 'It is in hand. All the compounds are guarded, and enforcers are deployed.'

'Do they know why this is happening?'

Annarovea gave him a dry look. 'Of course not.'

'Good,' Olgeir said.

Throughout, the governor had performed with calm competence. All of her staff had done so. As far as any of them could tell, panic had yet to hit the hive spires. Even if those being evacuated guessed the true reason for the orders, loose talk had not yet penetrated far out of the confines of the regiments. Keeping control of information was a specialism of Imperial command cadres, one of the very few things they had improved upon in ten thousand years of planetary administration.

Annarovea leaned heavily against the balcony railing. Half a kilometre away, shrouded in mist and steam, another lifter took off and lurched up into the sky, trailing columns of smog like tentacles.

'I don't enjoy watching this,' she said. 'My world, stripping itself bare.' She looked back at him. 'Would you have done this on Fenris?'

Olgeir's mind instantly went back to the Fang. He envisioned the immense fortress carved out of the solid matter of the planet's core, the ranks of ship-killer batteries on the flanks of the Asaheim peaks, the orbital fleets, the Great Companies stationed in the halls of the Mountain, the beasts that dwelled in the shadows, the Revered Fallen sleeping in the deepest holds.

It felt ludicrous even to consider the proposition of evacuation *there* – Fenris was one of the most heavily defended worlds in the Imperium. For all that, the *Festerax* was a truly unique threat, one spawned from the nightmares of the Eye itself. Could even the Chapter's massed warships have stopped it out in the void? If not, and it somehow made orbit, would the brutal logic that governed Kefa's fate also have extended to the home world of the Wolf King?

'They are different worlds,' he said, eventually.

Annarovea pushed free of the balcony and started to walk, back and forth, getting some circulation going in night-stiff limbs. She'd long discarded her ceremonial gown and now wore gilt body armour shrouded in a royal blue cloak.

'You know we can pick it up on the long-range augurs now?' she asked.

Olgeir nodded.

'Soon other stations will detect it,' she said. 'The comm-chatter will begin. We won't be able to keep the truth to ourselves.'

Olgeir turned to her. 'You trust your staff?'

'I do.'

'All of them?'

'I picked them myself.'

Olgeir grunted, and turned back to the view. Another bloat-bellied levi-athan was coming into land, replacing the carrier that had last taken off. More smoke spilled across the rockcrete, thick and oil-black as it mingled with strands of drifting mist.

'Morfol, your commissar,' he said. 'He wants to fight. Every part of his training demands it, and he is a fine example of his breed. We have six more hours. He could cause problems.'

'Ah, but that is why you're here, is it not? To keep us in line.' A trace of bitterness entered Annarovea's clipped voice. 'Forgive me, lord, but it won't matter to you much longer. As soon as you have our regiments safely pulled away, you'll be back into the void.'

Olgeir regarded her again, surprised. 'Will you leave, then?' he asked. 'You could take any ship you want.'

Annarovea lifted her chin proudly. 'In six hours, I'll be on my command throne. If the spore-clouds come, I'll marshal what remains of my armies and we'll burn them wherever they land. I'll fight the changelings every step of the way when they come for us. The last thing they'll see, when they break into the command spire, is an Imperial aquila standing guard over an uncorrupted, duly appointed leader. Then I'll set off the hive-atomics, and take as many of the bastards down with me as I can.'

Olgeir suppressed an approving smile. He didn't wish to insult her with condescension.

'A fine strategy,' he said. 'I will be there with you.'

Annarovea looked at him disbelievingly. 'You? Why?'

'I am not leaving, governor. My task is not done, and I do not leave until it is.' He drew in a long breath of Kefa's acrid air. 'Believe me, I am not here to goad you on, governor. I am here to protect you. This is my fate now – caught up with yours.'

'*Protect* me?'

'The news will be out by now.' As Olgeir spoke, the mist boiled away from the vista before him. The hazy outlines of spires grew firmer amid the drift-ing clouds. 'My Wolf Guard tells me the prospect of death does strange things to mortal minds. Perhaps you can trust your staff, perhaps not. In case not, I am here.'

Annarovea stared at him. For a moment it looked like she might burst out laughing, or perhaps flare into anger. In the end, she just shook her head.

'Twenty-four hours ago,' she said, 'I was planning an inspection mission of the ore refineries in the south. The prospect bored me immensely – seven days of touring industrial facilities in the company of tithe officials. Up until then, this world had never known a major assault by the Archenemy. It had never even been visited by one of the Adeptus Astartes. Boredom was the worst I had to fear.' She smiled grimly. 'And now I have a Wolf of Fenris as a chaperone, and a nightmare – a *real* nightmare – is about to be unleashed upon us all. Things change quickly.'

'They do. You regret that?'

Annarovea rolled her shoulders. Every move she made was tight with stress, but she was keeping herself together.

Out on the apron, more lifters came and went, transporting their precious contents into the temporary safety of the void.

The sunlight continued to grow stronger. The chronos kept ticking over.

'Ask me in six hours,' she said.

Vuokho shuddered, struck hard by more las-beams, and ducked down towards the nadir of the battle-sphere. More cracks shot across the armour-glass of the cockpit, and the engines began to labour.

'Maintain power for main thrust,' snarled Jorundur, pulling the gunship away from a ruinous thicket of incoming projectile fire. 'Blood of Russ, if you keep anything going, keep the drives going.'

The flight crew worked as hard as ever. Once aboard, Ingvar had taken the co-pilot's chair alongside Jorundur, with the mortals placed further back at the gunner's and navigator's stations. The metal cage around them rattled and screamed, flexing every time another impact came in.

'We're coming out,' said Ingvar calmly, running forward scans on the vessel's augur array. His armour was still caked in slowly drying fluids, making him look like some butcher's remnant amid all the naked steel.

The *Festerax*'s profile fell away behind them, though it still swelled in the rear viewers like some grotesque planetoid. Ahead of them, the void boiled with the lattice and turmoil of discharged weapons-fire.

Heimdall could be detected over to starboard-zenith, though it was moving chronically slowly. Its thrusters glowed black-red, looking more like wounds than drives, and the evidence of the beating it had taken was painfully obvious. Ahead glittered the opulent profile of *Vindicatus*, its own drives flaring up for launch.

'I need more speed, brother,' murmured Ingvar, watching the Grand Cruiser complete its pre-burn cycle. Any moment now the main thrusters would ignite, beginning the acceleration that would take it far out of range. *Heimdall* wouldn't catch it then, not in its half-crippled state.

'You find it, then,' hissed Jorundur, pulling out of another dive just as a phalanx of torpedoes scythed past ahead of them. The volume of fire was diminishing with every kilometre they put between them and the hulk's edge, but the hulk was still more than capable of knocking them out of the void with a full hit.

Ingvar ran another scan. *Vindicatus* was getting under way – grindingly slowly, but its momentum would soon pick up.

'Get me the link,' he said.

'What link?' grunted Jorundur, fully occupied with keeping *Vuokho* out of the many paths of destruction.

'Callia.'

Jorundur snatched the comm-bead from the socket in his gorget and threw it at Ingvar before hauling on the control column again.

Ingvar caught the bead, implanted it, and activated the channel.

'You are moving, Sister,' he voxed as the connection crackled into life.

'Nothing I can do about that,' came Callia's voice. 'Aiming to board? You don't have long – the shields are compromised in zone forty-five five. You can detect that?'

Ingvar checked the readings. There was a window – a small one. 'It will be difficult,' he said.

'I might be able to mask your approach. They are all scanning *Heimdall*.'

'Do what you can.'

Ingvar cut the link, just as the gunship slewed violently in a patch of projectile fire. The whole structure rattled as the ship was flung around further. As Jorundur worked to right it again, *Vindicatus* picked up speed, its engines suddenly blazing like stars.

'Full burn, brother,' insisted Ingvar, watching as the prize began to escape.

Jorundur looked up at the real-view portals, made a quick calculation, and pulled out a whole raft of levers.

'It'll shake us apart,' he warned.

'We will not get another chance.'

Jorundur fed the last sliver of power to the main drives, and *Vuokho* kicked into attack speed.

All manoeuvring subtlety disappeared as the gunship shot directly for its target. *Vindicatus*'s hull raced towards them, its fearsome macrocannon-studded flanks looming rapidly into sharp detail.

'You have Callia's coordinates?' asked Ingvar, gripping the sides of his command throne. Jorundur was right – the whole cockpit felt like it was splitting open.

'The target is *moving*,' muttered Jorundur, nudging the muzzle a fraction to the left. 'This is *complicated*.'

Two-thirds of the way along the ventral flank, a docking bay was opening. Gusts of venting atmosphere glistened as the doors slid apart, sparking as they interfered with the ragged edges of the void shields on either side.

'Like a needle through leather,' grunted Jorundur, fighting with the controls.

Vuokho was coming in too low, driven down by the final barrage from the plague-hulk's wall of las-fire. Jorundur pulled the nose up, though the momentum of the thrust still carried them in on the edge of destruction.

Ingvar felt a rush of endorphins, like combat-fervour. He leaned forwards in the throne, staring at the speed-blurred edges of the Grand Cruiser.

'They are not firing,' he said.

'By the time they have a fix,' said Jorundur with some satisfaction, twisting the gunship up for the final thrust, 'we'll be inside the shields.'

Vuokho gave a last judder before the engines delivered what was needed. Clean as a thrown spear, the gunship blasted into the shadow of *Vindicatus*. Callia was as good as her word, and they streaked through the gap in the void shields towards the opening launch bay.

'Hard landing coming,' warned Jorundur, suddenly kicking in reverse thrust.

Ingvar was thrown forward against his throne restraints. Terminal-sounding clangs resounded from deep within the Thunderhawk's tortured frame, and a thin snap echoed out from above the cockpit. He got a blurred impression of bulkheads rushing to meet them, picked out in crimson and bronze, before *Vuokho* slewed through the gap.

Jorundur aimed the gunship as well as he had ever done. By rights, an entry at that speed, in those conditions, carrying that much damage, should have smeared them across the side of *Vindicatus* in a thousand glowing shards of adamantium. Somehow, though, he managed to hit the aperture without clipping the edge, fast enough to evade sentry guns tracking them but with just enough room to brake once inside the atmosphere bubble.

'*Skítja*,' Jorundur muttered, physically wrestling with the last responsive sections of the command console.

Vuokho skidded round sharply, nearly tumbling over on its axis before righting drunkenly. *Vindicatus*'s gravity field clamped down strongly, slamming the gunship's twisted undercarriage hard against the flight deck. A soaring roof and colonnaded walls enclosed them, all picked out in smog-blackened gold leaf.

The rear wall of the hangar raced towards them, half obscured by the cloud of sparks and smoke kicked out by *Vuokho*'s driving progress. It looked very, very solid.

'Brother...' began Ingvar.

'I *see it*,' snapped Jorundur, activating the air-brakes and diverting all remaining power to the retro-thrusters. Huge gouts of flame surged out, arresting the suicidal momentum. The Thunderhawk's undercarriage gouged long trails into the hangar floor, though even that only part-slowed the charge.

They hit the wall with a heavy crack of ceramite breaking. Power lines shorted across the roof, sparking like fountains, and the thrones rocked on their mounts.

The main drives whined down, clanking eerily as broken components rattled around in their casings. The entire structure steamed, and smoke rose from the console, coupled with the acrid smell of metal burning.

For a moment, no one said anything. Then Jorundur turned to Ingvar.

'So I got us in,' he said. 'Now what?'

Ingvar reached for his bolter.

'You and me,' he said. 'To the bridge.'

'Tell me what you see,' said the Mycelite.

Baldr tried to twist around, to determine where the voice came from.

Nothing happened. He didn't move. He had no neck left to move, nor a head to swivel. The visual field before him was like nothing he'd ever experienced. He saw a shimmering wall of colour, moving in clots and streaks across a deeper well of luminous cloud. Motes of darkness skated over that tapestry – hard, sharp things that violated the beauty of the spectacle.

He found himself wanting to remove those motes, to restore the vista to unbroken splendour.

'I do not know,' he said.

His voice was just an echo. He had no lips to move, no tongue to form the words. They spun in existence like thoughts, and yet they were not just mental figments – they were words, spoken to another intelligence.

'You do,' said the Mycelite, his voice echoing in his mind. 'Use your eyes. Think. Tell me what you see.'

Baldr tried to relax. A feeling of astonishing power coursed through his veins. Except he had no veins – just the vague after-image of a body, like a faint echo still ringing in his consciousness.

He tried to move again, and this time something changed. His gaze altered, adjusting, zooming in a little. The tapestry flexed and bent, though the motes remained in place. There were three of them – three dark little clots of movement. If he had arms, he would have reached out to swipe them clear.

'I see the universe,' he said, not knowing where the words came from.

'Just so,' said the Mycelite, 'and you see the depths beneath it.'

Baldr recognised the truth of that immediately. He saw the relatedness of it all – the swirls of colour and the bluffs and wells of light. It was endlessly moving, turning like water, stretching and changing.

It was infinite. It was compelling.

'The *warp*,' he said, the word catching in his mind.

'You see it better than I,' said the Mycelite, delighted. 'You are something truly new, Baldr Fjolnir. How could your Priests have tested for this taint? It did not exist, not until now. But these are the Times of Accomplishment, and all is changing. Doors are unlocking that have remained shut since before the Corpse-Lord took us into the stars. You are just the *start*. Thousands will follow. Though will many be as powerful? I doubt it'

Baldr hardly listened. His gaze roved across the tapestry, then alighted on the three motes of darkness. Two of them were much larger than the third. As he watched, the tiny speck made its way towards the largest, and disappeared into it. Without knowing how, he began to realise what he was seeing.

'Ships,' he said. 'I am seeing the void.'

'They are the ships that besiege the *Festerax*. Tiny things, are they not?'

'Where is the hulk?'

'The *hulk*?' came the Mycelite's voice, amused. 'A poor name for this magnificent thing. You can guess, I think.'

Baldr's mind probed further into the tapestry. He saw the outlines of the other ships, blurred as if by heat. They swam amid the glory and the infinitude, fragmentary and insubstantial. It felt as if he could reach out, just extend an arm, and pluck them from the void.

'I *am* the hulk,' he said, once again letting the truth come to him. 'I am this ship.'

The Mycelite sounded pleased. 'That is it. You are the ship. Flex your muscles. Use your gift.'

Baldr began to see how things were ordered. His perspective was from the core of the great vessel. He could feel the torpedo tubes as if they were his arteries, the fuel cells as if they were his hearts. The universe surrounded him, cold and vacuous, but also rich and magnificent. He floated on the face of the deep, conscious, immense, eternal.

At the back of his mind, like an old memory, he felt other things stirring. Aside from the Mycelite, he half heard different voices whispering. They were oddly familiar – the words made a kind of sense to him.

God-marked.

'How are you... doing this?' Baldr asked, unable to fight back against the sensations flooding through him but not quite overwhelmed by them. 'I have a–'

'Yes, your collar. It holds you back. You feel that? If we could break it, then the link would be complete.'

'It will not break.'

'Give it time.'

Baldr felt a sudden pang. He was talking to the Mycelite like he might talk to any of his brothers. The fury had gone, the contempt had gone. He knew he ought to feel both those things, but somehow the will to defy had dissipated.

Part of that was sorcery, he knew. He could still taste the stink of it, hanging like vomit at the back of his throat. But only a part. Something else called to him.

He was being shown another way of being. He began to remember the dreams he'd had on Ras Shakeh while his body repaired.

He remembered the Dark Garden. He'd walked among those twilight groves, breathing in the spores and the poisons.

He had seen the goddess there, locked in her cage of iron. Her eyes had been rimmed with tears, her pale skin running with fever.

He had wanted to reach out, to press a cooling hand against her brow.

'You were *unlocked* by us, Baldr,' said the Mycelite, as if able to sense what he was thinking. 'You were fertile soil, but you still needed the seed. We gave it to you.' Just as before, his voice had an edge of tenderness to it. 'You are *home* now.'

Baldr ought to have recoiled at that, just as he had done when the Mycelite had run his diseased hand down his cheek.

But he didn't.

'I can control this,' Baldr said, feeling the thousands upon thousands of interlocking ship-systems unfolding in his mind. 'I can make it move. I can keep it alive.'

'Not quite,' warned the Mycelite. 'The collar was well made. It holds us back, but you will learn. There is time.'

Baldr felt a tremor of unease then. The *Festerax* was not as it should be. The vast structure was riddled with infections, but that was its natural state – the contagions made it stronger.

We will be its disease.

He couldn't remember who had said that. He couldn't even remember why he had ever come to the *Festerax*. But something wasn't right. There was a presence at the heart of the vessel, at *his* heart.

'There are intruders,' he said. 'To be purged.'

The Mycelite agreed. 'There are,' he said. 'Do you know what must be done to purge them?'

Baldr thought on that. He had no idea how to exert his will over the ship. There were huge structures within it – he could feel them. They could be made to move, to crush, to stifle, but only with the correct command.

'I do not,' he said, slowly. His mind moved in a fog, as if emerging from sleep. Ahead of him, he could see the glorious void glow and shimmer.

'But... I can learn.'

CHAPTER EIGHTEEN

The engine-gates loomed, now less than thirty metres away. The fires set before them roared into new and terrible shapes, throwing lurid light across a battlefield of swinging shadows. The enemy had been driven back, but their numbers remained. There was no end to them – they poured out from hidden arches, the vaults above and the pits beneath, an infinite tide of corrupted humanity.

Njal wasted none of his power on them. Fatigue was beginning to weigh on his arms, driving like lead through his veins. His throat was bloody and raw from the death-oaths he swore, his arms flared with pain from the effort of hurling storm-fire at the endless tides of ruin. He could feel the psychic tsunami of hatred crashing against him, surging against his own will and seeking to hammer it down.

The foul breath of the Dark Wolf lapped across his shoulder, as close as it had ever been. He could sense the purring growls behind him, catching up. Every exercise of runecraft summoned it closer, the avatar of his own destruction.

I sense you, now. You are on my heels.

They could have no understanding of this, those who did not walk the path of the runes. For outsiders, the power he wielded was nothing but dabbling in the shallows of the warp, just like any trickster or fallen sorcerer. Njal had heard the arguments a thousand times, and had read the same in a hundred proscribed manuscripts.

You are no different. You are warp-weavers, just as we are. All rivers meet at the same source, and our damnations are the same.

They were wrong. The whispers were wrong. Njal had seen the world-soul, raging in the heart of darkness. He had heard the low growls in the nether-world, and seen the pairs of eyes glowing in the afterdark. He had felt the power that would consume him in the end, dissipating his soul into the raging tempest that would break at the galaxy's end.

The power he wielded was of a different order, one tempered and purified by the mystical symmetries of the hunt and the wild. Those who had never known Fenris could disbelieve it all they liked. It changed nothing.

Somewhere deep in the soul of the storm, the Dark Wolf's fangs bared, as yellow and decayed as the bones of the earth.

'*Fenrys!*' Njal thundered, feeling his own fangs bare in symmetry.

He thrust his staff forward, and wild-edged coruscation surged around him once more, lighting up the eternal night in blood-edged silver. Storm-wind rushed to his aid, swirling about him in accelerating eddies. Flames bloomed out, catching on the backs of the hordes before him and flaring into roaring life. Fork-shaped gouts of fire leapt from his staff tip, lashing into the smog-shrouded vaults above. Great cracks opened at his feet, zigzagging across the pitted deck before spewing torrents of magma. His Terminator plate glowed deep red, thick as blood-clots, and the runes seared the dark like brands.

Fenris was a world of ice, but it was also a world of fire. Through sheer force of will, Njal had dragged the Summer of Flame into the enginarium chamber, and the devastation was as complete there as it was on his violent home world.

Ranks of mutant soldiers were hurled from their feet by the squalls and thrown, aflame, into the pits, where the forge-fires leapt up to welcome them. More were impaled by the sheets of red lightning rippling across the battlefield. The whole chamber swelled with the rip and tear of the racing winds, and fires latched on to the bare metal, making the fevered atmosphere shake.

Njal strode forth, his staff held high and his pelts snapping in the rune-summoned gales. The mortal enemy fell back before him, cowering and scrambling. Even to look on him in such an unleashed state was enough to burst corrupted eyeballs and tear open tainted flesh.

The engine-gates drew near, towering over all else and lit by their own vast furnaces. Njal felt the magma-heat thundering away before him, hot as a brand against his skin.

There was little in the enemy host capable of standing before him then, let alone fighting him. In his wake came the Wolves, swift and brutal in vengeance, already reaching for the thermal charges that would be hurled into the depths of the fusion reactors.

But between them stood the last line of defence – the Traitor Marines. Dragged into the combat at last as their minions withered away, the bloated leviathans strode down from their portals, each one carrying scythes or hefting massive organ-guns with carved daemon-head muzzles. Night-wing, circling high above the combat, ran scans on each and filtered the results back to Njal's armour systems. The Plague Marines were riddled with corrosion, their ancient bodies fused and integrated into a bizarre mix of tumescent organs and semi-bionic components. By rights, none of them should have been able to draw breath, let alone fight, but Njal knew well enough how utterly deadly they were.

The Plague Marines converged on Njal, advancing fearlessly into the inferno even as the flames whipped and curled around them. Njal's body-guard raced to intercept them, and the two forces crashed together. The fighting became truly vicious then, with no quarter given on either side – Traitors were hammered into the burning iron floor; Wolves were crushed under cloven boots, their hearts ripped out on the curve of Hel-forged blades.

Three huge scythe-bearers broke the cordon of Njal's bodyguards, eviscerating the Wolves in their path before lumbering on at him. The warriors' scythes glowed pale green, bleeding corpse-light into the fervid air. They were fearsome things, forged on some long-damned plague world and tempered with the malice of daemonic metalwrights.

Njal smiled savagely, and opened his fist.

Forks of blood-red lightning leapt out, slamming into their prey and spraying magma like the maw of a volcano. The flaming rune-magic blazed wildly as it came into contact with the fell metals, but it gripped tight, wrapping around the blade-edges in tight snarls.

The scythes exploded, sending circular blast-waves shuddering out. The Plague Marines weathered the rain of magma, reaching for bolters and meltaguns. They opened fire, loosing a volley of bolts and atomised energy straight at him. Njal felt searing heat as the molecular tech gnawed into the ceramite, stripping away the outer layers in a haze of fizzing smoke, followed by the hammering rain of shells exploding across his tortured armour. A second volley impacted hard, smashing him back several paces and ripping into his already battered plate.

Njal spat out a curse, and drew on fresh power. He spun around, whirling hard and driving the fire-winds into a vortex of speed. The Traitor Marines kept firing, but now their shells were sucked into the whirlwind and sprayed out wildly. Still surrounded by the flame-edged gale, Njal advanced again, gripping his staff two-handed and preparing the next blast.

The Plague Marines met the onslaught defiantly. The meltagunner opened fire again. His comrades kept up the barrage of bolter shots, shouldering into the fury of the gales.

Njal angled his staff at the leader, and poured all his battle-fury into a single word.

'*Skemmdarvargur.*'

His staff erupted. The space before him disappeared into a furnace of bestial energies, snarling and tearing at the bit like a leashed pack of hunting dogs. Somewhere buried in all the rampaging light and noise, the vague shapes of jaws could be half made out, latching on to the enemy and biting down. Arched backs plunged, powered by spectral, thick-pelted limbs. In a tornado of roars and snarls, the galloping predator-shapes surged ahead, sweeping aside any resistance. The three Plague Marines were swept away, deluged by the roiling fire-tide and slammed back into the pits whence they had come.

Panting with exhaustion, Njal let the furnace burn out. The winds, the flames, the lightning-shards, all of it ripped away and howled off into oblivion.

In front of him, a gorge of pure scorched devastation stretched off towards the gates. The bodies of the Plague Marines had been ripped apart, now little more than scraps of necrotic flesh and burning armour-pieces. Dozens more bodies were twisted and contorted all along the length of the carved-out furrow, still racked by the last sparks and flickers of the lightning that had killed them.

They can disbelieve it all they like, thought Njal grimly, surveying the ruin. *It changes nothing.*

Then he strode out, crushing the remnants of his enemies under his boots. Around him, surviving Grey Hunters regrouped and followed him back into battle. The toll had been horrendous, but enough still fought to gain the gate. The hordes screamed, and pushed back, but there was panic lacing their hatred now.

Step by step, stride by bloody stride, the Wolves were closing on the target.

On Kefa Primaris, word had got out. It had been impossible to hide the movements of so many ships, and attempts by the high command to shut down the city-wide comm-channels had been only partially successful.

Once the data from short-range planetary augurs came in, panic began to spread. Whispers ran from hab to hab, speaking of Guard officers summoned from their cells in the middle of the night, and of an enemy fleet making its way into orbit above them. The story got about that Annarovea had already left the planet, and that every voidcraft in-system was primed to leave, stranding the planet to the mercy of whatever ravening force was heading for the drop-zones.

Not all the details were correct, but the gist was close enough. The people of Kefa Primaris knew something terrible was about to happen, and they could see that their rulers were abandoning them to it.

In the face of all that, no amount of deference would hold them back. They took to the comm-stations, demanding action. They marched out of the manufactories, massing in crowds at the main hive intersections. They besieged the Adeptus Arbites control points in the core spire, unperturbed by the frequent vox-casts warning them to return to their assigned zones and get back to work.

As the morning wore on and the official response continued to be muted, the levels of disorder grew. Broadcast reassurances that all was in hand had no effect – they could see the data from unofficial augur screeds, and they could see with their own eyes the long trail of off-world traffic from the Guard garrisons.

With three hours until the *Festerax* was due to reach orbit, the crowds began to reinforce one another, pooling into larger groups and marching up from the lower levels. Most were menial workers from the big production lines, hardened by a lifetime of labour in the manufactory levels. Their overseers needed to be brutal to keep them in line at the best of times; now, as often as not, they marched alongside them.

Olgeir watched the incoming datafeeds from the vantage of the governor's private chambers. Annarovea's domain was a slender tower jutting from the northern flank of the main command spire, set just below the landing stages and astropathic pylons at the very summit. The entire tower had been cordoned off, and was guarded by the last remnants of her personal protective unit – blue-armoured soldiers wearing blank, reflective helms and carrying heavy-calibre autoguns.

The governor herself sat in her throne, surrounded by mobile pict units and shuffling attendants. The incoming tide of data brought no reassuring messages. The plague-hulk's speed had not diminished. Time was running out to get the last of the big troop carriers away, and many regiments were struggling to get to their launch-points in time. Low-level disorder was becoming widespread, with transport arteries blocked and convoys slowed. Shots had been fired over at the Bedelo training yards in order to secure the base perimeter, something that had only inflamed passions further.

Olgeir said nothing. Annarovea had a hundred other demands on her limited time, and he had no wish to add to them.

He turned his attention to the spire schematics. The intricate network of corridors and levels rotated slowly before him, picked out in the glowing lines of a hololith. Flashpoints were marked with a skull-rune, based on reports from the hard-pressed enforcers down in the depths. Slowly, the markers were creeping up the height of the spire.

He accessed pict-feeds from the upper-spire security net. The scenes were much the same wherever he looked – mobs running down transit lanes, looting or storming control points. The pict-feed had no audio track, and so he watched the eerily silent images of a world collapsing under the weight of mass hysteria.

He switched to the hab-levels immediately below the command dome. In one scene, he saw enforcers being driven back by a huge crowd. In another, he saw spire Guard units opt not to fire on a similarly massive mob, abandoning their barricades as the rabble charged them.

The tide of disorder was getting perilously close. As Olgeir studied the various incoming strands, he noticed how well organised they were. Their movements were coordinated expertly, flanking command points before taking them, isolating bottlenecks until they could be overwhelmed with force of numbers.

He scanned over to a different bank of pict screens. The story was the same everywhere – enforcers abandoning their posts or being overrun. As he pored over the feed, Olgeir noticed a familiar face at the forefront of the closest disturbances.

He zoomed in, correcting the image for distortion. Slowly, the features clarified.

Morfol.

Olgeir reached for his bolter, turning it to check the ammo-counter.

'You are not thinking of using that, I hope?' came Annarovea's concerned voice from the throne. She had seen the same thing.

Olgeir turned to face her. 'Your commissar seems to have forgotten his vows,' he said.

'Or is he the only one who remembers them?'

Annarovea looked fragile, yet defiant. Imperial governors were taught that their greatest and final duty was to fight and die to defend their worlds, and Olgeir knew that every sinew of Annarovea's body strained to call the Guard units back.

'You gave the order, governor,' said Olgeir quietly. 'You cannot take it back now. He must be stopped.'

'He is a good man.'

'He could be a saint. That means nothing.'

The populace were acting just as herd animals did when panicked – stampeding for an exit, any exit. It had been bound to happen, sooner or later, but Morfol had stirred them too soon. The commissar could not be allowed to jeopardise the void-lift – there were still three hours. A lot of carriers could be got away in that time, but only if anarchy were postponed for a little longer.

'I'm going down,' Olgeir said, walking over to the doors leading to the main hive transit shafts.

'My troops can handle him,' said Annarovea. The protest was weak – she had more than enough on her mind without worrying about trying to rein in a Space Wolf.

'Evidently not,' said Olgeir, reaching the gates and gesturing for the guards to let him pass.

'No slaughter, though,' called out the governor. 'Not unless you have to.'

Olgeir turned to face her. He was aware, as always, of how he looked – the scraggly beard, the metal studs in his tattooed flesh, the grim panoply of kill-markers and bone-totems covering his heavy battleplate.

Annarovea's face was drawn with anxiety. It was not for herself – it was for the world she had built, patiently and faithfully, and which now teetered on the edge of annihilation.

There was nothing he could say to that. He was *built* for slaughter. It was his only function, and the sole reason he had stayed on Kefa. If the enforcers could not stop Morfol, then that left only one option.

So he said nothing, but strode through the blast-doors and into the antechamber beyond.

From below, far below, he could already detect weapons-fire.

Vindicatus was racing. Once fully powered, the Grand Cruiser had phenomenal motive power, and Delvaux was happy to push it as hard as he could.

With the ignition of the main drives, the plague-hulk fell swiftly away aft. The *Festerax* was now barely a figment of the sensor-net, and it felt good to be out of its shadow. *Heimdall* had stayed in pursuit for a little while, before falling back again, its engines glowing over-hot. The Wolves' early bravery had cost them dear, and their teeth had been drawn.

Delvaux relaxed a little in his throne. He'd tensed up after the order was given, desperate to pull away before the decision reached the ears of Stormcaller. While the crew struggled to key up the void engines, he'd drummed his fingers impatiently, gnawed at by the fear that they would come for him.

On Fenris, the oathbreaker is lower than a beast.

Now, at last, they had ripped clear. Stormcaller would either die on the plague-hulk or remain too far behind to impede him. *Vindicatus* would arrive at Kefa Primaris well ahead of the deadly spore-pods, ready to immolate the planet and deprive the enemy of the army it sought.

It had been determined. There was no turning back. A great victory was at hand, a decisive stroke, and forever his name would be associated with it.

Not all men would have had the stomach to give the order. Those who did so were the elect, the chosen, the ones for whom greatness beckoned.

'Do we have the planet on our forward scopes yet?' he asked, trying to take his mind off the thought – even hypothetically – of pursuit.

'Not visual, lord,' replied Harryat, standing down below the throne dais, on a platform just above the sensor pits. Officers of his command staff came and went, handing him data-slate after data-slate to sign off on. 'You may inspect the augur schematic, if you wish.'

Delvaux narrowed his eyes. Was Harryat being curt with him? Was that disrespect in his voice? It was hard to tell. The captain spoke in an officious manner that gave nothing away.

Delvaux's eyes scanned across the expanse of the command bridge. Battle Sisters of Nuriyah's command were stationed at all the strategic points. The crew, from servitor up to tech-priest, were busy at their work. The low hum of conversation and data-exchange was just as it ever was.

Still, the nerves were there. There were thousands on the ship. Some of them could be plotting against him. Many of them could. Perhaps he should order Klaive to run a purge, once the business was over. You could never be too careful.

'Yes, I will take a look,' Delvaux said, adjusting his robes.

Harryat gestured to one of the sensorium operators, and a moment later a translucent schematic shimmered into existence at Delvaux's eye level. The *Festerax* was indicated with a red rune, and glowed softly to the right of his visual field. Kefa Primaris was marked out by a large blue circle, and stood on the very left. Between them, bisecting a long curved trajectory-line, was *Vindicatus*, approximately a third of the way between the two bodies. Even as Delvaux watched, the glyph blinked a little further along the line.

'And we are travelling at maximum speed?' he demanded.

'We are, lord.'

Delvaux grunted. He'd have liked to see the distances shrinking faster. He could feel his stomach beginning to knot. Tension always made his innards flare.

He was about to order the hololith away, when a warning rune lit up on the arm of his throne. He gazed down at it for a moment, unsure what it referred to.

'Do we have a problem?' he asked, almost to himself.

Harryat went over to a console, and consulted a bank of optical pict screens. 'Are you sure?' the captain muttered, speaking to the operator.

'Sure of what?' asked Delvaux. 'Captain, you will address your queries to me.'

Harryat ignored him, absorbed in what he was seeing, and ran another test. Just as he did so, more runes lit up on Delvaux's throne.

He knew what those ones meant.

'Nuriyah,' Delvaux voxed, trying to keep his voice steady.

The Battle Sister was already on the move, striding over from her station and calling a squad to her side. Her flamer-arm cast off its ceremonial drapery, and the feeder-nozzle kindled with a spurt of blue.

Harryat looked up at the throne. 'No response from checkpoints in outer security zone,' he reported. 'Weapons discharge in antechambers sixty-six and seventy-one.'

By then, Delvaux could see the results for himself, transmitted to his personal retinal implant. Something was heading towards the bridge, and it was moving very fast.

He is hunted unto the ends of the world.

How had they got on board?

Delvaux twisted around in his seat, growing alarmed. Squads of Battle Sisters were running now, heading for the entry points to lock them down. Sister Callia, one of those who had been taken from de Chatelaine's old force, was jogging towards one of the side entrances along with eight of her warriors, their bolters already drawn.

'Where is Klaive?' Delvaux blurted, speaking to no one in particular, running an increasingly panicked gaze over the command bridge. The black-robed confessor was nowhere to be seen.

A warning klaxon sounded. The faint sound of bolter explosions was now audible, growing louder with each moment.

'Seal the bridge!' cried Harryat, striding up from his position at the sensor station. He pulled a slim projectile pistol from the holster at his waist and released the safety. 'Do it now – full lock-down.'

There were many entrances and exits into the command space – at least eight visible from the throne dais. Immediately, all of them were shuttered by thick blast-doors that slammed down from their housings. The power supply switched to a separate generator, making the lights fade to a dull red. Proximity scanners whined into life, sending out faint bleeps as the augur equipment probed the spaces behind the sealed doors.

Delvaux felt his heart thumping hard, and swallowed thickly. The bridge contained over fifty Battle Sisters in full armour. They stood before each barred entrance, their weapons trained on the blast-doors. Several hundred armed guards in Ecclesiarchy body armour backed them up or stood sentry on the high terraces. The two Penitent Engines behind his throne were fully primed and armed, and each one of those was surely a match for a whole pack of Space Wolves.

In the distance, the sound of muffled bolt crashes grew louder. He thought he could hear, just on the edge of detection, something like snarling, and the hairs on the back of his arms rose.

'How soon before we reach Kefa?' he demanded.

Harryat looked up at him. That time, it was unmistakable – a faint blush of contempt. When this was over, the man would have to go.

'One hour, nineteen minutes,' Harryat replied.

'You can keep us secure for that long?'

'Depends who's trying to get in.'

'Do you venerate the soul of the Immortal Emperor?' snapped Delvaux. 'Do you love His Church with all your being? Do you wish to see the will of the Holy Ministorum enacted here?'

Harryat fixed Delvaux with his practised look of stony forbearance. 'I do, lord.'

'Then do your duty. Increase velocity two points beyond safety margins. We will not be derailed. We will not be deflected.'

Delvaux's thick lips pressed into a determined grimace.

'That world *will* burn.'

CHAPTER NINETEEN

Ingvar raced through the final chamber before reaching *Vindicatus*'s bridge. Jorundur loped alongside him, axe in hand. The two of them had made it up twenty levels and two kilometres in, killing silently and swiftly, before the alarm had been raised. After that, the fighting had escalated quickly. Ecclesiarchy-trained guards were well equipped and fanatically loyal, and the ship had a whole series of automatic defence mechanisms that had kicked into life once their progress had been discovered.

The Battle Sisters, though, were the real problem. On Ras Shakeh, Ingvar had observed how well the ones under de Chatelaine had fought. Those on the Cardinal's ship were no different, and once they had responded to the warning klaxons screaming out on every level, things had slowed up.

'I can't enjoy it,' voxed Jorundur, panting as he ran.

'What?'

'Killing them. I'd started to see them...' Jorundur snorted sourly, as if disgusted with himself, 'as allies.'

'Some still are,' said Ingvar, just as the doorway loomed before them.

The chamber around them was dark, lit only by devotional lumens that floated somewhere high in incense-clouded arches. Vast graven images of saints and primarchs stood in two files all along the main processional corridor, draped in shadow and wearing sombre, dull-eyed expressions. Ingvar hadn't been able to resist a grim smile when passing Russ's likeness. The Imperial sculptor had made him tall, noble, clean-shaven.

Perhaps he was, Ingvar had thought.

Just as they reached the ornate doorway leading to the bridge, bolt-ignitions whooshed out. Ingvar instantly dived over to his left, Jorundur to the right. The rounds pumped through the air where they'd just been.

Ingvar found the cover of a statue's plinth and spun around, rising to one knee to fire back, but his pursuers were already moving, darting into the cover of the statues ten metres back. He caught a faint glimpse of crimson power armour before the darkness swallowed them.

'Nuriyah's,' he voxed. 'Bring them down.'

By then Jorundur had reached cover of his own. He stowed his axe, unlocked his bolter, and began to creep forwards.

Ingvar ran a scan, but something in the ship's counter-offensive systems was dampening his helm-systems. He shut the proximity detector down and used his own hunt-sense.

Four of them. No, five. Spread out, moving behind the cover of the statues. Three this side, two the other.

Just as if he'd been stalking live prey on Fenris, he put himself in the mind of the enemy.

They'll break from Jorundur's side – fast and low. They need to draw us out.

He slunk forwards, still in the plinth's shadow. Every second that passed gave the Cardinal more time to prepare, to summon more defenders, but impatience could not be allowed to ruin this – Adepta Sororitas were serious opponents.

'Brother,' he voxed to Jorundur, 'stay in cover.'

'You are serious?'

'Stay in cover.'

Ingvar waited another two heartbeats, still in the shadows, his hyper-acute eyesight peering into the gloom ahead. He had to judge it to perfection.

Now.

He burst into movement just before they did. If he'd gone any earlier, they would have had a clear shot. As it was, two of them broke cover ahead of him, hampering the sight-lines of those behind.

Ingvar pounced on the foremost, loosing rounds from his bolter even as he swung *dausvjer*. His snarling blade lashed into the stomach of the lead Sister, cracking open her power armour and doubling her over.

The second made it into combat, wielding a chainsword two-handed and screaming devotional screeds. She was fast, and dragged the whining blades into Ingvar's side before he could bring his own blade to parry. He resisted the instinct to pull away, and let his armour take the damage. Staying close, he punched out heavily with his sword arm. The Sister's helm snapped back, her neck nearly broken, and she staggered away. Ingvar stumbled as he went after her, feeling hot blood running down from the wound where the chainsword had bitten.

Jorundur tore past him then, using Ingvar's fight to shield him as he ran down the remaining Battle Sisters. He sprayed a thick wall of bolts before him that blasted into the statues' bases and blew them apart. In a hail of spinning stone fragments, the Sisters were flushed out, firing back steadily and trying to retreat back down the long chamber.

Jorundur downed one of them, but was hit by return fire. More bolt-shells thudded in, exploding across his amour in a wave of sparks, and he lost his footing.

By then Ingvar had finished off the stricken Sister with a sharp stab to the throat and was adding his own volleys to Jorundur's. He sprinted at the two final adversaries, crashing into them both and forcing them to switch to close combat.

They were quick enough, but it did them little good. Ingvar's greater speed and bulk swept them aside – one beheaded with a savage slash from his power sword, the other run through with the same blade. The final Battle

Sister jerked and twitched on the sword as the energy field ran through her body, gurgling with trapped blood in her helm, before going limp.

Ingvar hurled the corpse aside before going to Jorundur. The old warrior got to his feet. His whole body bristled with irritation.

'Lucky shots,' he muttered.

Ingvar checked the data scrolling down his retinal feed. He'd taken a deep hit, but the blood was clotting and the skin already closing over.

'We are out of time,' Ingvar said, drawing out a krak grenade and heading for the blast-doors.

Jorundur joined him. 'Kraks won't dent those doors,' he said.

Ingvar primed the charge. 'Any better ideas?'

Jorundur activated the comm-bead which Ingvar had returned to him earlier. 'In position, Sister,' he voxed.

'Location noted,' came Callia's voice. 'The bridge is locked down – you'll need to come in fighting.'

'How many are with you?'

'Eight. More once the bolts are flying.' She paused. 'There are two Engines here, and a lot of guards.'

'It won't help him,' growled Jorundur. He glanced at Ingvar, who slammed a fresh magazine into the bolter and nodded. 'Open the doors.'

'Emperor be with you,' said Callia, and cut the link.

Ingvar and Jorundur pulled back to the walls on either side of the door, bolters held ready.

Ingvar could feel his wounds flaring painfully. Jorundur didn't look in much better shape – his armour was pocked and scored from shell-impacts.

This will be interesting.

Then, with a squeal and grind of metal on metal, the doors began to slide apart.

Gunnlaugur hardly noticed Njal forging his way towards the engine-gates. The lightning storm roared ahead, devouring and annihilating, and it barely registered. His every thought was consumed by the fight he'd initiated – he was locked into it, his mind fixed in total concentration.

No one else got close. The severity of the combat was so complete, so total, that even the most rabid of the mutants shied away. Three weapons swung and twisted in double-helix counter-movements, each pattern locked with the other. Gunnlaugur wielded his thunder hammer heavily, knowing how hard the hits needed to be in order to register with such an enemy. The Plague Marine champion responded equally savagely, slicing and slamming with the twin scythes embedded in his arms. For one of his Legion, he was swift, and the scythes danced a deadly series of sweeping figures.

The impacts, when they came, were crushing. Gunnlaugur was nearly floored by a sudden backhand lunge, barely keeping his feet before pushing back. The champion struggled to match the Wolf Guard's brutal skill with *skulbrotsjór*, and both his shoulder-guards were cracked nearly open. Whenever the addled ceramite took a hit, though, it closed over like scabrous flesh, morphing instantly into a hard defensive carapace. The Traitor's body absorbed punishment by sucking the force out of every blow. It felt like punching into water – the energy of the strike would just dissipate, spreading out across the creature's fleshy, yielding torso.

Broken slivers of battleplate were smashed clear. The last of Gunnlaugur's pelts was ripped away, hacked from his back by the scythes. The Death Guard's feeder-tubes and toxin-vials were shattered, spraying noxious fluids in blood-spattered streaks across both combatants.

Gunnlaugur whirled around, using the hammer to build up momentum, and sent a thundering blow ringing from the Death Guard's right arm. Ceramite cracked, cobwebbing out from the strike and rippling like crude oil. The Traitor withdrew steadily, wheezing through a dented rebreather, before pushing back. His left-hand scythe shot out, driving deep into Gunnlaugur's opposing arm. The blade entered at the elbow, severing armour cables and biting deep into the flesh.

Gunnlaugur roared again – this time from pain – and he lost his grip on the hammer. The huge weapon clanged to the ground, rolling to the edge of a smoke-laced pit and teetering on the edge.

The Traitor champion pressed his advantage immediately, rushing at Gunnlaugur with both blades aimed at his hearts. The long curved edges ran with shimmering green energies, poised to hammer clean through his ravaged breastplate.

Gunnlaugur surged forwards, both hands extended, eluding the twin blades as they came for him and seizing the champion by his throat. Hit hard, the Death Guard's balance went, and he stumbled back. Gunnlaugur followed up, squeezing up through the creature's gorget and driving the ceramite collar into the skin beneath.

The Death Guard hacked at him, choking, desperate to loosen the grip. The scythes rose and fell, slicing more chunks from Gunnlaugur's armour plate. The Wolf Guard took more wounds – a deep laceration across his left shoulder, a savage chop at his right flank – but he kept up the pressure.

The pain became excruciating. More blows came in, increasingly frantic, trying to deflect him, to knock him off-balance, to send him slamming to the ground. Gunnlaugur exerted all his remaining power into the twin-handed choke-hold, feeling the Traitor weaken at last. The scythe strikes grew more desperate, but the strength behind them ebbed.

Gunnlaugur gasped, tasting blood on his fangs as his armoured fingers twisted deeper. Cords severed, muscles ripped. With an agonised choke, the Traitor champion went limp at last. Gunnlaugur released the pressure, and the huge body thudded heavily onto its back, scythe-arms splayed. By then, the Plague Marine's neck was nothing more than a bloody, mucus-slick swamp.

Gunnlaugur sunk to his knees, exhausted. His entire body felt harrowed. His right arm fountained blood. He drew in deep breaths, fighting the well of dizziness that threatened to overcome him.

All around him, the enemy was in full retreat. Mutants were being driven like cattle, screaming as they were herded into the fire-shafts. He heard Haflói's whoops of triumph, cutting like clear ice through the tumult.

The enemy was broken. Njal had forged far ahead and secured the portals into the fusion chambers. The last of the Plague Marines were fighting a rearguard action, but the remaining Wolves had the initiative, and were not about to release it.

He grasped his elbow with his left fist. The bloodflow was slowing at last as clotting agents flooded the wound. His right hand felt numb and heavy, and he could no longer flex his fingers.

Grunting, he clambered to his feet again and retrieved his hammer. Hefting it in his good hand, he limped after his brothers. Up ahead, the gates towered over him. Blasphemous scripts ran around the iron frames.

Hafloí staggered up to him. He was bloody and battered, but his raw exuberance still radiated in his every movement. He was exhausted, just as they all were, but the savage spirit had not been extinguished yet.

'Good hunting, *vaerangi!*' he said, brandishing the severed helm of a Plague Marine in one fist.

Gunnlaugur grunted wearily. He had done well. They had all performed mighty feats – worthy of a song around firelight if they ever made it out again.

'That it is,' he growled, recovering some of his poise. With every second, the miracle of his genhanced physiology countered the heavy wounds he'd taken. 'And not over yet.'

At the vanguard, Njal was forcing the passage of the gates. The Rune Priest was still enveloped in a corona of raw flame. Lightning flickered around him, licking and twisting up against the frame of the central portal. Beyond the dark outlines of blackened iron, the air was raw-red. The heat was incredible, bleeding out of grilles the size of Titans. Vast exchangers hung on chains from the heights, thundering away as power coursed through them.

Hafloí and Gunnlaugur limped up to Njal's position, joining all the surviving Wolves at the portals – fifteen Hunters. The diminished warband assembled around Njal. Before them rose the main fusion reactor shell. Pillars of adamantium sheathed a heart of boiling liquid flames. The glowing innards of the reactor flared brighter, throwing bars of garnet-red light across the heart of the enginarium.

'Charges,' ordered Njal, drawing a spherical device from his belt.

Gunnlaugur, Hafloí and the others did likewise. They had all brought a heavily shielded thermal charge, each one capable of setting off a ruinous chain reaction if deployed within the heart of something as massive and plasma-rich as a starship engine.

Njal levelled his staff at the engine housing, and sent a bolt leaping towards it. The metal casing buckled, cracked, and melted, leaving a ragged-edged hole. From within, all that could be made out was the shimmer and blur of extreme energies.

'One hour,' ordered Njal, setting his chrono.

Gunnlaugur followed suit, just as they all did. It briefly crossed his mind that an hour was a ludicrously short time for them to get back to the Caestus assault rams – it had taken longer than that to fight their way in – but the mission demanded it, and there was no time to spare if the hulk were to be destroyed before reaching Kefa.

Njal turned to them all, looking across the assembled warriors. Already the howls of fresh defenders could be heard from the depths, ready to surge back out from whatever temporary holes they had found to shelter in.

Njal held his thermal charge up. Behind him, the swell and spit of the reactor silhouetted his armoured bulk.

'This is what we came for,' he said. 'Russ guide their path.'

Then he turned, and with an almighty heave, sent the first charge spinning into the depths of the reactor.

The voices were growing louder. Some of them seemed to welcome Baldr's presence in their midst, some of them were hostile. For all that, he could not catch the words properly. They sounded familiar, with inflections he thought he ought to recognise, but the chatter was just too diffuse to latch on to.

As more time went on, it became harder to distinguish his own thoughts from the babble around him. Even the Mycelite's soft tones half blended into the morass, just one more part of the *Festerax*'s gestalt consciousness.

'They are invaders,' the Mycelite assured him. 'You can drive them out.'

For a moment, Baldr wondered why *he* was needed to do this. The Mycelite was a powerful sorcerer – could he not do this himself? Were there not a thousand corrupted souls on board the plague-hulk who could have taken his place? What was so unique, and precious, about him?

That troubling thought, though, was soon buried, and replaced with desire. Baldr found that he *wanted* to act. The interlopers felt like a wound lodged deep in his own flesh, barbed and hooked. The pain of their presence was a real, physical pain. If he had been a mortal, he would have drawn a blade and excised them.

But he was no longer a mortal. He was the *Festerax*, the majestic scion of the Plaguefather, just a part of the infinite tide that would sweep away the rotten Imperium and bring an end to the fruitless striving, the endless scheming, the millennial violence.

It had been going on too long. The universe needed *rest*, repose from the struggle. It needed to slip back into the wet embrace of decay and gracefully slide into obsolescence. That was its fate anyway – to resist it further was, as the Mycelite had taught him, to usher needless pain into a reality already ringing with it.

'You know what to do,' came the Mycelite's voice again, half buried in the psychic hubbub.

'I do not,' replied Baldr. His senses were foggy, much as they had been before the attack in the gorge on Ras Shakeh. He felt, deep down, as if something were terribly, horribly wrong, but it was impossible to remember just what it was. All he could sense with any certainty was the matter of the ship around him – its vast spars, its thousands of interlocking chambers, its immense weapons arrays and its gargantuan engines, all swelling with nigh-on infinite power. His mind stretched out through it all, creeping like a cancer into every part.

'You do,' insisted the Mycelite. 'Use your gifts. Search for the source of the pain.'

Baldr did as he was asked. He withdrew into himself, blocking out the spectral chatter from the *Festerax* as best he could, delving into the network of sensor readings and physical sensations that constituted his new nervous system.

His mind swept through it all, running down twisting passageways and abyssal transit shafts. He moved through the colossal birthing chambers where new mutations were spawned from rows of cylindrical pods. He soared across forge-chambers where munitions were hammered into being on endless segmented conveyor belts. He ghosted amid the rendering plants where the flesh of a million conquered subjects was boiled down in greasy tanks, ready to be piped to the stomachs of limitless armies. He lingered in the spore vaults where thousands upon thousands of torpedoes waited to be sent out into the void, ready to start the cycle of death and rebirth all over again.

The pain was in none of those places. Only when he reached the ship's ancient core, where the reactors belched and roared, did he feel the sharp stab return.

They were *there* – the parasites, clawing their way towards his innards. He heard their voices raised in fury and triumph, and felt the bite of tiny weapons stabbing at his flesh.

For a moment, something made him hesitate. One of the voices made his hearts stop – it brought the terror rushing back, and for a moment he could almost grasp at the source of his doubts.

'Good,' said the Mycelite, soothingly. 'You have found them. Now flex your muscles.'

The doubt faded. Baldr realised he could do it. He felt a burning sensation, and remembered the collar he had once worn about his neck, but it was not enough to prevent him. A well of astonishing, exhilarating power surged up, frothing and surging. He directed his mind towards the interlopers, suddenly seeing how they could be destroyed.

If he had had lips, he would have smiled. As it was, the entirety of the *Festerax* seemed to shake with renewed energy.

From somewhere, he knew the word.

'*Skemmdarvargur,*' he breathed, and the rune-curse was echoed by a thousand new voices in his mind.

The last charge had just been flung into the furnace when it happened. Green-tinged energies suddenly lanced down from the enginarium roof, far out of visual range and lost in swirling clouds of soot.

Spears of warp-matter slammed down among the Wolves, whipping and virulent. Arik, one of Fellblade's pack, was impaled on the shimmering shafts. He jerked, prone, for a few moments, before his body exploded outwards, showering the engine chamber with armour-chunked gore.

Two more warriors were caught in secondary tendrils of aetheric power, their breastplates smashed in a bloody stab of warp-kinetics. The rest of the warband fell back, aiming bolters up at the hidden source of the deluge. Only Njal remained in place, still burning with stormlight. The Rune Priest met the incoming warp-spears with fires of his own, and the engine chamber rang and spat with the messy impacts of rival wyrd-work.

Gunnlaugur drew back with the others, unable to fight whatever power had been unleashed. They need to *move* – to finish the task and get off the hulk before it ripped itself apart. He tensed, ready to race to Njal's position.

'Stay back!' warned Njal, fighting the rain of esoteric fire. More aether-lances crashed down around him, spraying madly as they hit his protective aegis. The heat, already febrile, ramped up further, making his outline blur.

Njal launched a counter-attack, throwing twisting columns of razor-edged lightning high into the heights. Huge explosions rang out, bringing down arch-sections in crashing clouds. The two rival energies surged against one another, filling the entire chamber with a lurid mix of silver and green. The matched spheres of energy pushed against one another, swelling, flickering and striving. Njal was driven to his knees. Gunnlaugur and the others could only watch, their weapons held ready but with no living foe to take on.

Eventually, grindingly, Njal's spirit asserted itself. His neon-white pillars of storm-fire punctured the blooms of corruption, tearing clear shafts through the raging storm. He stood again, one fist raised in defiance, the other holding the skull-staff. With a resounding clap, he summoned a roll of thunder and sent it sweeping up into the distant roof. The whole structure shuddered, shaken to its rotten foundations. The rain of corruption roared and raged, and more debris showered down over the growling enginarium machines.

Finally, the rain of tainted power guttered out, as if shoved bodily back into the warp. Great clangs rose up from the depths, and the howl of ancient winds echoed for a few heartbeats more before sinking back into silence.

Njal sank to one knee again, breathing heavily. Gunnlaugur rushed over to him. The Rune Priest seemed drawn from effort.

'The ship,' Njal rasped.

'What of it?' asked Gunnlaugur, crouching beside him.

'It is the *ship*.'

Gunnlaugur didn't understand. 'We can–' he began, but Njal cut him short.

'You will do nothing,' said the Rune Priest. 'I know where it is. I *felt* it.' He looked up, searching into the infinite darkness above them. Dimly, the outlines of great buttresses and stairwells could be made out, twisting into shadow. 'It will crush us all.'

Gunnlaugur looked over his shoulder. Twelve Wolves stood around them, all of them battle-ravaged. Beyond their slender defensive line, the sound of mutant activity was already beginning to creep back into aural range. The enemy had been blooded, its champions slaughtered, but its near-limitless numbers had only been curtailed.

'Go,' said Njal. 'The assault rams can be reached. We have done what we came for.'

'The hunt is not complete.'

Njal chuckled grimly. 'You fight like the Slayer, *vaerangi*, but you cannot fight this, so save your hammer for another dawn.' The smile disappeared. '*Go*. I will not order it again.'

'How will you get out?' Gunnlaugur asked.

'You have less than an hour,' growled Njal, summoning Nightwing to his shoulder.

Giving in to the inevitable, Gunnlaugur saluted Njal, fist-on-chest in the Fenrisian way. Then he turned, gathered the survivors together and shook the gore from *skulbrotsjór*. He was the only pack-leader left alive, and the rest of the Hunters, their armour scored and their blades cracked, looked close to exhaustion.

'To me, then,' he snarled, already focusing on the road ahead. It would be a bloody path. 'To the Caestus.'

CHAPTER TWENTY

Olgeir raced down nine spire-levels, picking up support from those of Annarovea's security staff still at their stations as he went. He was obliged to silence a knot of half-hearted agitators up in the exclusive protected zone, but the real disorder was still in the ranks below, drawn from the hab-units that sheltered the skilled worker cadres.

He eventually reached a wide assembly chamber just below the main portals to the upper spire. It was a natural defensive position, with wide fire-lanes opening up across a huge semicircular auditorium. Dozens of entrances opened out into the lower levels of the auditorium, but only one gate-cluster guarded the summit, where the turbo-shafts leading up into the higher spire had been sited. Crowds had assembled at the base of the auditorium, and they were already moving up the aisles towards the summit.

Olgeir emerged from the upper portal, flanked by a dozen blue-armoured spire guards. They had their weapons drawn, but for the time being he kept his own bolter lowered. Thus far, his presence alone had been enough to deter even the most desperate of rioters, and he had no appetite for killing more than necessary.

'Do not fire unless I give the word,' he ordered his escort, taking up position under the upper gate's lintel.

The guards crouched into firing positions around him, training their projectile weapons on the crowd below. The mob kept approaching, more slowly now, clambering up over the rows of empty seating with their eyes fixed on the prize ahead.

Olgeir watched them come. There must have been thousands assembled, with many more filtering into the auditorium from the low-level entrances. The closest were less than fifty metres away, though the sight of a Space Wolf standing guard above them slowed them down.

'That is *enough!*' roared Olgeir, his helm-enhanced voice echoing across the vast space. The crowd's progress halted. 'Go back. Leave this place. You will not be allowed to travel higher.'

Olgeir looked across the front ranks of the mob. They were not soldiers. Their faces were uncovered, exposing fearful, desperate expressions. They had never been given any reason but fear and duty to serve their masters in the elite spire heights, and once a greater fear had penetrated their minds, that coercive force lost much of its deadening power.

Olgeir saw hab-workers, menials, minor Administratum officials, medicae field staff and pedagogues among them. They all wore the same panicky pallor. The jet-black armour of Adeptus Arbites enforcers could be made out further back in the press of bodies. That was surprising – they had a reputation for incorruptibility. Then again, when the entire world was teetering on the brink of annihilation, perhaps even their heavy conditioning could be suborned.

'Do not listen to him,' came a new voice.

Olgeir's eyes snapped onto the source. All around him, a dozen weapons trained on the same point.

A lone figure strode up from the lower levels of the auditorium. He advanced up the long central aisle, and the crowds parted to allow him passage.

Morfol.

The lord commissar was wearing what looked like some kind of carapace armour draped in robes of oily black and bearing the death mask emblem of the Imperium. He was accompanied by a retinue of heavily armed enforcers together with a small cadre of Guard soldiers. More armed troops, marching in disciplined ranks, followed behind.

'Come no closer, commissar,' warned Olgeir, resisting the urge to aim his bolter.

Morfol halted at the forefront of his ramshackle army. The light of certainty burned in his eyes. Olgeir had seen that light in a hundred other commissars on a hundred other worlds, and had always admired it.

'Or you will do what to me, Angel of the Emperor?' Morfol asked. His words carried to all corners of the huge space, broadcast by vox-emitters in his armoured collar. 'You will end me? You think I fear that?' He turned to address his followers. 'There is nothing to fear in death. There is *everything* to fear in cowardice.' Morfol knew his craft, and the crowd began to shuffle forwards once more. 'An enemy is coming. We see it on the augurs. The Emperor – as He must ever will it – demands that we *fight*. If the governor will not do it, if her newfound bodyguard will not, then *we* must.'

The lord commissar's words were infectious. As Olgeir watched, the front rank moved, climbing up over the rows of seats. Fear still shone in their wide eyes, but there was something else there, too – a dogged, desperate determination.

Morfol was a powerful orator. He was courageous, too, and marched with them, drawing a chainblade as he came.

Olgeir knew he could take Morfol out with a single shot, but that would enrage the others and vindicate his words. He knew he could hold the high gate virtually indefinitely against such opposition, but that would provoke huge bloodshed and tie up the spire completely.

As he hesitated, Annarovea's comm-signal blinked into life.

'My lord, a ship approaches orbital range,' said the governor, her voice reproachful.

Olgeir's grip on his bolter tightened by a fraction. 'Impossible,' he replied, glancing at his retinal chrono. 'Too soon.'

'It's not the one we've been tracking – it is a Grand Cruiser, it doesn't respond to hails, and it's ignoring the troop carriers in orbit. Its shields are raised.'

Olgeir backed up towards the high gate, keeping his weapon trained on the advancing Morfol. The lord commissar pushed on fearlessly.

'That ship is not here to help,' Olgeir warned.

'Does it not have Navy-level ordnance?' Annarovea's voice was tight with suspicion.

'It is a Ministorum ship, governor. They will not speak to you.'

'I can recall the Guard regiments. We have been hasty – we gave up on defence too soon.'

'Do *not* do it.' Olgeir felt his frustration rising. The mob was inching closer, climbing towards the gate with ever-more determined steps. 'Listen. Even if they could stop this thing, they will not. I say it again: they are not here to help.'

When Annarovea replied, her exasperation was evident. 'Then why *are* they here?'

Olgeir immediately imagined the life-eater torpedoes being readied for launch. It would be a quicker death, but just as agonisingly pointless as the plague. What had happened? Had Njal sanctioned Delvaux to run ahead? Or had the mission already failed?

By then, Morfol was less than twenty metres away from him, shouting out encouragement to his followers and waving his chainblade to beckon them on. Every movement he made exemplified that damned Commissariat certainty.

'I will return as soon as I can, governor,' voxed Olgeir. 'Until then, maintain the troop-lift. Do nothing to slow it.'

He cut off the comm-link, and burst into motion, charging down from the gate and leaping at Morfol. The commissar had no time to react – he tried to get his chainblade into position, but Olgeir swatted it aside. Then the Space Wolf's gauntlet was clamped around Morfol's neck, lifting him into the air one-handed.

Morfol glared back, still defiant, mastering his fear. 'Like I... said,' he gasped, his hands scrabbling uselessly against Olgeir's grip, 'I do not fear... death. Kill me here, and there are... thousands more.'

The crowd had fallen back when Olgeir charged, but now they edged forwards again, caught between fear, uncertainty and their lingering sense of outrage.

'Kill you?' hissed Olgeir, his eyes boring into the mortal's own. 'I could kill you with a twist of my fingers. I could kill every soul in this room and not one blade would come close to touching me. But why would I? You are *irrelevant*. You talk of duty, but I have already told you what you must do. If you will not listen, then you damn yourself.'

Morfol was struggling for breath by then, and Olgeir released his grip by a fraction. The mob around them kept its position, held rapt by the scene before it.

'If those spores land on this world,' Olgeir went on, 'you will have all the fighting you could ever wish for. Believe me, I would fight alongside you then. Do not be fooled, there can be no victory. Unlike some of my brothers, the prospect of a glorious death for no purpose does not fill my hearts with joy, but I would fight until the last breath nonetheless.'

Morfol was listening. His eyes bulged, his forehead was shiny with sweat, but he listened.

'Until then, there is only *one* duty – to get as many living souls off this world as we can. Your governor understands this, your generals understand it. You are charged with discipline on this world, lord commissar. Why do you not understand?'

For a few seconds longer, Morfol remained defiant. Then his bloodshot eyes ran across Olgeir's war-plate. He saw the tokens of a dozen campaigns, and the marks made by an extended lifetime of unbroken service. He saw the bloodstains, still uncleared from the fighting on the comm-station, and the heavy marks of use on his weapons.

The resolve went out of him. Olgeir released him, and Morfol fell to his knees, heaving in deep breaths.

Olgeir turned to the crowd. 'I told you to leave,' he growled.

Those closest fell back, cowed by the low threat-note in his voice. Bereft of Morfol's leadership, their will became fragile. Some looked to the commissar, but he no longer met their gaze. Instead, Morfol stared up at Olgeir, a mix of humiliation and resolve on his bruised face.

'How long have we got?' he asked.

'Less than three hours,' said Olgeir. 'Use the time wisely. It might be all you have left.'

Then he turned on his heel, and strode back to the upper gate where his escort still waited. Their guns remained trained on the crowds below, but Olgeir doubted they would be needed now.

As he walked, he made a record of Morfol's locator-ident. If the spores started to fall, he would track him down again. He had a sense the commissar might be a good man to fight alongside when all the other barricades had fallen.

That done, he reopened the comm-link to Annarovea.

'The spire is secure, governor,' he voxed, reaching the gate. 'I am coming back up.'

Baldr shuddered, and drew in a painful breath. It was air – real air. He was using his lungs again, and the body that housed them was his own.

The Mycelite's foetid grotto surrounded him once more, as dark and clammy as it had been before. The Plague Marine gazed up at him, and his withered features were twisted into a smile.

'Well done,' he said.

As soon as he heard the words, Baldr realised what he had done. The horror of it cut him to the core, and he raged against his bonds, thrashing and kicking out. The glutinous matter around him flexed by a finger's width, cracking where his right leg pushed against it.

The Mycelite remained calm, watching him with the keen interest of a guardian watching a child.

'It will do you no good to fight it,' the Plague Marine told him, shuffling back over to where he had been seated. 'Memory will fade again. You will become the ship, the ship will become you.' His smile drifted away. 'Imagine it – mightier than any of your brothers, mightier than any of mine. You will be something new.'

The fog of deception felt weaker now. Baldr's hatred was stronger, driving his body against its bonds. 'I will not do that again,' he swore.

'Evidence tends to the contrary.'

'I will fight you.'

The Mycelite shrugged. 'You cannot sustain your resistance.' He ran his withered hands up the length of his staff. 'The *collar*, though. The remaining obstacle. We must find some way to circumvent that.'

'I felt them reach the target,' said Baldr, clinging to the one sliver of hope. 'They have planted their charges. That ends the game.'

The Mycelite looked equivocal. 'Nothing in this vessel is beyond you. Your mind can travel down communications conduits and drift through cogitator wafers. You can manipulate matter, divert energies. Eliminating a few thermal devices from your fusion cores will be trivial.'

Baldr pushed against the material around him once again. It didn't shift at all.

'I will not do it,' Baldr said again.

'You will.'

'You are exhausted. You cannot force me again.'

The Mycelite looked up at him with an expression of genuine affection on his etiolated face. 'Ah, but the Grandfather has been kind. To even *witness* you – that would have been enough, but to be the guide to your ascension... That is more than I know how to compass.' He got to his feet again and hobbled up to Baldr, leaning on the staff two-handed. The Mycelite's breath was sweet with corruption.

'Perhaps you wonder why you are so important,' the Mycelite said. 'Perhaps it has occurred to you that I myself am a sorcerer, and that there are many others on this vessel who are touched by the Eye's gifts. Perhaps, you are telling yourself, this whole thing is a deception, and it is not *you* who is important at all. Perhaps that gives you some hope.'

Baldr regarded him scornfully. 'I will not do it,' he said for a third time, issuing the words like a litany against destruction.

'But I cannot command this vessel like you do,' the Mycelite went on. 'No one can. The talent you command is not something any of my Legion could ever match. Shall I tell you why, nightjar? We are interlopers, that is why, merely passengers. You, on the other hand, are where you belong.'

Baldr spat at him again, trying not to listen.

'You call this ship the *Festerax*,' said the Mycelite, sounding amused. 'I've always liked the name, but I did not give it.'

As the Mycelite spoke, cracks of blue light began to run down the inner walls of the grotto. Clumps of fungus fell away, plopping wetly on the floor. A great sigh ran across the chamber's roof, as if huge and rusty metal beams were being hauled into new formations.

'All things are corrupted by time. Thoughts, deeds, words. They all twist in the aether, mutating as the whim of the gods demands.'

Whole sections of the grotto's roof suddenly lifted away, pulled clear by massive cantilevers. A chill blue light flooded in, exposing swathes of pale fungi trembling in the dark. The temperature plummeted. Baldr narrowed his eyes against the sudden glare. The Mycelite's chamber was just a part of a larger structure, one that was being revealed as the shell around them unravelled.

'*Festerax* is a forgivable slip,' the Mycelite went on, 'a melding of similar sounds. It was merely luck, or perhaps fate, that made it possible.'

The last of the chamber's roof swung away, pulled clear on vast chain lengths. The chill illumination exposed Baldr's position for the first time – he was bound by stone-hard lengths of organic matter, as tough as oak and covered in veinous growths. The binding roots that supported him had engulfed a platform of stone.

A towering ceiling soared away above him, half lost in a miasma of pale blue fog. Thick-boled columns of granite supported ranks of gothic arches, all of which enclosed a teardrop-shaped platform of dusty marble. There were terraces beyond that, rows of sensor stations. In the seamy distance soared an armourglass viewing portal.

It was a command bridge.

'The *Festerax* is truly massive,' said the Mycelite, looking up in appreciation as the last vestiges of his fungus chamber unfolded themselves. In the cold light, he was hunched and diminished. 'But its core, as such hulks always are, is a single vessel. Wrecks and void-corpses were added to it, piling atop one another and bound by the will of gods and daemons, and so the original was lost, buried amid the vastness of what had been accumulated by time.'

Baldr recognised the things around him. He saw runes carved into the granite, thick with dust. He saw iron-rimmed doorways running around the chamber's edge, gaping blindly into nothingness. He saw command stations, each one manned by skeletal figures in pearl-grey fatigues. The crew were long dead, and their mummified cadavers slumped motionlessly in their seats.

'You know these things?' asked the Mycelite, hobbling across the filth-strewn marble towards the closest corpse. 'Perhaps you recognise their voices? They were speaking to you, Baldr. You recognised the language, even if you could not hear all the words. They have been here for nine thousand years.' He chuckled mournfully, and pulled the corpse's chair around. A dust-dry skull wobbled on a bony neck. 'I am afraid they are all quite mad. It is a long time to be locked in here, never quite being allowed to die.'

Baldr looked on grimly. The bodies all bore the age-faded livery of kaerls. Some of them seemed to have fused with their old machines, locked together in a desiccated embrace of entropy. All wore expressions of terror on their frozen faces.

'So that is why *you* must be the one to command the *Festerax*,' said the Mycelite, shuffling back over to him. 'You are on the command throne. The bound souls will only listen to you. This *ship* will only listen to you. If you learn to hear them, they will tell you why. They will tell you that only a Son of Russ could ever pilot this vessel, and not just any Son of Russ, but one marked out by the bounteous masters of the warp. They will tell you that *this* is the core, the heart of it all.'

He drew closer, wheezing as he leaned on his staff.

'They will tell you the ship's name was never *Festerax*, but *Frostaxe*, and that it last plied the void unsullied when the primarchs lived among men.' The Mycelite shot Baldr a wry smile. 'Perhaps you now also see the truth of what I was telling you: we are all the *same*, Baldr Fjolnir. We draw from the same source, we are prey to the same corruptions.'

He laughed – a foul sound, dredged up from a withered throat.

'You are home,' he said. 'The voices will drag you back in, and you will learn to listen. This has always been your home, and it has always been calling you.'

With a wrench of hollow insight, Baldr felt the truth of it then. He *had* heard the voices. He could still hear them, like after-echoes of a recited saga. They would whisper to him until his mind cracked and he joined them in eternal confinement, buried alive at the core of the plague-raddled Hel-ship.

He would give in. The Mycelite's deceptions would spin their veils of decay again, and his mind would once more join the choir of those locked forever in the *Frostaxe*'s tomb-cold soul. It could not be resisted, not forever.

'Time is short,' the Mycelite whispered, gazing into Baldr's eyes with an intense, almost infatuated, look. 'Soon we will go in again, you and I. You will purge the disease from your glorious, eternal body. After that, you will destroy the last of your brothers. You will not need to emerge. You will never need to emerge.'

His soft eyes glistened in the dark.

'Then we will be alone again, you and I, and with all the time in creation.'

Ingvar and Jorundur charged straight into a hail of las-fire and bolter-rounds. Callia and her squad of Battle Sisters were on either side of the doorway, hunkered down behind overturned cogitator stands and firing steadily ahead.

The two Wolves joined them. Ingvar crashed down beside Callia, his bolter kicking in his right hand as he added his own barrage to hers.

'My thanks, Sister,' he voxed.

'Bring him down,' she replied stonily. 'I need no more than that.'

The Cardinal's enormous throne was more than sixty metres away. Once clear of the piles of half-demolished cogitator units, the route to it had almost no cover. Though taken by surprise by Callia's rapid change of allegiance, the rest of the command bridge's defenders were rallying, laying down disciplined walls of suppressive fire while others advanced through the maze of sensor pits beyond the throne. Ingvar could see Sisters of Nuriyah's retinue among them, accompanied by more Ecclesiarchy troops. There must have been dozens of them, all told. Once they brought all their guns to bear, there would be few hiding places across the expanse of the bridge.

Ingvar glanced up towards the throne. Delvaux cowered there, his outline blurred by a personal shield-generator. He seemed to be shouting something, and Ingvar caught the familiar outline of his jowly face trembling.

Before he could see any more, though, the view was obscured by the two Penitent Engines striding into range. One was still on the far side of the throne, turning clumsily amid a squeal and roar of gears. The other lurched into range, venting flames from both extended weapon-arms. Circular saws mounted on either fist accelerated into whirls of adamantium, sending sparks spinning through the gouts of crimson.

'We do this quick, or not at all,' said Ingvar, gauging the distance to the throne. A rapid sprint would bring him into strike-range of Delvaux's throat within seconds, but he'd have to survive a punishing amount of fire.

Callia nodded. 'We'll break left, laying down covering fire. You can do the rest?'

Ingvar glanced over at Jorundur, who was hunched behind the broken remains of a sensor-unit and firing two-handed. The Old Dog nodded towards him. 'Say the word.'

'Then now,' Ingvar ordered.

Callia and the rest of the Battle Sisters leapt clear of their cover and advanced over towards the left flank of the battlefield, running hard and firing all the while. One Sister was hit while out in the open, going down in a whirl of smashed armour and blood-spray, but the rest made it to the doubtful security of a comm-station – a semicircular array of battered machinery rising from the bridge's polished floor. As the Battle Sisters ran, they drew whole swathes of tracer fire towards their position.

A few seconds later, Ingvar and Jorundur burst out, heading straight out into the open. Ingvar fired one-handed, laying down a withering rain of bolt-shells. Jorundur stayed on his shoulder, adding to the hail of rounds. Exposed Ecclesiarchy troops were blown away, lost in the tumbling haze of blasted marble and exploding rockcrete.

Ingvar sprinted low and fast, relying as before on hunt-sense rather than armour-sensors. He swerved unconsciously around an incoming blast from a heavy projectile weapon and powered onwards, never breaking stride.

'I'll take the Engine,' voxed Jorundur, racing towards the first lumbering war machine.

Ingvar nodded, and raced directly for the throne. He veered away from the worst of the incoming fire, but a shell ricocheted off his shoulder-guard, nearly sending him sprawling. He fired back, suppressing the worst of the barrage, and then the throne loomed up ahead, half screened by the whirl of blown dust and debris.

To his right, he was dimly aware of Jorundur taking on the Penitent Engine – he could hear the roars of fury and the sharp clash of metal on metal. He sensed the incoming presence of Nuriyah and the main body of Delvaux's defenders. In a few more heartbeats they'd be on him, and then things would get difficult.

He pounced away from a line of solid-round projectiles and leapt up at the throne's dais. Clouds of dust ripped away, and for an instant he saw

Delvaux's fat face glaring down at him in terror. Shielding still glittered between them, but that would never be enough to keep the Gyrfalkon from his prey.

Ingvar bounded up the steps, firing at the shield cover to rip it clear while activating *dausvjer* with his free hand. The blade-edge flared with energy, sensing an imminent kill.

Then, just as he was about to leap, hidden compartments on the throne's base swivelled open, revealing twin lines of autogun-barrels.

Too late, Ingvar tried to arrest his ascent and dive away. The guns opened up with an echoing volley, blasting him from the dais and sending him skidding across the pocked marble floor. He spun around, his vision blurry and flecked with red, before returning fire, strafing the throne's base and silencing the concealed batteries.

By then, though, time had run out. He felt a shadow fall across him, and looked up, twisting to avoid the hammer of incoming fire.

The second Penitent Engine towered over him, its flamers active and its saws whirling. There was no escape, and no room to move – before he could so much as raise his blade the war machine had extended its arms, raising them like some savage champion of pagan worlds, before plunging them down.

Gunnlaugur ran from the enemy.

He wanted to turn. Every fibre of his being yearned to stop the headlong race to the assault rams, swivel on his heel and bring his hammer to bear again. It had felt good, to be unleashed once more. He had remembered what it was like to command again – free of doubt, free of dissension.

And now he was haring through the endless gloom as if fear meant something to him.

He could have laughed, though the sound would have been bitter.

We race for the landing stages like whipped curs.

Every second that passed brought the thermal charges closer to ignition. The amount of destructive potential now laid in the churning heart of the hulk was chilling to contemplate – those charges would crack the enginarium's shell as easily as Gunnlaugur's fists might crack a skull.

The pack remained close on his heels. He could hear their strained, throaty breathing even through their armour. They were near the end of their strength, driven to extremity by the long, punishing, non-stop combat.

'*Faster!*' he thundered, giving them no quarter.

And they responded. They squeezed a morsel more energy from burning muscles, and their ragged breaths grew even more strained. They did not run because they feared what was on their heels. They did it because *he* had ordered it, and because their pride was now to live up to his demands.

I am vaerangi again, thought Gunnlaugur, and, despite everything, that kindled a spark of pride within him.

More corridors wound away ahead, cloaked deep in eternal night, twisting like entrails through the unimaginable vastness. Already he could sense fresh filth scurrying to cut them off – to clog the narrow ways with their own dead, to claw at them and lock them within the ship that would soon be their death-pyre.

He checked the chrono. It ticked down mercilessly. He could no longer detect Njal. He did not know if Ingvar and Jorundur still lived. He did not know whether Olgeir had made it to Kefa, and if anything had been salvaged from that world. All he knew for certain was what he could *smell* – frantic hatred from the ship around him, grim determination from his brothers behind him.

From somewhere, from some place lodged deep within his warrior's soul, he dredged up a sliver of additional energy. His strides lengthened by a fraction, his hammer swung further, his wounds cried at him more intensely.

'For the oathbreaker!' he bellowed. 'We will *live*, if for no other cause than to rip his faithless heart out!'

And amid the dark, running hard to keep up with the Wolf Guard's furious progress, his brothers roared the same vow, using it to fuel them, to drive them onwards in hatred.

For the oathbreaker.

The pain was phenomenal. It did not merely strike at his body – it raked across his soul, chilling it, scraping it into near-oblivion. Each time Njal delved into the source, the frigid grasp of agony became more acute, as if he were being shoved beneath pack-ice and held down there. Actinic fire rippled across him, caught and twisted by the elemental power unleashed within. He was racing, hurtling up through the heart of darkness, propelled by will alone in defiance of the law of the universe.

There was no possibility of withdrawal. There was no time left to use his mortal body as the others did. He had been forced to haul on the deepest fragments of runecraft, to turn his very body into an instrument, to send it soaring just as Nightwing did.

The raven cawed and circled around him, pushing higher, spiralling up through the myriad levels that constituted the *Festerax*'s upper reaches.

Njal followed it. He was already far above the enginarium and still climbing fast. Lightning flared and snapped, buoying him like a rising flood. He streaked upwards, tearing along vertical shafts gouged through the vessel's core, and the rune-storm boomed in his wake, roiling with soul-summoned thunder.

Decks passed by like dreams, lost in shadows. He caught only glimpses of their interiors. There were colossal arches leading to unknowable regions of utter darkness, unimaginably vast pillars holding up grotesque halls of plague-devices, pulsing energy fields throwing lurid green light across the gaping chasms. Some of those chambers might have lain undisturbed for millennia. Secrets might have been set down in those foetid halls, secrets that could change the course of the war, or summon back a golden age for humanity, or expose the forbidden secrets of the ten-thousand-year Imperium.

Or there might be nothing – nothing but ruin and disease, festering forever amid shadows that never lifted and air that never stirred.

Njal surged up through it all, his totems clattering against his armour, his staff-skulls rippling in the headwind. He was drawing near to the source. He could *feel* it, lodged like a canker in his mind.

I have faced this thing before.

Even amid his pain, the thought intrigued him. No mortal had ever set foot in this hulk and lived. There was no enemy within it that he could have met in combat before.

And yet. Something about the spears of warp-power that had eviscerated his warriors had borne the tang of dreadful familiarity. He swooped past a lattice of intersecting buttresses, ascending more rapidly now as momentum built. The air became less furiously hot. He saw moisture glistening on the surfaces of the iron and stone around him. Growths, shaggy like beards of moss, hung from every spar and brace-beam.

Nightwing called out, now just a few dozen metres above him. The raven had flown unerringly towards the target.

Njal drew deep on the runes, and thundered after it. He raced up a long well of iron, a narrow shaft that closed down nigh to the width of his armour plate, before bursting out into a vast spherical chamber above.

The sphere was kilometres in diameter, half drowned in abyssal shadows and dank with nebulae of drifting spores. Arcs of green-tinged fulguration cracked and shivered across the cyclopean gulf. Above him, suspended on hundreds of bone-like spars and tendrils, hung a warship. It was part melded to the concave walls around it, lodged like a thrown blade in a wound. Enormous conduits connected the warship's hull to the greater mass of the *Festerax* around it, many throbbing with electrical currents or swelling with seething liquids.

Njal immediately recognised the profile. Despite millennia of decay and damage, he saw the gunmetal-grey of the armour plates. He saw the knot-work icons etched above the ventral gunwales, and the vessel's name picked out in gold-edge runes.

Frostaxe.

Nightwing screamed at the obscenity of it, pinning its wings back and tearing towards the starship. Njal followed the raven up, and the shadow of the starship's hull fell across him. He saw many ways in, gaping holes in the once-proud exterior. Even as he did so, he sensed the malign force cradling within it, as old and maleficent as the gods of ruin.

And I am already weakened.

The Dark Wolf growled then, stirred by the enormous discharge of rune-power keeping Njal aloft. The Rune Priest thrust upwards towards the nearest breach, and grasped the shredded adamantium with both hands.

For a moment he hung above the gulf, his muscles flaring with pain. The chrono inside his helm ticked down, marking the shrinking window before the charges ignited. He looked down, seeing his boots suspended over the yawning void.

Enough.

He dragged himself up and into the carcass of the warship. Hauling his bulk onto the ironwork structure, he reached intact decking and stood once again on firm ground. He unlocked his staff and kindled the skull-tip with silver light.

Nightwing had already flown ahead, twisting up through the decks towards its target. Njal saw what it saw, and so the way was marked out like a trail of twine through the labyrinth.

'So be it,' snarled Njal, setting off into the shadows. 'To the core.'

CHAPTER TWENTY-ONE

Ingvar stared up at the Penitent Engine. There was no time to do anything but get his sword into the path of the spinning fist-blades, but he knew he would not be able to stop them. He glared up towards the agonised pilot of the machine, determined at least to face death head on.

The machine's linen-shrouded face gazed down at him, the features hidden but for a static scream marked on the fabric. It was de Chatelaine. The circular saws continued to whirr and the muzzles of the flame-cannons gouted pre-burst smoke.

Then it turned aside.

Ingvar watched the massive Engine sweep its weapons away from him and take a stride towards the throne. He heard Delvaux screaming for it to halt. Bolter-fire sparked and ricocheted from de Chatelaine's metal exo-skeleton, but it was far too sporadic to halt her.

Ingvar leapt to his feet, opening up with his own bolter. Battle Sisters advancing behind the cover of the Penitent Engine were mown down, struck by his shells as they turned their fire on their own war machine.

'Withdraw!' shrieked Delvaux, his voice shrill with panic. All his cor-pulent self-assurance vanished, replaced by a frantic, wide-eyed terror. 'I *command* you – withdraw!'

By then de Chatelaine had reached her target. Her flamethrower arms opened up, flooding the throne with crimson immolation. Delvaux cried out in pain, thrashing about on his seat while still trying to clamber out of harm's way.

But there would be no salvation for him. De Chatelaine plunged both chainfists down on the Cardinal's flabby form, shredding his body into a whirl of flying gore and flesh-scraps. The screaming only lasted seconds before Delvaux's torso was torn into strips, spraying the marble and gold-leaf in a curtain of thick, lumpy red.

Ingvar mounted the dais steps again, firing all the while. The bridge's defenders hesitated, shocked by the death of the Cardinal. The rain of bolter-shells faltered for a moment, and the battle suddenly hung in the balance.

'Take down the remaining Engine,' Ingvar voxed Callia. Jorundur was still fighting it, and the duel was an unequal one.

Then Ingvar set off, sprinting out from the throne and towards the shocked figure of Nuriyah. She stood motionless, her flamer-arm held limp, staring at the ruins of the throne.

It was all the time Ingvar needed. He streaked across the bridge deck, his blade lashing with energy, and threw himself through the air towards her. By the time she saw him come at her, the chance to defend herself was gone. She spun round, lifting the blackened muzzle of her pyromaniac augmetic, but Ingvar had already whipped *dausvjer* round at her neck.

The blade sliced clean through, cutting precisely between gorget and helm. With a snap of released disruptor-essence, Nuriyah's head flew through the air, tracing a line of blood in its toppling wake, before thudding heavily to the marble and rocking to a standstill.

Ingvar hit the ground hard, cracking the deck beneath his feet before whirling to face the remaining defenders.

'Enough!' shouted Callia over the bridge-wide vox.

The balance of power had shifted. De Chatelaine's Penitent Engine was still busy smashing the last pieces of Delvaux's throne into molten scrap. The other Engine had been disabled by Jorundur with the assistance of Callia's squad. The rest of the Battle Sisters were now leaderless and divided, since many had come over to Callia's side already.

The last of the incoming fire faded away in a series of banging echoes. The bridge's defenders began to emerge from behind devastated sections of cover, hands raised.

'This is still an Ecclesiarchy vessel,' announced Callia, taking control with all the resolve she had displayed in Hjec Aleja. 'Resume your stations, remove the bridge lock-down. Transmit messages to all decks that Cardinal Delvaux has been relieved of command and *Vindicatus* is now under the control of the Fiery...' Callia glanced over at de Chatelaine's rampaging Engine. 'Of the Wounded Heart.'

Ingvar looked over at Jorundur. The Old Dog gave him a weary nod from amid the ruins of the second Penitent Engine. He looked as battered as Ingvar had ever seen him, with his armour carved half open by the war machine's chainfists, but he still stood and still held a weapon.

That only left de Chatelaine. Her movements were becoming increasingly jerky. Delvaux's throne was now nothing more than a pile of bloody fragments, and still she hammered away at it. Her mechanisms, damaged by bolter-fire, began to overheat. The cantilevered arms flailed wildly. Something like a howl issued from her clamped-open lips, and the whole edifice of her iron exoskeleton began to totter.

Ingvar raced over to her just as the Engine fell, crashing onto its back amid the ruin of the throne dais. Columns of spark-filled exhaust twined up from her awkwardly twisted limbs. Her mortal body, shackled to the instruments of agony, twitched and bucked in its bonds.

Ingvar crouched beside her and pulled back the scrap of linen that covered her face. De Chatelaine's everlasting scream stared back at him. Blood ran from her eyes across scourged cheeks – the machine was pumping pain-amplifier chemicals into her body at a wildly punitive rate.

She was somehow defying it. With self-command bordering on the superhuman, de Chatelaine had overridden the dreadful straitjacket of the Penitent Engine's psychosis-inducing mechanisms. She had resisted the entire battery of control devices implanted into her shriven body, and, almost impossibly, turned the tools of the Ecclesiarchy against its own representative.

In a lifetime of combat across a thousand worlds, Ingvar had never seen mental strength quite that acute. Even now, as her body arched with pain, de Chatelaine was still fighting.

If Ingvar could have saved what remained of her, he would have done, but there was no living extraction from an Ecclesiarchy machine. He rested his bolter gently against her sweat-streaked temple.

'Be at rest, battle-sister,' he said. 'Your saga shall be sung in the Halls of Fenris.'

De Chatelaine's face remained contorted in agony, but something like understanding flashed momentarily in her eyes. For a second, gratitude mingled with the pain.

Then Ingvar fired. The spasms ceased immediately. The nerve-impulse units in the Penitent Engine registered the death of the host, and the last of its generators sputtered out. The chainfists wound down, the flamethrowers coughed out.

Ingvar stood up slowly, gazing down at de Chatelaine's body.

Callia walked up to him, followed closely by a limping Jorundur. Ahead of them all, glimpsed through the immense forward viewscreen, Kefa Primaris could now clearly be seen.

'The plague-hulk is on the augurs,' she said, checking her chrono. 'It is less than an hour away. Can your brothers–'

'They will kill it,' said Ingvar, turning away from the carnage over the throne. 'Have faith.'

'What of the life-eaters?' asked Jorundur.

'I have already given the order,' said Callia, moving to the sensor station just below the dais. She ran her fingers over the console. 'The torpedoes have been withdrawn. They will soon–'

She broke off again. Ingvar and Jorundur joined her at the console. Runes glowed across a cracked screen.

'This is impossible,' she said, glancing up at the curve of Kefa Primaris in the forward real-view portal.

Ingvar scanned the runes. 'They are still primed to fire.'

'I shut them down!' cried Callia.

Jorundur hefted his axe with fresh purpose. 'Is there an override? Some way to control them directly?'

'I don't know,' said Callia. 'Where's the ship's commander?'

Harryat was already dragging himself towards the console, clutching at a bloody patch over his shoulder and wincing from the pain. 'Ordnance control,' he said through gritted teeth. 'You can override from there, but you'd need full clearance. The Cardinal has gone. He couldn't–'

Ingvar looked at Jorundur, and the same thought flashed through their minds.

'Klaive,' he said. 'Give me a location.'

'Three levels down – I can shunt the coordinates to your armour. But you'll never reach it.'

'Do what you can from here,' growled Ingvar, already moving. 'Pull the ship out of orbit.'

Jorundur came with him, and the two Wolves broke into a run.

'He's the one you came for, isn't he?' Jorundur voxed as they sprinted back towards the bridge exits.

'He is the target,' confirmed Ingvar, picking up speed. 'But I want him alive.'

'That might be difficult.'

'*Alive.*'

Jorundur didn't reply immediately. When he did, his voice was dark.

'We'll see,' was all he said.

'You are afraid,' said Baldr.

The Mycelite looked up at him. 'Why do you say so?'

'Time runs out for you. Njal is still on the ship, and he hunts for you.'

The Mycelite would not be goaded. Everything about him remained as it had been – sad, stooped, drenched in soporific heaviness. 'He can destroy this ship,' he said. 'He can destroy me. It will only drag out the agony.'

He reached for his staff, and his fingers wrapped around the gnarled wood.

'I show you *mercy*,' he said. 'You understand this? Your Apothecaries administer battle-rites, do they not? To end the pain of your fallen? This is the same thing.'

Baldr examined the Plague Marine. The sorcerer's voice was weaker than it had been. Perhaps the effort of subduing Baldr's will had beaten the strength out of it. He could still feel the collar around his neck, biting into his flesh. When Njal had placed it on him, it had felt like a humiliation. Now it felt like a token of fate – a fragment of galactic luck, just as the skull-totem had been on Ras Shakeh.

'No more,' snapped the Mycelite. He reached out his clawed hand and rested it on Baldr's forehead. 'We do this again.'

The *Frostaxe*'s bridge shuddered away, and Baldr's mind immediately fell into the pit of darkness. For an instant, he felt the clammy touch of the Mycelite's skin on his, then nothing at all.

Colours swam out of the void, vivid and swirling. He sensed the movement of souls within his colossal body – the ship's body – running hard for the outer skin. He felt their desperation, not to survive, but to make their sacrifice worth something.

He felt the burning presence of the Stormcaller raging up through the chambers below, and wondered if the Mycelite knew that he was now very close.

Then Baldr felt the pricks of pain at his heart – the cluster of charges buried in the fusion reactor cores, ticking down within their shielded shells, poised to rip him apart in a supernova of destruction.

'Destroy them,' the Mycelite commanded, his voice floating in his mind – urgent now, persuasive.

Baldr knew that he could. Just as he had summoned fire to purge the inter-lopers from the inner enginarium, he knew he could douse the incipient inferno buried in those chambers of plasma. He could take each one in turn and shift them all into the void, where they would explode in silent puffs.

He wanted to do it. The instinct was as natural as plucking a thorn from one's flesh.

He reached out with his mind, delving into the plasma chambers. He saw the irritants, swimming in a luminescent mass – little dark spheres, glit-tering with heat shielding and ready to ignite. The urge to absorb them, to gather them up and fling them clear of danger, was virtually overwhelming. He cupped the closest of them in a ghostly hand, watching as the plasma around it slipped and slopped from invisible fingers.

'No,' he said.

He felt the power in Mycelite's voice immediately. 'You are the ship.'

It was difficult not to obey. It was crushingly, agonisingly hard.

But he could do it.

'No,' he said again, fighting to break free of the visions. He heard the other voices murmuring in half-aware fury, all of them struggling to drag him in with them, to consign him to the same incorporeal life they endured. They *were* mad, locked in debates of which they had no understanding.

Amid the struggle, the Mycelite's voice softened further.

'This gift is unique,' he said. 'It is new. Think on that. In ten thousand years there has been no one like you. The stars fade, and still such magni-ficence is created. Do not spurn this. You will be a god. You were always marked out for it, right from birth. The daemons of your ice-world knew it. They could feel it. You could feel it.'

Baldr remembered the wolf, the one that had stood before him in the dark, dripping wood. He remembered the amber eyes.

Why doesn't it move? Why doesn't it pounce?

He wavered. He felt the soul of the ship assert itself, surging up to swallow his own. He felt dizzy. Nausea piled in, welling up from the nigh-infinite volume of matter pressing down around him.

He reached for the charges again. He grasped them, enclosing them in an aura of suppression. All he had to do now was cast them away, scattering them into the void like a child throwing stones into the waves.

'Do it,' urged the Mycelite.

He would have done. The Mycelite's words had performed their work, and the last strands of Baldr's resistance flaked away. Given a free hand then, he would have nullified the threat from the devices before turning his wrath to those of his brothers still fleeing from the reach of his multifaceted mind. It would have been over, and all within the blink of an amber eye.

But then, just as Baldr's thoughts crystallised, the Mycelite's hold broke.

Baldr came around, snapped roughly back into reality. His eyes flick-ered open, watering from the harsh light. The *Frostaxe*'s darkened bridge danced with corposant, stirring up the dust of aeons and making the corpses shiver. Baldr shook his head, blinking hard and trying to shake off a crippling wave of nausea.

Bodies were moving ahead of him – huge bodies, wreathed in light and swaying amid a blur of torn reality. For a second Baldr thought he might have somehow died, and that his soul had been translated into an afterlife of insubstantial wraiths and spectral energy-flows.

Then his vision compensated, focus returned, and he saw the truth of it. The Mycelite had turned away from him, suddenly distracted by a new threat. Beyond the stooped and twisted form of the Plague Marine, Njal Stormcaller loomed dark and tall, his staff crackling and his armour-runes blazing.

'Ready your soul for damnation, Traitor,' Njal growled, summoning runefire to himself in iridescent streaks. 'Hel is upon you now.'

The impact sites flickered up on Gunnlaugur's helm-display. He gave the order, and the packs peeled away, each one heading for the loc-reading of a different Caestus assault ram. They had been forced to make calculations on the run, seeking out strong signals from undamaged vessels.

Given their losses, only three of the Caestus rams were needed. Gunnlaugur had run scans as the outer rim approached, and five had responded with live signals – four of them reporting battle-readiness. Each was sealed and locked down, their heavy ceramite armour protecting them from the predations of all but the most well-equipped and determined enemy.

Two packs of five split off, haring down the plunging tunnels towards the signals. The remaining four came with him, pressing ahead to the most distant of the loc-readings.

The target was almost open to the void – lodged in a vertical gouge in the hulk's flank the length of a starship comm-vane.

Gunnlaugur checked the chrono as he sprinted.

Sixteen minutes, and still ticking down. This was too close.

Hafloí's voice crackled over the comm, breathless and panting. 'Targets incoming.'

Gunnlaugur blinked to tactical, and watched the proximity markers crowd across his forward scan-field.

'*Skítja*,' he breathed. They were already clogging the tunnels ahead. Gunnlaugur's helm worked to give him numbers – two hundred, three hundred...

'*Break* them!' he voxed, slamming a fresh magazine into his bolter. It was his last.

The corridor echoed with the snap, thud and slide of ammo being replenished. Power weapons crackled into full-burn, sending neon flickers out across the dark.

Ten metres.

He spied the first pair of enemy eyes, glowing marsh-green.

'Allfather!' he roared, whirling his thunder hammer in one hand as the bolter kicked out shells with the other.

His brothers thundered their own battle-cries, tearing along in a tight knot of grey steel and ceramite. Then they crashed as one into the barricades, and the tunnel dissolved into fire and annihilation.

Olgeir burst into Annarovea's chambers. The governor turned to face him, her face flushed with anger.

'You *knew*,' she accused. 'It wasn't just you – there were other ships.'

Olgeir looked wearily around the chamber. The rest of the governor's staff glared back at him with censorious expressions – as far as they dared.

This mission was proving impossible to balance. There was no one to fight with honour, and no story to spin that would convince doubting souls.

'Nothing has changed,' he said.

'We cannot speak to the Ministorum vessel,' Annarovea said. 'Why is that?'

'You have a location fix?'

Annarovea pushed clear of her throne and strode over to a sensor station. Olgeir followed her. A glassy pict lens showed a rune-filled depiction of the immediate orbital zone. Troop-carriers making slow progress out of the system, hauling the precious human cargo beyond destruction's reach.

And then there was the Cardinal's ship. It was approaching deployment range, skirting the limit beyond which life-eater torpedoes would become unstoppable.

'Scan it,' he said.

Annarovea nodded towards an aide, who directed an augur-sweep towards *Vindicatus*.

'What do you see?' asked Olgeir.

'Extensive surface damage,' reported the aide. 'Its course is erratic. Engines seem slow to correct.'

'That ship took on the plague-hulk,' Olgeir told Annarovea. 'You can see the results. If it tries to do so again, it will be destroyed.' He studied the data scrolling across the pict screen. 'Run a weapons analysis.'

The aide adjusted the scope of the scan. 'There is a power build-up along the lower hull. Sporadic, but growing.'

Olgeir nodded grimly. 'Torpedo batteries.' He turned to Annarovea. 'The commander of that ship has the power to erase all life on this world. He will do it if he sees the plague-hulk reaching deployment range. Better to strip a planet of life than risk it supplying soldiers to the enemy. That's the calculation.'

Annarovea went pale. 'I do not–'

'There is *no help*, governor. Launch your fighters at it, if it will make you feel any better, but that is an Ecclesiarchy Grand Cruiser, so do not fool yourself they will do more than scratch its shields.'

Annarovea seemed to shrink in her armour. Fatigue, and hopelessness, were catching up with her, and she struggled to find a reply.

Just then, an alarm sounded from one of the watch-stations on the far side of the chamber. An officer leapt up.

'First signal, lords,' he reported.

'Put it through,' said Annarovea.

The pict screen updated. A new icon appeared on the extreme edge of orbital space, moving slowly but purposively. Unlike the troop carriers and *Vindicatus*, it had no standard fleet-identifier.

'So that is the hulk,' said Annarovea, quietly.

Olgeir nodded.

'What do we do?' she asked. Her self-possession had left her. She was no longer angry, no longer defiant. In the space of a single day, her armouries had been stripped bare, her citizens were rioting, and two vessels with the power to destroy every living thing on the planet were powering steadily into strike positions.

Olgeir drew in a long breath. 'How many regiments did you evacuate?' he asked.

'Four. Five, perhaps, if those carriers clear orbit in time.'

Olgeir forced a smile. Despite everything, Annarovea had done well. Kefa Primaris had done well. The forces already void-lifted were worth having – an Imperial commander could make use of such numbers.

'Then we've done all we were asked to,' he said.

'There's nothing else?' Her voice betrayed quiet desperation. 'Nothing at all?'

Olgeir crossed his arms, and watched the icons tick across the visual field. He thought of Gunnlaugur, and Ingvar, and the rest of the pack, and how much he would have preferred to be fighting alongside them. If they still fought, that was.

'Nothing, governor,' he confirmed. 'Now all we have to do is wait.'

CHAPTER TWENTY-TWO

Ingvar and Jorundur raced to the location shunted to them by Harryat, streaking through chambers thick with incense and fogged in confusion. Ecclesiarchy officers stared at them as they passed, paralysed by shock. Callia's orders had been issued, but still a few looked ready to fight them, as if the whole thing were some kind of elaborate sham.

Ingvar ignored them. The two Wolves tore down transit shafts and barrelled along corridors. As they went, warning lumens kicked in, heralding the imminent launch of the life-eater missiles. The entire structure around them shuddered as, somewhere below them, vast void-doors opened up ready to expose the launching tubes inside.

Ingvar swung around a right-angle corner. Twenty metres ahead stood two thick blast-doors chevroned in yellow and black.

'Krak charges,' voxed Ingvar, pulling two from his belt while still running. 'Zero delay.'

Jorundur did the same, and they hurled the four grenades directly at the doors. The charges went off as they hit, exploding in a hail of splinters, doing just enough to weaken the structure. Ingvar and Jorundur smashed into it, travelling at full tilt.

The door's centre-line crashed open, sending both panels barrelling inwards. The control chamber was small – about fifteen metres across – and octagonal. Each wall was lined with cogitator equipment and towering pict screens glowing with pre-launch runes.

Klaive spun round to face them, his face even paler than usual. He reached for the lever that would complete the launch protocol.

By mortal standards, his movements were quick.

Jorundur's bolt-round hit him on the shoulder, sending him slamming into the far wall. Jorundur followed up quickly, reaching for a knife. He grabbed Klaive's tumbling body and plunged the knife down, pinning the confessor to the floor with the blade.

Klaive screamed, twisting like a fish out of water. Ingvar made for the control panels. He shut down the launch orders one by one, restoring the safety protocols and issuing the commands to close the launch tubes.

'This is the Emperor's holy work!' shrieked Klaive, his features twisted by anger rather than pain. 'The Cardinal ordained it! You will burn for this!'

'Certainly,' muttered Ingvar, closing down the last of the launch systems and walking over to where Klaive lay prone.

The confessor's face showed nothing but fury. His red-lined eyes bulged, and he strained against the pin of the dagger, robes darkening with the stain of his blood.

Then the noise of running boots echoed down the corridor outside. The *Vindicatus*'s crew was catching up, and a dozen soldiers in crimson cara-pace armour formed up beyond the wreckage of the blast-doors.

Jorundur pulled his dagger free of Klaive's shoulder and walked slowly back towards the exit. As he did so, he hefted his bolter casually in the other hand. 'Get back,' he warned the guards, his voice catching with a low threat-note.

'They won't let you kill me,' spat Klaive, gazing up at Ingvar with perfect contempt. 'You can't take on the entire ship.'

Ingvar grabbed him by the throat and hauled him to his feet. 'You really think that?'

Jorundur activated the private channel to Callia, still functioning despite all the damage his armour had taken. 'Sister. Your life-eaters are disabled.'

'Good,' Callia replied, her voice distracted, as if uneasy about what she had to say. 'Then you will return to the bridge.'

Jorundur looked at Ingvar. 'The bridge?'

Ingvar checked his chrono, and suddenly understood. 'The *Festerax*,' he said.

'Lords, your place is here,' Callia went on. 'I shall look forward to your presence beside me as we end this.'

'They have detected the plague-hulk,' repeated Ingvar. 'It still lives. If we leave this chamber, they will rearm the life-eaters.'

Outside the doors, the Ecclesiarchy troops waited. More were joining them each second, unclamping weapons as they took up position along the length of the corridor.

'It is the *only way*,' urged Klaive, whispering into Ingvar's earpiece as if he could be swayed by rhetoric. 'You know it, and Callia knows it. The Storm-caller has failed. Loose vengeance on the world below! Better to burn than be damned.'

Jorundur cut the link to Callia, then took up position standing across the broken doorway. He emitted a low growl, vox-augmented, making the Ecclesiarchy troops back away a few paces.

But they didn't withdraw. They kept their weapons lowered, and held position.

Ingvar ran through the options. If the *Festerax* still burned through the void, if the Wolves kill-team had been destroyed, then Callia was right. Delvaux had broken the oath by disengaging early, but the fate of Kefa still hung by a thread.

'Don't even think of it, brother,' warned Jorundur, facing outwards at the gathering squads of crimson-armoured troops. 'Olgeir is down there.'

Klaive began to chuckle softly.

'You won't hold out forever. They'll break in eventu-'

Ingvar punched Klaive, breaking his nose and knocking him out cold. The confessor slumped in his grasp.

Ingvar hadn't been plagued by visions of the Deathwatch for a long time, but he remembered Callimachus then. He remembered the agonies they had unleashed to strip worlds of life in the face of the oncoming hive fleets. He remembered when the order had come in, and how long he had struggled over it.

Back then he couldn't have prevented it even if he'd wanted to. It had been their mission, the one they'd sworn to execute. It was abhorrent, and even the Ultramarine had blenched, but it had been the *mission*.

This was different. Ingvar had seen what happened to those on Ras Shakeh. The Ministorum, for all Delvaux's sadism, was right about Kefa Primaris – the world could not be allowed to incubate an army of trillions.

Jorundur looked over his shoulder. 'Gyrfalkon?'

Ingvar shoved Klaive to the floor, placing him well back. Then he unlocked his bolter.

'Njal will do it yet,' he said, defiantly, joining Jorundur in standing guard over the doorway. 'Until then, this chamber is ours.'

'Good,' Jorundur said, checking his ammo-counter. 'For a moment there, brother, you had me worried.'

For the first time since Baldr had awoken, he witnessed surprise on the face of the Mycelite. The Plague Marine's shock was quickly followed by an elated smile, as if he had got used to a nigh-eternal life of utter certainty and was now pleased to find that some unexpected events were still possible.

Njal's expression was unreadable under his helm. The Rune Priest's armour was dark with burned-on blood and slime. The heavy covering of animal skins had been ripped away, and the skulls hanging from chains at his waist were black with the patina of war.

Baldr could hear Njal breathing heavily through his vox-grille. His psyber-raven still accompanied him, hovering accusingly over his shoulder-guards in what looked like an oddly protective formation.

How had he fought his way to this place? What hunt-sense had he used to navigate through the endless dark of the hulk? From his mind-excursions through the plague-ship's interior, Baldr knew better than perhaps anyone just how huge and labyrinthine the *Festerax* was.

Then he remembered his forced actions at the enginarium, and guessed the cold truth.

'The Priest,' remarked the Mycelite, backing away slowly, clutching his staff two-handed as if it were some kind of shield. 'You have been gnawing through my ship like a cancer, and now you're here.'

Njal circled the sorcerer warily. His gaze flickered up at Baldr briefly, and the movement halted.

'You no longer have any claim on him,' the Mycelite said. 'You waste what you do not understand.'

Njal gripped his staff more tightly. Baldr felt the build-up of storm-power, making the air thicken and shudder.

'This ends now,' said Njal.

The Mycelite lost his smile. 'You are weakened, Priest. You have poured your soul out in my kingdoms, and now you have nothing left.'

Njal's gaze moved to Baldr a second time, as if trying to fathom whose side he was on, before the staff rose higher.

'We shall see,' Njal snarled.

The chamber suddenly filled with the hard clap and grind of thunder. Wind howled through the command bridge, sweeping away the withered fungus that coated the walls. Shards of silver leapt out from the metal underneath, snaking and lashing around Njal's staff.

The Mycelite buckled down, crouching low to weather the storm. His own staff surged with a sick green light, and a stench like vomit flared up in the shimmering air.

Baldr raged at his bonds, desperate to shake free of the shackles that bound him to the throne. Njal angled his staff at the Mycelite, and a corona of neon-white energy slammed into the sorcerer's hunched body. The light smashed crazily away from him, flaring and bouncing across the bridge's ruined expanse.

The Mycelite reeled from the impact, muttering half-heard words as he retreated. Njal advanced after him, and the fusty atmosphere curdled with more electric discharge.

The Rune Priest was about to launch another bolt when he suddenly stumbled. He whirled around, blazing with magnesium-bright coruscation, to see a grey-skinned cadaver clawing at his armour. Njal slammed the staff down, and his assailant exploded in a spinning cloud of dust and stone-dry flesh.

By then, the crew of the *Frostaxe* were moving. They dragged themselves up from their seats and skittered across the bridge decking. They made no sound save for the shuffle of bone on metal, and their milky eyes revealed nothing but a faint sheen of pale green.

Njal snarled, and hurled fresh bolts of rune-fire into their midst. The corpses burst open in droves, sending severed limbs cartwheeling across the empty thrones. The cadavers kept coming, clustering at the Rune Priest. They clambered up service hatches and dragged themselves through intersection orifices. Soon the bridge was full of them, swarming like bacilli on a plate.

Baldr kept tearing at his bonds. Powerless, he watched the tide of the dead rear up, clawing at the Rune Priest and threatening to overwhelm him. Njal reaped a swathe with his glittering staff tip, crying out words of power, shattering bones and bursting atrophied lungs.

As the corpses piled in, the Mycelite summoned up a fresh vortex of foul, green-laced energy. He let loose, slamming a clot of boiling warp-essence into Njal's breastplate.

The Rune Priest was hurled backwards through the knots of living dead, crashing into a command station and smashing the ancient cogitator units. The Mycelite's energy bolt clamped on to him like a slick of oil, worming its way into the cracks of his Terminator plate.

Nightwing plummeted, going for the sorcerer's eyes. The Mycelite screamed at it, flailing his staff wildly. The skull-tip connected, sending the psyber-raven careening across the bridge.

Njal righted himself, sending more crushed corpses cracking into the deck, but his armour was now covered in a writhing cloak of green-black mucus. It smeared across the ceramite, dragging him down, extending slobbering tendrils into every joint. The putrid warp-essence boiled and seethed, growing like a living thing, bubbling and multiplying into a cascade of soul-draining, matter-burning filth.

The Mycelite hobbled towards Njal, all the time whispering words of ruin. Spectral figures shimmered into life around him, their faces glowing with an unhealthy, ravening pallor. The ghosts launched themselves at Njal, still besieged by clusters of undead and bogged down by the dragging weight of the sorcerer's noxious bile. They were monstrous and misshapen – every phantasm that had ever haunted the *Frostaxe*'s corrupted bridge, from the echoes of daemon-kin to the plague-infested troops who had first stormed the Wolves' ancient defences. They shrieked as they swooped, reaching out for the Rune Priest with translucent arms. Njal's staff banished them into glassy fragments, but every time they impacted, he weakened further. His enormous shoulders bowed, he dropped to one knee, and his cries of defiance cracked into hoarseness.

The Mycelite hobbled up to him, his gnarled staff now burning freely with fell energies. Fresh waves of the phosphorescent mucus crashed across the Rune Priest, blistering as the armour corroded beneath it. The undead kept on coming, clawing and tearing, fixed on Njal like predators on a stricken prey-beast.

Baldr felt his hearts hammer with rage. His bonds fixed him tight, forcing him to watch powerlessly as the Stormcaller was beaten down. His mind strained at its bonds, desperate to do *something*, and he felt a sudden kick of power unlocking deep within him. The sensation burned furiously, surging into his limbs and locking them rigid in their bonds.

His collar suddenly flared white-hot, and the pain became agonising. Baldr roared out, and spurs of lightning escaped from between his fangs. Power ramped up within him, out of control, swelling into a pain-filled nightmare.

He felt a dark presence unravel within his soul – a wolf, black-coated with yellow eyes, vast and silent. He saw its jaws open, and curved fangs glint wetly.

Why doesn't it move? Why doesn't it pounce?

'The collar!' Baldr cried, forcing the words out as his body was seized by uncontrollable spasms.

Njal looked up then. His red helm-lenses shone fiercely, staring at Baldr from beneath a swirling tempest of warp-energies. He was stricken, hammered down by the Mycelite's art and prone for the killing blow.

The withered plague-sorcerer loomed over him, his staff held high, and a vortex of lurid green aether-matter crackled into life. The emerald plasma leaked pure *sickness* as it spiralled around the skull-tip, ready to finish what the undead had started.

476 CHRIS WRAIGHT

'The scalp of the Stormcaller,' murmured the Mycelite, a strain of pure malice entering his soft voice for the first time.

Njal's staff-fires, doused by torrents of corroding warp-oil, guttered away. The last of the storm-lightning crackled out across his runic armour. He stared up at the Mycelite, still on his knees.

He only issued one word.

'*Shatter,*' he rasped.

And with an eye-burning snap, Baldr's collar broke in two.

Hafloí could hardly see from fatigue. His limbs worked mechanically, chopping and hacking with automatic, nerve-conditioned skill. He'd long since run out of ammo and so had switched to his axe. If the enemy had been any more potent than the mutant filth that swilled around every bilge of the vast ship, he might have been in trouble. As it was, the killing had become a test of pure endurance.

He could feel both his hearts hammering at an insane speed. His helm-display listed a whole plethora of red warning-indicators, each one of them screaming for him to slacken his rate of movement. With a grim smile, Hafloí realised the truth – he was fighting himself to death.

The Grey Hunters around him were in scarce better shape. All carried wounds from the ferocious battle at the enginarium. Two more had been lost, dragged down as they tried to cut their way free of the mutant mobs. Such deaths were the worst of all, slain by foes unworthy of anything but contempt.

Hafloí set his jaw, ignoring the blood running down the inside of his battered helm, and dug deeper. Somehow, his limbs kept working, driven down solely by excess hyperadrenaline and combat-stimms. The Caestus was less than thirty metres away, though it might as well have been on the far side of the solar system – the space between was crammed with swarms of plague-damned, whose only remaining task was to keep the intruders from escaping the Hel they had created.

Hafloí was so absorbed in the fighting, was so intent on staying on his feet, that he barely heard the first explosion. It was low – right on the edge of his enhanced auditory range, and far, far away.

The mutants heard it, though. Whether because they were used to the myriad creaks and clangs of the *Festerax*, or through some warp-bound sixth sense, they responded immediately. What little formation they had broke. Some started screaming, not with their usual battle-rage, but with a frantic fear.

A second boom rocked the chamber, far louder this time, like the distant grind of thunderheads in the Asaheim peaks. Every structure around them – the corkscrew pillars, the sagging roofline, the rockcrete floor – trembled as if shaken by a giant hand.

The mutants began to scatter. Some fought on, but many started to scamper for cover, as if there were anywhere to hide from what was to come.

Hafloí, exhausted, checked his chrono.

It read zero. Down in the reactor cores, in the heart of the boiling inferno in the enginarium depths, the charges were going off. The fire would be racing after them, boiling up through the infinite shafts and kindling the methane. In his mind's eye, Hafloí saw the colossal wave of pure destruction welling up towards them, churning and destroying as it came. It would take mere moments to reach them.

His exhausted head lifted. Urgent energy stirred in his ravaged body once more. He could see the target now – half lost amid the melted panels of the chamber wall and skewed at a steep angle.

He kicked out, breaking the spine of a mutant who was too mind-addled to retreat, then joined his brothers in the race.

As the collar fell away, Baldr's power erupted into life. Fulguration screamed out from him, roaring like an unleashed avalanche. The throne exploded around him, breaking into a thousand pieces. His bonds were hurled aside, burning with silver-edged fire. He rose into the air, his arms outstretched, surrounded by a halo of pure, devastating power.

Baldr swept his gaze across the horde of undead. He clenched his fists, and they blew apart in a rippling wave of torn flesh and bone. The ghosts screamed out of existence, howling as they were banished back to the underverse.

He surged then towards the Mycelite, who was already backing away. Baldr opened up his clenched gauntlet, and a column of raging silver coruscation lanced out, slamming into the sorcerer and hurling him across the bridge. The Mycelite tried to respond, to fight back against the deluge, but Baldr's fury was unstoppable. The power flooded out of him, wild and feral, vomiting out of his soul from where it had been confined for too long. The fires broke open the Mycelite's armour, revealing a hunchbacked, milk-fleshed body beneath. The sorcerer screamed, locked in the thundering aegis of silver fire, and his staff shattered.

Baldr swooped down on him, both fists blazing. The Mycelite cowered. Gouts of black smoke roiled up his broken armour as the exposed skin was consumed in the fire.

Baldr drew his right fist back, coiling up yet more power in his clenched gauntlet. The Mycelite tried to raise his arms in some kind of defence, but Baldr punched straight through them, breaking the creature's wrists and driving the bone-fragments deep into his age-withered face.

He kept on punching, pouring out his wrath on the one who had imprisoned him. He remembered killing his own kind while lost in the warp-dream, and his cry of anguish echoed around the bridge. The blows rained down, smashing and cracking in a hail of anger-driven strikes.

With a wet snap, the Mycelite's neck broke. A huge explosion boomed out, and the entire chamber was consumed in a driving wind, flickering with ghoulish lights like the flashing eyes of the dead.

Then the tempest died. Baldr's own fires went out, leaving him standing on the decking amid the last echoes of the horrific outpouring. He swayed on his feet, suddenly feeling hollow. Black stars crowded his vision, and he felt his awareness sliding away.

Njal, his armour still coated in the last of the foul warp-bile, staggered to his feet. The remains of the Mycelite lay before them both, a blackened husk of scorched flesh. For a moment, it was all Baldr could do just to look on it. The hatred did not diminish. He felt *sick*, dragged back into the corruption he had worked so hard to fight off.

The null-collar lay behind him, lifeless and inert. With dreadful realisation, Baldr saw how completely he had damned himself. There could be no doubt now.

I am awakened, he thought, just as the wave of blackness rose up to engulf him.

The deck rippled like a wave, breaking open into fire-edged plates. A flash of deep red flame briefly surged up and was swiftly doused. More booms rang out from a long way down, growing far louder. Haflói heard secondary sounds follow in their wake – a sustained roar, like the tide coming in.

The pack tore through the remaining resistance and reached the Caestus. Embarkation ramps slammed down, whining on impact-stressed pistons. Gunnlaugur clanged up the interior towards the cockpit.

'Five seconds,' he ordered.

Haflói was the last one in before the ramp pulled closed again. It bolted shut and the brace-clamps slotted into place. From outside, a great, sighing snap heralded the bifurcation of the chamber's structural underpinning, followed by a rain of dislodged rubble from the roof.

The Caestus pushed off clumsily, buoyed by a surge from its retro-thrusters. Metal debris slewed from its outer hull as it turned on a cushion of super-heated exhaust. A supporting column collapsed close by, shattering as it hit the undulating floor.

Then the main engines kicked in. Haflói had barely reached for the restraint harness when the motive force hit, throwing him hard against the vessel's metal interior. A booming growl of thruster-fire filled the space, and the assault ram powered for the open void again.

By instinct, Haflói routed his helm-feed to the craft's anterior real-viewer. At first, the feed showed nothing but fire and static. Then, as the Caestus picked up speed and raced beyond the hull perimeter, the colours and shapes fell into cohesion.

He saw the flanks of the *Festerax* rear up behind them, stretching away in every direction. The outer shell had been dark and mottled on the way in, like a clenched fist of rotten iron. Now it burned and flared like the surface of a star.

As he watched, whole sections of fused starship-carcasses were consumed by vast, silent explosions. Rivers of magma spontaneously burst from cracks in the plague-hulk's flanks. The vista reeled, collapsing and expanding as colossal reservoirs of toxic gases at the ship's heart ignited. Voidships that had remained lodged tight for centuries were suddenly blasted loose, before disintegrating in spiralling orgies of destruction.

Haflói watched it in silence, slumped against the shuddering sides of the Caestus. He watched the *Festerax* slowly shrink in the viewers as the Caestus shot away from the impact site. He watched the chain reactions pick up force, blasting massive chunks of matter out into the void. He registered the phenomenal build-up of heat and pressure within the heart of the hulk.

The *Festerax* was dying, carved apart by the insanely rapid reactions boiling away in its bowels. A vessel of such magnitude would still take a while to die, but die it would, condemned by its own internal, infernal chemistry.

'*Heimdall*,' came Gunnlaugur's voice over the pack-comm. 'Hunt is complete. We are out, running hot. Loc-reading needed.'

There was a crackle, and then the link solidified. 'We detect two Caestus rams outbound, lord. Can you confirm?'

A pause. 'Scan for a third. Hulk void-weapons are disabled. Come in and get us.'

'Understood, lord. Do you have the Stormcaller among you?'

Another pause. 'No. You detect his loc-reading?'

'Negative.'

Hafloí heard Gunnlaugur's curse over the shared comm-loop. It sounded bone-weary, as if all his strength had been left behind on the battlefield.

'Keep scanning,' he ordered.

Then the link cut.

Njal limped over to Baldr, catching him before he crashed to the deck. The Hunter's face was as pale as death, his eyes rimmed with blood. The destruction of the collar had left a bloody weal around his neck.

Baldr looked blearily around him. The command bridge was shaking, rocked by titanic movements. The sound of vast, echoing booms roiled up from below them.

'The charges...' he rasped.

Njal dragged him back to his feet. A badly damaged Nightwing flapped heavily on to his shoulder.

'*Heimdall*,' the Rune Priest said, running rapid checks on his Terminator teleport homer.

'Too... far,' gasped Baldr.

More echoing crashes sounded. Cracks suddenly jagged across the bridge decking, opening up flame-filled fissures. The remnants of ancient armour-glass shattered, sending crystal rain showering across the dust.

'You forget who you are with,' growled Njal, preparing his mind for the trial.

More spars fell from the roof of the bridge, disintegrating into heaps of glowing ash as they hit the floor.

A gout of pure magma suddenly shot up through the ruined decking, less than a metre away, foaming and raging. More booms resounded, making the whole chamber shake.

Njal activated the teleport mechanism. A sphere of warp-frosted silver burned out, enclosing them both in a perfect orb of glittering iridescence.

The floor of the *Frostaxe*'s bridge gave way entirely, dissolving into a steaming, frothing sea of molten plasma. More magma-streamers jutted upwards, crashing into the chamber's roof and slicing clean through it. The entire bridge tottered, slewed, then imploded, buoyed up only by the glowing swell of liquid energy beneath.

For a few seconds, the ruined body of the Mycelite was the only thing to resist it, remaining intact amid the orange tide like a cork bobbing on the waves. Flames scorched across the ancient ceramite, stripped clear the layers of filth that a lifetime of corruption had generated. The emblem of Mortarion's proud Legion flashed clean again – a death's head enclosed in a dark star-pattern.

Then the sweep of destruction overtook it all, subsuming the chamber in molten ruin. The residual fungus crackled and crisped. The ancient corpses blazed like torches, accompanied by the impotent screams of their maddened souls.

Then the last of the superstructure fell away, the brace-beams cut free of the shaft's walls, and the Mycelite's domain was finally overcome by the fiery death of the *Festerax*.

CHAPTER TWENTY-THREE

Ingvar held his ground. From beyond the broken blast-doors, the Ecclesiarchy troops held theirs. He could sense their unwillingness to open fire, but neither were they going anywhere.

Jorundur radiated steady belligerence. The earlier combat seemed to have provoked the darker side of his nature, and Ingvar knew he would have no qualms about laying into any mortals daring to cross the threshold.

Ingvar could smell Klaive's blood in the air. The confessor was still unconscious, his body stretched out on the deck. There were so many questions. What had he been doing on Ras Shakeh? What secrets had he swept up with him, lifting them into the sanctuary of *Vindicatus* and away from prying eyes? Surely he'd taken any sensitive material with him, the kind of thing Bajola had warned him about. Klaive was the link – the reason the Ecclesiarchy had come to the isolated world in such numbers.

He needed to get him away, a place where he could ask the questions directly and without fear of interruption.

Do you know the name Hjortur Bloodfang?

Why was he killed?

And the most pressing:

What is the Fulcrum?

Every second they waited there, locked in a stalemate of mutual suspicion, the window for action shrunk a little further. And yet, if the two of them forced their way out, the Ministorum would respond and Delvaux's last order would be enacted.

The fate of an entire world, versus the truth of a lone murder. Not much of a choice.

Ingvar turned to Jorundur. 'Any signal?'

'Nothing.'

'We are wasting time.'

'Nothing's wasted.'

Jorundur wasn't going to move. Ingvar envied his certainties. 'Hand me the comm-bead,' he said. 'I want to speak to her.'

Jorundur unclipped the device from his gorget and passed it over. As Ingvar held it in his hand, it snapped into life.

'News, my lord,' came Callia's voice. 'Your Rune Priest has done it. The hulk is breaking up.'

Ingvar felt a surge of raw relief. 'My thanks, Sister. And you?'

'We're heading out of orbit. *Heimdall* is moving into range. We detected two boarding craft docking.'

Some survived, then.

'Our place is there, Sister,' he said.

'Your gunship is where you left it, and I have ordered it not to be touched. I remember how... particular your brother is about that.'

Ingvar checked to see if his armour's comm system backed her tidings up. Initially, his helm-display showed nothing. Then, with some distortion, a message flickered up on his retinal feed.

'Hunt complete,' came the burst, bearing *Heimdall*'s security mark. 'All warriors to return to *Heimdall*. Repeat: all warriors to *Heimdall*.'

Ingvar found himself wondering who had authorised that message. Had Gunnlaugur got out alive? Had Njal?

Ahead of them, in the corridor beyond the broken doors, the soldiers stood down, holstering weapons and standing to attention. They looked relieved.

'Can you get *Vuokho* moving again?' Ingvar asked Jorundur.

The Old Dog issued a low warning growl, which was all the answer he was ever going to give, and stomped off.

Ingvar reached for the still unconscious Klaive and hauled him, one-handed, from the deck. As the confessor was dragged up from the floor, his eyes flickered open briefly.

'Best you stay asleep,' hissed Ingvar coldly. 'When you next wake, things will look a lot worse.'

Annarovea was the first to receive the sensor readings. She pored over the pict screen, her face lit green by the runes flickering across it. As she took in the data, her grip on the console edge gradually relaxed. She pushed back in her chair and looked up at Olgeir.

'They're moving off,' she said.

Olgeir studied the readings for himself. *Vindicatus* had changed course, pulling higher. The power build-up along its flanks reduced, indicating that the torpedo launches had been cancelled. Soon the ship would be out of launch-range.

In addition, the hulk's trajectory had slowed radically. It no longer barrelled along on a direct course for the planet, but seemed to have blurred into a whole smear of indistinct sensor-ghosts.

'Can we get a hololith of that?' he asked.

Annarovea gave the order, and a cloud of red wireframes spun into life above the sensor station. The translucent edifice rippled for a while, struggling to latch on to an incoming feed, then started to rotate more surely.

'Throne,' breathed Annarovea, rapt. 'They killed it.'

The hololith showed the *Festerax* breaking into huge chunks. Mighty explosions rippled through the canyons between segments, showing up as patches of grainy white noise amid the glittering lith-lines. As the behemoth tore itself apart, its approach slowed, skewing it off-course. As the process continued, what was left of the ship would be eaten up before it reached orbit. The molten remains would tumble off into the deep void, the residual toxins freezing into inertness.

Annarovea stirred into action. With the threat of immediate annihilation averted, her earlier air of command returned.

'Broadcast this signal on all channels,' she ordered. 'Report that the incoming anomaly has been destroyed before reaching orbit. Reassure all citizens that order will shortly be restored. Repeat earlier commands restricting movement, and remind the populace that any citizens participating in disorder will face the full sanction of emergency law.'

Her officials hurried to comply, and soon the city-wide vox-casters were blaring the message out, accompanied by images of the *Festerax*'s lingering death.

Annarovea turned to face Olgeir. 'Your comrades...'

Olgeir continued staring at the hololith. For a moment, it looked as if the plague-hulk carcass was all that remained.

Then his helm-comm activated. 'Hunt complete. All warriors to return to *Heimdall*. Repeat: all warriors to *Heimdall*.'

As the message completed, the ravaged outline of Stormcaller's ship appeared within the sensor ambit, far behind *Vindicatus* but nonetheless moving under her own power.

Olgeir drew in a deep breath. Something remained to be salvaged, then.

'You may recall your troops now, governor,' he said, closing the comm-link.

'The orders are already sent,' said Annarovea. 'The first carriers will make planetfall in a few hours.'

'That should give you all you need to restore order.'

'It will take a while.'

'That it will.'

'And you?'

'I have my summons.'

Annarovea bowed. 'Very well. You must attend to your duties. But...' She paused, as if struggling to find the words. 'My thanks, lord. When you arrived–'

'Noted, governor,' said Olgeir. He let a smile crack across his scarred face. 'It is good to endure the storm.'

Heimdall's bridge was a mess. Cables hung in loops from the battered roof-arches, many sparking with unstaunched electrics. A whole section of the rear tactical area was in ruins, with both servitors and mortal crew trapped in the rubble. The command throne had survived relatively intact, as had the control stations ahead and below it, though the main forward viewscreen was scored deeply from repeated impacts.

Gunnlaugur stood on the rockcrete platform before the throne, his arms crossed, staring out at the scene before him. The surviving members of the kill-teams surrounded him, including Haflói and the two Thunderhawk pilots who'd remained on *Heimdall*. There was no sign of Njal.

'Detect anything yet?' he demanded of Derroth, *Heimdall*'s shipmaster.

The *Festerax* was gone. Its messy demise was clearly visible from the real-viewers. The burning remains looked like some huge asteroid being ripped apart by blood-red tectonic movements.

'We are working, lord,' said Derroth.

Gunnlaugur's combat-euphoria ebbed slowly. The incoming flight on damaged Caestus rams had been nightmarish, contending with stuttering engines, a mauled landing stage and *Heimdall*'s own erratic movements through space. On reaching safety, Gunnlaugur and the others had made their way straight to the command level.

There was no sign of Stormcaller, and no reliable link to Kefa Primaris. The *Festerax*'s huge burning ruins stood between them and the planet, playing havoc with their surviving systems.

'Then he is lost,' said Gunnlaugur, his voice grim. 'What news from *Vindicatus*?'

'Moving to high anchor,' replied Derroth, running a weary hand across his cropped hair. '*Vuokho* is inbound, and will dock soon.'

Gunnlaugur nodded. Ingvar had survived, so it seemed, and was bringing something with him. The Gyrfalkon had sounded animated over the comm, which boded well.

'So be it,' Gunnlaugur said, turning to his battle-brothers. 'We have–'

His words died as soon as the first stab of warp-energy snaked out across the centre of the bridge decking.

Gunnlaugur backed away from it. The bridge crew cleared a wide space around the empty command throne, opening it up as the air shook and shimmered.

Worm-like slivers of actinic matter snaked across the marble, joining up and twisting into slithering whips of power. The temperature suddenly plummeted, sending a fractured skin of hoarfrost shooting across exposed metalwork. There was a hard, echoing bang, the stench of ozone, then a vivid flash of magnesium-white.

When the blast cleared, two figures stood at its heart. One was Njal, the other was Baldr. Both were covered from head to boot in a thin layer of steaming ice, and residual warp-energies danced across their armour. Njal's battleplate had brutal rents in the ceramite, as if mauled by some huge beast.

'Stormcaller!' cried one of the crew, his voice filled with a savage, unlooked-for joy.

Gunnlaugur had no time to react. His shock at seeing Njal on the bridge was only matched by that at seeing Baldr again. No teleport signal had been detected, and no locus had been issued. The Rune Priest had guided himself, somehow fighting through the vagaries of the warp to emerge, with pinpoint accuracy, back in the world of matter.

'Did we kill it?' growled Njal, his voice thick with effort. 'Does it burn?'

Recovering himself, Gunnlaugur bowed clumsily. 'It burns, lord,' he said.

Out in the void, secondary explosions continued to go off, radiating silently like the birth of new and strange stars.

Njal twisted his helm free, revealing a harrowed, fatigue-hollow face. His blue eyes scrutinised the fallout.

'Deploy the gunships again,' he rasped from a hoarse throat. 'Scan for movement in the wreckage. Any signs of life, notify me. Signal *Vindicatus* and request it remains in contact. Signal the surface and inform the Governor. We cannot relax yet.'

As all eyes were on Njal, Baldr suddenly fell to his knees. His ice-pale face was streaked with blood, and his eyes were glassy.

Before any kaerls could reach him he had crashed to the metal plating, out cold. Haflof hurried to his side, but Njal held up a warning hand.

'No!' he commanded darkly. 'Do not go near him.' The Rune Priest turned to Gunnlaugur. 'The fault is mine. He should never have been taken back.'

Njal stalked over to Baldr's prone body and stooped over him, holding out an open palm, as if scanning for residual corruption.

No one moved. Gunnlaugur waited with the rest of them, powerless to intervene. They all watched the Rune Priest, not daring to interrupt.

Eventually, Njal straightened. His expression was mixed: grim, marked by a weary, duty-driven reluctance.

'He lives?' asked Gunnlaugur, already fearing what the response would be.

'He lives,' said Njal. 'As do I, and that counts for something.'

Nightwing turned its gimlet eye towards Gunnlaugur.

'But there is no doubt now,' Njal went on. 'He invoked the storm. He has the blood of our packs on his claws. I was wrong. I was badly wrong.' The Rune Priest's voice was tight with loathing. 'Suffer not the witch to live,' he said, bitterly. 'There can be no other judgement.'

The words hit Gunnlaugur like blows. Such was the iron law of Fenris, and it was just, and sanctified by millennia, but it made the verdict no less hard to hear.

He bowed his head stiffly.

'As you command it,' Gunnlaugur said, forcing the words out, 'it will be done.'

Vuokho came in hard, skidding across the flight deck apron as the thrusters gave out. Just as it had been since the void-battle over Ras Shakeh, the gunship remained on the verge of destruction, held together seemingly by Jorundur's will and little else.

Gunnlaugur watched it land. The assault ramp slammed down and Ingvar stomped down to deck level.

'Old Dog?' Gunnlaugur asked, as the void-deck crew raced towards the gunship with fire-dousing gear.

'Looking after our guest,' said Ingvar, wryly. 'The confessor, brother. I have him.'

Gunnlaugur raised an eyebrow. 'They let you take him?'

'We did not ask.'

Ingvar radiated zeal – his hunt-sense was palpable. Ever since Bajola's death he'd been obsessed with this quest.

Gunnlaugur couldn't match the euphoria, not any more.

'What is it, brother?' Ingvar asked.

'Come with me,' Gunnlaugur said, turning and walking towards *Heimdall*'s interior. Ingvar fell in alongside him.

'You heard what happened?' Gunnlaugur asked.

'We detected the *Festerax*'s destruction.'

'After that?'

'Nothing. *Vuokho*'s instruments barely function.'

'Baldr lives. Njal retrieved him.'

'He's... How?'

'I do not know. Njal discovered him at the hulk's heart. Baldr used the way of the storm.' Gunnlaugur shot Ingvar a bleak look. 'It happened again.'

Ingvar shook his head furiously. 'He was *recovered.*'

'Obviously not.'

'Did he use sorcery? Was it corruption, like before?'

Gunnlaugur shrugged. 'What does it matter?'

'It means *everything.*' Ingvar stopped walking, and gripped Gunnlaugur's arm. 'We knew he had changed. It was bound to come back, but what was he *like?* Was he corrupted?'

'I know not. Njal has ruled, brother.'

'I do not care what Njal has ruled! Damn you – he is one of *us.* What do *you* rule?'

Gunnlaugur shook his head. The certainties that had flooded back to him in the heart of combat were now dissipated. He knew nothing of the ways of the runes, and that blunted his instincts. 'I do not know.'

'We brought him *back.*' Ingvar's voice rang with certainty. 'We made him whole again. Njal should never have taken him on the hulk. It was too soon, and we both knew it.'

Those words had the ring of truth to them – Baldr *had* recovered. Whatever had been done to him on that ship might have affected any of them.

'Maybe so, but it is over now, brother,' said Gunnlaugur, unwilling to follow the path this was leading down.

'Where is he held?'

'Do not even think that.'

'Just tell me.'

'The apothecarion,' said Gunnlaugur, angrily. 'And when he wakes, judgement will be served. He is guarded.'

'Where is Heavy-hand?'

'Inbound on *Hlaupnir.*'

Ingvar started to walk again, his strides full of purpose. 'We cannot let this go, brother,' he said. 'You brought him back in. He was restored.'

Gunnlaugur went after him. 'There is nothing we can do.'

'You said it yourself: he's one of us. He's Járnhamar.'

'Then *say* it, brother,' said Gunnlaugur, feeling both cornered and shamed by Ingvar's fervour. 'What do you propose?'

Ingvar turned to face him. His grey eyes glittered with fresh purpose.

'Just listen,' he began.

CHAPTER TWENTY-FOUR

Bjargborn stirred as the locks to the chamber clicked. Others around him looked up, roused from whatever torpor they had sunk into.

For hours there had been no contact. *Heimdall*'s structure had continued to creak and crack, though the worst of the impacts had ceased a long time ago. Bjargborn had been pleased enough just to be alive to hear it – the cruiser had evidently weathered a hard period of void-combat. In the dreary hours that followed, however, when no word came down to them of any change in their status, his spirits had flagged. A dour mood had descended across the chamber as his warriors did their best to keep occupied.

The enforced inactivity was enervating. There must have been things they could have done on the ship – repairs to be made, gun-stations to man. They were all experienced soldiers, many of them drawn from *Undrider*'s specialist ranks, and they were withering away.

But when the lock clicked, Bjargborn snapped back into old habits immediately.

'Prepare,' he ordered, pulling his tunic straight and brushing down his grey fatigues.

By the time the doors opened, the entire space had resumed a semblance of military order, with troops standing to attention alongside the ranks of still-warm bunks.

Ingvar entered, and sought out Bjargborn. 'Rivenmaster,' he said. 'You have been patient.'

Bjargborn bowed. His pulse was racing. He found himself praying for a combat mission. 'We're needed?' was all he said.

Ingvar closed the door behind him. The Space Marine was as brutally massive as ever, but something about his movements was almost... furtive.

'You should never have been kept here,' he said, his voice low. 'Forgive us. The fighting has been hard.'

'Anything,' said Bjargborn. 'We'll do anything. Just say the word.'

'How many of you are primary ship-crew?'

'Most. Between us, there isn't a starship-system we can't cover.'

'A warp-runner will soon be docking in berth two. Its designation is *Hlaup-nir*, and it requires a full crew replacement. It is smaller than *Undrider*, but burns well enough through the void. We will be travelling on it for some time.'

Bjargborn nodded. 'I can organise the work details. How long do we have?'

'Under an hour,' said Ingvar. 'Work details can wait. I want your troops armed and combat-ready, then make your way to the hangar straightaway. We launch as soon as the engines are primed.'

Bjargborn hesitated. 'Of course,' he said. 'Can I ask–'

'Do you trust me?'

Bjargborn thought back to Hjec Falama. He had been raised and trained to obey the orders of a Sky Warrior without question, and before him stood the one who had delivered them from a slow death in the plague-wastes.

'It wounds me that you would ask, lord,' he said.

'I need that trust,' Ingvar said. 'You will answer to Járnhamar, just as before. We are going to be out on our own for a while. There may be other mortals on *Heimdall* who do not see things the same way. You understand me?'

Bjargborn did. Such things were, and always had been, the way of the Fang. Wolf Lords left for hunts, Lone Wolves split from the Great Companies. The *outrider* was a part of the Canis Helix's heritage – the urge to charge off across the ice alone, splitting from the herd and pursuing whatever wyrd had fallen upon him.

'I understand you.'

'Olgeir will bring the ship in. Do whatever he commands. We will be loading *Vuokho*. That will be difficult – manpower will be required. Do not attempt to enter the gunship – it contains sanctioned cargo.' Ingvar fixed Bjargborn with a significant look. 'You will be a shipmaster again. That suits you better than...' He looked around him. 'This.'

'By your will,' grinned Bjargborn.

'*Hlaupnir*'s current crew will be discharged. You will replace them. If there is any confusion or resistance, you will end it. No deadly force unless necessary – these are our people. But we *will* leave on that ship.'

'Understood. Weapons?'

'I will see to it the armoury is unlocked within ten minutes. You will do the rest. Take only what is necessary – we are not here to weaken *Heimdall*. Anything else?'

Bjargborn looked at his fellow kaerls. There was nothing but enthusiasm in their expressions, and that was reassuring. They had survived amid a living, boiling nightmare with nothing but saviour-pod rations and a blind faith that their masters would, sooner or later, come looking for them. That faith had been rewarded, cementing a bond of loyalty that was stronger than adamantium.

'Nothing at all, lord,' said Bjargborn, flexing his fingers in anticipation. 'We live to serve.'

Gunnlaugur strode down the corridor towards the apothecarion. The conduits were not busy this far down – most of the crew were engaged in urgent repair work or the recovery of weapon systems. Njal had ordered a quick turnaround prior to entering orbit alongside *Vindicatus*. He had much on his mind: the re-establishment of a working relationship with Ecclesiarchy forces in-system, proper contact with the Guard regiments on Kefa, a restoration of *Heimdall*'s fighting capability.

That was fortunate. If things had been less frenetic, a chance of slipping through the net would never have presented itself.

He rounded the last corner. Arjen, a Hunter of Bloodhame's pack, stood guard outside the doors. He was helmless, but two kaerls in full combat-gear were with him, each bearing an autogun. The doors were locked and braced, cutting off access to the cell beyond.

Gunnlaugur emerged into the open.

'No closer, *vaerangi*,' said Arjen warily, raising his bolter.

'Does he live still?' asked Gunnlaugur, keeping his hands well away from his weapons.

'No idea. Leave, now. Njal will–'

Gunnlaugur held his ground. 'He is my warrior.'

'Not any more.'

Gunnlaugur took a step closer. 'Just a look, brother. A final word. You would wish for the same, if he were of your pack.'

Arjen aimed straight at Gunnlaugur's chest. 'One more step.'

Gunnlaugur held Arjen's gaze. They had fought together for a long time in the depths of the hulk, but he had no doubt at all that Arjen would fire.

He backed off, slowly, keeping his hands in the open. 'So you say.'

Just then, there was a crash from inside the apothecarion, steel clanging heavily on steel. Arjen's head snapped round. He reached for the door release.

Gunnlaugur responded instantly, whipping his bolter from his belt and opening up. Bolt-rounds hit Arjen's shoulder, throwing him back against the doors with a heavy crash.

The kaerls fired back, and a rain of projectiles pinged and ricocheted from Gunnlaugur's armour.

Arjen recovered quickly, sweeping his own bolter back into a firing angle. Just as he did so, the doors slid open from the far side, revealing Hafloí standing under the lintel with his bolt pistol already aimed.

He fired twice, sending Arjen slamming towards the far corridor wall. Gunnlaugur pounced after him, switching to fists. As the wounded Arjen tried to right himself, Gunnlaugur hammered him hard – once, twice, then a third time.

Still he wouldn't go down. Snarling, Gunnlaugur thumped down both balled fists, nearly taking his head clean off.

That finally did it. Arjen slumped to the floor, his face a mask of blood. By then one of the kaerls had already been immobilised by Hafloí, but the second had managed to flee, running down the corridor, firing behind him erratically.

He ran straight into the emerging grey cliff-face of Ingvar's power armour, and bounced painfully from the unyielding ceramite. Ingvar swung out with a half-strength backhand swipe, throwing the mortal to the deck. He didn't get up.

'Swiftly,' said Gunnlaugur, moving into the apothecarion.

Baldr was restrained on the metal slab, just as on Ras Shakeh, shackled at the ankles, wrists and neck by thick adamantium loops. He was still unconscious, though he showed none of the signs of the Red Dream, nor of the deep sickness that had plagued him on Ras Shakeh. A rune-totem hung from the ceiling above him, no doubt left by Njal to stifle any recurrence of maleficarum, and a new collar had been fitted around his neck to dampen his innate powers.

A lone ceiling panel rested on the floor where Hafloí had dislodged it. In the hole above, ragged edges of cut metal still glowed red from where he had used a melta-blade to gain access from the chamber above.

Ingvar followed Gunnlaugur in, drawing *dausvjer* as he came. 'This will be quickest,' he said, activating the blade's energy field.

Hafloí moved to cover the open doorway, keeping his bolter trained on the corridor outside. Ingvar worked quickly, slicing through the bonds without cutting into the flesh below. As he did so, Baldr stirred.

'Remain calm, brother,' said Gunnlaugur.

Baldr looked like he barely understood. As Ingvar severed the last of the shackles, he looked around himself groggily. 'What happened?' he muttered.

Gunnlaugur grabbed him by the arm and roughly hauled him from the bunk, righting him to prevent him crashing face-first to the deck. Ingvar seized his other arm, propping him up. The three of them stumbled back into the corridor, supporting Baldr's armoured weight between them.

Hafloí went ahead, scanning for movement.

'You need to stand,' said Ingvar, trying to right Baldr. 'Can you do that?'

Baldr swayed a little, but kept his feet. 'Where are we going?' he asked, his speech still slurred.

'Now walk. Our orders are to take you to *Hlaupnir*.'

'Stormcaller...' started Baldr, frowning in confusion.

'They are his orders,' snapped Gunnlaugur. 'We have little time.'

The habit of pack-command kicked in, and Baldr started to shamble forwards. With every step, a little more fluency returned. By the time he'd reached the end of the first long corridor, his gait was more or less normal.

As Gunnlaugur strode along beside him, he reflected on the risk they were taking. There was no possibility of stealth – they had to brazen it out, trusting to speed, to the servility of the kaerls, and to the fact that anyone likely to recognise Baldr's armour markings was either on the bridge or engaged in fresh combat preparation.

If that assumption proved wrong, punishment would be swift, merciless, and unavoidable.

'Keep moving, brother,' he muttered through gritted teeth, resisting the urge to push Baldr along or pick up the pace. 'It is all you have to do. Keep moving.'

Olgeir strode down *Hlaupnir*'s main embarkation ramp and onto the floor of the docking berth.

It was still active with refit-teams and servitors. The turnaround he'd been asked to make had been ludicrously tight, even without the added

complication of a full crew-switch. Thraid and the rest of the ship's complement had obeyed without question, of course – they were used to sudden
redeployments across the Chapter vessels as the needs of war dictated –
but the numbers involved were a challenge.

Bjargborn's detachment were now on board and prepping the ship for
launch. *Vuokho* had been lifted into the vessel's lone hangar, fuel had been
taken on, the engines given a final, though cursory, check.

They were good to go. For all that, Olgeir remained tense. Gunnlaugur's
orders had come with no warning, and though he guessed the reasons for
it, that didn't mean he liked them.

This will damn us. There will be no way back from this.

He heard a heavy series of thuds behind him, and turned to see Jorundur heading down the ramp after him.

'You know what's in there, don't you?' Jorundur asked.

Olgeir shook his head.

'The Cardinal's confessor,' said Jorundur. 'That's our cargo.'

'*Skítja*,' muttered Olgeir.

He checked his chrono again. Any minute now, Thraid would be reporting for duty. He'd be looking up at his superior officer, confused that he
wasn't expected. Data-slates would be retrieved, and discrepancies would
be noted. Then it would become apparent that he hadn't been ordered to
leave *Hlaupnir* at all, and Njal would be alerted.

All it would take would be a lock-command placed over the berth's void-
gate.

'Where *are* they?' Olgeir breathed. 'If this doesn't happen soon–'

His comm-bead blinked. The ident-rune was Rasek, *Heimdall*'s void-deck
controller, one of many kaerl officers overseeing the movement of the
various gunships and landers stowed in the cruiser's hangars.

'What is it?' Olgeir asked.

'Apologies, lord. I have word from Derröth, requesting your presence on
the command deck. Did you receive it? The Stormcaller is waiting.'

'I got the message. Tell Derroth we have a problem shutting down the
drives on *Hlaupnir*. It will not take long.'

'A problem? Do you have sufficient servitor cover, lord?'

Olgeir could sense the uncertainty in the man's voice. There was no reason
for him to oversee any repairs – he was not an obsessive like Jorundur, and
there were many more pressing tasks for a Sky Warrior to undertake.

'Tell Derroth five minutes.' He cut the link. 'He will start the process now,'
he growled to Jorundur. 'The checks will begin.'

Jorundur chuckled darkly. 'How long have we got?'

'I'm going on board. We need to get those engines fired.'

Jorundur was about to join him when a set of cargo-lift doors in the nearside walls suddenly slid open. Both of them spun around, instinctively going
for their weapons.

Ingvar, Gunnlaugur and Baldr emerged, hurrying across the hangar deck.

'Let us *leave*, Heavy-Hand,' Gunnlaugur ordered. '*Now.*'

* * *

Njal stood on *Heimdall*'s command bridge. Kefa Primaris hung in the forward viewer, far huger than it had been during the final living hours of the *Festerax*. Its dirty grey surface was clearly visible through the bands of drifting cloud, as were the looming silhouettes of Guard troop carriers steadily making their way back to orbital berth-points.

Wreckage of the destroyed plague-hulk still registered on the augurs. Every chunk was tracked and investigated lest it be carrying some vestige of spoor-matter. Even a tiny amount could still prove ruinous, should it somehow survive the entry into Kefa's atmosphere.

He remembered the final moments aboard the *Frostaxe*. He remembered the horror, the chill grasp around his hearts. He remembered Baldr's fury. *God-marked.*

The law was immutable. It was the Chapter's only lasting defence against corruption. It was whispered among the ignorant that no Son of Russ had ever fallen to the service of the Great Enemy, and that the Rout alone retained the purity of the early Imperium in its Helix-strengthened veins.

Njal knew the falsity of that. Wolves had succumbed, whether through lust for battle, or power, or via the cruel arts of the enemy. Njal knew the tally of such lost souls. He knew their names, and what their wyrd had become.

Vigilance had to be eternal, unbending and relentless. Njal had already failed in that regard once.

I recognise my error. Even I am not above that.

His gaze shifted, passing up from the curve of the hive world to where *Vindicatus* hung, magnificent even in the wake of the damage it had taken. Callia, its new commander, was a woman he could work with. They were both warriors, and that bred a certain understanding.

That was well, for the war had only just started. There would be more incursions, more contagion-fleets, each one designed to cripple worlds, to sap the strength from the sector defences, to strip the productive capacity of every system between the Shakeh worlds and the Cadian perimeter. More plague-ships were ploughing through the void, and more Imperial vessels were burning across the warp in response. With a ponderous, uncertain trajectory, the war-sphere was expanding. There was no telling how many more hulks had been roused from the heart of the Eye, or what strength of Death Guard still marched across the sea of stars.

And at the centre of it, somewhere, was the architect. The Traveller. The master of the *Terminus Est*. He was hidden for now, but it would not stay that way forever.

That would be the real test, the one besides which all others would pale.

'My lord,' came Derroth's voice from close by. 'Did you authorise a launch?'

Njal snapped out of his thoughts. 'I did not.'

Derroth was standing amid the semi-functioning wreckage of a sensor station, surrounded by maintenance servitors. The forward scanners were only giving intermittent readings, and for the time being the bridge crew was relying on a range of short-scope real-viewers.

'A docking berth is open. We have an unauthorised departure.' Derroth looked up at him, shocked. '*Hlaupnir.*'

Njal swept down from his vantage and seized a pict-feed. The screen showed a clear departure vector. The ship was already moving fast.

'Who is on that ship?' he asked.

'Unknown. I just tried to raise them.'

Foreboding suddenly kindled. Nightwing flapped agitatedly on its mount. Njal opened a comm-channel to Arjen, and the link seethed emptily.

Njal swore. He turned to Eir, the most senior of the Wolves still on the bridge. 'Go to the apothecarion. Take others with you. If they are still there, pin them and keep them alive until I reach you.'

Eir stalked off. Njal didn't watch him go – he guessed it was already futile. 'Can we target the ship?' he asked.

Derroth was already working on it. 'We've barely any weapons left, lord,' he said, apologetically.

'*Find some.*'

By then, Njal could see *Hlaupnir* for himself through the main forward real-view portal. It was powering away at full speed, curving back round in the void. He didn't need to run trajectory analysis to know where it was going – straight for the system's Mandeville point.

'I can give you a limited macrocannon burst,' announced Derroth. 'But the window is closing.'

As Njal watched *Hlaupnir* thrusting away from the planet, an incoming transmission came in from *Vindicatus*.

'My lord Stormcaller,' came Callia's voice. 'We are tracking a rapid acceleration from a ship in your flotilla. Is all well?'

It would not do to have the Ecclesiarchy alerted to division within his ranks. Njal indicated to Derroth to stand the macrocannon crews down. *Heimdall* was already running on uncertain power – loosing a broadside at his own craft risked plunging the ship deeper into crisis.

'All is well, Sister,' replied Njal, working hard to keep the fury out of his voice. 'Chasing down a few stray scents.'

'Understood. One other thing: we have received long-range signals from the Ministorum battle-group *Rasumova*. It will be here in two weeks. There are other markers, but the provenance is yet unknown.' Her voice was triumphant, as well it might be, given her rapid elevation. 'Praise the Emperor. His armies gather.'

Njal's eyes remained locked on the diminishing outline of *Hlaupnir*. He knew who was on it.

Their name will be stricken from all sagas.

'So they do,' said Njal. 'We will confer again soon, Sister.'

Njal cut the link. Derroth was still waiting for an order.

'I can divert power for a single strike,' the shipmaster said. 'One shot. I've inlaid targeting coordinates.'

Njal considered that. He envisaged the lone streak of energy, lancing through the void. He saw the explosion, tumbling through space just as the *Festerax* had done.

He almost gave the command.

He closed his eyes.

+Hear this, Fjolnir,+ he sent, casting his mind-voice out after the wake of the fleeing system-runner. +You know the precipice on which you stand. You know the depths to which you can fall.+

He couldn't tell if the message had found its target. Just making the attempt, though, at least gave a channel for his anger to run down.

+I may have been wrong about you. We all may have been wrong. But if we were not, and if you fall – then I will *hunt* you. I will not let my laxity plague the stars.+

His words spilled into the uncaring void.

+If the time comes, if the touch of corruption stirs, you know what to do. You still have that power, even when all others fail. *Use* it.+

The sending finished. All that was left of *Hlaupnir* on the viewer was a brilliant point of light in the far distance.

Njal watched it for a few moments longer. None of the crew dared interrupt him.

Then, finally, Nightwing extended its wings again, and cawed bleakly. That was enough to break the spell. Njal drew in a deep breath.

'Enough of this. They are gone.'

He turned back to the command bridge, still in semi-disarray, and faced the thousand tasks that still awaited him. It would not be long before battle called again, and *Heimdall* would have to be ready.

'Vox the governor,' he said, wearily. 'We have much to discuss.'

EPILOGUE

Hlaupnir ran smoothly through the warp. Just as they had said, the vessel was fast. Its lines were cleaner than the old *Undrider*, and it rattled and creaked less as the aether-gales thrust it further and further from Kefa Primaris.

Baldr limped towards the ship's rather makeshift Annulus chamber – a cramped space set near the rear of the main structure. His body had made a swift recovery from the exertions on *Festerax*, though it was hard to shake the images that still crowded his waking thoughts. Every so often, as he moved his head, or when he blinked, the shrivelled visage of the Mycelite would stare back at him. He still saw those dark, sympathetic eyes staring at him in the dark, and felt the clammy fingertips that had traced a line down his cheek.

He still wore the second collar that Njal had fixed on him, and had no wish to remove it. For as long as he wore it, the risk of his power creeping back was dampened. Perhaps, in time, that state would become permanent, allowing him to fight as he had once done – carefree, untrammelled, his mind locked on the physical and untroubled by thoughts of the immaterial.

Perhaps, he thought. *In time.*

Ingvar was waiting for him outside the low doorway to the Annulus chamber.

'Recovered?' the Gyrfalkon asked him.

'You lied,' Baldr said. 'About Njal. I would not have come, if I'd known.'

'Which is why we lied. The others are waiting.'

'Why take the risk, brother?' asked Baldr, staying where he was. 'You have seen what I can do.'

'You are one of us. That is reason enough.' Ingvar pulled the door open, revealing the chamber beyond. 'There will be a cure. The galaxy is full of secrets. I have seen more than any of you – have some faith.'

Ingvar's voice betrayed the clarity of a certain mind. Baldr couldn't share it.

The two of them entered the Annulus chamber. Gunnlaugur, Jorundur, Olgeir and Hafloí were already there, standing in a loose circle around the stones. Fires burned in alcoves behind them, dully illuminating the iron outlines of sacred runes.

'Recovered?' asked Gunnlaugur.

They all asked the same thing. It felt as if they'd been enquiring after his physical state ever since landing on Ras Shakeh. That would have to change – he was a warrior, cast in the image of Russ, not some sickly patient to be chaperoned through what remained of his service.

'I am restored,' Baldr said, taking his place.

The others all looked at him, each giving away his own thoughts as they did so.

Gunnlaugur had his pride back, no doubt earned in the fiery heart of the plague-hulk. He stood taller, adopting the unconscious swagger of a *vaerangi*, and the danger – that old, unmatchable danger – had returned to his eyes. Ingvar, too, looked more at ease than he had done. His place had been found again, one of the pack, one of the Rout, and the dark temper that had marred his return had retreated. The bad blood boiling away between them had ebbed, and the prospect of their blades being wielded together in unity was a vision for a hunter to salivate over.

Jorundur and Hafloí had changed little. The Old Dog had spent his time since launch in the repair bays, slowly reconstructing *Vuokho* and lamenting the paucity of tools at his disposal. Hafloí had been badly scarred by the fighting on the hulk, though he already looked stronger for it. Like a blade tempered in the fire, he was rapidly growing sharper. A few more battles like that one, and he'd be as battered and hard-beaten as the rest of them.

Olgeir was the only one not to meet his eye. Baldr knew the reason – he had ever counselled against Baldr's return, and for good reason. There was no malice there, just belief in the law of the Chapter. The distrust would just have to be borne, until such time as one of them, Ingvar or Olgeir, was proved right over what had been done.

'So the step has been taken,' said Gunnlaugur, addressing them all. 'We are on our own. Get used to *Hlaupnir*.'

'Where are we headed?' asked Hafloí, his voice giving away his unease. He still had the weakest ties of brotherhood with the others, despite all that had changed since his arrival.

'Klaive will be our guide,' said Ingvar. He extended his hand, turning it palm-up to reveal a small golden cherub's head, less than a finger's-width in diameter. 'Soon we will have names, and locations, and access to the truth.'

'What truth?'

'The truth of the Fulcrum.'

Hafloí didn't look satisfied. He turned to Gunnlaugur, as if the Wolf Guard were likely to order them back, undoing everything and seeking Njal's rare forgiveness. 'We're running from the war,' he said, disapprovingly.

'There are many wars,' said Gunnlaugur. 'We have a new hunt, no less dangerous than the one we had before.'

'This is blood-debt,' said Ingvar. 'We are bound to honour it.'

An uneasy silence fell. Olgeir said nothing. Jorundur, of all of them, seemed the most content. He had always liked running out on the margins.

'It will be *done*, brothers,' Ingvar went on. 'Hjortur's shade cries out for vengeance. It will be restitution. It will be–'

'Absolution,' said Baldr, realising at last what was being proposed. 'A way back.'

'Perhaps,' said Ingvar, defiantly. 'If we take this to completion, then why should we not return?'

Again, silence fell. The only sounds were the faint crackle of burning coals and the low, ever-present grind of the warp engines.

'Then we are resolved,' said Gunnlaugur. 'We hunt across the sea of stars, never resting, never halting, until we claim the head of Hjortur's killer and bring it back to the Fang. I swear my soul to this, and may Morkai take it if I turn aside.'

Gunnlaugur drew his thunder hammer and extended it over the central stone. The others all did likewise, pulling axes or sword-blades from scabbards and joining them in a six-pointed circle. One by one, they swore the vow, binding their souls to the new hunt.

Baldr was the last. With the eyes of his brothers on him, he spoke the words.

'I swear it,' he said, feeling the weight of the other blades resting on his.

The weapons withdrew. The braziers continued to burn, the engines continued to growl. It was almost as if nothing had changed, but they knew, they all knew, that everything had.

Ingvar looked at him. 'This is the beginning, brother,' he said confidently. 'This is the greatest test.'

Baldr nodded, trying to believe it. In his mind, though, Njal's words still rang clear, the ones that he alone had heard, just before *Hlaupnir* had reached the jump-points.

If the time comes, if the touch of corruption stirs, you know what to do. You still have that power, even when all others fail. Use it.

'The beginning,' he replied, forcing a smile.

All around them, the walls of the Annulus trembled slightly as warp-gusts shook the ship. *Hlaupnir* powered onwards, forging a path deeper into the aether, leaving the Kefa system behind.

Ahead of them, vast and unknowable, stood the open void. Somewhere out there lay the object of the hunt.

For now, though, they flew blind – alone, adrift, and guided only by fate.

THE
HELWINTER GATE

PROLOGUE

It was a world of witches.

It had to be. You could see its sure corruption, even from far out in the void – a churn and a crash of devilish seas, seething, impossible, a place no mortal could live without making some kind of forbidden bargain. Even the most boastful warrior might do that, eventually, when death stared at him from every angle, crowding out the room for escape and giving the lie to talk of honour.

He stared at the viewers, watching the world turn, watching its hateful white glare in the darkness. If he could have reached out, stretched a hand through the ship's hull and into the void, curling his fingers around it, crushing it, he would have done. When he had been a child, schooled by pious instructors who taught him eternal truths, he had imagined faith would give him that power. He had thought that if you believed strongly enough, your body would grow larger and taller, until you could tower above the spire-tops and extend a hand up for the stars themselves, gathering them like fistfuls of dust. He remembered staring into the green eyes of Sister Lukba and telling her, solemnly, that the day of power would come for him.

She hadn't contradicted him. Children must have told her such things all the time – the pious ones, the ones who took things to heart. She had ignored it. Or maybe she had believed it too.

So he'd clung to the certainty, after a fashion, even when adulthood came and drove out most other childish conceits. It was true – you could reach out to clutch the stars and harvest them, albeit through the medium of voidships and battle cruisers. You could crush worlds, so long as you had sufficient arms and armour under command. These were the things that faith delivered – iron and adamantium, las-fire and bomb-blast – and they were not to be scorned, for they were His instruments.

But not all worlds were made the same. Some were holy, some were profane. Some were weak, some were strong. And some, like this one, were of their own kind entirely. A world of witches.

'My lord,' said the ship's master, Buta Avelina, looking up at him in alarm.

He knew what she was going to tell him. He did not know why she kept on relaying it all out loud, as if he were not plugged into the same nodes as her, and could not see just the same dispositions and movements and destructions.

He narrowed his eyes, gripping the arms of his iron command throne. He felt fused to it, his sweat-soaked robes stuck to the metal. His eyes never left the high-arched realviewers ahead, the armaglass cracked into webs of silver by repeated impacts. He felt the deck under his boots shudder again. He saw debris fall from the bridge roof, clanking into servitor pits and sensor galleries.

'My lord,' Avelina said again, more urgently.

All she wanted was certainty. He could have ordered her into the Eye of Terror and she would have obeyed without hesitation, just as long as his voice was firm and his gaze remained solid. She was painfully young, for one given such heavy responsibility. Then again, she, like him, placed every store in the power of faith. Faith was evidenced by certainty. Let doubt in, just for a moment, and nothing at all could be relied upon.

Just then, though, and for the first time in his life, all he felt was emptiness. He stared at the distant ice-world, drinking in its wickedness, and knew that he would never set foot on it. He would never breathe in its tainted air, nor witness the mountains themselves, the ones that so much had been written about – the ones, it was said, that He Himself had carved open and raised into a fortress without peer, now desecrated by the degenerates that squatted in its halls.

To withdraw now, though, after so much had been sacrificed... well, that was not in his nature, and had never been.

'Maintain assault,' he said softly. 'Maintain current positions, maintain pressure. Deploy the reserves.'

Avelina looked at him the whole time, rocking in her throne as the impacts rained in. 'If we deploy–'

'Deploy the reserves,' he said insistently, not angry with her, just resolute.

So she did. She passed the order to the principal comms officers, who sent it out over the secure grid to the assembled ships' masters and the squadron commanders and the three canonesses. Even amid all the destruction and the interference, the commands got through. The surviving operatives were still doing their duty, still processing orders and updating tactical summaries as their thrones fell apart under them and their rune-lenses fizzed and blew out.

He watched the results.

The cruiser *His Scrutiny* pulled away port-zenith, its flanks burning in jets of expelled oxygen, its torpedo bays emptying in dazzling scatters of light. The heavy assault carrier *Sin of Compromise* maintained its anchor point above the battle-sphere, still operating at something like half capacity, surrounded now by haloes of competing las-fire. Schools of void-fighters wheeled and plummeted, duelling between the giants amid puffs of explosive flame. The Order of the Wounded Heart's flagship, *Succession of Purity*, pushed ahead, fully committing now, its spine blackened and its towers crushed but its gunlines still firing. The Order of the White Rose had occupied the port flank, and its clustered ships were taking a bad beating. The Fiery Tear's squadrons were doing better out on starboard-nadir, but that would only attract more pain the longer this went on.

The reserves went in. Three cruisers sailed in the colours of his own diocese – violet and gold, with the chalice motif under a six-spiked coronet. Those were supported by nine waves of Furies and a smattering of Order Thunderhawks, plus the slower-moving hulks of twelve gunboats in anonymous dun-grey trim.

And then there was his own vessel, the centrepiece of the fleet, his magnificent barque, carved out of the blackness in curves of extravagant gold and crimson, its prow decorated with blindfolded angels, its keel underslung with a heavy lance battery that would have been the pride of any Navy line battle cruiser. The *Righteous Flail* it was called, and entire worlds had burned under its bombardments.

Not this one, though. For all the pomp and wrath, for all the diligence of the deckhands and the zeal of the Battle Sisters, this was a planet of madness and devilry, of beast-melded humanity, a stain on the conscience of the species. Its defenders came hard out of the void, howling and hammering. They flew their heavy voidcraft like lunatics, making reckless manoeuvres that, if they didn't result in catastrophic self-destruction, caused havoc among the more orthodox Ecclesiarchy formations. They sent their boarding tubes smashing into the undersides of the capital ships, weaving through defensive las-grids before crunching deep into the decks within. Once inside, they clawed and hacked their way towards the engines, the shield-generators, the reactors, almost impossible to stop, hard even to locate. The *Valorous Blade* had already been crippled that way, its heart chewed out by the fanatics running rampant through its innards, its colossal hull fallen away and listing. Others were in the process of being devoured. Sooner or later the beasts would hit the *Righteous Flail* too.

They had too many ships, far too many for a compliant Chapter, spiralling out of the sun's glare in flocks, offering yet more proof of their deviance. There was something unhinged about the exuberance of it. Other heretics fought with zeal, but these... he did not even know what to call them, now. They gave themselves a hundred names, he knew, each more prideful than the last, but he no longer had words for them himself. Maybe it was their perversions that made them mad – the energy of debased souls desperate to avoid being uncovered. Or maybe they were just baresarks after all, for all the legends spoke of deeper cunning lying under the surface of pelts and chain-hung fangs. Only monsters, self-damned monsters.

It couldn't last. Always, always, he kept his eyes fixed on the ice-world in the viewers, the circle of blue-white against the dark, even as his fleet crumpled into ashes around him. Three Orders had not been enough. Maybe ten could not have done it. Maybe no force of any size could withstand this, head-on, in full view, arms openly displayed.

'My lord,' said Avelina, in just the same way as before, turning to look at him again, seeing the incontrovertible evidence of death tallies and damage reports.

He switched his private comm-feed to the sensor-vessel he'd sent in under the shadow of the burning *Succession of Purity*. For many hours now, this had been the most important vessel in the fleet, too small to attract attention, running dark, stuffed with augurs, a mote of pure black amid the roiling fires of the void.

'Do you have it yet?' he asked.

The response came back amid waves of distortion. Unmarked it may have been, but it was still blown about by the storms he had sent it into. *'Scans are complete, lord. Analysis can begin on your command.'*

'You got everything? You're sure?'

'Everything. They do not seem to be... careful.'

That made sense. They would want the names to be discoverable. It was a matter of prestige to them – this adversary was slain by *me*; *I* did these things.

'Very good. Withdraw immediately. Do not allow yourself to be detected. I shall maintain cover for the next standard hour.' The link cut out. Immediately, he shifted in his throne, and turned his attention to Avelina. What had to happen next pained him – of course it did – but not as much as it might have done. A battle might last moments, or it might last decades, that was the lesson here. 'Annomark,' he said.

She blinked. 'Annomark?'

'You heard me. In full, please.'

She consulted her systems, just briefly, confused, but still obedient. 'Local system 8-76-02. Imperial standard M41.886.'

'Thank you.' Then he stood. He gathered his robes about him, donned his mitre again. He switched his vox-emitter to broadband, splayed out not just to the thousands of crew on the *Righteous Flail*, but the hundreds of thousands across the entire fleet. 'Remember this date, my sisters and brothers!' he said. 'You followed my order to come here, knowing the dangers. You have fought with faith and fury, just as He demands. We tested them hard, forcing them out, and now the prize lies within our eyesight. Many said we would never get this far. They were wrong. Your faith has proved that.'

The deck continued to bounce and buckle. More cracks wrinkled across the high balustrades.

'And I know you would have fought to the end, had I commanded it,' he told them. 'But it is no true devotion to squander sacred resources on a quest that cannot be completed. Three weeks of toil we have already given to this, spilling both our blood and theirs, and still we come no closer to planetfall. They do not see reason – they do not understand compromise. To force the issue now would result in devastation, depriving the Imperium of servants who have duties elsewhere.'

He swallowed. This was hard to say. It was hard even to countenance.

'So the order is to withdraw. I say it again, the order is to withdraw. All capital vessels assume positions for fighting retreat, all subsidiary vessels make for dock immediately or head directly for out-system muster.'

It was the right thing to do. It was the only thing to do. It didn't make the decision any less bitter. He felt the damp weight of his robes, the things that gave him his authority, and their burden was like an accusation, the mark of his hubris.

'But mark this,' he said, his eyes never leaving that circle of bright white. 'Names have been taken. His vengeance against the faithless knows no limit or exhaustion. I vow it here – a sanctified curse that shall never fade, never cease, never be undone. That, at least, is something they should understand.'

It was still failure. No defiance could mask that. Only the future could see salvation for this enterprise, for his reputation and for the sanctity of his greater mission. He would have to trust, of course, but he would also have to sacrifice. The road ahead, just as it had to be, was strewn with thorns.

'We will return,' he said, eyes fixed on the world he had come to sanction. 'In whatever manner He ordains, and as the Immortal Throne is the witness to my words, judgement will be served.'

I
THE BLADE OF NAXIAN

CHAPTER ONE

The *Blade of Naxian* ran hard through the void. It was a good ship, one of the best Hera Soteqa had ever served on, and that was something to cling on to in such times. Everything else seemed to be falling apart, lost in the confusion of contradictory astropathic screaming. She could almost see the break-up in the chain of command unfolding before her eyes. It was hellish, unusual, something to keep you awake in the hot night. She'd spoken to the priest about it. 'It will pass,' he'd told her. She didn't believe him. He didn't seem overly sure, either.

Finally, though, some solid orders had come in. Someone, somewhere, had got a grip, and assets were being mobilised. The *Blade of Naxian* was one of them, and now it was racing towards the Klaat System's Mandeville horizon, ready for translation out towards Admiral Freer's muster at Coronis Agathon. The Defender-class light cruiser would be a small but useful part of what looked like a serious conglomeration – cruisers, battle cruisers, even a few line battleships, they said – that had been plucked and swiped from every Navy rotation in the subsector.

Something was up. No one said what it was. Probably no one, not even the *Blade*'s bridge-captain, Avilo, knew. Orders would be given at Coronis Agathon, they said, and then at least a few of them would know a little more.

Soteqa hurried down the long corridor, her boot heels clacking on newly cleaned panels. As comms officer senioris, her place was on the command bridge, but too many things needed attending to in the hours before they attempted the warp crossing, and most of those she preferred to oversee in person. She'd already spent too long down in the depths of the augur-coils, trying to get some sense out of lexmechanics, making sure that by the time the frenzy of incoming data started up the machine-spirits would be primed and ready. Mno-8, the tech-priest, had detained her for a frustratingly long time over some anomalies on the ranged scans, something the priest thought pointed to a sensor malfunction, but which looked to her like typical Martian fussiness.

Still, she'd raised a report and sent it up to the bridge augur-monitors. Then she'd headed back along the vessel's central core transit route, taking a mag-train sternwards and disembarking at the fourth cargo hold. That still left a long walk down a series of high-vaulted corridors, all of them utilitarian, gleaming, scoured every rotation by hard-driven menial crews and servitor gangs. The entire ship was tightly run, but this section was given special attention. Soteqa passed three separate checkpoints before reaching her final destination, every one manned by squads of armsmen bearing lascarbines and siege-shields. As she went through each point, the atmosphere became colder by a few degrees. By the time she reached the last set of blast-doors, pocked with ancient scour-marks, she felt the cold sink into her bones.

A different breed of guard waited for her at the threshold – four sour-looking characters in nightshade robes carrying electro-staves. They had the eye-within-an-I icon of the Adeptus Astra Telepathica inked onto their foreheads, and their skin was the shade of translucent grey that told of lives spent within sealed cells without natural light.

'By His grace, lieutenant-commander,' the foremost of them said, speaking in that dry whisper that they all seemed to use. The speaker was a woman, stick-thin under her robes, with thin lips and dark shadows around her eyes. 'You wish to consult him before we make the transition.'

'That would be appreciated,' Soteqa said.

The woman inclined her head, stepped aside and keyed in a code on the lock-panel. The heavy doors juddered open, letting strangely scented air waft out – something charred, or maybe spoiled.

The chamber on the far side had once been a storage area, capable of taking standard trade-modules or tethered vehicles on loading claws. The main deck was more than six hundred yards across, the roof ninety feet up. In normal times, it would have rung to the echoing clang of lifters on tracks, underpinned by the smells of engine oil and the glare of arc-lumens. Now it felt like another world – a mist-wreathed, fabric-enclosed echo of a fine Terran princeling's apartments. Elaborate ironwork partitions had been raised, each of them decorated with glyphs in hard-to-discern patterns. The deck itself hummed, not from the buried thunder of the plasma drives, but from subtler harmonics, rhythms that few mortals found easy to endure. The cold became oppressive.

Soteqa picked her way through a tangle of cables, some as thick as her body, all of them rimed with frost. A maze of doorways led off in many directions, all bleeding a fine mist. Attendants in uniform black livery padded to and fro bearing scrolls, datatubes, brass siphons. A faint sound made the air throb – a murmuring, as if a thousand sleepers were mouthing something unintelligible as they dreamed.

The complex had been constructed four years ago, while the *Blade of Naxian* underwent a scheduled refit in the Naval dockyards of Mholo. It had since been refined, then further extended, until it had become as integral a part of the ship's body as the engines, power plants or gun decks. Truth be told, the facility was now the principal reason anyone, Admiral Freer included, cared about the *Blade of Naxian*.

Soteqa pushed further in, reaching a basalt-clad chamber with a steep roofline and High Gothic inscriptions carved on the walls. The deck was hidden under stone flags, and candles flickered on metal sconces. They liked their little touches of home, did the choir.

Talek was waiting for her there, tethered to his throne, his dried-up face peering at her from under a heavy dark cowl. He wore the same black robes as his staff, though translucent tubes ran out from under his cuffs and squirmed their way into banks of instrumentation arranged in a wide arc around him. Lenses glowed in the murk, bleeding out a pale green light. Auto-quills scratched away on thick bundles of vellum, fed by slow, clunking machinery. He sat amongst it all, tethered by it, nourishing it.

'Lieutenant-commander,' said Lervio Talek, master of the ship's astropathic relay node. 'Welcome.'

'Apologies for the disruption,' Soteqa replied. 'I know you're busy.'

'No need. You wish to check on our progress before we cross the veil.'

'It's been difficult.'

Talek let slip a sour chuckle. 'That is one word for it.' He shuffled in his throne, and the web of tubes jangled. 'We lost another one, four hours ago. A promising astropath, one with a long future of service ahead of her. Burned out, burned up. Such a waste. I finalised her training myself.'

Soteqa could have told him similar stories from her own crew – ratings going insensible from fatigue, officers opening void-hatches and walking calmly out into the airlocks. Perhaps, though, those working in this strange place did suffer more than the rest. She could hardly imagine what they witnessed with their empty eye-sockets, lined up in their tight rows, bound with iron fetters, forced to dream the raw stuff of madness for hour after hour.

'There have been storms before,' she said. 'But I need to know–'

'If this is truly worse. If it is a different order. Yes, I believe so. I believe it is.' He sniffed, and for a moment Soteqa caught a glimpse of a pale grey cheek under the cowl's shadow. 'We get fragments, only fragments, and they all tell me the same thing. It is like a tapestry, the warp. If it is calm, you see the pattern on its surface. If it is disturbed, the pattern is rumpled. If it becomes too disturbed, the only pattern *is* the disturbance.'

'And now?'

'I see things never taught me by my instructors on Terra. Maybe they never existed before. So, it is true, I think some great event is coming. Maybe just in this sector. Maybe in all sectors. That is the problem, of course – we cannot see far ahead of ourselves. We send our messages, and only get back faint echoes. I sometimes wonder if we are the only ship left. The only people left alive in all creation. Alone in the dark.'

Soteqa had little time for such talk. 'With respect, that's–'

'Nonsense. I know. But I am an old man. My imagination runs away with me.'

'So what are we heading into?'

'A wall of fire. On the far side of it, I see nothing. On this side of it, I see hosts gathering, like crows flying ahead of the storm. I wonder that they can follow their orders, or that they can even hear them. Many will not make it. The structure of the warp will become more violent. Massed hull-translations will be extremely perilous.'

'You know, then, what lies beyond the muster.'

'I do not.'

'But what is the gossip?'

He laughed – an amphibian croak. '*Gossip?* We are not schola students, commander. We are the soul-bound, the ether-scryers. When we confer, it is because we have something to–'

He suddenly broke off. He inclined his head to one side, as if listening.

Just as he did so, an alert throbbed at Soteqa's collar. It was red – she would have to attend it.

'We will speak again,' she said. 'But, for now, I emphasise the importance of this. The relay – *your* relay – was placed on this ship precisely because fixed planetary nodes were becoming unreliable. We cannot know for sure that the messages in your archive have been received by anyone else at all, and that makes me worried. They might be more valuable than we understand.'

He looked at her. Or, at least, she thought he looked at her – you could never tell just what was going on under that heavy fabric hood.

'I understand perfectly, commander,' he said. 'But you are needed elsewhere. The danger has, I think, caught up with us.'

Mno-8 was angry. Few things made him angry. Much of his emotional life had been burned away when they had first delved into his skull and started to replace the folds of fleshy matter with more reliable wafer banks. After that, he'd learned to adjust to the muffled existence of a senior tech-priest, one close to the Omnissiah, a being of logic and cold calculation.

But it hadn't all gone. Being disregarded, being talked down to – *that* still made him angry. Few people dared to do it. He knew, on some level, that Soteqa hadn't meant it, either. She was stressed, her mind racing down a whole gamut of alleys, and she hadn't wanted to spend her valuable time with him among the flickering augur banks. Still, she'd been curt. And, for some reason, whereas he could ignore or overlook a whole host of other human failings, that spiked his emotion-injectors.

So he clattered down the corridor, his mechadendrites flailing, his red cloak snagging on the metal grilles. The entire ship was racing, creaking, banging, flying along as if caught in a blast of real-world wind. Captain Avilo was clearly desperate to get into the warp, and yet – and *yet* – no one was listening to the real threat-indicators. On another day, there would be much less haste, but then this kind of madness was contagious, and the un-fixed humans suffered from it worse than his people. The armsmen needed to be dragged out of their garrison-units and training halls and sent to the deck intersections. It needed to happen now.

He burst into the chamber, squeezing his overextended bulk through the access hatch before emerging on the far side like an arachnid splaying out from its burrow.

The crew looked up, startled. Twenty of them, all in dark-blue Navy trim, half-buried among the analogue lenses of cogitator nodes. One of them got up from her station – the senior operator here, Calja Yui, just a level or two below Soteqa in the arcane hierarchy of the upper decks.

'My lord tech-priest,' she started. 'Can I help–'

Mno-8 held up a warning dendrite, then slotted three of his power claws into input jacks lodged in a rack over the line of augur stations. One of his cortex-bundles negotiated with the gaggle of machine-spirits who squatted within the chamber network, while another took over the hololith projection unit.

'Listen,' he croaked, using the vox-emitter stuck just under his clavicle, since his jaw was long gone. 'Observe.'

A schematic whirled into ghostly life, glowing eerily amid the gloom of the comms-chamber. Yui did as she was bid, and looked at it. A big blob of light traced a slender arc between two points. One was the hive world of Klaat, the nondescript anchorage they'd just spent three months at, pressing new crew, filling the cavernous promethium bunkers, dealing with a never-ending procession of dignitaries and officials trying to find out what was going on with their protection details and trade-route escorts. The second was the Mandeville limiter, a specific horizon marked with very old runes indeed – humans had given those phenomena the same basic names since their discovery, long before the dawn of the Imperial Age. The arc traced from one to the other, speeding away from Klaat and almost intersecting with the first rune.

'Yes?' asked Yui. 'You show me only what every other lens in this place shows me.'

'*Observe*,' said Mno-8 again, rattling a serpentine dendrite with a turbo-hammer at its terminus. 'The plasma-wake correction at 25-6-4. Observe.'

Realspace augurs used a number of techniques to give signals staff the data they required. Much of the actual knowledge behind their construction was buried in STCs so old that few truly comprehended them, but some use-factors were still well understood – that plasma drives operating at full burn created distortion fields that required compensation, lest the input retinas overload and blow into static. The hololith suspended between the two of them displayed all the telltale indicators of such compensation – lines of blocky image correction, flickering like faulty lumens in a storm.

To her credit, Yui did her best. She looked in the right places. 'I see noth–'

'At 25-6-4. This is chronomark minus four. We are accelerating into the present. Observe.'

She narrowed her eyes. Soteqa had done the same, though not for long enough. Her deputy lingered a little longer.

'Just a sensor artefact,' she said, eventually.

'Negative.'

'We see them all the time. It's tracking our velocity and course exactly.'

Mno-8 swept up to her, elevating to his full height, which placed his gold skullcap near the iron-plate chamber roof.

'Until chronomark minus two,' he growled. 'When it disappears.'

'Which you'd expect. We are at preliminary translation approach – the shutdown cascade has started.'

'Standard Naval procedure. Only, this is well known. A hostile, one with advanced scanner tech and extreme speed, could use that knowledge. They could use it to get in close.'

'Anything coming in on that path would have to be tiny. And anyway, no pilot could fly the course.'

'No *human* pilot.' Mno-8's cloak shuddered as his many limbs rearranged themselves under it. 'The Archenemy is everywhere. We know this. We have seen the signs in every subsector. Why do you not see the danger? One of my fallen brothers, using some devious archeotech, could conceivably–'

He broke off. Yui looked up. The hull had just boomed, as if it had hit something solid, something unyielding. No alarms went off. The *Blade of Naxian* just kept running, bolting, haring along.

'What was that?' Yui asked, suddenly looking worried.

'Maybe nothing,' said Mno-8 grimly. 'Or maybe, just maybe, your sensor artefact has now become strangely solid.'

CHAPTER TWO

Two hours before translation.

Armsman Sergeant Kaster was already running, his squad at his heels, some of them with their armour still only half pulled on. The klaxons had sounded just as he'd been preparing to stow his equipment for the veil crossing. They had come off rotation, and he had been looking forward to getting a few hours head-down in the bunk, just enough to ward off the worst of the warp sickness that would otherwise see him bilious for weeks.

Then the damned alarms had gone off, screaming out through the dorm chambers, startling those who had already hung their armour in the lockers and racked their lasrifles in the armoury and were halfway towards blessed unconsciousness. He'd started shouting as soon as he'd heard the first alarm, sent jolting right back into the old habits of command, his body reacting instantly, scrabbling for boots, tunic, jacket, helm, armoury access-wafers.

And now he was sprinting, still pulling at the clasps across his chest, feeling the lasrifle clang against his breastplate in its shoulder-strap. His mind was fuzzy, and he struggled to pull the data off his helm's order-distributor. Smoke was everywhere, pouring out of vents, clogging the passages.

'Enginarium!' he shouted, passing on the little he'd managed to pick out clearly. 'Deck forty-six, sector six! Something's headed for the enginarium!'

The more he ran, the faster his mind worked. The *Blade of Naxian* had only been boarded three times during his time in service. The last incursion had been a nasty one – some kind of Traitor Guard rabble, launched from an Archenemy frigate that had proved stubbornly hard to kill. He'd never found out what they called themselves, but he still remembered what they'd done to their faces, how they'd screamed when they died, how they'd smelled. He thought of those faces sometimes, especially when they were into the warp, but never by choice.

Behind him, thirty-two troopers did their best to keep up. All over the sector, across every deck, hundreds more would be racing to station, trying to sort out where and what the garrison captains wanted them to do, looking for something to shoot at.

'Hells,' grunted Xasta, his corporal, her tunic half-unbuttoned to reveal the flak armour beneath, her big boots slamming on the deck as she ran. 'Two hours. They'll be dropping the shutters any moment.'

'Not if this is major action,' Kaster panted. 'And they've mobilised everyone. I think it's a big one.'

Being an armsman on a light cruiser was often an exercise in drudgery. You manned your station, you kept your watches, you knocked heads together whenever the ratings got stir-crazy or gained access to an alcohol stash. By edict, Navy troops were forbidden from taking part in major planetary landings, an old tradition that wasn't always well enforced, but it did mean they rarely got off the decks alongside their Astra Militarum counterparts. Their battles, when they came, were sudden and close to home – an insurrection in the bilge-quarters, an attack on a Naval anchorage, a boarding action. And then everything kicked off, in confined corridors and compartments, the las-fire flashing and the hull rattling around them.

The klaxons started to make his ears ring.

'Sector bulkheads up ahead!' Kaster shouted. 'Verdian squad with me, Bolax squad – tie those access corridors down.'

Xasta's squad peeled right, skidding down into positions along two separate incoming transitways, both scored with rail tracks and lit overhead with strip-lumens that barely pierced the smoky gloom. The armsmen hunkered behind what cover there was – two huge buffer stops, two lifter platforms for the incoming trains, a service trench running transverse under the rails. Kaster's squad carried on, running past the railhead and into a larger chamber reinforced with heavy adamantium beams. At the far end of that chamber was a high wall, studded with blast-panels and warning chevrons. Alert beacons whirled red-amber overhead. Every exposed surface seemed to be trembling.

Beyond the wall, beyond more layers of steel and rockcrete ballast, was one of many approaches to the enginarium – that sprawling mass of chamber after chamber, hall after cavernous hall, all stuffed with iron-work monsters that bled plasma and thundered promethium. The entire complex was working at full tilt, making everything shudder and shake, steam and gout.

The bulkhead was intact – a heavy slide-door cast from a single slab of adamantium, locked down by six large bolts and covered with the flickering gauze of an impact field. Kaster barely had time to slither down into a narrow alcove in the left-hand wall before more frantic reports started to fizz into his earpiece. Alerts seemed to be coming from all over the deck-sector, from twenty different pinch points at once, but that had to be mistaken – nothing moved that fast, not with the entire garrison mobilised to repel incomers.

'Ready weapons!' Kaster ordered, swinging his own lasrifle into position, angling it back the way they'd come, covering the bulkhead approach. 'Wait for my lead!'

The corridor stretched away, empty and vibrating. To Kaster's left, where the railhead broke out, he could hear the clatter of Xasta's troops drawing arms. His lungs ached, his heart was pumping. The corridor was getting smokier. The lumens flickered, the deck hummed, his earpiece buzzed with half-intelligible chatter.

He checked the vox-channel to Xasta, nestled the lasrifle's stock into his shoulder and let his finger slip over the trigger. He could hear his own breathing, hot and fast inside his closed helm.

Then the lumens blew.

They all went at once, sending glass splinters cascading in a freeze-frame second of blinding light before darkness raced up the corridor. Kaster's helm-visor adjusted a second later, and then he opened fire. Every one of his troops did the same, letting loose with unaimed las-beams, scoring the blackness ahead with hard lines of neon, lighting the darkness with over-lapping flashes.

His breathing was now frantic – something was making him want to scream, to run away, but he couldn't see anything yet, just the pure dark, the lattice of las-bolts, the boom of the engines, the churn of smog, the throaty roar of plasma hurtling down feeder lines.

Then there was another roar, an animal roar, swelling up out of the murk, louder than the engines, loosed by something sprinting up the corridor towards them, something huge, something horrifyingly fast, cloaked in trails of smoke and bleeding blackness. Kaster fired and fired, his finger sweaty on the trigger, hitting nothing, catching only a fractured outline, ragged, jagged, leaping from wall to floor, bounding up, eating the ground, before the shadow crashed headlong into all of them.

Kaster was caught on the side of his helm, a strike heavier than lead, hurling him hard into the wall. He bounced off the steel plate, black stars spinning, before hitting the deck. Blood splattered across the inside of his visor. He blinked it away, and saw one of his squad sail through the air, limbs flailing.

He tried to get up, but his arms wouldn't straighten. The chamber seemed to lurch around him, churned by some dark clot at its centre, a raging sin-gularity, making him groggy with motion-blur. He saw a fiery maw open up at the bulkhead, pouring flame and fury at the door, dousing everything in a blaze of light and noise, before the portal blew away, clanging from its shorn bolts then tumbling away into a pall of red-edged smoke. The ragged mass leapt through the gap, plunging inward, onward, burrowing down towards the engines themselves.

Xasta was shouting. Someone else was screaming. The lumens were still out. He could only vaguely see the outlines of his troops, slumped in the smog, prone.

'Enginarium breached!' he blurted out, over the open comm. 'Deck forty-six, sector six! Bulkheads open, one hostile inside chamber!'

He tried to get up again, and failed again. He started to register the pain in his arms, then saw which way his left elbow joint now turned, and that made him suddenly nauseous.

Xasta dropped down beside him. She was panting. 'What in the–'

'Enginarium breach!' he shouted, hoarse with frustration. He was terri-fied. Why was he terrified? 'Hostile inside the chamber!'

'What *was* that thing?'

'No idea. No idea.'

She seemed to be the only one still standing, though her open jerkin was dark with blood. She swallowed, hoisted her lasrifle, and made to go after the shadow.

'Don't be a fool!' he hissed. 'We need *support*.'

'The Emperor protects,' she replied, before charging off into the shadows.

They were all shouting at him.

Bridge-Captain Avilo let them rant. He stayed seated in the command throne, hands folded in front of him, watching the tactical hololiths coldly. An hour and a half to go before they hit the jump-points. It was all very poor timing.

'Two reports of enginarium breach!' shouted his comms officer secundus, a jumpy man called Fygar Hoult. 'No, three! Three reports of enginarium breach!'

It would have been good to have Soteqa up here with him, Avilo thought. She was good in a crisis. A little stressy, perhaps, prone to overthinking, but good when the augurs were playing up and everyone else was flying blind.

'Another sighting!' called out Ivi Hertha, another of Soteqa's crew, stuck down in the sensor pits with a couple of milk-eyed servitors and a few scared menials. 'Rear spine sectors, looks like heading down-level, sectors fifty-six to fifty-seven, going *very fast*.'

Avilo said nothing. The data was streaming in, flooding the cogitators, sent in by panicked squads all operating in the near dark. He could have panicked too, if he had chosen to, and roared out orders, pulling the ship out of its trajectory and aborting the warp jump. An inexperienced captain might have done that. Avilo himself might have done it, once, before he'd seen something of void-war and its many traps.

Something had got on board. Something fast, something capable of getting past the close-hull sensors, something that seemed to be chewing its way without much difficulty towards two distinct objectives – the enginarium, and the Geller field generators. That indicated that the enemy, whoever they were, wanted to keep him from making the jump. And that in turn made Avilo extremely disinclined to halt the countdown. Never give an enemy what it wants, not unless you have to.

The chrono was still running.

'Do we have visuals yet?' he asked calmly.

'Negative,' reported one of Hoult's staff, a young woman with her wrist plugged into a whole cluster of augur-feeds. 'They're killing the power supplies, knocking out the lumens, then hitting their targets. I get armsmen shouting down the comm, then nothing.'

'The further in they go,' Avilo said, 'the fewer places they'll have to hide. Any troops yet to mobilise?'

'Negative, captain,' replied Kai Zort, the garrison commander, standing just a few feet from the throne in full armour and looking like he badly wanted to get into the action himself. 'All forces now converging on reported enemy locations. We know where they came in, we know where they're going. They're cut off.'

Avilo smiled coldly. 'You don't seem to have had much luck in stopping them so far, though, do you? Throw the reserves in too, if you have any left.' He turned his attention to Hoult. 'How did they do it?'

'I don't know.'

'Speculate, please.'

Hoult scratched his chin, looking harried. 'There's still nothing on the augurs. But then we've started the shutdowns. Our voids are up, so no teleports.' He shook his head, mystified. 'Something small? Locked to the hull now, maybe, inside sensor range?'

'Why wasn't it seen?'

'It should have been.'

'I know that. I asked why it wasn't.'

'Pre-jump is... difficult. Something might, ah, have been missed.'

Avilo shot him a withering look. The *Blade of Naxian* was a ship of the Emperor's fleet. Its crew were trained in Navy scholas, then tempered by heavy-duty rotations. They made a significant warp jump every few months. If something had indeed been missed, then the punishments would be crushing.

The chrono ticked over. Every ranged augur showed the Mandeville sectors crowding in, racing towards them. There were tolerances in those calculations, grey areas. They could pull an early transition, leaving the materium before the scheduled moment. That carried risks, but if something alien was clamped to their hull, the sudden wrench would also smash it apart, stranding the boarders.

Avilo sat back, pressing his fingers together. The bridge was in turmoil, but, as ever, he remained calm. You had to remain calm.

'Maintain course,' he ordered. 'Increase speed to one hundred and ten per cent of safe maximum. Begin shutter descent and Geller activation protocols.' He stared up at the forward viewers. 'One way or another, we're breaking into the warp. If our guests decide to come with us, we will deal with them in there.'

CHAPTER THREE

Soteqa ran as fast as she could, but it was hard to pick a path with the lumens out and cables strewn everywhere. Whatever had come through this section had charged like a Taurox down the corridors, ripping up the panels and exposing the ironwork substructure underneath. She could hear muffled shouting – over the comm, up ahead, down on the decks below. Fresh smoke poured out of damaged air-filtration units, swilling over the decking before sinking down the grille-vents.

Mno-8 had left her a dozen messages, each one ruder than the last. None of what he said was helpful, just vindictive, so she concentrated on what she was getting from the deck watch-sergeants.

She'd pulled her laspistol out, but hadn't had cause to use it so far. She ran past crew members either cowering in terror or prone on the floor, their uniforms bloody, none of whom had been able to tell her what was doing the damage or where it'd gone, so she just followed the trail of destruction.

She should have waited for backup, no doubt – called one of Zort's squads to her side, worked out where she was best placed, got some direction from Avilo. Trying to get to the heart of things alone felt both stupid and necessary. Stupid, because whatever had hit them wasn't going to be troubled by a lone woman with a laspistol. Necessary, because they were on the cusp of entering the warp, and it was hard not to feel this was her fault. She should have listened to the tech-priest. He was irritating, to be sure, and full of pointless blather, but she should have listened.

It got harder to breathe, even using her helm's filters. The corridor ahead was choked thick, lit only by the sparking fronds of a few ripped power lines. She skirted the worst of the debris, chest tight, jaw locked. During her many years on the *Blade of Naxian* the ship had been boarded six times. The last one had been nasty – a proscribed cult called the Void Shards, the true nature and origin of which had been kept from the ranks. It had been bloody work to excise them, and she'd played her part. But now – *now* – Throne of Terra, she was startled by everything, her breathing was rapid and shallow, her skin was soaking. This was real fear. It was hard to say just *why* – some kind of foul magick? The enemy deployed such arts, she knew. The priests always warned of them. Or maybe just the evidence in front of her – the rank destruction, the casual demolition of structures designed to endure full-scale void-war encounters.

She kept running, swerving around a tight corner and heading down towards the outer skin of the Geller containment sector, where the air prickled with heavy static even in normal times. Avilo hadn't changed course, and the chrono was getting dangerously close to marking the point of no return. From somewhere high up, she thought she even heard the chimes marking the cycle-up of the warp drives.

Madness. What was Avilo thinking? If they couldn't get them out now, how were they going to do it when out of realspace? Was he *that* wedded to the muster timetables? For what reason?

She checked her position on her helm's flickering tactical scanner. Something was blinking further ahead, in and out, as if the trackers were struggling to hold on to it. Panting now, she went after it, clambering up a ladder to the next deck and then racing down an access tube that stank from spilled oil.

She'd hoped to have encountered some armsmen squads by now, troops she could round up and drag along with her, but the few she'd come across had been in bloody heaps, knocked out or thrown aside like chaff in an agro-thresher. Not dead, though, she thought. Blasted aside, smashed out of contact, unconscious and battered, but not, as far as she could tell, shot or sliced open. It was as if a massive clenched fist had somehow rolled down the corridors, unheeding of everything but its target, grinding its way inward without thought of anything else. Amid all the sweat and fear of her pursuit, she could reflect on the eerie strangeness of it – no gunfire, no explosions, just the smoke, the damage, the clamour of the plasma drives and the trail of violence to follow in the dark.

She was deep in the Geller sector now. The walls crackled with displaced energy, the atmosphere was taut with static. Very few of the crew ever came down here in normal times. The sector had its own breed of enginseers, its own caste of tech-priests, its own menials in bottle-green robes and brass-chased rebreathers. All knew how essential it was – attempt to make a warp jump while the generators were offline or damaged, and you might as well have orchestrated your own suicide.

Then it came in again – the sensor-signal, ahead, static now, right on the cusp of the core itself, the regions protected with layers of adamantium plating and ether-dampening coils. The access tube led her straight to it – if she kept moving on her current trajectory, she'd get a shot at it.

She scampered down the cramped space, bent double, feeling her thighs burn. The end was blocked with a rickety-looking iron grille, and she shouldered it aside before skidding into the chamber beyond, slithering down to her haunches and swinging her laspistol up.

Everything sang. The air hummed, the surfaces reverberated, sparks fizzed and spat from smashed machinery. Ahead of her was the portal leading into the core itself, still barred and locked, marked with warning runes and overwatched with a brace of wall-mounted las-barrels, all gouged out. The chamber itself was deserted, though the three other access hatches were open, gaping into darkness.

For a moment, she was mystified – the signal had led her here, straight to one of the key Geller access points, an ideal place from which to infiltrate the sanctum beyond. She cautiously stood up, tracking slowly with her las-pistol, jumping at every shift in the shadows that hung thickly against the chamber walls.

It smelled strange. Under all of the stinks of the ship, there was something else, something that fed her fear, made her want to run.

It was then that she looked up, only to see that the chamber roof was gone. Where there should have been a mass of struts and pipework, there was a gaping hole, sparking and gouting, going up and up until her helm's visor gave up trying to penetrate the murk. It was a vertical column, carved through the decks, running arrow-straight, thick with that strange scent.

Whatever it was, then, it hadn't penetrated to the objective. It had blazed a path straight towards the Geller core, blasting aside any resistance, and had then turned aside at the last moment and churned upward to...

Her stomach suddenly lurched with realisation.

'Fools,' she said to herself, speaking out loud, cursing herself for not realising it sooner. The invaders were causing extravagant amounts of disruption, setting off every tripwire and smashing everything they encountered, shouting out their presence and scaring the entire garrison witless. But the guards had been immobilised, not slaughtered. The Geller field remained intact. The plasma drives were still burning.

She turned on her heels, tracking back towards the centre of the destroyer, to where the fast transit conduits were, she hoped, still operating. As she ran, veering around more ripped-up deck-plates and spilled equipment lockers, she put an urgent vox-burst into Avilo's channel.

'Terminate translation!' she shouted. 'Repeat – terminate translation! They're not here for the ship!'

Xasta had rarely been scared on duty before. She had grown up in the ganger warrens of Phoenox IX, and knew how to handle herself. She'd been hunting, and had been hunted, long before the Navy had pressed her, given her a gun and a uniform and made her natural inclinations more defined. She'd always known she had been made for her career, and also knew that she'd one day overtake Kaster in the chain of command. Maybe his injuries had been serious. Maybe she'd have to step up early.

Still, she was scared now. It was something about the smell, she thought – hard to pin down, hard even to detect, but *there*, like a pheromone, lodging in her nostrils, making her hands shake even as she gripped the lasrifle. She found herself murmuring prayers as she ran through the darkness, ones that she barely remembered the words to. It didn't make her feel much better. She'd never been religious anyway, and this felt like a poor moment to start.

All around her, the outer enginarium regions churned and boomed. There were few true walls in this place, just giant masses of clustered pipes, roaring with coolants or hissing with confined steam. The decking was a metal mesh that exposed huge drops below, chasms that fell for level after level between the machinery piles. The air was hot, as were the surfaces around her. Most edges were tarnished with ancient smuts, all save the valves and the regulators, which gleamed as brightly as the first day they had left the production halls on whichever forge world had birthed the *Blade of Naxian*.

Signs of damage were fewer in here – whatever had gnawed through the outer layers of the ship had started going more carefully. Or maybe the structures were so solid that they had withstood the storm better – she couldn't be sure.

It was up ahead. She couldn't see it yet, not through the curtains of hot smog, nor detect its heat signature amid the furious energy wells around her, but she knew it was there, just out of eyesight, running in the dark.

She hesitated, coming to a halt, trying to keep her panting under control. She looked up, down, back the way she'd come, sweeping every inch of tangled machinery with her rifle's muzzle. There were a thousand places to hide in here. But why would it hide? Nothing about this made very much sense, other than the fear, the raw fear, bleeding from every corner and from every deck-plate.

She almost turned back, then. Not because the panic had become too much – never that – but because she thought she must have taken a wrong turn, lost it amid the labyrinths of tubes and processors. She might be able to get a shot if she headed up a level or two, tried to angle down into some of those trenches.

Then she froze. Directly in front of her, half-lost behind curls of drifting smoke, something moved. She was staring at a wall of circuitry and valve-work, layered with brass sheaths and iron piston heads, a facade on a mighty through-conduit of some kind, one that thundered with shunting fuel. Now the wall was coming down at her, unravelling, ready to disintegrate and bury her.

But it wasn't the wall – it was something within it, a portion of it, uncurling, dark grey and black, a creature that had been lodged deep within its complexity, burrowed like a void-beast and hidden perfectly within all the overlapping plates and pipes.

Xasta aimed her lasrifle and tensed her finger on the trigger, blinking hard to get a solid image. She almost fired. It wouldn't have made much difference if she had, in all likelihood, though she still pulled back at the very last moment.

After that, she just stood immobile. There wasn't much else to do. A hundred questions raced through her mind, none of them with ready answers.

The thing emerging in front of her was man-shaped, only greater, and clad in heavy armour. In its basic profile it was like the devotional images she'd been forced to pore over after being pressed, the ones with red- and blue-armoured warriors with the livery of ancient Chapters on their curved shoulder-guards. Those pictures had been presented on glistening colour plates, always in heroic poses, standing victorious against a backdrop of vast planetary battles. She could remember some of the High Gothic rubrics that had accompanied those pictures – *Ad Gloriam Imperium Terra Adeptus Astartes, Angelus Mortis, Humanitas Superbus, Bellatores Extremis.*

This thing was not like them. It was dirty, its armour stained. Once, its exterior might have been a mottled white, though it had darkened heavily with burns. In place of Imperial imagery, its thick plates were encrusted with crude scratchings, like the scrawls of a child. Once out in the open, it stood in a semi-crouch, as if poised to leap at her. It carried a double-headed axe in one enormous gauntlet. A bolt pistol was strapped to its belt in a leather holster. A strange, half-audible sound purred out from a long-sloped vox-grille, like thick-furred breathing, or maybe a scraped metallic laugh. It seemed to occupy all the space in front of her, swelling up, drinking it in, consuming every bit of it.

It could kill her without a thought, that she knew. It could destroy everything in the chamber, and all the ones beyond. It might take more than a hundred armsmen to bring it down. Coming after it had been as stupid as Kaster had told her. But, still – she found that her heart was pumping hard, as hard as it had ever done.

This was a fighter.

'Come, then!' she snarled, aiming at its throat, fighting to keep panic from making her voice rise. 'If you wish to slay me, approach. But, by the Throne Eternal, I shall do my utmost to end you.'

And then, there could be no doubt about it – the creature was laughing. Not with scorn, though – more like an amused chuckle, buried under many layers of armour and vox-filters.

'Good!' it said. 'Good. Tell me your name.'

The voice was something else. Gruffer than a mortal man's, deeper, as if hauled up from the belly of the engines around her. She could almost hear the fangs clicking together under the helm, the snicker of a red tongue flickering around the words.

'Corporal-at-Arms Xasta Delbacha, fighting complement of His voidship *Blade of Naxian*.'

'That name shall be remembered. Now move aside – we stand on the edge of the veil. I like you, but I do not wish to traverse it with you.'

She stayed where she was. 'I shall not permit you to harm my ship.'

'We're not here for your ship.'

Holding forth with this... *thing* was difficult. Part of her wanted nothing more than to sprint away from it, screaming. She had been drilled in the wiles of the Archenemy, as well as the sorcery its servants were said to employ. Now she felt it for real, making her skin crawl and her jaw ache. But this feeling wasn't like it had been with that dross they'd cleared out back at the time of the last boarding, the ones who had sliced their eyelids off and shrieked with pleasure even when they were being cut down. It felt nothing like that. Foul, perhaps. Terrifying. But not like that.

'Why are you here, then?'

It moved closer to her, towering over her, its armour running with tendrils of smoke. In the gloom, the lenses of its helm glowed murkily. She could see the damage on the plates, up closer – the hack-marks, the claw-scrapes.

'Me? Just one false trail.'

'Then you're... traitors?'

Again, the laugh, this time with a harder edge. 'Not really.' It looked away from her then, up into the mass of cabling, where the engine-lines shook and hammered. 'Just fools of fate. Like all of us, eh?'

It moved again, ready to shove its way past her, to lope off to wherever its strange mission took it. There was nothing she could do to stop it. Ludicrously, her lasrifle was still pointed straight at its chest. Not that it paid any attention to that.

'You'll have a name,' she said, a last attempt to salvage something. 'If you're not the enemy, you'll have a name. Something I'll know.'

When it looked down at her, with that huge helm with its savage slant-eyes and snarl-muzzle, she had the distinct impression that something was smiling underneath, something wild and dangerous, something cut adrift, violent, cunning, but alive like very little else she had ever encountered.

'Haflói, of the Wolves of Fenris,' it said. 'Tell your daughters you met me in this place, that you stood up, didn't run, then lend them some of that courage. I'll sleep easier, knowing your breed guards the Allfather's fleets.'

Then it was gone, brushing past her, slipping back into the smoke, going fast, going silent. She got a final whiff of that fear-fragrance, like a musk in the night, then nothing.

It took her a while to move again, after that. She stood in the hot darkness, trembling. The lasrifle remained pointed at the same spot, now empty, held rigid, two-handed.

Several seconds passed before she summoned the self-command to vox control.

'Sector command,' she said numbly. 'Hostile sighted.'

'Acknowledged, corporal. Maintain tracking – support incoming to your location.'

'No point. It's... no, *he's* gone back the way he came.'

Silence. *'Uh. Repeat that?'*

But by then she'd holstered her sidearm again. She started walking. 'He's gone back the way he came. The engines weren't the target. I think we've been played.'

Then she started to grin. A woman might live for a thousand years and not witness what she just had. She'd been right to keep going.

'Magnificent, eh?' she said. 'Recommend... just letting them go. No sense more bones being broken.'

CHAPTER FOUR

Fifteen minutes until translation.

Every protocol had been activated, the shutters had clanged down, the plasma drives were burning themselves out, the warp drives were as hot as a sun's surface. This was it.

And still they were shouting, still counselling him to pull out. Avilo wasn't sure if that was possible now, but it would have made little difference even if it were. His mind had been made up two hours ago.

He sat forward in the command throne, clenching his fists. The lurch would come soon, the wrench out of the physical, the one that made every organ in your body feel like it had been rotated about its axis and stuffed back in again.

'More sightings!' shouted Hertha, clearly struggling to keep up with the frequency of reports. 'Heading hullwards!'

'Calm yourself!' Avilo said sternly. 'Tactical overview, if you please, or kindly hold your tongue.'

Hertha glared at him, stung by that, but then turned to the lenses. 'Engine integrity at ninety-five per cent, Geller field at operational maximum. Damage containment squads spread across all affected decks.'

'So where are our guests?'

Hertha took a while to respond. 'It seems that... they're gone.'

'Gone?'

'As I said, lord. Gone.'

He almost laughed out loud. Was this some kind of sick joke, played on him by the scanner crews? But then he'd heard the shouts of panic over the comm himself, seen the jumpy vid-captures of bloodied armsmen limping away from engagements.

The chrono kept cycling down. The *Blade of Naxian*'s approach velocity was far higher than it should have been.

'So, can someone make sense of all this for me?' he demanded. 'Or are we going to break the veil in a state of madness?'

It fell to Hoult's staff officer to give him something he could use. 'Analysis of sightings indicates two lines of attack, moving swiftly towards the engines and Geller field generators,' she said, speaking quickly and firmly. 'Both attacks were successful, with all defences neutralised, including the reinforcements assigned once the trajectories were known.'

'But we are still moving,' Avilo noted. 'Field integrity is still perfect.'

She looked up at him, her expression blank. 'They have withdrawn, it seems. Back the way they came. No further damage reported.'

For a moment, he had nothing to say. It made no sense. Why board a ship, overcome its defences, and then leave it again? Unless...

'Captain!' came Soteqa's frantic voice over the comm. *'The target is not the ship! Repeat – the target is not the ship! Recommend full-stop, come about and resumption of soak-scanning till we run them down.'*

Avilo glanced at the augur metrics. That would be difficult. The warp drives were already very hot.

'Negative, commander,' he voxed back. 'Course is set, course will be maintained.'

'Respectfully, captain, urge reconsideration! Whatever vessel they used must be tiny. We will have the power to disable it in the voi–'

Avilo cut the feed. As he had often observed, Soteqa was prone to outbursts, caused by the stress she seemed to carry with her at all times. That little example would have been overheard by others on the bridge. He would have to consider what punishment was appropriate. Maybe demotion.

He settled back into his throne. He could no longer see the stars through the realviewers, only the thick lead bars of the warp shutters. The chimes for veil-entry were already clanging. The priests were already praying. The lower-deck ratings were strapped in, no doubt mumbling prayers of their own.

'Zort, as soon as we're on the other side, oversee remaining operations,' he ordered, calm as ever. 'If any intruders remain, you know what to do.'

He *would* be at the muster. His reputation depended on it. He had promised as much to Freer, who had even deigned to make personal communication on the matter. Every macrocannon counted, he had been told. This was the big one, the one they had been predicting for years. Coronis Agathon was only the start. He knew where they would end up.

The chrono ticked down towards the translation point. Just seconds now.

'By His will, we traverse the void!' Avilo called out, just as he always did – a little superstition. This had been a distraction, a dangerous episode, one thankfully over. They could deal with the aftermath later. What counted now was keeping his promises.

The deck shivered, the chimes reached their zenith. More warning lumens flashed on, and copper-sunk runes engraved in the arches overhead suddenly blazed red.

And, with that, the *Blade of Naxian* crashed out of physical existence and went spinning hard into the eternal ether.

It took Soteqa a long time to reach the relay node again. The lumens were still down, every corridor seemed to be knee-high in wreckage. A few squads of armsmen lingered here and there, bloodied and stunned, though not many – Zort had redirected almost all of them to the enginarium and Geller generators. Now that the plasma drives had been powered down the decks shook a little less, but the warp drives had a resonance all of their own, one that sent subtler harmonics eddying through the ship's structure.

No one liked being in the warp. Humanity didn't belong there, Geller field or no, and it made everything a lot more difficult. Soteqa's head was already beginning to thump, a hot wash of blood that got stuck in her eyes and wouldn't leave her, she knew, until they reached Coronis Agathon.

Still, she was in better shape than Talek. When she finally picked her way through the smashed portals, stepping over the contorted bodies of the guards, and found him half sitting up against the flanks of his own cogitators, he grinned at her from a bloodied, toothless mouth. His cowl had been thrown back, revealing his scrawny white-grey pate ringed with a scraggly tonsure. One hand was clasped over a raised knee, the other looked to have been broken. A few cables still clung to their jacks, though most had been ripped out.

'I tried to stop them,' he said ruefully. 'That may have been a mistake.'

She squatted down in front of him. 'What did they take?'

'Everything.' He coughed up some more blood. He was a very old man, and they hadn't been gentle with him. 'I mean, the records. They left the scryers in place. That is something.'

'Had the scrolls been interpreted yet?'

'Some of them. Some were proving difficult. Others were awaiting our judgement. They took them all, though, complete or not.'

'So, can they–'

'Yes, I think so. Fleet movements, dispositions, orders. They'll have it all.'

'In cipher, I take it.'

Talek remained sufficiently self-possessed to look affronted. 'Of course. Triple-lock standard Naval encryption.'

'So it'll be useless to them,' she said. 'Unless they know what they need to do to break it.'

Talek tried to raise himself higher, and Soteqa helped him, hooking her hands under his armpits. He weighed very little. 'I know who they were,' he said, wiping his split lower lip with the cuff of his sleeve. 'They'd killed the lights, but we're all blind in here anyway. I heard enough – whispers from the comm-beads inside their armour. It wasn't Gothic. It was Juvyka. Only one Chapter in the Imperium uses that cant.'

'So they weren't the enemy?'

'Come, now. If they had been the enemy, death would have been the very best outcome for us. They were just noisy, creating a mess to ease the path to their objective.'

Soteqa turned around and leaned wearily back against the wall. 'This is confusing me, master. Everything about this is confusing me. If they were Adeptus Astartes, they would already have access to this material.'

'Yes, you would think so, would you not? Very strange. But they were not in the mood to explain themselves, and time was short. They hit us at just the right moment, just when all eyes were on the translation.'

Soteqa winced. 'I tried to halt that. The captain will not be pleased.'

'Aye, he's a cold one. But you were right to do it, commander – we might have got them, had we remained in realspace long enough to run out the guns.'

'I don't think he cares. I think all he's worried about is stroking Freer's lapels for him.'

Talek laughed, sourly. 'That is the galaxy we are in now, commander. The walls are breaking. I told you that myself, not that you didn't already guess it.'

'Yet, when I asked you what was going on before, you told me nothing.'

Talek lost his gummy smile, and folded what remained of his hands in his lap. 'Maybe because I do not wish to believe it myself,' he said. 'I see a single world, over and over again, the linchpin of all our hopes. And if we are going there, in such numbers, then I cannot believe it portends anything other than destruction, and on a scale that we have never yet seen.'

Soteqa said nothing. She had to get back to the bridge, report to Avilo, but something in the way Talek spoke made her linger.

'I'll know the name of this world, won't I?' she said.

'All know it.'

'And you're sure of it?'

'I feel it in the ether. That is not quite the same thing.'

'Someone out there clearly trusted your scryings, though.' Soteqa got up, looking around her at the wreckage. A few dazed menials were beginning to creep back into the chamber, flinching nervously as if the interlopers might still be waiting behind a slide-door. It would take a long time to get the ship back into shape and ready for combat again.

'Don't mind the tech-priest, will you,' Talek told her. 'I doubt much could have stopped them, even if we'd known they were incoming.'

'Oh, I won't,' said Soteqa, making her way grimly back to the exit portals. 'He'll have more than sensor-protocols to worry about soon. If you're right, and if we're truly heading where you think we're heading, then we all will.'

II
AMETHYST SUZERAINE

CHAPTER FIVE

Torek Bjargborn walked down the ship's corridor, his leather boots soft on the steel decking. All around him, just as ever, were the noises of the vessel, the myriad sounds that permeated every part of it at every hour, never ceasing, rarely slowing – the grind of the deep drives, the hum of the lumen banks, the reverberation of the atmosphere processors. Some experienced void-mariners learned to mask those sounds out, over time. He had never done so. In his berth during the noctis-shift, he would lie on his bunk, hearing them all. There was a comfort in that. He had been in the void for so long now that he missed the noises when they weren't there. Like a child in the womb, they surrounded him, giving definition to his life, to the phases of his duty-watches, to his sense of self.

The last time he'd been away from that environment was over a year ago, during the mission to Ras Shakeh. Back then, he had held an honoured rank in the Rout – a ship's master, commander of a frigate-class warship decked out in the steel-grey livery of the Wolves of Fenris. He had commanded thousands, making use of a strenuous training that had lasted decades, an artisan of the deep dark. He had known how to coax just a little more from the plasma drives when in close combat. He had known how to resolve disputes between armed menials on rival decks, something that could easily spill over into bloodshed if not clamped down on. He had known how to speak to the lowliest cargo-handler as well as hold his own with the masters themselves, the sacred warriors from the storm-lashed Mountain, the greatest of his home world's savage creations. This was his life, his gift, his duty.

And then, on Ras Shakeh, that had all been taken away. The ship he'd commanded had been destroyed, and he had only made it to the saviour pods at the very last moment, running ahead of a wall of fire the whole way. He'd plummeted from the tubes, whistling down through an atmosphere that just got hotter and hotter until he was thrown out on the baking sands of an arid, loathsome dust bowl. He could still remember the shock of breaking out of the capsule, his tunic bloody, his eyes streaming from the white sun. He had drawn in a breath of the air, tasted the dust at the back of his scorched throat, and thought that death was no more than a heartbeat away.

He had been wrong about that. Ras Shakeh had not been the end for him, though it had been for many of his crew, either lost within the wreckage of his vessel as it came apart, or sent crashing into the wastes of that harsh world, far from help or refuge. Somehow, he had dragged himself from one day to the next, one hour to the next, resting in the heat of the day, moving in the cool of the night. He had made his way into ruined cities, before discovering what had ruined them, then retreated back to the gasping desert, grabbing scant supplies where he could, always thirsty, always hungry. Eventually he had found other Fenrisian survivors, here and there, all as wretched as him, some with their weapons, some with little more than rags on their back. Once together again, they had been able to start to think about survival. They had told themselves over and over who they were, who had taught them, what their training demanded of them.

'Ice and iron,' they would say, marching under the cold of the stars. 'The people of Russ.'

Even then, it had felt like death had only been postponed. The same forces that had killed his ship infested the planet below. They had turned the living of Ras Shakeh into a mockery of the dead, riddling them with disease, making them walk again even as their sinews rotted to strings and their muscles fell from the bone. Bjargborn had had to fight, just as everyone from the ship had done, husbanding scarce ammunition and power packs, taking care not to get bitten or spat on, staying together and watching out, every second, all the time, for the corrupted to come at them again. The only supplies were in the cities, but the only safety was in the wastes. So they had hung on grimly, treading that impossible razor edge, doing what they had to, to keep breathing from one day to the next, one hour to the next.

And they would have died, sooner or later, because the planet was almost entirely gone by then, sunk deep into contagion, more than halfway towards becoming nothing but a plaything for unspeakable powers. They had fought on because there was nothing else to do – despair had no meaning, and there was no bargaining with such degraded enemies. None of them had complained, not even Aerold, because they had been schooled from childhood to know that this was the way of a violent galaxy, that death in combat was the proper fate for the people of Russ, and that the only true victory was bravery and the only true failure cowardice.

But it had not come to that, at least not for him. The mortal crew from his old ship were not the only ones to have survived, it turned out. Seven others had done so, all of them members of that immortal breed, the sons of the primarch, clad in armour forged in the molten guts of the Mountain and bearing weapons marked with the runes of eternity. When Bjargborn had been found by the warrior called Gyrfalkon, that had marked the end of the worst terror. After that, the people of Russ had been able to fight truly again, with a victory within sight and carrying hope for more than just a noble demise. And so fight they had done, keeping every vow, staying at the side of those who had delivered them, bound after that by both the old ties of duty and a new, fiercer devotion.

Now Torek Bjargborn was back on a ship again, surrounded once more by the rhythms and the sounds of an iron-bound womb. He had been restored to his rank and function, taking command of hundreds, holding the power of life and death over the crew, bending them to his will and that of the masters he served.

Except that this was no slate-drab warship of Fenris, lean and rangy, manned exclusively by scions of the ice. It was called the *Amethyst Suzeraine*, and it was a bronze-and-crimson battle-galleon with a host of stories all of its own. Fate had been strange. After further battles, further struggles against corruption, they had all become fugitives again, both hunted and hunting, cast adrift into another wasteland, only one far vaster and colder than the plague world of Ras Shakeh. Bjargborn had never questioned the decisions his masters had made to bring them there, not even in his own heart. They had their reasons, and he trusted them. Even if he had not owed his life to the Wolves, he would still have obeyed their orders, and so they were renegades now, all of them, subject to no authority but their own, and guided by no purpose other than vengeance.

It would all come right in the end, though. The Allfather still watched over His servants. The Hand of Russ still protected his people. Only the details of that providence were unclear.

Bjargborn reached his destination – a heavy steel door lined with bronze. It had been kept polished to a high sheen by the ship's old crew, who despite being a gaggle of rogues and outlaws still took a certain pride in their customs. He admired that, and saw no reason to prevent them keeping up appearances. He had even begun to find some aspects of the galleon's interior appealing, in a gaudy, knockabout kind of way.

He pressed the access lever, and the locks clicked open. On the far side, through a safety airlock, one of the big internal hangars yawned away. Most of the other hangars held a ramshackle collection of sub-warp vessels in them, many in no fit shape to take to the void. This one had only two occupants. The first was a Thunderhawk gunship, blackened from repeated scorchings, looking serviceable but carrying some fearsome scars along its flanks. It bore the name *Vuokho* in silver runes scratched under the cockpit. The second was a system runner, a sleek-lined hunter-killer, more than six times as big as the gunship and with limited warp capability in its own right. It bore the name *Hlaupnir*.

The system runner stood silently, its engines cold, its armaglass portals under wraps and its intakes masked. *Vuokho*, by contrast, still steamed from its recent return from action. Its panels had been sprung open, its tanks exposed and plugged with tubes. Like some huge medicae experiment, it was splayed open for examination, prepped for full refuel, re-equip, refit and turnabout. Servitors limped under its hull, hangar menials pulled at panel-locks and plugged in remote augurs. This was a practised process, something that they had all done a hundred times before, but still they were overlooked the whole time by an exacting judge.

Bjargborn came to stand alongside that judge, the one his battle-brothers called the Old Dog – not a name he would ever have employed himself. The warrior's birth name was Jorundur Erak, which he wore alongside the further title Kaerlborn. Almost all aspirants to the Space Wolves came from the open ice, from the tribes that battled for survival under hostile skies, though a few, now and again, through tortuous circumstances, might be born of the Mountain's own mortal population.

Perhaps that explained his temper, which was darker than that of his brothers. Perhaps that explained his hollow-eyed face, sallower than the norm, the deep black circles under his eyes. Perhaps that explained his facility for the mechanical tools of his trade, particularly the sacred Chapter vehicles, which he nurtured with a care that bordered on the obsessional. Or perhaps all that was just the way the Allfather had made him, and his origins meant nothing much at all.

Now Jorundur was observing keenly, his armoured hands clasped atop the haft of a long-handled axe, his long grey hair hanging lankly over a time-worn breastplate. His hooked nose protruded, his angular, beardless chin jutted. His golden irises glinted, missing nothing.

'A successful hunt,' Bjargborn offered, folding his arms and studying the Thunderhawk's battered chassis.

Jorundur grunted. 'I feel like I've been keeping this damn thing flying since we left Fenris. At least it didn't take much punishment this time – we were in and out of there before they knew much about it.'

'That must be satisfying.'

'It worries me, shipmaster, that's what it does.' He turned his piercing eyes to Bjargborn. 'I'm a damned fine pilot. I have no illusions about that. But there are other fine pilots in existence, and if we can do that to a Navy ship, be sure that the enemy can too. It worries me. The Imperium has become as slack as an old *gothi*'s bag of bones.'

Bjargborn thought that was probably unfair. Jorundur was more than a fine pilot – the Grey Hunter was the best he had ever served alongside. In addition, previous raids had given the pack details of the *Blade of Naxian*'s precise scanner-harmonics, something that had been very hard won and gave them a huge advantage. In any case, the manoeuvre he had pulled – tracing the exact path of anticipated augur-resonances, then darting in at the hull just before the pre-jump cascades shut down the close-range sensors – was more than fine flying. It had been next to impossible. Perhaps the Imperial crew should have done better than they had done, but Bjargborn, knowing what he did of the warriors he served, was inclined to cut them a little slack.

'They must have had other things on their minds,' he said.

Jorundur looked away, nodding ruefully, remaining silent. It was hard to argue with that. In the months since the pack's flight from the Chapter's writ, things had become markedly worse. No volume of space was free of strife now, both from the increasingly significant incursions by warbands of the Archenemy and from those old scourges of the Imperium, xenos corsairs and human outlaws. No one could be in any doubt that this was not just an incremental deterioration – it was a build-up to something decisive. These were the ragged stormbirds flying ahead of the lightning, in greater flocks than anyone had ever seen before.

'I came to ask if you required anything of me, lord,' Bjargborn said, changing the subject.

Jorundur smiled sourly. 'More servitors? I'd take those, if you had them.' Then he shook his head, and resumed his vigil over the Thunderhawk's refuelling. 'No, but with my thanks, shipmaster. I have no idea at all where we are headed next, nor what our esteemed battle leader has planned for us, so I can't think yet what I may require of you. When that changes, I'll let you know.'

Bjargborn bowed. 'The Hand of Russ, then,' he said. 'I remain at your service.'

He withdrew, going back the way he'd come. As he walked into the network of corridors again, he let slip a half-smile. This ship was a strange one, full of archaic devices and chambers he'd barely explored, even after over a year as its master. The pack was a strange one too, a jumble of misaligned warriors thrown together in defiance of Chapter custom, a mongrel bunch that had somehow managed to forge themselves into something that hunted with a lethal efficiency.

But hunted what? That was the real question, the one that, despite all the raids and all the void-strikes, he had no perfect answer to. The masters did not tell him all their secrets, nor did he often know the destination for the *Amethyst Suzeraine* before he was ordered to kindle the warp drives and lay in an immediate course.

And that was perfectly fine. Torek Bjargborn had been a dead man, to all intents and purposes, stranded on a world of eye-burning heat and endless plague, before fate had intervened. Everything after that, as far as he was concerned, was a gift from the outstretched hand of the primarch himself.

The tangle of the wyrd would unwind in good time. It always did.

Higher up, nearer the summit of the command bridge, another chamber had been locked fast. The single doorway was barred with heavy beams, and those were overlaid with motion-detector fields linked to auto-las-fire emplacements.

Inside, the place was as contradictory as any within that piebald ship. It had once been some kind of cartolith chamber, perhaps, or maybe an archive. The interior space was large, more than thirty yards long and twelve across, with white marble floors and walls lined with yard after yard of shelving. Bronze-bolted suspensors threw a warm light across dusty writing-slopes. Candles flickered atop skull-candelabras, their bone fixings streaked with lines of encrusted wax.

Amid all that dusty finery, the harder edge of Fenris could now also be found. Tattered war-standards hung at the far end of the long chamber, their leathery surfaces punched through with bullet holes and edged with scorches. A brace of ceremonial weapons hung from thick chains – axes, short blades, spears with knapped flint heads. Iron braziers had been set up close to the atmosphere filters, and now smouldered gently from a pile of whitened embers.

Ingvar Orm Eversson, the one they called Gyrfalkon, leaned his weight on the edge of one of several huge map-tables, and narrowed his grey eyes. Even out of armour, the pressure of his touch made the tabletops creak. Piles of vellum lay before him, ruffled through and sifted, some still bearing the security seals of the Adeptus Astra Telepathica. The script on them all was, without exception, spidery and dense, running to line after line of hand-written observations and interpretations.

Ingvar had enviable powers of concentration and retention, but even for him, studying such material for hours became wearisome. The screeds of star-speakers were not meant to be read by those outside their secretive order. An astropathic engagement was not like a comm-burst – a purely mechanical transmission of sounds and images. It was more like a process of divination, a skilled interpretation of dreams. Only a soul-bound psyker could undertake such work in relative safety, for it plumbed the depths of the warp itself, a place where sentient nightmares waited for the unwary mind. Whenever those savants withdrew from their meditations, their souls bruised and their empty eye-sockets throbbing, they dictated their find-ings, which were then vetted, interpreted, subjected to esoteric cleansing rites, and cross-referenced with other testimonies from the same warp-duct. What emerged, eventually, was counsel fit for the ears of void-ship captains and army generals, written in language even a mortal could understand.

The material Ingvar read was not like that. The sheets had been plun-dered from the records chambers of an astropathic relay node, plucked in some cases from under the noses of the working scribes. It was raw, unfil-tered, like half-set rockcrete. Much truth was in the parchment sheaves, maybe more than would ever end up in the final products, but it was hard to get at, and the more you studied the tiny curls of black ink, the more it felt like you were staring into some after-echo of the ether itself, tugging at your sanity and making your mind sicken.

He sighed, and started to read again, only to be interrupted by the clunk of the locks deactivating outside. He turned as the door opened, and saw his pack leader stooping to enter.

Gunnlaugur, the one called Skullhewer, had trouble with many of the portals on the voidship. The vessel had been built and crewed for mortal dimensions, and in comparison to a Navy ship had few concessions to the Imperium's larger breeds of defenders. Gunnlaugur was also out of armour, but still had to narrow his shoulders to squeeze through the door's rim. Only Olgeir Heavy-Hand was greater in stature, and the entire ship had long since got used to hearing him swearing violently as he cracked into yet another bulkhead. Gunnlaugur was not so effusive – he only let rip when in combat, and until then his voice was a deep growl, held in check like a dam holding back a torrent. His thick grey beard, knotted and plaited, tumbled down a barrel chest, and his scarred face and bald pate glinted under the lumens.

'How goes it, brother?' Gunnlaugur asked.

Ingvar pushed the parchment away and straightened. He rolled his shoul-ders, flexing muscles designed to be in constant motion, not stuffed away in records chambers. 'There's something here. I get glimpses, things I don't fully understand. But there's something here.'

Gunnlaugur came over to look at the collected records. Stashes from earlier raids – Imperial outposts, Militarum convoys, even a few enemy warbands – were stacked up in messy heaps on other tables. It made the chamber smell musty, like confinement. He flexed his right hand, testing a wound he'd picked up on the *Blade of Naxian*. Not from a defender, mind – he'd punched through a security hatch made of thicker steel than he'd expected.

'Jorundur was furious,' Gunnlaugur said.

'You amaze me. Why, this time?'

'That it was all so easy. The sector is falling apart, and we can peel open a voidship like that. He thinks the enemy will do the same.'

Ingvar shrugged. 'We had their schematics. They were distracted. Jorundur flies like a daemon. When it comes to real void-combat, they'll handle it.'

'They'd better.' Gunnlaugur looked up at the arched roof, then down the long rows of bundled vellum. 'You know, when we took this ship, I disliked it. I'm quite fond of it now. When this is all over, I think we should keep it.'

Ingvar chuckled. 'And the crew?'

'They'd get used to us. A lot of them already have.'

That was true. The *Amethyst Suzeraine* had belonged to a man named Rasmu Collaqua, a corsair of considerable skill and extravagant cruelty who had been the terror of a whole belt of worlds running across half the subsector. In normal times, his activities would have been tightly curtailed by Naval patrols, but they had been overstretched even before the recent incursions, and so his plunder had gone largely unopposed. He'd become very rich, then powerful, then daring. It had been his misfortune, and the subsector's fortune, to detect a lone system runner deep in the void, dependant on short-range warp hops and crammed with a clearly desperate crew. As Gunnlaugur had remarked to Collaqua before he was executed under ancient laws against void-piracy, no one had forced him to attack a Space Wolves ship. If his knowledge of Chapter livery hadn't been quite so poor, he might still be alive now, spreading his particular brand of misery a little further afield, and the *Hlaupnir* might still be hunting for another suitable vessel to take over.

Since the galleon had been taken, most of the old crew had come to terms with the change of ownership. They were driven harder than before, that was true, and the senior positions were all taken by Bjargborn's kaerls, but the rations arrived on time now, and Collaqua's old coterie of untouchable thugs had been culled. In the months since capture, the *Amethyst Suzeraine* had become a little bit more like a regular ship of the Adeptus Astartes – a rough place, still riddled with its own share of scarcity and violence, but effective, well maintained, alert. It had decent gunnery crews, and an enginarium that functioned well enough. It wouldn't last too long against a proper battleship, but it had kept them all alive for a while now. Gunnlaugur wasn't alone – most of them, even Jorundur, had started to like it.

Ingvar pushed his vellum pile to one side. 'Then you don't regret it yet?' he asked.

Gunnlaugur grunted. 'I regret plenty. But breaking him out of that cell? Ach, no. They'd have killed him, whatever was found. If running was the price of keeping the pack together, it was worth paying.'

'It wasn't just for Baldr.'

That was also true. There were two reasons that the pack, still calling itself Járnhamar despite everything that had taken place, had fled from the jurisdiction of the Chapter. The first was the presence within their number of a warrior named Baldr Fjolnir, a Grey Hunter who had begun to exhibit signs of psychic power on the world of Ras Shakeh. As a result of an attack by an enemy sorcerer, he had been briefly transformed into a vessel of malign energies, something that had nearly consumed him entirely. On his recovery, Njal Stormcaller, the greatest of the Chapter's Rune Priests, had shackled him with a null-collar to dampen his powers, intending to take him back to Fenris for full examination. Believing that this would result in his inevitable death, Gunnlaugur and Ingvar had sprung Baldr from his cell aboard the Stormcaller's ship and broken clear on the *Hlaupnir*, running into the deep void even as it was tracked by the *Heimdall*'s great guns.

If that had been the prime catalyst for the exodus, though, then there was also another one. Ras Shakeh had not only harboured fallen warriors of the ancient enemy. It had been a shrine world, one steeped in the institutions of the Holy Ecclesiarchy. Járnhamar had fought alongside members of the Sisters of Battle, all of whom had resisted the destruction of their sacred places with characteristic fury. And yet, that resistance had not all been about defiance. It had been about deception, too – the harbouring of secrets that should never have been left to moulder in the sands. Whether by fate or by chance, it was Ingvar who had stumbled across it – a list of names, all warriors of the Space Wolves, marked for destruction. Among those names was Hjortur Bloodfang, a Wolf Guard who had once fought with the pack, and who had been high in the favour of both Berek Thunderfist and the current lord of the Great Company, Ragnar Blackmane himself.

Much remained unknown. The Sister who had confided in Ingvar was now dead. All tangible records had been destroyed in the fighting. The scope of the list was unknown, and no physical copy of it survived. Had Járnhamar been annihilated on Ras Shakeh, as had looked likely more than once, then the document's existence would never have come to light at all.

But the pack had not been annihilated. It lived still, it hunted still, and now it thirsted for vengeance. Knowing the danger of discovery, more forces from the Ecclesiarchy had landed on Ras Shakeh, determined to recover any scraps that might lead to incrimination. In the fighting that had followed, Ingvar had captured a man named Klaive, a confessor to cardinals and a servant of senior forces within the Church. Since then, this Klaive had been their prisoner, the only link they had with the shadowy organisation that had responsibility for the death of Hjortur, and their one hope of running it down.

Klaive, though, had not known very much. The minds behind the list, whoever they were, had been careful, keeping information carefully sequestered at the highest levels. Even those who worked on their behalf had known almost nothing about those they sent their reports to, only that they were perfectly capable of delivering summary punishment if things went wrong.

And so the hunt had become one that had stretched out across time and space on a stolen corsair's galleon, a series of raids and infiltrations, slowly gathering hints and whispers, ones that only Klaive could confirm or deny were relevant, until a picture began to emerge in slowly solidifying detail, one that would lead to the architects, if only they could be reached before another tide of destruction carried all before it.

If that hunt might be thought indulgent, when whole sectors around the *Amethyst Suzeraine* were dissolving into ruin, then that meant little to the pack, who remained warriors of their unforgiving home world, where an oath was binding for life and the quest for vengeance against a wrong committed could last for all eternity. The stars themselves might burn out, the last fortresses might fall into ruins, and still that fire would burn, driving them, goading them, until either absolution was achieved or they died in the attempt to find it.

'Tell me, then,' Gunnlaugur said. 'What have you got?'

Ingvar drew in a long breath: part weariness, part in acknowledgement that this might be, just as it had been so often before, something or nothing, or just another link in an endless chain. 'A scrap to take to the rat,' he said. 'I was going to speak to him when I'm done here. You wish to come too?'

Gunnlaugur smiled grimly, a gesture that managed to convey far more danger than amusement.

'Show me what you've uncovered,' he said. 'We'll go together.'

CHAPTER SIX

Olgeir, the one they called Heavy-Hand, trudged back towards the rearward chambers. Those had been taken by the Space Wolves for their own soon after seizing the ship, and much of Collaqua's old finery had been stripped from the walls, thrown into the furnaces where it belonged. Now the surfaces were plain again, though some marks from Fenris had appeared here and there – carvings and rune-etchings, made by the kaerls going about their duties. Give them long enough, Olgeir thought, and they'll turn this creaking hulk into a proper ship of war.

He still wore his battleplate. During the raid on the Imperial cruiser, he'd stayed with Jorundur to guard the point where the Thunderhawk *Vuokho* had clamped itself to the hull. It had been his expertise with meltas that had got them inside, once the gunship had slipped beneath the void shields. After that, he'd maintained position inside the cat's cradle of beams and molten struts he'd created, just in case the insertion position was pinpointed and swarms of armsmen had dared to try to take it back.

It hadn't happened. Just as intended, the rapid incursions, all sent off in different directions, had kept the ship's guardians pinned on the back foot. Gunnlaugur had carved a path towards the Geller field generators, Baldr and Haflói towards the main engines, leaving Ingvar to slip more quietly towards the real prize of the astropathic relay node. The only mortals who had come anywhere near Olgeir were half-stunned bilge-filth, limping out of the fire-edged shadows to see what had rocked the foundations of their hidden kingdom. Once they'd seen him standing sentinel, motionless in the dark with his heavy bolter primed, they'd scuttled off soon enough.

The whole thing had taken almost no time at all. It had been a precision strike, thanks to Jorundur's skills and the pack's customary speed and power. And yet, Olgeir had had just enough time, alone amid the distant crashes and cries of alarm, to reflect on how many times they'd done this, on how many fortresses and starships. Sometimes the battles had been even more straightforward than that one. Sometimes the firefights had been vicious. One assault on an innocuous-looking frigate had uncovered a warband of Heretic Astartes from the Emperor's Children Legion, and getting out of the place alive had taken every scrap of ability and luck they possessed.

This was all Imperial space, nominally controlled and protected by the Allfather's limitless forces, and yet it felt like a trap lurked under every stone.

It was a tightening, a narrowing, the unmistakeable shrinkage down to a singularity – a great contest for control.

And yet here they were – not on Fenris, being told where they would be sent by the lords of the Fang, but scratching around in a stolen vessel that still stunk of its past crimes, sniffing at dregs ripped from the archives of other vagabonds and oligarchs. Olgeir had no idea how things stood with Fenris. None of the pack did. Perhaps the High King had dispatched his Great Companies already, guided by the visions of the Rune Priests, for some great feat of arms yet to come. Perhaps the death world was even under assault itself.

But a vow was a vow. Olgeir had sworn it, just as all the others had. You never let a pack-brother's fate lie in the hands of others. And if there was, as the Gyrfalkon told them, cause for blood-debt, then that had to be seen through. He knew that. He agreed with it.

Still, it remained the case that Baldr was far from cured. None of them knew what might aid him. Since leaving the Stormcaller's ships behind them, all they had encountered was war, and ruined worlds, and an Imperium in increasing states of panic and collapse. If it had not been a warrior of the Rout who had sickened, then he would never have been taken back – he would have been left, like so many thousands of loyal Imperial fighters, to die alone, lest contagion infect those whose bodies were still pure.

And even then, after it had first happened, Olgeir had argued against it. Alone of his brothers, he had wanted the taint kept away, lest *maleficarum* find its way into the closed circle of brotherhood. He hadn't done it lightly. Watching what had happened to Baldr on Ras Shakeh had been horrifying, a vision of corruption that still haunted his dreams. The Grey Hunter had been utterly changed, almost unrecognisable, riddled and sore-encrusted, overflowing with a crazed mix of storm-magick and deeper malignancy. He had killed unthinkingly, destroying everything that crossed his path, vomiting out raw ether and gazing blindly from eyes that saw nothing real. Amid the confusion and clamour of the final assault, he had struck out at enemy and pack-mate alike, throwing Olgeir aside with a blast of black-edged lightning that had left weals that still failed to heal, before loping off into the screaming night, more warp beast than mortal.

It had been Ingvar who had brought Baldr back from the edge of madness. It had been Ingvar who had argued most forcefully for his return, making the case to Skullhewer, convincing the others, until only Olgeir remained in doubt, just as he still was. Thus was the Law of the Chapter broken, exiling them all, risking damnation. All they could do now was see the matter out, hoping Gunnlaugur's judgement would be proved right.

The thought of all that made him morose, which was not in his nature. He pushed it out of his mind. Better to concentrate on what they had retained, which was considerable. The tension between Ingvar and Gunnlaugur, once rivals in spirit as well as arms, had abated. Unity had returned, tempered by combat, something that mattered to this pack of misaligned individuals, drawn from all across the Chapter in defiance of convention – just one more sign of how desperate things had become. This was the path they had chosen, and only one course of action remained – to see it to its end.

Olgeir reached the chamber they had turned into a makeshift armoury. In place of the racks of lasweaponry used by Collaqua's corsairs, there were now vaults for reverently maintained bolters, powerblades, combat knives. The pack had only been able to take what it could grab at short notice, so more equipment had been wrenched out from other places during other raids. Some of the survivors from the *Undrider* had been from the ship's forge, and so the gaps in their capability had gradually been repaired, what had been damaged was patched up, what remained was maintained. Even so, they had to be careful. Their stocks of ammunition, grenades and power packs had to be eked out, used wisely.

He twisted his helm, breaking the atmosphere seals and letting the *Amethyst Suzeraine*'s air in. He lifted the armour-piece in both hands, turning its face towards him, and took a look at it. It was an old unit, scoured and marked from many mortal lifetimes of constant combat. In places, the slate-grey warpaint had been scraped off, revealing steely ceramite underneath. The runes he had first engraved on it were faded now, illegible in many places. He reached out with a finger, tracing the line of the lenses, remembering how he had felt when first given it by the Iron Priest, how untouched it had been then, glinting in the light of braziers, a harbinger of the destruction he would later wreak.

'Taken damage?' came a familiar voice from behind him.

Olgeir put the helm down, ran his fingers through his lacquered hair and beard, spilling the streaked grey mass of plaits out across his gorget-collar. 'Not a scratch,' he grunted. 'You?'

Haflói, who had yet to be given a pack-name that had stuck, stomped across the armoury deck, his own bleached-white helm carried under his arm, the rest of his battleplate smeared with lines of engine oil. The Blood Claw looked a little less raw than when he'd first made his introduction to the pack on Fenris. It might have been Olgeir's imagination, but the messy thatch of red hair looked to have faded a little, his fangs to have lengthened.

Yes, probably his imagination. He hadn't been fighting with them for that long.

'Same. They were damned slow.' Haflói threw his helm down on a long bench and began to prepare for the removal of the rest of his armour. 'One of them caught up with me, though. An armsman.' He chuckled. 'She just aimed her lasgun at me, daring me to run at her. I could have knocked her into the fuel intakes, and she just stood there. Morkai, but she had mjod in her veins. I'll put her name in the annals, just like I said I would. Just stood there.'

The Blood Claw seemed to be in a good mood. He usually was – sometimes Olgeir had to remind himself how raw Haflói was, how fresh from aspirant training. All he wanted to do was fight, burn off the aggression he'd been pumped full of, learn how to do it more completely and expertly. Olgeir had seen the way Haflói studied the rest of them when they were in combat, and knew that after every raid he'd gone down to the training pens to hammer home the lessons. It was working, too – he'd always been dangerous, but the gap between what he could do and what the rest of them could was closing now.

'You don't ever get weary of this?' Olgeir asked idly, exposing the nodules on his armour where the drills would go in.

'The raids? I'd like some better prey. Something I can actually kill. But it's better than combat-servitors.'

'I just wonder, sometimes. You didn't ask for any of it.'

'*Hja*, what are you, my nursemaid now?'

'A long time away from the Chapter, that's all.'

'Good.' Hafloí grinned. 'I like it. It's proper hunting. I still remember what it was like, on the ice. You're too old for that, but I still do.' He pulled a chain of pelts from his shoulders, ones that had suffered badly and looked more like scuffed leather than fur. 'You could go anywhere, you remember that? You just looked up at the white cloud, and the white snow, and the wind was clawing at your skin, and you could take on any horizon. All you wanted was a scent, and then you'd be running.'

'Aye, I remember. And the hunger that gnawed at your guts, too.'

'Kept you sharp, though.'

'It did, that.'

Hafloí shrugged. 'It's just the same now. I don't care why. I just like an open sky.'

'Fair enough.'

A team of kaerls arrived then, trailed by a gang of armour-servitors. They carried heavy equipment with them – drills, ratchets, vials of sacred oils and lubricants. Removing battleplate properly could take a while, and was accompanied by quasi-mystical rites that derived from both Fenris and Mars. Olgeir stretched his arms out, activated the joint-unlocks, and made to move into the inner chamber, where the plates would be hoisted off, one by one, then taken to the forge decks for checks and reconditioning.

'Don't get sloppy, though,' he said, walking off under the archway. 'You're still raw as all Hel.' He left to the sound of more laughter – the kind of lung-deep chortling that said, *for now, greybeard.*

Three servitors, four kaerl menials and a lexmechanic were waiting for him inside, all looking up, tools out, expectant. This would be the highlight of their duty-shift, the chance to perform to the best of their ability. For him, it marked the end of another brief burst of activity, another flex of a body designed to do nothing but kill.

'Begin,' he told them, and let his mind zone out.

Baldr Fjolnir had removed his own armour as soon as he'd disembarked from *Vuokho*, and now wore robes of hard-spun grey with a heavy cloak thrown over his shoulders. He left the unrestricted decks, the ones where kaerls and the corsair crew mingled, travelling up guarded elevator shafts before emerging into another world of subdued lighting and unfamiliar fragrances. Unlike the rest of the ship, these chambers were decorated with both taste and extravagance, and bore neither the mark of a pirate captain nor a war-pack of the Adeptus Astartes. The metal decks were covered over with plush rugs, the pressed-panel walls hung with fine tapestries. Brass bowls smouldered with josticks, making the air in the walkways hazy. You could still hear the distant grind of the engines, feel the tremble under-foot, but in most other respects it felt like leaving a voidship altogether, and somehow stumbling into a Terran noble's private apartments.

And that, in a sense, was exactly what he had done, for these chambers were within the purview of Mamzel Judit van Kliis, the *Amethyst Suzeraine*'s resident Navigator. She had served Collaqua, and after his execution had continued to guide the ship just as before. It turned out that her relation-ship with her previous employer had been less than cordial, based on an unspecified blackmail threat concerning some obscure crime committed either by her or by a related branch of her minor house. She had shed no tears from her human eyes when Collaqua's death was reported to her, instead professing a perfect willingness to serve her new masters, which suited all concerned. It may have been true, of course, that no other ship would have taken her, but since the *Hlaupnir* had not carried a Navigator of its own, being too small for anything but the shortest and slowest warp jumps, Gunnlaugur had not attempted to be choosy. Since then, she had performed well. Navigators on Imperial Navy vessels were driven horrifically hard by the demands of their crews, burning out fast and often. Navigators for corsair princes, it turned out, had it slightly easier. Mamzel van Kliis cer-tainly seemed in fine health and spirits.

No other inhabitant of the galleon had anything approaching a sensi-tivity to the warp. There were no astropaths on board, nor any psykers in the mortal crew. Only she, in her recondite and irritable way, had any-thing explicit to do with the realm of dreams. And so it had turned out that she and Baldr, for this reason and others, had spoken together often. For his part, he felt the need of it – the desire to find another soul whose only instinct was not to recoil instantly when any mention was made of malefi-carum, psykerdom or witchery. What she got out of the exchanges was more of a mystery. It was probable, he thought, that she was merely lonely, stuck up in her isolated citadel at the summit of the galleon's hunched spine, her only other company being a cadre of mournful-looking menials and the baleful gaze of the living ether itself.

So when Baldr appeared, opening a dark wooden door set in an iron frame and stooping to enter, she looked up from her writing desk, put down her quill, placed her hands in her lap, and smiled.

'Ah,' she said. 'Back again, then?'

Baldr moved over to a long couch set beside her desk. Even in armour, he travelled more quietly than his brothers; out of it, he was like a grey ghost. He was leaner than they were. He was even leaner than he used to be, too. The null-collar sat around his neck now, the second one the Stormcaller had given him – a bone torc at his throat, capped with iron dragon's jaws. It looked a fragile thing, something a Space Marine could shatter with a twist of two fingers, and yet it held the power of life and death over him as surely as the gravity of a sun holds its planet. To remove it was to end him. To retain it was to cripple him.

He sat heavily. 'We ran it close,' he said. 'But you brought us in near enough, just before they made translation. Gunnlaugur sends his thanks.'

Van Kliis laughed. She stood up, and came to sit next to him. The mismatch in size was comical. Even beside an unaugmented human she would have been tiny, stick-thin, her withered old skin pulled tight and heavily rouged. She wore plentiful jewellery, some of it attached hard to the bone, and wore a silk gown with a crimson dragon pattern. She limped when she walked, and smelled strongly of both common incense and exotic alcohol. Her forehead was safely bound up with a lace-edged bandana of gold damask.

'The angry one barely knows I'm up here,' she said, patting him on the knee affectionately. 'Only you come. Is good. I'd miss it, if you didn't. How is it, now?'

Baldr placed his hands together. The flesh was calloused, greyer than it should have been. 'The weight of it grows. With every journey we make, I feel the pressure gathering.' He drew in a breath. 'Like a storm front, behind my eyes.'

Van Kliis tutted. 'Your rune-wizard built a dam. But you are a river. Which will prove stronger? That is question, eh? You never try to take it off?'

Baldr smiled wryly. 'More than once. The last time, I woke up a day later, the floor of my chamber covered in blood. I didn't think I had that much inside me.' He shrugged. 'He put it on me. For all I know, only he can take it off.'

'Your brothers, they never thought of that.'

'No, they did. They judged the risks – certain death, or an uncertain future. I owe them for the chance. Now I have to find a way to make it worth something.'

'Not easy.'

'No, not even if I knew what I was looking for.'

Van Kliis sniffed. 'You make it harder, you know that? Ever since you come on this ship, I see it. You go on, and on, you talk of your ways, your ways. You pretend you are different, and so need something different to cure your sickness. You are no different. Not to me.' She leaned towards him. '*Mutants*. What we both are. I am sanctioned. Are you? I don't know. You don't know. But admit the first step. Then, the rest will follow.'

Baldr looked down at his hands. 'The enemy told me the same thing. Everyone says the same thing.' He smiled again, the same dry smile. 'All others tell the truth, so they wish us to believe. Only the Sons of Russ tell themselves lies.'

'Ach, now you are pitying yourself.'

'No, just stating the fact. It looks simple, from the outside. But from the inside...' He struggled for the words. 'What Njal does, I could *feel* it. The character of it. It was different, both to what the enemy does, and to what I can do.'

'When your collar is broken.'

'Aye.'

'Then you're something new.'

'I've been told that too. Who knows?'

'It is your problem.'

'That it is.' He clenched one hand into a fist. 'But I will not let it weaken the pack. I must fight now, with them, on this hunt, whether or not the secret can be uncovered.'

'Or until it kills you.' She studied him carefully. 'And it is killing you now, I see that clearly. If I opened my Seeing Eye now, I would perceive it all the more. The Seethe is at the edges of your soul. It is straining to get out, but it cannot. You are locked into your disease.'

He slumped into thought. 'If I had a weapon, any other weapon, I would know how to use it. An axe, a blade, a bolter. I never doubt with them, not for a moment. But this – even if I could unlock it, should I?'

'You talk to your brothers about this?'

Baldr chuckled. 'Aye, we talk. They all saw me transformed. They know the dangers.'

'What do they say?'

'Just what you say. Just what I say. We are all in the dark.'

Van Kliis carried on looking at him. Her gaze was uncannily unwavering, like a small child's. Perhaps they were all like that, the star-scryers, made that way by their occupation.

'All right, then. If you have no useful counsel from them, take some from me. You will *know*. You will know when the moment comes, because there are no accidents with the Seethe. It found you, according to some design. Whose design? The enemy's, maybe. Or maybe not, because they do not control everything. But here is the thing – you will not find this thing by looking for it. You will catch the truth, out of the corner of your eye. That is what we do. We see what is on the edge, and are content that we cannot bring everything into focus. Be like us. Do not be such a hunter.'

Baldr listened carefully. He had learned to do that, with her. 'Everything I have ever been,' he said. 'Everything I ever wanted to be. It is to keep the prey in my sight. To run it down. To kill it, for myself, for the safety of my people.'

Van Kliis laughed, and patted him on the knee again. 'I know! Maybe you're capable of changing. Maybe not. But I tell you the truth of the Seethe. Take it, leave it, the choice is yours.'

Then she lost her smile.

'But it will kill you soon,' she said sternly. 'Very soon. So make your choice, whatever it is, and hold fast to it.'

CHAPTER SEVEN

Another chamber, further down now, buried between giant enginarium housings. It was always hot in that place – enough to make its occupant sweat, though not enough, probably, to cause serious damage. The walls were unadorned iron, the floor cracked tiles. A single lumen hung in the centre of the ceiling. It was noisy there – a grind of machine against machine that never stopped, and got worse whenever the *Amethyst Suzeraine* was in the void.

A single figure occupied the chamber, and had done for several months. Before that, he had been a prisoner in the brig of the *Hlaupnir*, an even more cramped existence. Before that, he had been confessor to Cardinal Delvaux, a powerful figure of intrigue in that man's court. He had eaten well, drunk well, slept in rooms inlaid with gold on plush mattresses. So, things had changed.

In his earlier life, he had been feared. Delvaux had been a ruthless commander of considerable military power, a man who had given little thought to the destruction of entire worlds if it would further his prospects within the diocesan hierarchy. Ausrach Klaive had been at his side the whole time, offering counsel, gently suggesting policy, volunteering to oversee interrogations in the lightless depths of the cardinal's many strongholds.

That was then. Now, he was skinnier. His exquisite robes had been taken from him, and he wore the same dirty shift as all the other bilge-level inhabitants. His skin, which had always been pale, was now as white as bone, tinged grey at the edges, under his eyes, around his thin mouth. His bare ankles had heavy manacles clamped on to them, connected to a length of chain that was fastened to a ring on the wall. He had a table, a single chair, a hard cot, a tray for food and drink. When he sickened, he was treated. From time to time, he was even taken out, walked around the lower decks on a tight leash, just to keep his muscles from wasting away. Other than that, this was now his entire world, three yards by three yards, far out into the void, surrounded on all sides by those who wished to see him dead.

It could have been worse. He could have been captured by a savage Chapter.

Ingvar and Gunnlaugur entered the chamber one after the other, squeezing their way in before unfurling those long, powerful limbs. Klaive shrunk back.

'Greetings, rat,' said Gunnlaugur cheerfully.

Klaive scowled, and said nothing.

Ingvar went over to the cot and sat on it, making the steel frame flex. Gunnlaugur reached out for the chain and gave it a yank. 'You haven't been interfering with this tether, have you?'

Klaive snorted. 'With what?'

'He's an enterprising soul,' said Ingvar to his pack leader. 'Maybe we should have taken his fingernails out.'

Gunnlaugur chuckled heartily. 'Don't tempt me, brother.'

Klaive didn't have the energy to look disgusted. At the beginning of his captivity, he had railed against his gaolers, cursing them as heretics and daemon-worshippers and genetic deviants. The Space Wolves had let him shout himself hoarse – it was nothing they hadn't heard before – and gradually his fighting spirit had exhausted itself.

Perhaps that early bluster had been about bravado, about steeling himself for the excruciation he confidently expected would come. Klaive had been a torturer in Delvaux's service, and like all such enthusiastic pain-givers, had assumed that all others would be like him, if given the chance. But it never had. The wounds he had taken during his abduction had been staunched – roughly, it was true – and he had been left to recover for a week or two. When the questions had come, they had been brought forcefully, relentlessly, giving him little rest, but no hands were raised against him.

Perhaps, if he had not chosen to give up what he knew, that would have changed. He never put it to the test – he knew there was no way out, no escape from his captors unless they got what they wanted. Klaive was a devout man, one who had always believed in the sanctity of the eternal Church, but he also wanted to live. In truth, his involvement with the Fulcrum had never been very extensive – it had been just one of a number of initiatives he had been party to – so telling them what he knew had carried little price. Just some communications he'd had, some documents he'd seen, meagre things.

'So what is it this time?' he asked sullenly.

Ingvar sat forward, placing his huge hands together and interlocking the fingers. Despite everything, Klaive had never got used to dealing with these outsized versions of the human – their ludicrous musculature, their permanent stench of violence. 'We're very close, now,' he said. 'Right on his tail.'

'Good for you.'

'You can take the credit, rat,' Gunnlaugur added, leaning back against the facing wall. 'Let's see if I remember this right. The Ecclesiarchy codes you gave us led to the raid on Xeres IX, which got us the details of the sector fleet movements. And that let us hit the *Tyrantian Eternus*, which got us the first sniff of the Fulcrum's location. Though that was wrong, or it had moved on, we still did some satisfying damage. Remember that?'

Klaive stared at his calloused hands. 'I don't even know that the Fulcrum is a single person,' he mumbled. 'I told you that.'

'We know it's a person,' said Ingvar. 'Everything we've intercepted tells us that.'

'It's how your people organise,' Gunnlaugur added. 'No one knows much, not individually, but it all stops at one single point. That's a weakness.'

Klaive shot him a sour, mirthless smile. 'And the Wolves of Fenris know all about organisation.'

'We've been close to it since then, haven't we?' said Gunnlaugur. 'We know we have. You know it, too. It must give you warm feelings of joy, knowing we're so near to the heart of it.'

Klaive shook his head. 'It's all pointless,' he muttered. 'You're wasting your strength on something that doesn't matter any more.'

'It mattered to you, on Ras Shakeh,' said Ingvar. 'Why else destroy the records?'

'Orders.'

'From the Fulcrum?'

'From my contact. Whoever that was.'

Gunnlaugur watched Klaive intently. 'Someone thought it was worth sending you and Delvaux to that planet. Despite everything happening in this sector, they arranged to send you in force. And they had the power to do it.'

'We had tracked the Archenemy fleet. We knew about the *Festerax*.'

'You knew nothing of it, not until we did,' Gunnlaugur replied.

'You did Delvaux's bidding, right up to the end,' said Ingvar. 'You would have destroyed an entire world, even after he was dead and the threat had been ended. I never understood that.'

'Because they *deserved* to die!' Klaive shot back. 'Just as you deserve to die. All who do not cleave to sacrifice, when called on, deserve it. Delvaux was a pious man. A good man. He saw the threat to the sector, and moved to end it.'

Gunnlaugur let slip a low growl. 'He was a monster. You could have held him back.'

'You credit me with too much influence. Anyway, I had no wish to. I only wished to do my duty.'

'You were using him,' said Ingvar coldly. 'He rose, you rose. Only, you got too close to the sun, and now you've been burned.'

'So we come to your present situation,' said Gunnlaugur. 'You gave us enough, a little here, a little there. The rest we did our-selves. And the *Blade of Naxian* was a good target. We have fragments of astropathic readings from across the entire subsector. Want to know what's in them, rat?'

Klaive looked down at his knuckles again. 'Is that a genuine question?'

'You know some of it already,' said Ingvar. 'Major fleet build-ups, every-where you look. You were just ahead of the curve. The Sororitas are mustering all their Convents between here and Ophelia.'

'Just like the Militarum,' said Gunnlaugur. 'Just like the Navy.'

'Just like the Adeptus Astartes,' Klaive said acidly. 'Those who remember their duty, anyway.'

'They're all heading one way,' said Ingvar. 'Coronis Agathon. Tallander. Mortijia. Lopax. Those are worlds on the approaches to the Cadian Gate, its feeder systems, the string of citadels running around the borders of the Eye itself. We saw it for ourselves at Kefa – the walls are crumbling out here. Now the Imperium is responding.'

'We looked at the call signs for its fleets, and got an idea of where they're going,' said Gunnlaugur. 'We can read a lot, rat, using the ciphers you were able to help us with. We gained a picture of a whole range of movements.'

'But not everything,' said Ingvar. 'Some codes were new. There's a single world, one that's been calling for aid for months. Nothing's coming. The last we could make out was that it had been marked as abandoned. It's not the only one. They're having to choose what they can defend, and what they can't.'

'All except one squadron,' said Gunnlaugur. 'It's using an Ecclesiarchy ident, and it should be heading for the muster at Mortijia. But it isn't. It's heading towards this world. The one that's already been written off by everyone else.'

Klaive reached up to scratch the skin at the nape of his neck. 'Then that's something you'll want to hunt down,' he said wearily.

'Definitely,' said Ingvar. 'We unlocked this using the same codes you used for your old transmissions, so someone on that squadron is picking up things you used to pick up.'

'Do pass on my regards, when you find them.'

'Oh, we will,' said Ingvar. 'But we need something from you first.'

'We have everything but the name,' said Gunnlaugur. 'There's no standard void-locator, just a sequence in an embedded Ecclesiarchy code line. We know it's not on a designated front line for the coming push, but that leaves a lot of void to cover. Wherever it is, this place isn't important enough to register elsewhere.'

'Except for this one squadron,' said Ingvar, 'who are taking a big risk to get there.'

Klaive shook his head. 'We've been down this path before,' he muttered. 'A hint of something, a whisper of something. You run it down, you destroy what you find, and still we're stuck out here, chasing shadows.'

Ingvar glanced at Gunnlaugur, and laughed. 'He thinks this has been random.'

'So he does,' said the Wolf Guard, his mouth twitching with his own amusement. 'Then again, I guess he doesn't see much of what we do, from down here.'

'Every hit we've made,' said Ingvar, turning back to Klaive, 'every raid, every ship taken, we've learned a little more.'

'Jorundur likes to analyse patterns,' said Gunnlaugur. 'He's a strange soul, but he's good at it. See, we all are – it's nothing more than what we used to do, when we could smell our prey on the wind. You close off paths, you circle inward. Soon there aren't that many places left to run to.'

'They're using your codes, rat,' said Ingvar. 'They're heading into a gale that everyone else is running away from.'

'My gut tells me this is the one,' said Gunnlaugur. 'Flushed out by the breaking storm, given to us by fortune. Only, fate is a wily old crone – she gives with one claw and takes with another.'

'That world will be ashes soon,' said Ingvar. 'Hence the need for haste. You know the old cartograph coding. You can do just one more thing for us.'

'We just need a name.'

'Then all this will be over.'

Then they said nothing more. Then they waited.

Klaive stared at the floor. Despite what he'd said, he had a sense they were right. The Fulcrum, whatever it truly was, could not have remained hidden forever once the search for it became determined. Its hope had been to stay entirely secret, something that its targets would never even look for. That had been the reason he'd been ordered to that hellish desert world in the first place – to clamp down on any possibility of discovery, given the presence of old communications there that should have been destroyed a long time ago.

It would have been easy to become bitter. But for that oversight, he would no doubt still have been at Delvaux's side, perhaps masterminding the diocesan contribution to this gathering warfront, with all its opportunities for advancement. Then again, the will of the Emperor was made manifest in unusual ways. He'd managed to preserve himself thus far. For as long as he lived, as long as he breathed, there still might be a route back to salvation.

He had outlived Delvaux. He had survived the assault on the plague ship when so many others, including some among the Wolves themselves, had not. So this wasn't over yet. The closer this got to the end, the more chance of a change in fortune. He had some reasons to hope for that, after all.

So he looked up.

'I'll need to see what you've found,' he said. 'Then I'll give you what I can.'

By the time Bjargborn reached the *Amethyst Suzeraine*'s command bridge, the place was a good deal less tense than it had been a few hours ago. While *Vuokho* had been out on the assault, augur operators had been glued to their lenses, watching for any sign that the *Blade of Naxian* might muster enough of a defence to repel its boarders, ready to train broadsides on a retreating gunship. The chance had been small, but the crew had been ready to light the plasma drives and move into gun range. No one had wanted that – the galleon probably would have suffered badly in the exchanges – so it had been welcome news when the Thunderhawk had speared back into sensor range, intact and with its full complement of interlopers on board.

The command throne was empty. Only Jorundur, or on occasion Gunnlaugur, occupied that seat, placed high up on a dais of marble and ouslite. All the sensor pits were occupied, though, mostly with officers taken from Bjargborn's old command. They wore a decent approximation of their old grey tunics, patched up and mingled with other scraps of fabric they'd had to grab since leaving the Stormcaller's protection.

The bridge-space echoed that sense of mingled origins. The ironwork was elaborate – a tiered series of carved galleries and balustrades in brass plate, all of it decked with statuary of a flamboyant nature. Those of the original crew who still worked the bridge were decked out in their old uniforms – crimson-sashed jerkins and polished leather boots – and a few of Collaqua's old looted paintings still hung in the alcoves. With the warp shutters up, the full extent of the gaudy armaglass viewpane-array was visible, hanging over them like a collection of crystal bubbles edged in gold. That fixture alone must have emptied out a chunk of the old pirate's treasury.

Bjargborn took his position in the shipmaster's throne, set in the rank just below the command seat, and reviewed the bulletins waiting for him. Most were in a form he knew well enough – terse information bursts in the Fenrisian style.

The right arm of the throne held a lithcaster, and he activated a holo-projection of the final report he'd asked for, on the state of the macrocannon batteries. Those were the *Amethyst Suzeraine*'s best armaments, the ones Collaqua had no doubt paid through the nose for, and the one element of its offensive capabilities that matched up to a decent-sized military vessel. They had originally been kitted out for disruption shells – ideal for a commander who wished to disable his prey for boarding, rather than destroy it. That was less useful in a situation where you might want to punch holes through enemy armour plate, so the resident tech-cadres had been busy converting as many as possible to carry adamantium-core shells. The conversion work was demanding and difficult, and Bjargborn had kept a close eye on it. Given enough time, given enough effort, he'd turn the galleon into a proper warship yet.

'I hope you're pleased with what we've accomplished,' came a voice at his shoulder.

He looked up to see Ejika Suaka standing there. As his operations chief on the bridge, she was wearing a close approximation of a Fenrisian uniform, but the impression only went so far. She was dark-skinned, with black glossy hair tied up in a sharp bun. The tattoo of corsair allegiance was still visible on her left cheek, and her fingers carried the gold rings of her previous occupation.

'Four units ready for test-firing,' Bjargborn said, glancing back at the holo-lith report. 'Eight more undergoing conversion. That's decent progress.'

Suaka bowed. 'I've overseen it personally.'

'My masters will only be pleased when they see the results.'

'Give the word, and we can commence the tests. Hopefully make them happier still.'

Suaka was a dutiful officer. That was why she was still alive, and why she had been kept in service. The galleon was a big, old ship, with plenty of crannies and idiosyncrasies to catch out the unwary, and more than once her experience had been essential.

Bjargborn looked up at her. 'Enjoy your labours, do you, lieutenant?'

'Why do you ask, lord?'

'We've been... demanding.'

Suaka shrugged. 'I've served plenty of masters in my time. I worked on an Imperial merchantman before this, you knew that? The *UV-56-A*, a big hauler, out on the Gorgon Sounds. And before that, on a supply tender to a schola majoris. That wasn't so different to this.'

'But you were freer, before.'

'Freer, but not safer.' Her eyes flickered over to the silos, where the mixed crews were working hard. 'It was a fearful ship,' she said, her voice lower.

'Some loved Collaqua, most hated him. The coin was good, when it came in, but that didn't make up for the beatings. All in all, most are happy to see him gone.'

'Including you.'

'I was always one of the faithful, lord. I never liked what we were doing. Then again, you don't have to like it, do you? Just keep your head down.'

Bjargborn grunted. That was probably true. She'd gone along with it, though, no doubt to keep herself alive. He couldn't approve, even if he understood.

'I'm waiting for our next set of orders,' he told her. 'The last I heard, the masters were entering conclave, so those may arrive soon. But know this – wherever we're heading, this ship needs to be able to land a harder punch. That means faster gunline roll-out, faster plasma power-up. We're not preying on the soft and slow any more, lieutenant.'

'Understood, lord.'

'So we'll schedule those cannon tests for deployment in one hour, standard Terran. Can the crews handle it?'

'I'll make sure they can.'

'Start at once.'

Suaka made the aquila, bowed, and headed off to start the process. Once she was gone, Bjargborn settled into his throne and reviewed the rest of the bulletins. Things were progressing more or less as he might have hoped, and even Jorundur would be pleased if the armaments work came in on schedule. But it would still be hard, if the fighting became more than sporadic. Even the *Undrider*, that universally disliked scrapheap of a Chapter frigate, had delivered more punishment than this vessel could, and that had been manned by an experienced void-war crew.

The hololith reports flicked across in front of his eyes, one after the other.

'We'll be ready, when the order comes,' he murmured to himself, as much for reassurance than out of any conviction. 'By Russ, we'll have to be.'

CHAPTER EIGHT

The pack had done what they could to create an Annulus Chamber. The old trappings had been ripped out, the decking made bare, the lumens torn from their moorings. Stone slabs from the *Hlaupnir* had been hauled up from the hangars, mortared into place, lit with flame. The icon of the Chapter, the snarling wolf's head, had been engraved onto the circular table at the room's centre, and the warhammer battle-standard of the pack hung in the shadows. Six long spears stood behind each of the thrones, their shafts fastened to stone columns with lengths of leather, their blade-sockets bearing hunt-totems of the old ice.

At least the chamber smelled right – burning coals, ancient stone, the musk of long-weathered pelts. If the fires had been roaring higher, if the mix of aromas had included raw meat and mjod, then it might just have passed for one of the Mountain's many deep-delved halls, the kind of place a battle company might meet to rake over past victories or plan future raids.

No menials were present at this gathering, only the Wolves themselves. Gunnlaugur had the place of honour, facing the chamber's lone entrance from across the tabletop. Ingvar was at his right hand, Jorundur his left. Olgeir, Hafloí and Baldr occupied the remaining seats. In the flicker of brazier light, their features were as varied as their natures – the Blood Claw pale and vivid, the Old Dog as dark as the chamber's deep recesses.

The centre of the table held a lithcaster, which bled out a deep red glow. A system schematic shimmered at eye level, each node marked with runes.

'The rat knew just enough,' said Gunnlaugur, placing his scarred hands before him on the tabletop. 'He could unlock the codes we couldn't, and gave us a name.' He gestured towards the largest of the translucent spheres. 'Ojada VII. Mining world, heavily populated, colonised some time in M36, very productive.'

'How far?' asked Olgeir.

'A few days, if we flay the warp drives,' Gunnlaugur said.

'And it's already under attack?' asked Jorundur.

'Everything in the subsector is. From what we know, it's not being relieved.'

Jorundur pursed his lips thoughtfully. 'That's a major world. A productive one. Hel, how bad have things got, if they're letting it go?'

'Maybe they judge it can hold out,' said Ingvar.

Hafloí spat a laugh. 'Not for long. You've seen what's gathering out there.'

'So you think the prey's on that world?' asked Olgeir, looking directly at Gunnlaugur.

The Wolf Guard nodded. 'Everything we've learned, everything we've run down since leaving Kefa, has pointed us in this direction. The rat got us this close, and what we took from the astropath relay delivered the rest.' He pushed his hands upward, sliding his elbows along the tabletop. 'We knew it wouldn't be a shrine world. The fragments we had from the *Tyrantian* told us that – if the Fulcrum had once used an Ecclesiarchy planet, it went underground a long time ago.'

'But a *mining* world,' said Hafloí.

'Good cover,' said Ingvar. 'Big enough to hide a major facility. It has regular void traffic – heavy, frequent, mostly bound for forge worlds or hive worlds. There'll be cities, cathedrals, plentiful tech, access to ships. And yet, who would go there looking for anything but ore?'

'The enemy would,' said Olgeir.

'Ach, they're burning everything between here and Lopax,' said Gunnlaugur. 'And that makes this urgent – we delay now, and they'll bury the secret.'

'If the secret's even still there,' said Jorundur.

'Aye, it may have run already,' said Gunnlaugur. 'But we know how many others were caught out by the moving battlefronts, unable to retreat before the enemy overwhelmed them. The squadron that's headed there – it has the look of something summoned to get them out.'

'There's always room for doubt,' said Ingvar. 'But, right now, we have nothing better.'

Olgeir laughed. 'And nowhere better to be.'

Hafloí grinned back at him. 'Sure about that? The Idelion Cluster is within spitting distance, and there'd be plenty of nice things to hit in there.'

Throughout the exchanges, Baldr had said nothing. He stared at the tabletop, ignoring the hololith. 'So, what would be the plan?' he asked quietly.

'We attempt to overtake this squadron,' said Gunnlaugur. 'If we can board it, we can find out what its tasking is. Though, if we're right about where it is, we'll be lucky to reach it before it gets to Ojada. In that case, we'll just have to improvise.'

Jorundur shot a crooked smile. 'Precise, as ever.'

'Time is of the essence,' said Gunnlaugur. 'If we do this, we do it now. So I need to know now if any of you wish to speak against it.'

No one said anything. Baldr kept his eyes locked on the table's surface.

'So be it,' said Gunnlaugur, placing his hands apart and clenching his fists. 'We light the engines. May the Hand of Russ guide us to the enemy.'

After that, things moved quickly. Orders were sent up to Bjargborn, and the countdown to warp translation begun. Alert klaxons began to sound, the crew hastened to their stations and the shutters slammed down across the viewports on every deck. Jorundur headed to the command bridge to take control of the ship once the word was given to cross the veil, while the rest of the pack made their way to the armoury. Once their battleplate had been reconditioned and given the necessary rites, it would all be clamped back on again soon enough. The warp was no place to linger unguarded.

Ingvar waited outside the Annulus Chamber until Baldr made his exit, after which he followed him down the corridor.

'Brother!' he called.

Baldr halted, turned and waited.

'You said little, back there,' Ingvar said.

'What was there to say?' Baldr replied, smiling wryly. 'He just wanted to put a seal on it.'

'Maybe. But if you have doubts...'

'None.' Baldr clapped a hand on Ingvar's shoulder. 'This is what we've been hunting for since we were on our own.'

'It's the route back to the Chapter. It's what we need, to regain our honour and our place.'

'I understand that.'

'We root this corruption out, expose the poison. They'll have to weigh our words. We give them this, then they–'

'Then they let me live.' Baldr laughed. 'Maybe. I still don't think they'd take back a witch, even if you'd saved Grimnar's neck itself.'

'You're no witch.'

'Sure of that, are you?'

Ingvar looked at him seriously. 'If I thought it, for a moment, I'd be holding the blade at your neck myself.'

'I have no such certainty.' Baldr started to walk again, heading directly to his chambers and the arming menials. 'You worry that all this has distracted from the search for a cure. Do not. We never knew where to look for that, only hoping that time and freedom would somehow deliver. This, though – *this* is before us, in our line of sight. We have to take it.'

Ingvar came with him. 'I have not given up on finding one.'

'I know you haven't.'

'And I believe them to be linked. Nothing happens except by fate. The desert world – the plague-bearers, the Sisters. We were positioned there to find these things.'

'You think that, brother?' He shook his head. 'You'd make a better gothi than me. Not everything is scored out by the wyrd.'

'This is. There has been a curse on us, an ill shadow hanging at our backs. I'd see it lifted.'

Baldr stopped walking. 'The moment I saw that world's name, read it in the runes over the table, I knew it was the place. I *knew* it. What does that tell you? That I can interpret your curse, or that it works through me? Either way, we have to go.' He smiled again, coldly. 'If these traitors exist, I'll be glad to slay them alongside you. But do not expect it to lift the blight. That is too ancient, and we are just a part of it.'

'It is the wyrd.'

'Believe that, if you want to.'

'I do.'

And then he was moving again. Ingvar didn't follow him. He watched the movement of bone-plates under the cloak, definition that should have been hidden under thick layers of muscle. The sickness could not be hidden now.

'You'll believe it too, brother, by the end,' Ingvar called after him. 'If a vow was ever worth swearing, I promise you that.'

III
FIRE OVER WATER

CHAPTER NINE

It took more than a few days. The warp fought them, just as it always seemed to do now – pushing back, writhing away, dropping down into chasms with no base before rising into spiky clusters that risked dashing the ship's prow into slivers.

The *Amethyst Suzeraine* had not been made for such arduous crossings. The orders given to van Kliis were specific, and she obeyed them to the letter, keeping the trajectory as close to optimum as she could. That meant the galleon ran into punishment quickly, straining the Geller field generators and making the entire structure crack, squeal and groan. The Fenrisians in the crew, used to tough runs through the ether, took it all in their stride, laughing to one another about the claws they could hear skittering down the far side of the hull-plates. The pressed menials took it harder, praying often, succumbing to warp-sickness, clinging on to railings and fervently wishing for the stage to finish quickly.

Gunnlaugur stayed in comms contact with van Kliis throughout, listening carefully to the bursts of information she emitted, studying every snippet of analytical data that slid down the lenses.

'I can hardly see the Beacon,' she'd reported at one stage, something that had given greater than usual cause for alarm. 'It's as if... no, that's not possible. Ah, see. There it is again.' A long silence. 'Throne. But look at... what's that? Behind it? No. But I don't...'

She broke off after that, and never elucidated what she'd meant by it all. The comms bursts subsequently became less frequent, and when her few reports did come in, her voice was often strained, as if choked.

'Are we going to have to drop out?' Jorundur asked Gunnlaugur grimly, on the seventh day.

The Wolf Guard remained static in the throne, glaring at the warp shutters as they shuddered. 'No,' he said. 'Not yet.'

It would have to happen soon, though. Injuries mounted, particularly in the lower decks, and those injuries soon turned into casualties. Bjargborn had organised patrols after day four, then stepped them up, finally requesting assistance from the Wolves themselves to keep order. The ether had a way of seeping into a vessel, particularly one as leaky and ancient as the *Amethyst Suzeraine*. A Geller field kept the worst of its manifestations out, but it didn't stop the dreams, or the visions, or the more prosaic effects of sleep deprivation and constant tension.

Out of all of them, it fell hardest on Baldr. The pressure behind his eyes, already intense, just kept building up. He volunteered for as many of the patrols as possible, knowing that sleep was impossible, wishing to keep his body moving, his mind focused on anything other than his waking nightmares. At times, when alone in the flickering darkness of the lower levels, he would reach out to the curve of the inner hull walls, pressing a finger against the ridged adamantium, feeling the distant thrum from outside. If you stayed there long enough, still enough, you might begin to think you could hear words, repeated, over and over again, spoken to you and no one else.

But it couldn't last forever. The warp drives kept on thundering, pushing the ship through the waves and eddies, smashing its lumpen prow onward, ever onward, as if by force of will alone. Soon the chronometers began to align, and the reports from the Navigator's sanctum started up again. The eighth day saw the worst of the resistance fade, and the orders to make ready for realspace given. The pack assembled, taking up combat stations. The armouries were thrown open, and Bjarg-born's troops equipped themselves. Then came the final few hours, the worst waiting of all, as the ship shook harder than ever and the seconds clicked down towards the wrench of realspace entry.

For that, Jorundur took his place in the command throne, assuming control of the galleon's course and speed. Gunnlaugur and the rest of the pack assembled on the dais around him, fully armoured. Bjargborn, Suaka and the rest of the bridge crew assumed their stations in the lower levels, manning the augur banks and weapons arrays. Down in the hangars, both *Vuokho* and the *Hlaupnir* were prepped and made ready, their engines warmed up and tanks filled. The galleon's gun-crews were placed on high alert – the *Amethyst Suzeraine* had no lance-level weapons, but its ranked macrocannon batteries now delivered a reasonable level of punishment at serviceable reload speeds, and the void shields were in good order.

'Steady...' murmured Gunnlaugur, watching the chronos clatter down.

'All systems report ready for re-entry,' intoned Bjargborn calmly, his eyes fixed on the battery of lenses around him. 'Plasma drives keyed for ignition. Stand by for warp drive decoupling.'

'Final notice – do you have anything for me?' Gunnlaugur voxed to van Kliis, isolated in her sanctum high up on the galleon's top ridge.

'All obscured,' the Navigator replied. *'Nothing but shadows on the far side. We won't be alone, though.'*

Jorundur cursed under his breath, placing both hands on the arms of the throne, letting his fingers slot into the connectors from where he could deliver immediate course correction vectors. 'How nice.'

'Plasma drives fired up,' Bjargborn reported. 'Decoupling commencement on my mark.'

'Here we go...' growled Gunnlaugur, his hands curled around the shaft of his thunder hammer.

Routine translation alarms broke out, a screaming chorus that swept over the bridge balconies. The ship bucked, as if hitting a huge wave of solid material, before skidding around on its axis and making the grav-compensators shriek. Everything boomed, the decks vibrated, the engines spasmed.

And then they were out. The shift in momentum was immediate – a lurch into physical movement, something that felt completely different to warp travel, a resumption of an explicable state, the vice of natural laws reasserting themselves.

'Shutters up!' Gunnlaugur commanded, bracing himself against the swinging deck movements. 'Full power to void shields, run out gunlines.'

'Get me close augurs,' Jorundur ordered Suaka, who was already working hard to calculate trajectories.

The cogitators blurted into life, filling the lenses up with cascades of runes and schematics. The warp shutters jerked open, spilling red-tinged sunlight across the deck canopies. From far below, the rhythmic thud of the warp drives gave way to the raw burn of the plasma drives. The hideous pressure of unreality lifted from every soul on the ship, as welcome as the emptying of thunderheads after a long drought. Realviewers sparked into life, generating magnified images of the spatial volumes around them, and the truth of van Kliis' prediction swam into view.

The void ahead was full. It was jam-packed, choked up, rammed with movement and fire. Everything was whirling, spiralling, like the aftermath of some colossal explosion. Debris tumbled towards them, some of it clouds of micro-fragments, some pieces as large as hab-blocks.

'Down, down, down!' ordered Jorundur, sending the *Amethyst Suzeraine* into a steep dive, before kicking in a twist that made the ship's structure lurch back the other way.

Wreckage hit the void shields with heavy smacks, exploding into smaller pieces as the barriers flexed under stress. Something absolutely massive – the exposed plasma-train of a starship, possibly – rolled overhead, narrowly missing taking the galleon's topmost spires off. Jorundur pulled off more tight manoeuvres, sliding through the debris clouds, before feeding more power to the burners and sending the *Amethyst Suzeraine* surging straight ahead.

'It's not all wreckage,' Bjargborn announced, diligently filtering through the riot of signals even as the ship plunged and tilted to avoid them. 'We have incoming intact units, weapons powered, tracking our position.'

Gunnlaugur said nothing. He could see the same augur-readings, and could process them far faster. More than three hundred ships were threading their way through the confusion, running hard, a whole gamut of types and displacements. Many were system runners little different to the *Hlaup-nir* – short-range craft with the bare minimum warp capacity. Others were absolute leviathans – mass conveyers, troop carriers, Chartist-registered haulers, even what looked like an ancient colony ship. They were all surging towards the Mandeville gates – the points of safe entry to the warp – but in such concentrations, with so many major gravity wells moving in such relative proximity, it was carnage.

'Away, away,' muttered Jorundur, hauling the galleon hard-starboard to bring them out of contact with a looming troop carrier. For a heart-stopping few moments they were running alongside the vast craft, barely a few hundred yards off its flanks, skidding across its vertiginous hull so close you could see the regiment sigils on the access portals.

'Weapons discharge detected,' Suaka called out over the increasing hubbub on the bridge. 'Not aimed at us – range six hundred miles, bearing two-forty-five...'

'They're mauling each other,' grunted Jorundur, working hard to bring the galleon up into a steep climb before it smashed headlong into another oncoming hauler. The volume of ships was thinning, but slowly. Three system runners shot past, tilting on their axes before haring down narrowing chasms of free space. Jorundur applied more power, nudging them up and out of the worst congestion.

Just as he did so, on the extreme edge of the sprawling ship-clusters, faster-moving blips appeared on the sensor grids.

'Get me a look at those,' Gunnlaugur ordered.

'Void-fighters,' Bjargborn replied. 'Recognise nineteen Swift-death-pattern, thirty Fury interceptors, various call signs, coming in fast into starboard-ahead quadrant.'

'Registering Imperial Navy attack wing idents from all squadrons,' Suaka added.

'They're not Navy,' said Ingvar, glancing at the incoming data. 'Whatever they're telling you.'

'Aye, Archenemy presence confirmed,' Bjargborn called out. 'They're going for the carriers.'

'Moving to intercept,' said Jorundur.

'Belay that,' snapped Gunnlaugur. 'We're not here for them – remain on course.'

Everything was moving rapidly, a vast orbital ballet of lumbering void-giants surrounded by darting small fry. From their vantage it all looked random and purposeless, until Jorundur succeeded in threading the ship further out from the Mandeville horizon and patterns began to emerge.

Almost everything was trying to get away. The carriers were packed with living souls, civilian and military. The biggest of them were heavily armed and escorted by gunships and fighter wings, but many more were fending for themselves with doubtful armaments and no support. A pitiful few Navy craft appeared to be attempting to impose some kind of order, but they were hopelessly overwhelmed. Amid all of that, predators had scented blood and closed in, strafing and lancing into the fringes of the vast conglomerations. Every few moments, a big hauler would break from the pack and go for the Mandeville horizon, calculating its position furiously to avoid proximal mass distortions. Those that got the gamble right would tear into the ether amid snarls of crackling warp energies. Those that got it wrong would blow themselves into scrap, their crews smeared across a half-formed mess of tortured physics.

The *Amethyst Suzeraine* was virtually the only ship trying to go in the other direction, to crunch its way through the spiralling shoal of desperate vessels and break clear for the planet itself. Anything else that wasn't trying to get away was either sensor-blind and drifting, or was commanded by an enemy that grew stronger with each new arrival.

'Additional incoming hostile targets,' Bjargborn went on. 'Signals indicate battle cruiser-class vessel on the cusp of materialisation.'

'You heard the pack leader,' said Jorundur. 'Full burn, dead ahead.'

'Can you pick up the target squadron in all this?' Ingvar asked. 'Any Ecclesiarchy idents?'

'Negative, lord,' replied Suaka, working hard at her station. 'If they've not been destroyed already, they must be far ahead of us.'

'Then keep running,' ordered Gunnlaugur darkly. 'We get to Ojada, then we fight.'

It felt hollow to leave a combat zone without firing a shot. Getting out of the engagement, once the initial shock of re-entry had been handled by Jorundur, hadn't proved hard, but watching the embattled ships shrink in the realviewers, knowing that only a fraction of them would make it to their translation points, was unpleasant.

Olgeir hadn't said a word during the engagement itself, and said nothing once Jorundur had found a path out of it and cranked up the galleon to its turgid top speed. He'd watched the firefights from a distance, like all the others, suppressing the urge to leap into a gunship and start taking out enemy void-fighters.

The same thing had happened to him on Kefa Primaris, where he'd been compelled to order an evacuation rather than help the planet defend itself. Every engagement he could remember since then had been a similar exercise in damage limitation – getting out before the enemy could come back at them, making compromises rather than unfurling their claws. This world, at least, promised to deliver a true confrontation, albeit one with an adversary who had remained elusive for too long.

He hefted his heavy bolter, cradling it two-handed. Just like every piece of equipment the pack used, it was battle-burned, chipped, scratched and worn at the edges. After each encounter, every time, he'd taken it apart, stripped it down, cleaned its sacred components and spoken the words of warding over them, just as the Iron Priests had taught him. The weapon had a spirit of its own, one that Olgeir respected, recognised and nurtured. Just like him, the bolter wanted to sing. It wanted to unlock its throat against an enemy worthy of its prestige.

Sigrún, it was called. It had been called that for longer than Olgeir had carried it, though it had been in his hands for so long now that he thought of it as his own. Many of those in the Chapter had inherited weapons – Ingvar's blade was the most ancient that he knew of – and they all understood that, on death, they would be passed on to the next wielder. The Wolves of Fenris tended many threads of history that stretched back to the dawn of the Imperium. Some were sagas, memorised and recited by the *skjalds* in the firelit halls. Some were Dreadnoughts, including the most revered of them all, buried deep in the vaults of the Mountain in perpetual ice and shadow.

And some were blades, bolters and storm shields, each one bathed in the blood of a thousand enemies of mankind, brought out of the armouries time and again, the loss of any of which was felt as keenly as the wielder's.

'Soon, now,' he found himself mouthing, to himself as much as the weapon-spirit.

The run into Ojada itself was not long. The galleon's sensors detected dozens more vessels streaming away from the system, all heading for the closest Mandeville geometry. Some of them even swept past in magnified visual range – a series of personnel conveyers in drab dark green, what looked like a gun-cutter with Arbites livery. Ranged augurs isolated many more lifeless hulks, powered down and drifting with puncture wounds along their flanks. Debris was everywhere, peppering the planetary approaches in steadily intensifying layers.

'Getting first major signals,' Suaka reported, just as the sensors locked on to the planetary mass and Jorundur adjusted the inward trajectory. 'Several thousand in motion – siphoning now.'

Soon the augurs were locking on to the planet and magnifying it onto the lenses. Olgeir looked up at the images, just as the rest of the pack did.

It was a red world, an angry world, barred with dark cloud-streaks, looking as if it were on fire itself. The scopes zoomed and refined, picking out clusters of warships in high orbit, tiny black specks against the glowing atmosphere below. Pinprick flashes of light flickered across the globe – lances firing, or ship-cores igniting. Cords of debris spun around the tortured planetscape, coalescing into orbital rings.

'Widespread fires on the surface,' Bjargborn reported, hunched over the sensor-feed with the furthest reach. 'Planet is an ocean world, it seems, but promethium pipelines have been severed, and the slicks are growing.'

Olgeir studied the feeds intently. 'Those cities – are they... floating?'

'Appear to be, lord,' Suaka said, analysing more opening vid-feeds. 'Or maybe rig-mounted.'

'I've seen the pattern before,' Jorundur said, his brow creasing with concentration as he boosted the galleon in closer. 'Refinery-cities built over water, like on Atreus Aiaxa. If the sea's on fire, though, that'll test things.'

'Get me more on what's in orbit,' Gunnlaugur ordered.

The sensor crews delved into the data, pulling sense out of the mass of signals. 'Heavy damage to defence plates,' Suaka reported. 'Several downed, six still in position. Debris makes it hard to pinpoint vessel numbers, but lance-fire extensive. This battle is still very much in progress.'

'Anything with an Ecclesiarchy call sign?' asked Ingvar.

'Plenty, but nothing matching the designation yet,' said Bjargborn.

'Could the squadron have been destroyed?' asked Gunnlaugur.

'No, they're here,' said Baldr quietly.

Olgeir turned sharply to look at his battle-brother, and saw only certainty on his face. For a moment, he wondered if Baldr had somehow got that damned collar off and unleashed his full, strange potential, but there it was, nestled between his breastplate and helm-seal, the iron tips glinting under the bridge lumens.

Everyone had become so... *relaxed* about it, as if the potential for harm had just gone away. But they'd all seen it – they'd all seen what he had become. Even now, on the cusp of battle, his doubts remained, nagging at him, just as they had since the first outbreak on Ras Shakeh.

No time to voice them now, though.

'Bring us in closer,' ordered Gunnlaugur. 'If they're in orbit, we'll take them there. Concentrate all sensors on that signature – I want it found.'

'Unless we're very lucky,' Olgeir said, 'they'll have made their landings already.'

'We haven't been lucky so far,' said Ingvar.

'Just get it into our sights,' said Gunnlaugur. '*Hlaupnir*'s prepped – we'll make planetfall if we need to.'

The *Amethyst Suzeraine* barrelled onward, smacking into thickening clots of wreckage, zeroing in on the distant point of light, which became a glowing disc, which became the uprushing arc of a world in its death throes.

Suaka gave a running commentary throughout the approach. The real-viewers firmed up images as the distances shrunk, throwing out a picture of planetwide wholesale destruction. By the time they reached true-visual range, three of the beleaguered orbital plates swam into view, their hearts burning, their reactors venting, their pockmarked surfaces blistered and cracked apart. Ships buzzed around them – racing escorts, lumbering battle cruisers, darting tenders, a whole raft of unclassified minor warships with lascannons ablaze. About a third of those bore sigils marking them as Ojada's defenders, with some arcane Mechanicus arks among them, but the clear majority wore the defaced aspect of traitor vessels – looted Militarum carriers, renegade galleons akin to the *Amethyst Suzeraine*, commandeered Navy ships hastily daubed with icons of proscribed factions, and – most imposing of all – the spike-ridged profile of true Chaos warcraft, bristling with brass-mouthed gunlines and spitting lurid energy-beams into the atmosphere below.

That atmosphere was burning. Up close, Olgeir saw the huge swaths of smoke ringing the planet's hemisphere, swept across its face by superheated winds, spiked with crackles of lightning. Through ragged gaps in the choking mask, the surface could be glimpsed – underlit red from the fires, hissing with steam and smog, the lights of its huge cities still shining – just – amid the roiling darkness.

'We are being targeted, lord,' Bjargborn warned as they shot in closer. Weapons-lock detectors began to blink across a number of augur-lenses.

'Let the void shields take the chaff,' Gunnlaugur ordered. 'Alert me if we get the attention of something serious. Where's our damned target?'

'Filtering signals, lord,' replied Suaka. 'The channels are overloading – working on it.'

'Filter faster,' growled Jorundur, pushing the galleon into a steeper approach vector. 'This is going to get difficult quickly.'

The available paths ahead were silting up. Ojada's ravaged hemisphere raced towards them, now filling the lower half of the viewers, the curve of its horizon flattening out. As it did so, the warships gnawing over its still-warm corpse spun into visual detail – racing wings of void-fighters, their thrusters flaring blue-white; formations of frigates and destroyers, their sides alight with coordinated las batteries; the lone shadows of major battleships, lit up with the brilliant flash of lances or lost behind the ripple of macrocannon broadsides. The scene was eye-watering in its intensity, the sheer black of the void backdrop sizzling with hard-edged flares and detonations.

'We've got someone's attention,' Bjargborn confirmed, swinging his throne around to highlight an incoming warship.

Olgeir glanced at the lens. The pinpointed ship was big, ugly, skeletal, forged from night-dark iron with a raised spine of vivid silver. Its prow might once have been a regular Imperial ploughshare profile, but had been hammered into an immense death's head, the eye sockets kindled with blue flame that streaked out into void as it turned. Its rangy flanks looked like the ribs of an emaciated canid, draped with heavy lengths of chain and studded with snarling cannon-mouths. Gaping thrusters left ink-blots of spidery pollution in its wake, lit from within by the final spark-ing of whatever foul discharge its infernal engines had created. Its precise allegiance was impossible to gauge – it carried no insignia, not even a sigil of the ancient Fallen Legions, just a mass of twisted metal tormented into a parody of mortal bone.

'Can we kill that?' Ingvar asked.

'It looks slow,' said Jorundur, burning the engines hard to keep the dis-tance between them from shrinking. 'Working on a targeting lock.'

'There'll be softer targets for it, if killing's all it wants,' said Gunnlaugur. 'Keep moving. Hel's teeth, where's *our* target?'

'I have something now, lord,' Suaka reported. 'Nine hundred miles, bearing twenty-four-four–'

'Key it in,' Gunnlaugur growled. 'Get us into cannon range.'

The *Amethyst Suzeraine* kicked on, tilting steeply to port before boost-ing hard. Behind them, still a long way off, the death's-head craft slipped into pursuit. Other ships began to pick up on their position, too, though the sheer volume of firefights all around them meant that few were able to do anything about it.

'Getting true-visual-feeds now, lord,' announced Bjargborn, his hands busy on the dials.

The deck rocked as something hit them. Amber alerts flashed on from the void shield read-outs.

'Maintain course,' Gunnlaugur ordered. 'Show me what you've got.'

A brace of lenses mounted high above the first tier of sensor pits flickered into life, showing a zoomed-in segment of the orbital battle. Even with the cogitators working hard to improve the images, the depictions were grainy and dim, little more than a collection of blobs swinging and blurring.

Then they clarified, at least a little.

'That's it,' Ingvar said, clenching his fists.

It had to be an Ecclesiarchy vessel. No other institution decorated their warships with such ludicrous sweeps of gold and crimson. It was a bloated thing, vaned and sparred, a serious battleship equipped with both ship-killing lances and ostentatious close-range batteries. It had waded into the warzone accompanied by a whole suite of escort craft, all of which were busy laying down a furious corona of las-fire. Even as Olgeir watched, the squadron was moving steadily northwards across Ojada's surface, drawing heavy fire from the dozens of enemy ships within range.

'Call signs confirmed,' Suaka called out. 'Description matches that given by the prisoner. Main vessel is the *Immaculate Destiny*. Supporting escorts *Purity of Action*, *Obsidian Mitre* and *Merited Judgement* identified – other idents incoming.'

The *Amethyst Suzeraine* rocked again, smacked in its midriff by what felt like a torpedo scatter. The lattice-prickle of las-fire began to spread across the realviewers, and more incoming sensor-blips clustered on the mid-range augur fields.

'Target all weapons when in range,' Gunnlaugur said. 'Get a lock on the upper hull. We can ignore the escorts – they're already busy.'

Olgeir looked at the lenses doubtfully. They were still a long way off, but everything he'd seen suggested that the *Immaculate Destiny* outgunned them easily. It would have been a difficult task to get in close at the best of times, and the full-scale orbital war raging around them made it even harder.

He was about to speak, suggesting another tack, when the images changed. The *Immaculate Destiny* briefly disappeared behind a huge flash of light, followed by a blistering column of energy spearing down to the world below. Anything caught in that burning column was smashed apart in a cascade of explosions, clearing a well of space all the way down to the surface. A split second after that, docking doors on the underside of the ship yawned open, and a brace of heavily armoured landers emerged, falling fast.

'Can we lock on yet?' Gunnlaugur asked.

'Just a few seconds...' grunted Jorundur, working frantically even as more impacts skittered the galleon's viewfinders sideways. 'Teeth of Russ – just a *few seconds*...'

The landers plummeted, dropping like stones through the tumbling void-wreckage, their undersides reddening fast until they looked more like meteors than manned vessels.

Gunnlaugur swore loudly, striding over to an augur-lens and wrenching it round to take a closer look. 'Mark where they went! Get a clear fix!'

'Aye, lord,' Suaka acknowledged, hunching over her station, her fingers a blur of movement.

'We can't take that ship on, Skullhewer,' said Olgeir, seeing his chance. 'Not easily. But we can follow those.'

Gunnlaugur looked back up at him, his ragged mouth splitting into a wide grin. 'Aye, Heavy-Hand, that we can. So start moving – I'll want Sigrún with me too.'

CHAPTER TEN

Four of them ran from the command bridge to the hangars – Gunnlaugur, Ingvar, Olgeir and Baldr. By the time they reached the lower level, the kaerls had made everything ready. The fuel lines had been withdrawn from the *Hlaupnir*, the hangar doors were opening to the void, warning klaxons were blaring and the aprons were cleared of personnel.

Ingvar sprinted across the deck, his blade swinging at his belt. Hafloí hadn't been happy about staying on the galleon with the Old Dog, but the whelp had learned to bite his tongue when given an order. In any case, things were unlikely to be uneventful on board – the hard-round impacts just kept coming in, clattering against the void shields, gathering in intensity. As soon as the system runner was away, Jorundur would be forced to fight his way clear, and that would keep the entire crew busy.

Ingvar reached the system runner and leapt up through the open crew hatch, seizing a handhold and throwing himself into the access berth. Gunnlaugur was a few paces ahead of him, charging up a ladder and making for the bridge. The *Hlaupnir* had felt absurdly cramped during the first few weeks of the hunt, but now was crewed sparsely – two dozen of Bjargborn's troops, a few servitors, the four Space Wolves. That made it trim, lean, something that could react quickly and still pack a punch. You wouldn't want to attempt a warp jump with that complement, but a planetary descent, hot and hard, that was a different matter.

Baldr was the last one in. The hatch slammed closed behind them, the locks spun tight and the atmosphere seals sucked rigid. The decks thrummed, then shivered as the manoeuvring thrusters ramped up. By the time Ingvar reached the bridge, the *Hlaupnir* was off the apron, swivelling around, making ready to boost clear of the hangar and out into the void.

The system runner's bridge itself was small – room enough for twenty, maybe, if you stuffed them in. Gunnlaugur occupied the stone-hewn command throne; the remainder of the operational stations were taken by kaerls, strapped in and armoured up. A sloping armaglass canopy stretched away overhead, barred with iron and already glistening with hololithic tactical read-outs. The whole place was bare, stripped down, utilitarian, just like a Fenrisian ship should be.

Olgeir hauled himself up through the floor-level hatch just as the engines blasted into full pitch, and was nearly thrown back into the rear bulkheads.

'Watch your step, brother,' Baldr said helpfully, coming up behind him.

The acceleration was wrenching, throwing them clear of the *Amethyst Suzeraine*'s side and deep into the orbital apocalypse. Gunnlaugur swung the nose down, and Ojada's burning atmosphere swelled up in the forward viewers. Ingvar caught a final view of the galleon as it peeled away, its void shields swimming with energy discharge, before everything turned into a criss-cross splash pattern of las-fire and plasma impacts.

He grasped his way over to Gunnlaugur, staggering against the heavy pitch of the deck and gripping the handholds. 'You still have the fix on them?' he asked.

Gunnlaugur nodded, face hidden behind his full armour. 'Interference heavy,' he growled. 'But they're not getting away.'

The *Hlaupnir* blasted to its full velocity, screaming planetwards like a shivered spear, leaving behind a whole gaggle of gunships that had started to take an interest in it. It headed straight down, nose first, boosting hard through the smack and skid of las-fire impacts. Ingvar finally reached his throne and thunked into it, hauling on the restraints to keep himself from being hurled back across the steepling deck.

The view ahead was burning up – first in gouts of rippling flame, then streamers of it, then a solid curtain that roared and licked across the armaglass. The vessel bounced and shook as the atmosphere thickened, tearing at the void shields. Collisions continued to rain in, though it was impossible to tell whether they were debris or the last desperate shots from the orbital zone.

'Hel! Signal lost,' Gunnlaugur spat, grappling with the controls. 'But I've got a rough lock – we'll come down close.'

Even as he spoke, the *Hlaupnir* pulled out of its vertical descent, switching to turbines and sliding into a shallower atmospheric run. The hard pull of gravity tilted, vying with the colossal inertia of the engine switch, making every rivet and fitting on the bridge rattle in its housings.

'Morkai's teeth,' breathed Olgeir, staring out of the realviewers as the vista cleared. 'They've made a mess.'

Flames still gusted and ripped across the armaglass, which now offered the first, tattered glimpses of the world beyond. A vivid orange atmosphere bloomed above them, striated with thick palls of oil-fuelled clouds. The planetscape was a storm of turbulence – lead-dark oceans boiling into columns of steam, ranks of lightning crackling through the roil like dancing star fields. Rig-cities loomed up around them on every side, marching off to the smoke-thick horizon, towers of blackened iron marked by layer upon layer of lumens and marker lights, colossal artificial cliffs that belched and spat with industrial burn-off.

The water, slathered in heavy slicks of promethium, shimmered like magma. The rigs all bore huge gouges in their flanks, exposing the extravagant complexity of their innards. Many sections had come down entirely, sliding into the oily waters as they fell apart, sending out tidal surges that crashed into the next rig along in bursts of spark-laced spray.

Atmospheric craft, thick flights of them, zipped and swerved through it all, strafing, spinning, loosing barrages of missiles into any intact fortress walls. Some bore Imperial livery – the Ojada defence forces, sundry military orders – but they were outnumbered many times over by the bizarre craft of the invaders. These were like junkyard rejects, vomiting out smuts, clad in overlapping plates of rust, slapped with vivid icons of heretic warbands and crowned with broken horns, spikes and hooks. Further off, up in the ruined crowns of the mighty rigs, heavier landers were coming down from orbit, shielded by coronas of covering las-fire, their swollen bellies full of warriors ready to be disgorged into the seething torment.

'This world is already dead,' said Baldr.

'Not quite,' said Ingvar, studying the scanners keenly. 'Just enough left for someone to come hunting.'

Olgeir's senses were alive now, his skin tingling. Getting out of the warp and back onto a world of air and fire would always do that, kindling the instincts that he'd been born with. He could already sense them – the agents of the Ecclesiarchy, out there, lost to vision amid the fire and smog, but *there* nonetheless, amid the listing rigs, come to salvage something from the wreckage just as they had done on Ras Shakeh. He could almost taste their presence on the air, just as he had once tasted the presence of beasts on the ice, just a spear-throw away, just a sword-thrust, just the reach of a hand.

'Target rig ahead,' Gunnlaugur announced, bringing the *Hlaupnir* down three hundred feet from the boiling seas. 'That's where I lost them.'

The system runner screamed along at full speed, carving a deep furrow in the waters beneath and throwing up a wall of spray. Fighters latched on and tried to keep up, but were left far behind as they angled to fire. Ahead of them, vast as a hive city, the rig swelled into clarity, smoke-shrouded and bleeding, towering into the burning atmosphere like some sacrificial volcano. Its gigantic supporting piers were lashed with the storm-swell, half lost in a sliding torrent of foam and fire-flecks. Its lower decks billowed with ash. Higher up, enormous sections had been cut out, as if by a jagged knife, stripping out a bewildering landscape of tortured rebar and twisted scaffolding. The giant oil processors were still churning, sucking up fuel from the undersea crust and piping it to the refineries, even as the entire world around them sunk into ruin.

Gunnlaugur didn't slow until the very last moment. The *Hlaupnir* careered towards the open flanks of the rig, finally pulling up just as it seemed he would crash them straight into the outer shell. The engines howled, the world swung on its axis, and for a second they were staring straight up the towering edge itself, gazing high into orange skies.

Then he killed the forward power and activated the manoeuvring thrusters, spinning the *Hlaupnir* over and sending the system runner dropping back sharply towards the rig's edge. A huge supporting spar passed overhead, then another, and then they were inside, under darkness, slowing rapidly as the city's structure swallowed them up. The retros activated, and Gunnlaugur zeroed in on a landing platform. The *Hlaupnir*, its hull steaming and scorched, hovered for a second, grinding to a halt, before he brought it down in a whine of turbines and thrown-up dust.

Gunnlaugur leapt out of the throne and onto his feet, hammer already in hand. Ingvar and the rest did the same, throwing off the restraints, weaponing up, ramming home magazines, kindling disruptor fields.

'Follow me in,' Gunnlaugur told them, his snarling voice alive with relish. 'And let the murder-make begin.'

The death's head kept on coming.

'Skítja,' spat Jorundur, working to haul the galleon out of cannon range. 'It's got its jaws into us now.'

It wasn't the only ship after them – a hundred lesser craft were zeroing in, loosing missiles, spitting las-batteries, trying to carve a piece of them off into the void – but the skull-faced cruiser was by far the most dangerous. Bjargborn's gunners had started to return fire in earnest by then, loosing strikes whenever anything got too close. They were good, and Bjargborn had worked hard at training them. But still, the targets just kept mounting up, and after a while that pressure would become too much to handle.

Jorundur liked flying. He liked flying a Thunderhawk, and he liked flying a battleship. The principles were different, the techniques were very different, but you could still take the same pleasure in it. This, though – this hunk of heavy metal, gravid, wallowing – was nothing like pleasure. It was torture just getting it to move where you wanted it to move, like wading through quicksand. It had been built for preying on the weak, for feasting on the dregs of inter-system trade. It was big, to be sure, and its hull was as thick as grox-hide, but just then he'd have traded all that bulk for some more powerful drives, for some agility, for just a sliver of tautness.

'Full spread, away port-nadir!' Bjargborn ordered, speaking directly to the gunnery master down in the lower decks. 'Clear us some space there, then keep the close cycles going.'

The rest of the bridge crew shouted over one another as the decks shook and banged, spraying orders down the comm-lines, their eyes fixed to the batteries of lenses that fizzed with the ship's vital signs and sensor-spreads, their hands dancing across input-boards.

And through it all, the death's head kept on coming.

'Keep me something in the tubes for that monster,' Jorundur told Bjargborn, struggling to get the *Amethyst Suzeraine* to roll around to where he wanted it. It felt like a stray hit had damaged the drives somehow, though most of the void shields were still holding. 'We need some distance, we need some time.'

'Ecclesiarchy squadron holding position,' said Haflói, standing beside Jorundur's throne. 'Its firepower's rolling out now.'

'So it is,' mused Jorundur. He'd guessed the Ecclesiarchy battleship would withdraw once its landers had made planetfall, but instead it was staying put, hovering over the landing sites like a vast golden vulture, its escorts clustered around. The *Immaculate Destiny* was the largest ship in the immediate void-volume by some distance, and when it opened fire, it detonated an impressive amount of plasma. It hadn't launched one of its orbital barrages again, but its regular broadsides were still huge enough to overload the realviewers when they went off, sending the lenses white and racing with static. 'Keep at range from that thing,' he ordered Suaka, feeding a slice more power to the plasma drives to kick out along the orbital zone. 'Treat as just another hostile – track the macrocannons, and report if you detect a lock.'

All the time, the death's head kept on coming. It was barging through the ship-clusters now, breaking a corvette across its prow as it advanced, heedless of the damage it took as the smaller craft's spine cracked and disintegrated. The cruiser looked strangely withered amid all the carnage, like a skin-stretched cadaver, its profile limned with corpse-light, its bony flanks strewn with wreckage. Its gun decks were open and firing, gaping with silvermawed cannons, spewing more of that ink-blot filth into the void as it came.

'Analysis, shipmaster,' Jorundur said, maintaining course but preparing to make a change.

'Pattern unknown, lord,' Bjargborn replied. 'My guess – only a guess – Heretic Astartes, battle cruiser-class.'

Jorundur nodded. 'Pain waiting for us on the inside too, then.' He shot a series of commands down to the enginarium, and pulled up a hololith of the volume immediately below. 'It'll launch boarders, if we let it. Prepare hard drop to five-six, on my mark, then loose main volley aft.'

Suaka looked up sharply. 'Lord, that will–'

'Course laid in, lord,' Bjargborn reported, giving her a hard glare. 'Ready for hard drop.'

The death's head picked up speed, shrugging off a raking scatter of solid rounds from a half-destroyed Ojada defence frigate before boosting clearly into transmit range. It was firing rapidly now, blasting a path through the tumbling debris with its forward batteries, making ready to strike.

'Launches detected!' Suaka cried. 'Boarding torpedoes incoming, eight signals, hull-breaking speeds.'

'Eight of them,' murmured Hafloí dryly, hefting his axe. 'They must rate us highly.'

'Attempting to get a lock...' reported Bjargborn. 'Hel. They're moving too fast.'

'Don't bother – they'll outpace a tracking augur,' Jorundur said. 'Just keep the drop primed.'

For a few seconds more, the *Amethyst Suzeraine* raced along at near full speed, plasma drives burning hard, taking the ship skating across the cap of Ojada's troposphere. The pursuing boarding torpedoes closed in quickly, corkscrewing through the firebursts. With its deadly cargo dispatched, the death's-head cruiser pivoted, rolling around and upwards to bring its cannon batteries to bear. Any moment now, it would open fire, smashing the *Amethyst Suzeraine*'s void coverage open and clearing a path for the incoming boarding parties. All the while, the torpedoes scythed in closer, closer, closer...

'Mark!' shouted Jorundur.

Bjargborn hit the controls, and the ship's power suddenly snapped out. Retros ignited, and the galleon smacked to a halt as if it had been stunned. It jolted, nose-down, then collapsed like a thrown anvil straight into the planet's gravity well.

Jorundur was yanked forward in his throne, Hafloí nearly hurled into the servitor pits. A cable severed, lashing across the upper galleries in a welter of sparks, and a whole rank of cogitators smashed loose of their moorings, crunching across the deck in a steel-denting cascade.

The galleon dived, all forward momentum killed, its main thrusters cold. The torpedoes, locked in by their machine-spirits, swooped after it, homing in on the tumbling mass ahead of them. A second later, and the *Amethyst Suzeraine* hit the upper atmosphere, scraping along it like a plough thrust deep into frost-tight earth. A plume of fire blazed out from the lower hull, flaring up around its flanks and surging into the semi-void. The boarding torpedoes activated crisis protocols and tried to pull out, battling hard against the sudden gravity-wrench.

'Torpedoes away aft!' Jorundur roared, fighting to keep his seat as the entire bridge shook around him. 'Full volley, maximum spread, away, away!'

Bjargborn had been hurled from his command seat by then, but scrambled back across a pitching deck and threw himself on the control lever, driving it open. The order sequence shot down to the launch bays, and the pre-targeted volley swooshed out of the rear tubes.

The torpedoes ignited as soon as they hit the wall of re-entry fire rearing up behind the plummeting galleon. As their warheads detonated, the torrent of flame bloomed into a gigantic plasma-field, a raging inferno that atomised everything within its rapidly expanding borders. The pursuing boarding tubes punched through the field, exploding into fragments as the extreme heat blew their casings apart.

'Now pull up!' Jorundur shouted. 'Get me full burn now, pull us out!'

The drives whined, shaking the entire vessel down, popping rivets and shivering brace-beams. For a moment it felt like they'd gone too far, that the planet would swallow them up and break them up across its tortured skylines, but then the old ship's thick hull came into its own, shielding them from the friction-burn just long enough, keeping the engines going, buying time for the wheezing old drives to propel them back into the true-void and hurl them up and out of danger.

Behind them, the plasma effect blew out almost as soon as it had started – a burst of intensity that had fried the galleon's rear quarters in a flash of sun-hot energies almost as badly as the boarding torpedoes it had been kindled to take out.

'Status,' demanded Jorundur, adjusting position within the throne.

'All boarding tubes destroyed,' called out Suaka, gripping her vibrating station with both hands. 'Heavy damage taken to keel sections and thruster arrays. Void generators blown on three sectors – attempting to compensate.'

Jorundur could see the alert runes for himself. 'Keep us moving. Ready defensive broadside – that thing won't have given up.'

It hadn't. Through the haze of las-beams and plasma, it ground its way after them, diving fast now, keeping its ranks of guns trained on them the whole time. It might have been a trick of the flickering light, but it almost looked angrier, driven into some higher pitch of rage by the loss of its precious warriors.

'Fire at will, master,' Jorundur ordered, watching the death's head rapidly gain ground. 'See if we can knock the grin off its bony face.'

Bjargborn relayed the orders, and the *Amethyst Suzeraine*'s nearside batteries went off, kicking the ship with its recoil and sending a broad spread into the void. Most shells flew wide or high, but a scatter impacted, wreathing the cruiser in kaleidoscopic curtains of void-stress.

'Counter build-up detected,' Bjargborn warned.

'Brace!' Jorundur called out.

The response, when it came, was horrific. The battle cruiser's arsenal was serious – adamantium-tipped shells, close-packed, well aimed and delivered. The sensors briefly registered the scale of the incoming pain, and then the volleys impacted, hammering across the rear void shields in a close sequence of crunching impacts.

The lumens blew, plunging them into darkness, before reserve units flickered back on. The bridge tilted crazily, thrown wildly as the entire structure listed. Warning klaxons blared, signalling systems failures across a whole range of decks, and half the lenses went dark.

'Critical augur failures,' Suaka called out. 'Losing full spectrum, both close and ranged.'

'Confirmed, lord,' said Bjargborn, sounding groggy, as if he'd taken a hit himself. 'We'll be running blind in moments.'

'Can you correct?' Jorundur demanded.

'Not from here,' Suaka said, unstrapping herself from her throne and getting up. 'Permission to take command in the sensorium – I could do something from there.'

'Go.' Jorundur glanced up at the realviewers, still clogged with ships and explosions, overshadowed by the looming orb of Ojada's fiery atmosphere. One by one, his tactical lenses were going dark, robbing him of the spatial computations he needed. 'As of now, I'm open to suggestions.'

'The battleship,' Hafloí said, gesturing through the realviewers towards the huge profile of the Ecclesiarchy vessel, still close in absolute terms and now wreathed in a furious firefight of its own. Enemy ships were streaming towards it like rats out of a sewer, but it was giving as good as it got, lighting up the void with blistering counter-barrages.

'It'll take us out itself,' Jorundur muttered, 'likely as not.'

'Any better ideas?' Hafloí countered.

The moment of indecision lasted just a fraction of a second. That was all Jorundur needed in order to assess the vectors, the odds, the likelihoods. Just as he did that, as if to ram home the message, a secondary salvo hit, slamming hard along the ship's ventral spars, blowing the lumens a second time and reducing the bridge to combat-lighting.

'Lay in an intercept course,' he spat grimly. 'I guess we'll see just what grade of bastards are on that thing.'

CHAPTER ELEVEN

The air stank of oil, the metal decks stank of oil, the people stank of oil. Those who had survived the onslaught now thronged across the gantries and the gang-ramps to the waiting shuttles, their robes and tabards filthy with it, their skin caked, their fingers greasy.

Even in normal times, the rig-city was acrid from the processors, but now, with the smog in the skies and the fires coming up from the ocean itself, there was no escape. Throats were scorched, eyes burned, skin blistered. Fresh slicks oozed out from cracked pipelines and burning cataracts fell down hab-levels, sluicing through the access grilles before slithering out over the tormented seas.

It took only moments for the pack to discover the name of their site – rig-station U56, designation Augedes, part of the major chain of processor cities running along the deep submarine trench below. The place was gigantic, composed of level after level after level, rising up in a confused cat's cradle of ironwork and steel-lattice, all spiralling about the huge central machine core. Like all the other stations, it had a single function – to suck promethium up from the planet's crust, to shunt it into the giant refinery coils, to crack it and split it and send the various grades foaming out into the receiving tanks, all ready to be piped to waiting cargo lifters for transport off-world. The necessary appendages of human life – hab-blocks, refectories, chapels, morgues – were strictly secondary to that, clinging to the edges of the enormous machine like limpets, strung around it on scaffolds and extrusions, rising in dizzying terraces over the turbulent seas as the pumps wheezed and the chem-stations bubbled.

Once inside, Baldr felt the weight of desperate humanity about him keenly, pressing on his mind like a fog. Since touching down, the pack had moved fast, breaking out from the landing site and pushing inward and upward. Aside from the roar of both surf and flame, the dominant sound was screaming, from above, from below, from all around. The entire population of the rig was trying to get out now. Most large transports must have left already, and those that remained were the unlucky or the dutiful, who had either stayed at their stations voluntarily or had been too slow or ignorant to see the apocalypse coming.

The pack broke up into a narrow plaza, surrounded by steep layers of manufactoria, all still working, gaining a view both up and down. Below them, dizzyingly far below, was the churning sea, sending columns of steam and smoke surging up the chasms between the levels. Above them were the high eyries of the defence towers and the landing stages, all now under sustained attack. Even as he watched, a swell-bellied personnel carrier was cracked open just after take-off. Its human cargo spilled out into the hot air, tumbling like chaff into the distant waves.

Remnants of defensive perimeters remained intact, strung around the major command towers, but it was clear that these would be overrun within hours unless reinforcements arrived. The only ships that touched down now, though, were those of the enemy, eager for the slaughter that they had been promised. All that remained, for the pack, was to race through it all, seeking out a landing station big enough to take the drop-ships they'd spied from orbit, clearing their minds of everything but the objective.

Hard, though, to hear all those screams, echoing down the open shafts and access-wells. Hard to let them fight on, without standing beside them, even for a single hour of defiance, just as they had done at the Mandeville point. It eroded the soul, this constant evasion – the time to stand and fight could not come soon enough.

Gunnlaugur set the pace, leading from the front, charging down the clanging gantries with his hammer swinging around him.

'Higher up,' he voxed, crashing through a half-blown hatch and thudding up a steep flight of stairs. 'Getting big clusters on the augur now, maybe twelve decks – could be them.'

They ran together, keeping tight, keeping close. The levels became claustrophobic – a maze of pipes and valves and thick girders, all hissing and overloading and threatening to burst apart with every heavy footfall. The decks were open mesh-metal, the roofs the same, so that one moment it felt like being buried inside an endless mountain of dark iron, and the next you were exposed to the tearing, howling elements, teetering on the edge of a sheer precipice with nothing but bowing steel plate between you and oblivion.

'Heat signatures ahead,' Ingvar reported, running just behind Gunnlaugur.

'You're getting a heat trace, in this?' replied Olgeir sceptically, lumbering at the rear with Sigrún ready to unload.

'Confirmed,' rasped Gunnlaugur, reaching a cracked gothic arch at the end of a long corridor. 'Our first taste of what's still here.'

They moved out onto a long open gallery perched high on the eastern flank of the rig. Along the left-hand side ran a sheer cliff of criss-crossed steel plates, many blown open to reveal machine-entrails leaking smoke from within. An empty deck stretched away down the centre, gaping with holes and strewn with the wreckage of vehicles and refinery control-stations. The right flank overhung the ocean, three hundred yards down, and petered out into a tattered wilderness of sprung rebar and rubble.

A barricade comprised of bullet-riddled rockcrete blocks, burned-out tank chassis and scorched metal piles had been strung across the central deck, less than six feet high, overlooked by the squat hulks of three gun towers. Around two hundred Ojada defence force troops hunkered down in the debris, their backs pressed up against the barricade wall. They were dirty, ragged, their dun-orange uniforms torn, their helmets dented. A few Chimera transports huddled in the lee of the gun towers. Mortar teams were unloading shells, but they had the exhausted look of soldiers getting ready to repel another push, possibly for the last time.

The four Space Wolves burst in among them, prompting startled yells of alarm and a hasty clatter of raised lasrifles.

'Do not be foolish,' Gunnlaugur snapped at the nearest of them, a woman who looked about to panic-fire into his chest. 'Get your commander.'

She blinked, froze for a second, then got her commander.

He proved to be a short, stocky man with a bloodied uniform and five-day-old beard on his blunt chin. He called himself Colonel-Inferior Jete Nefort, and was too fatigued to register more than a token surprise at four of the Emperor's Holy Angels suddenly appearing in the midst of his unit's engagement.

'I didn't know–' he started.

'You don't need to,' said Gunnlaugur, towering over him, his gauntlets still laced with the filigree snarls of Skulbrotsjór's active disruptor field. 'What's your tasking?'

Nefort ran a weary glove through his thick hair. 'Orders to hold the landing stages – there, up on the platform limit-ridge. We did it for three days, enough to get most of the carriers out intact, but then the enemy came through in numbers, and pushed us back. We're to hold here for relief.' He smiled dryly. 'I don't think that's coming.'

'And now?'

'Nothing. Comms dead since last night. We'll hold the line as long as we have a few power packs left. Nowhere else to go now but the sea.'

As the two of them spoke, Baldr and Ingvar both moved up to the barricade and peered through a wide rent at the summit. The long open central deck stretching away from them was disfigured with craters. A line of Administratum buildings had once run down the middle of it, fifty yards off, but all were roofless shells now. Beyond those, more wreckage, more shattered buildings, a severed pipeline, another burned-out gun tower, all overshadowed by the high uniform structure on the left flank. Baldr's helm zoomed in, sweeping across the debris for targets. Eventually he found them – eight hundred yards out, clustering for the moment behind their own defensive lines: multiple infantry bands in unidentifiable livery, at least four battle tanks with old Militarum insignias scratched out, a couple of troop carriers idling, some tracked artillery pieces being loaded. The troops were shrouded in machine-fumes, but were clearly making ready to push up the central avenue.

'We can take those,' Ingvar reported over the pack vox.

'There's something else,' said Baldr, without meaning to.

Ingvar looked at him sharply. 'What, brother?'

He didn't know. He didn't even know why he'd said it. The pain in his head, at his neck, was vivid, and getting worse.

'Nothing,' he said, hefting his bolter, falling back from the barricade. 'Forget it. This is the right path.'

Ingvar looked like he wanted to ask more, but Gunnlaugur came up to them with Nefort in tow, eager to press on.

'What's at the end of this deck?' Gunnlaugur asked. 'Your landing stages?'

'Affirmative,' Nefort replied. 'This is – was – the evac point for this sector, but they're using it now.'

'Could it handle an orbital lifter?'

'Doubtful. But three levels up, past the evac point, then you've got the main dock stage for the whole rig. That could, if it's still there.'

Gunnlaugur nodded. 'Get your troops together, load up all the kit you can carry.' He motioned towards Olgeir and the others in battle-sign. 'We'll get you back up there – if there's transports intact, we'll get you on them too.'

'Aye, lord!' Nefort blurted, his weary face lighting up with sudden hope.

'I want schematics, tac-readings, cartoliths – anything you've got for the next five levels up.'

'You're going further in?'

Gunnlaugur laughed. 'Just show me what you've got. Then we clear out this filth.'

Klaive lay on the cot, his hands clasped across his chest, mouthing words from the catechisms. He knew them all, of course, but it was only recently that he'd begun to really believe them. You could go a long way in the Church without ever really believing very much at all, as long as you knew the right answers to the right questions, and always looked the part.

Now, though, he'd been forced to confront his own mortality, over and over again. He'd had time to think about the things he'd done, the bodies he'd trodden over, the tombs he'd sealed up. He didn't regret much of it, not even now, except for the last few decisions he'd made – staying at Delvaux's side once the decision had been taken to make an example of Kefa Primaris, underestimating how far the Wolves would go to avenge a perceived wrong.

Still, there was no changing the past. They'd kept him alive, and so he'd made use of the time, recalling everything he'd learned in the seminaries, putting it into a kind of order in his mind, attempting to make fresh sense of it. And it helped, after a while. For the first time ever, he began to see how the doctrines of the faith might appeal to the weak. He'd always despised the observant masses – their desperation, their clinging to relics and rumours of miracles – but, once put for a while in their position, he could understand a little more of how they thought.

He'd always believed in the Emperor, of course, and seen himself as doing the Throne's work. Only now he could think of it as more personal, less about the grim calculus of world-death and sector-survival, more about divine intervention into the lives of His servants.

Now, his little world shook around him. Now, rust-flakes skittered across the metal plates of his cell as the *Amethyst Suzeraine* underwent its own form of purgatory. The ship had been attacked many times during his captivity. On some of those occasions he'd firmly believed death had come for him, and his mouthed benedictions had all been drawn from the Preparedness for Ascension manuals. This time felt different – more certain, more final. The impacts were so frequent, so close-packed, that it seemed impossible they'd last more than another hour or two.

This world, then, would likely be the one to end him. He'd even guided his captors here, so that had a kind of grim irony to it. Was there absolution for sins in life? Maybe, if there were, then this was his. He'd ended so very many souls, and been implicated in so very many exercises of dubious virtue, but perhaps this was a shabby kind of redemption, the only one he likely deserved.

And, of course, it looked probable that the Wolves were all going to die here, too. So that was doubly satisfying.

Then his cell door suddenly clanked. He raised his head – the bang had sounded nothing like the combat-noises from the hull, more like something set right outside.

He shuffled into a seated position, gingerly lowering his reddened ankles to the deck. If he'd had a weapon, he'd have reached for it.

Another clunk, then a high-pitched whine, then a flash of light under the door's edge. The lock-panel – a hunk of iron the size of his head – emitted a puff of smoke and shunted open. The hatch creaked on its hinges, revealing a woman bearing the garb of Collaqua's old corsair crew.

'What do you want?' he asked, shuffling back against the wall, guessing that they'd sent her to ensure he met his demise before the ship did.

'Servant of the Divine Emperor,' the woman said, hurrying inside and heaving the hatch closed behind her. Then she turned, made a fervent aquila, and bowed. 'I've been waiting for a long time. Ever since I discovered who they'd brought on board with them.'

Klaive tensed. If she was going to kill him, he'd rather she just got on with it. 'Oh?'

'Bad enough to have to work for that pirate dog,' she spat, with feeling. 'Worse, to take orders from these strutting beasts. I used to work for the scholas, you see? That was honourable work. I'd always dreamed of getting out, doing it again. Of putting it all right.'

'Forgive me, mamzel. I do not think I–'

'I am Ejika Suaka,' she said, speaking quickly, keeping her voice low. 'Listen. We do not have much time. I have shut down the augurs, but they'll be back up soon. There's a saviour pod primed and ready on deck seventy-eight. Here's a gun. Oh – your bonds. I've got the release here.'

She rummaged around in the backpack she'd pulled the autopistol from, and extracted a lock-breaker. It made short work of the manacles, and soon he was rubbing his ankles, trying to get blood back into them.

'They wouldn't understand the blasphemy they committed. I'd always wince, when they spoke about you, and they never noticed it. I'm sorry. For all of it.'

It was all so hard to process. It was all so totally unexpected. He hadn't even prayed for something like this, not for months.

'You have done well, my child,' he said, feeling like he had to extemporise. What did she think he was, exactly? Some sort of saint? 'I feel absolutely sure you were meant to do this.'

She smiled at him briefly, guiltily, handed him a ration pack, a set of overalls and a void-kit. 'I don't hate them. They're ignorant, that's all. But I had the chance, and I had to take it.'

Klaive got up, pulled the overalls on, checked out the weapon. 'I sensed you coming for me. In my dreams. Even in our darkest moments, we are never alone. But, tell me, child – this is blessed, good work, but I confess that I do not see everything clearly. We are at war, right now, is that correct? What did you intend next?'

'There's an Ecclesiarchy squadron, static off the starboard quadrant. The Wolves will make for it now, because they have no choice. Launch now, the pod can make it across. It'll be away before they notice a thing. You'll be safe.'

Holy Throne. She'd worked it all out. Of course, he might be blown to atoms on the crossing, or annihilated by the Ecclesiarchy's own guns before he got within range to hail, but it was worth a try. Anything was better than rotting in this corroding shit-heap while the Space Wolves' own hubris saw it torn apart.

He reached for her, clasped her hand, squeezed it.

'Perfect,' he told her warmly. 'But are you not worried, sister? For yourself, once they discover what you have done here?'

For the first time, she looked perplexed. 'Why would they?' she asked. 'I'm coming with you.'

His heart sank. Why did the simpletons, the needy, the soul-weak, always need to cling to him like this? Why couldn't they perform their service, and leave? What had he ever done to deserve this lingering, cloying company of fools?

Plenty, of course. He'd done plenty.

He smiled broadly, and squeezed her hand again.

'Just what I hoped you would say,' he told her. 'So now, let us go – they will surely be on our heels in moments.'

CHAPTER TWELVE

Gunnlaugur liked this world. He liked the way it smelled, he liked its elemental violence. It would have been good to linger here, to make a stand, crack some skulls while the lightning fell and the fires burned. The whole place would fall soon, of course – that had already been decided – but the Space Wolves had always enjoyed a fate-filled stand, one that etched a worthy doom onto the sagas. It mattered not how you lived, but how you died – was it a *good* death? Were you standing, at the end, roaring defiance? Did your enemies lie in heaps at your feet? That was how Gunnlaugur intended to go, looking his foes in the eye, beckoning them to come again, to test claw against hammer one last time.

To be deprived of such an end was the only fate worthy of fearing. That was why this hunt meant so much. If Ingvar was right, and Gunnlaugur was sure he was, then many of his Chapter brothers had died for nothing, their threads cut by an enemy who had never showed his face. That had to be avenged, even if it cost the pack everything in the process. The name of Fenris might be hated, might be scorned, but could never be mocked.

He vaulted over the barricade, thudding hard into the deck beyond, immediately powering into the run that would bring him to the enemy. Behind him, Baldr followed close, running hard, shedding for a moment the stricken aura he'd taken on. They were both out on the right flank of the long deck, skirting the edge of the long drop into nothingness, speeding through a broken landscape of torn-up battlements and deck-plates.

At the precise same moment, Ingvar and Olgeir had broken out on the left flank, hugging the deep shadow of the rig's soaring bulk. None of them had their disruptors kindled, and they went silently, keeping low, tearing across the ground like the smoke-gusts that went before and behind them.

Nefort had broken cover much earlier, and his troops were still advancing up the centre, racing between gaps in the plentiful cover, securing ground and regrouping before breaking out again. Their approach, though serviceably stealthy, had been detected by the enemy almost as soon as it had started. The renegades had responded instantly, cranking up their armour and trundling forward, each mobile piece flanked by jogging infantry platoons. The tanks moved up into shell range quickly, and started to pulverise the remains of the buildings in their path, angling their guns low and turning the deck into a maelstrom of flying masonry.

That suited the Space Wolves fine. The curtains of dust that surged up hid their advance. They tore past Nefort's advance on either side, keeping well wide of their positions, before powering onwards towards the oncoming enemy.

Once they arrived, the traitors never stood a chance. Fully occupied with targeting the ranks of Ojada troopers ahead of them, the pincer movement from out of the smog caught them entirely unprepared. Gunnlaugur pounced first, setting Skulbrotsjór alight as he emerged from clouds of grey, blowing the dust apart as the energy field snapped into snarling existence. Baldr sprinted close at his shoulder, carrying his rune-carved power sword. Neither of them would waste a bolt on this calibre of enemy unless they had to. Ingvar and Olgeir broke out from the opposite side, similarly bearing blades. Given the signal, Nefort's squads abandoned caution for a full-frontal advance, sweeping up through the wreckage to concentrate their las-fire into the centre of the enemy advance.

Gunnlaugur swung the hammer left to right, sweeping three startled enemy troopers from their feet and hurling them, broken, out over the rig's edge. He opened his throat as he did so, roaring both hatred and challenge at them, making the debris shake underfoot.

Baldr darted ahead of him, slashing with what looked like wild blade-movements, but that were angled with optimal precision. He broke through a knot of cultist fighters, slaying them quickly and driving a path towards the closest of the tanks.

The enemy were dressed in Imperial uniforms, a mix of them, some that might once have been Militarum, others that were worker-drab or vehicle crew, motley and torn, defaced with stitched-on emblems of foul patrons. Their faces, where visible, were sore-encrusted or bloated, distorted and scar-crossed, mutilated with metalwork or carved open down to the bone. Their death cries were like bird's calls, or abattoir beasts under the knife, and their stench penetrated even over the fug of spilled oil.

Gunnlaugur killed another fighter with a second swipe, then more, then more, taking pleasure in each cleaving of atrophied flesh. Skulbrotsjór flew freely around him, tracing heavy arcs, leaving streamer-trails of gore that cooked out on the crackling disruptor-flare.

He and Baldr reached the first tank at the same time, neither speaking to one another, just reacting the way they always did – with instinct, aligning around one another, blades blurred from speed and heft. A gunner in the high turret tried to angle his machine-cannon at Baldr, who leapt up, one foot on the chassis, wrenching the barrel from its mount and flinging it aside. Gunnlaugur slammed his thunder hammer into the nearside tracks, driving them inward, before reaching in with a free fist and hauling the segment-chain free of the housing, causing the entire vehicle to keel over on its axis.

They didn't even need to use grenades. Baldr clambered across the tank's roof, ripping open panels to get at the crew below. Gunnlaugur smashed his way down to the promethium tanks, using his thunder hammer's energy field to ignite the reservoir. By the time the two of them were done, loping onwards to the next target, the tank had blown itself apart, sending heavy metal components spinning high into the air.

There was nowhere for the enemy to go. The deck was a mess of collapsed masonry, hindering a retreat. In any case, they couldn't possibly move fast enough – when they tried, they were run down, hauled back, necks broken, spines snapped. Nefort's las-barrage kept them pinned while the Wolves did the real killing, rampaging through the lines with a hunger born of long void-confinement. Soon the rubble was painted red, the artillery pieces reduced to scrap, the vehicles hollowed out, the avenue to the landing stages cleared.

Only at the end of it did the pack unite again, joining up on the far side of the apron, their armour glistening and their weapons sizzle-hot.

'*Hjá!*' cried Olgeir, flexing his powerful arms, throwing them wide and laughing savagely. 'By my bones, that was fighting.'

'Aye, you looked like you were enjoying yourself,' said Ingvar, amused, shaking down his own blade.

Nefort's forces caught up, marching gingerly across territory they'd recently conceded, looking shocked to see that it still existed at all. The landing stages appeared reasonably intact, though the corpses of Ojada troopers hung from the perimeter palisades in clusters, stripped of their uniforms, many showing clear signs of excruciation. A few atmospheric transports still stood on the far edge, enough to take what remained of Nefort's command off the rig.

'Now get out, colonel,' Gunnlaugur told him, once he had made his way into their midst. 'Get out, get off-world if you can.'

Nefort hesitated, as if trying to work out if that was some kind of trick – a test of devotion, the kind of thing a commissar might pull. But it only took a glance upward, out to where the rest of the burn-off spires thundered and the crowds poured, screaming, across the disintegrating viaducts and crosswalks, to see that the rig-city above them was already overrun.

He swallowed, stood as tall as he could, and made the aquila. 'May the Throne preserve you, lord.'

Then his troops were running and hobbling towards the remaining transports, dragging their wounded and their rationcrates with them.

'They'll be lucky to get five miles,' said Olgeir, watching them go.

'Maybe,' said Baldr. 'But they've been lucky once already.'

Gunnlaugur stalked across the apron, towards the inner perimeter, where the jutting landing pads branched off from the main trunk of the rig-city's bulk. He looked at the terraces of the main spire running up and up, all of them spewing smoke. Viaducts led inward, both up and down, connecting with the stacked terraces and platforms within. The haze of battle made it hard to pick out details, but the scale of the destruction was clear enough. Even as they watched, a big control nexus on the far side of the high spire imploded, its inner decks collapsing, the entire structure sliding down into the sea in a riot of flame and spewed-out dust.

'The main terminals should be up ahead,' said Gunnlaugur, his helm-lenses cycling through the filth, zooming and augmenting. 'Five levels, northern sector, beyond that processor column.'

It was hard to imagine anything much remaining intact so high up, but then the Ecclesiarchy had sent down some heavy transports, with enough firepower, perhaps, to keep the hordes at bay for a few hours yet.

'Running short on time,' said Ingvar. 'Do you have a clear path?'

Gunnlaugur did – Nefort's cartoliths gave him a rapid ascent, one that took them right to the heart of the orbital receptor platforms. But he wasn't looking at that – he was looking at Baldr, who had moved past the perimeter, going stealthily, his hackles up.

'What have you seen?' Gunnlaugur asked.

For a moment, Baldr said nothing. He stood, motionless, appearing as if he was drinking in the vista of ruin before him, soaking up the madness of it. Gunnlaugur half-expected him to start walking again, like some revenant, dream-stumbling onward. He almost reached for his weapon, just as Olgeir was already doing.

But then Baldr spoke – clearly, no slurring, entirely himself.

'Quadrant five-six-three,' he said. 'I almost missed it.'

Gunnlaugur zoomed in on the coordinates, his armour-systems locking on and filtering the muck from the viewfield. Even then, it was hard to make out at first – a grainy mess of overlapping image-gauzes.

But then he got it. He saw what it was, where it was, where it was going, what it had already done. Within moments it would be between them and the objective, carving its way upward, the first, perhaps, of very many due to arrive here. It was as hateful to him as anything that drew breath, the breathing, walking embodiment of everything he had been schooled to loathe. Just watching it move – its glossy armour, its heavy tread, its sapphire lens-glow – made his fangs itch.

'Just one of them, you think?' said Ingvar, his voice a low growl. 'It's going our way.'

This made things harder. The longer they remained in this place, the harder they would get.

'Heavy-Hand, Fjolnir, take it out,' Gunnlaugur ordered. 'Gyrfalkon, come with me. Let's finish this.'

Bjargborn toiled as hard as he had ever toiled. Jorundur was pushing them all remorselessly, but then he needed to – this void-battle had turned into a bruising, grinding horror show in all directions. Every passing moment saw another ship either destroyed or withdraw crippled, most of them Imperial. The only reason the *Amethyst Suzeraine* was still alive was its late arrival to the carnage, and that meagre advantage was slipping away fast.

Jorundur shouted out orders from his throne while the bridge bounced and boomed around them all. The armaglass flashed from the detonations in the void, sending shadows swinging crazily across the cracked decks. Servitors carried on mutely, just as always, but the human crew were starting to lose their composure, yelling down order-tubes or slamming their fists in frustration on the control consoles.

Ahead of them, looming larger than before, was the Ecclesiarchy squadron, an island of stability in a turbulent sea of destruction. The warships were holding formation admirably, dishing out huge quantities of defensive las-fire. Their captain must have had nerves of steel to remain at anchor in such a frenzied warzone, but then they certainly had the guns to back up their position, at least for the time being.

Bjargborn had already implemented Jorundur's principal orders, giving the ship what it need to bring them racing hard under the squadron's shadow. The *Amethyst Suzeraine*'s plasma drives were still firing, albeit erratically, and their slingshot momentum from the troposphere manoeuvre had sent them barrelling along at a cracking rate, just enough to keep the pursuing barrage from their death's-head pursuer from tearing the weakened aft hull-plates off. Now he was working furiously on the augur arrays, trying to coax more than rudimentary sensor coverage back.

And it was only then that he saw it. The impacts had been real, the damage to the void shields had been real, but – yes, he was sure of it – the disruption to the sensors hadn't been.

'Lieutenant?' he voxed urgently.

Nothing came back. That wasn't interference. She'd turned her commbead off.

Bjargborn ran a quick locator-trace, and got nothing back. Then he overrode the malfunction alerts she'd put into the grid, and the *Amethyst Suzeraine*'s augur coverage started to flicker back into life, one array after the other.

'Thank the Allfather,' Jorundur grunted, as the lenses relit around him. 'Track for incoming major projectiles, but keep us boosting.'

But Bjargborn couldn't do that. He had a sick, cold feeling growing in the pit of his stomach. He had to find her. Deck by deck, he ran the anomaly checks.

'Shipmaster!' Jorundur called to him. 'Acknowledge, then enact.'

Bjargborn stood up, twisting around so he could address the throne directly. 'She's taken him, lord. They're headed for the saviour-pod decks.'

It was all he needed to say. Hafloí was running even before he'd finished the sentence, his heavy bootfalls making the decks shiver. Jorundur glared back, outraged, his voice instantly curdling with fury. 'Hel's teeth! Shut the launch decks down, then! Shut them all down!'

Of course, Bjargborn couldn't do that, not immediately. Suaka had known more about the ship's systems than anyone – that had been why they had kept her on – and every control-link on the bridge was disabled.

So he started to run himself, tearing after Hafloí, nearly losing his footing as the deck pitched and yawed, scrambling towards the rear archway and the maglevs down to the operations decks. His heart was already beating faster than before. Should he have suspected her? She'd never given any kind of hint of treachery – had she?

You don't have to like it, do you? she'd said. *Just keep your head down.*

But why do it? Why do anything to preserve that rat? Why risk a life for someone so evidently odious, so unconnected with her life and duties, when she had been treated well – something she'd admitted herself?

The questions crowded in his mind as he coursed through the decks, piling into an elevator and sending it racing down the access shafts. Every corridor was crowded with bodies running from one station to another, calling out orders, hauling munitions or equipment from station to station. The lumens kept blowing as the power fluctuated, and the entire hull-structure felt just a hair's breadth away from coming apart around him. The impacts kept landing – great booms that ran the length of the ship, testament to the continued pounding they were taking from outside. Bjargborn had seen the state of the surviving void shields before leaving his station, and dreaded to think how much longer they would hold out. Either Jorundur piloted them into some kind of refuge soon, or the rat might be the only one of them to get out of this thing alive.

The elevator clanged to a halt, the doors jerked open, and he was running again, sprinting along a narrow companionway before tumbling down into a wider corridor, one with twin rows of lumen-glowing hatches down the left-hand side complete with ladders, handholds and dispatch levers. The atmosphere-breach alarms were already going off, which gave him a further twinge of panic.

He reached an intersection and skidded around it, just in time to see Hafloí smashing his armoured fist against a bulkhead in frustration. A woman lay on the deck, the remains of her head blasted across the metalwork. Bjargborn didn't need to recognise the features to know who it was.

You fool, Suaka.

One of the pods was missing, its tube's access hatch sealed but whistling still from the decompression at its terminus.

Hafloí rounded on him. 'Too late,' he snarled.

Bjargborn grabbed a status-lens from the wall-panel and punched up a read-out. 'One saviour pod launched. Coordinates set from here. It's code-locked to the *Immaculate Destiny*.'

Hafloí mag-locked his axe to his thigh-plate, clunked his palm against a release-valve, and headed for the next pod along. 'You can replicate that tasking, yes?'

Bjargborn stared at him. 'Replicate that... I mean, yes. Yes, I can, lord.'

'Do it.' Hafloí wrenched open the tube's hatch, and fresh warning alarms blared out.

'Lord, there is no guarantee that–' He stopped then. What was the point? The master would know the risks more than him – Bjargborn's only function was to serve. 'By your will.'

'What in Hel, whelp?' he heard Jorundur's caustic voice over the comm.

'I'm going after it,' Hafloí replied coolly, clambering into the pod's entry hatch before cutting the link. The last Bjargborn saw before the hatch rammed closed was the helm, still bleached pale, smeared with ash and rune-outlines, strobing under the interior lumens of the pod cockpit as it counted down to launch.

He returned to the control panel, ensuring that Hafloí's pod had the same trajectory and machine-spirit taskings as the rat's had. As he keyed in the instructions, he reflected that Suaka had probably done just the same thing, only moments earlier, the last action she'd ever taken.

He pressed home the final sequence, twisted the valves closed and hit the enact rune. The pod's tube housing hissed wildly, the air inside the launch capillary venting rapidly, before the burners on the far side of the locked hatch ignited. With a thud of releasing clamps, the pod was loosed, thundering down the tube in a riot of thruster-flare and out of the hull.

Bjargborn drew in a deep breath. 'The Hand of Russ,' he murmured. 'May it surely guard you.'

CHAPTER THIRTEEN

The two of them ran swiftly from the evac-point, Ingvar and Gunnlaugur, climbing fast from the transport stage and heading up into the tangled maze of the rig's interior. It didn't take long to encounter more traitor fighters, kitted out much as the others had been, all in the process of looting or slaughter. The Space Wolves killed them where they found them, but did not linger over it. The levels passed in rapid succession – burned-out hab-units in bleak rows butted up against ferrocrete supporting columns, deserted pumping stations crammed with rows of chronos and pressure-valves, wind-blasted observer platforms ringed with thick pipe-runs and churning mixer-silos. They raced up creaking metal ladders, hand over hand, ever upwards, ever inwards, the salt-edged storm wind following them in and vying with the hot blasts from the inner fires.

Eventually they emerged high up on the northern edge of the rig-city. An open vista yawned away before them – an unimpeded view of the fire-edged ocean and its ranks of darkened platforms, all buffeted by the crash of wind-whipped waves, all surrounded by mixed columns of steam and smoke. The aerial combat had lessened in intensity as the defenders were winnowed out. Even as they watched, a pair of Ojada defence fighters ploughed into the water, exploding on impact and scattering wreckage across the glowing slicks. One by one, the rigs were becoming pyres.

Directly ahead of them was a far broader and more substantial set of landing platforms – octagons of raw ferrocrete more than three hundred yards across, overlooked by a brace of fortified control towers and ringed with high flaywire-tipped defensive parapets. Six heavy military-grade landers stood out in the open, still steaming from their orbital journey, tied down with cabling and guarded by several dozen soldiers in crimson armour with gilt detailing and high helms. Those guards looked well armed, carrying what looked like Militarum-issue lasrifles. A few of them had flamers, others projectile weapons.

About fifty more of them were occupied on the extreme far edge of the compound. Beyond those far walls, the screams and shrieks of onrushing traitors could just be heard over the engine-growl and gale-whine. To the left-hand side, the view of the open sky was blocked by the largest of the control towers – a many-tiered, blocky, slit-windowed bunker culminating in a mass of sensor vanes and twin-linked lascannons.

Ingvar slid down into cover, keeping his head low and his body pressed against a thick upright in the compound's perimeter fence. Gunnlaugur did the same behind another column, scanning through the slats.

'Frateris Militia?' he said. 'Or armsmen from the battle cruiser?'

Ingvar let his helm zoom in closer, cycling from one guard to the next. 'Too well armed for militia. Unless they're getting more brazen than ever.'

'No one's keeping an eye on them, this far out.'

Gunnlaugur glanced over to his left, to the main tower. The only obvious access was a broad gateway studded with guns, security lumens, hovering servo-skulls and more crimson-armoured guards. A series of troop carriers, also liveried in red and gold, lumbered under the arch, waved through by more of the guards. A brace of gun-servitors stalked jerkily in the lee of the sloping walls, their shoulder-mounted cannons tracking silently.

'It'll take some time to chew through all that,' Ingvar said, his thumb shifting up to his blade's energy field trigger.

'I don't see another way in.'

'Agreed. So how do you want to run this?'

Before Gunnlaugur could answer, a huge explosion rocked the northern edge of the compound. The shrieks of the rampaging traitors grew in volume, and more detonations went off beyond the far gun towers. Ingvar craned to get a look, and saw the linked lascannons swivelling to get a shot away northwards. As the neon beams scythed out, orders were shouted, and personnel carriers swivelled around, rumbling straight towards the source of the disturbance. Several guard squads, including one that had been stationed under the shadow of the gates, broke from their patrol routes and raced northwards.

'I guess we take what fate hands us,' Gunnlaugur said, thumbing his thunder hammer into life and leaping to his feet.

Ingvar moved with him, taking two frag grenades from his belt and hurling them over the perimeter. They sailed past the moored landers and exploded some distance beyond them, rocking the deck and sending rolling balls of flame out over the rockcrete. That diverted the attention of the already-depleted compound guards, prompting more yelled orders and hurried redeployment, by which time Gunnlaugur was smashing his way through the fencing. Skulbrotsjór, its heavy head blazing, made short work of the defence-plates. Once the fixings were shattered, Gunnlaugur shouldered through the remains, pushing clear onto the far side in a shower of rubble and metal splinters.

They covered the ground rapidly to the gates. Servo-skulls detected them the instant they were through the perimeter, and a flurry of raking las-fire broke out in their direction, skipping and pinging off the deck. The Space Wolves veered between it, swerving around the worst before reaching the first of the gate's defenders. Ingvar danced around a slow-moving gun-servitor, selling it a swerve before jinking back and smashing his gauntlet into its blank face. Gunnlaugur careered into two of the armsmen at once, breaking legs with a low swipe of his thunder hammer then swinging down to crunch through twin breastplates.

The remaining guards retreated, signalling the alarm and calling for backup.

Their panicked las-fire couldn't all be evaded, but it was too slow, too erratic, singeing their armour but never slowing them. Ingvar and Gunnlaugur had fought alongside one another for decades, and knew one another's movements so perfectly that they almost became a single target for the enemy – a combined entity that moved in a dazzle-pattern of plasma-blur and whirling blades. Just then, they fought as they had done in the years before their long separation, free of any thought but slaying.

As they reached the gate, the guards attempted to lower the blast-doors. Ingvar switched to a brief bolter-blast to clear the approach while Gunnlaugur took out the panel operators. Then they were inside, sprinting through the dark, into a low-roofed interior that smelled, like everywhere else on that rig, of blood and oil in equal measure.

It wasn't long before they saw the bodies. Crimson-armoured guards, just like the ones they were still fighting, sprawled out on the decks in bloody piles. Those still standing fought back, where they could, but in the dark confines of the interior the Wolves were ferocious and gave them no quarter. Strewn amid the bodies of the armsmen were other corpses, harder to spot in the gloom, wearing what looked like black, close-fitting carapace battleplate.

'What is this, now?' Gunnlaugur asked, lashing Skulbrotsjór into a squad of retreating guards before rampaging down a long antechamber after them. 'Archenemy? Already inside?'

Ingvar returned to bladework, his sword flaring in the shadows. He stole a few glances at the flash-framed corpses on the deck. There were many fewer of the black-clad warriors, and their livery was strange – highly engineered plates, lined with thin edges of silver, evidence of unusual weapons in their gauntlets. There weren't many of them. Had they been fighting alongside the armsmen? *Against* them? They didn't look anything like the traitor rabble encountered so far, but you could never be sure – the enemy possessed warriors from a thousand worlds and a thousand warbands.

'Something's strange here,' was all he said, driving onward, focusing his mind on the deadly movement of his blade, keeping the momentum going.

'Aye, that it is,' grunted Gunnlaugur, breaking through into an assembly area – a vaulted chamber riven with las-blast marks and blasted supporting beams – and racing onward towards a steep set of bloodied stairs. Light bled down from the level above, and the sounds of movement, and shouting, and guns opening up in desperate volleys. Nefort's cartoliths identified the level above as the command centre, the heart of the complex. 'Not far, now. We pick up the pace.'

Despite it all, Ingvar smiled to himself then. They were already tearing through the resistance at a truly blistering rate, streaking towards the location they had burned planetwards to find. Gunnlaugur's impatience to end this, given the carnage they had already inflicted, felt almost obsessional.

But then Ingvar shared that obsession too. He had been the first to succumb to it, out in the hot sands of another doomed world, and it had been through him that the entire pack now shared it. Now, finally, he could dare to hope that they were drawing close to its source, to the fountainhead of it all, the place where the secret had started, and the place where it would be extinguished.

So all he said was, 'Aye, vaerangi,' a note of tight eagerness catching in his throat, and the rate of murder duly increased.

Olgeir charged down the gang-ramp, his boots resounding from the stressed metal, his shoulder-guards scraping under the low roof above him. Baldr came just behind, sprinting to keep up.

Neither of them spoke. Both had switched to bolters. They ignored those they witnessed on the way down, whether rampaging cultist or fleeing Imperial citizen. Only one living soul held their attention.

The release of combat had, for a time, been something like joy. To wield weapons, to slay the foes of the Allfather – this was why they had been made. They needed to exercise those muscles, to keep sharp, to kindle the war-spirits that had been fused deep into their blood and soul. The traitor rabble they had cleansed from the evac-point had been nothing more than that – an exercise, a way to stretch their limbs and loosen their joints.

This was different. Now, every movement was made with perfect deliberation. Their twin hearts both beat hard, flooding their systems with hyperadrenaline. When the moment came, there would be no joy now, only intense hatred, perfect concentration.

Olgeir swerved around the corner at the base of the ramp and careered along another enclosed corridor. A few mortals trying to go the other way were barged aside at speed, flung into the inner walls as if hit by a skidding groundcar.

'I have a fix,' Baldr voxed.

'So do I,' Olgeir replied, his voice a tight snarl. 'It's reached the bridge.'

They were so high up by then that the rig structure was like a crown of thorns around them – interlaced pinnacles of comm-spires and hab-towers, all strung together by a network of high-slung bridges and maglev tracks. Some of the interconnectors were flimsy, traversed only by chain-tethered servitors as the winds screamed around them, but others were heavy-beamed viaducts, crammed with ground traffic in normal times, their walkways stuffed with crowds of shuffling workers. One of these was the intercept point, the route leading from the burning interior out to the orbital landing platforms – a many-arched ferrocrete bridge, multi-laned, stack-tiered, overlooked by high towers and swathed in thick clouds of acrid smoke.

Now it was desolate, punched with craters, its asphalt surface broken up like choppy waves. Blackened vehicle chassis peppered the deck surface, some private units, some empty personnel carriers. A ruined tank was embedded in the viaduct's structure some way down, teetering over the steep drop, its engine compartment still on fire. Warriors rampaged across the viaduct, scuttling in ramshackle units from cover-point to cover-point, all of them wearing ragged traitor uniforms. None of those were worth a damn – they were the chaff of this invasion, the disposable fodder sent down to overwhelm mortal defences.

But among them came a different proposition entirely. It was taller even than the Wolves, bloated upward and outward by long exposure to fell energies. Its armour plate was ancient, cracked and changed, but still bearing the surface colour of its long allegiance – turquoise, marred by discolouration, semi-glossy like antique shellac. The icon of the hydra was still visible on its thick shoulder-guard, picked out in faded white ink. It carried a fine-looking bolt pistol in one fist, embellished with ivory chasing and glowing from its heat-outtake. It carried a short-bladed power axe in the other, which crackled with a thick sleeve of disruptor energy. It advanced ponderously, its cloven hooves making the asphalt crease.

The mortal warriors kept well away from it – those in front ran harder, those behind hung back. The very air about it seemed charged, as if quickened with radiation or thickened with spores. Its movements occasionally blurred, not from speed, but from something uncanny in its aura – a shift, maybe, fractionally, into a shadow-realm of broken possibilities.

Olgeir charged straight at it, never missing a beat. Baldr switched out left, running just as hard as before. Both opened fire with their bolters, dousing it in a drum roll of hits and surrounding its armour in messy splash-patterns of blown sparks.

It fired back instantly, snapping off rounds that made both of them swerve and duck. Even while smothered in a rain of mass-reactive impacts, it somehow kept firing, never making any effort to evade, just marching onward. Olgeir saw the lacquer blasted off its armour, gouging lines of grey-silver ceramite, but still it waded onward, clad in a jump-cut cloak of interference. It looked to be half shifting in and out of existence – shrouding, stuttering, lurching a hand's breadth to one side, then jerking forward, back, stooping or rising.

'Blades,' Baldr said, weaving his way through the vicious rain of bolt-shells.

'Aye, make it bleed,' Olgeir agreed, mag-locking Sigrún and drawing his own short-handled axe.

The gap between them shrank to nothing. The creature stowed its bolt pistol and brought up its own axe, a master-crafted piece that left a smear of heat-shimmer in the air behind it. The three blades clashed into a pyramid of explosive energy, throwing out a blast wave that sent the ash bouncing for twenty yards in all directions.

Olgeir put all his strength into the blow – two-handed, heavy as lead bars, aimed at the creature's neck-joint. Baldr swiped in low, driving at the cabling under the breastplate. Impossibly, the enemy managed to block both, the outline of its arm flickering as if on a faulty vid-feed, before it threw them both off and came back at them.

The creature's own blows were perfectly aimed, fast, just as heavy as theirs, surrounded in that corona of diffusion that made them hard to pick, hard to defend. Olgeir and Baldr hacked and parried, their limbs pumping, stepping back, leaning in, dropping to a knee before powering back up, going for the opening. The three of them created an enclosed vortex of movement, fast as thought, making the outside universe an irrelevance of sluggish ineptitude. This was pure Astartes combat, uncompromising, motivated by powerful and eternal hatreds.

The flurry of blows was titanic. The decks flew to slivers under them, the smoke clouds were driven into whirling threads. Two of the fighters operated purely on the physical plane, but the third had something else, something esoteric, something that made its orientation strange, its movements somehow super-positioned.

That gave it the edge. After a blistering exchange in which its armour was lacerated by a diagonal down-drag from Olgeir, it seemed to shift horizontally by a blade's-width, adjusted posture in a microsecond, raised its arms, then crashed its axe-head down.

The blade hit Olgeir on the shoulder-guard in a cataclysm of released energy, throwing him backwards. Olgeir braced to kill the momentum, but the ground beneath him cracked open, riven by wriggling slivers of force. He teetered for a fraction of a second before an entire section of the deck collapsed, taking him down amid a billowing plume of thrown-out dust and flame.

Baldr had to shift fast to avoid being sucked down too, fighting all the while, keeping the creature at bay with a whirr of parries. The collar at his neck was burning now, searing through his armour as if it were made of silk rather than ceramite.

The creature fought on, hammering at him, slicing at him, pushing him back, step by step, manoeuvring him closer, closer to the looming edge. And then, for the first time, something other than ragged breathing came out of its slanted vox-grille.

'Son of Russ,' it said, the voice a bizarre mix of machine-grind and saliva-thick slurring. 'You should *not* be here.'

Baldr fought back. His arms were flooded with lactic acid, his twin hearts thudding hard and fast. He was aware of the drop behind him, and felt the deck flex underfoot as the impacts weakened it. It was all he could to evade annihilation, let alone shift the contest back to firmer ground.

'You must be *lost*,' the creature said, musingly, its limbs still punching, scything, jittering. 'You must have been lost for a long time.'

Baldr's heels grazed up against the viaduct's kerb, and he felt the whistle of the wind at his back. One more strike would send him over. He tried to resist the crushing weight, to find a way through, to turn the tide. As he did so, his vision began to shake, to rip away at the edges.

'But I was not *lost*, Son of Russ,' the creature said, giving away neither pleasure nor sorrow, just a kind of intoxicated slide of words over words, as if reeled from some infernal machine-feed. 'I was *there*. On your mountains. On your *ice floes*. Would you like to see what we *did* to them?'

The collar went white-hot then, blotting out the light from all other sources, throwing out snaking whips of pale flame. Baldr had to fight to retain consciousness, let alone resist the flurries of incoming blows from the axe. Visions started to crowd in, pushing out the real world, overlapping and cycling in mad succession.

'We did *this*, Son of Russ,' the creature hissed, pressing in for the kill. 'We did *this*.'

Baldr roared in pain and fury, kicking back, putting everything into one final, desperate push. His sword-blade shattered the visions, plunging through them like glass, finally biting deep. Thrown off balance by the unexpected breakthrough, he thrashed onwards, trying to press the advantage.

'Ware your blade, brother!' roared Olgeir, looming back up out of the vision-tendrils, covered in rubble-dust and with a half-severed shoulder-guard. 'I'm not gone yet.'

Baldr didn't have time to wonder how Olgeir was back, nor why he was back, so just fought on, angling his onrushing sword-edge so as not to take out his own battle-brother.

But it was Olgeir who did the real damage, crunching his gauntlet out and catching the creature full in the face, followed by a succession of close-range axe-strikes that tore clean into its witch-forged armour. That broke the spell, stilling the visions and banishing the strange dislocation effects, enabling both of them to pile in further, never giving it a moment to recover, ripping out cables, slashing through connective membranes, releasing gouts of the foul gases that fermented within its ruined shell, stamping on it as it tried to rise, hacking down, slamming down, again, again, until the blood ran black from its ravaged, exposed flesh and the last gurgled heaves for air gave out.

Finally, panting heavily, sheened in sweat, the two of them stood over the broken corpse. Olgeir dropped to one knee, hauling in breaths.

'Eye of Morkai!' he chuckled. 'Just one hand-grip! That's all I had. On another day, I'd still be falling.'

Baldr couldn't laugh. His collar had stopped raging, but the pain remained, seared on the flesh of his neck. Worse than that, he could hardly see. The creature's projections still crowded over one another in his mind, as vivid as if real.

He lowered himself down, leaning onto his hands, shaking his head from side to side, trying to clear them.

'Brother,' said Olgeir, suddenly serious. 'Are you injured?'

For a few moments, he couldn't speak. All he could see were the boiling seas, the silver lightning in ice-dark skies, the laughter on the frozen wind.

'It is gone,' he gasped, balling his fists, trying to recover, his nostrils full of the stench of the dead traitor that lay before him. 'All gone. Ruins.'

'What is?'

Baldr looked up at him, feeling sick with the horror of it, sick with the certainty that it was true. 'Fenris. They've sacked Fenris.'

CHAPTER FOURTEEN

He had genuinely hesitated over killing her.

It would have been safer, probably, to keep her alive for the crossing, seeing as how she had known so much about the ship and its systems. Right at the end, as she'd completed the machine-spirit incantation and inputted the trajectory data, he'd stayed his hand, looking at the way she was concentrating so hard, her eyes bright with the certainty of what she was doing. From their brief snatches of conversation on the hurried route down to the saviour-pod banks, he'd learned more of her life and character. She had always been devoted, he discovered. She'd read the catechisms in private, learning them by heart, becoming convinced that one day she would find a way to put them into practice. It must have been hard to have lived that life under the corsair captain. It must have been almost as hard to have done so under the rule of the Space Wolves, who had never cared much for orthodox devotion. So that was all very impressive. He wasn't blind to such considerations. He admired her. And, in all likelihood, he owed her his life.

In the end, though, you had to make the hard choices. Once he got to the *Immaculate Destiny* – assuming he made it – it would look strange to be in the company of a random, non-Ecclesiarchy officer. He would have to explain why she was with him. She might want to talk for herself. And that would make things complicated – he wasn't sure yet how he was going to explain his presence in Ojada, or how it would go with the authorities on the battleship, who might have been drawn from any one of a hundred different factions within the labyrinthine Church hierarchy. It was too much of a risk to keep her, just in case she said or did something stupid.

Still, she had died for a just cause. Her soul was with the Emperor now, and all he had really done was hasten that process. It was a shame, of course, something he could genuinely regret a little, but unquestionably the correct thing to have done.

Right now, however, he had other things on his mind. The saviour pod was a tiny thing – a capsule of metal barely sixty feet long. He was strapped in tightly to a long ridge running down its centre, his limbs bound against metal clasps and his neck padded. Even so, the experience was horrendous – the centrifugal forces were colossal as the pod corkscrewed and twisted its way towards the objective, auto-avoiding explosions and incoming fire-lanes the whole time. It felt like his internal organs would be shaken loose, his teeth scattered across the low-grav interior, his knuckles rubbed raw. Months of confinement had eroded what little physical condition he'd originally possessed, and he felt like he might pass out at any moment, or vomit, or both.

He couldn't see anything. There were no viewscreens, just a few tiny rune-displays telling him things he couldn't understand. He could hear nothing but the roar of the directional thrusters, feel nothing other than the buck and slew of the pod's progress. It was like being locked inside some uniquely awful sensory-deprivation chamber. For all he knew, the rest of the galaxy had ceased to exist, leaving only this echoing, vibrating, roaring hell-room.

In truth, though, the transit time was only short. Saviour pods travelled at impressive speeds for as long as their fuel cells lasted, aimed at making planetfall as quickly as possible. The void distance between the *Amethyst Suzeraine* and the *Immaculate Destiny* was, by the time of launch, not great. Though buffeted by proximal plasma-bursts, soon it was racing into contact with the battleship, all the while broadcasting the cipher-codes Klaive had given Suaka, the ones identifying the occupant as being a high-ranking Ecclesiarchy official in need of assistance. Without that, the certainty was that the saviour pod would have either been shot out of the void or smashed across void shields.

He tried to relax, to unclench his rattling teeth, to keep his fingers from fusing to the handholds. At any moment, he expected to feel the hot rush of flame, followed by the icy oblivion of space.

Neither occurred. The first he knew of the change was an alteration in engine-pitch – a huge rise in volume, as if the thrusters had passed through a narrow tunnel. Then came the shuddering, bone-jarring deceleration, followed by a crunching halt that sent his head driving back into the padding. After that came alarms, the muffled sound of shouts, boots clanging overhead, the whine of cranes and drills. He felt nausea rise up in his gorge, and struggled to keep from vomiting. He blinked hard, trying to remain fully conscious, flexing his aching muscles inside the restraints.

The hatch was twisted open, and two guards wearing crimson battleplate piled inside. One, dressed in a captain's uniform, pointed a laspistol at his forehead, the other scanned the interior for other occupants.

'Code-sequence,' the captain ordered.

Klaive told him, trying to make his voice more than a strangled squeak, hoping he'd remembered it correctly. The guard paused for a few seconds, evidently sending a request for confirmation higher up, then nodded.

They pulled him out of his restraints, looking warily at his dirty overalls and general state of dishevelment. He was given something for his nausea, a cup of water, then moved onto a mag-train for transmission to the upper levels.

'Your pod's origin-point was unmarked,' the captain told him as the unit rattled down the tunnels. 'It was almost destroyed, even with the codes received. Where did you eject from?'

By then, Klaive was beginning to recover himself a little. The next few moments were important. He was a confessor of the Imperial Cult, a figure of heft and dignity, counsellor to cardinals and canonesses. If he was to survive, then chart a course to redemption, he would have to act like it.

'I will speak to your commander only,' Klaive said, not deigning to look at the man. 'Until then, remain silent.'

The captain hesitated, and for a moment looked like he might press the issue. Eventually, though, he turned away, gazing stonily ahead, saying nothing. The mag-train juddered onward in silence after that. Habits of deference in the Ecclesiarchy ran deep.

Klaive was taken higher up, escorted at every stage by a platoon of armsmen. He took a look at their insignia when he got the chance – he didn't recognise it, but that meant very little. This was clearly the personal ship of a cardinal, and there were thousands of those, all powerful in their own right, some commanding huge fleets and military assets. If he'd had to guess, he'd have said they were of the Terran Holy Synod rather than the Ophelian division, perhaps close to the Throneworld itself. The equipment he saw was good, and the forces mustered were significant. Unlike the *Amethyst Suzeraine*, which clanged like an empty censer every time it was hit, the *Immaculate Destiny* appeared to be weathering the storm well, with barely a sign of the riotous destruction going on outside penetrating to its cavernous interior.

That all changed when they reached the highest tier of the command bridge. The space was huge, thronged with hundreds of staff working in tight-packed ranks. A great armaglass roof yawned away above the operational decks, barred with lead and crystal, giving a panoramic view of the carnage over Ojada. Ships wheeled and dived before them, some burning, some discharging weapons, all surrounded with flashes and plumes of light. The stricken planet itself occupied the lower third, an arc of blood-blotched orange laced with black bars of soot and ash. The decks underfoot trembled at regular intervals as the battle cruiser opened fire, briefly outshining all other light-sources as its gun decks were unleashed.

Armsmen were everywhere, all decked out in the crimson and gold. Klaive was escorted up a wide flight of marble steps to where the whitestone command throne stood under a wall of gold-leaf statuary. Candles burned in iron stands, throwing warm, flickering illumination across the finery. Heavy embroidered drapes hung down from frames in the high vaults, all depicting scenes from the lives of saints and martyrs. Priests moved reverently among the crew, followed by hovering skulls and shuffling incense servitors, murmuring benedictions as they went.

Ahead of the throne stood the battle cruiser's senior counsellors and commanders – more than thirty men and women decked out in absurdly elaborate ceremonial armour. His escort brought him into the heart of the group, presenting him to the one obviously in charge.

'My lord cardinal,' the armsman captain said, bowing low. 'The occupant of the saviour pod. Confessor, this is Cardinal Axith Orquemond.'

The man he addressed was nearly a head taller than all those around him. He wore heavy golden armour, finely made and decorated, giving a bulk and presence only a little less than a Space Marine. A thick velvet cloak, trimmed with ermine, hung from broad shoulder-guards, and a longsword in an ebon scabbard hung at his belt. He went unhelmed, and his bald head was earth brown, with tight features and pale green eyes.

He was a warlike man, clearly; a man more at home in the thick of battle than the cloisters of a cathedral. Many cardinals were like that, given the times they lived in. Delvaux had not been. When this one spoke, his voice was calm, almost scholarly in its precision, but the self-command it betrayed was absolute.

'Confessor,' Orquemond said, inclining his severe head a little. 'Throne be praised that we could preserve you.'

Klaive bowed low, just as the captain had done. He had to go carefully, here. 'You are the veritable instrument of providence, my lord cardinal. I give Him thanks for it.'

Orquemond regarded him carefully. His eyes remained narrowed, as if gauging a possible threat. His gauntlet, encrusted with jewels, remained close to the hilt of his greatblade. 'As you can see,' he said, 'we are fully engaged here. I had to lower a section of shielding to bring you in, and that was not done lightly.'

'My sincere thanks.'

'Perhaps, then, you might tell me what you are doing here.'

'Assuredly,' said Klaive, beginning the charade. 'I was sent here on the orders of Canoness Alexis de Chatelaine. My ship was detained in the warp for many weeks, losing a third of its crew. By the time we arrived, we were unprepared for what awaited us. We attempted to make planetfall, but sustained heavy damage. I was among those who attempted escape, once it became clear just how extensive the battle was becoming. I must assume that the ship that brought me – the *Glorious Resolve* – has been destroyed, and that the majority of saviour pods were also lost. I take it, lord, that mine was the only one you tracked?'

'We briefly picked up another, but the signal was lost.' Everything about the cardinal's demeanour remained wary, suspicious. 'So what was your business here?'

Klaive let a sorrowful droop colour his features briefly. 'As it has been for many years, my lord – war. The canoness was preparing to mobilise her forces, but ran critically short of supplies. Her chamber's promethium reserves were depleted. I was sent to negotiate a preferential rate of supply, making use of Cult prerogatives. It grieves me to observe that my mission was always destined to be futile.'

Orquemond's eyes never left his. 'You had no idea that war had reached this world.'

'None, my lord.'

'Yet you must have known that there was risk. The entire sector is in turmoil.'

'There is always risk, my lord. The canoness knew it, too. I must hope that she has found a way to serve, in my absence. It seems that all worlds are engulfed, now.'

'That they are. No generation of mankind has seen the like.'

Klaive glanced up at the armaglass panes again, seeing the battle raging beyond the void shields – a silent procession of ship-kills and orbital launches. The fury and scale of it was breathtaking. It was hard to imagine that the *Amethyst Suzeraine* could last long in its embrace. Perhaps it had already been annihilated, and his long nightmare of subjugation was definitively over. At any rate, even if the galleon somehow lasted a little longer, it could hardly trouble this magnificent battleship.

'And, so, my lord,' he ventured carefully, 'can I assume that your presence here is of a similar nature? Are you here to turn back the tide of invasion?'

Orquemond's mouth turned up a little – just a fraction, the merest hint of dark humour. 'You are no strategist, I see. We are fighting at this moment for survival. If we do not leave Ojada within four hours, escape will become impossible. Everything we have is currently focused on keeping a path open, here, in this place.'

Of course, Klaive knew that already. He knew why they had come here, and what they planned to do. Only the names and the particulars were still a mystery. He decided to push his luck, and press a little more.

'Forgive me, my lord. I do not understand.'

At that, the cardinal beckoned for him to move closer to the edge of the marble dais. His various counsellors and adjutants moved to make room, and soon Klaive was staring out at the view planetwards, unimpeded and in perfect focus. Targeting hololiths were imposed on the realviewer's field, picking out a single location on the surface – a rig-city. Various picter lenses mounted all across the dais sent image-feeds from ground level.

'Maybe it was providence that brought you here indeed, confessor,' said Orquemond. 'One of our brothers of the Church is on that world, under siege within his citadel – His Holiness Cardinal Astra Leon Chirastes, once commander of one of our finest battle groups, latterly given over to his own endeavours. We have come for him, risking destruction. In truth, we did not know what state Ojada would be in when we set off. Some believed it would have been spared desecration and that we would be free to reach him unimpeded. Others feared, rightfully as it turned out, that we would arrive to find it in flames. We have cut it fine, that is sure, but just on the right side of the blade. Throne willing, we shall leave here with our mission complete.'

Leon Chirastes. Klaive knew the name, if only by reputation. Once one of the greatest of the Synod, talked of as a possible delegate to the Council of Cardinals on Terra, a driven man with a reputation for decisive martial action. Decades ago, it had seemed possible he would come to dominate the politics of the Church, only for his flame to suddenly gutter out, as if extinguished by some vengeful, hidden fist.

'Then I am glad to be here to witness your action, my lord,' he said, not having to feign his eagerness this time. 'Thank the Throne you have arrived to take him to safety.'

At that, Orquemond smiled again, though this time with even less evident humour. He stared up at the viewscreens, a hard expression on his hard face.

'Take him to safety?' he asked. 'No, I do not think you understand, confessor. We are not here to evacuate him. Chirastes is a renegade, one who has jeopardised a century's worth of careful labour in pursuit of his own private obsession. I am here to punish him. Even now my troops are closing in, preparing to bring him back to me in chains. I plan to look into his eyes as I pass judgement. I plan to discover the full extent of the damage he has done before I end him, here, on this ship.'

Klaive didn't know what to say to that. He just stood, stupidly, following the cardinal's gaze as the viewscreens ticked over with fresh evidence of combat. This was a surprise. It made things more precarious. He needed to think, to plan again, and hope he hadn't incriminated himself already.

'He is defending what remains of his kingdom,' Orquemond went on. 'The extraction is taking longer than I'd hoped, despite the resources expended on it. Still, there are only two outcomes now. Either my troops detain him within the current standard hour, enabling the Emperor's Justice to be served in person, or I shall light the orbital lasers and destroy the city from here.'

Jorundur kept the drives at full burn, angling and tilting to evade the worst of the beating that he was being handed. Every passing minute brought another echoing smack that made the combat-lumens shake. His void coverage was down to minimal now, meaning that a solid hit from virtually anything would strip them of the last protection they could rely on.

He was so focused on the flight for survival that he barely noticed Bjargborn's return to his station, reeling across the listing deck and throwing himself into his throne.

'Close augurs back online!' the rivenmaster shouted.

'That fool's launched himself out of a pod-tube, then?' Jorundur asked.

'He believed he could overtake the prisoner, lord,' Bjargborn replied, swivelling on his throne's supports and patching in a fresh tracker.

'He'll do nothing but blow himself to Morkai's kingdom,' Jorundur sighed. 'Try to locate the pod, if you can.'

The *Amethyst Suzeraine* dived down steeply, heading towards the nadir of the battle-sphere, before pulling out and twisting away to port, barely evading the latest salvo from the death's-head battle cruiser. The distance between the two ships was now very tight – soon they would be out of space to make any kind of useful evasions.

'Broadcast Imperial idents on all open channels,' Jorundur ordered to his comms staff, who were proving slow to react in the absence of Suaka. 'I want that Church battleship to know just who we are.'

The Ecclesiarchy squadron was right up ahead now, ringed with its concentric circles of fire, rocked by the volume of incoming ordnance but still doling out plenty of its own. Despite everything going on around it, it hadn't moved at all – just weathered the storm. That felt strange. Even if it was here for an evacuation, it could have pulled up higher, maintaining comms, keeping itself intact and ready for a fast system exit. For some reason, the captain was maintaining station, just where he had been when he'd fired the initial orbital laser barrage.

Still, that made things a little easier for him, at least. A few hundred miles less to survive before they put things to the test.

'Gunnery deck, I need maximum spread, full complement aft,' he voxed. 'What can you give me?'

'Reloading, lord!' came the frantic reply from the lower decks. In the background, Jorundur could hear the echoing booms of the breeches closing. *'Aiming to deliver volley within twenty seconds!'*

That might well be too long. 'Make it ten. Your target vectors have been dispatched.'

Jorundur glanced at the ranged tactical lens. The death's-head battle cruiser was coming about again, aiming to cut them off from their escape route. It was going for broke now, flaying its drives to get into strike position. Ahead and above were the bellies of the Ecclesiarchy ships, dominated by the vast hull of the battleship itself. They were dark against the distant void, lit into silhouettes by the firestorms around them.

'Old Dog!' came the crackling voice of Hafloí over the comm. He was barely audible, his words a hiss of static amid the roar of interference.

'You damned fool!' Jorundur thundered. 'Where in Hel are you? Get back on board before I-'

'Too late,' came the reply. *'Managed to... lower decks, somewhere... no tactical, but flew blind for a... voids down, got inside, now... aim to get to bridge.'*

Before Jorundur could reply, the gunnery master succeeded in launching his volley, and a brace of shells flew aft, targeted at the death's head's prow as it turned. The intention was not to cripple it – they had no power for that, now – but to signal to the observers on the *Immaculate Destiny* where their allegiance was.

The shells impacted, mangling the pursuer's voids for a moment or two and jolting it off course by a mark.

'You're on the Church ship?' Jorundur demanded, pulling up the damage reports as he reset the *Amethyst Suzeraine*'s trajectory again. Now it was about speed.

'... lower decks, I think. Smells... yes, it's bad. Going... main bridge level.'

'All engines, maximum burst!' Jorundur called out to Bjargborn. 'Hammer them, everything we have, and ignore the tolerances.'

The ship responded instantly, leaping as if kicked. They surged up towards the Ecclesiarchy squadron, ignoring the hits they took, no time left for evasive action, just thundering to the goal as if all the hounds of Hel were on their heels. As they went, the tactical alerts all went red.

'Massive power build-up reported!' Bjargborn shouted. 'They've got their shot!'

'Outrun it!' growled Jorundur, gripping the arms of the throne. The Ecclesiarchy ships were just spitting distance away – in a second the *Amethyst Suzeraine* would be beyond them, screened by their huge rows of active guns. 'Blood of Russ, *move!*'

Then the void went white. The full barrage loosed – a colossal, rolling, eye-burning wall of neon that flooded every oculus and overloaded the few augurs that had staggered back up to full capacity. For a moment even Jorundur winced, his eyes closing, his fists clenching. The impact would be horrendous – it would crunch the hull inward and shear the last of the void shield units from their moorings, even if they were lucky.

But it never hit. The barrage had been real enough, but it hadn't come from the death's head – it had come from four of the Ecclesiarchy escorts, all firing in concert. The *Amethyst Suzeraine* slingshotted under their formation, darting like a thrown bolas across their displacement shadow.

Ice and iron, thought Jorundur grudgingly. That had been an incredible shot, exceptionally orchestrated.

'Now bring us up, slow us down,' he ordered, switching to the rear sensors. 'Keep us on the far side of those gunlines.'

The traitor battle cruiser had been savaged, caught in a crossfire of expertly deployed lance strikes. Its spine was broken, the grinning skull-face across its prows cracked into pieces. Gas vented all along its blackened length, punctuated by internal explosions. Even as Jorundur watched, it began to lose power, falling away towards Ojada's gravity well. Its hunt was over.

On another day, he might have thought of that as an unworthy kill, relying on the firepower of a doubtful ally rather than take on the enemy alone. But then, his ship was a stolen rust-hulk, a pirate's plaything turned into a half-serious warship at best, and the real objective lay on the planet below, so there was a limit to how bad he could feel about it.

A coded hail came in to the throne's private lens, shunted up from the ship's main receiver matrix.

'Unidentified privateer,' it read, marked at the top with Ecclesiarchy runes. *'Maintain your distance and heading, do not interfere with our deployment. Come within strike range, and the next volley will be for you.'*

'Fair enough,' Jorundur said to himself, calculating the vectors to comply. All he wanted to do now was shelter for a moment in their shadow, using their bulk and prowess to keep them all alive just a little longer. 'Shipmaster, ensure we maintain relative position. Inform me at once if you pick up another targeting lock.'

And then he was back to Hafloí, trying to raise his locator amid a welter of interference.

'Whelp!' he shouted down the link, not entirely sure he had been heard. 'Do *not* attempt to locate the rat! You hear me? Stay where you are, or get off that damn ship! We need its guns, we need its eyes elsewhere. I don't care about Klaive, just do nothing to make them angry!'

It wasn't clear whether any of that had got through. Jorundur glanced up at the realviewers, over to where the vast shadow of the battleship hung in the void. He thought of Hafloí crawling around in its bilges, and shuddered. Damn Blood Claws – more bone in their heads than brains.

'How are our augurs?' he asked Bjargborn.

'Partial recovery, lord,' came the reply. 'A few systems knocked out during the run in, but I'm working on them.'

'Can you raise the vaerangi yet?'

'Working on it, lord.'

Then Jorundur slumped back in the throne, watching the orbital battle rage around them. For the moment, he'd done what he needed to – they were in the lee of a greater power, shielded from the worst of the storm. He was under no illusion that the respite was anything less than temporary – more predators were out there, and in numbers that would overwhelm even the battleship above them – but all Gunnlaugur had asked for was a little time.

He couldn't take his eyes off the *Immaculate Destiny*. It still hadn't moved, not an inch, even as the tempest raged around it. That bothered him. And the more he looked, the more he was bothered.

'Why so static, then?' he murmured, drumming his fingers on the throne's arm. 'What am I missing, here?'

CHAPTER FIFTEEN

Gunnlaugur broke into the command centre, vaulting up the last of the stairs and bursting through an already wrecked doorway. As he crossed the threshold, he seamlessly switched to his bolter, a move Ingvar silently echoed.

The centre was a large hexagonal space, more than forty yards in diameter, near the very summit of the observation tower, its walls floor-to-ceiling armaglass. A central column dominated, ringed with display lenses and clicking sensor banks. Spiral stairs led up to a higher level, screened by metal-mesh panels. The decking was thick ferrocrete, utilitarian and blast-resistant. The external firestorm howled around them, making the structure creak, pressing against the glass as if trying to force its way in.

Bodies were everywhere, broken across cogitator housings, twisting into the gaps between equipment racks. Most were in the crimson livery of the armsmen, a few wore black carapace plate. Las scorches marked every surface, leaving long streak-patterns across the glass and plasteel. Now there could be no doubt – they were fighting each other. The armsmen were trying to get to the foot of the stairs, the more heavily armoured troops were trying to stop them. Numbers were against the defenders – only four of them remained, crouching low on the screened inside curve of the stairwell, versus more than thirty of the armsmen, huddled in the lee of overturned desk-units and sensor stations, ready to burst out for the final push.

In the face of that, Gunnlaugur hesitated, just for a microsecond. He took in the pattern of the carapace-units on the defenders, the silver lining on every plate, the twin powerblades that they each carried, the close-faced helms that gave nothing away, the tiny golden-cherub icons lodged on their right breast.

'Clear them *all* out,' he growled, opening up with his bolter.

Ingvar joined him, and together they sprayed mass-reactive shells across the entire breadth of the chamber. The percussive stream blew the housings apart, punched through the armaglass, cut up the armsmen's flak-plate, blasted the deck-plates into powdery chunks. The Space Wolves ran straight through the explosive blooms, making for the stairs amid the chorus of cut-short screams and secondary detonations.

Unprepared, the armsmen were cut down in the first wave. The exposed carapace-plate guards did little better – three were blown off their feet as the shells hit, smacked back into the central column before the explosions shredded them open. By the time Gunnlaugur reached the spiral stairs, only one remained, reeling from the shock waves and scrambling for shelter. Gunnlaugur snapped off a final shot, aimed at his head.

He evaded it. Somehow, moving faster than any of the others had, the sable warrior dropped to one side, letting the bolt fly past his helm to impact on the plasteel casing. Then he was up again, blades in both hands, launching himself at the Wolf Guard. Gunnlaugur swung the bolter at him heavily, aiming to crunch his helm-face inward, but the warrior moved too fast again, ducking under the swipe and flickering his blades up into Gunnlaugur's midriff.

Gunnlaugur twisted away, out of the path of one cutting edge, but the second sliced into his armour, biting an inch deep as the energy field flared. He spun back to punch into the warrior's face, but his helm blew apart as Ingvar's bolt-shell speared through it.

'Slowing down, vaerangi?' Ingvar asked, amused.

Gunnlaugur, spattered with gore and armour-pieces, spat out a curse, shoving the headless body aside. In truth, he hadn't been slow – the warrior had been fast. Extremely fast, more so than any unaugmented human body had a right to be. 'What *are* these things?' he growled, vaulting up the stairs.

'I've seen their sigil before,' said Ingvar, racing up after him. 'When all this started.'

They ran up the spiral stair, boots clanging on the plasteel treads, before emerging into a large, high-roofed chamber, now right at the very top of the tower.

It was different to all the others, as dark as the interior of a chapel. The deck was circular, the windows narrow slits. The floor was thickly carpeted, the walls were hung with drapes. Its ceiling was vaulted in the Imperial gothic style, and granite statues of saints stood in shadowy alcoves, lit by the guttering light of racked candles. A huge altar stood on the far side of the room. It looked rare and expensive – the kind of thing you might find in the heart of a cathedral on a shrine world, not on an industrial planet on the edge of destruction. Bookcases lined the walls, each of them stuffed with reams of leather-bound tomes. Opposite the altar, close to where the Space Wolves had emerged, stood another statue – an idealised cherub, cast in pure gold, carrying a sheaf of arrows in its youthful hand.

The place was bizarre. The internal fashioning was mostly orthodox Imperial cult, but interspersed with strange objects – xenos artefacts, archeotech held in glittering stasis fields, hololith recordings playing softly, over and over. Weapons hung in the gloomy recesses. Some of those looked very old. A disturbing number of them seemed to be of Fenrisian origin. Indeed, the more Gunnlaugur looked, the more artefacts from Fenris he saw – armour-pieces, nameplates from Chapter warships, rune-tablets and animal totems locked in glass cabinets. It was as if the place were some kind of esoteric collector's den, a grim museum of plunder, all fused with the austere iconography of the Ecclesiarchy.

A man knelt before the altar. He was powerfully built, clad in robes of black and silver that pooled around him. A second figure, a woman in similar black-and-silver garb, stood next to him carrying a long ceremonial sword. Ingvar and Gunnlaugur trained their bolters, one for each, but neither fired. From below, the only sounds filtering up were the whine of the wind and the muffled crackle of distant fires. Fighting still raged in the compound outside, but for the moment the four of them were alone in the chamber.

'Get up,' said Gunnlaugur.

The woman looked at him. For a moment, the man didn't move. Gunnlaugur edged to his left, getting a better view, and saw that he was praying, his lips moving soundlessly. Once the kneeling figure had completed whatever ritual he was engaged in, his eyes opened. He slowly got to his feet, placing a hand on the floor to steady himself, breathing heavily. He turned, adjusting his robes over his broad frame. When he caught sight of the two of them, his face registered a brief flicker of surprise.

'You,' he murmured, then smiled wryly. 'Perhaps, though, it had to be.'

The woman looked old, or maybe ill. She had a slim figure that the black robes hung loosely from. Her long hair was pulled back from her face, making her profile severe. The sword she carried was more relic than weapon, and she did not look capable of wielding it in more than a token fashion.

The man's skin was a dark bronze-brown, his eyes blue. His hair was cut short against his scalp, exposing old scars across his forehead, the back of his neck. He wore the chasuble and stole of a high priest of the Imperial cult, though not in any colours Gunnlaugur had ever observed before. Every piece of fabric in the place was glossy black and silver, a combination that shimmered strangely in the candlelight.

The man's expression was manic. His jawline was far too tight, he was sweating, and the veins at his neck bulged. He didn't seem to blink much, if at all. A cursory scan revealed that he wasn't carrying a weapon of his own. Gunnlaugur lowered his, locking it against his armour. Ingvar kept his bolter trained on the woman.

'Your name,' Gunnlaugur ordered.

'I'd have thought you'd know it.' The man clasped twitchy hands together in front of his waist. 'Leon Chirastes. Cardinal astra, for what that was ever worth, but I suppose they've taken that from me too, now. So it's just Leon, now. Or Ser Chirastes. Take your pick.'

'What has happened here?'

Chirastes gave a jerky shrug. 'They caught up with me. You caught up with me. I've had hunters on my scent for so long now I've forgotten what it was like to live freely.' He grinned at the woman. 'Glad it's over now, eh, Buta? You start a thing. You're full of energy. The years go on, and it traps you, but you have to see it through, because you made an oath. Oaths, oaths, oaths. We said we'd do something, so that make us move, makes us work. Even the Archenemy has that disease, eh? Why else do they keep coming at us, century after century? I think some of them must be sick of it, too. Oaths, though. Oaths.'

Gunnlaugur ran a secondary scan. The man's heartbeat was erratic, his vital signs were overloaded. He had augmetics riddled through his body, though most of them looked to be dormant or defective. 'We came a long way to find you.'

'I'll wager you did.'

'And now you're coming with us.'

Chirastes shook his head emphatically. 'I'm going nowhere.'

'It was not a request,' said Ingvar.

'And that was not defiance,' said Chirastes. 'I'll be dead in moments. Acherosa is a powerful poison, and I was sure to take plenty of it. I didn't want Axith getting his grubby fingernails into me. You wouldn't, either. All I wished for, in this place, was to complete the Rites of Ascendence, accompanied by Buta here. And I couldn't even be left alone to finish that! So much for a lifetime of service.'

Ingvar let slip a snarl of frustration. 'We *will* have our answers.'

'Oh, you can have those now,' Chirastes said, more sweat running down his forehead. 'You can have as many of those as you wish – if, that is, the good Cardinal Orquemond lets this place linger intact for just a few more moments. If there's time, I'll tell you just whatever you wish to learn. I want to tell you. I've been *burning* to tell someone. Just look around you – you can see that it was always about you.'

He moved a little closer to Ingvar, limping visibly, the skin around his neck darkening as he moved.

'And all because you have no *soul*, Son of Russ,' he said. 'You are a devil, a phantom. It matters not what you know, because you are not even human. You are a mockery, a mistake, a throwaway. As a confessor, you make a poor one, but you are all I have, so there we are. You are far too late, if you wish to halt what I have I done. All has already been accomplished. The oath is settled, and I can go in peace.'

The woman's expression never changed during all that – it was hollow. Chirastes, on the other hand, looked exultant, his gaze feverish.

'I *beat* you,' he said, jabbing a finger up at Ingvar's chest. 'It's all that matters now, and when the annals come to be written, that is what they'll say. I beat you.'

'What do you mean, *sacked?*' Olgeir demanded. 'How can you know that?'

The viaduct was still full of moving bodies – men and women scampering through the ruins, hunting either for plunder or sanctuary – but neither of the Wolves paid them any attention. The corpse of the traitor lay some way off, already beginning to degrade following the removal of whatever dark magicks had been keeping it together for so long.

Olgeir's arm ached from the wrench of carrying his whole weight, even briefly. Catching the handhold on the edge of the sinkhole in the viaduct's main deck had stopped him from dropping right down into the burning heart of the rig, but it had still taken all his strength to haul himself back up to the surface. His pulse was fast and hard still, his blood vessels throbbing.

Baldr's collar was black, like an extinguished coal. Just like Olgeir, he'd taken damage from the creature – his armour was gouged and blasted, the steel-grey covering scraped away in patches. He was having trouble breathing. Eventually, though, he dragged himself up to his feet, shaking his head to clear it, panting.

'I... saw it,' he said bleakly.

'You saw what it showed you.'

'It showed me things it had seen.'

'They *lie*.'

Baldr turned on him. 'Aye, they lie. They lie and they lie, but this one... it was *there*.'

'How can you know that?'

Baldr hesitated. 'You know how.'

'I thought that collar kept you from–'

'It does. Most of the time.' Baldr wearily reached for his blade, began to clean the filth off it. 'But it grows weaker. And, somehow, stronger. It fights me, and one of us will break, in the end.' He slid the sword back into its scabbard. 'So I *know* things, whatever the Stormcaller might have hoped for, and I know now that Fenris is in ruins. You hear me, Heavy-Hand? Ruins.'

Contemplating such an image stretched the boundaries of the possible. Fenris was eternal. One of the Rout might die, his pack might perish, even Grimnar would go, one day, but the world would remain, the Mountain would remain, the fixed point around which the entire universe revolved.

Until, that was, the Time of Ending. Until the return of the primarch, when all would be cast into the proving fire.

'So tell me everything,' Olgeir said.

'I do not understand it all,' Baldr said haltingly. 'Many forces were there, I think. I could see the stink of maleficarum on the storm. Imagery of our greatest enemy, it must have been, but they were not alone. Scraps of warbands, fragments of the old Legions, they were there with the one-eyed traitor. The seas were boiling, the Mountain was ringed with flame. I saw... maybe, I saw Midgardia cast into the sun. I saw it go, the weregild for the whole system. And then, when that was done, I saw black ships make planetfall, right down onto the ice, their bellies opened up. I saw the tribes marching into them.'

'Never. Lies.'

'How would you know, brother? We were not there.'

'And neither was that thing.'

'We were *here*.' Now Baldr's tone became harder. 'Running down this stale spoor, heedless of anything else. And for what? Vendetta? Some cure for this damned hex-collar? You should have left me for Njal while you could.'

Olgeir snorted. 'That was never an option. You'd be dead by now, and we'd be scrubbing off the meat-boards in the Aett, dreaming of getting off-world again.'

'So you never even questioned it?'

'Aye, I questioned it.' Olgeir shook the blood from his own axe. 'I asked from the very start – I told Gunnlaugur you'd infect us all. When I came back from Kefa, I told him the same thing. I was always worried. It matters to me, purity. It matters that we're different to that... thing. It's a long way to fall, brother. We all know how far.'

He remembered the unseeing eyes, then. The black-edged lightning, the glow of green around sickening flesh, the unbridled power that blasted and scoured through the hot night. Old wounds twinged under his armour, ones given him by the very warrior who stood before him now – or, at least, the thing that had taken his name.

Baldr looked him right in the eye. 'Then maybe you were right.'

'Ach, what does it matter now?' Olgeir pulled the pelts around his shoulder. 'We all made the oath, and that's an end to it. Gods, quit your whining – we all had enough of it from the Gyrfalkon when he came back, but at least he grew out of it. Decisions were made. We stand by them.'

'Fenris is laid waste. It's where we should have been.'

'Hah.' Olgeir tied his axe back to his belt. 'We are where we are. That's what fate *is*. Couldn't be otherwise. And never believe a word you hear from a traitor.' He drew in a long breath, filling his lungs with oil-laced hot air. 'Enough. We need to get back to Gunnlaugur.'

Baldr looked over at the corpse of the traitor. 'So what'll you tell him?'

'That we did as he asked,' Olgeir replied, starting to move out. 'Nothing more to say.'

CHAPTER SIXTEEN

The battle hadn't stopped. New attack waves screamed in, driving under the bow waves of las-fire to streak up and into the defensive cordons. Fighters led the charge – Furies, mostly, refitted and defaced but still lethal. Those were followed by their escort-class mother ships, then the heavier gun-barques, and then, further out but coming closer all the time, the big beasts, the ones that could do the real damage.

Jorundur spent the whole time shouting orders out, making himself hoarse to ensure the crew were in the right places and doing the right things. The void shields needed to be restored across all hull sections, the fires in the aft bilge decks needed to be put out, the cannon decks needed fast reloading, the plasma drives needed to be rapidly cooled before they were stoked again. All the while, the las-batteries were kept busy, and the need for constant evasion remained acute.

'Move us closer under that one – which is it?' he called out.

'The *Purity of Action*, lord,' Bjargborn intoned, occupied with a dozen of his own tasks.

The Ecclesiarchy frigate, a high-prowed, capable vessel with longer than usual broadside-flanks, was rapidly becoming bogged down by the sheer volume of incoming strikes. A few more precision hits might start to give it serious trouble.

'All guns, target that ship's attackers,' Jorundur ordered. 'I want them to know we're an ally.'

'More hails from the *Immaculate Destiny*, lord,' reported Tjade, Suaka's replacement at principal comms. 'They still want details of our complement and registration.'

'Give them nothing,' Jorundur snapped. 'Fake a transmission blow-out, if you have to, and let me know *the instant* you get wind of a target lock.'

They were playing a delicate game. The Ecclesiarchy squadron, for all its prowess, couldn't remain in its position for more than a couple of hours more before it started taking too much damage. If their commanders hadn't had so much to deal with, no doubt they'd have been asking more questions of the unmarked galleon that had burst into their formation at such reckless speed. All Jorundur could do was help keep their attention on the main enemy, stay out of trouble, make himself the least of their many problems.

'Raking spreads ready, lord!' called out the gunnery liaison officer.

'Good,' said Jorundur. 'Fire at will, sustained barrage.'

What was left of the *Amethyst Suzeraine*'s lascannons spat out against the *Purity of Action*'s attackers, taking down a wing of Furies and crippling what looked like some heavily modified torpedo-barques. The line guns kept firing after that, roll after roll of ship-crippling shells.

Once the attack-pattern had its momentum, he turned to the most urgent matter of all. 'Anything yet from the surface? Anything at all?'

Bjargborn shook his head. 'If they transmitted while we were augur-blind, it'll be lost. I've been trying to track them, but the rigs are all on fire, there are sensor-baffles everywhere...'

'I don't need excuses – just any data you've got.'

'Shunting raw vid-transmit from the vaerangi's helm-feed, then,' Bjargborn said. 'Just a few seconds, picked up by the auto-scanners before they went dark.'

Jorundur swivelled round to one of the throne's lenses as the data scanned onto the surface. It was hard to make out – a jumble of data-distorted phosphor that panned and jumped as violently as Gunnlaugur had been moving at the time. Jorundur narrowed his eyes, analysing what he could of it. He saw bodies, lots of them, their torsos bearing signs of laceration from power-blades. Some were in the uniform of Ecclesiarchy naval armsmen, the kind they'd become very familiar with over the past few months. Even amid all the interference, he could see that the Space Wolves hadn't killed those troops – the cuts weren't the kind of whole-body-severing slash that an Astartes swipe delivered, but shorter jabbing actions. He could see no cultists or renegade warriors at all.

The feed cut out. Jorundur sat back, his mind working hard. Something was wrong with the whole set-up down there.

'Give me close visual on the battleship,' he ordered.

Bjargborn complied, shunting a range of tactical profiles of the *Immaculate Destiny* over to the throne's lens racks.

'Absolutely motionless,' Jorundur said, half to himself, half to Bjargborn. 'Would you maintain that position, rivenmaster, in all of this?'

'They have troops on the surface,' Bjargborn offered.

'With their own very capable transports. Get me a view of its underside, close as you can.'

Bjargborn complied, and soon Jorundur was staring at the empty funnels of six heavy orbital lasers, the ones that had been used to smash a path through the battlezone for the landers. The conical barrels were gigantic, protruding from the under-hull plates like iron volcanos. They were all active, too – their feeder mechanisms alight with lumen-points, their power plants clearly primed for maximum drain.

'Skítja, that thing's got a geo-lock,' Jorundur muttered. 'Rivenmaster – can you raise the pack?'

'Negative, lord. Will keep trying.'

'Tell them to get out. All of them, now.' Then he was trying to get a fix on Haflói. Three times, nothing came back but empty static. The fourth time, his transponder told him he had a weak tether. 'Whelp – I hope to Hel you can hear this. If you're still on that thing – if you're still *alive* – forget about Klaive.'

He took a deep breath. This was going to be tight.

'Here's what you have to do.'

He still winced with every impact. It didn't matter that the *Immaculate Destiny* was far bigger than the Space Wolves' old galleon and far more capable of defending itself, he still jumped whenever he felt the deck underfoot jolt badly.

Klaive was not a warrior. He never had been. He'd been a functionary to warriors, sure, and had always been happy to inflict a bit of pain when it was necessary, but this, *this* – plunging right into the three-dimensional heart of a rampaging void-battle, with the rivets popping and the gantries buckling – this wore his nerves away.

He tried to concentrate. He was surrounded by dangerous people, people whom just moments earlier he'd thought of as certain allies. For as long as they had no idea of the true reason for his presence in Ojada, his safety remained precariously intact. All he had to do was keep the pretence going until he could get back out of the system, just long enough for him to jump ship again and make his way to somewhere his name wasn't known and his rank might carry more weight.

But if they managed to somehow get this Chirastes up here alive, up to where he could look at Klaive, possibly recognise his face from a report, or a name, or a code word, maybe give the game away... well then, that would be difficult. Best to hope that the Wolves did his dirty work for him, prevented the man's escape, necessitated the use of those cherished orbital laser banks to wipe all the evidence away before the world itself passed into the hands of the enemy.

It was ironic, to be so beholden to his old gaolers. On another day, with his blood pressure a little lower, he might have smiled at the chance.

'So, my lord,' Klaive said, opting to talk, to keep Orquemond's mind occupied. 'Are you permitted to tell me what this man has done? It must have been serious, to bring you halfway across the sector after him.'

Orquemond looked irritated. 'To be sure, I do not wish to be here. Worlds across the Imperium are falling like leaves in winter, they say. The guns of this ship should be heading towards a fortress we may yet hold.' He shook his head wearily. 'And yet. The law is the law, as is my responsibility to uphold it. Chirastes passed into madness a long time ago, and the deaths of many faithful souls lie at his door.'

Another shattering impact, somewhere off the port bows, made the bridge-deck drum. The lumens flashed, and indistinct crashes sounded from a long way up in the bridge-roof's structure. Throughout it all, the cardinal remained almost entirely unmoved.

'Chirastes was zealous,' he said. 'Too zealous. Not for the truth, mind, which is something to be commended, but he never learned that the prosecution of heresy is the patient task of years. To rush to judgement, taking no care whose houses are burned, jeopardises the very foundations of our order. He would run every sniff of impropriety down, wherever it led, heeding no advice and accepting no counsel. And so, when he learned of alleged forbidden practices of the ice-world of Fenris, he had to launch an investigation.' Orquemond sighed. 'He had to do it. He couldn't have helped himself, even though it was always a fool's errand, doomed to failure. The Wolves do not yield, they do not comply, and they do not forgive. When he pressed the matter, his ships were destroyed, his agents killed. And still he did not give up. He truly thought he could bring them to heel. Somehow – and I have to be impressed about this – he raised a fleet drawn from three separate Orders of the Sororitas, in addition to the power he'd built in his own name. He went to war.' Orquemond chuckled darkly. 'He went to war with a First Founding Chapter. If that is not the definition of madness, then I do not know what is.'

And just then, Klaive suddenly remembered where he'd heard the name. The Fenris Incident. They still spoke about it, in hushed tones, within the Ecclesiarchy conclaves and scholae. But that had been more than a century ago. The detailed records had been, as you would expect, thoroughly expunged, and what remained was sealed into the most exclusive of vaults. For himself, he'd never quite believed that it had happened, and had begun to think of it as some kind of instructional myth, a warning of overreach to give to the young acolytes.

'If that had been the end of the matter,' Orquemond said, 'he'd have lost his reputation, nothing more. After three weeks of intense conflict, during which the assets of the Church sustained terrible damage, he made his escape. And after that, if you believe the official histories, he left the Ecclesiarchy altogether, forfeiting his position and privileges, a wiser yet much weaker man.'

'Clearly, though, that was a lie.'

Orquemond gave him a sly look. 'They say he's operated within the Church's structures ever since. That was why it took so long for us to find him. Most of those who still took his order never knew his history. They saw the cardinal's badge on the vellum, and did what it told them. Even once we began to investigate him ourselves, we ran into the sand at every turn – no names were ever given, no chain of command. Operatives didn't know the names or ranks of those they reported to, only the destination for their material. Even when faced with the instruments, they would insist on that ignorance. No one ever said that Chirastes was a simpleton. Only that he was a maniac.'

Klaive began to feel even more uncomfortable. That was exactly how it had been. The orders had come down from on high, using all the right passcodes and verification seals. No names, no details. It was why he had been of so little use to the Wolves, at least at the start of his captivity.

'To what end, though?' he asked. 'All this?'

'Continuing his war,' said Orquemond. 'Doing by stealth what he could no longer do openly. It has been taking place for decades, under our noses, under *their* noses. Indeed, if they ever learned what has happened, make no mistake – all our throats would be liable for the axe-edge.'

'But, my lord... the Wolves. They are undeniably... extreme.'

'Maybe so. I have no love for Space Marines myself, of any breed. But they are the Emperor's creations, sanctified in the holy canon, and it does not fall to any one of us to undo what He has created. Fenris may be a haunt of monsters beyond reason for all I know, but unless we are given lawful instruction from the Throneworld itself, sanctified and examined by the highest authority, its denizens cannot be touched.'

'Then how did you find all this out?'

Orquemond raised his eyebrows ironically. 'With difficulty. Tracks had been covered well. The few static installations his cabal controlled were emptied even as we discovered news of their existence. As the current war grew worse, he must have sent out hundreds of his people, scouring it all, burning the order-trails, working hard lest the confusion of battle unearthed what he had worked to keep secret. But he was commanding entire armies, confessor. Even in an Imperium as vast as ours, even with so many eyes elsewhere, that was always going to be hard to conceal.'

Klaive felt another pang of unease. He had been one of those agents. His orders on Ras Shakeh had been just those – to destroy the identified archives before they were taken by either the enemy or the Imperials. He'd never even known what was in them, just that they had to go. You didn't ask questions, in his position – that was the surest route to danger. Still, hearing it all laid out like that, it was hard to not feel foolish. Even guilty.

He was about to ask more, pushing his luck as far as it would go, when reports from the bridge operatives started to filter back in numbers. Orquemond held up a hand, silencing him, and listened carefully. As he did so, orders were shouted down the long crew-trenches, and several of the cowled counsellors bowed low before hurrying away to new taskings.

'What is happening?' Klaive asked, mostly to himself, but Orquemond glanced at him a final time before heading back towards the command throne.

'I am afraid that we are out of time, confessor,' the cardinal said, his voice heavy with disappointment. 'My troops on the surface advise that resistance has been stronger than hoped, and that they are now under attack from elements of the enemy. It will either take more time to bring him in, or more landings, neither of which I am prepared to countenance.'

He climbed the low steps before settling himself in the throne, his hands falling across the control panels set in each arm.

'We have done what we can,' he said grimly. 'You will miss the chance to meet Chirastes in person, confessor, but at least you will witness the final ending of his insurrection, which may give some satisfaction.'

More klaxons began to sound, not indicating damage this time, but instead the preparations for orbital strike, something that consumed colossal power and would require the diversion of supply from many other subsystems.

'There's no alternative?' Klaive asked, attempting to sound more disappointed than relieved.

'None at all,' said Orquemond, flipping open the protective guard on the panel and readying the controls for firing. 'This ends now.'

CHAPTER SEVENTEEN

It felt strangely deflating, to see him standing there, the object of so much long-cherished hatred – on death's edge, unrepentant, gloating.

Ingvar studied Chirastes carefully as he spoke, watching for any sign of deception, a hook, something he could use to provoke the violence that he had always assumed he would unleash in this moment. He wanted to fight him, hurt him, avenge the deaths the man had caused. And yet here they all were, locked in a darkened chamber at the summit of a doomed refinery-spire, deprived of even that meagre satisfaction, condemned to listen only to more stories.

It reminded him of the deflation he had felt after his long service with the Deathwatch came to an end – not the realisation that the Imperium's enemies were greater in number than anyone could imagine, but that the Imperium was one such enemy itself, like a serpent eating its own tail, consuming its brightest progeny before they could ever come to fruition. Every soul in the room, all four of them, had sworn oaths to the Allfather. They all still cleaved to those oaths, in all honesty, and yet here they were, their blades drawn but unused, rehearsing loathings that had been born more than a century ago, all in the sterile language of diplomats.

'Tell us everything,' Gunnlaugur said, his voice thick with his own suppressed fury.

And the man did. He wanted to. He could barely wait to spill the details, unravelling it all, listing the injuries he had done them. He wished to boast, whether to them or to himself. As Ingvar listened, he registered the other danger – the place was comms-blind, sealing them in, away from the reach of both Jorundur and Olgeir. They could not afford to linger in such a state for long, especially given the parlous state of the rig-city outside these walls. Still, they had come a long way for this – if knowledge was all they were destined to take away from it, that was a little better than nothing.

'I am the knife in your side,' Chirastes crowed. 'The punishment for your many sins. The hidden thorn that tears your flesh.'

'You ordered the death of Hjortur Bloodfang,' said Gunnlaugur.

'Hjortur Ageir Hvat, called Bloodfang, Wolf Guard. Yes, I made that happen.'

'And others of the Chapter.'

'Many others, yes.'

'Why?'

Chirastes laughed, a fragile sound, and a thin trickle of blood ran down from the corner of his mouth. 'Because you all deserve death. You understand that? All of you. I know what you practise, on that hell-world of yours. I know what your shamans preach, and what heresies ferment in the stinking hovel you call your Mountain. It was the labour of a lifetime to learn it. When I told others, they were shocked. They all said the same thing – why is this tolerated? Why do we burn minor heretics in hive-sumps, when there's a whole planet of the corrupted sitting in plain view! And, you know, I could never answer them. In the end, once you've run out of excuses, you have to act. So, a long time ago now, I came to your world.'

Ingvar listened, not just to the words, but to the things the man gave away with them. Chirastes wasn't affecting this – he really believed that the exercise was over, and that he'd already won. His eyes were bright – too bright. And yet, there was a residual fear under the crazed bravado, a nugget of it, buried deep, something that had yet to emerge.

'At first,' Chirastes went on, the words tumbling out, 'I came with nothing more than a delegate-fleet – the kind of thing the protocols lay down. That would have been enough, on most worlds. I'd have made planetfall with my entourage, and we'd have looked around for a while. Maybe we'd have left, satisfied. But you couldn't even allow that, could you? You were so thirsty for a fight, so proud of your false sanctity, that my agents came back to me in body-capsules. Sending a message, I guessed. That you were above any authority, even one speaking on behalf of the Imperial cult itself. Clumsy. Brutal. And stupid. That kind of thing might work out in your undeveloped, forgotten slush-pools, but it doesn't play well in more civilised climes. So we had to come again.'

Gunnlaugur looked at Ingvar. 'The Incursion of Fools,' he said.

'Sounds like it.' Ingvar's gaze never left Chirastes. 'This was 886, your calendar, yes?'

'So that's what you call it. Ha. I'm surprised you even keep records.'

'We remember plenty,' said Gunnlaugur. 'It was a petty war. None of those who fought it celebrate.'

'No, they don't, and no, they can't!' laughed Chirastes. 'Because they're *all dead*.' Then he broke into coughing. By the time he stopped, panting hard, his chin was mottled with blood. 'Three weeks of war. Three weeks, dashing ourselves into splinters on your defences. We soon realised we couldn't win. We couldn't even punish you. So what was left to do? Run off, our tails between our legs? No, we still had tools. We could take names. We could tap your comms, and find out who was there, who was doing this to us. So that's how we used the time. We bled ourselves out, and all for that. By the time I left your world, my ships burning and breaking apart, I knew who had done this to us. I knew who the guilty were. And that wasn't the end. It was just the start.'

'How many?' asked Ingvar.

'All of them,' said Chirastes. 'Every battlefield commander, every squad leader.'

'Impossible,' said Gunnlaugur.

'Really? You know the fates of all your brothers?' He chuckled bloodily. 'You die so very often, Space Marine. That is the problem. You are always at war, rushing from one world to the next. These times have been hard for you, I think. And you never turn down a chance for bloodletting. That's your other weakness.' He wiped his chin with the sleeve of his robe, leaving a dark smear. 'So how do you think Hjortur died? Fighting against the green-skins? Yes, that was how it looked, but we were there, alongside him. And so you never questioned it, because how many hundreds of your kind have the greenskins killed over the centuries? Could you even count them?' For a moment, the sardonic edge left his expression, and he looked momenta-rily thoughtful. 'All that was left was deception. To come alongside you, fight *with* you. Until the moment came to give the real order.'

Ingvar could feel the weight of his blade in his hand, and the itch to use it was so strong now. 'This could not all have been done in secret.'

'It was very difficult,' Chirastes admitted. 'An entire administration kept in the dark as to its true purpose. Commands given without attribution, records cleaned up or destroyed, whole regiments of soldiers kept igno-rant. But you forget that one thing we do so expertly in this Imperium is to follow orders. I learned that well in my old life – you could tell a cleric to saw his own arm off, if you had the right credentials, and he'd do it. We make it impossible to question, we make it a crime to doubt, and thus we till the ground for such hidden work.'

'Even so,' said Gunnlaugur. 'We're not easy to kill.'

'No, you're not! You're *damned hard* to kill, every one of you! I had to spend my entire fortune to create an army capable of it. I could once count planets in my possession like another man counts ration-slips. They're all gone now, all used up. Maybe you encountered one of my hunters before you reached me here. They're good, aren't they? As good as I could make them. They still die, of course. But even if a hundred of them are put down, it only takes one to get close enough. That was exactly what I built their units for – to get one close enough.'

And then Chirastes, staggered, falling to one knee, breathing heavily. The woman, the one he'd called Buta, reached out to take his arm. Neither of the Space Wolves moved.

'You attacked us,' said Gunnlaugur, almost incredulous. '*You* came to *our* world.'

'It is a hell-world.'

'You never set foot on it.'

'What do you have to hide on it, then? Why keep it shrouded?'

'We do not hide,' said Ingvar quietly, contemptuously. 'Wherever there is battle, we are there. We do not ask for understanding, let alone affection, only that our own realm remains in our own hands.'

'There *is* no realm, save for His! That is the lesson! You tell yourself these stories, you make yourselves into the heroes of your own tedious sagas, and you never *examine*. You never look at what you believe, what you *do*. What is the point of preserving an Imperium at all, if its heart is rotten? None! You should *all* be excised! If I'd had the strength for it, I'd have done it myself!'

Chirastes' invective came to a breathless halt, and he panted hard. 'As it was, I struck a blow. A modest one, in the scheme of things, but a blow nonetheless. I beat you. I beat you.'

And that, for Ingvar, was the worst of it. To discover that the Fulcrum, which had seemed for so long like something put in place by powerful and malign forces of the Archenemy, was in truth the lone project of a bitter, damaged man, one who had squandered a system-spanning fortune just to gain a personal slice of revenge, cheapened everything.

'And yet, we endure,' Ingvar said. 'You have wasted your time alive, cardinal. Fenris is unchanged. The Chapter still fights.'

Chirastes raised an eyebrow. 'Sure of all that, are you?' Then he coughed up more blood, the fingers of his planted hand splaying out across the deck. Buta knelt down, winding an arm under his chest.

'Get away from him,' Gunnlaugur told her, taking up his bolter.

She stared up at him for a moment, then stared at Ingvar.

'Go, Buta,' Chirastes rasped. 'Let them do what they came to do. It is the kind of thing they understand. I suppose I have given them every reason to be angry.'

She finally let him go, limping away and sheltering next to the altar. From outside, back down the corridors, noises of voices being raised in alarm filtered up the stairwell.

Chirastes looked straight up at the muzzle of Gunnlaugur's bolter. His flushed, drug-ravaged face twitched.

'I guessed that one of you would find me, one day,' he said. 'What a blessing, though, to have it happen now, when all is already–'

Gunnlaugur fired once, putting the bolt straight through the man's smile and into the decking beyond. Headless, Chirastes' body thunked heavily over.

Ingvar aimed his bolter at the woman.

'Wait,' said Gunnlaugur, holding up a hand. 'Did you take the same poison?'

She nodded. 'What part did you play?'

It looked like she was trying to reply, but her words died in her throat. She stared at Ingvar, then back at Gunnlaugur, her hands shaking.

Ingvar moved in closer. 'It wasn't the whole truth, was it?'

Still she couldn't answer. Her eyes widened, the veins on her temple throbbed. Gunnlaugur's finger slipped from the trigger with a faint click of ceramite.

'There's something else,' he said. 'Take her. We're leaving.'

The journey in the saviour pod had been exhilarating. Hafloí had barely used the shackle-restraints on the crossing, instead hanging on one-handed as the tube had pirouetted and spiralled through the maelstrom. His sensor load-out had been minimal – just a single lens with some rudimentary local-void schematics that flickered and scrolled madly. Bjargborn had done a good job, though, locking the machine-spirit on to the rat's trajectory. After the long rush through the delivery tube, the saviour pod had shot through the bloom of exploding starships on all sides, screaming across the narrow gulf between the *Amethyst Suzeraine* and the *Immaculate Destiny*.

Still, it had always been a dangerous thing to attempt. Just on the wrong side of foolhardy, probably. If Hafloí had thought about it a little more, he might never have got inside. Klaive's pod was no doubt able to broadcast Ecclesiarchy access codes during its passage, giving the receiving ship what it needed to lower a section of void shields and bring it inside safely. Hafloí had none of that – just the hope that he could ride fast within the rat's trail, staying close enough to slip under the screens and somehow penetrate the hull when the moment came.

Of course, it hadn't worked out like that. The rat had had too great a head start, and despite Hafloí overloading the pod's thrusters to catch up, the lead capsule had vanished from the scopes just moments before he was was lined up to crash straight into the uprushing battleship. With its tether lost, the saviour pod had spun wildly off course. Hafloí had fought hard with the basic controls, pulling the tube out of its suicidal plunge and hauling it back onto something like a stable trajectory. The battleship's towering sides had whirled around in the tiny realviewer, rapidly coming into focus and displaying its ranks upon ranks of active cannon-mouths.

For an uncomfortable few seconds, it had seemed inevitable that he'd be smashed against those gunwales. It had taken a huge effort to swing the pod's nose under the closing void-aegis, tearing close in against the ship's gilt-edged flanks, before he'd found enough power to boost clean between the physical bulk of the hull perimeter and the glittering energy field of the shields. His fuel counter had ticked away, the thrusters had started to cough, and still there was nowhere to bring it in – the hangar doors were all shut, and a saviour pod was far from having the forward armour to punch through the outer plates unaided. He'd swung it in as close as he could, scouring the artificial landscape as if it were an asteroid's crust, pulled towards it all the time by unstoppable momentum.

And then, right at the end, the opportunity had come. An incoming las-barrage had smacked into the battleship, five hundred yards ahead, ripping through a damaged void shield sector and driving deep into the hull beyond. Solid plates had blown outward, kicked from their bracings by internal explosions. Hafloí had pounced immediately, diving into the heart of the explosion, yanking the control levels as far as they'd go. The viewscreens had gone a wild amber-red, overwhelmed by the firestorm, before the entire pod crashed to a bone-creaking halt, lodged within the crumbling remnants of the semi-demolished wall section.

Hafloí had moved out immediately, hauling the pod's damaged hatch open and pulling himself upward into a world of howling, shrieking, streaming fire. His helm had gone instantly haywire in the extreme heat – a mix of jumping, static-laced half-images – and he'd clambered, semi-blind, in and through a disintegrating tangle of melting struts and brace-beams, going as swiftly as he could before the liquid flame-tide engulfed his armour completely. He had eventually spilled out into an internal corridor, blackened and smoking, hauling flesh-charring breaths through an overloaded vox-filter.

After that, he'd been able to run again, dragging himself away from the flames and the wreckage, eventually staggering to a working bulkhead, piling through it and locking it behind him. Smoke had been everywhere, pouring out of the air vents, pooling on the deck. Lumens had flashed, and he'd heard the drumbeat of the big guns firing from the decks above him. Soon he'd penetrated a long way down, deep within the bilge levels where everything stank of promethium, rust and human waste.

Sure enough, the first inhabitants he saw were the lowest level of rating, their uniforms little more than rags, their pale skin caked in dirt and grease. He emerged into a narrow feeder-route, the walls open to the coolant tubes that hissed and gurgled along its length. As soon as they saw him, they screamed and ran, falling over one another to scrabble for the nearest ladder hatch.

Hafloí roared out load, enjoying the sound of his vox-enhanced battle cry echoing madly in the confined space, going after them with his arms out wide, flames still flickering on his pelts, his armour a riotous mix of bleached white and burned black.

He didn't make a serious effort to catch them, but one of them did drop a locator-slate in her hurry to get away, so he swooped to pick it up. He quickly pulled up a schematic of the decks above and below, and saw that he'd come in a long way down. That was probably a good thing, in that there wouldn't be many well-armed guards, but also a bad thing, as it meant he'd have a long slog to work his way up towards the rat. For that, he'd need to get to the command levels, the kind of place you'd bring an honoured guest.

He started to run. He made his way upwards and inwards, working hard, driving the mortal crew ahead of him as he traced a direct route. None of them stopped to fight – they must have thought they'd roused some daemon of the outer hells – though he knew that once he was up into the main operational levels things would get trickier.

And then he heard from Jorundur. Somehow, despite the fire damage in his helm-unit and the ongoing las-storm raging between the ships outside, the Old Dog got a comm-burst through. Hafloí almost refused to take it, guessing that it would just be a barrage of curses and demands for him to get back to the ship.

'Skítja,' he breathed, eventually, and listened.

As soon as it was over, he turned on his heels, switching back, upping the pace from a jog to a sprint. He tore back through the gantries and the crawl-ways, his burned armour scraping and dinking against the close press of ironwork, his vision fogged with smoke, his boots slipping on the oily decks.

The locator-slate gave him the route he needed, but several of the access tunnels had collapsed or were blocked with dumped heavy machinery. The deep levels were like forgotten mine-workings – dark, clogged, treacherous. He quickly ran into more crew, some of them wearing blast-protection for emergency repair work, some armed and clearly looking for him. He smashed them aside quickly, brutally, not pausing to make sure of the kill, just to do enough to get past, to keep going, to speed up.

Soon both his hearts were pumping, his skin flushed. He skidded on the decks again, slamming into a press of bilge-pumps, before careering down a steep slope and swinging around a tight corner. The air was getting hotter again, and every surface was thick with vibration. From up ahead, he could hear the growing roar of something big, like an exchanger or a power convertor.

He ran into a chamber full of cowled technicians, and had to waste precious time smashing two against the hatch frame and knocking out a third before he could move on. Las-bolts snapped and whistled after him, aimed from some hidden vantage above, but he had no time to return fire, just to race further in, faster and faster.

By the time he reached his destination, he could already feel the colossal build-up of energy, making the hairs on his skin raise and static flickers zip from his armour. He plunged down a long goods-track and spun out straight into a whole gaggle of heavily armed ratings. He lashed out to cripple two of them before ploughing onward, charging into a high-roofed chamber painted with hazard stripes and echoing from numerous alarms. He fired his bolt pistol to shatter the far doorway's lock-panel then shoulder-barged through it.

Las-fire zeroed in at him, from behind, from ahead, from balconies up above. On either side were sheer ironwork walls, all clogged with active devices encrusted with the Cog Mechanicus and shedding steam-tendrils like tears. Big lifter platforms hissed upwards, propelled by polished steel pistons bearing gangs of robed menials and servitors. Above them rose a mighty access shaft, soaring up through many decks, shimmering from imprisoned energies within tight bundles of black-rimmed cabling. The huge space was crammed tight with both crew ratings and armsmen. Some panicked as he crunched his way in among them; others fought back, dragging his momentum down.

The deck ahead gave way after about fifty yards, after which the floor dropped away to nothing – exposed to the void, the breathable atmosphere kept inside only through the use of stasis fields. The first of the giant orbital laser barrels protruded down into the well, a broad curve of pure adamantium that looked more like the outer skin of a hab-tower than a weapon. It was glowing already, its innards flaring blue-white behind heavy grilles, its control vanes flashing for imminent discharge.

The main barrel was far too huge for Hafloí to take out directly. The volume of las-fire aimed at him was starting to cause problems – he was exposed, and there were hundreds of armed troops in that cavernous space. Swerving to avoid the worst of the incoming bolts, he leapt up to one of the floor-level platforms, cleared out the deck with his bolt pistol pumping, then punched the release lever. The platform clattered upward swiftly as Hafloí reached for the krak grenades at his belt. He took two and set both to detonate at close to zero-count. As the platform reached the first stage of the access shaft, he leapt upward and outward, propelling himself across the wide chasm amid a hail of flying las-bolts.

He crashed heavily straight into the thick power cabling. It swayed drunkenly from the impact, and he stuffed the krak canisters into the thicker primary conduits, then shoved himself back away, dropping hard to the deck some twenty yards below. Even before he hit, the krak grenades went off, exploding in a wild snap of released energy and sending the severed cables flailing around him like whips. The breakage immediately set off emergency klaxons, and more tech-menials poured into the chamber from access hatches set high into the walls. The power-feed to the lasers stuttered, flickered, then blew completely, fusing a long line of tank-sized capacitors and sending shrapnel flying horizontally across the chamber.

Hafloí was now completely surrounded. Squads of armsmen advanced on him warily, firing steadily, scoring hits now that drilled into his armour and knocked him from side to side like a kicked marionette. Lexmechanics backed them up, bringing to bear strange weapons he didn't even recognise. Behind them were gun-servitors, and right at the back of the whole lot came nastier creations – walker-cages carrying industrial lasers and spinning metal-cutters. All the while the severed cables kept thudding down before lashing across the desk and sending spark clouds flying.

'Hel's *eyes*,' he grunted, spraying a wide scatter of bolts to send the nearest armsmen scurrying back into cover. 'Far too many.'

He bludgeoned his way back towards the relative sanctuary of the nearest access tunnels, fighting through knots of armsmen and taking more las-hits across his battered plate. They scattered before his frontal assault, but then came after him in droves, trying to bring him down with dense flurries of ranged fire, much of which impacted and made him stagger.

Hafloí piled through the first hatch he reached, then scrambled up the narrow crawl-way. Once he was a few yards up inside it, he turned and emptied his bolt magazine back at the closest of his pursuers. While they were still screaming he slammed home a fresh magazine and picked up speed again.

They had a lock on him now. They'd just keep coming, squad after squad, and sooner or later the numbers would tell. He had to get out now – find a shuttle, find a boarding torpedo, anything.

'I've bought the pack some time,' he voxed to Jorundur as he ran, hearing with some satisfaction the continuing explosions from the power lines behind him. 'But that's all they'll get – tell them to get out, and get out *now*.'

CHAPTER EIGHTEEN

The visions never left him. As he ran, Baldr was assailed by them – fantastical vistas of ice sheets melted by blue-tinged flames, of spectral daemons fighting with ghosts in the night skies, of the crusts of Midgardia tilting and erupting and bubbling into lakes of magma. He blinked furiously, determined to concentrate on the very real spectacle of ruin around him, but the dream-images just kept crowding in, jostling the real world aside.

Olgeir was right, of course – the enemy lied. And yet, the pack had been away from the Chapter for long enough. They had seen enough evidence of the erosion of Imperial control in every corner of the void, like an upheaved continent slowly slipping into the sea, fraying at the edges, boulder by boulder, until the land itself sighed under the waves. Maybe all citadels were broken, now. Maybe all worlds were on fire.

Some of his brothers might welcome that. Weary of the long grind, they would roar to greet the Wolftime, glad at last to be fighting in something decisive, something that promised to drown the greyness of reality in the blood of the brave. Baldr could not share that eagerness. For him, the fight had always been about more than prestige – it had been about the preservation of something, the cherishing of uniqueness. The enemy ushered in nothingness, annihilation, the disintegration of stable matter into a soup of screaming daemon-fodder. In the background of every heretical vision he had ever witnessed, that future was there, underpinning it, undermining it. The Heretic Astartes he had killed alongside Olgeir knew it, too – they all knew that truth. Every boast they made, every taunt, it was all empty, deep down, because that final goal could never be erased or forgotten. They were the heralds of emptiness, not just traitors to the Imperium, but traitors to their species, trading temporary glory for eternal extinguishment.

'I can't raise Gunnlaugur,' Olgeir muttered breathily, running at his side, leaping up stairs three at a time to reach the ramps to the landing stages. 'I don't think the Old Dog has, either.'

Baldr said nothing, just ran. Ahead were the walls to the orbital drop-zones, now burning freely. One of the Ecclesiarchy landers was trying to take off amid a veritable storm of las-fire, its thrusters leaking smoke and its stabilisers already kicking it askew. Warriors swarmed over every ground-level surface, virtually all renegades of some kind or another, hunting the last few of the world's defenders or merely seeking out plunder.

But then, just as they reached the gates, they caught sight of Gunnlaugur and Ingvar coming the other way. Gyrfalkon had a human female slumped over his shoulder, but it hadn't slowed him down much – both of them were moving fast, loping over the rubble.

'Vaerangi!' Olgeir called out. 'Word from Jorundur! He's–'

'I know,' Gunnlaugur shouted back. 'Just got through to us, too. Time's up, it seems.'

Baldr swivelled to follow Gunnlaugur's lead, and all four of them charged back down towards the rig's eastern galleries, following the route they'd taken earlier. As they did so, explosions rocked the command tower above them, blowing out the armaglass in clouds of spinning crystal.

He looked up at the skies. The clouds were still racing, flecked with black and crimson, swirled by the firestorms and prickling with lightning, but now there was something else – a quickening, a greater stirring. The patch of storm-cover over the very apex of the rig's pinnacles was darkening, thickening up. Something was affecting the atmosphere above it. He'd seen similar patterns on other worlds, and knew what was causing it.

Ingvar came up alongside him, running freely despite the extra weight on his shoulder. 'You ended the traitor?'

Baldr nodded. 'Heavy-Hand did,' he grunted. 'With some help.'

'What was it doing there?'

In all the frenzy of activity, amid all the fighting, Baldr had not even thought about that. Most of the forces crawling all over the rig were routine mortal filth, and a true Heretic Astartes had once been a rare thing to encounter. Strange, perhaps, that it should have chosen this rig, out of all the possible other ones, on which to make its landing.

'Who knows?' he said. 'It won't be going anywhere else.'

Ingvar stared at him for a moment, before turning his attention back to the chase. The decking felt looser underfoot now, as if the foundations of the city were disintegrating.

Baldr could have asked questions of his own just then. He could have asked if Ingvar had found the answers he sought in that tower, and who the woman was he'd brought out of its destruction, and if they'd discovered what so many Ecclesiarchy troops were doing among the ruins.

But instead he just glanced up again, briefly, to where the clouds had darkened again. The air was already heavier – a drawing of breath before the deluge, the sigh of the retreating surf before the tsunami.

'We're not going to make it, are we?' he murmured, the words slipping out, despite himself.

'We damned well are,' Ingvar growled back. 'Stop looking up, run harder.'

'What happened?' asked Klaive, who had expected to feel the jolt of the orbital lasers powering up, followed by the pillars of energy lancing down through the clouds below. Instead, the command bridge was in uproar, with menials shouting over one another and order-tubes clattering with fresh canisters.

No one was listening to him. Orquemond looked furious, and bellowed a series of invective-laced commands to his orderlies in the tiers below. Far above them all, the view from the armaglass fractured as repeated las-strikes stressed the void shields. Klaive bustled towards the cardinal, wondering whether he dared interrupt him, then decided that he didn't. As the deck pitched, he teetered back across to a vacant terminal, and punched up a status report. Most of what he saw didn't make much sense to him, but it was clear that a power drain had just knocked out the orbital batteries. From the way the crew was reacting, it didn't feel like a mere equipment malfunction, more like a full-blown mechanical crisis.

He shuffled along to the adjacent terminal, occupied by an operative with lieutenant-commander stripes on her shoulder and a hard look of concentration on her face.

'What's going on?' he asked.

She shot him an irritated glance. 'Who in all the hells are you?'

'Confessor to cardinals, little sister,' Klaive replied coldly. 'Watch your tongue and follow an order.'

He didn't look the part, he knew, but he sounded it, and she wasn't foolish enough to challenge him. 'Something's taken out a power-feed to the lasers. We're rerouting, but it's not an easy operation.'

'Something?'

'No one knows. Just... something.'

At that, Klaive suddenly felt a tight twinge in the pit of his stomach. They couldn't have followed him over. It was impossible. The cardinal had closed the void shield aperture once his own saviour pod had been salvaged, sealing them in. And yet, if something else had hit the hull...

'What ships do we have in close range?' he asked.

She gave him a bewildered look. 'I don't see how–'

'Answer the damn question. What ships are within strike range of this one?'

She switched to a local augur scan, which picked out a hundred vessel-idents, all rolling and swaying around one another. The largest displacements were the squadron's capital ships, the smallest were the interceptor wings. Somewhere in between was a loose collection of intermediate vessels, most with Ojada idents, sheltering from the apocalypse for as long as they could. Only one of those had no definite name-descriptor – just a class identifier and some comm-hail protocol blips.

'What's that one?'

'Unknown. It joined the defence of the *Purity of Action*, so it's been left alone, but I can't get more data.' She shrugged. 'Looks like a corsair's old junk heap. Refusing all hails.'

The Wolves. They were still in close – he'd assumed they would have broken for cover elsewhere rather than risk taking a beating from the Ecclesiarchy's guns. Klaive spun away from her, scrambling back to the command dais, now heedless of Orquemond's disapproval.

'You have to target that ship, my lord!' he shouted, vaulting up the steps. 'The galleon, two points down from the *Purity of Action* – you have to knock it out!'

The cardinal shot him an irritated glance. 'Stand down, confessor,' he warned. 'This is not the time for–'

'It is *not* an ally! By the grace of the Throne, target it!'

Orquemond's face flushed. 'Enough!' he snapped. 'Never again tell me what to do on my own bridge, or rank be damned and I'll have you thrown through the void-locks.' He turned his attention back to the control banks around him. 'We are almost out of time. Gunnery-master – how stands the main array?'

A man seated at a bulky lens-terminal just below the throne, his face hidden behind a bulbous augmetic filter and his hands trailing impulse-cables, looked up briefly. 'Restoration imminent, my lord. Final rerouting connections are being applied, then you may fire at will.'

'Tell me the instant you get clearance. Any word on what caused the power drop?'

'Nothing concrete, lord. All lower decks are now flooded with armsmen – we'll isolate it.'

Klaive balled his fists, standing impotently on the dais amid the torrent of data streaming down the lenses. His palms were sweaty. This sanctuary no longer felt safe at all. Should he make another break for it? There was nowhere to go. If the cardinal managed to get a shot away soon, destroying the last remnants of the Fulcrum on Ojada as well as the Wolves on the surface, that was still the best chance of getting disentangled from this thing. Once the battleship was safely back in the warp, whatever had followed him on board could surely be dealt with. Surely. The main thing was to keep the charade going – he had lapsed badly by panicking.

Just as he was about to slink back away, though, the gunnery-master banged his cable-laced fist on the console in triumph.

'We have it, lord!' the man cried, relieved. 'Full power restored – you may fire whenever you wish.'

Orquemond's eyes lit up again, this time with relish.

'Do it now,' he snarled. 'Turn that city to atoms.'

You could feel it before you saw it – a quickening, a downdraught of heat, a speckling in the cloud cover. A full orbital strike was such a stupendous expenditure of energy that even its targeting beams played havoc in the upper atmosphere. As Gunnlaugur tore along he could almost count the seconds trickling away. The tumult around him – the screams and shouts, the collapsing structures, the crackle of promethium fires – they melted into the background, just things to veer around or vault over. Everything was about speed, now – keep running, keep moving, get to the ship.

They had cut it too fine, but then this thing had always been a half-crazed quest, a deliberate race into the furnace with the hope that secrets could still be pulled from the ashes. He didn't regret it. To pull the trigger on that man, even if it had been the most basic of kills, the most skill-free, had at least closed the loop. Never let a murder go unavenged – that maxim was older than the Chapter itself, something that the tribes of Fenris had held sacred even in the long, empty years before the Allfather had come among them.

So there was satisfaction there, amid everything else. A task complete, a debt settled. He'd taken some records from the chamber – a few scrolls and scrits grabbed before they'd had to get out – and that would no doubt throw further light on what Chirastes had done. Of course, reading those would only prove possible if he survived, and that was by no means certain.

He shot a glance at Ingvar as the two of them leapt from a derelict balcony and crunched to the deck below. Somehow he managed to keep the woman from snapping her spine as he landed – a deft manoeuvre at speed.

'She's awake?' he asked, his boots echoing in the tunnel that enclosed them as they pushed on.

'Out cold,' Ingvar told him, his breathing heavy and rapid. 'Alive, though.'

'Tough.'

The four of them raced onward, recognising structures they'd passed earlier, or spotting fresh gaping holes in the decks where pillars had gone down. Eventually they reached the hall where the *Hlaupnir* had landed, still full of its cavalcade of wrecks and debris. A few gangs of desperate looters were attacking the ship, trying to force their way on board. The kaerls left to guard it had mobilised to drive them off, and even before the Space Wolves turned up were doing a good job of it. As soon as they saw the pack speeding towards them, they retreated inside and fired up the engines.

Gunnlaugur didn't waste any time on taking out the looters. He charged through a bunch of them at the foot of the opening gang-ramp, backhanding one aside before thudding up and into the hull. From there, he hauled himself up through the access column, clambered rapidly up the short ladder, swept out through the hatch and dumped himself into the command throne.

'Emergency launch, no delay,' he snarled, hitting the atmospheric-seal lever and swinging the throne around on its column. As he did so, the kaerls already in position activated the main thrusters, flooding the hall with fire and immolating the few looters still trying to hammer their way inside. Olgeir and Baldr strapped themselves in for the ascent – Ingvar must have gone below with the female. Gunnlaugur assumed direct control, boosting the mainline power even as the ship swung around, aiming for the ragged exit in the rig's outer flank.

The entire place started to shake. The rockcrete below them buckled, rippling up and down like threshed grain. Supporting girders snapped, pinging apart and showering the burning void with blown rivets.

'Here it comes...' murmured Olgeir, his fists clamped to the arms of his throne.

The air shimmered, first a blip, then a rapid acceleration, a ramping up of light and heat. The walls around them glowed red, then orange, then bright yellow.

Gunnlaugur levelled the *Hlaupnir*'s prow at the gap and smacked the lever up to full power. The vessel boosted forward, blazing up to maximum velocity as the walls around them burned white-hot. The cavern disintegrated, melting and popping and atomising into a seething gas-ball even as they raced through it.

'Teeth of Russ,' Baldr observed calmly. 'Look at the hull temperature.'

Gunnlaugur didn't look at the hull temperature. He kept the engines roaring, rocketing them out of the inferno and into a world of dazzling, coruscating, retina-searing light. The orbital laser-beam was hundreds of yards in diameter, a tremendous column of destruction that enveloped everything, obliterating all other sources of heat and energy and subsuming them within its exclusive and terrible embrace. The forward viewers went white, the augur-lenses went white, the atmospheric controllers screamed, the engines shrieked from overload.

And then they were out, shooting clear of the annihilation-horizon, the ship's back aflame and streaming plasma like a comet. Only then did Gunnlaugur risk a quick glance at the rear viewers before powering the ship out over the open seas.

The heart of the laser-beam was impossible to stare at directly, even for Astartes eyes. Its edges thundered, jutting straight down into the oceans and kicking up vast columns of superheated steam. The rig-city's structure could just be made out within its perimeter – blurred from heat-shake, a mere gauze of pale grey amid the liquid neon of the pure energy lance. It was crumpling, collapsing, sliding into ruin, melting and re-forming even as its terraces and decks and pumping stations toppled and imploded and dissolved. For an instant, its profile was shakily visible, wobbling like an apparition, still vast even in its state of dissolution.

Then the main reactor core detonated. A gigantic ball of flame flared up, fuelled and goaded by the laser-column, swelling like the heart of some earth-locked sun, racing out in a circumference of radiant energy. The *Hlaupnir* was caught up in the shock wave, hurled like a toy across the smouldering oceans, its compensators overloaded and its atmospheric turbines spluttering. It spun head over aft, whirling crazily. For a horrific moment its prow was aimed right into the promethium-slapped waves.

Gunnlaugur killed the power to all but the directional burners, swinging the ship's axis back into line and sending it skating low against the waves like a flat stone. Furnace-hot winds howled past them, whipping up the ocean-burn and fanning the flames into sheets of raw effervescence.

He yanked the control lever, bringing the nose up just as the hurricane blew itself out and the laser-beam finally snapped out of existence. The *Hlaupnir* angled steeply, climbing fast, its outer plates still streaking with smoke but its hull intact. For a few moments the hellscape below remained visible – a seascape of churning fire, marked by the charred remains of the rig-city, now just a skeleton of metal struts tossed about by the turbulent foam. An enormous wall of water radiated out from its epicentre, the summit two hundred yards tall, already crashing into the closest rigs and threatening to bring them down in turn.

But then the *Hlaupnir* broke into the smog clouds, and the realviewers were obscured again. The ship rattled and shook, still racing, keeping the velocity high in preparation for the firing of the void drives.

Olgeir let out a long, low whistle, then chuckled heartily.

'Fine flying, Skullhewer,' he said.

Gunnlaugur didn't smile. He kept both hands on the controls, poised for breaking cloud cover and re-entering the orbital kill-zone. Russ only knew what they'd find when they emerged into that.

'Save it,' he growled. 'We're not out yet.'

CHAPTER NINETEEN

'Get a lock on the system runner!' Jorundur bellowed, hammering out a series of secondary commands on his console. 'The moment you see it, send a protective spread to nadir. And someone, anyone, get me a fix on the whelp's position.'

The *Amethyst Suzeraine* was moving, ponderously, uncertainly, shifting for position among the crowded orbital ballet. The Ecclesiarchy ships were still in close proximity, though they were taking a dreadful battering by then, and the formation had started to fracture. The gigantic *Immaculate Destiny*, its work done, was beginning to come round, its prow and underside flashing from las-hits, its mighty plasma drives keying up for ignition.

He still had no precise lock on Hafloí. The *Hlaupnir*, for all he knew, had been destroyed in the orbital energy beam – everything coming out of Ojada was now a howl of empty static, and even the realviewers were blurred and shaky. The Archenemy ships, sensing blood, were flocking in now, targeting anything still headstrong or foolish enough to remain in orbit. The galleon had to get out, and get out soon, or nothing but wreckage would mark its brief presence here.

'*Hlaupnir* sighted!' Bjargborn announced triumphantly, flagging up the approach vector. 'Keying in intercept course now.'

'Very good,' growled Jorundur, trying not to betray too much relief. 'Maintain free firing, all flanks – it'll get hotter before we're clear.'

So it did. The Ecclesiarchy squadron was leaving now, pulling up and away, its escorts tilting over to gain an angle before boosting hard. Even as they completed their manoeuvre, one of the smaller destroyers was caught in heavy crossfire, its shields overloaded. Spears of las-fire slid under its hull-plates, buckling them and disabling the engines. It started to list back towards the gravity well, crippled and failing.

'Keep us moving,' Jorundur ordered, watching as half a dozen Archenemy vessels started to slide into strike range. It was hard to keep up with them all – every scope was crammed. 'As soon as we get them, full burn out of here.'

Heavy hits started to come in – coordinated strikes that made the void-array shriek and threatened to pierce through to the hull. Jorundur kept things in motion, dropping down steadily before rolling away aft. The seconds counted down, each one grinding by turgidly, too slowly, agonisingly. At any moment, he expected to hear the crack and squeal of something major breaking.

And then he saw it – trailing fire, hurtling up out of the atmosphere, its sleek lines scorched black but its drives still firing.

'Bring it in!' he cried.

'Lord, we are close to the–'

'I know damn well where we are – *bring it in*.'

For the second time, the *Amethyst Suzeraine* dropped dangerously near to the roof of the world's atmosphere, this time with its retro thrusters blazing furiously. A brace of enemy fighters, launched from a nearby gun-carrier, swooped down after it, but that couldn't be helped. Jorundur kept his eyes locked on the augurs, trying to gauge the absolute last moment to effect the transfer. At the back of his mind, nearly out of sensor range now, he was aware of the *Immaculate Destiny* fighting its way clear of the orbital battle-sphere, dragging dozens of enemy ships with it.

'Rear shields down on my mark,' he warned, counting down to the moment, watching the hull temperature rise. 'Hangar doors open, reception crews on standby...'

The enemy fighters tilted in close, raking them with hard-round fire, causing the entire ship to shake. He ignored them, leaving the response to the overworked gunnery crews. The chronos rattled down, the augurs tracked the incoming *Hlaupnir*, the damage counters ticked up, and up, and up...

'Mark!' Jorundur shouted.

Void shields crackled out across the hangar maws, immediately exposing the hull to fresh strikes. The *Hlaupnir* hurtled up towards the gap, rolling over at the last moment to line up with the cantilevered door panels, then blasting inside.

'Away!' roared Jorundur. 'Shields up, full power to plasma-lines! Get us out of this Hel-damned system!'

'Arvus-class shuttle incoming on starboard bow-sector,' Bjargborn reported calmly, even as the *Amethyst Suzeraine* began to pick up speed.

'From the Church battleship?'

'Aye, lord.'

Jorundur swung round towards a ranged lens-feed to get a closer look. It was flying erratically, as if it had shipped some damage to its engines, and its cockpit was cracked and leaking oxygen. 'Any hails?'

'Comms unit seems to be down. No audex, but I'm getting a strange pattern from the lumens. It may be nothing.'

Jorundur took a look. The shuttle was flashing in semi-random patterns, as if its electrical systems were totally shot.

Except the patterns weren't random at all – he suddenly recognised the Juvyka battle-cant sequences.

Op-en th-e do-ors y-ou pi-ece of skít–

'Get it inside,' ordered Jorundur, a wave of relief washing over him. 'That's the last one – then we're gone.'

The galleon creaked around again, swinging up and away from the raging troposphere. The fighters followed it, dogging them like ragged crows, but the gunnery crews were still managing to pick them off here and there, limiting the carnage they could cause. The Ecclesiarchy ships had powered up to full escape velocity, leaving behind their own trail of wreckage in the void. There would be no reckoning with them, now – the galleon had no hope of catching them. The rat had got away, and despite everything they had achieved, that stung him badly.

A few seconds later, they caught up with the damaged Arvus, taking more las-strikes and projectile-hits all the while. Gunnlaugur hailed him from the hangar as soon as it was in visual range, ordering immediate system-exit, which was both a relief and an irritation, because he was already going as fast as he could. The Arvus limped in under the cover of a final massed volley from the rear gunners. The macrocannons were by then almost out of mainline ammunition, but they spat out what they had left in a display of impressive petulance, taking out four more racing fighters before having to switch to lascannons and heavy bolters.

'Full speed, now!' Jorundur thundered, swinging back around to gauge the congestion ahead. Even as the *Amethyst Suzeraine* lumbered up to its grinding straight-line velocity, he was counting the threats, judging the angles, trying to thread a path that would get them away from the doomed world. 'All vectors set for Mandeville horizon, let's stay intact for just a little longer, eh?'

He heard the tramp of boots from behind him. Before he turned to face the returning pack, his comm-line crackled open with a burst from Hafloí.

'Took your time, didn't you?' he said, sounding breathless and annoyed.

'Amazed you got out at all,' Jorundur replied. 'I'm guessing you didn't track down the rat.'

'No chance.'

'Then he got away. Damn it all.'

The comm-feed hissed with what sounded like a chuckle.

'Maybe, maybe not. I couldn't leave without giving them something to chew over.'

He had made it. He had got away.

The *Immaculate Destiny* sailed through the warp, along with most of the escorts it had brought to Ojada. Klaive didn't know what its course was now. He knew very little about Orquemond's intentions, only that the cardinal had been deeply disappointed not to have had Chirastes brought to him in person, and regarded the destruction of the renegade from distance as close to a total defeat.

For Klaive, though, it was perfect. The Wolves, locked on their creaky, useless galleon, had been unable to get close enough to exact the revenge they surely wished for. One of them, it was true, must have somehow got on board the battleship and attacked the orbital lasers, but it was clear that the interloper had either been killed or had been forced to flee again – he'd heard it muttered that a shuttle was missing from the reserve pool. It had been a long time now since the ship had broken the veil, and the damage was steadily being repaired. Finally, he was able to relax, just a little. Finally, he was able to turn his mind to what came next.

He had to get off the *Immaculate Destiny* as soon as he could. His story had been constructed under duress, and wouldn't stand up to much scrutiny. He would speak to Orquemond, when he could, and explain that he needed to return to his previous duties. A shuttle to take him to the closest Ecclesiarchy facility would be quite sufficient, and after that he could make his own arrangements. Once back within the bosom of the Church, he would be able to draw on his private accounts again, make contact with his old network of associates. Some of Delvaux's remaining allies would no doubt be willing to help, if he made it worth their while.

It would be best, he thought, to forget about the Fulcrum altogether. It was finished now, its last station wiped out and its mastermind dead. The Wolves had nothing more to hunt, and the Church had nothing more to fear. He would have to move on, to find new patrons and new causes. As soon as he was away from Orquemond, free of association with the whole damned business, things would get easier again.

They had already started to improve. The crew had found him new robes, had arranged for a cadre of menials to see to his needs, and had appointed comfortable chambers for him on the command levels. Since the ship had entered the warp, he had been left largely to his own devices. The time had been filled well – he had feasted on the exquisite meals prepared in the senior refectories, perused the fine collection of devotional books in the cardinal's private library, started to plot out the course back towards greatness.

It was seven days before Orquemond paid him a visit again. Klaive had just finished another extensive supper, taken in his private rooms, and was pondering retiring for a period of rest. Orquemond arrived without warning, entering the chamber with four armsmen and a women in a black tunic and bodyglove.

'By His immortal will,' said the cardinal, inclining his head a little in greeting. 'I see you are enjoying our hospitality, confessor.'

Klaive stood up, dabbing at his chin. Orquemond was a powerful presence even out of his battle-armour. The armsmen all had their lasguns drawn. The woman hung back, said nothing, but he didn't like the look of her at all.

'You have been most generous, lord,' Klaive replied. 'I trust that all is well?'

'Perfectly. Though the damage in the lower levels was remarkable. It seems, contrary to all sense, that a single warrior must have got on board. Extraordinary. I am still uncertain how it was done, or even why. Do you have a theory?'

Klaive began to get uncomfortable. The tone of the man's voice was unmistakable – he'd used it himself, many times, but only when interrogating a suspect. 'None at all. Though the servants of the Archenemy can be powerful, their objectives hard to fathom.'

'Quite so. It was for that reason that I ordered a forensic examination of the damaged areas. I had to be sure that I was not being somehow made a fool of.' Orquemond held out his hand, and an armsman gave him a small piece of metal. Klaive only had to glance at it to see what it was – a data-slug, capable of holding hours of testimony. 'This was the only thing we managed to retrieve. It was left in plain sight, just where we were likely to stumble across it. Curious, isn't it? Left just where we lost that shuttle, amid all the wreckage of the outer blast-doors.'

Klaive couldn't take his eyes off it. A sick taste was beginning to ferment in his mouth. He tried to think of something to say, but no words would come.

'There is a lot stored here,' Orquemond said. 'Would you like to listen to a portion of it? Very well.'

He clicked a switch, and a crackling audex-feed began to play.

'I don't even know that the Fulcrum is a single person. I told you that.'

Orquemond clicked it closed. 'There's much more. It seems they recorded every conversation they ever had with you. And one of them, no doubt displeased that you tried to escape their care, felt obliged to leave a copy here.'

Klaive's vision began to waver. He felt nauseous. He looked at the woman again.

'This whole business has left me angry,' Orquemond said. 'It has soured my mood. And yet, just when all seems darkest, He has ways of rewarding the faithful. I wished to learn the truth of the Fulcrum, and thought I had been denied it. Now, though, I find that illumination was always waiting, handed to me, so to speak, on a plate.'

The nausea grew. 'I know almost nothing, lord,' he tried feebly. 'You will see this, if you listen to what is on that thing. I could tell them very little.'

Orquemond nodded to an armsman, who shut the doors and locked them. The woman took a step towards him, withdrawing something metallic and barbed from her tunic.

'Perhaps they didn't press you hard enough,' Orquemond said. 'My servants are very diligent – they have a way of getting to the truth, no matter the... messiness encountered on the way.'

The woman began to unfold more instruments, never making eye contact with him. Two of the armsmen moved to stand beside him. They had shackles in their hands.

Klaive felt like weeping. He had been so close.

'You don't need to do this, my lord,' he tried. 'I could just... talk.'

Orquemond smiled at him – as cold and humourless a gesture as it was possible to imagine. 'But you have already lied so completely to me, confessor. I do not like that. And, as I said, this thing has placed me in a foul mood.'

Klaive barely noticed as he was forced back onto the chair, the shackles closed over his wrists. The woman finished her preparations, and started to move the tip of the steel barb towards him.

'I wanted Chirastes, but you will do,' said Orquemond, fixing him with a final, acid stare before turning to the woman. 'Interrogator, you may begin when ready.'

IV
THE DEAD OF FENRIS

CHAPTER TWENTY

Gunnlaugur had been right – the woman was tough. As Ingvar looked down at her, he found himself increasingly impressed.

She was old, by mortal standards – maybe more than a century old. The skin around her face was tight, as if she'd undergone rejuvenat on more than one occasion, though those effects were fraying now. She was thin, with signs of malnourishment, and had clearly not been in good health even before the suicide pact with her master. The poison she'd taken on Ojada was working its way through her body rapidly, shutting down her organs, turning her blood to gel, blocking up her lungs.

The two of them were alone in a private compartment of the *Amethyst Suzeraine*'s medical bay. The walls, deck and ceiling had been scrubbed clean prior to their arrival, and now gleamed whitely under twin strip lumens. The woman lay on a hard cot, her head propped up with a rough bolster. The ship's medicae staff had done what they could when he'd brought her in, and Ingvar had briefly held out some hope that she might be revived. Eventually, though, the chief officer, a competent man from Collaqua's old crew, had shaken his head.

'Acherosa,' he'd said grimly. 'Horrible stuff.'

After that, they'd made her as comfortable as they could, and left the two of them alone. She had a morphex line inserted into her arm, as well as numbing agents prepped and ready in vials.

She should have died on the passage up from Ojada, by rights. Something was keeping her alive – force of will, maybe. Bajola had been the same, Ingvar remembered. There was something about the coming of the moment, the final moment, that did it to all of them. They always wanted to talk.

'He didn't tell us the truth, did he?' Ingvar said.

There was so much he wanted to ask her. Everything about the discovery of Chirastes had been frustrating – that they'd been too late to properly enact revenge, that there was still so much they didn't know. If time had not been so pressing, he'd have wished to extract every last morsel of information from her – the Fulcrum's history, its modes of operation, its bases of operations.

The woman smiled weakly. 'He didn't lie,' she croaked. 'He never really lied. Not even to me.'

'Then he left something out.'

She closed her eyes. 'Why do you think there's anything more to say? You are a devil. My life has been devoted to hurting you.'

'*His* life was. Maybe yours was too, in the beginning.' Ingvar watched her carefully throughout. 'But I saw the way you were with him. I think you've been doing this for a very long time. Long enough to ask why your whole existence was wasted on one man's obsessions. He kept the faith, right up to the end, because he had to. I'm not sure you did.'

The woman smiled, then opened her bloodshot eyes again. 'Quite the philosopher. I hoped you were going to rage at me, barbarian.'

'I can, if you want. Or you can use this time to salvage something.'

'And give you what you need.'

'Just the truth. Imagine it – you could go the Allfather with your soul eased.'

'The *Allfather.*' She shook her head, a dismissive movement, heavy with pain and contempt. 'Blasphemy. All of it, blasphemy. That was what started this.'

'Did you never think, just for a moment, that by harming us, you were harming the Emperor's work?'

'A work may be corrupted. Perhaps you were purer, long ago, when He first made you.'

'We have never changed. That's one thing even our enemies agree on – we were fighting His wars even before there was a Church.'

'There was always a Church.'

Ingvar sighed. 'You wish to debate history with me? Now?' He stretched out, reaching to grip the edge of her cot, leaning on the frame. 'What is your name?'

'Buta Avelina.'

'You were his deputy, yes? His most senior commander?'

'By the end, yes.'

'So how did you do it?'

Avelina's expression flickered. Her knuckles whitened as she clutched the blanket. 'Like he said. We tried going to war, and failed. So we did what we had to, in secret.'

'But you needed whole regiments. You couldn't have hidden those.'

'The regiments weren't hidden. They were Astra Militarum, Navy, defence forces. They operated in plain sight, under normal chains of command. Most of their troops were untampered with. A few – sometimes dozens, sometimes hundreds – were ours. The ones we'd built and trained. They were inserted carefully, over decades. Even they didn't know much, not until the imprint-commands were given.' She swallowed painfully. 'Then they only had one objective. One they'd die to reach. That was the pattern. In the heat of battle – always major engagements, the bigger the better – we'd work to place auxiliaries in the right position. Move alongside you. They'd only deploy when we told them, and only when the target was exposed. That was the hardest part of our work – monitoring, making the judgement on when to activate. Chirastes blew his entire fortune to build that predictive capacity. He could have been master of a whole diocese. Maybe master of much more. In the end, though, seeing you suffer was more important.'

Was there an edge of bitterness in her voice, then? Or just the pain having its effect?

'A waste,' he murmured.

'Was it?' She shrugged a little. 'How long have you hunted us, in your turn?'

'Wrong us, and we will surely come after you.'

'And, as far as Leon saw it, you committed the original crime.'

Her voice was getting weaker. Debates over who had started the vendetta, and for what cause, seemed more futile than ever. 'So the work was complete, was it? Your funds were all expended, your troops all gone?'

'The coin was spent, yes. We made ourselves paupers, hunted eventually by our own people. I began to wonder who would reach us first – them, you, or neither. As fate would have it, you both did.'

'But you haven't answered me. Were all your armies extinguished?'

She hesitated. Her gaze shifted, almost like a schola girl caught in some minor wrongdoing. Ingvar wondered how much damage to her mind had been done over the long years of secrecy. Maybe she might have been genuinely impressive, once. Now she was ruined, burned out, and she must have known it.

'Ojada was the last base,' she said reluctantly. 'The last place we had regiments under our influence. All the Hunters we still controlled, they were in those units, training there, waiting for the command to activate.'

'Why? Chirastes said he'd reached the end of the list.'

'He had. Or, at least, by the time you reached us. The programme had become harder to operate. We used to control an entire fleet. A huge fleet! It was all gone, used up. Everything was difficult – we were reliant on agents in the Ojada Administratum. Those regiments had been earmarked for the defence of that planet. They should have been present, when the enemy arrived. It took a lot of effort to get them posted off-world. You can imagine why.'

'You moved them? To where?'

'To where the last name on the list would be. The last one. Leon was adamant he had to get them all. So we got the regiments sent away, added to the sector musters. Once they did their work, everything would be accomplished. They've gone now. Maybe you even passed their troop carriers on your way in-system. Ha! Imagine that. You would have gone straight past them, thinking they were evacuating.'

She was fading quickly now. Her gaze was unfocused, her skin had turned grey.

'Where were they going?' he asked. 'What was the name he gave them?'

'You are devils,' she slurred, smiling. 'And you have been duly punished.'

Ingvar wanted to grab her then, to shake her by the shoulders, but that would have snapped her spine. He moved closer, not to threaten her, just to hear what she said. As her life slipped away, so did the last chance for information.

'You can see me here in front of you,' he said. 'You can see truly that I am no devil. You know, in your soul, that you have made a terrible mistake, and that it has consumed your whole life. You have a chance – a last chance – to make partial amends, as your final breaths come, if you choose it.'

'I never broke a vow.'

'All I need is a name. The last one Chirastes wanted.'

She shot him a strange look then. 'You and he are the same, I think. I might have served you the same way, had I been born on your witch-world. Think on that.' The last colour bled from her cheeks. 'Then I might have destroyed myself for another useless cause, and wasted my promise for another tyrant.'

Ingvar's eyes never left hers. She was slipping away, and nothing he could say made much difference now.

'Ah, I see him now,' she murmured. 'I see him amid the choirs of angels. I see the golden veil lifting.' Then, strangest of all, she winked at him – a sly gesture, one that indicated there was still some spark there, some hint of the woman she had been a long time ago. 'Not really. I don't want to see him ever again. I just want to rest, now. I want it all to be over. It's been a long time, consumed by this. And it wasn't even my revenge. We all just followed orders.'

She looked at him directly, her expressions suddenly clarifying – the clarity of the moment before death, when the transition between worlds was imminent and visible, like a cliff-edge into oblivion.

'Blackmane,' she said, with some satisfaction. 'Blackmane Thunderfist. That's the last one. That's the one he had to get.'

'So, tell me how it was.'

Gunnlaugur sat in the throne in his quarters. It was a heavy stone piece, ripped out of the *Hlaupnir*'s innards and bolted to the deck of the *Amethyst Suzeraine*. The granite was carved with runes, some so old that the figures had almost worn away, though the Fenrisian knotwork would still be made out, snaking its way under the armrests and up to the crown. On either side, braziers burned low, making the walls shift and flicker.

The only other occupant was Olgeir. He'd removed his helm and scraped the lacquer out of his beard. His armour still bore the signs of combat – a blackened dent in his shoulder-guard – and would be removed soon for attention at the forge.

'A dreg of the old Legions,' Olgeir said. 'It had some tricks. They didn't prove sufficient.'

'And Fjolnir?'

'He was very helpful.'

'He didn't... waver?'

Olgeir looked at him carefully. 'He has been master of himself since we pulled him out from under Njal's nose. You know that.'

'But still.' Gunnlaugur shifted against the cold stone. He had to resist the urge to drum his fingers, to move again. He was restless. Impatience already tore at him, to be moving again, to shift to the next sniff of quarry. Now that they were back in the warp, every emotion was heightened. 'The creature was corrupted. Proximity to that, well...'

'Is that why you sent him with me? To see if he could handle it?'

Gunnlaugur raised an eyebrow, genuinely surprised. 'You think I'd do that? No. It had to be removed, that was all.'

And that was true. At least, it was what he told himself was true. In battle, with the rush of events and the need for decision, it might have been a little different – you couldn't always reconstruct, after the action.

'So why was it there?'

'Not much time to ask it questions,' Olgeir said, amused. 'Baldr might know more.'

'I'll speak to him, then.'

'They're everywhere, vaerangi. The old Legions. Like acid-spiders spilled from a nest. You know what I think? I think they're going where they want to now, taking advantage of the collapse. It didn't need a reason – it was just there, picking at the meat on the bones.'

'Aye.' Gunnlaugur drew in a long breath. 'Aye, that seems to be the way. A time of trial. Maybe it'll burn itself out, like all the others. Or maybe not, this time.'

Olgeir looked uncomfortable.

'Anything else you want to tell me, Heavy-Hand?' Gunnlaugur asked.

For a moment, it didn't look like there was. 'You really should speak to Baldr,' he said, eventually. 'But it… told him things. About Fenris. About fighting there.'

'Fighting.'

'It told him the home world had been ravaged.'

Gunnlaugur laughed. 'It saw this with its own eyes, did it?' He shook his head. 'And then somehow ended up here, running down promethium caches on a random rig-city? Come, now. They *lie*, brother.'

'That's what I told him.'

'But you're not convinced.'

Again, the hesitation. 'We've been away a long time. No tidings, no contact. I don't know… You said it yourself – this feels like an acceleration.'

Gunnlaugur shook his head. 'Aye, but some things are unshakable, at least until Russ returns. This creature hadn't seen any sign of him, on its travels?'

'We'll have to go back at some stage,' said Olgeir.

'That's the intention.'

'So did you get enough? You killed the one you needed to, ended the hunt?'

Gunnlaugur smiled darkly. 'We killed the one we needed to. As for the hunt, I don't know. I need to study what we took from the chamber. Gyrfalcon's speaking to the last survivor. He has a way with mortals – I'd put coin down on him finding something else.' He sat forward in the throne, adjusting his weight over the stone, clasping his gauntlets together. 'I know you wish to return, brother. I know what it means to you, to us all. And we will do it, when we have certainty. When I can bring something with us, to show them why we had to leave. Anything less, and they'd be within their rights to have our heads, no?'

'But what might we find waiting, vaerangi, if we leave it too late?'

Gunnlaugur's smile vanished.

'I'll make the judgement,' he said. 'When all is done, when all is known. Not before.'

If he was honest, Bjargborn hadn't really expected to see Haflói again. Even by the standards of his masters, launching a saviour pod on a ship-to-ship transfer during a void-battle had been ambitious. Once the galleon was back into the warp, he'd wanted to see the evidence for himself, just to check that there wasn't some cruel trick being played on them all. Down in the main hangar, when the shuttle's doors were opened up, he'd tensed, in case vengeful Ecclesiarchy armsmen had spilled out into the hangars. In the end, though, Haflói had limped down onto the rock-crete, alone, his pelts sheared away and his armour looking like it had been for a spell in a blast-furnace.

The Blood Claw had pulled his helm off, shaken his red hair, and grinned. 'Quite a ride,' he'd said.

In truth, though, he'd been badly injured. A single lasgun posed little threat to a Space Marine, but hundreds of them, aimed at close quarters, could do real damage. When the menials got him out of his armour, the extent of that damage became obvious. Much of his plate had been carved up badly, with joints seared away and control cables severed. A few more well-aimed beams, and he'd never have made it back.

Jorundur had been pleased to see Haflói return, greeting him with a slightly warmer grunt than usual. Gunnlaugur had ordered him down to the medicae bay to get himself patched up. Only once he was on his way, barely able to stay on his feet, did the Wolf Guard clap his hand on the warrior's lacerated shoulder-guard.

'You did well,' he'd said, his mouth twitching into a crooked smile. 'When all this is over, maybe, we might not send you back.'

After that, Bjargborn was detained with duties on the command bridge – mostly clearing up the mess Suaka had created. Jorundur said nothing to him about that. It hadn't been Bjargborn's sole responsibility to keep an eye on her, or anyone else, but the chain of command did stop with him, at least with regard to the baseline-human tiers of the crew. Sooner or later the discussion would have to be had. Were there signs that were missed? How many others from the old corsair ranks were liable to snap under pressure? Could they still trust any of them?

Once he completed the urgent tasks on the bridge, he headed down to the medicae levels. After any engagement there were casualties to tally up, task-squads to reassign, assessments of worker fitness to be made. He travelled down the long mag-train track, disembarked at the medicae level and made for the sealed hatchway. Once inside, he worked his way along the rows of cots, noting whether each occupant was likely to pull through, keeping half an eye on the bustling medicae staff and checking how quickly they were burning through the scarce supplies. The cots were already fully occupied, and those unlucky enough to be brought in late were now lying on the deck-floor with drips pinned up on the walls or splinted limbs waiting for proper reset. It smelled bad, as all medicae wards did in such conditions – a mix of chems and bodily waste, poorly filtered by the overworked air processors.

Hafloí could have demanded a chamber to himself and they'd have given it to him. Instead, he stood in a corner next to a supply-gurney, stripped of his armour, surrounded by half-conscious invalids and bustling menials, doing his own repair-work. As Bjargborn approached, he seemed to be finishing up, snipping the last of the sutures from his self-sewn lacerations and dropping the heavy-duty needles back into the steel dishes. He smiled broadly up as Bjargborn approached.

'Rivenmaster!' he said. 'Glad you came.'

Bjargborn bowed. 'I am just glad to see you alive, lord.'

Hafloí shrugged, a gesture of magnificent ambivalence. The absence of any kind of fear, any kind of concern for physical safety – it could still take you aback, sometimes. 'So what happened? With that officer?'

'I do not know.' Immediately, Bjargborn felt the guilt rush back, the acute sense of failure. 'I have a team looking through her quarters, but I do not think they will find much. If there was fault on my part, then–'

'Ach, forget that.' Hafloí sluiced down the last laceration with some counterseptic, then flexed his arm, testing his stitching. 'They're not of the ice. You know what I mean? Not like we are. They're weak. Gunnlaugur knows it. You've done a damned good job knocking some shape into them, and he won't forget it.' He reached for a length of bandage and wrapped it around his forearm. 'Anyway, this won't last forever. Given a bit of luck, we'll be back on a proper warship soon. One you can take some pride in commanding.' He tied the fabric off. The bruises on his skin were already looking less lurid. 'How does that sound, eh? A real *drekkar*, one with a crew that knows how to follow an order.'

It sounded good. It was all Bjargborn wanted, now – to get off this creaking hulk and resume service in the way he'd been trained. At times, including just then, he yearned for it so badly it hurt. 'When the moment comes,' he said, keeping all that emotion in check, just as always, 'I'll give thanks to the Allfather.'

Hafloí laughed, limping back down the aisle between the cots, swinging his arms to shake off the last stiffness.

'It'll come, rivenmaster,' he said. 'I'm going to speak to Skullhewer now. If he got what he wanted down there, we'll be headed home sooner than you think. I can see this being the last voyage we ever take in this rust-heap.'

Bjargborn watched him go. Then he looked around him, at the mix of kaerls and non-Fenrisians, crammed together in a gaudy chamber with more decoration than useful medical function.

'One way or another, that may be true,' he said to himself, before stirring, and getting back to work.

CHAPTER TWENTY-ONE

They met in the Annulus Chamber again, just as before. The fires had been stoked, making the walls glow a deep red. The distant thrum of the warp drives made the place echo, and from outside the walls the muffled clamour and clank of the starship's many internal systems could be picked up.

Gunnlaugur waited for Haflói to take his place, the last of the pack to do so, then leaned forward, elbows grazing the granite.

'So, it wasn't what we expected,' he said. 'Yes, there was a list. A list of those within the Chapter, all marked for assassination. And yes, they'd had some success with it. But it was a product of madness, not design.'

All of them listened, Ingvar most intently. He'd had a chance to look at some of the scrolls retrieved from Ojada, but only Gunnlaugur had read them all.

'It's been going on for decades,' the Wolf Guard went on. 'Ever since the Incursion of Fools. Remember that, from the sagas? I still remember them laughing about it in the Hall of Fire. Empty laughs, I thought. No one came out of that with much honour. I'm glad it was before my time.'

'That's what started it?' Olgeir asked doubtfully.

'Aye. Just one soul, humiliated by what we did to him, willing to kill his own prospects to get revenge. That's who we killed on Ojada. Maybe he might have been more impressive, back when he controlled fleets, but down there he was just a ranter, curled up around his bitterness. Slaying him was like slaying a sickened dog.'

'He didn't have the support of the Church,' Ingvar added. 'No part of it, not knowingly. He was acting alone. Even they wanted it over, once they realised he was still active.'

'They may be bastards,' said Gunnlaugur, 'but they're not all insane. He was.'

Haflói laughed then, a low cynical chuckle. 'All this trouble. How did he do it?'

'He was a cardinal astra, when he was anybody,' said Gunnlaugur. 'Once, he could build entire armies. We encountered some of his creations on the planet. They don't look like much, but they can fight. Once he had those, he started putting them into Militarum regiments, getting them sent to warzones where we were active. They'd deploy as close as they could, right at the heart of the fighting, with a single name imprinted on their minds.

648

Then, when everything was blurred by battle-confusion, they'd strike. Afterwards, their target was just one more casualty. Chirastes would move on to the next one.'

Jorundur frowned. 'That's not possible,' he said. 'The deaths would have been picked up.'

'Who was looking?' Gunnlaugur countered. 'Only those in squad command during the incursion were targeted, and that's from one hundred and fourteen years ago. How many warriors from the packs would you expect to make it that long? Hel, we've lost more warriors in single battles and never stopped to ask how they all died.'

'Hjortur was one,' said Ingvar. 'They made it look like greenskins, and we never questioned it, because others did die that day to ork claws. Chirastes didn't care whether we knew he was taking revenge – it only mattered that *he* did.'

'I can't believe it,' said Olgeir. 'How did they even get hold of this list?'

Gunnlaugur smiled grimly. 'I scoured the scrolls for that. It seems they compiled it while in orbit about Fenris, the one and only time they were there. Some comms must have been intercepted during the fighting, and Chirastes hung around long enough to extract transcripts. My guess is that's all they ever had. Everything else, everything they did, came from that.'

'Those would have been in battle-cant,' said Baldr.

'Hard to break, but not impossible,' said Ingvar. 'If you had decades to work at it.'

'But they didn't get it all right,' said Gunnlaugur. 'They were guessing about some of the data. See, I found a reference to Svengar Brokenaxe in the scrolls. They killed him, so the records claim, thirty years ago during a joint campaign in the Artaf Rho System. I don't know if they really did kill him there. But I do know that he couldn't have been part of the Incursion of Fools – he wasn't even born then. So maybe they mistranslated a message, or got a name mixed up, or someone in their administratum just had to put something on a report. I don't know. But don't assume we're dealing with all-powerful conspirators, here. This was a damaged man, crushing his own future to lash out at an enemy who barely knew he existed. It was a mess. A poisonous mess.'

'But it's over now, right?' asked Hafloí. 'You killed him, you got the records? The debt's settled.'

'Almost,' said Ingvar. 'Ojada was the only base they still used. Their final cache of warriors was there, saved up for the last name of all. If we'd got there a few days earlier, we'd have found them in place – members of the system Militarum garrisons, stationed to defend rig production.'

'Chirastes got them sent off-world,' said Gunnlaugur. 'Gods only know how, but they're all in the warp now. He lied to us, even at the end – he hadn't finished.'

'Just one name was left,' said Ingvar. 'Blackmane Thunderfist.'

Silence fell.

'Who?' asked Haloí.

'The old jarl, Berek?' asked Olgeir.

'Or Ragnar?' asked Jorundur.

'Like I said,' said Gunnlaugur, a sour smile on his features. 'A mess.'

'That's the name the survivor gave me,' said Ingvar. 'She died before I could ask her any more. She wouldn't have known the whole truth, I guess, even if she'd lived – Chirastes was a master at telling his servants almost nothing.'

'Berek was at the battle in 886,' said Gunnlaugur. 'I remember him talking of it in the Hall of Fire, back when I was a Blood Claw. Hjortur was there too, before he made Wolf Guard. It was part of a whole recital of the sagas, and they didn't dwell on that engagement, but they couldn't just leave it out. I remember thinking that Thunderfist must have been instrumental in the defence, somehow. Maybe it was one of things that got him made Wolf Lord. I don't know. He'd have preferred to have been remembered for other things, I reckon.'

Olgeir started to chuckle, a deep rumble in his thick throat. 'So what are we supposed to think, now? That this man was behind Berek's death, too?'

'No,' said Ingvar firmly. 'The jarl's body was recovered. We know who killed him – Ragnar heard the boasts from the killer's own lips, and the death was avenged in the open, warrior to warrior.'

'Then they are after Ragnar,' said Baldr. 'And that is another mistake – the Young King was not alive either during the Incursion.'

'But he shares the name Thunderfist,' said Gunnlaugur. 'Something that could have been used on the battle-comms during the assault. It has always seemed a strange coincidence to me – one name given to a Wolf Lord after a bionic, shared with the tribal mark of his successor. Fate, maybe, but what could Chirastes know of that? All he had was battle-cant cipher, and he had to apply it to the Chapter as it stood. Berek has been dead for years. By the time Thunderfist came up on the list, maybe the name he was deliberately saving until last, the one he hated more than any other, it was borne by another.'

'The deeds of Ragnar are talked of halfway across the galaxy,' said Ingvar. 'They know he is a Wolf Lord, honoured among us, just as Berek was. Mistaken or not, they have enough to find the one they seek.'

Jorundur leaned back in his throne. 'Can you be sure, though? This seems like mistake after mistake.'

'The regiments have been sent,' said Gunnlaugur. 'I've read the manifests – five hundred thousand troopers of the Ojada Perennials, bound for the void. One unit within that, the Fourteenth Advanced Armoured, contains more than five hundred Fulcrum Hunters, virtually all they had left, all primed with the order to kill Blackmane Thunderfist.'

Olgeir exhaled loudly. 'Five hundred!' he snorted. 'Morkai, that wouldn't be enough. Not for Ragnar.'

'Not in open battle, maybe,' said Ingvar. 'But that would not be how it would happen. They would be up close, fighting alongside one another. You know how it is, once things start. Comms get drowned, orders are forgotten. Any warrior may become isolated, and that is when they will strike, all at once, against a target unprepared for it.'

'And they're good,' warned Gunnlaugur. 'We got a taste of it down there.

Given cover, given surprise, they're dangerous. Chirastes knew his time was running out – he staked everything he had on this working, the last piece of his long game.'

'So we go home, now,' said Hafloí firmly, looking at his brothers for support. 'We go back now, we take the proof. That's what we wanted, was it not? A way back? Something to give them?'

'Ragnar is not on Fenris,' said Baldr quietly.

All eyes turned to him.

'And how could you know that?' asked Hafloí.

'Because Fenris has already been consumed by this war.' Baldr's face, as so often, looked pained. He didn't lift his gaze, but spoke to the stone. 'There's nothing left to fight for, there. So he has moved on, to where we were always destined to meet him again.'

Olgeir looked uncomfortable, Jorundur still sceptical.

'We could take a safe guess at where Chirastes sent those regiments, even if we had no data,' said Gunnlaugur. 'We've all seen the pattern of violence growing.'

'And yet, the creature even told me,' said Baldr. 'Not the one on Ojada – the one on the plague-hulk, months ago. It'll start on Cadia, it said. And every night since then, I've been watching the hour come closer, feeling it turn slowly from prophecy into reality. That world is calling everyone, now.'

'The Helwinter Gate,' said Ingvar. 'The fortress at the world's end.'

'It's where the troops were dispatched,' said Gunnlaugur. 'The very last item in the records, and the final piece of intelligence Chirastes' agents collected before the Fulcrum was dissolved. We know how it works from here onwards – the orders are sent ahead, the bribes are already paid, the arguments already made. The Hunters end up deployed wherever the Blackmanes fight, right until the moment comes and the trigger is pulled. Chirastes never needed to be there – he just needed to put the pieces in place.'

'Then we send that message,' said Olgeir. 'We go hunting, find an astropath relay, just like we've been doing all this time. Get tidings to the jarls.'

'No message of ours would ever reach them,' said Ingvar. 'Who would be listening? The bloodtide has already broken – every ship heading towards the Gate will soon be overwhelmed. If we wish to stop this, we need to go after them.'

'Those ships are ahead of us,' said Jorundur. 'The routes already plotted. You really think we can catch them?'

'We can catch anything,' said Gunnlaugur.

'The warp's in torment,' said Hafloí doubtfully.

'It can still be read,' said Baldr. 'Van Kliis is good.'

Hafloí turned to Baldr. 'And what of you, then? We said we wouldn't go back until we had both our targets accounted for.'

'We're not going back,' Baldr replied calmly. 'We're keeping going. This is just another step on the road.'

'So we have no choices here,' said Gunnlaugur. 'If they land on Cadia, get to their destination–'

'Vaerangi, you've seen the same things we've seen,' said Olgeir wearily.

'The fleets moving, the *size* of them, all in the same direction. This isn't a brawl like the one we just crashed – this is the cataclysm the Priests have been muttering about for years. If we go there, if we even get there, we'll be a pebble amid the landslide. This ship will last just a few moments in a real battle. And somehow, in those few moments, we'd have to locate these regiments, get down to the surface alive, overtake them, eliminate the hidden killers before the rest of the Imperial divisions in the warzone, Ragnar at their head, tear us apart for traitors.'

Ingvar smiled. 'That's the plan, aye.'

Jorundur shook his head. 'Madness.'

'Agreed,' said Gunnlaugur. 'But necessary. You all know what the Young King means. You know what store the gothi have placed in him. Chirastes was working for himself, but the greater enemy won't scruple to make use of such delusion. We have to try.'

'Then this council is not about debate,' said Olgeir. 'You have your decision, and you merely wish us to ratify it.'

'You can say your piece, Heavy-Hand,' said Gunnlaugur. 'I'll listen.'

'But my vote is to go,' said Ingvar urgently. 'We risked everything to chase down this scent. We can't turn aside now, just when we discover what it means.'

'True,' said Baldr. 'The fates have been drawing us there since we left Fenris on the *Undrider*. Now that we know the truth, we have to be there.'

Hafloí laughed. 'Aye, and it'll be a real fight, something worth scratching over your grave-marker. What's the matter, old one? Shying away from proper combat?'

Olgeir shot him a warning glare, but Jorundur spoke next. 'If we did it, it'd have to be done fast,' he said, grim-faced as ever, clearly working through the possibilities. 'Heavy-Hand is right – this ship won't last long in a major encounter. We'd have to use it to get to a drop-point, bail for *Vuokho*, trust to speed and luck to get us through the orbital kill-layer.'

Ingvar nodded. 'The *Hlaupnir* might last a little longer. Bjargborn and the faithful deserve a chance to cut free, if they can take it. The rest of the crew... well, they've already proved their dubious value.'

'All that can be determined later,' said Gunnlaugur. 'For now, Heavy-Hand, speak. Speak openly.'

Olgeir frowned deeply, rubbing the flesh of his temples with his fingertips. He looked over at Ingvar, then at Baldr, as if gauging who to blame most. Then he stretched back in his throne, his huge shoulders uncurling, and smiled wryly.

'I never turned down the chance to bear a blade,' he said. 'I'll break the skull of any who say it, whether they're in the pack or no. And if I could stand before Ragnar again, a warrior of his company with no shame, then I'll take it. I'd cross the maw of Hel to be there.'

Gunnlaugur nodded. 'Understood.'

'You give the orders. We follow them. That's the way of it, and I have no complaint. But, when this is done, and if any of us are still alive by then, I won't pretend that I don't wish to see an end to this.' He never looked at

Baldr while speaking. 'We belong in the company, if they'll take us back. We belong in the Rout.'

'That's what we all want,' said Gunnlaugur. 'By doing this, we give ourselves the chance to make it happen.' Then he turned to the others. 'We know where this will end now. That is better. If we die there, we die as part of something important. If we live, we'll tell of this deed in the Hall of Fire forever. What more could we wish for?'

He placed his hands together on the Annulus surface, a chink of ceramite against fire-warmed stone.

'So be it – enough talking,' he said. 'We light the drives, and sail for Helwinter.'

Afterwards, once the others had left, Gunnlaugur and Ingvar remained behind.

'I remember when you came back to the pack,' Gunnlaugur said, after a while.

Ingvar smiled wryly. 'When I'd drunk the spoiled beer of the Imperium. And thought it made me wiser than Ulrik.'

'It might do us all some good, to spend time outside. Maybe we might understand a little more why these things keep happening.'

'Let them hate, so long as they fear.'

'One of your Ultramarine's sayings?'

'Callimachus spent a lot of time quoting. I think they drill it into the whelps, on Macragge.'

Gunnlaugur chuckled, then looked moodily at the makeshift Annulus. 'I wasn't jesting. It's become ridiculous. Hjortur would never have recognised it – slay them all, he'd say – but we're on the edge of doom, and still the Imperium finds ways to try to damage us. One day, someone will tally up just how many institutions we've infuriated, and begin to wonder whether it's not them. Maybe it's us.'

Ingvar shrugged. 'The Dark Angel, the one I served with, he never failed to tell me that we'd be exterminated, one day.'

'Ever fight him?'

'Got close to it, a few times.'

Gunnlaugur looked rueful. 'Shame you didn't break his head.'

'Ah, though, I started to believe it, after a while,' Ingvar said. 'I started to think we were the outliers. You can't help it, when you're surrounded by the Inquisition, all the time, and you see the way they speak about you, look at you. Hel, we've had inquisitors after us, too – greater powers than this cardinal.'

'What changed your mind?'

'Coming back.' Ingvar smiled. 'An inquisitor is a twisted thing. A cardinal, much the same. Their blood's thin, their arms weak. We think that we're hated, because we think the whole Imperium is made of such creatures, but it isn't. They're the scum-layer at the surface. The billions and billions, the unnumbered, the ones who build the cities and crew the voidships, they're different. They drink. They fight. They admire a good blade and laugh at the weak or the vain. They're like us. We forget that.'

'Maybe we do.'

'I mean it. Talk to a Guardsman, sometime. Tell them to name the Holy Primarchs. They'll know the name of Sanguinius. If they're pious, maybe a few more. And they respect all those names. But then mention Russ, and see them smile. See them grin, like he's looking down on them. And if you're in the trenches with blood falling out of the sky, ask them who they'd rather have going over the top with them – a Blood Claw who'll die roaring, or a Dark Angel who never said a word to them the whole time.'

Gunnlaugur thought on that. 'Like I said. It would do us some good, to do what you did.'

'Don't envy it, brother. I lost a lot. I had to come home, to remember it.'

'I wasn't sure how I felt about that, at the time.'

'Aye. And it's led to all this, now.'

'It was always going to.'

'Sounds like something Fjolnir would say.'

At that, Gunnlaugur's expression clouded. 'And there's the other riddle,' he said. 'We're no closer to healing him. What did I think – we'd stumble over the Tree of Life, just waiting for us to pluck an apple?' He shook his scarred head. 'That's the piece we need to solve, before we go back.'

Ingvar nodded. 'But he wants to go. He wants to do all these things. Maybe it's the road he needs to take – and if any of us knows the truth of that, he will.'

'Every time we've encountered the enemy, ones who know true malefi-carum, he's been changed. That's why we've kept to the shadows for so long. But here – Cadia – there'll be witchery there like nowhere else in the galaxy. That troubles me.'

'The strongest poison can be the most potent cure.'

'Another one of your Macragge sayings?'

'No. Just a slender hope.'

Gunnlaugur sighed. 'Aye. That may be all we have left.'

CHAPTER TWENTY-TWO

Once the course had been set, the *Amethyst Suzeraine* fell into its plotted warp route. The crew tensed on the first jump, ready for the hull to clang and the shutters to rattle. And yet, even though the transition brought the usual mix of nausea and disorientation at first, things settled down. Hours went by, and nothing important broke. Maintenance teams worked on the damage from the void-action, and were surprised to find that the welding took, and the lumens stayed on, and no one smashed their forehead into the hull-plates while screaming about the claws coming for them all.

The hours turned into days. Stages passed, one after the other, each without major incident. The ship's forges stayed busy, repairing weapons and doing what they could to patch up the Space Wolves' armour. Wounded crew members recovered, and went back to work. The ship's complement was down, but not catastrophically so. Bjargborn's teams even had some time to look at the gun-galleries again, using what they'd learned over Ojada to hone the systems further.

Each member of the pack used the time in different ways. Jorundur drew up battle plans for entry into the Cadia System, going over every angle obsessively. Ingvar, affected almost as much by warp transit as a mortal was, cleared his mind by studying the scrolls from Ojada. Olgeir and Gunnlaugur sparred for hours in the training-pens, hammering away at one another to keep their muscles sharp. Hafloí joined them often, but also spent time on his own, charging down the near-empty corridors in the bilge decks as if hunting invisible shadow-creatures. It was a time of waiting, of enforced calm before the storm, all locked within the narrow confines of the galleon's creaking carcass.

For Baldr, the time passed surprisingly calmly. He'd expected to feel the usual pangs on entry to the empyrean – the augmentation of the pressure on his temples, the chattering of half-heard voices forever crowding out his thoughts. Instead, there was nothing but the physical environment around him, solid, unaffected, dependable.

'You seem improved, brother,' Ingvar told him.

And that was true. Though, given the circumstances, that was strange in itself.

Given the tranquillity of the passage, even van Kliis left her sanctum on occasion. Baldr knew when she was out of seclusion as soon as she withdrew to her private chambers. Inevitably, he made his way there in the end. When he entered her rooms, she gave him her usual smart, knowing smile, and gestured to the couch. She looked better than she often did, though the rigours of a long warp passage always took their toll, drying her skin, tightening it over the bone, deepening the wrinkles further.

'You wish to know why the passage is so tranquil,' she said, tottering to a sideboard where two pewter goblets stood on a salver with a decanter. She poured herself one, knowing better than to offer a goblet to her guest.

'Maybe just luck,' Baldr said.

'Ha! A jest, I am guessing.' She returned to the couches, and sat opposite him. She wore a turquoise gown this time, one that hung a little too loosely. She swirled the liquid in the goblet, then took a long swig. 'Storms have been bad for so long, I wondered if they would ever go.'

'Every passage we've taken since Fenris has been hard.'

'Yes, yes. And getting worse.' Van Kliis tutted. 'See, though, they call the Seethe an ocean. And they're right! It has currents, tides, swells. A ship can founder on them, if alone. The more alone, the worse it is. The Presences, they flock, come up from the depths. Like sharks sniffing blood.' She took another draught. 'Is not better, this way. Is worse. But, here it is. There are thousands of ships out there. *Thousands*. I see them, in the pinnacle. Like stars in the void, all with their trails of soul-fire. So many, so many. They are carving the Seethe up, splintering it. The Presences can't track them all. There are wakes piled on wakes – it makes everything flat. Never seen anything like it before.' She leaned forward, resting spindly elbows on spindly knees. 'Went to Sol quadrant, once. Longest traverse I ever took. Saw the Throneworld itself, from a distance, only in the warp. Like a dirty pit, it was. Thought I'd never see so many warp-wakes again, all churning, churning, making it hard to gauge anything. But this. Ha! This. This is off the charts. They're going fast, like we are, carving the ether into slivers.'

'What can you tell of them?' asked Baldr. 'Imperial?'

'Some. Most, from my viewpoint. But this on the right side of Eye. On the other side? Fagh. I suspect *huge* numbers. Huge. Maybe more than ever.' She chuckled. 'I was bored, before. Thought I'd die out here, tracking merchant convoys. I should thank you. If you could see it, you would like it. Thousands of trails, in the Seethe, like lines of pearls thrown across velvet. It is very beautiful.'

Baldr laughed, and a little of the weariness seemed to lift from his features. 'So that's what's calming the warp. Too many ships, all going the same way.'

Van Kliis' expression hardened. 'Do not be fooled. Cannot last. Put all those souls in same place, at same time, and it'll cause rupture. Enemy knows this. High Lords know this. If they still come, then things are desperate. We are heading into big storm.'

'We know it.'

'And you want to go faster.'

'I could help you with that.'

For the first time, van Kliis looked genuinely shocked. 'I don't know what you mean.'

'I see them too. The ships. All of them.' Baldr placed his hands together calmly. 'I see the energies around them, and the vortex they're heading into. I could help you.'

Van Kliis didn't say anything. She took another swig, then stared at him quizzically. 'Maybe your dreams are just strange. And anyway, is forbidden. I don't care for much of the orthodox code, but some things are sacred.' She tapped her forehead, just next to where her jewelled bandana concealed her Seeing Eye. 'This alone. Everything else, very dangerous.'

Baldr shrugged. 'As you wish. But maintain speed. Gunnlaugur wants us there ahead of anything else from Ojada.'

'On this ship?' Van Kliis laughed sourly. 'I know why, though. Your only hope is that troop transports are slow. Maybe it'll be enough. Maybe not. I can't tell. So many lights, so many lights.' She looked at him again. 'So why you call it that, anyway? The... what is it? Helwinter Gate?'

Baldr smiled. 'We are a people of sagas. That place has been in them since the days of Russ.' The smile disappeared. 'Helwinter is the end. It is the grip that never lets up, it is the strangling of life. The Gate is shut, holding it back. If it endures, then life endures. If it breaks, then the storm is all that remains. So the skjalds say, anyway.'

'And you wish to go there.'

'Aye. And if you get us there in time, you'll have served us beyond all call of duty.'

She gave him a sidelong smirk. 'My last work, eh? Before this sailing tomb is finally blown into pieces? I think so.'

'Maybe. Maybe not.' Baldr leaned in closer. 'It'll happen quickly. We may all be destroyed in the first few moments, but the system runner is being made ready for evacuation. You know where it's berthed? Get down to the hangars, as soon as we break the veil.'

'That thing you people arrived on?' Van Kliis chuckled. 'How would that help?'

'It's fast, it's small. Rivenmaster Bjargborn has orders to take the Fenrisian crew, plus a few others who've given loyal service. That's all it'll be able to take. It has limited warp capability, enough to get you clear of the system, with some luck.'

'A large slice of luck, I'd say.' She shook her head, still smiling. 'You have been a good friend to me, Baldr of Fenris. Better than any captain I've worked for. Imagine that! Perhaps I could get used to your stink, and your lack of taste. Perhaps I could ignore what you think about your rune-magick, and just forgive the ignorance. Perhaps all that could happen.'

Baldr shrugged. 'You'd have to survive, first.'

'As would you.'

'There are worthy goals other than survival.'

'And other perils, other than death.'

Baldr got up. 'Make your preparations now. There will be no time once we arrive – just move, go swiftly, gather no possessions.'

'Except my dresses. And the jewel-box from Hyperia.'

Baldr laughed. 'Essential items.'

'They are. To me.' She looked up at him. 'I will bring us in as tightly as I can. Sweet through the Seethe, as close as is possible. I'll do it for you, as I wouldn't have done for that old man. I'll give you every chance.'

'I know it. Thank you.'

'And may His Eye be on us all.'

Baldr nodded seriously, then turned to leave. 'It'll need to be,' he said.

The days counted down, a remorseless procession, marked only by the ship's internal chronos. The closer they got, the more time Jorundur and Gunnlaugur spent preparing for the system entry. They'd huddle together up in the command bridge, sometimes alone, sometimes with other members of the crew, going over the sequence of events.

'I'd have liked an astropath reading,' Jorundur said, on the final occasion before they broke the veil. 'Just one. Something to tell us what we're running into.'

Gunnlaugur grunted his agreement. The activities of the bridge went on in the tiers below – the steady click and hum of the systems in operation – but on the command dais it was just the two of them, their faces underlit green from hololiths.

'Aye. Still, we can make our guesses.'

Jorundur switched the throne's lithcaster to an image of the Cadia System. 'I spoke to the Navigator. She tells me the warp-wakes into Cadia are all still active, moving to the Mandeville horizon before dropping in sequence back to realspace. That indicates the Imperium still holds the ingress points. We should be able to translate intact, if nothing else. I'd be surprised if we weren't able to run the gauntlet to the planet itself, too – everything's going one way, and we'll be no one's principal target. It'll be in orbit. That'll be where we have our problems.'

'Everyone's primed,' said Gunnlaugur. 'I'll take the bridge, Gyrfalkon with me. Fjolnir will run augur sweeps to locate those troop carriers. Olgeir will tap into the Chapter comm-net, if we can still access it, to get the locator for Ragnar's company. We'll break for *Vuokho* together, once we get any kind of lock. In the meantime, you and the whelp will secure the hangars, ensure the *Hlaupnir* is primed for evacuation along with the Thunderhawk. Bjargborn knows his duty, and the kaerls are all prepared.'

'The rest of the crew won't be fooled for long,' said Jorundur.

'We can manage that. You'll pilot *Vuokho*, once we break for the void. With any luck, we'll at least have a geo-locator to follow by then. If not, we'll just have to take our best guess.'

'What do you know of the planet?'

'Not much. Terran-sized, standard atmospherics, standard grav. The greatest fortress-world in the galaxy, they say.'

'They say that about many places.'

'And we don't know what state it'll be in.' Gunnlaugur balled his fists, then relaxed them, as if flexing to grip his hammer already. 'We don't know what's attacked it, save that every fleet between here and the Hearthworld has been mobilised to meet it. We don't know why Ragnar was sent there. We don't know who else went. Hel, we don't know much.'

'We don't need to. Once we're in the thick of it, everything will become clear. It always does.'

Gunnlaugur snorted a laugh. 'You must spend time in different warzones to me.'

'We only have one task. That simplifies things.'

'True. Make planetfall, concentrate on that, then we can see how things look.' He gazed up at the closed warp shutters. They were less noisy than usual, as if the forces raging past them were weakened, somehow. 'Never known it so calm. Not going somewhere like this.'

Jorundur shrugged. 'The gods like their games.'

'Ulrik has been talking about it for decades. All the Priests have. You start to think they're just addicted to gloom. You start to think that maybe they always talked that way. But now I think they saw this coming, and didn't dare give it the name it deserves.' Gunnlaugur's expression hardened. 'A Black Crusade? I wondered if I'd ever live to see one.'

'Not something to aspire to, Skullhewer.'

'But I wouldn't want to miss it. I wouldn't want it to be known that the Gate was breaking open, and I wasn't there. I've had this dark hope in my soul, ever since we began this thing. That it was the time. That our age was the hardest one, and the greatest battles were for this generation.' He laughed, low and self-aware. 'You listen to the sagas, and all they tell you is that things were mightier in the past. The primarchs walked among us, the Emperor's light still lingered. I want to think they're wrong. I want to think that no battles were ever greater than these, and that we – *we* – face the hardest tests ever to come before humanity. And when I go to the All-father at last, my battles over, I want to hold my head up, look the dead of Fenris in the eye, and feel I belong among them.'

Jorundur shot him a dry look. 'You know what I think, vaerangi? I think you should leave the speeches to the skjalds. We get down there, we slay these skít-eating traitors, we somehow persuade Grimnar not to have our heads put on spikes, then we get back to how it's always been.' He stretched out his arms expansively. 'Mjod and meat in the fire-halls. A little sleep. Then back to some other dirt-streaked war.'

Gunnlaugur laughed. 'You'll enjoy it when you get there,' he said, getting up from the throne. 'How long before we break in-system?'

'Six hours.'

'Good. I'll give Heavy-Hand another bout in the pens. Don't study the vectors too much up here – I want you to get at least some rest before this all kicks off.'

'I'll be ready.'

'Aye. See that you are.'

They cut it fine, to prepare the last of the armour. The ship's forges were ill-equipped for working with ceramite, and most of the heavy tooling had been hauled over from the *Hlaupnir*. No menials from Collaqua's complement had ever been permitted to touch it – only kaerls, working alongside servitors and the scattering of lexmechanics that had been taken from the

Fenrisian ship. They did what they could, honing, welding, scraping the worst of the grime from the plate and splicing replacement panels into the ground-out defects. Power armour was a sacred and complex thing, its systems only partially understood even by the greatest of the Iron Priests, and so to work in such a way was a kind of blasphemy in itself, made necessary by privation. Only the runework could be maintained as it was on Fenris, painstakingly repaired and embellished by the warriors themselves.

A long time ago, Hafloí had hardly seen the point of it. In his tribe, before ascension, the rudimentary runic scripts had all been etched by the gothi, while the warriors and hunters had barely troubled themselves to learn the basics of the craft. Once in the Mountain, all that had changed. The transformation of the body was accompanied by a transformation of the mind, and every Blood Claw learned the sacred marks, and their significance, and what they could do to a weapon, or a shield, or a ship. The runes ceased to be vague scratchings made to appease the gods of storm and murder, and became totems of a deeper magick – roots that penetrated down to the Underverse itself and tapped its power.

So he'd learned to make them himself, after a fashion. Not in the way that a true master would, labouring for years at the forge with hammer and chisel. Still, he improved with every attempt, marking the rims of his pauldrons, the curved panels of greaves, scoring the names of those he had killed, or the places where the wyrd had given him fortune. Now that his plate had been cleaned and rededicated, the marks were visible again, an angular necklace of glyphs that looped and jagged across the storm-grey surface.

He looked at each piece as it was hauled up by menials, ready to be hoisted and clamped into place. The firelight edged each mark with blood-red, a procession of names and places, plucked from battles and given a kind of immortality.

Ingvar stood beside him, his own armour being put into place, its surface even more encrusted with wounds. Like real bodies, battleplate picked up scars and defects over time, its surface pocking and coarsening. The Grey Hunter's armour was darker, older, eroded, just like its wearer.

'Feeling ready?' Ingvar asked, face lit up with flashes from the drill-sparks.

On another day, Hafloí might have resented the question. Would Ingvar have asked Heavy-Hand the same thing? They all still saw him as the whelp, the new blood sent to bolster their numbers as the death toll wreaked havoc on the Chapter's old customs.

And yet, maybe that was not what had been meant. They did address him differently, these days. The jibes were still there, but more guarded, hedged with a kind of respect. So perhaps he didn't need to rise to them, aggressively defending his right to be there.

'I don't know,' he said, feeling the sensor-bulbs on the underside of the armour-panel slide into his carapace jacks.

Ingvar looked at him. 'You don't know?'

Hafloí shifted his shoulder, letting the menials lower the pauldron down on chain-carries. 'What do you want me to say? That all I can think of is covering myself in the blood of the enemy? No. I don't know. I've seen many worlds. But this is... Cadia.' He grinned. 'You think I've got bone behind my eyes. But I know what it means. This one can't be lost.'

'That's not up to us.'

'It is, if we're there.'

'We'll be a very small part.'

'Only if we fail.'

Then it was Ingvar's turn to receive his right pauldron, clanking on its chains, heavy as a mortal man. 'Ever met Blackmane?' he asked.

'No. I mean, I saw him, in the Hall of Fire, at the gatherings, like everyone does. I watched him.'

'What did you think?'

Haflói thought on that. 'That he was trying to be something. Or not be something. That he was carrying it, whatever it was, the whole time.'

Ingvar extended his hands, taking the gauntlets up and letting the menials slot the power-feeds into the under-skin nodes. 'I spoke to him, just before leaving. I thought he looked tired. Maybe because I was tired myself. I've seen him fight, though. That's a thing to witness.' He chuckled in appreciation. 'Skullhewer is the most dangerous Wolf Guard I've ever known. He'll be jarl himself, one day. But he'll always be older than Blackmane was, because Ragnar is something else, and that talent won't come around again.'

'They say that about a lot of warriors.'

'Aye, maybe. But Ragnar is... the future. Snuff that out, and what do we have? The weight of our ancestors, judging us forever.' He turned his fist, testing the connections, working one finger at a time. 'Count yourself lucky, Grey Hunter. You're in the greatest of the Great Companies, the one that'll redeem us.'

Haflói saw them lift his helm up, ritually, the lexmechanic sprinkling it with oils. 'What did you just call me?'

'Just what you are. We can stop pretending now, I think.'

Haflói's helm descended, a hollow crown, studded with fine archeotech, threaded with gold and iron. It settled into place with a faint hiss and click, immediately shrouding his vision with the filigree of combat awareness.

'It doesn't work like that,' Haflói said. 'It's too quick.'

Ingvar's helm was lowered next, masking his face behind the snarl-grille of armour. 'It worked like that for Ragnar. We're not under the Codex – what did rules ever mean to us, anyway?' He stepped down from the mounting-cradle, ready for the final rivets and the last dousings of sacred unguents. 'Your name, your deeds. They're the same thing. If you didn't deserve it, you wouldn't be called it.'

Haflói felt the minute shudder as the armour's power systems completed their loops and kicked into action. It was always the same – a tiny flood of endorphins, knowing what you could do, now, with that which you had been given.

He almost pushed back again. He still felt young. His hair bore streaks of red. It could have been years, decades, before his designation changed. It was too soon. All too soon.

Before he spoke, though, an alert came through, pinging into his newly attached retinal-feed. Ingvar, who had just taken up his blade in a fresh-fitted gauntlet, evidently got it too. He looked up at Hafloí, his helm-lenses flaring.

'So here it is,' he said. 'The world's end.'

V
THE HELWINTER GATE

CHAPTER TWENTY-THREE

There was no smashing of lumens, no shattering of armaglass, no cracking of steel, just a kick and a slide, a shift from one register to another, like a heel skipping down a step before landing on solid earth. The *Amethyst Suzeraine*, racing at full speed, transitioned smartly from the otherworld to the real one, spinning out of the empyrean and boosting hard into the tangible void.

The augurs unfolded, the lenses started to clog with data, and Gunnlaugur immediately started issuing orders from his vantage on the command throne.

'Down, down, starboard, then down again!' he roared at astrogation, before swivelling around to tactical. 'Activate all gun decks, unroll the gunwales, target at will.'

All across the bridge, voices quickly rose in urgency, shouting, calling over one another.

'Shields up! Full spread, full power!'

'Shut down Geller-feeds on my mark! Clear those lines for the plasma drives!'

'Where are the ranged sensors, starboard-zenith? Get them up! Get them up!'

The oculus shutters furled in a rattle, showering the decks with rust-flakes. The steady rhythm of the warp drives gave way to the more staccato beat of the realspace engines. Positioned at crew stations across the high dais, Ingvar, Olgeir and Baldr each fell to their tasks, all of them presiding over a team of kaerls working furiously at machine banks. Bjargborn occupied his usual station, a semicircular pit just down from the main throne, speaking calmly and continually into vox-tubes while he adjusted the dials on his many consoles.

Ahead of the ship, picked out harshly in the light of Cadia's near star, the void was speckled with ship-outlines. Most of those were hundreds of thousands of miles distant, but even so they mottled the deeps in swathes of grey and gold – whole formations, whole convoy-lines, spiralling fast towards a single unseen point. A nearspace void-volume flashed and tore open again, and another ship crashed into the realm of the senses, its flanks streaming with corposant. Then another, and another, all of them igniting plasma drives immediately, kicking on, blazing as fast as their engines would allow.

These things were not the rabble and scatter that had assaulted Ojada – these were main-sequence battleships, colossal and imposing, their spines crested with cathedrals and their flanks lined with armour-mauling guns. Just one of those craft would have been enough to subdue most worlds, at most times, but now there were hundreds of them, driving through the darkness like miniature planetoids in their own right, proud and majestic, bristling to their pinnacles with armaments and poised attack-wings.

'Eye of Russ,' breathed Olgeir, looking up briefly to get a better view of the gathering around them. 'Never seen so many.'

'Full burn, fast as you can,' ordered Gunnlaugur. 'Keep us out of range of those broadsides, and transmit Imperial-pattern marker-hails on all open channels. We don't *look* legitimate, so we might as well sound it.'

The *Amethyst Suzeraine* boosted harder, its battered drives banging and roaring. It was soon outpaced by the gigantic Naval ships around it, all of which ignored the galleon off their prows in favour of the true target ahead. Everything was going the same way, a lone sweep of tremendous energy that tore and surged from the Mandeville entry points and barrelled onward. Even as the galleon throttled hard, another titan of the deeps burst into reality less than two hundred miles above it, crashing through realspace like an anvil thrust into water, its immense, cliff-like sides going on and on and on before the sun-hot thrusters finally appeared and the rift closed behind it.

'Heavy grav-turbulence in all directions,' reported the master of astrogation, working hard to compensate. 'Mass-locators are off the scale – augurs overloading.'

By then Olgeir and Baldr were scouring carefully for signals, either for the Ojada carriers or for any sign of a Fenrisian deployment.

'Nothing in Juvyka yet,' Olgeir reported. 'Hel, there must be a billion comm-lines operating – we'll be lucky even to latch on to an Astartes code-sequence.'

'No sign of the carriers,' confirmed Baldr. 'Widening scan range.'

Gunnlaugur glanced briefly at Ingvar. 'As expected,' he said.

'More than I ever dreamed of,' murmured Ingvar.

'We're not even that close yet.'

The galleon careered onward, scraping the top edge of its velocity range yet still regularly overtaken by the leviathans gearing up to full attack speed. The bigger ships were already shifting into formation, spreading out across the heavens in clusters of overlapping gunlines, expertly rolling and shifting to fall into preordained displacement-wells. Almost all of them bore the livery of the Imperial Navy, with ploughshare muzzles and high gothic bridge fortifications. A few had the blood-red hides of the Mechanicus, including some absolutely monstrous arks bearing arcane weapons that Gunnlaugur had no descriptions for. Right on the edge of the cavalcade, far out of visual range, were scarce sensor-blips indicating battle-barge-class ships, though those were all from recent-Founding, Codex-compliant Chapters.

'First engagements!' shouted a comms officer from below.

A few seconds later, and the reports started to pile in – radiation-sources, hundreds of them, then thousands, spreading across the forward quadrants like a cancer. The Navy vessels carried on regardless, clearly expecting the signals. Picter-lenses across the bridge flashed warnings as the sensor banks picked up lance-ignitions in apocalyptic quantities.

'Stay low to the main plane,' Gunnlaugur commanded, pulling up a schematic of the system run-in. 'Those heavy concentrations at forty-five-six – keep well clear. Bring us in on a parabola, maintain full speed.'

The viewers ahead began to pulse with light, first blooms of angry red, then orange and yellow, spreading out, until a galaxy of false novas were igniting and flaring. A cluster of them spread like a ragged wound across the void, growing rapidly, a vortex of ignited plasma and las-beams with tendrils and clusters and spots of its own, like some miniature nebula rocked by the birth pangs of tiny stars.

The closer they got, the more the battle-sphere resembled some massive, inchoate sea of flame, rotating in stately procession around a hidden epicentre. The voidships were black spots against it, blurred by heat and distance, all of them unloading their fearsome batteries into the already raging conflagration.

'Nothing from Fenris,' repeated Olgeir.

'We know they're here,' said Ingvar, checking his own scan-array.

'We know they were *due* here,' corrected Gunnlaugur. 'That's all.'

Now the ranges were diminishing rapidly, and things were coming into full, bloody focus. The ship-swarms were bewildering in size, stretching out in all directions, numbers and velocities straining the cogitator-counters. Everything was wrapped in curtains of gauzy weapons-fire – coronas of backwash and impact-flare, explosions that sent debris-plumes bursting through gravity-eddies and into crazily flung wreckage arms that had started to orbit in long straggling flails. The first hard impacts peppered the forward void shields – not shells yet, just flecks of annihilated adamantium plate.

'Entering Cadian gravity well,' Bjargborn announced calmly. 'Major engagements now on realviewers with zero magnification, spread across all planetary zones. No designated targets located.'

The planet itself was still hidden, though more by the ferocious energies being unleashed than by distance. The viewers struggled with the intense luminosity of it, rendering jerky, broken-up images of broadside flashes and cannon-discharges. The lenses were tightly crowded, bursting, crammed. Every profile was enormous – veritable mountainsides of ship-metal, wheeling and plunging and unloading in a dazzling choreography of orchestrated murder.

'Skate us over the polar regions,' ordered Gunnlaugur. 'The more ground we cover, the more chance we–'

And then it came in – the first smack of true ordnance, a jarring crack that sent the *Amethyst Suzeraine* reeling athwartships. That was followed by a dozen more, crashing lower down and stressing the void generators all across the main hull structure. Enemy vessels started to turn, to swivel, to gain better attack-lines.

'Multiple weapon-locks!' shouted a menial in the close-augur station. 'Most angles, *all* angles, now closing at speed.'

'Return fire,' growled Gunnlaugur. 'Anything that lights its guns, pay it back.'

The galleon's broadsides started to retaliate, loosing in rolling bursts, surrounding the ship with a flimsy aegis of thrown projectiles. At the same time, the ship itself began to jink and dive, swapping straight-line speed for a more unpredictable flight pattern, doing what it could to mimic genuine evasion patterns. Amid the rolling blooms of fire, vast occluded shapes clarified into dark, jagged outlines – gigantic shadows against the flame, ridged and spiked and hanging with iron edifices, their cannons carved into screaming rip-maws, their backs hunched, their engines burning blood red. Those structures were ancient, designs that were old even at the birth of the Imperium, now corrupted and degraded by the long acidic effects of the Eye of Terror. Their weapons were hoary with senescence but also made maliciously effective by the daemon-craft bound up in the barrels. The ships' bridge-lights shone like living eyes, hinting at the horrors contained within, all enclosed and contained and wrapped-up by dark pinnacles and towers and vanes, corroded and blackened by the dubious favour of cruel intelligences. Hangar doors opened, squadrons spilled out, yet more motes of black over the fiery abyss.

'Drop further, drop harder!' ordered Gunnlaugur, studying the pain they were already taking. 'Those monsters can't follow us all the way down.'

The *Amethyst Suzeraine* dipped again, spiralling hard into the Cadian gravity well until the bright edge of the planet itself swelled up, circled by streamers of smoke, its jewel-like visage marred by savage wounds. Overhead, more giant battleships crashed into close contact, hammering at one another with epoch-ending weaponry, vomiting clouds of smaller craft that buzzed and bit like insects. Three Retribution-class battleships slid magisterially into the void-volume, each one surrounded by dozens of escorts, liberally throwing out lance-fire, only to be met by four Despoiler-class opponents, themselves surrounded by cloaks of racing fighters. The two groups met, sending out tectonic shock waves as cores detonated and drivetrains overloaded, and yet it was only one of dozens of similar clashes across the planet's tortured horizon-curve, just another region of ripped-up space. It was impossible to process it all, to focus on it – too overwhelming, too *complete*.

'I can't read a damned *thing*,' growled Olgeir, smacking a fist on his console's housing. 'Augurs are half scrambled.'

'Anything on the carriers?' demanded Gunnlaugur, keeping half an eye on the fast-rising damage-counters.

'Negative, vaerangi,' reported Baldr. 'There must be a hundred troopships still sending out landers in this sector alone, but nothing with the right idents.'

'Ventral void-array close to failure,' warned Bjargborn.

'Incoming fighters!' cried another menial. 'Forty signals, more beyond them!'

The bridge rocked as another hard-round strike-sequence landed, punching up from below. Those had the heavy, thuddy feel of torpedo impacts, and the picter screens went briefly offline in static-hails before zigzagging back into shaky focus. The decks bounced, the bulkheads cracked open, and lines of corroded debris clattered down from the heights.

'Evacuation vessels prepped and ready,' came Jorundur's voice over the pack-comm. *'Hangars secured. For now.'*

Gunnlaugur's eyes narrowed. More impacts came in, flexing the void shields further, and the first of the fighter wings entered visual range. The volume of it all was ludicrous – beyond ludicrous. Far above them, something passed across the upper battle-sphere, so colossal that it briefly overwhelmed the augur grid and sent insane signals down to the processors.

'Full spread fore,' Gunnlaugur ordered. 'Those fighters are the priority – take as many down as you can. Heavy-Hand – what do you have for me?'

'Maybe something,' Olgeir muttered, his hands dancing across the controls. 'Over the terminator, reception poor, but it sounds like garbled Blackmanes battle-cant. Get me closer, I might be able to filter it.'

The ship shuddered again, slammed sideways by a sequence of strikes that shorted the shield generators and showered the lower tiers with sparks. For a moment it felt like they were plummeting, but then the inertial controls kicked in again, and the grav-generators coughed back to full power. An armaglass panel shattered, setting off blaring alarms before the auto-shutters rattled down and the airlocks slammed closed.

'Get that geo-lock,' Gunnlaugur growled. 'We won't make it much further.'

Ahead of them, part masked by other ships, a gaudy battle cruiser with golden chasing and a sapphire prow was turning, sliding through a hurricane of shell-hits to come about in front of them. Its gunlines crackled with blue-edged flame, and there was something decidedly unwholesome about the way it moved.

'If that thing targets us...' Ingvar began, but then his attention was abruptly taken up with another signal.

'Fjolnir – anything?' asked Gunnlaugur.

Baldr shook his head. 'Either landed, destroyed, or out of range.'

'Then we're running out of time,' said Gunnlaugur, getting up. 'We'll take Heavy-Hand's geo-lock and trust to fate.'

The enemy fighters screamed into range then, spreading apart as they scored the void, and unloading at them. Bjargborn's gunners took a few of them out, blowing them up into flying clouds of burning metal, but most fizzed past unscathed, smashing long wounds in the void shields as they went. The generators flickered, for an instant leaving the entire ship unprotected, and the bridge-lumens dimmed. More fighters cut in close, raking down the ventral lines, blowing up hull-segments and sending the wreckage spewing like spittle.

'Auxiliary power!' roared Gunnlaugur to all bridge stations, before switching to the pack-comm. 'Prepare to evacuate.'

Ingvar's gaze was still locked on the battle cruiser ahead, a lone static point amid the whirl and swing of ship-death. Its weapons were zeroing.

'Vaerangi, that thing's got our mark,' he warned.

'Aye, that's why we're leaving,' said Gunnlaugur.

'But it's not the only one.' Ingvar gestured to another ship, higher up in the galleries of voidcraft, holding position amid a raging circlet of plasma gouts. It was an Adeptus Astartes strike cruiser in the cobalt and bronze of Ultramar. It had already carved its way through a thicket of less capable craft and was holding station while hurling out a huge amount of las-fire. 'I recognise the ident.'

'And?'

'Give me just a moment. One moment.'

Gunnlaugur hesitated, only taking a second to absorb the positions of the battle cruiser, the fighters, the strike cruiser, the hundreds of signals beyond. More impacts were coming in – streaming towards them across the scopes, each of them apt to crack the defences open and leave them ripe for instant destruction. The decks resounded again, shaken like drum skins, and very soon the last slivers of void-coverage would blink out.

'You have it,' he said. 'Make it count.'

Brother-Sergeant Callimachus of Parmenio stood on the bridge of the *Resolve's Arrow*, watching the carnage unfold.

The veteran sergeant was used to void-war. He'd spent much of his long service on the bridges of battleships, dealing out death from afar. For a few decades, it was true, his assignment away from the Chapter had meant that his combat record had become more a matter of close engagements, fought at squad-level, learning a fresh range of skills and honing them until he excelled at them all. On his return, though, his greatest pleasure had been to take the helm again, to feel the living heartbeat of a great ship underfoot, to marshal its strength in the cause of the Imperium and to witness the enemies of mankind burning up in the light of its vengeful fires.

It hadn't been easy to return from the Deathwatch. Some of his brothers still maintained that he'd been changed by the experience. For a few of them, steeped so deeply in the Codex that any non-Ultramarine was halfway to a heretic already, that was enough to mark him as suspect forever. Perhaps that was why service in the Cadian Honour Company had appealed so much. Over time, the few furtive glances of suspicion had died away. He was, as he had always been, a true son of the primarch. His calmness under pressure had not altered, his manners had not been blunted, his effectiveness had never been called into question.

Now, of course, even such lingering doubts, insofar as they remained, had become entirely irrelevant – the entire Chapter had been mobilised, every asset was deployed, and the tactical squads were all at war, from Ultramar itself to the edge of the Eye and beyond. The neophytes were hurled into the thick of it, just as much as the veterans. No reserves were held back, no husbanding of resources could be made. That was just as the primarch had ordained in his writings – some situations called for prudence, others for unbridled aggression. Reality itself was under threat, now – Tigurius himself had warned of it – and so restraint had to be cast aside.

So it was that the *Resolve's Arrow* had made for the void, one of the principal strike vessels of the Honour Company's specialised arsenal. It had been a proud sailing, one that in normal times would have dominated almost anything it was sent against, but here, in this place, it was just a fragment of the far vaster forces already assembled.

'By Terra's Throne,' his adjutant, Serro, had breathed on entry to the Cadian furnace. 'This is the end of all things.'

Callimachus hadn't replied. He was not in the habit of making small talk while in command of a strike cruiser. He had prepared diligently, and unfolded his careful plans as soon as they reached the raging battlezone. He had his orders – to effect the landings of the squads his ship carried, to shepherd the attack runs of the frigates that would secure the orbital strike-zones allocated to him, to keep the void-volume cleared of enemy vessels and support the main thrust of the Aurora Chapter battle-barge *Artamenas*.

All those things had been done, and were being done, or would soon be done, and yet now, rammed into the middle of the butchery, it was hard not to think that Serro was right. Surely, this was the end. Or maybe a beginning. Either way, when all these fires were finally extinguished, the galaxy could not possibly be the same again.

'Final attack-squads securely on surface, lord,' reported his master of signals, keeping her voice up to remain audible over the crashes and booms of the void-battle around them. 'All vehicles and pods deployed as ordered, actions commencing.'

'Very good,' said Callimachus calmly, moving over to a hololith column to examine the tactical situation in the void. 'You may relay that to Captain Echion, pass on the geo-locators for the landings, then open a channel to the *Artamenas* when it reaches the rendezvous locus.'

For a few seconds, perhaps, a hiatus had opened up. The strike cruiser would continue its barrage against the ships around it, reinforcing the Imperial lines and doing what it could to hurt the enemy advance, but until the battle-barge made contact, its primary tasking was dormant.

And then, almost as if ordained by some higher power, his comm-feed crackled. That line should never have opened again – it was a throwback, one that he had sworn never to speak of to another soul. The very fact that it still operated was something of a surprise to him. Then again, power armour was a marvellous thing, something to venerate and never take for granted.

It could have been any of them. The Dark Angel. The Blood Angel. The Angel Puissant, the Executioner or the Iron Shade. But of course it wasn't them. It was the one who had caused him the most trouble, been the most difficult, and in the end had been the one he remembered more than any other.

'Son of Russ,' said Callimachus, speaking over the private channel. 'You just can't leave me alone, it seems.'

'*My apologies,*' replied Ingvar. '*I know how much procedure matters to you. I'd ask how things were, if that weren't already painfully obvious.*'

'Are you on that... *ship*?'

'*Not for long. We're making planetfall. All we have is our Thunderhawk. We'll never cross the orbital fire-lanes. So consider this a plea for aid.*'

'We're somewhat busy.'

'*I can see that.*'

Callimachus found himself smiling under his helm. The old accent, clipped by the Fenrisian ice. They never spoke Gothic very well, did the Wolves. 'It will need to be now.'

'*Suits us fine. It'll be another debt I owe you.*'

'One day I'll ask you why you're on that ridiculous vessel.'

'*If we make it through this, I'll be pleased to tell you.*'

Callimachus' crew were looking at him. A series of queries had queued up on his system, all of them needing urgent attention. 'If you can launch within the next thirty seconds,' he said, 'you'll have a necklace of fire around you so close it'll warm even your frozen hide.'

'*Thank you, brother. May Russ guide your hand.*'

'He won't need to. This is a civilised ship.'

The link cut. Callimachus, still smiling, turned to face his master of ordnance, who failed to hide the disquiet on his grizzled face.

'Do not look so dismayed, master,' Callimachus told him. 'Ready the orbital batteries, and listen carefully. I have a specific, and most interesting, task for you.'

CHAPTER TWENTY-FOUR

When the order came, they moved as one. The pack, the kaerls, the few members of Collaqua's crew who'd merited a chance at survival. Every station was immediately abandoned, the occupants leaping up, reaching for stowed void-gear, running for the exit hatches.

Those not in on the plan stared up blankly at them, unable to process what was happening. The bridge was already failing by then, hammered and battered beyond tolerance, its panels crumbling and its cogitators fusing. By the time the brightest of them had realised that this was a full-scale evacuation, it was too late. The Space Wolves and their trained crew were too fast, too organised, racing through the hatches before spinning the locks closed behind them.

Once Gunnlaugur had given the word, Jorundur, Hafloí and the kaerls stationed in the hangars activated the outer door releases and shredded the last of the void-coverage over the exits. The *Hlaupnir* and *Vuokho* both powered up, engines roaring and access-ramps slamming down. The vacuum outside was as bright as magma, eerily lit up with the silent, blazing frenzy of the orbital battle. The kaerls arrived first, sprinting through the access hatches and stumbling across the rockcrete apron. They all piled inside the *Hlaupnir*, instantly taking up their allotted places at the guns or in the enginarium. The assortment of non-Fenrisians, van Kliis among them, trailing a rattling casket of her essential luggage, were bundled inside next, before the main doors cantilevered closed and the thrusters started spitting.

Bjargborn was last to take his place, running across the hangar floor alongside the pack. He paused at the base of the ladder leading up to the system runner's cockpit, and turned to face his masters.

'I'd go down there with you, if you'd let me!' he shouted over the gathering whine of the engines.

'Do *not* linger!' Gunnlaugur shouted back. 'Get clear of the system, make for safety! I'll expect to find you on Fenris when we return!'

Hafloí saluted him. 'Stay alive, rivenmaster! You're too good to be wasted in this mess.'

And then Bjargborn was gone, clambering up inside the final hatch before the thrusters lifted the *Hlaupnir* up and pivoted it around its centre of gravity. Heavy hit-slams crashed in from outside, as the enemy fighters spat everything they had at the already-listing *Amethyst Suzeraine*. Sections of the outer hull splintered off just as the system-runner boosted clear, ducking hard-starboard to evade the tumbling debris, then spearing out into the maelstrom.

By then the Space Wolves were taking their positions inside the Thunderhawk – Jorundur in the pilot's seat, Gunnlaugur beside him as co-pilot. Olgeir took the gunner's position, with Ingvar on navigation. Jorundur swung them up and around, tilting steeply to avoid a collapsing support-column. Geysers of ignited promethium erupted from the storage tanks under the hangar floor, driving up the rockcrete slabs and sending girders flying. Several chunks hit the Thunderhawk's undercarriage, knocking it hard to one side.

'I really don't want this ship to be my tomb...' muttered Hafloí.

'Curb your mouth, whelp, or I'll make sure it is,' spat Jorundur, before kicking up to full power and sending the Thunderhawk thundering out towards the hangar doors.

The lintel collapsed, blown apart by repeated las-strikes, but *Vuokho* just scraped under it, ducking down at the end before Jorundur pulled it into a vicious climb. Tongues of flame surged after them, before reaching the void shield limiter and gusting out. For a second, the heavily damaged *Amethyst Suzeraine* loomed large in the rear viewers before *Vuokho* rolled hard to starboard and plunged like a rock towards the atmosphere below.

The surrounding battleships, which had looked gigantic before, now seemed almost comically huge – great gods of the void, battling one another with arcs of lightning and flame while their minions scrapped and feuded in their shadows. The view from the Thunderhawk's forward portals was congested – ship after ship after ship, all firing, all in motion, fuelling the curtains of plasma that shimmered across the debris-strewn void like the auroras of the frozen north.

A lone Thunderhawk was far below the attention-profile of a battleship, but presented a tempting morsel to the many smaller hunters prowling in the chasms between them. Almost immediately after blasting clear of the ravaged galleon, Jorundur's console started to flash red with incoming target-locks.

'You mentioned you had a plan, Gyrfalkon,' Jorundur remarked dryly, throwing the gunship into a vertical dive and thrusting straight for atmospheric entry.

'Keep to this trajectory,' replied Ingvar, glancing at the sensor readings showing the *Hlaupnir* arrowing away from the battle-sphere at speed, as well as the *Amethyst Suzeraine* beginning to break up under sustained bombardment. He swept his ranged oculus-finder upward, scanning past a hundred other ships before locating the *Resolve's Arrow* high up in the void-volume, still motionless, its heavy guns still unlit.

Then they were struck – las-bolts, raking across their flanks, jarring the gunship's descent and pushing it out of kilter.

'Fighters, coming in fast,' Gunnlaugur growled, switching to the lascannons and sending a brace of beams back out at them. 'Lots of them.'

Jorundur battled to keep them hurtling true, wrenching the controls to tilt the Thunderhawk around its longitudinal axis. His task was made harder by a flail of solid-round fire that scratched and dinked along the chassis roof, blowing a control cable and cutting into the armour plates. Torpedoes locked on, prompting warning alerts from every control station.

'Where's that damned fire-supp–' he began furiously.

Then the realviewer scopes went yellow. All of them, all at once.

Ingvar laughed out loud. Callimachus had always been a fine shot, but this was almost too much, like he was showing off for old times' sake.

The Thunderhawk shot down a hollow tube of raging las-fire, an empty column formed from the precise circular firing of planet-facing cannons. Everything caught across the energy perimeter – shells, missiles, even fighter-hulls – was ripped apart, cut into pieces with the precision of an industrial shaper-beam. Briefly cocooned from the inferno outside, *Vuokho* roared planetwards, free to boost up to full speed without making evasive manoeuvres.

The fusillade lasted mere seconds – anything longer would have risked a burn-out of even a strike cruiser's batteries – but it was enough. Within moments, the Thunderhawk had cleared the worst of the orbital kill-zone and plunged hard into the outer troposphere below. The viewers turned red, fuelled this time by friction, dousing the hurtling vessel in crackling flame. *Vuokho* started to buck and kick, knocked about by the sudden rise in pressure, just as the *Resolve's Arrow*'s las-beams guttered out.

'Switching to turbines!' shouted Jorundur, slamming the control lever over and preparing to arrest the dive. 'This'll be bumpy!'

It was no understatement – *Vuokho* hit the thickening atmosphere hard, slamming into it as if into solid earth. The entire structure creaked, and alarm-runes flashed across the cockpit ceiling. A panel blew, sending sparks bouncing across the cockpit, and one of the atmospheric drives started to gust internal flames.

'Skítja!' cursed Jorundur, killing the fuel lines to the engine and making the entire gunship list hard to the left. Cloud banks, themselves underlit with burning, raced up towards them before blundering across the prow and making the vessel shake jarringly. For a few moments more, there was nothing at all on the realviewers – just a dirty orange fog shot through with flying grit and shivered-metal slivers – before they plunged out of the other side, and then, for the first time, saw Cadia with their own eyes.

A wide plain opened up before them, stretching in almost unbroken uniformity towards a haze-hidden horizon. Maybe once it had been verdant, but now it was choked with dust, a drifting screen of brown-grey that rolled and boiled as if alive. For miles in every direction, armies marched. Whole divisions of mobile armour thundered across the dust-pans, throwing up high plumes in their wake. Infantry detachments laboured in their debris-shadow, just minuscule specks against the vista, but in such numbers that it seemed as if the earth itself were liquifying. Atmospheric craft shot overhead and around them, strafing and darting, while heavier assault carriers hung against the horizon, firing at targets below in steady burn-lines.

In the far distance, isolated artificial mountains could just about be perceived in the gauzy twilight, twinkling with faint lumen-beams and flash-lit with the constant drumbeat of explosions. These were the famed kasrs, the immense fortress-cities that dotted the entire planetary surface, and in which the majority of the population lived. All those within visual range were clearly under assault, the fixed points in the continent-spanning maelstrom that had hit this world. The long pipelines and causeways that linked the kasrs were the focal points of the plains conflict, grappled over by regiments and Chapters, pummelled by ranged artillery and stalked by hovering gun-platforms. Further off were truly monstrous war machines – Titans, marching against the burning horizon in attack-gangs, towering over all else on the battlefield, their outsized frames bracketed with constant weapons impacts.

'I have that geo-lock,' said Gunnlaugur grimly. 'We're a long way off.'

Jorundur brought the Thunderhawk down lower, steering away from the worst concentrations of fighting and aiming for a ridge of wind-sheared granite running north-east. Even as he did so, the volume of the clashes below ramped up further, vying with the booming roar of the engines to fill the cockpit.

'*Trying to make sense of the tactical data,*' reported Baldr over the vox. '*Comm-channels overloaded, every scope hit with lag. It's going to be hard to navigate in this.*'

'Weapons-lock detected,' added Ingvar, shunting the vectors to Jorundur. 'Our little descent didn't go unnoticed.'

'We've lost a lascannon, too,' said Olgeir. 'Burned out on the way down.'

Jorundur snorted in wry amusement, yanked the controls down, and sent *Vuokho* skimming rapidly towards ground level.

'Shot-up, half burned to slag, badly outnumbered and already lost,' he muttered. 'This has started well.'

They came under fire almost immediately. Baldr felt the impacts down in the crew bay, surrounded by equipment taken over from the galleon – heaps of sensor-boxes wired together and bolted to the deck, crates of supplies and ammunition boxes, making the lower compartment cramped even with their small crew complement.

He ignored the booms from outside, and concentrated on the tactical lenses and their phosphor swirls. The problem wasn't the lack of signals, but the overwhelming number of them. Every comm-line was clogged by a dozen incompatible feeds on the same frequency. Every so often he got a snatch of something coherent before another desperate vox-impression overwrote it. Some of the dialogue was Imperial, in a whole range of Gothic dialects and battle-codes, all distorted by distance and interference, not to mention cipher-overlays. Some was from enemy transmissions, which sounded like a glut of growling and bestial grunts. He painstakingly noted regiment names and positions where they were audible, gleaning what he could from the confused and overlapping bulletins. Hafloí worked at a terminal next to him, rocking with the swaying of the gunship, similarly trying to make sense of the hundreds of scans.

'Hel, this is hateful,' Hafloí muttered, punching the side of his lens-housing to clarify the image.

But it wasn't. Not for Baldr. For the first time in an age, his mind was clear.

The further they travelled across the Cadian landscape, despite the barrage of incoming fire and the noises of combat from outside, the more that clarity increased. It was as if a weight had been lifted from him. His vision was no longer clouded by bloody visions, his thought-processes no longer slowed down by the constant pain behind his eyes. He operated faster than he had since awakening on the *Hlaupnir*, his fingers working more surely, his judgement steadier.

'Still nothing from Olgeir's fix,' he replied, extending the augur ranges and trying to get a latch on to anything solid. 'We could be hundreds of miles off course.'

'If we're lucky,' said Hafloí.

As they travelled further, though, the broader picture emerged in greater detail. The battlezone was immense, stretching far across the straggling lowlands of the entire continental mass. The kasrs were numerous in all directions, though studded concentratedly along a ridgeline where the land started to rise towards a mountainous interior. Imperial and traitor forces alike had landed across the exposed landscape and were vying for advantage, trying to gain supremacy there and push on towards the strategic kasr networks. It was clear that the enemy was in the ascendant through all of that, mostly due to overwhelming numbers, particularly in the north-west, but the fighting remained at a pitch of furious intensity. This was total war – in the void, on the land, in the cities, out in the wastes.

Baldr studied the hololiths intently, his eyes scanning rapidly over the mess of glowing dots and vector indicators, backed up by the constant half-intelligible chatter over the vox-lines. Patterns emerged, first as vague tangles, then sharpening up. It felt as if there were visual cues in the scanlines, virtually perceptible but elusive, lurking out of the corner of one eye, only to fall into blurry indistinctness when you looked directly.

After a while Hafloí tired of the sensor work, and clambered up towards the command section. That left Baldr in the dark, absorbed, lost to his study. The Thunderhawk continued to take a beating, and the engine pitch changed from a steady thrum into something more throttled and broken. The deck swung around, almost throwing him from his seat, but he worked on through it, trying to unpick the truths that lay in the augur readings.

Eventually, after what felt a long stint in the air, Baldr felt the camber of the deck change, and the guttering engine-tone told him they were rising fast. The hard-edged noise of weapons-fire fell away, replaced by the howl of external winds. The gunship banked, then swung around, then banked again, then started its familiar descent-sequence.

Baldr got up from his station, staggered as a sudden gust hit them, then picked his way along the tight accessway towards the flank access-hatch. By the time he reached it, Jorundur had brought the Thunderhawk down onto solid ground with a dusty thump. The external lumens were doused, the engines powered down. Even the internal lighting reduced, turning everything a sullen red. As the stressed metal ticked and clanged, cooling rapidly, Gunnlaugur's voice was the first over the pack-comm.

'That's enough for now. Fjolnir – tell me what you've got.'

Baldr opened the hatch. Cool night air wafted in, acrid with spilt fuel and burning. The gunship was perched high up, wedged onto a narrow ledge on the eastern shoulder of the ridgeline he'd scanned from the air. He jumped down from the metal foothold, his boots crunching on loose earth. The rest of the pack made their descent from the steaming hull of the gunship. Jorundur and Olgeir immediately busied themselves with repairs, cranking open panels and delving into the smoking engine bays. Baldr turned to look at the view east.

They had crossed the spine of the ridge, clearing the jagged summits and dropping hard into the lee of broken peaks. The patch of level ground they'd found was less than thirty yards across – Jorundur had performed a minor miracle to bring them down at all. The ground fell away steeply ahead of them, dropping hard into ravines cloaked in shadow. The darkness had crept across the landscape, though no stars were visible under the all-encompassing smog layers, and the far horizon was lit with flashes. The noises of combat – mortar crumps, engine growls – could be heard coming from all directions. When the northern sky erupted with a particularly vindictive set of rolling explosions, the distant silhouettes of the kasrs were briefly visible – stark black cones against a seething fabric of flame – before being swallowed by the darkness again.

Baldr breathed in the air. Despite the stink of battle, it had an invigorating edge to it. In other circumstances, at another time, this might have been a good world – one with clean winds and ice on the peaks.

'It's everywhere,' he said, just as Gunnlaugur came to stand beside him.

'The fighting?'

'Aye. I've picked up signals from the southern polar region, the equator, out in the oceans. They're not taking any chances.'

Gunnlaugur grunted, and stared moodily into the firelit distance. 'We can't stay here long. Old Dog took out four flyers, but more'll be back.'

'For just one gunship?'

'Like you say. They're not taking any chances. Pick up anything we can use?'

'I'm not sure. Nothing from the Ojada ships – they might be down, they might not be. For a moment I thought I caught a mention of something from an Imperial set of dispatches. They spoke of Wolves of Fenris taking positions in one of the kasrs. I couldn't catch a name – there are hundreds of them. Kasr Alloc? Kasr Revok? I don't know. Our cartographs can't be relied on. It's something, though. A mention.'

Gunnlaugur nodded. 'Olgeir's geo-lock is north-east. That's where we're headed. You agree?'

'Aye. The fighting's heavier up there, the further you go. It's where Ragnar would be.'

'That he would.' Then Gunnlaugur looked at him. 'But... you. You sound different.'

'I like the air here.'

Gunnlaugur snorted. 'Smells foul to me.'

'Foul enough. But, underneath it... well, there's something strange about this world.'

Just as Baldr spoke, a whole raft of munitions went off along the eastern horizon, a long way away, vast enough to briefly expose a second mountain range. In one bowl-shaped valley between the peaks, a single slender stone pillar was briefly lit up, angular, artificial, isolated. Its flanks were black, and it rose up into the night like a giant needle.

Gunnlaugur saw it too. He grunted non-committally. 'For as long as it lasts.' Then he clapped his gauntlet-palm against Baldr's arm. 'But I'm glad it agrees with you, brother.'

Baldr kept staring into the dark, where the obelisk had been illuminated, just for a moment. 'How long has the Imperium held this place?' he asked thoughtfully.

'Njal might know,' said Gunnlaugur, turning away, not sounding too concerned. 'But let us hope, for your sake, *he's* not here.'

'So we're moving again?'

'Within the hour. Old Dog needs to shore up some damage, then we'll need coordinates.'

'I'll work on it.'

CHAPTER TWENTY-FIVE

Jorundur was as good as his word – within the hour, they were airborne again, boosting from the narrow eyrie, pitching down the steep slope then angling upward. They went north-north-east, hugging the high shelf of land to their left, keeping as low as the terrain allowed.

Gunnlaugur remained as co-pilot, letting the Old Dog do what he did best. It was an impressive thing to witness, the way he shifted and slid the huge chunk of metal, over a hundred tons of solid armoured gunship, making it as agile as a *konungur* in the snow.

It had started to rain – not precipitation, but a dirty cloud of ash filtering down from the heavens. Jorundur kept *Vuokho*'s lumens doused, relying on his eyesight to guide him, and so the view ahead was almost completely dark, marred by the smudge and smear of grey flecks striking the view-screen. Every so often an explosion in the distance would illuminate the cliffs on either side – stark white impressions of vertical rock-plates and scraggly pines, already beginning to die back as the atmosphere poisoned – and the extent to which Jorundur was hugging the mountainsides became briefly apparent.

'This can't last,' Jorundur said eventually.

'What can't?'

'Flying.' He suddenly yanked on the control columns, and the gunship scraped past an outcrop in the dark, missing it by a yard or two. 'We'll be off the scopes in here, but once we hit open terrain...'

'Aye, I know it. We'll get as far as we can.'

'And then what? Run the rest of the way?'

'If we have to.'

Jorundur snorted.

'You think this is a fool's hunt,' Gunnlaugur said.

'Ach, no. I just want to find him again. The Young King.' He chuckled darkly. 'This has always been a mongrel pack, thrown together, the scraps discarded from the rest. It'd be nice to make it count. I'd like to be the ones that haul his gilded arse out of the fire.'

Gunnlaugur laughed. 'Aye. That'd be good.'

More ash flew against the viewers, clogging up against the jerking wipers, leaving long grey streaks against the armaglass. Something big was on fire, somewhere. Maybe the entire world was.

'Once we're clear of these peaks, we'll see kasrs,' Gunnlaugur said. 'If they're still defended, we could set down, get access to come cartographs that tell us something.'

Jorundur glanced at the ranged augurs, most of which flashed error-runes. 'Or maybe they'll be as blind as we are.' He adjusted some dials, and a few flickery ghost images blinked across the lens before juddering out. 'Sensor-baffles, overlapping, some theirs, some ours. Orbital satellites down, a million ships coming in and out of the warp at once. It's a miracle we can get anything. It'll come down to snouts on the ground, soon enough. What we can see with our eyes, feel with our hands.'

'Just like back on the ice.'

'But dirtier.'

'And if time wasn't so pressing–'

'You'd enjoy this. Aye, I would too.'

Gunnlaugur looked at him steadily. 'First Fjolnir, now you. What's happened to your mood?'

Jorundur laughed, just as bleakly as ever, but with some humour under it all. 'I don't know. Maybe it's that damned whelp, shaking things up. Maybe Gyrfalkon getting his spirit back. Or maybe this is the end of all things, and we're flying into it with a shot-to-pieces gunship, just to be there. All very amusing.'

Gunnlaugur shook his head, mystified. 'Well. Glad it's having an effect.'

They flew on, running hard, staying low, even as the crevices and ravines began to bottom out and the crags fell away. In the extreme distance, the skies began to lighten – they were approaching dawn, a grey, washed-out return of the light. As they left the cover of the mountains, the plains stretched away ahead of them again. It might once have been agricultural land – miles of open fields tended by industrial cultivator-haulers – but now the dust had swallowed it up, choking the irrigation channels and rolling in palls across the ruins of the buildings. Some gigantic pipelines were still intact, snaking their way alongside transport arteries, casting long shadows in the half-light.

The environment didn't stay empty for long. A fortified bastion wall, already part destroyed, bisected the dust-fields running west-east, and beyond that the land started to climb again in terraces towards a cluster of three large kasrs. Columns of smoke drifted with the wind from multiple sources across those terraces, feeding the plumes of smuts and dirt that made the air filthy. Tiny against the vast landscape, massed columns of troop carriers were heading towards the lead kasr, rumbling along with their own smokestacks belching, flanked by trudging columns of infantry. The advance was ragged, strung-out, undisciplined. That alone would have given away the allegiance of the fighters, but the plethora of tattered banners, strung with skeletons and still-twitching corpses, removed any doubt. They limped and shuffled their way past the burning carcasses of vehicles, bombed-out gun emplacements, debris-stacked trenches. Heavy tracked armour ground its way alongside them, set a few miles north, escorted by more infantry phalanxes and gun-walkers.

'Keep out of sight as long as you can,' said Gunnlaugur, studying the formations carefully, trying to gauge numbers, possible warband-signifiers, whether anything was still resisting them.

The gunship dropped down even lower, taking advantage of the flattening landscape, skating across the dust-blasted fields of trodden wheat, almost brushing against the stalks with its descenders.

The lead kasr drew closer, its high walls lit by the first direct rays of grey sunlight. The fortress-city was as vast as they all were, a colossal pile of rock-crete turrets and interlocking retaining walls, all designed purely for defence, crusted with artillery and masked by the faint glitter of active void shields. Its skirts were aflame – a ruddy, ember-like glow that made it seem as if the earth was scored apart down to the lava. Defence lasers and wall-mounted cannons blasted a steady rhythm of defiance, carefully timed, well orchestrated. Something within that city was still operational, then, however desperate the situation was in its lower reaches.

The skies ahead started to fill – convoys of lifters hauling materiel up to the front, escorted by hovering squadrons of ornithopters and gunships. Flashes and blasts peppered the cloud bank beyond the kasr's high pro-file, indicating ongoing aerial combat. A gang of fighter-bombers speared past close enough to register on the gunship's tactical augurs, but seemed to ignore them, powering off towards the beleaguered kasr, leaving lines of smog behind them almost as thick as physical tails.

'We'll have to angle north soon, vaerangi,' Jorundur warned, as the plains slipped below them and the worst signs of fighting began to slide out of scanner range. 'Cartoliths show a transitway running back from that kasr-line, heading up-country. That'll be a target, and we can't avoid it.'

'Understood.' Gunnlaugur switched to the pack-channel. 'Heavy-Hand – prepare yourself.'

'As always,' Olgeir replied from the gunner's station, reaching up to acti-vate the battle cannon's power-feed.

As the kasr fell away to the west, Jorundur gently banked the gunship, bringing them around in a wide loop and dipping the left-hand wingtips. He applied more speed, gradually ramping the velocity up close to max-imal, all the while skimming along as low as he dared.

The landscape became wilder, harder, scoured as much by the elements as by the ravages of the war. Nothing productive had ever grown on these plains, and the jagged thrusts of naked rock vied with filth-encrusted veg-etation stands, stringy and hard-cased. The elevation began to drop again, steadily but surely, towards what looked like a wide river catchment.

Just as Jorundur completed his course corrections, the first alarms began to sound.

'Damn,' he said, punching in more commands and flicking a lens over to a more fine-grained sweep. 'We've been picked up.'

Ingvar's voice came over the comm from the navigation-station. 'Three signals, matching course, gunship-class.'

Gunnlaugur glanced at the readings. 'Storm Eagles,' he muttered.

'Aye – patterns match. They're on our scent.'

Jorundur maintained his course and speed, pushing the engine-load a little higher, but the gap between them and the chasing gunships began to close quickly. All of the vessels had a similar top speed, but *Vuokho* had taken a beating during the descent and the turbines were still operating at below full capacity. 'They'll be on us in a few minutes,' he said.

'Pick your moment, then,' Gunnlaugur replied.

For a few more tense moments, Jorundur blazed a course due north, thundering across the empty wilderness. Three blips on the scanner crawled closer and closer, boosting just as hard as they did, staying in close formation.

Right as the gap shrunk almost into gun range, Jorundur slammed on the air brakes and hauled the controls upward. The gunship lurched, its nose shearing up, before Jorundur restored full power and *Vuokho* shot higher, swinging round tightly and bringing the battle cannon to bear on the approaching gunships.

The Storm Eagles – painted in a lurid mix of red and black and daubed with profane sigils, their spines ridged and their chassis broken up with almost organic growths – instantly broke formation and fanned out three ways, blurting out noxious smoke as their engines whined.

Olgeir fired, launching a salvo from the battle cannon that almost blew the rear end of the lead Storm Eagle clean off. He followed up with lascannon fire, using the one that still functioned, and Jorundur corkscrewed after the prey. The first few las-salvos flew wide, but Jorundur anticipated a switchback from the enemy pilot and dived in close to give Olgeir a split-second perfect target. The gunner didn't waste it, sending a vicious spitting flurry of las-bolts slamming into the smaller gunship's cockpit, punching through metal and shattering the armaglass into flying clouds of bloody debris.

That finished it off, though by then the other two attackers had swept round and brought their own guns to bear. Heavy bolters opened up in unison, hurling mass-reactive shells in quadruple fire-lanes. Jorundur banked hard, but couldn't evade them all, and the right-hand crew bay was mauled amid a long welter of sparks and chips, the plates driven in, dented and cracked.

'Skítja!' Jorundur cursed, killing the power again to lose altitude, then twisting up and around to give Olgeir something to aim at.

The pilots of the Storm Eagles stayed tight, using their superior manoeuvrability to spiral away from the las-bolts while raking with more bolter-fire. One of them launched a scatter of missiles that whistled in very close, and only a desperate jink by Jorundur prevented one from blowing its way straight into the crew bay.

By then Baldr and Hafloí were on the Thunderhawk's own heavy bolters, both firing freely, swinging the barrels around to target the incoming gunships. All three flyers raced, ducked and spun across the empty landscape, duelling their way north as the valley walls dropped down further. The silver-grey of a large river glistened below, half a mile wide, locked between rock-crete embankments, now a mire of oil slicks and smouldering wreckage.

'Imperial positions two miles due east,' Ingvar reported. 'Make those, we might get some cover.'

Jorundur plunged down towards the mist-wreathed surface of the water,

driving hard along it, the bolt-streams thudding out behind, before shooting back up towards the north bank and tilting to give Olgeir another shot.
The lascannon fired, nearly impaling the closer of the two gunships but
failing to shake either one off.

'They're not giving up...' muttered Gunnlaugur, peering through the drifting clouds, trying to see what lay ahead.

Jorundur piled on the straight-line power, streaking out of a rolling mist
bank to expose a long bridge spanning the river. It was low-slung, wide and
heavyset – eight lanes wide for ground-traffic and embedded rail, lined
with artillery towers and monumental defence bastions. Both ends of the
bridge terminated in a sprawl of buildings, refineries, river-docks and industrial complexes. The north side seemed relatively intact, if badly damaged,
whereas the southern bank was a burning set of ruins. Artillery lances and
mortar fire arced from one side to the other, the impact-flashes reflecting
dully in the sluggish water below.

Just as the bridge came into view, the Storm Eagles drew alongside on
either flank and launched a pincer-strike of bolt-shells. Jorundur climbed
immediately, but a cluster of projectiles hit under the cockpit, blowing out
a stabiliser unit and briefly sending the Thunderhawk careering towards the
water. Jorundur righted with difficulty, still speeding towards the bridge,
then jinked around and sent the gunship listing belly-up, rolling the lascannon wing right into the path of the further Storm Eagle.

Olgeir fired, striking true this time, and the bolt-stream blew clean through
the gunship's tail, sending it somersaulting through the air. The Storm Eagle
hurtled onward and earthward, whining out of control, before colliding
with one of the bridge's support piers and exploding in a smear of ignited
engine fuel.

But that left the other one. Closing in fast, it fired a second missile, and
at that range it wasn't going to miss. The missile cut straight into the rear
engines, blowing the turbine from its housing and destroying the entire tail
section of the Thunderhawk.

The gunship reeled, the remaining two engines screamed, and everything lurched crazily, almost upending and smashing into the northern
embankment.

'Hel's *eyes*!' Jorundur cursed, pulling with all his strength to arrest the dive.
Just as he did so, the cannons on the bridge swivelled round and targeted
the remaining Storm Eagle, blowing it out of the sky with a combined strike
that sent debris smacking into the carriageways and tearing up the asphalt.

Vuokho was still out of control, though, slewing wildly, rotating around its
axis with its damaged engines gouting. The G-forces in the cockpit became
crushing, slamming the occupants against their restraints. Gunnlaugur,
gripping his throne arms hard, got a snatched glimpse of the bridge's edge
flashing by before the river's surface raced up to meet them.

'Brace!' he roared, just as the gunship's own alarms reached a blaring
climax. Jorundur attempted to pull up, but the momentum was too strong
now. A panel in the cockpit blew in, flooding the interior with thick black
smoke.

Then they hit. The Thunderhawk smashed sideways-on into a bridge column, cracking open down the middle before being dumped into the water and sending a thick, flotsam-crammed bow wave surging up to the embankments. The engines briefly went wild, churning the slurry into foam before their intakes clogged and the turbines blew out.

By then the Wolves were already moving, snapping out of the restraints and kicking hard against the fast-sinking structure. Gunnlaugur hit the emergency door releases, and every working hatch and gang-ramp blew open in a cloud of bubbles. They piled out, kicking upwards, using the rapidly descending gunship chassis as a platform to boost themselves before it dragged them down to the riverbed.

Ingvar managed to get a grip on a bridge support, hauling himself out of the churning muck. He grabbed hold of Olgeir, and the two of them clambered up onto a ledge, each covered in oil and slime. Hafloí and Baldr were both swept downstream, their heavy armour carrying them to the silty bottom, and had to drag themselves out on foot. Last of all were Jorundur and Gunnlaugur, caught up in the wreckage of the cockpit as it disintegrated, finally trudging up through the mud and grit like nightmares of the Fenrisian deep. As they staggered to the edge of the embankment, waist-deep in churning, greasy water, the bridge loomed up over them, dark against the steel-grey sky. The sound of engines revving and guns firing came from its upper levels, echoed by the ongoing fire from the cannons mounted on the carriageway's rim.

Jorundur turned, staring at the wreckage of the Thunderhawk. If his helm had been off, his expression would have been distraught. He said nothing for a moment, just reached out with an empty gauntlet, as if he could somehow lift it back up. Then he let his arm fall, weakly, and shook his head.

'Ach,' he murmured. 'So that's that, then.'

Ingvar didn't try to make him feel better. There weren't any words, he knew. Jorundur would have an outlet for his rage soon enough, and it would only antagonise him to say something before that chance came.

He could feel the hot tingle of blood on the inside of his helm, and his ribs ached mightily. He strode up through the knee-high water, and took in the surroundings. The Thunderhawk had come down just under the bridge's shadow. The water couldn't be much more than ten feet deep at that point, so they'd be able to salvage much of their gear, the weapons, maybe some supplies. It'd be a big loss, though. Their ability to travel swiftly had been taken away, and there was still a long way to go to reach Olgeir's cartograph reference. Maybe trying to travel any distance by air had always been reckless, but it would still slow them.

It wore at his patience. More than any of the others, he had pushed for this, and now that the hunt was underway, he wanted to complete it. Every setback, every delay, it chipped away at the chance for success.

He looked up. A silt and gravel beach piled up ahead of him, lapped by the dark water, beyond which was a high embankment pocked with bullet holes. Soldiers were already scrambling down to meet him, all in the grey-green of the Cadian standing army. Beyond them rose a series of fortified positions, and beyond those were the high walls of the industrial buildings, gradually lightening into pale grey as the sun grappled its way further up across an overcast sky.

Ingvar shook the slime from his armour and stamped through the receding water. The first of the Cadians made the sign of the aquila, stared briefly at the site of the gunship's descent, and introduced herself.

'Lieutenant Alys Mordova,' she said snappily, a little wearily. 'Do you require help?'

Ingvar was used to baseline humans being overwhelmed by his presence. Perhaps the sight of them all trudging up out of a river, battered and covered in straggling weeds, dented the aura a little bit. More likely it was that these were just Cadians, a warlike people fighting on their own world – they'd seen too much to be easily awed.

'Ingvar of Fenris,' he replied, making the same sign. 'What is this place?'

'Ninth Crossing,' she said. 'On the route from the lowlands to the Inner Coronet, across the Namuva. You picked a good time to arrive, lord.'

'How long have you been here?'

'Six weeks.'

'Fighting, that long?'

'The whole time.'

'Show me.'

By that time, the rest of the pack was emerging from under the bridge's lee. Gunnlaugur and Jorundur stayed further back, lost in some animated discussion, probably about what could be salvaged. Hafloí looked a little dazed, as if he'd taken a big hit on the way down. Olgeir and Baldr seemed unscathed.

Ingvar allowed Mordova to lead him up a steep set of plascrete steps set into the embankment wall. They reached a crow's nest outpost piled with sandbags and protruding anti-aircraft guns. From there, the ground level rose steeply away from the river until they were on a wide riverine path that ran for a few miles along the northern bank. In normal times it might have been empty and windswept – a place to walk after a shift at the manufactorum, or to stage parades for Sanguinala – but now it was crammed with bodies. Flakboard and cinderblock installations had created a makeshift township of medicae units, refectories, armouries, the whole panoply of facilities needed by an army in the field. Behind them rose the more solid walls of the many manufactoria, their hole-blown roofs occupied by snipers and portable augur-teams.

'We were ordered to hold the bridge,' Mordova said. 'We occupied both banks until a few days back, when they overran the south side, right up to the crossing.'

'They?'

Mordova smiled wryly behind her helm's visor. 'You want me to name them? Whichever set of soulless bastards it is this week. They've come across at us three times. Each time, they got a little further.'

They walked up another set of stairs, taking them up to the point where the bridge met the embankment. The majority of the Cadians were deployed at the intersection – a broad area over fifty yards wide, where the multi-lane highway met the transitways to the northern half of the settlement. Now the entire area, once a bustling junction, was dug up, fortified with long rows of heavy rockcrete barriers and pillboxes, overwatched by prefabricated gun towers and fixed artillery positions. Tanks, more than twenty of them, were set hull-down amid piles of sandbags, their long barrels pointing out at the empty crossing. The infantry squads, all holed up in cover, must have numbered several hundred, and Ingvar could see Sentinel walkers and reserve troop carriers waiting in the streets just beyond, ready to move forward when needed.

Three banners, all of them ripped and shot-at and ragged, hung from the high wall facing the crossing – the double eagle of the Imperium, the ivory standard of Cadia with a skull set against a blue background, and a black-and-purple cross with a death's head at the centre – the sign of whatever regiment it was that had been stationed to Ninth Crossing.

Mordova took him to the officer in command, a colonel called Irisa Borsch, who might have been in his thirties but looked a lot older. His uniform was dirty but his armour and weapon were in good shape, just like those of his troops.

'My lord,' he said as Ingvar ducked under the lintel of his pillbox entrance. Every member of his staff in the cramped interior made a diligent, if cursory, bow in Ingvar's direction. 'We saw your transport take fire. Do you need anything?'

'Your lieutenant already offered,' said Ingvar. 'What is the situation?'

The officers stood round a long table piled with physical maps and dataslates. A few battered cogitators, lithcasters and comms-boxes stood up against the far wall, connected to the power-jacks with a tangle of thick cabling. The lumens flickered, and it was cold.

'This is the last crossing in the sector we still hold,' Borsch said. 'They've moved three divisions up towards the interior north of here, but it's a long way round. So they'd like this one too. We were holding both banks fine. Until those... *things* came.'

'Heretic Astartes,' volunteered the regimental commissar, a thick-boned woman with a pale complexion. 'I believe that is the correct term.'

Borsch looked at her distastefully. 'Whatever they are. They're hard to put down. We're meant to have support, *massive* support, because this is supposedly a priority for sector command, but it's two weeks late now, and we're not going anywhere. So that's the situation.'

As the colonel spoke, Olgeir walked into the pillbox, having to stoop lower to get in. Ingvar glanced at him, and voxed the question.

'Skullhewer's dragging some salvage out,' Olgeir replied over the packcomm. 'But the gunship's not coming back up.'

'We're due to meet up with our people,' said Ingvar to Borsch, 'but our augurs have been down since planetfall. Any intelligence on Adeptus Astartes deployments north of here? The Wolves of Fenris? Or our supporting regiments, from Ojada?'

Borsch leaned over to the comms officer, who shook her head, then went to rummage through a sheaf of code-books and order dockets.

'We can look into it,' Borsch said doubtfully. 'But it'll take time.'

As the words left his mouth, a distant crash sounded, far away to the south. A few trickles of dust fell from the pillbox roof, and alert runes blinked on across one of the cogitators. Vox-chatter immediately started up, and two of the guards in the room saluted and vaulted up the stairs to the exit.

'And now they're trying again,' said Ingvar, feeling the perennial impatience start up again. He sent an urgent message to Gunnlaugur, then drew his power sword. 'Which means, I guess, that we'll be here a little longer.'

CHAPTER TWENTY-SIX

They came in a howling charge, stumbling over one another, the dross and the fanatics, driven ahead of the main advance to soak up las-fire and waste valuable bullets. The grey sun was fully up by then, illuminating a scrum of poorly armoured, poorly armed fanatics, their exposed skin punctured and stretched, their faces tattooed and stitched into tapestries of raw, ruddy flesh. They stretched across the entire width of the transitway, thousands of them, running wildly, their limbs flapping and flailing. Some carried little more than wrenches and power hammers. They screamed, throwing their hairless heads back and ululating crazily, hollering languages that they had not known until dark whispers from dark mouths taught it to them. The air itself seemed to recoil from their words, pressurising as they ran through it, making the whole ragged advance shake with a kind of heatwash.

The Cadians were well drilled, used to dealing with waves of such attacks, and didn't throw ammunition away in speculative shots. The tanks opened fire once the crowds had rolled up close enough, sending shrapnel rounds into the front ranks. When those exploded, the carnage was prodigious, felling whole rows of cultists at once and making those behind topple over. That slowed them, but only until the frenzied press of bodies behind managed to trample the dying underfoot and continue the rampage.

Three more times the tanks fired, each time causing similar mayhem, and each time failing to do much more than winnow out the most reckless and least fortunate. All the while, the Cadian infantry waited behind their barricades, lasguns resting on the top of the sandbags, fingers on the triggers, listening for the order. Dust billowed up, shrouding the onslaught like an allied army of ghosts. It became hard to make out much beyond the first few ranks of the oncoming horde, but occasionally glimpses came of larger, slower outlines in the middle of that giant mass, jogging with ominous certainty amid the wild sprints of the slave-rabble around them.

When the command finally came in, the troopers opened up as one, flooding the bridge deck with targeted barbs of neon-white las-bolts. The volume and rate of fire were exemplary, and more cultists smacked to the deck, their chests shot through or their limbs winged. Closer still, and hard rounds joined the slaughter, fired by gunnery teams operating tripod-mounted cannons with ammo-loops churning through the mechanism. Closer again, and frag grenades were sent sailing high over the heads of the mob, set to explode as they struck the deck, blasting further holes in the wayward onward charge, spraying blood and armour-fragments across the already rubble-strewn asphalt.

Gunnlaugur heard it all. The rest of the pack heard it all. None of them saw it take place. It would have been hard to see anything much from their vantage, hanging underneath the bridge's main deck, their limbs coiled around cross-braced steel supports, waiting for the drum of boots overhead to indicate that the vanguard of the assault had passed them. They were arranged on either side of the structure – Gunnlaugur, Baldr and Jorundur on the left, Ingvar, Olgeir and Hafloí on the right – hidden in the lattice of metalwork that supported the bridge's heavy upper rockcrete blocks.

Gunnlaugur deactivated his helm's auditory enhancements, placed the ceramite against the bridge's structure so that the reverberations passed straight through, and listened. The rhythms were erratic, scattered, no coordination, broken up by the barrages from the defenders some four hundred yards back at the intersection.

He gripped the metal more tightly. Having to delay progress north was an irritation, possibly a dangerous one, but there was no real alternative – he didn't want *Vuokho* being taken before they had stripped it out, and the defenders deserved a chance to hold their position. Besides, Jorundur was in a dangerous mood following the destruction of his beloved gunship – giving him the chance to work off some of that fury had its benefits.

Still, he could have ordered the pack to keep moving. They could have commandeered a vehicle from the Cadians and left the Imperial troops to it, no doubt saving time and certainly minimising risk to themselves. Would that have been the right decision? Perhaps, but it would have been shabby and craven. They'd ducked too many stands already in the cause of speed, and had always known they'd have to fight at some stage. This was as good a place as any to start.

Mention Russ, and see them smile, Ingvar had said. It'd be nice, if possible, to have that proven.

Suddenly the bootfalls changed in tone – slower, heavier, making the bridge-structure flex.

'Now,' he voxed, and sprang into motion.

The others reacted instantly, swinging up and round, climbing over the outer railings and vaulting across, activating blades and bolters. They plunged right into the thick of the horde, out of range of the defenders' ongoing gun-volleys but close enough to the mob's vanguard to cripple its onward momentum. Olgeir opened up with Sigrún, clearing a bloody swathe ahead of him and sending broken bodies flying in all directions. Baldr, Haploí and Jorundur let loose with their bolters too, blowing lanes open through the press. Ingvar followed up with his power sword, crackling with its pale light. Gunnlaugur kindled the energy-arcs over his thunder hammer and joined in, smashing two traitors bodily over the bridge's edge before launching into another knot further in.

The attacks caused panic in the cultists, generating screams of fear on top of the frenzy, but that was not why the Wolves had waited. Just ahead of them, advancing steadily through their cluster-shield of lesser fighters, were the real targets – five Heretic Astartes, blood-bronze giants steeped in ancient corruption, their armour stained and blistered, their weapons already snarling, their corrupted helms glowing with unearthly light. Their battleplate was cracked and befouled, but under all the hard-baked ichor and filth you could just about make out a deep crimson colouration, chipped and scratched to the ceramite, adorned with brass and gold and hung with clanking loops of bleached skulls. They spoke, but the words were unintelligible – just a bestial set of barks and spittle-thick grunts, mockeries of the humanity they had possessed in another age.

As soon as the Wolves emerged, those grunts changed – the warriors of the World Eaters bellowed with pleasure, crunching over their own lackeys to engage, revving their chainswords and pulling out daemon-bound blades. Their boots tore the asphalt up, their amplified vox-blasts made the air shake and unprotected eardrums burst. None of them used ranged weapons, preferring a brace of blunt-edged blades already slick with gore. They moved incredibly fast when they wanted to, like runaway juggernauts, but that swaggering power was matched by a raw battle-cunning – an instinctual awareness of everything around them, honed by many mortal lifetimes of endless combat.

The Space Wolves emptied their magazines at them, and Olgeir managed to blast one into a pulpy mess with his heavy bolter before the gap between them closed to nothing. After that, the combat became a matter of close-pressed bladework. Gunnlaugur crunched Skulbrotsjór into the churning chainblade of their champion – a colossal monster with arching horns over a brass-mouthed helm. The World Eaters and Space Wolves tore into one another, hacking and hammering, ripping up the bridge structure around them and throwing aside the broken bodies of cultists caught up in the carnage. Gunnlaugur smashed his hammer head down again, then again, its energy field spitting as the disruptor-charge splashed across his opponent's crushing blade-swipes. He could hear Olgeir thundering away close at hand, and caught glimpses of Baldr and Ingvar fighting in tandem against a single raging World Eater, energy-scraps flying wildly around them as their blows struck home.

Now that they were close, he could smell nothing but the enemy – their burned-metal, coppery foulness, their corrupted breath stinking of death, their stimm-chem backwash that stuck in his nostrils. Their roars were animal roars, like maddened beasts, dredged up from throats thick with acidic spittle. They were phenomenally strong, their muscles boosted and twisted by corruption, their very armour screaming at him as fractured faces winked and flashed in what remained of the reflective lacquer. There was no trickery, no sham illusions. Just naked aggression, boosted and distended, bound up in bodies hammered into sacred weapons for a god of unbridled anger.

Gunnlaugur saw Hafloí whirl into the thick of things, whooping and spinning his blades, his youthful energy matching the sleet-cold hardness of the Grey Hunters around him. The pack had the numbers, now – the edge that should prove decisive, given the momentum of the ambush attack – but then he heard the cry, ahead of him, strangled with loathing and anguish, rawer than any other in the pack.

'Old Dog!' Gunnlaugur bellowed, driving forward with his warhammer and plunging it straight through the champion's exposed gorget. The plasma-flare exploded, ripping the helm from its cables and sending the huge body crashing to the deck in a welter of boiling blood. Even before the corpse had thudded to the deck he was leaping across it, barging through a reeling clot of cultists. Ingvar had also broken free from combat, racing through the mob to where the cry had come from.

Jorundur had pushed ahead too far, driven by his own rage, caution forgotten. Gunnlaugur caught up, only to see a World Eater driving a pair of powerblades up through Jorundur's chest, both of them emerging out the other side just under the shoulder blades. The old warrior roared in pain, blood suddenly gouting from his damaged helm-seal, drowning his cries. The World Eater withdrew his locked swords, and Jorundur's lifeless body thunked to the deck, arms clattering limply among the other piled bodies.

Gunnlaugur screamed in wild anger, throwing himself bodily at the traitor. He slashed once, twice, blistering hammer-throws that had every ounce of his strength behind them. The World Eater, caught off balance, tried to parry and had both forearms smashed. Gunnlaugur crunched him backwards with a shoulder-barge, pulled the thunder hammer up and then hurled it down, sending the snarling head crashing into the traitor's helm and driving deep into his chest.

Ingvar joined him, hacking in a berserk frenzy, lashing out as if he wished to carve up the entire bridge. Gunnlaugur heard Olgeir's hurled invective, followed by a deafening barrage from Sigrún that mowed down the cultists for yards around. Baldr and Haflói were still fighting, finishing off the final two World Eaters one apiece, but all Gunnlaugur could see just then was Jorundur's broken body, as wrecked as *Vuokho*, ripe to be trodden down in the melee and lost amid the onward tide of combat.

He opened his throat, flying at the enemy ahead of him, carving them up, pummelling them back, spraying their broken corpses in all directions. He and Ingvar hacked a gore-streaked path right into the heart of the horde, backed up by a still-raging Olgeir's tempestuous barrages from the heavy bolter. All he wanted to do just then was find more of them, more slaves to these Dark Gods, more faithless members of the Old Legions, warriors that he could break his fury across and douse it in their deaths. There were bound to be more of them somewhere in that mob, maybe a few, maybe dozens, and if he had to slaughter his way through every last benighted mortal to get at them, then he would.

The Space Wolves must have cut their way to the very centre of the bridge, maddened, unstoppable, slaying in heaps, before the war-horns blared. Even over the screams and the shouts of combat, even across the steady drum of the Cadian guns, those colossal vox-emitters boomed out, shattering the last glass in the windows of the buildings on either bank.

Gunnlaugur looked up, startled out of his rampage. A Titan was striding up the river, the waters boiling against its knee sections, its smokestacks pouring out black smog, its weapon arms slowly coming to bear on the southern bank. It was Imperial, Reaver-class, towering over the buildings around it. Its battle-standards swung heavily as its mighty piston-driven legs waded through the dirty surf. On the southern shore, making almost as much noise, came a support-pack of Warhounds in the same gold-and-blue livery. By their marks, they were of the Legio Gryphonicus, an old and storied Imperial icon. The distinctive helms of supporting skitarii infantry units could just be made out advancing at the feet of the god-machines, filtering through the ruins on the shoreline, making their way steadily towards the point where the bridge made landfall.

That was enough, finally, to break the resolve of the enemy, and the wavering advance became a frantic retreat. Cultists scrambled and twisted to fall back, running over one another in their desperation to get back to the ruins and break west, away from the advance of the Titans. The Warhounds were swiftly coming in range, and their mega-bolters were whining up to fire. The Reaver angled its colossal gatling blaster into the ruins, and its barrels clunked audibly into position.

Gunnlaugur heard cheers rising from the north bank, followed by the unrestrained discharge of Cadian weaponry. He knew he could push on, now, if he chose to. Under the cover of the Titans' guns, the pack could slice through the retreating enemy like a dagger through fat, hunting down the true warriors in the heart of the rabble, the ones he burned so hard to slay. The rest of the pack were already moving, hacking running cultists down, thirsting for blood-vengeance.

'Hold!' he roared, lofting his thunder hammer high and sending the energy field flaring.

They turned to face him one by one, first Ingvar and Olgeir, then Baldr, then, last of all, the whelp.

Gunnlaugur felt wretched, as if the fire in his blood had turned to lead, weighing him down. Even as he spoke, the god-machines unloaded their weaponry, igniting the southern shore in fireballs of pure destruction.

'That's enough,' he growled, dousing Skulbrotsjór's disruptor.

Then he turned heavily, and stalked back to where the body of the Old Dog lay, his mood as black as the clouds that rose up, one after the other, over the ruins.

The forces of the Machine-God did not linger. They swept up along the southern bank, driving the enemy westward, striding after them and giving them no respite. The Reaver made landfall, lurching up onto the embankment before absolutely pummelling what remained of the buildings beyond. With its Warhounds flanking it, it strode out west, blaring all the time, its massive feet crushing the rubble and its heavy weapon-arms swivelling.

An emissary from the Legio did cross the bridge to speak to the defenders and pass on dispatches from the sector command before scuttling back to join the skitarii. The robed creature didn't so much as glance at the Space Wolves as it passed them, its metallic-looking head hidden under a crimson cowl. Once it had departed, and the last of the Mechanicus transports had rumbled their way west, the entire place fell into an eerie quiet, still hanging with dust, the blood of the slain cooling against the rockcrete.

Ingvar didn't meet Gunnlaugur's gaze. He didn't feel like meeting the gaze of any of the pack. Once the fighting had stilled, the Wolf Guard went over to Jorundur to salvage what could be salvaged – his weapons, his helm, any rune-tokens or totems that might be taken back to Fenris. Olgeir and Baldr remained with him. They would carry the body back to the north bank, though after that it wasn't clear what could be done with it. It was impractical to take it with them, impossible to leave it to rot, its sacred gene-seed unharvested.

Hafloí just stood where he had been fighting, his blades still dripping, staring at the spot where Jorundur lay. Ingvar didn't attempt to speak to him. He trudged north, back towards the Cadian positions. A kind of sickness settled in his throat, the dull grief that always came with the death of a pack-member. It had been the same with Váltyr, when he had been slain – the aching sense of removal, as if a part of himself had been hacked away, leaving the wound exposed and throbbing. In time, and soon enough, they would mark his passing into the Underverse. They would laugh, remembering his foul temper and acid tongue. They would mark down his saga for recitation, including as many occasions where he had tripped up or injured himself as they could.

But not yet. For now, it was just the grief, deep and potent.

By the time he reached the intersection on the northern embankment, the Cadians had finished the remaining butchery, and had advanced out across the bridge with flamers to clear the remnants away. Ingvar made his way back to the command bunker, but Borsch had already emerged. They met once more in the open, with the sun now lowering again, lengthening the shadows across the sluggish river.

'My thanks, lord!' Borsch said, pulling his helm off and smiling broadly. 'You rendered us great service.'

Ingvar grunted, and wrenched his own helm from his head, running a gauntlet through his sweaty, dusty hair. His expression said all that needed to be said.

'So, then, do you... require anything?' the colonel asked haltingly, just as he had done before.

'We'll need to move now. As planned, without delay.'

'Arrangements have been made. I have troops converting a Taurox for your... requirements. The work's almost done – we've stripped out what we can, fuelled and serviced it. If you need more, then–'

'No, I'm sure it will suffice. Did you find anything about the deployments?'

'Not much.' Borsch looked apologetic. 'Our main systems have been out for a week or more. The comms officer remembers chatter on the grid about a push north of Kasr Belloc, and there was mention of Adeptus Astartes being involved. Maybe your kind – he can't be sure. Nothing on any regiments from Ojada.'

'Fine. We'll find them. Thank you.'

'Thank *you*. Titans or no, if you hadn't been here–'

Ingvar turned away. Out on the bridge, the rest of the pack was returning, Jorundur's body hoisted on their shoulders. Borsch stared at it.

'We won't be able to take him with us,' Ingvar said. 'Do you have a medicae vault here, secure, something you can guard?'

'We do.'

'I'll speak to my commander. We might have to leave the body with you. You said you were due to be relieved. When you are, if you are, it would have to be transported, protected, somewhere where the Adeptus Astartes have command posts. You understand? This is very important.'

'I do, lord. If it is within my power, it will be done.'

Ingvar nodded, watching grimly as the pack marched across the bridge.

'And then we'll be gone,' he said. 'But Throne be with you, colonel – you fought well here.'

 # CHAPTER TWENTY-SEVEN

The Taurox had been stripped of all but its essentials, mostly to make room for the Space Marines to fit inside without hunching. It was a weather-beaten old machine, with its regimental insignias half blasted off the metal, but Borsch had clearly found someone decent to service it, so the engine ran true enough. Its turret had twin autocannons fitted, the barrels cleaned and draped with machine-spirit benedictions.

By the time they left Ninth Crossing, heading up the transitway through the Imperial-occupied section, the sun was low in the sky. As the cloud cover darkened, the booms of combat became more vivid against the horizon. Most of the major impacts came from the north, the direction they were travelling in, making the underside of the clouds flash and flicker with internal fire. For a while the road was decent, albeit strewn with burned-out groundcars and troop carriers. The buildings on either side were empty-windowed and de-powered, but the walls still stood, with their carved aquilas and urban-sector number designations. Ninth Crossing wasn't much of a place – a semi-industrial outpost that was more check-point than true settlement – but it was still striking to see how completely the war had emptied it out.

Olgeir drove. After the Taurox left the city limits, the road got worse, pocked with mortar craters and transverse cracks, sending the transport bouncing and reeling.

No one said much. Ingvar stared at his clenched fists. Gunnlaugur still had a thunderous scowl etched across his scarred face.

For Baldr, the pain had begun to return. The further north they went, the worse it got. The fighting at the river had made little odds – he had been lost in the fury of it, that was true, but once it was over the pulse behind his temples had returned swiftly, incessant, nagging, impossible to avoid.

'I mean,' Hafloí said, after an hour or so. 'He was a rancid-tempered old hog, when he wanted to be.'

Olgeir chuckled at the wheel, driving the Taurox as fast as he dared, having to work to keep them on the road. 'Aye. That he was.'

Ingvar smiled thinly. Gunnlaugur remained silent.

They drove on into the night. Out in the wasteland, the dark became near absolute. A scrubland of dry brush and cracked earth ran away from them in all directions, flat, wind-scoured. More peaks rose up ahead of them, but they were a long way off. The only things to break the monotony were occasional tank-hulls, burned black and splayed open like ribcages, or the relics of downed flyers. The wind tore across them all, snatching at the tattered remains of straps and bindings and uniforms, fluttering in whispers against the blackened metal.

The pain got worse. Baldr sat with his back against the Taurox's chassis, eyes closed, trying to focus. From what he remembered from the Thunderhawk's scanners, they must be getting closer now, heading into whichever cauldron of combat Ragnar had opted to make his stand in. They would surely come across more enemy forces soon. All it would take would be for a flyer to spot them out in the open, lock on with an air-to-surface missile, and it would all be over.

Although, somehow, he knew it wouldn't be like that. The worse the pain got, the more his certainty returned. He'd been as blind as any of them to Jorundur's danger, back at the river where the heat behind his eyes had been easier. It all went together, it seemed – the pain, the foresight. The column must have had something to do with it – the pinnacle of dark stone he'd seen from afar. The further they left it behind, the harder things became.

Olgeir hit a divot, making the Taurox buck, smacking Baldr's head against the steel frame. A wave of hot agony flushed down his neck, and he grunted. Ingvar turned to look at him, gave him a quick glance of concern, but did not speak.

It was growing, building, pressurising. He clenched his fists, and felt the soul-ward jangle against his chest, tinking off the ceramite as the Taurox moved. Slowly, deliberately, he closed his eyes again.

'Brother...' said Hafloí, after more agonising time had passed.

He opened his eyes, and saw the glow. It wasn't intense, just a faint blush of pale light, like moonlight. It was coming from his neck.

All the others riding in the crew compartment were staring at it. In the night-dark, with the Taurox's lumens killed, it was the only thing lighting up the interior.

'Are you doing that?' Hafloí asked.

Baldr didn't know, not truly. But it felt unlikely. It felt that the null-collar was under stress, greater than it had ever been, trying to clamp down on the thing within him that just kept on growing, remorseless as gravity.

He began to feel nauseous, and the ache behind his eyes sharpened.

'We... need to stop,' he said.

He didn't even know where those words came from. Gunnlaugur, who had been listening into any comm-traffic the scanners could pick up, turned sharply towards him. 'We are running out of time,' he said.

'I know that. We have to stop.'

Ingvar checked his own handheld augur. 'There's something here. A mile off the road, over to the left.'

'What kind of thing?'

'Faint heat source. Strange pattern.'

Gunnlaugur hesitated for a moment, clearly unwilling to make a diversion.

He let slip a low snarl of frustration, then looked quizzically at Baldr. 'This is *needful*, brother?'

By then, there could be no doubt. The pain was becoming so bad that it was hard merely to move his jaw to answer. Baldr felt like he was caught in some giant invisible vice, simultaneously crushing, pulling and grinding him apart. Every second that passed made it worse, and he knew – in that same uncanny manner that marked all his certainties – that it had something to do with whatever Ingvar had detected out in the wilderness.

'We have,' he said again, forcing the words out, 'to stop.'

Gunnlaugur shook his head, wearily. 'Heavy-Hand – follow the signal.'

Olgeir did as he was ordered, swerving the Taurox off the transitway and sending it revving unevenly across the broken scrubland. The rest of them put their helms back on, silently, grimly, and reached for weapons.

It didn't take long to reach the source of the signal. Olgeir pulled up a hundred yards ahead of it and killed the engine. The pack got out, hefting their bolters, and advanced slowly through the darkness.

By then, it was the deep of the night. The wind was cold and incessant, pulling at the scrub and the dusty soil. The landscape was still unremittingly flat, offering uninterrupted views in all directions. Aside from the occasional boulder or thorn-bush outcrop, nothing persisted in that strange place. The gusts of icy air eddied strangely, and lights glimmered and flickered against the scudding clouds. Some of those might have been reflective echoes of distant ordnance, but others were unusual – pearlescent, as fleeting as gas flares or starlight ripples over water.

Baldr had trouble focusing. He held his bolter two-handed, gripped ready to fire, but doubted he'd be able to do much good with it. In any case, this felt more for show than anything else – he sensed no great physical threat ahead, just something... strange.

They pressed on, keeping close together, treading carefully against the dry vegetation. Eventually, they reached a wide curve where the land fell away, as if gouged by a great ploughshare. The edges of the depression were crumbling and friable, but the descent was shallow.

'This is the place,' said Ingvar, putting the augur away. His voice was tight, just as it always became before sighting an enemy.

Gunnlaugur went ahead, peering down the slope. 'There's more up ahead,' he said. Even with his eyesight, it was hard to pick up much in the murk without using helm-lumens. 'Go watchfully.'

The pack edged down the scree, boots sinking into broken earth. It turned out to be a furrow rather than a crater, one heading north-west. As they moved along it, debris appeared – shards of some dull, non-reflective material. It looked like something broken off from a large vehicle, though not one used by either Imperial forces or the enemy.

Ingvar said it first, though they were all thinking the same thing. 'Xenos.'

The main body of the wreckage lay at the terminus of the furrow, driven down below ground level by more than twenty yards. By then the furrow had widened, and the earth was hot. The wind whipped up hard-to-place smells – almost like flowers, or alcohol, or maybe some exotic chem-mix.

The detritus piled up there, long shards like broken glass, but in sweeps and curves. The surfaces were all matt-black, though jewels had been embedded in the structure, glossy as jet. As far as it was possible to tell, this was the wreckage of a single vehicle, something large enough to survive descent from orbit, but clearly atmospheric-capable. Some of its vanes and spars were still more or less intact, jutting into the night sky like extravagant sculptures, though its engines were dormant and the fires of its descent were out.

A single figure lay on the ground before it. The Space Wolves advanced warily, guided by silent battle-sign from Gunnlaugur. Olgeir fell back a little, scanning over the ship-ruins with his heavy bolter. Hafloí climbed a little way up the slope on the far side. The rest of them came to stand before the prone xenos, all guns aimed squarely at it.

By then, Baldr felt like screaming. It was virtually silent in that place, but inside his head a chorus of half-intelligible voices shrieked, over and over, a choir of madness. Every time he moved his head, the world blurred, breaking up into overlaid shards of translucence. Merely holding position was a challenge.

The xenos looked straight at him, of course, ignoring the others. He or she – it was always hard to tell – was clad in close-fitting flight-armour, as black as its ship, overlaid with oil-dark robes. Just like the ship, the armour was studded with what looked like jewels – ovals of polished stone, ringed with thin lines of silver. It lifted its slender head, helmless and long-haired, and gave a pain-filled smile.

'Sons of the Wolf King,' she said, the timbre of her voice indicating that she was female.

'We should end it,' said Ingvar, clearly itching to kill the creature. Baldr could feel the belligerence from the others, too, but Ingvar's was the brightest flame.

'Hold, brother,' Baldr said. Then, to Gunnlaugur, 'Let it speak.'

'Only lies come from the mouth of a xenos,' protested Ingvar.

'It can do us no harm. Not like this.'

Gunnlaugur regarded the creature carefully. Baldr could see how close he was to opening fire. Everything in his body strained to do it. Only the circumstances, only Baldr's word, was keeping the alien alive.

Even for him, it was hard to look at that oddly elongated face – like a human's in so many ways, but utterly different in others – and not wish to break it open. Every part of his training, every part of the Imperial doctrines that he had been immersed in his whole life, urged him to extinguish the filth from existence. Perhaps the xenos felt the same way about them. Perhaps it, too, was holding off a last gasp of violence. Everything remained ratchet-tense, held in suspension, apt to explode at any moment.

Taking Gunnlaugur's silence for consent, at least provisionally, Baldr gradually lowered his bolter. His vision was by then so cloudy that the weapon had become almost useless anyway. The only illumination in the entire place was still his null-collar, now glowing like a half-forged sword pulled from the fires.

'Why are you here?' Baldr asked.

The xenos looked to be suffering at least as much as he was. One of her limbs was twisted at an impossible angle, the left-hand side of her body was stained with blood. Her breathing was shallow and rapid, her skin moon-pale. When she spoke, a thin black trickle ran from the corner of her mouth.

'The same reason you are,' she replied, the Gothic highly accented, but otherwise perfectly intelligible. 'First movement of the Rhana Dandra. We all have our roles to play.'

'Kill it,' hissed Ingvar.

Gunnlaugur held up a warning fist, letting Baldr continue.

'What happened to you?' he asked.

The xenos smiled weakly. 'Fate was cruel. As it has been, I see, for you.' Then, as the audible words were heard by all, a pulse of mind-communication, for him alone. +You are at the doors of annihilation, warrior. You know the truth of this.+

'I sensed you,' Baldr said. 'You were intended to be here.'

'No, not all things are planned, whatever Ulthran might tell you. This is coincidence. Or, if it is not, then its provenance escapes me.' She struggled to rise a little, but her arm gave out. She paused to control her breathing, then swallowed painfully. 'What did you think? That you were somehow... special?'

Baldr's collar twinged, almost making him cry out from the spasm of agony. 'Hardly. I am cursed. I seek a cure.'

The xenos nodded, as if to herself. 'Yes, I suppose it is a curse. Both a blessing and a curse.' Then she looked suddenly dismissive. 'But do not fool yourself. There is no cure. You yourself are under no particular curse, human. Or, rather, if you are, then your whole species is too. This is not about you. On every world of your dying empire, the kindling is already lit. Soon it will be a wildfire. Your kind are, at last, *waking up*.'

Baldr instantly recalled what Njal had told him. *A thousand stories reach my ears. Some talk of awakening.*

'All the same,' he said. 'It is maleficarum. It cannot be used.'

He half expected the xenos to show off her species' much-vaunted disdain then, as if that were a hopelessly simplistic complaint about a matter that was far too complex to couch in such terms. She didn't. In fact, though it was hard to read non-human expressions, she almost looked sympathetic.

'No, it cannot be used,' she said weakly. 'But, also, it must be. That is the great riddle.' She shifted painfully, and her too-wide eyes flickered warily towards the others. 'I know the struggle your kind have with... what do you call it? The warp. I know it. And you are wise to mistrust it. Some of my kind mock the efforts you make to keep it secret, keep it hidden. I do not. What right have we to laugh? We tried to answer the same riddle ourselves, and failed. Maybe there is no answer. Or maybe the answer changes. But the riddle itself – it is still spoken, every hour, with every living heartbeat, by all who draw breath.'

By then, the null-collar felt hot, even through his armour. He could feel his flesh searing, just one more spike of pain to add to the cacophony in his mind.

'Then perhaps it is best if the curse stays around my neck,' he said. 'To prevent the greater harm.'

'And so you will die,' the xenos said. 'Pointlessly, but that would be your choice.' Then, with a change of expression as sudden and complete as the other shifts in emotion, her face filled with fear. 'There are worse things than death, though. Many worse things.' She managed then to push herself up a little, to shuffle towards them. The movements were crippled, pathetic, and all of a sudden she seemed more supplicant than sage. 'You could help me, if you chose. Not to keep me alive – too late for that – but to... take something for me. Carry it with you, just for a little while, until it can be moved to a place of safety. You cannot imagine what that would mean, what agonies it would prevent.'

'Why would I do that?'

'Because I can end your pain, too,' she said, utterly seriously. 'I can set you free.'

'It cannot be trusted,' said Ingvar.

'Of course it can't,' said Gunnlaugur. 'That is not in question.'

'But it is here, in front of us,' said Olgeir doubtfully. 'What did we expect to come across?'

Hafloí said nothing, but glanced at Baldr. For the time being, Baldr was silent.

The pack had withdrawn a little way from the xenos. Olgeir kept his weapon trained on it, and all the rest remained armed and alert. They spoke over the pack-comm, keeping their words locked within their helms. As they debated, the alien creature closed her eyes, placed her remaining good hand over her chest, and tried to breathe.

'It is a warlock,' said Ingvar. 'A twister of fates. I've seen what they do to armies. To worlds.'

'As have I,' said Gunnlaugur, his growl giving away some irritation. 'It's not just the Deathwatch that fights xenos.'

'There's no strength left in it,' said Hafloí. 'Not that I can see. It'd say anything now, just to get what it wants.'

'Its jewel,' said Ingvar. 'That's what it wants you to take. Those things are more valuable than starships to them – I've seen them fight like daemons to retrieve them.'

'Other things covet them too,' said Gunnlaugur. 'Or so it is said.'

'So it's in no position to demand anything,' said Hafloí. 'We could take what we want, if we chose, then walk away. When did we start making bargains with such filth?'

'If we make an oath,' said Baldr quietly, 'we keep it.'

Gunnlaugur turned to face him. 'Then you wish to take the chance,' he said, almost accusingly.

'I'll do what you order, vaerangi,' said Baldr. 'But know this – I am dying, right now, right here. In the void, I can hold it back, just a little. For a little while, on this planet, the pain eased. But now it's back, and I can feel it tearing me apart. Njal never intended the collar to be permanent – it was something to keep the power in check while he took me back to Fenris. It's breaking up at the edges now. One of us will give out soon. Perhaps before we get to Ragnar. Maybe just after. I only say this to make the choice clear.'

Gunnlaugur grunted. He'd guessed at that for some time. They all had. Still, to hear it baldly stated, that was different. 'We all saw you,' he said carefully. 'When you were... not yourself. That is the danger.'

'Aye,' said Olgeir. 'It was always the danger, one we accepted at the time. We never knew what chance to end this would come our way, save that it would be just as perilous. It was always going to be.'

Baldr looked at him, grateful for the words. 'I didn't expect such counsel from you, brother,' he said.

Olgeir shrugged. 'Decisions were made. We stand by them.'

'The creature is terrified,' said Ingvar, his voice full of doubt. 'Hafloí speaks the truth – it will say anything, just to get what it wants. They are powerful, those witches, but can it do what it promises? Only Njal himself had the power to remove the collar, you said – even the monster on the plague-hulk couldn't, and that thing was steeped in sorcery.'

'Njal is not here,' said Baldr patiently. 'Even if he is on Cadia, I would be dead before we found him, or any other Priests of the Chapter. The xenos may be lying or deluded, but I see no other chances.' He turned back to Gunnlaugur. 'I'm not begging. If you forbid it, I'll offer my neck for the knife. But that is the choice. One way or another, time is up.'

Olgeir snorted. 'Then that settles it. What have we been doing, all this time, but searching for a cure? Let him die now, when one stands before us, we might as well have stayed on the *Heimdall*.'

An uneasy silence fell. Beyond the crater's ridge, the wind skipped and moaned.

'Gyrfalkon?' asked Gunnlaugur.

Ingvar didn't reply for a moment. 'I don't know what I expected to find,' he said, eventually. 'Only that something would come, and we would know it when we saw it.' He looked squarely at Baldr. 'If it was anything but *xenos*... I learned to hate them more than all else. But then maybe that is my fault to remedy.'

'It was you who made the argument on the *Heimdall*,' said Gunnlaugur. 'And you who brought him back inside the walls on Ras Shakeh.' Then he looked at Baldr. 'But, both times, it was I who gave the order. So Heavy-Hand is right – what would be the point of that risk, now, if we spurned the chance when it came? Danger is what we were made for.'

Baldr felt the collar around his neck suddenly flare, driving a sliver of heat into his chest, as if it somehow knew the way the argument was going. He clenched his jaw tighter, stifling the cry, and said nothing.

'Take the creature's stone, and let it do what it can,' Gunnlaugur said finally, his voice still betraying his deep uncertainty. 'We'll keep our weapons raised. Ruin or no ruin, death or vindication, we'll have an answer before the sun is up.'

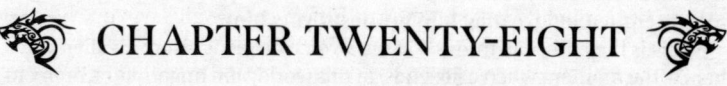# CHAPTER TWENTY-EIGHT

By the time they returned, the xenos was looking worse. Her pallor had faded, her eyes were ringed with grey. In places, her skin looked almost translucent.

Baldr stood before her. The rest of the pack resumed their original positions, guarding them both, weapons raised. It was a strange feeling, to sense the bolters of your own battle-brothers, aimed at you as much as they were on the xenos. Just in case.

'We accept the bargain,' Baldr said.

'You will take the spirit stone?' the xenos asked, her voice close to breaking. 'Keep it safe, ward it at all costs?'

'You have my word.'

'And return it to my people?'

'When we can.'

The xenos looked at him for a long time, as if her damaged eyes were capable of piercing through his mask and judging the truth of his words. 'Remove your helm.'

Baldr reached up and twisted it free. The cold night air washed over his skin, offering some level of relief from the fizzing ache across his face and neck.

'Tell me your name, son of the Wolf King,' the xenos said.

'Baldr, called Fjolnir.'

'And I am Caerlainn, of the people of Ulthanesh Shelwe. A name is important. Both will be needed.'

The collar throbbed, twitching like a living thing.

'So what needs to be done?' Baldr asked.

'Only contact.' She smiled, a pain-filled grimace. 'If it does not injure your pride too much, you will need to stoop.'

Baldr dropped to one knee. His bulk far surpassed the frail, slender creature lying before him, and he had to lower his head a long way before she was able to reach out for the collar.

'It will hurt, of course,' she said.

'Just begin.'

Her fingers made contact with the bone torc.

And everything disappeared. Everything snapped out of existence, save for the agony, which sharply increased. Baldr tried to straighten, to throw his head back and howl, but he couldn't move. It was as if his body had ceased to be entirely, save for a point of pain, a singular nexus. He saw nothing, heard nothing but the great roaring, like surf, or perhaps millions of voices, crashing onward, unending, merciless.

That might have gone on for hours, or just moments – he lost all sense of time and space, only the one reality of unbearable pain, ramping up, flooding his entire being, eating him up, destroying him.

+This is the end of all things,+ came a voice he recognised: an alien voice, hers. +The moment when a life ends, in this world, and lingers, for a moment, in the next. That is the pain you feel.+

He had no way to reply. Somewhere, on some plane of existence, he knew he had physical lips, locked apart in a rictus of anguish, but here, in the place he had been taken to, all he had was the kernel of himself, the spirit of fire, the soul he had always been, alone.

Then, just as suddenly as it had come, the agony cracked. A sound like ice grinding against ice shuddered through the darkness, and he had a sensation of falling, dropping fast, accelerating down a bottomless shaft into the depths of the Underverse, unable to reach out and grab anything to arrest it.

Slowly, the roaring died away, receding into a muffled silence. The sense of falling faded. Everything became cold, perfectly dark, perfectly still.

He looked down, and saw his hands, his body. He was not wearing armour. He was wearing furs, stitched leather, a ragged half-cloak, just as he had once worn when a hunter in the Ascurii. He was standing on a polished stone floor, featureless and black. Columns marched away into the darkness, cut from the same black stone. The place was frigid, echoing, empty.

He turned, and saw the xenos standing next to him. She didn't appear to be injured now. Her robes were different, too – pale white, like bleached bone, and traced with a fine golden lattice of runes. She had a broken torc in her hand, as well as a pendant with a shattered animal skull hanging from it.

'Both were destroyed,' she said. 'The first was killing you, the second was keeping you alive. This ward was on the verge of failing, so you had a day, maybe two, left.'

Her voice rebounded down the long, dark halls, before being swallowed up by the shadows. Out of the corner of his eye, Baldr thought he saw other things in the gloom, shifting, murmuring, but couldn't get a clear view.

'What is this place?'

'You call it Hel, I believe. But I am guessing – I do not see what you see. Not here.'

'Then, this is death.'

'Not yet. A place between life and death, perhaps. Once, my people could move between these many worlds at will. Now even we cannot escape, when the hour comes.'

He looked down at himself. The clothes he wore were just the same as they had been. They smelled the same as they had done in another life – the dry smell of old, cold animal hides. He had his axe at his belt, the same axe he had carried the day the beast had come for him in the endless forest, the one that had hesitated, that had let him live.

God-marked.

'So, it was easy to accomplish,' he said. 'In the end.'

The xenos laughed. 'Easy? No, not easy. For you, it was the work of a moment. For me, it took rather longer – and exhausted what remained of my physical form. We count ourselves masters of this craft, and yet... I was dying already, of course, but this action has sealed the compact.' She looked briefly haunted. 'You were unlocked by the enemy, I think, in the first instance. That will leave a trace. I cannot erase that entirely, so you must guard against what you do with your gift. Or curse. Whatever you choose to call it.'

'And you must stay here,' he said, knowing the truth of it even as the words left his mouth.

'My body is burned away. When you return, you will see nothing but a husk. I am the stone, now. The stone is me. Should you lose it, or see it destroyed, the pain you just felt will be mine to endure for eternity. Should you return it to my people, a chance remains to avoid that fate.' The xenos smiled dryly. 'Perhaps now you see why I was keen to strike the bargain.'

'But you trust me.'

'What choice do I have? But yes, I trust you. There is a certain kinship, amongst those who have been in such places.'

'So I see now that this was always ordained.'

'You see that, do you? Strange, that I do not. But maybe *you* were fated to be here for *me*, eh? You may not be the end in this, just the means. That is the great deception – to believe that *we* are the significant thing in any given nexus of events. Maybe you are, maybe you are not. My ability to tell has been... curtailed.'

Baldr felt no sorrow for the xenos. Ancient hatreds remained strong, whatever debt of honour now lay between them. 'Your thread is ended.'

'In this place, surely. But there are other worlds, human. Ones that you may glimpse soon, if you have the wit for it.'

Baldr's eyes flickered, half catching one of the denizens of the shadows. He almost recognised what it was, but then it was gone, evaporating into nothing. He felt uncomfortable, as if he were being tricked or deceived, and yet his senses had never been clearer. All his old training, all his old beliefs... they would either be needed more than ever, or would have to be cast aside. He needed guidance. Or maybe that was the last thing he needed. He needed to return to the source. Or maybe he needed to keep running, forever, further and further away.

'This is not an awakening,' he said. 'It is more like rebirth. I am a child again.'

'Something the masters of your race understand.'

'Hence their caution.'

'The craft in your containment device was great. If you had not been fighting it for so long, perhaps it would have been too great to overcome, even for me. But you had been consuming one another for a long time, and I do not think it was ever meant to be employed for such a span.' She looked down at the splintered bone pieces. 'It is a valiant thing, to try to hold back the tide. I admire the ambition of it. But it must fail, in the end. More of you will awaken, growing in number with every generation, until what is rare now becomes as common as breathing. It cannot be stopped. Maybe this will be the blaze that consumes you, just as it was for us, or maybe you will find a way to master it, but every species must take the test, sooner or later.'

Baldr reached up to touch his face, pressing his fingers into the flesh. It yielded more than he was used to. His bone structure was less pronounced, his muscles less hardened. He had forgotten just how fragile it was to be a human, before the Test of Morkai had changed him, so long ago.

'I will be an aberration,' he said.

'In the eyes of many.'

'It will cause strife.'

'Your Imperium already has plenty of that, I think.'

'We call it maleficarum. The craft of witches. Only the way of the storm is permitted, the craft of the old gothi, and even that is hedged with peril. That has always been what we were taught.'

'Then keep teaching it. I am not telling you it is false.' The xenos began to fade, then, her robes becoming translucent, then gauzy, then spinning into flurries of dust. 'All of it, all the way back to the origin, is stories. Endless stories, told and listened to by every mind and soul that has ever been. A story is neither true nor false, though it may be noble, or it may be base. Tell the story you must, either to yourself, or to those you encounter. Just be sure to believe in it, to live it, to act as if every word of it must have been, and could never have been otherwise. Nothing else exists. Nothing else remains. Just voices, speaking in the dark, building the worlds that we labour in, that we both destroy and preserve.'

She was almost gone now. In this place, she had no jewel at her breast, just a skein of golden light that spun and rippled in the murk.

'Hel is the home of the unworthy warriors, is it not?' she asked, her lips like snuffed candle-flames.

'That it is.'

'Then, when the time comes, Baldr of Fenris,' she said, in a voice no louder than a child's whisper, 'ensure that you do not return here. Your soul belongs, I foresee, in the Halls of Fire.'

When he opened his eyes, he saw the world again, its emptiness, its cold wind and its racing, burning skies. He saw his brothers, all of them staring at him. He saw the body of the xenos, lifeless now, its skin already hardening, becoming brittle.

It was darker, now. His collar was gone, and the only remaining light came from the firelit distance, in addition to the wisps of refracted ghostliness that shimmered in the cloud cover.

He lifted his hands, turning them, trying to assess how he felt.

A weight had gone. The pain, for the most part, had gone. What pain remained was like that of a healed wound – more wholesome, speaking of recovery. He knew without having to look that scar tissue ridged along his collarbone.

Of the collar itself, there was no sign – it was neither in pieces on the ground nor in the xenos' grasp. The soul-ward pendant, too, was gone.

'Speak to me,' said Gunnlaugur, aiming his bolt pistol at Baldr's head. It was a command, not a request, and made from wariness.

'I am myself,' Baldr said, slowly turning to face him, keeping his movements slow and obvious. 'Aye, I am myself.'

'What happened?' Ingvar asked.

'Did you not see it?'

'We saw nothing,' said Hafloí, sounding almost cheated. 'Just a flash of light, then you were standing again, and the creature was dead.'

'But you can see that the collar is gone,' said Baldr. 'And that I am restored.'

'And your... gift?' asked Olgeir, still the most suspicious of all.

Baldr thought on that. He didn't know how he was supposed to feel. It had been so long since he had lived without some nagging sense of wrongness, some cradled fear within him, that another way of being felt almost inconceivable.

What had changed? His body was the same. The corruption that had taken it over on Ras Shakeh, and then briefly on the plague-hulk, was burned away. Maybe those things had always been shams, or birth pangs, or something imposed by sorcery on top of a deeper change. The power that surged within him now felt colder, older, harder and more durable.

He let a pulse of it rise to the surface of his mind, and felt his fingers tingle in response. A faint blush of white-blue light spread across the palms of his hands, flickering for a moment, before he let it gust out.

He looked up. The world around him felt sharper, more defined, its depths deeper and its heights higher. When he moved his head, his hands, it felt as if he were moving through something more alive than air – something swimming with old thoughts and words and deeds.

All of it, all the way back to the origin, is stories.

And then, when he moved his attention further out, up past the wreck of the xenos ship and into the wastes beyond, he saw other things – souls moving, in anguish, being ripped from their bodies and sent screaming into the Underverse. They were like stars in galaxies, first thousands of them, and then, when he moved a little way beyond, millions. He could get lost in that vision. He could leave his body, move into that realm, immerse himself in the endless sea of consciousness, merge himself with it, forget everything but the wonder and the scope and the infinity of it...

He drew in a breath, blinked hard, clenched his fists. Physicality was his tether, his anchor.

'I will have to be careful,' he said, smiling dryly. He looked up at Olgeir. 'Keep vigilant, brother.'

Still, they hesitated. He couldn't blame them. He was now a source of almost infinite danger, a conduit into horror that they had been trained to revile and repulse since the first day of their ascended lives. Perhaps, at some level, they sensed it too – the fact that he had changed.

And yet, in truth, he had not changed. He had always been this way, ever since the beast in the woods had let him live. Like a shadow, this part of him had been following him ever since, stalking him in plain sight, waiting for the moment when it would rise up to embrace the rest of him.

'Just give me your word,' said Gunnlaugur. 'That must be enough, for now. Are you whole?'

Baldr looked him in the eye. 'I am.'

'Then can you see where he is?' asked Ingvar. 'Blackmane, the others? Do you know how to find them?'

Baldr smiled again. Maybe Njal could have done it. Maybe even the rawest aspirant in the Priests' training halls could have done it.

'Give me time, brother,' he said. 'I have only just woken up.'

They returned to the Taurox in silence. The last thing Baldr did before leaving the site of the crash was to take the black stone from the xenos' armour, just as he'd promised. That took a while – the jewel was artfully held in place by a narrow clasp-rim, and it needed a deft twist of his knife to prise it out. When he held it up for the first time it looked perfectly black and inert. After a few moments, when looking carefully, you could just make out a faint glimmer from its heart, a twist of light that danced for a moment on the edge of vision. Baldr stowed it carefully away, and the pack moved out.

When they reached the vehicle again, Ingvar rode with Gunnlaugur in the cab. The rest remained in the crew bay, separated from the driver's compartment by a single-skin metal wall. As they mounted up, Gunnlaugur voxed a private command to Olgeir.

'Stay watchful,' he said. 'The first sign of maleficarum, do not hesitate.'

Then they were driving again, crunching over the scrub and heading back towards the transitway. It was still the dead of night, almost silent save for the muffled crunches of explosives from far off. Gunnlaugur steered them back onto the asphalt, and then they were gunning along again, lumens still out, rocked by the ceaseless wind.

'So, what do you think?' asked Ingvar, after a while.

Gunnlaugur snorted. 'He hasn't grown claws and tried to chew our throats out.'

Ingvar chuckled darkly. 'Give it time.'

'You?'

Ingvar stared ahead into the night. The faint lights in the sky were growing in number, writhing as the wind blew, outlining the bulk and motion of the clouds. 'I want him to succeed. I'm aware of the danger of that.'

Gunnlaugur nodded. 'But it *feels* clean, for now. You know what I mean?'

'Aye. And he gives us another path to the target.'

'Once he learns how to use... whatever he's got.' Gunnlaugur glanced down the augur-box bolted on to the Taurox's serviceable dashboard. It was scanning through the frequencies, picking up a dozen new fixes at every sweep. None of them gave much information – just chatter from poorly encrypted streams, low-level stuff, or overlaid to the extent that the content was unreadable. 'Until then, we're relying on this rubbish. We're still using Olgeir's geo-lock to guide us, but even if it was correct from orbit, they've surely moved on now.'

'Then we're guessing.'

'A little. Here's what I can make out.' Gunnlaugur flicked the augur-lens to a cartolith, one that flickered over the dashboard as he drove. 'The line of kasrs on the high ground north of here – see? From what I've managed to pick up, I think they're gone now, broken. Hel, we can see the flames from here. If he was there, he'll have been pushed east.'

'Kasr Aver. Kasr Belloc. Kasr Morgev.' Ingvar scanned the cartolith. 'And taking the river crossing would have speeded movements up from the south of them. What about that range?'

'I've been tracking it. Sheer, if the scans are right. It's like the whole planet is a fortress.'

'A good place to defend.'

'Look.' Gunnlaugur pointed to a narrow gap in the range. Kasr Vasta had been sited there. 'We're getting intermittent Imperial signals from that location. Nothing from the others. If you wanted to halt an advance–'

'You'd do it there. Aye, you might at that. But can we make it?'

Gunnlaugur grunted. 'Maybe. But it'll get tighter, the closer we get.' He deactivated the cartolith. 'We'll still need him, I reckon. His... skills. I don't want to lose another warrior.'

Ingvar hesitated before replying. 'But you were right to support them. Back there.'

'Maybe.' His voice was sour. 'We'll have to do it again, but it's all lost time.'

'Time works against them, too. If the Hunters are there, they'll have to wait for the moment. It'll need to be perfect. They don't know we're coming for them. We have that.'

'But still, we should climb. Take the southern route up the pass entrance, the one that loops around the peak, see? You couldn't get Titans up there, no armour, even mobile infantry would struggle. This thing, though – it might just claw its way up, bringing us within a spit of the earthworks. And if it gives out, we can run.'

Ingvar laughed. 'Run.'

'What's the problem with that?'

'Nothing at all. It'll be just like home.'

'Less visible. Harder to track. Purer.'

Objects started to strike the forward viewscreen then – gobbets of blackness, like ash-flakes. Just a few to begin with, then more and more, as if it were raining. Some seemed to be semi-alight, like the drifting residue of some enormous fire. As the flecks fell in greater numbers, the sky began to lighten, not with the beams of the sun, but with something angrier, redder, closer to hand.

Gunnlaugur glanced at the Taurox's scanners. 'It's a long way off, what's doing that,' he murmured. 'Throne, though. It's big.'

The western horizon kept getting redder and redder. With the auditory delay of a thunderstorm, the roaring came later, just as dull, just as vast. Ingvar looked out at it through the left-hand viewport – a bloom of colour, intensifying, spreading, leaking across the entire night sky until the mountains ahead were silhouettes of pure black against a seething, bloody screen.

And then it broke through the clouds, burning furiously, descending at what looked like a stately pace, but must have been in truth a dizzying plummet. Its outline was indistinct, just a skeleton of metal enclosing a raging heart of fire, but you could still make out the distinctive elements of the voidship it had been – the curve of its bows, the pinnacles of its astrogation towers. It was coming down a long way away – miles and miles – and yet it was still visible against the thunderheads, a falling star, cut from the heavens, outshining all other atmospheric fires, a spear hurled down by the gods from their ongoing orbital struggle.

The scatter and thump of ash-clots grew thicker, stirred up by winds that were no longer natural. An artificial heat surge swept across the plains, ember-mottled, gathering pace, thick with wreckage shed by the collapsing void-giant. Beyond the mountains, the ravaged hull itself broke up further, splitting apart into separate iron comets under the inexorable tug of gravity, spreading vivid flame-tendrils across the skies like ink dropped into water.

And then the bulk of it passed out of view, sinking below the line of the distant peaks, trails of fire lingering to mark its passage, the storm that it had provoked still building in strength, carpeting the scrubland in ash and engine-toxins. The wind howled, buffeting the Taurox, caking its viewfinders in dust, before the first cracking, echoing noises of ultimate impact.

After that, the rising dust-palls finally obscured the fires, looming up in colossal, churning towers across the hidden landing sites, rising into the skies like some immense supporting pillar-cluster for the cloud banks overhead. The earth shook, hard, and the wiry plants swayed wildly as the aftershocks resonated. The booms went on and on, the sky filling with ever more filth and grime, red replaced with black.

It took a long time for the glow to subside, masked by the airborne grime, replaced amid the darkness by the smaller fire-flares of ongoing fighting. The wind lessened its howl, though it still carried flurries of ash, and the rad-counters on the dashboard clicked up to dangerous levels.

'A few more of those,' Ingvar said, 'and this world won't be recovering, whoever wins here.'

Gunnlaugur drove on, peering into the ashen murk ahead. 'I think we knew that,' he said. 'But this isn't about victory, is it?'

'Our own, it is.'

'Aye, our own. But, for this place...' He sighed deeply, a movement that made his huge chest rise and fall. 'We'll take the mountain road.'

CHAPTER TWENTY-NINE

The Taurox rattled and creaked as it left the marked road and began to climb up the scree-lanes and mountain tracks. A weak light filtered through the slit-windows of the crew compartment, but it never really amounted to much – the ash was now falling like rain, coating the gravel and rocks around them, turning everything a dirty black-grey. The wind remained turbulent, rocking the carrier as it laboured up the steep inclines.

Olgeir sat against the inner wall, watching it all through the slit-window. He watched the ash flakes stick to the outer armaglass panes. He watched the fuel tanks gradually empty and the engine temperature rise. He watched his brother Baldr, who sat opposite him.

No one said much. If Jorundur had been there, he might have offered some sarcastic remark about Skullhewer's driving, but he wasn't, and his presence was already missed. Hafloí was subdued, his body rocking with the Taurox as it moved. Eventually, he retrieved his axe and began to work on the haft, picking at the leather bindings with the tip of his knife and cleaning the muck from between them.

Olgeir wasn't sure how he felt. It was good to have Baldr back, without that hex-collar, looking more like himself. Even under armour, you could tell that the sickness was gone, for now – he sat erect, no longer slouching from fatigue. On the other hand, if he succumbed again, would he be so powerful now that none of them could oppose him? Would it affect his mind, his willingness to serve within the pack? Rune Priests did not, as a rule, attach themselves to any particular pack, but served the Chapter as a whole. If Baldr left, that would leave them just four-strong, getting close to minimum strength. Maybe, if they survived this, more fresh blood would have to be introduced, just as before. But that had always been an experiment, a violation of the old traditions made possible by desperation, and Olgeir found himself hoping it would soon be forgotten.

Hours passed, and the cabin felt increasingly cramped and stuffy. The ceiling had been designed for baseline human dimensions, and despite the hasty refit, it was still impossible to stretch out in it. The daylight remained weak, and with the interior lumens out the compartment stayed shadowy. The wind outside kept picking up, more every mile, until it was a continual keening moan outside, pushing against the Taurox, wearing at its war-battered exterior.

The temperature dropped quickly, and the ash-flakes began to mingle with dirty flurries of snow.

'So how do you feel, brother?' he asked eventually, looking straight at Baldr.

'Good,' Baldr replied. 'Better than for a long time.'

'Good,' said Olgeir, trying to keep the worst of the suspicion from his voice. 'No... issues?'

The wind roared louder, searing across the carrier and making it tilt alarmingly. Gunnlaugur had driven them hard up a steep slope, and they were among the high cliffs now.

Baldr didn't reply. He looked up suddenly, listening intently. 'The wind,' he murmured. 'Listen to that.'

Hafloí chuckled, working on his weapon. 'Never heard a gale before? Hel, you've forgotten where you came from.'

But it had become stronger now, raging. The ash-snow thumped against the exterior, almost like clenched fists banging. The moans became whines, high-pitched and whistling.

Baldr reached for the hilt of his sword, though didn't draw it. 'Axe ready, Heavy-Hand?' he asked.

For a moment, Olgeir had no idea why he was asking. There was barely room in the compartment to sit, let alone swing a blade.

'I don't–' he started.

But then, he smelled it. Smell was always first, the result of his enhanced physiology, the sense that kicked in ahead of all the others. The interior of the Taurox was full of smells – the heat of their bodies, the oils of the power armour, the rust of the panelling and the chem-traces from the promethium tanks and ammo boxes. But under that, subtle, almost totally masked, was something else – a musk, a stink, a breath of foulness.

He drew his axe, half stood, braced against the rocking of the carrier. 'What in the–'

Hafloí looked up sharply, alarmed, grabbing his own blade out of instinct. The howls from outside rose in volume again, sounding almost like the fractured wails of children, lost out in the storm.

'Those screams aren't the wind,' said Baldr, unclasping his axe. He got up as well, moving his head to one side, hunting for the source of the stink, the wrongness.

In the end, it came to find them. An arm, lissom, transparent, groping through the sealed access hatch. A mouth, opening in the midst of the chamber, split wide, then shimmering out of existence. The floor rippled, and another claw scratched its way in, scrabbling on the pressed-metal, skittering like a spider.

Olgeir stamped down on it, his boot passing through thin air and jarring against the panel. Hafloí swung at an apparition, striking it dead centre, and sailing on through, slicing into nothing.

The air inside boiled, spat, flexed. Body parts started to materialise, then collapse, then coalesce again. The Taurox's armour plates vibrated, fizzing as if heating up, though the temperature outside was frigid.

'Daemonkin,' hissed Olgeir, whirling around to square up to the fleeting image of a leering, stretched-out face, before it popped out of reality.

Baldr made no attempt to strike them, seemingly frozen into indecision. The Taurox barrelled onward – if the cab was affected, Gunnlaugur was not slowing down – and the screaming became all-encompassing. Haflói struck out again, a wild blow born of frustration, and sent his blade clanging against the forward bulkhead. Olgeir balled his fist, poised to reach out and grab the next vision to appear.

But there was nothing to seize, nothing to wrap fingers around – the creatures were trying to get at them, to instantiate, and failing. All that remained were impressions, snatches, like glimpses in broken mirrors. Another unreal face rushed into focus barely an arm's length in front of Baldr – eldritch, purple-blushed, needle-toothed, black-in-black eyes, distorted as if trying to force itself through molten glass. When it screamed at him, reality flexed, pulled out of symmetry, popping and wobbling and refracting. The shrieks echoed and overlapped, coming from multiple directions at once, before being snuffed out almost as soon as they arrived. The words were almost impossible to decipher – maybe they were in forbidden languages, or were just too blurred by their state, or were just gibberish.

'God-marked!' Olgeir heard, a single intelligible phrase amid all the squawks and howls. 'God-marked!'

Another translucent arm punched out of the reality-morass, going for Baldr's throat, just where the collar had once been. Its fingers stretched desperately, scrabbling to find purchase, long nails raking, a howl of frustration coming with it. Olgeir went to grab it, to break its wrist, but once more his gauntlet clutched at nothing. As his grip closed, though, he felt a spasm of pure cold ripple through his flesh. With a last agonised shriek, the spectral arm blew into pieces, and vanished.

One by one, the rest of the ghosts were sent wailing back into their own realm, the final slivers of pseudo-flesh winking out like sunlight on ice crystals, leaving nothing but the stench of them, and patches of glittering frost on the metal.

Baldr had remained static throughout, staring at the place where the hand had emerged, his axe unused.

Olgeir swept over to him, grabbing him by the shoulders and slamming him against the wall. 'You did *nothing!*' he growled. 'What is it, brother? Have you learned to fear them? Or love them?'

Baldr shook him off, and sat heavily back on the bench. 'I could have...' he began, then broke off.

'What were they?' Haflói demanded.

Baldr shook his head. 'Just... fragments. They wanted to come in. They couldn't.'

'You could have *fought* them,' Olgeir snarled. 'At least tried.'

Baldr looked up at him. 'And if I'd done it?' His voice flashed with anger. 'Shown you what I could do? Would that axe be at *my* neck, now?'

Olgeir glared at him for a moment longer, his blade still in his hand. He knew well enough that some of the anger was frustration, the desire to lash out, to hurt something, anything. Even so.

He turned away, his cheeks hot. 'Skullhewer,' he voxed. 'Did you just see something?'

'Aye,' came the reply. 'Only phantoms. We keep going.'

The snowfall was heavier by then, splatting and smearing over the slit-viewers, caking them with melting ash-clods. The Taurox had never so much as paused, grinding its way upward, onward, further towards the head of the pass.

'They can't break through,' Baldr muttered, looking down at his hands. Olgeir noticed that the palms of his gauntlets were still hot, glowing faintly. 'This world. There's something here. Something holding them back. I felt it earlier, when we saw the pillar. It's making them... furious.'

Olgeir gestured towards his gauntlets. 'So, were you about to...' he started.

'Aye.' Baldr pressed his hands together, hiding the evidence. 'I didn't know what it would do to you. To the transport.'

Olgeir stared at him a little longer, then backed down. He shackled his axe again, and stomped over to where a ladder led up to the gun turret station.

'Well, they know where we are, now,' he said, starting to climb. 'Best we get ready for more.'

Gunnlaugur kept going. The Taurox was struggling now, a combination of the altitude and the terrain, but it had been built for rugged survivability and somehow managed to haul its way further up the steep mountainside, crunching its way through rubble-packed stretches, glossy with ice. The gale kept getting worse, wrapping the vehicle in whirling flurries of dirty snow. The linked tracks slipped and skidded where the gravel was churned up to slush, but Gunnlaugur kept pushing it, barging aside the ash-choked remains of landslips and pouring on the power to blast up the increasingly harsh cambers. For a long time they'd been following trails, relatively wide and well trodden, but now they were up above the snowline, lost in a grey-out that buffeted and bludgeoned from all directions.

'Head of the pass approaching,' Ingvar reported, checking his stalker bolter over as the dashboard augurs blinked and flickered. 'Head for that ridge, ahead left, where the rocks divide.'

Gunnlaugur saw the place – a narrow cleft between giant shoulders of naked rock, choked with rubble. The snow flurries gusted and spiralled between them, as volatile as the dust clouds down on the plains. The Taurox would fit through the cleft, just, though beyond that the scanners didn't penetrate very far. According to the sketchy cartolith data, Kasr Vasta should have been less than five miles north of the turn, perched across the summit of the greater pass entrance, its walls straddling the gulf between mountains, though until he laid eyes on it himself Gunnlaugur placed little faith in expectation.

It stank in the cab, the residue of the apparitions that had scratched and ripped their way through the front windscreen. They hadn't done any real damage, being unable to make themselves fully physical, but their appearance had been so sudden that Gunnlaugur had almost sent the Taurox careering off the track and down into a snow-filled defile. Even after the initial shock had worn off, watching them try to instantiate, their claws raking at emptiness, their teeth glistening in semi-solidity, had been distracting.

'You think it's because of him?' Gunnlaugur asked, wrenching the wheel to bring the Taurox rollicking up the incline towards the cleft. 'That jewel he took? They were going for that?'

'Maybe,' said Ingvar, completing his checks and hefting the bolter in his right hand. With the other, he activated the release catch for the armaglass panel. 'As you suspected – intermittent signals from beyond the gap.'

The terrain was ideal for an ambush, and if the enemy had already advanced up the maw of the main pass then they would certainly have dispatched outriders to plug the smaller feeder routes on either flank. Gunnlaugur's hope was that any defences wouldn't be established yet – just skirmishers peeled off from the advance – and that they could fight their way through without getting bogged down for too long. Either way, they weren't going in blind, and Olgeir had already activated the autocannons on the Taurox's turret.

'Going in now,' Gunnlaugur announced over the pack-comm. 'We'll keep moving, so clear me a path.'

The Taurox pounded its way through the blizzard, rocking on the uneven terrain before driving clear through the cleft mouth. It blasted through deep drifts, bounced heavily on a hidden hard outcrop, then revved down the slope beyond, emerging into a steep-sided valley that ran zigzagging down towards a dense forest of firs. On either flank, broken cliff-edges reared up, their summits hidden by the ashen sleet and their flanks blackened by the deluge. Visibility was low – no more than a hundred feet in the shadows – and the Taurox's lumens were still out.

Gunfire broke out immediately, most from the right-hand flank, snapping and cracking against the Taurox's armoured hide. Gunnlaugur never let up, sending the carrier kicking on faster, its exhausts coughing and its engine labouring. He heard what sounded like Haflof's weapon discharge, launching bolt-shells up at the source of the incoming fire. A microsecond later, explosions some forty feet off into the murk blew whole segments of the cliffside apart.

Gunnlaugur swung the Taurox around a knife-sharp ridge, before pushing it down a long straight. Slushy gravel kicked up against the tracks and clattered against the underside. More shots came in, this time from both sides of the gap, launched from positions both high above and closer to ground level. They were solid rounds, mostly, but a few las-bolts flashed out of the gloom, raking across the long engine housing and scarring the armour plates.

Ingvar returned fire, as did Baldr from further back, and soon the Taurox was careening its way along a widening passage, its side blazing with sparks, under fire and trailing smoke.

'Heavy-Hand,' voxed Gunnlaugur, wrestling with the wheel. 'See those?'

'Aye, vaerangi,' came the deep voice over the comm. *'Just keep us moving – I'll handle the rest.'*

Vehicles were emerging up ahead now, skating and sliding out of cover and across the broken rockfields. They were scout groundcars – light armour, bulky tires and roof-mounted guns, lone drivers, fast but fragile. They opened fire immediately, sending erratically-aimed volleys scything out into storm. Some shots hit home, cracking and denting the Taurox's forward plates.

Olgeir replied, making the autocannons kick and roar. The barrels spat out twin lines of shells, blasting up the snowfields and causing the oncoming scout cars to tumble and cartwheel in a spin of mashed axles and blood-shattered windscreens.

More of them roared up the valley floor, driven wildly, sounding alert-klaxons to summon allies. They were sketchy things – metal frames hung together with chains and welded crossbars, their exposed engines leaking sparks and flame-gusts, gunners hanging off the rear, spiked bull-bars and bolted-on electro-packs. Their occupants had the look of every blood-cultist Gunnlaugur had ever slain – rampant crude tattoos, flesh-cutting, sutures and improvised body modifications. They all wore scraps and rags despite the perishing cold, their wide eyes staring under the influence of cheap combat drugs. Though they aimed poorly and drove like baresarks, there were lots of them, and more were on the way.

Gunnlaugur depressed the accelerator, using the momentum of the slide to power the Taurox even faster, ignoring the punishment it was taking from the uneven terrain. One of the scout-cars veered in too close, and he slammed directly into it, smashing it apart against the carrier's heavy bumpers. The Taurox lurched heavily as it crunched over the wreckage, nearly losing its grip before the tracks bit deep and it ploughed onward again.

By then Olgeir was firing freely, blasting at the oncoming vehicles and chewing mechanically through his ammo belts. The rest of pack continued to fire their bolters, each shot aimed perfectly even amid the wild movement of their platform, taking out both dug-in snipers and onrushing ground-cars. The wind whined down the valley, whipping up the smoggy discharge from overloaded engines.

'They've blocked the route ahead,' warned Ingvar, reloading calmly before getting back to it.

'Of course they have,' snarled Gunnlaugur, keeping the Taurox roaring.

The groundcars were swinging around now, scraping and tilting before bursting back along parallel to the speeding Taurox. They were far faster than the troop carrier, though fragile too – several of them hit obstacles and instantly exploded, their occupants flung through the air like paper dolls. The rain of fire rose in intensity – for every vehicle Olgeir took out, another would sweep into view, piling down the valley's steep sides and letting loose with a lasgun or heavy stubber. The Taurox took more damage, its armour plates dinked and chipped, its tracks cut up and its smokestacks holed.

The line of tree cover whooshed up to meet them, a thick dark fence on either side of the depression's floor. What passed for a track shot straight ahead, snow-sunk and scattered with loose stone. Where the track met the forest, a barricade had been constructed – a six-foot-high tangle of planks, trunks, girders and flaywire, hammered together across a width of forty feet and guarded by makeshift platforms stacked with fixed guns. The cultists were still constructing it, hauling up more beams to throw into the mix, preparing to drag more guns into place.

'That looks quite solid, vaerangi...' Ingvar observed, firing at an encroaching groundcar and blowing up its exposed fuel tank.

'Not as solid as us,' Gunnlaugur replied, keeping his boot solid on the accelerator.

Olgeir swung the turret around and sent a vicious barrage straight into the centre of the barricade, blowing apart the spars and metal plates. Return fire spattered back, gouging and sparking against the Taurox's armour. A scatter of bullets found their way under the damaged engine housing, chewing through cables and gaskets and releasing bursts of steam from under the long radiator grille. The barricade raced up out of the gloom, some defenders leaping from their positions, others grimly staying put and emptying their magazines at the onrushing giant. More hits found weak spots – a track section flew crazily out of kilter, the side hatch was dented, the fuel tank was speared, an upper-forward armour plate was sheared straight off.

'Impact!' Gunnlaugur roared.

The Taurox crashed into the barrier, throwing it open and sending debris hurtling through the air. Something heavy smashed into the engine housing, ripping up the cover and sending it clanging off the cab front. The entire vehicle tilted, almost thudding clean onto its side, before Gunnlaugur somehow righted it, slewing through a secondary wall of piled mud and flaywire and directing it back on track. A crunch, a sickening skid, a neck-jarring slam, and they were out the other side, trailing heavy lines of smoke, the engine howling.

Olgeir swung the turret around rearwards and sent shells punching out at any pursuers, blasting apart more groundcars and gunners. Something flammable – an ammo store, maybe – was hit, and the entire structure ballooned with flame, soaring up into the trees and kindling on the overhanging leaves.

The Taurox snarled on, wheezing and shedding, its engines half-blown and its damaged tracks slapping against the drivetrain. The descending slope got steeper, and its huge momentum dragged it onward, grinding through disintegrating earth and sending divots kicking up in clods. Rune alerts flashed all across the dashboard – imminent engine failure, overheating, structural collapse, the lot.

'That's it!' Gunnlaugur shouted, watching the signals slide beyond critical and feeling the controls stop responding. 'Prepare to bail!'

But the machine was still barrelling fast, sliding and skiing like a wounded beast, its controls blown and its inertia remorseless. Branches whipped and smacked against the windscreen and scraped down the smouldering flanks, blurred with snow-load and ash-fall. Gunnlaugur smacked his fist against the emergency door release, and the rear hatch blew open. Olgeir, Baldr and Haflói all scrambled out, plunging through the narrow aperture and landing heavily in the snow. Ingvar was next, breaking down the flimsy divide into the crew bay and leaping through the gap.

That left Gunnlaugur. Twisting awkwardly in the confined space, smacking his head and shoulders against the low ceiling, he somehow pushed out of the driver's position and thudded heavily onto the Taurox's floor. The entire vehicle was shaking itself to pieces by then, shuddering and shivering as the terrain broke its damaged structure up. It felt as if it was speeding up, or maybe dropping, as if the entire world had fallen away beneath it.

Gunnlaugur threw himself through the rear hatch and out into a world of flying slush and kicked-up earth. He crunched hard to the ground, rolled to evade a looming tree trunk and then scrambled back to his knees. Twisting around, looking out and up, he saw what had happened to the Taurox.

The slope had been steepening ever since they'd punched through the barricade. Twenty yards further down from where he'd landed, it gave out entirely, dropping over a vertical cliff-edge, one that boiled with cloud amid the ongoing blizzards. The Taurox went straight over the edge, its momentum carrying it well clear of the scrub and underbrush. The whole vehicle seemed to hang in the air for a split second before it dropped away, still leaking smoke and steam. A few heartbeats later, and a huge explosion blew the snow off the branches and made the trunks shiver.

By then, Ingvar and the others had caught up with him, loping through the trees.

'Cut it fine, eh, Skullhewer?' Olgeir remarked.

Gunnlaugur got up, shook himself down, reached for his mag-locked thunder hammer and strode closer towards the edge. The ground was churned deeply all the way, torn to pieces by the rampaging Taurox. As he got nearer, he saw just how steep the final drop was – the terrain fell away abruptly, a sheer rock face that carried on, unimpeded, for hundreds of feet before finally beginning to level out. The wreckage of the Taurox was distributed down the slope's lower half, burning freely.

That did not catch his attention, though. His gaze had already moved further out, beyond the cliffs and out into the blizzard-obscured void beyond. A wide gulf opened up, the far side of which was barely visible in the grey-out. A pair of gigantic peaks reared up against the murky skies, one high up on Gunnlaugur's right-hand side, the other across the gap. In between those summits, far below their current position, was a wide bowl-shaped depression, over a mile across. In normal times, it might have been a desolate place, eroded by the wind, the black stone rubbed raw. Now, it was crammed with movement – marching infantry columns, churning tank-lines, hovering gunships, the limping stride of Titans, artillery pieces being hauled by armoured tractors. The army filled the entire depression. Las-fire and bolter-blasts lit up the ranks at its heart, flickering in the daylight gloom of the storm, illuminating rank after rank of armoured troops, monstrous war-constructions, flame-filled battle-engines, hulking mutations. The wind shrieked and eddied over it all, snatching at the hundreds of battle-standards that swayed to the echoing beat of enormous, vox-distorted drums.

Most of them were already fighting. Higher up the valley, set hard under the shadow of the peaks themselves, was an immense earthwork, carved from the bones of the mountains and reinforced with rockcrete piers and adamantium strongpoints. Fires burned across it, many raging out of control, though through the palls of smoke las-fire still spat and flickered – not the slender bolts of individual lasguns, but the searing beams of fixed las-cannons. The concentration and rate of fire was impressive – volley after volley, spiking and latticing into the oncoming horde.

Above the besieged earthworks rose the bulk of the kasr, its sloping walls crowned with armoured battlements, its gun towers, its landing stages and its comms spires. Kasr Vasta filled the entire valley's width, blocking the path through the mountains. Every pinnacle of it was alight, either spewing defiant ordnance at the enemy below or raging with wildfires caused by incendiary strikes. Atmospheric craft of all kinds zipped and hovered through the turbulence, unloading missiles at ground-level targets or mobilising to engage in dogfights amongst the spires. The entire structure was semi-smothered in clouds of fumes, hissing walls of rapidly boiling slush, cascades of ash from the despoiled air, its vast promontories looming through the shrouds like the prows of ancient battle cruisers. Many of its long wall sections were still unbroken and fiercely defended, but others had been reduced to rubble. Infantry battalions surged across the still-hot stones, their armour glinting from the flames, stalked by heavier war machines that swaggered through the murk, ready to deliver their deadly payloads.

'They're inside the walls,' said Gunnlaugur grimly.

'Already,' said Olgeir. 'Those tunnels will be crawling.'

Baldr moved past them both, coming to stand on the very edge of the precipice. Ash fell heavily against his armour, darkening it and obscuring the sigils of both Fenris and the Imperium. He remained still for a long time, staring out at the wide vistas of destruction, completely silent.

'What is it, brother?' asked Gunnlaugur, eventually.

Baldr turned to face him.

'I can sense him.' He looked back, pointing towards the sprawling maze of the earthworks, the ruined terrain where attacker and defender struggled alike in the lightless shafts and warrens. 'Ragnar. He's there.'

CHAPTER THIRTY

They ran. Without another word being spoken, they activated their weapons and tore down the steep slope towards the walls.

Gunnlaugur carried his thunder hammer, its mighty head crackling with energy. Ingvar and Baldr bore their ancient power swords, similarly wreathed in ghost-like illumination, the edges of the runes glinting through the mass of plasma. Olgeir and Hafloí took up axes – short-handled, double-headed, the metal black against the snarl and spit of disruptor-flare.

The descent was precipitous – a series of near-vertical drops, two hundred yards down to the pass below, shadowed and crowded by the giant trunks of the pines. Fume-spoiled snow whirled and gusted around them, coating the naked rocks in greasy slime. The patches of open sky ahead were ablaze, throwing hard shadows back, lines of black that danced and swayed to the erratic rhythm of a million weapons being fired.

The sharp contrast – smoggy gloom, lit by the swing and flash of explosions – made the footing treacherous, but the pack ran as surely and swiftly as konungur, leaping from outcrop to outcrop, sliding down the scree-flumes, grabbing hold of branches and swinging down to handholds far below. Somewhere up in the tree cover there must have been the winding tracks the groundcars used to get up here, but they wasted no time trying to locate them, opting for the direct route.

Hafloí worked hard to keep up. Once spurred to action, a Grey Hunter was one of the fastest weapons in the Allfather's armoury – untiring, gifted with preternatural senses, tempered by decades of combat experience. Whatever Ingvar had said, Hafloí didn't feel like one of them, not just yet. Their footfalls were surer, their choices better. Where they crunched into snowfields then pounced onward, the whole manoeuvre virtually a single movement, he teetered and swerved to avoid being thrown headlong across the face of the drop. They were silent, single-minded, exacting, already totally lost in their expertise. He could feel his hearts pumping, his lungs aching from the frigid air. He wanted to whoop out loud, to howl at the coming enemy to fire his war-spirits, but that would have been a lone voice, snatched away by the wind, something to draw enemy fire before it needed to be drawn.

And yet, hard as it was, he kept pace. He concentrated furiously, gauging every drop, measuring every leap. The sensory overload was crushing – as hard as anything he'd undertaken on Fenris as an aspirant – and the firing hadn't even started yet, but he gritted his jaw and worked, driving himself, on, on, on. There was always something to learn, always a new test, always something to remind him that he wasn't quite there yet. He had wanted the others to treat him as an equal for a long time. Now that the day had come, he recognised the price of it.

'End of cover,' voxed Gunnlaugur, his thick voice panting. 'Enemy sighted.'

'Aye,' confirmed Ingvar. 'The Hand of Russ, brothers.'

They had raced down the slope terrifyingly quickly, dropping from the heights and down to where the steep valley walls began to level out across a cracked and exposed rock-floor. The trees thinned, their enormous trunks blackened from the fires, their foliage blasted away.

The point at which the terrain ended and the kasr's structure began was not clear. The citadel had been sculpted out of the stuff of the world's crust itself, raised over generations by terraformers and geomancers the likes of which no longer lived in the Imperium. The Space Wolves passed ventilation towers protruding from the ground long before they came into range of the enemy itself, edifices that demonstrated the extent to which the place sprawled and spread underground like some gigantic insect's nest, worming its tendrils into every cranny and shaft of the mountain's roots.

As the last of the trees swept past, though, and Hafloí finally emerged into the open again, the scale of what lay ahead became starkly apparent.

The kasr's grey walls shot high up ahead and on their right-hand side, swelling out against the storm-blown skies, so vast that the ramparts masked the peaks on the far side of the pass. The first of those true walls – the colossal rockcrete parapets more than fifty yards thick – was still far off, above them now, rearing like a tidal barrier against the inchoate press of the enemy. Below those parapets was the earthwork layer, the straggling maze of masonry defences, spread out like crumpled skirts, a labyrinth of choke points, kill-zones, switchbacks and dead ends, studded with pillboxes and fire-lanes and gun-bunkers, designed to slow an enemy, bog it down and drag on its limbs, so that the mighty gunlines mounted on the high pinnacles could pick them off amid the rubble.

This enemy, though, had already been at work for many days. The ground was ankle-deep in a bloody mix of gore and gravel, the air stinking of copper, the bunkers blown open and the pillboxes ruptured. The pack soon found themselves charging straight into a horror-landscape of piled corpses and discarded vehicles, stinking, burning, lit up with crashes and blasts of neon, before sinking into a fire-flecked perma-night of smoke and fyceline-smoulder. Cadian uniforms mingled with cultist garb, Chimera transports lay in ruins beside the carcasses of baroque creations that still wheezed and glimmered as if partially conscious.

The walls were all gone, in that place – smashed apart, torn open, trodden down. The price paid for the advance had been high, evidenced by the catastrophic damage all about them, but now the enemy was marching into the deep places unhindered, processing in disordered lines under the lintels of the tunnels, jogging or running or limping, staring about them-selves in either trepidation or battle-ecstasy or drug-delusion, goaded by electro-whips and roared injunctions from the monsters around them. They were a rabble, the lost and the damned, some of them Traitor Guard with snatches of their old uniforms still recognisable under layers of grime, some of them mutants with scaled skin, or horns, or extra eyes that jerked and swivelled uncannily. They were all yowling, though whether from fear or exultation, or both, it was impossible to say.

The Space Wolves smashed into the heart of those columns, breaking out of the night like steel shades, undetected until the last moment. They sprinted across the last of the natural landscape, hurling themselves into the enemy, spinning and lashing and flailing in an orgy of plasma-streaked violence.

'Fenrys!' cried Hafloí at last, the yell breaking from his throat, cutting through the roar of the battle like a knife into flesh.

He cracked his axe-head down onto the rusted helm of a hunched warrior, breaking her skull before she even knew what was upon her. Then he broke the ribs of a second, before slicing the arm from a third. All the time he was moving, dancing through them, slaying only to clear a path.

By then the others too had opened their throats, roaring out the war-curses of the old ice. Gunnlaugur was at the apex of the movement, a force of nature, gigantic and unleashed, his thunder hammer carving great swathes through the dross around it. Ingvar was a purer blade, moving so fast now that even Hafloí had trouble detecting where the next blow would come from. Olgeir was the most vocal of them all, hollering imprecations and denunciations like a gothi before a tribal enemy, his pelts flying about his armour as he slew.

Only Baldr was silent. Hafloí caught splintered glimpses of him as the fighting became complete – his helm, his blade rising, a fist punching, a boot treading down a shattered arm. The long shadows jerked around him like writhing daemons, wriggling across the blood-soaked mud as if desperate to escape.

Only moments later, as the pack surged towards the first of the blown-open tunnel-mouths, did Hafloí see why that was. As his head turned, as he shifted from lacerating a bestial goat-faced mutant towards a cowering cultist clad in a cloak of overlapping iron, he saw the shine, the glimmer, the afterburn. The entire battlefield was overlapped with light sources – the energy-weapons, the fires, the explosions – so you could miss it, if you weren't looking hard, but now Baldr himself was a source of illumination. His gauntlets were shining, glowing from within like white-hot ingots. His helm-lenses had gone from blood red to ice white. His every movement was slurred with afterglows, resonances that swelled and glistered in the gloom. And they were getting brighter.

'Brother...' Hafloí voxed to Ingvar, the closest one to hand.

'I see it,' Ingvar replied, hacking his way through a gang of badly corrupted mutants, pressing on, racing for the underground passages. 'Keep going.'

So they did. They crunched and bludgeoned and throttled their way through the enemy, slamming heads against the inside of the tunnel walls, trampling them, snapping limbs and spines under the heavy impact of their blades. They pushed on down, the greater battle around them closed off by the tunnel roofs, lost to the mayhem and struggle of the main overland thrust. Soon they were deep underground, burning a path through one of the many hundreds of subterranean channels, all of them clogged with enemy troops clawing their way through the stinking earth to get at the defenders. Here, too, were the signs of desperate combat – the burned-out strongpoints, the barricaded chambers, the embedded tanks with their broken barrels still aimed down the long, winding ways. The Cadians had fought like dogs to hold these places, and for every Imperial corpse there were four or five bodies from the enemy ranks. Some had been shot, others blown up, others torn into with fists, even fingers, prising open jaws or gouging into eye-sockets.

Gunnlaugur cleaved the road ahead, slaying with an almost feral abandon, but it was Baldr who guided them now.

'This way,' he'd vox, his manner strained, but controlled. 'The left fork.' Then, 'The higher slope.' Then, 'It's stronger now. Straight ahead.'

His voice was just as it had ever been – the quietest of them, the softest – but there was something else, now. Certainty? Anticipation? Hard to tell. Haflói didn't waste time trying to interpret, but carried on fighting. His axe-blade was heavy with gore, its energy field spitting from it, trailing acrid smoke with every swipe. The tunnels were cramped, narrow, with low roofs that kept them all stooping as they ran. The heat ramped up quickly, making the blackened masonry walls run with condensation. His breathing echoed within his helm, rapid and rhythmic, thudding out a beat as he killed again and again, punctuating every swing and thrust of his arms.

'Hjolda!' he hollered, lashing out to clear some space, to throw the filth from his presence, to send the faithless spinning back into the dark.

But more kept coming, slithering and skittering out of the cloying shadows, reaching for him now, to slow his axe-arm, to drag it down, to bury him under their screaming, shrieking weight. They were growing in stature and capability as the pack carved its way close to the real fighting, in numbers to weary him, to blunt his energy and drag him into the mire.

Onward, he said to himself, over and over, ignoring the burn in his muscles, the steady overloading of his axe's power unit, the ever increasing numbers that had noticed the incursion and came to meet it. *Onward*.

They fought together – that was the essential thing.

The enemy were greater in number, hemmed in, desperate, but each one of them was an individual, with nothing more at stake than their own survival, for another day, another hour, another minute. They had long since ceased to care about anything but a debased form of sensory existence. Honour counted for nothing, nor did oaths, nor fealty, nor the prestige of a good death. They were isolated even in their throngs, and when they were sent screaming into the Underverse, they wept with the panicked tears of those who had nothing to show for how they had lived.

That was the difference. Ingvar could feel his brothers around him, fighting for him even as he fought for them. They had been doing this for so long now that it was instinctive, needing no commands or forward planning.

He would move, and Baldr would move, and Olgeir would move, and it would be so seamless, so complete, so orchestrated, that every gesture and strike was multiplied and enhanced. Power armour was part of it, and their physical condition was another, but the unity they displayed, honed and tempered by the proving ground of endless battle, was what made them so perfectly deadly.

Even the Deathwatch had not been like this. They had worked so hard to integrate all the various doctrines and instincts over the half-century that Onyx Squad had been together, but even at the end, when they were as effective as they were ever going to be, there was never *this* – the unconscious sharing of battle-souls, merging and flowing like water over stone.

Jorundur should have been there, of course. His presence was missed – a hole in their formation, a cracked link in their shieldwall. The Old Dog had never been the fastest of them, nor the strongest, but his sheer cussed irascibility gave them something that could not be replaced. They missed Váltyr, too, even though he had been gone for a long time now. Every death, every removal from the pack, left its bitter trace. In the joy of fighting, you could forget that they were gone, for a moment, only realising it when the strike you had counted on wasn't there, or the parry you judged was coming never arrived.

But they had the purpose still, the one great goal, standing ahead of them, somewhere in the heart of that dark maze. To fight towards it, to burn a path through the shadow – there could be nothing worthier.

The tunnels branched and meandered, made deliberately confusing to slow down an invading army, but Baldr never hesitated once. Ingvar glanced at him when he could, watching the way his gauntlets shone now, blazing as brightly as his power sword. At first, Ingvar had thought that was a trick of the dark, some reflected plasma-flare, but after a while there could be no doubting it – the warrior's long-suppressed powers had risen to the surface, surrounding him in strands of wild corposant, flashing and crackling when his blade impacted. The kinetic effect was minimal – nothing like the pyrotechnics even a novice Rune Priest could summon at will – and yet it still lent Baldr a fraction greater killing-potential. It was impossible to ignore how much further the broken bodies of his victims flew when he struck them, or the greater damage his blows inflicted on their armour and helms.

'Make use of him,' Gunnlaugur growled, who had seen what the rest of them had. By now, the pack leader was fully immersed in combat, falling into his state of remorseless, rage-directed focus, flinging his thunder hammer in mighty parabolas that both crushed and severed.

So they did, allowing Baldr to guide them and take the brunt of the assault. They fell into a supporting formation, freeing him up, enabling his blade to whip across with greater abandon while they protected him against counterstrikes. The blood, mud and dust caked them all, splattering against their knuckles, vox-grilles, helm-lenses, but they just wiped it clear and carried on, never slowing, never pausing.

Soon, the earth-delved tunnels began to broaden out, to meet up with others, to enlarge. The roofs rose, supported by high arches and buttressed gates. They cut their way through the sites of what must have been ferocious battles – last stands at crossing-points and intersections, littered with vehicle wrecks and blasted-aside defence walls. The corpses became varied in their livery – many Cadian regiments, but others too from different sectors, their bloodied tunics crimson, blue, yellow, olive green, all trampled and ripped apart, dead hands clutching at spent lasguns and blunted knives. The noises of active fighting filtered down from ahead, echoing strangely in the confinement, a confusion of cracks and blares and the roar of hundreds of open mouths.

Ingvar had no idea where they were, only that they had been running for a long time, and must have traversed miles already, weaving in and out of the subterranean caverns and stone-bound arteries. He saw no Wolves lying amid the slain, nor any sign of the Ojada regiments there, just a motley collection of corpses taken from a hundred worlds, all brought to this single place to die.

The pack began to ascend again, fighting its way up a shallow incline. The ambient light grew, angry as lit coals, flickering against the raw-cut walls. Blurred shouting and percussive gunfire ramped up, flooding the routes ahead. Eventually, the pack broke into a high-arched chamber, still a long way underground, reinforced with thickset columns in marching ranks. The place appeared to be the meeting point of five other tunnels, out of which streams of cultists were pouring steadily, clawing at one another to break into the open and bring their knives into the faces of the hated defenders.

But here they were meeting resistance – the exit tunnel on the far side of the chamber was occupied by a mix of Cadian and other Militarum troops. These were dug in behind a row of rockcrete barriers, each a yard high and two feet thick, strung out across a gap roughly thirty yards wide. Las-fire spattered and flickered from all across the barricade, still in controlled volleys, punching into the onrushing mob. Heavier guns at either end of the redoubt chewed out a stream of solid rounds, mowing down dozens with every sweep. The body count in front of the barrier was piling up, though the first ranks of attackers were getting perilously close before the hail of fire knocked them down. Several of the defenders were already reaching for bayonets, anticipating the moment when the pressure would overrun them.

'Clear them out!' Gunnlaugur cried, plunging straight into the heart of the fighting.

Ingvar pounced after him, slicing and jabbing with his powerblade, cutting a bloody rift towards the Militarum position. The work was hard – there was precious little room to move, and in such confines even that rabble could do damage. Olgeir's sheer power helped them, there – he heaved enemy fighters bodily aside when he couldn't hack them down, throwing them back into their own ranks before launching himself at the next clutch. And, of course, there was Baldr, who blazed through it all like a star. He had become vocal over the vox by then, repeating the injunctions to keep moving, to take this or that junction, to increase the pace, and now he was repeating himself, saying things more than once, either to reinforce the message his senses were giving him, or because of the strain the headlong charge was placing on him.

'Through this,' he murmured, blasting a gang of cultists back into the rock walls and turning on more. 'Through this, then up, then left. Through this, then up. Through–'

They ground out their way to the barricades, shrugging off the smattering of friendly fire that lanced their way. It was Gunnlaugur who leapt over the summit of the defence line, crunching heavily among the defenders, some of whom staggered away from him, others squaring up to fight him, their senses addled by the confusion of the melee.

Ingvar joined him, shouting out warnings in Gothic to stand down, exposing the Chapter symbols on his armour. The others piled over the barricades next. Haflói and Olgeir immediately swivelled on their heels, drew bolters and sent shells cracking into the horde beyond. The defenders quickly seized the chance, took up positions and resumed the steady barrage of las-fire.

It wasn't obvious who was in charge – prone bodies were everywhere, and more than seven different regiments were fighting on the front rank alone. Beyond the fortified position, a wide tunnel ran off into the dark, through which soldiers were either limping back to the front or away from it, depending on the severity of their injuries.

Baldr didn't wait, but carried on running, shoving aside any who blocked his path. One luckless trooper was flung straight into Ingvar, and bounced off the Grey Hunter's armour before twisting around to see what he'd hit.

'What is this place?' Ingvar demanded.

The trooper's mouth fell open. 'Section fifty-six, front line halt-point.' He swallowed hard. 'Lord.'

'What's up ahead?'

The man looked nonplussed. 'I, er. More of... this.'

Ingvar turned, once again exposing the Wolf emblem on his armour. 'Seen this sign in combat, anywhere close?'

At that, he nodded warily. 'Yes. No. Not me. But they say the Wolves are fighting in the Third Gallery, holding the Undergate. I heard that.'

'And regiments from another world – Ojada. Heard of them?'

The man looked bewildered. Ingvar was about to ask him again, when Gunnlaugur suddenly sent out a warning shout.

Ingvar looked up, out across the barricade, and saw why. The mob was coming on again, warily now, but advancing nonetheless. They looked almost cowed, as if they were more scared of what was goading them than what they faced. And that made perfect sense, because what was behind them had now come into view, stalking out from the tunnels, unafraid, belligerent and brazen.

Ingvar didn't recognise their warband's colours. There were a thousand different splinter-gangs of the enemy, many destroyed almost as soon as they were founded, others that were nigh as ancient as the Legions themselves, and even the Inquisition could not catalogue them all. These ones had donned armour of dark green, edged with gold, and their helms were cast into dragon's heads and chimera-faces. Foul runes had been scratched onto the battleplate, dug in deep, and their pauldrons were hung with still-glossy skins that whispered and flapped as they moved. They carried bolters and chainswords – monstrous perversions of sacred weapons, twisted into animal-like forms by their fell warpsmiths. Their armour whined and shrieked, as if spirits of the slain were still trapped in the joints, and a cold stink of spoiled meat roiled ahead of them.

Olgeir and Hafloí immediately opened fire, ignoring the chaff to aim their bolt-shells at the real threat. The Heretic Astartes fired straight back, making use of the cover of the columns and the living shield of their mortal slaves, and soon the chamber was clanging again with the maelstrom of battle. Amid the dust and dark it wasn't clear just how many of them there were – at least four, maybe double that. It was likely that reinforcements were not far away.

Ingvar pushed his way to the barricade, drawing his own bolter, but Gunnlaugur's hand grabbed his wrist.

'No, brother,' he growled. 'No time.'

The Heretic Astartes advanced steadily, coming closer amid a hail of las-beams and bolt-streaks.

'They'll break through,' Ingvar protested. 'Then come after us.'

'Aye. I'll hold them.'

For a moment, Ingvar didn't think he was serious. He tried to move, to reach the barricade, to join the defence, but Gunnlaugur locked him fast. Gods, the Wolf Guard was strong.

'Fjolnir needs to keep going,' Gunnlaugur said. 'Ragnar is close now, you have to get him there. That's why we came here. Anything else... doesn't matter.'

Ingvar stared at him for a moment longer. He almost resisted again. He almost asked whether this was some gesture – some kind of atonement for Jorundur, for not being quick enough then – but banished the thought as quickly as it had come.

Gunnlaugur was right. If not checked, the traitors would overrun the barricade and run them down, force them to fight. The pack would have to turn, sooner or later, in a place where there might be no cover, no support, no hope. Here, at least, there was a chance to stall them for a little while.

Ingvar looked to find Baldr, but he was already out of sight. The chamber rang to the echoing report of gunfire, a chorus of overlapping strikes and splinters, ones that blew chunks out of the masonry supports and gouged lines in the rockcrete walls. Olgeir and Hafloí would have to be ordered to leave – given the chance to face the Archenemy, they'd not want to cede an inch of ground.

Ingvar turned back at Gunnlaugur. There was something about the way the Wolf Guard was, just then. Eager, maybe.

He pulled his arm back, stowed his bolter, reached for his blade.

'Aye, vaerangi,' he said. 'I'll get him there.'

CHAPTER THIRTY-ONE

He was surrounded, all the time, up close. Not by physical bodies – by minds, by souls, crowding at him, clamouring for him, reaching out spectral hands to drag him down.

Baldr knew that his body was in motion. To some degree, he retained full control of it – his limbs moved as they should do, his eyes witnessed the clamour and destruction, his mouth spoke and his hearts pumped. And yet, the divide between the worlds had thinned, blurring into a mist of time-fractured impressions and ghost-images. The souls of those he slew were like hot coals in an empty brazier-pan, glowing faintly, apt to be snuffed out by a gust of air or a smatter of water.

He saw the structure of the fortress towering away in semi-translucence like some gigantic hololith. The walls and the floors were hard to pinpoint, but the souls within it were not – they were points of fire, flickering, moving, whirling like a star field. They were beyond counting, and more streamed into combat with every moment, fuelling the inferno that made the foundations of the fortress shiver.

Not all those fires burned equally brightly. Most were dim and easily extinguished. A few raged with intensity, looking as if they might resist the rigours of the storm ahead, even flourish in it. Many of those souls fought for the enemy, and their auras were edged with strange resonances. Others were clearly defenders of the kasr, leading desperate charges to shore up defences and claw back lost ground. Baldr could sense types, too – mortal humans, those corrupted by the daemonic, those who had lived for mere decades and those whose threads were centuries old.

Most intensely of all, he felt his own self, his own essence, raging at the bonds his body placed on it. He could feel the pressure of the forces within, struggling to escape, to unleash. He could do it now, here, exploding at any point of his choosing and sweeping all resistance away. The spirits of the ice were snarling and unravelling, ancient war-gheists that had always been there, just sleeping, just suppressed, now unfettered and lusting for violence. They bore raiments that he recognised – ravens, serpents, dragons of the deep, and, most salient of all, the monstrous wolves, their fur matted with blood, their teeth long and yellow, their eyes as red as the world's end. Just keeping those avatars in check now took almost all his strength, pressing them down into the depths of his psyche, grasping them by the nape as they slavered and leapt.

'Ahead now,' he murmured, almost to himself, only dimly aware of Ingvar running at his side. His pack-brothers were like shades, their outlines lost in the darkness, only their souls strongly visible. Gyrfalkon's was stark and vivid, a cold star that burned in the gloom, made colder by his long years of exile. Olgeir's was huge and generous, though checked now by suspicion and doubt. Hafloí's was the brightest, the hottest, but also the most brittle. And, far off, he could still just make out Skullhewer's aura, the mightiest of them all, though obscured now, beset on all sides. How long could it last? Was it already on the road to annihilation, just to buy a little more time?

They were close, now. The vaults rose up around them, ever more immense, gathering themselves up towards the undergates and the mighty galleries, places where the fate of the kasr would be decided. He could feel Blackmane's presence, sense the furnace of his existence, hotter and more striking than any other, though also surrounded, also obscured, as if smothered by a hundred lesser entities, all trying to sink their claws into him and bring him down.

The beasts within him growled, opened their eyes, exposed their teeth. They could not be held back forever, not in this place, where the fury of ancient powers had already been let loose and the warp itself lapped at the corpse-thick shore. They knew where he was headed. They knew what was taking place within the walls and under the earth.

He needed to hold out a little longer. Just a little longer.

Time was running out, space was running out.

Just a little longer.

Olgeir ran too, his chest aching, his limbs aflame, his hearts thumping fast. The tunnels ahead still offered plenty in the way of prey – the barricade had been an incomplete barrier, one around which roving bands of cultists had managed to infiltrate via any number of other routes. Brutal battles still took place in the dark – Militarum forces grappling with enemy fighters, taking back some chambers before losing others, locked in a grim struggle for every inch of ground. Sounds of combat came from high bridges above, glimpsed as the pack ran across the base of great shafts, or from below, when they skirted pits that seemed to descend into the bowels of the planet itself.

They could not pause, they could not hesitate to support the beleaguered Imperial positions, only keep going, driven onward by Baldr's unerring other-sense. It sickened him to see the unravelling of the defences, the slow erosion of the entire kasr's vast foundations. It sickened him, if he was honest, to do so in the pale glow of witch-light. For that was what it was, in all truth – an echo of forbidden power, one that should have been placed in rigorous bonds, marshalled by the Rune Priests and judged every day for all the long years of aspirant training. Just being close to it, unbound and clearly fluctuating in intensity, tore at him. More than once he'd hefted his weapon, not against an enemy, but close to Baldr, just in case, just in case. And each time he'd pulled back, seeing his pack-brother's determination to master the power, his drive, the runes on his armour burning hard, one by one, just as they had done on Njal's own sacred battleplate, just as they did with every gothi who had earned the trust of the Chapter.

Now it was Ingvar who led them, guided by Fjolnir's increasingly obscure mutterings. Hafloí remained close, sprinting so hard Olgeir thought his hearts might burst, clearly determined not to slow them down in any way.

Olgeir tried not to think about Gunnlaugur. He'd seen how many traitors were coming for that redoubt, and how capable they'd looked, and how exhausted the mortal defenders were. Perhaps Skullhewer could hold it. Maybe he could hold it for hours. That had to be the hope – that it was the kind of choke point where a small band could keep the enemy at bay for long enough to be relieved. There must be many such places up ahead, down below, lost in the shadows.

So they had to find Ragnar. They had to find him soon, so they could turn and fight, look the enemy in the eyes, stand some ground. He had no idea if they were close. Every rock wall looked much the same to him, every turn and every drop. It got steadily hotter, steadily more humid, steadily louder.

He swung his axe, keeping his arm loose, itching to propel it properly in a killing stroke.

Keep going, he breathed to himself, jaw clenched, racing through the dark. *Keep going.*

They were only a little less strong than he was, only a little less powerful and a little less swift. He still didn't know what their precise allegiance was, and nor did it matter much to him – they were the most hateful of a hateful breed, the ones who had been given everything and had thrown it away. They had been the best of the Imperium, its signal defenders and its champions, and now they had turned against their creators in the vain hope of getting something greater from their malicious patrons.

So Gunnlaugur fought harder, just then, than he had ever done. His blows were heavier, his strikes were aimed with more venom, his resolution was more complete. As he tore into them, he opened his throat, hurling imprecations and war-curses, roaring himself hoarse on them, declaiming the fate of the heretic in tones that would have made Ulrik himself proud.

At the start, he had done it to rouse himself, to fortify himself, to summon up that primal battle-rage that all sons of Fenris thrived on. The war-words had power locked in them, and had done for as long as the tribes had grappled with one another across the heaving floes. After the Allfather had come, and they had swapped their clinker-built warships for giant voidcraft, they had found the same words still resonated, still answered. Across a thousand new battlefields, the ancient hexes had been called out, lending heft to the axe-strike and precision to the sword-blow.

In the deep tunnels, his voice only boomed louder, echoing from the walls and roofs and swelling in volume. Skulbrotsjór's hammer head whirled, strung-out with blood and gore, resonating to the drumbeat of his unlocked fury. He stood tall, scorning cover, striding out, shrugging off hits even as he smashed his way through ceramite and bone.

'Heidur Rus!' he bellowed, his vox-grille augmenting the sound and making it deafening. 'For the honour of Fenrys!'

At the start he hadn't noticed, so wrapped up was he in his own private onslaught, that the effect was not felt just by the enemy, but that the mortal troops at the barricade responded, too. One by one, they started to shout out their own battle cries, ones drawn from a dozen different regiments. Many of the cries were not even in Gothic, but came from whichever world the warriors had been plucked from. It was a cacophony, overlapping and discordant, almost impossible to hear over the strident bellows coming from the Wolf Guard's vox-grille.

But it changed things. It generated resolve. The Militarum troops kept their discipline, using the cover of the barriers and the columns, but they no longer cowered. Their chants rose up, sending each las-bolt or bullet flying towards the mobs beyond with just a little more spite than before. With Gunnlaugur raging at their head, they held the line, concentrating all their fire on the lumbering Heretic Astartes, drowning them in las-beams, overloading them with emptied magazines before reaching for more. For a few brief, glorious moments, the entire traitor advance reeled against the combined zeal of the Imperial defenders.

It couldn't last. As spirit-stirring as it had been, the numbers were still against them. True Space Marines, corrupted or no, were very hard to kill through mortal efforts, and with the near-limitless support of their slave-troops, the tide was always apt to turn. The green-and-gold monsters weathered the worst of it, then came straight back, wading through the hail of projectiles and moving inexorably into strike range. They weren't mindless – they used cover too, where they could – but where that failed them their thick armour plates absorbed tremendous punishment, allowing them to lumber up to full speed and charge for the barricade.

And so, for all the bravery of the Militarum soldiers, it was Gunnlaugur who resisted the longest. He pushed back against the attackers, throwing his body into the lines of danger, spewing his death-oaths at the enemy and smashing their blades aside with the greater heft of his thunder hammer. His armour blazed with the ricochets of glancing bolt-hits, his pelts flickered with flames as the propellants ignited. He drove the hammer head through the helm of the first one to confront him, driving the creature's breastplate inward and slicing the gold ornaments from the lacquer. The next one managed to blood him, sending a poison-edge blade arcing up under his outstretched arms. For that, the traitor's torso was slammed down and his neck was broken.

More Heretic Astartes loomed up out of the flame-edged smog-mire, their advance a whisper of corroded servos, their twisted helms leering in the shifting light. The soldiers on the barricade were picked off by the hail of incoming fire, crushed by the toppling of the heavy blocks, overrun, overmanned. The diminishing cadre of survivors fought on through it all, cleaving to their champion, using his bulk and energy to shield them from the worst of the onslaught before darting out, when they could, to open fire or draw a desperate bayonet.

'Fenrys hjolda!' Gunnlaugur roared on, slaying another of the traitor monsters, carving him open before throwing the corpse down to the dirt. His arms flared with lactic feedback, his armour sloshed with blood. Sweat ran freely down the inside of his helmet, pooling around his neck. Another strike landed, driving the point of a powerblade into his collarbone. A bolt strike blew his knee-guard off, fracturing the bone beneath.

He felt no pain. Every muscle still strained, every strike was still full-hearted. He spun around, twisting on an ankle to generate kinetic force. He swerved away from a bolt-shell before driving back into close attack. More traitors came at him, one after the other, then in twos and threes, closing him down, shutting down his space to move.

His support died away. The Militarum positions were finally swamped, the cultist hordes rushing the last redoubts and hacking at the bodies of the Imperial dead. That left the tunnels beyond open, but none of the Heretic Astartes took the option – they came at Gunnlaugur, determined to bring him down before they moved further into the kasr's underbelly.

The chrono in the inside of his helm ticked over, showing the time he had bought. It might not be enough. It might never be enough. Unlike Baldr, he had no precise idea of how far the pack needed to travel. All that remained was to fight on, to hold the portal, to defy the enemy.

'For the Allfather!' he thundered, his throat filled with blood now. 'For Leman of the Russ!'

He saw them now, the dead of Fenris, judging him, weighing his valour in the iron scales. All eyes were on him, assessing whether he would pass into the Halls of Fire, worthy of a place at the long hearth-table.

His hammer shaft cracked, extinguishing the disruptor-field, so he used it as a club. His breastplate was blown open, his greaves dented. A fist reached out for his neck, to throw him down, but he smashed it away, knowing that to lose his footing would be the end.

He could no longer see how many were coming for him. He had no knowledge of how many he had already killed. All that remained was to keep going, to stay upright, to block their advance. Time blurred around him. Space dimmed into a blood-screen that washed everything in red. A great heaviness sank across his arms, and he felt a creeping coldness in his damaged leg.

And then came the blow that he knew he couldn't evade – a mighty sweep from the enemy's curved blade, aimed at his head, too low to duck beneath and too fast to pull away from. It raced out at him in slow motion, glinting in the darkness like a jewel.

Defiance remained. He bared his fangs, clenched his fists, and howled out his fury, his hatred, and his raw, elemental joy.

For the Allfather, he told himself as the impact came. *For Leman of the Russ.*

CHAPTER THIRTY-TWO

He both hated and loved this world.

It was not beautiful. Not like Fenris was beautiful – violent, savage and ever-changing. This world was static, locked down by its mighty solidity, held in chains by its endless lines of fortresses and causeways. When he had first arrived, the air had still been clear, exposing a cold and wind-torn land of high veldts and plateaus. Even when the enemy had made planet-fall in earnest, and the atmosphere was spoiled, there had still been plenty to admire. Its people, most of all, who fought like beasts to hold on to their home.

And yet, now that all was coming to its inevitable end, it was hard not to hate. The bone-weariness did that – the ache down to the marrow, caused by the long weeks of constant battle, bleeding into months, forever falling back, yielding ground, hurting the enemy but never defeating it. He had almost lost track of the names of the kasrs. They looked much the same from underground, where the worst of the infantry fighting always was. The tunnels had been created to slow the advance, and so they had, turning the blaze of kinetic warfare into the heavy grind of attrition. And that was hateful, too, in the end. When you saw your battle-brothers slain under piles of low-grade brawlers, or saw them buried alive by rockslides, or took orders from a distant high command that could only result in more disaster, it was hard to feel anything but loathing for the entire place, and a desire for this to be over, one way or another, whatever the outcome.

That feeling never lasted. He was too good for that, too wedded to combat. They all were. Olvec, and Alrydd, and the rest – his Great Company, his packs, his people. They shook themselves down, wiped the blood from their blades, swept the dust from their pelts and faces, and started again. The fires still burned. Even in defeat, even at the moment of death, you could still roar.

He remembered speaking to Ulrik, back when the Slayer was still fighting alongside them.

'Which skjald called this place the Helwinter Gate?' he'd asked.

'No idea,' the Priest had replied.

'It's a bad name.'

'Tell me why.'

'The Helwinter has an end. When its fury is gone, new life returns.' He'd stared out at the burning shoreline, the pyres of the coastal kasr-line, watching the enemy landers fight their way to the lowland drop-points. 'There will be no recovery from this.'

Ulrik had laughed. 'So mournful, Ragnar. You'll be singing a happier tune when you get your teeth into them.'

And so it had proved, at the start. The Blackmanes had charged into the fray with their wonted zeal, slaying heavily, blunting the assaults and driving the invaders back into the blood-foamed sea. Cadians had even started chanting their name, so they told him. Asking to be stationed alongside them. *The Blackmanes. The war-dogs of Fenris. The mad ones.*

They had been under-strength even before the first deployments. Every pack in the Chapter was under-strength – plenty had been annihilated entirely, or reduced to Lone Wolves stalking through the rubble in search of vengeance. The rot had been there for a long time, a product of the age of Endless War, forcing them to improvise, to make do, to cobble packs together from the remnants of others and throw them straight into the grinder. That alone was hard to preside over. A pack was a sacred thing – the best of them lasted for mortal generations, only slowly winnowing down until the greatest of their members eventually succumbed to Morkai's axe. Now, though, they were burning too quickly through the ranks. With Fenris itself still smouldering, it wasn't even clear where new aspirants would come from. The lords of the Chapter, Grimnar and Njal and Ulrik, they made plans and drew up stratagems and declaimed great speeches in the Halls of Fire, but even they must have felt the treads of doom coming up behind them.

'All that counts is to fight,' Ulrik had said.

'So long as one of us remains,' Ragnar had replied dryly.

They did that. They fought the long defeat, pulling back up from the coast and heading ever eastwards, up into the high peaks, the iron-and-stone barrier that offered the best chance to hold them. After a gruelling march, with the skies blackening and the rain of fire from orbit never ceasing, they had finally made their stand at Kasr Vasta, as ordered, where three Chapters of the Adeptus Astartes and thirty-two regiments had drawn together to keep the pass from falling.

The enemy had been hard on their heels the whole time. The packs had barely had time to re-equip and take up positions before the sound of the approaching armies rolled up the pass, heralded by the filthy snow that blew ahead of the coming storm. Initially the defence had been ordered and organised, but as the earthworks were steadily overrun the lines of control and communication began to falter. The forces of the Astra Militarum and the Navy were capable of handling the ranged conflict – the artillery lines and the airborne battles – but when the outer perimeter was breached and fighters started to infiltrate the tunnels then the Space Marines came into their own.

Ragnar had been hunting ever since. A familiar pattern emerged – the packs were split up, sent into battle at the head of separate Militarum regiments. That spread them thin, but made sure that no sections of the earthworks were without Astartes guidance. The underworld of Kasr Vasta stretched for miles in all directions, and soon tens of thousands of troops were fighting in the deep chasms, their resolve stiffened by the Blood Claws and Grey Hunters at their head.

One by one, as the hidden ways were bloodied and blasted, with controlled collapses and frequent counter-offensives failing to halt the remorseless onslaught, Ragnar had sent his own Wolf Guard to staunch the failing sections. One by one they'd left, loping off through the shadows to deliver reinforcements to distant sectors. With comm-links uncertain over any distance, and ever greater numbers of Heretic Astartes entering combat, the tactic had its dangers, but it made the most of their limited numbers and prevented total collapse among the mortal contingents.

By the time of the withdrawal to the Third Gallery, only a dozen warriors of the Rout remained physically at his side. The Cadian 457th and 56th they had been fighting with were exhausted, their ammunition gone and their morale shot. Promised reinforcements from other regiments never arrived – either destroyed elsewhere or diverted to some other battlefront within the kasr's confines. The prospect of attempting to hold the vital Undergate approaches with such fatigued and shell-shocked troops was grim, and so he'd been forced to contemplate pulling the packs back, ready to make a stand where it could count for something.

In the event, he hadn't needed to. A crackling, static-laced order had come in, straight from the sector command, announcing auxiliary battalions, fresh off the transports, heading his way. He didn't recognise the name of the world in question, but that wasn't surprising – a thousand different planets had sent their tithe of soldiers. Though unexpected, the news was welcome – it offered the chance, not just to hold the position, but to push further out, maybe even forge a path back towards the Second Gallery and the feeder tunnels up to the Outer Wall. He was being sent thousands of soldiers, with the promise of more on the way, all fully supplied and in combat-ready shape.

'Maybe we can turn this thing around,' he'd said to Alrydd, the last of his Guard still fighting at his side.

'If they give us the tools,' Alrydd had replied.

When they had arrived, his optimism had increased further. The battalions were well drilled, well armed, and looked up for a fight. Their Chimeras had rumbled down the tunnels, coming to a juddering halt amid the debris of the Third Gallery's smoke-blackened chambers. Ragnar had gone to greet their commander, a man named Brinn, from a mining world out in one of the Cadian approach subsectors.

'I wish to take the fight to the invader,' Ragnar had told him. 'Can you support me?'

Brinn had looked overjoyed. 'We can, lord, and look forward to it. All units are ready for your order.' And then he had paused, as if hesitant or embarrassed to ask for some kind of favour. 'If I may, my own battalion, the Fourteenth Advanced Armoured, is built for this work. It would be an honour... it would be *the* honour, if we could accompany you in the vanguard. We have been blooded, we have been trained. You would not be disappointed in what we can do.'

Ragnar had smiled. It made a change, to be faced with enthusiasm, after so long having to cajole and bolster desperate fighters at the end of their strength.

'Then fight with me, commander,' he'd said. 'And let us test that boast together.'

The Undergate was a colossal complex – a sprawling and semi-ruined underworld of steadily larger chambers, each connected to the other via a network of tunnels and bridges. The greatest of the halls were lofty and echoing, more than three hundred feet high and many hundreds of yards long. Those places had raged for days with some of the fiercest fighting. Large infantry divisions, mobile armour, even Scout-class Titans could be brought to bear in those places, and some of the engagements had been as brutal and extended as any battle pitched in the open air.

Almost all the terrain up to the Third Gallery had been ceded, with Ragnar's forces the last to hold out. The subterranean halls were full of the enemy now, crawling up like rats in the gloom, gathering themselves for the push up into the kasr's higher levels.

With reinforcements in play, though, Ragnar's response could be direct. One central hall in particular, a vast domed space at the meeting point of five separate access-routes, was of critical importance to both the attackers and the defenders. Hold that, and you could hope to dictate terms. Lose it, and you had no control at all over the movements out of the tunnels. The place was situated half a mile from the Blackmanes' command point and more than two hundred yards down, where the naked rock was still visible across the turbolaser-carved wall surfaces, hot and streaming with condensation.

A few hours was all it took to prepare – to dispatch the ravaged Cadian regiments back to their resupply stations, then refuel and arm the newcomers. Ragnar and the few remaining Space Wolves eschewed transports, preferring to lope back to the front on foot, but the Militarum regiments piled into their troop carriers and halftracks, slamming the hatches closed and filling the chambers with exhaust fumes as the engines spluttered back to life.

Then they were moving, going fast, needing to use both speed and surprise to have a chance of retaking the objective. Ragnar ran with Alrydd and three of the packs, dispatching the rest to spearhead other battalions. Each division of the mining world's troops numbered several hundred, operating fairly autonomously, making them ideal for the confined world of tunnel-warfare. Their armour livery was pale grey with orange chevrons. Their infantry units wore close-fitting flak armour with closed-faced helms and carried standard lasguns. The 14th Advanced Armoured would have been better described as mobile infantry – they had use of Chimera transports, supported by a range of light tanks and tracked gun platforms – but they moved fast, and responded to orders promptly.

As soon as Ragnar started running, setting off down the slope as the carriers revved up to follow, he felt the old spikes of anticipation flare again. He could only be morose when standing still – when on the move, when his blood was pumping and his chainsword activated, the war-spirits kindled again, fuelling him, goading the latent anger that only ever slept lightly below the surface.

Alrydd began to chuckle, swinging his blade as he ran, his long limbs striding out. 'Good to be on the front foot again, jarl,' he said.

'Aye,' Ragnar snarled, narrowing his eyes, trying to pick out the first of the enemy. 'For once.'

It did not take long to find them. The column vanguard swept into a large, derelict chamber dominated by a wrecked line-up of pumping stations and atmosphere processors. The place was occupied by cultists, some of whom were dug in, others intent on scavenging whatever they could from the shattered machinery around them. Even as Ragnar and his Wolves charged into the heart of them, lashing out with blade and axe-head, the Chimeras ground to a halt and discharged their occupants. The Ojada troops scrambled for cover, thunking down heavily across the rockcrete and opening up with las-bolts, surrounding the onrushing Space Marines with a wave of supporting fire. Caught between the ferocity of the close-range assault and the volume of las-impacts, the enemy fell back in disarray, cut to shreds then felled as they ran.

Even before the chamber had been cleared out, Ragnar found himself laughing – a release, a discharge of pent-up energy, a feral joy in the exercise of arms. He sent Frostfang whirling, biting deep into corrupted limbs, carving up armour plates, slicing through weapon-barrels and making the magazines explode.

'*Fenrys hjolda!*' he cried out, pushing on, driving the rabble into the tunnels beyond, sending them screaming and scampering and limping back into the dark.

From there, the ways divided, splitting up like blood vessels in a body, looping and curling, diving and rising. There would be no choke points to defend between there and the domed chamber – they would have to flush out every enemy from every tunnel, sweeping down them in one distributed movement, before coalescing again where the arteries gathered together. At every intersection, Ragnar would dispatch one of his own to lead a splinter charge, taking a battalion or two of the Ojada forces with him. The last to go was Alrydd, racing off at the head of a line of trundling Chimeras and calling out wild war-curses as he disappeared into the dark.

Brinn never missed a step. His troops were, just as he had promised, the best of the Ojadans, rapidly disembarking whenever ordered, moving on again swiftly when required. They were robust, surviving some shots that looked as if they might have felled a Cadian trooper, and aggressive to boot. They stuck together, used the terrain well, rotated their squads, pressed hard even without the command.

Half a mile to go. Ragnar checked his close-range tactical display, showing the split-up battalions snaking through the labyrinth. The tunnels ahead were filling again with enemy troops – mostly cultists, but he caught the telltale stink of deeper corruption among them: psykers, mutants, infernal war-engines, surely Heretic Astartes too, muscling their way to the front rank. This would be as hard as any pitched battle faced so far – getting to the dome intact would be a challenge, even if the rest of the pack all made their targets and the Ojadans continued to impress.

The walls narrowed, coming within thirty feet of one another, and the troop carriers began to struggle over the wreckage.

'Permission to disembark, lord?' came a vox-hail from Brinn in the lead Chimera.

Ragnar gave him the assent-signal without looking back, roving ahead of the lead carrier and trying to plot a route. He heard the vehicles shudder to a halt, one after the other, followed by the tramp of massed boots. The tunnel was speckled with the swinging light of helm-lumens, the slam and snap of power packs being replaced and activated. Twenty carriers had pulled up, with thirty more drawing up close behind, together holding more than five hundred warriors, all now on foot and advancing.

He felt the change, just a moment before it happened. The hairs on his neck went up, a chill ran across his spine. It was always the same – the uncanny awareness of threat, the sense that had saved his life a hundred times over.

He spun around, chainsword raised, and was hit by a hurricane of las-bolts. He deflected some, his armour repelled more, but his furs and totems were blasted off the ceramite, scoured away in a withering rain of well-aimed beams. Troopers were leaping towards him through the storm, lashing out with glowing combat-blades, surrounded by a glittering aegis of more las-fire from behind.

There was no time, no warning, no chance to demand answers. They were coming for him, fast, low, in numbers, racing up the tunnel floor like a plague of rats fleeing a sewer. Ragnar pulled his bolt pistol out and rapid-fired into the mob, downing ten of them before the magazine clicked empty. He lashed out with his chainblade, clearing a tight semicircle ahead of him, before scrambling back through the debris, reloading as he went.

They came after him, leaping over their own dead, firing in controlled bursts. Some on the front ranks had been wounded by the blade, their armour cut open to reveal a close-fitting mesh of black metal underneath. He shot more down, but the tide kept coming, spilling and rolling in a smear of limbs. Grapples shot out – long chains with snare-hooks and electro-shock fields – which he slashed out of the air, retreating all the while. More shots lanced in, some pinging off his battleplate, some drilling deep, burning through plates and searing into the flesh underneath. The volume of fire was intense, all of it carefully aimed from the flanks, leaving just enough space for advance troops to sprint up in close.

Shock turned to anger. Ragnar bellowed in wild fury, dropping his shoulder before crashing back into the heart of the onrushing mob. He swiped out again, cutting deep into the front rank and taking out three more fighters. He loosed bolts directly into the throat of a fourth, showering both of them in blood as the shell detonated. A lesser enemy might have broken under that charge, thrown back in disarray as the Wolf rampaged among them, but these were made of tougher material – they held their ground, maintaining the storm of las-bolts, sending more warriors racing ahead to engage up close, tying him down, closing out the space, suffocating him.

More strikes snapped in, cracking a helm-lens, scoring his right pauldron, shivering his torso-plate. Ragnar punched hard again, dropping a fighter before swivelling around and gunning his chainsword into the stomach of a second.

His rage didn't blind him to the odds. There were too many of them. He could kill at twice this rate, and still come nowhere close to dropping them all before they found a weak spot and did more serious damage. They crowded the tunnel ahead, making it impossible to clear a path back the way he'd come. Disengaging left him open to those electro-grapples, and even if he outpaced them, the true enemy was surely advancing up the tunnels to meet them, closing off any escape. He opened a vox-line, only to hear the muffled hum of a jammer on the channel.

How had they known the frequency for that? For how long had this thing been planned?

'Faithless!' he spat, tearing into them with all his matchless anger, hurling a broken-backed trooper straight up into the rock-roof before cutting two more down with a savage backslash of Frostfang. 'Honourless, soulless!'

They never replied. Not so much as a shout left their lips now. As if a switch had been thrown, they swarmed at him in silence, a single orchestrated movement that swept up out of the dark, ready to drown him. The las-bolts flew, the blades flashed, and a dozen gauntlets reached out, desperate to haul him down and finish the job. A chain-length whipped around his blade-arm, weighing it down. A power-knife plunged up into his armpit joint, puncturing the muscle, before he swatted its owner away.

As if in sudden premonition, Ragnar's mind briefly flashed back to Fenris, to the night-storms of the wide oceans, the fury of the endless, frigid tempest where battles raged in an endless cycle between tribes forever on the edge of annihilation. He would have given anything just then to have his old companions at his side, even if the odds still counted against them, just to fight back to back in the ancient way, blades whirling in counterpoint, roaring out both defiance and denunciation.

'Heidur Rus!' he thundered, crashing anew into the traitors, smashing them aside in a last, final, bruising heave.

And, against all hope, the call was answered.

'Hjá, jarl!'

The battle-shout came from more than one throat, a cry that echoed down the long tunnel. Four figures sprinted into view, grey against the black of the tunnel's edge, fighting hard, laying about them with blade and bolter. One was huge, bellowing every war-curse known to the Chapter and opening up with a heavy bolter that shredded and pulverised. Another looked raw and pale for a Grey Hunter, but fought in their manner nonetheless, slaying expertly with a short-handled axe. The third moved faster and more surely than either of them, and his rune-carved power sword would have been recognised by even the rawest aspirant of the Chapter. All of them fought furiously towards Ragnar, hewing a path through the assassins, creating panic in the rearguard and breaking up their disciplined onslaught.

But it was the fourth who dominated. It was hard to lay eyes on him.

Hard even to see what kind of thing he was, only that he carried the icons of Fenris along with him in a ghost-grey tide, flickering and shimmering, caught between the world of the senses and the world of dreams. He was greater in stature than he should have been, though still in the form of a Sky Warrior, his gauntlets snarling with ice-white lightning, his eyes flaring. Creatures bounded alongside him, spectral and fractured – clouds of ravens, as thick as curdled storm fronts, swooping and ripping with translucent beaks. Greater beasts roared within the miasma – all creatures of the Fenrisian bestiary, the hunters and the hunted, thick hides and snarling maws, loping, panting, ripping into the stunned warriors and mauling them apart. Some were shaggy and gigantic, others sleek and long-limbed, and at the forefront, as ever, was the greatest of them all – the hulking blackmane of legend, yellow-eyed, bloody-fanged, slavering through the carnage as if summoning the end of all worlds.

Ragnar recognised the pungent tang of the wyrd, the same tingling aura created by the gothi when they invoked the storm. Maybe it was rawer, a little wilder and more strident here, but it was the same basic thing. Njal himself might have been proud of the terror created in that tunnel, the screams and the growls, the wind-howl and the lightning-snap.

He took full advantage, launching back into the enemy and adding to the slaughter. Caught between the devastation of the gothi's art and the physical fury of the Grey Hunters, the assassins' discipline broke at last, making them easy prey. Frostfang whirled, carving into the reeling knots of a suddenly desperate enemy, while the looming blades of the Grey Hunters made quick work of those at the rear.

What followed was butchery – brutal and blunt-edged, swept up in the swirl of the gothi's rampaging wyrd-beasts. Ghostly they might have been, but they were still capable of dealing out real damage. They swept up and around Ragnar's own strikes, the ravens swooping in the lee of his flying pelts, the serpents coiled about his striding boots, the wyrd-wolves pouncing in the shadow of his chainsword. He felt as if he were immersed in magicks, his blood boiling with them, lending strength to his every blow and burning the pain from his wounds.

As the revenants swirled and dived, he fought his way to the side of the Grey Hunter, one whose armour-marks he recognised from a long time ago, and they slew together in the heart of the witch-light-flickered darkness.

'Gyrfalkon,' he panted, working his blade fast and hard. 'It has been a while.'

The Grey Hunter carried on fighting, his movements unrestrained and lavish, as if energies held back for an eternity had suddenly been let loose.

'You told me to keep the edge of my sword sharp,' Ingvar replied, sending it whistling into the neck of an exposed traitor. 'I did as I was ordered.'

CHAPTER THIRTY-THREE

The fighting never truly stopped, after that. Five hundred trained killers took a while to purge from existence, even with the help of Baldr's horde of storm-magicked allies. The noises of combat had drawn the attention of the real enemy, and while the Fulcrum Hunters still fought their desperate rearguard action, the first outriders of a greater invading army were already filtering up the winding tunnels towards them. Baldr's wyrd-beasts tumbled through the dark like crashing waves, flushing out the last resistance in a surge of dream-cast fragments, just in time for the first of the Heretic Astartes to arrive.

Given all that, there was no time for explanations. Ingvar fought at the side of the Young King, and was soon given a reminder of just how deadly the jarl was when given freedom to move. Shadowed by the spectral beast-spirits, he was nigh-unstoppable – like a vision out of the ancient myths, pulled from a time before the Imperium had stamped its mark on the mountains. Ingvar had to try not to laugh out loud for pleasure, at times, seeing some of the truly ludicrous strikes, bleeding with force and speed, driven by arms that had no equal in the Chapter, save for Grimnar himself.

With the destruction of the Ojada Hunters, the comms-lines opened up again, enabling Ragnar to call for aid from the rest of the packs. Many of the Wolf Guard were still close by, advancing down adjacent tunnels or digging into proximate chambers, so sped back to join the fighting. They left behind their accompanying units of Ojada troopers, all of whom were likely as loyal as any other regiment, but there was no chance to make that judgement before fresh combat overtook them again.

As the enemy vanguard advanced up through the tunnels, Baldr plunged straight at them, his armour lit up from within and searing with a crown of white-blue flame. He had become unresponsive to orders by then, still surrounded by the translucent packs of dream-beasts, now consumed with the scent of a greater and more corrupted foe. The great blackmane-ghost prowled around him protectively, slavering and leaping up if any came close. Hafloí tried, and was driven back. After that, they left him alone, lost in his world of vengeance.

All thought of taking the Second Gallery was long gone. At best the objective was now to stay alive, summon genuine auxiliaries, try to keep a grip on the territory they still held, staunch the losses.

'Skullhewer fights alone!' Ingvar shouted to Ragnar.

'Where?' Ragnar called back, busy now with a Heretic Astartes in World Eaters colours.

'Section fifty-six – if it stands.'

Ragnar didn't reply at once. Ingvar understood why – they were barely surviving as it was, and splitting away to dart back into the deeper tunnels would scatter what little cohesion they had left.

'We make for the Third Gallery!' Ragnar shouted back, finally. 'Hold that. After that, if fate allows, we'll go for him.'

It was the best he was going to get. More invaders ground their way towards them, thirsting for blood and despoliation. More reinforcements arrived at their rear, running hard to answer Ragnar's summons, and the fighting retreat began. There would be no respite now, no chance for glory or explanation, only more grim defiance, more weapon-work and desperate bloodletting.

But the pack was no longer alone – that was something. When they uttered their battle cries, their voices were matched with others of their kin now, all hurling the imprecations of the old ice into the faces of those destined to die under their sacred blades.

'Fenrys hjolda!' Ingvar roared, and the Wolves of Fenris, the blood of Asaheim, his sworn-kin and shield-brothers, roared it back with him.

Baldr could feel the tethers loosening, the ties binding him to the world of the senses stretching out like overworked sinews.

The beasts around him shook out the throats of the enemy, drank in the blood of the slain before pouncing on to their next prey. They were pure savagery – as pitiless as the world that had bred them. Every move they made found an echo in his own body – when they were struck, he felt it; when they killed, his soul rejoiced. It was exhilarating, a rush of power the like of which he had never experienced before.

But it was dangerous, too. With each fresh moment of soul-fury, Baldr's core self became a little weaker, a little more distant. The spirit of the blackmane, that was the most powerful one – a truly dark and monstrous presence that swelled up with every kill, pregnant with rune-curses, swollen with hunt-magick. Would it devour him, too, if he let it? Would it carry on forever, if he failed to call it back?

He could still hear the war cries of his brothers, but now as if from underwater, lost among the growls and snarls around him. When he killed, it was almost without thinking, almost unconscious – a release of wild energy from a wellspring that could never now be blocked.

Just as before, his mind's eye began to cut loose then, to see the entire citadel as it soared above them. He witnessed the souls within it, layer upon layer of them, all struggling with their own life-and-death duels, hundreds of them at every moment, the slain sent wailing off into dissolution, the living moving immediately to their next contest.

He didn't hold back. He let his perspective rove further, higher up, beyond the kasr and the mountains and out across the burning wastes. He saw clashes that dwarfed this one – whole maniples of god-machines grappling amid raging electric storms, legions of unholy engines crashing into super-heavy formations as the ash-rain fell. He heard the yammering of the daemonkin as they pushed, pushed, pushed against the geometries that held them out, and understood the pattern of the enemy attack, and what they were trying to undo.

His perspective raced forward, reeling in time and space, accelerating towards the final event that could no longer be prevented. He even saw it happen, a glimpse of the future that drew in the threads of causality around it like a black hole – the great ship, the black star, the void-fortress of the Despoiler himself, sent crashing through the atmosphere and into the planet. He saw the world's crust broken, the fractured mantle tilting up, the winds of a true Helwinter searing across the globe as blood-magma bubbled in the spreading wound.

The battle would be lost. The Gate would break. Any victories they achieved here – an enemy champion slain, a hero saved – would be set against that failure. And in the wake of that, a greater terror lay, one that would reach out across the entire galaxy before its rampage was halted.

'Brother!'

The voice was tiny against the background roar of annihilation, coming as if from a long way off.

'Brother!

His vision guttered away. In its place was the earth around him, the shadows and the blood and the screams of mortals. Gyrfalkon was calling out, just as he had done before.

Baldr looked down at his gauntlets. They were streaked with lightning now, crackling over the surface and slithering into the wrist-seals. Blood and corposant fizzed in pools across the rest of his armour. He was alive with magick, burning up from it, overloaded with it.

'Hold fast!' Ingvar cried, reaching out for him from across a wall of raging enemies. 'We must withdraw!'

He could already see himself doing it. He saw himself banishing the beasts that prowled around him, clearing a path back to his shield-kin, ready to serve again.

But, then, he knew what was coming now. The orders would be given, gathering up those who remained, sending them back to the Chapter warships, ready to take them away from a breaking world. Nothing could prevent that, not even Grimnar. And once back within the Chapter, the old problem would still remain.

Baldr held his right hand higher, closed the fingers of his fist, and time slowed to a halt, grinding as if the keel of a dragonship had run into the silt. The clamour of war slowly echoed away, replaced by an eerie, frozen stillness.

'Stormcaller hasn't forgotten,' he said, breaking the vice of quiet. 'I am... not what he would make me.'

Ingvar tried to move, prompting more growls from the flickering blackmane. 'This is what we wanted,' he managed to say. 'Return to us.'

'No.' When he spoke now, Baldr found himself marvelling at his own voice. It was deeper, more resonant, drawing on a lode that had been capped for a very long time. 'You can go back. You, and the others. Maybe one day, I will too. Not this day.'

Ingvar started to remonstrate again. They needed to find Gunnlaugur, he said. They needed to gather with the rest of the Great Company, forge some kind of defence, find a way to keep fighting. They needed to *explain*, to earn their path back to the hearthside.

Baldr looked about him, out across the static scene of battle. Ragnar, Hafloí and Olgeir were all locked in combat. The enemy surrounded them, filling the tunnel from wall to wall. Some of those warriors were very great. They were already pushing back against the eldritch bonds he had placed on them – soon the hiatus in violence would be ripped away. He could stay, if he chose to, and aid them.

But it was no longer his fight. Eventually, Ingvar seemed to give in to the inevitable. He had brought Baldr back to the pack once before. Not a second time.

'I am sorry,' Gyrfalkon said. 'Sorry that I doubted the xenos.'

Baldr nodded. 'But you were right, Gyrfalkon, from the very start. I feel the wyrd, now. I feel it in every sinew.' He made to turn back, then lingered for a final moment. 'It is a new dawn, brother. A fiery one. Who knows what we will see of it, when the sun is full-risen?'

And, with that, he let the world back in, allowed the curtain to be ripped away, and he was running again, slaying again, sweeping down the tunnel and into the dark, his spectral packs loping alongside him, the lightning snapping and sparking at his heels.

CHAPTER THIRTY-FOUR

Three weeks later, Kasr Vasta fell.

More battles followed, high up in the ice-flung peaks, then out across the exposed veldt, always falling back, always trying to salvage something before disaster overtook them. There was no want of zeal on the part of the defenders, only numbers, and only arms. The armada loosed upon Cadia was larger and more devastating than any force of conquest since the days of the Great Heresy, and there had only ever been the slightest chance of halting it. In the event, all their valour accomplished was a little delay, a brief window of time before the final apocalypse came. Armies were evacuated, weapon-hauls loaded onto cargo-haulers, treasures salvaged. That was something – a morsel of comfort to report back to Terra when the time came to tally the numbers – but in truth it was still a crushing defeat, the destruction of a bastion that had stood firm for a hundred centuries and which had no rival in either strength or prestige.

Had it not been for the Imperial Navy maintaining a tight grip on the void-lanes, that defeat would have been a rout. As it was, more ships arrived by the day, streaming into the Cadian battlezone from all across the Imperium, determined to prevent a single world's loss from cascading into total sector implosion. The Adeptus Astartes were at the forefront, pulling ships from their many far-flung warzones to aid in the staunching of the wound at the Eye's edge.

So it had been that the frigate-class warship *Dawnrunner* had entered the bleeding Cadian System as part of the final muster from the Space Wolves Chapter. It had been an auxiliary vessel for most of its short life, hastily refitted for full military service in the aftermath of the raids on Fenris. In normal times it would never have been pressed into active duty at all, but every asset was now being called on, however unsuitable or unready. Its crew were all kaerls, many of them taken from other, larger vessels, a few drawn directly from the already depleted ranks of the Mountain itself. Its weapons were untried, its engines temperamental. It was a disaster waiting to happen, from most points of view. From others, it was a blank slate – something to improve upon.

Ingvar had tried to convince himself of the latter approach ever since arriving on a war-battered shuttle, straight from the final planetary evacuations as the magma slithered over the battlefields and the continents broke apart. Ragnar had gifted the ship to Járnhamar in gratitude for what they had done. It was a typical jarl's gesture – in other ages, he would have had a golden torc or a jewelled sword-hilt.

So fierce had the fighting been, and so relentless, that little was ever said about the quest, or of the Fulcrum, or of the long game played by Chirastes. It would all come out in due course. Right now, as the sector stood on the brink of anarchy, the Chapter had more to worry about than the last-gasp obsessions of a deranged cardinal.

There had been one exchange, though, near the end, just as the atmosphere had started to burn and the world's strange protective aegis had finally begun to fail.

'I find myself in your debt, Grey Hunter,' Ragnar had said, grinning at him with bloodied fangs.

Ingvar had bowed. 'I am only glad we were there in time.'

'Aye. Just where you needed to be.' He had looked thoughtful. 'Any news of your gothi?'

Ingvar had shaken his head.

'Maybe for the best. Njal found out you'd come back. He'd like to talk to you. I told him you were busy. It might be wise for you to stay active for a while. He doesn't forgive easily.'

Ingvar had smiled dryly. 'I don't think we'll have trouble finding things to do.'

'No, I don't think you will.' He'd looked out at the skies of flame, the cloud banks that were now blood red and hurtling. 'They're calling this the end. The start of the final defeat.'

'The xenos called it Rhana Dandra. The battle at the world's end.'

'So what do you think of that, Gyrfalkon?'

He hadn't needed to consider his response. 'The end will come when Russ returns. Until then, we fight for victory. For the honour of our jarl and the crushing of his enemies.'

Ragnar had laughed. 'Well said. You know, when you first returned to Fenris...'

'I know. I got better.'

And that had been it. They had parted soon after, Ragnar to his retinue, Ingvar to his. Now, off-world again, on the bridge of the *Dawnrunner*, feeling the thrum of void-drives, knowing that the world he had fought for was laid waste, he tried to collect his thoughts.

He was alive. The pack, what remained of it, was back home, under the protection of their liege-lord once more. More battles lay ahead, now given to them as orders to accomplish rather than as a quest they undertook for their own reasons. It was as it should be. Some things, at least, had been restored.

He moved into the Annulus Chamber, took his seat, resting his gauntlets on the cold stone. The old pack banner hung over the circular tabletop. It was good to see it again. Just as his gaze ran across the thick fabric, his comm-bead pulsed.

'*My lord,*' came Torek Bjargborn's voice. '*We are ready to fire the plasma drives, on your command. Mistress van Kliis awaits orders for warp transit at your pleasure.'*

'Understood. You have everything you need?'

There was a slight pause before the reply. *'Absolutely everything, lord.'*

The shipmaster had done well to escape the inferno of Cadia in one piece. The *Hlaupnir* had been taken off his hands soon afterwards, but he seemed satisfied with what had replaced it.

Ingvar cut the link, just as the doors to the chamber slid open. Olgeir and Hafloí entered, the latter limping heavily, the former with a new scar to add to the lattice across his cheeks. They took their places around the Annulus. Both were exhausted still, driven into deep weariness by the weeks of battle. They would recover, of course, given a little time, and given something fresh to hunt.

'We have our orders?' Olgeir asked.

Ingvar nodded. 'We leave with the fleet. Regroup at Solar Mariatus. Grimnar's already there, they say.'

Hafloí stared at his hands moodily. 'Good for him.'

Ingvar knew how he felt. They had lost much. Váltyr first, then Jorundur, then Baldr – who was alive, he presumed, though far beyond their reach. It had been a grim tally, and that was before he even thought of–

The doors scraped open again, and a huge, ungainly melding of flesh and metal clunked inside, wrapped around with tubes and patched up with staples. Half of his frame was armoured in the usual fashion, half of it was still exposed bionics, provisionally powered with bolt-on energy units. Some flesh was exposed, especially above neck-level, though all of it was raw and scar-puckered. The body locked within the heart of all those augmetic pins and shackles should never have been let out of the apothecarion, not for months yet.

But Gunnlaugur, the one called Skullhewer, had never been good at following orders. As he came into the chamber, Ingvar and the others rose to their feet, causing him to growl in irritation.

'I'm not a damned vaerangi now,' he said, his voice a blood-wet snarl of overlapping vox-feeds. 'Remember? Ragnar had to give Stormcaller something to smooth it all over.'

Ingvar chuckled, and even Hafloí twitched a half-smile. 'Pack-leader, then,' he said.

'Aye.' Gunnlaugur sat awkwardly. Blood was welling at this throat, where a series of poorly fitted iron threads jutted into the skin. 'That'll do.'

The four of them sat down around the Annulus, just enough of them to make up a pack, all Grey Hunters now, their old differences scoured away.

'So, we did it,' said Olgeir.

'We came back,' said Hafloí.

'With Ragnar still alive, and as damned young and healthy-looking as ever,' said Gunnlaugur. 'Consider it a victory.'

'It was,' said Ingvar. 'We should remember that.'

'It cost us,' said Olgeir.

'Aye, that it did,' said Ingvar.

He looked over at the empty places. Of all of them, it was Baldr's that was the keenest loss. They had laboured for so long to keep him from death, believing it to be important, and now there was nothing to show for it, not even a weapon to hang in the armoury. Maybe one day, they would live to see the fruits of the seed that had been sown.

'Someone will need to fly the ship,' said Gunnlaugur, 'now that the Old Dog's gone.'

'I'll do it,' said Hafloí, looking at them all, as if daring any to gainsay him. 'I wanted *Vuokho*, but this'll be something.'

Olgeir chuckled. Despite the fatigue that still weighed on his broad shoulders, the tightness in his manner had ebbed. He had got what he wanted, and the deceptions were over. 'It's a good ship,' he said. 'With a good crew. A long time, since we had that.'

'And we'll be using it soon,' said Gunnlaugur. 'We won't linger at Solar Mariatus – the Despoiler's moving again, and there'll be fighting again before the month's out.'

'Good,' said Olgeir, with feeling. 'I have debts to settle now, more of them than before.'

'We all do,' said Hafloí.

Ingvar watched and listened. The unity of purpose was still there, deeper than ever now, forged hard by privation. The pack was smaller than it had been, but purer, like a diamond squeezed into shape amid the folds of the earth. One debt had been settled, but Olgeir was right – more vendettas had now been sworn. That story would never end – they would never run out of grievances to address, honour to be satisfied, oaths to be fulfilled. That was the way of them, and always had been, right from the very start.

'So what say you, Gyrfalkon?' asked Gunnlaugur, flexing his new augmetic fingers idly, scraping them over the stone. 'Is your soul at ease, now that the secrets are exposed and you have no more mysteries to plague us with?'

It was hard to know what to say to that. In part, it was. He was where he belonged, with a clear sky ahead and the promise of battle to come. A canker had been excised, the poison bled out. And yet, the Imperium's failure at Cadia would have repercussions. The Rune Priests were already speaking of a great chasm opening up amid the debris of the Helwinter Gate, a cleavage between worlds, one that risked casting a swath of the galaxy into darkness if it could not be staunched. Baldr's awakening spoke of more ruptures in the carefully watched old order – of souls flaring up into new life and power, a process that carried more danger with it than any physical war.

There were no ends, not truly, only brief pauses before the struggle began anew. The wise had always known it, and the brave had always welcomed it.

'My soul will be at ease when it feasts in the Halls of Fire,' Ingvar said. 'Until then, I have a blade, and a helm, and my pack-brothers at my side.'

He smiled.

'It is enough. Glory to Russ, it is enough.'

KRAKEN

He wore their names on his armour. The words had been graven deeply; a parting gift from the Iron Priest before he'd left Fenris. Nearly a centimetre deep, now crusted with the filth of years, just like the rest of him.

Eight names: four on the right side of his dented breastplate, four on the left. One was barely legible, scraped away by some massive, crunching impact a long time ago. The others were all faded, or obscured by burn marks, or bisected with scratches.

He remembered them all anyway. They came to him when he slept, whispering to him in old voices. He saw their faces, looming up out of the dark well of memory, their flesh still marked by tattoos, scars and studs. Sometimes they were angry, sometimes mournful. Their purpose in appearing, so he'd realised, was always the same: to urge him on, to stir him into action.

And so he never rested, not truly. He respected the demands of his vocation and kept moving. Oaths had been sworn, and they bound him more tightly than bands of adamantium. One world after another, blurring into a morass of sense impressions; some cold, some hot, all struggling, all playing their tiny part in the galaxy-wide war that had long since ceased to have boundaries.

It would have been easy to lose his sense of significance in all of that. It would have been easy, after twenty years of it, to give in to the darkness that lurked behind his eyes and forget the faces. He'd seen it happen to mortals. Their mouths drooped, their eyes went dull, even as they still clutched their weapons and made a show of walking toward the enemy. Then, as sure as ice follows fire, they died.

That was why he had the names put on his armour. The carvings would continue to fade or sustain damage, but some mark would always be there, some small impression to register what had once been lives as vital as his life.

And as long as there were marks to remind him, he would not slope off into despair. He would keep moving, seeking the final trial that would restore lost honour and still the whispers in the dark.

One world after another, blurring into a morass of sense impressions; some cold, some hot. None that made much of an impression on his sullen mind; since their wars gave no opportunity to achieve the goal he craved.

None, that was, until the last of them.

None of those worlds made an impression on Aj Kvara until, following the eddies of fate, he came to Lyses, and the raw beauty of it stirred even his old, cold soul.

Morren Oen shaded his eyes against the morning glare, squinting as the green light flashed from the waves. Fifty metres below him, the downdraft of the flyer's four rotors churned the water.

There shouldn't even have been water down there. There should have been several thousand tons of dirt-grey plasteel, designation Megaera VI, humming with life and machinery. There should have been lights blinking along the smoothly curved tidewalls to beckon the flyer down to land, and the low grind of algal processors working their way through the endless harvest.

Instead there was a thin skin of floating debris bobbing on the emerald water. He saw a plastic hopper tumble by, rolling amid a web of tangled fibres. Below the surface, there were dark shadows, perhaps the outlines the struts and flotation booms, still half-operative even after the main structure had gone down.

'Emperor,' he swore, sweeping the scene of devastation for something, some sign of resistance or survival.

Four other flyers hung low over the water, each one full of men with lasguns. They pointed their barrels uselessly down at the debris. Whatever had happened to Megaera VI had moved on long before they got there.

Preja Eim leaned a long way over the edge of the flyer's open-sided crew bay and took a few more picts. Her auburn hair fluttered in the warm breeze, catching on the upturned collar of her uniform.

'Have enough yet?' asked Oen, turning away from the view and leaning back against the juddering metal of his seat-back.

Eim carried on clicking.

'Information,' she said, her face screwed up in concentration. 'There might be something. Some clue.'

Oen looked at her wearily. She was so young. Her freckled skin looked healthy in the sun, almost translucent. Perhaps, once, he'd been as enthusiastic in his work.

For the first time since joining up, he felt too old. Forty years of service on Lyses, rising steadily through the ranks, had taken its toll. Rejuve was expensive, and he had other commitments that prevented him splashing out. And so he felt the skin of his jawline sag a little and his stomach bulge out over his heavy old regimental belt. Watching Eim made him feel worse. It reminded him of what he had been, and how long ago that was.

'Snap away,' he said. 'Don't think you'll get anything we haven't already scanned for.'

He looked out aimlessly, keeping his hand over his eyes. The curve of the ocean ran unbroken across the horizon, deep green and smooth. The pale rose sky shimmered above it, warmed by the diffuse light of both suns.

Oen was used to the view of open seas. All of Lyses was open seas. All of it, that was, except for the floating hubs, strewn across the endless ocean like motes of dust, separated by thousands of kilometres and gently drifting.

And they were being picked off, one by one. That thought, when he chose to entertain it, was quite thrillingly disquieting.

'Procurator,' came a voice over his earpiece.

'Go ahead,' said Oen, welcoming the distraction. Whatever news there was, it was unlikely to make him feel worse.

'Grid Nine have a comm-signal. Ship entering the orbital exclusion zone. The hails all check out, but they thought you ought to know.'

'Nice of them. Why, especially?'

'It's not in-system, nor Navy. They think it might be Adeptus Astartes, but they're not sure.'

At the mention of the magic triplet of syllables, *as-tar-tes*, Oen felt his heart miss a beat. He didn't know whether that was born of fear or excitement. Probably a bit of both.

'They're not sure? What are they not sure about?'

'Perhaps you'd better get back to Nyx, procurator. They're not going to try to stop it, and by the time you get back it'll be in geostat.'

'Fine. Keep them quiet until I get there. We're just about done here.'

The link broke. By then Eim had stopped taking picts and was looking intently at the wreckage.

'No signs of explosions,' she murmured, watching the pieces float by. 'It's like some giant hand just... pulled it apart.'

'Did you hear all that?' asked Oen, ignoring her. 'We're going back in. You can take another flyer out here if you want to keep at it.'

Eim looked at him, and her freckled face was wide-eyed. There was a strangely childlike look of desolation in them.

'What's doing this, procurator? Why can't we stop it?'

'If I knew that, do you not think I'd have ordered something more potent than overflights?' He smiled, trying to be reassuring, and knowing he'd probably failed. 'Listen, the distress signals have been picked up. Trust in grace, Eim. There's probably a whole company of Space Marines lining up on Nyx as we speak, and, believe me, there's no more impressive sight in the Emperor's own galaxy.'

He slumped in the chair in the reception chamber, leaning both hands on the only table, smelling like old meat. His scraggly beard spilled over the breastplate of his enormous armour, snarled and tangled. Grey streaks shot through it, making him look like an old, sick man.

Do they get old? thought Oen, observing him through the one-way plexiglass viewport in the corridor outside. *Would they die of age, if given long enough?*

Accounts of the newcomer's landing from atmospheric control had been garbled. One transmission implied that the newcomer had blasted his way through the upper defensive cordon without warning, while another, from a low-order servitor-controlled station, indicated nothing but impeccable orbital manners.

One way or another, though, he'd gotten through, and his ship, now standing five hundred metres up on the landing stages, was like nothing

Oen had ever seen – dirty, angular, covered in plasma burns and with a blocky aquila picked out in bronze on the sloping nose. It didn't look big enough for inter-system travel, though it must have been, since its occupant certainly wasn't from Lyses.

From the look of it the ship's crew was entirely composed of servitors. They were strange looking creatures, with clunking servos and spikes and animal bones hanging from their pearl-white flesh. They'd stayed on board the ship after the pilot had stomped down the landing ramp, which Oen couldn't be too sorry about. Not that the pilot was any less strange.

'I thought you said...' began Eim, gazing through the viewer, fascinated. Her query trailed off.

Oen knew what she meant.

'I've been told they vary,' he said, rather stiffly. 'The only picts I saw were from a rogue trader who'd run a squadron out through Ultramar. Those ones were... different.'

Eim nodded slowly, running her eyes over the bulky figure sitting at the metal desk on the other side of the viewport.

His head was bare and bald. A knotwork tattoo ran across the tanned flesh from behind one ear, over the skull and down toward one eye. His face seemed to have several metal studs in it, each one a slightly different shape. His armour was pale grey, like dirty snow, and had carvings all over it. The lettering wasn't standard Gothic – it was angular and close-typed, covered in marks and bisected with slashes like those made by animal claws.

Oen had imagined the armour of a Space Marine to be clean, polished and flawless, just like the ones in the devotional holos sent out by the Ecclesiarchy's Office of Truth Distribution. He'd imagined bronze shoulder-guards and bright cobalt breastplates glimmering under the white lumens.

He hadn't imagined the mess, and the dirt. He certainly hadn't imagined the smell.

'Finished gawping?'

Both Oen and Eim jumped. He'd spoken. The words were thickly accented, as if Low Gothic were a foreign language, and muffled by the dividing wall. He hadn't looked up. His strange yellow eyes remained fixed on his loosely clasped hands.

Oen readied himself, shot Eim a reassuring glance, and went round the corner to open the door. As he entered the room, the newcomer looked up at him.

'I'm sorry, lord,' said Oen, bowing before taking a seat opposite. 'Standard observational procedure. We have to be careful.'

The newcomer, massive in his armour, gazed at him with a profoundly disinterested expression on his savage face. He didn't smile. His scarred and tattooed features looked almost incapable of smiling.

'A pointless gesture,' he said quietly. 'If I'd wanted to kill you, you'd be dead already. But since you've started, observe away.'

Oen swallowed. The newcomer's voice was worryingly deep, underlined with a permanent, breathy growl and made eerie by the unusual pronunciation.

'Do you have, er, a designation? Something I can use for the reports?'

'A designation?'

'A title, lord. Something I can–'

The huge figure leaned back, and Oen could see the metal chair flex under the huge strain.

'I am a Space Wolf, Procurator Morren Oen,' he said. As he spoke, Oen caught sight of long, yellow fangs flashing out from behind the hairy lips. 'Have you heard of us?'

Oen shook his head meekly. He felt his heart beating a little too quickly. Something about the man in front of him made it very hard to retain composure.

Except he wasn't a *man*. Not like Oen was a man, anyway.

'Good,' said the newcomer. 'Probably for the best.'

Oen cleared his throat, trying to remain something close to professional.

'And your name, lord?'

'My name is Kvara.'

Oen nodded. He was aware he was gesturing too much, but he couldn't stop it.

'I'd expected… more of you.'

That had come out wrong. Kvara looked at him with amusement. His eyes were circles of gold. Animal's eyes, lodged in a lined, worn and battered face.

'You do not need more of us. One of us is more than enough.'

Oen nodded again.

'Quite so,' he said, casting around for something more intelligent to say.

Kvara stepped in then, tiring of Oen's stammering enquiries.

'The data in your sending was clear,' he said. As he spoke, he lifted a gauntlet and flexed the fingers of it absently. Oen stared at it, distracted by the casual, supple movement. 'You've lost five of your harvester stations in five local months. No survivors, no readings. Nothing but debris. Something is coming out of the water. A beast.'

Kvara let his gauntlet fall to the tabletop with a dull clang.

'I have hunted beasts before.'

'We've men assigned to this already,' Oen said. 'I'd hoped that–'

'That I might join them?' Kvara shook his head. 'No. Tell your men to stand down. In this, as in everything, I work alone.'

Oen looked up into the golden eyes, and thought about protesting. Perhaps this… *Space Wolf* didn't know how big a hub harvester was. Anything that could take down one of those things must be massive, far bigger than the flyer he'd returned to Nyx in. The security detail he'd had on alert for three months consisted of nine hundred men, and he'd been considering expanding it.

'I'm not sure–'

'You're not sure I can handle whatever it is you've got attacking your people,' said Kvara. 'You're not sure something looking as dishevelled and terrible as me could do much more than get himself killed.'

He leaned forward, and the metal of the table bowed under the pressure of his forearms. Oen recoiled, feeling the hot-meat breath wash over him.

'This is not about you, Morren Oen,' whispered Kvara, taking a cold pleasure in running his tongue around the words. 'This has nothing to do with you.'

Oen tried to hold the gaze from those animal eyes, and failed. He looked down at the rivets on the table, ashamed of himself.

'I need a flyer,' said Kvara, sitting back. 'Fastest you have. Then you can forget about me, and forget about your problem.'

Oen nodded for a third time. Being in the presence of Kvara was intensely tiring. He found himself happy to do almost anything to get the encounter over with.

'It will be done, lord,' he said, knowing that, whatever he'd expected to get out of that first meeting, he'd failed badly. 'I'll get straight on it.'

Eim looked sympathetic as Oen emerged from the room. She placed a hand lightly on his shoulder.

'How'd it go?'

Oen shrugged and smiled wryly.

'Not what I expected,' he said, shaking off the hand and walking down the corridor. He went quickly, keen to be out of there. 'Though I don't really know what I thought would happen.'

Eim trotted after him, looking up anxiously.

'How many of them have come?'

'Just him.'

'You're joking.'

'No.'

Eim snorted.

'I'll get the 'paths sending again.'

'That may not be necessary.'

'Of course it'll be necessary,' said Eim, scowling. 'We need men. There must be Guard somewhere within range – they'd send a whole company soon enough if they thought tithe production was about to fall.'

Oen halted, looking thoughtful. Now that he was out of Kvara's intimidating presence, he was beginning to think more clearly.

'He doesn't think he needs help.'

'That's his problem. I mean, did you *see* what he looked like?'

'Right up close,' said Oen, ruefully. 'It wasn't pretty.'

Eim shook her head irritably.

'*One*!' she snorted. 'I didn't think they ever worked on their own. I thought they came in squads – you know, like you see on the holos.'

Oen shrugged.

'So did I,' he said. 'Maybe different types have different ways. He's a Space Wolf. Heard of them?'

Eim shook her head.

'Nice name,' she said. 'Suits his looks.'

'Careful what you say,' warned Oen, looking over his shoulder and back down the corridor. 'His hearing's very good.'

'Okay, okay.' Eim sighed, and ran a weary hand through her hair. 'But, procurator, this is the last thing we needed. We lose another hub, and we'll miss the next quota even if I keep the crews on triple rotation. For a minute there I was daring to hope we'd find a way out of this.'

This time it was Oen who put a reassuring hand on her shoulder.

'You never know,' he said. 'He may be more impressive than he looks.'

He leaned closer to her, and lowered his voice.

'He's taking a flyer out, soon as I can requisition one,' he said, covering his mouth. 'And, whatever he says, I want it tracked and a team placed ready for rapid deployment, just in case he finds anything. Can you do that?'

Eim shot him a tolerant, affectionate look.

'Sure I can,' she said. 'Just in case.'

The flyer skimmed low over the ocean, casting a deep green shadow on the waves. Kvara drove it hard, irritated by the lack of the explosive speed he was used to. One engine was already burning close to capacity, and the dashboard in front of him was active with red warning runes.

Kvara ignored them and concentrated on the view from the cockpit. Lyses stretched away in every direction, formless and empty, a wasteland of pure water and pure sky. The first sun was up, and the arc of the atmosphere was bleached salmon pink. The ocean was calm, veined with lines of white where the massive swells rolled under him.

It was pristine. In an Imperium where the hand of man fell heavily on everything it touched, Lyses was a rare jewel. In its inviolability it reminded Kvara of Fenris. On the death world, everything below the Asaheim parallel was barely touched by humanity. Lyses was more benign, but had the same vast, untouched quality.

Despite everything, that spoke to his soul. It had been a long time since anything had done that, and he found the experience, on the whole, uncomfortable.

There is one objective left, one mission, one task. Remember it.

He pushed the flyer down further, skimming it barely a man's height above the waves. Spray flashed down the sleek flanks of the machine, spinning and frothing as he banked around in a long arc. Then he powered it up, sweeping along the trajectory the procurator had given him. For a moment, just a moment, he could have been back on a *drekkar*, relishing the steep pitch and yaw of the heavy wooden hull as it ploughed through the endlessly violent seas of his home.

But Lyses was too beautiful for that. Too beautiful, and too forgiving.

Below him, the algal blooms began to intensify. Deep green and cloudy, they hung just below the surface, bathed by the light of the sun. They extended for hundreds of kilometres, a vast mat of nutrient-rich matter, stuffed with proteins.

It was for them that mankind had come to Lyses, to suck up the endless stream of life-giving algae, to process it into foodstuffs ready to be transported off-world to the famished hives and forges elsewhere in the sector. Hub harvesters, mobile floating industrial behemoths, prowled the waters endlessly, slowly ploughing furrows through the infinite bounty, dragging it up and packing it into billions upon billions of dried and pressed pellets ready for transport to gigantic processing manufactoria on other planets.

According to the records Kvara had accessed in Nyx, Lyses hadn't had a serious security incident for over five hundred years. The harvesters had just kept on going, criss-crossing the ocean, working the algae and scooping it into their maw-like hoppers, as if it would go on forever.

But nothing lasted forever – everything decayed, everything was tainted.

Kvara allowed himself a grunt of cynical satisfaction. A world without strife was an affront to his battle-hardened sensibilities. All that could exist in such a place was softness, and softness opened the door to corruption.

The blooms grew ever thicker as the flyer sped on. The green darkened, forming a solid mass under the waves. If things had been working properly, he guessed, it would never have been left to become so overgrown.

A green rune blinked on the forward scanner. Kvara sat back in the pilot's seat, cramped in his bulky armour, and watched the ruin of the hub approach. He came in low, observing the way the broken struts still speared up from the waves.

The harvester had been massive. Wreckage littered the surface for a square kilometre or more, floating on the gentle swell or lodged in thick knots of algae. Kvara applied the air brakes, swivelling the engines forward to arrest his speed and achieve a low hover. He flicked a dial on the dashboard, and the bubble-cockpit slid back.

Warm, softly fragranced air rolled over him. The smell of the algae was rich and faintly sweet. Kvara hauled himself out of the seat and leaned over the side. His weight caused the flyer to tip violently and the engines whined as they compensated.

He narrowed his eyes, poring over the debris. No burn marks or signs of explosions marked the surfaces. Where the plasteel was broken, it looked like it had been snapped cleanly. Other pieces had the jagged evidence of claw-rakes on them.

Kvara studied each piece carefully, spending time observing the angle of the impacts, the force used, the frequency of them.

Is it worthy? Is it enough?

Early signs were promising. He felt a tremor of excitement in his hearts, and swiftly suppressed it. There had been too many disappointments for him to start thinking along those lines.

Keeping the cockpit-bubble open, Kvara sat back in the pilot's seat and started a slow circle of the wreckage. As he did so, he abstracted his mind from the particular, and drifted into the general.

There were huge channels gouged through the algae blooms, marking the passage of something truly massive. Though there were several of them, Kvara had the sense that only one beast had made them.

Prey.

He closed his eyes, just as he would have done on Fenris where the spirits of hunter and hunted intertwined closely, haunting the high mountain airs and staining the unbroken snow.

I see you. I see your path. I will follow it, and then comes the test.

He saw the trail of the beast in his mind, just as if it were a herd of *konungur*, twisting away into possible futures. He saw it plunge down into the frigid depths, as dark as the void of space, writhing along the jagged ocean floor.

He opened his eyes. Below him, a wide furrow in the algal carpet stretched off into the distance, jagging back and forth.

I see you.

Kvara nudged the flyer after it, following the trail. As he did during every hunt, he put himself in the mind of his prey, imagining the mental processes of the beast and the strange, sluggish thoughts in that giant mind. He had learned to do it with such acuity that, for a moment at least, he might have been one himself.

As he travelled, his certainty grew. He powered the flyer back into full propulsion.

Kvara sat back, eyes half-closed, the warm wind racing past him. He let his instincts play loose, running down the prey, chasing after it as if a physical scent had lodged in his nostrils.

It was the same then as it had always been. For a moment, the hunt took over, the quest became everything.

In simpler, harsher times, that was all there had been.

In the past that was now faded and hard to recall, he had lived for nothing else.

I see you.

The *drekkar* took a heavy hit and buckled over to starboard. It rolled across the heavy, gun-grey sea, lashed by the torrential rain. The deluge lanced down from the low cloud line, spears of liquid that bounced and rattled from the deck.

Everything moved. Waves crashed against the high flanks and cascaded down the deck, as cold as mountain-ice and hard as bullwhips. The masts screamed against the rigging, taut with ice crystals and shivering.

'I see you!' roared Thenge, bounding up to the prow with his long, white pelt in tow.

Olekk and Regg followed him, clasping tight to the railing, their boots slipping on the sodden deck-boards. Each one of them carried a long spear in their hands, crowned with a biting edge ground out of the iron by the priests.

Lighting flickered across the northern sky, followed by the crack, roll and boom of thunder.

Fenrys was angry, just as ever, and the seas boiled with that anger.

Aj Kvara hung from the high foremast by one hand, swaying far out over the water as the ship tilted and tipped. He hadn't seen anything but the driving rain and riot of moving water.

He swore to himself, and hurried down the rigging. If Thenge had seen something from the prow, then his eyes had been the keener. That was bad. Kvara's youth was supposed to be his advantage.

Then, before he was halfway to the deck, the sea off to port boiled up in a mass of bubbles and lashing, slapping fronds.

'Here it comes!' yelled Rakki, his voice high with excitement. From somewhere else in the longship, furious laughter broke out. Kvara dropped to the deck, grabbed a spear and raced to the side.

Ahead of them, breaking the surface a dozen fathoms off, something vast and black slipped above the turmoil of the waves before sloping back down again. Kvara saw a glossy shell, pock-marked with barnacles, rolling away from the pursuing hunters and diving smoothly. A geyser of water puffed up as the beast exhaled and drew in more air.

'*Hvaluri*!' roared Olekk, laughing like the others.

Kvara felt excitement spur up within him, and he leaned further over, craning for another glimpse. The *drekkar* carried over thirty warriors. Taking a *hvaluri* would feed them and their families for weeks, as well as providing much else of value to the tribe.

'Faster!' Kvara shouted, up at old Rakki who was master of the ship.

The big man, one-eyed and scar-faced, glared back at him from the tiller. 'You hunt!' he blurted, outraged. 'I sail!'

The creature broke the surface again, closer that time, sweeping up through the choppy water and letting out a muffled bellow of anger.

Maggr was still up in the rigging, and was first to throw. His spear shot down through the rain, spinning on its axis. It hit hard, burying the jagged iron blade deep into the *hvaluri*'s armoured hide. The beast roared and went down again.

'*Hjolda*!' Maggr bellowed, balling his fists and sending his face red with fervour.

Other spears shot down, missing the target and splashing into the walls of moving water.

Kvara bided his time, waiting for the *hvaluri* to surface again. The ship slipped steeply down a precipitous leading wave, wallowing at the base of it before climbing up the next one. The deck rolled and swung like a berserker's axe-lunge, testing the warriors' precarious footing. They braced themselves against the ropes, edging closer to the tilting side of the ship, peering into the storm-lashed murk for a glimpse of the prey they hunted.

'Round left!' bellowed Thenge, getting frustrated and reaching for a second throwing spear.

The *drekkar* shivered as its prow came across, buffeted by the crashing seas. The skinsails, those had hadn't been furled against the storm, stretched out taut, making the ship race through the spray like a loosed crossbow bolt.

'I have it!' crowed Olekk, leaping up on to the sharply pitching rail and taking aim.

Something long and sinuous flashed out of the water, lashing across at Olekk with spiked barbs and dragging him over.

There was no scream. He was gone in an instant, pulled down into the icy depths from which no living man ever returned.

Kvara ran across the deck, springing up to where Olekk had been standing. He had a brief glimpse of black tentacles thrashing in the water, covering a foaming patch of dark red before that was swept astern by the racing sea.

He hurled his spear down, but the edge of the ship bucked wildly, sending his aim wide.

'*Skítja*,' he swore, jumping down and reaching for another spear.

Then the *drekkar* shuddered heavily, as if something vast had hit it from below. Thenge lost his footing and sprawled across the deck like a drunkard. The whole ship shot up, briefly thrown clear of the waves, before crashing back down again, snapping whole lengths of rigging and making the loose ropes flail like scourges.

Maggr jumped from the broken ropes, still flushed from his success, and barrelled up to the prow, leaping over the grappling form of Thenge.

'Ha!' he crowed, grabbing two throwing spears and taking the lead warrior's place.

Kvara chuckled at the presumption of it, leaping away from the rolling edge and grabbing a fresh spear of his own.

Everyone was still laughing and roaring – the ragged, caustic laugh of hunters gripped by the manic touch of the kill-urge. The whole ship was febrile with it, spilling over with savage, raw energy.

'I *want* this kill,' spat Kvara. His blond hair had come loose of its plaits, and lashed round his clean, ruddy face in the wind. He grinned as he spoke, and his white teeth flashed in the storm.

'Then throw quicker, lad,' said Maggr, taking up a spearing position and scouring the churning waves.

It came up again then, huge and glistening. Kvara saw a single eye the size of his chest, as round as the moon and grey like an oyster. It glared at them, burning with bestial hatred and fury.

He didn't hesitate. Fast as a whip-snap, Kvara hurled the spear. It whistled through the air, striking straight through the heart of the eye. The shaft trembled, and it lodged fast.

The *hvaluri* bellowed, its roars making the water drum and vibrate, before rolling heavily away from the boat.

'It won't go down!' shouted Thenge, back on his feet and braced for another throw. 'Not now!'

Kvara raced to fetch another spear. His heart was thumping with glorious, brutal energy. Every muscle ached, every sinew was taut, but his heart sang.

I speared the eye! I did it!

The creature reared up, thundering out of the boiling sea, throwing water across its hunched, gnarled back in huge tumbling sheets.

'*Morkai!*' swore Regg, hurling a spear at it and somehow managing to miss.

The beast was massive, at least the size of the *drekkar* and much, much heavier. It thrashed around in a wallow of agony, the spears still protruding from its body. A huge shell of barnacle-crusted blackness rolled around, crowned with spines and bone-ridges. A mass of tentacles flashed out from under the skirts of the shell, twisting and writhing like a nest of prehensile tongues. Spray shot out, splattering against the masts and cascading down on to the warriors.

'Too close!' warned Rakki, heaving on the tiller.

The ship came round, but not quickly enough. Tentacles shot out, latching on to the railings and dragging the *drekkar* back. It tilted heavily, listing over nearly to the tipping point.

Thenge lost his footing again, raging and cursing as he slipped down the

steepling deck. A tentacle spun out, clamping on to his ankle and gripping tight. He grabbed his axe from his belt and hacked down, severing it
cleanly and freeing himself.

Other warriors charged, hurling their spears at the exposed underbelly
of the beast. Some of the blades bit deep, disappearing into the forest of
thrashing members, provoking fresh roars of pain. The sea frothed with a
thick black sludge as the monster began to bleed. Some of it splashed out
across Kvara's face, hot and salty.

'It'll drag us down!' shouted Rakki, toiling uselessly at the tiller.

More tentacles latched on to the ship, some reaching all the way across
to the far side. The *drekkar* listed further, and water began to lap across the
lower edge of the deck, washing up across the already drenched planks.

Thenge raced over to the nearest tendril, hacking away with his axe. He
cut through it sharply, but two more fronds quickly whipped across. All
across the ship, warriors swapped their throwing spears for short-handled
axes and began chopping frantically at the strangling lengths of tentacle.
Even as they worked, the ship slipped further down, dragged through the
mountainous swell by the wounded beast.

Kvara drew his throwing arm back, only to feel a viscous, slimy wall of
flesh hit him full in the face. He crashed back heavily, cracking his head
on something unyielding on the way down. He had the blurred impression of a black tube the width of his arm snaking across his field of vision
and falling over him. A hot wash of pain ran through his skull, and he felt
blood running down the back of his neck.

Acting on instinct, he swept up his spear, still grasped in his right hand,
shoving the blade of it up through the tentacle. It carved through sweetly,
separating it into two pieces. The broken-off end continued to writhe on
its own, jerking and spasming across the sodden wood.

Kvara staggered to his feet. The ship was going down. Waves rushed up
the tilted deck, flooding into the hold below. For every tentacle the warriors
slashed apart, more shot out, wrapping the *drekkar* in a morass of dripping, slippery tendrils.

'*Hjolda!*' he roared, grabbing his axe from his belt and throwing his arms
back in challenge.

The beast loomed up at him, sweeping up out of the waves and roaring
its own booming call of anger.

Kvara sprinted down the listing deck, leaping over the bodies of the
fallen and veering past the flickering ends of searching tentacles, ignoring
the hammering pain in his head. He ran straight at the huge domed shell,
hacking away the snaking tubes of meat as they swept into his path.

It felt like he was running down a cliff-edge, straight into the depths of the
bottomless ocean. He could see the bulk of the *hvaluri* below him, wallowing in a messy broth of broken spars and bloody water.

He leapt, flying away from the ship and through the air, plummeting
for a moment, his long hair streaming behind him and his axe held high.

Then he landed, crunching on to the shell of the beast, feeling the hard
surface flex from the impact.

He nearly skidded straight across it and over the far side, but managed to clutch at a bone-ridge with his trailing hand. He yanked to a halt, nearly blinded with spray and buffeted by the gusting wind.

The creature let out a deafening roar and hauled itself further out of the boiling sea. Tentacles shot up, trailing across its shell, reaching out to rip him from its back and hurl him into the water.

Kvara pulled himself to his knees, balancing precariously on the bucking, rolling curve, hacking at any tentacles that reached him. Blood still ran from his head wound, making him dizzy. Through the clouds of spray, he could just make out the *drekkar* rolling away, righting itself as the hold of the tentacles was released.

Kvara batted away a flailing length of tentacle, then slammed the axe-head down. It cracked open the shell, plunging deep into the translucent, sticky matter beneath.

The beast bellowed, thrashing and yawing in the waves. Jets of black ink spouted up, splashing across Kvara's chest. He pulled the axe free, drew it up and chopped down again. The blade cracked open a new wound, shattering the beast's armoured covering and tearing up the soft flesh beneath. More ink welled up, boiling hot and fizzing.

Kvara kept attacking it, ripping up the outer layers and burying the axe-head deep into the yielding blubber beneath. The tentacles lashed out, feebly now. The cries of the beast became plaintive rather than angry. Gouts of black murk pumped from its wounds, turning the roiling waves dark and viscous.

Kvara heard a heavy crunch close by. He looked up and saw Thenge by his side, scrabbling for purchase on the shell before getting to his knees. The big warrior grinned at him, an axe in each hand.

'Brave work, pup!' he laughed, whirling the blades in his hands before hacking them down. 'We'll make you a man yet!'

Then the two of them got to work, gripping the tilting shell and hacking it open, burrowing down, slicing through the hide of the beast, breaking up what remained of the hard barrier between them and the pulpy mass beneath. Out of the corner of his eye, Kvara saw the grappling hooks fly out from the *drekkar*, latching on the foundering creature, ready to haul it to the side of the ship. Other warriors were preparing to make the leap across, brandishing hooks and cleavers.

Kvara kept his head down after that, working hard. His pain at the back of his head wouldn't abate, though it didn't stop him working.

Amid all of it, he still grinned. He couldn't help himself. The flush of victory ran through his veins, keeping his arms moving and giving his legs the strength to hold him in position.

This is my kill, he thought as he hacked away furiously, trying not to let his stupid, childish grin show too much.

My kill.

A day later and the storm lessened in its fury, though the seas ran hard for much longer. The *drekkar* made heavy work of it, labouring in the deep swell. The central mast still stood but much of the rigging had been ripped away. Several holes had been punched below the waterline, and no matter how fast the crew bailed it out, the bilges sloshed with seawater where the makeshift repairs had been hammered on.

Aside from Olekk, three other warriors had been dragged over the edge. That was a heavy toll for the tribe, through the scale of the prize compensated for that. The meat of the *hvaluri* would keep them fed for many months once the women had smoked and salted it. The tough shell would provide tools for them and the beast's blood would be distilled into both fuel and food.

The ship ran low in the water, laden down with every piece of hide and blubber the warriors could fit aboard. It stank of the sea, acrid and salty, but no one minded that. It was a good haul, worth setting out across the blade-dark ocean for.

As they neared home Thenge sat with Kvara in the prow, chewing on a long piece of sinew and letting the grease run down his beard.

'Feeling better?' he asked good-naturedly.

Kvara nodded. He'd broken his arm on the leap back to the ship after the *hvaluri* had given up the fight, much to the raucous amusement of the rest of the crew. Even after it had been bound up with a rough splint, it still ached – not that he would ever show it.

His head was the worst of it. He didn't dare to get it looked at by the priests. The blood still oozed thickly from the wound, and the pain grew with every passing hour. His vision was beginning to blur. It wasn't healing.

'I mean what I say,' said Thenge, jabbing his finger at the blond warrior. 'That was brave. The test of manhood awaits, and you're ready.'

Kvara took up a string of sinew himself and chewed on it.

'Not sure?' asked Thenge.

'I'll do it,' he said. 'Not now.'

Thenge snorted.

'Why wait?'

Kvara looked away from him, down the longship where the rest of the crew laboured. They were his people, the ones he'd lived with all his short life. They'd never made him feel anything less than part of their world. The test of manhood – the long, solitary hunt across the icy wastes, daunted him. He didn't fear death, and certainly didn't fear danger, but something about the ordeal made him hang back.

He would do it, but not soon. The time wasn't right.

'I don't know,' he said, truthfully enough. He took another bite of the sinew, feeling the slippery flesh slide around his mouth. The action of eating dulled the pain slightly. 'I'm not ready.'

He looked up then, up at the grey walls of cloud that shrouded Fenrys. In a rare break, where the sheets of occlusion gave way slightly, he thought he saw something up there, shadowing them. A huge bird, perhaps, but its profile was strangely angular. It seemed to hang motionless in the air.

'Perhaps you're not ready to be out on your own,' said Thenge, resignedly.

Kvara nodded, not really paying attention. His head was getting worse. The clouds closed back together, hiding whatever it was that he'd seen.

'Yes,' he said. 'Perhaps that's right.'

Kvara ran his finger over the names on his armour. The snow-grey metal was softened in Lyses's warm light. Even the blade marks, the scorches and the dents looked a little less jagged.

He didn't need to read the names in order to remember them. They were carved on to his mind just as deeply as they were etched into the ceramite.

Mór, his thick-set face framed by black, dense sideburns. Dark hair, pale skin, like a vision of an underverse spectre with the sardonic humours to match.

Grimbjard Lek, the polar opposite. Sunny, blond, his mouth twitching up into a wicked smile at the first excuse. He'd killed with a smile on his face, that one, glorying the Allfather with every swing of his axe.

Vrakk, the one they'd all called Backhand, bulky and blunt with his power-fist thrumming, a dirty fighter but useful enough to make up for it.

Aerjak and Rann, brothers-in-arms, inseparable and possessed of that uncanny awareness of the other's state. Kvara had always had Aerjak down for the Rune Priests. He'd had a strange way about him, something tied to the wyrd, for all the good it had done him on Deneth Teros.

Frorl, the blade-master, swinging his frostblade with that unconscious, mocking ease, disdaining ranged weapons for the thrill of disruptors and steel-edge.

Rijal Svensson, wiry and fast, quick to anger and equally quick to laugh, his nose broken so many times that it had almost been not worth bothering with. He'd never accepted augmetic replacements, preferring to keep the stub of gristle and bone-shards in place to remind him not to get carried away.

Finally, Beorth, the quiet one. Only happy when hoisting his heavy bolter into position or at the controls of something huge and slung with big guns. He'd have been a Long Fang before he made Grey Hunter, if they'd let him. He'd laughed rarely, never sharing the coarse jokes the rest of them let spill from their profane lips, but when he had done, that rolling, rich, mirthful rumble had made Kvara grin unconsciously along with him.

Beorth had been the hardest, out of all of them. He'd been the one they'd never noticed unless he wasn't there.

Kvara let his armoured finger trace out the names, clicking softly as it passed over the runic grooves.

Perhaps you're not ready to be out on your own.

A warning light blinked on the dashboard. Kvara snapped out of his memories and took in the data.

The hub was in visual range and racing towards him fast. It was a small installation, a few hundred metres in diameter on the surface and crowned with a couple of comms towers, a few landing stages and a squat ops centre. Lights still blinked at the summit, flashing piercingly in the heat of day. The algae stretched away from it, sparse in patches and thick in others. Four lines of oily smoke rose from the harvester processing nodes, indicating that it was still working.

Kvara's face wrinkled in disapproval. He could smell the thick stench of promethium already, a low-grade variant, greasy and sour.

His armoured fingers ran over the console, keying in the landing codes from the databank Oen had uploaded to the flyer. A pict over to his left immediately updated with the response. The protective cover of one of the landing stages withdrew, unfurling like an iron rosebud, and he banked the flyer towards it.

Nothing obviously wrong.

He touched the flyer down on the platform and jumped down from the open cockpit. Smoke poured from one of the engines, and the others wound down slowly, as if their bearings had been ground away.

Kvara strode across the apron, unconsciously checking his weapons. The bolt pistol at his waist was fully loaded and primed with the appropriate blessing. Blood, his own blood, ceremonially stained the muzzle. Across his back was strapped Djalik, his blade. It was a short, stabbing sword, notched and serrated along one of the cutting edges and with inset runes lodged under the bronze-lined hilt. Over the years the metal had been dulled with burns from the weapon's disruptor field, making it as dark as charcoal.

Kvara sniffed the air, going watchfully. Everything was quiet. The installation barely moved on the placid waters. The warm wind blew across the towers and manufactoria units, washing over the grey plasteel in an endless, placid sigh.

Ahead of him, two doors slid soundlessly open, opening the way into the hub's interior. Orange lights blinked on, illuminating a bare, clean corridor. Everything smelled of the algae – a mulchy, briny tang that lingered at the back of the throat.

Kvara paused before entering, taking a final look across the hub. Aside from the low growl of automating processors, all was calm. The green waters lapped softly at the flanks of the harvester, a hundred metres down from the landing platforms.

Where are the men?

Reluctantly, having got used to the clean, unfiltered taste of the air, Kvara retrieved his battered helm from its mag-lock and screwed it in place. The balmy atmosphere of Lyses disappeared, replaced by the filtered, sterile environment of his armour-shell.

Kvara took up his bolt pistol, and breathed a prayer, the same prayer he'd uttered during every quest since Deneth Teros.

Allfather, deliver me from safety and bring me into peril.

Then he walked inside.

'Where is he now?'

'Alecto XI. He's landed.'

'That's a long way from the last site. Have we got anything from the crew?'

'Nothing. Not a thing.'

'When was the last transmit?'

'Uh, hang on.'

Eim steadied herself against the sway of the flyer. It was a big one, capable of spending several days out over the water and accommodating a full assault company. She didn't like using craft that big – their judder and yaw, as well as the fuel-tinged air, made her nauseous, and the grunts got restive cooped up in the holds.

'We don't have anything from them for six days, ma'am.'

Eim turned to the comms officer and raised an eyebrow.

'Why wasn't that picked up? They're meant to be checking in daily.'

The comms officer, a grey-faced man with deep-sunk eyes and an unfortunate overbite, shrugged apologetically.

'There are a lot to monitor.'

Eim swore and rubbed her eyes with the balls of his fists. Throne of Earth, she felt tired. Oen would owe her for this when she got back.

'Okay, run a scan. Check for anything.'

'I can't see... whoa. I really don't know... what is that?'

Eim pushed him aside and leaned over the augur console. As she watched the shapes clarify, she felt a sudden, cold thrill shudder through her body.

'How close are we to him?'

'A long way. Procurator Oen insisted on a range of–'

'Forget that. We're going in. Signal Nyx, but don't wait for a response.'

She turned away from the comms officer and looked out across the cramped bridge space. Other officers looked up from their stations. Their expressions had switched from mild boredom into nervous expectation.

'Get the men armed and ready to deploy,' she said, speaking to the company commander, a squat, low-browed man called Frehis Aerem. 'All squads, assault order, ready to drop on my word.'

Eim looked back at the console before he'd had a chance to respond. As she watched the augur line sweep round for another pass, she felt her heart start to thump faster within her chest.

'Damn you, Oen,' she muttered, shaking her head as she watched the data stream in. 'You let him go out there – this is on *your* conscience.'

The corridors were quiet and lit only by dim orange light. Every metre of them was pristine, scrubbed clean and glistening. Octagonal hatches appeared at regular intervals along the walls, all closed. Kvara tried one of the handles, and it clicked against the bolt lock. He punched through the mechanism, cracking the handle, and the hatch swung open.

The chamber on the far side was empty. There was a desk, two metal chairs, a scale model of the harvester station on a sideboard. More orange light flickered from a semi-functional lumen, catching the jewels in a cheap devotional image of some primarch or other. No one was inside and, from the sterile smell of it, no one had been inside for some time.

Kvara turned back, walking through the network of corridors. Despite his heavy boots, his footfalls were soft. The power armour hummed – a low, grinding noise at the edge of mortal hearing – the only thing that broke the dense fog of silence.

Kvara paused, inclining his head, listening carefully. For a second, there was a trace sound, right on the edge of his audible range. Nothing he could latch on to, and not enough data for the helm to augment.

He started walking again, keeping his pistol held high. The grey hair along the back of his neck stood erect, brushing against the collar of his armour. He could feel his thick blood pumping vigorously around his bulky frame. His awareness had sharpened up, causing his muscles to loosen and his pupils to dilate. He heard his own breathing resonate within the helm, close and hot.

I come for you. You know I am here.

At the end of the corridor was another intersection. He waited again, watching, listening, absorbing.

Show yourself.

The lights blew.

The corridor plunged into darkness. Something raced up out of the shadows, phenomenally fast, scrabbling on the metal floor as it came.

In the nanosecond before Kvara's helm compensated, it swerved around the corner and out at him. A hellish face, obscenely long and crested, lashed up out of the dark.

Kvara loosed two bolts, aiming fast. They impacted with a crack and flash of light, shattering a brittle shell. High screams, alien screams, echoed from the walls.

More of them arrived, leaping over the fallen outrider. Jointed limbs clattered over metal, flashing ice-white as more bolt-flares lit them up. They came in a tangled rush, jostling each other, jaws wide and biting.

Kvara pulled back, firing all the time. His arm moved only by fractions, picking out target after target, cracking apart the growing swarm of xenos creatures. The intersection clogged quickly with smashed shells and oozing pulp, but he kept coolly firing.

Just as the ammo counter ran down, the onslaught ceased. The last of the chittering screams died away, leaving a pile of twisted, snapped and cracked shells in front of him.

Kvara ejected the old magazine, slammed a fresh one into the pistol housing and drew his blade with his left hand. Djalik's disruptor field fizzed into life, throwing an electric blue aura out from the cutting edge.

He strode out into the intersection, wading through a swamp of broken, twitching carcasses, watching for more of the xenos to come at him.

He knew what they were. He'd fought such beasts on a dozen worlds.

Hormagaunts, the Imperium called them.

Kvara liked fighting tyranids. Unlike Traitors, for whom he could feel nothing but a blind, disgusted fury, or the greenskins, which were contemptible, tyranids were a force he could respect.

They were pure. They suffered from neither fear nor corruption nor fatigue. Like the native beasts of his own world, they lashed out with an unsullied primal aggression, driven to kill out of hammered-in instinct and never stopping until death took them or the task was completed.

They saw him as prey. He saw them as prey. That made things even.

Ahead of Kvara the corridor opened out into a wide, square room. Banks of equipment were arranged in long rows, all still clean and unsullied. Across them lay the bodies of the hub's crew, very much not clean and unsullied.

They had been ripped open. Their bodies, what was left of them, hung in glistening loops of gristle and sinew all across the room. A few had tried to get out, running for the double doors on the far side of the space. The trails of blood, as thick and dark as engine oil, didn't reach very far. The corpses still had looks of horrified surprise on their faces – those, at any rate, who still had faces.

Kvara swept the room with his pistol. The lights were still down, and his helm picked the outlines of the bodies in fuzzy grey light.

He sensed them coming before his armour's equipment did. A skittering, scraping run, muffled by the closed doors to the corridor beyond, punctuated by the high-pitched rattle of xenos vocal cords. They were racing toward him – dozens of them, maybe more.

Kvara grinned.

The doors burst apart, thrown aside by a press of straining bodies. Blurred xenos outlines, skeletal and reptilian, swarmed through the gap and into the room, screaming at him with stretched-wide jaws, pouring over the surfaces in a rolling wave of needle-teeth and hooked claws.

'*Fenrys!*'

Kvara charged straight back at them, leaping over a slumped pile of eviscerated bodies and bringing his blade round in a wide, blistering arc. He hurled himself into the tide, loosing volleys of bolt-fire that flashed out in the dark like storm lightning.

They came on, lashing out at him, and he shattered their talons. They leapt up to maul him, and he broke their snapping jaws. He spun round, shifting from one foot to another, punching out, slicing back with the blade, firing all the while. Scrawny xenos bodies smashed apart, bursting open and spraying fluid across his whirling, gyrating armour.

More of them poured in through the broken doors, streaming into the chamber and leaping up to make contact with him. They bounded over the bodies of their own dead, desperate to draw blood.

Kvara smashed his pistol-hand round, caving in a swollen xenos skull, before sending two more rounds spinning into two more targets, jabbing up with the blade and hauling it back through the entrails of another flailing monster.

They were all over him, tearing and screaming, but he was faster, bigger and stronger. As they howled with agonised frustration, he grunted with coarse satisfaction. His gauntlets were heavy and sticky with fluids, but he kept them moving. The liquid splattered over his breastplate, dousing the graven names under layers of filth.

He had been bred to do this. There was nothing left for him but this. Only in such work could his soul find a measure of peace even as his body pushed itself to the extremes of performance.

He was back where he belonged. Back in the fight.

* * *

'Kvara!'

Mór's voice was strained over the comm, broken up by the crackle of ordnance. Huge, thumping crashes distorted the feed.

'Position, brother,' snapped Kvara, running hard, feeling the sweat run down his temple.

'Rann... all gone...'

And that was it. The comm spat a fog of static. Kvara kept running, keeping his head low, weaving through the rubble. Solid rounds fizzed over his head, impacting against the rockcrete and showering him with rubble.

Blood of Russ – where are they?

He sensed a detonation to his left, and leapt clear. The already ruined wall exploded, hurling out an orb of fire and rusty shrapnel. The blast wave threw him from his feet, slamming him into the nearside bulwark. His armour crunched through it, tearing up the stone and showering him in dust.

'Position!' he spat, righting himself and breaking into a run again.

Nothing but hissing came over the comm. The fractured sky of Deneth Teros rumbled with electric storms, and a fork of violet lightning licked the burning horizon.

'Lek. Svensson. *Position.*'

He ducked down again and starting to run. Above him, huge artillery trails lanced between the shells of the spires, exploding in a cacophony of overlaid, shuddering booms.

The static mocked him, and he blinked the feed closed. Far ahead of him, the city core was tearing itself apart. A vast hab-spire, hundreds of metres tall and crested with jagged towers, toppled over with eerie, magisterial slowness. Already broken open by a hundred major impacts, the walls imploded as it crashed down amongst the ruins, throwing up a bow wave of burning dust. The screams of those inside were lost in the ripping, flickering wind, burned away by the igniting promethium in the air.

Kvara raced across a narrow transit corridor, dodging the smoking craters and leaping over the lines of barbed stranglewire. Explosive rounds followed him, puffing up as they hit the tarmac. Since he'd left Vrakk, coughing up his own blood in the gutter with his lower body on the other side of the street, Kvara's tactical display had showed nothing but interference. The location runes of his pack all showed blank.

We're being torn apart.

He spotted movement, right on the edge of his left visual field, and swerved after it. Something – something big – ducked under a huge, low-hanging metal beam.

Kvara fired. The bolts screamed off into the fire-flecked murk, exploding as they demolished the beam in a cloud of spinning metal shards.

Then he was running again, leaping past smoking mortar holes and sweeping around smouldering heaps of twisted slag. He hadn't killed it. He'd have known if he had killed it.

Warned by some inner sense, he skidded to a halt, dropping down to a crouch.

A ball of plasma seared out of the gloom, missing by centimetres, slamming into the wall behind him. Kvara lurched forward, feeling the heat as another plasma bolt flew across his back.

He rolled to one side, bringing up his pistol and firing blind. The bolts connected with something, there was a shrill shriek, and the plasma torrent ceased.

Kvara sprang up, bounding after the source of the noise, ducking and swooping across the broken ground. As he went, his senses processed a thousand minor events in every direction – Guardsmen howling and weeping with fear and pain, juddering fire from dug-in positions over by the refineries, the grind and crack of armoured formations coming up from the transit hub along what remained of the Joslynssbahn. He processed those sounds, but did nothing about them. Everything was focussed on the elusive shadow, the shape that stayed one step ahead, the shape that had come among them and summoned blood.

Kvara tore round the shell of a burned-out Chimera, tasting the sweet taste of the hunt in his cloyed saliva.

Ahead, two hundred metres, he saw it again, dark between clouds of engine smoke. Huge, edged with spikes, loping like a maddened devil of the Helwinter. Corruption rolled from its carapace in a stink of oily shadow.

It turned, and eyes the colour of newborn flesh blazed at him.

Kvara fired as he ran, loosing a rolling column of explosive rounds and zigzagging through the broken remnants of the 576th Armoured Falchions.

The bolts connected, and the creature rocked back on huge, cloven feet. It cast aside a charred and broken plasma cannon and reached for a glittering blade. A scream sliced through the air, echoing in nightmarish polyphony.

Kvara didn't slow down. The pistol clicked empty, and he cast it aside, drawing up his blade Rothgeril and activating the lashing disruptors.

The thing he faced had once been a man. After that, it had been a Space Marine. After that, it had become a living altar of sadism, a prophet of the darkest corner of insanity and depravity in a galaxy already drenched in it.

Its armour, a grotesque blasphemy of Tactical Dreadnought plate, had burst out and split from the pulsing flesh beneath. Translucent tumours swelled up in the cracks, glowing and leaking and trembling. A face – part helm-grille, part skeletal rictus – grinned out from under a cowl of whip-curl bronze snakes. Eldritch energy rippled across the warped ceramite like meltwater. Blood flecked and speckled the pale pink tracery, boiling and hissing as the raw ether touched it and recoiled.

Kvara swung the blade low, driving it with frightening speed and precision. He could sense the acuity of his own movements, and gloried in it. Every nanometre of his body was straining for the kill. His hearts thudded, his blood raged, his lungs burned with a cleansing pain.

The blades clashed, and a boom of power discharged, throwing Kvara back and blunting his charge. The monster reared over him, pulling its pulsing sword-edge round for another blow.

Kvara pulled away, opening up a narrow space and spinning round to build up fresh momentum. The creature sliced its own blade across at him, tearing the very air itself asunder and leaving a trail of agonised matter in its wake.

Kvara ducked under it, feeling the charged edge tear a chunk from his backpack. He thrust up, ignoring the sickly stench of filth that poured from the corrupted horror, grabbing the hilt of Rothgeril two-handed.

The sword bit deep, blazing like a field of stars as it crashed through the distorted ceramite and warp-addled flesh.

Then it was hauled away, dragged from his hands by a wrench so hard that Kvara lost his feet and was dragged, face-down, into the ash and dust of the ruined city. He recovered instantly, rolling away to evade the downward killing plunge before jumping back to his feet and backing away, disgusted at how easily his weapon had been taken from him.

Now the creature held two swords. One, its own, blazed with sick, overripe energy. The other, Kvara's, held upside-down by the blade-tip. The beast's long fingers squeezed through the furious disruptor field, bleeding dark purple blood where Rothgeril's biting edge sunk deep into its twisted flesh.

It laughed, and the sound was like the screaming of children.

Weaponless, Kvara clenched his gauntlets and snarled, ready for the onslaught. The creature was nearly twice his height, mutated and imbued with the essence of the Ruinous Powers. The Grey Hunter gazed up at it through red helm lenses, fearless and desperate, judging whether any blow he landed could do any damage to such a monster, tensing to sell his life with as much blood and fire as could still be mustered.

But not yet. A hurricane of heavy bolter fire slammed into the towering monster, smashing up the twisted armour and churning deep into the rose-pink muscle. It reeled, flailing against the bludgeoning hail of exploding projectiles.

Beorth limped out of the roiling clouds, his underslung bolter thundering from his two-handed grip. The comm-link was still a hiss of nothing. In broken bursts, Kvara could only hear a strangled, desperate sound from Beorth's feed.

The man, the big man, was *roaring*.

'A blade, brother!' shouted Kvara, stretching out a hand imploringly.

Beorth ignored him. He strode toward the staggering creature, firing all the while, ripping the armour-shell free of its sickening sigils and unholy signs. His own armour was as black as night, burned and rent open, and blood still poured from a dozen mortal wounds. He walked on regardless, massive and implacable, pouring a steady stream of withering, searing destruction from the red-hot muzzle of his huge weapon.

The monster waded through it, clawing at the bolts even as they punched into it, blowing shards from its armour and spraying plumes of purple. It staggered toward Beorth, screaming the whole time in a paroxysm of outrage and madness.

Then it leapt, streaming out in trails of blood and shell-discharge, arms outstretched and jaws open. It crashed into Beorth, knocking them both to the ground and rolling over. It savaged at his neck, tore at the cracks in his armour, stamped down with cloven hooves on to his prone limbs.

Kvara raced after them, pouncing on to the back of the creature. He grabbed the ornate lip of its armour and heaved, pulling it away from Beorth.

The horror snarled and lashed round, trying to throw him off. Kvara clung on, digging his fingers deep into the exposed flesh under the ceramite, tearing it up and pulling it out in strips.

Beorth clambered back to his feet, drawing his blade. The heavy bolter thudded to the floor, spent and smoking.

The creature of Chaos threw Kvara off, hurling him to one side and swinging the twin swords down at his prone body. Kvara rolled away, evading them by centimetres, before Beorth charged back, slashing with his own combat blade, whirling and dancing with all the skill of Frorl.

Together, the two of them rocked back and forth, hacking and blocking. The Traitor was reeling now, weeping blood in rivulets down its shattered armour. Beorth's left arm hung limply by his side, awkwardly twisted, his every move radiating agony.

Kvara lurched to his feet in time to witness his brother's sword knocked away with a vicious swipe from the Traitor's warp-tainted blade. It spun away, glittering in the firelight, clattering across the stone. Spurred on by desperation, Kvara scrambled after it, grabbing the hilt just as it came to rest.

He whirled back round, only to see the creature break Beorth's neck with a final, horrifying lunge. The huge warrior was hoisted into the air and cast aside with a sickening crunch of bone.

Then it turned to Kvara, and grinned.

Kvara ignited the disruptor on Beorth's blade, barely noticing the runes signifying 'Djalik' along the blade. It felt light in his hand, balanced the way a combat sword should be.

'For the Allfather,' Kvara breathed softly, staring at the murderer of his pack, sensing the death-spirit locked tight in the killing blade.

The creature charged at him, both swords flailing, but its movements were jerky and erratic. Massive wounds had opened out across its body from Beorth's onslaught, all bleeding torrents.

Kvara darted forward, ducking under the first incoming swipe before jabbing up with the point of Djalik, twisting as the edge punched up through the outstretched chin of the Traitor.

The point cleaved cleanly, thrusting up through bone and brain. The monster, impaled on the lashing, spitting energy blade, jerked like a marionette, lashing out blindly with its twin weapons.

Huge fists battered Kvara, buffeting him from either side, but he remained firm. He fed power to Djalik's disruptors, and the creature's head bulged, cracked, and exploded.

A rain of pulp and bone shot outward, blinding Kvara and sending him reeling backwards again. Disorientated, he stumbled, landing heavily on his back. A sharp pain radiated from his side, and he caught sight of the Traitor's blade lodged in his torso. Runes flashed red across his helm display, giving him a tediously thorough summary of just how badly hurt that made him.

The headless body of the Traitor toppled, thudding dully against the tortured earth of Deneth Teros. Tendrils of warp-matter flickered across its ruined corpse, dancing like grave-sprites.

Still on his back, Kvara grabbed hold of the corrupted blade, gritted his teeth, and pulled. It came free with a wet squelch, dragging strands of muscle and skin with it through the jagged gash in his armour. He could feel the poison in the wound already, hot and boiling away like a swarm of insects. He tried to rise, and failed. Blood was leaking out of him freely, defying the clotting agents in his body. His vision blurred, going black, and his head fell back against the hot soil.

Above him, the sky was scored with trails of fire. As if from far away, he heard the rush and clamour of warfare. The ground trembled underfoot as huge war engines trundled toward one another. High up in the dark skies, black silhouettes of drop-ships hung, shaky in the heatwash from their labouring engines.

Kvara watched it all mutely, feeling paralysis creep up to his lips. He could feel his consciousness slipping away, even as his ravaged body rallied against the poison frothing in his blood.

'Position...' he murmured, automatically, repeating the word he'd used so often over the last hour, feeling the bitter futility of it even as his mind lost its grip on the world of the senses.

Beorth was dead. Vrakk was dead. Rann and Aerjak had died together, just as they had surely been fated to do. The pack – all of them – were dead.

Kvara felt a solitary tear of rage run down his burned cheek. He wanted to take his helm off, to taste the air of the world that had done this, but his hands no longer obeyed his commands.

Night closed in on him, the night of oblivion. The last thing he saw was the helm display, functional and stark. The eight runes, eight identifier marks, were all blank, like empty holes into the void.

All dead.

The thought burned at his mind even as it retreated in nothingness. It stabbed at him, far sharper than the wound in his side, sharper than the many wounds across his battle-worn body, sharper than the knowledge, coming to him even as lost everything else, that he was equal to the poisons, and that this would not be the last fight he would live to see.

That didn't matter. For the first time since coming off the ice and taking the Helix, that didn't matter.

Nothing mattered.

All dead.

'This is your choice.'

'I have made it.'

'Not yet. You need more time.'

'My decision won't change.'

'It may. I've seen it before.'

The eyes in the dark were red and slanted. If he had died, he would have expected eyes like those.

But he hadn't died, not physically. The eyes behind those lenses were like his. They were sunk deep into a black wolf skull mask with teeth set around the helm-grille.

Around him, the isolation chamber of the *Vrafnki* hummed with the grind of sub-warp travel. He didn't know where it was going, or how long it would be in transit. Much still had to be explained to him, though he was in no hurry to ask for information.

'It's a privilege, not a right,' said the Rune Priest, though less harshly than he might have done.

Kvara let his head sink back to the metal surface of the medicae cot. Every part of him still ached. His blood felt painfully hot, as if he'd been given a transfusion of molten lead.

'With all respect, lord,' he said, working his swollen lips painfully, 'I don't believe you. It's never been refused.'

For a moment, the skull mask remained static. Then a low, grating chuckle broke out from behind the black armour.

'Maybe.'

The mask drew closer, looming over him, coming to within a few centimetres of his face. Kvara looked up through the translucent mask of the medicae shroud with the one eye that still worked. He felt the soft pulse of the machinery around him, cycling his blood, working his hearts, filling his lungs, keeping him shackled to life.

'What do you think taking the lone path will be like, Hunter?' he asked. 'How long do you think it will take to find a prize big enough to extinguish your grief? When we pulled you from the ice, as near to death as you are now, you'd killed a *hvaluri*. How much bigger would your beast have to be, Aj Kvara, before its death would be enough?'

Kvara smiled grimly.

'When I was a child, I dreamed of killing a *krakken*. That's what I thought it took to become a Sky Warrior.'

'Then you are a fool. The *krakken* cannot be killed.'

'But Jarl Engir–'

'The *krakken* cannot be killed. It will tear at the roots of the world for eternity, weakening them, making them frail.'

The Rune Priest withdrew his skull mask. Kvara closed his eye. He felt the drugs in his system dragging him back to unconsciousness, and fought against it.

'It can be killed,' he said, feeling his words slur. 'I know it, and you know it. Everything that lives can be killed.'

He kept moving, heading down, ever down, fighting through the hormagaunts as they swarmed up from the lower levels, relishing every wave of them as they crashed and broke against his armour. Djalik was slick with their fluid, as was the muzzle of his bolt pistol, now dangerously low on ammunition.

The creatures had come from below. They'd run up the sensor shafts from the underwater sections, fast and silent. The human crew would have had no warning – no time even to send off a panicked transmission before the living wall of teeth and claws ripped into them. Before Kvara had arrived they'd been dispersing again, falling back down in scattered packs, making way for the monster whose appearance they'd heralded. Only his intervention had stirred them again, rousing them back into the slavering, indignant fury they'd shown before.

Now, once again, their numbers had been thinned. Kvara wheeled around smoothly, knocking three of the creatures bodily into the chamber walls. Two thumped wetly against the plasteel, slumping to the floor. The other managed to get up, and he grabbed it, snapping its neck with a contemptuous twist.

The floor rocked as something collided with the outside wall. The collisions were getting more violent, and he braced himself against them. A hormagaunt, one of the last remaining, skittered into the chamber and threw itself at him. Kvara cracked his fist into its oncoming jaws, not bothering to use the blade.

The chamber lurched again, and a crack snaked across the wall. Kvara backed away from it, running a quick check over his armour's integrity seals, knowing full well that he was several hundred metres below sea level.

The structure around him groaned and the walls began to bulge inwards. The cracks grew, as if something huge and prehensile had wrapped itself around the chamber and was pulling tight.

Kvara braced himself, gauging from the creaks and snaps of breaking struts how big the thing outside was.

The walls bulged further, breaking into a lattice of fractures, then broke. Seawater, opaque with bubbles, cascaded in, hitting him hard and knocking him off balance. Kvara thrust himself upward, kicking out against the sudden influx, rotating in the torrent and lashing out with his blade. Its edge connected with something viscous and mobile, snagging on it before cutting through.

He kept moving, pushing out from the rapidly disintegrating walls, powering through the rushing water. More tendrils snaked inside, thrashing after him. As he moved, he fought against a dizzying whirl of disorientation. Everything was in motion, frothing and racing. Water poured rapidly into what remained of the chamber's outer casing, rushing up to waist-height, then shoulder-height, then over his head.

Through a blurred curtain of moving water Kvara saw a huge length of sucker-clad skin race past him, ripping away a length of armour-casing from the hub's exterior. He kicked himself toward it. As he pushed off the crumbling floor gave way entirely, dissolving into a bubbling foam of broken mesh and cladding. More water bloomed up from under it, chasing out the last of the chamber's air in a glistening bubble.

Kvara brought Djalik round in a curve, aiming at the tentacle snaking through the breach. The blade sliced into it cleanly, and a huge cry echoed throughout the water – a shuddering, booming bellow of pain.

Then the last remnants of the chamber caved in, bringing with them a fresh deluge of churning, bloody water from all directions. Kvara ducked down under a collapsing wall section, lurching away from it in slow motion even as he fell down deeper, supported now by nothing but collapsing struts and spars. He tumbled into the centre of the zone of destruction, dragged further into the abyss as the metal around him was crushed and whipped into nothing more than splinters.

The last of the air shot up in columns of glittering silver, leaving him plummeting through rapidly darkening seawater. His helm-visor partially compensated, rendering the scene around him into a riot of false-colour targets.

Kvara spun away from the forest of needle-thin sensor prongs jutting below the disintegrating harvester, still falling rapidly, still trying to get some kind of lock on the creature that was doing this. He had a vague impression of something vast moving just above him. He spun cumbersomely on to his back and fired upward. The bolts shot through the water leaving long trails of bubbles. A series of muffled thuds rang out and impact shocks rippled through the water.

Then Kvara hit the algae. He was dragged into a sticky, cloying morass of thick vegetation. It grasped at him, pulling on his limbs. He twisted around again, slicing out with his blade to clear it, still falling deeper. He reached out with his bolter-arm, ready to fire upward again, only to have a tentacle shoot down and lash round his wrist, wrenching it out of position.

With a violent jerk, he stopped falling. The algae rolled away from him and more tendrils snaked down, grabbing him and pulling him back up. He cut himself free, only for more suckers to grab on. Kvara felt his second heart thumping hard. His breath echoed, fast and regular, in the enclosed space of his helm.

He looked up, and saw the creature in full for the first time. A huge serrated crest of armour reared up in the gloom, ridged and pocked with barnacles. Jaws protruded from under the crest, lined with flashing lines of needle teeth. A massive torso, segmented and flexible, hung down from a spike-ringed neck. Tentacles flowed out from joints along the torso, writhing in the water as if they had sentience of their own. A long tail trailed back into the depths, terminated with a scorpion-like sting. The beast's hide was glossy and streamlined, and it moved through the water with a ponderous, muscular grace.

As Kvara stared up at it, struggling against the tendrils that clutched at him, its huge jaws opened to reveal several flicking tongues, each one the length of his forearm. Six multi-jointed arms uncurled out from the forest of tentacles, stretching out to grab at him. As Kvara saw the claws extend toward him, he remembered the shattered pieces of plasteel floating on the water.

He wrenched his bolt pistol free of the tentacles and fired straight at the creature's looming face. The rounds shot off through the water, leaving trails of bubbles in their wake.

With a mighty whiplash movement, the leviathan surged away from them, evading the projectiles with a sinuous ease. While it was moving, Kvara brought his blade to bear, severing the tendrils that still bound him and breaking free of their hold.

He dropped deeper, spinning around as his heavy armour dragged him down. The creature swam around and swept down after him, undulating through the blooms of algae like a colossal sea-serpent of Fenrisian myth.

Kvara tried to control his cartwheeling descent and failed. The thick liquid dragged at his limbs and the turbulence buffeted him. The wrecked hub was now far above him and out of his eyeline. Even with his helm lenses compensating, it was hard to make out much through the murk other than the vast serrated shadow pursuing him.

Then he reached the bottom. The sea floor rushed up at him, dark and jagged. Huge rocks, each as sharp as butcher's knives and many metres high, cut up into the fog of algae. Kvara arched his back, missing the tip of the nearest stalagmite by a finger's width. He spun away from it and collided with the flank of another one. As he rebounded clear, he managed to mag-lock his blade and stretch out with his free hand. His fingers clutched at the sharp edge of another rock column and he clamped his gauntlet tightly over the rock. His body swung after it, crashing into the unyielding stone and grinding to a standstill.

The stalagmite held him, and his boots lodged firm against a narrow ledge on the stone. Locking himself in place with his free hand, Kvara swung his pistol up again and loosed another volley of bolts.

The creature had been close on his tail the whole time – too close to evade the point-blank shots. The bolts span into its bony crest, detonating once they penetrated the hard casing and exploding with a series of blunt thuds. The beast screamed and jerked sharply back up, sending a back-draught of water washing over him.

He spotted the tail sweeping round at him almost too late. Kvara pressed himself back against the rock-edge and the bulbous sting swam past just in front of him, lashing furiously as it passed.

Then the creature was coming at him again, surging through the water, multiple arms outstretched. Kvara squeezed the trigger again, but the pistol jammed.

Spitting a curse, he let it drop and brought his blade up. His movements were as fast as he could make them in the thick soup of algae, but still too slow, too cumbersome. The first tentacles clamped on to his weapon-arm, pinning him back to the rock. Then more shot out, wrapping themselves around his midriff. They squeezed tight, and Kvara felt his breastplate flex under the pressure.

A clawed hand reached for him, aimed at his head. Kvara managed to pull himself out of its path, wrestling hard against the drag of the tendrils. The beast's talons smashed into the rock behind him, shattering it and sending a cloud of dust floating out and up.

Kvara felt the first crack on his armour even before the warning runes started to flash. It ran transverse across the list of names on his right side, breaking up the inscriptions.

Then the creature went for him again, this time at his torso. Kvara kicked back against the rock, pushing himself upwards. He wrenched his blade-arm free and lashed out at the tendrils around him, briefly clearing a space to operate in. He struck deep, cutting into solid flesh and staining the water with the beast's dark blood, before rolling away and down, sliding down the sheer rock in a flurry of kicked-up dust.

But the beast was far faster, and the abyss was its element. It shot after him, moving with unhurried undulations. The creature's outstretched claws grasped at him, gouging new rents in the ceramite of his backpack where they made contact. More warning indicators flared red across his lens display.

Kvara rolled clumsily on to his back, swinging his blade round and slashing at the scrabbling talons. The beast clutched its claws back up away from the flashing blade before punching them back down after it had swept across. Talons punched down, through Kvara's guard, cutting into his trailing leg like a stud being shot into leather.

Kvara grimaced, wrenching his leg away as the flesh punctured. The leg-plate cracked open, leaving clouds of blood in the water behind him. Valves shut closed at his knee socket and his armour's greave filled with water as the rents in the ceramite spun apart.

The creature swooped in closer, black against the shadow of the deep waters. Off-balanced and unsighted, Kvara crashed and wheeled down the sheer face of the pinnacle. He hit a jutting outcrop in mid-spin that arched his spine and sent him reeling in the opposite direction. Then he collided with another wall of rock face-first, cracking his weakened breastplate further. For a second he could see nothing but flashes of red light. He swung out blindly as he fell further and the sword bit into pursuing claws, darkening the water with the beast's oil-black blood.

Then his boots connected with something solid and his dizzying plummet thumped abruptly to a halt. His vision cleared, though he could feel blood running down the inside of his helm. The cracks in his plate were leaking water and it sloshed around, freezing and pressurised, in the cavities between his skin and the armour.

He was lodged in a narrow cleft between two sheer peaks of rock. Frustrated for a moment, the beast scratched frantically at the pinnacles above him, pulling them apart to get at him. One elongated talon stabbed down clean through the gap, carving through the protection of his upraised sword-arm and severing it nearly clean through.

Kvara roared with pain, watching helplessly as his blade floated free of his control. Blood ballooned out from the wound, pluming in jets through the water.

Another claw shot down through the narrow cleft, reaching for his head and shoulders. Dizzy with pain and incipient shock, Kvara only just managed to punch up with his good hand. His gauntlet closed over the incoming talons and he twisted, using his whole body to leverage the manoeuvre. The talons ripped free, and the creature roared in turn, sending pulsating shivers radiating through the water.

By then Kvara's armour had sealed off the severed vambrace. His blood had already started clotting, and his vision had cleared. Above him, the huge creature withdrew its tentative strikes and broke into a frenzy of pain-filled destruction. Its tail crashed round, demolishing the fragile peaks of the two pinnacles. Another pass, and the last of his protection would be ripped away. His sword-arm was useless, his armour was compromised, and his weapons were gone.

Kvara pulled two krak grenades from his belt and primed them. He clutched them both in his good hand and crouched down, coiled to spring.

Something like elation coursed through his heavily damaged body – the elation felt by a master swordsman having at last met his match in battle. The beast had the measure of him. It was worthy.

I have found it.

Its tail crashed back across, demolishing the pinnacles on either side of the cleft, exposing him again to the full wrath of the wounded creature. When the debris cleared, Kvara just had time to see an enraged, bleeding face hurtling straight at him. It was obscenely stretched, utterly alien, devoid of anything but animal hatred and a primal lust for the coming kill.

Kvara pounced, propelling himself upward into the oncoming jaws, holding the twin grenades tightly in his one working gauntlet and thrusting them forward. The beast snapped its jaws closed out of instinct, ripping Kvara's arm off at the shoulder.

He bellowed with pain. Dark stars exploded before his eyes, quickly lost in a blur of shock and agony. He saw his own blood stream out in a long, viscous trail as he fell back, hanging in the water like a slick of promethium. He felt more water rushing into the breaches in his battle-plate, cracking open the ravaged protection and sending him tumbling back down into the shadow of the rock-cleft.

Above it all was the face of the beast, grinning with alien malice, triumphant and malevolent. It came in close, its teeth stained with his blood, ready to finish him.

Then the grenades went off.

Kvara was hurled down against the rock as the twin booms rocked the sea floor. The creature spasmed and bulged as the explosions tore through its innards. A shockwave swept out from the epicentre of the blast carrying scraps of flesh and carapace with it and carpeting the stark rock needles. The swirling mass of tentacles seemed to implode, shrinking back in toward the bony ridge of the creature's spine before going suddenly limp. A long, echoing scream resonated through the water, hanging there until the beast, flailing for a moment longer in a desperate attempt to climb on to life, slumped immobile.

It still hung, buoyant and huge, drifting a little on the cold, dark currents, before beginning to tilt away, trailing lines of gore from its punctured torso.

With what little awareness that remained to him, Kvara gazed up at it. Though wracked by pain and feeling the frigid clutch of unconscious rush up to grasp him, he could still marvel at the beast's size.

My kill.

Kvara's head fell back on to the rock. Water had got into his helm, which was slowly filling up. Pain throbbed throughout his whole body, acute and blinding. He felt heady with stimms and adrenaline. Before they did their work, dragging him into the oblivion of the Red Dream, he only had one more thought – a correction –recognising the nature of the beast he had killed and the significance it possessed. The voices no longer echoed in his mind, and he could no longer see them as they had been. Death, next to that, seemed of little consequence.

Our kill.

The wound in his head never healed. He became sick, then dizzy, falling over the deck as the *drekkar* pitched with the winter sea. They laughed at him right until the time he couldn't get up.

Kvara saw the world through a mist of confusion, nauseous and slurring. The sea went flat, and the wind came hurling down from the heavens in a blaze of fire and smoke.

He cried out for Thenge, looking for the big man through the rushing noise. Thenge wasn't there. In his place stood a giant wearing a black metal skin and the mask of a wolf. His dried pelt cloak shook in the downdraught and he carried a skull-topped staff.

I am dead. This is the spectre of Morkai.

He felt hands reach out for him – human hands. He was pulled on to some kind of stretcher. He recognised the smell of those hands. Preja Eim, perhaps, the human female who had stood outside the interrogation chamber. Where was her superior, the man called Oen? There were others there, clad in environment suits and talking in low voices.

This is not real. I am not on Fenris.

The *drekkar* reeled, nearly sending him into the sea. He managed to lift his head, and saw the shaky outline of a huge metal casket in the sky. It was as grey as the clouds, and hung above the ship in defiance of all law. Gigantic rings of bronze thundered with flame, breaking through the storm and making the air shake with heat.

The giant with the black metal skin made a gesture, and more metal-clad warriors leapt down from the hovering casket. They wore snow-grey armour with runes hammered into it and none of their faces were visible. They lumbered up to Kvara, walking smoothly even as the ship plunged through the swell.

I have killed the krakken, and it has killed me. Now they come to take me to Halls of the Slain.

Kvara felt the water drain from his helm. In the distance, sounding as if still underwater, drills rang out, removing the surviving sections of battle-plate. Lights flashed painfully in his eyes, surgical and piercing. He heard voices with the accent of Lyses Gothic coming in and out of hearing. A man came to the forefront, his forehead creased with concern.

That is Oen. He fears me still. What is he doing here?

They took him up into the hovering casket of fire. The pain in his head grew worse. Kvara looked down from his impossible position for a final time, seeing his own blood on the decks below. Then, at last, he saw Thenge and the others, huddled at the far end of the ship, gazing up, open-mouthed.

They were afraid. He had never seen them afraid of anything before.

Huge doors closed with an echoing clang, sealing him in. The lights dimmed. He heard the sound of medicae equipment being dragged closer.

Someone leaned over him. It might have been the black wolf-mask. It might have been the man Oen.

It didn't matter. They both said the same thing.

'You will not die, warrior.'

'Could you not have got here quicker?'

'Throne, Preja, I do have other things to worry about.'

'He's scaring the hell out of everybody.'

'I don't doubt it. Is he up and walking?'

'No, he can't get up. But he's still fething scary, procurator.'

Oen walked as fast as he could down the corridors of the medicae unit, ignoring the nervous glances from the apothecary's staff as he went. Eim trotted along at his side, irritable and tense.

'What has he said?'

'He wants his armour. He wants to know what we've done with his ship.'

'And you told him?'

'That he can have it, and that we left it the hell alone.'

'Good.'

The pair of them reached the secure ward. Two sentries in full assault armour stood guard outside. They saluted briskly before opening the metal-banded doors.

The ward was spacious enough, but its lone occupant made it seem cramped. He lay on his back, his huge limbs barely fitting onto the reinforced slab of plasteel that served as a bed. Wires ran from his chest, his face and his limbs. One arm had been severed just below the shoulder and the stump was crowned with a metal cap.

As they entered, Kvara lifted his head. Even after so long, his face was still swollen with bruises. He looked at Oen and Eim with those strange, luminous gold eyes.

'I came as soon as I could, lord,' said Oen, bowing.

Eim stood to one side, chewing her lip nervously.

The Space Wolf took a long time to speak. When he did, his thick, growling voice had gone. His throat shook, and the sound that emerged was little more than a pale whisper.

'How long?' he rasped.

'Two standard months,' said Oen. 'I'm told you've been in some kind of deep coma. We've done what we can, so I'm glad to see you awake again.'

Kvara ran his eyes over the wires jutting from his body, and grunted.

Oen watched him carefully. Kvara looked even more ravaged than he had done on arrival. His long hair and beard hung in grey straggles over the edge of the cot. His massive barrel chest, covered in scars and tattoos, rose and fell under a thin coverlet. His skin was studded with metal devices, none of which the surgeons had made any attempt to investigate. They'd been terrified of doing anything invasive to him and had been half-appalled, half-fascinated by his outlandish physiology. As far as Oen could tell from their reports, the Space Marine had essentially cured himself.

'You recovered the creature?' Kvara asked. His eyes met Oen's blearily. Even with Kvara in such a state, the procurator found it hard to meet that gaze.

'What was left of it, lord. The remains are preserved.'

'The head?'

'I... er, the what?'

'Did you retrieve the head?'

'We did.'

Kvara let his head fall back. His breath was ragged and shallow.

Oen looked at Eim, who shrugged. He had no idea what to say.

'My armour,' said Kvara. His voice had slurred, as if he were fighting against sleep. 'Where is it?'

'Here, lord,' said Eim, motioning over to the far corner of the room. 'We brought it here, just as you asked, when you were sleeping.'

Kvara lifted his head again with difficulty, screwing his eyes up and peering out as if through a thick fog.

The armour had been hung on a reinforced metal scaffold. Even the broken pieces had been mounted on the rig, each one carefully hoisted into place by a team of engineers who'd been every bit as reverent and afraid as the surgeons.

The breastplate hung in the centre. Where once the surface had been covered in eight lines of runes, it was now almost bare. A series of huge impacts had scoured the surface clear, wearing away the grey paint and boring deep into whatever material it had been constructed out of. The curved surface glinted sharply in the light of the medicae chamber, as raw as newly-tempered steel.

'The names,' whispered Kvara, looking at it intently.

'Your pardon?'

Then the Space Wolf issued a dry, cracking chuckle. It seemed to pain him, and he looked away from the armour and back at Oen.

'Come here, mortal,' he ordered.

His throat dry, Oen shuffled closer. Kvara winced as he turned his head, exposing a pair of fangs between chapped lips.

'How did you locate me?' he asked.

Oen swallowed.

'I disobeyed your instruction, and your movements were tracked. By the time our flyers arrived, you'd destroyed the creature.'

Kvara nodded.

'I should add,' said Oen haltingly, remembering how he'd felt when Kvara's body had been retrieved, 'that we're sorry. We came too late. But, you should know, we did what we could for you. You were never alone. We couldn't keep up with you, but you were never alone.'

Kvara smiled at that. Unlike the weary, sardonic smile he'd worn on arrival at Lyses, the gesture was natural, almost human.

'Never alone,' he echoed thoughtfully.

Oen swallowed again, uncertain of what to say to that. An uneasy silence fell over the chamber.

'I don't expect you to understand the ways of my kind, human,' said Kvara at last, his voice low. 'I don't expect you to understand why I came here, nor why I must take the head of that beast back to Fenris, nor what that will mean for the blood-debt of my pack.'

His bestial eyes shone wetly as he spoke.

'Their names have been erased, and it eases the torment of my soul. But we'll remember them in the sagas for as long as such songs are remembered. And among them, in the position of honour, will be yours, human. Take that as you will, but there are those in the galaxy who would see it as a compliment.'

Out of the corner of his eye, Oen saw Eim raise her eyebrows and give a little shrug. He tried to think of something suitably polite to respond with.

It was difficult. For all the reputation of the Adeptus Astartes, the reality of them was hard to come to terms with. Perhaps the Space Wolves were a minor Chapter, a fringe example of the species with more eccentricities than the others. Maybe the other ones he'd seen on the devotional holos with their gleaming cobalt armour and gold-lined pauldrons looked down on them as quaint or inferior.

By the time Oen had thought of something, though, Kvara seemed to have drifted back into an exhausted sleep, and to say anything further felt rather superfluous. For the sake of form, though, Oen bowed courteously and gave his reply.

'That's very kind, lord,' he said. 'What a nice tradition.'

He had learned to use his new body out in the wilds of Asaheim, and it gave him the strength and poise of a demigod. Even out of his armour he could withstand the biting air of the Fang with barely a flicker of discomfort. He had been changed, dragged beyond himself and into the realm of legend.

For all that, the first time he met them his tongue felt thick and useless. He'd never been much of a talker, and they already knew one another as well as mortal brothers. He envied the way they were with each other – easy, casual, close.

'So they've sent us a whelp,' said the one they called Mór, scowling at him as he entered the hearth chamber with his false-confident strut.

The one they called Lek laughed at that, grinding the edge of his axe with a whetstone. He stopped the wheel and pushed a loose strand of blond hair back behind his ear.

'So they have.'

Vrakk, Aerjak and Rann looked up from their game of bones. Vrakk shook his head wearily and went back to it. Aerjak and Rann exchanged a knowing smile, but said nothing.

'Can you use a blade, whelp?' asked Frorl, walking up to him and whirling a practice-sword expertly in his left hand.

'Of course he can't,' snorted Svensson, wrinkling his ruined nose sceptically. 'He's just been pulled off the ice.'

He felt his anger rising at that. Since the changes in his blood, he could be made angry so quickly. The Rune Priest had warned him of that, but still he struggled to control it. Perhaps he would never control it. Perhaps, having been shown the realm of the gods and his place within it, he would still stumble at the final hurdle.

'He'll learn,' said the big one, the one they called Beorth.

Of all of them, he was first to clap his hand on his shoulder. His rough palm fell heavily, like a blow, and he staggered.

'You'll learn, won't you, whelp?'

He looked into Beorth's eyes, and saw the calm, effortless strength there.

'Don't call me whelp,' he said, holding Beorth's gaze.

'Oh?' Beorth looked amused. 'What do you want to be called?'

'Brother.'

Vrakk snorted, still engrossed in his game.

'You have to earn that,' he said.

Aj Kvara didn't look at him. He looked at Beorth, whose hand still rested on his shoulder.

The big warrior seemed like he was going to say something, then paused. He looked down at Kvara, who was still bristling with youth and anger and uncertainty.

'Perhaps you will,' he said. 'For now, though, you need to learn to fight.'

Beorth grinned, and pulled out his blade. It was a short, stabbing sword, notched and serrated along one of the cutting edges and with inset runes lodged under the bronze-lined hilt.

'Let me show you,' he said.

ABOUT THE AUTHOR

Chris Wraight is the author of the Horus Heresy novels *Warhawk, Scars and The Path of Heaven*, the Primarchs novels *Leman Russ: The Great Wolf* and *Jaghatai Khan: Warhawk of Chogoris*, the novellas *Brotherhood of the Storm, Wolf King* and *Valdor: Birth of the Imperium*, and the audio drama *The Sigillite*. For Warhammer 40,000 he has written the Space Wolves books *Blood of Asaheim, Stormcaller* and *The Helwinter Gate*, as well as the Vaults of Terra trilogy, *The Lords of Silence* and the Dawn of Fire novel *Sea of Souls*. Additionally, he has many Warhammer novels to his name, and the Warhammer Crime novel *Bloodlines*. Chris lives and works in Bradford-on-Avon, in south-west England.

YOUR
NEXT READ

THE LION: SON OF THE FOREST
by Mike Brooks

The Lion. Son of the Emperor, brother of demigods and primarch of the Dark Angels.
Awakened. Returned. And yet… lost.

An extract from
The Lion: Son of the Forest
by Mike Brooks

I

The river sings silver notes: a perpetual, chaotic babble in which a fantastically complex melody seems to hang, tantalising, just out of reach of the listener. He could spend eternity here trying to find the heart of it, without ever succeeding, yet still not consider the time wasted. The sound of water over stone, the interplay of energy and matter, creates a quiet symphony that is both unremarkable and unique. He does not know how long he has been here, just listening.

Nor, he realises, does he know where *here* is.

The listener becomes aware of himself in stages, like a sleeper passing from the deepest, darkest depths of slumber, through the shallows of semi-consciousness where thought swirls in confusing eddies, and then into the light. First comes the realisation that he is not the song of the river; that he is in fact separate from it, and listening to it. Then sensation dawns, and he realises he is sitting on the river's bank. If there is a sun, or suns, then he cannot see them through the branches of the trees overhead and the mist that hangs heavily in the air, but there is still light enough for him to make out his surroundings.

The trees are massive, and mighty, with great trunks that could not be fully encircled by one, two, perhaps even half a dozen people's outstretched arms. Their rough, cracked bark pockmarks them with shadows, as though the trees themselves are camouflaged. The ground beneath their branches is fought over by tough shrubs: sturdy, twisted, thorny things strangling each other in the contest for space and light, like children unheeded at the feet of adults. The earth in which they grow is dark and rich, and when the listener digs his fingers into it, it smells of life, and death, and other things besides. It is a familiar smell, although he cannot say from where, or why.

His fingers, he realises as they penetrate the ground, are armoured. His whole body is armoured, in fact, encased in a great suit of black plates with the faintest hint of dark green. This is a familiar sensation, too. The armour feels like a part of him – an extension, as natural as the shell of any crustacean that might lurk in the nooks and crannies of the river in front of him. He leans forward and peers down into the still water next to the bank, sheltered from the main flow by an outcropping just upstream. It becomes an almost perfect mirror surface, as smooth as a dream.

The listener does not recognise the face that looks back at him. It is deeply lined, as though a world of cares and worries has washed over it like the river water, scoring the marks of their passage into the skin. His hair is pale, streaked with blond here and there, but otherwise fading into grey and white. The lower part of his face is obscured by a thick, full beard and moustache, leaving only the lips bare; it is a distrustful mouth, one more likely to turn downwards in disapproval than quirk upwards in a smile.

He raises one hand, the fingers still smeared with dirt, before his face. The reflection does the same. This is surely his face, but the sight sparks no memory. He does not know who he is, and he does not know where he is, for all that it feels familiar.

That being the case, there seems little point in remaining here.

The listener gets to his feet, then hesitates. He cannot explain to himself why he should move, given the song of the river is so beautiful. However, the realisation of his lack of knowledge has opened something inside him, a hunger which was not there before. He will not be satisfied until he has answers.

Still, the river's song calls to him. He decides to walk along the bank, following the flow of the water and listening to it as he goes, and since he does not know where he is, one direction is as good as the other. There is a helmet on the bank, next to where he was sitting. It is the same colour as his armour, with vertical slits across the mouth, like firing slits in a wall. He picks it up, and clamps it to his waist with a movement that feels instinctual.

He does not know for how long he walks. Time is surely passing, in that one moment slips into another, and he can remember ones that came before and consider the concept of ones yet to come, but there is nothing to mark it. The light neither increases nor decreases, instead remaining an almost spectral presence which illuminates without revealing its source. Shadows lurk, but there is no indication as to what casts them. The walker is unperturbed. His eyes can pierce those shadows, just as he can smell foliage, and he can hear the river. There is no soughing of wind in the branches, for the air is still, but the moist air carries the faint hooting, hollering calls of animals of some kind, somewhere in the distance.

The river's course begins to flatten and widen. The walker follows it around a bend, then comes to a halt in shock.

On the far bank stands a building.

It is built of cut and dressed stone, a dark blue-grey rock in which brighter specks glitter. It is not immense – the surrounding trees tower over it – but it is solid. It is a castle of some kind, a fortress, intended to keep the unwanted out and whatever people and treasures lie within safe from harm. It is neither new and pristine, nor ancient and weathered. It looks as though it has always stood here, and always shall. And on the wide, calm water in front of it sits a boat.

It is small, wooden, and unpainted. It is large enough for one person, and indeed one person is sitting in it. The walker's eyes can make him out, even at distance. He is old, and not old in the same way as the walker's face is. Time has not lined his features, it has ravaged them. His cheeks are sunken, his limbs are wasted; skin that was once clearly a rich chestnut now has an ashen patina, and his long hair is lifeless, dull grey, and matted. However, that grey head supports a crown: little more than a circlet of gold, but a crown nonetheless.

In his hands, swollen of knuckle and weak of grip, he holds a rod. The line is already cast into the water. Now he sits, hunched over as though in pain, a small, ancient figure in a small, simple boat.

The walker does not stop to wonder why a king would be fishing in such a manner. He is aware of the context of such things, but he does not know from where, and they do not matter to him. Here is someone who might have some answers for him.

'Greetings!' he calls. His voice is strong, rich and deep, although rough around the edges from age or disuse, or both. It carries across the water. The old king in the boat blinks, and when his eyes open again, they are looking at the walker.

'What is this place?' the walker demands.

The old king blinks again. When his eyes open this time, they are focused on the water once more. It is as though the walker is not there at all, a dismissal of minimal effort.

The walker discovers that he is not used to being ignored, and nor does he appreciate it. He steps into the water, intending to wade across the river so the king cannot so easily dismiss him. He is unconcerned about the current: he is strong of limb, and knows without knowing that his armour is waterproof, and that should he don his helmet he will be able to breathe even if he is submerged.

He has only gone a few steps, in up to his knees, when he realises there are shadows in the water: large shadows that circle the small boat, around and around. They do not bite on the line, and nor do they capsize the craft in which the fisher sits, but either could be disastrous.

Moreover, the walker realises, the king is wounded. The walker cannot see the wound, but he can smell the blood. A rich, copperish tang tickles his nose. It is not a smell that delights him, but neither does he find it repulsive. It is simply a scent, one that he is able to parse and understand. The king is bleeding into the water, drip by drip. Perhaps that is what has drawn the shadows to this place. Perhaps they would have been here anyway.

Some of the shadows start to peel away, and head towards the walker.

The walker is not a being to whom fear comes naturally, but nor is he unfamiliar with the concept of danger. The shadows in the water are unknown to him, and move like predators.

+Come back to the bank.+

The walker whirls. A small figure stands on the land, swathed in robes of dark green, so that it nearly blends into the background against which it stands. It is the size of a child, perhaps, but the walker knows it to be something else.

It is a Watcher in the Dark.

+Come back to the bank,+ the Watcher repeats. Although its communication can hardly be called a voice – there is no sound, merely a sensation inside the walker's head that imparts meaning – it feels increasingly urgent nonetheless. The walker realises that he is not normally one to turn away from a challenge, but nor is he willing to ignore a Watcher in the Dark. It feels like a link, a connection to what came before, to what he should be able to remember.

He wades back, and steps up onto the bank. The approaching shadows hesitate for a moment, then circle away towards the king in his boat.

+They would destroy you,+ the Watcher says. The walker understands that it is talking about the shadows. There are layers to the feelings in his head now, feelings that are the mental aftertaste of the Watcher's communication. Disgust lurks there, but also fear.

'Where is this place?' the walker asks.

+Home.+

The walker waits, but nothing else is forthcoming. Moreover, he understands that there will not be. So far as the Watcher is concerned, that is not simply all the information that is required, but all that is available to give.

He looks out over the water, towards the king. The old man still sits hunched over, rod in his hands, blood leaking from his wounds one drip at a time.

'Why does he ignore me?'

+You did not ask the correct question.+

The walker looks around. The shadows in the water are still there, so it seems foolish to try to cross. However, he has seen no bridge over the river, nor another boat. He has no tools with which to build such a craft from the trees around him, and the knowledge of how to do so does not come easily to his mind. He is not like some of his brothers, for whom creation is natural...

His brothers. Who are his brothers?

Shapes flit through his mind, as ephemeral as smoke in a storm. He cannot get a grip, cannot wrestle them into anything that makes sense, or anything onto which his reaching mind can latch. The peace brought about by the song of the river is gone, and in its place is uncertainty and frustration. Nonetheless, the walker would not return to his former state. To knowingly welcome ignorance is not his way.

He catches a glimpse of something pale, a long way off through the trees, but on his side of the river. He begins to walk towards it, leaving the river behind him – he can always find it again, he knows its song – and making his way through the undergrowth. The plants are thick and verdant, but he is strong and sure. He ducks under spines, slaps aside strangling tendrils reaching out for anything that passes, and avoids breaking the twigs, which would leak sap so corrosive it might damage even his armour.

He does not wonder how he knows these things. The Watcher said that this was home.

The Watcher itself has been left behind, but it keeps reappearing, stepping out of the edge of shadows. It says nothing; not until the walker passes through a thicket of thorns and finally gets a clearer view of what he had seen.

It is a building, or at least the roof of one; that is all he can see from here. It is a dome of beautiful pale stone, supported by pillars. Whereas before he had been finding his own route through the forest, now there is a clear path ahead, a route of short grass hemmed in on either side by bushes and tree trunks. It curves away, rather than arrowing straight towards the pale building, but the walker knows that is where it leads.

+Do not take that path,+ the Watcher cautions him. +You are not yet strong enough.+

The walker looks down at this tiny creature, barely knee-high to him, then breathes deeply and rolls his shoulders within his armour. He presumes he had a youth, given he now looks old. Perhaps he was stronger then. Nonetheless, his body does not feel feeble.

+That is not the strength you will need.+

The walker narrows his eyes. 'You caution me against anything that might help me make sense of my situation. What would you have me do instead?'

+Follow your nature.+

The walker breathes in again, ready to snap an answer, for he finds he is just as ill-disposed towards being denied as he is to being ignored. However, he pauses, then sniffs.

He sniffs again.

Something is amiss.

He is surrounded by the deep, rich scent of the forest, which smells of both life and death. However, now his nose detects something else: a rancid undercurrent, something that is not merely rot or decay – for these are natural odours – but far worse, far more jarring.

Corruption.

This is something wrong, something twisted. It is something that should not be here: something that should not, in fact, exist at all.

The walker knows what he must do. He must follow his nature.

The hunter steps forward, and starts to run in pursuit of his quarry.

II

He flows over the ground, each step sure and certain and placed to perfection. Walking is second nature and not something about which he has to think, but running awakens something within him. This sense of urgency, this sense of a goal towards which he is striving; it provides focus and clarity, and makes him not only more aware, but also more aware of his own awareness. He realises that he perceives the forest in a new way: not as a homogenous landscape, but as terrain. The ground on which tracks will be left, the plants that will show the signs of a body passing, the thickets where a predator might wait in ambush and those in which lurking would lead only to becoming a meal for the plant itself: these things are as clear to him as words upon a page.

This *is* his home, and nothing can hide from him here.

The scent leads him onwards, as distinct as a wrong note in a symphony, and strengthening as he closes on it. The Watcher is forgotten, as are the king in the boat and the shadows in the water. He is hunting beasts through the trees, just as he used to long ago, back before...

Back before what?

The hunter slows, his focus disrupted for a moment by another flash of something that is not even memory, but perhaps the shadow of one. He does not remember what came before, but he remembers that there was something to remember, which is both welcome and infuriating. All he knows is that he hunted like this in the past.

He shakes himself. Memory will return when it returns, *if* it returns. For now, he still has a quarry to chase down. He presses on, still following the scent of corruption.

The hunter is not certain when the forest begins to change character, for there was never before any way with which to mark the time except by counting his own breaths or heartbeats. However, at some point he becomes aware that the mist is thinning. The light around him has a source now, high up and to his left, and he can feel the heat of this sun upon his scalp; it is a thick heat, a wet heat, the type that reaches into the throat and threatens to clog the airways. The trees are different, as well: they are still tall, still towering, but this is no longer a world of massive, low-hanging branches. Now their crowns splay out far above him, and their trunks are bare apart from the climbing plants that seek to scale their neighbours to snatch a glimpse of light for themselves. The air is alive with the chittering of insects, and the hunter can no longer hear the song of the river. He pauses and reaches down into the ground once more, this time coming up with a fistful of mouldering leaves. They carpet the ground, thick and brown, and do not easily give up the prints of those who have passed over them before; not like soft earth does, the tracker's friend.

The hunter does not know where he is now, any more than he truly knew where he was before, but he knows that this is somewhere else. He is no longer home.

The scent of corruption is still strong, though. Stronger, even. The hunter is drawn forwards, pressing on through this new undergrowth: purplish ferns, pale roots trailing down from above, hanging vines, and plants he does not know with broad, glossy leaves edged with spikes. He does not feel the same connection to this forest, but he is closing on his quarry and he will not lose it once he is this near, no matter his surroundings.

There is movement up ahead. The hunter can hear the faint creaking of stems, as his quarry passes through the brush. He begins to build a picture of what he is following. It is large, certainly, for it cannot avoid making some noise as it moves. It feels like a predator, too; its movements sound like his own, designed not to alert prey to its approach, rather than something going about its own business. He can smell the faint tang of offal and rotting meat, such as might be caught between a hunter's jaws, or smeared across its snout where it has fed on a carcass.

A large, dangerous predator. The hunter removes his helmet from where it is clamped to his belt and, with a strange familiarity of movement despite being unable to remember having ever done it before, lowers it over his head.

The helmet clicks into place, making an airtight seal. Displays power up instantly, and the hunter finds himself looking at read-outs detailing his armour's power reserves, the external temperature, humidity levels and atmospheric composition, and even the day length of the world he is on – eighteen point five-four hours – as estimated from the infinitesimal movement of the local star in the sky above him. Without knowing how he knows what to do, he blinks through the vision options available to him: standard, polarised, infra-red, thermal-imaging, and on and on.

He settles on the standard vision. Everything has its place, but he will have no need of enhancements for this. He sets the air intakes to open, allowing himself to still experience the scents of this world, and moves back into the hunt. Even clad in his armour, thick though it is, he has no problem moving stealthily. The suit responds intuitively to him, as though it is a second skin. He does not pause to ponder this. It feels as natural as breathing.

He inhales, and detects the odour of his prey. There is no wind in this dense understorey, so he has little concern about his own scent giving him away.

He inhales again, double-checking. His armour, feverishly analysing his surroundings, offers up a breakdown of molecular concentrations and pheromone trails which overlays his vision like ghostly fluorescent trails. He is not mistaken.

There is more than one predator, and they have split up, to the left and right as he looks at it.

The hunter scans the ground, but the leaf litter is as obstinate as before and refuses to divulge its secrets. Is he following two predators, or more? Even his senses, sharp though they are, have limits. Still, hesitation is not his way. He follows the trail that leads to his left, balancing speed with stealth. If he slays this corrupted beast, whatever it may turn out to be, he will need to do it quickly enough to then retrace his steps and pick up the scent of its pack mates. He blinks a command and the audio receptors on his helmet increase in sensitivity, ready to warn him if anything chooses to hunt him while he is on the trail of his quarry.

He does not hear clawed feet or muscled bodies converging on him through the undergrowth, but he does detect something else from up ahead: voices. Human voices. Not the eerie sensation of the Watcher in the Dark's communication, where meaning suddenly arrived in his head, but true voices like his own – not quiet, not stealthy, but broadcasting their position to all with ears to hear them. If the hunter is certain of anything, it is that his quarry has both the ears to hear them, and the intention of doing harm.

He breaks into a sprint, all his own stealth forgotten as he smashes through tangling underbrush. He hurdles the giant trunk of a fallen tree just in time to hear a scream, and see a monstrous shape sheathed in scales of irides-cent green spring towards a huddle of humans.

The hunter launches himself into a leap, a black-armoured arrow powered by superhuman muscle and sinew. He strikes the beast in the flank with his knee, and feels rib bones the width of his wrist crack from the force of the impact. The beast sprawls onto its side with a roaring scream, its pounce cut short, but the hunter has no time to finish the job before the undergrowth rustles and two more creatures emerge on the far side of the humans.

There are three humans: two adults, and a child. All three are unkempt, dressed in ragged clothes, and the two adults sport growths of facial hair which appear to owe more to lack of grooming opportunity than to cultural significance or personal choice. The child is prepubescent, of an as-yet indeterminable gender, with long straggly hair, and eyes wide and white in a dirty face. The hunter sees this within the space of a moment as he glances past them. The humans are weak, tired, and scared, of little value as allies in this struggle, and as likely to freeze in fear as they are to respond to instruction. He dismisses them, and springs over their heads.

The predators are a different matter altogether. They each stand taller than a human at the shoulder, but the similarities between them taper off at that point. The one the hunter struck down to begin with had a scaled hide, but one of these others has purplish-green fur interspersed with patches of scales, and the third's skin appears to have hardened into chitinous carapace in many places. They all have long jaws lined with sharp teeth, but one has additional tusks that protrude below its chin, and another has large, ridged horns that curl back from above its eyes.

The hunter comes down from his leap with his hands clasped together to form one giant fist, and lands them in a titanic blow directly between those horns.

The predator's head is driven down into the forest floor so fast that the rest of its body does not have time to keep up, and its rump is still standing as the hunter rolls away and turns towards the third creature. This one faces him and opens its mouth, but no roar of rage or aggression emerges. Instead a long, thickly muscled tongue lashes out to cover the space between them, some thirty feet or more, and the tip of it engulfs the hunter's right hand with a hideous sucking noise.

Strength means little without leverage. The hunter does not have time to set his feet before he is hauled off them by the tongue, and wrenched through the air towards the creature who has snared him. He draws back his free fist, determined to turn his headlong flight into an attack, but he is smashed out of the air by a massive, clawed paw a moment before he can strike his blow.

He is pinned face down on the ground, and he automatically shuts his helmet's air intakes to prevent himself from inhaling dust or dirt. Then his concerns become more immediate, as the creature draws his hand into its mouth with its ensnaring tongue and bites down on his arm at the elbow.

The force is tremendous, and could have easily snapped a regular human in two at the waist. The hunter's armour withstands it, although red warning icons flash up into his vision to let him know how close it is to giving way. The beast shakes its head to and fro, trying to achieve through wrenching and tearing what it could not manage through direct force alone, and nearly tears the hunter's shoulder out of its socket in the process. He grits his teeth, waits for half a second to get his timing right, and hauls his arm back out of the beast's jaws in the moment that it starts to shake its head back the other way, and its grip on his limb slackens ever so slightly.

The hunter's arm scrapes free. The predator's teeth leave grooves in the smooth surface of his vambrace, then snap shut as the resistance disappears. In doing so, they sever the creature's own tongue, which still envelops the hunter's fist.

The beast screams in self-inflicted pain, and lifts its paw from the hunter's back to claw at its own mouth, from which dark blood is leaking between its teeth. The hunter springs up, shaking the tongue tip loose. Without the muscle contractions to hold it in place, it is no more than a fleshy cylinder which flops wetly onto the forest floor.

The beast lunges for him, at least two tons of flesh driving behind a fanged maw, which opens to engulf the hunter. This time, however, he has the chance to set himself. He spreads his arms wide and his fingers close for a moment on the tips of its jaws, just as he shifts his weight and twists his torso. His muscles tense, and the servos in his armour spring into action to support them.

The hunter pivots, and uses the beast's own momentum to send it spinning through the air into its horned companion, which is only now rising to its feet after being stunned by the hunter's blow. The two predators collide and collapse into a thrashing, howling pile of limbs and tails.

All of this has taken perhaps ten seconds since the hunter first leaped over the terrified humans. He has been aware of their shrieks and gasps as he struggled with the predators, but only now does he turn back to them. They are still where he left them, their arms full of sticks: not weapons, but firewood they have collected. They are small, and weak, and unable to defend themselves against threats such as this. The hunter supposes that he might easily consider them pathetic. Perhaps he did, once, in whatever existence he had before, if he had dwelled too long on the differences between him and them.

Now, he sees only lives that need his protection. He is strong and they are weak, and therefore he will lend them his strength until they no longer need it.

The animal whose ribs he cracked is struggling back to its feet with the resilience of the wild. The hunter sees the hunger in its eyes. Its desire for flesh to eat is no more malicious than the mutations that have turned its tail into a scorpion's stinger, or the vines that constrict the trees around which they grow so tightly that the tree dies, or the fungi that grow into their victims' brains and kill them by bursting out through their skulls. It is the nature of humanity to see the fate the wild has in store for them, and cheat it. Here and now, the hunter is that cheat.

'Stay out of my way!' he shouts, the first words he has directed at the humans. He does not intend them as hostile – they are supposed to be a warning for the humans to keep their distance from the struggle – but they shrink away from him anyway with a new, sharper fear. He dismisses their reaction. There will be time enough to clarify things when he has dealt with the predators, and his primary purpose is to make them stay clear. He does not, at this point, particularly care what their rationale is for obeying him.

He sprints at the wounded beast, which snarls and lashes out at him with its stinger. The hunter catches it behind the venom bulb with one hand, and rips the weapon off with his other. The predator howls again and wrenches backwards, and blood spurts from the severed trunk to spray across the hunter's faceplate, clogging and obscuring his eye-lenses. He wipes at them, but hard, shiny armour can only smear fluids ineffectually. He can still hear the beasts around him, but hearing alone will not be sufficient to win him this fight.

He drops the stinger and reaches up, pops the neck seal expertly, and removes his helmet. He throws it towards the humans and shouts, 'Clean that!' He does not have time to see whether they scramble to obey his order or shrink from the helmet as though it is a grenade, because the now stingless beast is coming at him again.

He steps slightly to the side, and punches upwards. The uppercut crashes into its lower jaw, and is powerful enough to knock the beast off its feet and flip it over, causing its onrushing mass to miss him and come to a slumped halt in the leaf litter. The hunter pounces on it, seizes its head, and wrenches, pitting his strength against the resistance of its neck muscles and spine. It is a brief struggle: the predator's neck snaps, and when the hunter releases its head it drops limply to the ground.

That leaves two.

He picks up the severed stinger and moves to attack. The other beasts have disentangled themselves, not without a couple of snaps at each other, and spread out to flank him. The one with the severed tongue roars at him, which is its last mistake. The hunter hurls the stinger into its mouth, and the barb pierces the roof of it. The venom bulb discharges automatically, pumping toxins into its bloodstream. The creature stiffens, falls to the ground and begins to thrash, no more immune to its pack mate's venom than their prey would be.

That leaves one.

The final predator charges the hunter, faster than even he is prepared for. It ducks its horned head low and swipes upwards at the last moment, hammering its weapons into his chest. He is lifted off his feet and sent flying gracelessly through the air, the ground and the sky rapidly swapping places as he tumbles. Perhaps he would have recovered his equilibrium sufficiently to land on his feet, or perhaps not, but the sudden intervention of a tree trunk renders it a moot point. He strikes hard enough to splinter the wood, and falls to the ground.

His armour has held, but it will not stand up to many more impacts of such force. He clambers back to his feet, a little short of breath, a little shaken, and with his hearts pounding. This too is a familiar sensation, but familiarity with mortal peril does not bring any guarantee of survival. Lessons can be learned, and adjustments made, but each struggle is contested on its own merits.

The predator has forgotten about the humans. Now it only has eyes for the hunter, this thing that has stepped into its territory and challenged it. Whether it considers him to be a rival seeking to claim its food for himself,